# ELEMENTS
# OF·FICTION

# ELEMENTS OF FICTION

## REVISED CANADIAN EDITION

Edited by
Robert Scholes & Rosemary Sullivan

Toronto
OXFORD UNIVERSITY PRESS

Oxford University Press
70 Wynford Drive, Don Mills, Ontario M3C 1J9

Toronto   Oxford   New York
Delhi   Bombay   Calcutta   Madras   Karachi
Kuala Lumpur   Singapore   Hong Kong   Tokyo
Nairobi   Dar es Salaam   Cape Town
Melbourne   Auckland

and associated companies in
Berlin   Ibadan


**Canadian Cataloguing in Publication Date**
Main entry under title:
Elements of fiction: an anthology
Rev. Canadian ed.

ISBN 0-19-540656-7

1. Fiction — 19th century.   2. Fiction — 20th century.
I. Scholes, Robert, 1929–   II. Sullivan, Rosemary.

PN6120.2.E44 1988        808.83        C88-093439-5

# ACKNOWLEDGEMENTS

Sherwood Anderson. "I'm a Fool" from *The Portable Sherwood Anderson*, edited by Horace Gregory. Copyright 1922 copyright renewed 1950 by Eleanor Copenhaver Anderson. Reprinted by permission of Viking Penguin Inc.

Margaret Atwood. "The Grave of the Famous Poet" from *Dancing Girls* by Margaret Atwood. Used by permission of the Canadian Publishers, McClelland and Stewart, Toronto.

Isaac Babel. "Guy de Maupassant." Reprinted by permission of S.G. Phillips, Inc. from *The Collected Works of Isaac Babel*. Copyright © 1955 by S.G. Phillips, Inc.

John Barth. "Lost in the Funhouse" from *Lost in the Funhouse* by John Barth. Copyright © 1968 by John Barth. Reprinted by permission of Doubleday, a division of Bantam, Doubleday, Dell Publishing Group, Inc.

Ann Beattie. "Janus" from *Where You'll Find Me*. Copyright © 1986 by Iron & Pity, Inc. The story first appeared in the New Yorker. Reprinted by permission of Linden Press, a division of Simon & Schuster, Inc.

Sandra Birdsell. "The Wednesday Circle" is reprinted by permission from *Night Travellers* (Turnstone Press), copyright Sandra Birdsell, 1982.

Jorge Luis Borges. "The Lottery in Babylon" translated by John M. Fein, from Jorge Luis Borges, *Labyrinths*. Copyright © 1962 by New Directions Publishing Corporation. Reprinted by permission of New Directions.

Elizabeth Bowen. "The Demon Lover" copyright 1946 and renewed 1974 by Elizabeth Bowen. Reprinted from *The Collected Stories of Elizabeth Bowen* by Elizabeth Bowen by permission of Alfred A. Knopf, Inc.

Kay Boyle. "Winter Night" copyright 1946 by New York Magazine, Inc. from the book *Fifty Stories* by Kay Boyle. Reprinted by permission of Doubleday, a division of Bantam, Doubleday, Dell Publishing Group Inc.

Morley Callaghan. "Ancient Lineage" from *Morley Callaghan's Stories* by Morley Callaghan. Reprinted by permission of Macmillan of Canada A Division of Gage Publishing Limited.

Italo Calvino. "Meiosis" from *Zero* by Italo Calvino, translated by William Weaver. Reprinted by permission of Roslyn Targ Literary Agency.

Raymond Carver. "Cathedral" from *Cathedral* by Raymond Carver. Copyright © 1983 by Raymond Carver. Reprinted by permission of Alfred A. Knopf, Inc.

John Cheever. "The Swimmer" from *The Stories of John Cheever*, by John Cheever. Copyright © 1964 by John Cheever. Reprinted by permission of Alfred A. Knopf, Inc.

Anton Chekhov. "Heartache" from *The Portable Chekhov*, edited by Avrahm Yarmolinsky Copyright 1947, Copyright © renewed 1975 by Avrahm Yarmolinsky Reprinted by permission of Viking Penguin Inc.

Julio Cortazar. "Blow-up" from *End of the Game and Other Stories*, by Julio Cortazar, translated by Paul Blackburn. Copyright © 1967 by Random House, Inc. Reprinted by permission of Pantheon Books, a Division of Random House, Inc.

Timothy Findley. "Dinner Along the Amazon" from *Dinner Along the Amazon* by Timothy Findley. Copyright © Pebble Productions, 1984. Reprinted by permission of Penguin Books Canada Limited and the author.

F. Scott Fitzgerald. "Babylon Revisited" (copyright 1931 by the Curtis Publishing Company; copyright renewed) from *Taps at Reveille*. Copyright 1935 by Charles Scribner's Sons; copyright renewed. Reprinted with the permission of Charles Scribner's Sons.

Mavis Gallant. "The Ice Wagon Going Down the Street" © Mavis Gallant from *Home Truths*. Reprinted by permission of Macmillan of Canada, A Division of Canada Publishing Corporation.

Gabriel Garcia-Marquez. "Tuesday Siesta" from *No One Writes to the Colonel* by Gabriel Garcia-Marquez. Copyright © 1968 in the English translation by Harper & Row, Publishers, Inc. Reprinted by permission of the publisher.

Nikolai Gogol. "The Overcoat" from *The Diary of a Madman and Other Stories* by Nikolai Gogol, as translated by Andrew R. McAndrew. Copyright © 1960 by Andrew R. McAndrew. Reprinted by arrangement with NAL Penguin, Inc. New York, New York.

Ernest Hemingway. "Hills Like White Elephants" in *Men Without Women*. Copyright 1927 by Charles Scribner's Sons; copyright renewed. Reprinted with the permission of Charles Scribner's Sons.

Jack Hodgins. "Separating" from *Spit Delaney's Island* by Jack Hodgins. Reprinted by permission of Macmillan of Canada A Division of Gage Publishing Limited.

James Joyce. "The Boarding House" and "Clay" from *Dubliners* by James Joyce. Copyright © 1967 by the Estate of James Joyce. Reprinted by permission of Viking Penguin Inc.

# Preface to the Canadian Edition

*Elements of Fiction: An Anthology,* edited by Robert Scholes, was first published in 1981. The present edition, adapted for a Canadian audience, includes twelve new stories by Canadian authors. The aim and structure of this book remain essentially the same. As Professor Scholes writes in his original preface, the book is intended to help the reader toward an enriched experience of fiction and includes representative selections from the full spectrum of the short-story tradition.

The Canadian stories, ranging from early historical realism of the nineteenth-century story to modern metafiction, have been inserted into the overall chronological ordering of the book by authors' birth dates. Readers will discover that, rather than isolated from European and American writing, Canadian authors work in the same fictional styles as their contemporaries. Stephen Leacock, like other writers of his generation (such as O. Henry, Kipling and Stephen Crane), writes in a realistic mode for the sheer delight of the yarn, with a slight moral edge to his deflationary humor. Morley Callaghan and Sinclair Ross follow the European tradition of realism created by Tolstoy and perfected by Chekhov, a tradition that dominates the twentieth-century short story through the work of Joyce and Hemingway. These writers are interested in a spare fiction that makes an impression of objective description, rejecting as "literary" anything that distracts attention from the protagonist to the writer.

The Canadian short-story form is perhaps at its most subtle in the hands of Mavis Gallant, Anne Hébert and Alice Munro, who explore delicate shifts in the minds of characters in complex psychological situations. Writers like Margaret Atwood and Jack Hodgins share the same vision of the story as Flannery O'Connor and John Updike, writing carefully crafted stories that use symbolic detail but with such skill that the artifice never obtrudes. A ruthless honesty that is the root of much ironic humor also characterizes their style.

The Canadian story moves into the arena of metafiction with the works of Rudy Wiebe and Leon Rooke, where the boundary between history and fiction is erased and the compulsion is to write fiction about fiction. Here readers find themselves in the labyrinth where fact and fiction, object and subject, merge until reality itself becomes a fictional game.

This edition has been compiled on the assumption that Canadian students will wish to read the fiction writers of their own culture in the context of the European and American traditions. They will find that these writers are Canadian in the sense in which Mavis Gallant speaks of herself: "I would be Canadian even if Canada ceased to exist, because it is a part of being myself." Yet as writers, Canadians participate in the stylistic conventions of their time, giving their deepest commitment to the craft of fiction. Students might best approach this book as Professor Scholes suggests: with a recognition that the aesthetic experience of a story goes beyond critical analysis into something more rewarding—"a kind of consummation—an embrace."

Rosemary Sullivan

# A Note on the Revised Canadian Edition

Although some critics had predicted the demise of the short story as a literary form, the genre continues to develop. The current edition has been updated to reflect some of these changes. We have added stories by three Canadian writers who have come into prominence in recent years—Timothy Findley, Bharati Mukherjee, and Sandra Birdsell— and included the nineteenth-century writer Sara Jeannette Duncan, whose stories, out of print since 1903, were only recently rediscovered. We have also included two of the best among the new American practitioners of the genre: Raymond Carver and Ann Beattie. Finally, the early stories by Mavis Gallant and Leon Rooke have been replaced by ones that are more representative of their work. I would like to thank all the users of the book who have offered suggestions over the years as to changes they would wish to see, and who have pointed out errors in the first edition that have now been corrected. Updating a book is always a pleasure, particularly where the short story is concerned; it confirms one's belief in the strength of the genre.

# Contents

## 3. The Modern Novella

# 1
# THE
# ELEMENTS
# OF
# FICTION

# The Elements of Fiction

## FICTION, FACT, AND TRUTH

A fiction is a made-up story. This definition covers a lot of territory. It includes the homemade lies we tell to protect ourselves from annoying scrutiny, and the casual jokes we hear and re-tell as polite (or impolite) conversation, as well as great visionary works of literature like Milton's *Paradise Lost* or the Bible itself. Yes, I am saying that the Bible is fiction; but before you either bristle with smug piety or nod with complacent skepticism, read a few words more. The Bible is fiction because it is a made-up story. This does not mean that it necessarily lacks truth. Nor does it mean that the Bible may not contain fact. The relation between fact and fiction is by no means as simple as one might think; and, since it is very important to an understanding of fiction, it must be considered with some care.

Fact and fiction are old acquaintances. They are both derivatives of Latin words. Fact comes from *facere*—to make or do. Fiction comes from *fingere*—to make or shape. Plain enough words, one would think—not necessarily loaded with overtones of approval or disapproval. But their fortunes in the world of words have not been equal. Fact has prospered. In our ordinary conversation, "fact" is associated with those pillars of verbal society, "reality" and "truth." "Fiction," on the other hand, is known to consort with such suspicious characters as "unreality" and "falsehood." Still, if we look into the matter, we can see that the relation of "fact" and "fiction" with "the real" and "the true" is not exactly what appears on the surface. Fact still means for us quite literally "a thing done." And fiction has never lost its meaning of "a thing made." But in what sense do things done or things made partake of truth or reality? A thing done has no real existence once it has been done. It may have consequences, and there may be many records that point to its former existence (think of the Civil War, for

3

example); but once it is done its existence is finished. A thing made, on the other hand, exists until it decays or is destroyed. Once it is finished, its existence begins (think of a Civil War story like Stephen Crane's *Red Badge of Courage*, for example). Fact, finally, has no real existence, while fiction may last for centuries.

We can see this rather strange relation between fact and fiction more clearly if we consider one place where the two come together: the place we call history. The word "history" itself hides a double meaning. It comes from a Greek word that originally meant inquiry or investigation. But it soon acquired the two meanings that interest us here: on the one hand, history can mean "things that have happened"; on the other, it can refer to "a recorded version of things that are supposed to have happened." That is, history can mean both the events of the past and the story of these events: fact—or fiction. The very word "story" lurks in the word "history," and is derived from it. What begins as investigation must end as story. Fact, in order to survive, must become fiction. Seen in this way, fiction is not the opposite of fact, but its complement. It gives a more lasting shape to the vanishing deeds of men.

But this is, in fact, only one aspect of fiction. We *do* think of it also as something quite different from historical records or mere data. We think of it not just as made but as made-up, a non-natural, unreal product of the human imagination. It is helpful to see fiction in both the ways outlined here. It can be very factual, maintaining the closest possible correspondence between its story and things that have actually happened in the world. Or it can be very fanciful, defying our sense of life's ordinary possibilities.

Taking these two extremes as the opposite ends of a whole spectrum of fictional possibilities, between the infra-red of pure history and the ultra-violet of pure imagination, we can distinguish many shades of coloration. But all are fragments of the white radiance of truth, which is present in both history books and fairy tales, but only partly present in each—fragmented by the prism of fiction, without which we should not be able to see it at all. For truth is like ordinary light, present everywhere but invisible, and we must break it to behold it. To fracture truth in a purposeful and pleasing way—that is the job of the writer of fiction, with whatever shades from the spectrum he or she chooses to work.

## FICTION: EXPERIENCE AND ANALYSIS

Though fiction itself has a real existence—a book has weight and occupies space—our experience of fiction is unreal. When we are reading a story we are not "doing" anything. We have stopped the ordinary course of our existence, severed our connections with friends and family, in order to withdraw temporarily into a private and unreal world. Our experience of fiction is more like dreaming than like our normal waking activity. It makes us physically inert yet exercises our imagination. In terms of our performing any action in it, this special world is absolutely unreal, whether we are reading a history book or a science fiction story. We can do nothing to affect either the Battle of Waterloo or the War of the Worlds. And yet, in a way, we participate. We are engaged and involved in the events we are reading about, even though powerless to alter them. We *experience* the events of a story, but without the consequences—emerging from Rudy Wiebe's *The Temptations of Big Bear,* for example, without a scratch on our bodies. Emotionally, however, and intellectually, we are different. We have experienced something.

All discussion of literature, all classes and instruction in literary matters, can have only one valid end: to prepare us for our part in the literary experience. Just as the dull routine exercises and repetitious practice for an athletic event or a dramatic performance are devoted to the end of physical and mental readiness for the actual game or play, exercises in literature are preparations for the act of reading. The successful athlete must do much "instinctively," moving faster than thought to make the most of his time. The painstaking analysis of "game movies" by football coach and players, the searching criticism of each player's reactions to every situation, the drill to counteract past errors—all these wait upon the test of the game itself. Then ability, experience, and training will reveal their quality. It is similar with reading. Classroom, teacher, the artificially assembled anthology—all these must give place to that final confrontation between individual reader and story. Except that this is not a struggle like an athletic contest, but something more intimate and more rewarding. Ideally, it is a kind of consummation—an embrace.

Everything that follows in this section is intended to help readers toward an enriched experience of fiction. Such special terminology as is presented is presented not because critical terminology is an important object of study. Its acquisition is not an end in itself. We learn terminology in order to analyze more accurately. We learn the process of analysis in order to read better.

# THE SPECTRUM OF FICTION

The fictional spectrum mentioned earlier can be of use in the analysis of fiction, so long as we remember that it is just a metaphor, a handy linguistic tool to be discarded when it becomes more of a hindrance to understanding than a help. In terms of this metaphor, you will remember, it was possible to think of fiction as resembling the spectrum of color to be found in ordinary light, but in the fictional spectrum the ends were not infra-red and ultra-violet but history and fantasy.

Now only a recording angel, taking note of all the deeds of men without distorting or omitting anything, could be called a "pure" historian. And only a kind of deity, creating a world out of his own imagination, could be called a "pure" fantasist. Both ends of the spectrum are invisible to mortal eyes. All history recorded by men becomes fictional. All human fantasy involves some resemblance—however far-fetched—to life. For the student of fiction, then, the *combination* of historical and imaginative materials becomes crucial. This is so because our understanding of fiction depends on our grasping the way in which any particular work is related to life.

Life itself is neither tragic nor comic, neither sentimental nor ironic. It is a sequence of sensations, action, thoughts, and events that we try to tame with language. Every time we say a word about our existence we are engaged in this taming process. An art like fiction is a highly developed method of domestication, in which life is not merely subdued but is asked to perform tricks as well. The tricks, if well done, please us in a very complicated way. In the first place they *please* because their order and intelligibility are a welcome relief from the confusions and pressures of daily existence. In the second place this artificial order may be mastered by us and used to help *make sense of our own experience.* Having read Hemingway, Lawrence or Munro, we will begin to recognize certain situations in our existence as having a family resemblance to situations we have encountered in the pages of Lawrence, Munro or Hemingway.

Literature offers us an "escape" from life, but also provides us with new equipment for our inevitable return. It offers us an "imitation" of life. It helps us understand life, and life helps us understand fiction. We recognize aspects of ourselves and our situations in the more ordered perspectives of fiction, and we also see ideal and debased extremes of existence—both possible and impossible—that are interesting in themselves and interestingly different from our own experience. Fiction interests us because of the complicated ways in which it is at once like and unlike life—which is what we mean when we call it an "imitation." Our experience of fiction, then, involves both pleasure and understanding. We may think of understanding either as a result of the pleasurable experience of fiction or as a necessary preliminary to that pleasure. But no matter how we view the complicated relation between pleasure and understanding, we must recognize that the two are inseparable in the reading of fiction.

Now it happens that education has more to do with understanding than with pleasure. This is regrettable, perhaps, but unavoidable. In our study of fiction, then, we must concentrate on understanding, and hope that plea·· sure will follow because of the connection between the two. Understanding a work of fiction begins with recognizing what kind of fiction it is. This is where the notion of a spectrum becomes useful. We can adjust to the special qualities of any given work more readily if we begin it with a clear and flexible view of fictional possibilities.

Any attempt to give every shade of fiction a place would be cumbersome and misleading. What we want is a rough scale only, with the primary possibilities noted and located in relation to one another. Between the extremes of history and fantasy on such a scale we might locate two major points of reference something like this:

history            realism            romance            fantasy

"Realism" and "romance" are names of the two principal ways that fiction can be related to life. Realism is a matter of perception. The realist presents his impressions of the world of experience. A part of his vocabulary and other technical instruments he shares with the social scientists—especially the psychologists and sociologists. The realistic writer seeks always to give the reader a sense of the way things are, but he feels that a made-up structure of character and event can do better justice to the way things are than any attempt to copy reality directly. The realist's truth is a bit more general and typical than the reporter's fact. It may also be more vivid and memorable.

Romance is a matter of vision. The romancer presents not so much his impressions of the world as his ideas about it. The ordinary world is seen at a greater distance, and its shape and color are deliberately altered by the lenses and filters of philosophy and fantasy. In the world of romance, ideas are allowed to play less encumbered by data. Yet, though "what is" often gives way in romance to "what ought to be" or "might be," *ought* and *might* always imply what *is* by their distortion of it.

Realism and romance are not absolutely different: they share some qualities between them. Realism itself is more romantic than history or journalism. (It is not reality, after all, but *realism*.) And romance is more realistic than fantasy. Many important works of fiction are rich and complicated blends of romance and realism. In fact, it is possible to say that the greatest works are those that successfully blend the realist's perception and the romancer's vision, giving us fictional worlds remarkably close to our sense of the actual, but skillfully shaped so as to make us intensely aware of the meaningful potential of existence.

## FICTIONAL MODES AND PATTERNS

The usefulness of the concept of a fictional spectrum will depend upon our ability to adapt it to various works of fiction. Such adaptation will inevitably require a certain amount of complication. The additional concepts of fictional modes and patterns will be a step in that direction. The spectrum assumed that romance diverges from realism in one way only, along that line which leads from history to fantasy. But it is possible to see this divergence in a more complete way by observing that there are actually two quite different modes of what we have been calling romance.

We may begin by noting that there are two obvious ways that reality can be distorted by fiction, that it can be made to appear better or worse than we actually believe it to be. These distortions are ways of seeing certain aspects of reality more clearly at the expense of others. They can present a "true" picture of either the heroic or the debased side of human existence. A fictional work that presents a world better than the real world is in the mode of romance. A work that presents a fictional world worse than the real world is in the mode of anti-romance, or satire. Because they represent certain potentialities that we recognize as present in our world, both these distorted views depend on our sense of the actual to achieve their effects.

The world of romance emphasizes beauty and order. The world of satire emphasizes ugliness and disorder. The relations between individual characters and these distorted worlds constitute a crucial element of fiction, for these relations determine certain patterns or master plots that affect the shaping of the particular plot of every story. One of these master patterns deals with the kind of character who begins out of harmony with his world and is gradually educated or initiated into a harmonious situation in it. This pattern may operate in either the ordered world of romance or the chaotic world of satire, but the same pattern will have a quite different effect on us when we observe it working out in such different situations. Education that adapts the inept or foolish character for a role in the orderly world presents a comic rise that we observe with approval and pleasure. An initiation into a world of ugliness and disorder, however, amounts to corruption, an ironic rise to what Milton called a "bad eminence"; and we react with disapproval and disgust. (For some reason we find both reactions pleasurable.)

Another master pattern reverses this process of accommodation and presents us with change of another sort: the character who begins in harmony with his world but is finally rejected or destroyed by it. Again, depending on our view of the world presented, we react differently. The heroic figure who falls from his position in the orderly world through some flaw in his character is *tragic*. The lowly creature whose doom is the result of his unfortunate virtue or delicacy is *pathetic*. His fall is, ironically, a kind of rise. (It is traditionally assumed, for complicated reasons, that tragedy is superior to pathos. That assumption is not made here. These patterns are presented as descriptions only, not evaluations.)

The *comic* rise and the *tragic* fall are straightforward because the values of the orderly world represent human virtue raised to a heroic power. The *satiric* rise and *pathetic* fall are ironic because of the inverted values of the debased world. Satire and pathos debase the world in order to criticize it. Tragedy and comedy elevate it to make it acceptable. The two romantic patterns promote resignation. The two satiric patterns promote opposition.

One other pair of fictional patterns may be added to the two already considered. When characters begin and end in a harmonious relation to their respective worlds, the fictional pattern is one not of change but of movement. The characters will have adventures or encounters but will not make any fundamental change in themselves or their relation to the world around them. In this kind of story the hero himself will not be as important as the things he meets. In the romantic world the adventures of the hero will take the form of a quest or voyage that ends with his triumphant return and/or his marriage to the heroine. This pattern moves us to admiration of the wonderful, offering us more of an escape from the actual than a criticism of it. In the satiric world the adventures of a born anti-hero or rogue will parody the quest pattern, often reflecting the chaos of the debased world by becoming endless themselves. Stories of this kind are likely to end when the rogue heads for new territory or another tour of the familiar chaos. This picaresque pattern moves us to recognition and acceptance of the chaotic.

Thus, we have distinguished three pairs of fictional patterns, or six kinds in all: the comic and the satiric rise; the tragic and the pathetic fall; the heroic (romantic) and the anti-heroic (picaresque) quest. But we have done this only with regard to the fantasy worlds of romance and satire, leaving open the question of what happens as these patterns are introduced into a more realistic fictional universe. What happens is, naturally, very complicated indeed. These neat, schematic distinctions fade; the various patterns combine and interact; and values themselves are called into question: rise and fall, success and failure—all become problematic. And this problematic quality is one of the great sources of interest in realistic fiction. Realism uses the familiar patterns of education, expulsion, and quest, but often in such a way as to call into question the great issues of whether the education is beneficial, the expulsion or death justified, the quest worthwhile. Our recognition of the traces of traditional patterns in realistic fiction will be of use, then, mainly in helping us to see what questions are being raised.

Viewed historically, realism developed later than romance and satire; thus it will be useful for us to see realistic fiction as combining the elements of its predecessors in various ways. It would be a mistake, however, to think of realism as superseding the earlier forms just because it uses some of their elements in a new way. In fact, the development of realism has led to a kind of counterflow of realistic elements into the older forms of fiction, reinvigorating them with its problematical qualities. The reader of contemporary fiction in particular will require the flexibility of response that can be attained by careful attention to the workings of traditional patterns in modern fiction. But our discernment of these patterns in any work of fiction will depend on our grasp of the specific elements of that work. We must be alert to the way that *its* characters, *its* plot, and *its* point of view adapt the traditional elements we have been considering.

# PLOT

Fiction is movement. A story is a story because it tells about a process of change. A person's situation changes. Or the person is changed in some way. Or our understanding of the person changes. These are the essential movements of fiction. Learning to read stories involves learning to "see" these movements, to follow them, and to interpret them. In the classroom we often—perhaps too often—put our emphasis on interpretation. But you cannot interpret what you cannot see. Thus, before getting into more complicated questions of interpretation, we want to give the plainest and most direct advice possible about how to perceive and follow fictional plotting. This advice includes things to be done while reading and things to be done after a first reading. A good story may be experienced pleasurably many times, and often a second or third reading will be more satisfying in every respect than the first time through.

1. *Look at beginnings and endings.* Movement in fiction is always movement *from* and *to*. A grasp of the start and the finish should lead to a sense of the direction taken to get *from* start *to* finish.

2. *Isolate the central characters.* The things that happen in fiction happen *to* somebody. A few major characters or even a single central character may be the real focus of our concern. Explore the situation of the major characters (or central character) at the beginning and at the end of the story. The nature of the changes revealed by this exploration should begin to suggest what the story is all about.

3. *Note the stages in all important changes.* If a character has moved from one situation to another, or one state of mind to another, the steps leading to the completed change should be illuminating. Through them the reader can get to "how" and "why." But, as always, "what" comes first.

4. *Note the things working against the movement of the story.* Usually, the interest of a story may be seen as the product of two forces: the things that work to move it toward its end, and those that work against that movement, delaying its completion. If the story moves toward a marriage, for example, consider what things delay the happy occasion. When we see the obstacles clearly, we should have a better sense of the direction of the plot itself.

5. *In a long story or novel, consider the various lines of action.* A complex fiction is likely to involve a number of actions, each with its own central character. The actions may or may not interact. The central character in one line of action may be insignificant in another. By isolating the various lines of action and separating them from one another in our

thoughts, we should gain a better sense of those things that connect them. Often these connections will lead us to thematic relations that cast a direct light on the meaning of the whole fiction.

6. *Note carefully characters or events that seem to make no contribution to plot or movement.* This negative advice is a way of moving from the plot to the meaning of a story. Often elements that are not important in the plot have a special thematic importance.

# CHARACTER

The greatest mistake we can make in dealing with characters in fiction is to insist on their "reality." No character in a book is a real person. Not even if he is in a history book and is called Louis Riel. Characters in fiction are *like* real people. They are also unlike them. In realistic fiction, which includes most novels and short stories, writers have tried to emphasize the lifelikeness of their characters. This means that such writers have tried to surround these characters with details drawn from contemporary life. And they have tried to restrict the events of their narrative to things likely to happen in ordinary life. As a result, the writers of realistic fiction have had to abandon certain kinds of plots that are too fanciful for characters supposed to typify ordinary life. Such writers have tried to draw the reader away from his interest in the movement of fiction and to lead him toward an interest in character for its own sake.

Using the newly developed ideas we have learned to call psychology and sociology, the realistic writers have offered us instruction in human nature. The motivation of characters, the workings of conscience and consciousness, have been made the focal point of most novels and short stories. Perhaps the most extreme movement in this direction has been the development of the stream of consciousness technique, through which fiction writers offer us a version of mental process at the level where impressions of things seen and heard converge with confused thoughts and longings arising from the subconscious mind. In reading this kind of fiction we must check the validity of its characterization against our own sense of the way people behave. The best realists always offer us a shock of recognition through which we share their perception of human behavior.

It may be useful for us to think of character as a function of two impulses: the impulse to individualize and the impulse to typify. Great and memorable characters are the result of a powerful combination of these two impulses. We remember the special, individualizing quirks—habitual patterns of speech, action, or appearance—and we remember the way the character represents something larger than himself. These individualizing touches are part of the storyteller's art. They amuse us or engage our sympathy for the character. The typifying touches are part of a story's meaning. In realistic fiction a character is likely to be representative of a social class, a race, a profession; or he may be a recognizable psychological type, analyzable in terms of this or that "complex" or "syndrome." Or he may be a mixture of social and psychological qualities. In allegorical fiction the characters are more likely to represent philosophical positions. In a story of adventure we will encounter types belonging to the traditional pattern of romantic quest: hero, heroine, villain, monster.

The important thing for a reader to remember about characterization is that there are many varieties—and many combinations of the varieties. An adventure story may have an important realistic or allegorical dimension that will be observable in its characterizations. Characters in realistic novels may also be meaningful as illustrations of philosophical ideas or attitudes. As readers we must be alert and ready to respond to different kinds of characterization on their own terms. A story by Jorge Luis Borges and a story by James Joyce are not likely to yield equally to the same kind of reading. It is the reader's business to adapt himself to whatever fictional world he enters. It is the writer's business to make such adaptation worthwhile.

## MEANING

More often than not, when we talk about a story after our experience of it, we talk about its meaning. In the classroom, "What is the theme of this work?" is a favorite question. This interpretive aspect of literary analysis is the most difficult, we should say, for the reason that in order to attempt it we must not only look carefully at the work itself but also look away from the work toward the world of ideas and experiences. Discovering themes or meanings in a work involves us in making connections between the work and the world outside it. These connections *are* the meaning. The great problem for the interpreter, then, becomes that of the validity of the thematic materials he discovers. Are these ideas *really* there? we want to know. Are they being "read out" of the story or "read into" it? Is any given set of connections between story and world necessarily implied by the story itself or are they arbitrarily imposed by an overly clever interpreter?

A story is always particular, always an instance. How do we properly move from any given instance to a general notion? When is it legitimate to conclude from the presence of a husband and wife in a story (for example) that the story is "about" marriage—that it makes a statement or raises a question about this aspect of human relations? It is impossible to provide a single method that will always work. In fact, as T. S. Eliot once observed, "There is no method except to be very intelligent." But there are certain procedures that will frequently prove helpful, even for the very intelligent.

If we isolate everything that is not just narration, description, or dialogue, some clues are likely to appear in a story. The title of a work is often a striking instance of this kind of material. Sometimes it will point our thinking about the work in a particular direction, or it will emphasize for us the importance of a particular element in the work. Like the title, passages in the writing that are themselves commentary or interpretation are of especial importance for thematic discussion.

Often, however, interpretive passages will not be presented directly by a narrator, with all his authority behind them. They will be spoken instead by a character, and this means that we must assess the reliability of the character before we decide to accept his interpretation as valid. Sometimes the narrator will be characterized to the extent that we must question even *his* reliability. In similar ways narration and description may also be colored by thematic materials. A character or a scene may be presented by the author so as to lead us toward a certain way of thinking about the materials presented. A school called "Dotheboys Hall" or a teacher named "Gradgrind" is presented to us with a name that carries some not too subtle advice as to how we are to understand the presentation.

In less obvious cases, where the author refrains from direct commentary, we must look for subtler clues. Patterns of repetition, ironic juxtaposition, the tone of the narration—devices like these must lead us to the connections between the particular world of the book and the generalized world of ideas. And the more delicate and subtle the story is, the more delicate our interpretation must be. Thus, taking care that our interpretation is rooted in the work itself is only one aspect of the problem.

The other aspect involves the outside knowledge that the interpreter brings to the work. If the story is realistic it will be understood best by those readers whose experience has equipped them with information about the aspect of reality toward which the story points. This does not mean that one must have lived the life of a French-Canadian spinster to understand "The House on the Esplanade." But these stories do depend on the reader's having some understanding of injustice and prejudice, and some sense of the way impersonal social forces can act destructively upon individuals and even whole groups of human beings.

Often a realistic story may point to an aspect of life we have encountered but never understood, and the fiction may help us clarify and order that experience. D. H. Lawrence's story "The Rocking-Horse Winner" can teach us something about personal relations, but Lawrence requires us to bring some experience of family life to that story, for without that it must remain virtually meaningless for the reader. Fantasy and adventure are the principal ingredients of the child's literary diet, for the reason that the child lacks the experience that would make realism meaningful to him, and he lacks the learning necessary for the interpretation of complex allegorical fiction.

Often, however, allegorical fiction takes the form of fantasy or adventure, so that it can be read by the child "at one level" and by the adult on two.

Jonathan Swift's *Gulliver's Travels* has been read in that way for over two centuries. D. H. Lawrence's "The Rocking-Horse Winner" is an exciting story about a boy with a kind of magical power, but it is also a criticism of an excessively materialistic society. Leon Rooke's "A Bolt of White Cloth" may seem to be just a strangely imagined vision of an itinerant merchant who sells magic cloth, and yet it asks to be read as a commentary on the need, in our modern alienating world, for the simple virtues of love. We call such modern allegories "fabulation," and we recognize their ancient ancestors in the simple fable and the homely parable. These two early forms of fiction will be discussed in the next part of this section, and a number of examples of modern fabulation will be found in the anthology of short stories that concludes our study of fiction.

Fiction generates its meanings in innumerable ways, but always in terms of some movement from the particular characters and events of the story to general ideas or human situations suggested by them. The reader comes to an understanding of a fictional work by locating the relevant generalities outside the work and fitting them to the specific instances within the work. The process of understanding can be crudely represented as a sequence something like this:

1. The reader determines whether the work points mainly toward experience itself (i.e., is "realistic"), or toward ideas about experience (i.e., is "allegorical"), or is self-contained.

2. Using the clues in the work, the reader sifts his or her store of general notions drawn from experience or systematic thought to find those appropriate to the specific materials of the story.

3. He or she checks back against the story to test the relevance of the general notions summoned up.

4. He or she seeks for the way the story refines, qualifies, questions, or reinforces those notions.

Something like the process described—performed not a single time but in rapid oscillation into the work and back out—should leave the reader with an understanding of the story and with an enriched store of general notions that he has been led to develop in order to understand. In addition to acquiring new notions, the reader may have refined his attitudes toward his old notions and toward experience itself. Fiction is justified not as a means of conveying ideas but as a means of generating attitudes toward ideas. The meaning of fiction must finally be seen in terms of emotions directed toward impressions of experience or toward ideas about life.

# POINT OF VIEW: PERSPECTIVE AND LANGUAGE

Point of view is a technical term for the way a story is told. A stage play normally has no particular point of view: no one stands between the audience and the action. But if we *read* a play, the stage directions—the words of someone who is not a character—provide the beginnings of a special point of view. A story told all in dialogue would be similarly without a point of view. But as soon as a descriptive phrase is added—such as "he said *cruelly*" or "she *whined viciously*"—we begin to have a special viewpoint. A voice outside the action is reaching us, shaping our attitude toward the events being presented. In our experience of fiction, the attitude we develop toward the events presented, and our understanding of those events, will usually be controlled by the author through his or her technical management of point of view.

For convenience we may divide the subject of fictional viewpoint into two related parts—one dealing with the nature of the storyteller in any given fiction, the other dealing with his language. Obviously the two are not really separate. Certain kinds of narration require certain kinds of language—Duddy Kravitz must talk like Duddy Kravitz—but we may consider them apart for analytical purposes.

The nature of the storyteller is itself far from a simple matter. It involves such things as the extent to which he is himself a character whose personality affects our understanding of his statements, and the extent to which his view of events is limited in time and space or in his ability to see into the minds of various characters. The complications and refinements in fictional point of view can be classified at considerable length. But for the reader the classifications themselves are less important than his awareness of many possibilities. The reader's problem comes down to knowing how to take the things presented to him. This means paying special attention to any limitations in the narrator's viewpoint. If the viewpoint in the story is "partial"—in the sense of incomplete or in the sense of biased—the reader must be ready to compensate in appropriate ways.

The language of narration presents a similar problem for the reader—that is, a problem of adjustment and compensation. Of all the dimensions of language that can be considered, two are especially important for the reader of fiction. Both these dimensions may be seen as ways in which wit—or artistic intelligence—operates through language. One has to do with *tone*, or the way unstated attitudes are conveyed through language. The other has to do with *metaphor*, or the way language can convey the richest and most delicate kinds of understanding by bringing together different images and ideas. Consider first this small passage from Virginia Woolf's novel *Mrs. Dalloway:*

> But Sir William Bradshaw stopped at the door to look at a picture. He looked
> in the corner for the engraver's name. His wife looked too. Sir William
> Bradshaw was so interested in art.

What is the tone of this? Sarcastic, I should say. The paragraph asks us
to be critical of the Bradshaws, but it does not do so directly. It uses the
indirection of verbal irony in which the real meaning is different from the
apparent sense of the words. The last sentence might be read aloud with a
drawn-out emphasis on the word "soooo." How do we know this? How do
we supply the appropriate tone of voice for words that we see on the page
but do not hear prounounced? We pay attention to the clues given. In *Mrs.
Dalloway* the Bradshaws appear in a similar light several times; so that by
this, their last appearance, we have been prepared to regard them unsym-
pathetically. But just on the strength of these four sentences we should be
able to catch the tone.

The banal "Dick and Jane" sentence patterns reinforce the banality of an
approach to art by way of the artist's name. Sir William looks not at the
picture itself but at the signature. The implication of this action is that (a) he
cannot tell who the artist is by considering the work alone, and (b) he
attaches too much importance to the name. His interest in art is fraudulent.
Thus, the statement that he is "so" interested in art conflicts with both the
actions narrated and the tone of the narration. We resolve the conflict by
reading the sentence as *ironic,* meaning the opposite of what it seems to say,
and acquiring thereby a sarcastic tone. The way his wife's behavior mechanically mimics his own adds another satiric dimension to the little scene.
As an earlier passage in the novel has revealed, she has no life of her own
but has been reduced by him to the status of an object:

> Fifteen years ago she had gone under. It was nothing you could put your
> finger on; there had been no scene, no snap; only the slow sinking,
> water-logged, of her will into his.

Thus, the short sentence—"His wife looked too"—picks up the earlier
statement about the "submersion" of her will in his, and reminds us of it
with satiric brevity. Catching the tone of a passage is a matter of paying
attention to clues in sentence pattern and choice of words, and also of
keeping in mind the whole context of the story we are reading. The more
we read a particular author, the better we become at catching her tone—at
perceiving the emotional shades that color the sense of her words.

The second passage quoted from *Mrs. Dalloway* (which comes first in the
book) is also a good introductory example of a writer's use of metaphor. The
expression "gone under" has been used often enough to refer to defeat or
failure—so often, in fact, that it is quite possible to use it without any sense
that it is metaphorical. But actually the notion of drowning—going under
water to the point of death—is present in the expression. A writer who, like

Virginia Woolf, is sensitive to metaphor, can pick up the submerged (!) implications of such an expression and use them to strengthen her meaning: "the slow sinking, water-logged, of her will into his." The metaphor—which implicitly compares her to a floating object and him to the engulfing waters—conveys a sense of how slowly and inexorably this process has taken place, and it generates in us an appropriate feeling of horror at a human being's lingering destruction.

Similar metaphors can be used in different ways. In another part of the same novel, Virginia Woolf employs the metaphor of drowning in a related but distinct context. When Peter Walsh, who wanted to marry Clarissa Dalloway in his youth, returns from India to tell her that he is in love with a young woman whom he intends to marry, Mrs. Dalloway reacts in this way:

> "In love!" she said. That he at his age should be sucked under in his little bow-tie by that monster! And there's no flesh on his neck; his hands are red; and he's six months older than I am! her eye flashed back to her; but in her heart she felt, all the same, he is in love. He has that, she felt; he is in love.

Love is seen here as a monstrous whirlpool that sucks people under. It is dangerous and destructive: one loses one's identity when sucked in by that monster. But it is also heroic to be involved in such dangerous matters. While her "eye" tells Mrs. Dalloway that Peter is unheroic and even ridiculous, with his little bow tie and skinny neck, her "heart" accepts the heroism of this venture. It is absurd to "be sucked under" in a "little bow-tie," but it is also intensely real: "He has that, she felt; he is in love." By comparing these two metaphors of drowning we can see more accurately certain dimensions of Virginia Woolf's view of marriage: it involves a submergence or submission, but a violent conquest by an emotional whirlpool is superior to a "slow sinking, water-logged," of one will into another. We need not go outside the novel to understand this discrimination, but when we learn or remember that in a state of depression Ms. Woolf took her own life by drowning, we get a hint of why this metaphor has such intensity in her hands.

These uses of the metaphor of drowning are actually just brief examples of the way metaphorical possibilities can be exploited in the language of fiction. We present now a fuller example of metaphorical development, for the student to explore. Marcel Proust's multi-volume novel, *The Remembrance of Things Past*, is constructed upon the recovery of the past in the memory of the central character and narrator, Marcel. The process of recollection is described in a famous passage in which, on being given a piece of cake (a *madeleine*) dipped in tea, Marcel suddenly finds that the taste of this morsel has brought to mind much that he had forgotten. In the part of this passage quoted here, Marcel first discusses the persistence of sensations of taste and smell, and then considers the manner in which recollection can emerge from these sensations. The passage should be read with an eye to the metaphors (including similes) operative in it:

> But when from a long-distant past nothing subsists, after the people are dead, after the things are broken and scattered, still, alone, more fragile, but with more vitality, more unsubstantial, more persistent, more faithful, the smell and taste of things remain poised a long time, like souls, ready to remind us, waiting and hoping for their moment, amid the ruins of all the rest; and bear unfaltering, in the tiny and almost impalpable drop of their essence, the vast structure of recollection.
>
> And once I had recognised the taste of the crumb of madeleine soaked in her decoction of lime-flowers which my aunt used to give me (although I did not yet know and must long postpone the discovery of why this memory made me so happy) immediately the old grey house upon the street, where her room was, rose up like the scenery of a theatre, to attach itself to the little pavilion, opening on to the garden, which had been built out behind it for my parents (the isolated panel which until that moment had been all that I could see); and with the house the town, from morning to night and in all weathers, the Square where I was sent before luncheon, the streets along which I used to run errands, the country roads we took when it was fine. And just as the Japanese amuse themselves by filling a porcelain bowl with water and steeping in it little crumbs of paper which until then are without character or form, but, the moment they become wet, stretch themselves and bend, take on colour and distinctive shape, become flowers or houses or people, permanent and recognisable, so in that moment all the flowers in our garden and in M. Swann's park, and the water-lilies on the Vivonne and the good folk of the village and their little dwellings and the parish church and the whole of Combray and of its surroundings, taking their proper shapes and growing solid, sprang into being, town and gardens alike, from my cup of tea.

While it is not my intention to encroach too much on what should be matter for the student's consideration and discussion, I should point out two of the principal metaphors in the passage and offer a suggestion or two about them. The first is the comparison of the smell and taste of things to "souls" in whose "essence" a shape or structure is housed. Proust is here using an ancient Greek notion of the soul as an essence that gives its shape to the body it inhabits. The second, the final metaphor of the passage, takes the form of an extended analogy: *"just as* the Japanese . . . *so* in that moment. . . ."  In examining Proust's use of this particular metaphor, the student might begin by considering the ways in which the metaphor is appropriate to the situation—that is, to both the eating of a cake dipped in tea and the ensuing recovery of the past. Beyond that, he might consider how the Japanese paper metaphor is related to the soul metaphor, and how both of these are related to the theatrical simile ("like the scenery") that links them.

Finally, this consideration of metaphor should lead back to an awareness of tone. Though this passage is a translation from the original French, it captures the tone of the original with high fidelity. How would you describe this tone? How should the passage sound if read aloud? What is the function of the repeated use of "and" in the last sentence (which is the last sentence in a whole section of the book)? How is the tone related to the metaphoric structure and the meaning of the passage? In sum, how do these two most important dimensions of the art of language—tone and metaphor—operate in this passage to control the response of a sensitive and careful reader?

In getting at this question the student might try to paraphrase the passage without its metaphors and tonal qualities. Considering such a paraphrase, he might then ask to what extent the meaning *is* paraphrasable, and to what extent the meaning requires the images and rhythms of the passage itself.

## DESIGN: JUXTAPOSITION AND REPETITION IN THE STRUCTURE OF FICTION

When we look at a painting up close, we can see its details clearly and the texture of its brush strokes, but we cannot really see it as a whole. When we back away, we lose our perception of these minute qualities but gain, with this new perspective, a sense of its design. Similarly, as we read a story, we are involved in its details. And in a story we are involved especially because we experience it as a flow of words in time, bringing us impressions and ideas, moving us emotionally and stirring us intellectually. It is natural to back away from a painting and see it as a whole. But it is less natural and more difficult to get a similar perspective on a book. We can never "see" it all at once. Yet design is an important part of the writer's art, and a sense of design is essential to a full reading experience.

Design in fiction takes many forms, but these may be seen as mainly of two kinds. One has to do with juxtaposition: with what is put next to what in the arrangement of the story. The other has to do with repetition: with images, ideas, or situations that are repeated—often with interesting variations—in the course of the narrative. Juxtaposition is more important in some kinds of fiction than it is in others. If a single action is presented in a simple, chronological arrangement, the order of events is not likely to assume any special significance. But if the action is rearranged in time so that we encounter events out of their chronological sequence—through flashbacks or some other device—the order should be given some attention. We must look for reasons behind this manipulation of chronology by the author. Why has he chosen to place this particular scene from the "past" next to this particular scene in the "present"? Similarly, if we are following two actions in one story, now one and now the other, we should look for reasons why an incident from one sequence should be placed next to a particular incident in the other.

Often we will find interesting parallels: similar situations that amount to a kind of repetition with variation. If character A gets into a situation and takes one kind of action, while character B, in a similar situation, takes a different action, we should be able to compare the two and contrast their distincitve behavior, thus learning more about both. This kind of comparison can also lead us quite properly to generalizations about the meaning of a work.

Significant kinds of repetition occur also in sections of a story that are not placed next to one another. This kind of repetition is an important element of design, and serves to tie separate parts of a story together, enriching and strengthening the whole structure. Structure in fiction is a very complicated notion, because it involves so many factors. We can think of structure in one sense as the elements that shape our experience as we move through the story. In this sense structure is close to plot. We can also think of structure as the elements that enable us to see a meaningful pattern in the whole work. In this sense structure is close to design. For if plot has to do with the dynamics or movement of fiction, design has to do with the statics of fiction—the way we see a whole story after we have stopped moving through it. When we become aware of design in reading, so that one part of a story reminds us of parts we have read earlier, we are actually involved in a movement counter to our progress through from beginning to end. Plot wants to move us along; design wants to delay our movement, to make us pause and "see." The counteraction of these two forces is one of the things which enrich our experience of fiction.

Design is often a matter of the repetition of images or metaphors. In considering the metaphors of drowning in *Mrs. Dalloway,* we have already begun an examination of the way metaphoric design can tie together quite different characters and situations. Now we present a striking example of a rather different use of repetition in the design of a story. This is a case in which two episodes in the life of the same character—separated both by pages of our reading and by weeks in the life of the character—are brought together into powerful contrast by means of repetition with variation.

At the end of the second chapter of James Joyce's novel *A Portrait of the Artist as a Young Man,* the young man of the title, Stephen Dedalus, has been led by the urgings of physical desire into the arms of a prostitute. This is the last paragraph of that chapter:

> With a sudden movement she bowed his head and joined her lips to his and he read the meaning of her movements in her frank uplifted eyes. It was too much for him. He closed his eyes, surrendering himself to her, body and mind, conscious of nothing in the world but the dark pressure of her softly parting lips. They pressed upon his brain as upon his lips as though they were the vehicle of vague speech; and between them he felt an unknown and timid pressure, darker than the swoon of sin, softer than sound or odour.

By the end of the third chapter, Joyce has taken Stephen Dedalus through a period of disgust, remorse, and repentance. In the last paragraphs of the chapter we find Stephen receiving Holy Communion:

He knelt before the altar with his classmates, holding the altar cloth with them over a living rail of hands. His hands were trembling, and his soul trembled as he heard the priest pass with the ciborium from communicant to communicant.

—*Corpus Domini nostri.*

Could it be? He knelt there sinless and timid: and he would hold upon his tongue the host and God would enter his purified body.

—*In vitam eternam. Amen.*

Another life! A life of grace and virtue and happiness! It was true.

—*Corpus Domini nostri.*

The ciborium had come to him.

In the last sentence of the second chapter, Stephen felt the woman's tongue, pressing through her kiss—"an unknown and timid pressure." In the last lines of the third chapter, his tongue receives the body of Our Lord. Could the contrast be made more striking, or more rich in emotional and intellectual implications? Design here is powerfully carrying out Joyce's intention, which is to make us see Stephen poised between sinful and holy extremes, both of which attract him powerfully but neither of which can hold him finally—as the later chapters demonstrate. The focus on tongues in these two episodes is the crucial repeated element that makes the contrast Joyce wishes. And in the context of the whole story, it reminds us that tongues are not only for kissing or receiving the sacrament. They are also instruments of expression. Stephen ultimately must strive to express himself as an artist of languages, using his gift of tongues. In these two episodes, Stephen has been passive, the receiver. Later he will learn to speak out.

What we have been considering is the way that an object—in this case the tongue—can by its use in a fictional design acquire a metaphorical value that points in the direction of meaning. When this happens, the object becomes a symbol. The process of symbolism will be examined further in the commentary on "Clay" below.

# Early Forms of Fiction

## KINDS OF STORY

Long before the modern novel and short story developed, human beings were telling one another stories, acting them and singing them, too. When systems of writing were developed, stories began to be recorded for future times. In this brief section we present some illustrative examples of the ancestors of modern fiction, since modern works of fiction usually offer us a combination of elements that were more distinctly separated in these earlier forms. In order to isolate these elements for inspection, we include, first, three different kinds of story: the myth, the fable (or parable), and the tale; followed by examples of three different types of characterization.

In the study of fiction it is never really possible to separate plot from character. After all, a character *is* what he or she does; and a story must be about *someone*. In the most primitive forms of fiction—myth and legend—it is impossible to say whether the character or the plot is the center of interest, since the character is known specifically for the action that defines his or her mythic or legendary status. In more sophisticated forms, as we shall see later on, character can be presented in terms of description, analysis, and a few illustrative actions, without anything like a complete story being required.

## Myth

Myths are expressions in narrative form of the deepest human concerns. The myths of primitive peoples are closely associated with their religious beliefs and tribal values. The Orpheus myth presented here is based on ancient celebrations of the fertility/sterility cycle that follows the annual march of the seasons. But the myth has already been given a personal touch; it is also the story of any husband mourning the loss of a beloved wife, a story of death and bereavement.

The following two versions of the Orpheus myth are, first, the plainest possible telling (by C. S. Lewis) of the events that compose the myth; and, second, a modern translation of the sophisticated Roman poet Ovid's elaboration of the mythic story. Taken together, the two versions allow us to see how different the "same story" may appear when it is told differently. Some people prefer the plain version; others, the fancy one. Ask yourself which one you prefer. Can you locate any specific parts of Ovid's version that seem to you especially effective or, on the other hand, too elaborate for your taste? Do you find anything lacking in the plain version?

## C. S. LEWIS
1898–1963
### Orpheus

There was a man who sang and played the harp so well that even beasts and trees crowded to hear him. And when his wife died he went down alive into the land of the dead and made music before the King of the Dead till even he had compassion and gave him back his wife, on condition that he led her up out of that land without once looking back to see her until they came out into the light. But when they were nearly out, one moment too soon, the man looked back, and she vanished from him forever.

## OVID
43 B.C.–?A.D.17
### Orpheus

From there Hymen, clad in his saffron robes, was summoned by Orpheus, and made his way across the vast reaches of the sky to the shores of the Cicones. But Orpheus' invitation to the god to attend his marriage was of no avail, for though he was certainly present, he did not bring good luck. His expression was gloomy, and he did not sing his accustomed refrain. Even the torch he carried sputtered and smoked, bringing tears to the eyes, and no amount of tossing could make it burn. The outcome was even worse than the omens foretold: for while the new bride was wandering in the meadows, with her band of naiads, a serpent bit her ankle, and she sank lifeless to the ground. The Thracian poet mourned her loss; when he had wept for her to the full in the upper world, he made so bold as to descend through the gate of Taenarus to the Styx, to try to rouse the sympathy of the shades as well. There he passed among the thin ghosts, the wraiths of the dead, till he reached Persephone and her lord, who holds sway over these dismal regions, the king of the shades. Then, accompanying his words with the music of his lyre, he said:

"Deities of this lower world, to which all we of mortal birth descend, if I have your permission to dispense with rambling insincerities and speak the simple truth, I did not come here to see the dim haunts of Tartarus, nor yet to chain Medusa's monstrous dog, with its three heads and snaky ruff. I came because of my wife, cut off before she reached her prime when she trod on a serpent and it poured its poison into her veins. I wished to be strong enough to endure my grief, and I will not deny that I tried to do so; but Love was too much for me. He is a god well-known in the world above; whether he may be so here too, I do not know, but I imagine that he is familiar to you also and, if there is any truth in the story of that rape of long ago, then you yourselves were brought together by Love. I beg you, by these awful regions, by this boundless chaos, and by the silence of your vast realms, weave again Eurydice's destiny, brought too swiftly to a close. We mortals and all that is ours are fated to fall to you, and after a little time, sooner or later, we hasten to this one abode. We are all on our way here, this is our final home, and yours the most lasting sway over the human race. My wife, like the rest, when she has completed her proper span of years will, in the fullness of time, come within your power. I ask as a gift from you only the enjoyment of her: but if the fates refuse her a reprieve, I have made up my mind that I do not wish to return either. You may exult in my death as well as hers!"

As he sang these words to the music of his lyre, the bloodless ghosts were in tears: Tantalus made no effort to reach the waters that ever shrank away, Ixion's wheel stood still in wonder, the vultures ceased to gnaw Tityus' liver, the daughters of Danaus rested from their pitchers, and Sisyphus sat idle on his rock. Then for the first time, they say, the cheeks of the Furies were wet with tears, for they were overcome by his singing. The king and queen of the underworld could not bear to refuse his pleas. They called Eurydice. She was among the ghosts who had but newly come, and walked slowly because of her injury. Thracian Orpheus received her, but on condition that he must not look back until he had emerged from the valleys of Avernus, or else the gift he had been given would be taken from him.

Up the sloping path, through the mute silence they made their way, up the steep dark track, wrapped in impenetrable gloom, till they had almost reached the surface of the earth. Here, anxious in case his wife's strength be failing and eager to see her, the lover looked behind him, and straightway Eurydice slipped back into the depths. Orpheus stretched out his arms, straining to clasp her and be clasped; but the hapless man touched nothing but yielding air. Eurydice, dying now a second time, uttered no complaint against her husband. What was there to complain of, but that she had been loved? With a last farewell which scarcely reached his ears, she fell back again into the same place from which she had come.

At his wife's second death, Orpheus was completely stunned. He was like that timid fellow who, when he saw three-headed Cerberus led along, chained by the middle one of his three necks, was turned to stone in every limb, and lost his fear only when he lost his original nature too: or like Olenus and hapless Lethaea, once fond lovers, now stones set on well-watered Ida, all because Lethaea was too confident in her beauty, while Olenus sought to take her guilt upon his own shoulders, and wished to be considered the culprit. In vain did the poet long to cross the Styx a second time, and prayed that he might do so. The ferryman thrust him aside. For seven days, unkempt and neglected, he sat on the river bank, without tasting food: grief, anxiety and tears were his nourishment. Then he retired to lofty Rhodope and windswept Haemus, complaining of the cruelty of the gods of Erebus.

## Fable and Parable

The fable and parable are ancient forms of fiction that share two important elements. They are very short, and they are allegorical in nature. That is, they tell, very briefly, a story about one thing while really directing attention to something else. Thus, there are always "two levels" to the fable and parable—a *literal* level and a *figurative* level.

In the fables of Aesop (a Greek of very ancient times) the literal level always involves animals, and the figurative level always points toward some aspect of human social behavior. Aesop invariably concludes his fable with a moral generalization that brings home the figurative point made by the fable. Jesus, on the other hand, usually bases his parables on some ordinary human action. He tells an anecdote about human behavior which is intended to illustrate a moral or spiritual truth at the figurative level. As Jesus explains in the Parable of the Sower, a parable has a hidden meaning that can function as a kind of test. Those who are enlightened will understand. Those who are not, will fail to comprehend. If and when they finally see the light, they will join the enlightened.

These little allegorical fictions are related to such truly primitive forms as the riddle. In ancient rituals, initiation often involved the answering of riddles as a qualification test for admission to the inner circle. The parable works in somewhat the same way. The fable, on the other hand, is a more socialized form: it is related to the primitive proverb—and, indeed, many a "moral" attached to the end of a fable also circulates on its own as a maxim or proverb.

You could, for instance, invent a story to go before such familiar sayings as "Look before you leap" or "He who hesitates is lost." You could also retell the stories of Aesop and Jesus so as to make different points from those made in the originals. You might even suggest alternatives to the morals or spiritual values regularly attached to the fables and parables presented here. Kurt Vonnegut (whose modern fable "Harrison Bergeron" you may read later in this volume) has rather impudently suggested, for instance, that the whole life story of Jesus may be read as a fable leading to a moral like this one: You shouldn't hassle a kid whose family has connections. Could you rewrite or reinterpret the fables or parables presented here, or invent others of your own?

# FABLES OF AESOP
*c.* 620–*c.* 560 B.C.
## The Wolf and the Mastiff

A Wolf, who was almost skin and bone—so well did the dogs of the neighborhood keep guard—met, one moonshiny night, a sleek Mastiff, who was, moreover, as strong as he was fat. Bidding the Dog good-night very humbly, he praised his good looks. "It would be easy for you," replied the Mastiff, "to get as fat as I am if you liked." "What shall I have to do?" asked the Wolf. "Almost nothing," answered the Dog. They trotted off together, but, as they went along, the Wolf noticed a bare spot on the Dog's neck. "What is that mark?" said he. "Oh, the merest trifle," answered the Dog; "the collar which I wear when I am tied up is the cause of it." "Tied up!" exclaimed the Wolf, with a sudden stop; "tied up? Can you not always then run where you please?" "Well, not quite always," said the Mastiff; "but what can that matter?" "It matters much to me, " rejoined the Wolf, and, leaping away, he ran once more to his native forest.

*Moral: Better starve free, than be a fat slave.*

## The Dog in the Manger

A Dog was lying in a Manger full of hay. An Ox, being hungry, came near and was going to eat of the hay. The Dog, getting up and snarling at him, would not let him touch it. "Surly creature," said the Ox, "you cannot eat the hay yourself, and yet you will let no one else have any."

*Moral: People often grudge others what they cannot enjoy themselves.*

## The Fox and the Grapes

A famished Fox saw some clusters of ripe black grapes hanging from a trellised vine. She resorted to all her tricks to get at them, but wearied herself in vain, for she could not reach them. At last she turned away, beguiling herself of her disappointment and saying: "The Grapes are sour, and not ripe as I thought."

*Moral: It is easy to despise what we cannot have.*

# PARABLES OF JESUS
1–34 A.D.

## The Sower and the Seed

And when much people were gathered together, and were come to him out of every city, he spake by a parable: A sower went out to sow his seed: and as he sowed, some fell by the way side; and it was trodden down, and the fowls of the air devoured it. And some fell upon a rock; and as soon as it was sprung up, it withered away, because it lacked moisture. And some fell among thorns; and the thorns sprang up with it, and choked it. And other fell on good ground, and sprang up, and bare fruit an hundredfold. And when he had said these things, he cried, He that hath ears to hear, let him hear. And his disciples asked him, saying, What might this parable be? And he said, Unto you it is given to know the mysteries of the kingdom of God: but to others in parables; that seeing they might not see, and hearing they might not understand. Now the parable is this: The seed is the word of God. Those by the way side are they that hear; then cometh the devil, and taketh away the word out of their hearts, lest they should believe and be saved. They on the rock are they, which, when they hear, receive the word with joy; and these have no root, which for a while believe, and in time of temptation fall away. And that which fell among thorns are they, which, when they have heard, go forth, and are choked with cares and riches and pleasures of this life, and bring no fruit to perfection. But that on the good ground are they, which in an honest and good heart, having heard the word, keep it, and bring forth fruit with patience.

These excerpts are from the King James version of the Gospel according to Luke, chapters 8, 10, and 15.

## The Good Samaritan

And, behold, a certain lawyer stood up, and tempted him, saying, Master, what shall I do to inherit eternal life? He said unto him, What is written in the law? how readest thou? And he answering said, Thou shalt love the Lord thy God with all thy heart, and with all thy soul, and with all thy strength, and with all thy mind; and thy neighbour as thyself. And he said unto him, Thou hast answered right: this do, and thou shalt live. But he, willing to justify himself, said unto Jesus, And who is my neighbour? And Jesus answering said, A certain man went down from Jerusalem to Jericho, and fell among thieves, which stripped him of his raiment, and wounded him, and departed, leaving him half dead. And by chance there came down a certain priest that way: and when he saw him, he passed by on the other side. And likewise a Levite, when he was at the place, came and looked on him, and passed by on the other side. But a certain Samaritan, as he journeyed, came where he was: and when he saw him, he had compassion on him, and went to him, and bound up his wounds, pouring in oil and wine, and set him on his own beast, and brought him to an inn, and took care of him. And on the morrow when he departed, he took out two pence, and gave them to the host, and said unto him, Take care of him; and whatsoever thou spendest more, when I come again, I will repay thee. Which now of these three, thinkest thou, was neighbour unto him that fell among the thieves? And he said, He that shewed mercy on him. Then said Jesus unto him, Go, and do thou likewise.

## Three Parables on Lost and Found

Then drew near unto him all the publicans and sinners for to hear him. And the Pharisees and scribes murmured, saying, This man receiveth sinners, and eateth with them.

And he spake this parable unto them, saying, What man of you, having an hundred sheep, if he lose one of them, doth not leave the ninety and nine in the wilderness, and go after that which is lost, until he find it? And when he hath found it, he layeth it on his shoulders, rejoicing. And when he cometh home, he calleth together his friends and neighbours, saying unto them, Rejoice with me; for I have found my sheep which was lost. I say unto you, that likewise joy shall be in heaven over one sinner that repenteth, more than over ninety and nine just persons, which need no repentance.

Either what woman having ten pieces of silver, if she lose one piece, doth not light a candle, and sweep the house, and seek diligently till she find it? And when she hath found it, she calleth her friends and her neighbours together, saying, Rejoice with me; for I have found the piece which I had lost. Likewise, I say unto you, there is joy in the presence of the angels of God over one sinner that repenteth.

And he said, A certain man had two sons: and the younger of them said to his father, Father, give me the portion of goods that falleth to me. And he divided unto them his living. And not many days after the younger son gathered all together, and took his journey into a far country, and there wasted his substance with riotous living. And when he had spent all, there arose a mighty famine in that land; and he began to be in want. And he went and joined himself to a citizen of that country; and he sent him into his fields to feed swine. And he would fain have filled his belly with the husks that the swine did eat: and no man gave unto him. And when he came to himself, he said, How many hired servants of my father's have bread enough and to spare, and I perish with hunger! I will arise and go to my father, and will say unto him, Father, I have sinned against heaven, and before thee, and am no more worthy to be called thy son: make me as one of thy hired servants. And he arose, and came to his father. But when he was yet a great way off, his father saw him, and had compassion, and ran, and fell on his neck, and kissed him. And the son said unto him, Father, I have sinned against heaven, and in thy sight, and am no more worthy to be called thy son. But the father said to his servants, Bring forth the best robe, and put it on him; and put a ring on his hand, and shoes on his feet: and bring hither the fatted calf, and kill it; and let us eat, and be merry: for this my son was dead, and is alive again; he was lost, and is found. And they began to be merry. Now his elder son was in the field: and as he came and drew nigh to the house, he heard musick and dancing. And he called one of the servants, and asked what these things meant. And he said unto him, Thy brother is come; and thy father hath killed the fatted calf, because he hath received him safe and sound. And he was angry, and would not go in: therefore came his father out, and intreated him. And he answering said to his father, Lo, these many years do I serve thee, neither transgressed I at any time thy commandment: and yet thou never gavest me a kid, that I might make merry with my friends: but as soon as this thy son was come, which hath devoured thy living with harlots, thou hast killed for him the fatted calf. And he said unto him, Son, thou art ever with me, and all that I have is thine. It was meet that we should make merry, and be glad: for this thy brother was dead, and is alive again; and was lost, and is found.

# The Tale

The tale is a complete story that exists for its own sake, because it is "a good story." Even though it may make a point or illustrate an argument, and thus be reduced to a kind of fable or parable, there is always something about its own form that justifies it for us whether it has a moral or not. The tale, of all the ancient forms of story, is also the most deeply rooted in everyday life. The tale turns on points of human behavior, and thus tends to focus on the things that move people most immediately: love, money, and social position.

Of all the early forms of short fiction, the tale is the one most concerned to produce an emotional reaction in an audience. The simplest tales call for either laughter or tears from their audience. More complicated fictions call for both—or something in between that partakes of both. The greatest tales seem always to have an ironic dimension. They exploit the difference between what humans hope for and what they get, or between what they say and what they do, producing either the pathetic irony of frustrated dreams or the ironic comedy of satire and ridicule.

More modern fictions have been frequently based upon the difference between what a character thinks to be true about the world and what is actually the case. Such an ironic gap between appearance and reality may lead to the realistic story of education. The ancient tales seldom if ever took this form. Most of them were in fact simple stories of hopes and wishes fulfilled, like many fairy tales. But the two tales included for examination here are not so simple. Although both have "happy endings," neither is a simple story of wish fulfillment.

The tale began as an oral form, and both examples here preserve some oral quality. The first, taken from the *Satyricon* of the first-century (A.D.) Roman courtier Petronius, is presented as a story that proves a point, but it is also considered a real anecdote, of "something that happened in our own time." In the hands of Petronius the tale reveals its connection to the ancient form of the joke, as well as to the fable and parable. The second, taken from the *Decameron* of Giovanni Boccaccio (a Florentine of the fourteenth century), is also presented as a story told aloud to an audience. And it, too, is said to be a real story about real people. In Boccaccio's case, this "reality" is insisted upon even more, through the device of naming a real person, known to the audience, who is alleged to be the authority for the tale's authenticity.

The hundred stories of the *Decameron* are presented as being told to one another by a group of ladies and gentlemen, to while away the time they must spend in the country avoiding a siege of plague in the city of Florence. The stories were called *novelli*, or novels, by Boccaccio, since they were supposed to be "new" or "novel" stories set in contemporary places, rather than traditional tales retold. Many of them, however, were far from new, but Boccaccio modernized them as best he could, and the very best, like the tale included here, he must have shaped himself.

The word "novel" became the word for short story in all the Romance languages, as opposed to the word "romance," which meant long story. When the English took over these words, they made a different distinction, designating both "novel" and "romance" as terms for long fictions in prose, but thinking of the novel as being closer to ordinary life—more realistic— and romance as extraordinary or fantastic. But the *novello* of Boccaccio is the ancestor not of the modern novel but of the modern short story. It is just a step from "Federigo and Giovanna" to certain stories of Maupassant —but it took humanity almost five centuries to manage that little step.

# PETRONIUS
First century A.D.
## The Widow of Ephesus

Meanwhile Eumolpus, our spokesman in the hour of danger and the author of our present reconciliation, anxious that our gaiety should not be broken, began, in a sudden movement of silence, to gibe at the fickleness of women, the wonderful ease with which they became infatuated, their readiness to abandon their children for their lovers, and so forth. In fact, he declared, no woman was so chaste or faithful that she couldn't be seduced; sooner or later she would fall head over heels in love with some passing stranger. Nor, he added, was he thinking so much of the old tragedies and the classics of love betrayed as of something that had happened in our own time; in fact, if we were willing to hear, he would be delighted to tell the story. All eyes and ears were promptly turned to our narrator, and he began:

Once upon a time there was a certain married woman in the city of Ephesus whose fidelity to her husband was so famous that the women from all the neighboring towns and villages used to troop into Ephesus merely to stare at this prodigy. It happened, however, that her husband one day died. Finding the normal custom of following the cortege with hair unbound and beating her breast in public quite inadequate to express her grief, the lady insisted on following the corpse right into the tomb, an underground vault of the Greek type, and there set herself to guard the body, weeping and wailing night and day. Although in her extremes of grief she was clearly courting death from starvation, her parents were utterly unable to persuade her to leave, and even the magistrates, after one last supreme attempt, were rebuffed and driven away. In short, all Ephesus had gone into mourning for this extraordinary woman, all the more since the lady was now passing her fifth consecutive day without once tasting food. Beside the failing woman sat her devoted maid, sharing her mistress' grief and relighting the lamp whenever it flickered out. The whole city could speak, in fact, of nothing else: here at last, all classes alike agreed, was the one true example of conjugal fidelity and love.

In the meantime, however, the governor of the province gave orders that several thieves should be crucified in a spot close by the vault where the lady was mourning her dead husband's corpse. So, on the following night, the soldier who had been assigned to keep watch on the crosses so that nobody could remove the thieves' bodies for burial suddenly noticed a light blazing among the tombs and heard the sounds of groaning. And prompted by a natural human curiosity to know who or what was making those sounds, he descended into the vault.

But at the sight of a strikingly beautiful woman, he stopped short in terror, thinking he must be seeing some ghostly apparition out of hell. Then, observing the corpse and seeing the tears on the lady's face and the scratches her fingernails had gashed in her cheeks, he realized what it was: a widow, in inconsolable grief. Promptly fetching his little supper back down to the tomb, he implored the lady not to persist in her sorrow or break her heart with useless mourning. All men alike, he reminded her, have the same end; the same resting place awaits us all. He used, in short, all those platitudes we use to comfort the suffering and bring them back to life. His consolations, being unwelcome, only exasperated the widow more; more violently than ever she beat her breast, and tearing out her hair by the roots, scattered it over the dead man's body. Undismayed, the soldier repeated his arguments and pressed her to take some food, until the little maid, quite overcome by the smell of the wine, succumbed and stretched out her hand to her tempter. Then, restored by the food and wine, she began herself to assail her mistress' obstinate refusal.

"How will it help you," she asked the lady, "if you faint from hunger? Why should you bury yourself alive, and go down to death before the Fates have called you? What does Vergil say?—

> Do you suppose the shades and ashes of the dead are by such sorrow touched?

No, begin your life afresh. Shake off these woman's scruples; enjoy the light while you can. Look at that corpse of your poor husband:

doesn't it tell you more eloquently than any words that you should live?"

None of us, of course, really dislikes being told that we must eat, that life is to be lived. And the lady was no exception. Weakened by her long days of fasting, her resistance crumbled at last, and she ate the food the soldier offered her as hungrily as the little maid had eaten earlier.

Well, you know what temptations are normally aroused in a man on a full stomach. So the soldier, mustering all those blandishments by means of which he had persuaded the lady to live, now laid determined siege to her virtue. And chaste though she was, the lady found him singularly attractive and his arguments persuasive. As for the maid, she did all she could to help the soldier's cause, repeating like a refrain the appropriate line of Vergil:

If love is pleasing, lady, yield yourself to love.

To make the matter short, the lady's body soon gave up the struggle; she yielded and our happy warrior enjoyed a total triumph on both counts. That very night their marriage was consummated, and they slept together the second and the third night too, carefully shutting the door of the tomb so that any passing friend or stranger would have thought the lady of famous chastity had at last expired over her dead husband's body.

As you can perhaps imagine, our soldier was a very happy man, utterly delighted with his lady's ample beauty and that special charm that a secret love confers. Every night, as soon as the sun had set, he bought what few provisions his slender pay permitted and smuggled them down to the tomb. One night, however, the parents of one of the crucified thieves, noticing that the watch was being badly kept, took advantage of our hero's absence to remove their son's body and bury it. The next morning, of course, the soldier was horror-struck to discover one of the bodies missing from its cross, and ran to tell his mistress of the horrible punishment which awaited him for neglecting his duty. In the circumstances, he told her, he would not wait to be tried and sentenced, but would punish himself then and there with his own sword. All he asked of her was that she make room for another corpse and allow the same gloomy tomb to enclose husband and lover together.

Our lady's heart, however, was no less tender than pure. "God forbid," she cried, "that I should have to see at one and the same time the dead bodies of the only two men I have ever loved. No, better far, I say, to hang the dead than kill the living." With these words, she gave orders that her husband's body should be taken from its bier and strung up on the empty cross. The soldier followed this good advice, and the next morning the whole city wondered by what miracle the dead man had climbed up on the cross.

# GIOVANNI BOCCACCIO
1313–1375
## Federigo and Giovanna

It is now my turn to speak, dearest ladies, and I shall gladly do so with a tale similar in part to the one before, not only that you may know the power of your beauty over the gentle heart, but because you may learn yourselves to be givers of rewards when fitting, without allowing Fortune always to dispense them, since Fortune most often bestows them, not discreetly but lavishly.

You must know then that Coppo di Borghese Domenichi, who was and perhaps still is one of our fellow citizens, a man of great and revered authority in our days both from his manners and his virtues (far more than from nobility of blood), a most excellent person worthy of eternal fame, and in the fullness of his years delighted often to speak of past matters with his neighbors and other men. And this he could do better and more orderly and with a better memory and more ornate speech than anyone else.

Among other excellent things, he was wont to say that in the past there was in Florence a young man named Federigo, the son of Messer Filippo Alberighi, renowned above all other young gentlemen of Tuscany for his prowess in arms and his courtesy. Now, as most often happens to gentlemen, he fell in love with a lady named Monna Giovanna, in her time held to be one of the gayest and most beautiful women ever known in Florence. To win her love, he went to jousts and tourneys, made and gave feasts, and spent his money without stint. But she, no less chaste than beautiful, cared nothing for the things he did for her nor for him who did them.

Now as Federigo was spending far beyond his means and getting nothing in, as easily happens, his wealth failed and he remained poor with nothing but a little farm, on whose produce he lived very penuriously, and one falcon which was among the best in the world. More in love than ever, but thinking he would never be able to live in the town any more as he desired, he went to Campi where his farm was. There he spent his time hawking, asked nothing of anybody, and patiently endured his poverty.

Now while Federigo was in this extremity it happened one day that Monna Giovanna's husband fell ill, and seeing death come upon him, made his will. He was a very rich man and left his estate to a son who was already growing up. And then, since he had greatly loved Monna Giovanna, he made her his heir in case his son should die without legitimate children; and so died.

Monna Giovanna was now a widow, and as is customary with our women, she went with her son to spend the year in a country house she had near Federigo's farm. Now the boy happened to strike up a friendship with Federigo, and delighted in dogs and hawks. He often saw Federigo's falcon fly, and took such great delight in it that he very much wanted to have it, but did not dare ask for it, since he saw how much Federigo prized it.

While matters were in this state, the boy fell ill. His mother was very much grieved, as he was her only child and she loved him extremely. She spent the day beside him, trying to help him, and often asked him if there was anything he wanted, begging him to say so, for if it were possible to have it, she would try to get it for him. After she had many times made this offer, the boy said:

"Mother, if you can get me Federigo's falcon, I think I should soon be better."

The lady paused a little at this, and began to think what she should do. She knew that Federigo had loved her for a long time, and yet had never had one glance from her, and she said to herself:

"How can I send or go and ask for this falcon, which is, from what I hear, the best that ever flew, and moreover his support in life? How can I be so thoughtless as to take this away from a gentleman who has no other pleasure left in life?"

Although she knew she was certain to have the bird for the asking, she remained in embarrassed thought, not knowing what to say, and did not answer her son. But at length love for her child got the upper hand and she determined that to please him in whatever way it might be, she would not send, but go herself for it and bring it back to him. So she replied:

"Be comforted, my child, and try to get better somehow. I promise you that tomorrow morning I will go for it, and bring it to you."

The child was so delighted that he became a little better that same day. And on the morrow the lady took another woman to accompany her, and as if walking for exercise went to Federigo's cottage, and asked for him. Since it was not the weather for it, he had not been hawking for some days, and was in his garden employed in certain work there. When he heard that Monna Giovanna was asking for him at the door, he was greatly astonished, and ran there happily. When she saw him coming, she got up to greet him with womanly charm, and when Federigo had courteously saluted her, she said:

"How do you do, Federigo? I have come here to make amends for the damage you have suffered through me by loving me more than was needed. And in token of this, I intend to dine today familiarly with you and my companion here."

"Madonna," replied Federigo humbly, "I do not remember ever to have suffered any damage through you, but received so much good that if I was ever worth anything it was owing to your worth and the love I bore it. Your generous visit to me is so precious to me that I could spend again all that I have spent; but you have come to a poor host."

So saying, he modestly took her into his house, and from there to his garden. Since there was nobody else to remain in her company, he said:

"Madonna, since there is nobody else, this good woman, the wife of this workman, will keep you company, while I go to set the table."

Now, although his poverty was extreme, he had never before realised what necessity he had fallen into by his foolish extravagance in spending his wealth. But he repented of it that morning when he could find nothing with which to do honour to the lady, for love of whom he had entertained vast numbers of men in the past. In his anguish he cursed himself and his fortune and ran up and down like a man out of his senses, unable to find money or anything to pawn. The hour was late and his desire to honour the lady extreme, yet he would not apply to anyone else, even to his own workman; when suddenly his eye fell upon his falcon, perched on a bar in the sitting room. Having no one to whom he could appeal, he took the bird, and finding it plump, decided it would be food worthy such a lady. So, without further thought, he wrung its neck, made his little maid servant quickly pluck and prepare it, and put it on a spit to roast. He spread the table with the whitest napery, of which he had some left, and returned to the lady in the garden with a cheerful face, saying that the meal he had been able to prepare for her was ready.

The lady and her companion arose and went to table, and there together with Federigo, who served it with the greatest devotion, they ate the good falcon, not knowing what it was. They left the table and spent some time in cheerful conversation, and the lady, thinking the time had now come to say what she had come for, spoke fairly to Federigo as follows:

"Federigo, when you remember your former life and my chastity, which no doubt you considered harshness and cruelty, I have no doubt that you will be surprised at my presumption when you hear what I have come here for chiefly. But if you had children, through whom you could know the power of parental love, I am certain that you would to some extent excuse me.

"But, as you have no child, I have one, and I cannot escape the common laws of mothers. Compelled by their power, I have come to ask you—against my will, and against all good manners and duty—for a gift, which I know is something especially dear to you, and reasonably so, because I know your straitened fortune has left you no other pleasure, no other recreation, no other consolation. This gift is your falcon, which has so fascinated my child that if I do not take it to him, I am afraid his present illness will grow so much worse that I may lose him. Therefore I beg you, not by the love you bear me (which holds you to nothing), but by your own nobleness, which has shown itself so much greater in all courteous usage than is wont in other men, that you will be pleased to give it me, so that through this gift I may be able to say that I have saved my child's life, and thus be ever under an obligation to you."

When Federigo heard the lady's request and knew that he could not serve her, because he had given her the bird to eat, he began to weep in her presence, for he could not speak a word. The lady at first thought that his grief came from having to part with his good falcon, rather than from anything else, and she was almost on the point of retraction. But she remained firm and waited for Federigo's reply after his lamentation. And he said:

"Madonna, ever since it has pleased God that I should set my love upon you, I have felt that Fortune has been contrary to me in many things, and have grieved for it. But they are all light in comparison with what she has done to me now, and I shall never be at peace with her again when I reflect that you came to my poor house, which you never deigned to visit when it was rich, and asked me for a little gift, and Fortune has so acted that I cannot give it to you. Why this cannot be, I will briefly tell you.

"When I heard that you in your graciousness desired to dine with me and I thought of your excellence and your worthiness, I thought it right and fitting to honor you with the best food I could obtain; so, remembering the falcon you asked me for and its value, I thought it a meal worthy of you, and today you had it roasted on the dish and set forth as best I could. But now I see that you wanted the bird in another form, it is such a grief to me that I cannot serve you that I think I shall never be at peace again."

And after saying this, he showed her the feathers and the feet and the beak of the bird in proof. When the lady heard and saw all this, she first blamed him for having killed such a falcon to make a meal for a woman; and then she inwardly commended his greatness of soul which no poverty could or would be able to abate. But, having lost all hope of obtaining the falcon, and thus perhaps the health of her son, she departed sadly and returned to the child. Now, either from disappointment at not having the falcon or because his sickness must inevitably have led to it, the child died not many days later, to the mother's extreme grief.

Although she spent some time in tears and bitterness, yet, since she had been left very rich and was still young, her brothers often urged her to marry again. She did not want to do so, but as they kept on pressing her, she remembered the worthiness of Federigo and his last act of generosity, in killing such a falcon to do her honor.

"I will gladly submit to marriage when you please," she said to her brothers, "but if you want me to take a husband, I will take no man but Federigo degli Alberighi."

At this her brothers laughed at her, saying:

"Why, what are you talking about, you fool? Why do you want a man who hasn't a penny in the world?"

But she replied:

"Brothers, I know it is as you say, but I would rather have a man who needs money than money which needs a man."

Seeing her determination, the brother, who knew Federigo's good qualities, did as she wanted, and gave her with all her wealth to him, in spite of his poverty. Federigo, finding that he had such a woman, whom he loved so much, with all her wealth to boot, as his wife, was more prudent with his money in the future, and ended his days happily with her.

## TYPES OF CHARACTER

One of the major lines of development in the history of fiction may be traced in the examples presented here. As humans have developed their knowledge of the social and psychological forces conditioning human behavior, they have learned to write about people with greater insight into the motives behind their actions. Of course, the more we have discovered about the extent to which human actions are indeed conditioned by forces beyond our control, the less heroic our fictional characters have become.

If we think of Orpheus, that mythic hero whose story was presented earlier, as the most ancient kind of characterization, we can trace a steady movement in types of character from ancient times to the modern era. First, the mythic figures, who can deal even with the gods face to face; then heroes, whose brave deeds affect the fate of kingdoms; then social types, such as one might encounter on the street or at home; and, finally, individuals who are unique. This is not a simple progression through time: the Germanic and Scandinavian peoples (including the Anglo-Saxons) were still writing a heroic kind of fiction a thousand years after sophisticated Greeks had developed characterizations of different social types. But the general tendency is clear: a movement from heroic figures, defined by their valorous deeds, toward social and psychological portraiture.

When English and French writers of the seventeenth century rediscovered ways of writing about social types and historic individuals, the features of characterization that we recognize in the realistic modern novel and short story were finally achieved, and a recognizably modern fiction could begin its development. As we shall see later on, this development culminated in the fictional achievements of the nineteenth and twentieth centuries.

## Legendary Hero

The Legendary Hero is to be found in the writings of certain historians who emphasize battlefield heroics in their histories. These writers are poised between the world of myth and the world of science, between fantastic invention and sober recording. Their heroes in a sense are actual historical personages, in that people bearing those names may well have lived and even been present at the events described. But the deeds recounted are so colored by myth and epic poetry that no modern historian dares to accept them uncritically.

The first historian represented here is the Greek Herodotus (fifth century B.C.), called the "father of history" because he was the first to call his writing *Histories* (or, more literally, *Inquiries*) and to attempt a kind of historical research—not easy in a world with few written records of the past. He has also been called, by later historians, the "father of lies." Our second historian is the Roman, Livy (first century B.C.) who, like Herodotus, loved a good story whether it was entirely accurate or not.

The tendency to make legendary heroes out of more ordinary or more complicated human beings did not die with the fall of Rome. It was one of the most powerful forces operating in European literature during the Middle Ages, and it is still powerful wherever folk literature flourishes. Historians and folklore scholars have shown how strongly the popular image of figures like Madeleine de Verchères or General Custer was colored by the same heroic pattern you will find in the stories of Leonidas and Horatius. And whenever a modern folk singer tries to cash in on an actual event, the result is likely to be a song about a figure cast in the old heroic mold, made into a "legend in his own time."

## HERODOTUS
Fifth Century B.C.

## Leonidas

The Greeks at Thermopylae had their first warning of the death that was coming with the dawn from the seer Megistias, who read their doom in the victims of sacrifice; deserters, too, came in during the night with news of the Persian flank movement, and lastly, just as day was breaking, the look-out men came running from the hills. In council of war their opinions were divided, some urging that they must not abandon their post, others the opposite. The result was that the army split: some dispersed, contingents returning to their various cities, while others made ready to stand by Leonidas. It is said that Leonidas himself dismissed them, to spare their lives, but thought it unbecoming for the Spartans under his command to desert the post which they had originally come to guard. I myself am inclined to think that he dismissed them when he realized that they had no heart for the fight and were unwilling to take their share of the danger; at the same time honor forbade that he himself should go. And indeed by remaining at his post he left a great name behind him, and Sparta did not lose her prosperity, as might otherwise have happened; for right at the outset of the war the Spartans had been told by the Delphic oracle that either their city must be laid waste by the foreigner or a Spartan king be killed. The prophecy was in hexameter verse and ran as follows:

Hear your fate, O dwellers in Sparta of the wide spaces;
Either your famed, great town must be sacked by Perseus' sons,
Or, if that be not, the whole land of Lacedaemon
Shall mourn the death of a king of the house of Heracles,
For not the strength of lions or of bulls shall hold him,
Strength against strength; for he has the power of Zeus,
And will not be checked till one of these two he has consumed.

I believe it was the thought of this oracle, combined with his wish to lay up for the Spartans a treasure of fame in which no other city should share, that made Leonidas dismiss those troops; I do not think that they deserted, or went off without orders, because of a difference of opinion. Moreover, I am strongly supported in this view by the case of the seer Megistias, who was with the army—an Acarnanian, said to be of the clan of Melampus—who foretold the coming doom from his inspection of the sacrificial victims. He quite plainly received orders from Leonidas to quit Thermopylae, to save him from sharing the army's fate. He refused to go, but he sent his only son, who was serving with the forces.

Thus it was that the confederate troops, by Leonidas' orders, abandoned their posts and left the pass, all except the Thespians and the Thebans who remained with the Spartans. The Thebans were detained by Leonidas as hostages very much against their will; but the Thespians of their own accord refused to desert Leonidas and his men, and stayed, and died with them. They were under the command of Demophilus the son of Diadromes.

In the morning Xerxes poured a libation to the rising sun, and then waited till it was well up before he began to move forward. This was according to Ephilates' instructions, for the way down from the ridge is much shorter and more direct than the long and circuitous ascent. As the Persian army advanced to the assault, the Greeks under Leonidas, knowing that they were going to their deaths, went out into the wider part of the pass much further than they had done before; in the previous days' fighting they had been holding the wall and making sorties from behind it into the narrow neck, but now they fought outside the narrows. Many of the invaders fell; behind them the company commanders plied their whips indiscriminately, driving the men on. Many fell into the sea and were drowned, and still more were trampled to death by their friends. No one could count the number of the dead. The Greeks, who knew that the enemy were on their way round by the mountain track and that death was inevitable, put forth all their strength and fought with fury and desperation. By this time most of their spears were broken, and they were killing Persians with their swords.

In the course of that fight Leonidas fell, having fought most gallantly, and many distinguished Spartans with him—their names I have learned, as those of men who deserve to be remembered; indeed, I have learned the names of all the three hundred. Amongst the Persian dead, too, were many men of high distinction, including two brothers of Xerxes, Habrocomes and Hyperanthes, sons of Darius by Artanes' daughter Phratagune. Artanes, the son of Hystaspes and grandson of Arsames, was Darius' brother; as Phratagune was his only child, his giving her to Darius was equivalent to giving him his entire estate.

There was a bitter struggle over the body of Leonidas; four times the Greeks drove the enemy off, and at last by their valour rescued it. So it went on, until the troops with Ephialtes were close at hand; and then, when the Greeks knew that they had come, the character of the fighting changed. They withdrew again into the narrow neck of the pass, behind the wall, and took up a position in a single compact body—all except the Thebans—on the little hill at the entrance to the pass, where the stone lion in memory of Leonidas stands today. Here they resisted to the last, with their swords, if they had them, and, if not, with their hands and teeth, until the Persians, coming on from the front over the ruins of the wall and closing in from behind, finally overwhelmed them with missile weapons.

Of all the Spartans and Thespians who fought so valiantly the most signal proof of courage was given by the Spartan Dieneces. It is said that before the battle he was told by a native of Trachis that, when the Persians shot their arrows, there were so many of them that they hid the sun. Dieneces, however, quite unmoved by the thought of the strength of the Persian army, merely remarked: "This is pleasant news that the stranger from Trachis brings us: if the Persians hide the sun, we shall have our battle in the shade." He is said to have left on record other sayings, too, of a similar kind, by which he will be remembered. After Dieneces the greatest distinction was won by two Spartan brothers, Alpheus and Maron, the sons of Orsiphantus; and of the Thespians the man to gain the highest glory was a certain Dithyrambus, the son of Harmatides.

The dead were buried where they fell, and with them the men who had been killed before those dismissed by Leonidas left the pass. Over them is this inscription, in honor of the whole force:

Four thousand here from Pelops' land
Against three million once did stand.

The Spartans have a special epitaph; it runs:

Go tell the Spartans, you who read:
We took their orders, and are dead.

For the seer Megistias there is the following:

Here lies Megistias, who died
When the Mede passed Spercheius' tide.
A prophet; yet he scorned to save
Himself, but shared the Spartans' grave.

The columns with the epitaphs inscribed on them were erected in honor of the dead by the Amphictyons—though the epitaph upon the seer Megistias was the work of Simonides, the son of Leoprepes, who put it there for friendship's sake.

# LIVY

59 B.C.–A.D. 17

## Horatius

On the approach of the Etruscan army, the Romans abandoned their farmsteads and moved into the city. Garrisons were posted. In some sections the city walls seemed sufficient protection, in others the barrier of the Tiber. The most vulnerable point was the wooden bridge, and the Etruscans would have crossed it and forced an entrance into the city, had it not been for the courage of one man, Horatius Cocles—that great soldier whom the fortune of Rome gave to be her shield on that day of peril. Horatius was on guard at the bridge when the Janiculum was captured by a sudden attack. The enemy forces came pouring down the hill, while the Roman troops, throwing away their weapons, were behaving more like an undisciplined rabble than a fighting force. Horatius acted promptly: as his routed comrades approached the bridge, he stopped as many as he could catch and compelled them to listen to him. "By God," he cried, "can't you see that if you desert your post escape is hopeless? If you leave the bridge open in your rear, there will soon be more of them in the Palatine and the Capitol than on the Janiculum." Urging them with all the power at his command to destroy the bridge by fire or steel or any means they could muster, he offered to hold up the Etruscan advance, so far as was possible, alone. Proudly he took his stand at the outer end of the bridge; conspicuous amongst the rout of fugitives, sword and shield ready for action, he prepared himself for close combat, one man against an army. The advancing enemy paused in sheer astonishment at such reckless courage. Two other men, Spurius Lartius and Titus Herminius, both aristocrats with a fine military record, were ashamed to leave Horatius alone, and with their support he won through the first few minutes of desperate danger. Soon, however, he forced them to save themselves and leave him; for little was now left of the bridge, and the demolition squads were calling them back before it was too late. Once more Horatius stood alone; with defiance in his eyes he confronted the Etruscan chivalry, challenging one after another to single combat, and mocking them all as tyrants' slaves who, careless of their own liberty, were coming to destroy the liberty of others. For a while they hung back, each waiting for his neighbor to make the first move, until shame at the unequal battle drove them to action, and with a fierce cry they hurled their spears at the solitary figure which barred their way. Horatius caught the missiles on his shield and, resolute as ever, straddled the bridge and held his ground. The Etruscans moved forward, and would have thrust him aside by the sheer weight of numbers, but their advance was suddenly checked by the crash of the falling bridge and the simultaneous shout of triumph from the Roman soldiers who had done their work in time. The Etruscans could only stare in bewilderment as Horatius, with a prayer to Father Tiber to bless him and his sword, plunged fully armed into the water and swam, through the missiles which fell thick about him, safely to the other side where his friends were waiting to receive him. It was a

noble piece of work—legendary, maybe, but destined to be celebrated in story through the years to come.

For such courage the country showed its gratitude. A statue of
Horatius was placed in the Comitium, and he was granted as much
land as he could drive a plough round in a day. In addition to public
honours many individuals marked their admiration of his exploit in
the very hard times which were to follow, by going short themselves
in order to contribute something, whatever they could afford, to his
support.

## The Social Type

The word "characters" was used by the Greek writer Theophrastus (fourth
century B.C.) to describe his collection of sketches of typical Athenian social
types. The sketches that have come down to us are comic and satirical,
apparently designed for recitation at parties and other social functions. They
are fictional in two senses. First, they are slightly exaggerated portraits, and,
second, they represent a "type" of behavior rather than the actions of any
individual person. The exaggeration, in fact, comes from the putting together of so many similar traits as the sketch of a single character. Yet each
trait represents a kind of actual behavior. The types represented by Theophrastus are not social types in the sense of being defined by class or trade;
they are behavioral types who violate the standards of good manners in
some particular way.

In seventeenth-century England there was a great revival of "Character"-
making. The inspiration for this came from the rediscovery of the work of
Theophrastus himself, but the nature of the English Characters changed the
form somewhat. In the two samples presented here (modernized a bit but
quite faithful to the originals), you will find the work of Thomas Overbury
and some friends of his, which sees each Character as linked to a particular
profession or trade. One question to ask in considering these is how the
Overburian Character differs from the Theophrastian. Another is how au-
thentically historical these Characters may be. Are these types confined to
ancient Athens and the England of three centuries ago? Or do they represent human functions sufficiently universal to be recognized today? Would
it be possible to produce contemporary imitations of Theophrastus or Overbury? Overbury's own definition of a Character offers some clues as to how
to proceed:

> . . . it is a picture (real or personal) quaintly drawn in various colors, all of
> them heightened by one shadowing.
>     It is a quick and soft touch of many strings, all shutting up in one musical
> close. It is wit's descant [variation] on any plain song.

# THEOPHRASTUS
Fourth century B.C.
## The Rough

Roughness is coarse conduct, whether in word or act. The rough takes an oath lightly and is insensible to insult and ready to give it. In character he is a sort of town bully, obscene in manner, ready for anything and everything. He is willing, sober and without a mask, to dance the vulgar cordax[1] in comic chorus. At a show he goes around from man to man and collects the pennies, quarrelling with the spectators who present a pass and therefore insist on seeing the performance free.

He is the sort of man to keep a hostelry,[2] or brothel, or to farm the taxes. There is no business he considers beneath him, but he is ready to follow the trade of crier, cook, or gambler. He does not support his mother, is caught at theft and spends more time in jail than in his home. He is the type of man who collects a crowd of bystanders and harangues them in a loud brawling voice; while he is talking, some are going and others coming, without listening to him; to one part of the moving crowd he tells the beginning of his story, to another part a sketch of it, and to another part a mere fragment. He regards a holiday as the fittest time for the full exhibition of his roughness.

He is a great figure in the courts as plaintiff or defendant. Sometimes he excuses himself on oath from trial but later he appears with a bundle of papers in the breast of his cloak, and a file of documents in his hands. He enjoys the role of generalissimo in a band of rowdy loaters; he lends his followers money and on every quarter collects a penny interest per day. He visits the bakeshops, the markets for fresh and pickled fish, collects his tribute from them, and stuffs it in his cheek.

1. Lewd dance
2. Innkeepers were in ill-repute in antiquity.

## The Gross Man

Grossness is such neglect of one's person as gives offense to others. The gross man is one who goes about with an eczema, or white eruption, or diseased nails, and says that these are congenital ailments; for his father had them, and his grandfather, too, and it would be hard to foist an outsider upon their family. He's very apt to have sores on his shins and bruises on his toes, and to neglect these things so that they grow worse.

His armpits are hairy like an animal's for a long distance down his sides; his teeth are black and decayed. As he eats, he blows his nose with his fingers. As he talks, he drools, and has no sooner drunk wine than up it comes. After bathing he uses rancid oil to anoint himself; and when he goes to the marketplace, he wears a thick tunic and a thin outer garment disfigured with spots of dirt.

When his mother goes to consult the soothsayer, he utters words of evil omen; and when people pray and offer sacrifices to the gods he lets the goblet fall, laughing as though he had done something amusing. When there's playing on the flute, he alone of the company claps his hands, singing an accompaniment and upbraiding the musician for stopping so soon.

Often he tries to spit across the table,—only to miss the mark and hit the butler.

# THOMAS OVERBURY
1581–1613
## A Mere Scholar

A mere scholar is an intelligible ass, or a silly fellow in black that speaks sentences more familiarly than sense. The antiquity of his University is his creed, and the excellency of his College (though but for a match of football) is an article of his faith. He speaks Latin better than his mother tongue, and is a stranger in no part of the world but in his own country. He does usually tell great stories of himself to small purpose, for they are commonly ridiculous, be they true or false. His ambition is that he either is, or shall be, a graduate, but if he ever gets a fellowship, he has then no fellow. In spite of all logic he dare swear and maintain it, that a cuckold and a townsman are *termini convertibles*,[1] though his mother's husband be an Alderman. He was never begotten (as it seems) without much wrangling, for his whole life is spent in *Pro & Contra*.[2] His tongue goes always before his wit, like a gentleman-usher, but somewhat faster. That he is a complete gallant in all points, from head to toe, witness his horsemanship and the wearing of his weapons. He is commonly long-winded, able to speak more with ease than any man can hear with patience.

University jests are his universal discourse, and his news the demeanor of the Proctors. His phrase, the apparel of his mind, is made up of diverse shreds like a cushion, and when it goes plainest

1. I.e., that a deceived husband and a man who lives in town are identical concepts.
2. Disputation

has a rash outside and rough linings. The current of his speech is closed with an *"ergo,"* and whatever be the question, the truth is on his side. 'Tis a wrong to his reputation to be ignorant of anything, and yet he knows not that he knows nothing. He gives directions for husbandry from Virgil's *Georgics;* for cattle, from his *Bucolics;* for warlike strategems, from his *Aeneid* or Caesar's *Commentaries.* He orders all things by the book, is skillful in all trades, and thrives in none. He is led more by his ears than his understanding, taking the sound of words for their true sense. His ill luck is not so much in being a fool, as in being put to such pains to express it to the world; for what in others is natural, in him (with much ado) is artificial. His poverty is his happiness, for it makes some men believe that he is none of fortune's favorites. That learning which he has, was in his youth put in backwards like an enema, and 'tis now like ware mislaid in a peddler's pack: he has it, but knows not where it is. In a word, he is the index of a man, and the title page of a scholar, or a Puritan in morality; much in profession, nothing in practice.

## A Jailer

Is a creature mistaken in the making, for he should be a tiger. But the shape being thought too terrible, it is covered, and he wears the mask of a man, yet retains the qualities of his former fierceness, currishness, and ravenousness. Of that red earth of which he was fashioned, this piece was the basest. Of the rubbish which was left and thrown aside came a jailer. Or if God had something else to do than to regard such trash, his descent, then, is more ancient but more ignoble, for he comes of the race of those angels that fell with Lucifer from heaven, whither he never (or hardly ever) returns. Of all his bunches of keys not one has the power to open that door. For a jailer's soul stands not upon those two pillars that support heaven (justice and mercy), it rather sits upon those two footstools of hell, wrong and cruelty. He is a judge's slave, a prisoner is his. In this they differ: he is a voluntary one, the other compelled. He is the hangman of the law with a lame hand, and if the law gave him all his limbs perfect, he would strike those on whom he is glad to fawn. In fighting against a debtor he is a creditor's second, but observes not the laws of the dueller's code, for his play is foul and he takes base advantages. His conscience and his shackles hang up together and are made very nearly of the same metal, saving that the one is harder than the other and has one property greater than iron, for it never melts. He distills money out of the poor's tears, and grows fat by their curses. No man coming to the practical part of hell can discharge it better, because here he does nothing but study the theory of it. His house is a picture of hell, and the original of the Letters Patent of his office stand exemplified there. A chamber of lousy beds is better worth to him than the best acre of corn-land in England. Two things are hard to him (nay, almost impossible), *viz:* to save all his prisoners that none ever escape, and to be saved himself. His ears are stopped to the cries of others, and God's to his. And good reason, for lay the life of a man in one scale, and his fees in another—he will lose the first to find the second. He must look for no mercy (if he desires justice to be done to him) for he shows none; and I think he cares less, because he knows heaven has no need of jailers. The doors there want no porters, for they stand ever open. If it were possible for all creatures in the world to sleep every night, he only and a Tyrant cannot. That blessing is taken from them, and this curse comes instead: to be ever in fear, and ever hated. What estate can be worse?

## The Historical Personage

As we have seen, the earliest historians were interested especially in presenting heroic figures taken from a legendary past. Even in ancient times, however, certain writers made a serious effort to describe the events of their own times and to record the lives of important people for posterity. Little more than a century after Livy wrote, Tacitus, his fellow Roman, produced a brilliant study of Imperial Rome, which, though it is heightened with the colors of rhetoric, is also valuable as documentation of Rome in the time of Nero. We have excerpted from the *Annals* of Tacitus two passages dealing with the life and death of Seneca, a famous playwright and philosopher, who had been Nero's tutor and became his victim. Even in a modern translation we can appreciate how Tacitus used language to create dramatic scenes and to color events and situations with his own harshly ironical view of life.

The other two portraits of individuals presented here are modern English translations from the eighteenth-century French *Memoirs* of Louis de Rouvroy, Duc de Saint-Simon. Less formal than Tacitus, and less dramatic, Saint-Simon offers posterity intimate sketches of life at the court of Louis XIV. The portraits or sketches of Saint-Simon were written roughly a century after the Characters of the Englishman Thomas Overbury. It will be in instructive to compare the work of Overbury and Saint-Simon, to see what distinguishes the memoir-sketch of an actual historical personage from the invented character-type produced by Overbury and his friends. Certainly, in both cases, we find a fierce delight in capturing the unpleasant detail, but the methods are interestingly different. And, taken together, they show very clearly where the realistic characterizations of modern fiction have their roots.

# TACITUS

55(?)–117(?) A.D.

## Seneca

Burrus' death undermined Seneca's influence. Decent standards carried less weight when one of their two advocates was gone. Now Nero listened to more disreputable advisers. These attacked Seneca, first for his wealth, which was enormous and excessive for any subject, they said, and was still increasing; secondly, for the grandeur of his mansions and beauty of his gardens, which outdid even the emperor's; and thirdly, for his alleged bids for popularity. They also charged Seneca with allowing no one to be called eloquent but himself. "He is always writing poetry," they suggested, "now that Nero has become fond of it. He openly disparages the emperor's amusements, underestimates him as a charioteer, and makes fun of his singing. How long must merit at Rome be conferred by Seneca's certificate alone? Surely Nero is a boy no longer! He is a grown man and ought to discharge his tutor. His ancestors will teach him all he needs." Seneca knew of these attacks. People who still had some decency told him of them. Nero increasingly avoided his company.

Seneca, however, requested an audience, and when it was granted, this is what he said. "It is nearly fourteen years, Caesar, since I became associated with your rising fortunes, eight since you became emperor. During that time you have showered on me such distinctions and riches that, if only I could retire to enjoy them unpretentiously, my prosperity would be complete.

"May I quote illustrious precedents drawn from your rank, not mine? Your great-great-grandfather Augustus allowed Marcus Agrippa to withdraw to Mytilene, and allowed Gaius Maecenas the equivalent of retirement at Rome itself. The one his partner in wars, the other the bearer of many anxious burdens at Rome, they were greatly rewarded, for great services. I have had no claim on your generosity, except my learning. Though acquired outside the glare of public life, it has brought me the wonderful recompense and distinction of having assisted in your early education.

"But you have also bestowed on me measureless favours, and boundless wealth. Accordingly, I often ask myself: 'Is it I, son of a provincial non-senator, who am accounted a national leader? Is it my unknown name which has come to glitter among ancient and glorious pedigrees? Where is my old self, that was content with so little? Laying out these fine gardens? Grandly inspecting these estates? Wallowing in my vast revenues?' I can only find one excuse. It was not for me to obstruct your munificence.

"But we have both filled the measure—you, of what an emperor can give his friend, and I, of what a friend may receive from his emperor. Anything more will breed envy. Your greatness is far above all such mortal things. But I am not; so I crave your help. If, in the field or on a journey, I were tired, I should want a stick. In life's journey, I need just such a support.

"For I am old and cannot do the lightest work. I am no longer equal to the burden of my wealth. Order your agents to take over my property and incorporate it in yours. I do not suggest plunging myself into poverty, but giving up the things that are too brilliant and dazzle me. The time now spent on gardens and mansions shall be devoted to the mind. You have abundant strength. For years the supreme power has been familiar to you. We older friends may ask for our rest. This, too, will add to your glory—that you have raised to the heights men content with lower positions."

The substance of Nero's reply was this. "My first debt to you is that I can reply impromptu to your premeditated speech. For you taught me to improvise as well as to make prepared orations. True, my great-great-grandfather Augustus permitted Agrippa and Maecenas to rest after their labors. But he did so when he was old enough to assure them, by his prestige, of everything—of whatever kind—that he had given them. Besides, he certainly deprived neither of the rewards which they had earned from him in the wars and crises of Augustus' youthful years. If my life had been warlike, you too would have fought for me. But you gave what our situation demanded: wisdom, advice, philosophy, to support me as boy and youth. Your gifts to me will endure as long as life itself! My gifts to you, gardens and mansions and revenues, are liable to circumstances.

"They may seem extensive. But many people far less deserving than you have had more. I omit, from shame, to mention ex-slaves who flaunt greater wealth. I am even ashamed that you, my dearest friend, are not the richest of all men. You are still vigorous and fit for State affairs and their rewards. My reign is only beginning. Or do you think you have reached your limit? If so you must rank yourself below Lucius Vitellius, thrice consul, and my generosity below that of Claudius, and my gifts as inferior to the lifelong savings of Lucius Volusius Saturninus (II).

"If youth's slippery paths lead me astray, be at hand to call me back! You equipped my manhood; devote even greater care to guiding it! If you return my gifts and desert your emperor, it is not your unpretentiousness, your retirement, that will be on everyone's lips, but *my* meanness, your dread of *my* brutality. However much your self-denial were praised, no philosopher could becomingly gain credit from an action damaging to his friend's reputation."

Then he clasped and kissed Seneca. Nature and experience had fitted Nero to conceal hatred behind treacherous embraces. Seneca expressed his gratitude (all conversations with autocrats end like that). But he abandoned the customs of his former ascendancy. Terminating his large receptions, he dismissed his entourage, and rarely visited Rome. Ill-health or philosophical studies kept him at home, he said. . . .

Seneca's death followed. It delighted the emperor. Nero had no proof of Seneca's complicity but was glad to use steel against him when poison had failed. The only evidence was a statement of Antonius Natalis that he had been sent to visit the ailing Seneca and complain because Seneca had refused to receive Piso. Natalis had conveyed the message that friends ought to have friendly meetings; and Seneca had answered that frequent meetings and conversations would benefit neither, but that his own welfare depended on Piso's.

A colonel of the Guard, Gavius Silvanus, was ordered to convey this report to Seneca and ask whether he admitted that those were the words of Natalis and himself. Fortuitously or intentionally, Seneca had returned that day from Campania and halted at a villa four miles from Rome. Towards evening the officer arrived. Surrounding the villa with pickets, he delivered the emperor's message to Seneca as he dined with his wife Pompeia Paulina and two friends. Seneca replied as follows: "Natalis was sent to me to protest, on Piso's behalf, because I would not let him visit me. I answered excusing myself on grounds of health and love of quiet. I could have had no reason to value any private person's welfare above my own. Nor am I a flatterer. Nero knows this exceptionally well. He has had more frankness than servility from Seneca!"

The officer reported this to Nero in the presence of Poppaea and Tigellinus, intimate counsellors of the emperor's brutalities. Nero asked if Seneca was preparing for suicide. Gavius Silvanus replied that he had noticed no signs of fear or sadness in his words or features. So Silvanus was ordered to go back and notify him of the death-sentence. According to one source,[1] he did not return by the way he had come but made a detour to visit the commander of the Guard, Faenius Rufus; he showed Faenius the emperor's orders asking if he should obey them; and Faenius, with that ineluctable weakness which they all revealed, told him to obey. For Silvanus was himself one of the conspirators—and now he was adding to the crimes which he had conspired to avenge. But he shirked communicating or witnessing the atrocity. Instead he sent in one of his staff-officers to tell Seneca he must die.

Unperturbed, Seneca asked for his will. But the officer refused.

1. Fabius Rusticus

Then Seneca turned to his friends. "Being forbidden," he said, "to show gratitude for your services, I leave you my one remaining possession, and my best: the pattern of my life. If you remember it, your devoted friendship will be rewarded by a name for virtuous accomplishments." As he talked—and sometimes in sterner and more imperative terms—he checked their tears and sought to revive their courage. Where had their philosophy gone, he asked, and that resolution against impending misfortunes which they had devised over so many years? "Surely nobody was unaware that Nero was cruel!" he added. "After murdering his mother and brother, it only remained for him to kill his teacher and tutor."

These words were evidently intended for public hearing. Then Seneca embraced his wife and, with a tenderness very different from his philosophical imperturbability, entreated her to moderate and set a term to her grief, and take just consolation, in her bereavement, from contemplating his well-spent life. Nevertheless, she insisted on dying with him, and demanded the executioner's stroke. Seneca did not oppose her brave decision. Indeed, loving her wholeheartedly, he was reluctant to leave her for ill-treatment. "Solace in life was what I commended to you," he said. "But you prefer death and glory. I will not grudge your setting so fine an example. We can die with equal fortitude. But yours will be the nobler end."

Then, each with one incision of the blade, he and his wife cut their arms. But Seneca's aged body, lean from austere living, released the blood too slowly. So he also severed the veins in his ankles and behind his knees. Exhausted by severe pain, he was afraid of weakening his wife's endurance by betraying his agony—or of losing his own self-possession at the sight of her sufferings. So he asked her to go into another bedroom. But even in his last moments his eloquence remained. Summoning secretaries, he dictated a dissertation. (It has been published in his own words, so I shall refrain from paraphrasing it.)

Nero did not dislike Paulina personally. In order, therefore, to avoid increasing his ill-repute for cruelty, he ordered her suicide to be averted. So, on instructions from the soldiers, slaves and ex-slaves bandaged her arms and stopped the bleeding. She may have been unconscious. But discreditable versions are always popular, and some took a different view—that as long as she feared there was no appeasing Nero, she coveted the distinction of dying with her husband, but when better prospects appeared life's attractions got the better of her. She lived on for a few years, honorably loyal to her husband's memory, with pallid features and limbs which showed how much vital blood she had lost.

Meanwhile Seneca's death was slow and lingering. Poison, such as was formerly used to execute State criminals at Athens, had long been prepared; and Seneca now entreated his well-tried doctor, who was also an old friend,[1] to supply it. But when it came, Seneca drank it without effect. For his limbs were already cold and numbed against the poison's action. Finally he was placed in a bath of warm water. He sprinkled a little of it on the attendant slaves, commenting that this was his libation to Jupiter. Then he was carried into a vapor-bath, where he suffocated. His cremation was without ceremony, in accordance with his own instructions about his death—written at the height of his wealth and power.

1. Annaeus Statius

# DUC DE SAINT-SIMON
1675–1755

## Two Portraits

*Princesse d'Harcourt*

The Princesse d'Harcourt was a sort of personage whom it is good to make known, in order better to lay bare a Court which did not scruple to receive such as she. She had once been beautiful and gay; but though not old, all her grace and beauty had vanished. The rose had become an ugly thorn. At the time I speak of she was a tall, fat creature, mightily brisk in her movements, with a complexion like milk-porridge; great, ugly, thick lips, and hair like tow, always sticking out and hanging down in disorder, like all the rest of her fittings out. Dirty, slatternly, always intriguing, pretending, enter-prising, quarrelling—always low as the grass or high as the rainbow, according to the person with whom she had to deal: she was a blonde Fury, nay more, a harpy: she had all the effrontery of one, and the deceit and violence; all the avarice and the audacity; moreover, all the gluttony, and all the promptitude to relieve herself from the effects thereof; so that she drove out of their wits those at whose house she dined; was often a victim of her confidence; and was many a time sent to the devil by the servants of M. du Maine and M. *le Grand*. She, however, was never in the least embarrassed, tucked up her petticoats and went her way; then returned, saying she had been unwell. People were accustomed to it.

Whenever money was to be made by scheming and bribery, she was there to make it. At play she always cheated, and if found out stormed and raged; but pocketed what she had won. People looked upon her as they would have looked upon a fishfag, and did not like to commit themselves by quarrelling with her.

Sometimes the Duchesse de Bourgogne used to send about twenty Swiss guards, with drums, into her chamber, who roused her from her first sleep by their horrid din. Another time—and these scenes were always at Marly—they waited until very late for her to go to bed and sleep. She lodged not far from the post of the Captain of the Guards, who was at that time the Maréchal de Lorges. It had snowed very hard, and had frozen. Madame la Duchesse de Bourgogne and her suite gathered snow from the terrace which is on a level with their lodgings; and, in order to be better supplied, waked up to assist them, the Maréchal's people, who did not let them want for ammunition. Then, with a false key, and lights, they gently slipped into the chamber of the Princesse d'Harcourt; and, suddenly drawing the curtains of her bed, pelted her amain with snowballs. The filthy creature, waking up with a start, bruised and stifled in snow, with which even her ears were filled, with disheveled hair, yelling at the top of her voice, and wriggling like an eel, without knowing where to hide, formed a spectacle that diverted people more than half an hour: so that at last the nymph swam in her bed, from which the water flowed everywhere, slushing all the chamber. It was enough to make one die of laughter.

She was very violent with her servants, beat them, and changed them every day. Upon one occasion, she took into her service a strong and robust chambermaid, to whom, from the first day of her arrival, she gave many slaps and boxes on the ear. The chambermaid said nothing, but after submitting to this treatment for five or six days, conferred with the other servants; and one morning, while in her mistress's room, locked the door without being perceived, said something to bring down punishment upon her, and at the first box on the ear she received, flew upon the Princesse d'Harcourt, gave her no end of thumps and slaps, knocked her down, kicked her, mauled her from her head to her feet, and when she was tired of this exercise, left her on the ground, all torn and disheveled, howling like a devil.

### Madame de Montespan

On Wednesday, the 27th of May, 1707, at three o'clock in the morning, Madame de Montespan, aged sixty, died very suddenly at the waters of Bourbon. Her death made much stir, although she had long retired from the Court and from the world, and preserved no trace of the commanding influence she had so long possessed. I need not go back beyond my own experience, and to the time of her reign as mistress of the King. I will simply say, because the anecdote is little known, that her conduct was more the fault of her husband than her own. She warned him as soon as she suspected the King to be in love with her; and told him when there was no longer any doubt upon her mind. She assured him that a great entertainment that the King gave was in her honor. She pressed him, she entreated him in the most eloquent manner, to take her away to his estates of Guyenne, and leave her there until the King had forgotten her or chosen another mistress. It was all to no purpose; and Montespan was not long before repentance seized him; for his torment was that he loved her all his life, and died still in love with her—although he would never consent to see her again after the first scandal.

At last God touched her. Her sin had never been accompanied by forgetfulness; she used often to leave the King to go and pray in her cabinet; nothing could ever make her evade any fast-day or meagre day; her austerity in fasting continued amidst all her dissipation. She gave alms, was esteemed by good people, never gave way to doubt or impiety; but she was imperious, haughty and overbearing, full of mockery, and of all the qualities by which beauty with the power it bestows is naturally accompanied. Being resolved at last to take advantage of an opportunity which had been given her against her will, she put herself in the hands of Père de la Tour, that famous General of the Oratory. From that moment to the time of her death her conversion continued steadily, and her penitence augmented.

Little by little she gave almost all she had to the poor. She worked for them several hours a day, making stout shirts and such things for them. Her table, that she had loved to excess, became the most frugal; her fasts multiplied; she would interrupt her meals in order to go and pray. Her mortifications were continued; her chemises and her sheets were of rough linen, of the hardest and thickest kind, but hidden under others of ordinary kind. She unceasingly wore bracelets, garters, and a girdle, all armed with iron points, which oftentimes inflicted wounds upon her; and her tongue, formerly so dangerous, had also its peculiar penance imposed on it.

She received the last sacrament with an ardent piety. The fear of death which all her life had so continually troubled her, disappeared suddenly, and disturbed her no more. She died, without regret, occupied only with thoughts of eternity, and with a sweetness and tranquility that accompanied all her actions.

Madame de Montespan was bitterly regretted by all the poor of the province, amongst whom she spread an infinity of alms, as well as amongst others of different degree.

# Two Stories and Commentaries

## INTRODUCTION

These two stories are intended to illustrate something of the range and variety of modern short fiction. The commentaries illustrate ways in which the procedures outlined at the beginning of this section may be employed in the reading of specific texts. They may also be thought of as developments or refinements of those procedures. In preparing them I have sought not to put the stories mechanically through every analytical process mentioned earlier, but rather to fit the relevant and useful procedures to the appropriate aspects of each story.

In the anthology section ahead, students and teachers will find an even greater range of fiction for discussion and study. The examples of analysis offered here should suggest approaches that may apply to other stories but should not be allowed to limit the analytical procedures applied to the stories to come. Every discussion of a story must be adapted to that particular story. There is no single analytical method that works for everything. In considering these examples of critical analysis, it might be especially appropriate to ask why each discussion takes the form it does, emphasizing the aspects of the story it does, and whether it leaves out anything important about the story it treats.

## GUY DE MAUPASSANT

1850–1893

### Moonlight

His warlike name well suited the Abbé Marignan.[1] He was a tall thin priest, full of zeal, his soul always exalted but just. All his beliefs were fixed; they never wavered. He sincerely believed that he understood his God, entered into His plans, His wishes, His intentions.

As he strode down the aisle of his little country church, sometimes a question would take shape in his mind: "Now why has God done that?" He would seek the answer stubbornly, putting himself in

1. The Battle of Marignan (1515) was a great and bloody victory for Francis I and France.

Translated by R.S., with valuable advice and criticism from Peter Clothier and the students in his University of Iowa Translation Workshop.

God's place, and he nearly always found it. He was not one of those who murmur with an air of pious humility, "O Lord, your designs are impenetrable!" He would say to himself: "I am the servant of God, I should know His purposes, and if I don't know them I should divine them."

Everything in nature seemed to him created with an absolute and admirable logic. The "why" and the "because" always balanced out. Dawns existed to make waking up a pleasure, days to ripen the crops, rain to water them, evening to prepare for slumber, and the night was dark for sleeping.

The four seasons were perfectly fitted to all the needs of agriculture; and it would never have occurred to the priest to suspect that nature has no intentions at all, and that, on the contrary, every living thing has bowed to the hard necessities of times, climates, and matter itself.

But he hated women, he hated them unconsciously and despised them by instinct. He often repeated the words of Christ: "Woman, what have I to do with thee?" and he added, "You'd think that not even God himself was happy with that particular piece of work." Woman for him was precisely that child twelve times unclean of whom the poet speaks. She was the temptress who had ensnared the first man and who still continued her damnable work—a weak creature, dangerous, curiously disturbing. And even more than her devilish body he hated her loving soul.

He had often felt the yearning affection of women, and, even though he knew himself invulnerable, he was exasperated by this need to love which always trembled in them.

God, in his opinion, had made woman only to tempt man and test him. Thus man should approach her with great care, ever fearful of traps. She was, in fact, even shaped like a trap, with her arms extended and her lips parted for a man.

He was indulgent only of nuns, made inoffensive by their vows; and he treated even them severely, because he felt stirring in the depths of their fettered hearts—those hearts so humbled—that eternal yearning which still sought him out, even though he was a priest.

He felt it in their gaze—more steeped in piety than that of monks—in their religious ecstasy tainted with sex, in their transports of love for Christ, which infuriated him because it was woman's love, fleshly love. He felt it—this wicked yearning—even in their docility, in the sweetness of their voices in talking to him, in their lowered eyes, and in their submissive tears when he rebuffed them rudely.

And he shook out his soutane on leaving the gates of a convent and strode quickly away as though fleeing from danger.

He had a niece who lived with her mother in a little house nearby. He was determined to make her a Sister of Charity.

She was pretty, light-headed, and impish. When the Abbé preached, she laughed; and when he got angry at her she kissed him eagerly, clasping him to her heart while he tried instinctively to escape this embrace which nevertheless gave him a taste of sweet happiness, waking deep within him those paternal impulses which slumber in every man.

Often he spoke to her of God—of his God—while walking beside her along country lanes. She scarcely listened but looked at the sky, the grass, the flowers, with a lively joy which showed in her eyes. Sometimes she leaped to catch some flying thing and brought it back to him, crying: "Look, uncle, how pretty it is. I want to pet it." And this impulse to "pet bugs" or nuzzle lilac blossoms disturbed, annoyed, sickened the priest, who discerned in it that ineradicable yearning which always springs up in the female heart.

Then, it happened that one day the sacristan's wife, who kept house for the Abbé Marignan, cautiously told him that his niece had a lover. The news shocked him terribly and he stopped, choking, with his face full of soap, for he was busy shaving.

When he recovered so that he could think and speak, he shouted: "It is not true, you are lying, Mélanie!"

But the good woman put her hand on her heart: "May the Good Lord strike me dead if I'm lying, M. le Curé. She goes out there every night, I tell you, as soon as your sister's in bed. They meet down by the river. You've only to go and watch there between ten and midnight."

He stopped scraping his chin and started walking up and down violently, as he always did in his hours of solemn meditation. When he tried to finish shaving he cut himself three times between the nose and the ear.

All day he was silenced, swollen with indignation and rage. To his fury as a priest, confronted by love, the invincible, was added the exasperation of a strict father, of a guardian, of a confessor fooled, cheated, tricked by a child. He shared that self-centered feeling of suffocation experienced by parents whose daughter tells them she has—without them and despite them—chosen a husband.

After dinner he tried to read a bit, but he could not get into it. He got more and more exasperated. When ten o'clock struck he took down his walking stick, a formidable oaken cudgel he always used when making his evening rounds to visit the sick. And he smiled as he looked at this big club, whirling it about fiercely in his great countryman's fist. Then, suddenly, he raised it and, gritting his teeth, brought it down on a chair, knocking its splintered back to the floor.

He opened the door to go out, but stopped on the sill, surprised by a splendor of moonlight such as he had rarely seen.

And, endowed as he was with an exalted spirit—such as those poetical dreamers the Fathers of the Church might have had—he was immediately distracted, moved by the glorious and serene beauty of the pale night.

In his little garden, all bathed in soft light, the ordered ranks of his fruit trees traced on the path the shadows of their slender limbs, lightly veiled with foliage, while the giant honeysuckle, clinging to the wall of the house, exhaled a delicious, sugary breath that floated through the calm clear air like a ghostly perfume.

He began to breathe deeply, drinking the air as a drunkard drinks wine, and he took a few slow, dreaming, wondering steps, almost forgetting his niece.

When he reached the open country, he stopped to contemplate the fields all flooded with tender light, bathed in the delicate and languid charm that calm nights have. Incessantly the frogs gave out their short metallic note, and distant nightingales, inspiring dream not thought, blended their unstrung tune—a rapid throbbing music made for kisses—with the enchantment of the moonlight.

The Abbé pressed on, losing heart, though he could not tell why. He felt feeble, suddenly drained; he wanted to sit down, to stay there, to contemplate, to admire God in His handiwork.

Below, following the undulations of the little river, a tall line of poplars wound like a snake. A fine mist, a white vapor which the moonbeams pierced and turned to glowing silver, hung around and above the banks wrapping the whole tortuous watercourse in a sort of delicate and transparent gauze.

The priest halted again, struck to the depths of his soul by an irresistible wave of yearning.

And a doubt, a vague disturbance, came over him. He sensed within himself another of those questions he sometimes posed.

Why had God done this? Since the night is intended for sleep, for unconsciousness, for repose, for oblivion, why make it more charming than the day, sweeter than dawn or evening? And why this slow and seductive moon, which is more poetic than the sun and seems intended by its very delicacy to illumine things too fragile and mysterious for daylight, why should it come to make the shadows so transparent?

Why should the loveliest of songbirds not go to sleep with the others but linger on to sing in the disturbing shade?

Why this half-veil thrown over the world? Why this thrill in the heart, this stirring of the soul, this languor of the flesh?

Why this display of delights that men never see, since they are asleep in their beds? For whom was it intended, this sublime spectacle, this flood of poetry poured from the sky over the earth?

And the Abbé found no answer.

But then, down below, on the edge of the fields, under the vault of trees drenched with glowing mist, two shadows appeared, walking side by side.

The man was taller and held the neck of his lover and sometimes kissed her forehead. Their sudden appearance brought the still countryside to life, and it enfolded the young lovers like a setting divinely made for them. They seemed, the pair, a single being, the being for whom this calm and silent night was intended, and they moved toward the priest like a living answer, the answer to his question, flung back by his Master.

He stood still, his heart pounding in confusion, and he felt as if he were looking at a biblical scene, like the love of Ruth and Boaz, like the accomplishment of the will of God as presented in one of the great scenes of holy scripture. In his head echoed verses of the Song of Songs: the passionate cries, the calls of the flesh, all the ardent poetry of this poem that seethes with passionate yearning.

And he said to himself: "Perhaps God has made such nights to veil the loves of men with ideal beauty."

He recoiled before the couple who kept walking arm in arm. It was certainly his niece. But he asked himself now if he was not on the verge of disobeying God. Must not God permit love since He lavished upon it such visible splendor?

And he fled, distraught, almost ashamed, as if he had entered a temple where he had no right to be.


## A Commentary

This tale is essentially realistic. The events are ordinary, the geography recognizable; the characters can be assigned to a particular time, place, religion, and class. But the imposition of a pattern on this realistic material moves it in the direction of comic romance. It contains no detail presented for its own sake or as documentation of a way of life. Every piece of information given to us contributes to the comic pattern of the plot. We can see this if we consider the central character and what we know about him.

In this uncomplicated tale the Abbé Marignan is not only the central character, he is almost the only character. His niece and the housekeeper, Mélanie, exist only to the extent that they contribute to the Abbé's story.

And the Abbé's story, if we consider its beginning and end, is a story of education, of a change in attitude. The change involves a dramatic shift in the priest's view of women and love.

The story falls naturally into three sections of nearly equal length, of which the first is entirely devoted to the presentation of the Abbé's character. Even here a striking selectivity prevails. We learn about two facets of this character only: one is the nature of the priest's religious belief, presented in the first paragraph and elaborated in the next three; the other is the priest's attitude toward women and love, presented in the fourth paragraph and elaborated in the next five. These two attributes are absolutely vital to the story because his attitude toward love must be changed— this is what the story is "about"—and his religious belief is the lever by means of which the change is accomplished. All the information in the first four paragraphs prepares us for the priest's mental process as we follow it in the closing paragraphs of the story.

If we accept the justice of the priest's comic education, we accept with it a particular view of life. There is a touch of satire as well as comedy in this tale. The priest's view of the workings of the universe is being subjected to an ironic scrutiny that is implicit in the way the story is worked out, and is almost explicit in the point of view from which the story is told. Even the priest's name, Marignan, is touched with irony for those who recognize what it alludes to, since the victor of the Battle of Marignan, Francis I, was defeated and captured in his next campaign, as the Abbé is in *his* little struggle.

Exactly what is our perspective on the events of this little tale? We look into the mind of the Abbé but we do not see things from his point of view. The narrator has his own perspective which is revealed to us by the allusion to the Battle of Marignan and by other means. Consider the fourth paragraph:

> The four seasons were perfectly fitted to all the needs of agriculture; and it would never have occurred to the priest to suspect that nature has no intentions at all, and that, on the contrary, every living thing has bowed to the hard necessities of times, climates, and matter itself.

Up to the semicolon, we are receiving a report on the priest's view—actually a continuation of the preceding paragraph. But after the semicolon, we are being given another view of the world, one which "would never have occurred" to the Abbé himself. This other viewpoint—the narrator's—is in direct opposition to the priest's. Where the Abbé sees God's intentions everywhere, the narrator sees a nature without plan or purpose but still determining the quality of existence. There is a touch of naturalism in this view (a satiric hint of a chaotic, destructive world), which is counteracted by the purposeful pattern of the story itself.

The narrator's views are closest to the surface in this paragraph, but once we are alert to them we can see them operating more subtly elsewhere. In the very first paragraph, for instance, the last two sentences are so emphatic in their repetition that they acquire a somewhat mocking tone. In them we learn not only that the priest's views are "fixed," but also that they "never wavered." We learn that the Abbé entered not only into God's "plans," but also into "His wishes, His intentions." This underlining of the rigidity and presumption of the priest's beliefs prepares us for his comeuppance and at the same time makes us unconsciously begin to wish for it.

Some of the metaphors used by the narrator also enrich the meaning of the work. The last sentence employs a simile which is appropriate and ironic. The priest flees from this love scene "as if he had entered into a temple where he had no right to be." The word "entered" (*pénétré*), of course, echoes ironically the penetration of the priest into God's designs, and is an interesting example of such designed repetition, but this penetration in the last sentence of the story is part of a metaphoric structure—an analogy introduced by the expression "as if." The key word in the simile is "temple." The priest does not flee from a scene that outrages religion in order to take sanctuary in his church. In a comic reversal he flees from a scene which is itself religious, as he now understands it, and where he is the infidel profaning holy ground. This image of the temple, we should also note, has been prepared for by our first sight of the two lovers, under the "vault" of the trees.

Other metaphors operate with comparable subtlety. Consider the priest's first vision of this scene, as he pauses above it and looks at the winding river and the poplars lining its banks. The narrator, in describing the trees, says they "wound like a snake" (*serpentait*). He must have chosen this expression specifically to remind us of a similar idyllic love scene—the Garden of Eden—which also had its serpent. The suggestion is delicate and rich. The priest usually thinks of woman as "the temptress who had ensnared the first man," but in this scene nature itself and finally God seem to have conspired to surround this "sin" with beauty. And the Abbé enters a world in which he is as much an alien as the devil in paradise, though his intention is not to tempt but to prevent a fall.

Although this story is essentially a plot, it is not without design. The early sample of the Abbé's reasoning process is repeated at the end with its startling new conclusion that God "must permit love." And the temple simile in the last sentence reminds us of two related scenes: the Abbé striding so confidently down the aisle of his own church, and the Abbé leaving a convent of nuns with that same stride, after having shaken its contaminating dust of femininity off his soutane. He, who had been too pure to accept these nuns as his spiritual equals, is finally seen as profaning a temple of love. The design and the tone reinforce in various subtle ways the irony of the plot. The strength of this little story lies in the way all these elements cooperate to achieve its comic effect.

# JAMES JOYCE
## 1882–1941
## Clay

The matron had given her leave to go out as soon as the women's tea was over and Maria looked forward to her evening out. The kitchen was spick and span: the cook said you could see yourself in the big copper boilers. The fire was nice and bright and on one of the side-tables were four very big barmbracks. These barmbracks seemed uncut; but if you went closer you would see that they had been cut into long thick even slices and were ready to be handed round at tea. Maria had cut them herself.

Maria was a very, very small person indeed but she had a very long nose and a very long chin. She talked a little through her nose, always soothingly: Yes, my dear, and No, my dear. She was always sent for when the women quarrelled over their tubs and always succeeded in making peace. One day the matron had said to her:

—Maria, you are a veritable peace-maker!

And the sub-matron and two of the Board ladies had heard the compliment. And Ginger Mooney was always saying what she wouldn't do to the dummy who had charge of the irons if it wasn't for Maria. Everyone was so fond of Maria.

The women would have their tea at six o'clock and she would be able to get away before seven. From Ballsbridge to the Pillar, twenty minutes; from the Pillar to Drumcondra, twenty minutes; and twenty minutes to buy the things. She would be there before eight. She took out her purse with the silver clasps and read again the words A Present from Belfast. She was very fond of that purse because Joe had brought it to her five years before when he and Alphy had gone to Belfast on a Whit-Monday trip. In the purse were two half-crowns and some coppers. She would have five shillings clear after paying tram fare. What a nice evening they would have, all the children singing! Only she hoped that Joe wouldn't come in drunk. He was so different when he took any drink.

Often he had wanted her to go and live with them; but she would have felt herself in the way (though Joe's wife was ever so nice with her) and she had become accustomed to the life of the laundry. Joe was a good fellow. She had nursed him and Alphy too; and Joe used to often say:

—Mamma is mamma but Maria is my proper mother.

After the break-up at home the boys had got her that position in the Dublin by Lamplight laundry, and she liked it. She used to have such a bad opinion of Protestants but now she thought they were very nice people, a little quiet and serious, but still very nice people to live with. Then she had her plants in the conservatory and she liked looking after them. She had lovely ferns and wax-plants and, whenever anyone came to visit her, she always gave the visitor one or two slips from her conservatory. There was one thing she didn't like and that was the tracts on the walls; but the matron was such a nice person to deal with, so genteel.

When the cook told her everything was ready she went into the women's room and began to pull the big bell. In a few minutes the women began to come in by twos and threes, wiping their steaming hands in their petticoats and pulling down the sleeves of their blouses over their red steaming arms. They settled down before their huge mugs which the cook and the dummy filled up with hot tea, already mixed with milk and sugar in huge tin cans. Maria superintended the distribution of the barmbrack and saw that every woman got her four slices. There was a great deal of laughing and joking during the meal. Lizzie Fleming said Maria was sure to get the ring and, though Fleming had said that for so many Hallow Eves, Maria had to laugh and say she didn't want any ring or man either; and when she laughed her grey-green eyes sparkled with disappointed shyness and the tip of her nose nearly met the tip of her chin. Then Ginger Mooney lifted up her mug of tea and proposed Maria's health while all the other women clattered with their mugs on the table, and said she was sorry she hadn't a sup of porter to drink it in. And Maria laughed again till the tip of her nose nearly met the tip of her chin and till her minute body nearly shook itself asunder because she knew that Mooney meant well though, of course, she had the notions of a common woman.

But wasn't Maria glad when the women had finished their tea and the cook and the dummy had begun to clear away the tea-things! She went into her little bedroom and, remembering that the next morning was a mass morning, changed the hand of the alarm from seven to six. Then she took off her working skirt and her house-boots and laid her best skirt out on the bed and her tiny dress-boots beside the foot of the bed. She changed her blouse too and, as she stood before the mirror, she thought of how she used to dress for mass on Sunday morning when she was a young girl; and she looked with quaint affection at the diminutive body which she had so often adorned. In spite of its years she found it a nice tidy little body.

When she got outside the streets were shining with rain and she was glad of her old brown raincloak. The tram was full and she had to sit on the little stool at the end of the car, facing all the people, with her toes barely touching the floor. She arranged in her mind all she was going to do and thought how much better it was to be independent and to have your own money in your pocket. She hoped they would have a nice evening. She was sure they would but she could not help thinking what a pity it was Alphy and Joe were not speaking. They were always falling out now but when they were boys together they used to be the best of friends: but such was life.

She got out of her tram at the Pillar and ferreted her way quickly among the crowds. She went into Downes's cake-shop but the shop was so full of people that it was a long time before she could get herself attended to. She bought a dozen of mixed penny cakes, and at last came out of the shop laden with a big bag. Then she thought what else would she buy: she wanted to buy something really nice. They would be sure to have plenty of apples and nuts. It was hard to know what to buy and all she could think of was cake. She decided to buy some plumcake but Downes's plumcake had not enough almond icing on top of it so she went over to a shop in Henry Street. Here she was a long time in suiting herself and the stylish young lady behind the counter, who was evidently a little annoyed by her, asked her was it wedding-cake she wanted to buy. That made Maria blush and smile at the young lady; but the young lady took it all very seriously and finally cut a thick slice of plumcake, parcelled it up and said:

—Two-and-four, please.

She thought she would have to stand in the Drumcondra tram because none of the young men seemed to notice her but an elderly gentleman made room for her. He was a stout gentleman and he wore a brown hard hat; he had a square red face and a greying moustache. Maria thought he was a colonel-looking gentleman and she reflected how much more polite he was than the young men who simply stared straight before them. The gentleman began to chat with her about Hallow Eve and the rainy weather. He supposed the bag was full of good things for the little ones and said it was only right that the youngsters should enjoy themselves while they were young. Maria agreed with him and favoured him with demure nods and hems. He was very nice with her, and when she was getting out at the Canal Bridge she thanked him and bowed, and he bowed to her and raised his hat and smiled agreeably; and while she was going up along the terrace, bending her tiny head under the rain, she thought how easy it was to know a gentleman even when he has a drop taken.

Everybody said: O, here's Maria! when she came to Joe's house. Joe was there, having come home from business, and all the children had their Sunday dresses on. There were two big girls in from next door and games were going on. Maria gave the bag of cakes to the eldest boy, Alphy, to divide and Mrs Donnelly said it was too good of her to bring such a big bag of cakes and made all the children say:

—Thanks, Maria.

But Maria said she had brought something special for papa and mamma, something they would be sure to like, and she began to look for her plumcake. She tried in Downes's bag and then in the pockets of her raincloak and then on the hallstand but nowhere could she find it. Then she asked all the children had any of them eaten it—by mistake, of course—but the children all said no and looked as if they did not like to eat cakes if they were to be accused of stealing. Everybody had a solution for the mystery and Mrs Donnelly said it was plain that Maria had left it behind her in the tram. Maria, remembering how confused the gentleman with the greyish moustache had made her, coloured with shame and vexation and disappointment. At the thought of the failure of her little surprise and of the two and fourpence she had thrown away for nothing she nearly cried outright.

But Joe said it didn't matter and made her sit down by the fire. He was very nice with her. He told her all that went on in his office, repeating for her a smart answer which he had made to the manager. Maria did not understand why Joe laughed so much over the answer he had made but she said that the manager must have been a very overbearing person to deal with. Joe said he wasn't so bad when you knew how to take him, that he was a decent sort so long as you didn't rub him the wrong way. Mrs Donnelly played the piano for the children and they danced and sang. Then the two next-door girls handed round the nuts. Nobody could find the nutcrackers and Joe was nearly getting cross over it and asked how did they expect Maria to crack nuts without a nutcracker. But Maria said she didn't like nuts and that they weren't to bother about her. Then Joe asked would she take a bottle of stout and Mrs Donnelly said there was port wine too in the house if she would prefer that. Maria said she would rather they didn't ask her to take anything: but Joe insisted.

So Maria let him have his way and they sat by the fire talking over old times and Maria thought she would put in a good word for Alphy. But Joe cried that God might strike him stone dead if ever he spoke a word to his brother again and Maria said she was sorry she had mentioned the matter. Mrs Donnelly told her husband it was a great shame for him to speak that way of his own flesh and blood but Joe said that Alphy was no brother of his and there was nearly being a row on the head of it. But Joe said he would not lose his temper on account of the night it was and asked his wife to open some more stout. The two next-door girls had arranged some Hallow Eve games and soon everything was merry again. Maria was delighted to see the children so merry and Joe and his wife in such good spirits. The next-door girls put some saucers on the table and then led the children up to the table, blindfolded. One got the prayer-book and the other three got the water; and when one of the next-door girls got the ring Mrs Donnelly shook her finger at the blushing girl as much as to say: *O, I know all about it!* They insisted then on blindfolding Maria and leading her up to the table to see what she would get; and, while they were putting on the bandage, Maria laughed and laughed again till the top of her nose nearly met the tip of her chin.

They led her up to the table amid laughing and joking and she put her hand out in the air as she was told to do. She moved her hand about here and there in the air and descended on one of the saucers. She a felt a soft wet substance with her fingers and was surprised that nobody spoke or took off her bandage. There was a pause for a few seconds; and then a great deal of scuffling and whispering. Somebody said something about the garden, and at last Mrs Donnelly said something very cross to one of the next-door girls and told her to throw it out at once: that was no play. Maria understood that it was wrong that time and so she had to do it over again: and this time she got the prayer-book .

After that Mrs Donnely played Miss McCloud's Reel for the children and Joe made Maria take a glass of wine. Soon they were all quite merry again and Mrs Donnelly said Maria would enter a convent before the year was out because she had got the prayer-book. Maria had never seen Joe so nice to her as he was that night, so full of pleasant talk and reminiscences. She said they were all very good to her.

At last the children grew tired and sleepy and Joe asked Maria would she not sing some little song before she went, one of the old songs. Mrs Donnelly said *Do, please, Maria!* and so Maria had to get up and stand beside the piano. Mrs Donnelly bade the children be quiet and listen to Maria's song. Then she played the prelude and said *Now, Maria!* and Maria, blushing very much, began to sing in a tiny quavering voice. She sang *I Dreamt that I Dwelt*, and when she came to the second verse she sang again:

I dreamt that I dwelt in marble halls
    With vassals and serfs at my side
And of all who assembled within those walls
    That I was the hope and the pride.
I had riches too great to count, could boast
    Of a high ancestral name,
But I also dreamt, which pleased me most,
    That you loved me still the same.

But no one tried to show her her mistake; and when she had ended her song Joe was very much moved. He said that there was no time like the long ago and no music for him like poor old Balfe, whatever other people might say; and his eyes filled up so much with tears that he could not find what he was looking for and in the end he had to ask his wife to tell him where the corkscrew was.

## A Commentary

I can remember vividly my first encounter with "Clay," and this is partly why I have included it here. I was a freshman in college, and my roommate handed me the anthology they were using in his English class and asked me what I made of one story that baffled him. The story was "Clay," and I remember that it baffled me as well. It was not like the stories I knew and admired—by Poe, O. Henry, Maupassant. It seemed to me to have no plot and to be about nothing in particular. By one of those ironies that operate in life as well as in art, I have since devoted a good deal of my time to studying Joyce. So "Clay" is here both because I know it well and respect it and because I can remember so well what it was like not to understand it.

Like "Moonlight" it is realistic, dealing with ordinary people and situations. It is, in fact, much more concerned to document a kind of reality than to tell a crisp and comic tale. It is more realistic than "Moonlight" and more pathetic than comic in its effect. As the Abbé Marignan's story is amusing, Maria's is sad. And as his story is one of education, hers is one of revelation. He *learns* from his experience; she *is revealed* to us through her experience, but without any increase in awareness on her part. The Abbé's day, after all, is an extraordinary one in his life. Maria's is merely typical. Nothing of great importance happens in it. This is one reason why "Clay" can be so baffling. It is hard to "see" a story in it, since nothing of any consequence happens. Nevertheless, it is a story, and it will respond to a careful consideration of its elements.

To begin with the matter of plot, it is not easy to find one in "Clay," but one is there all the same. Part of it has to do with the Halloween game that Maria and the others play. The game is not explained but there are enough clues in the story for us to reconstruct its method. We first hear of the game while Maria is still at the laundry:

> There was a great deal of laughing and joking during the meal. Lizzie Fleming said Maria was sure to get the ring and, though Fleming had said that for so many Hallow Eves, Maria had to laugh and say she didn't want any ring or any man either; and when she laughed her grey-green eyes sparkled with disappointed shyness and the tip of her nose nearly met the tip of her chin.

Later, Maria plays the game at her brother's house, so that, taken together, the two scenes make the beginning and end of a line of action in the story. And, since the title points directly toward the second of these scenes, we are surely right to consider it important. In this scene we first learn more about the operation of the game, as the children and the next-door girls play it:

> The next-door girls put some saucers on the table and then led the children up to the table, blindfolded. One got the prayer-book and the other three got the water; and when one of the next-door girls got the ring Mrs Donnelly shook her finger at the blushing girl as much as to say: *O, I know all about it!*

And later, after the game has gone "wrong" once and been played over, Maria is gently teased by Mrs Donnelly also:

> ... Mrs Donnelly said Maria would enter a convent before the year was out because she had got the prayer-book.

The game, as we can reconstruct it from the clues in these three passages, is a simple, fortunetelling affair. A blindfolded person chooses among three saucers and the choice indicates the future event. The ring indicates marriage, the prayerbook foretells entering the Church, and the water—we are not told, but I should guess a sea voyage. In reading this story we must continue to perform exactly this kind of reconstruction. Where Maupassant told us everything he wanted us to know in the most direct way possible, Joyce is *in*direct, making us do a good deal of interpretive labor ourselves. But having figured out the game, we must now arrive at an understanding of its significance in Maria's story.

At the beginning of this line of action, Maria was teased by Lizzie Fleming about being "sure to get the ring"—which would mean marriage. At the end she is teased about having got the prayerbook, which means a life of chaste seclusion from the world. But between these moments, Maria has actually made her real selection:

> They led her up to the table amid laughing and joking and she put out her hand out in the air as she was told to do. She moved her hand about here and there in the air and descended on one of the saucers. She felt a soft wet substance with her fingers and was surprised that nobody spoke or took off her bandage. There was a pause for a few seconds; and then a great deal of scuffling and whispering. Somebody said something about the garden, and at last Mrs Donnelly said something very cross to one of the next-door girls and told her to throw it out at once: that was no play. Maria understood that it was wrong that time and so she had to do it over again: and this time she got the prayer-book.

By calling his story "Clay," Joyce made sure that we would be able to understand this episode and its significance, even though Maria herself, from whose point of view we are perceiving things, never realizes what substance she has encountered. The next-door girls have played a trick on her by putting clay into one of the saucers. We know what the ring, prayerbook, and water signify in this game. But clay is not regularly a part of it. Its significance is a matter for our interpretation. Clearly, we will not be far wrong if we associate it with death, realizing that Maria is not likely to marry or enter a convent, but certainly is destined to die and become clay—as are we all. Clay is the substance out of which the first man was made. It conveys the essence of human frailty. Indeed, "that was no play." The clay intrudes on this Halloween scene like a ghostly presence, reminding us of the reality of death and decomposition. Thus, with some scrutiny, this strand of the action becomes both clear and meaningful. But at least one other must be accounted for. If we are to grasp the entire story we must understand such episodes as Maria admiring her body in the mirror, Maria responding to the "colonel-looking gentlemen," Maria losing her plumcake, and Maria mistaking the verses of her song.

Since the mistake in singing is the very last thing in "Clay," we might well consider it for possible revelations. What mistake does Maria make? "When she came to the second verse she sang again: . . . . But no one tried to show her her mistake." She repeats the first verse, which is to say, she leaves out the second. What does she leave out? The omitted second verse goes this way:

> I dreamt that suitors sought my hand,
>   That knights on bended knee,
> And with vows no maiden heart could withstand,
>   They pledged their faith to me.
> And I dreamt that one of that noble band,
>   Came forth my heart to claim,
> But I also dreamt, which charmed me most,
>   That you loved me all the same.

Joyce could have told us what was in this verse that Maria omitted, but he chose simply to leave out what she left out and include the verse she repeated. He made sure we knew she had left something out, but he did not tell us its nature. As with the game, he insists that we do the work of interpretation, which in this case includes research into "I Dreamt that I Dwelt," so that we can supply the missing verse. He continually requires us to share the work of constructing this story in order to understand it. But what does the missing verse tell us? It tells us that Maria unconsciously rebelled at singing "suitors sought my hand"; that a subject such as "vows that no maiden heart could withstand" bothered her enough that she repressed it and "forgot" the second verse. Can we relate this to the other episodes in the story?

When Lizzie Fleming teased her and predicted she would "get the ring,"

Maria "had to laugh and say she didn't want any ring or man either." But she adorns her "nice tidy little body," and she gets so flustered by an inebriated "colonel-looking gentleman" that she misplaces her plumcake while talking to him. In its very different way from Maupassant's, Joyce's story is also about feminine *tendresse*, or "yearning." The missing verse fits into this pattern perfectly. Maria is a reluctant spinster, homely as a Halloween witch, with the tip of her nose nearly meeting the tip of her chin. She feels superior to the "common" women who work in the *Dublin by Lamplight* laundry (a title intended to suggest that the laundresses have been reclaimed from a distinctly "fallen" status), but she takes several drinks when Joe "makes" her. Her appetites are more like those of the "common" women than she would admit. All in all, she is a pathetic figure—a "peacemaker" whose "children" have quarreled so bitterly that she is powerless to reconcile them, and whose suspicions that the children ate her missing plumcake turn them temporarily against her and perhaps lead to the trick by the next-door girls. Clay certainly, common clay.

The title of this story points much more insistently toward its meaning than does the title of "Moonlight" (though the French title, "Clair de lune," is stronger than its English equivalent in suggesting a metaphoric "light" in the sense of mental illumination). Like the title of "Moonlight," the title of "Clay" points toward something that is present in the story, but this clay of Joyce's story is more richly and subtly meaningful than Maupassant's moonlight. The substance, clay, acquires metaphorical suggestions of mortality and common human weakness. The object in the story—that dish of clay in the Halloween game—becomes a symbol for these complicated qualities. And symbolism is the richest and most complicated of metaphorical processes.

Metaphorical possibilities range from the simple and straightforward simile to the symbol. The simile indicates precisely the nature of the comparison it makes with words like "as" and "so." But the symbol opens out from an object or image in the direction of an unspecified meaning. We should add that though the meaning of a symbol is extensive and not precisely limited, this meaning is always directed and controlled in some way. A symbol in a work of fiction, like the clay in this story, cannot be made to "mean" anything we happen to associate with the word "clay." Only those associations both suggested by the substance clay and actually related to Maria's fictional situation belong in our interpretation of the story. Meanings like "mortality" and "common weakness" are traditionally associated with clay in Western tradition, from the Bible on, and clay is used to symbolize similar things in other cultures as well. But we must demonstrate a connection between these traditional meanings and the story in order to establish their appropriateness. Plot, character, and symbol work together to shape our final understanding of the story.

We should note in passing that "Clay" is a special kind of short story in that it is actually part of a sequence of stories put together by its author for a purpose beyond that realizable in any single short piece. In this case, Joyce called his sequence *Dubliners* and meant it as a representation of life in his native city of Dublin. In its proper setting, the meaning of "Clay" chimes with the meaning of the other stories, as Maria's spinsterhood and common humanity are echoed by and contrasted with the situations and qualities of other Dubliners. But even though it gains in resonance when placed in *Dubliners*, "Clay" is sufficient to be of interest by itself.

Aside from its central symbol, Joyce is sparing of metaphor in "Clay." But he is very careful about his control of tone. The tone he establishes at the beginning never falters. How should it be described? "The kitchen was spick and span. . . . The fire was nice and bright." What kind of prose is this? Or consider the short fourth paragraph:

> And the sub-matron and two of the Board ladies had heard the compliment. And Ginger Mooney was always saying what she wouldn't do to the dummy who had charge of the irons if it wasn't for Maria. Everyone was so fond of Maria.

The syntactical pattern of "And . . . and . . . . And" is just one facet of the excessive simplicity of this prose. It is echoed by the quality of cliché that we find in phrases like "spick and span" or "nice and bright." Though Maria herself is not telling this story to us, the narrator is using language closely approaching her own. That is one reason why any striking use of metaphor has been ruled out. Complicated sentences, complex words, and brilliant turns of phrase are all inappropriate here. Joyce said once that he had written *Dubliners* in a style of "scrupulous meanness." That expression is exactly appropriate to the style of "Clay."

In the paragraph we are considering, this linguistic situation is actually somewhat like the one in the first paragraph quoted from *Mrs. Dalloway* in the section on point of view (see p. 114 above): simple, even banal language; and a "so" in the last sentence. Is the tone of the two paragraphs—or of the two "so's"—exactly the same? I think not. The excessive simplicity of Virginia Woolf's prose at this point is entirely devoted to mockery of Sir William Bradshaw. But Joyce's simplicity is in considerable part devoted to giving us Maria's own view of her situation. Her view is undoubtedly limited. Everyone is not *so* fond of her as she would like to think. But we are not really standing off from her and subjecting her to an ironic scrutiny. We are *with* her to some extent here, as well as detached from her. The paragraph in *Mrs. Dalloway* is almost pure satire. The paragraph in "Clay" is pathos mainly, with perhaps a slight admixture of satire.

All the way through the story, Joyce keeps very close not only to a style of language appropriate to Maria, but also to Maria's perspective. Only rarely, as when Maria responds to Lizzie's teasing, does he tell us directly something she could not perceive herself. And there, when he tells us her "eyes sparkled with disappointed shyness," he is giving us an important clue to the "disappointed" quality of her spinsterhood. Usually he avoids such direct transcendence of Maria's perspective and makes us do the work of inference ourselves. Even at the end, when he tells us something that Maria does not know—that she has left out a verse of the song—he does not tell us what is in the verse, for to do so would take us too far from her perspective. By holding us so close to the viewpoint of his central character, Joyce makes it necessary for us to infer a good deal in order to achieve a distance from her sufficient to focus on her with the clarity of detachment. In effect, he makes us see Maria with a double vision, engaged and detached, sympathetic and ironic. And not only Maria but the other characters as well must be seen in this way. Joe, at the close of the story, weeping so much he cannot find the corkscrew to open another bottle, could be seen as a caricature only—another drunken, sentimental, stage Irishman. But Joe's booze-induced sentimentality is also genuine warmth—a mixture of the genuine and the spurious which is, for better or worse, very common in life. Joyce leaves the evaluation to us.

The comic clarity of Maupassant does make, in a sense, a better story. The delicacy and complexity of Joyce make a more realistic one. Fortunately, we do not have to choose between one and the other. We can have both ways, and many more, whenever we want.

Design in "Clay" is mainly a matter of the organization of parts to bear on the revelation of Maria's common disappointments. The central symbol of the clay itself, which is established in the story's climactic episode, is the pivot around which everything else turns. The story appears to us to be almost a plotless, designless "slice of life," and we have to look carefully to note the care of its construction. Actually, design operates much more powerfully in *Dubliners* as a whole than in any single story. The arrangement of stories was very carefully worked out by Joyce to achieve certain juxtapositions, and the stories are designed so that each contains elements that repeat and echo their counterparts in the others. The larger any work is, the more important plot and design become as elements of coherence. A collection of stories, which has no plot, must depend extensively on design for its structural interconnections. But Joyce preferred design to plot, and his longest narratives, *Ulysses* and *Finnegans Wake,* are scantily plotted and elaborately designed.

You will encounter another story from *Dubliners* in the anthology section that follows. At that point, it should be interesting to see how the two stories work together, treating similar thematic materials with a similar technique—yet managing to be entirely unique.

# 2

# THE
# MODERN
# SHORT
# STORY

# Introduction

The short stories in this collection have been arranged in chronological order (by their authors' birth years). They need not, of course, be read in that order, but they are presented that way because the short story as a form has a history, and this history is part of the development of Western Civilization over the past two centuries. A very brief sketch of the author's life is provided before each story, primarily because readers like to know who is talking to them. There is a personal dimension to reading which cannot and need not be suppressed. Our understanding of a story—or any act of communication—is in fact aided by our knowledge of its origin. This is why literary history is a proper part of literary study.

The modern short story emerges with the rise of literary realism in the nineteenth century. This is not to say that the short story is exclusively realistic—for it is not—but that it is a form influenced by realism. The first stories in the following collection (by Hawthorne, Melville, and Gogol) still have something of the moral fable about them: a whiff of the unnatural, a hint of allegory. Poe, of course, who could be very unnatural when he felt like it, is busy here founding a new super-rational kind of fiction: the detective story. After these beginnings come the founders of realism in France and Russia: Flaubert and Tolstoy—but you may notice how Tolstoy uses a fabulous element, the communicative horse, Strider, to generate his realistic perspective.

With Maupassant in France and Chekhov in Russia the form of the realistic short story is perfected: brief, pointed, ironic. At this point in its history the short story becomes truly short, selecting a moment or a few moments out of a life rather than recounting it at length. Chekhov's "Heartache" is an extreme but perfect example of this. The form developed by Maupassant and Chekhov was to become the dominant strain in the short story for the next century. O. Henry, Kipling, Joyce, Lawrence, Mansfield, Porter, Babel, Callaghan, Hemingway, Boyle, Ross, Olsen, Lessing, Updike—they are all children of Maupassant or Chekhov, or both.

But other things are going on, too. The impulse to tell fables never dies, as the stories here by Kipling, Wells, Bowen, Nabokov, Borges, Leacock, Vonnegut, Wiebe and Atwood amply demonstrate. (The same writers, of course, sometimes work in both the fabulous and realistic modes, or mix them together.) In the twentieth century a new impulse becomes identifiable: the desire to write fiction about fiction, or "metafiction." The stories here by Cortázar, Böll, Calvino, Barth, and Rooke are all metafictional, exploring the relationship between fact and fiction, which modern philosophy and science have made problematical.

We often think of "science fiction" as a modern form, too, and many of the writers in this collection have been identified in that way: Wells and Vonnegut regularly, Borges and Calvino occasionally. Their works in this collection, however, show them to be involved with the same possibilities of realism, fabulation, and metafiction as the other writers. The label "science fiction" has more to do with attitude and subject matter than with the formal possibilities of fiction.

All categories, of course, are limited in their usefulness. The blending of realism, fabulation, and metafiction in many of these stories is elaborate and subtle: a challenge to the tact and skill of the reader. To simply assign a work to a particular type or mode of fiction would often be a drastic error. Even the most fantastic of these fictions has something to do with reality and even the most realistic is not to be confused with life itself. In reading the short story we must learn about life and art—both—or risk not learning about either.

# NATHANIEL HAWTHORNE
## 1804–1864

Born in Salem, Massachusetts, at a time when the American revolution was still living history and the Puritan heritage of Salem was very much alive, Hawthorne absorbed its preoccupation with sin and its remembrance of witch-hunts. Four years at Bowdoin College in Maine, a job at the Boston Custom House, and a short stay at Brook Farm—an idealistic commune that ran into practical problems—broadened his horizons, but his best work came from brooding over the past more than from observation of the present. He called his short fiction "tales" and his longer works "romances," insisting that his imagination have a certain latitude in which to work. He knew what he was about. *The Scarlet Letter* (1850) has become a classic of world literature and many of his shorter tales have proved equally durable.

## My Kinsman, Major Molineux

After the kings of Great Britain had assumed the right of appointing the colonial governors, the measures of the latter seldom met with the ready and generous approbation which had been paid to those of their predecessors, under the original charters. The people looked with most jealous scrutiny to the exercise of power which did not emanate from themselves, and they usually rewarded their rulers with slender gratitude for the compliances by which, in softening their instructions from beyond the sea, they had incurred the reprehension of those who gave them. The annals of Massachusetts Bay will inform us, that of six governors in the space of about forty years from the surrender of the old charter, under James II, two were imprisoned by a popular insurrection; a third, as Hutchinson inclines to believe, was driven from the province by the whizzing of a musket-ball; a fourth, in the opinion of the same historian, was hastened to his grave by continual bickerings with the House of Representatives; and the remaining two, as well as their successors, till the Revolution, were favored with few and brief intervals of peaceful sway. The inferior members of the court party, in times of high political excitement, led scarcely a more desirable life. These remarks may serve as a preface to the following adventures, which chanced upon a summer night, not far from a hundred years ago.[1] The reader, in order to avoid a long and dry detail of colonial affairs, is requested to dispense with an account of the train of circumstances that had caused much temporary inflammation of the popular mind.

It was near nine o'clock of a moonlight evening, when a boat crossed the ferry with a single passenger, who had obtained his conveyance at that unusual hour by the promise of an extra fare. While he stood on the landing-place, searching in either pocket for the means of fulfilling his agreement, the ferryman lifted a lantern, by the aid of which, and the newly risen moon, he took a very accurate survey of the stranger's figure. He was a youth of barely eighteen years, evidently country-bred, and now, as it should seem, upon his first visit to town. He was clad in a coarse gray coat, well worn, but in excellent repair; his under garments were durably constructed of

---

1. The time of this tale is the eve of the American revolution. The place is Boston.

leather, and fitted tight to a pair of serviceable and well-shaped limbs; his stockings of blue yarn were the incontrovertible work of a mother or a sister; and on his head was a three-cornered hat, which in its better days had perhaps sheltered the graver brow of the lad's father. Under his left arm was a heavy cudgel formed of an oak sapling, and retaining a part of the hardened root; and his equipment was completed by a wallet, not so abundantly stocked as to incommode the vigorous shoulders on which it hung. Brown, curly hair, well-shaped features, and bright, cheerful eyes were nature's gifts, and worth all that art could have done for his adornment.

The youth, one of whose names was Robin, finally drew from his pocket the half of a little province bill of five shillings, which, in the depreciation in that currency, did but satisfy the ferryman's demand, with the surplus of a sexangular piece of parchment, valued at three pence. He then walked forward into the town, with as light a step as if his day's journey had not already exceeded thirty miles, and with as eager an eye as if he were entering London city, instead of the little metropolis of a New England colony. Before Robin had proceeded far, however, it occurred to him that he knew not whither to direct his steps; so he paused, and looked up and down the narrow street, scrutinizing the small and mean wooden buildings that were scattered on either side.

"This low hovel cannot be my kinsman's dwelling," thought he, "nor yonder old house, where the moonlight enters at the broken casement; and truly I see none hereabouts that might be worthy of him. It would have been wise to inquire my way of the ferryman, and doubtless he would have gone with me, and earned a shilling from the Major for his pains. But the next man I meet will do as well."

He resumed his walk, and was glad to perceive that the street now became wider, and the houses more respectable in their appearance. He soon discerned a figure moving on moderately in advance, and hastened his steps to overtake it. As Robin drew nigh, he saw that the passenger was a man in years, with a full periwig of gray hair, a wide-skirted coat of dark cloth, and silk stockings rolled above his knees. He carried a long and polished cane, which he struck down perpendicularly before him at every step; and at regular intervals he uttered two successive hems, of a peculiarly solemn and sepulchral intonation. Having made these observations, Robin laid hold of the skirt of the old man's coat, just when the light from the open door and windows of a barber's shop fell upon both their figures.

"Good evening to you, honored sir," said he, making a low bow, and still retaining his hold of the skirt. "I pray you tell me whereabouts is the dwelling of my kinsman, Major Molineux."

The youth's question was uttered very loudly; and one of the barbers, whose razor was descending on a well-soaped chin, and another who was dressing a Ramillies wig, left their occupations, and came to the door. The citizen, in the mean time, turned a long-favored countenance upon Robin, and answered him in a tone of excessive anger and annoyance. His two sepulchral hems, however, broke into the very centre of his rebuke, with most singular effect, like a thought of the cold grave obtruding among wrathful passions.

"Let go my garment, fellow! I tell you, I know not the man you speak of. What! I have authority, I have—hem, hem—authority; and if this be the respect you show for your betters, your feet shall be brought acquainted with the stocks[2] by daylight, tomorrow morning!"

Robin released the old man's skirt, and hastened away, pursued by an ill-mannered roar of laughter from the barber's shop. He was at first considerably surprised by the result of his question, but, being a shrewd youth, soon thought himself able to account for the mystery.

"This is some country representative," was his conclusion, "who has never seen the inside of my kinsman's door, and lacks the breeding to answer a stranger civilly. The man is old, or verily—I might be tempted to turn back and smite him on the nose. Ah, Robin, Robin! even the barber's boys laugh at you for choosing such a guide! You will be wiser in time, friend Robin."

He now became entangled in a succession of crooked and narrow streets, which crossed each other, and meandered at no great distance from the water-side. The smell of tar was obvious to his nostrils, the masts of vessels pierced the moonlight above the tops of the buildings, and the numerous signs, which Robin paused to read, informed him that he was near the centre of business. But the streets were empty, the shops were closed, and lights were visible only in the second stories of a few dwelling-houses. At length, on the corner of a narrow lane, through which he was passing, he beheld the broad countenance of a British hero swinging before the door of an inn, whence proceeded the voices of many guests. The casement of one of the lower windows was thrown back, and a very thin curtain permitted Robin to distinguish a party at supper, round a well-furnished table. The fragrance of the good cheer steamed forth into the outer air, and the youth could not fail to recollect that the last remnant of his travelling stock of provision had yielded to his morning appetite, and that noon had found and left him dinnerless.

"Oh, that a parchment three-penny might give me a right to sit down at yonder table!" said Robin, with a sigh. "But the Major

2. The stocks were an outdoor engine of imprisonment.

will make me welcome to the best of his victuals; so I will even step
boldly in, and inquire my way to his dwelling."

He entered the tavern, and was guided by the murmur of voices
and the fumes of tobacco to the public-room. It was a long and low
apartment, with oaken walls, grown dark in the continual smoke,
and a floor which was thickly sanded, but of no immaculate purity.
A number of persons—the larger part of whom appeared to be mar-
iners, or in some way connected with the sea—occupied the wooden
benches, or leather-bottomed chairs, conversing on various matters,
and occasionally lending their attention to some topic of general
interest. Three or four little groups were draining as many bowls of
punch, which the West India trade had long since made a familiar
drink in the colony. Others, who had the appearance of men who
lived by regular and laborious handicraft, preferred the insulated
bliss of an unshared potation, and became more taciturn under its
influence. Nearly all, in short, evinced a predilection for the Good
Creature in some of its various shapes, for this is a vice to which, as
Fast Day sermons of a hundred years ago will testify, we have a long
hereditary claim. The only guests to whom Robin's sympathies inclined him were two or three sheepish countrymen, who were using
the inn somewhat after the fashion of a Turkish caravansary; they
had gotten themselves into the darkest corner of the room, and
heedless of the Nicotian atmosphere, were supping on the bread of
their own ovens, and the bacon cured in their own chimney-smoke.
But though Robin felt a sort of brotherhood with these strangers, his
eyes were attracted from them to a person who stood near the door,
holding whispered conversation with a group of ill-dressed associates. His features were separately striking almost to grotesque-
ness, and the whole face left a deep impression on the memory. The
forehead bulged out into a double prominence, with a vale between;
the nose came boldly forth in an irregular curve, and its bridge was
of more than a finger's breadth; the eyebrows were deep and
shaggy, and the eyes glowed beneath them like fire in a cave.

While Robin deliberated of whom to inquire respecting his kinsman's dwelling, he was accosted by the innkeeper, a little man in a
stained white apron, who had come to pay his professional welcome
to the stranger. Being in the second generation from a French Prot-
estant, he seemed to have inherited the courtesy of his parent nation; but no variety of circumstances was ever known to change his
voice from the one shrill note in which he now addressed Robin.

"From the country, I presume, sir?" said he, with a profound
bow. "Beg leave to congratulate you on your arrival, and trust you
intend a long stay with us. Fine town here, sir, beautiful buildings,
and much that may interest a stranger. May I hope for the honor of
your commands in respect to supper?"

"The man sees a family likeness! the rogue has guessed that I am related to the Major!" thought Robin, who had hitherto experienced little superfluous civility.

All eyes were now turned on the country lad, standing at the door, in his worn three-cornered hat, gray coat, leather breeches, and blue yarn stockings, leaning on an oaken cudgel, and bearing a wallet on his back.

Robin replied to the courteous innkeeper, with such an assumption of confidence as befitted the Major's relative. "My honest friend," he said, "I shall make it a point to patronize your house on some occasion, when"—here he could not help lowering his voice—"when I may have more than a parchment three-pence in my pocket. My present business," continued he, speaking with lofty confidence, "is merely to inquire my way to the dwelling of my kinsman, Major Molineux."

There was a sudden and general movement in the room, which Robin interpreted as expressing the eagerness of each individual to become his guide. But the innkeeper turned his eyes to a written paper on the wall, which he read, or seemed to read, with occasional recurrences to the young man's figure.

"What have we here?" said he, breaking his speech into little dry fragments. " 'Left the house of the subscriber, bounden servant, Hezekiah Mudge,—had on, when he went away, gray coat, leather breeches, master's third-best hat. One pound currency reward to whosoever shall lodge him in any jail of the providence.' Better trudge, boy; better trudge!"

Robin had begun to draw his hand towards the lighter end of the oak cudgel, but a strange hostility in every countenance induced him to relinquish his purpose of breaking the courteous innkeeper's head. As he turned to leave the room, he encountered a sneering glance from the bold-featured personage whom he had before noticed; and no sooner was he beyond the door, than he heard a general laugh, in which the innkeeper's voice might be distinguished, like the dropping of small stones into a kettle.

"Now, is it not strange," thought Robin, with his usual shrewdness,—"is it not strange that the confession of an empty pocket should outweigh the name of my kinsman, Major Molineux? Oh, if I had one of those grinning rascals in the woods, where I and my oak sapling grew up together, I would teach him that my arm is heavy though my purse be light!"

On turning the corner of the narrow lane, Robin found himself in a spacious street, with an unbroken line of lofty houses on each side, and a steepled building at the upper end, whence the ringing of a bell announced the hour of nine. The light of the moon, and the lamps from the numerous shop-windows, discovered people promenading on the pavement, and amongst them Robin had hoped to recognize his hitherto inscrutable relative. The result of his former inquiries made him unwilling to hazard another, in a scene of such publicity, and he determined to walk slowly and silently up the street, thrusting his face close to that of every elderly gentleman, in search of the Major's lineaments. In his progress, Robin encountered many gay and gallant figures. Embroidered garments of showy colors, enormous periwigs, gold-laced hats, and silver-hilted swords glided past him and dazzled his optics. Travelled youths, imitators of the European fine gentlemen of the period, trod jauntily along, half dancing to the fashionable tunes which they hummed, and making poor Robin ashamed of his quiet and natural gait. At length, after many pauses to examine the gorgeous display of goods in the shop-windows, and after suffering some rebukes for the impertinence of his scrutiny into people's faces, the Major's kinsman found himself near the steepled building, still unsuccessful in his search. As yet, however, he had seen only one side of the thronged street; so Robin crossed, and continued the same sort of inquisition down the opposite pavement, with stronger hopes than the philosopher seeking an honest man, but with no better fortune. He had arrived about midway towards the lower end, from which his course began, when he overheard the approach of some one who struck down a cane on the flag-stones at every step, uttering at regular intervals, two sepulchral hems.

"Mercy on us!" quoth Robin, recognizing the sound.

Turning a corner, which chanced to be close at his right hand, he hastened to pursue his researches in some other part of the town. His patience now was wearing low, and he seemed to feel more fatigue from his rambles since he crossed the ferry, than from his journey of several days on the other side. Hunger also pleaded loudly within him, and Robin began to balance the propriety of demanding, violently, and with lifted cudgel, the necessary guidance from the first solitary passenger whom he should meet. While a resolution to this effect was gaining strength, he entered a street of mean appearance, on either side of which a row of ill-built houses was straggling towards the harbor. The moonlight fell upon no passenger along the whole extent, but in the third domicile which Robin passed there was a half-opened door, and his keen glance detected a woman's garment within.

"My luck may be better here," said he to himself.

Accordingly, he approached the door, and beheld it shut closer as he did so; yet an open space remained, sufficing for the fair occupant to observe the stranger, without a corresponding display on her part. All that Robin could discern was a strip of scarlet petticoat, and the occasional sparkle of an eye, as if the moonbeams were trembling on some bright thing.

"Pretty mistress," for I may call her so with a good conscience, thought the shrewd youth, since I know nothing to the contrary,— "my sweet pretty mistress, will you be kind enough to tell me whereabouts I must seek the dwelling of my kinsman, Major Molineux?"

Robin's voice was plaintive and winning, and the female, seeing nothing to be shunned in the handsome country youth, thrust open the door, and came forth into the moonlight. She was a dainty little figure, with a white neck, round arms, and a slender waist, at the extremity of which her scarlet petticoat jutted out over a hoop, as if she were standing in a balloon. Moreover, her face was oval and pretty, her hair dark beneath the little cap, and her bright eyes possessed a sly freedom, which triumphed over those of Robin.

"Major Molineux dwells here," said this fair woman.

Now, her voice was the sweetest Robin had heard that night, yet he could not help doubting whether that sweet voice spoke Gospel truth. He looked up and down the mean street, and then surveyed the house before which they stood. It was a small, dark edifice of two stories, the second of which projected over the lower floor, and the front apartment had the aspect of a shop for pretty commodities.

"Now, truly, I am in luck," replied Robin, cunningly, "and so indeed is my kinsman, the Major, in having so pretty a housekeeper. But I prithee trouble him to step to the door; I will deliver him a message from his friends in the country, and then go back to my lodgings at the inn."

"Nay, the Major has been abed this hour or more," said the lady of the scarlet petticoat; "and it would be to little purpose to disturb him to-night, seeing his evening draught was of the strongest. But he is a kind-hearted man, and it would be as much as my life's worth to let a kinsman of his turn away from the door. You are the good old gentleman's very picture, and I could swear that was his rainy-weather hat. Also he has garments very much resembling those leather small-clothes. But come in, I pray, for I bid you hearty welcome in his name."

So saying, the fair and hospitable dame took our hero by the hand; and the touch was light, and the force was gentleness, and though Robin read in her eyes what he did not hear in her words, yet the slender-waisted woman in the scarlet petticoat proved stronger than the athletic country youth. She had drawn his half-willing footsteps nearly to the threshold, when the opening of a door in the neighborhood startled the Major's housekeeper, and, leaving the Major's kinsman, she vanished speedily into her own domicile. A heavy yawn preceded the appearance of a man, who, like the Moonshine of Pyramus and Thisbe, carried a lantern, need-lessly aiding his sister luminary in the heavens. As he walked sleepily up the street, he turned his broad, dull face on Robin, and displayed a long staff, spiked at the end.

"Home, vagabond, home!" said the watchman, in accents that seemed to fall asleep as soon as they were uttered. "Home, or we'll set you in the stocks by peep of day!"

"This is the second hint of the kind," thought Robin. "I wish they would end my difficulties, by setting me there to-night."

Nevertheless, the youth felt an instinctive antipathy towards the guardian of midnight order, which at first prevented him from ask-ing his usual question. But just when the man was about to vanish behind the corner, Robin resolved not to lose the opportunity, and shouted lustily after him,—

"I say, friend! will you guide me to the house of my kinsman, Major Molineux?"

The watchman made no reply, but turned the corner and was gone; yet Robin seemed to hear the sound of drowsy laughter steal-ing along the solitary street. At that moment, also, a pleasant titter saluted him from the open window above his head; he looked up, and caught the sparkle of a saucy eye; a round arm beckoned to him, and next he heard light footsteps descending the staircase within. But Robin, being of the household of a New England clergy-man, was a good youth, as well as a shrewd one; so he resisted temptation, and fled away.

He now roamed desperately, and at random, through the town, almost ready to believe that a spell was on him, like that by which a wizard of his country had once kept three pursuers wandering, a whole winter night, within twenty paces of the cottage which they sought. The streets lay before him, strange and desolate, and the lights were extinguished in almost every house. Twice, however, little parties of men, among whom Robin distinguished individuals in outlandish attire, came hurrying along; but, though on both occa-sions, they paused to address him, such intercourse did not at all enlighten his perplexity. They did but utter a few words in some language of which Robin knew nothing, and perceiving his inability to answer, bestowed a curse upon him in plain English and has-tened away. Finally, the lad determined to knock at the door of every mansion that might appear worthy to be occupied by his kinsman, trusting that perseverance would overcome the fatality that had hitherto thwarted him. Firm in this resolve, he was passing beneath the walls of a church, which formed the corner of two streets, when, as he turned into the shade of its steeple, he en-countered a bulky stranger, muffled in a cloak. The man was proceeding with the speed of earnest business, but Robin planted himself full before him, holding the oak cudgel with both hands across his body as a bar to further passage.

"Halt, honest man, and answer me a question," said he, very resolutely. "Tell me, this instant, whereabouts is the dwelling of my kinsman, Major Molineux!"

"Keep your tongue between your teeth, fool, and let me pass!" said a deep, gruff voice, which Robin partly remembered. "Let me pass, or I'll strike you to the earth!"

"No, no, neighbor!" cried Robin, flourishing his cudgel, and then thrusting its larger end close to the man's muffled face. "No, no, I'm not the fool you take me for, nor do you pass till I have an answer to my question. Whereabouts is the dwelling of my kinsman, Major Molineux?"

The stranger, instead of attempting to force his passage, stepped back into the moonlight, unmuffled his face, and stared full into that of Robin.

"Watch here an hour, and Major Molineux will pass by," said he.

Robin gazed with dismay and astonishment on the unprecedented physiognomy of the speaker. The forehead with its double prominence, the broad hooked nose, the shaggy eyebrows, and fiery eyes were those which he had noticed at the inn, but the man's complexion had undergone a singular, or more properly, a twofold change. One side of the face blazed an intense red, while the other was black as midnight, the divison line being in the broad bridge of the nose; and a mouth which seemed to extend from ear to ear was black or red, in contrast to the color of the cheek.[3] The effect was as if two individual devils, a fiend of fire and a fiend of darkness had united themselves to form this infernal visage. The stranger grinned in Robin's face, muffled his party-colored features, and was out of sight in a moment.

"Strange things we travellers see!" ejaculated Robin.

He seated himself, however, upon the steps of the church-door, resolving to wait the appointed time for his kinsman. A few moments were consumed in philosophical speculations upon the species of man who had just left him; but having settled this point shrewdly, rationally, and satisfactorily, he was compelled to look elsewhere for his amusement. And first he threw his eyes along the street. It was of more respectable appearance than most of those into which he had wandered; and the moon, creating, like the imaginative power, a beautiful strangeness in familiar objects, gave some-

---

3. The disguise of an Indian in war paint was much used by the early revolutionaires, as in the Boston tea party.

thing of romance to a scene that might not have possessed it in the light of day. The irregular and often quaint architecture of the houses, some of whose roofs were broken into numerous little peaks, while others ascended, steep and narrow, into a single point, and others again were square; the pure snow-white of some of their complexions, the aged darkness of others, and the thousand sparklings, reflected from bright substances in the walls of many; these matters engaged Robin's attention for a while, and then began to grow wearisome. Next he endeavored to define the forms of distant objects, starting away, with almost ghostly indistinctness, just as his eye appeared to grasp them; and finally he took a minute survey of an edifice which stood on the opposite side of the street, directly in front of the church-door, where he was stationed. It was a large, square mansion, distinguished from its neighbors by a balcony, which rested on tall pillars, and by an elaborate Gothic window, communicating therewith.

"Perhaps this is the very house I have been seeking," thought Robin.

Then he strove to speed away the time, by listening to a murmur which swept continually along the street, yet was scarcely audible, except to an unaccustomed ear like his; it was a low, dull, dreamy sound, compounded of many noises, each of which was at too great a distance to be separately heard. Robin marvelled at this snore of a sleeping town, and marvelled more whenever its continuity was broken by now and then a distant shout, apparently loud where it originated. But altogether it was a sleep-inspiring sound, and, to shake off its drowsy influence, Robin arose, and climbed a window-frame, that he might view the interior of the church. There the moonbeams came trembling in, and fell down upon the deserted pews, and extended along the quiet aisles. A fainter yet more awful radiance was hovering around the pulpit, and one solitary ray had dared to rest upon the open page of the great Bible. Had nature, in that deep hour, become a worshipper in the house which man had builded? Or was that heavenly light the visible sanctity of the place,—visible because no earthly and impure feet were within the walls? The scene made Robin's heart shiver with a sensation of loneliness stronger than he had ever felt in the remotest depths of his native woods; so he turned away and sat down again before the door. There were graves around the church, and now an uneasy thought obtruded into Robin's breast. What if the object of his search, which had been so often and so strangely thwarted, were all the time mouldering in his shroud? What if his kinsman should glide through yonder gate, and nod and smile to him in dimly passing by?

"Oh that any breathing thing were here with me!" said Robin.

Recalling his thoughts from this uncomfortable track, he sent them over forest, hill, and stream, and attempted to imagine how that evening of ambiguity and weariness had been spent by his father's household. He pictured them assembled at the door, beneath the tree, the great old tree, which had been spared for its huge twisted trunk and venerable shade, when a thousand leafy brethen fell. There, at the going down of the summer sun, it was his father's custom to perform domestic worship, that the neighbors might come and join with him like brothers of the family, and that the wayfaring man might pause to drink at that fountain, and keep his heart pure by freshening the memory of home. Robin distinguished the seat of every individual of the little audience; he saw the good man in the midst, holding the Scriptures in the golden light that fell from the western clouds; he beheld him close the book and all rise up to pray. He heard the old thanksgivings for daily mercies, the old supplications for their continuance, to which he had so often listened in weariness, but which were now among his dear remembrances. He perceived the slight inequality of his father's voice when he came to speak of the absent one; he noted how his mother turned her face to the broad and knotted trunk; how his elder brother scorned, because the beard was rough upon his upper lip to permit his features to be moved; how the younger sister drew down a low hanging branch before her eyes; and how the little one of all, whose sports had hitherto broken the decorum of the scene, understood the prayer for her playmate, and burst into clamorous grief. Then he saw them go in at the door; and when Robin would have entered also, the latch tinkled into its place, and he was excluded from his home.

"Am I here, or there?" cried Robin, starting; for all at once, when his thoughts had become visible and audible in a dream, the long, wide, solitary street shone out before him.

He aroused himself, and endeavored to fix his attention steadily upon the large edifice which he had surveyed before. But still his mind kept vibrating between fancy and reality; by turns, the pillars of the balcony lengthened into the tall, bare stems of pines, dwindled down to human figures, settled again into their true shape and size, and then commenced a new succession of changes. For a single moment, when he deemed himself awake, he could have sworn that a visage—one which he seemed to remember, yet could not absolutely name as his kinsman's—was looking towards him from the Gothic window. A deeper sleep wrestled with and nearly overcame him, but fled at the sound of footsteps along the opposite pavement. Robin rubbed his eyes, discerned a man passing at the foot of the balcony, and addressed him in a loud, peevish, and lamentable cry.

"Hallo, friend! must I wait here all night for my kinsman, Major Molineux?"

The sleeping echoes awoke, and answered the voice; and the passenger, barely able to discern a figure sitting in the oblique shade of the steeple, traversed the street to obtain a nearer view. He was himself a gentleman in his prime, of open, intelligent, cheerful, and altogether prepossessing countenance. Perceiving a country youth, apparently homeless and without friends, he accosted him in a tone of real kindness, which had become strange to Robin's ears.

"Well, my good lad, why are you sitting here?" inquired he. "Can I be of service to you in any way?"

"I am afraid not, sir," replied Robin, despondingly; "yet I shall take it kindly, if you'll answer me a single question. I've been searching, half the night, for one Major Molineux; now, sir, is there really such a person in these parts, or am I dreaming?"

"Major Molineux! The name is not altogether strange to me," said the gentleman, smiling. "Have you any objection to telling me the nature of your business with him?"

Then Robin briefly related that his father was a clergyman, settled on a small salary, at a long distance back in the country, and that he and Major Molineux were brothers' children. The Major, having inherited riches, and acquired civil and military rank, had visited his cousin, in great pomp, a year or two before; had manifested much interest in Robin and an elder brother, and, being childless himself, had thrown out hints respecting the future establishment of one of them in life. The elder brother was destined to succeed to the farm which his father cultivated in the interval of sacred duties; it was therefore determined that Robin should profit by his kinsman's generous intentions, especially as he seemed to be rather the favorite, and was thought to possess other necessary endowments.

"For I have the name of being a shrewd youth," observed Robin, in this part of his story.

"I doubt not you deserve it," replied his new friend, good-naturedly; "but pray proceed."

"Well, sir, being nearly eighteen years old, and well grown, as you see," continued Robin, drawing himself up to his full height, "I thought it high time to begin in the world. So my mother and sister put me in handsome trim, and my father gave me half the remnant of his last year's salary, and five days ago I started for this place, to pay the Major a visit. But, would you believe it, sir! I crossed the ferry a little after dark, and have yet found nobody that would show me the way to his dwelling; only, an hour or two since, I was told to wait here, and Major Molineux would pass by."

"Can you describe the man who told you this?" inquired the gentleman.

"Oh, he was a very ill-favored fellow, sir," replied Robin, "with two great bumps on his forehead, a hook nose, fiery eyes; and, what struck me as the strangest, his face was of two different colors. Do you happen to know such a man, sir?"

"Not intimately," answered the stranger, "but I chanced to meet him a little time previous to your stopping me. I believe you may trust his word, and that the Major will very shortly pass through this street. In the mean time, as I have a singular curiosity to witness your meeting, I will sit down here upon the steps and bear you company."

He seated himself accordingly, and soon engaged his companion in animated discourse. It was but of brief continuance, however, for a noise of shouting, which had long been remotely audible, drew so much nearer that Robin inquired its cause.

"What may be the meaning of this uproar?" asked he. "Truly, if your town be always as noisy, I shall find little sleep while I am an inhabitant."

"Why, indeed, friend Robin, there do appear to be three or four riotous fellows abroad to-night," replied the gentleman. "You must not expect all the stillness of your native woods here in our streets. But the watch will shortly be at the heels of these lads and"—

"Ay, and set them in the stocks by peep of day," interrupted Robin, recollecting his own encounter with the drowsy lantern-bearer. "But, dear sir, if I may trust my ears, an army of watchmen would never make head against such a multitude of rioters. There were at least a thousand voices went up to make that one shout."

"May not a man have several voices, Robin, as well as two complexions?" said his friend.

"Perhaps a man may; but Heaven forbid that a woman should!" responded the shrewd youth, thinking of the seductive tones of the Major's housekeeper.

The sounds of a trumpet in some neighboring street now became so evident and continual, that Robin's curiosity was strongly excited. In addition to the shouts, he heard frequent bursts from many instruments of discord, and a wild and confused laughter filled up the intervals. Robin rose from the steps, and looked wistfully towards a point whither people seemed to be hastening.

"Surely some prodigious merry-making is going on," exclaimed he. "I have laughed very little since I left home, sir, and should be sorry to lose an opportunity. Shall we step round the corner by that darkish house, and take our share of the fun?"

"Sit down again, sit down, good Robin," replied the gentleman, laying his hand on the skirt of the gray coat. "You forget that we must wait here for your kinsman; and there is reason to believe that he will pass by, in the course of a very few moments."

The near approach of the uproar had now disturbed the neighborhood; windows flew open on all sides; and many heads, in the attire of the pillow, and confused by sleep suddenly broken, were protruded to the gaze of whoever had leisure to observe them. Eager voices hailed each other from house to house, all demanding the explanation, which not a soul could give. Half-dressed men hurried towards the unknown commotion, stumbling as they went over the stone steps that thrust themselves into the narrow foot-walk. The shouts, the laughter, and the tuneless bray, the antipodes of music, came onwards with increasing din, till scattered individuals, and then denser bodies, began to appear round a corner at the distance of a hundred yards.

"Will you recognize your kinsman, if he passes in this crowd?" inquired the gentleman.

"Indeed, I can't warrant it, sir; but I'll take my stand here, and keep a bright lookout," answered Robin, descending to the outer edge of the pavement.

A mighty stream of people now emptied into the street, and came rolling slowly towards the church. A single horseman wheeled the corner in the midst of them, and close behind him came a band of fearful wind-instruments, sending forth a fresher discord now that no intervening buildings kept it from the ear. Then a redder light disturbed the moon-beams, and a dense multitude of torches shone along the street, concealing, by their glare, whatever object they illuminated. The single horseman, clad in a military dress, and bearing a drawn sword, rode onward as the leader, and, by his fierce and variegated countenance, appeared like war personified; the red of one cheek was an emblem of fire and sword; the blackness of the other betokened the mourning that attends them. In his train were wild figures in the Indian dress, and many fantastic shapes without a model, giving the whole march a visionary air, as if a dream had broken forth from some feverish brain, and were sweeping visibly through the midnight streets. A mass of people, inactive, except as applauding spectators, hemmed the procession in; and several women ran along the sidewalk, piercing the confusion of heavier sounds with their shrill voices of mirth or terror.

"The double-faced fellow has his eye upon me," muttered Robin, with an indefinite but an uncomfortable idea that he was himself to bear a part in the pageantry.

The leader turned himself in the saddle, and fixed his glance full upon the country youth, as the steed went slowly by. When Robin had freed his eyes from those fiery ones, the musicians were pass-

ing before him, and the torches were close at hand; but the unsteady brightness of the latter formed a veil which he could not
penetrate. The rattling of wheels over the stones sometimes found
its way to his ear, and confused traces of a human form appeared at
intervals, and then melted into the vivid light. A moment more, and
the leader thundered a command to halt: the trumpets vomited a
horrid breath, and then held their peace; the shouts and laughter of
the people died away, and there remained only a universal hum,
allied to silence. Right before Robin's eyes was an uncovered cart.
There the torches blazed the brightest, there the moon shone out
like day, and there, in tar-and-feathery dignity,[4] sat his kinsman,
Major Molineux!

He was an elderly man, of large and majestic person, and strong,
square features, betokening a steady soul; but steady as it was, his
enemies had found means to shake it. His face was pale as death,
and far more ghastly; the broad forehead was contracted in his
agony, so that his eyebrows formed one grizzled line; his eyes were
red and wild, and the foam hung white upon his quivering lip. His
whole frame was agitated by a quick and continual tremor, which
his pride strove to quell, even in those circumstances of overwhelming humiliation. But perhaps the bitterest pang of all was when his
eyes met those of Robin; for he evidently knew him on the instant,
as the youth stood witnessing the foul disgrace of a head grown
gray in honor. They stared at each other in silence, and Robin's
knees shook, and his hair bristled, with a mixture of pity and terror.
Soon, however, a bewildering excitement began to seize upon his
mind; the preceding adventures of the night, the unexpected appearance of the crowd, the torches, the confused din and the hush
that followed, the spectre of his kinsman reviled by that great multitude,—all this, and more than all, a perception of tremendous ridicule in the whole scene, affected him with a sort of mental inebriety.
At that moment a voice of sluggish merriment saluted Robin's ears;
he turned instinctively, and just behind the corner of the church
stood the lantern-bearer, rubbing his eyes, and drowsily enjoying
the lad's amazement. Then he heard a peal of laughter like the
ringing of silvery bells; a woman twitched his arm, a saucy eye met
his, and he saw the lady of the scarlet petticoat. A sharp, dry cachin-
nation appealed to his memory, and, standing on tiptoe in the
crowd, with his white apron over his head, he beheld the courteous
little innkeeper. And lastly, there sailed over the heads of the multitude a great, broad laugh, broken in the midst by two sepulchral

---

4. In this rough punishment a man was stripped naked, covered with hot tar, and
sprinkled with feathers. It was frequently visited upon those suspected of resisting
the revolution.

hems; thus, "haw, haw, haw,—hem, hem,—haw, haw, haw, haw!"

The sound proceeded from the balcony of the opposite edifice, and thither Robin turned his eyes. In front of the Gothic window stood the old citizen, wrapped in a wide gown, his gray periwig exchanged for a nightcap, which was thrust back from his forehead, and his silk stockings hanging about his legs. He supported himself on his polished cane in a fit of convulsive merriment, which manifested itself on his solemn old features like a funny inscription on a tombstone. Then Robin seemed to hear the voices of the barbers, of the guests of the inn, and of all who had made sport of him that night. The contagion was spreading among the multitude, when all at once, it seized upon Robin, and he sent forth a shout of laughter that echoed through the street,—every man shook his sides, every man emptied his lungs, but Robin's shout was the loudest there. The cloud-spirits peeped from their silvery islands, as the congregated mirth went roaring up the sky! The Man in the Moon heard the far bellow. "Oho," quoth he, "the old earth is frolicsome tonight!"

When there was a momentary calm in that tempestuous sea of sound, the leader gave the sign, the procession resumed its march. On they went, like fiends that throng in mockery around some dead potentate, mighty no more, but majestic still in his agony. On they went, in counterfeited pomp, in senseless uproar, in frenzied merriment, trampling all on an old man's heart. On swept the tumult, and left a silent street behind.

. . . . . . . . . . .

"Well, Robin, are you dreaming?" inquired the gentleman, laying his hand on the youth's shoulder.

Robin started, and withdrew his arm from the stone post to which he had instinctively clung, as the living stream rolled by him. His cheek was somewhat pale, and his eye not quite as lively as in the earlier part of the evening.

"Will you be kind enough to show me the way to the ferry?" said he, after a moment's pause.

"You have, then, adopted a new subject of inquiry?" observed his companion, with a smile.

"Why, yes, sir," replied Robin, rather dryly. "Thanks to you, and to my other friends, I have at last met my kinsman, and he will scarce desire to see my face again. I begin to grow weary of a town life, sir. Will you show me the way to the ferry?"

"No, my good friend Robin,—not to-night, at least," said the gentleman. "Some few days hence, if you wish it, I will speed you on your journey. Or, if you prefer to remain with us, perhaps, as you are a shrewd youth, you may rise in the world without the help of your kinsman, Major Molineux."

# EDGAR ALLAN POE
## 1809–1849

Though he was born in Boston, Poe spent his early years in Virginia. His parents, who were in show business, died when he was very young, leaving him in the care of a family named Allan, whose name became part of his own. He started college at the University of Virginia, but was soon expelled for excessive drinking and gambling. (The room he lived in there is now reverently preserved and exhibited to visitors.) After two years in the army he again tried college—this time the U.S. Military Academy at West Point—but with a similar result. After this his short life followed a similar pattern until its end. But despite his excesses, which made it difficult for him to hold a steady job, he won a number of literary prizes and produced a body of ingenious poetry, fiction, and criticism that has proved both fascinating and influential. In particular he argued for a "unity of effect" in literary works, and he followed his own formulas, occasionally with spectacular results. He made the tale of terror his own, and also had a major influence on the development of the detective story.

# The Purloined Letter

> Nil sapienatiæ odiosius acumine nimio.[1]
> *Seneca*

At Paris, just after dark one gusty evening in the autumn of 18—, I was enjoying the twofold luxury of meditation and a meerschaum, in company with my friend, C. Auguste Dupin, in his little back library, or book-closet, *au troisième*, No. 33 *Rue Dunôt, Faubourg St. Germain*.[2] For one hour at least we had maintained a profound silence; while each, to any casual observer, might have seemed intently and exclusively occupied with the curling eddies of smoke that oppressed the atmosphere of the chamber. For myself, however, I was mentally discussing certain topics which had formed matter for conversation between us at an earlier period of the evening; I mean the affair of the Rue Morgue, and the mystery attend-

---

1. Nothing is more offensive to the wise than an excess of trickery.
2. On the third floor above the ground in a fashionable district in Paris.

ing the murder of Marie Rogêt.[3] I looked upon it, therefore, as something of a coincidence, when the door of our apartment was thrown open and admitted our old acquaintance, Monsieur G——, the Prefect of the Parisian police.

We gave him a hearty welcome; for there was nearly half as much of the entertaining as of the contemptible about the man, and we had not seen him for several years. We had been sitting in the dark, and Dupin now arose for the purpose of lighting a lamp, but sat down again, without doing so, upon G.'s saying that he had called to consult us, or rather to ask the opinion of my friend, about some official business which had occasioned a great deal of trouble.

"If it is any point requiring reflection," observed Dupin, as he forbore to enkindle the wick, "we shall examine it to better purpose in the dark."

"That is another of your odd notions," said the Prefect, who had the fashion of calling everything "odd" that was beyond his comprehension, and thus lived amid an absolute legion of "oddities."

"Very true," said Dupin, as he supplied his visitor with a pipe, and rolled toward him a comfortable chair.

"And what is the difficulty now?" I asked. "Nothing more in the assassination way I hope?"

"Oh, no; nothing of that nature. The fact is, the business is *very* simple indeed, and I make no doubt that we can manage it sufficiently well ourselves; but then I thought Dupin would like to hear the details of it because it is so excessively *odd*."

"Simple and odd," said Dupin.

"Why, yes; and not exactly that either. The fact is, we have all been a good deal puzzled because the affair *is* so simple, and yet baffles us altogether."

"Perhaps it is the very simplicity of the thing which puts you at fault," said my friend.

"What nonsense you *do* talk!" replied the Prefect, laughing heartily.

"Perhaps the mystery is a little *too* plain," said Dupin.

"Oh, good heavens! who ever heard of such an idea?"

"A little *too* self-evident."

"Ha! ha! ha!—ha! ha! ha!—ho! ho! ho!" roared our visitor, profoundly amused, "oh, Dupin, you will be the death of me yet!"

"And what, after all, *is* the matter on hand?" I asked.

"Why, I will tell you," replied the Prefect, as he gave a long, steady, and contemplative puff, and settled himself in his chair. "I will tell you in a few words; but, before I begin, let me caution you that this is an affair demanding the greatest secrecy, and that I

3. These are the subjects of previous detective stories by Poe.

should most probably lose the position I now hold, were it known that I confided it to any one."

"Proceed," said I.

"Or not," said Dupin.

"Well, then; I have received personal information, from a very high quarter, that a certain document of the last importance has been purloined from the royal apartments. The individual who purloined it is known; this beyond a doubt; he was seen to take it. It is known, also, that it still remains in his possession."

"How is this known?" asked Dupin.

"It is clearly inferred," replied the Prefect, "from the nature of the document, and from the non-appearance of certain results which would at once arise from its passing *out* of the robber's possession— that is to say, from his employing it as he must design in the end to employ it."

"Be a little more explicit," I said.

"Well, I may venture so far as to say that the paper gives its holder a certain power in a certain quarter where such power is immensely valuable." The Prefect was fond of the cant of diplomacy.

"Still I do not quite understand," said Dupin.

"No? Well; the disclosure of the document to a third person, who shall be nameless, would bring in question the honor of a personage of most exalted station; and this fact gives the holder of the document an ascendancy over the illustrious personage whose honor and peace are so jeopardized."

"But this ascendancy," I interposed, "would depend upon the robber's knowledge of the loser's knowledge of the robber. Who would dare—"

"The thief," said G., "is the Minister D——, who dares all things, those unbecoming as well as those becoming a man. The method of the theft was not less ingenious than bold. The document in question—a letter, to be frank—had been received by the personage robbed while in the royal *boudoir*. During its perusal she was suddenly interrupted by the entrance of the other exalted personage from whom especially it was her wish to conceal it. After a hurried and vain endeavor to thrust it in a drawer, she was forced to place it, open as it was, upon a table. The address, however, was uppermost, and, the contents thus unexposed, the letter escaped notice. At this juncture enters the Minister D——. His lynx eye immediately perceives the paper, recognizes the handwriting of the address, observes the confusion of the personage addressed, and fathoms her secret. After some business transactions, hurried through in his ordinary manner, he produces a letter somewhat similar to the one in question, opens it, pretends to read it, and then places in in close juxtaposition to the other. Again he converses, for some fifteen minutes, upon the public affairs. At length, in taking leave, he takes also from the table the letter to which he had no claim. Its rightful owner saw, but, of course, dared not call attention to the act, in the presence of the third personage who stood at her elbow. The minister decamped; leaving his own letter—one of no importance—upon the table."

"Here, then," said Dupin to me, "you have precisely what you demand to make the ascendancy complete—the robber's knowledge of the loser's knowledge of the robber."

"Yes," replied the Prefect; "and the power thus attained has, for some months past, been wielded, for political purposes, to a very dangerous extent. The personage robbed is more thoroughly convinced, every day, of the necessity of reclaiming her letter. But this, of course, cannot be done openly. In fine, driven to despair, she has committed the matter to me."

"Than whom," said Dupin, amid a perfect whirlwind of smoke, "no more sagacious agent could, I suppose, be desired, or even imagined."

"You flatter me," replied the Prefect; "but it is possible that some such opinion may have been entertained."

"It is clear," said I, "as you observe, that the letter is still in the possession of the minister; since it is this possession, and not any employment of the letter, which bestows the power. With the employment the power departs."

"True," said G.; "and upon this conviction I proceeded. My first care was to make thorough search of the minister's hotel;[4] and here my chief embarrassment lay in the necessity of searching without his knowledge. Beyond all things, I have been warned of the danger which would result from giving him reason to suspect our design."

"But," said I, "you are quite *au fait* in these investigations. The Parisian police have done this thing often before."

"Oh, yes; and for this reason I did not despair. The habits of the minister gave me, too, a great advantage. He is frequently absent from home all night. His servants are by no means numerous. They sleep at a distance from their master's apartment, and, being chiefly Neapolitans, are readily made drunk. I have keys, as you know, with which I can open any chamber or cabinet in Paris. For three months a night has not passed, during the greater part of which I have not been engaged, personally, in ransacking the D—— Hotel. My honor is interested, and, to mention a great secret, the reward is enormous. So I did not abandon the search until I had become fully satisfied that the thief is a more astute man than myself. I fancy that

---

4. "Hotel" in the French sense: a large building; in this case a private house in the city.

I have investigated every nook and corner of the premises in which it is possible that the paper can be concealed."

"But is it not possible," I suggested, "that although the letter may be in possession of the minister, as it unquestionably is, he may have concealed it elsewhere than upon his own premises?"

"This is barely possible," said Dupin. "The present peculiar condition of affairs at court, and especially of those intrigues in which D— —is known to be involved, would render the instant availability of the document—its susceptibility of being produced at a moment's notice—a point of nearly equal importance with its possession."

"Its susceptibility of being produced?" said I.

"That is to say, of being *destroyed*," said Dupin.

"True," I observed; "the paper is clearly then upon the premises. As for its being upon the person of the minister, we may consider that as out of the question."

"Entirely," said the Prefect. "He has been twice waylaid, as if by footpads, and his person rigidly searched under my own inspection."

"You might have spared yourself this trouble," said Dupin. "D— —, I presume, is not altogether a fool, and, if not, must have anticipated these waylayings, as a matter of course."

"Not *altogether* a fool," said G., "but then he is a poet, which I take to be only one remove from a fool."

"True," said Dupin, after a long and thoughtful whiff from his meerschaum, "although I have been guilty of certain doggerel myself."

"Suppose you detail," said I, "the particulars of your search."

"Why, the fact is, we took our time, and we searched *everywhere*. I have had long experience in these affairs. I took the entire building, room by room; devoting the nights of a whole week to each. We examined, first, the furniture of each apartment. We opened every possible drawer; and I presume you know that, to a properly trained police-agent, such a thing as a *'secret'* drawer is impossible. Any man is a dolt who permits a 'secret' drawer to escape him in a search of this kind. The thing is *so* plain. There is a certain amount of bulk—of space—to be accounted for in every cabinet. Then we have accurate rules. The fiftieth part of a line could not escape us. After the cabinets we took the chairs. The cushions we probed with the fine long needles you have seen me employ. From the tables we removed the tops."

"Why so?"

"Sometimes the top of a table, or other similarly arranged piece of furniture, is removed by the person wishing to conceal an article; then the leg is excavated, the article deposited within the cavity, and the top replaced. The bottoms and tops of bedposts are employed in the same way."

"But could not the cavity be detected by sounding?" I asked.

"By no means, if, when the article is deposited, a sufficient wadding of cotton be placed around it. Besides, in our case, we were obliged to proceed without noise."

"But you could not have removed—you could not have taken to pieces *all* articles of furniture in which it would have been possible to make a deposit in the manner you mention. A letter may be compressed into a thin spiral roll, not differing much in shape or bulk from a large knitting-needle, and in this form it might be inserted into the rung of a chair, for example. You did not take to pieces all the chairs?"

"Certainly not; but we did better—we examined the rungs of every chair in the hotel, and, indeed, the jointings of every description of furniture, by the aid of a most powerful microscope. Had there been any traces of recent disturbance we should not have failed to detect it instantly. A single grain of gimlet-dust, for example, would have been as obvious as an apple. Any disorder in the gluing—any unusual gaping in the joints—would have sufficed to insure detection."

"I presume you looked to the mirrors, between the boards and the plates, and you probed the beds and the bedclothes, as well as the curtains and carpets."

"That of course; and when we had absolutely completed every particle of furniture in this way, then we examined the house itself. We divided its entire surface into compartments, which we numbered, so that none might be missed; then we scrutinized each individual square inch throughout the premises, including the two houses immediately adjoining, with the microscope, as before."

"The two houses adjoining!" I exclaimed; "you must have had a great deal of trouble."

"We had; but the reward offered is prodigious."

"You included the *grounds* about the houses?"

"All the grounds are paved with brick. They gave us comparatively little trouble. We examined the moss between the bricks, and found it undisturbed."

"You looked among D——'s papers, of course, and into the books of the library?"

"Certainly; we opened every package and parcel; we not only opened every book, but we turned over every leaf in each volume, not contenting ourselves with a mere shake, according to the fashion of some of our police officers. We also measured the thickness of every book-*cover*, with the most accurate admeasurement, and applied to each the most jealous scrutiny of the microscope. Had any of the bindings been recently meddled with, it would have been utterly impossible that the fact should have escaped observation. Some five or six volumes, just from the hands of the binder, we carefully probed, longitudinally, with needles."

"You explored the floors beneath the carpets?"

"Beyond doubt. We removed every carpet, and examined the boards with the microscope."

"And the paper on the walls?"

"Yes."

"You looked into the cellars?"

"We did."

"Then," I said, "you have been making a miscalculation, and the letter is *not* upon the premises, as you suppose."

"I fear you are right there," said the Prefect. "And now, Dupin, what would you advise me to do?"

"To make a thorough research of the premises."

"That is absolutely needless," replied G——. "I am not more sure that I breathe than I am that the letter is not at the hotel."

"I have no better advice to give you," said Dupin. "You have, of course, an accurate description of the letter?"

"Oh, yes!"—And here the Prefect, producing a memorandum-book, proceeded to read aloud a minute account of the internal, and especially of the external, appearance of the missing document. Soon after finishing the perusal of this description, he took his departure, more entirely depressed in spirits than I had ever known the good gentleman before.

In about a month afterward he paid us another visit, and found us occupied very nearly as before. He took a pipe and a chair and entered into some ordinary conversation. At length I said:

"Well, but G., what of the purloined letter? I presume you have at last made up your mind that there is no such thing as overreaching the Minister?"

"Confound him, say I—yes; I made the re-examination, however, as Dupin suggested—but it was all labor lost, as I knew it would be."

"How much was the reward offered, did you say?" asked Dupin.

"Why, a very great deal—a *very* liberal reward—I don't like to say how much, precisely; but one thing I *will* say, that I wouldn't mind giving my individual check for fifty thousand francs to any one who could obtain me that letter. The fact is, it is becoming of more and more importance every day; and the reward has been lately doubled. If it were trebled, however, I could do no more than I have done."

"Why, yes," said Dupin, drawlingly, between the whiffs of his meerschaum, "I really—think, G., you have not exerted yourself—to the utmost in this matter. You might—do a little more, I think, eh?"

"How?—in what way?"

"Why—puff, puff—you might—puff, puff—employ counsel in the matter, eh?—puff, puff, puff. Do you remember the story they tell of Abernethy?"

"No; hang Abernethy!"

"To be sure! hang him and welcome. But, once upon a time, a certain rich miser conceived the design of spunging upon this Abernethy for a medical opinion. Getting up, for this purpose, an ordinary conversation in a private company, he insinuated his case to the physician, as that of an imaginary individual.

" 'We will suppose,' said the miser, 'that his symptoms are such and such; now, doctor, what would *you* have directed him to take?'

" 'Take!' said Abernethy, 'why, take *advice*, to be sure.' "

"But," said the Prefect, a little discomposed, "I am *perfectly* willing to take advice, and to pay for it. I would *really* give fifty thousand francs to any one who would aid me in the matter."

"In that case," replied Dupin, opening a drawer, and producing a check-book, "you may as well fill me up a check for the amount mentioned. When you have signed it, I will hand you the letter."

I was astounded. The Prefect appeared absolutely thunder-stricken. For some minutes he remained speechless and motionless, looking incredulously at my friend with open mouth, and eyes that seemed starting from their sockets; then apparently recovering himself in some measure, he seized a pen, and after several pauses and vacant stares, finally filled up and signed a check for fifty thousand francs, and handed it across the table to Dupin. The latter examined it carefully and deposited it in his pocket-book; then, unlocking an *escritoire*, took thence a letter and gave it to the prefect. This functionary grasped it in a perfect agony of joy, opened it with a trembling hand, cast a rapid glance at its contents, and then, scrambling and struggling to the door, rushed at length unceremoniously from the room and from the house, without having uttered a syllable since Dupin had requested him to fill up the check.

When he had gone, my friend entered into some explanations.

"The Parisian police," he said, "are exceedingly able in their way. They are persevering, ingenious, cunning, and thoroughly versed in the knowledge which their duties seem chiefly to demand. Thus, when G—— detailed to us his mode of searching the premises at the Hotel D——, I felt entire confidence in his having made a satisfactory investigation—so far as his labors extended."

"So far as his labors extended?" said I.

"Yes," said Dupin. "The measures adopted were not only the best of their kind, but carried out to absolute perfection. Had the letter been deposited within the range of their search, these fellows would, beyond a question, have found it."

I merely laughed—but he seemed quite serious in all that he said.

"The measures, then," he continued, "were good in their kind, and well executed; their defect lay in their being inapplicable to the case and to the man. A certain set of highly ingenious resources are, with the Prefect, a sort of Procrustean bed, to which he forcibly adapts his designs. But he perpetually errs by being too deep or too shallow for the matter in hand; and many a school-boy is a better reasoner than he. I knew one about eight years of age, whose success at guessing in the game of 'even and odd' attracted universal admiration. This game is simple, and is played with marbles. One player holds in his hand a number of these toys, and demands of another whether that number is even or odd. If the guess is right, the guesser wins one; if wrong, he loses one. The boy to whom I allude won all the marbles of the school. Of course he had some principle of guessing; and this lay in mere observation and admeasurements of the astuteness of his opponents. For example, an arrant simpleton is his opponent, and holding up his closed hand, asks, 'Are they even or odd?' Our school-boy replies, 'Odd,' and loses; but upon the second trial he wins, for he then says to himself: 'The simpleton had them even upon the first trial, and his amount of cunning is just sufficient to make him have them odd upon the second; I will therefore guess odd';—he guesses odd, and wins. Now, with a simpleton a degree above the first, he would have reasoned thus: 'This fellow finds that in the first instance I guessed odd, and, in the second, he will propose to himself, upon the first impulse, a simple variation from even to odd, as did the first simpleton; but then a second thought will suggest that this is too simple a variation, and finally he will decide upon putting it even as before. I will therefore guess even';—he guesses even, and wins. Now this mode of reasoning in the school-boy, whom his fellows termed 'lucky,'—what, in its last analysis, is it?"

"It is merely," I said, "an identification of the reasoner's intellect with that of his opponent."

"It is," said Dupin; "and, upon inquiring of the boy by what means he effected the *thorough* identification in which his success consisted, I received answer as follows; 'When I wish to find out how wise, or how stupid or how good, or how wicked is any one, or what are his thoughts at the moment, I fashion the expression of my face, as accurately as possible, in accordance with the expression of his, and then wait to see what thoughts or sentiments arise in my mind or heart, as if to match or correspond with the expression.'

This response of the school-boy lies at the bottom of all the spurious profundity which has been attributed to Rochefoucault, to La Bougive, to Machiavelli, and to Campanella."

"And the identification," I said, "of the reasoner's intellect with that of his opponent, depends, if I understand you aright, upon the accuracy with which the opponent's intellect is admeasured."

"For its practical value it depends upon this," replied Dupin; "and the Prefect and his cohort fail so frequently, first, by default of this identification and, secondly, by ill-admeasurement, or rather through non-admeasurement, of the intellect with which they are engaged. They consider only their *own* ideas of ingenuity; and, in searching for any thing hidden, advert only to the modes, in which *they* would have hidden it. They are right in this much—that their own ingenuity is a faithful representative of that of the *mass*; but when the cunning of the individual felon is diverse in character from their own, the felon foils them, of course. This always happens when it is above their own, and very usually when it is below. They have no variation of principle in their investigations; at best, when urged by some unusual emergency—by some extraordinary reward—they extend or exaggerate their old modes of *practice*, without touching their principles. What, for example, in this case of D——, has been done to vary the principle of action? What is all this boring, and probing, and sounding, and scrutinizing with the microscope, and dividing the surface of the building into registered square inches—what is it all but an exaggeration *of the application* of the one principle or set of principles of search, which are based upon the one set of notions regarding human ingenuity, to which the Prefect, in the long routine of his duty, has been accustomed? Do you not see he has taken it for granted that *all* men proceed to conceal a letter, not exactly in a gimlet-hole bored in a chair-leg, but, at least, in *some* out-of-the-way hole or corner suggested by the same tenor of thought which would urge a man to secrete a letter in a gimlet-hole bored in a chair-leg? And do you not see also, that such *recherchés* nooks for concealment are adapted only for ordinary occasions, and would be adopted only by ordinary intellects; for, in all cases of concealment, a disposal of the article concealed—a disposal of it in this *recherché* manner,—is, in the very first instance, presumable and presumed; and thus its discovery depends, not at all upon the acumen, but altogether upon the mere care, patience, and determination of the seekers; and where the case is of importance—or, what amounts to the same thing in the political eyes, when the reward is of magnitude,—the qualities in question have *never* been known to fail. You will now understand what I meant in suggesting that, had the purloined letter been hidden anywhere within the limits of the Prefect's examination—in other words, had the principle of its concealment been comprehended within the principles of the Prefect—its discovery would have been a matter altogether beyond question. This functionary, however, has been thoroughly mystified; and the remote source of his defeat lies in the supposition that the Minister is a fool, because he has acquired renown as a poet. All fools are poets; this the Prefect *feels*; and he is merely guilty of a *non distributio medii* in thence inferring that all poets are fools."

"But is this really the poet?" I asked. "There are two brothers, I know; and both have attained reputation in letters. The Minister I believe has written learnedly on the Differential Calculus. He is a mathematician, and no poet."

"You are mistaken; I know him well; he is both. As poet *and* mathematician, he would reason well; as mere mathematician, he could not have reasoned at all, and thus would have been at the mercy of the Prefect."

"You surprise me," I said, "by these opinions, which have been contradicted by the voice of the world. You do not mean to set at naught the well-digested idea of centuries. The mathematical reason has long been regarded as *the* reason *par excellence*."

" 'Il y a à parier,' " replied Dupin, quoting from Chamfort, " 'que toute idée publique, toute convention reçue, est une sottise, car elle a convenu au plus grand nombre.'[5] The mathematicians, I grant you, have done their best to promulgate the popular error to which you allude, and which is none the less an error for its promulgation as truth. With an art worthy a better cause, for example, they have insinuated the term 'analysis' into application to algebra. The French are the originators of this particular deception; but if a term is of any importance—if words derive any value from applicability— then 'analysis' conveys 'algebra' about as much as, in Latin, *'ambitus'* implies 'ambition,' *'religio'* 'religion,' or *'homines honesti'* a set of *honorable* men."

"You have a quarrel on hand, I see," said I, "with some of the algebraists of Paris; but proceed."

"I dispute the availability, and thus the value, of that reason which is cultivated in any especial form other than the abstractly logical. I dispute, in particular, the reason educed by mathematical study. The mathematics are the science of form and quantity; mathematical reasoning is merely logic applied to observation upon form and quantity. The great error lies in supposing that even the truths of what is called *pure* algebra are abstract or general truths. And this error is so egregious that I am confounded at the universal-

5. "The odds are that any public idea or accepted opinion is stupid, because it has suited the majority of people."

ity with which it has been received. Mathematical axioms are *not* axioms of general truth. What is true of *relation*—of form and quantity—is often grossly false in regard to morals, for example. In this latter science it is very usually *un*true that the aggregated parts are equal to the whole. In chemistry also the axiom fails. In the consideration of motive it fails; for two motives, each of a given value, have not, necessarily, a value when united, equal to the sum of their values apart. There are numerous other mathematical truths which are only truths within the limits of *relation*. But the mathematician argues from his *finite truths*, through habit, as if they were of an absolutely general applicability—as the world indeed imagines them to be. Bryant, in his very learned 'Mythology,' mentions an analogous source of error, when he says that 'although the pagan fables are not believed, yet we forget ourselves continually, and make inferences from them as existing realities.' With the algebraists, however, who are pagans themselves, the 'pagan fables' *are* believed and the inferences are made, not so much through lapse of memory as through an unaccountable addling of the brains. In short, I never yet encountered the mere mathematician who would be trusted out of equal roots, or one who did not clandestinely hold it as a point of his faith that $x2 + px$ was absolutely and unconditionally equal to $q$. Say to one of these gentlemen, by way of experiment, if you please, that you believe occasions may occur where $x2 + px$ is *not* altogether equal to $q$, and, having made him understand what you mean, get out of his reach as speedily as convenient, for, beyond doubt, he will endeavor to knock you down.

"I mean to say," continued Dupin, while I merely laughed at his last observations, "that if the Minister had been no more than a mathematician, the Prefect would have been under no necessity of giving me this check. I knew him, however, as both mathematician and poet, and my measures were adapted to his capacity, with reference to the circumstances by which he was surrounded. I knew him as a courtier, too, and as a bold *intriguant*. Such a man, I considered, could not fail to be aware of the ordinary policial modes of action. He could not have failed to anticipate—and events have proved that he did not fail to anticipate—the waylayings to which he was subjected. He must have foreseen, I reflected, the secret investigations of his premises. His frequent absences from home at night, which were hailed by the Prefect as certain aids to his success, I regarded only as *ruses*, to afford opportunity for thorough search to the police, and thus the sooner to impress them with the conviction to which G——, in fact, did finally arrive—the conviction that the letter was not upon the premises. I felt, also, that the whole train of thought, which I was at some pains in detailing to you just now, concerning the invariable principle of policial action in searches for articles concealed—I felt that this whole train of thought would necessarily pass through the mind of the minister. It would imperatively lead him to despise all the ordinary *nooks* of concealment. *He* could not, I reflected, be so weak as not to see that the most intricate and remote recess of his hotel would be as open as his commonest closets to the eyes, to the probes, to the gimlets, and to the microscopes of the Prefect. I saw, in fine, that he would be driven, as a matter of course, to *simplicity*, if not deliberately induced to it as a matter of choice. You will remember, perhaps, how desperately the Prefect laughed when I suggested, upon our first interview, that it was just possible this mystery troubled him so much on account of its being so *very* self-evident."

"Yes," said I, "I remember his merriment well. I really thought he would have fallen into convulsions."

"The material world," continued Dupin, "abounds with very strict analogies to the immaterial; and thus some color of truth has been given to the rhetorical dogma, that metaphor, or simile, may be made to strengthen an argument as well as to embellish a description. The principle of the *vis inertiæ*, for example, seems to be identical in physics and metaphysics. It is not more true in the former, that a large body is with more difficulty set in motion than a smaller one, and that its subsequent *momentum* is commensurate with this difficulty, than it is, in the latter, that intellects of the vaster capacity, while more forcible, more constant, and more eventful in their movements than those of inferior grade, are yet the less readily moved, and more embarrassed, and full of hesitation in the first few steps of their progress. Again: have you ever noticed which of the street signs, over the shop doors, are the most attractive of attention?"

"I have never given the matter a thought," I said.

"There is a game of puzzles," he resumed, "which is played upon a map. One party playing requires another to find a given word— the name of town, river, state, or empire—any word, in short, upon the motley and perplexed surface of the chart. A novice in the game generally seeks to embarrass his opponents by giving them the most minutely lettered names; but the adept selects such words as stretch, in large characters, from one end of the chart to the other. These, like the over-largely lettered signs and placards of the street, escape observation by dint of being excessively obvious; and here the physical oversight is precisely analogous with the moral inapprehension by which the intellect suffers to pass unnoticed those considerations which are too obtrusively and too palpably self-evident. But this is a point, it appears, somewhat above or beneath the understanding of the Prefect. He never once thought it probable, or possible, that the minister had deposited the letter immediately beneath the nose of the whole world, by way of best preventing any portion of that world from perceiving it.

"But the more I reflected upon the daring, dashing, and discriminating ingenuity of D——; upon the fact that the document must always have been *at hand*, if he intended to use it to good purpose; and upon the decisive evidence, obtained by the Prefect, that it was not hidden within the limits of the dignitary's ordinary search—the more satisfied I became that, to conceal this letter, the minister had resorted to the comprehensive and sagacious expedient of not attempting to conceal it at all.

"Full of these ideas, I prepared myself with a pair of green spectacles, and called one fine morning, quite by accident, at the Ministerial hotel. I found D—— at home, yawning, lounging, and dawdling, as usual, and pretending to be in the last extremity of *ennui*. He is, perhaps, the most really energetic human being now alive—but that is only when nobody sees him.

"To be even with him, I complained of my weak eyes, and lamented the necessity of the spectacles, under cover of which I cautiously and thoroughly surveyed the whole apartment, while seemingly intent only upon the conversation of my host.

"I paid especial attention to a large writing-table near which he sat, and upon which lay confusedly, some miscellaneous letters and other papers, with one or two musical instruments and a few books. Here, however, after a long and very deliberate scrutiny, I saw nothing to excite particular suspicion.

"At length my eyes, in going the circuit of the room, fell upon a trumpery filigree card-rack of pasteboard, that hung dangling by a dirty blue ribbon, from a little brass knob just beneath the middle of the mantelpiece. In this rack, which had three or four compartments, were five or six visiting cards and a solitary letter. This last was much soiled and crumpled. It was torn nearly in two, across the middle—as if a design, in the first instance, to tear it entirely up as worthless, had been altered, or stayed, in the second. It had a large black seal, bearing the D—— cipher *very* conspicuously, and was addressed, in a diminutive female hand, to D——, the minister himself. It was thrust carelessly, and even, as it seemed, contemptuously, into one of the uppermost divisions of the rack.

"No sooner had I glanced at this letter than I concluded it to be that of which I was in search. To be sure, it was, to all appearance, radically different from the one of which the Prefect had read us so minute a description. Here the seal was large and black, with the D—— cipher; there it was small and red, with the ducal arms of the S—— family. Here, the address, to the minister, was diminutive and feminine; there the superscription, to a certain royal personage, was markedly bold and decided; the size alone formed a point of correspondence. But, then, the *radicalness* of these differences, which was excessive; the dirt; the soiled and torn condition of the paper, so inconsistent with the *true* methodical habits of D——, and so suggestive of a design to delude the beholder into an idea of the worthlessness of the document;—these things, together with the hyperobtrusive situation of this document, full in the view of every visitor, and thus exactly in accordance with the conclusions to which I had previously arrived; these things, I say, were strongly corroborative of suspicion, in one who came with the intention to suspect.

"I protracted my visit as long as possible, and, while I maintained a most animated discussion with the minister, upon a topic which I knew well had never failed to interest and excite him, I kept my attention really riveted upon the letter. In this examination, I committed to memory its external appearance and arrangement in the rack; and also fell, at length, upon a discovery which set at rest whatever trivial doubt I might have entertained. In scrutinizing the edges of the paper, I observed them to be more *chafed* than seemed necessary. They presented the *broken* appearance which is manifested when a stiff paper, having been once folded and pressed with a folder, is refolded in a reversed direction, in the same creases or edges which had formed the original fold. This discovery was sufficient. It was clear to me that the letter had been turned, as a glove, inside out, re-directed and re-sealed. I bade the minister good-morning, and took my departure at once, leaving a gold snuff-box upon the table.

"The next morning I called for the snuff-box, when we resumed, quite eagerly, the conversation of the preceding day. While thus engaged, however, a loud report, as if of a pistol, was heard immediately beneath the windows of the hotel, and was succeeded by a series of fearful screams, and the shoutings of a terrified mob. D—— rushed to a casement, threw it open, and looked out. In the meantime I stepped to the card-rack, took the letter, put it in my pocket, and replaced it by a *fac-simile*, (so far as regards externals) which I had carefully prepared at my lodgings—imitating the D—— cipher, very readily, by means of a seal formed of bread.

"The disturbance in the street had been occasioned by the frantic behavior of a man with a musket. He had fired it among a crowd of women and children. It proved, however, to have been without ball, and the fellow was suffered to go his way as a lunatic or a drunkard. When he had gone, D—— came from the window, whither I had followed him immediately upon securing the object in view. Soon afterward I bade him farewell. The pretended lunatic was a man in my own pay."

"But what purpose had you," I asked, "in replacing the letter by a *fac-simile?* Would it not have been better, at the first visit, to have seized it openly, and departed?"

"D——," replied Dupin, "is a desperate man, and a man of nerve. His hotel, too, is not without attendants devoted to his interests. Had I made the wild attempt you suggest, I might never have left the Ministerial presence alive. The good people of Paris might have heard of me no more. But I had an object apart from these considerations. You know my political prepossessions. In this matter, I act as a partisan of the lady concerned. For eighteen months the Minister has had her in his power. She has now him in hers—since, being unaware that the letter is not in his possession, he will proceed with his exactions as if it was. Thus will he inevitably commit himself, at once, to his political destruction. His downfall, too, will not be more precipitate than awkward. It is all very well to talk about the *facilis descensus Averni;*[6] but in all kinds of climbing, as Catalani said of singing, it is far more easy to get up than to come down. In the present instance I have no sympathy—at least no pity—for him who descends. He is that *monstrum horrendum*, an unprincipled man of genius. I confess, however, that I should like very well to know the precise character of his thoughts, when, being defied by her whom the Prefect terms 'a certain personage,' he is reduced to opening the letter which I left for him in the card-rack."

"How?" did you put any thing particular in it?"

"Why—it did not seem altogether right to leave the interior blank—that would have been insulting. D——, at Vienna once, did me an evil turn, which I told him, quite good-humoredly, that I should remember. So, as I knew he would feel some curiosity in regard to the identity of the person who had outwitted him, I thought it a pity not to give him a clew. He is well acquainted with my MS.,[7] and I just copied into the middle of the blank sheet the words—

>" '——       ——Un dessein si funeste,
>S'il n'est digne d'Atrée, est digne de Thyeste.'[8]

They are to be found in Crébillon's 'Atrée.' ' "

6. "The easy descent to Hell" as described by Vergil in *The Aeneid*.
7. MS—handwriting.
8. "A scheme so horrible,/If it is unworthy of Atreus, is worthy of Thyestes." The allusion is to a particularly revolting episode of revenge in Greek mythology.

# NIKOLAI GOGOL
## 1809–1852

Born in the Russian Ukraine, in the town of Sorochintsky, Gogol was a sickly and unattractive child. His father, a small landowner and amateur playwright, and his mother, a mystically religious woman, gave him a lot of attention until he was twelve, and then sent him away to a boarding school, where he was known as "the mysterious dwarf." After his father died in 1825, his health improved and he began writing under the influence of the great Russian poet Pushkin. He passed the civil service examinations and held various jobs, some involving secret service. He also taught history at a girls' boarding school. In 1836 he wrote a comedy, *The Inspector General*, which was felt to be dangerously critical of the government, and he left the country for a more or less permanent exile in Rome. During the rest of his life he worked on his important novel, *Dead Souls*. He wrote his influential story "The Overcoat" in 1840. With this work Gogol opened the way to Russian realism, so that Tolstoy could say of himself and the other Russian realists, "We all come out of 'The Overcoat.' "

# The Overcoat

Once, in a department . . . but better not mention which department. There is nothing touchier than departments, regiments, bureaus, in fact any caste of officials. Things have reached the point where every individual takes an insult to himself as a slur on society as a whole. It seems that not long ago a complaint was lodged by the police inspector of I forget which town, in which he stated clearly that government institutions had been imperiled and his own sacred name taken in vain. In evidence he produced a huge volume, practically a novel, in which, every ten pages, a police inspector appears, and what's more, at times completely drunk. So, to stay out of trouble, let us refer to it just as *a department*.

And so, once, *in a department*, there worked a clerk. This clerk was nothing much to speak of: he was small, somewhat pockmarked, his hair was somewhat reddish and he even looked somewhat blind. Moreover, he was getting thin on top, had wrinkled cheeks and a complexion that might be aptly described as hemorrhoidal. But that's the Petersburg climate for you.

As to his civil-service category (for first a man's standing should be established), he was what is called an eternal pen-pusher, a lowly ninth-class clerk, the usual butt of the jeers and jokes of those writers who have the congenial habit of biting those who cannot bite back.

The clerk's name was Shoenik. There is no doubt that this name derives from shoe but we know nothing of how, why, or when. His father, his grandfather, and even his brother-in-law wore boots, having new soles put on them not more than three times a year.

His first name was Akaky, like his father's, which made him Akaky Akakievich. This may sound somewhat strange and contrived but it is not contrived at all, and, in view of the circumstances, any other name was unthinkable. If I am not mistaken, Akaky Akakievich was born on the night between the 22nd and the 23rd of March. His late mother, an excellent woman and the wife of a clerk, had made all the arrangements for the child's christening, and, while she was still confined to her bed, the godparents arrived: the worthy Ivan Yeroshkin, head clerk in the Senate, and Arina Whitetumkin, the wife of a police captain, a woman of rare virtue.

The new mother was given her pick of the following three names for her son: Mochius, Sossius, and that of the martyr, Hotzazat. "That won't do," Akaky's late mother thought. "Those names are . . . how shall I put it . . ." To please her, the godparents opened the calendar at another page and again three names came out: Strifilius, Dulius, and Varachasius.

"We're in a mess," the old woman said. "Who ever heard of such names? If it was something like Varadat or Varuch, I wouldn't object . . . but Strifilius and Varachasius . . ."

So they turned to yet another page and out came Pavsicachius and Vachtisius.

"Well, that's that," the mother said. "That settles it. He'll just have to be Akaky like his father."

So that's how Akaky Akakievich originated.

And when they christened the child it cried and twisted its features into a sour expression as though it had a foreboding that it would become a ninth-class clerk.

Well, that's how it all happened and it has been reported here just to show that the child couldn't have been called anything but Akaky.

No one remembers who helped him get his appointment to the department or when he started working there. Directors and all sorts of chiefs came and went but he was always to be found at the same place, in the same position, and in the same capacity, that of copying clerk. Until, after a while, people began to believe that he must have been born just as he was, shabby frock coat, bald patch, and all.

In the office, not the slightest respect was shown him. The porters didn't get up when he passed. In fact, they didn't even raise their eyes, as if nothing but an ordinary fly had passed through the reception room. His chiefs were cold and despotic with him. Some head clerks would just thrust a paper under his nose without even saying, "Copy this," or "Here's a nice interesting little job for you," or some such pleasant remark as is current in well-bred offices. And Akaky Akakievich would take the paper without glancing up to see who had put it under his nose or whether the person was entitled to do so. And right away he would set about copying it.

The young clerks laughed at him and played tricks on him to the limit of their clerkish wit. They made up stories about him and told them in front of him. They said that his seventy-year-old landlady beat him and asked him when the wedding would be. They scattered scraps of paper which they said was snow over his head. But with all this going on, Akaky Akakievich never said a word and even acted as though no one were there. It didn't even affect his work and in spite of their loud badgering he made no mistakes in his copying. Only when they tormented him unbearably, when they jogged his elbow and prevented him from getting on with his work, would he say:

"Let me be. Why do you do this to me? . . ."

And his words and the way he said them sounded strange. There was something touching about them. Once a young man who was new to the office started to tease him, following the crowd. Suddenly he stopped as if awakened from a trance and, after that, he couldn't stand the others, whom at first he had deemed decent people. And for a long time to come, during his gayest moments, he would suddenly see in his mind's eye the little, balding clerk and he would hear the words, "Let me be. Why do you do this to me?" and within those words rang the phrase, "I am your brother." And the young man would cover his face with his hands. Later in life, he often shuddered, musing about the wickedness of man toward man and all the cruelty and vulgarity which are concealed under refined manners. And this, he decided, was also true of men who were considered upright and honorable.

It would be hard to find a man who so lived for his job. It would not be enough to say that he worked conscientiously—he worked with love. There, in his copying, he found an interesting, pleasant world for himself and his delight was reflected in his face. He had his favorites among the letters of the alphabet and, when he came to them, he would chuckle, wink and help them along with his lips so that they could almost be read on his face as they were formed on his pen.

Had he been rewarded in proportion with his zeal, he would,

perhaps to his own surprise, have been promoted to fifth-class clerk. But all he got out of it was, as his witty colleagues put it, a pin for his buttonhole and hemorrhoids to sit on.

Still, it would be unfair to say that no attention had ever been paid him. One of the successive directors, a kindly man, who thought Akaky Akakievich should be rewarded for his long service, suggested that he be given something more interesting than ordinary copying. So he was asked to prepare an already drawn-up document for referral to another department. Actually, all he had to do was to give it a new heading and change some of the verbs from the first to the third person. But Akaky Akakievich found this work so complicated that he broke into a sweat and finally, mopping his brow, he said:

"Oh no, I would rather have something to copy instead."

After that they left him to his copying forever. And aside from it, it seemed, nothing existed for him.

He never gave a thought to his clothes. His frock coat, which was supposed to be green, had turned a sort of mealy reddish. Its collar was very low and very narrow so that his neck, which was really quite ordinary, looked incredibly long—like the spring necks of the head-shaking plaster kittens which foreign peddlers carry around on their heads on trays. And, somehow, there was always something stuck to Akaky Akakievich's frock coat, a wisp of hay, a little thread. Then too, he had a knack of passing under windows just when refuse happened to be thrown out and as a result was forever carrying around on his hat melon rinds and other such rubbish.

Never did he pay any attention to what was going on around him in the street. In this he was very different from the other members of the pen-pushing brotherhood, who are so keen-eyed and observant that they'll notice an undone strap on the bottom of someone's trousers, an observation that unfailingly molds their features into a sly sneer. But even when Akaky Akakievich's eyes were resting on something, he saw superimposed on it his own well-formed, neat handwriting. Perhaps it was only when, out of nowhere, a horse rested its head on his shoulder and sent a blast of wind down his cheek that he'd realize he was not in the middle of a line but in the middle of a street.

When he got home he would sit straight down to the table and quickly gulp his cabbage soup, followed by beef and onions. He never noticed the taste and ate it with flies and whatever else God happened to send along. When his stomach began to feel bloated, he would get up from the table, take out his inkwell, and copy papers he had brought with him from the office. And if there weren't any papers to copy for the office, he would make a copy for his own pleasure, especially if the document were unusual. Unusual, not for the beauty of its style, but because it was addressed to some new or important personage.

Even during those hours when light has completely disappeared from the gray Petersburg sky and the pen-pushing brotherhood have filled themselves with dinner of one sort or another, each as best he can according to his income and his preference; when everyone has rested from the scraping of pens in the office, from running around on their own and others' errands; when the restless human being has relaxed after the tasks, sometimes unnecessary, he sets himself; and the clerks hasten to give over the remaining hours to pleasure—the more enterprising among them rushes to the theater, another walks in the streets, allotting his time to the inspection of ladies' hats; another spends his evenings paying compliments to some prettyish damsel, the queen of a small circle of clerks; another, the most frequent case, goes to visit a brother clerk, who lives somewhere on the third or fourth floor, in two small rooms with a hall of a kitchen and some little pretensions to fashion, a lamp or some other article bought at great sacrifice, such as going without dinner or outside pleasures—in brief, at the time when all clerks have dispersed among the lodgings of their friends to play a little game of whist, sipping tea from glasses and nibbling biscuits, inhaling the smoke from their long pipes, relaying, while the cards are dealt, some bit of gossip that has trickled down from high society; a thing which a Russian cannot do without whatever his circumstances, and even, when there's nothing else to talk about, telling once again the ancient joke about the commandant to whom it was reported that someone had hacked the tail off the horse of the monument to Peter the First—in a word, when everyone else was trying to have a good time, Akaky Akakievich was not even thinking of diverting himself.

No one had ever seen him at a party in the evening. Having written to his heart's content, he would go to bed, smiling in anticipation of the morrow, of what God would send him to copy.

Thus flowed the life of a man who, on a yearly salary of four hundred rubles, was content with his lot. And perhaps it would have flowed on to old age if it hadn't been for the various disasters which are scattered along life's paths, not only for ninth-class clerks, but even for eighth-, seventh-, sixth-class clerks and all the way up to State Councilors, Privy Councilors, and even to those who counsel no one, not even themselves.

In Petersburg, there's a formidable enemy for all those who receive a salary in the neighborhood of four hundred rubles a year.

The enemy is none other than our northern cold, although they say it's very healthy.

Between eight and nine in the morning, at just the time when the streets are filled with people walking to their offices, the cold starts to mete out indiscriminately such hard, stinging flicks on noses that the wretched clerks don't know where to put them. And when the cold pinches the brows and brings tears to the eyes of those in high positions ninth-class clerks are completely defenseless. They can only wrap themselves in their threadbare overcoats and run as fast as they can the five or six blocks to the office. Once arrived, they have to stamp their feet in the vestibule until their abilities and talents, which have been frozen on the way, thaw out once again.

Akaky Akakievich had noticed that for some time the cold had been attacking his back and shoulders quite viciously, try as he might to sprint the prescribed distance. He finally began to wonder whether the fault did not lie with his overcoat. When he gave it a good looking-over in his room he discovered that in two or three places—the shoulders and back—it had become very much like gauze. The cloth was worn so thin that it let the draft in, and, to make things worse, the lining had disintegrated.

It must be noted that Akaky Akakievich's overcoat had also been a butt of the clerks' jokes. They had even deprived it of its respectable name, referring to it as the old dressing gown. And, as far as that goes, it did have a strange shape. Its collar shrank with every year, since it was used to patch other areas. And the patching, which did not flatter the tailor, made the overcoat baggy and ugly.

Having located the trouble, Akaky Akakievich decided to take the cloak to Petrovich, a tailor who lived somewhere on the fourth floor, up a back stairs, and who, one-eyed and pockmarked as he was, was still quite good at repairing clerks' and other such people's trousers and frock coats, provided he happened to be sober and hadn't other things on his mind.

We shouldn't, of course, waste too many words on the tailor, but since it has become the fashion to give a thorough description of every character figuring in a story, there's nothing to be done but to give you Petrovich.

At first he was called just Grigory and was the serf of some gentleman or other. He began to call himself Petrovich when he received his freedom and took to drinking rather heavily on all holidays, on the big ones at first and then, without distinction, on all church holidays—on any day marked by a little cross on the calendar. In this he was true to the traditions of his forefathers, and when his wife nagged him about it, he called her impious and a German. Now that we've mentioned his wife, we'd better say a word or two about her, too. But unfortunately very little is known about her, except that Petrovich had a wife who wore a bonnet instead of a kerchief, but was apparently no beauty, since, on meeting her, it occurred to no one but an occasional soldier to peek under that bonnet of hers, twitching his mustache and making gurgling sounds.

Going up the stairs leading to Petrovich's place, which, to be honest about it, were saturated with water and slops and exuded that ammonia smell which burns your eyes and which you'll always find on the back stairs of all Petersburg houses—going up those stairs, Akaky Akakievich was already conjecturing how much Petrovich would ask and making up his mind not to pay more than two rubles.

The door stood open because Petrovich's wife was cooking some fish or other and had made so much smoke in the kitchen that you couldn't even see the cockroaches. Akaky Akakievich went through the kitchen without even seeing Mrs. Petrovich and finally reached the other room, where he saw Petrovich sitting on a wide, unpainted wooden table, with his legs crossed under him like a Turkish pasha.

He was barefoot, as tailors at work usually are, and the first thing Akaky Akakievich saw was Petrovich's big toe, with its twisted nail, thick, and hard like a tortoise shell. A skein of silk and cotton thread hung around Petrovich's neck. On his knees there was some old garment. For the past three minutes he had been trying to thread his needle, very irritated at the darkness of the room and even with the thread itself, muttering under his breath: "It won't go through, the pig, it's killing me, the bitch!" Akaky Akakievich was unhappy to find Petrovich so irritated. He preferred to negotiate when the tailor was a little under the weather, or, as his wife put it, "when the one-eyed buzzard had a load on." When caught in such a state, Petrovich usually gave way very readily on the price and would even thank Akaky Akakievich with respectful bows and all that. True, afterwards, his wife would come whining that her husband had charged too little because he was drunk; but all you had to do was to add ten kopeks and it was a deal.

This time, however, Petrovich seemed to be sober and therefore curt, intractable, and likely to charge an outrageous price. Akaky Akakievich realized this and would have liked to beat a hasty retreat, but the die was cast. Petrovich had fixed his one eye on him and Akaky Akakievich involuntarily came out with:

"Hello, Petrovich."

"Wish you good day, sir," said Petrovich and bent his eye toward Akaky Akakievich's hands to see what kind of spoil he had brought him.

"Well, Petrovich, I've come . . . see . . . the thing is . . . to . . ."

It should be realized that Akaky Akakievich used all sorts of prepositions, adverbs and all those meaningless little parts of speech when he spoke. Moreover, if the matter were very involved, he generally didn't finish his sentences and opened them with the words: "This, really, is absolutely, I mean to say . . ." and then nothing more—he had forgotten that he hadn't said what he wanted to.

"What is it then?" Petrovich asked, looking over Akaky Akakievich's frock coat with his one eye, the collar, the sleeves, the back, the tails, the buttonholes, all of which he was already acquainted with, since, repairs and all, it was his own work. That's just what tailors do as soon as they see you.

"Well, it's like this, Petrovich . . . my cloak, well, the material . . . look, you can see, everywhere else it's very strong, well, it's a bit dusty and it looks rather shabby, but it's not really . . . look, it's just in one place it's a little . . . on the back here, and here too . . . it's a little worn . . . and here on this shoulder too, a little—and that's all. There's not much work . . ."

Petrovich took Akaky Akakievich's old dressing gown, as his colleagues called it, spread it out on the table and looked it over at length. Then he shook his head and, stretching out his hand, took from the window sill a snuffbox embellished with the portrait of a general, though just what general it was impossible to tell since right where his face used to be there was now a dent glued over with a piece of paper. Taking some snuff, Petrovich spread the overcoat out on his hands, held it up against the light and again shook his head. Then he turned the overcoat inside out, with the lining up, and shook his head again. Then, once more, he removed the snuffbox lid with its general under the piece of paper, and, stuffing snuff into his nose, closed the box, put it away, and finally said:

"No. It can't be mended. It's no use."

At these words, Akaky Akakievich's heart turned over.

"But why can't it be, Petrovich?" he said in the imploring voice of a child. "Look, the only trouble is that it's worn around the shoulders. I'm sure you have some scraps of cloth . . ."

"As for scraps, I suppose I could find them," Petrovich said, "but I couldn't sew them on. The whole thing is rotten. It'd go to pieces the moment you touched it with a needle."

"Well, if it starts to go, you'll catch it with a patch . . ."

"But there's nothing for patches to hold to. It's too far gone. It's only cloth in name—a puff of wind and it'll disintegrate."

"Still, I'm sure you can make them hold just the same. Otherwise, really, Petrovich, see what I mean . . ."

"No," Petrovich said with finality, "nothing can be done with it. It's just no good. You'd better make yourself some bands out of it to wrap round you legs when it's cold and socks aren't enough to keep you warm. The Germans thought up those things to make money for themselves."—Petrovich liked to take a dig at the Germans whenever there was a chance.—"As to the overcoat, it looks as if you'll have to have a new one made."

At the word "new" Akaky Akakievich's vision became foggy and the whole room began to sway. The only thing he saw clearly was the general with the paper-covered face on the lid of Petrovich's snuffbox.

"What do you mean a *new* one?" he said, talking as if in a dream. "I haven't even got the money . . ."

"A new one," Petrovich repeated with savage calm.

"Well, but if I really had to have a new one, how would it be that . . ."

"That is, what will it cost?"

"Yes."

"Well, it will be over one hundred and fifty rubles," Petrovich said, pursing his lips meaningfully. He liked strong effects, he liked to perplex someone suddenly and then observe the grimace that his words produced.

"A hundred and fifty rubles for an overcoat!" shrieked the poor Akaky Akakievich, shrieked perhaps for the first time in his life, since he was always noted for his quietness.

"Yes, sir," said Petrovich, "but what an overcoat! And if it is to have marten on the collar and a silk-lined hood, that'll bring it up to two hundred."

"Please, Petrovich, please," Akaky Akakievich said beseechingly, not taking in Petrovich's words or noticing his dramatic effects, "mend it somehow, just enough to make it last a little longer."

"No sir, it won't work. It would be a waste of labor and money."

Akaky Akakievich left completely crushed. And when he left, Petrovich, instead of going back to his work, remained for a long time immobile, his lips pursed meaningfully. He was pleased with himself for having upheld his own honor as well as that of the entire tailoring profession.

Akaky Akakievich emerged into the street feeling as if he were in a dream. "So that's it," he repeated to himself. "I never suspected it would turn out this way . . ." and then, after a brief pause, he went on: "So that's it! Here's how it turns out in the end, and I, really, simply couldn't have foreseen it." After another, longer pause, he added: "And so here we are! Here's how things stand. I in no way expected . . . but this is impossible . . . what a business!" Muttering thus, instead of going home, he went in the opposite direction, without having the slightest idea of what was going on.

As he was walking, a chimney sweep brushed his dirty side against him and blackened his whole shoulder; a whole bucketful of lime was showered over him from the top of a house under construction. But he noticed nothing and only when he bumped into a watchman who, resting his halberd near him, was shaking some snuff out of a horn into his calloused palm, did he come to a little and that only because the watchman said:

"Ya hafta knock my head off? Ya got the whole sidewalk, ain'tcha?"

This caused him to look about him and turn back toward home. Only then did he start to collect his thoughts and to see his real position clearly. He began to talk to himself, not in bits of phrases now but sensibly, as to a wise friend in whom he could confide.

"Oh no," he said, "this wasn't the moment to speak to Petrovich. Right now he's sort of . . . his wife obviously has given him a beating . . . that sort of thing. It'd be better if I went and saw him Sunday morning. After Saturday night, his one eye will be wandering and he'll be tired and in need of another drink, and his wife won't give him the money. So I'll slip him a quarter and that will make him more reasonable and so, for the overcoat . . ." Thus Akaky Akakievich tried to reassure himself, and persuaded himself to wait for Sunday.

When that day came, he waited at a distance until he saw Petrovich's wife leave the house and then went up. After his Saturday night libations, Petrovich's eye certainly was wandering. He hung his head and looked terribly sleepy. But, despite all that, as soon as he learned what Akaky Akakievich had come about, it was as if the devil had poked him.

"It can't be done," he said. "You must order a new one."

Here Akaky Akakievich pressed the quarter on him.

"Thank you," Petrovich said. "I'll drink a short one to you, sir. And as to the overcoat, you can stop worrying. It's worthless. But I'll make you a first-rate new one. That I'll see to."

Akaky Akakievich tried once more to bring the conversation around to mending, but Petrovich, instead of listening said:

"I'll make you a new one, sir, and you can count on me to do my best. I may even make the collar fastened with silver-plated clasps for you."

At this point Akaky Akakievich saw that he'd have to have a new overcoat and he became utterly depressed. Where was he going to get the money? There was of course the next holiday bonus. But the sum involved had long ago been allotted to other needs. He had to order new trousers, to pay the cobbler for replacing the tops on his boots. He owed the seamstress for three shirts and simply had to have two items of underwear which one cannot refer to in print. In fact, all the money, to the last kopek, was owed, and even if the director made an unexpectedly generous gesture and allotted him, instead of forty rubles, a whole forty-five or even fifty, the difference would be a drop in the ocean of the overcoat outlay.

It is true Akaky Akakievich knew that, on occasions, Petrovich slapped on heaven knows what exorbitant price, so that even his wife couldn't refrain from exclaiming:

"Have you gone mad, you fool! One day he accepts work for nothing, and the next, something gets into him and makes him ask for more than he's worth himself."

But he also knew that Petrovich would agree to make him a new overcoat for eighty rubles. Even so, where was he to find the eighty? He could perhaps scrape together half that sum. Even a little more. But where would he get the other half? . . . Let us, however, start with the first half and see where it was to come from.

Akaky Akakievich had a rule: whenever he spent one ruble, he slipped a copper into a little box with a slot in its side. Every six months, he counted the coppers and changed them for silver. He'd been doing this for a long time and, after all these years, had accumulated more than forty rubles. So this came to one half. But what about the remaining forty rubles?

Akaky Akakievich thought and thought and decided that he would have to reduce his regular expenses for an entire year at least. It would mean going without his evening tea; not burning candles at night, and, if he absolutely had to have light, going to his landlady's room and working by her candle. It would mean, when walking in the street, stepping as carefully as possible over the cobbles and paving stones, almost tiptoeing, so as not to wear out the soles of his boots too rapidly, and giving out his laundry as seldom as possible, and, so that it shouldn't get too soiled, undressing as soon as he got home and staying in just his thin cotton dressing gown, which, if time hadn't taken pity on it, would itself have collapsed long ago.

It must be admitted that, at first, he suffered somewhat from these restrictions. But then he became accustomed to them somehow and things went smoothly again. He even got used to going hungry in the evenings, but then he was able to feed himself spiritually, carrying within him the eternal idea of his overcoat-to-be. It was if his existence had become somehow fuller, as if he had married and another human being were there with him, as if he were no longer alone on life's road but walking by the side of a delightful companion. And that companion was none other than the overcoat itself, with its thick padding and strong lining that would last forever. In some way, he became more alive, even stronger-minded, like a man who has determined his ultimate goal in life.

From his face and actions all the marks of vacillation and indecision vanished.

At times, there was even a fire in his eyes and the boldest, wildest notions flashed through his head—perhaps he should really consider having marten put on the collar? The intensity of these thoughts almost distracted his attention from his work. Once he almost made a mistake, which caused him to exclaim—true, very softly—"Oof!" and to cross himself.

At least once each month he looked in on Petrovich to discuss the overcoat—the best place to buy the material, its color, its price . . . Then, on the way home, a little worried but always pleased, he mused about how, finally, all this buying would be over and the coat would be made.

Things went ahead faster than he had expected. Beyond all expectations, the director granted Akaky Akakievich not forty, not forty-five, but a whole sixty rubles. Could he have had a premonition that Akaky Akakievich needed a new overcoat, or had it just happened by itself? Whatever it was, Akaky Akakievich wound up with an extra twenty rubles. This circumstance speeded matters up. Another two or three months of moderate hunger and he had almost all of the eighty rubles he needed. His heartbeat, generally very quiet, grew faster.

As soon as he could, he set out for the store with Petrovich. They bought excellent material, which is not surprising since they had been planning the move for all of six months, and a month had seldom gone by without Akaky Akakievich dropping into the shop to work out prices. Petrovich himself said that there was no better material to be had.

For the lining they chose calico, but so good and thick that, Petrovich said, it even looked better and glossier than silk. They did not buy marten because it was too expensive. Instead they got cat, the best available—cat which at a distance could always be taken for marten. Petrovich spent two full weeks on the overcoat because of all the quilting he had to do. He charged twelve rubles for his work—it was impossible to take less; it had been sewn with silk, with fine double seams and Petrovich had gone over each seam again afterwards with his own teeth, squeezing out different patterns with them.

It was—well, it's hard to say exactly which day it was, but it was

probably the most solemn in Akaky Akakievich's life, the day Petrovich finally brought him the overcoat. He brought it in the morning,
just before it was time to go to the office. There couldn't have been a
better moment for the coat to arrive, because cold spells had been
creeping in and threatened to become even more severe. Petrovich
appeared with the coat, as befits a good tailor. He had an expression
of importance on his face that Akaky Akakievich had never seen
before. He looked very much aware of having performed an important act, an act that carries tailors over the chasm which separates
those who merely put in linings and do repairs from those who
create.

He took the overcoat out of the gigantic handkerchief—just fresh
from the wash—in which he had wrapped it to deliver it. The han-
derkerchief he folded neatly and put in his pocket, ready for use.
Then he took the coat, looked at it with great pride and, holding it
in both hands, threw it quite deftly around Akaky Akakievich's
shoulders. He pulled and smoothed it down at the back, wrapped it
around Akaky Akakievich, leaving it a little open at the front. Akaky
Akakievich, a down-to-earth sort of man, wanted to try out the
sleeves. Petrovich helped him to pull his arms through and it turned
out that with the sleeves too it was good. In a word, it was clear that
the coat fitted perfectly.

Petrovich didn't fail to take advantage of the occasion to remark
that it was only because he did without a signboard, lived in a small
side street, and had known Akaky Akakievich for a long time that
he had charged him so little. On Nevsky Avenue, nowadays, he
said, they'd have taken seventy-five rubles for the work alone. Akaky
Akakievich had no desire to debate the point with Petrovich—he
was always rather awed by the big sums which Petrovich liked to
mention to impress people. He paid up, thanked Petrovich, and left
for the office wearing his new overcoat.

Petrovich followed him and stood for a long time in the street
gazing at the overcoat from a distance. Then he plunged into a
curving side street, took a short cut, and reemerged on the street
ahead of Akaky Akakievich, so that he could have another look at
the coat from another angle.

Meanwhile, Akaky Akakievich walked on, bubbling with good
spirits. Every second of every minute he felt the new overcoat on his
shoulders and several times he even let out a little chuckle of inward
pleasure. Indeed, the overcoat presented him with a double advantage; it was warm and it was good. He didn't notice his trip at all
and suddenly found himself before the office building. In the
porter's lodge, he slipped off the overcoat, inspected it, and entrusted it to the porter's special care.

No one knows how, but it suddenly became general knowledge in the office that Akaky Akakievich had a new overcoat and that the old dressing gown no longer existed. Elbowing one another, they all rushed to the cloakroom to see the new coat. Then they proceeded to congratulate him. He smiled at first, but then the congratulations became too exuberant, and he felt embarrassed. And when they surrounded him and started trying to persuade him that the very least he could do was to invite them over one evening to drink to the coat, Akaky Akakievich felt completely at a loss, didn't know what to do with himself, what to say or how to talk himself out of it. And a few minutes later, all red in the face, he was trying rather naively to convince them that it wasn't a new overcoat at all, that it wasn't much, that it was an old one.

In the end, a clerk, no lesser person than an assistant to the head clerk, probably wanting to show that he wasn't too proud to mingle with those beneath him, said:

"All right then, I'll do it instead of Akaky Akakievich. I invite you all over for a party. Come over to my place tonight. Incidentally, it happens to be my birthday today."

Naturally the clerks now congratulated the head clerk's assistant and happily accepted his invitation. Akaky Akakievich started to excuse himself, but he was told that it would be rude on his part, a disgrace, so he had to give way in the end. And later he was even rather pleased that he had accepted, since it would give him an opportunity to wear the new coat in the evening too.

Akaky Akakievich felt as if it were a holiday. He arrived home in the happiest frame of mind, took off the overcoat, hung it up very carefully on the wall, gave the material and the lining one more admiring inspection. Then he took out that ragged item known as the old dressing gown and put it next to the new overcoat, looked at it and began to laugh, so great was the difference between the two. And long after that, while eating his dinner, he snorted every time he thought of the dressing gown. He felt very gay during his dinner, and afterwards he did no copying whatsoever. Instead he wallowed in luxury for a while, lying on his bed until dark. Then, without further dallying, he dressed, pulled on his new overcoat and went out.

It is, alas, impossible to say just where the party-giving clerk lived. My memory is beginning to fail me badly and everything in Petersburg, streets and houses, has become so mixed up in my head that it's very difficult to extract anything from it and to present it in an orderly fashion. Be that as it may, it is a fact that the clerk in question lived in a better district of the city, which means not too close to Akaky Akakievich.

To start with, Akaky Akakievich had to pass through a maze of deserted, dimly lit streets, but, toward the clerk's house, the streets became lighter and livelier. More pedestrians began flashing by more often; there were some well-dressed ladies and men with beaver collars. And, instead of the drivers with their wooden, fretworked sledges studded with gilt nails, he came across smart coachmen in crimson velvet caps, in lacquered sledges, with bearskin lap rugs. He even saw some carriages darting past with decorated boxes, their wheels squeaking on the snow.

Akaky Akakievich gazed around him. For several years now he hadn't been out in the evening. He stopped before the small, lighted window of a shop, staring curiously at a picture of a pretty woman kicking off her shoe and thereby showing her whole leg, which was not bad at all; in the background, some man or other with side whiskers and a handsome Spanish goatee was sticking his head through a door leading to another room. Akaky Akakievich shook his head, snorted, smiled and walked on. Why did he snort? Was it because he had come across something that, although completely strange to him, still aroused in him, as it would in anyone, a certain instinct—or did he think, as many clerks do, along the following lines: "Well, really, the French! If they were after something . . . that sort of thing . . . then, really! . . ." Maybe he didn't even think that. After all, one can't just creep into a man's soul and find out everything he's thinking.

At last he reached the house in which the head clerk's assistant lived. And he lived in style, on the second floor, with the staircase lighted by a lantern. In the hall, Akaky Akakievich found several rows of galoshes. Amidst the galoshes, a samovar was hissing and puffing steam. All around the walls hung overcoats and cloaks, some with beaver collars and others with velvet lapels. The noise and talk that could be heard through the partition became suddenly clear and resounding when the door opened and a servant came out with a tray of empty glasses, a cream jug, and a basket of cookies. It was clear that the clerks had arrived long before and had already drunk their first round of tea.

Akaky Akakievich hung his coat up and went in. In a flash, he took in the candles, the clerks, the pipes, the card tables, while his ears were filled with the hubbub of voices rising all around him and the banging of chairs being moved. Awkwardly, he paused in the middle of the room, trying to think what to do. But he had been noticed and his arrival was greeted with a huge yell. Immediately everybody rushed out into the hall to have another look at his new overcoat. Akaky Akakievich felt a bit confused, but, being an uncomplicated man, he was rather pleased when everyone agreed that it was a good overcoat.

Soon, however, they abandoned him and his overcoat and turned their attention, as was to be expected, to the card tables.

The din, the voices, the presence of so many people—all this was unreal to Akaky Akakievich. He had no idea how to behave, where to put his hands, his feet, or, for that matter, his whole body. He sat down near a card table, stared at the cards and peeked in turn into the faces of the players. In a little while he got bored and began to yawn, feeling rather sleepy—it was long past his usual bedtime. He wanted to take leave of the host, but they wouldn't let him go. He really had to toast his new overcoat with champagne, they insisted. They made Akaky Akakievich drink two glasses of champagne, after which he felt that the party was becoming gayer, but nevertheless he was quite unable to forget that it was now midnight and that he should have gone home long ago.

In spite of everything his host could think up to keep him, he went quietly out into the hall, found his overcoat, which to his annoyance was lying on the floor, shook it, carefully removed every speck he could find on it, put it on and walked down the stairs and out into the street.

The street was still lighted. Some little stores, those meeting places for servants and people of every sort, were open, while others, although closed, still showed a long streak of light under their doors, which indicated that the company had not yet dispersed and that the menservants and maids were finishing up their gossip and their conversations, leaving their masters perplexed as to their whereabouts.

Akaky Akakievich walked along in such a gay mood that, who knows why, he almost darted after a lady who flashed by him like a streak of lightning, every part of her body astir with independent, fascinating motion. Still, he restrained himself immediately, went back to walking slowly and even wondered where that compulsion to gallop had come from.

Soon there stretched out before him those deserted streets which, even in the daytime, are not so gay, and, now that it was night, looked even more desolate. Fewer street lamps were lit—obviously a smaller oil allowance was given out in this district. Then came wooden houses and fences; not a soul around, nothing but glistening snow and black silhouettes of the low, sleeping hovels with their shuttered windows. He came to the spot where the street cut through a square so immense that the houses opposite were hardly visible beyond its sinister emptiness.

God knows where, far away on the edge of the world, he could see the glow of a brazier by a watchman's hut.

Akaky Akakievich's gay mood definitely waned. He could not

suppress a shiver as he stepped out into the square, a foreboding of evil in his heart. He glanced behind him and to either side—it was like being in the middle of the sea. "No, it's better not to look," he thought, and walked on with his eyes shut. And when he opened them again to see if the other side of the square was close, he saw instead, standing there, almost in front of his nose, people with mustaches, although he couldn't make out exactly who or what. Then his vision became foggy and there was a beating in his chest.

"Why, here's my overcoat," one of the people thundered, grabbing him by the collar.

Akaky Akakievich was just going to shout out "Help!" when another brought a fist about the size of a clerk's head up to his very mouth, and said:

"You just try and yell . . ."

Akaky Akakievich felt them pull off his coat, then he received a knee in the groin. He went down on his back and after that he lay in the snow and felt nothing more.

When he came to a few minutes later and scrambled to his feet, there was no one around. He felt cold and, when he realized that the overcoat was gone, desperate. He let out a yell. But his voice didn't come close to reaching the other side of the square.

Frantic, he hollered all the way across the square as he scrambled straight toward the watchman's hut. The watchman was standing beside it, leaning on his halberd, and gazing out across the square, wondering who it could be running toward him and shouting. At last Akaky Akakievich reached him. Gasping for breath, he began shouting at him—what sort of a watchman did he think he was, hadn't he seen anything, and why the devil had he allowed them to rob a man? The watchman said he had seen no one except the two men who had stopped Akaky Akakievich in the middle of the square, who he had thought were friends of his, and that instead of hollering at the watchman, he'd better go and see the police inspector tomorrow and the inspector would find out who had taken the overcoat.

Akaky Akakievich hurried home; he was in a terrible state. The little hair he had left, on his temples and on the back of his head, was completely disheveled, there was snow all down one side of him and on his chest and all over his trousers. His old landlady, hearing his impatient banging on the door, jumped out of bed, and, with only one shoe on, ran to open up, clutching her nightgown at the neck, probably out of modesty. When she saw the state Akaky Akakievich was in, she stepped back.

When he told her what had happened, she threw up her hands

and said that he should go straight to the borough Police Commissioner, that the local police inspector could not be trusted, that he'd just make promises and give him the runaround. So it was best, she said, to go straight to the borough Commissioner. In fact, she even knew him because Anna, her former Finnish cook, had now got a job as a nanny at his house. And the landlady herself often saw him driving past their house. Moreover, she knew he went to church every Sunday and prayed and at the same time looked cheerful and was obviously a good man. Having heard her advice, Akaky Akakievich trudged off sadly to his room and somehow got through the night, though exactly how must be imagined by those who know how to put themselves in another man's place.

Early the next morning, he went to the borough Commissioner's. But it turned out that he was still asleep. He returned at ten and again he was told he was asleep. He went back at eleven and was told that the Commissioner was not home. He tried again during the dinner hour but the secretaries in the reception room would not let him in and wanted to know what business had brought him. For once in his life Akaky Akakievich decided to show some character and told them curtly that he must see the Commissioner personally, that they'd better let him in since he was on official government business, that he would lodge a complaint against them and that then they would see.

The secretaries didn't dare say anything to that and one of them went to call the Commissioner. The Commissioner reacted very strangely to Akaky Akakievich's story of the robbery. Instead of concentrating on the main point, he asked Akaky Akakievich what he had been doing out so late, whether he had stopped off somewhere on his way, hadn't he been to a house of ill repute. Akaky Akakievich became very confused and when he left he wasn't sure whether something would be done about his overcoat or not.

That day he did not go to his office for the first time in his life. The next day he appeared, looking very pale and wearing his old dressing gown, which now seemed shabbier than ever. His account of the theft of his overcoat touched many of the clerks, although, even now, there were some who poked fun at him. They decided on the spot to take up a collection for him but they collected next to nothing because the department employees had already had to donate money for a portrait of the Director and to subscribe to some book or other, on the suggestion of the section chief, who was a friend of the author's. So the sum turned out to be the merest trifle.

Someone, moved by compassion, decided to help Akaky Akakievich by giving him good advice. He told him that he had better not go to his local inspector because, even supposing the inspector wanted to impress his superiors and managed to recover the coat, Akaky Akakievich would still find it difficult to obtain it at the police station unless he could present irrefutable proof of ownership. The best thing was to go through a certain important personage who, by writing and contacting the right people, would set things moving faster. So Akaky Akakievich decided to seek an audience with the important personage.

Even to this day, it is not known exactly what position the important personage held or what his duties consisted of. All we need to know is that this important personage had become important quite recently and that formerly he had been an unimportant person. And even his present position was unimportant compared with other, more important ones. But there is always a category of people for whom somebody who is unimportant to others is an important personage. And the personage in question used various devices to play up his importance: for instance, he made the civil servants of lower categories come out to meet him on the stairs before he'd even reached his office; and a subordinate could not approach him directly but had to go through proper channels. That's the way things are in Holy Russia—everyone tries to ape his superior.

They say that one ninth-class clerk, when he was named section chief in a small office, immediately had a partition put up to make a separate room, which he called the conference room. He stationed an usher at the door who had to open it for all those who came in, although the conference room had hardly enough space for a writing table, even without visitors. The audiences and the manner of our important personage were impressive and stately, but quite uncomplicated. The key to his system was severity. He liked to say: "Severity, severity, severity," and as he uttered the word for the third time, he usually looked very meaningfully into the face of the person he was talking to. True, it was not too clear what need there was for all this severity since the ten-odd employees who made up the whole administrative apparatus of his office were quite frightened enough as it was. Seeing him coming, they would leave their work and stand to attention until he had crossed the room. His usual communication with his inferiors was full of severity and consisted almost entirely of three phrases: "How dare you!" "Who do you think you're talking to?" and "Do you appreciate who I am?" Actually, he was a kindly man, a good friend and obliging, but promotion to a high rank had gone to his head, knocked him completely off balance, and he just didn't know how to act. When he happened to be with equals, he was still a decent fellow, and, in a way, by no means stupid. But whenever he found himself among those who were below him—even a single rank—he became impossible. He fell silent and was quite pitiable, because even he himself realized that he could have been having a much better time. Sometimes he was obviously longing to join some group in a lively conversation, but he would be stopped by the thought that he would be going too far, putting himself on familiar terms and thereby losing face. And so he remained eternally in silent, aloof isolation, only occasionally uttering some monosyllabic sounds, and, as a result, he acquired a reputation as a deadly bore.

It was to this important personage that Akaky Akakievich presented himself, and at a most unpropitious moment to boot. That is, very unpropitious for him, although quite suitable for the important personage. The latter was in his office talking gaily to a childhood friend who had recently come to Petersburg and whom he hadn't seen for many years. This was the moment when they announced that there was a man named Shoenik to see him.

"Who's he?" the personage wanted to know.

"Some clerk," they told him.

"I see. Let him wait. I am not available now."

Here it should be noted that the important personage was greatly exaggerating. He was available. He and his friend had talked over everything imaginable. For some time now the conversation had been interlaced with lengthy silences, and they weren't doing much more than slapping each other on the thigh and saying:

"So that's how it is, Ivan Abramovich."

"Yes, indeed, Stepan Varlamovich!"

Still Akaky Akakievich had to wait, so that his friend, who had left the government service long ago and now lived in the country, could see what a long time employees had to wait in his reception room.

At last, when they had talked and had sat silent facing each other for as long as they could stand it, when they had smoked a cigar reclining in comfortable armchairs with sloping backs, the important personage, as if he had just recalled it, said to his secretary who was standing at the door with papers for a report:

"Wait a minute. Wasn't there a clerk waiting? Tell him to come in."

Seeing Akaky Akakievich's humble appearance and his wretched old frock coat, he turned abruptly to face him and said: "What do you want?"

He spoke in the hard, sharp voice which he had deliberately developed by practicing at home before a mirror an entire week before he had taken over his present exalted position.

Akaky Akakievich, who had felt properly subdued even before this, felt decidedly embarrassed. He did his best, as far as he could control his tongue, to explain what had happened. Of course, he added even more than his usual share of phrases like "that is to say" and "so to speak." The overcoat, he explained, was completely new and had been cruelly taken away from him and he had turned to the important personage, that is to say, come to him, in the hope that he would, so to speak, intercede for him somehow, that is to say, write the Superintendent of Police or, so to speak, someone, and find the overcoat.

For some unimaginable reason the important personage found his manner too familiar.

"My dear sir," he answered sharply, "don't you know the proper channels? Do you realize whom you're addressing and what the proper procedure should be? You should first have handed in a petition to the office. It would have gone to the head clerk. From him it would have reached the section head, who would have approached my secretary and only then would the secretary have presented it to me. . . ."

"But, Your Excellency," said Akaky Akakievich, trying to gather what little composure he had and feeling at the same time that he was sweating terribly, "I, Your Excellency; ventured to trouble you because secretaries, that is to say . . . are, so to speak, an unreliable lot. . . ."

"What, what, what?" demanded the important personage. "Where did you pick up such an attitude? Where did you get such ideas? What is this insubordination that is spreading among young people against their chiefs and superiors?"

The important personage, apparently, had not noticed that Akaky Akakievich was well over fifty. Thus, surely, if he could be called young at all it would only be relatively, that is, to someone of seventy.

"Do you realize to whom you are talking? Do you appreciate who I am? Do you really realize, do you, I'm asking you?"

Here he stamped his foot and raised his voice to such a pitch that there was no need to be an Akaky Akakievich to be frightened.

And Akaky Akakievich froze completely. He staggered, his whole body shook, and he was quite unable to keep his feet. If a messenger hadn't rushed over and supported him, he would have collapsed onto the floor. They carried him out almost unconscious.

And the important personage, pleased to see that his dramatic effect had exceeded his expectations, and completely delighted with the idea that a word from him could knock a man unconscious, glanced at his friend to see what he thought of it all and was pleased to see that the friend looked somewhat at a loss and that fear had extended to him too.

Akaky Akakievich remembered nothing about getting downstairs and out into the street. He could feel neither hand nor foot. In all his life he had never been so severely reprimanded by a high official, and not a direct chief of his at that. He walked open-mouthed through a blizzard, again and again stumbling off the sidewalk. The wind, according to Petersburg custom, blew at him from all four sides at once, out of every side street. In no time it had blown him a sore throat and he got himself home at last quite unable to say a word. His throat was swollen and he went straight to bed. That's how severe the effects of an adequate reprimand can be.

The next day he was found to have a high fever. Thanks to the generous assistance of the Petersburg climate, the illness progressed beyond all expectations. A doctor came, felt his pulse, found there was nothing he could do and prescribed a poultice. That was done so that the patient would not be deprived of the beneficial aid of medicine. The doctor added, however, that, by the way, the patient had another day and a half to go, after which he would be what is called kaput. Then, turning to the landlady, the doctor said:

"And you, my good woman, I'd not waste my time if I were you. I'd order him the coffin right away. A pine one. The oak ones, I imagine, would be too expensive for him."

Whether Akaky Akakievich heard what for him were fateful words, and, if he heard, whether they had a shattering effect on him and whether he was sorry to lose his wretched life, are matters of conjecture. He was feverish and delirious the whole time. Apparitions, each stranger than the last, kept crowding before him. He saw Petrovich and ordered an overcoat containing some sort of concealed traps to catch the thieves who were hiding under his bed, so that every minute he kept calling his landlady to come and pull out the one who had even slipped under his blanket. Next, he would ask why his old dressing gown was hanging there in front of him when he had a new overcoat. Then he would find himself standing before the important personage, listening to the reprimand and repeating over and over: "I am sorry, Your Excellency, I am sorry."

Then he began to swear, using the most frightful words, which caused his old landlady to cross herself in horror; never in her life had she heard anything like it from him, and what made it even worse was that they came pouring out on the heels of the phrase, "Your Excellency." After that he talked complete nonsense and it was impossible to make out anything he was saying, except that his disconnected words kept groping for that lost overcoat of his. Then, at last, poor Akaky Akakievich gave up the ghost.

They did not bother to seal his room or his belongings because there were no heirs and, moreover, very little to inherit—namely, a bundle of goose quills, a quire of white government paper, three pairs of socks, a few buttons that had come off his trousers, and the old dressing-gown coat already mentioned. God knows whom they went to; even the reporter of this story did not care enough to find out.

They took Akaky Akakievich away and buried him. And Petersburg went on without him exactly as if he had never existed. A creature had vanished, disappeared. He had had no one to protect him. No one had ever paid him the slightest attention. Not even that which a naturalist pays to a common fly which he mounts on a pin and looks at through his microscope. True, this creature, who had meekly borne the office jokes and gone quietly to his grave, had had, toward the end of his life, a cherished visitor—the overcoat, which for a brief moment had brightened his wretched existence. Then a crushing blow had finished everything, a blow such as befalls the powerful of the earth. . . .

A few days after his death, a messenger from his office was sent to his lodgings with an order summoning him to report immediately; the chief was asking for him. But the messenger had to return alone and to report that Akaky Akakievich could not come.

"Why not?" he was asked.

"Because," the messenger said, "he died. They buried him four days ago."

That is how the department found out about Akaky Akakievich's death, and the next day a new clerk sat in his place: he was much taller and his handwriting was not as straight. In fact, his letters slanted considerably.

But who would have imagined that that was not the end of Akaky Akakievich, that he was fated to live on and make his presence felt for a few days after his death as if in compensation for having spent his life unnoticed by anyone? But that's the way it happened and our little story gains an unexpectedly fantastic ending. Rumors suddenly started to fly around Petersburg that a ghost was haunting the streets at night in the vicinity of the Kalinkin Bridge. The ghost, which looked like a little clerk, was purportedly searching for a stolen overcoat and used this pretext to pull the coats off the shoulders of everyone he met without regard for rank or title. And it made no difference what kind of coat it was—cat, beaver, fox, bearskin, in fact any of the furs and skins people have thought up to cover their own skins with.

One of the department employees saw the ghost with his own eyes and instantly recognized Akaky Akakievich. However, he was so terrified that he dashed off as fast as his legs would carry him and so didn't get a good look; he only saw from a distance that the ghost was shaking his finger at him. Complaints kept pouring in, and not only from petty employees, which would have been understandable. One and all, even Privy Councilors, were catching chills in their backs and shoulders from having their overcoats peeled off. The police were ordered to catch the ghost at any cost, dead or alive, and to punish him with due severity as a warning to others. And what's more, they nearly succeeded.

To be precise, a watchman caught the ghost red-handed, grabbed it by the collar, in Kiryushkin Alley, as it was trying to pull the coat off a retired musician who, in his day, used to tootle on the flute. Grabbing it, he called for help from two colleagues of his and asked them to hold on to it for just a minute. He had, he said, to get his snuff-box out of his boot so that he could bring some feeling back to his nose, which had been frostbitten six times in his life. But it was evidently snuff that even a ghost couldn't stand. The man, closing his right nostril with his finger, had hardly sniffed up half a fistful into the left when the ghost sneezed so violently that the three watchmen were blinded by the resulting shower. They all raised their fists to wipe their eyes and, when they could see again, the ghost had vanished. They even wondered whether they had really held him at all. After that, watchmen were so afraid of the ghost that they felt reluctant to interfere with live robbers and contented themselves with shouting from a distance: 'Hey you! On your way!"

And the clerk's ghost began to haunt the streets well beyond the Kalinkin Bridge, spreading terror among the meek.

However, we have completely neglected the important personage, who really, in a sense, was the cause of the fantastic direction that this story—which, by the way, is completely true—has taken. First of all, it is only fair to say that shortly after poor Akaky Akakievich, reduced to a pulp, had left his office, the important personage felt a twinge of regret. Compassion was not foreign to him—many good impulses stirred his heart, although his position usually prevented them from coming to the surface. As soon as his visiting friend had left the office, his thoughts returned to Akaky Akakievich. And after that, almost every day, he saw in his mind's eye the bloodless face of the little clerk who had been unable to take a proper reprimand. This thought was so disturbing that a week later he went so far as to send a clerk from his office to see how Akaky Akakievich was doing and to find out whether, in fact, there was any way to help him. And when he heard the news that Akaky Akakievich had died suddenly of a fever, it was almost a blow to him, even made him feel guilty and spoiled his mood for the whole day.

Trying to rid himself of these thoughts, to forget the whole unpleasant business, he went to a party at a friend's house. There he found himself in respectable company and, what's more, among people nearly all of whom were of the same standing so that there was absolutely nothing to oppress him. A great change came over him. He let himself go, chatted pleasantly, was amiable, in a word, spent a very pleasant evening. At supper, he drank a couple of glasses of champagne, a well-recommended prescription for inducing good spirits. The champagne gave him an inclination for something special and so he decided not to go home but instead to pay a little visit to a certain well-known lady named Karolina Ivanovna, a lady, it seems, of German extraction, toward whom he felt very friendly. It should be said that the important personage was no longer a young man, that he was a good husband, the respected father of a family. His two sons, one of whom already had a civil-service post, and his sweet-faced sixteen-year-old daughter, who had a slightly hooked but nevertheless pretty little nose, greeted him every day with a "Bonjour, Papa." His wife, a youngish woman and not unattractive at that, gave him her hand to kiss and then kissed his. But although the important personage was quite content with these displays of family affection, he considered it the proper thing to do to have, for friendship's sake, a lady friend in another part of the city. This lady friend was not a bit prettier or younger than his wife, but the world is full of such puzzling things and it is not our business to judge them.

So the important personage came down the steps, stepped into his sledge, and said to the coachman:

"To Karolina Ivanovna's."

Wrapping his warm luxurious fur coat around him, he sat back in his seat. He was in that state so cherished by Russians, in which, without your having to make any effort, thoughts, each one pleasanter than the last, slip into your head by themselves.

Perfectly content, he went over all the most pleasant moments at the party, over the clever retorts that had caused that select gathering to laugh. He even repeated many of them under his breath and, still finding them funny, laughed heartily at them all over again, which was natural enough. However, he kept being bothered by gusts of wind which would suddenly blow, God knows from where or for what reason, cutting his face, throwing lumps of snow into it, filling the cape of his coat like a sail and throwing it over his head, so that he had to extricate himself from it again and again.

Suddenly the important personage felt someone grab him violently from behind. He turned around and saw a small man in a worn-out frock coat. Terrified, he recognized Akaky Akakievich, his face as white as the snow and looking altogether very ghostly indeed. Fear took over completely when the important personage saw the ghost's mouth twist and, sending a whiff of the grave into his face, utter the following words:

"I've caught you at last. I've got you by the collar now! It's the coat I need. You did nothing about mine and hollered at me to boot. Now I'll take yours!"

The poor important personage almost died. He may have displayed force of character in the office and, in general, towards his inferiors, so that after one glance at his strong face and manly figure, people would say: 'Quite a man," but now, like many other mighty-looking people, he was so frightened that he began to think, and not without reason, that he was about to have an attack of something or other. He was even very helpful in peeling off his coat, after which he shouted to the coachman in a ferocious tone:

"Home! As fast as you can!"

The coachman, hearing the ferocious tone which the important personage used in critical moments and which was sometimes accompanied with something even more drastic, instinctively ducked his head and cracked his whip, so that they tore away like a streak. In a little over six minutes the important personage was in front of his house. Instead of being at Karolina Ivanovna's, he was somehow staggering to his room, pale, terrified, and coatless. There he spent such a restless night that the next morning, at breakfast, his daughter said:

"You look terribly pale this morning, Papa."

But Papa was silent, and he didn't say a word to anyone about what had happened to him, or where he had been or where he had intended to go. This incident made a deep impression upon him. From then on his subordinates heard far less often: "How dare you!" and "Do you know whom you're talking to?" And even when he did use these expressions it was after listening to what others had to say.

But even more remarkable—after that night, Akaky Akakievich's ghost was never seen again. The important personage's overcoat must have fitted him snugly. At any rate, one no longer heard of coats being torn from people's shoulders. However, many busybodies wouldn't let the matter rest there and maintained that the ghost was still haunting certain distant parts of the city. And, sure enough, a watchman in the Kolomna district caught a glimpse of the ghost behind a house. But he was rather a frail watchman. (Once an ordinary, but mature, piglet, rushing out of a private house, knocked him off his feet to the huge delight of a bunch of cabbies, whom he fined two kopeks each for their lack of respect—then he spent the proceeds on tobacco.) So, being rather frail, the watchman didn't dare to arrest

the ghost. Instead he followed it in the darkness until at last it
stopped suddenly, turned to face him, and asked:

"You looking for trouble?"

And it shook a huge fist at him, much larger than any you'll find
among the living.

"No," the watchman said, turning away.

This ghost, however, was a much taller one and wore an enormous mustache. It walked off, it seems, in the direction of the
Obukhov Bridge and soon dissolved into the gloom of night.


# HERMAN MELVILLE
1819–1891

A native New Yorker, Melville went to the Albany Academy and the Albany
Classical School, then taught school in Massachusetts, and in little towns
around Albany. In 1839 he began his break with conventional, shorebound
life by signing on a ship to Liverpool. In 1841 he signed on the whaler
Acushnet bound for the South Seas. He jumped ship there, lived in Tahiti,
made a whaling cruise on another vessel, and finally came home as a sailor
in the U.S. Navy. Like his character Ishmael, he could say, "A whale ship
was my Yale College and my Harvard." On his return he began to write
seriously, publishing novels about the South Seas and sailing, culminating
in Moby Dick (1851). He never made enough money from his writing to
support himself and his family. Ultimately, like Hawthorne, whom he admired, he got a job in a Customs House, where he worked quietly for
twenty years of increasing obscurity, writing very little. When he died in
New York City in 1891, his last masterwork, Billy Budd, was unpublished
and remained so for over thirty years. Now that tale, along with a few
others and Moby Dick itself, are appreciated as they never were during
Melville's lifetime.


## Bartleby, the Scrivener: A Story of Wall-Street

I am a rather elderly man. The nature of my avocations, for the last
thirty years, has brought me into more than ordinary contact with
what would seem an interesting and somewhat singular set of men,
of whom, as yet, nothing, that I know of, has ever been written—I
mean, the law-copyists, or scriveners. I have known very many of
them professionally and privately, and, if I pleased, could relate
divers histories, at which good-natured gentlemen might smile, and
sentimental souls might weep. But I waive the biographies of all

other scriveners, for a few passages in the life of Bartleby, who was a scrivener, the strangest I ever saw, or heard of. While, of other law-copyists, I might write the complete life, of Bartleby nothing of that sort can be done. I believe that no materials exist, for a full and satisfactory biography of this man. It is an irreparable loss to litera-ture. Bartleby was one of those beings of whom nothing is ascer-tainable, except from the original sources, and, in his case, those are very small. What my own astonished eyes saw of Bartleby, *that* is all I know of him, except, indeed, one vague report, which will appear in the sequel.

Ere introducing the scrivener, as he first appeared to me, it is fit I make some mention of myself, my *employés*, my business, my chambers, and general surroundings; because some such descrip-tion is indispensable to an adequate understanding of the chief character about to be presented. Imprimis: I am a man who, from his youth upwards, has been filled with a profound conviction that the easiest way of life is the best. Hence, though I belong to a profession proverbially energetic and nervous, even to turbulence, at times, yet nothing of that sort have I ever suffered to invade my peace. I am one of those unambitious lawyers who never address a jury, or in any way draw down public applause; but, in the cool tranquillity of a snug retreat, do a snug business among rich men's bonds, and mortgages, and title-deeds. All who know me, consider me an eminently *safe* man. The late John Jacob Astor, a personage little given to poetic enthusiasm, had no hesitation in pronouncing my first grand point to be prudence; my next, method. I do not speak it in vanity, but simply record the fact, that I was not unem-ployed in my profession by the late John Jacob Astor; a name which, I admit, I love to repeat; for it hath a rounded and orbicular sound to it, and rings like unto bullion. I will freely add, that I was not insensible to the late John Jacob Astor's good opinion.

Some time prior to the period at which this little history begins, my avocations had been largely increased. The good old office, now extinct in the State of New York, of a Master in Chancery, had been conferred upon me. It was not a very arduous office, but very pleas-antly remunerative. I seldom lose my temper; much more seldom indulge in dangerous indignation at wrongs and outrages; but I must be permitted to be rash here and declare, that I consider the sudden and violent abrogation of the office of Master in Chancery, by the new Constitution, as a—premature act; inasmuch as I had counted upon a life-lease of the profits, whereas I only received those of a few short years. But this is by the way.

My chambers were up stairs, at No. — Wall Street. At one end, they looked upon the white wall of the interior of a spacious sky-light shaft, penetrating the building from top to bottom.

This view might have been considered rather tame than otherwise, deficient in what landscape painters call "life." But, if so, the
view from the other end of my chambers offered, at least, a contrast,
if nothing more. In that direction, my windows commanded an
unobstructed view of a lofty brick wall, black by age and everlasting
shade; which wall required no spy-glass to bring out its lurking
beauties, but, for the benefit of all near-sighted spectators, was
pushed up to within ten feet of my window-panes. Owing to the
great height of the surrounding buildings, and my chambers being
on the second floor, the interval between this wall and mine not a
little resembled a huge square cistern.

At the period just preceding the advent of Bartleby, I had two
persons as copyists in my employment, and a promising lad as an
office-boy. First, Turkey; second, Nippers; third, Ginger Nut. These
may seem names, the like of which are not usually found in the
Directory. In truth, they were nicknames, mutually conferred upon
each other by my three clerks, and were deemed expressive of their
respective persons or characters. Turkey was a short, pursy Englishman, of about my own age—that is, somewhere not far from sixty.
In the morning, one might say, his face was of a fine florid hue, but
after twelve o'clock, meridian—his dinner hour—it blazed like a
grate full of Christmas coals; and continued blazing—but, as it
were, with a gradual wane—till six o'clock, P.M., or there-abouts;
after which, I saw no more of the proprietor of the face, which,
gaining its meridian with the sun, seemed to set with it, to rise,
culminate, and decline the following day, with the like regularity
and undiminished glory. There are many singular coincidences I
have known in the course of my life, not the least among which was
the fact, that, exactly when Turkey displayed his fullest beams from
his red and radiant countenance, just then, too, at that critical moment, began the daily period when I considered his business capacities as seriously disturbed for the remainder of the twenty-four
hours. Not that he was absolutely idle, or averse to business then;
far from it. The difficulty was, he was apt to be altogether too energetic. There was a strange, inflamed, flurried, flighty recklessness of
activity about him. He would be incautious in dipping his pen into
his inkstand. All his blots upon my documents were dropped there
after twelve o'clock, meridian. Indeed, not only would he be reckless, and sadly given to making blots in the afternoon, but, some
days, he went further, and was rather noisy. At such times, too, his
face flamed with augmented blazonry, as if cannel coal had been
heaped on anthracite. He made an unpleasant racket with his chair;
spilled his sand-box; in mending his pens, impatiently split them all
to pieces, and threw them on the floor in a sudden passion; stood
up, and leaned over his table, boxing his papers about in a most

indecorous manner, very sad to behold in an elderly man like him. Nevertheless, as he was in many ways a most valuable person to me, and all the time before twelve o'clock, meridian, was the quickest, steadiest creature, too, accomplishing a great deal of work in a style not easily to be matched—for these reasons, I was willing to overlook his eccentricities, though, indeed, occasionally, I remonstrated with him. I did this very gently, however, because, though the civilest, nay, the blandest and most reverential of men in the morning, yet, in the afternoon, he was disposed, upon provocation, to be slightly rash with his tongue—in fact, insolent. Now, valuing his morning services as I did, and resolved not to lose them—yet, at the same time, made uncomfortable by his inflamed ways after twelve o'clock—and being a man of peace, unwilling by my admonitions to call forth unseemly retorts from him, I took upon me, one Saturday noon (he was always worse on Saturdays) to hint to him, very kindly, that, perhaps, now that he was growing old, it might be well to abridge his labors; in short, he need not come to my chambers after twelve o'clock, but, dinner over, had best go home to his lodgings, and rest himself till tea-time. But no; he insisted upon his afternoon devotions. His countenance became intolerably fervid, as he oratorically assured me—gesticulating with a long ruler at the other end of the room—that if his services in the morning were useful, how indispensable, then, in the afternoon?

"With submission, sir," said Turkey, on this occasion, "I consider myself your right-hand man. In the morning I but marshal and deploy my columns; but in the afternoon I put myself at their head, and gallantly charge the foe, thus"—and he made a violent thrust with the ruler.

"But the blots, Turkey," intimated I.

"True; but, with submission, sir, behold these hairs! I am getting old. Surely, sir, a blot or two of a warm afternoon is not to be severely urged against gray hairs. Old age—even if it blot the page—is honorable. With submission, sir, we *both* are getting old."

This appeal to my fellow-feeling was hardly to be resisted. At all events, I saw that go he would not. So, I made up my mind to let him stay, resolving, nevertheless, to see to it that, during the afternoon, he had to do with my less important papers.

Nippers, the second on my list, was a whiskered, sallow, and, upon the whole, rather piratical-looking young man, of about five-and-twenty. I always deemed him the victim of two evil powers—ambition and indigestion. The ambition was evinced by a certain impatience of the duties of a mere copyist, an unwarrantable usurpation of strictly professional affairs, such as the original drawing up of legal documents. The indigestion seemed betokened in an occasional nervous testiness and grinning irritability, causing the teeth to audibly grind together over mistakes committed in copying; unnecessary maledictions, hissed, rather than spoken, in the heat of business; and especially by a continual discontent with the height of the table where he worked. Though of a very ingenious mechanical turn, Nippers could never get this table to suit him. He put chips under it, blocks of various sorts, bits of pasteboard, and at last went so far as to attempt an exquisite adjustment, by final pieces of folded blotting-paper. But no invention would answer. If, for the sake of easing his back, he brought the table-lid at a sharp angle well up towards his chin, and wrote there like a man using the steep roof of a Dutch house for his desk, then he declared that it stopped the circulation in his arms. If now he lowered the table to his waistbands, and stooped over it in writing, then there was a sore aching in his back. In short, the truth of the matter was, Nippers knew not what he wanted. Or, if he wanted anything, it was to be rid of a scrivener's table altogether. Among the manifestations of his diseased ambition was a fondness he had for receiving visits from certain ambiguous-looking fellows in seedy coats, whom he called his clients. Indeed, I was aware that not only was he, at times, considerable of a ward-politician, but he occasionally did a little business at the Justices' courts, and was not unknown on the steps of the Tombs. I have good reason to believe, however, that one individual who called upon him at my chambers, and who, with a grand air, he insisted was his client, was no other than a dun, and the alleged title-deed, a bill. But, with all his failings, and the annoyances he caused me, Nippers, like his compatriot Turkey, was a very useful man to me; wrote a neat, swift hand; and, when he chose, was not deficient in a gentlemanly sort of deportment. Added to this, he always dressed in a gentlemanly sort of way; and so, incidentally, reflected credit upon my chambers. Whereas, with respect to Turkey, I had much ado to keep him from being a reproach to me. His clothes were apt to look oily, and smell of eating-houses. He wore his pantaloons very loose and baggy in summer. His coats were execrable; his hat not to be handled. But while the hat was a thing of indifference to me, inasmuch as his natural civility and deference, as a dependent Englishman, always led him to doff it the moment he entered the room, yet his coat was another matter. Concerning his coats, I reasoned with him; but with no effect. The truth was, I suppose, that a man with so small an income could not afford to sport such a lustrous face and a lustrous coat at one and the same time. As Nippers once observed, Turkey's money went chiefly for red ink. One winter day, I presented Turkey with a highly respectable-looking coat of my own—a padded gray coat, of a most comfortable warmth, and which buttoned straight up from the knee to the neck. I thought Turkey would appreciate the favor, and abate his rashness and obstreperousness of afternoons. But no; I verily believe that buttoning himself up in so downy and blanket-like a coat had a pernicious effect upon him—upon the same principle that too much oats are bad for horses. In fact, precisely as a rash, restive horse is said to feel his oats, so Turkey felt his coat. It made him insolent. He was a man whom prosperity harmed.

Though, concerning the self-indulgent habits of Turkey, I had my own private surmises, yet, touching Nippers, I was well persuaded that, whatever might be his faults in other respects, he was, at least, a temperate young man. But, indeed, nature herself seemed to have been his vintner, and, at his birth, charged him so thoroughly with an irritable, brandy-like disposition, that all subsequent potations were needless. When I consider how, amid the stillness of my chambers, Nippers would sometimes impatiently rise from his seat, and stopping over his table, spread his arms wide apart, seize the whole desk, and move it, and jerk it, with a grim, grinding motion on the floor, as if the table were a perverse voluntary agent, intent on thwarting and vexing him, I plainly perceive that, for Nippers, brandy-and-water were altogether superfluous.

It was fortunate for me that, owing to its peculiar cause—indigestion—the irritability and consequent nervousness of Nippers were mainly observable in the morning, while in the afternoon he was comparatively mild. So that, Turkey's paroxysms only coming on about twelve o'clock, I never had to do with their eccentricities at one time. Their fits relieved each other, like guards. When Nippers's was on, Turkey's was off; and *vice versa*. This was a good natural arrangement under the circumstances.

Ginger Nut, the third on my list, was a lad, some twelve years old. His father was a carman, ambitious of seeing his son on the bench instead of a cart, before he died. So he sent him to my office, as student at law, errand-boy, cleaner and sweeper, at the rate of one dollar a week. He had a little desk to himself, but he did not use it much. Upon inspection, the drawer exhibited a great array of the shells of various sorts of nuts. Indeed, to this quick-witted youth, the whole noble science of the law was contained in a nut-shell. Not the least among the employments of Ginger Nut, as well as one which he discharged with the most alacrity, was his duty as cake and apple purveyor for Turkey and Nippers. Copying law-papers being proverbially a dry, husky sort of business, my two scriveners were fain to moisten their mouths very often with Spitzenbergs, to be had at the numerous stalls nigh the Custom House and Post Office. Also, they sent Ginger Nut very frequently for that peculiar cake—small, flat, round, and very spicy—after which he had been named by them. Of a cold morning, when business was but dull, Turkey would gobble up scores of these cakes, as if they were mere wafers—indeed, they sell them at the rate of six- or eight for a penny—the scrape of his pen blending with the crunching of the crisp particles in his mouth. Of all the fiery afternoon blunders and flurried rashnesses of Turkey, was his once moistening a ginger-cake between his lips, and clapping it on to a mortgage, for a seal. I came within an ace of dismissing him then. But he mollified me by making an oriental bow, and saying—

"With submission, sir, it was generous of me to find you in stationery on my account."

Now my original business—that of a conveyancer and title hunter, and drawer-up of recondite documents of all sorts—was considerably increased by receiving the Master's office. There was now great work for scriveners. Not only must I push the clerks already with me, but I must have additional help.

In answer to my advertisement, a motionless young man one morning stood upon my office threshold, the door being open, for it was summer. I can see that figure now—pallidly neat, pitiably respectable, incurably forlorn! It was Bartleby.

After a few words touching his qualifications, I engaged him, glad to have among my corps of copyists a man of so singularly sedate an aspect, which I thought might operate beneficially upon the flighty temper of Turkey, and the fiery one of Nippers.

I should have stated before that ground-glass folding-doors divided my premises into two parts, one of which was occupied by my scriveners, the other by myself. According to my humor, I threw open these doors, or closed them. I resolved to assign Bartleby a corner by the folding-doors, but on my side of them, so as to have this quiet man within easy call, in case any trifling thing was to be done. I placed his desk close up to a small side-window in that part of the room, a window which originally had afforded a lateral view of certain grimy back-yards and bricks, but which, owing to subsequent erections, commanded at present no view at all, though it gave some light. Within three feet of the panes was a wall, and the light came down from far above, between two lofty buildings, as from a very small opening in a dome. Still further to a satisfactory arrangement, I procured a high green folding screen, which might entirely isolate Bartleby from my sight, though not remove him from my voice. And thus, in a manner, privacy and society were conjoined.

At first, Bartleby did an extraordinary quantity of writing. As if long famishing for something to copy, he seemed to gorge himself on my documents. There was no pause for digestion. He ran a day and night line copying by sunlight and by candle-light. I should have been quite delighted with his application, had he been cheerfully industrious. But he wrote on silently, palely, mechanically.

It is, of course, an indispensable part of a scrivener's business to verify the accuracy of his copy, word by word. Where there are two or more scriveners in an office, they assist each other in this examination, one reading from the copy, the other holding the original. It is a very dull, wearisome, and lethargic affair. I can readily imagine that, to some sanguine temperaments, it would be altogether intolerable. For example, I cannot credit that the mettlesome poet, Byron, would have contentedly sat down with Bartleby to examine a law document of, say five hundred pages, closely written in a crimpy hand.

Now and then, in the haste of business, it had been my habit to assist in comparing some brief document myself, calling Turkey or Nippers for this purpose. One object I had, in placing Bartleby so handy to me behind the screen, was to avail myself of his services on such trivial occasions. It was on the third day, I think, of his being with me, and before any necessity had arisen for having his own writing examined, that, being much hurried to complete a small affair I had in hand, I abruptly called to Bartleby. In my haste and natural expectancy of instant compliance, I sat with my head bent over the original on my desk, and my right hand sideways, and somewhat nervously extended with the copy, so that, immediately upon emerging from his retreat, Bartleby might snatch it and proceed to business without the least delay.

In this very attitude did I sit when I called to him, rapidly stating what it was I wanted him to do—namely, to examine a small paper with me. Imagine my surprise, nay, my consternation, when, without moving from his privacy, Bartleby, in a singularly mild, firm voice, replied, "I would prefer not to."

I sat awhile in perfect silence, rallying my stunned faculties. Immediately it occurred to me that my ears had deceived me, or Bartleby had entirely misunderstood my meaning. I repeated my request in the clearest tone I could assume; but in quite as clear a one came the previous reply, "I would prefer not to."

"Prefer not to," echoed I, rising in high excitement, and crossing the room with a stride. "What do you mean? Are you moon-struck? I want you to help me compare this sheet here—take it," and I thrust it towards him.

"I would prefer not to," said he.

I looked at him steadfastly. His face was leanly composed; his gray eye dimly calm. Not a wrinkle of agitation rippled him. Had there been the least uneasiness, anger, impatience or impertinence in his manner; in other words, had there been anything ordinarily human about him, doubtless I should have violently dismissed him from the premises. But as it was, I should have as soon thought of turning my pale plaster-of-paris bust of Cicero out of doors. I stood gazing at him awhile, as he went on with his own writing, and then reseated myself at my desk. This is very strange, thought I. What had one best do? But my business hurried me. I concluded to forget the matter for the present, reserving it for my future leisure. So, calling Nippers from the other room, the paper was speedily examined.

A few days after this, Bartleby concluded four lengthy documents, being quadruplicates of a week's testimony taken before me in my High Court of Chancery. It became necessary to examine them. It was an important suit, and great accuracy was imperative. Having all things arranged, I called Turkey, Nippers and Ginger Nut, from the next room, meaning to place the four copies in the hands of my four clerks, while I should read from the original. Accordingly, Turkey, Nippers and Ginger Nut had taken their seats in a row, each with his document in his hand, when I called to Bartleby to join this interesting group.

"Bartleby! quick, I am waiting."

I heard a slow scrape of his chair legs on the uncarped floor, and soon he appeared standing at the entrance of his hermitage.

"What is wanted?" said he, mildly.

"The copies, the copies," said I, hurriedly. "We are going to examine them. There"—and I held towards him the fourth quadruplicate.

"I would prefer not to," he said, and gently disappeared behind the screen.

For a few moments I was turned into a pillar of salt, standing at the head of my seated column of clerks. Recovering myself, I advanced towards the screen, and demanded the reason for such extraordinary conduct.

"Why do you refuse?"

"I would prefer not to."

With any other man I should have flown outright into a dreadful passion, scorned all further words, and thrust him ignominiously from my presence. But there was something about Bartleby that not only strangely disarmed me, but, in a wonderful manner, touched and disconcerted me. I began to reason with him.

"These are your own copies we are about to examine. It is labor saving to you, because one examination will answer for your four papers. It is common usage. Every copyist is bound to help examine his copy. Is it not so? Will you not speak? Answer!"

"I prefer not to," he replied in a flute-like tone. It seemed to me that, while I had been addressing him, he carefully revolved every statement that I made; fully comprehended the meaning; could not gainsay the irresistible conclusion; but, at the same time, some paramount consideration prevailed with him to reply as he did.

"You are decided, then, not to comply with my request—a request made according to common usage and common sense?"

He briefly gave me to understand, that on that point my judgment was sound. Yes: his decision was irreversible.

It is not seldom the case that, when a man is browbeaten in some unprecedented and violently unreasonable way, he begins to stagger in his own plainest faith. He begins, as it were, vaguely to surmise that, wonderful as it may be, all the justice and all the reason is on the other side. Accordingly, if any disinterested persons are present, he turns to them for some reinforcement for his own faltering mind.

"Turkey," said I, "what do you think of this? Am I not right?"

"With submission, sir," said Turkey, in his blandest tone, "I think you are."

"Nippers," said I, "what do *you* think of it?"

"I think I should kick him out of the office."

(The reader of nice perceptions will here perceive that, it being morning Turkey's answer is couched in polite and tranquil terms, but Nippers replies in ill-tempered ones. Or, to repeat a previous sentence, Nippers's ugly mood was on duty, and Turkey's off.)

"Ginger Nut," said I, willing to enlist the smallest suffrage in my behalf, "what do *you* think of it?"

"I think, sir, he's a little *luny*," replied Ginger Nut, with a grin.

"You hear what they say," said I, turning towards the screen, "come forth and do your duty."

But he vouchsafed no reply. I pondered a moment in sore perplexity. But once more business hurried me. I determined again to postpone the consideration of this dilemma to my future leisure. With a little trouble we made out to examine the papers without Bartleby, though at every page or two Turkey deferentially dropped his opinion, that this proceeding was quite out of the common; while Nippers, twitching in his chair with a dyspeptic nervousness, ground out, between his set teeth, occasional hissing maledictions against the stubborn oaf behind the screen. And for his (Nippers's) part, this was the first and the last time he would do another man's business without pay.

Meanwhile Bartleby sat in his hermitage, oblivious to everything but his own peculiar business there.

Some days passed, the scrivener being employed upon another lengthy work. His late remarkable conduct led me to regard his ways narrowly. I observed that he never went to dinner; indeed, that he never went anywhere. As yet I had never, of my personal knowledge, known him to be outside of my office. He was a perpetual sentry in the corner. At about eleven o'clock though, in the morning, I noticed that Ginger Nut would advance toward the opening in Bartleby's screen, as if silently beckoned thither by a gesture invisible to me where I sat. The boy would then leave the office, jingling a few pence, and reappear with a handful of gingernuts, which he delivered in the hermitage, receiving two of the cakes for his trouble.

He lives, then, on ginger-nuts, thought I; never eats a dinner, properly speaking; he must be a vegetarian, then, but no; he never eats even vegetables, he eats nothing but ginger-nuts. My mind then ran on in reveries concerning the probable effects upon the human constitution of living entirely on ginger-nuts. Ginger-nuts are so called, because they contain ginger as one of their peculiar constituents and the final flavoring one. Now, what was ginger? A hot, spicy thing. Was Bartleby hot and spicy? Not at all. Ginger, then, had no effect upon Bartleby. Probably he preferred it should have none.

Nothing so aggravates an earnest person as a passive resistance. If the individual so resisted be of a not inhumane temper, and the resisting one perfectly harmless in his passivity, then, in the better moods of the former, he will endeavor charitably to construe to his imagination what proves impossible to be solved by his judgment. Even so, for the most part, I regarded Bartleby and his ways. Poor fellow! thought I, he means no mischief; it is plain he intends no insolence; his aspect sufficiently evinces that his eccentricities are involuntary. He is useful to me. I can get along with him. If I turn him away, the chances are he will fall in with some less indulgent employer, and then he will be rudely treated, and perhaps driven forth miserably to starve. Yes. Here I can cheaply purchase a delicious self-approval. To befriend Bartleby; to humor him in his strange wilfulness, will cost me little or nothing, while I lay up in my soul what will eventually prove a sweet morsel for my conscience. But this mood was not invariable with me. The passiveness of Bartleby sometimes irritated me. I felt strangely goaded on to encounter him in a new opposition—to elicit some angry spark from him answerable to my own. But, indeed, I might as well have essayed to strike fire with my knuckles against a bit of Windsor soap. But one afternoon the evil impulse in me mastered me, and the following little scene ensued:

"Bartleby," said I, "when those papers are all copied, I will compare them with you."

"I would prefer not to."

"How? Surely you do not mean to persist in that mulish vagary?"
No answer.

I threw open the folding-doors near by, and, turning upon Turkey and Nippers, exclaimed:

"Bartleby a second times says, he won't examine his papers. What do you think of it, Turkey?"

It was afternoon, be it remembered. Turkey sat glowing like a brass boiler; his bald head steaming; his hands reeling among his blotted papers.

"Think of it?" roared Turkey. "I think I'll just step behind his screen, and black his eyes for him!"

So saying, Turkey rose to his feet and threw his arms into a pugilistic position. He was hurrying away to make good his promise, when I detained him, alarmed at the effect of incautiously rousing Turkey's combativeness after dinner.

"Sit down, Turkey," said I, "and hear what Nippers has to say. What do you think of it, Nippers? Would I not be justified in immediately dismissing Bartleby?"

"Excuse me, that is for you to decide, sir. I think his conduct quite unusual, and, indeed, unjust, as regards Turkey and myself. But it may only be a passing whim."

"Ah," exclaimed I, "you have strangely changed your mind, then—you speak very gently of him now."

"All beer," cried Turkey; "gentleness is effects of beer—Nippers and I dined together to-day. You see how gentle I am, sir. Shall I go and black his eyes?"

"You refer to Bartleby, I suppose. No, not to-day, Turkey," I replied; "pray, put up your fists."

I closed the doors, and again advanced towards Bartleby. I felt additional incentives tempting me to my fate. I burned to be rebelled against again. I remembered that Bartleby never left the office.

"Bartleby," said I, "Ginger Nut is away; just step around to the Post Office, won't you?" (it was but a three minutes' walk) "and see if there is anything for me."

"I would prefer not to."

"You *will* not?"

"I *prefer* not."

I staggered to my desk, and sat there in a deep study. My blind inveteracy returned. Was there any other thing in which I could procure myself to be ignominousy repulsed by this lean, penniless wight?—my hired clerk? What added thing is there, perfectly reasonable, that he will be sure to refuse to do?

"Bartleby!"

No answer.

"Bartleby," in a louder tone.

No answer.

"Bartleby," I roared.

Like a very ghost, agreeably to the laws of magical invocation, at the third summons, he appeared at the entrance of his hermitage.

"Go to the next room, and tell Nippers to come to me."

"I prefer not to," he respectfully and slowly said, and mildly disappeared.

"Very good, Bartleby," said I, in a quiet sort of serenely-severe self-possessed tone, intimating the unalterable purpose of some terrible retribution very close at hand. At the moment I half intended something of the kind. But upon the whole, as it was drawing towards my dinner-hour, I thought it best to put on my hat and walk home for the day, suffering much from perplexity and distress of mind.

Shall I acknowledge it? The conclusion of this whole business was, that it soon became a fixed fact of my chambers, that a pale young scrivener, by the name of Bartleby, had a desk there; that he copied for me at the usual rate of four cents a folio (one hundred words); but he was permanently exempt from examining the work done by him, that duty being transferred to Turkey and Nippers, out of compliment, doubtless, to their superior acuteness; moreover, said Bartleby was never, on any account, to be dispatched on the most trivial errand of any sort; and that even if entreated to take upon him such a matter, it was generally understood that he would "prefer not to"—in other words, that he would refuse point-blank.

As days passed on, I became considerably reconciled to Bartleby. His steadiness, his freedom from all dissipation, his incessant industry (except when he chose to throw himself into a standing revery behind his screen), his great stillness, his unalterableness of demeanor under all circumstances, made him a valuable acquisition. One prime thing was this—*he was always there*—first in the morning, continually through the day, and the last at night. I had a singular confidence in his honesty. I felt my most precious papers perfectly safe in his hands. Sometimes, to be sure, I could not, for the very soul of me, avoid falling into sudden spasmodic passions with him. For it was exceeding difficult to bear in mind all the time those strange peculiarities, privileges, and unheard-of exemptions, forming the tacit stipulations on Bartleby's part under which he remained in my office. Now and then, in the eagerness of dispatching pressing business, I would inadvertently summon Bartleby, in a short, rapid tone, to put his finger, say, on the incipient tie of a bit of red tape with which I was about compressing some papers. Of course, from behind the screen the usual answer, "I prefer not to," was sure to come; and then, how could a human creature, with the common infirmities of our nature, refrain from bitterly exclaiming upon such perverseness—such unreasonableness? However, every added repulse of this sort which I received only tended to lessen the probability of my repeating the inadvertence.

Here it must be said, that, according to the custom of most legal gentlemen occupying chambers in densely-populated law buildings, there were several keys to my door. One was kept by a woman residing in the attic, which person weekly scrubbed and daily swept and dusted my apartments. Another was kept by Turkey for convenience sake. The third I sometimes carried in my own pocket. The fourth I knew not who had.

Now, one Sunday morning I happened to go to Trinity Church, to hear a celebrated preacher, and finding myself rather early on the ground I thought I would walk round to my chambers for a while. Luckily I had my key with me; but upon applying it to the lock, I found it resisted by something inserted from the inside. Quite surprised, I called out; when to my consternation a key was turned from within; and thrusting his lead visage at me, and holding the door ajar, the apparition of Bartleby appeared, in his shirt-sleeves, and otherwise in a strangely tattered deshabille, saying quietly that he was sorry, but he was deeply engaged just then, and—preferred not admitting me at present. In a brief word or two, he moreover added, that perhaps I had better walk round the block two or three times, and by that time he would probably have concluded his affairs.

Now, the utterly unsurmised appearance of Bartleby, tenanting my law-chambers of a Sunday morning, with his cadaverously gentlemanly *nonchalance*, yet withal firm and self-possessed, had such a strange effect upon me, that incontinently I slunk away from my own door, and did as desired. But not without sundry twinges of impotent rebellion against the mild effrontery of this unaccountable scrivener. Indeed, it was his wonderful mildness chiefly, which not only disarmed me, but unmanned me, as it were. For I consider that one, for the time, is a sort of unmanned when he tranquilly permits his hired clerk to dictate to him, and order him away from his own premises. Furthermore, I was full of uneasiness as to what Bartleby could possibly be doing in my office in his shirt-sleeves, and in an otherwise dismantled condition of a Sunday morning. Was anything amiss going on? Nay, that was out of the question. It was not to be thought of for a moment that Bartleby was an immoral person. But what could he be doing there—copying? Nay again, whatever might be his eccentricities, Bartleby was an eminently decorous person.

He would be the last man to sit down to his desk in any state approaching to nudity. Besides, it was Sunday; and there was something about Bartleby that forbade the supposition that he would by any secular occupation violate the proprieties of the day.

Nevertheless, my mind was not pacified; and full of a restless curiosity, at last I returned to the door. Without hindrance I inserted my key, opened it, and entered. Bartleby was not to be seen. I looked round anxiously, peeped behind his screen; but it was very plain that he was gone. Upon more closely examining the place, I surmised that for an indefinite period Bartleby must have ate, dressed, and slept in my office, and that too without plate, mirror, or bed. The cushioned seat of a rickety old sofa in one corner bore the faint impress of a lean, reclining form. Rolled away under his desk, I found a blanket; under the empty grate, a blacking box and brush; on a chair, a tin basin, with soap and a ragged towel; in a newspaper a few crumbs of ginger-nuts and a morsel of cheese. Yes, thought I, it is evident enough that Bartleby had been making his home here, keeping bachelor's hall all by himself. Immediately then the thought came sweeping across me, what miserable friendlessness and loneliness are here revealed! His poverty is great; but his solitude, how horrible! Think of it. Of a Sunday, Wall Street is deserted as Petra; and every night of every day it is an emptiness. This building, too, which of week-days hums with industry and life, at nightfall echoes with sheer vacancy, and all through Sunday is forlorn. And here Bartleby makes his home; sole spectator of a solitude which he has seen all populous—a sort of innocent and transformed Marius brooding among the ruins of Carthage!

For the first time in my life a feeling of overpowering stinging melancholy seized me. Before, I had never experienced aught but a not unpleasing sadness. The bond of a common humanity now drew me irresistibly to gloom. A fraternal melancholy! For both I and Bartleby were sons of Adam. I remembered the bright silks and sparkling faces I had seen that day, in gala trim, swan-like sailing down the Mississippi of Broadway; and I contrasted them with the pallid copyist, and thought to myself, Ah, happiness courts the light, so we deem the world is gay; but misery hides aloof, so we deem that misery there is none. These sad fancyings—chimeras, doubtless of a sick and silly brain—led on to other and more special thoughts, concerning the eccentricities of Bartleby. Presentiments of strange discoveries hovered round me. The scrivener's pale form appeared to me laid out, among uncaring strangers, in its shivering winding-sheet.

Suddenly I was attracted by Bartleby's closed desk, the key in open sight left in the lock.

I mean no mischief, seek the gratification of no heartless curiosity, thought I; besides, the desk is mine, and its contents, too, so I will make bold to look within. Everything was methodically arranged, the papers smoothly placed. The pigeon-holes were deep, and removing the files of documents, I groped into their recesses. Presently I felt something there, and dragged it out. It was an old bandanna handkerchief, heavy and knotted. I opened it, and saw it was a saving's bank.

I now recalled all the quiet mysteries which I had noted in the man. I remembered that he never spoke but to answer; that, though at intervals he had considerable time to himself, yet I had never seen him reading—no, not even a newspaper; that for long periods he would stand looking out, at his pale window behind the screen, upon the dead brick wall; I was quite sure he never visited any refectory or eating-house; while his pale face clearly indicated that he never drank beer like Turkey, or tea and coffee even, like other men; that he never went anywhere in particular that I could learn; never went out for a walk, unless, indeed, that was the case at present; that he had declined telling who he was or whence he came, or whether he had any relatives in the world; that though so thin and pale, he never complained of ill-health. And more than all, I remembered a certain unconscious air of pallid—how shall I call it?—of pallid haughtiness, say, or rather an austere reserve about him which had positively awed me into my tame compliance with his eccentricities, when I had feared to ask him to do the slightest incidental thing for me, even though I might know, from his long-continued motionlessness, that behind his screen he must be standing in one of those dead-wall reveries of his.

Revolving all these things, and coupling them with the recently discovered fact, that he made my office his constant abiding place and home, and not forgetful of his morbid moodiness; revolving all these things, a prudential feeling began to steal over me. My first emotions had been those of pure melancholy and sincerest pity; but just in proportion as the forlornness of Bartleby grew and grew to my imagination, did that same melancholy merge into fear, that pity into repulsion. So true it is, and so terrible, too, that up to a certain point the thought or sight of misery enlists our best affections; but, in certain special cases, beyond that point it does not. They err who would assert that invariably this is owing to the inherent selfishness of the human heart. It rather proceeds from a certain hopelessness of remedying excessive and organic ill. To a sensitive being, pity is not seldom pain. And when at last it is perceived that such pity cannot lead to effectual succor, common sense bids the soul be rid of it.

What I saw that morning persuaded me that the scrivener was the victim of innate and incurable disorder. I might give alms to his body; but his body did not pain him; it was his soul that suffered, and his soul I could not reach.

I did not accomplish the purpose of going to Trinity Church that morning. Somehow, the things I had seen disqualified me for the time from church-going. I walked homeward, thinking what I would do with Bartleby. Finally, I resolved upon this—I would put certain calm questions to him the next morning, touching his history, etc., and if he declined to answer them openly and unreservedly (and I supposed he would prefer not), then to give him a twenty dollar bill over and above whatever I might owe him, and tell him his services were no longer required; but that if in any other way I could assist him, I would be happy to do so, especially if he desired to return to his native place, wherever that might be, I would willingly help to defray the expenses. Moreover, if, after reaching home, he found himself at any time in want of aid, a letter from him would be sure of reply.

The next morning came.

"Bartleby," said I, gently calling to him behind his screen.

No reply.

"Bartleby," said I, in a still gentler tone, "come here; I am not going to ask you to do anything you would prefer not to do—I simply wish to speak to you."

Upon this he noiselessly slid into view.

"Will you tell me, Bartleby, where you were born?"

"I would prefer not to."

"Will you tell me *anything* about yourself?"

"I would prefer not to."

"But what reasonable objection can you have to speak to me? I feel friendly towards you."

He did not look at me while I spoke, but kept his glance fixed upon my bust of Cicero, which, as I then sat, was directly behind me, some six inches above my head.

"What is your answer, Bartleby?" said I, after waiting a considerable time for a reply, during which his countenance remained immovable, only there was the faintest conceivable tremor of the white attenuated mouth.

"At present I prefer to give no answer." he said, and retired into his hermitage.

It was rather weak of me I confess, but his manner, on this occasion, nettled me. Not only did there seem to lurk in it a certain calm disdain, but his perverseness seem ungrateful, considering the undeniable good usage and indulgence he had received from me.

Again I sat ruminating what I should do. Mortified as I was at his behavior, and resolved as I had been to dismiss him when I entered my office, nevertheless I strangely felt something superstitious knocking at my heart, and forbidding me to carry out my purpose, and denouncing me for a villain if I dared to breathe one bitter word against this forlornest of mankind. At last, familiarly drawing my chair behind his screen, I sat down and said: "Bartleby, never mind, then, about revealing your history; but let me entreat you, as a friend, to comply as far as may be with the usages of this office. Say now, you will help to examine papers to-morrow or next day: in short, say now, that in a day or two you will begin to be a little reasonable:—say so, Bartleby."

"At present I would prefer not to be a little reasonable," was his mildly cadaverous reply.

Just then the folding-doors opened, and Nippers approached. He seemed suffering from an unusually bad night's rest, induced by severer indigestion than common. He overheard those final words of Bartleby.

"*Prefer not*, eh?" gritted Nippers—"I'd *prefer* him, if I were you, sir," addressing me—"I'd *prefer* him; I'd give him preferences, the stubborn mule! What is it, sir, pray, that he *prefers* not to do now?"

Bartleby moved not a limb.

"Mr. Nippers," said I, "I'd prefer that you would withdraw for the present."

Somehow, of late, I had got into the way of involuntarily using this word"prefer" upon all sorts of not exactly suitable occasions. And I trembled to think that my contact with the scrivener had already and seriously affected me in a mental way. And what further and deeper aberration might it not yet produce? This apprehension had not been without efficacy in determining me to summary measures.

As Nippers, looking very sour and sulky, was departing, Turkey blandly and deferentially approached.

"With submission, sir," said he, "yesterday I was thinking about Bartleby here, and I think that if he would but prefer to take a quart of good ale every day it would do much towards mending him, and enabling him to assist in examining his papers."

"So you have got the word, too," said I, slightly excited.

"With submission, what word, sir?" asked Turkey, respectfully crowding himself into the contracted space behind the screen, and by so doing, making me jostle the scrivener. "What word, sir?"

"I would prefer to be left alone here," said Bartleby, as if offended at being mobbed in his privacy.

"*That's* the word, Turkey," said I—"*that's* it."

"Oh, *prefer?* oh yes—queer word. I never use it myself. But, sir, as I was saying, if he would but prefer—"

"Turkey," interrupted I, "you will please withdraw."

"Oh certainly, sir, if you prefer that I should."

As he opened the folding-door to retire, Nippers at his desk caught a glimpse of me, and asked whether I would prefer to have a certain paper copied on blue paper or white. He did not in the least roguishly accent the word "prefer." It was plain that it involuntarily rolled from his tongue. I thought to myself, surely I must get rid of a demented man, who already has in some degree turned the tongues, if not the heads of myself and clerks. But I thought it prudent not to break the dismission at once.

The next day I noticed that Bartleby did nothing but stand at his window in his dead-wall revery. Upon asking him why he did not write, he said that he had decided upon doing no more writing.

"Why, how now? what next?" exclaimed I, "do no more writing?"

"No more."

"And what is the reason?"

"Do you not see the reason for yourself?" he indifferently replied.

I looked steadfastly at him, and perceived that his eyes looked dull and glazed. Instantly it occurred to me, that his unexampled diligence in copying by his dim window for the first few weeks of his stay with me might have temporarily impaired his vision.

I was touched. I said something in condolence with him. I hinted that of course he did wisely in abstaining from writing for a while; and urged him to embrace that opportunity of taking wholesome exercise in the open air. This, however, he did not do. A few days after this, my other clerks being absent, and being in a great hurry to dispatch certain letters by the mail, I thought that, having nothing else earthly to do, Bartleby would surely be less inflexible than usual, and carry these letters to the post-office. But he blankly declined. So, much to my inconvenience, I went myself.

Still added days went by. Whether Bartleby's eyes improved or not, I could not say. To all appearance, I thought they did. But when I asked him if they did, he vouchsafed no answer. At all events, he would do no copying. At last, in reply to my urgings, he informed me that he had permanently given up copying.

"What!" exclaimed I; "suppose your eyes should get entirely well—better than ever before—would you not copy then?"

"I have given up copying," he answered, and slid aside.

He remained as ever, a fixture in my chamber. Nay—if that were possible—he became still more of a fixture than before. What was to be done? He would do nothing in the office; why should he stay there? In plain fact, he had now become a millstone to me, not only useless as a necklace, but afflictive to bear. Yet I was sorry for him. I speak less than truth when I say that, on his own account, he occasioned me uneasiness. If he would but have named a single relative or friend, I would instantly have written, and urged their taking the poor fellow away to some convenient retreat. But he seemed alone, absolutely alone in the universe. A bit of wreck in the mid-Atlantic. At length, necessities connected with my business tyrannized over all other considerations. Decently as I could, I told Bartleby that in six days' time he must unconditionally leave the office. I warned him to take measures, in the interval, for procuring some other abode. I offered to assist him in this endeavor, if he himself would but take the first step towards a removal. "And when you finally quit me, Bartleby," added I, "I shall see that you go not away entirely unprovided. Six days from this hour, remember."

At the expiration of that period, I peeped behind the screen, and lo! Bartleby was there.

I buttoned up my coat, balanced myself; advanced slowly towards him, touched his shoulder, and said, "The time has come; you must quit this place; I am sorry for you; here is money; but you must go."

"I would prefer not," he replied, with his back still towards me.

"You *must*."

He remained silent.

Now I had an unbounded confidence in this man's common honesty. He had frequently restored to me sixpences and shillings carelessly dropped upon the floor, for I am apt to be very reckless in such shirt-button affairs. The proceeding, then, which followed will not be deemed extraordinary.

"Bartleby," said I, "I owe you twelve dollars on account; here are thirty-two, the odd twenty are yours— Will you take it?" and I handed the bills towards him.

But he made no motion.

"I will leave them here, then," putting them under a weight on the table. Then taking my hat and cane and going to the door, I tranquilly turned and added—"After you have removed your things from these offices, Bartleby, you will of course lock the door—since every one is now gone for the day but you—and if you please, slip your key underneath the mat, so that I may have it in the morning. I shall not see you again; so good-bye to you. If, hereafter, in your new place of abode, I can be of any service to you, do not fail to advise me by letter. Good-bye, Bartleby, and fare you well."

But he answered not a word; like the last column of some ruined temple, he remained standing mute and solitary in the middle of the otherwise deserted room.

As I walked home in a pensive mood, my vanity got the better of my pity. I could not but highly plume myself on my masterly management in getting rid of Bartleby. Masterly I call it, and such it must appear to any dispassionate thinker. The beauty of my procedure seemed to consist in its perfect quietness. There was no vulgar bullying, no bravado of any sort, no choleric hectoring, and striding to and fro across the apartment, jerking out vehement commands for Bartleby to bundle himself off with his beggarly traps. Nothing of the kind. Without loudly bidding Bartleby depart—as an inferior genius might have done—I *assumed* the ground that depart he must; and upon that assumption built all I had to say. The more I thought over my procedure, the more I was charmed with it. Nevertheless, next morning, upon awakening, I had my doubts—I had somehow slept off the fumes of vanity. One of the coolest and wisest hours a man has, is just after he awakes in the morning. My procedure seemed as sagacious as ever—but only in theory. How it would prove in practice—there was the rub. It was truly a beautiful thought to have assumed Bartleby's departure; but, after all, that assumption was simply my own, and none of Bartleby's. The great point was, not whether I had assumed that he would quit me, but whether he would prefer so to do. He was more a man of preferences than assumptions.

After breakfast, I walked down town, arguing the probabilities *pro* and *con*. One moment I thought it would prove a miserable failure, and Bartleby would be found all alive at my office as usual; the next moment it seemed certain that I should find his chair empty. And so I kept veering about. At the corner of Broadway and Canal Street, I saw quite an excited group of people standing in earnest conversation.

"I'll take odds he doesn't," said a voice as I passed.

"Doesn't go?—done!" said I, "put up your money."

I was instinctively putting my hand in my pocket to produce my own, when I remembered that this was an election day. The words I had overheard bore no reference to Bartleby, but to the success or non-success of some candidate for the mayoralty. In my intent frame of mind, I had, as it were, imagined that all Broadway shared in my excitement, and were debating the same question with me. I passed on, very thankful that the uproar of the street screened my momentary absent-mindedness.

As I had intended, I was earlier than usual at my office door. I stood listening for a moment. All was still. He must be gone. I tried the knob. The door was locked. Yes, my procedure had worked to a charm; he indeed must be vanished. Yet a certain melancholy mixed with this: I was almost sorry for my brilliant success. I was fumbling under the door mat for the key, which Bartleby was to have left there for me, when accidentally my knee knocked against a panel, producing a summoning sound, and in response a voice came to me from within—"Not yet; I am occupied."

It was Bartleby.

I was thunderstruck. For an instant I stood like the man who, pipe in mouth, was killed one cloudless afternoon long ago in Virginia, by summer lightning; at his own warm open window he was killed, and remained leaning out there upon the dreamy afternoon, till some one touched him, when he fell.

"Not gone!" I murmured at last. But again obeying that wondrous ascendancy which the inscrutable scrivener had over me, and from which ascendancy, for all my chafing, I could not completely escape, I slowly went down stairs and out into the street, and while walking round the block, considered what I should next do in this unheard-of perplexity. Turn the man out by an actual thrusting I could not; to drive him away by calling him hard names would not do; calling in the police was an unpleasant idea; and yet, permit him to enjoy his cadaverous triumph over me—this, too, I could not think of. What was to be done? or, if nothing could be done, was there anything further that I could *assume* in the matter. Yes, as before I had pro-spectively assumed that Bartleby would depart, so now I might re-trospectively assume that departed he was. In the legitimate carry-ing out of this assumption, I might enter my office in a great hurry, and pretending not to see Bartleby at all, walk straight against him as if he were air. Such a proceeding would in a singular degree have the appearance of a home-thrust. It was hardly possible that Bart-leby could withstand such an application of the doctrine of assump-tions. But upon second thoughts the success of the plan seemed rather dubious. I resolved to argue the matter over with him again.

"Bartleby," said I, entering the office, with a quietly severe ex-pression, "I am seriously displeased. I am pained, Bartleby. I had thought better of you. I had imagined you of such a gentlemanly organization, that in any delicate dilemma a slight hint would suf-fice—in short, an assumption. But it appears I am deceived. Why," I added, unaffectedly starting, "you have not even touched that money yet," pointing to it, just where I had left it the evening previous.

He answered nothing.

"Will you, or will you not, quit me?" I now demanded in a sud-den passion, advancing close to him.

"I would prefer *not* to quit you," he replied, gently emphasizing the *not*.

"What earthly right have you to stay here? Do you pay any rent? Do you pay my taxes? Or is this property yours?"

He answered nothing.

"Are you ready to go on and write now? Are your eyes recovered? Could you copy a small paper for me this morning? or help examine a few lines? or step round to the post-office? In a word, will you do anything at all, to give a coloring to your refusal to depart the premises?"

He silently retired into his hermitage.

I was now in such a state of nervous resentment that I thought it but prudent to check myself at present from further demonstrations. Bartleby and I were alone. I remembered the tragedy of the unfortunate Adams and the still more unfortunate Colt in the solitary office of the latter; and how poor Colt, being dreadfully incensed by Adams, and imprudently permitting himself to get wildly excited, was at unawares hurried into his fatal act—an act which certainly no man could possibly deplore more than the actor himself. Often it had occurred to me in my ponderings upon the subject that had that altercation taken place in the public street, or at a private residence, it would not have terminated as it did. It was the circumstance of being alone in a solitary office, up stairs, or a building entirely unhallowed by humanizing domestic associations—an uncarpeted office, doubtless, of a dusty, haggard sort of appearance—this it must have been, which greatly helped to enhance the irritable desperation of the hapless Colt.

But when this old Adam of resentment rose in me and tempted me concerning Bartleby, I grappled him and threw him. How? Why, simply by recalling the divine injunction: "A new commandment give I unto you, that ye love one another." Yes, this it was that saved me. Aside from higher considerations, charity often operates as a vastly wise and prudent principle—a great safeguard to its possessor. Men have committed murder for jealousy's sake, and anger's sake, and hatred's sake, and selfishness' sake, and spiritual pride's sake; but no man, that ever I heard of, ever committed a diabolical murder for sweet charity's sake. Mere self-interest, then, if no better motive can be enlisted, should, especially with high-tempered men, prompt all beings to charity and philanthropy. At any rate, upon the occasion in question, I strove to drown my exasperated feelings towards the scrivener by benevolently construing his conduct. Poor fellow, poor fellow! thought I, he don't mean anything; and besides, he has seen hard times, and ought to be indulged.

I endeavored, also, immediately to occupy myself, and at the same time to comfort my despondency. I tried to fancy, that in the course of the morning, at such time as might prove agreeable to him, Bartleby, of his own free accord, would emerge from his hermitage and take up some decided line of march in the direction of the door. But no. Half-past twelve o'clock came; Turkey began to glow in the face, overturn his inkstand, and become generally obstreperous; Nippers abated down into quietude and courtesy; Ginger Nut munched his noon apple; and Bartleby remained standing at his window in one of his profoundest dead-wall reveries. Will it be credited? Ought I to acknowledge it? That afternoon I left the office without saying one further word to him.

Some days now passed, during which, at leisure intervals I looked a little into "Edwards on the Will," and "Priestley on Necessity." Under the circumstances, those books induced a salutary feeling. Gradually I slid into the persuasion that these troubles of mine, touching the scrivener, had been all predestinated from eternity, and Bartleby was billeted upon me for some mysterious purpose of an all-wise Providence, which it was not for a mere mortal like me to fathom. Yes, Bartleby, stay there behind your screen, thought I; I shall persecute you no more; you are harmless and noiseless as any of these old chairs; in short, I never feel so private as when I know you are here. At last I see it, I feel it; I penetrate to the predestinated purpose of my life. I am content. Others may have loftier parts to enact; but my mission in this world, Bartleby, is to furnish you with office-room for such period as you may see fit to remain.

I believe that this wise and blessed frame of mind would have continued with me, had it not been for the unsolicited and uncharitable remarks obtruded upon me by my professional friends who visited the rooms. But thus it often is, that the constant friction of illiberal minds wears out at last the best resolves of the more generous. Though to be sure, when I reflected upon it, it was not strange that people entering my office should be struck by the peculiar aspect of the unaccountable Bartleby, and so be tempted to throw out some sinister observations concerning him. Sometimes an attorney, having business with me, and calling at my office, and finding no one but the scrivener there, would undertake to obtain some sort of precise information from him touching my whereabouts; but without heeding his idle talk, Bartleby would remain standing immovable in the middle of the room. So after contemplating him in that position for a time, the attorney would depart, no wiser than he came.

Also, when a reference was going on, and the room full of lawyers and witnesses, and business driving fast, some deeply-occupied legal gentleman present, seeing Bartleby wholly unemployed, would request him to run round to his (the legal gentleman's) office and fetch some papers for him. Thereupon, Bartleby would tranquilly decline, and yet remain idle as before. Then the lawyer would give a great stare, and turn to me. And what could I say? At last I was

made aware that all through the circle of my professional acquaintance, a whisper of wonder was running round, having reference to
the strange creature I kept at my office. This worried me very much.
And as the idea came upon me of his possibly turning out a long-
lived man, and keep occupying my chambers, and denying my authority; and perplexing my visitors; and scandalizing my professional reputation; and casting a general gloom over the premises;
keeping soul and body together to the last upon his savings (for
doubtless he spent but half a dime a day), and in the end perhaps
outlive me, and claim possession of my office by right of his perpetual occupancy: as all these dark anticipations crowded upon me
more and more, and my friends continually intruded their relentless
remarks upon the apparition in my room; a great change was
wrought in me. I resolved to gather all my faculties together, and
forever rid me of this intolerable incubus.

Ere revolving any complicated project, however, adapted to this
end, I first simply suggested to Bartleby the propriety of his permanent departure. In a calm and serious tone, I commended the idea to
his careful and mature consideration. But, having taken three days
to meditate upon it, he apprised me, that his original determination
remained the same; in short, that he still preferred to abide with
me.

What shall I do? I now said to myself, buttoning up my coat to the
last button. What shall I do? what ought I to do? What does conscience say I *should* do with this man, or, rather, ghost. Rid myself
of him, I must; go, he shall. But how? You will not thrust him, the
poor, pale, passive mortal—you will not thrust such a helpless creature out of your door? you will not dishonor yourself by such cruelty? No, I will not, I cannot do that. Rather would I let him live and
die here, and then mason up his remains in the wall. What, then,
will you do? For all your coaxing, he will not budge. Bribes he
leaves under your own paper-weight on your table; in short, it is
quite plain that he prefers to cling to you.

Then something severe, something unusual must be done. What!
surely you will not have him collared by a constable, and commit
his innocent pallor to the common jail? And upon what ground
could you procure such a thing to be done?—a vagrant, is he? What!
he a vagrant, a wanderer, who refuses to budge? It is because he
will *not* be a vagrant, then, that you seek to count him *as* a vagrant.
That is too absurd. No visible means of support: there I have him.
Wrong again: for indubitably he *does* support himself, and that is
the only unanswerable proof that any man can show of his possessing the means so to do. No more then. Since he will not quit me, I

must quit him. I will change my offices; I will move elsewhere, and give him fair notice, that if I find him on my new premises I will then proceed against him as a common trespasser.

Acting accordingly, next day I thus addressed him: "I find these chambers too far from the City Hall; the air is unwholesome. In a word, I propose to remove my offices next week, and shall no longer require your services. I tell you this now, in order that you may seek another place."

He made no reply, and nothing more was said.

On the appointed day I engaged carts and men, proceeded to my chambers, and, having but little furniture, everything was removed in a few hours. Throughout, the scrivener remained standing behind the screen, which I directed to be removed the last thing. It was withdrawn; and, being folded up like a huge folio, left him the motionless occupant of a naked room. I stood in the entry watching him a moment, while something from within me upbraided me.

I re-entered, with my hand in my pocket—and—and my heart in my mouth.

"Good-bye, Bartleby; I am going—good-bye, and God some way bless you; and take that," slipping something in his hand. But it dropped upon the floor, and then—strange to say—I tore myself from him whom I had so longed to be rid of.

Established in my new quarters, for a day or two I kept the door locked, and started at every footfall in the passages. When I returned to my rooms, after any little absence, I would pause at the threshold for an instant, and attentively listen, ere applying my key. But these fears were needless. Bartleby never came nigh me.

I thought all was going well, when a perturbed-looking stranger visited me, inquiring whether I was the person who had recently occupied rooms at No.—Wall Street.

Full of forebodings, I replied that I was.

"Then, sir," said the stranger, who proved a lawyer, "you are responsible for the man you left there. He refuses to do any copying; he refuses to do anything; he says he prefers not to; and he refuses to quit the premises."

"I am very sorry, sir," said I, with assumed tranquillity, but an inward tremor, "but, really, the man you allude to is nothing to me—he is no relation or apprentice of mine, that you should hold me responsible for him."

"In mercy's name, who is he?"

"I certainly cannot inform you. I know nothing about him. Formerly I employed him as a copyist; but he has done nothing for me now for some time past."

"I shall settle him, then—good morning, sir."

Several days passed, and I heard nothing more; and, though I often felt a charitable prompting to call at the place and see poor Bartleby, yet a certain squeamishness, of I know not what, withheld me.

All is over with him, by this time, thought I, at last, when, through another week, no further intelligence reached me. But, coming to my room the day after, I found several persons waiting at my door in a high state of nervous excitement.

"That's the man—here he comes," cried the foremost one, whom I recognized as the lawyer who had previously called upon me alone.

"You must take him away, sir, at once," cried a portly person among them, advancing upon me, and whom I knew to be the landlord of No.—Wall Street. "These gentlemen, my tenants, cannot stand it any longer; Mr. B——," pointing to the lawyer, "has turned him out of his room, and he now persists in haunting the building generally, sitting upon the banisters of the stairs by day, and sleeping in the entry by night. Everybody is concerned; clients are leaving the offices; some fears are entertained of a mob; something you must do, and that without delay."

Aghast at this torrent, I fell back before it, and would fain have locked myself in my new quarters. In vain I persisted that Bartleby was nothing to me—no more than to any one else. In vain—I was the last person known to have anything to do with him, and they held me to the terrible account. Fearful, then, of being exposed in the papers (as one person present obscurely threatened), I considered the matter, and, at length, said, that if the lawyer would give me a confidential interview with the scrivener, in his (the lawyer's) own room, I would, that afternoon, strive my best to rid them of the nuisance they complained of.

Going up stairs to my old haunt, there was Bartleby silently sitting upon the banister at the landing.

"What are you doing here, Bartleby?" said I.

"Sitting upon the banister," he mildly replied.

I motioned him into the lawyer's room, who then left us.

"Bartleby," said I, "are you aware that you are the cause of great tribulation to me, by persisting in occupying the entry after being dismissed from the office?"

No answer.

"Now one of two things must take place. Either you must do something, or something must be done to you. Now what sort of business would you like to engage in? Would you like to re-engage in copying for some one?"

"No; I would prefer not to make any change."

"Would you like a clerkship in a dry-goods store?"

"There is too much confinement about that. No, I would not like a clerkship; but I am not particular."

"Too much confinement," I cried, "why, you keep yourself confined all the time!"

"I would prefer not to take a clerkship," he rejoined, as if to settle that little item at once.

"How would a bar-tender's business suit you? There is no trying of the eye-sight in that."

"I would not like it at all; though, as I said before, I am not particular."

His unwonted wordiness inspired me. I returned to the charge.

"Well, then, would you like to travel through the country collecting bills for the merchants? That would improve your health."

"No, I would prefer to be doing something else."

"How, then, would going as a companion to Europe, to entertain some young gentleman with your conversation—how would that suit you?"

"Not at all. It does not strike me that there is anything definite about that. I like to be stationary. But I am not particular."

"Stationary you shall be, then," I cried, now losing all patience, and, for the first time in all my exasperating connection with him, fairly flying into a passion. "If you do not go away from these premises before night, I shall feel bound—indeed, I *am* bound—to—to—to quit the premises myself!" I rather absurdly concluded, knowing not with what possible threat to try to frighten his immobility into compliance. Despairing of all further efforts, I was precipitately leaving him, when a final thought occurred to me—one which had not been wholly unindulged before.

"Bartleby," said I, in the kindest tone I could assume under such exciting circumstances, "will you go home with me now—not to my office, but my dwelling—and remain there till we can conclude upon some convenient arrangement for you at our leisure? Come, let us start now, right away."

"No: at present I would prefer not to make any change at all."

I answered nothing; but, effectually dodging every one by the suddenness and rapidity of my flight, rushed from the building, ran up Wall Street towards Broadway, and, jumping into the first omnibus, was soon removed from pursuit. As soon as tranquillity returned, I distinctly perceived that I had now done all that I possibly could, both in respect to the demands of the landlord and his tenants, and with regard to my own desire and sense of duty, to benefit Bartleby, and shield him from rude persecution. I now strove to be entirely care-free and quiescent; and my conscience justified me in the attempt; though, indeed, it was not so successful as I could have wished. So fearful was I of being again hunted out by the incensed

landlord and his exasperated tenants, that, surrendering my business to Nippers, for a few days, I drove about the upper part of the
town and through the suburbs, in my rockaway; crossed over to
Jersey City and Hoboken, and paid fugitive visits to Manhattanville
and Astoria. In fact, I almost lived in my rockaway for the time.

When again I entered my office, lo, a note from the landlord lay
upon the desk. I opened it with trembling hands. It informed me
that the writer had sent to the police, and had Bartleby removed to
the Tombs as a vagrant. Moreover, since I knew more about him
than any one else, he wished me to appear at that place, and make a
suitable statement of the facts. These tidings had a conflicting effect
upon me. At first I was indignant; but, at last, almost approved. The
landlord's energetic, summary disposition, had led him to adopt a
procedure which I do not think I would have decided upon myself;
and yet, as a last resort, under such peculiar circumstances, it
seemed the only plan.

As I afterwards learned, the poor scrivener, when told that he
must be conducted to the Tombs, offered not the slightest obstacle,
but, in his pale, unmoving way, silently acquiesced.

Some of the compassionate and curious by-standers joined the
party; and headed by one of the constables arm-in-arm with Bartleby, the silent procession filed its way through all the noise, and
heat, and joy of the roaring thoroughfares at noon.

The same day I received the note, I went to the Tombs, or, to
speak more properly, the Halls of Justice. Seeking the right officer, I
stated the purpose of my call, and was informed that the individual
I described was, indeed, within. I then assured the functionary that
Bartleby was a perfectly honest man, and greatly to be compassion-
ated, however unaccountably eccentric. I narrated all I knew, and
closed by suggesting the idea of letting him remain in as indulgent
confinement as possible, till something less harsh might be done—
though, indeed, I hardly knew what. At all events, if nothing else
could be decided upon, the alms-house must receive him. I then
begged to have an interview.

Being under no disgraceful charge, and quite serene and harmless
in all his ways, they had permitted him freely to wander about the
prison, and, especially, in the inclosed grass-platted yards thereof.
And so I found him there, standing all alone in the quietest of the
yards, his face towards a high wall, while all around, from the
narrow slits of the jail windows, I thought I saw peering out upon
him the eyes of murderers and thieves.

"Bartleby!"

"I know you," he said, without looking round—"and I want nothing to say to you."

"It was not I that brought you here, Bartleby," said I, keenly pained at his implied suspicion. "and to you, this should not be so vile a place. Nothing reproachful attaches to you by being here. And see, it is not so sad a place as one might think. Look, there is the sky, and here is the grass."

"I know where I am," he replied, but would say nothing more, and so I left him.

As I entered the corridor again, a broad meat-like man, in an apron accosted me, and, jerking his thumb over his shoulder, said— "Is that your friend?"

"Yes."

"Does he want to starve? If he does, let him live on the prison fare, that's all."

"Who are you?" asked I, not knowing what to make of such an unofficially speaking person in such a place.

"I am the grub-man. Such gentlemen as have friends here, hire me to provide them with something good to eat."

"Is this so?" said I, turning to the turnkey.

He said it was.

"Well, then," said I, slipping some silver into the grubman's hands (for so they called him), "I want you to give particular attention to my friend there; let him have the best dinner you can get. And you must be as polite to him as possible."

"Introduce me, will you?" said the grub-man, looking at me with an expression which seemed to say he was all impatience for an opportunity to give a specimen of his breeding.

Thinking it would prove of benefit to the scrivener, I acquiesced; and, asking the grub-man his name, went up with him to Bartleby.

"Bartleby, this is a friend; you will find him very useful to you."

"Your sarvant, sir, your sarvant," said the grub-man, making a low salutation behind his apron. "Hope you find it pleasant here, sir; nice grounds—cool apartments—hope you'll stay with us some time—try to make it agreeable. What will you have for dinner to-day?"

"I prefer not to dine to-day," said Bartleby, turning away. "It would disagree with me; I am unused to dinners." So saying, he slowly moved to the other side of the inclosure, and took up a position fronting the dead-wall.

"How's this?" said the grub-man, addressing me with a stare of astonishment. "He's odd, ain't he?"

"I think he is a little deranged," said I, sadly.

"Deranged? deranged is it? Well, now, upon my word, I thought that friend of yourn was a gentleman forger; they are always pale and genteel-like, them forgers. I can't help pity 'em—can't help it, sir. Did you know Monroe Edwards?" he added, touchingly, and paused. Then, laying his hand piteously on my shoulder, sighed, "He died of consumption at Sing-Sing. So you weren't acquainted with Monroe?"

"No, I was never socially acquainted with any forgers. But I cannot stop longer. Look to my friend yonder. You will not lose by it. I will see you again."

Some few days after this, I again obtained admission to the Tombs, and went through the corridors in quest of Bartleby; but without finding him.

"I saw him coming from his cell not long ago," said a turnkey, "maybe he's gone to loiter in the yards."

So I went in that direction.

"Are you looking for the silent man?" said another turnkey, passing me. "Yonder he lies—sleeping in the yard there. 'Tis not twenty minutes since I saw him lie down."

The yard was entirely quiet. It was not accessible to the common prisoners. The surrounding walls, of amazing thickness, kept off all sounds behind them. The Egyptian character of the masonry weighed upon me with its gloom. But a soft imprisoned turf grew under foot. The heart of the eternal pyramids, it seemed, wherein, by some strange magic, through the clefts, grass-seed, dropped by birds, had sprung.

Strangely huddled at the base of the wall, his knees drawn up, and lying on his side, his head touching the cold stones, I saw the wasted Bartleby. But nothing stirred. I paused; then went close up to him; stooped over, and saw that his dim eyes were open; otherwise he seemed profoundly sleeping. Something prompted me to touch him. I felt his hand, when a tingling shiver ran up my arm and down my spine to my feet.

The round face of the grub-man peered upon me now. "His dinner is ready. Won't he dine to-day, either? Or does he live without dining?"

"Lives without dining," said I, and closed the eyes.

"Eh!—He's asleep, ain't he?"

"With kings and counselors," murmured I.

\*       \*       \*

There would seem little need for proceeding further in this history. Imagination will readily supply the meagre recital of poor Bartleby's interment. But, ere parting with the reader, let me say, that if this little narrative has sufficiently interested him, to awaken curiosity as to who Bartleby was, and what manner of life he led prior to the present narrator's making his acquaintance, I can only reply, that in such curiosity I fully share, but am wholly unable to gratify it. Yet here I hardly know whether I should divulge one little item of rumor, which came to my ear a few months after the scrivener's decease. Upon what basis it rested, I could never ascertain; and hence, how true it is I cannot now tell. But, inasmuch as this vague report has not been without a certain suggestive interest to me, however sad, it may prove the same with some others, and so I will briefly mention it. The report was this: that Bartleby had been a subordinate clerk in the Dead Letter Office at Washington, from which he had been suddenly removed by a change in the administration. When I think over this rumor, hardly can I express the emotions which seize me. Dead letters! does it not sound like dead men? Conceive a man by nature and misfortune prone to a pallid hopelessness, can any business seem more fitted to heighten it than that of continually handling these dead letters, and assorting them for the flames? For by the cart-load they are annually burned. Sometimes from out the folded paper the pale clerk takes a ring—the finger it was meant for, perhaps, moulders in the grave; a bank-note sent in swiftest charity—he whom it would relieve, nor eats nor hungers any more; pardon for those who died despairing; hope for those who died unhoping; good tidings for those who died stifled by unrelieved calamities. On errands of life, these letters speed to death.

Ah, Bartleby! Ah, humanity!

# GUSTAVE FLAUBERT
## 1821–1880

Flaubert was born in Rouen, France, where his father had an important medical practice. After studying law in Paris, he returned home and devoted himself to writing. His major efforts were dedicated to making fiction an art form comparable to poetry. Writing and rewriting, seeking the exact word for every situation, he produced a remarkable series of letters on the art of fiction (mostly written to his beloved Louise Colet). The publication of these letters set a model for literary seriousness which was of great importance to later writers such as Henry James, Joseph Conrad, and James Joyce. Flaubert's carefully wrought fiction became a standard for other writers, while his realistic detail and cynical values made his work scandalous in the eyes of many. He was obliged to defend his most famous novel, *Madame Bovary* (1859), in court; but aside from this he led a quiet life, troubled by a kind of epilepsy, until his death.

# A Simple Soul

For half a century the housewives of Pont-l'Evêque had envied Madame Aubain her servant Félicité. For a hundred francs a year, she cooked and did the housework, washed, ironed, mended, harnessed the horse, fattened the poultry, made the butter and remained faithful to her mistress—although the latter was by no means an agreeable person.

Madame Aubain had married a comely youth without any money, who died in the beginning of 1809, leaving her with two young children and a number of debts. She sold all her property excepting the farm of Toucques and the farm of Geffosses, the income of which barely amounted to 5,000 francs; then she left her house in Saint-Melaine, and moved into a less pretentious one which had belonged to her ancestors and stood back of the market-place. This house, with its slate-covered roof, was built between a passage-way and a narrow street that led to the river. The interior was so unevenly graded that it caused people to stumble. A narrow hall separated the kitchen from the parlour, where Madame Aubain sat all day in a straw armchair near the window. Eight mahogany chairs stood in a row against the white wainscoting. An old piano, standing beneath a barometer, was covered with a pyramid of old books and boxes. On either side of the yellow marble mantelpiece, in Louis XV style, stood a tapestry armchair. The clock represented a temple of Vesta; and the whole room smelled musty, as it was on a lower level than the garden.

On the first floor was Madame's bed-chamber, a large room papered in a flowered design and containing the portrait of Monsieur dressed in the costume of a dandy. It communicated with a smaller room, in which there were two little cribs, without any mattresses. Next, came the parlour (always closed), filled with furniture covered with sheets. Then a hall, which led to the study, where books and papers were piled on the shelves of a book-case that enclosed three quarters of the big black desk. Two panels were entirely hidden under pen-and-ink sketches, gouache landscapes and Audran engravings, relics of better times and vanished luxury. On the second floor, a garret-window lighted Félicité's room, which looked out upon the meadows.

She arose at daybreak, in order to attend mass, and she worked without interruption until night; then, when dinner was over, the dishes cleared away and the door securely locked, she would bury the log under the ashes and fall asleep in front of the hearth with a rosary in her hand. Nobody could bargain with greater obstinacy, and as for cleanliness, the lustre on her brass sauce-pans was the envy and despair of other servants. She was most economical, and when she ate she would gather up crumbs with the tip of her finger, so that nothing should be wasted of the loaf of bread weighing twelve pounds which was baked especially for her and lasted three weeks.

Summer and winter she wore a dimity kerchief fastened in the back with a pin, a cap which concealed her hair, a red skirt, grey stockings, and an apron with a bib like those worn by hospital nurses.

Her face was thin and her voice shrill. When she was twenty-five, she looked forty. After she had passed fifty, nobody could tell her age; erect and silent always, she resembled a wooden figure working automatically.


## II

Like every other woman, she had had an affair of the heart. Her father, who was a mason, was killed by falling from a scaffolding. Then her mother died and her sisters went their different ways; a farmer took her in, and while she was quite small, let her keep cows in the fields. She was clad in miserable rags, beaten for the slightest offense and finally dismissed for a theft of thirty sous which she did not commit. She took service on another farm where she tended the poultry; and as she was well thought of by her master, her fellow-workers soon grew jealous.

One evening in August (she was then eighteen years old), they persuaded her to accompany them to the fair at Colleville. She was immediately dazzled by the noise, the lights in the trees, the brightness of the dresses, the laces and gold crosses, and the crowd of people all hopping at the same time. She was standing modestly at a distance, when presently a young man of well-to-do appearance, who had been leaning on the pole of a wagon and smoking his pipe, approached her, and asked her for a dance. He treated her to cider and cake, bought her a silk shawl, and then, thinking she had guessed his purpose, offered to see her home. When they came to the end of a field he threw her down brutally. But she grew frightened and screamed, and he walked off.

One evening, on the road leading to Beaumont, she came upon a wagon loaded with hay, and when she overtook it, she recognised Théodore. He greeted her calmly, and asked her to forget what had happened between them, as it "was all the fault of the drink."

She did not know what to reply and wished to run away.

Presently he began to speak of the harvest and of the notables of the village; his father had left Colleville and bought the farm of Les

Écots, so that now they would be neighbors. "Ah!" she exclaimed. He then added that his parents were looking around for a wife for him, but that he, himself, was not so anxious and preferred to wait for a girl who suited him. She hung her head. He then asked her whether she had ever thought of marrying. She replied, smilingly, that it was wrong of him to make fun of her. "Oh! no, I am in earnest," he said, and put his left arm around her waist while they sauntered along. The air was soft, the stars were bright, and the huge load of hay oscillated in front of them, drawn by four horses whose ponderous hoofs raised clouds of dust. Without a word from their driver they turned to the right. He kissed her again and she went home. The following week, Théodore obtained meetings.

They met in yards, behind walls or under isolated trees. She was not ignorant, as girls of well-to-do families are—for the animals had instructed her;—but her reason and her instinct of honour kept her from falling. Her resistance exasperated Théodore's love and so in order to satisfy it (or perchance ingenuously), he offered to marry her. She would not believe him at first, so he made solemn promises. But, in a short time he mentioned a difficulty; the previous year, his parents had purchased a substitute for him; but any day he might be drafted and the prospect of serving in the army alarmed him greatly. To Félicité his cowardice appeared a proof of his love for her, and her devotion to him grew stronger. When she met him, he would torture her with his fears and his entreaties. At last, he announced that he was going to the prefect himself for information, and would let her know everything on the following Sunday, between eleven o'clock and midnight.

When the time drew near, she ran to meet her lover.

But instead of Théodore, one of his friends was at the meeting-place.

He informed her that she would never see her sweetheart again; for, in order to escape the conscription, he had married a rich old woman, Madame Lehoussais, of Toucques.

The poor girl's sorrow was frightful. She threw herself on the ground, she cried and called on the Lord, and wandered around desolately until sunrise. Then she went back to the farm, declared her intention of leaving, and at the end of the month, after she had received her wages, she packed all her belongings in a handkerchief and started for Pont-l'Evêque.

In front of the inn, she met a woman wearing widow's weeds, and upon questioning her, learned that she was looking for a cook. The girl did not know very much, but appeared so willing and so modest in her requirements, that Madame Aubain finally said:

"Very well, I will give you a trial."

And half an hour later Félicité was installed in her house.

At first she lived in constant anxiety that was caused by "the style of the household" and the memory of "Monsieur," that hovered over everything. Paul and Virginia, the one aged seven, and the other barely four, seemed made of some precious material; she carried them pig-a-back, and was greatly mortified when Madame Aubain forbade her to kiss them every other minute.

But in spite of all this, she was happy. The comfort of her new surroundings had obliterated her sadness.

Every Thursday, friends of Madame Aubain dropped in for a game of cards, and it was Félicité's duty to prepare the table and heat the foot-warmers. They arrived at exactly eight o'clock and departed before eleven.

Every Monday morning, the dealer in second-hand goods, who lived under the alley-way, spread out his wares on the sidewalk. Then the city would be filled with a buzzing of voices in which the neighing of horses, the bleating of lambs, the grunting of pigs, could be distinguished, mingled with the sharp sound of wheels on cobble-stones. About twelve o'clock, when the market was in full swing, there appeared at the front door a tall, middle-aged peasant, with a hooked nose and a cap on the back of his head; it was Robelin, the farmer of Geffosses. Shortly afterwards came Liébard, the farmer of Toucques, short, rotund and ruddy, wearing a grey jacket and spurred boots.

Both men brought their landlady either chickens or cheese. Félicité would invariably thwart their ruses and they held her in great respect.

At various times, Madame Aubain received a visit from the Marquis de Grémanville, one of her uncles, who was ruined and lived at Falaise on the remainder of his estates. He always came at dinner-time and brought an ugly poodle with him, whose paws soiled the furniture. In spite of his efforts to appear a man of breeding (he even went so far as to raise his hat every time he said "My deceased father"), his habits got the better of him, and he would fill his glass a little too often and relate broad stories. Fécilité would show him out very politely and say: "You have had enough for this time, Monsieur de Grémanville! Hoping to see you again!" and would close the door.

She opened it gladly for Monsieur Bourais, a retired lawyer. His bald head and white cravat, the ruffling of his shirt, his flowing brown coat, the manner in which he took snuff, his whole person, in fact, produced in her the kind of awe which we feel when we see extraordinary persons. As he managed Madame's estates, he spent hours with her in Monsieur's study; he was in constant fear of being compromised, had a great regard for the magistracy and some pretensions to learning.

In order to facilitate the children's studies, he presented them with an engraved geography which represented various scenes of the world: cannibals with feather head-dresses, a gorilla kidnapping a young girl, Arabs in the desert, a whale being harpooned, etc.

Paul explained the pictures to Félicité. And, in fact, this was her only literary education.

The children's studies were under the direction of a poor devil employed at the town-hall, who sharpened his pocket-knife on his boots and was famous for his penmanship.

When the weather was fine, they went to Geffosses. The house was built in the centre of the sloping yard; and the sea looked like a grey spot in the distance. Félicité would take slices of cold meat from the lunch basket and they would sit down and eat in a room next to the dairy. This room was all that remained of a cottage that had been torn down. The dilapidated wall-paper trembled in the drafts. Madame Aubain, overwhelmed by recollections, would hang her head, while the children were afraid to open their mouths. Then, "Why don't you go and play?" their mother would say; and they would scamper off.

Paul would go to the old barn, catch birds, throw stones into the pond or pound the trunks of the trees with a stick till they resounded like drums. Virginia would feed the rabbits and run to pick the wild flowers in the fields, and her flying legs would disclose her little embroidered pantalettes. One autumn evening, they struck out for home through the meadows. The new moon illumined part of the sky and a mist hovered like a veil over the sinuosities of the river. Oxen, lying in the pastures, gazed mildly at the passing persons. In the third field, however, several of them got up and surrounded them. "Don't be afraid," cried Félicité; and murmuring a sort of lament she passed her hand over the back of the nearest ox; he turned away and the others followed. But when they came to the next pasture, they heard frightful bellowing.

It was a bull which was hidden from them by the fog. He advanced towards the two women, and Madame Aubain prepared to flee for her life. "No, no! not so fast," warned Félicité. Still they hurried on, for they could hear the noisy breathing of the bull close behind them. His hoofs pounded the grass like hammers, and presently he began to gallop! Félicité turned around and threw patches of grass in his eyes. He hung his head, shook his horns and bellowed with fury. Madame Aubain and the children, huddled at the end of the field, were trying to jump over the ditch. Félicité continued to back before the bull, blinding him with dirt, while she shouted to them to make haste.

Madame Aubain finally slid into the ditch, after shoving first Virginia and then Paul into it, and though she stumbled several times she managed, by dint of courage, to climb the other side of it.

The bull had driven Félicité up against a fence; the foam from his muzzle flew in her face and in another minute he would have disembowelled her. She had just time to slip between two bars and the huge animal, thwarted, paused.

For years, this occurrence was a topic of conversation in Pontl'Evêque. But Félicité took no credit to herself, and probably never knew that she had been heroic.

Virginia occupied her thoughts solely, for the shock she had sustained gave her a nervous affliction and the physician, M. Poupart, prescribed the salt-water bathing at Trouville. In those days, Trouville was not greatly patronised. Madame Aubain gathered information, consulted Bourais, and made preparations as if they were going on an extended trip.

The baggage was sent the day before on Liébard's cart. On the following morning, he brought around two horses, one of which had a woman's saddle with a velveteen back to it, while on the crupper of the other was a rolled shawl that was to be used for a seat. Madame Aubain mounted the second horse, behind Liébard. Félicité took charge of the little girl, and Paul rode M. Lechaptois's donkey, which had been lent for the occasion on the condition that they should be careful of it.

The road was so bad that it took two hours to cover the eight miles. The two horses sank knee-deep into the mud and stumbled into ditches; sometimes they had to jump over them. In certain places, Liébard's mare stopped abruptly. He waited patiently till she started again and talked of the people whose estates bordered the road, adding his own moral reflections to the outline of their histories. Thus, when they were passing through Toucques, and came to some windows draped with nasturtiums, he shrugged his shoulders and said: "There's a woman, Madame Lehoussais, who, instead of taking a young man—" Félicité could not catch what followed; the horses began to trot, the donkey to gallop, and they turned into a lane; then a gate swung open, two farm-hands appeared and they all dismounted at the very threshold of the farm-house.

Mother Liébard, when she caught sight of her mistress, was lavish with joyful demonstrations. She got up a lunch which comprised a leg of mutton, tripe, sausages, a chicken fricassée, sweet cider, a fruit tart and some preserved prunes; then to all this the good woman added polite remarks about Madame, who appeared to be in better health, Mademoiselle, who had grown to be "superb," and Paul, who had become singularly sturdy; she spoke also of their deceased grandparents, whom the Liébards had known, for they had been in the service of the family for several generations.

Like its owners, the farm had an ancient appearance. The beams of the ceiling were mouldy, the walls black with smoke and the windows grey with dust. The oak sideboard was filled with all sorts of utensils, plates, pitchers, tin bowls, wolf-traps. The children laughed when they saw a huge syringe. There was not a tree in the yard that did not have mushrooms growing around its foot, or a bunch of mistletoe hanging in its branches. Several of the trees had been blown down, but they had started to grow in the middle and all were laden with quantities of apples. The thatched roofs, which were of unequal thickness, looked like brown velvet and could resist the fiercest gales. But the wagon-shed was fast crumbling to ruins. Madame Aubain said that she would attend to it, and then gave orders to have the horses saddled.

It took another thirty minutes to reach Trouville. The little caravan dismounted in order to pass Les Ecores, a cliff that overhangs the bay, and a few minutes later, at the end of the dock, they entered the yard of the Golden Lamb, an inn kept by Mother David.

During the first few days, Virginia felt stronger, owing to the change of air and the action of the sea-baths. She took them in her little chemise, as she had no bathing suit, and afterwards her nurse dressed her in the cabin of a customs officer, which was used for that purpose by other bathers.

In the afternoon, they would take the donkey and go to the Roches-Noires, near Hennequeville. The path led at first through undulating grounds, and thence to a plateau, where pastures and tilled fields alternated. At the edge of the road, mingling with the brambles, grew holly bushes, and here and there stood large dead trees whose branches traced zigzags upon the blue sky.

Ordinarily, they rested in a field facing the ocean, with Deauville on their left, and Havre on their right. The sea glittered brightly in the sun and was as smooth as a mirror, and so calm that they could scarcely distinguish its murmur; sparrows chirped joyfully and the immense canopy of heaven spread over it all. Madame Aubain brought out her sewing, and Virginia amused herself by braiding reeds; Félicité wove lavender blossoms, while Paul was bored and wished to go home.

Sometimes they crossed the Toucques[1] in a boat, and started to

---

1. This is the river Touques, which separates Deauville and Trouville. The village of Touques, which the family passed through on the way to Trouville, is a short distance inland.

hunt for sea-shells. The outgoing tide exposed star-fish and sea-urchins, and the children tried to catch the flakes of foam which the wind blew away. The sleepy waves lapping the sand unfurled themselves along the shore that extended as far as the eye could see, but where land began, it was limited by the downs which separated it from the "Swamp," a large meadow shaped like a hippodrome. When they went that way, Trouville, on the slope of a hill below, grew larger and larger as they advanced, and, with all its houses of unequal height, seemed to spread out before them in a sort of giddy confusion.

When the heat was too oppressive, they remained in their rooms. The dazzling sunlight cast bars of light between the shutters. Not a sound in the village, not a soul on the sidewalk. This silence intensified the tranquility of everything. In the distance, the hammers of some calkers pounded the hull of a ship, and the sultry breeze brought them an odour of tar.

The principal diversion consisted in watching the return of the fishing-smacks. As soon as they passed the beacons, they began to ply to windward. The sails came down on two of their three masts, and with their fore-sails swelled up like balloons they glided over the waves and anchored in the middle of the harbour. Then they crept up alongside of the dock and the sailors threw the quivering fish over the side of the boat; a line of carts was waiting for them, and women with white caps sprang forward to receive the baskets and embrace their men-folk.

One day, one of them spoke to Félicité, who, after a little while, returned to the house gleefully. She had found one of her sisters, and presently Nastasie Barette, wife of Léroux, made her appearance holding an infant in her arms, another child by the hand, while on her left was a little cabin-boy with his hands in his pockets and his cap on his ear.

At the end of fifteen minutes, Madame Aubain bade her go.

They always hung around the kitchen, or approached Félicité when she and the children were out walking. The husband, however, did not show himself.

Félicité developed a great fondness for them; she brought them a stove, some shirts and a blanket; it was evident that they exploited her. Her foolishness annoyed Madame Aubain, who, moreover did not like the nephew's familiarity, for he called her son "thou";[2]—and, as Virginia began to cough and the season was over, she decided to return to Pont-l'Evêque.

---

2. The French have two forms of address, *vous*, which means "you," and *tu*, which we translate "thou." *Tu* is used by superiors talking to inferiors and also between close friends or family members. All others use *vous*.

Monsieur Bourais assisted her in the choice of a school. The one at Caen was considered the best. So Paul was sent away and bravely said good-bye to them all, for he was glad to go to live in a house where he could have boy companions.

Madame Aubain resigned herself to the separation from her son because it was unavoidable. Virginia brooded less and less over it. Félicité missed the noise he made, but soon a new occupation diverted her mind; beginning at Christmas, she accompanied the little girl to her catechism lesson every day.

### III

After she had made a curtsey at the threshold, she would walk up the aisle between the double lines of chairs, open Madame Aubain's pew, sit down and look around.

Girls and boys, the former on the right, the latter on the left-hand side of the church, filled the stalls of the choir; the priest stood beside the reading-desk; on one stained window of the side-aisle the Holy Ghost hovered over the Virgin; on another one, Mary knelt before the Child Jesus, and behind the altar, a wooden group represented Saint Michael felling the dragon.

The priest first read a condensed lesson of sacred history. Félicité encountered Paradise, the Flood, the Tower of Babel, the blazing cities, the dying nations, the shattered idols; and out of this she developed a great respect for the Almighty and a great fear of His wrath. Then, when she listened to the Passion, she wept. Why had they crucified Him who loved little children, nourished the people, made the blind see, and who out of humility, had wished to be born among the poor, in a stable? The sowings, the harvests, the wine-presses, all those familiar things which the Scriptures mention, formed a part of her life; the word of God sanctified them; and she loved the lambs with increased tenderness for the sake of the Lamb, and the doves because of the Holy Ghost.

She found it hard, however, to think of the latter as a person, for was it not a bird, a flame, and sometimes only a breath? Perhaps it is its light that at night hovers over swamps, its breath that propels the clouds, its voice that renders church-bells harmonious. And Félicité worshipped devoutly, while enjoying the coolness and the stillness of the church.

As for the dogma, she could not understand it and did not even try. The priest discoursed, the children recited, and she went to sleep, only to awaken with a start when they were leaving the church and their wooden shoes clattered on the stone pavement.

In this way, she learned her catechism, her religious education having been neglected in her youth; and thenceforth she imitated all

Virginia's religious practices, fasted when she did, and went to confession with her. At the Corpus-Christi Day they both decorated an altar.

She worried in advance over Virginia's first communion. She fussed about the shoes, the rosary, the book and the gloves. With what nervousness she helped the mother dress the child!

During the entire ceremony, she felt anguished. Monsieur Bourais hid part of the choir from view, but directly in front of her, the flock of maidens, wearing white wreaths over their lowered veils, formed a snow-white field, and she recognised her darling by the slenderness of her neck and her devout attitude. The bell tinkled. All the heads bent and there was a silence. Then, at the peals of the organ the singers and the worshippers struck up the Agnus Dei; the boys' procession began; behind them came the girls. With clasped hands, they advanced step by step to the lighted altar, knelt at the first step, received one by one the Host, and returned to their seats in the same order. When Virginia's turn came, Félicité leaned forward to watch her, and through that imagination which springs from true affection, she at once became the child, whose face and dress became hers, whose heart beat in her bosom, and when Virginia opened her mouth and closed her lids, she did likewise and came very near fainting.

The following day, she presented herself early at the church so as to receive communion from the curé. She took it with the proper feeling, but did not experience the same delight as on the previous day.

Madame Aubain wished to make an accomplished girl of her daughter; and as Guyot could not teach English nor music, she decided to send her to the Ursulines at Honfleur.

The child made no objection, but Félicité sighed and thought Madame was heartless. Then, she thought that perhaps her mistress was right, as these things were beyond her sphere. Finally, one day, an old *fiacre* stopped in front of the door and a nun stepped out. Félicité put Virginia's luggage on top of the carriage, gave the coachman some instructions, and smuggled six jars of jam, a dozen pears and a bunch of violets under the seat.

At the last minute, Virginia had a fit of sobbing; she embraced her mother again and again, while the latter kissed her on her forehead, and said: "Now, be brave, be brave!" The step was pulled up and the *fiacre* rumbled off.

Then Madame Aubain had a fainting spell, and that evening all her friends, including the two Lormeaus, Madame Lechaptois, the ladies Rochefeuille, Messieurs de Houppeville and Bourais, called on her and tendered their sympathy.

At first the separation proved very painful to her. But her daughter wrote her three times a week and the other days she, herself, wrote to Virginia. Then she walked in the garden, read a little, and in this way managed to fill out the emptiness of the hours.

Each morning, out of habit, Félicité entered Virginia's room and gazed at the walls. She missed combing her hair, lacing her shoes, tucking her in her bed, and the bright face and little hand when they used to go out for a walk. In order to occupy herself she tried to make lace. But her clumsy fingers broke the threads; she had no heart for anything, lost her sleep and "wasted away," as she put it.

In order to have some distraction, she asked leave to receive the visits of her nephew Victor.

He would come on Sunday, after church, with ruddy cheeks and bared chest, bringing with him the scent of the country. She would set the table and they would sit down opposite each other, and eat their dinner; she ate as little as possible, herself, to avoid any extra expense, but would stuff him so with food that he would finally go to sleep. At the first stroke of vespers, she would wake him up, brush his trousers, tie his cravat and walk to church with him, leaning on his arm with maternal pride.

His parents always told him to get something out of her, either a package of brown sugar, or soap, or brandy, and sometimes even money. He brought her his clothes to mend, and she accepted the task gladly, because it meant another visit from him.

In August, his father took him on a coasting-vessel.

It was vacation time and the arrival of the children consoled Félicité. But Paul was capricious, and Virginia was growing too old to be thee-and-thou'd, a fact which seemed to produce a sort of embarrassment in their relations.

Victor went successively to Morlaix, to Dunkirk, and to Brighton; whenever he returned from a trip he would bring her a present. The first time it was a box of shells; the second, a coffee-cup; the third, a big doll of ginger-bread. He was growing handsome, had a good figure, a tiny moustache, kind eyes, and a little leather cap that sat jauntily on the back of his head. He amused his aunt by telling her stories mingled with nautical expressions.

One Monday, the 14th of July, 1819 (she never forgot the date), Victor announced that he had been engaged on a merchant-vessel and that in two days he would take the steamer at Honfleur and join his ship, which was going to start from Havre very soon. Perhaps he might be away two years.

The prospect of his departure filled Félicité with despair, and in order to bid him farewell, on Wednesday night, after Madame's dinner, she put on her pattens and trudged the four miles that separated Pont-l'Evêque from Honfleur.

When she reached the Calvary,[3] instead of turning to the right, she turned to the left and lost herself in coal-yards; she had to retrace her steps; some people she spoke to advised her to hasten. She walked helplessly around the harbour filled with vessels, and knocked against hawsers. Presently the ground sloped abruptly, lights flitted to and fro, and she thought all at once that she had gone mad when she saw some horses in the sky.

Others, on the edge of the dock, neighed at the sight of the ocean. A derrick pulled them up in the air and dumped them into a boat, where passengers were bustling about among barrels of cider, baskets of cheese and bags of meal; chickens cackled, the captain swore and a cabin-boy rested on the railing, apparently indifferent to his surroundings. Félicité,who did not recognise him, kept shouting: "Victor!" He suddenly raised his eyes, but while she was preparing to rush up to him, they withdrew the gang-plank.

The packet, towed by singing women, glided out of the harbour. Her hull squeaked and the heavy waves beat up against her sides. The sail had turned and nobody was visible;—and on the ocean, silvered by the light of the moon, the vessel formed a black spot that grew dimmer and dimmer, and finally disappeared.

When Félicité passed the Calvary again, she felt as if she must entrust that which was dearest to her to the Lord; and for a long while she prayed, with uplifted eyes and a face wet with tears. The city was sleeping; some customs officials were taking the air; and the water kept pouring through the holes of the dam with a deafening roar. The town clock struck two.

The parlour of the convent would not open until morning, and surely a delay would annoy Madame; so, in spite of her desire to see the other child, she went home. The maids of the inn were just arising when she reached Pont-l'Evêque.

So the poor boy would be on the ocean for months! His previous trips had not alarmed her. One can come back from England and Brittany; but America, the colonies, the islands, were all lost in an uncertain region at the very end of the world.

From that time on, Félicité thought solely of her nephew. On warms days she feared he would suffer from thirst, and when it stormed, she was afraid he would be struck by lightning. When she harkened to the wind that rattled in the chimney and dislodged the tiles on the roof, she imagined that he was being buffeted by the

3. The Calvary is a hill with a Christian monument, near the Ursuline convent school.

same storm, perched on top of a shattered mast, with his whole body bent backward and covered with sea-foam; or,—these were recollections of the engraved geography—he was being devoured by savages, or captured in a forest by apes, or dying on some lonely coast. She never mentioned her anxieties, however.

Madame Aubain worried about her daughter.

The sisters thought that Virginia was affectionate but delicate. The slightest emotion enervated her. She had to give up her piano lessons. Her mother insisted upon regular letters from the convent. One morning, when the postman failed to come, she grew impatient and began to pace to and fro, from her chair to the window. It was really extraordinary! No news for four days!

In order to console her mistress by her own example, Félicité said:

"Why, Madame, I haven't had any news for six months!"—

"From whom?"—

"Why—from my nephew."

"Oh, yes, your nephew!" And shrugging her shoulders, Madame Aubain continued to pace the floor as if to say: "I did not think of it.—Besides, I do not care, a cabin-boy, a pauper!—but my daughter—what a difference! just think of it!—"

Félicité, although she had been reared roughly, was very indignant. Then she forgot about it.

It appeared quite natural to her that one should lose one's head about Virginia.

The two children were of equal importance; they were united in her heart and their fate was to be the same.

The chemist informed her that Victor's vessel had reached Havana. He had read the information in a newspaper.

Félicité imagined that Havana was a place where people did nothing but smoke, and that Victor walked around among negroes in a cloud of tobacco. Could a person, in case of need, return by land? How far was it from Pont-l'Evêque? In order to learn these things, she questioned Monsieur Bourais. He reached for his map and began some explanations concerning longitudes, and smiled with superiority at Félicité's bewilderment. At last, he took his pencil and pointed out an imperceptible black point in the scallops of an oval blotch, adding: "There it is." She bent over the map; the maze of coloured lines hurt her eyes without enlightening her; and when Bourais asked her what puzzled her, she requested him to show her the house Victor lived in. Bourais threw up his hands, sneezed, and then laughed uproariously; such ignorance delighted his soul; but Félicité failed to understand the cause of his mirth, she whose intelligence was so limited that she perhaps expected to see even the picture of her nephew!

It was two weeks later that Liébard came into the kitchen at market-time, and handed her a létter from her brother-in-law. As neither of them could read, she called upon her mistress.

Madame Aubain, who was counting the stitches of her knitting, laid her work down beside her, opened the letter, started, and in a low tone and with a searching look said: "They tell you of a— misfortune. Your nephew—."

He had died. The letter told nothing more.

Félicité dropped on a chair, leaned her head against the back and closed her lids; presently they grew pink. Then, with drooping head, inert hands and staring eyes she repeated at intervals:

"Poor little chap! poor little chap!"

Liébard watched her and sighed. Madame Aubain was trembling. She proposed to the girl to go to see her sister in Trouville.

With a single motion, Félicité replied that it was not necessary.

There was a silence. Old Liébard thought it about time for him to take leave.

Then Félicité uttered:

"They have no sympathy, they do not care!"

Her head fell forward again, and from time to time, mechanically, she toyed with the long knitting-needles on the work-table.

Some women passed through the yard with a basket of wet clothes.

When she saw them through the window, she suddenly remembered her own wash; as she had soaked it the day before, she must go and rinse it now. So she arose and left the room.

Her tub and her board were on the bank of the Toucques. She threw a heap of clothes on the ground, rolled up her sleeves and grasped her bat; and her loud pounding could be heard in the neighbouring gardens. The meadows were empty, the breeze wrinkled the stream, at the bottom of which were long grasses that looked like the hair of corpses floating in the water. She restrained her sorrow and was very brave until night; but, when she had gone to her own room, she gave way to it, burying her face in the pillow and pressing her two fists against her temples.

A long while afterward, she learned through Victor's captain, the circumstances which surrounded his death. At the hospital they had bled him too much, treating him for yellow fever. Four doctors held him at one time. He died almost instantly, and the chief surgeon had said:

"Here goes another one!"

His parents had always treated him barbarously; she preferred not to see them again, and they made no advances, either from forgetfulness or out of innate hardness.

Virginia was growing weaker.

A cough, continual fever, oppressive breathing and spots on her cheeks indicated some serious trouble. Monsieur Poupart had advised a sojourn in Provence. Madame Aubain decided that they would go, and she would have had her daughter come home at once, had it not been for the climate of Pont-l'Evêque.

She made an arrangement with a livery-stable man who drove her over to the convent every Tuesday. In the garden there was a terrace, from which the view extends to the Seine. Virginia walked in it, leaning on her mother's arm and treading the dead vine leaves. Sometimes the sun, shining through the clouds, made her blink her lids, when she gazed at the sails in the distance, and let her eyes roam over the horizon from the chateau of Tancarville to the lighthouses of Havre. Then they rested in the arbour. Her mother had bought a little cask of fine Malaga wine, and Virginia, laughing at the idea of becoming intoxicated, would drink a few drops of it, but never more.

Her strength returned. Autumn passed. Félicité began to reassure Madame Aubain. But, one evening, when she returned home after an errand, she met M. Boupart's coach in front of the door; M. Boupart himself was standing in the vestibule and Madame Aubain was tying the strings of her bonnet. "Give me my foot-warmer, my purse and my gloves; and be quick about it," she said.

Virginia had congestion of the lungs; perhaps it was desperate.

"Not yet," said the physician, and both got into the carriage, while the snow fell in thick flakes. It was almost night and very cold.

Félicité rushed to the church to light a candle. Then she ran after the coach which she overtook after an hour's chase, sprang up behind and held on to the straps. But suddenly a thought crossed her mind: "The yard had been left open; supposing that burglars got in!" And down she jumped.

The next morning, at daybreak, she called at the doctor's. He had been home, but had left again. Then she waited at the inn, thinking that strangers might bring her a letter. At last, at daylight she took the coach from Lisieux.

The convent was at the end of a steep and narrow street. When she arrived about at the middle of it, she heard strange noises, a funeral knell. "It must be for some one else," thought she; and she pulled the knocker violently.

After several minutes had elapsed, she heard footsteps, the door was half opened and a nun appeared. The good sister, with an air of compunction, told her that "she had just passed away." And at the same time the tolling of Saint-Léonard's increased.

Félicité reached the second floor. Already at the threshold, she caught sight of Virginia lying on her back, with clasped hands, her mouth open and her head thrown back, beneath a black crucifix inclined toward her, and stiff curtains which were less white than her face. Madame Aubain lay at the foot of the couch, clasping it with her arms and uttering groans of agony. The Mother Superior was standing on the right side of the bed. The three candles on the bureau made red blurs, and the windows were dimmed by the fog outside. The nuns carried Madame Aubain from the room.

For two nights, Félicité never left the corpse. She would repeat the same prayers, sprinkle holy water over the sheets, get up, come back to the bed and contemplate the body. At the end of the first vigil, she noticed that the face had taken on a yellow tinge, the lips grew blue, the nose grew pinched, the eyes were sunken. She kissed them several times and would not have been greatly astonished had Virginia opened them; to souls like these the supernatural is always quite simple. She washed her, wrapped her in a shroud, put her into the casket, laid a wreath of flowers on her head and arranged her curls. They were blond and of an extraordinary length for her age. Félicité cut off a big lock and put half of it into her bosom, resolving never to part with it.

The body was taken to Pont-l'Evêque, according to Madame Aubain's wishes; she followed the hearse in a closed carriage.

After the ceremony it took three quarters of an hour to reach the cemetery. Paul, sobbing, headed the procession; Monsieur Bourais followed, and then came the principal inhabitants of the town, the women covered with black capes, and Félicité. The memory of her nephew, and the thought that she had not been able to render him these honours, made her doubly unhappy, and she felt as if he were being buried with Virginia.

Madame Aubain's grief was uncontrollable. At first she rebelled against God, thinking that he was unjust to have taken away her child—she who had never done anything wrong, and whose conscience was so pure! But no! she ought to have taken her South. Other doctors would have saved her. She accused herself, prayed to be able to join her child, and cried in the midst of her dreams. Of the latter, one more especially haunted her. Her husband, dressed like a sailor, had come back from a long voyage, and with tears in his eyes told her that he had received the order to take Virginia away. Then they both consulted about a hiding-place.

Once she came in from the garden, all upset. A moment before (and she showed the place), the father and daughter had appeared to her, one after the other; they did nothing but look at her.

During several months she remained inert in her room. Félicité scolded her gently; she must go on living for her son and also for the other one, for "her memory."

"Her memory!" replied Madame Aubain, as if she were just awakening, "Oh! yes, yes, you do not forget her!" This was an allusion to the cemetery where she had been expressly forbidden to go.

But Félicité went there every day. At four o'clock exactly, she would go through the town, climb the hill, open the gate and arrive at Virginia's tomb. It was a small column of pink marble with a flat stone at its base, and it was surrounded by a little plot enclosed by chains. The flower-beds were bright with blossoms. Félicité watered their leaves, renewed the gravel, and knelt on the ground in order to till the earth properly. When Madame Aubain was able to visit the cemetery she felt very much relieved and consoled.

Years passed, all alike and marked by no other events than the return of the great church holidays: Easter, Assumption, All Saints' Day. Household happenings constituted the only data to which in later years they often referred. Thus, in 1825, workmen painted the vestibule; in 1827, a portion of the roof almost killed a man by falling into the yard. In the summer of 1828, it was Madame's turn to offer the hallowed bread; at the time, Bourais disappeared mysteriously; and the old acquaintances, Guyot, Liébard, Madame Lechaptois, Robelin, old Grémanville, paralysed for a long time, passed away one by one. One night, the driver of the mail in Pont-l'Evêque announced the Revolution of July. A few days afterward a new sub-prefect was nominated, the Baron de Larsonnière, ex-consul in America, who, besides his wife, had his sister-in-law and her three grown daughters with him. They were often seen on their lawn, dressed in loose blouses, and they had a parrot and a negro servant. Madame Aubain received a call, which she returned promptly. As soon as she caught sight of them, Félicité would run and notify her mistress. But only one thing was capable of arousing her: a letter from her son.

He could not follow any profession as he was absorbed in drinking. His mother paid his debts and he made fresh ones; and the sighs that she heaved while she knitted at the window reached the ears of Félicité who was spinning in the kitchen.

They walked in the garden together, always speaking of Virginia, and asking each other if such and such a thing would have pleased her, and what she would probably have said on this or that occasion.

All her little belongings were put away in a closet of the room which held the two little beds. But Madame Aubain looked them over as little as possible. One summer day, however, she resigned herself to the task and when she opened the closet the moths flew out.

Virginia's frocks were hung under a shelf where there were three dolls, some hoops, a doll-house, and a basin which she had used. Félicité and Madame Aubain also took out the skirts, the handkerchiefs, and the stockings and spread them on the beds, before putting them away again. The sun fell on the piteous things, disclosing their spots and creases formed by the motions of the body. The atmosphere was warm and blue, and a blackbird trilled in the garden; everything seemed to live in happiness. They found a little hat of soft brown plush, but it was entirely moth-eaten. Félicité asked for it. Their eyes met and filled with tears; at last the mistress opened her arms and the servant threw herself against her breast and they hugged each other, giving vent to their grief in a kiss which equalized them for a moment.

It was the first time that this had ever happened, for Madame Aubain was not of an expansive nature. Félicité was as grateful for it as if it had been some favour, and thenceforth loved her with animal-like devotion and a religious veneration.

Her kind-heartedness developed. When she heard the drums of a marching regiment passing through the street, she would stand in the doorway with a jug of cider and give the soldiers a drink. She nursed cholera victims. She protected Polish refugees, and one of them even declared that he wished to marry her. But they quarrelled, for one morning when she returned from the Angelus she found him in the kitchen coolly eating a dish which he had prepared for himself during her absence.

After the Polish refugees, came Colmiche, an old man who was credited with having committed frightful misdeeds in '93. He lived near the river in the ruins of a pig-sty. The urchins peeped at him through the cracks in the walls and threw stones that fell on his miserable bed, where he lay gasping with catarrh, with long hair, inflamed eyelids, and a tumour as big as his head on one arm.

She got him some linen, tried to clean his hovel and dreamed of installing him in the bake-house without his being in Madame's way. When the tumour broke, she dressed it every day; sometimes she brought him some cake and placed him in the sun on a bundle of hay; and the poor old creature, trembling and drooling, would thank her in his broken voice, and put out his hands whenever she left him. Finally he died; and she had a mass said for the repose of his soul.

That day a great joy came to her: at dinner-time, Madame de Larsonnière's servant called with the parrot, the cage, and the perch and chain and lock. A note from the baroness told Madame Aubain that as her husband had been promoted to a prefecture, they were leaving that night, and she begged her to accept the bird as a remembrance and a token of her esteem.

For a long time the parrot had been on Félicité's mind, because he came from America, which reminded her of Victor, and she had approached the negro on the subject.

Once even, she had said:

"How glad Madame would be to have him!"

The man had repeated this remark to his mistress who, not being able to keep the bird, took this means of getting rid of it.


IV

He was called Loulou. His body was green, his head blue, the tips of his wings were pink and his breast was golden.

But he had the tiresome tricks of biting his perch, pulling his feathers out, scattering refuse and spilling the water of his bath. Madame Aubain grew tired of him and gave him to Félicité for good.

She undertook his education, and soon he was able to repeat: "Pretty boy! Your servant, sir! I salute you, Marie!" His perch was placed near the door and several persons were astonished that he did not answer to the name of "Jacquot," for every parrot is called Jacquot. They called him a goose and a log, and these taunts were like so many dagger thrusts to Félicité. Strange stubbornness of the bird which would not talk when people watched him!

Nevertheless, he sought society; for on Sunday, when the ladies Rochefeuille, Monsieur de Houppeville and the new habitués, On-froy, the chemist, Monsieur Varin and Captain Mathieu, dropped in for their game of cards, he struck the window-panes with his wings and made such a racket that it was impossible to talk.

Bourais's face must have appeared very funny to Loulou. As soon as he saw him he would begin to roar. His voice re-echoed in the yard, and the neighbors would come to the windows and begin to laugh, too; and in order that the parrot might not see him, Monsieur Bourais edged along the wall, pushed his hat over his eyes to hide his profile, and entered by the garden door, and the looks he gave the bird lacked affection. Loulou, having thrust his head into the butcher-boy's basket, received a slap, and from that time he always tried to nip his enemy. Fabu threatened to wring his neck, although he was not cruelly inclined, notwithstanding his big whiskers and tattooings. On the contrary, he rather liked the bird and, out of devil-try, tried to teach him oaths. Félicité, whom his manner alarmed, put Loulou in the kitchen, took off his chain and let him walk all over the house.

When he went downstairs, he rested his beak on the steps, lifted his right foot and then his left one; but his mistress feared that such feats would give him vertigo. He became ill and was unable to eat. There was a small growth under his tongue like those chickens are sometimes afflicted with. Félicité pulled it off with her nails and cured him. One day, Paul was imprudent enought to blow the smoke of his cigar in his face; another time, Madame Lormeau was teasing him with the tip of her umbrella and he swallowed the tip. Finally he got lost.

She had put him on the grass to cool him and went away only for a second; when she returned, she found no parrot! She hunted among the bushes, on the bank of the river, and on the roofs, without paying any attention to Madame Aubain who screamed at her: "Take care! you must be insane!" Then she searched every garden in Pont-l'Evêque and stopped the passers-by to inquire of them: "Haven't you perhaps seen my parrot?" To those who had never seen the parrot, she described him minutely. Suddenly she thought she saw something green fluttering behind the mills at the foot of the hill. But when she was at the top of the hill she could not see it. A hod-carrier told her that he had just seen the bird in Saint-Melaine, in Mother Simon's store. She rushed to the place. The people did not know what she was talking about. At last she came home, exhausted, with her slippers worn to shreds, and despair in her heart. She sat down on the bench near Madame and was telling of her search when presently a light weight dropped on her shoulder—Loulou! What the deuce had he been doing? Perhaps he had just taken a little walk around town!

She did not easily forget her scare; in fact, she never got over it. In consequence of a cold, she caught a sore throat; and some time afterward she had an ear-ache. Three years later she was stone deaf, and spoke in a very loud voice even in church. Although her sins might have been proclaimed throughout the diocese without any shame to herself, or ill effects to the community, the curé thought it advisable to receive her confession in the vestry-room.

Imaginary buzzings also added to her bewilderment. Her mistress often said to her: "My goodness, how stupid you are!" and she would answer: "Yes, Madame," and look for something.

The narrow circle of her ideas grew more restricted than it already was; the bellowing of the oxen, the chime of the bells no longer reached her intelligence. All things moved silently, like ghosts. Only one noise penetrated her ears; the parrot's voice.

As if to divert her mind, he reproduced for her the tick-tack of the spit in the kitchen, the shrill cry of the fish-vendors, the saw of the carpenter who had a shop opposite, and when the door-bell rang, he would imitate Madame Aubain: "Félicité! go to the front door."

They held conversations together, Loulou repeating the three phrases of his repertory over and over, Félicité replying by words that had no greater meaning, but in which she poured out her feelings. In her isolation, the parrot was almost a son, a lover. He climbed upon her fingers, pecked at her lips, clung to her shawl, and when she rocked her head to and fro like a nurse, the big wings of her cap and the wings of the bird flapped in unison. When clouds gathered on the horizon and the thunder rumbled, Loulou would scream, perhaps because he remembered the storms in his native forests. The dripping of the rain would excite him to frenzy; he flapped around, struck the ceiling with his wings, upset everything, and would finally fly into the garden to play. Then he would come back into the room, light on one of the andirons, and hop around in order to get dry.

One morning during the terrible winter of 1837, when she had put him in front of the fire-place on account of the cold, she found him dead in his cage, hanging to the wire bars with his head down. He had probably died of congestion. But she believed that he had been poisoned, and although she had no proofs whatever, her suspicion rested on Fabu.

She wept so sorely that her mistress said: "Why don't you have him stuffed?"

She asked the advice of the chemist, who had always been kind to the bird.

He wrote to Havre for her. A certain man named Fellacher consented to do the work. But, as the diligence driver often lost parcels entrusted to him, Félicité resolved to take her pet to Honfleur herself.

Leafless apple-trees lined the edges of the road. The ditches were covered with ice. The dogs on the neighbouring farms barked; and Félicité, with her hands beneath her cape, her little black sabots and her basket, trotted along nimbly in the middle of the sidewalk. She crossed the forest, passed by the Haut-Chêne and reached Saint-Gatien.

Behind her, in a cloud of dust and impelled by the steep incline, a mail-coach drawn by galloping horses advanced like a whirlwind. When he saw a woman in the middle of the road, who did not get out of the way, the driver stood up in his seat and shouted to her and so did the postilion, while the four horses, which he could not hold back, accelerated their pace; the two leaders were almost upon her; with a jerk of the reins he threw them to one side, but, furious at the incident, he lifted his big whip and lashed her from her head to her feet with such violence that she fell to the ground unconscious.

Her first thought, when she recovered her senses, was to open the basket. Loulou was unharmed. She felt a sting on her right cheek; when she took her hand away it was red, for the blood was flowing.

She sat down on a pile of stones, and sopped her cheek with her handkerchief; then she ate a crust of bread she had put in her basket, and consoled herself by looking at the bird.

Arriving at the top of Ecquemanville, she saw the lights of Honfleur shining in the distance like so many stars; further on, the ocean spread out in a confused mass. Then a weakness came over her; the misery of her childhood, the disappointment of her first love, the departure of her nephew, the death of Virginia; all these things came back to her at once, and, rising like a swelling tide in her throat, almost choked her.

Then she wished to speak to the captain of the vessel, and without stating what she was sending, she gave him some instructions.

Fellacher kept the parrot a long time. He always promised that it would be ready for the following week; after six months he announced the shipment of a case, and that was the end of it. Really, it seemed as if Loulou would never come back to his home. "They have stolen him," thought Félicité.

Finally he arrived, sitting bolt upright on a branch which could be screwed into a mahogany pedestal, with his foot in the air, his head on one side, and in his beak a nut which the naturalist, from love of the sumptuous, had gilded. She put him in her room.

This place, to which only a chosen few were admitted, looked like a chapel and a second-hand shop, so filled was it with devotional and heterogeneous things. The door could not be opened easily on account of the presence of a large wardrobe. Opposite the window that looked out into the garden, a bull's-eye opened on the yard; a table was placed by the cot and held a wash-basin, two combs, and a piece of blue soap in a broken saucer. On the walls were rosaries, medals, a number of Holy Virgins, and a holy-water basin made out of a cocoanut; on the bureau, which was covered with a napkin like an altar, stood the box of shells that Victor had given her; also a watering-can and a balloon, writing-books, the engraved geography and a pair of shoes; on the nail which held the mirror, hung Virginia's little plush hat! Félicité carried this sort of respect so far that she even kept one of Monsieur's old coats. All the things which Madame Aubain discarded, Félicité begged for her own room. Thus, she had artificial flowers on the edge of the bureau, and the picture of the Comte d'Artois in the recess of the window. By means of a board, Loulou was set on a portion of the chimney which advanced into the room. Every morning when she awoke, she saw him in the dim light of dawn and recalled bygone days and the smallest details of insignificant actions, without any sense of bitterness or grief.

As she was unable to communicate with people, she lived in a sort of somnambulistic torpor. The processions of Corpus-Christi

Day seemed to wake her up. She visited the neighbours to beg for candle-sticks and mats so as to adorn the temporary altars in the street.

In church, she always gazed at the Holy Ghost, and noticed that there was something about him that resembled a parrot. The likeness appeared even more striking on a colored picture by Espinal, representing the baptism of our Saviour. With his scarlet wings and emerald body, it was really the image of Loulou. Having bought the picture, she hung it near the one of the Comte d'Artois so that she could take them in at one glance.

They associated in her mind, the parrot becoming sanctified through the neighbourhood of the Holy Ghost, and the latter becoming more lifelike in her eyes, and more comprehensible. In all probability the Father had never chosen as messenger a dove, as the latter has no voice, but rather one of Loulou's ancestors. And Félicité said her prayers in front of the coloured picture, though from time to time she turned slightly toward the bird.

She desired very much to enter in the ranks of the "Daughters of the Virgin." But Madame Aubain dissuaded her from it.

A most important event occurred: Paul's marriage.

After being first a notary's clerk, then in business, then in the customs, and a tax collector, and having even applied for a position in the administration of woods and forests, he had at last, when he was thirty-six years old, by a divine inspiration, found his vocation: registrature! and he displayed such a high ability that an inspector had offered him his daughter and his influence.

Paul, who had become quite settled, brought his bride to visit his mother.

But she looked down upon the customs of Pont-L'Evêque, put on airs, and hurt Félicité's feelings. Madame Aubain felt relieved when she left.

The following week they learned of Monsieur Bourais's death in an inn. There were rumours of suicide, which were confirmed; doubts concerning his integrity arose. Madame Aubain looked over her accounts and soon discovered his numerous embezzlements; sales of wood which had been concealed from her, false receipts, etc. Furthermore, he had an illegitimate child, and entertained a friendship for "a person in Dozulé."

These base actions affected her very much. In March, 1853, she developed a pain in her chest; her tongue looked as if it were coated with smoke, and the leeches they applied did not relieve her oppression; and on the ninth evening she died, being just seventy-two years old.

People thought that she was younger, because her hair, which she wore in bands framing her pale face, was brown. Few friends regretted her loss, for her manner was so haughty that she did not attract them. Félicité mourned for her as servants seldom mourn for their masters. The fact that Madame should die before herself perplexed her mind and seemed contrary to the order of things, and absolutely monstrous and inadmissible. Ten days later (the time to journey from Besançon), the heirs arrived. Her daughter-in-law ransacked the drawers, kept some of the furniture, and sold the rest; then they went back to their own home.

Madame's armchair, foot-warmer, work-table, the eight chairs, everything was gone! The places occupied by the pictures formed yellow squares on the walls. They had taken the two little beds, and the wardrobe had been emptied of Virginia's belongings! Félicité went upstairs, overcome with grief.

The following day a sign was posted on the door; the chemist screamed in her ear that the house was for sale.

For a moment she tottered, and had to sit down.

What hurt her most was to give up her room,—so nice for poor Loulou! She looked at him in despair and implored the Holy Ghost, and it was this way that she contracted the idolatrous habit of saying her prayers kneeling in front of the bird. Sometimes the sun fell through the window on his glass eye, and lighted a great spark in it which sent Félicité into ecstasy.

Her mistress had left her an income of three hundred and eighty francs. The garden supplied her with vegetables. As for clothes, she had enough to last her till the end of her days, and she economised on the light by going to bed at dusk.

She rarely went out, in order to avoid passing in front of the second-hand dealer's shop where there was some of the old furniture. Since her fainting spell, she dragged her leg, and as her strength was failing rapidly, old Mother Simon, who had lost her money in the grocery business, came every morning to chop the wood and pump the water.

Her eyesight grew dim. She did not open the shutters after that. Many years passed. But the house did not sell or rent. Fearing that she would be put out, Félicité did not ask for repairs. The laths of the roof were rotting away, and during one whole winter her bolster was wet. After Easter she spit blood.

Then Mother Simon went for a doctor. Félicité wished to know what her complaint was. But, being too deaf to hear, she caught only one word: "Pneumonia." She was familiar with it and gently answered:—"Ah! like Madame," thinking it quite natural that she should follow her mistress.

The time for the altars in the street drew near.

The first one was always erected at the foot of the hill, the second in front of the post-office, and the third in the middle of the street. This position occasioned some rivalry among the women and they finally decided upon Madame Aubain's yard.

Félicité's fever grew worse. She was sorry that she could not do anything for the altar. If she could, at least, have contributed something toward it! Then she thought of the parrot. Her neighbors objected that it would not be proper. But the curé gave his consent and she was so grateful for it that she begged him to accept after her death, her only treasure, Loulou. From Tuesday until Saturday, the day before the event, she coughed more frequently. In the evening her face was contracted, her lips stuck to her gums and she began to vomit; and on the following day, she felt so low that she called for a priest.

Three neighbors surrounded her when the dominie administered the Extreme Unction. Afterwards she said that she wished to speak to Fabu.

He arrived in his Sunday clothes, very ill at ease among the funereal surroundings.

"Forgive me," she said, making an effort to extend her arm, "I believed it was you who killed him!"

What did such accusations mean? Suspect a man like him of murder! And Fabu became excited and was about to make trouble. "Don't you see she is not in her right mind?"

From time to time Félicité spoke to shadows. The women left and Mother Simon sat down to breakfast.

A little later, she took Loulou and holding him up to Félicité:

"Say good-bye to him, now!" she commanded.

Although he was not a corpse, he was eaten up by worms; one of his wings was broken and the wadding was coming out of his body. But Félicité was blind now, and she took him and laid him against her cheek. Then Mother Simon removed him in order to set him on the altar.

V

The grass exhaled an odour of summer; flies buzzed in the air, the sun shone on the river and warmed the slated roof. Old Mother Simon had returned to Félicité and was peacefully falling asleep.

The ringing of bells woke her; the people were coming out of church. Félicité's delirium subsided. By thinking of the procession, she was able to see it as if she had taken part in it. All the schoolchildren, the singers and the firemen walked on the sidewalks, while in the middle of the street came first the custodian of the church with his halberd, then the beadle with a large cross, the teacher in charge of the boys and a sister escorting the little girls; three of the smallest ones, with curly heads, threw rose leaves into the air; the deacon with outstretched arms conducted the music; and two incense-bearers turned with each step they took toward the Holy Sacrament, which was carried by M. le Curé, attired in his handsome chasuble and walking under a canopy of red velvet supported by four men. A crowd of people followed, jammed between the walls of the houses hung with white sheets; at last the procession arrived at the foot of the hill.

A cold sweat broke out on Félicité's forehead. Mother Simon wiped it away with a cloth, saying inwardly that some day she would have to go through the same thing herself.

The murmur of the crowd grew louder, was very distinct for a moment and then died away. A volley of musketry shook the window-panes. It was the postillions saluting the Sacrament. Félicité rolled her eyes and said as loudly as she could:

"Is he all right?" meaning the parrot.

Her death agony began. A rattle that grew more and more rapid shook her body. Froth appeared at the corners of her mouth, and her whole frame trembled. In a little while could be heard the music of the bass horns, the clear voices of the children and the men's deeper notes. At intervals all was still, and their shoes sounded like a herd of cattle passing over the grass.

The clergy appeared in the yard. Mother Simon climbed on a chair to reach the bull's-eye, and in this manner could see the altar. It was covered with a lace cloth and draped with green wreaths. In the middle stood a little frame containing relics; at the corners were two little orange-trees, and all along the edge were silver candlesticks, porcelain vases containing sun-flowers, lilies, peonies, and tufts of hydrangeas. This mound of bright colours descended diagonally from the first floor to the carpet that covered the sidewalk. Rare objects arrested one's eye. A golden sugar-bowl was crowned with violets, earrings set with Alençon stones were displayed on green moss, and two Chinese screens with their bright landscapes were near by. Loulou, hidden beneath roses, showed nothing but his blue head which looked like a piece of lapis-lazuli.

The singers, the canopy-bearers and the children lined up against the sides of the yard. Slowly the priest ascended the steps and placed his shining sun on the lace cloth. Everybody knelt. There was deep silence; and the censers slipping on their chains were swung high in the air. A blue vapour rose in Félicité's room. She opened her nostrils and inhaled it with a mystic sensuousness; then she closed her lids. Her lips smiled. The beats of her heart grew fainter and fainter, and vaguer, like a fountain giving out, like an echo dying away;—and when she exhaled her last breath, she thought she saw in the half-opened heavens a gigantic parrot hovering above her head.

# LEO TOLSTOY
## 1828-1910

Leo Tolstoy, the man who became the greatest of realistic novelists, was born a nobleman on his parents' considerable estate, Yasnaya Polyana, in the province of Tula, Russia. His early career was unpromising, as he devoted his years at the University of Kazan to drinking and gambling. In his twenties he joined the Russian army, where his experience of battle and suffering during the Crimean War led to his first serious writing, the *Sevastopol Sketches*. After his army service and travel in Western Europe, he settled down to regular writing, producing his two great novels, *War and Peace* in 1869 and *Anna Karenina* in 1876. Always, he loved to provide a fresh perspective on life by presenting things through the innocent eyes of a young person, a child, or even an animal. In his later years, an interest in religion came to dominate his thought and his writing, to the point that he would sometimes leave home seeking a purer life. On his last such trip he died in a railroad station.

## Strider: The Story of a Horse

### I

Higher and higher receded the sky, wider and wider spread the streak of dawn, whiter grew the pallid silver of the dew, more lifeless the sickle of the moon, and more vocal the forest. People began to get up, and in the owner's stable-yard the sounds of snorting, the rustling of litter, and even the shrill angry neighing of horses crowded together and at variance about something, grew more and more frequent.

"Hold on! Plenty of time! Hungry?" said the old huntsman, quickly opening the creaking gate. "Where are you going?" he shouted, threateningly raising his arm at a mare that was pushing through the gate.

The keeper, Nester, wore a short Cossack coat with an ornamental leather girdle, had a whip slung over his shoulder, and a hunk of bread wrapped in a cloth stuck in his girdle. He carried a saddle and bridle in his arms.

The horses were not at all frightened or offended at the horse-man's sarcastic tone: they pretended that it was all the same to them and moved leisurely away from the gate; only one old brown mare, with a thick mane, laid back an ear and quickly turned her back on him. A small filly standing behind her and not at all concerned in the matter took this opportunity to whinny and kick out at a horse that happened to be near.

"Now then!" shouted the keeper still louder and more sternly, and he went to the opposite corner of the yard.

Of all the horses in the enclosure (there were about a hundred of them) a piebald gelding, standing by himself in a corner under the penthouse and licking an oak post with half-closed eyes, displayed least impatience.

It is impossible to say what flavour the piebald gelding found in the post, but his expression was serious and thoughtful while he licked.

"Stop that!" shouted the groom, drawing nearer to him and put-ting the saddle and a glossy saddle-cloth on the manure heap beside him.

The piebald gelding stopped licking and without moving gave Nester a long look. The gelding did not laugh, nor grow angry, nor frown, but his whole belly heaved with a profound sigh and he turned away. The horseman put his arm round the gelding's neck and placed the bridle on him.

"What are you sighing for?" said Nester.

The gelding switched his tail as if to say, "Nothing in particular, Nester!" Nester put the saddle-cloth and saddle on him, and this caused the gelding to lay back his ears, probably to express dissatis-faction, but he was only called a "good-for-nothing" for it and his saddle-girths were tightened.

At this the gelding blew himself out, but a finger was thrust into his mouth and a knee hit him in the stomach, so that he had to let out his breath. In spite of this, when the saddle-cloth was being buckled on he again laid back his ears and even looked round. Though he knew it would do no good he considered it necessary to show that it was disagreeable to him and that he would always express his dissatisfaction with it. When he was saddled he thrust forward his swollen off foot and began champing his bit, this too for some reason of his own, for he ought to have known by that time that a bit cannot have any flavour at all.

Nester mounted the gelding by the short stirrup, unwound his long whip, straightened his coat out from under his knee, seated himself in the manner peculiar to coachmen, huntsmen, and horse-men, and jerked the reins. The gelding lifted his head to show his readiness to go where ordered but did not move. He knew that before starting there would be much shouting and that Nester, from the seat on his back, would give many orders to Váska, the other groom, and to the horses. And Nester did shout: "Váska! Hullo, Váska. Have you let out the brood mares? Where are you going, you devil? Now then! Are you asleep? . . . Open the gate! Let the brood mares get out first!" and so on.

The gate creaked. Váska, cross and sleepy, stood at the gate-post holding his horse by the bridle and letting the other horses pass out. The horses followed one another and stepped carefully over the straw, smelling at it: fillies, yearling colts with their manes and tails cut, suckling foals, and mares in foal carrying their burden heedfully passed one by one through the gateway. The fillies sometimes crowded together in twos and threes, throwing their heads across one another's backs and hitting their hoofs against the gate, for which they received a rebuke from the grooms every time. The foals sometimes darted under the legs of the wrong mares and neighed loudly in response to the short whinny of their own mothers.

A playful filly, directly she had got out at the gate, bent her head sideways, kicked up her hind legs, and squealed, but all the same she did not dare to run ahead of old dappled Zhuldýba who at a slow and heavy pace, swinging her belly from side to side, marched as usual ahead of all the other horses.

In a few minutes the enclosure that had been so animated became deserted, the posts stood gloomily under the empty penthouse, and only trampled straw mixed with manure was to be seen. Used as he was to that desolate sight it probably depressed the piebald gelding. As if making a bow he slowly lowered his head and raised it again, sighed as deeply as the tightly drawn girth would allow, and hobbling along on his stiff and crooked legs shambled after the herd, bearing old Nester on his bony back.

"I know that as soon as we get out on the road he will begin to strike a light and smoke his wooden pipe with its brass mountings and little chain," thought the gelding. "I am glad of it because early in the morning when it is dewy I like that smell, it reminds me of much that was pleasant; but it's annoying that when his pipe is between his teeth the old man always begins to swagger and thinks himself somebody and sits sideways, always sideways—and that side hurts. However, it can't be helped! Suffering for the pleasure of others is nothing new to me. I have even begun to find a certain equine pleasure in it. Let him swagger, poor fellow! Of course he can only do that when he is alone and no one sees him—let him sit sideways!" thought the gelding, and stepping carefully on his crooked legs he went along the middle of the road.

II

Having driven the horses to the riverside where they were to graze, Nester dismounted and unsaddled. Meanwhile the herd had begun gradually to spread over the untrampled meadow, covered with dew and by the mist that rose from it and the encircling river.

When he had taken the bridle off the piebald gelding, Nester scratched him under the neck, in response to which the gelding expressed his gratitude and satisfaction by closing his eyes. "He likes it, the old dog!" muttered Nester. The gelding however did not really care for the scratching at all and pretended that it was agreeable merely out of courtesy. He nodded his head in assent to Nester's words, but suddenly Nester, quite unexpectedly and without any reason, perhaps imagining that too much familiarity might give the gelding a wrong idea of his importance, pushed the gelding's head away from himself without any warning and, swinging the bridle, struck him painfully with the buckle on his lean leg, and then without saying a word went up the hillock to a tree-stump beside which he generally seated himself.

Though this action grieved the piebald gelding he gave no indication of it, but leisurely switching his scanty tail sniffed at something and, biting off some wisps of grass merely to divert his mind, walked to the river. He took no notice whatever of the antics of the young mares, colts, and foals around him, who were filled with the joy of the morning; and knowing that, especially at his age, it is healthier to have a good drink on an empty stomach and to eat afterwards, he chose a spot where the bank was widest and least steep, and wetting his hoofs and fetlocks, dipped his muzzle in the water and began to suck it up through his torn lips, to expand his filling sides, and from pleasure to switch his scanty tail with its half bald stump.

An aggressive chestnut filly, who always teased the old fellow and did all kinds of unpleasant things to him, now came up to him in the water as if attending to some business of her own but in reality merely to foul the water before his nose. But the piebald gelding, who had already had his fill, as though not noticing the filly's intention quietly drew one foot after the other out of the mud in which they had sunk, jerked his head, and stepping aside from the youthful crowd started grazing. Sprawling his feet apart in different ways and not trampling the grass needlessly, he went on eating without unbending himself for exactly three hours. Having eaten till his belly hung down from his steep skinny ribs like a sack, he balanced himself equally on his four sore legs so as to have as little pain as possible, especially in his off foreleg which was the weakest, and fell asleep.

Old age is sometimes majestic, sometimes ugly, and sometimes pathetic. But old age can be both ugly and majestic, and the gelding's old age was just of that kind.

He was tall, rather over fifteen hands high. His spots were black, or rather they had been black, but had now turned a dirty brown. He had three spots, one on his head, starting from a crooked bald patch on the side of his nose and reaching half-way down his neck. His long mane, filled with burrs, was white in some places and brownish in others. Another spot extended down his off side to the middle of his belly; the third, on his croup, touched part of his tail and went half-way down his quarters. The rest of the tail was whitish and speckled. The big bony head, with deep hollows over the eyes and a black hanging lip that had been torn at some time, hung low and heavily on his neck, which was so lean that it looked as though it were carved of wood. The pendant lip revealed a blackish, bitten tongue and the yellow stumps of the worn lower teeth. The ears, one of which was slit, hung low on either side, and only occasionally moved lazily to drive away the pestering flies. Of the forelock, one tuft which was still long hung back behind an ear; the uncovered forehead was dented and rough, and the skin hung down like bags on his broad jaw-bones. The veins of his neck had grown knotty and twitched and shuddered at every touch of a fly. The expression of his face was one of stern patience, thoughtfulness, and suffering.

His forelegs were crooked to a bow at the knees, there were swellings over both hoofs, and on one leg, on which the piebald spot reached half-way down, there was a swelling at the knee as big as a fist. The hind legs were in better condition, but apparently long ago his haunches had been so rubbed that in places the hair would not grow again. The leanness of his body made all four legs look disproportionately long. The ribs, though straight, were so exposed and the skin so tightly drawn over them, that it seemed to have dried fast to the spaces between. His back and withers were covered with marks of old lashings, and there was a fresh sore behind, still swollen and festering; the black dock of his tail, which showed the vertebrae, hung down long and almost bare. On his dark-brown croup—near the tail—was a scar, as though of a bite, the size of a man's hand and covered with white hair. Another scarred sore was visible on one of his shoulders. His tail and hocks were dirty because of chronic bowel troubles. The hair on the whole body, though short, stood out straight. Yet in spite of the hideous old age of this horse one involuntarily paused to reflect when one saw him, and an expert would have said at once that he had been a remarkably fine horse in his day. The expert would even have said that there was only one breed in Russia that could furnish such breadth of bone, such immense knees, such hoofs, such slender cannons, such a well-shaped neck, and above all such a skull, such eyes—large, black, and clear—and such a thoroughbred network of veins on head and neck, and such delicate skin and hair.

There was really something majestic in that horse's figure and in the terrible union in him of repulsive indications of decrepitude, emphasized by the motley colour of his hair, and his manner which expressed the self-confidence and calm assurance that go with beauty and strength. Like a living ruin he stood alone in the midst of the dewy meadow, while not far from him could be heard the tramping, snorting and youthful neighing and whinnying of the scattered herd.

### III

The sun had risen above the forest and now shone brightly on the grass and the winding river. The dew was drying up and condensing into drops, the last of the morning mist was dispersing like tiny smoke-clouds. The cloudlets were becoming curly but there was as yet no wind. Beyond the river the verdant rye stood bristling, its ears curling into little horns, and there was an odour of fresh verdure and blossom. A cuckoo called rather hoarsely from the forest, and Nester, lying on his back in the grass, was counting the calls to ascertain how many years he still had to live. The larks were rising over the rye and the meadow. A belated hare, finding himself among the horses, leaped into the open, sat down by a bush, and pricked his ears to listen. Váska fell asleep with his head in the grass; the fillies, making a still wider circle about him, scattered over the field below. The old mares went about snorting and made a shiny track across the dewy grass, always choosing a place where no one would disturb them. They no longer grazed but only nibbled at choice tufts of grass. The whole herd was moving imperceptibly in one direction.

And again it was old Zhuldýba who, stepping sedately in front of the others, showed the possibility of going farther. Black Múshka, a young mare who had foaled for the first time, with uplifted tail kept whinnying and snorting at her bluish foal; the young filly Satin, sleek and brilliant, bending her head till her black silky forelock hid her forehead and eyes, played with the grass, nipping off a little and tossing it and stamping her leg with its shaggy fetlock all wet with dew. One of the older foals, probably imagining he was playing some kind of game, with his curly tail raised like a plume, ran for the twenty-sixth time round his mother, who quietly went on grazing, having grown accustomed to her son's ways, and only occasionally glanced askance at him with one of her large black eyes.

One of the very youngest foals, black, with a big head, a tuft sticking up in astonishment between his ears, and a little tail still twisted to one side as it had been in his mother's womb, stood motionless, his ears pricked and his dull eyes fixed, gazing at the frisking and prancing foal—whether admiring or condemning him it is hard to say. Some of the foals were sucking and butting with their noses, some—heaven knows why—despite their mothers' call were running at an awkward little trot in quite the opposite direction as if searching for something and then, for no apparent reason, stopping and neighing with desperate shrillness. Some lay on their sides in a row, some were learning to eat grass, some again were scratching themselves behind their ears with their hind legs. Two mares still in foal were walking apart from the rest and while slowly moving their legs continued to graze. The others evidently respected their condition, and none of the young ones ventured to come near to disturb them. If any saucy youngsters thought of approaching them, the mere movement of an ear or tail sufficed to show them all how improper such behaviour was.

The colts and yearling fillies, pretending to be grown up and sedate, rarely jumped or joined the merry company. They grazed in a dignified manner, curving their close-cropped swan-like necks, and flourished their little broom-like tails as if they also had long ones. Just like the grown-ups they lay down, rolled over, or rubbed one another. The merriest group was composed of the two- and three-year old fillies and mares not yet in foal. They almost always walked about together like a separate merry virgin crowd. Among them you could hear sounds of tramping, whinnying, neighing, and snorting. They drew close together, put their heads over one another's necks, sniffed at one another, jumped, and sometimes at a semi-trot, semi-amble, with tails lifted like an oriflamme, raced proudly and coquettishly past their companions. The most beautiful and spirited of them was the mischievous chestnut filly. What she devised the others did; wherever she went the whole crowd of beauties followed. That morning the naughty one was in a specially playful mood. She was seized with a joyous fit, just as human beings sometimes are. Already at the riverside she had played a trick on the old gelding, and after that she ran along through the water pretending to be frightened by something, gave a hoarse squeal, and raced full speed into the field so that Váska had to gallop after her and the others who followed her. Then after grazing a little she began rolling, then teasing the old mares by dashing in front of them, then she drove away a small foal from its dam and chased it as if meaning to bite it. Its mother was frightened and stopped grazing, while the little foal cried in a piteous tone, but the mischievous one did not touch him at all, she only wanted to frighten him and give a performance for the benefit of her companions, who watched her escapade approvingly. Then she set out to turn the head of a little roan horse with which a peasant was ploughing in a rye-field far beyond the river. She stopped, proudly lifted her head somewhat to one side, shook herself, and neighed in a sweet, tender, long-drawn voice. Mischief, feeling, and a certain sadness were expressed in that call. There was in it the desire for and the promise of love, and a pining for it.

"There in the thick reeds is a corn-crake running backwards and forwards and calling passionately to his mate; there is the cuckoo, and the quails are singing of love, and the flowers are sending their fragrant dust to each other by the wind. And I too am young and beautiful and strong," the mischievous one's voice said, "but it has not yet been allowed me to know the sweetness of that feeling, and not only to experience it, but no lover—not a single one—has ever seen me!"

And this neighing, sad and youthful and fraught with feeling, was borne over the lowland and the field to the roan horse far away. He pricked up his ears and stopped. The peasant kicked him with his bast shoe, but the little horse was so enchanted by the silvery sound of the distant neighing that he neighed too. The peasant grew angry, pulled at the reins, and kicked the little roan so painfully in the stomach with his bast shoes that he could not finish his neigh and walked on. But the little roan felt a sense of sweetness and sadness, and for a long time the sounds of unfinished and passionate neighing, and of the peasant's angry voice, were carried from the distant rye-field over to the herd.

If the sound of her voice alone so overpowered the little roan that he forgot his duty, what would have happened had he seen the naughty beauty as she stood pricking her ears, breathing in the air with dilated nostrils, ready to run, trembling with her whole beautiful body, and calling to him?

But the mischievous one did not brood long over her impressions. When the neighing of the roan died away she gave another scornful neigh, lowered her head, and began pawing the ground, and then she went to wake and to tease the piebald gelding. The piebald gelding was the constant martyr and butt of those happy youngsters. He suffered more from them than at the hands of men. He did no harm to either. People needed him, but why should these young horses torment him?

IV

He was old, they were young; he was lean, they were sleek; he was miserable, they were gay; and so he was quite alien to them, an outsider, an utterly different creature whom it was impossible for them to pity. Horses only have pity on themselves and very occasionally on those in whose skins they can easily imagine themselves to be. But was it the old gelding's fault that he was old, poor, and ugly?

One might think not, but in equine ethics it was, and only those were right who were strong, young, and happy—those who had life still before them, whose every muscle quivered with superfluous energy,' and whose tails stood erect. Maybe the piebald gelding himself understood this and in his quiet moments was ready to agree that it was his fault that he had already lived his life, and that he had to pay for that life, but after all he was a horse and often could not suppress a sense of resentment, sadness, and indignation when he looked at those youngsters who tormented him for what would befall them all at the end of their lives. Another cause of the horses' lack of pity was their aristocratic pride. Every one of them traced back its pedigree, through father or mother, to the famous Creamy, while the piebald was of unknown parentage. He was a chance comer, purchased three years before at a fair for eighty assignat rubles.

The chestnut filly, as if taking a stroll, passed close by the piebald gelding's nose and pushed him. He knew at once what it was, and without opening his eyes laid back his ears and showed his teeth. The filly wheeled round as if to kick him. The gelding opened his eyes and stepped aside. He did not want to sleep any more and began to graze. The mischief-maker, followed by her companions, again approached the gelding. A very stupid two-year-old white-spotted filly who always imitated the chestnut in everything went up with her and, as imitators always do, went to greater lengths than the instigator. The chestnut always went up as if intent on business of her own and passed by the gelding's nose without looking at him, so that he really did not know whether to be angry or not, and that was really funny.

She did the same now, but the white-spotted one, who followed her and had grown particularly lively, bumped right against the gelding with her chest. He again showed his teeth, whinnied, and with an agility one could not have expected of him, rushed after her and bit her flank. The white-spotted one kicked out with all her strength and dealt the old horse a heavy blow on his thin bare ribs. He snorted heavily and was going to rush at her again but bethought himself and drawing a deep sigh stepped aside. The whole crowd of young ones must have taken as a personal affront the impertinence the piebald gelding had permitted himself to offer to the white-spotted one and for the rest of the day did not let him graze in peace for a moment, so that the keeper had to quieten them several times and could not understand what had come over them.

The gelding felt so offended that he went up himself to Nester when the old man was getting ready to drive the horses home and felt happier and quieter when he was saddled and the old man had mounted him.

God knows what the gelding was thinking as he carried old Nester on his back: whether he thought bitterly of the pertinacious and merciless youngster or forgave his tormenters with the contemptuous and silent pride suited to old age. At all events he did not betray his thoughts till he reached home.

That evening, as Nester drove the horses past the huts of the domestic serfs, he noticed a peasant horse and cart tethered to his porch: some friends had come to see him. When driving the horses in he was in such a hurry that he let the gelding in without unsaddling him and, shouting to Váska to do it, shut the gate and went to his friends. Whether because of the affront to the white-spotted filly—Creamy's great-grand-daughter—by that "mangy trash" bought at the horse fair, who did not know his father or mother, and the consequent outrage to the aristocratic sentiment of the whole herd, or because the gelding with his high saddle and without a rider presented a strangely fantastic spectacle to the horses, at any rate something quite unusual occurred that night in the paddock. All the horses, young and old, ran after the gelding, showing their teeth and driving him all round the yard; one heard the sound of hoofs striking against his bare ribs, and his deep moaning. He could no longer endure this, nor could he avoid the blows. He stopped in the middle of the paddock, his face expressing first the repulsive weak malevolence of helpless old age, and then despair: he dropped his ears, and then something happened that caused all the horses to quiet down. The oldest of the mares, Vyazapúrikha, went up to the gelding, sniffed at him, and sighed. The gelding sighed too . . . .

v

In the middle of the moonlit paddock stood the tall gaunt figure of the gelding, still wearing the high saddle with its prominent peak at the bow. The horses stood motionless and in deep silence around him as if they were learning something new and unexpected. And they had learnt something new and unexpected.

This is what they learnt from him . . .

*First Night*

Yes, I am the son of Affable I and of Bába. My pedigree name is Muzhík, and I was nicknamed Strider by the crowd because of my long and sweeping strides, the like of which was nowhere to be found in all Russia. There is no more thoroughbred horse in the world. I should never have told you this. What good would it have done? You would never have recognized me: even Vyazapúrikha, who was with me in Khrénovo, did not recognize me till now. You would not have believed me if Vyazapúrikha were not here to be my witness, and I should never have told you this. I don't need equine sympathy. But you wished it. Yes, I am that Strider whom connoisseurs are looking for and cannot find—that Strider whom the count himself knew and got rid of from his stud because I outran Swan, his favourite.

When I was born I did not know what *piebald* meant—I thought I was just a horse. I remember the first remark we heard about my colour struck my mother and me deeply.

I suppose I was born in the night; by the morning, having been licked over by my mother, I already stood on my feet. I remember I kept wanting something and that everything seemed very surprising and yet very simple. Our stalls opened into a long warm passage and had latticed doors through which everything could be seen.

My mother offered me her teats but I was still so innocent that I poked my nose now between her forelegs and now under her udder. Suddenly she glanced at the latticed door and lifting her leg over me stepped aside. The groom on duty was looking into our stall through the lattice.

"Why, Bába has foaled!" he said, and began to draw the bolt. He came in over the fresh bedding and put his arms round me. "Just look, Tarás!" he shouted, "what a piebald he is—a regular magpie!"

I darted away from him and fell on my knees.

"Look at him—the little devil!"

My mother became disquieted but did not take my part; she only stepped a little to one side with a very deep sigh. Other grooms came to look at me, and one of them ran to tell the stud groom.

Everybody laughed when they looked at my spots, and they gave me all kinds of strange names, but neither I nor my mother understood those words. Till then there had been no piebalds among all my relatives. We did not think there was anything bad in it. Everybody even praised my strength and my form.

"See what a frisky fellow!" said the groom. "There's no holding him."

Before long the stud groom came and began to express astonishment at my colour; he even seemed aggrieved.

"And who does the little monster take after?" he said. "The general won't keep him in the stud. Oh, Bába, you have played me a trick!" he addressed my mother. "You might at least have dropped one with just a star—but this one is all piebald!"

My mother did not reply but as usual on such occasions drew a sigh.

"And what devil does he take after—he's just like a peasant-horse!" he continued. "He can't be left in the stud—he'd shame us. But he's well built—very well!" said he, and so did everyone who saw me.

A few days later the general himself came and looked at me, and again everyone seemed horrified at something, and abused me and my mother for the colour of my hair. "But he's a fine colt—very fine!" said all who saw me.

Until spring we all lived separately in the brood mares' stable, each with our mother, and only occasionally when the snow on the stable roofs began to melt in the sun were we let out with our mothers into the large paddock strewn with fresh straw. There I first came to know all my dear and my distant relations. Here I saw all the famous mares of the day coming out from different doors with their little foals. There was the old mare Dutch, Fly (Creamy's daughter), Ruddy the riding-horse, Wellwisher—all celebrities at that time. They all gathered together with their foals, walking about in the sunshine, rolling on the fresh straw and sniffing at one another like ordinary horses. I have never forgotten the sight of that paddock full of the beauties of that day. It seems strange to you to think, and hard to believe, that I was ever young and frisky, but it was so. This same Vyazapúrikha was then a yearling filly whose mane had just been cut; a dear, merry, lively little thing, but—and I do not say it to offend her—although among you she is now considered a remarkable thoroughbred she was then among the poorest horses in the stud. She will herself confirm this.

My mottled appearance, which men so disliked, was very attractive to all the horses; they all came round me, admired me, and frisked about with me. I began to forget what men said about my mottled appearance and felt happy. But I soon experienced the first sorrow of my life and the cause of it was my mother. When the thaw had set in, the sparrows twittered under the eaves, spring was felt more strongly in the air, and my mother's treatment of me changed.

Her whole disposition changed: she would frisk about without any reason and run around the yard, which did not at all accord with her dignified age; then she would consider and begin to neigh, and would bite and kick her sister mares, and then begin to sniff at me and snort discontentedly; then on going out into the sun she would lay her head across the shoulder of her cousin, Lady Merchant, dreamily rub her back, and push me away from her teats.

One day the stud groom came and had a halter put on her and she was led out of the stall. She neighed and I answered and rushed after her, but she did not even look back at me. The strapper, Tarás, seized me in his arms while they were closing the door after my mother had been led out.

I bolted and upset the strapper on the straw, but the door was shut and I could only hear the receding sound of my mother's neighing; and that neigh did not sound like a call to me but had another expression. Her voice was answered from afar by a powerful voice—that of Dóbry I, as I learned later, who was being led by two grooms, one on each side, to meet my mother.

I don't remember how Tarás got out of my stall: I felt too sad, for I knew that I had lost my mother's love forever. "And it's all because I am piebald!" I thought, remembering what people said about my colour, and such passionate anger overcame me that I began to beat my head and knees against the walls of the stall and continued till I was sweating all over and quite exhausted.

After a while my mother came back to me. I heard her run up the passage at a trot and with an unusual gait. They opened the door for her and I hardly knew her—she had grown so much younger and more beautiful. She sniffed at me, snorted, and began to whinny. Her whole demeanour showed that she no longer loved me.

She told me of Dóbry's beauty and her love of him. Those meetings continued and the relations between my mother and me grew colder and colder.

Soon after that we were let out to pasture. I now discovered new joys which made up to me for the loss of my mother's love. I had friends and companions. Together we learnt to eat grass, to neigh like the grown-ups, and to gallop round our mothers with lifted tails. That was a happy time. Everything was forgiven me, everybody loved me, admired me, and looked indulgently at anything I did. But that did not last long.

Soon afterwards something dreadful happened to me . . . .

The gelding heaved a deep sigh and walked away from the other horses.

The dawn had broken long before. The gates creaked. Nester came in, the horses separated. The keeper straightened the saddle on the gelding's back and drove the horses out.

**VI**

*Second Night*
As soon as the horses had been driven in they again gathered round
the piebald, who continued:

In August they separated me from my mother and I did not feel
particularly grieved. I saw that she was again heavy (with my
brother, the famous Usán) and that I could no longer be to her what
I had been. I was not jealous but felt that I had become indifferent to
her. Besides, I knew that having left my mother I should be put in
the general division of foals, where were kept two or three together
and were every day let out in a crowd into the open. I was in the
same stall with Darling. Darling was a saddle-horse, who was sub-
sequently ridden by the Emperor and portrayed in pictures and
sculpture. At that time he was a mere foal, with a soft glossy coat, a
swanlike neck, and straight slender legs taut as the strings of an
instrument. He was always lively, good-tempered, and amiable, always ready to gambol, exchange licks, and play tricks on horse or
man. Living together as we did we involuntarily made friends, and
our friendship lasted the whole of our youth. He was merry and
giddy. Even then he began to make love, courted the fillies, and
laughed at my guilelessness. To my misfortune vanity led me to
imitate him, and I was soon carried away and fell in love. And this
early tendency of mine was the cause of the greatest change in my
fate. It happened that I was carried away . . . Vyazapúrikha was a
year older than I, and we were special friends, but towards the
autumn I noticed that she began to be shy to me . . . .

But I will not speak of that unfortunate period of my first love; she
herself remembers my mad passion, which ended for me in the
most important change of my life.

The strappers rushed to drive her away and to beat me. That
evening I was shut up in a special stall where I neighed all night as
if foreseeing what was to happen next.

In the morning the General, the stud groom, the stablemen and
the strappers came into the passage where my stall was, and there
was a terrible hubbub. The General shouted at the stud groom, who
tried to justify himself by saying that he had not told them to let me
out but the grooms had done it of their own accord. The General
said that he would have everybody flogged, and that it would not
do to keep young stallions. The stud groom promised that he would
have everything attended to. They grew quiet and went away. I did
not understand anything, but could see that they were planning
something concerning me.

The day after that I ceased neighing for ever. I became what I am now. The whole world was changed in my eyes. Nothing mattered any more; I became self-absorbed and began to brood. At first everything seemed repulsive to me. I even ceased to eat, drink, or walk, and there was no idea of playing. Now and then it occurred to me to give a kick, to gallop, or to start neighing, but immediately came the question: Why? What for? and all my energy died away.

One evening I was being exercised just when the horses were driven back from pasture. I saw in the distance a cloud of dust enveloping the indistinct but familiar outlines of all our brood mares. I heard their cheerful snorting and the trampling of their feet. I stopped, though the cord of the halter by which the groom was leading me cut the nape of my neck, and I gazed at the approaching drove as one gazes at happiness that is lost for ever and cannot return. They approached, and I could distinguish one after another all the familiar, beautiful, stately, healthy, sleek figures. Some of them also turned to look at me. I was unconscious of the pain the groom's jerking at my halter inflicted. I forgot myself and from old habit involuntarily neighed and began to trot, but my neighing sounded sad, ridiculous, and meaningless. No one in the drove made sport of me, but I noticed that out of decorum many of them turned away from me. They evidently felt it repugnant, pitiable, indelicate, and above all ridiculous, to look at my thin expressionless neck, my large head (I had grown lean in the meantime), my long, awkward legs, and the silly awkward gait with which by force of habit I trotted round the groom. No one answered my neighing—they all looked away. Suddenly I understood it all, understood how far I was for ever removed from them, and I do not remember how I got home with the groom.

Already before that I had shown a tendency towards gravity and thoughtfulness, but now a decided change came over me. My being piebald, which aroused such curious contempt in men, my terrible and unexpected misfortune, and also my peculiar position in the stud farm which I felt but was unable to explain made me retire into myself. I pondered over the injustice of men, who blamed me for being piebald; I pondered on the inconstancy of mother-love and feminine love in general and on its dependence on physical conditions; and above all I pondered on the characteristics of that strange race of animals with whom we are so closely connected, and whom we call men—those characteristics which were the source of my own peculiar position in the stud farm, which I felt but could not understand.

The meaning of this peculiarity in people and the characteristic on which it is based was shown me by the following occurrence.

It was in winter at holiday time. I had not been fed or watered all day. As I learnt later this happened because the lad who fed us was drunk. That day the stud groom came in, saw that I had no food, began to use bad language about the missing lad, and then went away.

Next day the lad came into our stable with another groom to give us hay. I noticed that he was particularly pale and sad and that in the expression of his long back especially there was something significant which evoked compassion.

He threw the hay angrily over the grating. I made a move to put my head over his shoulder, but he struck me such a painful blow on the nose with his fist that I started back. Then he kicked me in the belly with his boot.

"If it hadn't been for this scurvy beast," he said, "nothing would have happened!"

"How's that?" inquired the other groom.

"You see, he doesn't go to look after the count's horses but visits his own twice a day."

"What, have they given him the piebald?" asked the other.

"Given it, or sold it—the devil only knows! The count's horses might all starve—he wouldn't care—but just dare to leave *his* colt without food! 'Lie down!' he says, and they begin walloping me! No Christianity in it. He has more pity on a beast than on a man. He must be an infidel—he counted the strokes himself, the barbarian! The general never flogged like that! My whole back is covered with wales. There's no Christian soul in him!"

What they said about flogging and Christianity I understood well enough, but I was quite in the dark as to what they meant by the words *"his* colt," from which I perceived that people considered that there was some connexion between me and the head groom. What the connexion was I could not at all understand then. Only much later when they separated me from the other horses did I learn what it meant. At that time I could not at all understand what they meant by speaking of *me* as being a man's property. The words *"my* horse" applied to me, a live horse, seemed to me as strange as to say "my land," "my air," or "my water."

But those words had an enormous effect on me. I thought of them constantly and only after long and varied relations with men did I at last understand the meaning they attach to these strange words, which indicate that men are guided in life not by deeds but by words. They like not so much to do or abstain from doing anything, as to be able to apply conventional words to different objects. Such words, considered very important among them, are *my* and *mine,* which they apply to various things, creatures, or objects: even to land, people, and horses. They have agreed that of any given thing only one person may use the word *mine*, and he who in this game of theirs may use that conventional word about the greatest number of things is considered the happiest. Why this is so I do not know, but it is so. For a long time I tried to explain it by some direct advantage they derive from it, but this proved wrong.

For instance, many of those who called me *their* horse did not ride me, quite other people rode me; nor did they feed me—quite other people did that. Again it was not those who called me *their* horse who treated me kindly, but coachmen, veterinaries, and in general quite other people. Later on, having widened my field of observation, I became convinced that not only as applied to us horses, but in regard to other things, the idea of *mine* has no other basis than a low, mercenary instinct in men, which they call the feeling or right of property. A man who never lives in it says "my house" but only concerns himself with its building and maintenance; and a trades-man talks of "my cloth business" but has none of his clothes made of the best cloth that is in his shop.

There are people who call land theirs, though they have never seen that land and never walked on it. There are people who call other people theirs but have never seen those others, and the whole relationship of the owners to the owned is that they do them harm. There are men who call women their wives; yet these women live with other men. And men strive in life not to do what they think right but to call as many things as possible *their own*.

I am convinced that in this lies the essential difference between men and us. Therefore, not to speak of other things in which we are superior to men, on this ground alone we may boldly say that in the scale of living creatures we stand higher than man. The activity of men, at any rate of those I have had to do with, is guided by words, while ours is guided by deeds.

It was this right to speak of me as *my horse* that the stud groom had obtained, and that was why he had the stable lad flogged. This discovery much astonished me and, together with the thoughts and opinions aroused in men by my piebald colour, and the thoughtful-ness produced in me by my mother's betrayal, caused me to become the serious and thoughtful gelding that I am.

I was thrice unfortunate: I was piebald, I was a gelding, and people considered that I did not belong to God and to myself, as is natural to all living creatures, but that I belonged to the stud groom.

Their thinking this about me had many consequences. The first was that I was kept apart from the other horses, was better fed, oftener taken out on the line, and was broken in at an earlier age. I was first harnessed in my third year. I remember how the stud groom, who imagined I was his, himself began to harness me with a crowd of other grooms, expecting me to prove unruly or to resist. They put ropes round me to lead me into the shafts, put a cross of broad straps on my back and fastened it to the shafts so that I could not kick, while I was only awaiting an opportunity to show my readiness and love of work.

They were surprised that I started like an old horse. They began to break me and I began to practise trotting. Every day I made greater and greater progress, so that after three months the general himself and many others approved of my pace. But strange to say, just because they considered me not as their own, but as belonging to the head groom, they regarded my paces quite differently.

The stallions who were my brothers were raced, their records were kept, people went to look at them, drove them in gilt sulkies, and expensive horse-cloths were thrown over them. I was driven in a common sulky to Chesménka and other farms on the head groom's business. All this was the result of my being piebald, and especially of my being in their opinion, not the count's, but the head groom's property.

To-morrow, if we are alive, I will tell you the chief consequence for me of this right of property the head groom considered himself to have.

All that day the horses treated Strider respectfully, but Nester's treatment of him was as rough as ever. The peasant's little roan horse neighed again on coming up to the herd, and the chestnut filly again coquettishly replied to him.

### VII

*Third Night*
The new moon had risen and its narrow crescent lit up Strider's figure as he once again stood in the middle of the stable yard. The other horses crowded round him:

The gelding continued:

For me the most surprising consequence of my not being the count's, nor God's, but the head groom's, was that the very thing that constitutes our chief merit—a fast pace—was the cause of my banishment. They were driving Swan round the track, and the head groom, returning from Chesménka, drove me up and stopped there. Swan went past. He went well, but all the same he was showing off and had not the exactitude I had developed in myself—so that directly one foot touched the ground another instantaneously lifted and not the slightest effort was lost but every atom of exertion carried me forward. Swan went by us. I pulled towards the ring and the head groom did not check me. 'Here, shall I try my piebald?" he shouted, and when next Swan came abreast of us he let me go. Swan was already going fast, and so I was left behind during the first round, but in the second I began to gain on him, drew near to his sulky, drew level—and passed him. They tried us again—it was the same thing. I was the faster. And this dismayed everybody. The general asked that I should be sold at once to some distant place, so that nothing more should be heard of me: "Or else the count will get to know of it and there will be trouble!" So they sold me to a horse-dealer as a shaft-horse. I did not remain with him long. An hussar who came to buy remounts bought me. All this was so unfair, so cruel, that I was glad when they took me away from Khrénovo and parted me for ever from all that had been familiar and dear to me. It was too painful for me among them. They had love, honour, freedom, before them! I had labour, humiliation; humiliation, labour, to the end of my life. And why? Because I was piebald, and because of that had to become somebody's horse . . . .

Strider could not continue that evening. An event occurred in the enclosure that upset all the horses. Kupchíkha, a mare big with foal, who had stood listening to the story, suddenly turned away and walked slowly into the shed, and there began to groan so that it drew the attention of all the horses. Then she lay down, then got up again, and again lay down. The old mares understood what was happening to her, but the young ones became excited and, leaving the gelding, surrounded the invalid. Towards morning there was a new foal standing unsteadily on its little legs. Nester shouted to the groom, and the mare and foal were taken into a stall and the other horses driven to the pasture without them.

VIII

*Fourth Night*
In the evening when the gate was closed and all had quieted down, the piebald continued:

I have had the opportunity to make many observations both of men and horses during the time I passed from hand to hand.
    I stayed longest of all with two masters: a prince (an officer of hussars), and later with an old lady who lived near the church of St. Nicholas the Wonder Worker.
    The happiest years of my life I spent with the officer of hussars.

Though he was the cause of my ruin, and though he never loved anything or anyone, I loved and still love him for that very reason.

What I liked about him was that he was handsome, happy, rich, and therefore never loved anybody.

You understand that lofty equine feeling of ours. His coldness and my dependence on him gave special strength to my love for him. "Kill me, drive me till my wind is broken!" I used to think in our good days, "and I shall be all the happier."

He bought me from an agent to whom the head groom had sold me for eight hundred rubles, and he did so just because no one else had piebald horses. That was my best time. He had a mistress. I knew this because I took him to her every day and sometimes took them both out.

His mistress was a handsome woman, and he was handsome, and his coachman was handsome, and I loved them all because they were. Life was worth living then. This was how our time was spent: in the morning the groom came to rub me down—not the coachman but the groom. The groom was a lad from among the peasants. He would open the door, let out the steam from the horses, throw out the droppings, take off our rugs, and begin to fidget over our bodies with a brush, and lay whitish streaks of dandruff from a curry-comb on the boards of the floor that was dented by our rough horseshoes. I would playfully nip his sleeve and paw the ground. Then we were led out one after another to the trough filled with cold water, and the lad would admire the smoothness of my spotted coat which he had polished, my foot with its broad hoof, my legs straight as an arrow, my glossy quarters, and my back wide enough to sleep on. Hay was piled onto the high racks, and the oak cribs were filled with oats. Then Feofán, the head coachman, would come in.

Master and coachman resembled one another. Neither of them was afraid of anything or cared for anyone but himself, and for that reason everybody liked them. Feofán wore a red shirt, black velveteen knickerbockers, and a sleeveless coat. I liked it on a holiday when he would come into the stable, his hair pomaded, and wearing his sleeveless coat, and would shout, "Now then, beastie, have you forgotten?" and push me with the handle of the stable fork, never so as to hurt me but just as a joke. I immediately knew that it was a joke and laid back an ear, making my teeth click.

We had a black stallion, who drove in a pair. At night they used to put me in harness with him. That Polkán, as he was called, did not understand a joke but was simply vicious as the devil. I was in the stall next to his and sometimes we bit one another seriously. Feofán was not afraid of him. He would come up and give a shout:

it looked as if Polkán would kill him, but no, he'd miss, and Feofán would put the harness on him.

Once he and I bolted down Smiths Bridge Street. Neither my master nor the coachman was frightened; they laughed, shouted at the people, checked us, and turned so that no one was run over.

In their service I lost my best qualities and half my life. They ruined me by watering me wrongly, and they foundered me . . . . Still, for all that, it was the best time of my life. At twelve o'clock they would come to harness me, black my hoofs, moisten my fore-lock and mane, and put me in the shafts.

The sledge was of plaited cane upholstered with velvet; the reins were of silk, the harness had silver buckles, sometimes there was a cover of silken fly-net, and altogether it was such that when all the traces and straps were fastened it was difficult to say where the harness ended and the horse began. We were harnessed at ease in the stable. Feofán would come, broader at his hips than at the shoulders, his red belt up under his arms: he would examine the harness, take his seat, wrap his coat round him, put his foot into the sledge stirrup, let off some joke, and for appearance sake always hang a whip over his arm though he hardly ever hit me, and would say, "Let go!" and playfully stepping from foot to foot I would move out of the gate, and the cook who had come out to empty the slops would stop on the threshold and the peasant who had brought wood into the yard would open his eyes wide. We would come out, go a little way, and stop. Footmen would come out and other coach-men, and a chatter would begin. Everybody would wait: sometimes we had to stand for three hours at the entrance, moving a little way, turning back and standing again.

At last there would be a stir in the hall: old Tíkhon with his paunch would rush out in his dress coat and cry, "Drive up!" (In those days there was not that stupid way of saying, "Forward!" as if one did not know that we moved forward and not back.) Feofán would cluck, drive up, and the prince would hurry out carelessly, as though there were nothing remarkable about the sledge, or the horse, or Feofán—who bent his back and stretched out his arms so that it seemed it would be impossible for him to keep them long in that position. The prince would have a shako on his head and wear a fur coat with a grey beaver collar hiding his rosy, black-browed, handsome face, that should never have been concealed. He would come out clattering his sabre, his spurs, and the brass backs of the heels of his overshoes, stepping over the carpet as if in a hurry and taking no notice of me or Feofán whom everybody but he looked at and admired. Feofán would cluck, I would tug at the reins, and respectably, at a foot pace, we would draw up to the entrance and stop. I would turn my eyes on the prince and jerk my thoroughbred head with its delicate forelock . . . . The prince would be in good spirits and would sometimes jest with Feofán. Feofán would reply, half turning his handsome head, and without lowering his arms would make a scarcely perceptible movement with the reins which I understand: and then one, two, three . . . with ever wider and wider strides, every muscle quivering, and sending the muddy snow against the front of the sledge, I would go. In those days, too, there was none of the present-day stupid habit of crying, "Oh!" as if the coachman were in pain, instead of the sensible "Be off! Take care!" Feofán would shout, "Be off! Look out there !" and the people would step aside and stand craning their necks to see the handsome gelding, the handsome coachman, and the handsome gentle- man . . . . I was particularly fond of passing a trotter. When Feofán and I saw at a distance a turn-out worthy of the effort, we would fly like a whirlwind and gradually gain on it. Now, throwing the dirt right to the back of the sledge, I would draw level with the occupant of the vehicle and snort above his head: then I would reach the horse's harness and the arch of his troyka, and then would no longer see it but only hear its sounds in the distance behind. And the prince, Feofán, and I would all be silent, and pretend to be merely going on our own business and not even to notice those with slow horses whom we happened to meet on our way. I liked to pass another horse but also liked to meet a good trotter. An instant, a sound, a glance, and we had passed each other and were flying in opposite directions.

The gate creaked and the voices of Nester and Váska were heard.


*Fifth Night*
The weather began to break up. It had been dull since morning and there was no dew, but it was warm and the mosquitoes were troublesome. As soon as the horses were driven in they collected round the piebald, and he finished his story as follows:


The happy period of my life was soon over. I lived in that way only two years. Towards the end of the second winter the happiest event of my life occurred, and following came my greatest misfor- tune. It was during carnival week. I took the prince to the races. Glossy and Bull were running. I don't know what people were doing in the pavilion, but I know the prince came out and ordered Feofán to drive onto the track. I remember how they took me in and placed me beside Glossy. He was harnessed to a racing sulky and I, just as I was, to a town sledge. I outstripped him at the turn. Roars of laughter and howls of delight greeted me.

When I was led in, a crowd followed me and five or six people offered the prince thousands for me. He only laughed, showing his white teeth.

"No," he said, "this isn't a horse, but a friend, I wouldn't sell him for mountains of gold. *Au revoir*, gentlemen!"

He unfastened the sledge apron and got in.

"To Ostózhenka Street!"

That was where his mistress lived, and off we flew . . . .

That was our last happy day. We reached her home. He spoke of her as *his*, but she loved someone else and had run away with him. The prince learnt this at her lodgings. It was five o'clock, and without unharnessing me he started in pursuit of her. They did what had never been done to me before—struck me with the whip and made me gallop. For the first time I fell out of step and felt ashamed and wished to correct it, but suddenly I heard the prince shout in an unnatural voice: "Get on!" The whip whistled through the air and cut me, and I galloped, striking my foot against the iron front of the sledge. We overtook her after going sixteen miles. I got him there but trembled all night and could not eat anything. In the morning they gave me water. I drank it and after that was never again the horse that I had been. I was ill, and they tormented me and maimed me—doctoring me, as people call it. My hoofs came off, I had swellings and my legs grew bent; my chest sank in and I became altogether limp and weak. I was sold to a horse-dealer who fed me on carrots and something else and made something of me quite unlike myself, though good enough to deceive one who did not know. My strength and my pace were gone.

When purchasers came the dealer also tormented me by coming into my stall and beating me with a heavy whip to frighten and madden me. Then he would rub down the stripes on my coat and lead me out.

An old woman bought me of him. She always drove to the Church of St. Nicholas the Wonder Worker, and she used to have her coachman flogged. He used to weep in my stall and I learnt that tears have a pleasant, salty taste. Then the old woman died. Her steward took me to the country and sold me to a hawker. Then I overate myself with wheat and grew still worse. They sold me to a peasant. There I ploughed, had hardly anything to eat, my foot got cut by a ploughshare, and I again became ill. Then a gipsy took me in exchange for something. He tormented me terribly and finally sold me to the steward here. And here I am.

All were silent. A sprinkling of rain began to fall.

IX

*The Evening After*

As the herd returned home the following evening they encountered their master with a visitor. Zhuldýba when nearing the house looked askance at the two male figures: one was the young master in his straw hat, the other a tall, stout, bloated military man. The old mare gave the man a side-glance and, swerving, went near him; the others, the young ones, were flustered and hesitated, especially when the master and his visitor purposely stepped among them, pointing something out to one another and talking.

"That one, the dapple grey, I bought of Voékov," said the master.

"And where did you get that young black mare with the white legs? She's a fine one!" said the visitor. They looked over many of the horses, going forward and stopping them. They noticed the chestnut filly too.

"That is one I kept of Khrénov's saddle-horse breed," said the master.

They could not see all the horses as they walked past, and the master called to Nester, and the old man, tapping the sides of the piebald with his heels, trotted forward. The piebald limped on one leg but moved in a way that showed that as long as his strength lasted he would not murmur on any account, even if they wanted him to run in that way to the end of the world. He was even ready to gallop and tried to do so with his right leg.

"There, I can say for certain that there is no better horse in Russia than this one," said the master, pointing to one of the mares. The visitor admired it. The master walked about excitedly, ran forward, and showed his visitor all the horses, mentioning the origin and pedigree of each.

The visitor evidently found the master's talk dull but devised some questions to show interest.

"Yes, yes," he said absent-mindedly.

"Just look," said the master, not answering a question. "Look at her legs. . . . She cost me a lot but has a third foal already in harness."

"And trots well?" asked the guest.

So they went past all the horses till there were no more to show. Then they were silent.

"Well, shall we go now?"

"Yes, let's go."

They went through the gate. The visitor was glad the exhibition was over and that he could now go to the house where they could eat and drink and smoke, and he grew perceptibly brighter. As he went past Nester, who sat on the piebald waiting for orders, the visitor slapped the piebald's crupper with his big fat hand.

"What an ornamented one!" he said. "I once had a piebald like him; do you remember my telling you of him?"

The master, finding that it was not his horse that was being spoken about, paid no attention but kept looking round at his own herd.

Suddenly above his ear he heard a dull, weak, senile neigh. It was the piebald that had begun to neigh and had broken off as if ashamed.

Neither the visitor nor the master paid any attention to this neighing, but went into the house.

In the flabby old man Strider had recognized his beloved master, the once brilliant, handsome, and wealthy Serpukhovskóy.

X

It kept on drizzling. In the stable yard it was gloomy, but in the master's house it was very different. The table was laid in a luxurious drawing-room for a luxurious evening tea, and at it sat the host, the hostess, and their guest.

The hostess, her pregnancy made very noticeable by her figure, her strained convex pose, her plumpness, and especially by her large eyes with their mild inward look, sat by the samovar.

The host held in his hand a box of special, ten-year-old cigars, such as he said no one else had, and he was preparing to boast about them to his guest. The host was a handsome man of about twenty-five, fresh-looking, well cared for, and well groomed. In the house he was wearing a new loose thick suit made in London. Large expensive pendants hung from his watch-chain. His gold-mounted turquoise shirt studs were also large and massive. He had a beard à la Napoléon III, and the tips of his moustache stuck out in a way that could only have been learned in Paris.

The hostess wore a dress of silk gauze with a large floral pattern of many colours, and large gold hair-pins of a peculiar pattern held up her thick, light-brown hair—beautiful though not all her own. On her arms and hands she wore many bracelets and rings, all of them expensive.

The tea-service was of delicate china and the samovar of silver. A footman, resplendent in dress-coat, white waistcoat and necktie, stood like a statue by the door awaiting orders. The furniture was elegantly carved and upholstered in bright colours, the wall-paper dark with a large flowered pattern. Beside the table, tinkling the silver bells on its collar, was a particularly fine whippet, whose difficult English name its owners, who neither of them knew English, pronounced badly.

In the corner, surrounded by plants, stood an inlaid piano. Everything gave an impression of newness, luxury, and rarity. Everything was good, but it all bore an imprint of superfluity, wealth, and the absence of intellectual interests.

The host, a lover of trotting races, was sturdy and full-blooded— one of that never-dying race which drives about in sable coats, throws expensive bouquets to actresses, drinks the most expensive wines with the most fashionable labels at the most expensive restaurants, offers prizes engraved with the donor's name, and keeps the most expensive mistresses.

Nikíta Serpukhovskóy, their guest, was a man of over forty, tall, stout, bald-headed, with heavy moustaches and whiskers. He must once have been very handsome but had now evidently sunk physically, morally, and financially.

He had such debts that he had been obliged to enter the government service to avoid imprisonment for debt and was now on his way to a provincial town to become the head of a stud farm, a post some important relatives had obtained for him.

He wore a military coat and blue trousers of a kind only a rich man would have had made for himself. His shirt was of similar quality and so was his English watch. His boots had wonderful soles as thick as a man's finger.

Nikíta Serpukhovskóy had during his life run through a fortune of two million rubles, and was now a hundred and twenty thousand in debt. In cases of that kind there always remains a certain momentum of life enabling a man to obtain credit and continue living almost luxuriously for another ten years.

These ten years were however coming to an end, the momentum was exhausted, and life was growing hard for Nikíta. He was already beginning to drink—that is, to get fuddled with wine, a thing that used not to happen, though strictly speaking he had never begun or left off drinking. His decline was most noticeable in the restlessness of his glance (his eyes had grown shifty) and in the uncertainty of his voice and movements. This restlessness struck one the more as it had evidently got hold of him only recently, for one could see that he had all his life been accustomed not to be afraid of anything or anybody and had only recently, through heavy suffering, reached this state of fear so unnatural to him.

His host and hostess noticed this and exchanged glances which showed that they understood one another and were only postponing till bedtime a detailed discussion of the subject, putting up meanwhile with poor Nikíta and even showing him attentions.

The sight of his young host's good fortune humiliated Serpukhovskóy, awakening a painful envy in him as he recalled his own irrecoverable past.

"Do you mind my smoking a cigar, Marie?" he asked, addressing the lady in the peculiar tone acquired only by experience—the tone, polite and friendly but not quite respectful, in which men who know the world speak to kept women in contradistinction to wives. Not that he wished to offend her: on the contrary he now wished rather to curry favour with her and with her keeper, though he would on no account have acknowledged the fact to himself. But he was accustomed to speak in that way to such women. He knew she would herself be surprised and even offended were he to treat her as a lady. Besides he had to retain a certain shade of a respectful tone for his friend's real wife. He always treated his friend's mistresses with respect, not because he shared the so-called convictions promulgated in periodicals (he never read trash of that kind) about the respect due to the personality of every man, about the meaninglessness of marriage, and so forth, but because all decent men do so and he was a decent, though fallen, man.

He took a cigar. But his host awkwardly picked up a whole handful and offered them to him.

"Just see how good these are. Take them!"

Serpukhovskóy pushed aside the hand with the cigars, and a gleam of offence and shame showed itself in his eyes.

"Thank you!" He took out his cigar-case. "Try mine!"

The hostess was sensitive. She noticed his embarrassment and hastened to talk to him.

"I am very fond of cigars. I should smoke myself if everyone about me did not smoke."

And she smiled her pretty, kindly smile. He smiled in return, but irresolutely. Two of his teeth were missing.

"No, take this!" the tactless host continued. "The others are weaker. Fritz, *bringen Sie noch einen Kasten*," he said; *dort zwei.*"[1]

The German footman brought another box.

"Do you prefer big ones? Strong ones? These are very good. Take them all!" he continued, forcing them on his guest.

He was evidently glad to have someone to boast to of the rare things he possessed, and he noticed nothing amiss. Serpukhovskóy lit his cigar and hastened to resume the conversation they had begun.

1. "Bring another box. There are two there."

"So, how much did you pay for Atlásny?" he asked.

"He cost me a great deal, not less than five thousand, but at any rate I am already safe on him. What colts he gets, I tell you!"

"Do they trot?" asked Serpukhovskóy.

"They trot well! His colt took three prizes this year: in Túla, in Moscow, and in Petersburg; he raced Voékov's Raven. That rascal, the driver, let him make four false steps or he'd have left the other behind the flag."

"He's a bit green. Too much Dutch blood in him, that's what I say," remarked Serpukhovskóy.

"Well, but what about the mares? I'll show Goody to you tomorrow. I gave three thousand for her. For Amiable I gave two thousand."

And the host again began to enumerate his possessions. The hostess saw that this hurt Serpukhovskóy and that he was only pretending to listen.

"Will you have some more tea?" she asked.

"I won't," replied the host and went on talking. She rose, the host stopped her, embraced her, and kissed her.

As he looked at them Serpukhovskóy for their sakes tried to force a smile, but after the host had got up, embraced her, and led her to the portière, Serpukhovskóy's face suddenly changed. He sighed heavily, and a look of despair showed itself on his flabby face. Even malevolence appeared on it.

The host returned and smilingly sat down opposite him. They were silent awhile.

XI

"Yes, you were saying you bought him of Voékov," remarked Serpukhovskóy with assumed carelessness.

"Oh yes, that was of Atlásny, you know. I always meant to buy some mares of Dubovítzki, but he had nothing but rubbish left."

"He has failed . . ." said Serpukhovskóy, and suddenly stopped and glanced round. He remembered that he owed that bankrupt twenty thousand rubles, and if it came to talking of being bankrupt it was certainly said that he was one. He laughed.

Both again sat silent for a long time. The host considered what he could brag about to his guest. Serpukhovskóy was thinking what he could say to show that he did not consider himself bankrupt. But the minds of both worked with difficulty, in spite of efforts to brace themselves up with cigars. "When are we going to have a drink?" thought Serpukhovskóy. "I must certainly have a drink or I shall die of ennui with this fellow," thought the host.

"Will you be remaining here long?" Serpukhovskóy asked.

"Another month. Well, shall we have supper, eh? Fritz, is it ready?"

They went into the dining-room. There under a hanging lamp stood a table on which were candles and all sorts of extraordinary things: syphons, and little dolls fastened to corks, rare wine in decanters, unusual hors-d'oeuvres, and vodka. They had a drink, ate a little, drank again, ate again, and their conversation got into swing. Serpukhovskóy was flushed and began to speak without timidity.

They spoke of women and of who kept this one or that, a gipsy, a ballet-girl, or a Frenchwoman.

"And have you given up Mathieu?" asked the host. (That was the woman who had ruined Serpukhovskóy.)

"No, she left me. Ah, my dear fellow, when I recall what I have got through in my life! Now I am really glad when I have a thousnd rubles, and am glad to get away from everybody. I can't stand it in Moscow. But what's the good of talking!"

The host found it tiresome to listen to Serpukhovskóy. He wanted to speak about himself—to brag. But Serpukhovskóy also wished to talk about himself, about his brilliant past. His host filled his glass for him and waited for him to stop, so that he might tell him about himself and how his stud was now arranged as no one had ever had a stud arranged before. And that his Marie loved him with her heart and not merely for his wealth.

"I wanted to tell you that in my stud . . ." he began, but Serpukhovskóy interrupted him.

"I may say that there was a time," Serpukhovskóy began, "when I liked to live well and knew how to do it. Now you talk about trotting—tell me which is your fastest horse."

The host, glad of an opportunity to tell more about his stud, was beginning, when Serpukhovskóy again interrupted him.

"Yes, yes," he said, "but you breeders do it just out of vanity and not for pleasure, not for the joy of life. It was different with me. You know I told you I had a driving-horse, a piebald with just the same kind of spots as the one your keeper was riding. Oh, what a horse that was! You can't possibly know: it was in 1842, when I had just come to Moscow; I went to a horse-dealer and there I saw a well-bred piebald gelding. I liked him. The price? One thousand rubles. I liked him, so I took him and began to drive with him. I never had, and you have not and never will have, such a horse. I never knew one like him for speed and for strength. You were a boy then and couldn't have known, but you may have heard of him. All Moscow was talking about him."

"Yes, I heard of him," the host unwillingly replied. "But what I wished to say about mine . . ."

"Ah, then you did hear! I bought him just as he was, witho'

pedigree and without a certificate; it was only afterwards that I got to know Voékov and found out. He was a colt by Affable I. Strider—because of his long strides. On account of his piebald spots he was removed from the Khrénov stud and given to the head keeper, who had him castrated and sold him to a horse-dealer. There are no such horses now, my dear chap. Ah, those were days! Ah, vanished youth!"—and he sang the words of the gipsy song. He was getting tipsy. "Ah, those were good times. I was twenty-five and had eight thousand rubles a year, not a single grey hair, and all my teeth like pearls. . . . Whatever I touched succeeded, and now it is all ended . . ."

"But there was not the same mettlesomeness then," said the host, availing himself of the pause. "Let me tell you that my first horses began to trot without . . ."

"Your horses! But they used to be more mettlesome . . ."

"How—more mettlesome?"

"Yes, more mettlesome! I remember as if it were to-day how I drove him once to the trotting races in Moscow. No horse of mine was running. I did not care for trotters, mine were thoroughbreds: General Chaulet, Mahomet, I drove up with my piebald. My driver was a fine fellow, I was fond of him, but he also took to drink. . . . Well, so I got there.

" 'Serpukhovskóy,' I was asked, 'When are you going to keep trotters?' 'The devil take your lubbers!' I replied. 'I have a piebald hack that can outpace all your trotters!' 'Oh no, he won't!' 'I'll bet a thousand rubles!' Agreed, and they started. He came in five seconds ahead and I won the thousand rubles. But what of it? I did a hundred versts[2] in three hours with a troyka of thoroughbreds. All Moscow knows it."

And Serpukhovskóy began to brag so glibly and continuously that his host could not get a single word in and sat opposite him with a dejected countenance, filling up his own and his guest's glass every now and then by way of distraction.

The dawn was breaking and still they sat there. It became intolerably dull for the host. He got up.

"If we are to go to bed, let's go!" said Serpukhovskóy rising, and reeling and puffing he went to the room prepared for him.

The host was lying beside his mistress.

"No, he is unendurable," he said. "He gets drunk and swaggers incessantly."

"And makes up to me."

"I'm afraid he'll be asking for money."

2. Nearly seventy miles.

Serpukhovskóy was lying on the bed in his clothes, breathing heavily.

"I must have been lying a lot," he thought. "Well, no matter! The wine was good, but he is an awful swine. There's something cheap about him. And I'm an awful swine," he said to himself and laughed aloud. "First I used to keep women, and now I'm kept. Yes, the Winkler girl will support me. I take money of her. Serves him right. Still, I must undress. Can't get my boots off. Hullo! Hullo!" he called out, but the man who had been told off to wait on him had long since gone to bed.

He sat down, took off his coat and waistcoat and somehow managed to kick off his trousers, but for a long time could not get his boots off—his soft stomach being in the way. He got one off at last, and struggled for a long time with the other, panting and becoming exhausted. And so with his foot in the boot-top he rolled over and began to snore, filling the room with a smell of tobacco, wine, and disagreeable old age.

XII

If Strider recalled anything that night, he was distracted by Váska, who threw a rug over him, galloped off on him, and kept him standing till morning at the door of a tavern near a peasant horse. They licked one another. In the morning when Strider returned to the herd he kept rubbing himself.

Five days passed. They called in a veterinary, who said cheerfully: "It's the itch; let me sell him to the gipsies."

"What's the use? Cut his throat, and get it done to-day."

The morning was calm and clear. The herd went to pasture, but Strider was left behind. A strange man came—thin, dark, and dirty, in a coat splashed with something black. It was the knacker. Without looking at Strider he took him by the halter they had put on him and led him away. Strider went quietly without looking round, dragging along as usual and catching his hind feet in the straw.

When they were out of the gate he strained towards the well, but the knacker jerked his halter, saying: "Not worthwhile."

The knacker and Váska, who followed behind, went to a hollow behind the brick barn and stopped as if there were something peculiar about this very ordinary place. The knacker, handing the halter to Váska, took off his coat, rolled up his sleeves, and produced a knife and a whetstone from his boot-leg. The gelding stretched towards the halter meaning to chew it a little from dullness, but he could not reach it. He sighed and closed his eyes. His nether lip hung down, disclosing his worn yellow teeth, and he began to drowse to the sound of the sharpening of the knife. Only his swo

len, aching, outstretched leg kept jerking. Suddenly he felt himself
being taken by the lower jaw and his head lifted. He opened his
eyes. There were two dogs in front of him; one was sniffing at the
knacker, the other was sitting and watching the gelding as if expecting something from him. The gelding looked at them and began to
rub his jaw against the arm that was holding him.

"Want to doctor me probably—well, let them!" he thought.

And in fact he felt that something had been done to his throat. It
hurt, and he shuddered and gave a kick with one foot, but restrained himself and waited for what would follow. . . . Then he felt
something liquid streaming down his neck and chest. He heaved a
profound sigh and felt much better.

The whole burden of his life was eased.

He closed his eyes and began to droop his head. No one was
holding it. Then his legs quivered and his whole body swayed. He
was not so much frightened as surprised.

Everything was so new to him. He was surprised and started
forward and upward, but instead of this, in moving from the spot
his legs got entangled, he began to fall sideways, and trying to take
a step fell forward and down on his left side.

The knacker waited till the convulsions had ceased, drove away
the dogs that had crept nearer, took the gelding by the legs, turned
him on his back, told Váska to hold a leg, and began to skin the
horse.

"It was a horse, too," remarked Váska.

"If he had been better fed the skin would have been fine," said
the knacker.

The herd returned down hill in the evening, and those on the left
saw down below something red, round which dogs were busy and
above which hawks and crows were flying. One of the dogs, pressing its paws against the carcass and swinging his head, with a
crackling sound tore off what it had seized hold of. The chestnut
filly stopped, stretched out her head and neck, and sniffed the air
for a long time. They could hardly drive her away.

At dawn, in a ravine of the old forest, down in an overgrown
glade, big-headed wolf cubs were howling joyfully. There were five
of them: four almost alike and one with a head bigger than his
body. A lean old wolf who was shedding her coat, dragging her full
belly with its hanging dugs along the ground, came out of the
bushes and sat down in front of the cubs. The cubs came and stood
round her in a semi-circle. She went up to the smallest, and bending
er knee and holding her muzzle down, made some convulsive
vements, and opening her large sharp-toothed jaws disgorged a

large piece of horseflesh. The bigger cubs rushed towards her, but she moved threateningly at them and let the little one have it all. The little one, growling as if in anger, pulled the horseflesh under him and began to gorge. In the same way the mother wolf coughed up a piece for the second, the third, and all five of them, and then lay down in front of them to rest.

A week later only a large skull and two shoulder-blades lay behind the barn; the rest had all been taken away. In summer a peasant, collecting bones, carried away these shoulder-blades and skull and put them to use.

The dead body of Serpukhovskóy, which had walked about the earth eating and drinking, was put under ground much later. Neither his skin, nor his flesh, nor his bones, were of any use.

Just as for the last twenty years his body that had walked the earth had been a great burden to everybody, so the putting away of that body was again an additional trouble to people. He had not been wanted by anybody for a long time and had only been a burden, yet the dead who bury their dead found it necessary to clothe that swollen body, which at once began to decompose, in a good uniform and good boots and put it into a new and expensive coffin with new tassels at its four corners, and then to place that coffin in another coffin of lead, to take it to Moscow and there dig up some long buried human bones, and to hide in that particular spot this decomposing maggotty body in its new uniform and polished boots, and cover it all up with earth.

# MARK TWAIN

## 1835–1910

Born in Florida, Missouri, with the name of Samuel Clemens, Twain was raised in Hannibal, a few miles away. He left school at the age of twelve and learned much of what he knew as an apprentice pilot on a Mississippi River steamer and in the frontier towns and mining camps of the American West. His gift for storytelling and writing was apparent early, so that he soon was able to support himself by writing articles and delivering lectures, which he continued to do throughout his life, using a pen name taken from the language of the river steamers. His greatest achievement was *Huckleberry Finn* (1884), a comic masterpiece that made him world famous. In his later years he moved to Connecticut, built a mansion in Redding, and produced a series of sinister and cynical works, the lightest and most tightly constructed of which was "The Man that Corrupted Hadleyburg."

# The Man That Corrupted Hadleyburg

I

It was many years ago. Hadleyburg was the most honest and upright town in all the region round about. It had kept that reputation
unsmirched during three generations, and was prouder of it than of
any other of its possessions. It was so proud of it, and so anxious to
insure its perpetuation, that it began to teach the principles of honest dealing to its babies in the cradle, and made the like teachings
the staple of their culture thenceforward through all the years devoted to their education. Also, throughout the formative years
temptations were kept out of the way of the young people, so that
their honesty could have every chance to harden and solidify, and
become a part of their very bone. The neighboring towns were
jealous of this honorable supremacy, and affected to sneer at Hadleyburg's pride in it and call it vanity; but all the same they were
obliged to acknowledge that Hadleyburg was in reality an incorruptible town; and if pressed they would also acknowledge that the
mere fact that a young man hailed from Hadleyburg was all the
recommendation he needed when he went forth from his natal town
to seek for responsible employment.

But at last, in the drift of time, Hadleyburg had the ill luck to
offend a passing stranger—possibly without knowing it, certainly
without caring, for Hadleyburg was sufficient unto itself, and cared
not a rap for strangers or their opinions. Still, it would have been
well to make an exception in this one's case, for he was a bitter man
and revengeful. All through his wanderings during a whole year he
kept his injury in mind, and gave all his leisure moments to trying
to invent a compensating satisfaction for it. He contrived many
plans, and all of them were good, but none of them was quite
sweeping enough; the poorest of them would hurt a great many
individuals, but what he wanted was a plan which would comprehend the entire town, and not let so much as one person escape
unhurt. At last he had a fortunate idea, and when it fell into his
brain it lit up his whole head with an evil joy. He began to form a
plan at once, saying to himself, "That is the thing to do—I will
corrupt the town."

Six months later he went to Hadleyburg, and arrived in a buggy at
the house of the old cashier of the bank about ten at night. He got a
sack out of the buggy, shouldered it, and staggered with it through
the cottage yard, and knocked at the door. A woman's voice said
"Come in," and he entered, and set his sack behind the stove in the

parlor, saying politely to the old lady who sat reading the *Missionary Herald* by the lamp:

"Pray keep your seat, madam, I will not disturb you. There—now it is pretty well concealed; one would hardly know it was there. Can I see your husband a moment, madam?"

No, he was gone to Brixton, and might not return before morning.

"Very well, madam, it is no matter. I merely wanted to leave that sack in his care, to be delivered to the rightful owner when he shall be found. I am a stranger; he does not know me; I am merely passing through the town tonight to discharge a matter which has been long in my mind. My errand is now completed, and I go pleased and a little proud, and you will never see me again. There is a paper attached to the sack which will explain everything. Good night, madam."

The old lady was afraid of the mysterious big stranger, and was glad to see him go. But her curiosity was roused, and she went straight to the sack and brought away the paper. It began as follows:

> TO BE PUBLISHED: or, the right man sought out by private inquiry—either will answer. This sack contains gold coin weighing a hundred and sixty pounds four ounces—

"Mercy on us, and the door not locked!"

Mrs. Richards flew to it all in a tremble and locked it, then pulled down the window shades and stood frightened, worried, and wondering if there was anything else she could do toward making herself and the money more safe. She listened awhile for burglars, then surrendered to curiosity and went back to the lamp and finished reading the paper:

> I am a foreigner, and am presently going back to my own country, to remain there permanently. I am grateful to America for what I have received at her hands during my long stay under her flag; and to one of her citizens—a citizen of Hadleyburg—I am especially grateful for a great kindness done me a year or two ago. Two great kindnesses, in fact. I will explain. I was a gambler. I say I WAS. I was a ruined gambler. I arrived in this village at night, hungry and without a penny. I asked for help—in the dark; I was ashamed to beg in the light. I begged of the right man. He gave me twenty dollars—that is to say he gave me life, as I considered it. He also gave me fortune; for out of that money I have made myself rich at the gaming table. And finally, a remark which he made to me has remained with me to this day, and has at last conquered me; and in conquering has saved the remnant of my morals: I shall gamble no more. Now I have no idea who that man was, but I

want him found, and I want him to have this money, to give away, throw away, or keep, as he pleases. It is merely my way of testifying my gratitude to him. If I could stay, I would find him myself; but no matter, he will be found. This is an honest town, an incorruptible town, and I know I can trust it without fear. This man can be identified by the remark which he made to me; I feel persuaded that he will remember it.

And now my plan is this: If you prefer to conduct the inquiry privately, do so. Tell the contents of this present writing to anyone who is likely to be the right man. If he shall answer, "I am the man; the remark I made was so-and-so," apply the test—to wit: open the sack, and in it you will find a sealed envelope containing that remark. If the remark mentioned by the candidate tallies with it, give him the money, and ask no further questions, for he is certainly the right man.

But if you shall prefer a public inquiry, then publish this present writing in the local paper—with these instructions added, to wit: Thirty days from now, let the candidate appear at the town hall at eight in the evening (Friday), and hand his remark, in a sealed envelope, to the Rev. Mr. Burgess (if he will be kind enough to act); and let Mr. Burgess there and then destroy the seals of the sack, open it, and see if the remark is correct: if correct, let the money be delivered, with my sincere gratitude, to my benefactor thus identified.

Mrs. Richards sat down, gently quivering with excitement, and was soon lost in thinkings—after this pattern: "What a strange thing it is! . . . And what a fortune for that kind man who set his bread afloat upon the waters! . . . If it had only been my husband that did it!—for we are so poor, so old and poor! . . ." Then, with a sigh—"But it was not my Edward; no, it was not he that gave a stranger twenty dollars. It is a pity, too; I see it now . . ." Then, with a shudder—"But it is a *gambler's* money! the wages of sin: we couldn't take it; we couldn't touch it. I don't like to be near it; it seems a defilement." She moved to a farther chair. . . . "I wish Edward would come, and take it to the bank; a burglar might come at any moment; it is dreadful to be here all alone with it."

At eleven Mr. Richards arrived, and while his wife was saying, "I am *so* glad you've come!" he was saying, "I'm so tired—tired clear out; it is dreadful to be poor, and have to make these dismal journeys at my time of life. Always at the grind, grind, grind, on a salary—another man's slave, and he sitting at home in his slippers, rich and comfortable."

"I am so sorry for you, Edward, you know that; but be comforted: we have our livelihood; we have our good name—"

"Yes, Mary, and that is everything. Don't mind my talk—it's just a moment's irritation and doesn't mean anything. Kiss me—there, it's all gone now, and I am not complaining any more. What have you been getting? What's in the sack?"

Then his wife told him the great secret. It dazed him for a moment, then he said:

"It weighs a hundred and sixty pounds? Why, Mary, it's for-ty thou-sand dollars—think of it—a whole fortune! Not ten men in this village are worth that much. Give me the paper."

He skimmed through it and said:

"Isn't it an adventure! Why, it's a romance; it's like the impossible things one reads about in books, and never sees in life." He was well stirred up now; cheerful, even gleeful. He tapped his old wife on the cheek, and said, humorously, "Why, we're rich, Mary, rich; all we've got to do is to bury the money and burn the papers. If the gambler ever comes to inquire, we'll merely look coldly upon him and say: 'What is this nonsense you are talking? We have never heard of you and your sack of gold before'; and then he would look foolish, and—"

"And in the meantime, while you are running on with your jokes, the money is still here, and it is fast getting along toward burglar-time."

"True. Very well, what shall we do—make the inquiry private? No, not that: it would spoil the romance. The public method is better. Think what a noise it will make! And it will make all the other towns jealous; for no stranger would trust such a thing to any town but Hadleyburg, and they know it. It's a great card for us. I must get to the printing office now, or I shall be too late."

"But stop—stop—don't leave me here alone with it, Edward!"

But he was gone. For only a little while, however. Not far from his own house he met the editor-proprietor of the paper, and gave him the document, and said, "Here is a good thing for you, Cox—put it in."

"It may be too late, Mr. Richards, but I'll see."

At home again he and his wife sat down to talk the charming mystery over; they were in no condition for sleep. The first question was, Who could the citizen have been who gave the stranger the twenty dollars? It seemed a simple one; both answered it in the same breath.

"Barclay Goodson."

"Yes," said Richards, "he could have done it, and it would have been like him, but there's not another in the town."

"Everybody will grant that, Edward—grant it privately, anyway. For six months, now, the village has been its own proper self once more—honest, narrow, self-righteous, and stingy."

"It is what he always called it, to the day of his death—said it right out publicly, too."

"Yes, and he was hated for it."

"Oh, of course; but he didn't care. I reckon he was the best-hated man among us, except the Reverend Burgess."

"Well, Burgess deserves it—he will never get another congregation here. Mean as the town is, it knows how to estimate *him*. Edward, doesn't it seem odd that the stranger should appoint Burgess to deliver the money?"

"Well, yes—it does. That is—that is—"

"Why so much that-*is*-ing? Would *you* select him?"

"Mary, maybe the stranger knows him better than this village does."

"Much *that* would help Burgess!"

The husband seemed perplexed for an answer; the wife kept a steady eye upon him, and waited. Finally Richards said, with the hesitancy of one who is making a statement which is likely to encounter doubt:

"Mary, Burgess is not a bad man."

His wife was certainly surprised.

"Nonsense!" she exclaimed.

"He is not a bad man. I know. The whole of his unpopularity had its foundation in that one thing—the thing that made so much noise."

"That 'one thing,' indeed! As if that 'one thing' wasn't enough, all by itself."

"Plenty. Plenty. Only he wasn't guilty of it."

"How you talk! Not guilty of it! Everybody knows he *was* guilty."

"Mary, I give you my word—he was innocent."

"I can't believe it, and I don't. How do you know?"

"It is a confession. I am ashamed, but I will make it. I was the only man who knew he was innocent. I could have saved him, and—and—well, you know how the town was wrought up—I hadn't the pluck to do it. It would have turned everybody against me. I felt mean, ever so mean; but I didn't dare; I hadn't the manliness to face that."

Mary looked troubled, and for a while was silent. Then she said, stammeringly:

"I—I don't think it would have done for you to—to— One mustn't—er—public opinion—one has to be so careful—so—" It was a difficult road, and she got mired; but after a little she got started again. "It was a great pity, but— Why, we couldn't afford it, Edward—we couldn't indeed. Oh, I wouldn't have had you do it for anything!"

"It would have lost us the good will of so many people, Mary; and then—and then—"

"What troubles me now is, what *he* thinks of us, Edward."

"He? *He* doesn't suspect that I could have saved him."

"Oh," exclaimed the wife, in a tone of relief, "I am glad of that. As long as he doesn't know that you could have saved him, he— he—well, that makes it a great deal better. Why, I might have known he didn't know, because he is always trying to be friendly with us, as little encouragement as we give him. More than once people have twitted me with it. There's the Wilsons, and the Wilcoxes, and the Harknesses, they take a mean pleasure in saying, 'Your friend Burgess,' because they know it pesters me. I wish he wouldn't persist in liking us so; I can't think why he keeps it up."

"I can explain it. It's another confession. When the thing was new and hot, and the town made a plan to ride him on a rail, my conscience hurt me so that I couldn't stand it, and I went privately and gave him notice, and he got out of the town and stayed out till it was safe to come back."

"Edward! If the town had found out —"

"*Don't!* It scares me yet, to think of it. I repented of it the minute it was done; and I was even afraid to tell you, lest your face might betray it to somebody. I didn't sleep any that night, for worrying. But after a few days I saw that no one was going to suspect me, and after that I got to feeling glad I did it. And I feel glad yet, Mary— glad through and through."

"So do I, now, for it would have been a dreadful way to treat him. Yes, I'm glad; for really you did owe him that, you know. But, Edward, suppose it should come out yet, some day!"

"It won't."

"Why?"

"Because everybody thinks it was Goodson."

"Of course they would!"

"Certainly. And of course *he* didn't care. They persuaded poor old Sawlsberry to go and charge it on him, and he went blustering over there and did it. Goodson looked him over, like as if he was hunting for a place on him that he could despise the most, then he says, 'So you are the Committee of Inquiry, are you?' Sawlsberry said that was about what he was. 'Hm. Do they require particulars, or do you reckon kind of a *general* answer will do?' 'If they require particulars, I will come back. Mr. Goodson; I will take the general answer first.' 'Very well, then, tell them to go to hell—I reckon that's general enough. And I'll give you some advice, Sawlsberry; when you come back for the particulars, fetch a basket to carry the relics of yourself home in.' "

"Just like Goodson; it's got all the marks. He had only one vanity: he thought he could give advice better than any other person."

"It settled the business, and saved us, Mary. The subject was dropped."

"Bless you, I'm not doubting *that*."

Then they took up the gold-sack mystery again, with strong interest. Soon the conversation began to suffer breaks—interruptions caused by absorbed thinkings. The breaks grew more and more frequent. At last Richards lost himself wholly in thought. He sat long, gazing vacantly at the floor, and by and by he began to punctuate his thoughts with little nervous movements of his hands that seemed to indicate vexation. Meantime his wife too had relapsed into a thoughtful silence, and her movements were beginning to show a troubled discomfort. Finally Richards got up and strode aimlessly about the room, plowing his hands through his hair, much as a somnambulist might do who was having a bad dream. Then he seemed to arrive at a definite purpose; and without a word he put on his hat and passed quickly out of the house. His wife sat brooding, with a drawn face, and did not seem to be aware that she was alone. Now and then she murmured, "Lead us not into t— . . . but—but—we are so poor, so poor! . . . Lead us not into. . . . Ah, who would be hurt by it?—and no one would ever know . . . . Lead us . . ." The voice died out in mumblings. After a little she glanced up and muttered in a half-frightened, half-glad way:

"He is gone! But, oh dear, he may be too late—too late . . . . Maybe not—maybe there is still time." She rose and stood thinking, nervously clasping and unclasping her hands. A slight shudder shook her frame, and she said, out of a dry throat, "God forgive me—it's awful to think such things—but . . . Lord, how we are made—how strangely we are made!"

She turned the light low, and slipped stealthily over and kneeled down by the sack and felt of its ridgy sides with her hands, and fondled them lovingly; and there was a gloating light in her poor old eyes. She fell into fits of absence; and came half out of them at times to mutter, "If we had only waited!—oh, if we had only waited a little, and not been in such a hurry!"

Meantime Cox had gone home from his office and told his wife all about the strange thing that had happened, and they had talked it over eagerly, and guessed that the late Goodson was the only man in the town who could have helped a suffering stranger with so noble a sum as twenty dollars. Then there was a pause, and the two became thoughtful and silent. And by and by nervous and fidgety. At last the wife said, as if to herself:

"Nobody knows this secret but the Richardses . . . and us . . . nobody."

The husband came out of his thinkings with a slight start, and gazed wistfully at his wife, whose face was become very pale; then he hesitatingly rose, and glanced furtively at his hat, then at his wife—a sort of mute inquiry. Mrs. Cox swallowed once or twice, with her hand at her throat, then in place of speech she nodded her head. In a moment she was alone, and mumbling to herself.

And now Richards and Cox were hurrying through the deserted streets, from opposite directions. They met, panting, at the foot of the printing office stairs; by the night light there they read each other's face. Cox whispered:

"Nobody knows about this but us?"

The whispered answer was:

"Not a soul—on honor, not a soul!"

"If it isn't too late to—"

The men were starting upstairs; at this moment they were over-taken by a boy, and Cox asked:

"Is that you, Johnny?"

"Yes, sir."

"You needn't ship the early mail—nor *any* mail; wait till I tell you."

"It's already gone, sir."

"*Gone?*" It had the sound of an unspeakable disappointment in it.

"Yes, sir. Timetable for Brixton and all the towns beyond changed today, sir—had to get the papers in twenty minutes earlier than common. I had to rush; if I had been two minutes later—"

The men turned and walked slowly away, not waiting to hear the rest. Neither of them spoke during ten minutes; then Cox said, in a vexed tone:

"What possessed you to be in such a hurry, *I* can't make out."

The answer was humble enough:

"I see it now, but somehow I never thought, you know, until it was too late. But the next time—"

"Next time be hanged! It won't come in a thousand years."

Then the friends separated without a good night, and dragged themselves home with the gait of mortally stricken men. At their homes their wives sprang up with an eager "Well?"—then saw the answer with their eyes and sank down sorrowing, without waiting for it to come in words. In both houses a discussion followed of a heated sort—a new thing; there had been discussions before, but not heated ones, not ungentle ones. The discussions tonight were a sort of seeming plagiarisms of each other. Mrs. Richards said:

"If you had only waited, Edward—if you had only stopped to think; but no, you must run straight to the printing office and spread it all over the world."

"It *said* publish it."

"That is nothing; it also said do it privately, if you liked. There, now—is that true, or not?"

"Why, yes—yes, it is true; but when I thought what a stir it would make, and what a compliment it was to Hadleyburg that a stranger should trust it so—"

"Oh, certainly, I know all that; but if you had only stopped to think, you would have seen that you *couldn't* find the right man, because he is in his grave, and hasn't left chick nor child nor relation behind him; and as long as the money went to somebody that awfully needed it, and nobody would be hurt by it, and—and—"

She broke down, crying. Her husband tried to think of some comforting thing to say, and presently came out with this:

"But after all, Mary, it must be for the best—it *must* be; we know that. And we must remember that is was so ordered—"

"Ordered! Oh, everything's *ordered*, when a person has to find some way out when he has been stupid. Just the same, it was *ordered* that the money should come to us in this special way, and it was you that must take it on yourself to go meddling with the designs of Providence—and who gave you the right? It was wicked, that is what it was—just blasphemous presumption, and no more becoming to a meek and humble professor of—"

"But, Mary, you know how we have been trained all our lives long, like the whole village, till it is absolutely second nature to us to stop not a single moment to think when there's an honest thing to be done—"

"Oh, I know it, I know it—it's been one everlasting training and training and training in honesty—honesty shielded, from the very cradle, against every possible temptation, and so it's *artificial* honesty, and weak as water when temptation comes, as we have seen this night. God knows I never had shade nor shadow of a doubt of my petrified and indestructible honesty until now—and now, under the very first big and real temptation, I—Edward, it is my belief that this town's honesty is as rotten as mine is; as rotten as yours is. It is a mean town, a hard, stingy town, and hasn't a virtue in the world but this honesty it is so celebrated for and so conceited about; and so help me, I do believe that if ever the day comes that its honesty falls under great temptation, its grand reputation will go to ruin like a house of cards. There, now, I've made confession, and I feel better; I am a humbug, and I've been one all my life, without knowing it. Let no man call me honest again—I will not have it."

"I—well, Mary, I feel a good deal as you do; I certainly do. It seems strange, too, so strange. I never could have believed it—never."

A long silence followed; both were sunk in thought. At last the wife looked up and said:

"I know what you are thinking, Edward."

Richards had the embarrassed look of a person who is caught.

"I am ashamed to confess it, Mary, but—"

"It's no matter, Edward, I was thinking the same question myself."

"I hope so. State it."

"You were thinking, if a body could only guess out *what the remark was* that Goodson made to the stranger."

"It's perfectly true. I feel guilty and ashamed. And you?"

"I'm past it. Let us make a pallet here; we've got to stand watch till the bank vault opens in the morning and admits the sack. . . . Oh dear, oh dear—if we hadn't made the mistake!"

The pallet was made, and Mary said:

"The open sesame—what could it have been? I do wonder what that remark could have been? But come; we will get to bed now."

"And sleep?"

"No: think."

"Yes, think."

By this time the Coxes too had completed their spat and their reconciliation, and were turning in—to think, to think, and toss, and fret, and worry over what the remark could possibly have been which Goodson made to the stranded derelict; that golden remark; that remark worth forty thousand dollars, cash.

The reason that the village telegraph office was open later than usual that night was this: The foreman of Cox's paper was the local representative of the Associated Press. One might say its honorary representative, for it wasn't four times a year that he could furnish thirty words that would be accepted. But this time it was different. His dispatch stating what he had caught got an instant answer:

Send the whole thing—all the details—twelve hundred words.

A colossal order! The foreman filled the bill; and he was the proudest man in the state. By breakfast time the next morning the name of Hadleyburg the Incorruptible was on every lip in America, from Montreal to the Gulf, from the glaciers of Alaska to the orange groves of Florida; and millions and millions of people were discussing the stranger and his money sack, and wondering if the right man would be found, and hoping some more news about the matter would come soon—right away.

## II

Hadleyburg village woke up world-celebrated—astonished—happy—vain. Vain beyond imagination. Its nineteen principal citizens and their wives went about shaking hands with each other, and beaming, and smiling, and congratulating, and saying *this* thing adds a new word to the dictionary—*Hadleyburg*, synonym for *incorruptible*—destined to live in dictionaries forever! And the minor and unimportant citizens and their wives went around acting in much the same way. Everybody ran to the bank to see the gold sack; and before noon grieved and envious crowds began to flock in from Brixton and all neighboring towns; and that afternoon and next day reporters began to arrive from everywhere to verify the sack and its history and write the whole thing up anew, and make dashing free-hand pictures of the sack, and of Richards's house, and the bank, and the Presbyterian church, and the Baptist church, and the public square, and the town hall where the test would be applied and the money delivered; and damnable portraits of the Richardses, and Pinkerton the banker, and Cox, and the foreman, and Reverend Burgess, and the postmaster—and even of Jack Halliday, who was the loafing, good-natured, no-account, irreverent fisherman, hunter, boys' friend, stray-dogs' friend, typical "Sam Lawson" of the town. The little, mean, smirking, oily Pinkerton showed the sack to all comers, and rubbed his sleek palms together pleasantly, and enlarged upon the town's fine old reputation for honesty and upon this wonderful endorsement of it, and hoped and believed that the example would now spread far and wide over the American world, and be epoch-making in the matter of moral regeneration. And so on, and so on.

By the end of a week things had quieted down again; the wild intoxication of pride and joy had sobered to a soft, sweet, silent delight—a sort of deep, nameless, unutterable content. All faces bore a look of peaceful, holy happiness.

Then a change came. It was a gradual change; so gradual that its beginnings were hardly noticed; maybe were not noticed at all, except by Jack Halliday, who always noticed everything; and always made fun of it, too, no matter what it was. He began to throw out chaffing remarks about people not looking quite so happy as they did a day or two ago; and next he claimed that the new aspect was deepening to positive sadness; next, that it was taking on a sick look; and finally he said that everybody was become so moody, thoughtful, and absent-minded that he could rob the meanest man in town of a cent out of the bottom of his breeches pocket and not disturb his revery.

At this stage—or at about this stage—a saying like this was dropped at bedtime—with a sigh, usually—by the head of each of the nineteen principal households: "Ah, what *could* have been the remark that Goodson made?"

And straightway—with a shudder—came this, from the man's wife:

"Oh, *don't!* What horrible thing are you mulling in your mind? Put it away from you, for God's sake!"

But that question was wrung from those men again the next night—and got the same retort. But weaker.

And the third night the men uttered the question yet again—with anguish, and absently. This time—and the following night—the wives fidgeted feebly, and tried to say something. But didn't.

And the night after that they found their tongues and responded—longingly:

"Oh, if we *could* only guess!"

Halliday's comments grew daily more and more sparklingly disagreeable and disparaging. He went diligently about, laughing at the town, individually and in mass. But his laugh was the only one left in the village: it fell upon a hollow and mournful vacancy and emptiness. Not even a smile was findable anywhere. Halliday carried a cigar box around on a tripod, playing that it was a camera, and halted all passers and aimed the thing and said, "Ready!—now look pleasant, please," but not even this capital joke could surprise the dreary faces into any softening.

So three weeks passed—one week was left. It was Saturday evening—after supper. Instead of the aforetime Saturday evening flutter and bustle and shopping and larking, the streets were empty and desolate. Richards and his old wife sat apart in their little parlor—miserable and thinking. This was become their evening habit now: the lifelong habit which had preceded it, of reading, knitting, and contented chat, or receiving or paying neighborly calls, was dead and gone and forgotten, ages ago—two or three weeks ago; nobody talked now, nobody read, nobody visited—the whole village sat at home, sighing, worrying, silent. Trying to guess out that remark.

The postman left a letter. Richards glanced listlessly at the superscription and the postmark—unfamiliar, both—and tossed the letter on the table and resumed his might-have-beens and his hopeless dull miseries where he had left them off. Two or three hours later his wife got wearily up and was going away to bed without a goodnight—custom now—but she stopped near the letter and eyed it awhile with a dead interest, then broke it open, and began to skim it over. Richards, sitting there with his chair tilted back against the wall and his chin between his knees, heard something fall. It was his wife. He sprang to her side, but she cried out:

"Leave me alone, I am too happy. Read the letter—read it!"

He did. He devoured it, his brain reeling. The letter was from a distant state, and it said:

> I am a stranger to you, but no matter: I have something to tell. I have just arrived home from Mexico, and learned about that episode. Of course you do not know who made that remark, but I know, and I am the only person living who does know. It was GOODSON. I knew him well, many years ago. I passed through your village that very night, and was his guest till the midnight train came along. I overheard him make that remark to the stranger in the dark—it was in Hale Alley. He and I talked of it the rest of the way home, and while smoking in his house.. He mentioned many of your villagers in the course of his talk—most of them in a very uncomplimentary way, but two or three favorably; among these latter yourself. I say "favorable"—nothing stronger. I remember his saying he did not actually LIKE any person in the town—not one; but that you—I THINK he said you—am almost sure—had done him a very great service once, possibly without knowing the full value of it, and he wished he had a fortune, he would leave it to you when he died, and a curse apiece for the rest of the citizens. Now, then, if it was you that did him that service, you are his legitimate heir, and entitled to the sack of gold. I know that I can trust to your honor and honesty, for in a citizen of Hadleyburg these virtues are an unfailing inheritance, and so I am going to reveal to you the remark, well satisfied that if you are not the right man you will seek and find the right one and see that poor Goodson's debt of gratitude for the service referred to is paid. This is the remark: "YOU ARE FAR FROM BEING A BAD MAN: GO, AND REFORM."
>
> HOWARD L. STEPHENSON.

"Oh, Edward, the money is ours, and I am so grateful, *oh*, so grateful—kiss me, dear, it's forever since we kissed—and we needed it so—the money—and now you are free of Pinkerton and his bank, and nobody's slave any more; it seems to me I could fly for joy."

It was a happy half-hour that the couple spent there on the settee caressing each other; it was the old days come again—days that had begun with their courtship and lasted without a break till the stranger brought the deadly money. By and by the wife said:

"Oh, Edward, how lucky it was you did him that grand service, poor Goodson! I never liked him, but I love him now. And it was fine and beautiful of you never to mention it or brag about it." Then, with a touch of reproach, "But you ought to have told *me*, Edward, you ought to have told your wife, you know."

"Well, I—er—well, Mary, you see—"

"Now stop hemming and hawing, and tell me about it, Edward. I always loved you, and now I'm proud of you. Everybody believes there was only one good generous soul in this village, and now it turns out that you—Edward, why don't you tell me?"

"Well—er—er— Why, Mary, I can't!"

"You *can't? Why* can't you?"

"You see, he—well, he—he made me promise I wouldn't".

The wife looked him over, and said, very slowly.

"Made—you—promise? Edward, what do you tell me that for?"

"Mary, do you think I would lie?"

She was troubled and silent for a moment, then she laid her hand within his and said:

"No . . . no. We have wandered far enough from our bearings— God spare us that! In all your life you have never uttered a lie. But now—now that the foundations of things seem to be crumbling from under us, we — we—" She lost her voice for a moment, then said, brokenly, "Lead us not into temptation. . . . I think you made the promise, Edward. Let it rest so. Let us keep away from that ground. Now—that is all gone by; let us be happy again; it is no time for clouds."

Edward found it something of an effort to comply, for his mind kept wandering—trying to remember what the service was that he had done Goodson.

The couple lay awake the most of the night, Mary happy and busy, Edward busy but not so happy. Mary was planning what she would do with the money. Edward was trying to recall that service. At first his conscience was sore on account of the lie he had told Mary—if it was a lie. After much reflection—suppose it *was* a lie? What then? Was it such a great matter? Aren't we always *acting* lies? Then why not *tell* them? Look at Mary—look what she had done. While he was hurrying off on his honest errand, what was she doing? Lamenting because the papers hadn't been destroyed and the money kept! Is theft better than lying?

*That* point lost its sting—the lie dropped into the background and left comfort behind it. The next point came to the front: *Had* he rendered that service? Well, here was Goodson's own evidence as reported in Stephenson's letter; there could be no better evidence than that—it was even *proof* that he had rendered it. Of course. So that point was settled. . . . No, not quite. He recalled with a wince that this unknown Mr. Stephenson was just a trifle unsure as to whether the performer of it was Richards or some other—and, oh dear, he had put Richards on his honor! He must himself decide whither that money must go—and Mr. Stephenson was not doubting that if he was the wrong man he would go honorably and find the right one. Oh, it was odious to put a man in such a situation—

ah, why couldn't Stephenson have left out that doubt! What did he want to intrude that for?

Further reflection. How did it happen that *Richards'* name remained in Stephenson's mind as indicating the right man, and not some other man's name? That looked good. Yes, that looked very good. In fact, it went on looking better and better, straight along—until by and by it grew into positive *proof*. And then Richards put the matter at once out of his mind, for he had a private instinct that a proof once established is better left so.

He was feeling reasonably comfortable now, but there was still one other detail that kept pushing itself on his notice: of course he had done that service—that was settled; but what *was* that service? He must recall it—he would not go to sleep till he had recalled it; it would make his peace of mind perfect. And so he thought and thought. He thought of a dozen things—possible services, even probable services—but none of them seemed adequate, none of them seemed large enough, none of them seemed worth the money—worth the fortune Goodson had wished he could leave in his will. And besides, he couldn't remember having done them, anyway. Now, then—now, then—what *kind* of a service would it be that would make a man so inordinately grateful? Ah—the saving of his soul! That must be it. Yes, he could remember, now, how he once set himself the task of converting Goodson, and labored at it as much as—he was going to say three months; but upon closer examination it shrunk to a month, then to a week, then to a day, then to nothing. Yes, he remembered now, and with unwelcome vividness, that Goodson had told him to go to thunder and mind his own business—*he* wasn't hankering to follow Hadleyburg to heaven!

So that solution was a failure—he hadn't saved Goodson's soul. Richards was discouraged. Then after a little came another idea: had he saved Goodson's property? No, that wouldn't do—he hadn't any. His life? That is it! Of course. Why, he might have thought of it before. This time he was on the right track, sure. His imagination mill was hard at work in a minute, now.

Thereafter during a stretch of two exhausting hours he was busy saving Goodson's life. He saved it in all kinds of difficult and perilous ways. In every case he got it saved satisfactorily up to a certain point; then, just as he was beginning to get well persuaded that it had really happened, a troublesome detail would turn up which made the whole thing impossible. As in the matter of drowning, for instance. In that case he had swum out and tugged Goodson ashore in an unconscious state with a great crowd looking on and applauding, but when he had got it all thought out and was just beginning to remember all about it, a whole swarm of disqualifying details

arrived on the ground: the town would have known of the circumstance, Mary would have known of it, it would glare like a limelight
in his own memory instead of being an inconspicuous service
which he had possibly rendered "without knowing its full value."
And at this point he remembered that he couldn't swim, anyway.

Ah—*there* was a point which he had been overlooking from the
start: it had to be a service which he had rendered "possibly without knowing the full value of it." Why, really, that ought to be an
easy hunt—much easier than those others. And sure enough, by
and by he found it. Goodson, years and years ago, came near marrying a very sweet and pretty girl, named Nancy Hewitt, but in some
way or other the match had been broken off; the girl died, Goodson
remained a bachelor, and by and by became a soured one and a
frank despiser of the human species. Soon after the girl's death the
village found out, or thought it had found out, that she carried a
spoonful of Negro blood in her veins. Richards worked at these
details a good while, and in the end he thought he remembered
things concerning them which must have gotten mislaid in his
memory through long neglect. He seemed to dimly remember that it
was *he* that found out about the Negro blood; that it was he that told
the village; that the village told Goodson where they got it; that he
thus saved Goodson from marrying the tainted girl; that he had
done him this great service "without knowing the full value of it,"
in fact without knowing that he *was* doing it; but that Goodson
knew the value of it, and what a narrow escape he had had, and so
went to his grave grateful to his benefactor and wishing he had a
fortune to leave him. It was all clear and simple now, and the more
he went over it the more luminous and certain it grew; and at last,
when he nestled to sleep satisfied and happy, he remembered the
whole thing just as if it had been yesterday. In fact, he dimly remembered Goodson's *telling* him his gratitude once. Meantime
Mary had spent six thousand dollars on a new house for herself and
a pair of slippers for her pastor, and then had fallen peacefully to
rest.

That same Saturday evening the postman had delivered a letter to
each of the other principal citizens—nineteen letters in all. No two of
the envelopes were alike, and no two of the superscriptions were in
the same hand, but the letters inside were just like each other in every
detail but one. They were exact copies of the letter received by Richards—handwriting and all—and were all signed by Stephenson, but
in place of Richards' name each receiver's own name appeared.

All night long eighteen principal citizens did what their caste-
brother Richards was doing at the same time—they put in their
energies trying to remember what notable service it was that they

had unconsciously done Barclay Goodson. In no case was it a holiday job; still they succeeded.

And while they were at this work, which was difficult, their wives put in the night spending the money, which was easy. During that one night the nineteen wives spent an average of seven thousand dollars each out of the forty-thousand in the sack—a hundred and thirty-three thousand altogether.

Next day there was a surprise for Jack Halliday. He noticed that the faces of the nineteen chief citizens and their wives bore that expression of peaceful and holy happiness again. He could not understand it, neither was he able to invent any remarks about it that could damage it or disturb it. And so it was his turn to be dissatisfied with life. His private guesses at the reasons for the happiness failed in all instances, upon examination. When he met Mrs. Wilcox and noticed the placid ecstasy in her face, he said to himself, "Her cat has had kittens"—and went and asked the cook: it was not so; the cook had detected the happiness, but did not know the cause. When Halliday found the duplicate ecstasy in the face of "Shadbelly" Billson (village nickname), he was sure some neighbor of Billson's had broken his leg, but inquiry showed that this had not happened. The subdued ecstasy in Gregory Yates's face could mean but one thing—he was a mother-in-law short: it was another mistake. "And Pinkerton—Pinkerton—he has collected ten cents that he thought he was going to lose." And so on, and so on. In some cases the guesses had to remain in doubt, in the others they proved distinct errors. In the end Halliday said to himself, "Anyway it foots up that there's nineteen Hadleyburg families temporarily in heaven: I don't know how it happened; I only know Providence is off duty today."

An architect and builder from the next state had lately ventured to set up a small business in this unpromising village, and his sign had now been hanging out a week. Not a customer yet; he was a discouraged man, and sorry he had come. But his weather changed suddenly now. First one and then another chief citizen's wife said to him privately:

"Come to my house Monday week—but say nothing about it for the present. We think of building."

He got eleven invitations that day. That night he wrote his daughter and broke off her match with her student. He said she could marry a mile higher than that.

Pinkerton the banker and two or three other well-to-do men planned country-seats—but waited. That kind don't count their chickens until they are hatched.

The Wilsons devised a grand new thing—a fancy-dress ball. They made no actual promises, but told all their acquaintanceship in confidence that they were thinking the matter over and thought they should give it—"and if we do, you will be invited, of course." People were surprised, and said, one to another, "Why, they are crazy, those poor Wilsons, they can't afford it." Several among the nineteen said privately to their husbands, "It is a good idea: we will keep still till their cheap thing is over, then *we* will give one that will make it sick."

The days drifted along, and the bill of future squanderings rose higher and higher, wilder and wilder, more and more foolish and reckless. It began to look as if every member of the nineteen would not only spend his whole forty thousand dollars before receiving day, but be actually in debt by the time he got the money. In some cases lightheaded people did not stop with planning to spend, they really spent—on credit. They bought land, mortgages, farms, speculative stocks, fine clothes, horses, and various other things, paid down the bonus, and made themselves liable for the rest—at ten days. Presently the sober second thought came, and Halliday noticed that a ghastly anxiety was beginning to show up in a good many faces. Again he was puzzled, and didn't know what to make of it. "The Wilcox kittens aren't dead, for they weren't born; nobody's broken a leg; there's no shrinkage in mother-in-laws; *nothing* has happened—it is an unsolvable mystery."

There was another puzzled man, too—The Rev. Mr. Burgess. For days, wherever he went, people seemed to follow him or to be watching out for him; and if he ever found himself in a retired spot, a member of the nineteen would be sure to appear, thrust an envelope privately into his hand, whisper "To be opened at the town hall Friday evening," then vanish away like a guilty thing. He was expecting that there might be one claimant for the sack,—doubtful, however, Goodson being dead—but it never occurred to him that all this crowd might be claimants. When the great Friday came at last, he found that he had nineteen envelopes.

### III

The town hall had never looked finer. The platform at the end of it was backed by a showy draping of flags; at intervals along the walls were festoons of flags; the gallery fronts were clothed in flags; the supporting columns were swathed in flags; all this was to impress the stranger, for he would be there in considerable force, and in a large degree he would be connected with the press. The house was full. The 412 fixed seats were occupied; also the 68 extra chairs which had been packed into the aisles; the steps of the platform were occupied; some distinguished strangers were given seats on the platform; at the horseshoe of tables which fenced the front and sides of the platform sat a strong force of special correspondents who had come from everywhere. It was the best-dressed house the town had ever produced. There were some tolerably expensive toilets there, and in several cases the ladies who wore them had the look of being unfamiliar with that kind of clothes. At least the town thought they had that look, but the notion could have arisen from the town's knowledge of the fact that these ladies had never inhabited such clothes before.

The gold sack stood on a little table at the front of the platform where all the house could see it. The bulk of the house gazed at it with a burning interest, a mouth-watering interest, a wistful and pathetic interest; a minority of nineteen couples gazed at it tenderly, lovingly, proprietarily, and the male half of this minority kept saying over to themselves the moving little impromptu speeches of thankfulness for the audience's applause and congratulations which they were presently going to get up and deliver. Every now and then one of these got a piece of paper out of his vest-pocket and privately glanced at it to refresh his memory.

Of course there was a buzz of conversation going on—there always is; but at last when the Rev. Mr. Burgess rose and laid his hand on the sack he could hear the microbes gnaw, the place was so still. He related the curious history of the sack, then went on to speak in warm tones of Hadleyburg's old and well-earned reputation for spotless honesty, and of the town's just pride in this reputation. He said that this reputation was a treasure of priceless value; that under Providence its value had now become inestimably enhanced, for the recent episode had spread this fame far and wide, and thus had focused the eyes of the American world upon this village, and made its name for all time, as he hoped and believed, a synonym for commercial incorruptibility. [*Applause.*] And who is to be the guardian of this noble treasure—the community as a whole? NO! The responsibility is individual, not communal. From this day forth each and every one of you is in his own person its special guardian, and individually responsible that no harm shall come to it. Do you—does each of you—accept this great trust? [*Tumultuous assent.*] Then all is well. Transmit it to your children and to your children's children. Today your purity is beyond reproach—see to it that it shall remain so. Today there is not a person in your community who could be beguiled to touch a penny not his own—see to it that you abide in this grace. [*"We will! we will!"*] This is not the place to make comparisons between ourselves and other communities—some of them ungracious toward us; they have their ways, we have ours; let us be content. [*Applause.*] I am done. Under my hand, my friends, rests a stranger's eloquent recognition of what we are; through him the world will always henceforth know what we are. We do not know who he is, but in your name I utter your gratutide, and ask you to raise your voices in endorsement."

The house rose in a body and made the walls quake with the thunders of its thankfulness for the space of a long minute. Then it sat down, and Mr. Burgess took an envelope out of his pocket. The house held its breath while he slit the envelope open and took from it a slip of paper. He read its contents—slowly and impressively— the audience listening with tranced attention to this magic document, each of whose words stood for an ingot of gold.

" 'The remark which I made to the distressed stranger was this: 'You are very far from being a bad man: go, and reform.' ' " Then he continued:

"We shall know in a moment now whether the remark here quoted corresponds with the one concealed in the sack; and if that shall prove to be so—and it undoubtedly will—this sack of gold belongs to a fellow citizen who will henceforth stand before the nation as the symbol of the special virtue which has made our town famous through the land—Mr. Billson!"

The house had gotten itself all ready to burst into the proper tornado of applause; but instead of doing it, it seemed stricken with a paralysis; there was a deep hush for a moment or two, then a wave of whispered murmurs swept the place—of about this tenor: '*Billson!* oh, come, this is *too* thin! Twenty dollars to a stranger—or *anybody*—*Billson!* Tell it to the marines!" And now at this point the house caught its breath all of a sudden in a new access of astonishment, for it discovered that whereas in one part of the hall Deacon Billson was standing up with his head meekly bowed, in another part of it Lawyer Wilson was doing the same. There was a wondering silence now for a while.

Everybody was puzzled, and nineteen couples were surprised and indignant.

Billson and Wilson turned and stared at each other. Billson asked, bitingly:

"Why do *you* rise, Mr. Wilson?"

"Because I have a right to. Perhaps you will be good enough to explain to the house why *you* rise?"

"With great pleasure. Because I wrote that paper."

"It is an impudent falsity! I wrote it myself."

It was Burgess's turn to be paralyzed. He stood looking vacantly at first one of the men and then the other, and did not seem to know what to do. The house was stupefied. Lawyer Wilson spoke up, now, and said:

"I ask the Chair to read the name signed to that paper."

That brought the Chair to itself, and it read out the name:

" 'John Wharton *Billson.'* "

"There!" shouted Billson. "What have you got to say for yourself, now? And what kind of apology are you going to make to me and to this insulted house for the imposture which you have attempted to play here?"

"No apologies are due, sir; and as for the rest of it, I publicly charge you with pilfering my note from Mr. Burgess and substituting a copy of it signed with your own name. There is no other way by which you could have gotten hold of the test-remark; I alone, of living men, possessed the secret of its wording."

There was likely to be a scandalous state of things if this went on; everybody noticed with distress that the shorthand scribes were scribbling like mad; many people were crying "Chair, Chair! Order! Order!" Burgess rapped with his gavel, and said:

"Let us not forget the proprieties due. There has evidently been a mistake somewhere, but surely that is all. If Mr. Wilson gave me an envelope—and I remember now that he did—I still have it."

He took one out of his pocket, opened it, glanced at it, looked surprised and worried, and stood silent a few moments. Then he waved his hand in a wandering and mechanical way, and made an effort or two to say something, then gave it up, despondently. Several voices cried out:

"Read it! Read it! What is it?"

So he began in a dazed and sleepwalker fashion:

" 'The remark which I made to the unhappy stranger was this: 'You are far from being a bad man. [The house gazed at him, marveling.] Go, and reform' " [*Murmurs:* "Amazing! what can this mean?"] This one," said the Chair, "is signed Thurlow G. Wilson."

"There!" cried Wilson, "I reckon that settles it! I knew perfectly well my note was purloined."

"Purloined!" retorted Billson. "I'll let you know that neither you nor any of your kidney must venture to—"

*The Chair.* "Order, gentlemen, order! Take your seats, both of you, please,"

They obeyed, shaking their heads and grumbling angrily. The house was profoundly puzzled; it did not know what to do with this curious emergency. Presently Thompson got up. Thompson was the hatter. He would have liked to be a Nineteener; but such was not for him: his stock of hats was not considerable enough for the position. He said:

"Mr. Chairman, if I may be permitted to make a suggestion, can both of these gentlemen be right? I put it to you, sir, can both have happened to say the very same words to the stranger? It seems to me—"

The tanner got up and interrupted him. The tanner was a disgruntled man; he believed himself entitled to be a Nineteener, but he couldn't get recognition. It made him a little unpleasant in his ways and speech. Said he:

"Sho, *that's* not the point! *That* could happen—twice in a hundred years—but not the other thing. *Neither* of them gave the twenty dollars!"

[*A ripple of applause.*]

Billson. *"I* did!"

Wilson. *"I* did!"

Then each accused the other of pilfering.

The Chair. "Order! Sit down, if you please—both of you. Neither of the notes has been out of my possession at any moment."

A Voice. "Good—that settles *that!*"

The Tanner. "Mr. Chairman, one thing is now plain: one of these men has been eavesdropping under the other one's bed, and filching family secrets. If it is not unparliamentary to suggest, I will remark that both are equal to it. [*The Chair.* "Order! Order!"] I withdraw the remark, sir, and will confine myself to suggesting that *if* one of them has overheard the other reveal the test-remark to his wife, we shall catch him now."

A Voice. "How?"

The Tanner. "Easily. The two have not quoted the remark in exactly the same words. You would have noticed that, if there hadn't been a considerable stretch of time and exciting quarrel inserted between the two readings."

A Voice. "Name the difference."

The Tanner. "The word *very* is in Billson's note, and not in the other."

Many Voices. "That's so—he's right!"

The Tanner. "And so, if the Chair will examine the test-remark in the sack, we shall know which of these two frauds— [*The Chair.* "Order!"]—which of these two adventurers— [*The Chair.* "Order! Order"]—which of these two gentlemen—[*Laughter and applause*]—is entitled to wear the belt as being the first dishonest blatherskite ever bred in this town—which he has dishonored, and which will be a sultry place for him from now out!" [*Vigorous applause.*]

Many Voices. "Open it!—open the sack!"

Mr. Burgess made a slit in the sack, slid his hand in and brought out an envelope. In it were a couple of folded notes. He said:

"One of these is marked, 'Not to be examined until all written communications which have been addressed to the Chair—if any—shall have been read.' The other is marked '*The Test.*' Allow me. It is worded—to wit:

" 'I do not require that the first half of the remark which was made to me by my benefactor shall be quoted with exactness, for it was not striking, and could be forgotten; but its closing fifteen words are quite striking, and I think easily rememberable; unless *these* shall be accurately reproduced, let the applicant be regarded as an impostor. My benefactor began by saying he seldom gave advice to anyone, but that it always bore the hallmark of high value when he did give it. Then he said this—and it has never faded from my memory: *"You are far from being a bad man—"* ' "

*Fifty Voices.* "That settles it—the money's Wilson's! Wilson! Wilson! Speech! Speech!"

People jumped up and crowded around Wilson, wringing his hand and congratulating fervently—meantime the Chair was hammering with the gavel and shouting:

"Order, gentlemen! Order! Order! Let me finish reading please." When quiet was restored, the reading was resumed, as follows:

" '*Go, and reform—or, mark my words—some day, for your sins, you will die and go to hell or Hadleyburg—*TRY AND MAKE IT THE FORMER.' "

A ghastly silence followed. First an angry cloud began to settle darkly upon the faces of the citizenship; after a pause the cloud began to rise, and a tickled expression tried to take its place; tried so hard that it was only kept under with great and painful difficulty; the reporters, the Brixtonites, and other strangers bent their heads down and shielded their faces with their hands, and managed to hold in by main strength and heroic courtesy. At this most inopportune time burst upon the stillness the roar of a solitary voice—Jack Halliday's:

"*That's* got the hallmark on it!"

Then the house let go, strangers and all. Even Mr. Burgess' gravity broke down presently, then the audience considered itself officially absolved from all restraint, and it made the most of its privilege. It was a good long laugh, and a tempestuously wholehearted one, but it ceased at last—long enough for Mr. Burgess to try to resume, and for the people to get their eyes partially wiped; then it broke out again; and afterward yet again; then at last Burgess was able to get out these serious words:

"It is useless to try to disguise the fact—we find ourselves in the presence of a matter of grave import. It involves the honor of your town, it strikes at the town's good name. The difference of a single word between the test-remarks offered by Mr. Wilson and Mr. Billson was itself a serious thing, since it indicated that one or the other of these gentlemen had committed a theft—"

The two men were sitting limp, nerveless, crushed; but at these words both were electrified into movement, and started to get up.

"Sit down!" said the Chair, sharply, and they obeyed. "That, as I have said, was a serious thing. And it was—but for only one of them. But the matter has become graver; for the honor of *both* is now in formidable peril. Shall I go even further, and say in inextricable peril? *Both* left out the crucial fifteen words." He paused. During several moments he allowed the pervading stillness to gather and deepen its impressive effects, then added: "There would seem to be but one way whereby this could happen. I ask these gentlemen—Was there *collusion?—agreement?*"

A low murmur sifted through the house; its import was, "He's got them both."

Billson was not used to emergencies; he sat in a helpless collapse. But Wilson was a lawyer. He struggled to his feet, pale and worried, and said:

"I ask the indulgence of the house while I explain this most painful matter. I am sorry to say what I am about to say, since it must inflict irreparable injury upon Mr. Billson, whom I have always esteemed and respected until now, and in whose invulnerability to temptation I entirely believed—as did you all. But for the preservation of my own honor I must speak—and with frankness. I confess with shame—and I now beseech your pardon for it—that I said to the ruined stranger all of the words contained in the test-remark, including the disparaging fifteen. [*Sensation.*]. When the late publication was made I recalled them, and I resolved to claim the sack of coin, for by every right I was entitled to it. Now I will ask you to consider this point, and weigh it well: that stranger's gratitude to me that night knew no bounds; he said himself that he could find no words for it that were adequate, and that if he should ever be able he would repay me a thousandfold. Now, then, I ask you this: Could I expect—could I believe—could I even remotely imagine—that, feeling as he did, he would do so ungrateful a thing as to add those quite unnecessary fifteen words to his test?—set a trap for me?—expose me as a slanderer of my own town before my own people assembled in a public hall? It was preposterous: it was impossible. His test would contain only the kindly opening clause of my remark. Of that I had no shadow of doubt. You would have thought as I did. You would not have expected a base betrayal from one whom you had befriended and against whom you had committed no offense. And so, with perfect confidence, perfect trust, I wrote on a piece of paper the opening words—ending with 'Go, and reform'—and signed it. When I was about to put it in an envelope I was called into my back office, and without thinking I left the paper lying open on my desk." He stopped, turned his head slowly toward Billson, waited a moment, then added: "I ask you to note this: when I returned, a little later, Mr. Billson was retiring by my street door." [*Sensation*]

In a moment Billson was on his feet and shouting:

"It's a lie! It's an infamous lie!"

*The Chair.* "Be seated, sir! Mr. Wilson has the floor."

Billson's friends pulled him into his seat and quieted him, and Wilson went on:

"Those are the simple facts. My note was now lying in a different place on the table from where I had left it. I noticed that, but attached no importance to it, thinking a draft had blown it there. That Mr. Billson would read a private paper was a thing which could not occur to me; he was an honorable man, and he would be above that. If you will allow me to say it, I think his extra word '*very*' stands explained; it is attributable to a defect of memory. I was the only man in the world who could furnish here any detail of the test-remark—by *honorable* means. I have finished."

There is nothing in the world like a persuasive speech to fuddle the mental apparatus and upset the convictions and debauch the emotions of an audience not practiced in the tricks and delusions of oratory. Wilson sat down victorious. The house submerged him in tides of approving applause; friends swarmed to him and shook him by the hand and congratulated him, and Billson was shouted down and not allowed to say a word. The Chair hammered and hammered with its gavel, and kept shouting:

"But let us proceed, gentlemen, let us proceed!"

At last there was a measurable degree of quiet, and the hatter said:

"But what is there to proceed with, sir, but to deliver the money?"

*Voices.* "That's it! That's it! Come forward, Wilson!"

*The Hatter.* "I move three cheers for Mr. Wilson, Symbol of the special virtue which—"

The cheers burst forth before he could finish; and in the midst of them—and in the midst of the clamor of the gavel also—some enthusiasts mounted Wilson on a big friend's shoulder and were going to fetch him in triumph to the platform. The Chair's voice now rose above the noise.

"Order! To your places! You forget that there is still a document to be read." When quiet had been restored he took up the document, and was going to read it, but laid it down again, saying, "I forgot; this is not to be read until all written communications received by me have first been read." He took an envelope out of his pocket, removed its enclosure, glanced at it—seemed astonished—held it out and gazed at it—stared at it.

Twenty or thirty voices cried out:

"What is it? Read it! Read it?"

And he did—slowly and wondering:

" 'The remark which I made to the stranger—[*Voices.* "Hello! how's this?"]—was this: "You are far from being a bad man. [*Voices.* "Great Scott!"] Go, and reform." ' [*Voice.* "Oh, saw my leg off!"'] Signed by Mr. Pinkerton the banker."

The pandemonium of delight which turned itself loose now was of a sort to make the judicious weep. Those whose withers were unwrung laughed till the tears ran down; the reporters, in throes of laughter, set down disordered pothooks which would never in the world be decipherable; and a sleeping dog jumped up, scared out of its wits, and barked itself crazy at the turmoil. All manner of cries were scattered through the din: "We're getting rich—*two* Symbols of Incorruptibility!—without counting Billson!" "*Three!*—count Shadbelly in—we can't have too many!" "All right—Billson's elected!" "Alas, poor Wilson—victim of *two* thieves?"

*A Powerful Voice.* "Silence! The Chair's fished up something more out of its pocket."

*Voices.* "Hurrah! It is something fresh? Read it! Read! Read!"

*The Chair* [*reading.*] " 'The remark which I made,' etc.: "You are far from being a bad man. Go," etc. Signed, Gregory Yates.' "

*Tornado of Voices.* "Four Symbols!" " 'Rah for Yates!" "Fish again!"

The house was in a roaring humor now, and ready to get all the fun out of the occasion that might be in it. Several Nineteeners, looking pale and distressed, got up and began to work their way toward the aisles, but a score of shouts went up:

"The doors, the doors—close the doors; no Incorruptible shall leave this place! Sit down, everybody!"

The mandate was obeyed.

"Fish again! Read! Read!"

The Chair fished again, and once more the familiar words began to fall from its lips— " 'You are far from being a bad man—' "

"Name! name! What's his name?"

"L. Ingoldsby Sargent."

"Five elected! Pile up the Symbols! Go on, go on!"

" 'You are far from being a bad—' "

"Name! name!"

"Nicholas Whitworth."

"Hooray! hooray! It's a symbolical day!"

Somebody wailed in, and began to sing this rhyme (leaving out "it's") to the lovely "Mikado" tune of "When a man's afraid, a beautiful maid—"; the audience joined in, with joy; then, just in time, somebody contributed another line:

"And don't you this forget—"

The house roared it out. A third line was at once furnished:

"Corruptibles far from Hadleyburg are—"

The house roared that one too. As the last note died, Jack Halliday's voice rose high and clear, freighted with a final line:

"But the Symbols are here, you bet!"

That was sung, with booming enthusiasm. Then the happy house started in at the beginning and sang the four lines through twice, with immense swing and dash, and finished up with a crashing three-times-three and a tiger for "Hadleyburg the Incorruptible and all Symbols of it which we shall find worthy to receive the hallmark tonight."

Then the shoutings at the Chair began again, all over the place:

"Go on! Go on! Read some more! Read all you've got!"

"That's it—go on! We are winning eternal celebrity!"

A dozen men got up now and began to protest. They said that this farce was the work of some abandoned joker, and was an insult to the whole community. Without a doubt these signatures were all forgeries—

"Sit down! Sit down! Shut up! You are confessing. We'll find *your* names in the lot."

"Mr. Chairman, how many of those envelopes have you got?"

The Chair counted.

"Together with those that have been already examined, there are nineteen."

A storm of derisive applause broke out.

"Perhaps they all contain the secret. I move that you open them all and read every signature that is attached to a note of that sort—and read also the first eight words of the note."

"Second the motion!"

It was put and carried—uproariously. Then poor old Richards got up, and his wife rose and stood at his side. Her head was bent down, so that none might see that she was crying. Her husband gave her his arm, and so supporting her, he began to speak in a quavering voice:

"My friends, you have known us two—Mary and me—all our lives and I think you have liked us and respected us—"

The Chair interrupted him:

"Allow me. It is quite true—that which you are saying, Mr. Richards; this town *does* know you two; it *does* like you; it *does* respect you; more—it honors you and *loves* you—"

Halliday's voice rang out:

"That's the hall-marked truth, too! If the Chair is right, let the house speak up and say it. Rise! Now, then—hip! hip! hip!—all together!"

The house rose in mass, faced toward the old couple eagerly filled the air with a snow-storm of waving handkerchiefs, and delivered the cheers with all its affectionate heart.

The Chair then continued:

"What I was going to say is this: We know your good heart, Mr. Richards, but this is not a time for the exercise of charity toward offenders. [*Shouts of "Right! right!"*] I see your generous purpose in your face, but I cannot allow you to plead for these men—"

"But I was going to—"

"Please take your seat, Mr. Richards. We must examine the rest of these notes—simple fairness to the men who have already been exposed requires this. As soon as that has been done—I give you my word for this—you shall be heard."

*Many Voices.* "Right!—the Chair is right—no interruption can be permitted at this stage! Go on!—the names!—the names!—according to the terms of the motion!"

The old couple sat reluctantly down, and the husband whispered to the wife, "It is pitifully hard to have to wait; the shame will be greater than ever when they find we were going to plead for *ourselves*."

Straightway the jollity broke loose again with the reading of the names.

" 'You are far from being a bad man—' Signature, 'Robert J. Titmarsh.'

" 'You are far from being a bad man—, Signature, 'Eliphalet Weeks.'

" 'You are far from being a bad man—, Signature, 'Oscar B. Wilder.' "

At this point the house lit upon the idea of taking the eight words out of the Chairman's hands. He was not unthankful for that. Thenceforward he held up each note in its turn, and waited. The house droned out the eight words in a massed and measured and musical deep volume of sound (with a daringly close resemblance to a well-known church chant)—" 'You are f-a-r from being a b-a-a-d

man.' " Then the Chair said, "Signature, 'Archibald Wilcox.' " And
so on, and so on, name after name, and everybody had an increasingly and gloriously good time except the wretched Nineteen. Now
and then, when a particularly shining name was called, the house
made the Chair wait while it chanted the whole of the test-remark
from the beginning to the closing words, "And go to hell or Hadleyburg—try and make it the for-or-m-e-r!" and in these special cases
they added a grand and agonized and imposing "A-a-a-a-men!"

The list dwindled, dwindled, dwindled, poor old Richards keeping tally of the count, wincing when a name resembling his own
was pronounced, and waiting in miserable suspense for the time to
come when it would be his humiliating privilege to rise with Mary
and finish his plea, which he was intending to word thus: ". . . for
until now we have never done any wrong thing, but have gone our
humble way unreproached. We are very poor, we are old, and have
no chick nor child to help us; we were sorely tempted, and we fell. It
was my purpose when I got up before to make confession and beg
that my name might not be read out in this public place, for it
seemed to us that we could not bear it; but I was prevented. It was
just; it was our place to suffer with the rest. It has been hard for us.
It is the first time we have ever heard our name fall from anyone's
lips—sullied. Be merciful—for the sake of the better days; make our
shame as light to bear as in your charity you can." At this point in
his reverie Mary nudged him, perceiving that his mind was absent.
The house was chanting, "You are f-a-r," etc.

"Be ready," Mary whispered. "Your name comes now; he has
read eighteen."

The chant ended.

"Next! next! next!" came volleying from all over the house.

Burgess put his hand into his pocket. The old couple, trembling,
began to rise. Burgess fumbled a moment, then said:

"I find I have read them all."

Faint with joy and surprise, the couple sank into their seats, and
Mary whispered:

"Oh, bless God, we are saved! He has lost ours—I wouldn't give
this for a hundred of those sacks!"

The house burst out with its "Mikado" travesty, and sang it three
times with ever-increasing enthusiasm, rising to its feet when it
reached for the third time the closing line:

"But the Symbols are here, you bet!"

and finishing up with cheers and a tiger for "Hadleyburg purity and
our eighteen immortal representatives of it."

Then Wingate, the saddler, got up and proposed cheers "for the cleanest man in town, the one solitary important citizen in it who didn't try to steal that money—Edward Richards."

They were given with great and moving heartiness; then somebody proposed that Richards be elected sole guardian and Symbol of the now Sacred Hadleyburg Tradition with power and right to stand up and look the whole sarcastic world in the face.

Passed, by acclamation. Then they sang the "Mikado" again, and ended it with:

"And there's *one* Symbol left, you bet!"

*A Voice.* "Now, then, who's to get the sack?"

*The Tanner (with bitter sarcasm).* "That's easy. The money has to be divided among the eighteen Incorruptibles. They gave the suffering stranger twenty dollars apiece—and that remark—each in his turn—it took twenty-two minutes for the procession to move past. Staked the stranger—total contribution, $360. All they want is just the loan back—and interest—forty thousand dollars altogether."

*Many Voices [derisively.]* "That's it! Divvy! Divvy! Be kind to the poor—don't keep them waiting?"

*The Chair.* "Order! I now offer the stranger's remaining document. It says: 'If no claimant shall appear [*grand chorus of groans*], I desire that you open the sack and count out the money to the principal citizens of your town, they to take it in trust [*cries of "Oh! Oh! Oh!"*], and use it in such ways as to them shall seem best for the propagation and preservation of your community's noble reputation for incorruptible honesty [*more cries*]—a reputation to which their names and their efforts will add a new and far-reaching luster.' [*Enthusiastic outburst of sarcastic applause.*] That seems to be all. No—here is a postscript:

" 'P.S.—CITIZENS OF HADLEYBURG: There *is* no test-remark—nobody made one. [*Great sensation.*] There wasn't any pauper stranger, nor any twenty-dollar contribution, nor any accompanying benediction and compliment—these are all inventions. [*General buzz and hum of astonishment and delight.*] Allow me to tell my story—it will take but a word or two. I passed through your town at a certain time, and received a deep offense which I had not earned. Any other man would have been content to kill one or two of you and call it square, but to me that would have been a trivial revenge, and inadequate; for the dead do not *suffer*. Besides, I could not kill you all—and, anyway, made as I am, even that would not have satisfied me. I wanted to damage every man in the place, and every woman—and not in their bodies or in their estate, but in their vanity—the place where feeble and foolish people are most vulnerable. So I disguised myself and came back and studied you. You were easy game. You had an old and lofty reputation for honesty, and naturally you were proud of it—it was your treasure of treasures, the very apple of your eye. As soon as I found out that you carefully and vigilantly kept yourselves and your children *out of temptation,* I knew how to proceed. Why, you simple creatures, the weakest of all weak things is a virtue which has not been tested in the fire. I laid a plan, and gathered a list of names. My project was to corrupt Hadleyburg the Incorruptible. My idea was to make liars and thieves of nearly half a hundred smirchless men and women who had never in their lives uttered a lie or stolen a penny. I was afraid of Goodson. He was neither born nor reared in Hadleyburg. I was afraid that if I started to operate my scheme by getting my letter laid before you you would say to yourselves, "Goodson is the only man among us who would give away twenty dollars to a poor devil"—and then you might not bite at my bait. But Heaven took Goodson; then I knew I was safe, and I set my trap and baited it. It may be that I shall not catch all the men to whom I mailed the pretended test secret, but I shall catch the most of them, if I know Hadleyburg nature. [*Voices.* "Right—he got every last one of them."] I believe they will even steal ostensible *gamble*-money, rather than miss, poor, tempted, and mistrained fellows. I am hoping to eternally and everlastingly squelch your vanity and give Hadleyburg a new renown—one that will *stick*—and spread far. If I have succeeded, open the sack and summon the Committee on Propagation and Preservation of the Hadleyburg Reputation.' "

*A Cyclone of Voices.* "Open it! Open it! The Eighteen to the front! Committee on Propagation of the Tradition! Forward—the Incorruptibles!"

The Chair ripped the sack wide, and gathered up a handful of bright, broad, yellow coins, shook them together, then examined them.

"Friends, they are only gilded disks of lead!"

There as a crashing outbreak of delight over this news, and when the noise had subsided, the tanner called out:

"By right of apparent seniority in this business, Mr. Wilson is Chairman of the Committee on Propagation of the Tradition. I suggest that he step forward on behalf of his pals, and receive in trust the money."

*A Hundred Voices.* "Wilson! Wilson! Wilson! Speech! Speech!"

*Wilson* [*in a voice trembling with anger.*] "You will allow me to say, and without apologies for my language, *damn* the money!"

*A Voice.* "Oh, and him a Baptist!"

*A Voice.* "Seventeen Symbols left! Step up, gentlemen, and assume your trust!"

There was a pause—no response.

*The Saddler.* "Mr. Chairman, we've got *one* clean man left, anyway, out of the late aristocracy; and he needs money, and deserves it. I move that you appoint Jack Halliday to get up there and auction off that sack of gilt twenty-dollar pieces, and give the result to the right man—the man whom Hadleyburg delights to honor—Edward Richards."

This was received with great enthusiasm, the dog taking a hand again; the saddler started the bids at a dollar, the Brixton folk and Barnum's representative fought hard for it, the people cheered every jump that the bids made, the excitement climbed moment by moment higher and higher, the bidders got on their mettle and grew steadily more and more daring, more and more determined, the jumps went from a dollar up to five, then to ten, then to twenty, then fifty, then to a hundred, then—

At the beginning of the auction Richards whispered in distress to his wife: "O Mary, can we allow it? It—it—you see, it is an honor reward, a testimonial to purity of character, and—and—can we allow it? Hadn't I better get up and—O Mary, what ought we to do?— what do you think we—" [*Halliday's voice. "Fifteen I'm bid!— fifteen for the sack!—twenty!—ah, thanks!—thirty—thanks again! Thirty, thirty, thirty!—do I hear forty?—forty it is! Keep the ball rolling, gentlemen, keep it rolling!—fifty!—thanks, noble Roman! going at fifty, fifty, fifty!—seventy!—ninety!—splendid!—a hundred!—pile it up, pile it up!—hundred and twenty—forty!—just in time!—hundred and fifty!— TWO hundred!—superb! Do I hear two h—thanks!—two hundred and fifty!—"*]

"It is another temptation, Edward—I'm all in a tremble—but, oh, we've escaped *one* temptation, and that ought to warn us to— [*"Six did I hear?—thanks!—six fifty, six f—*SEVEN *hundred!"*] And yet, Edward, when you think—nobody susp— [*"Eight hundred dollars!— hurrah!—make it nine!—this noble sack of virgin lead going at only nine hundred dollars, gilding and all—come! do I hear—a thousand!—gratefully yours!—did someone say eleven?—a sack which is going to be the most celebrated in the whole Uni—"*] O Edward" (beginning to sob), "we are *so* poor!—but—but—do as you think best—do as you think best."

Edward fell—that is, he sat still; sat with a conscience which was not satisfied, but which was overpowered by circumstances.

Meantime a stranger, who looked like an amateur detective gotten up as an impossible English earl, had been watching the evening's proceedings with manifest interest, and with a contented expression in his face; and he had been privately commenting to himself. He was now soliloquizing somewhat like this: "None of the Eighteen are bidding; that is not satisfactory; I must change that—the dramatic unities require it; they must buy the sack they tried to steal; they must pay a heavy price, too—some of them are rich. And another thing, when I make a mistake in Hadleyburg nature the man that puts that error upon me is entitled to a high honorarium, and someone must pay it. This poor old Richards has brought my judgment to shame; he is an honest man. I don't understand it, but I acknowledge it. Yes, he saw my deuces *and* with a straight flush, and by rights the pot is his. And it shall be a jackpot, too, if I can manage it. He disappointed me, but let that pass."

He was watching the bidding. At a thousand, the market broke; the prices tumbled swiftly. He waited—and still watched. One competitor dropped out; then another, and another. He put in a bid or two, now. When the bids had sunk to ten dollars, he added a five; someone raised him a three; he waited a moment, then flung in a fifty-dollar jump, and the sack was his—at $1,282. The house broke out in cheers—then stopped; for he was on his feet, and had lifted his hand. He began to speak.

"I desire to say a word, and ask a favor. I am a speculator in rarities, and I have dealings with persons interested in numismatics all over the world. I can make a profit on this purchase, just as it stands; but there is a way, if I can get your approval, whereby I can make every one of these leaden twenty-dollar pieces worth its face in gold, and perhaps more. Grant me that approval, and I will give part of my gains to your Mr. Richards, whose invulnerable probity you have so justly and so cordially recognized to-night; his share shall be ten thousand dollars, and I will hand him the money to-morrow. [*Great applause from the house.* But the "invulnerable probity" made the Richardses blush prettily; however, it went for modesty, and did no harm.] If you will pass my proposition by a good majority—I would like a two-thirds vote—I will regard that as the town's consent, and that is all I ask. Rarities are always helped by any device which will rouse curiosity and compel remark. Now if I may have your permission to stamp upon the faces of each of these ostensible coins the names of the eighteen gentlemen who—"

Nine-tenths of the audience were on their feet in a moment—dog and all—and the proposition was carried with a whirlwind of approving applause and laughter.

They sat down, and all the Symbols except "Dr." Clay Harkness got up, violently protesting against the proposed outrage, and threatening to—

"I beg you not to threaten me," said the stranger, calmly. "I know my legal rights, and am not accustomed to being frightened at bluster." [*Applause.*] He sat down. "Dr." Harkness saw an opportunity here. He was one of the two very rich men of the place and Pinkerton was the other. Harkness was proprietor of a mint; that is to say a popular patent medicine. He was running for the Legislature on one ticket and Pinkerton on the other. It was a close race and a hot one, and getting hotter every day. Both had strong appetites for money; each had bought a great tract of land, with a purpose; there was going to be a new railway, and each wanted to be in the Legislature and help locate the route to his own advantage; a single vote might make the decision, and with it two or three fortunes. The stake was large, and Harkness was a daring speculator. He was sitting close to the stranger. He leaned over while one or another of the other Symbols was entertaining the house with protests and appeals, and asked, in a whisper:

"What is your price for the sack?"

"Forty thousand dollars."

"I'll give you twenty."

"No."

"Twenty-five."

"No."

"Say thirty."

"The price is forty thousand dollars; not a penny less."

"All right, I'll give it. I will come to the hotel at ten in the morning. I don't want it known; will see you privately."

"Very good." Then the stranger got up and said to the house:

"I find it late. The speeches of these gentlemen are not without merit, not without interest, not without grace; yet if I may be excused I will take my leave. I thank you for the great favor which you have shown me in granting my petition. I ask the Chair to keep the sack for me until tomorrow, and to hand these three five-hundred-dollar notes to Mr. Richards." They were passed up to the Chair. "At nine I will call for the sack, and at eleven will deliver the rest of the ten thousand to Mr. Richards in person, at his home. Good night."

Then he slipped out, and left the audience making a vast noise, which was composed of a mixture of cheers, the "Mikado" song, dog-disapproval, and the chant, "You are f-a-r from being a b-a-d man—a-a-a a-men!"

### IV

At home the Richardses had to endure congratulations and compliments until midnight. Then they were left to themselves. They looked a little sad, and they sat silent and thinking. Finally Mary sighed and said:

"Do you think we are to blame, Edward—*much* to blame?" And her eyes wandered to the accusing triplet of big banknotes lying on the table, where the congratulators had been gloating over them and reverently fingering them. Edward did not answer at once; then he brought out a sigh and said hesitatingly:

"We—couldn't help it, Mary. It—well, it was ordered. *All* things are."

Mary glanced up and looked at him steadily, but he didn't return the look. Presently she said:

"I thought congratulations and praises always tasted good. But—it seemed to me, now—Edward?"

"Well?"

"Are you going to stay in the bank?"

"N-no."

"Resign?"

"In the morning—by note."

"It does seem best."

Richards bowed his head in his hands and muttered:

"Before, I was not afraid to let oceans of people's money pour through my hands, but—Mary, I am so tired, so tired—"

"We will go to bed."

At nine in the morning the stranger called for the sack and took it to the hotel in a cab. At ten Harkness had a talk with him privately. The stranger asked for and got five checks on a metropolitan bank—drawn to "Bearer"—four for $1,500 each, and one for $34,000. He put one of the former in his pocketbook, and the remainder, representing $38,500, he put in an envelope, and with these things he added a note, which he wrote after Harkness was gone. At eleven he called Richards house and knocked. Mrs. Richards peeped through the shutters, then went and received the envelope, and the stranger disappeared without a word. She came back flushed and a little unsteady on her legs, and gasped out:

"I am sure I recognized him! Last night it seemed to me that maybe I had seen him somewhere before."

"He is the man that brought the sack here?"

"I am almost sure of it."

"Then he is the ostensible Stephenson, too, and sold every important citizen in this town with his bogus secret. Now if he has sent checks instead of money, we are sold, too, after we thought we had escaped. I was beginning to feel fairly comfortable once more, after my night's rest, but the look of that envelope makes me sick. It isn't fat enough; $8,500 in even the largest banknotes makes more bulk than that."

"Edward, why do you object to checks?"

"Checks signed by Stephenson! I am resigned to take the $8,500 if it could come in banknotes—for it does seem that it was so ordered, Mary—but I have never had much courage, and I have not the pluck to try to market a check signed with that disastrous name. It would be a trap. That man tried to catch me; we escaped somehow or other; and now he is trying a new way. If it is checks—"

"Oh, Edward, it is *too* bad!" And she held up the checks and began to cry.

"Put them in the fire! Quick! We mustn't be tempted. It is a trick to make the world laugh at *us* along with the rest, and— Give them to *me*, since you can't do it!" He snatched them and tried to hold his grip till he could get to the stove; but he was human, he was a cashier, and he stopped a moment to make sure of the signature. Then he came near to fainting.

"Fan me, Mary, fan me! They are the same as gold!"

"Oh, how lovely, Edward! Why?"

"Signed by Harkness. What can the mystery of that be, Mary?"

"Edward, do you think—"

"Look here—look at this! Fifteen—fifteen—fifteen—thirty-four. Thirty-eight thousand five hundred. Mary, the sack isn't worth twelve dollars, and Harkness—apparently—has paid about par for it."

"And does it all come to us, do you think—instead of the ten thousand?"

"Why, it looks like it. And the checks are made to 'Bearer,' too."

"Is that good, Edward? What is it for?"

"A hint to collect them at some distant bank, I reckon. Perhaps Harkness doesn't want the matter known. What is that—a note?"

"Yes, It was with the checks."

It was in the "Stephenson" handwriting, but there was no signature. It said:

> I am a disappointed man. Your honesty is beyond the reach of temptation. I had a different idea about it, but I wronged you in that, and I beg pardon, and do it sincerely. I honor you—and that is sincere too. This town is not worthy to kiss the hem of your garment. Dear sir, I made a square bet with myself that there were nineteen debauchable men in your self-righteous community. I have lost. Take the whole pot, you are entitled to it.

Richards drew a deep sigh, and said:

"It seems written with fire—it burns so. Mary—I am miserable again."

"I, too. Ah, dear, I wish—"

"To think, Mary—he *believes* in me."

"Oh don't Edward—I can't bear it."

"If those beautiful words were deserved, Mary—and God knows I believed I deserved them once—I think I could give the forty thousand dollars for them. And I would put that paper away as representing more than gold and jewels, and keep it always. But now— We could not live in the shadow of its accusing presence, Mary."

He put it in the fire.

A messenger arrived and delivered an envelope.

Richards took from it a note and read it; it was from Burgess.

> You saved me, in a difficult time. I saved you last night. It was at cost of a lie, but I made the sacrifice freely, and out of a grateful heart. None in this village knows so well as I know how brave and good and noble you are. At bottom you cannot respect me, knowing as you do of that matter of which I am accused, and by the general voice condemned; but I beg that you will at least believe that I am a grateful man; it will help me to bear my burden.
> [Signed]                    BURGESS.

"Saved, once more. And on such terms!" He put the note in the fire. "I—I wish I were dead, Mary, I wish I were out of it all."

"Oh, these are bitter, bitter days, Edward. The stabs, through their very generosity, are so deep—and they come so fast!"

Three days before the election each of two thousand voters found himself in possession of a prized memento—one of the renowned bogus double eagles. Around one of its faces was stamped these words: "THE REMARK I MADE TO THE POOR STRANGER WAS—" Around the other face was stamped these: "GO AND REFORM. [SIGNED] PINKERTON." Thus the entire remaining refuse of the renowned joke was emptied upon a single head, and with calamitous effect. It revived the recent vast laugh and concentrated it upon Pinkerton; and Harkness's election was a walkover.

Within twenty-four hours after the Richardses had received their checks their consciences were quieting down, discouraged; the old couple were learning to reconcile themselves to the sin which they had committed. But they were to learn, now, that a sin takes on new and real terrors when there seems a chance that it is going to be found out. This gives it a fresh and most substantial and important aspect. At church the morning sermon was of the usual pattern; it was the same old things said in the same old way; they had heard them a thousand times and found them innocuous, next to meaningless, and easy to sleep under; but now it was different: the sermon seemed to bristle with accusations; it seemed aimed straight and specially at people who were concealing deadly sins. After church they got away from the mob of congratulators as soon as they could, and hurried homeward, chilled to the bone at they did not know what—vague, shadowy, indefinite fears. And by chance they caught a glimpse of Mr. Burgess as he turned a corner. He paid no attention to their nod of recognition! He hadn't seen it; but they did not know that. What could his conduct mean? It might mean—it might mean—oh, a dozen dreadful things. Was it possible that he knew that Richards could have cleared him of guilt in that bygone time, and had been silently waiting for a chance to even up accounts? At home, in their distress they got to imagining that their servant might have been in the next room listening when Richards revealed the secret to his wife that he knew of Burgess's innocence; next, Richards began to imagine that he had heard the swish of a gown in there at that time; next, he was sure he *had* heard it. They would call Sarah in, on a pretext, and watch her face: if she had been betraying them to Mr. Burgess, it would show in her manner. They asked her some questions—questions which were so random and incoherent and seemingly purposeless that the girl felt sure that the old people's minds had been affected by their sudden good fortune; the sharp and watchful gaze which they bent upon her frightened her, and that completed the business. She blushed, she became nervous and confused, and to the old people these were plain signs of guilt—guilt of some fearful sort or other—without doubt she was a spy and a traitor. When they were alone again they began to piece many unrelated things together and get horrible results out of the combination. When things had got about to the worst Richards was delivered of a sudden gasp, and his wife asked:

"Oh, what is it?—What is it?"

"The note—Burgess's note? Its language was sarcastic, I see it now." He quoted: " 'At bottom you cannot respect me, *knowing*, as you do, of *that matter* of which I am accused'—oh, it is perfectly plain, now, God help me! He knows that I know! You see the ingenuity of the phrasing. It was a trap—and like a fool, I walked into it. And Mary—?"

"Oh, it is dreadful—I know what you are going to say—he didn't return your transcript of the pretended test-remark."

"No—kept it to destroy us with. Mary, he has exposed us to some already. I know it—I know it well. I saw it in a dozen faces after church. Ah, he wouldn't answer our nod of recognition—*he* knew what he had been doing!"

In the night the doctor was called. The news went around in the morning that the old couple were rather seriously ill—prostrated by the exhausting excitement growing out of their windfall, the congratulations, and the late hours, the doctor said. The town was sincerely distressed; for these old people were about all it had left to be proud of, now.

Two days later the news was worse. The old couple were delirious, and were doing strange things. By witness of the nurses, Richards had exhibited checks—for $8,500? No—for an amazing sum—$38,500! What could be the explanation of this gigantic piece of luck?

The following day the nurses had more news—and wonderful. They had concluded to hide the checks, lest harm come to them; but when they searched they were gone from under the patient's pillow—vanished away. The patient said:

"Let the pillow alone; what do you want?"

"We thought it best that the checks—"

"You will never see them again—they are destroyed. They came from Satan. I saw the hell-brand on them, and I knew they were sent to betray me to sin." Then he fell to gabbling strange and dreadful things which were not clearly understandable, and which the doctor admonished them to keep to themselves.

Richards was right; the checks were never seen again.

A nurse must have talked in her sleep, for within two days the forbidden gabblings were the property of the town; and they were of a surprising sort. They seemed to indicate that Richards had been a claimant for the sack himself, and that Burgess had concealed that fact and then maliciously betrayed it.

Burgess was taxed with this and stoutly denied it. And he said it was not fair to attach weight to the chatter of a sick old man who was out of his mind. Still, suspicion was in the air, and there was much talk.

After a day or two it was reported that Mrs. Richards' delirious deliveries were getting to be duplicates of her husband's. Suspicion flamed up into conviction now and the town's pride in the purity of its one undiscredited important citizen began to dim down and flicker toward extinction.

Six days passed, then came more news. The old couple were dying. Richards' mind cleared in his latest hour and he sent for Burgess. Burgess said:

"Let the room be cleared. I think he wishes to say something in privacy."

"No!" said Richards: "I want witnesses. I want you all to hear my confession, so that I may die a man and not a dog. I was clean—artificially—like the rest and like the rest I fell when temptation came. I signed a lie, and claimed the miserable sack. Mr. Burgess remembered that I had done him a service, and in gratitude (and ignorance) he suppressed my claim and saved me. You know the thing that was charged against Burgess years ago. My testimony, and mine alone, could have cleared him, and I was a coward, and left him to suffer disgrace—"

"No—no—Mr. Richards, you—"

"My servant betrayed my secret to him—"

"No one has betrayed anything to me—"

—"and then he did a natural and justifiable thing, he repented of the saving kindness which he had done me, and he *exposed* me—as I deserved—"

"Never! —I make oath—"

"Out of my heart I forgive him."

Burgess's impassioned protestations fell upon deaf ears; the dying man passed away without knowing that once more he had done poor Burgess a wrong. The old wife died that night.

The last of the sacred Nineteen had fallen a prey to the fiendish sack; the town was stripped of the last rag of its ancient glory. Its mourning was not showy, but it was deep.

By act of the Legislature—upon prayer and petition—Hadleyburg was allowed to change its name to (never mind what—I will not give it away), and leave one word out of the motto that for many generations had graced the town's official seal.

It is an honest town once more, and the man will have to rise early that catches it napping again.

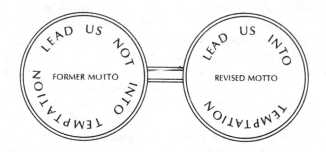

# AMBROSE BIERCE
## 1842–1913?

Bierce was born at a religious camp in the Western Reserve, Ohio. The Civil War gave him an opportunity to escape from poverty, and he accepted it eagerly, rising to an officer's rank, though paying for it by being wounded twice. Like Tolstoy, he began his serious writing by describing some of the horrors of war. He is best known for his cynical *Devil's Dictionary* (1911) and a few gems of fiction such as the one included here.

# An Occurrence at Owl Creek Bridge

### I

A man stood upon a railroad bridge in Northern Alabama, looking down into the swift waters twenty feet below. The man's hands were behind his back, the wrists bound with a cord. A rope loosely encircled his neck. It was attached to a stout cross-timber above his head, and the slack fell to the level of his knees. Some loose boards laid upon the sleepers supporting the metals of the railway supplied a footing for him and his executioners—two private soldiers of the Federal army, directed by a sergeant, who in civil life may have been a deputy sheriff. At a short remove upon the same temporary platform was an officer in the uniform of his rank, armed. He was captain. A sentinel at each end of the bridge stood with his rifle in the position known as "support," that is to say, vertical in front of the left shoulder, the hammer resting on the forearm thrown straight across the chest—a formal and unnatural position, enforcing an erect carriage of the body. It did not appear to be the duty of these two men to know what was occurring at the center of the bridge; they merely blockaded the two ends of the foot plank which traversed it.

Beyond one of the sentinels nobody was in sight; the railroad was lost to view. Doubtless there was an outpost further along. The other bank of the stream was open ground—a gentle acclivity crowned with a stockade of vertical tree trunks, loop-holed for rifles, with a single embrasure through which protruded the muzzle of a brass cannon commanding the bridge. Midway of the slope between bridge and fort were the spectators—a single company of infantry in line, at "parade rest," the butts of the rifles on the ground, the barrels inclining slightly backward against the right shoulder, the hands crossed upon the stock. A lieutenant stood at the right of the line, the point of his sword upon the ground, his left hand resting upon his right. Excepting the group of four at the center of the bridge not a man moved. The company faced the bridge staring stonily, motionless. The sentinels, facing the banks of the stream, might have been statues to adorn the bridge. The captain stood with folded arms, silent, observing the work of his subordinates but making no sign. Death is a dignitary who, when he comes announced, is to be received with formal manifestations of respect, even by those most familiar with him. In the code of military etiquette silence and fixity are forms of deference.

The man who was engaged in being hanged was apparently about thirty-five years of age. He was a civilian, if one might judge from his dress, which was that of a planter. His features were good—a straight nose, firm mouth, broad forehead, from which his long, dark hair was combed straight back, falling behind his ears to the collar of his well-fitting frock coat. He wore a mustache and pointed beard, but no whiskers; his eyes were large and dark grey and had a kindly expression which one would hardly have expected in one whose neck was in the hemp. Evidently this was no vulgar assassin. The liberal military code makes provision for hanging many kinds of people, and gentlemen are not excluded.

The preparations being complete, the two private soldiers stepped aside and each drew away the plank upon which he had been standing. The sergeant turned to the captain, saluted and placed himself immediately behind that officer who in turn moved apart one pace. These movements left the condemned man and the sergeant standing on the two ends of the same plank, which spanned three of the cross-ties of the bridge. The end upon which the civilian stood almost, but not quite, reached a fourth. This plank had been held in place by the weight of the captains; it was now held by that of the sergeant. At a signal from the former, the latter would step aside, the plank would tilt and the condemned man go down between two ties. The arrangement commended itself to his judgment as simple and effective. His face had not been covered nor his eyes bandaged. He looked a moment at his "unsteadfast footing," then let his gaze wander to the swirling water of the stream racing madly beneath his feet. A piece of dancing driftwood caught his attention and his eyes followed it down the current. How slowly it appeared to move! What a sluggish stream!

He closed his eyes in order to fix his last thoughts upon his wife and children. The water, touched to gold by the early sun, the brooding mists under the banks at some distance down the stream, the fort, the soldiers, the piece of drift—all had distracted him. And now he became conscious of a new disturbance. Striking through the thought of his dear ones was a sound which he could neither ignore nor understand, a sharp distinct metallic percussion like the stroke of blacksmith's hammer upon the anvil; it had the same ringing quality. He wondered what it was, and whether immeasurably distant or near by—it seemed both. Its recurrence was regular, but as slow as the tolling of a death knell. He awaited each stroke with impatience and—he knew not why—apprehension. The intervals of silence grew progressively longer; the delays became maddening. With their greater infrequency the sounds increased in strength and sharpness. They hurt his ear like the thrust of a knife; he feared he would shriek. What he heard was the ticking of his watch.

He unclosed his eyes and saw again the water below him. "If I could free my hands," he thought, "I might throw off the noose and spring into the stream. By diving I could evade the bullets, and, swimming vigorously, reach the bank, take to the woods, and get away home. My home, thank God, is as yet outside their lines; my wife and little ones are still beyond the invader's farthest advance."

As these thoughts, which have here to be set down in words, were flashed into the doomed man's brain rather than evolved from it, the captain nodded to the sergeant. The sergeant stepped aside.

## II

Peyton Farquhar was a well-to-do planter, of an old and highly-respected Alabama family. Being a slave owner, and, like other slave owners, a politician, he was naturally an original secessionist and ardently devoted to the Southern cause. Circumstances of an imperious nature which it is unnecessary to relate here, had prevented him from taking service with the gallant army which had fought the disastrous campaigns ending with the fall of Corinth,[1] and he chafed under the inglorious restraint, longing for the release of his energies, the larger life of the soldier, the opportunity for distinction. That opportunity, he felt, would come, as it comes to all in war time. Meanwhile he did what he could. No service was too humble for him to perform in aid of the South, no adventure too perilous for him to undertake if consistent with the character of a civilian who was at heart a soldier, and who in good faith and without too much qualification assented to at least a part of the frankly villainous dictum that all is fair in love and war.

One evening while Farquhar and his wife were sitting on a rustic bench near the entrance to his grounds, a grey-clad soldier rode up to the gate and asked for a drink of water. Mrs. Farquhar was only too happy to serve him with her own white hands. While she was gone to fetch the water, her husband approached the dusty horseman and inquired eagerly for news from the front.

"The Yanks are repairing the railroads," said the man, "and are getting ready for another advance. They have reached the Owl Creek bridge, put it in order, and built a stockade on the other bank. The commandant has issued an order, which is posted everywhere, declaring that any civilian caught interfering with the railroad, its bridges, tunnels, or trains, will be summarily hanged. I saw the order."

"How far is it to the Owl Creek bridge?" Farquhar asked.

"About thirty miles."

"Is there no force on this side the creek?"

---

1. Corinth, Mississippi.

"Only a picket post half a mile out, on the railroad, and a single sentinel at this end of the bridge."

"Suppose a man—a civilian and student of hanging—should elude the picket post and perhaps get the better of the sentinel," said Farquhar, smiling, "what could he accomplish?"

The soldier reflected. "I was there a month ago," he replied. "I observed that the flood of last winter had lodged a great quantity of driftwood against the wooden pier at this end of the bridge. It is now dry and would burn like tow."

The lady had now brought the water, which the soldier drank. He thanked her ceremoniously, bowed to her husband, and rode away. An hour later, after nightfall, he repassed the plantation, going northward in the direction from which he had come. He was a Federal scout.

### III

As Peyton Farquhar fell straight downward through the bridge, he lost consciousness and was as one already dead. From this state he was awakened—ages later, it seemed to him—by the pain of a sharp pressure upon his throat, followed by a sense of suffocation. Keen, poignant agonies seemed to shoot from his neck downward through every fiber of his body and limbs. These pains appeared to flash along well defined lines of ramification, and to beat with an inconceivably rapid periodicity. They seemed like streams of pulsating fire heating him to an intolerable temperature. As to his head, he was conscious of nothing but a feeling of fullness—of congestion. These sensations were unaccompanied by thought. The intellectual part of his nature was already effaced; he had power only to feel, and feeling was torment. He was conscious of motion. Encompassed in a luminous cloud, of which he was now merely the fiery heart, without material substance, he swung through unthinkable arcs of oscillation, like a vast pendulum. Then all at once, with terrible suddenness, the light about him shot upward with the noise of a loud plash; a frightful roaring was in his ears, and all was cold and dark. The power of thought was restored; he knew that the rope had broken and he had fallen into the stream. There was no additional strangulation; the noose about his neck was already suffocating him, and kept the water from his lungs. To die of hanging at the bottom of a river!—the idea seemed to him ludicrous. He opened his eyes in the blackness and saw above him a gleam of light, but how distant, how inaccessible! He was still sinking, for the light became fainter and fainter until it was a mere glimmer. Then it began to grow and brighten, and he knew that he was rising toward the surface—knew it with reluctance, for he was now very comfortable. "To be hanged and drowned," he thought, "that is not so bad; but I do not wish to be shot. No; I will not be shot; that is not fair."

He was not conscious of an effort, but a sharp pain in his wrist apprised him that he was trying to free his hands. He gave the struggle his attention, as an idler might observe the feat of a juggler, without interest in the outcome. What splendid effort!—what magnificent, what superhuman strength! Ah, that was a fine endeavor! Bravo! The cord fell away; his arms parted and floated upward, the hands dimly seen on each side in the growing light. He watched them with a new interest as first one and then the other pounced upon the noose at his neck. They tore it away and thrust it fiercely aside, its undulations resembling those of a water-snake. "Put it back, put it back!" He thought he shouted these words to his hands, for the undoing of the noose had been succeeded by the direst pang which he had yet experienced. His neck ached horribly; his brain was on fire; his heart, which had been fluttering faintly, gave a great leap, trying to force itself out at his mouth. His whole body was racked and wrenched with an insupportable anguish! But his disobedient hands gave no heed to the command. They beat the water vigorously with quick, downward strokes, forcing him to the surface. He felt his head emerge; his eyes were blinded by the sunlight; his chest expended convulsively, and with supreme and crowning agony his lungs engulfed a great draught of air, which instantly he expelled in a shriek!

He was now in full possession of his physical senses. They were, indeed, preternaturally keen and alert. Something in the awful disturbance of his organic system had so exalted and refined them that they made record of things never before perceived. He felt the ripples upon his face and heard their separate sounds as they struck. He looked at the forest on the bank of the stream, saw the individual trees, the leaves and the veining of each leaf—saw the very insects upon them, the locusts, the brilliant-bodied flies, the grey spiders stretching their webs from twig to twig. He noted the prismatic colors in all the dewdrops upon a million blades of grass. The humming of the gnats that danced above the eddies of the stream, the beating of the dragon flies' wings, the strokes of the water spiders' legs, like oars which had lifted their boat—all these made audible music. A fish slid along beneath his eyes and he heard the rush of its body parting the water.

He had come to the surface facing down the stream; in a moment the visible world seemed to wheel slowly round, himself the pivotal point, and he saw the bridge, the fort, the soldiers upon the bridge, the captain, the sergeant, the two privates, his executioners. They were a silhouette against the blue sky. They shouted and gesticulated, pointing at him; the captain had drawn his pistol, but did not fire; the others were unarmed. Their movements were grotesque and horrible, their forms gigantic.

Suddenly he heard a sharp report and something struck the water smartly within a few inches of his head, spattering his face with spray. He heard a second report, and saw one of the sentinels with his rifle at his shoulder, a light cloud of blue smoke rising from the muzzle. The man in the water saw the eye of the man on the bridge gazing into his own through the sights of the rifle. He observed that it was a grey eye, and remembered having read that grey eyes were keenest and that all famous marksmen had them. Nevertheless, this one had missed.

A counter swirl had caught Farquhar and turned him half round; he was again looking into the forest on the bank opposite the fort. The sound of a clear, high voice in a monotonous singsong now rang out behind him and came across the water with a distinctness that pierced and subdued all other sounds, even the beating of the ripples in his ears. Although no soldier, he had frequented camps enough to know the dread significance of that deliberate, drawling, aspirated chant; the lieutenant on shore was taking a part in the morning's work. How coldly and pitilessly—with what an even, calm intonation, presaging and enforcing tranquillity in the men—with what accurately-measured intervals fell those cruel words:

"'Attention, company . . . . Shoulder arms . . . . Ready . . . . Aim . . . Fire."

Farquhar dived—dived as deeply as he could. The water roared in his ears like the voice of Niagara, yet he heard the dulled thunder of the volley, and rising again toward the surface, met shining bits of metal, singularly flattened, oscillating slowly downward. Some of them touched him on the face and hands, then fell away, continuing their descent. One lodged between his collar and neck; it was uncomfortably warm, and he snatched it out.

As he rose to the surface, gasping for breath, he saw that he had been a long time under water; he was perceptibly farther down stream—nearer to safety. The soldiers had almost finished reloading; the metal ramrods flashed all at once in the sunshine as they were drawn from the barrels, turned in the air; and thrust into their sockets. The two sentinels fired again, independently and ineffectually.

The hunted man saw all this over his shoulder; he was now swimming vigorously with the current. His brain was as energetic as his arms and legs; he thought with the rapidity of lightning.

"The officer," he reasoned, "will not make that martinet's error a second time. It is as easy to dodge a volley as a single shot. He has probably already given the command to fire at will. God help me, I cannot dodge them all!"

An appalling plash within two yards of him, followed by a loud rushing sound, *diminuendo*,[2] which seemed to travel back through the air to the fort and died in an explosion which stirred the very river to its deeps! A rising sheet of water, which curved over him, fell down upon him, blinded him, strangled him! The cannon had taken a hand in the game. As he shook his head free from the commotion of the smitten water, he heard the deflected shot humming through the air ahead, and in an instant it was cracking and smashing the branches in the forest beyond.

"They will not do that again," he thought; "the next time they will use a charge of grape.[3] I must keep my eye upon the gun; the smoke will apprise me—the report arrives too late; it lags behind the missile. It is a good gun."

Suddenly he felt himself whirled round and round—spinning like a top. The water, the banks, the forest, the now distant bridge, fort and men—all were commingled and blurred. Objects were represented by their colors only; circular horizontal streaks of color—that was all he saw. He had been caught in a vortex and was being whirled on with a velocity of advance and gyration which made him giddy and sick. In a few moments he was flung upon the gravel at the foot of the left bank of the stream—the southern bank—and behind a projecting point which concealed him from his enemies. The sudden arrest of his motion, the abrasion of one of his hands on the gravel, restored him and he wept with delight. He dug his fingers into the sand, threw it over himself in handfuls and audibly blessed it. It looked like gold, like diamonds, rubies, emeralds; he could think of nothing beautiful which it did not resemble. The trees upon the bank were giant garden plants; he noted a definite order in their arrangement, inhaled the fragrance of their blooms. A strange, roseate light shone through the spaces among their trunks, and the wind made in their branches the music of æolian harps. He had no wish to perfect his escape, was content to remain in that enchanting spot until retaken.

A whizz and rattle of grapeshot among the branches high above his head roused him from his dream. The baffled cannoneer had fired him a random farewell. He sprang to his feet, rushed up the sloping bank, and plunged into the forest.

All that day he travelled, laying his course by the rounding sun. The forest seemed interminable; nowhere did he discover a break in it, not even a woodman's road. He had not known that he lived in so wild a region. There was something uncanny in the revelation.

2. A musical term for growing softer.
3. Grapeshot, a cluster of small pellets fired from a cannon.

By nightfall he was fatigued, footsore, famishing. The thought of his wife and children urged him on. At last he found a road which led him in what he knew to be the right direction. It was as wide and straight as a city street, yet it seemed untravelled. No fields bordered it, no dwelling anywhere. Not so much as the barking of a dog suggested human habitation. The black bodies of the great trees formed a straight wall on both sides, terminating on the horizon in a point, like a diagram in a lesson in perspective. Overhead, as he looked up through this rift in the wood, shone great golden stars looking unfamiliar and grouped in strange constellations. He was sure they were arranged in some order which had a secret and malign significance. The wood on either side was full of singular noises, among which—once, twice, and again—he distinctly heard whispers in an unknown tongue.

His neck was in pain, and, lifting his hand to it, he found it horribly swollen. He knew that it had a circle of black where the rope had bruised it. His eyes felt congested; he could no longer close them. His tongue was swollen with thirst; he relieved its fever by thrusting it forward from between his teeth into the cool air. How softly the turf had carpeted the untravelled avenue! He could no longer feel the roadway beneath his feet!

Doubtless, despite his suffering, he fell asleep while walking, for now he sees another scene—perhaps he has merely recovered from a delirium. He stands at the gate of his own home. All is as he left it, and all bright and beautiful in the morning sunshine. He must have travelled the entire night. As he pushes open the gate and passes up the wide white walk, he sees a flutter of female garments; his wife, looking fresh and cool and sweet, steps down from the verandah to meet him. At the bottom of the steps she stands waiting, with a smile of ineffable joy, an attitude of matchless grace and dignity. Ah, how beautiful she is! He springs forward with extended arms. As he is about to clasp her, he feels a stunning blow upon the back of the neck; a blinding white light blazes all about him, with a sound like the shock of a cannon—then all is darkness and silence!

Peyton Farquhar was dead; his body, with a broken neck, swung gently from side to side beneath the timbers of the Owl Creek bridge.

# GUY DE MAUPASSANT
## 1850–1893

Born Henri René Albert Guy de Maupassant, he grew up in Normandy, not far from Rouen, and went to school at the Rouen Lycée before entering government service. At the age of twenty he served in the Franco-Prussian War, and many of his finest stories came out of that experience. After the war he apprenticed himself to the older Flaubert. His greatest gifts were for the realistic short story, and he virtually perfected the form, producing nearly three hundred stories in a dozen years. Early in life he had contracted syphilis, for which there was no effective treatment at the time. In his forties he could no longer work, as the disease attacked his brain, ultimately reducing him to insanity before he died at the age of forty-three. His final condition is described in the story by Isaac Babel in this collection, called "Guy de Maupassant."

## The Diamond Necklace

She was one of those pretty, charming young ladies, born, as if through an error of destiny, into a family of clerks. She had no dowry, no hopes, no means of becoming known, appreciated, loved, and married by a man either rich or distinguished; and she allowed herself to marry a petty clerk in the office of the Board of Education.

She was simple, not being able to adorn herself; but she was unhappy, as one out of her class; for women belong to no caste, no race; their grace, their beauty, and their charm serving them in the place of birth and family. Their inborn finesse, their instinctive elegance, their suppleness of wit are their only aristocracy, making some daughters of the people the equal of great ladies.

She suffered incessantly, feeling herself born for all delicacies and luxuries. She suffered from the poverty of her apartment, the shabby walls, the worn chairs, and the faded stuffs. All these things, which another woman of her station would not have noticed, tortured and angered her. The sight of the little Breton, who made this humble home, awoke in her sad regrets and desperate dreams. She thought of quiet antechambers, with their Oriental hangings, lighted by high, bronze torches, and of the two great footmen in short trousers who sleep in the large armchairs, made sleepy by the heavy air from the heating apparatus. She thought of large drawing-rooms, hung in old silks, of graceful pieces of furniture carrying bric-à-brac of inestimable value, and of the little perfumed coquettish apartments, made for five o'clock chats with most intimate friends, men known and sought after, whose attention all women envied and desired.

When she seated herself for dinner, before the round table where the tablecloth had been used three days, opposite her husband who uncovered the tureen with a delighted air, saying: "Oh! the good potpie! I know nothing better than that—" she would think of the elegant dinners, of the shining silver, of the tapestries peopling the walls with ancient personages and rare birds in the midst of fairy forests; she thought of the exquisite food served on marvelous dishes, of the whispered gallantries, listened to with the smile of the sphinx, while eating the rose-colored flesh of the trout or a chicken's wing.

She had neither frocks nor jewels, nothing. And she loved only those things. She felt that she was made for them. She had such a desire to please, to be sought after, to be clever, and courted.

She had a rich friend, a schoolmate at the convent, whom she did not like to visit, she suffered so much when she returned. And she wept for whole days from chagrin, from regret, from despair, and disappointment.

One evening her husband returned elated bearing in his hand a large envelope.

"Here," he said, "here is something for you."

She quickly tore open the wrapper and drew out a printed card on which were inscribed these words:

> The Minister of Public Instruction and Madame George Ramponneau ask the honor of Mr. and Mrs. Loisel's company Monday evening, January 18, at the Minister's residence.

Instead of being delighted, as her husband had hoped, she threw the invitation spitefully upon the table murmuring:

"What do you suppose I want with that?"

"But, my dearie, I thought it would make you happy. You never go out, and this is an occasion, and a fine one! I had a great deal of trouble to get it. Everybody wishes one, and it is very select; not many are given to employees. You will see the whole official world there."

She looked at him with an irritated eye and declared impatiently·

"What do you suppose I have to wear to such a thing as that?"

He had not thought of that; he stammered:

"Why, the dress you wear when we go to the theater. It seems very pretty to me—"

He was silent, stupefied, in dismay, at the sight of his wife weeping. Two great tears fell slowly from the corners of her eyes toward the corners of her mouth; he stammered:

"What is the matter? What is the matter?"

By a violent effort, she had controlled her vexation and responded in a calm voice, wiping her moist cheeks:

"Nothing. Only I have no dress and consequently I cannot go to this affair. Give your card to some colleague whose wife is better fitted out than I."

He was grieved, but answered:

"Let us see, Matilda. How much would a suitable costume cost, something that would serve for other occasions, something very simple?"

She reflected for some seconds, making estimates and thinking of a sum that she could ask for without bringing with it an immediate refusal and a frightened exclamation from the economical clerk.

Finally she said, in a hesitating voice:

"I cannot tell exactly, but it seems to me that four hundred francs ought to cover it."

He turned a little pale, for he had saved just this sum to buy a gun that he might be able to join some hunting parties the next summer, on the plains at Nanterre, with some friends who went to shoot larks up there on Sunday. Nevertheless, he answered:

"Very well. I will give you four hundred francs. But try to have a pretty dress."

The day of the ball approached and Mme. Loisel seemed sad, disturbed, anxious. Nevertheless, her dress was nearly ready. Her husband said to her one evening:

"What is the matter with you? You have acted strangely for two or three days."

And she responded: "I am vexed not to have a jewel, not one stone, nothing to adorn myself with. I shall have such a poverty-laden look. I would prefer not to go to this party."

He replied: "You can wear some natural flowers. At this season they look very *chic*. For ten francs you can have two or three magnificent roses."

She was not convinced. "No," she replied, "there is nothing more humiliating than to have a shabby air in the midst of rich women."

Then her husband cried out: "How stupid we are! Go and find your friend Mrs. Forestier and ask her to lend you her jewels. You are well enough acquainted with her to do this."

She uttered a cry of joy: "It is true!" she said. "I had not thought of that."

The next day she took herself to her friend's house and related her story of distress. Mrs. Forestier went to her closet with the glass doors, took out a large jewel-case, brought it, opened it, and said: "Choose, my dear."

She saw at first some bracelets, then a collar of pearls, then a

Venetian cross of gold and jewels and of admirable workmanship. She tried the jewels before the glass, hesitated, but could neither decide to take them nor leave them. Then she asked:

"Have you nothing more?"

"Why, yes. Look for yourself. I do not know what will please you."

Suddenly she discovered, in a black satin box, a superb necklace of diamonds, and her heart beat fast with an immoderate desire. Her hands trembled as she took them up. She placed them about her throat against her dress, and remained in ecstasy before them. Then she asked, in a hesitating voice, full of anxiety:

"Could you lend me this? Only this?"

"Why, yes, certainly."

She fell upon the neck of her friend, embraced her with passion, then went away with her treasure.

The day of the ball arrived. Mme. Loisel was a great success. She was the prettiest of all, elegant, gracious, smiling, and full of joy. All the men noticed her, asked her name, and wanted to be presented. All the members of the Cabinet wished to waltz with her. The Minister of Education paid her some attention.

She danced with enthusiasm, with passion, intoxicated with pleasure, thinking of nothing, in the triumph of her beauty, in the glory of her success, in a kind of cloud of happiness that came of all this homage, and all this admiration, of all these awakened desires, and this victory so complete and sweet to the heart of woman.

She went home toward four o'clock in the morning. Her husband had been half asleep in one of the little salons since midnight, with three other gentlemen whose wives were enjoying themselves very much.

He threw around her shoulders the wraps they had carried for the coming home, modest garments of everyday wear, whose poverty clashed with the elegance of the ball costume. She felt this and wished to hurry away in order not to be noticed by the other women who were wrapping themselves in rich furs.

Loisel retained her: "Wait," said he. "You will catch cold out there. I am going to call a cab."

But she would not listen and descended the steps rapidly. When they were in the street, they found no carriage; and they began to seek for one, hailing the coachmen whom they saw at a distance.

They walked along toward the Seine, hopeless and shivering. Finally they found on the dock one of those old, noctural *coupés* that one sees in Paris after nightfall, as if they were ashamed of their misery by day.

It took them as far as their door in Martyr street, and they went wearily up to their apartment. It was all over for her. And on his part, he remembered that he would have to be at the office by ten o'clock.

She removed the wraps from her shoulders before the glass, for a final view of herself in her glory. Suddenly she uttered a cry. Her necklace was not around her neck.

Her husband, already half undressed, asked: "What is the matter?"

She turned toward him excitedly:

"I have—I have—I no longer have Mrs. Forestier's necklace."

He arose in dismay: "What! How is that? It is not possible."

And they looked in the folds of the dress, in the folds of the mantle, in the pockets, everywhere. They could not find it.

He asked: "You are sure you still had it when we left the house?"

"Yes, I felt it in the vestibule as we came out."

"But if you had lost it in the street, we should have heard it fall. It must be in the cab."

"Yes. It is probable. Did you take the number?"

"No. And you, did you notice what it was?"

"No."

They looked at each other utterly cast down. Finally, Loisel dressed himself again.

"I am going," said he, "over the track where we went on foot, to see if I can find it."

And he went. She remained in her evening gown, not having the force to go to bed, stretched upon a chair, without ambition or thoughts.

Toward seven o'clock her husband returned. He had found nothing.

He went to the police and to the cab offices, and put an advertisement in the newspapers, offering a reward; he did everything that afforded them a suspicion of hope.

She waited all day in a state of bewilderment before this frightful disaster. Loisel returned at evening with his face harrowed and pale; and had discovered nothing.

"It will be necessary," said he, "to write to your friend that you have broken the clasp of the necklace and that you will have it repaired. That will give us time to turn around."

She wrote as he dictated.

At the end of a week, they had lost all hope. And Loisel, older by five years, declared:

"We must take measures to replace this jewel."

The next day they took the box which had inclosed it, to the jeweler whose name was on the inside. He consulted his books:

"It is not I, Madame," said he, "who sold this necklace; I only furnished the casket."

Then they went from jeweler to jeweler seeking a necklace like the other one, consulting their memories, and ill, both of them, with chagrin and anxiety.

In a shop of the Palais-Royal, they found a chaplet of diamonds which seemed to them exactly like the one they had lost. It was valued at forty thousand francs. They could get it for thirty-six thousand.

They begged the jeweler not to sell it for three days. And they made an arrangement by which they might return it for thirty-four thousand francs if they found the other one before the end of February.

Loisel possessed eighteen thousand francs which his father had left him. He borrowed the rest.

He borrowed it, asking for a thousand francs of one, five hundred of another, five louis of this one, and three louis of that one. He gave notes, made ruinous promises, took money of usurers and the whole race of lenders. He compromised his whole existence, in fact, risked his signature, without even knowing whether he could make it good or not, and, harassed by anxiety for the future, by the black misery which surrounded him, and by the prospect of all physical privations and moral torture, he went to get the new necklace, depositing on the merchant's counter thirty-six thousand francs.

When Mrs. Loisel took back the jewels to Mrs. Forestier, the latter said to her in a frigid tone:

"You should have returned them to me sooner, for I might have needed them."

She did open the jewel-box as her friend feared she would. If she should perceive the substitution, what would she think? What should she say? Would she take her for a robber?

Mrs. Loisel now knew the horrible life of necessity. She did her part, however, completely heroically. It was necessary to pay this frightful debt. She would pay it. They sent away the maid; they changed their lodgings; they rented some rooms under a mansard roof.

She learned the heavy cares of a household, the odious work of a kitchen. She washed the dishes, using her rosy nails upon the greasy pots and the bottoms of the stewpans. She washed the soiled linen, the chemises and dishcloths, which she hung on the line to dry; she took down the refuse to the street each morning and brought up the water, stopping at each landing to breathe. And, clothed like a woman of the people she went to the grocer's, the butcher's, and the fruiterer's, with her basket on her arm, shopping, haggling to the last sou her miserable money.

Every month it was necessary to renew some notes, thus obtaining time, and to pay others.

The husband worked evenings, putting the books of some merchants in order, and nights he often did copying at five sous a page.

And this life lasted for ten years.

At the end of ten years, they had restored all, all, with interest of the usurer, and accumulated interest besides.

Mrs. Loisel seemed old now. She had become a strong, hard woman, the crude woman of the poor household. Her hair badly dressed, her skirts awry, her hands red, she spoke in a loud tone, and washed the floors with large pails of water. But sometimes, when her husband was at the office, she would seat herself before the window and think of that evening party of former times, of that ball where she was so beautiful and so flattered.

How would it have been if she had not lost that necklace? Who knows? Who knows? How singular is life, and how full of changes! How small a thing will ruin or save one!

One Sunday, as she was taking a walk in the Champs-Elysées to rid herself of the cares of the week, she suddenly perceived a woman walking with a child. It was Mrs. Forestier, still young, still pretty, still attractive. Mrs. Loisel was affected. Should she speak to her? Yes, certainly. And now that she had paid, she would tell her all. Why not?

She approached her. "Good morning, Jeanne."

Her friend did not recognize her and was astonished to be so familiarly addressed by this common personage. She stammered:

"But, Madame—I do not know— You must be mistaken—"

"No, I am Matilda Loisel."

Her friend uttered a cry of astonishment: "Oh! my poor Matilda! How you have changed—"

"Yes, I have had some hard days since I saw you; and some miserable ones—and all because of you—"

"Because of me? How is that?"

"You recall the diamond necklace that you loaned me to wear to the Commissioner's ball?"

"Yes, very well."

"Well, I lost it."

"How is that, since you returned it to me?"

"I returned another to you exactly like it. And it has taken us ten years to pay for it. You can understand that it was not easy for us who have nothing. But it is finished and I am decently content."

Madame Forestier stopped short. She said:

"You say that you bought a diamond necklace to replace mine?"

"Yes. You did not perceive it then? They were just alike."

And she smiled with a proud and simple joy. Madame Forestier was touched and took both her hands as she replied:

"Oh! my poor Matilda! Mine were false. They were not worth over five hundred francs!"

# ANTON CHEKHOV
## 1860–1904

Born in Taganrog, Russia, Chekhov was the son of a tradesman and grandson of a serf (peasant slave). After attending a local school, he went in 1879 to study medicine at the University of Moscow, where he supported himself by writing comic sketches for newspapers and magazines. After taking his medical degree in 1884, he began writing more seriously, publishing both stories and plays. When he married a young actress in 1901, he was already dying of tuberculosis. He moved to Yalta in the south and continued to write, finishing his dramatic masterpiece *The Cherry Orchard* in the year of his death. His hundreds of short stories made him, along with Maupassant, one of the two masters of the realistic short story in the nineteenth century.

# Heartache

"To whom shall I tell my sorrow?"[1]

Evening twilight. Large flakes of wet snow are circling lazily about the street lamps which have just been lighted, settling in a thin soft layer on roofs, horses' backs, peoples' shoulders, caps. Iona Potapov, the cabby, is all white like a ghost. As hunched as a living body can be, he sits on the box without stirring. If a whole snowdrift were to fall on him, even then, perhaps he would not find it necessary to shake it off. His nag, too, is white and motionless. Her immobility, the angularity of her shape, and the sticklike straightness of her legs make her look like a penny gingerbread horse. She is probably lost in thought. Anyone who has been torn away from the plow, from the familiar gray scenes, and cast into this whirlpool full of monstrous lights, of ceaseless uproar and hurrying people, cannot help thinking.

Iona and his nag have not budged for a long time. They had driven out of the yard before dinnertime and haven't had a single fare yet. But now evening dusk is descending upon the city. The pale light of the street lamps changes to a vivid color and the bustle of the street grows louder.

"Sleigh to the Vyborg District!" Iona hears. "Sleigh!"

Iona starts, and through his snow-plastered eyelashes sees an officer in a military overcoat with a hood.

"To the Vyborg District!" repeats the officer. "Are you asleep, eh? To the Vyborg District!"

1. From an old Russian song comparable to a Negro Spiritual.

As a sign of assent Iona gives a tug at the reins, which sends layers of snow flying from the horse's back and from his own shoulders. The officer gets into the sleigh. The driver clucks to the horse, cranes his neck like a swan, rises in his seat and, more from habit than necessity, flourishes his whip. The nag, too, stretches her neck, crooks her sticklike legs and irresolutely sets off.

"Where are you barging in, damn you?" Iona is promptly assailed by shouts from the massive dark wavering to and fro before him. "Where the devil are you going? Keep to the right!"

"Don't you know how to drive? Keep to the right," says the officer with vexation.

A coachman driving a private carriage swears at him; a pedestrian who was crossing the street and brushed against the nag's nose with his shoulder, looks at him angrily and shakes the snow off his sleeve. Iona fidgets on the box as if sitting on needles and pins, thrusts out his elbows and rolls his eyes like a madman, as though he did not know where he was or why he was there.

"What rascals they all are," the officer jokes. "They are doing their best to knock into you or be trampled by the horse. It's a conspiracy."

Iona looks at his fare and moves his lips. He wants to say something, but the only sound that comes out is a wheeze.

"What is it?" asks the officer.

Iona twists his mouth into a smile, strains his throat and croaks hoarsely: "My son, sir . . . er, my son died this week."

"H'm, what did he die of?"

Iona turns his whole body around to his fare and says, "Who can tell? It must have been a fever. He lay in the hospital only three days and then he died. . . . It is God's will."

"Get over, you devil!" comes out of the dark. "Have you gone blind, you old dog? Keep your eyes peeled!"

"Go on, go on," says the officer. "We shan't get there until tomorrow at this rate. Give her the whip!"

The driver cranes his neck again, rises in his seat, and with heavy grace swings his whip. Then he looks around at the officer several times, but the latter keeps his eyes closed and is apparently indisposed to listen. Letting his fare off in the Vyborg District, Iona stops by a teahouse and again sits motionless and hunched on the box. Again the wet snow paints him and his nag white. One hour passes, another . . .

Three young men, two tall and lanky, one short and hunchbacked, come along swearing at each other and loudly pound the pavement with their galoshes.

"Cabby, to the Police Bridge!" the hunchback shouts in a cracked voice. "The three of us . . . twenty kopecks!"

Iona tugs at the reins and clucks to his horse. Twenty kopecks is not fair, but his mind is not on that. Whether it is a ruble or five kopecks, it is all one to him now, so long as he has a fare. . . . The three young men, jostling each other and using foul language, go up to the sleigh and all three try to sit down at once. They start arguing about which two are to sit and who shall be the one to stand. After a long ill-tempered and abusive altercation, they decide that the hunchback must stand up because he is the shortest.

"Well, get going," says the hunchback in his cracked voice, taking up his station and breathing down Iona's neck. "On your way! What a cap you've got, brother! You won't find a worse one in all Petersburg—"

"Hee, hee . . . hee, hee . . ." Iona giggles, "as you say—"

"Well, then, 'as you say,' drive on. Are you going to crawl like this all the way, eh? D'you want to get it in the neck?"

"My head is splitting," says one of the tall ones. "At the Dukmasovs' yesterday, Vaska and I killed four bottles of cognac between us."

"I don't get it, why lie?" says the other tall one angrily. "He is lying like a trouper."

"Strike me dead, it's the truth!"

"It is about as true as that a louse sneezes."

"Hee, hee," giggles Iona. "The gentlemen are feeling good!"

"Faugh, the devil take you!" cries the hunchback indignantly. "Will you get a move on, you old pest, or won't you? Is that the way to drive? Give her a crack of the whip! Giddap, devil! Giddap! Let her feel it!"

Iona feels the hunchback's wriggling body and quivering voice behind his back. He hears abuse addressed to him, sees people, and the feeling of loneliness begins little by little to lift from his heart. The hunchback swears till he chokes on an elaborate three-decker oath and is overcome by cough. The tall youths begin discussing a certain Nadezhda Petrovna. Iona looks round at them. When at last there is a lull in the conversation for which he has been waiting, he turns around and says: "This week . . . er . . . my son died."

"We shall all die," says the hunchback, with a sigh wiping his lips after his coughing fit. "Come, drive on, drive on. Gentlemen, I simply cannot stand this pace! When will he get us there?"

"Well, you give him a little encouragement. Biff him in the neck!"

"Do you hear, you old pest? I'll give it to you in the neck. If one stands on ceremony with fellows like you, one may as well walk. Do you hear, you old serpent? Or don't you give a damn what we say?"

And Iona hears rather than feels the thud of a blow on his neck.

"Hee, hee," he laughs. "The gentlemen are feeling good. God give you health!"

"Cabby, are you married?" asks one of the tall ones.

"Me? Hee, hee! The gentlemen are feeling good. The only wife for

me now is the damp earth . . . Hee, haw, haw! The grave, that is! . . .
Here my son is dead and me alive . . . It is a queer thing, death comes
in at the wrong door . . . It don't come for me, it comes for my
son. . . ."

And Iona turns round to tell them how his son died, but at that point
the hunchback gives a sigh of relief and announces that, thank God,
they have arrived at last. Having received his twenty kopecks, for a
long while Iona stares after the revelers, who disappear into a dark
entrance. Again he is alone and once more silence envelops him. The
grief which has been allayed for a brief space comes back again and
wrenches his heart more cruelly than ever. There is a look of anxiety
and torment in Iona's eyes as they wander restlessly over the crowds
moving to and fro on both sides of the street. Isn't there someone
among those thousands who will listen to him? But the crowds hurry
past, heedless of him and his grief. His grief is immense, boundless. If
his heart were to burst and his grief to pour out, it seems that it would
flood the whole world, and yet no one sees it. It has found a place for
itself in such an insignificant shell that no one can see it in broad
daylight.

Iona notices a doorkeeper with a bag and makes up his mind to
speak to him.

"What time will it be, friend?" he asks.

"Past nine. What have you stopped here for? On your way!"

Iona drives a few steps away, hunches up and surrenders himself to
his grief. He feels it is useless to turn to people. But before five minutes
are over, he draws himself up, shakes his head as though stabbed by a
sharp pain and tugs at the reins . . . He can bear it no longer.

"Back to the yard!" he thinks. "To the yard!"

And his nag, as though she knew his thoughts, starts out at a trot.
An hour and a half later, Iona is sitting beside a large dirty stove. On
the stove, on the floor, on benches are men snoring. The air is stuffy
and foul. Iona looks at the sleeping figures, scratches himself and
regrets that he has come home so early.

"I haven't earned enough to pay for the oats," he reflects. "That's
what's wrong with me. A man that knows his job . . . who has enough
to eat and has enough for his horse don't need to fret."

In one of the corners a young driver gets up, hawks sleepily and
reaches for the water bucket.

"Thirsty?" Iona asks him.

"Guess so."

"H'm, may it do you good, but my son is dead, brother . . . did you
hear? This week in the hospital. . . . What a business!"

Iona looks to see the effect of his words, but he notices none. The
young man has drawn his cover over his head and is already asleep.

The old man sighs and scratches himself. Just as the young man was thirsty for water so he thirsts for talk. It will soon be a week since his son died and he hasn't talked to anybody about him properly. He ought to be able to talk about it, taking his time, sensibly. He ought to tell how his son was taken ill, how he suffered, what he said before he died, how he died. . . . He ought to describe the funeral, and how he went to the hospital to fetch his son's clothes. His daughter Anisya is still in the country. . . . And he would like to talk about her, too. Yes, he has plenty to talk about now. And his listener should gasp and moan and keen. . . . It would be even better to talk to women. Though they are foolish, two words will make them blubber.

"I must go out and have a look at the horse," Iona thinks. "There will be time enough for sleep. You will have enough sleep, no fear. . . ."

He gets dressed and goes into the stable where his horse is standing. He thinks about oats, hay, the weather. When he is alone, he dares not think of his son. It is possible to talk about him with someone, but to think of him when one is alone, to evoke his image is unbearably painful.

"You chewing?" Iona asks his mare seeing her shining eyes. "There, chew away, chew away. . . . If we haven't earned enough for oats, we'll eat hay. . . . Yes. . . . I've grown too old to drive. My son had ought to be driving, not me. . . . He was a real cabby. . . . He had ought to have lived. . . ."

Iona is silent for a space and then goes on: "That's how it is, old girl. . . . Kuzma Ionych is gone. . . . Departed this life. . . . He went and died to no purpose. . . . Now let's say you had a little colt, and you were that little colt's own mother. And suddenly, let's say, that same little colt departed this life. . . . You'd be sorry, wouldn't you?"

The nag chews, listens and breathes on her master's hands. Iona is carried away and tells her everything.


# SARA JEANNETTE DUNCAN

## 1861–1922

Born in Brantford, Canada West (Ontario), Duncan attended Toronto Normal School but soon abandoned teaching for a career as a journalist. She worked as editorial writer and book reviewer for the Washington *Post* (1885–6), and as a columnist for the Toronto *Globe* (1886–7) and the *Montreal Star* (1887–8). Ambitious to become a novelist, she set off in 1888 with a fellow journalist on a world tour. In India she met and married Everard Cotes, a museum entomologist, and lived with him in Calcutta and Simla (then the summer administrative capital of

India) for most of the next three decades. Her first book, *A Social Departure: How Orthodocia and I Went Round the World by Ourselves*, was published in London in 1890. Although she published twenty-two books, her reputation today rests on her novel *The Imperialist* (1904) and her short-story collection *The Pool in the Desert* (1903). The following is the title story from that volume.

## The Pool In The Desert

I knew Anna Chichele and Judy Harbottle so well, and they figured so vividly at one time against the rather empty landscape of life in a frontier station, that my affection for one of them used to seem little more, or less, than a variant upon my affection for the other. That recollection, however, bears examination badly; Judy was much the better sort, and it is Judy's part in it that draws me into telling the story. Conveying Judy is what I tremble at: her part was simple. Looking back—and not so very far—her part has the relief of high comedy with the proximity of tears; but looking closely, I find that it is mostly Judy, and what she did is entirely second, in my untarnished picture, to what she was. Still I do not think I can dissuade myself from putting it down.

They would, of course, inevitably have found each other sooner or later, Mrs. Harbottle and Mrs. Chichele, but it was I who actually introduced them; my palmy veranda in Rawul Pindi; where the teacups used to assemble, was the scene of it. I presided behind my samovar over the early formalities that were almost at once to drop from their friendship, like the sheath of some bursting flower. I deliberately brought them together, so the birth was not accidental, and my interest in it quite legitimately maternal. We always had tea in the veranda in Rawul Pindi, the drawing-room was painted blue, blue for thirty feet up to the whitewashed cotton ceiling; nothing of any value in the way of a human relation, I am sure, could have originated there. The veranda was spacious and open, their mutual observation had room and freedom; I watched it to and fro. I had not long to wait for my reward; the beautiful candor I expected between them was not ten minutes in coming. For the sake of it I had taken some trouble, but when I perceived it revealing I went and sat down beside Judy's husband, Robert Harbottle, and talked about Pharaoh's split hoof. It was only fair; and when next day I got their impressions of one another, I felt single-minded and deserving.

I knew it would be a satisfactory sort of thing to do, but perhaps it was rather more for Judy's sake than for Anna's that I did it. Mrs. Harbottle was only twenty-seven then and Robert a major, but he had brought her to India out of an episode too color-flushed to tone with English hedges; their marriage had come, in short, of his divorce, and as too natural a consequence. In India it is well known that the eye becomes accustomed to primitive pigments and high lights; the aesthetic consideration, if nothing else, demanded Robert's exchange. He was lucky to get a Piffer* regiment, and the Twelfth were lucky to get him; we were all lucky, I thought, to get Judy. It was an opinion, of course, a good deal challenged, even in Rawul Pindi, where it was thought, especially in the beginning, that acquiescence was the most the Harbottles could hope for. That is not enough in India; cordiality is the common right. I could not have Judy preserving her atmosphere at our tea-parties and gymkhanas. Not that there were two minds among us about "the case;" it was a preposterous case, sentimentally undignified, from some points of view deplorable. I chose to reserve my point of view, from which I saw it, on Judy's behalf, merely quixotic, preferring on Robert's just to close my eyes. There is no doubt that his first wife was odious to a degree which it is simply pleasanter not to recount, but her malignity must almost have amounted to a sense of humour. Her detestation of her cousin Judy Thynne dated much further back than Robert's attachment. That began in Paris, where Judy, a young widow, was developing a real vein at Julian's. I am entirely convinced that there was nothing, as people say, "in it," Judy had not a thought at that time that was not based on Chinese white and permeated with good-fellowship; but there was a good deal of it, and no doubt the turgid imagination of the first Mrs. Harbottle dealt with it honestly enough. At all events, she saw her opportunity, and the depths of her indifference to Robert bubbled up venomously into the suit. That it was undefended was the senseless mystery; decency ordained that he and Judy should have made a fight, even in the hope that it would be a losing one. The reason it had to be a losing one—the reason so immensely criticized—was that the petitioning lady obstinately refused to bring her action against any other set of circumstances than those to which, I have no doubt, Judy contributed every indiscretion. It is hard to imagine Robert Harbottle refusing her any sort of justification that the law demands short of beating her, but her malice would accept nothing of which the account did not go for final settlement to Judy Thynne. If her husband wanted his liberty, he should have it, she declared, at that price and no other. Major Harbottle did indeed deeply long for his liberty, and his interesting friend, Mrs. Thynne, had, one can only say, the most vivid commiseration for his bondage. Whatever chance they had of winning, to win would be, for the end they had at heart, to lose, so they simply abstained, as it were, from comment upon the detestable procedure which terminated in the rule absolute. I have often wondered whether the whole business would not have been more defensible if there had been on Judy's part any emotional spring for the leap they made. I offer my conviction that there was none, that she was only extravagantly affected by the ideals of the Quarter—it is a transporting atmosphere—and held a view of comradeship which permitted the reversal of the modern situation filled by a blameless correspondent. Robert, of course, was tremendously in love with her; but my theory is that she married him as the logical outcome of her sacrifice and by no means the smallest part of it.

It was all quite unimaginable, as so many things are, but the upshot of it brought Judy to Rawul Pindi, as I have said, where I for one thought her mistake insignificant compared with her value. It would have been great, her value, anywhere; in the middle of the Punjab it was incalculable. To explain why would be to explain British India, but I hope it will appear; and I am quite willing, remember, to take the responsibility if it does not.

Somers Chichele, Anna's son, it is absurd to think, must have been about fifteen then, reflecting at Winchester with the other "men" upon the comparative merits of tinned sardines and jam roll, and whether a packet of real Egyptians was not worth the sacrifice of either. His father was colonel of the Twelfth; his mother was still charming. It was the year before Dick Forsyth came down from the neighborhood of Sheikhbudin with a brevet and a good deal of personal damage. I mention him because he proved Anna's charm in the only conclusive way before the eyes of us all; and the station, I remember, was edified to observe that if Mrs. Chichele came out of the matter "straight"—one relapses so easily into the simple definitions of those parts—which she undoubtedly did, she owed it in no small degree to Judy Harbottle. This one feels to be hardly a legitimate reference, but it is something tangible to lay hold upon in trying to describe the web of volitions which began to weave itself between the two that afternoon on my veranda and which afterward became so strong a bond. I was delighted with the thing; its simplicity and sincerity stood out among our conventional little compromises at friendship like an ideal. She and Judy had the assurance of one another; they made upon one another the finest and often the most unconscionable demands. One met them walking at odd hours in queer places, of which I imagine they were not much aware. They would turn deliberately off the Maidan and away from the bandstand to be rid of our irrelevant bows; they did their duty by the rest of us, but the most egregious among us, the Deputy-Commissioner for selection, could see that he hardly counted. I thought I understood, but that may have been my fatuity; certainly when their husbands inquired what on earth they had been talking of, it usually transpired that they had found an infinite amount to say about nothing. It was a little worrying to hear Colonel Chichele and Major Harbottle describe their wives as "pals," but the fact could not be denied, and after all we were in the Punjab. They were pals too, but the terms were different.

People discussed it according to their lights, and girls said in pretty wonderment that Mrs. Harbottle and Mrs. Chichele were like men, they never kissed each other. I think Judy prescribed these conditions. Anna was far more a person who did as the world told her. But it was a poor negation to describe all that they never did; there was no common little convention of attachment that did not seem to be tacitly omitted between them. I hope one did not too cynically observe that they offered these to their husbands instead; the redeeming observation was their husbands' complete satisfaction. This they maintained to the end. In the natural order of things Robert Harbottle should have paid heavily for interfering as he did in Paris between a woman and what she was entitled to live for. As a matter of fact he never paid anything at all; I doubt whether he ever knew himself a debtor. Judy kept her temperament under like a current and swam with the tides of the surface, taking refreshing dips only now and then which one traced in her eyes and her hair when she and Robert came back from leave. That sort of thing is lost in the sands of India, but it makes an oasis as it travels, and it sometimes seemed to me a curious pity that she and Anna should sit in the shade of it together, while Robert and Peter Chichele, their titular companions, blundered on in the desert. But after all, if you are born blind—and the men were both immensely liked, and the shooting was good.

Ten years later Somers joined. The Twelfth were at Peshawur. Robert Harbottle was Lieutenant-Colonel by that time and had the regiment. Distinction had incrusted, in the Indian way, upon Peter Chichele, its former colonel; he was General Commanding the District and K.C.B. So we were all still together in Peshawur. It was great luck for the Chicheles, Sir Peter's having the district, though his father's old regiment would have made it pleasant enough for the boy in any case. He came to us, I mean, of course, to two or three of us, with the interest that hangs about a victim of circumstances; we understood that he wasn't a "born soldier." Anna had told me on the contrary that he was a sacrifice to family tradition made inevitable by the General's unfortunate investments. Bellona's bridegroom was not a role he fancied, though he would make a kind of compromise as best man; he would agree, she said, to be a war correspondent and write picturesque specials for the London halfpenny press. There was the humor of the poor boy's despair in it, but she conveyed it, I remember, in exactly the same tone with which she had said to me years before that he wanted to drive a milk-cart. She carried quite her half of the family tradition, though she could talk of sacrifice and make her eyes wistful, contemplating for Somers the limitations of the drill-book and the camp of exercise, proclaiming and insisting upon what she would have done if she could only have chosen for him. Anna Chichele saw things that way. With more than a passable sense of all that was involved, if she could have made her son an artist in life or a commander-in-chief, if she could have given him the seeing eye or the Order of the Star of India, she would not have hesitated for an instant. Judy, with her single mind, cried out, almost at sight of him, upon them both, I mean both Anna and Sir Peter. Not that the boy carried his condemnation badly, or even obviously; I venture that no one noticed it in the mess; but it was naturally plain to those of us who were under the same. He had put in his two years with a British regiment at Meerut—they nurse subalterns that way for the Indian army—and his eyes no longer played with the tinsel vision of India; they looked instead into the arid stretch beyond. This preoccupation conveyed to the Surgeon-Major's wife the suggestion that Mr. Chichele was the victim of a hopeless attachment. Mrs. Harbottle made no such mistake; she saw simply, I imagine, the beginnings of her own hunger and thirst in him, looking back as she told us across a decade of dusty sunsets to remember them. The decade was there, close to the memory of all of us; we put, from Judy herself downward, an absurd amount of confidence in it.

She looked so well the night she met him. It was English mail day; she depended a great deal upon her letters, and I suppose somebody had written her a word that brought her that happy, still excitement that is the inner mystery of words. He went straight to her with some speech about his mother having given him leave, and for twenty minutes she patronized him on a sofa as his mother would not have dreamed of doing.

Anna Chichele, from the other side of the room, smiled on the pair.

"I depend on you and Judy to be good to him while we are away," she said. She and Sir Peter were going on leave at the end of the week to Scotland, as usual, for the shooting.

Following her glance I felt incapable of the proportion she assigned me. "I will see after his socks with pleasure," I said. "I think, don't you, we may leave the rest to Judy?"

Her eyes remained upon the boy, and I saw the passion rise in them, at which I turned mine elsewhere. Who can look unperturbed upon such a privacy of nature as that?

"Poor old Judy!" she went on. "She never would be bothered with him in all his dear hobble-dehoy time; she resented his claims, the unreasonable creature, used to limit me to three anecdotes a week; and now she has him on her hands, if you like. See the pretty air of deference in the way he listens to her! He has nice manners, the villain, if he is a Chichele!"

"Oh, you have improved Sir Peter's," I said kindly.

"I do hope Judy will think him worth while. I can't quite expect that he will be up to her, bless him, she is so much cleverer, isn't she, than any of us? But if she will just be herself with him it will make such a difference."

The other two crossed the room to us at that, and Judy gaily made Somers over to his mother, trailing off to find Robert in the billiard-room.

"Well, what has Mrs. Harbottle been telling you?" Anna asked him.

The young man's eye followed Judy, his hand went musingly to his moustache.

"She was telling me," he said, "that people in India were sepulchers of themselves, but that now and then one came who could roll away another's stone."

"It sounds promising," said Lady Chichele to me.

"It sounds cryptic," I laughed to Somers, but I saw that he had the key.

I can not say that I attended diligently to Mr. Chichele's socks, but the part corresponding was freely assigned me. After his people went I saw him often. He pretended to find qualities in my tea, implied that he found them in my talk. As a matter of fact it was my inquiring attitude that he loved, the knowledge that there was no detail that he could give me about himself, his impressions and experiences, that was unlikely to interest me. I would not for the world imply that he was egotistical or complacent, absolutely the reverse, but he possessed an articulate soul which found its happiness in expression, and I liked to listen. I feel that these are complicated words to explain a very simple relation, and I pause to wonder what is left to me if I wished to describe his commerce with Mrs. Harbottle. Luckily there is an alternative; one needn't do it. I wish I had somewhere on paper Judy's own account of it at this period, however. It is a thing she would have enjoyed writing and more enjoyed communicating, at this period.

There was a grave reticence in his talk about her which amused me in the beginning. Mrs. Harbottle had been for ten years important enough to us all, but her serious significance, the light and the beauty in her, had plainly been reserved for the discovery of this sensitive and intelligent person not very long from Sandhurst and exactly twenty-six. I was barely allowed a familiar reference, and anything approaching a flippancy was met with penetrating silence. I was almost rebuked for lightly suggesting that she must occasionally find herself bored in Peshawur.

"I think not anywhere," said Mr. Chichele; "Mrs. Harbottle is one of the few people who sound the privilege of living."

This to me, who had counted Mrs. Harbottle's yawns on so many occasions! It became presently necessary to be careful, tactful, in one's implications about Mrs. Harbottle, and to recognize a certain distinction in the fact that one was the only person with whom Mr. Chichele discussed her at all.

The day came when we talked of Robert; it was bound to come in the progress of any understanding and affectionate colloquy which had his wife for inspiration. I was familiar, of course, with Somers's opinion that the Colonel was an awfully good sort; that had been among the preliminaries and become understood as the base of all references. And I liked Robert Harbottle very well myself. When his adjutant called him a born leader of men, however, I felt compelled to look at the statement consideringly.

"In a tight place," I said—dear me, what expressions had the freedom of our little frontier drawing-rooms!—"I would as soon depend on him as on anybody. But as for leadership—"

"He is such a good fellow that nobody here does justice to his soldierly qualities," said Mr. Chichele, "except Mrs. Harbottle."

"Has she been telling you about them?" I inquired.

"Well," he hesitated, "she told me about the Mulla Nulla affair. She is rather proud of that. Any woman would be."

"Poor dear Judy!" I mused.

Somers said nothing, but looked at me, removing his cigarette, as if my words would be the better of explanation.

"She has taken refuge in them—in Bob Harbottle's soldierly qualities—ever since she married him," I continued.

"Taken refuge," he repeated, coldly, but at my uncompromising glance his eyes fell.

"Well?" I said.

"You mean—"

"Oh, I mean what I say," I laughed. "Your cigarette has gone out— have another."

"I think her devotion to him splendid."

"Quite splendid. Have you seen the things he brought her from the Simla Art Exhibition? He said they were nice bits of color, and she has hung them in the drawing-room, where she will have to look at them every day. Let us admire her—dear Judy."

"Oh," he said, with a fine air of detachment, "do you think they are so necessary, those agreements?"

"Well," I replied, "we see that they are not indispensable. More sugar? I have only given you one lump. And we know, at all events," I added, unguardedly, "that she could never have had an illusion about him."

The young man looked up quickly. "Is that story true?" he asked.

"There was a story, but most of us have forgotten it. Who told you?"

"The doctor."

"The Surgeon-Major," I said, "has an accurate memory and a sense of proportion. As I suppose you were bound to get it from somebody, I am glad you got it from him."

I was not prepared to go on, and saw with some relief that Somers was not either. His silence, as he smoked, seemed to me deliberate; and I had oddly enough at this moment for the first time the impression that he was a man and not a boy. Then the Harbottles themselves joined us, very cheery after a gallop from the Wazir-Bagh. We talked of old times, old friendships, good swords that were broken, names that had carried far, and Somers effaced himself in the perfect manner of the British subaltern. It was a long, pleasant gossip, and I thought Judy seemed rather glad to let her husband dictate its level, which, of course, he did. I noticed when the three rode away together that the Colonel was beginning to sit down rather solidly on his big New Zealander; and I watched the dusk come over from the foot-hills for a long time thinking more kindly than I had spoken of Robert Harbottle.

I have often wondered how far happiness is contributed to a temperament like Judy Harbottle's, and how far it creates its own; but I doubt whether, on either count, she found as much in any other winter of her life except perhaps the remote ones by the Seine. Those ardent hours of hers, when everything she said was touched with the flame of her individuality, came oftener; she suddenly cleaned up her palate and began to translate in one study after another the language of the frontier country, that spoke only in stones and in shadows under the stones and in sunlight over them. There is nothing in the Academy of this year, at all events, that I would exchange for the one she gave me. She lived her physical life at a pace which carried us all along with her; she hunted and drove and danced and dined with such sincere intention as convinced us all that in hunting and driving and dancing and dining there were satisfactions that had been somehow overlooked. The Surgeon-Major's wife said it was delightful to meet Mrs. Harbottle, she seemed to enjoy everything so thoroughly; the Surgeon-Major looked at her critically and asked her if she were quite sure she hadn't a night temperature. He was a Scotchman. One night Colonel Harbottle, hearing her give away the last extra, charged her with renewing her youth.

"No, Bob," she said, "only imitating it."

Ah, that question of her youth. It was so near her—still, she told me once, she heard the beat of its flying, and the pulse in her veins answered the false signal. That was afterward, when she told the truth. She was not so happy when she indulged herself otherwise. As when she asked one to remember that she was a middle-aged woman, with middle-aged thoughts and satisfactions.

"I am now really happiest," she declared, "when the Commissioner takes me in to dinner, when the General Commanding leads me to the dance."

She did her best to make it an honest conviction. I offered her a recent success not crowned by the Academy, and she put it down on the table. "By and by," she said. "At present I am reading Pascal and Bossuet." Well, she was reading Pascal and Bossuet. She grieved aloud that most of our activities in India were so indomitably youthful, owing to the accident that most of us were always so young. "There is no dignified distraction in this country," she complained, "for respectable ladies nearing forty." She seemed to like to make these declarations in the presence of Somers Chichele, who would look at her with a little queer smile—a bad translation, I imagine, of what he felt.

She gave herself so generously to her seniors that somebody said Mrs. Harbottle's girdle was hung with brass hats. It seems flippant to add that her complexion was as honest as the day, but the fact is that the year before Judy had felt compelled, like the rest of us, to repair just a little the ravages of the climate. If she had never done it one would not have looked twice at the absurdity when she said of the powder-puff in the dressing-room, "I have raised that thing to the level of an immorality," and sailed in to dance with an uncompromising expression and a face uncompromised. I have not spoken of her beauty; for one thing it was not always there, and there were people who would deny it altogether, or whose considered comment was, "I wouldn't call her plain." They, of course, were people in whom she declined to be interested, but even for those of us who could evoke some demonstration of her vivid self her face would not always light in correspondence. When it did there was none that I liked better to look at; and I envied Somers Chichele his way to make it the pale, shining thing that would hold him lifted, in return, for hours together, with I know not what mystic power of a moon upon the tide. And he? Oh, he was dark and delicate, by nature simple, sincere, delightfully intelligent. His common title to charm was the rather sweet seriousness that rested on his upper lip, and a certain winning gratification in his attention; but he had a subtler one in his eyes, which must be always seeking and smiling over what they found; those eyes of perpetual inquiry for the exquisite which ask so little help to create it. A personality to button up in a uniform, good heavens!

As I begin to think of them together I remember how the maternal note appeared in her talk about him.

"His youth is pathetic," she told me, "but there is nothing that he does not understand."

"Don't apologize, Judy," I said. We were so brusque on the frontier. Besides, the matter still suffered a jocular presentment. Mrs. Harbottle and Mr. Chichele were still "great friends;" we could still put them next each other at our dinner-parties without the feeling that it would be "marked." There was still nothing unusual in the fact that when Mrs. Harbottle was there Mr. Chichele might be taken for granted. We were so broad-minded also, on the frontier.

It grew more obvious, the maternal note. I began positively to dread it, almost as much, I imagine, as Somers did. She took her privileges all in Anna's name, she exercised her authority quite as Lady Chichele's proxy. She went to the very limit. "Anna Chichele," she said actually in his presence, "is a fortunate woman. She has all kinds of cleverness, and she has her tall son. I have only one little talent, and I have no tall son." Now it was not in nature that she could have had a son as tall as Somers, nor was that desire in her eyes. All civilization implies a good deal of farce, but this was a poor refuge, a cheap device; I was glad when it fell away from her sincerity, when the day came on which she looked into my fire and said simply, "An attachment like ours has no terms."

"I wonder," I said.

"For what comes and goes," she went on dreamily, "how could there be a formula?"

"Look here, Judy," I said, "you know me very well. What if the flesh leaps with the spirit?"

She looked at me, very white. "Oh no," she said, "no."

I waited, but there seemed nothing more that she could say; and in the silence the futile negative seemed to wander round the room repeating itself like an echo, "Oh no, no." I poked the fire presently to drown the sound of it. Judy sat still, with her feet crossed and her hands thrust into the pockets of her coat, staring into the coals.

"Can you live independently, satisfied with your interests and occupations?" she demanded at last. "Yes, I know you can. I can't. I must exist more than half in other people. It is what they think and feel that matters to me, just as much as what I think and feel. The best of life is in that communication."

"It has always been a passion with you, Judy," I replied. "I can imagine how much you must miss—"

"Whom?"

"Anna Chichele," I said softly.

She got up and walked about the room, fixing here and there an intent regard upon things which she did not see. "Oh, I do," she said at one point, with the effect of pulling herself together. She took another turn or two, and then finding herself near the door she went out. I felt as profoundly humiliated for her as if she had staggered.

The next night was one of those that stand out so vividly, for no reason that one can identify, in one's memory. We were dining with the Harbottles, a small party, for a tourist they had with them. Judy and I and Somers and the traveller had drifted out into the veranda, where the scent of Japanese lilies came and went on the spring wind to trouble the souls of any taken unawares. There was a brightness beyond the foot-hills where the moon was coming, and I remember how one tall clump swayed out against it, and seemed in passionate perfume to lay a burden on the breast. Judy moved away from it and sat clasping her knees on the edge of the veranda. Somers, when his eyes were not upon her, looked always at the lily.

Even the spirit of the globe-trotter was stirred, and he said, "I think you Anglo-Indians live in a kind of little paradise."

There was an instant's silence, and then Judy turned her face into the lamplight from the drawing-room. "With everything but the essentials," she said.

We stayed late; Mr. Chichele and ourselves were the last to go. Judy walked with us along the moonlit drive to the gate, which is so unnecessary a luxury in India that the servants always leave it open. She swung the stiff halves together.

"Now," she said, "it is shut."

"And I," said Somers Chichele, softly and quickly, "am on the other side."

Even over that depth she could flash him a smile. "It is the business of my life," she gave him in return, "to keep this gate shut." I felt as if they had forgotten us. Somers mounted and rode off without a word; we were walking in a different direction. Looking back, I saw Judy leaning immoveable on the gate, while Somers turned in his saddle, apparently to repeat the form of lifting his hat. And all about them stretched the stones of Kabul valley, vague and formless in the tide of the moonlight . . .

Next day a note from Mrs. Harbottle informed me that she had gone to Bombay for a fortnight. In a postscript she wrote, "I shall wait for the Chicheles there, and come back with them." I remember reflecting that if she could not induce herself to take a passage to England in the ship that brought them, it seemed the right thing to do.

She did come back with them. I met the party at the station. I knew Somers would meet them, and it seemed to me, so imminent did disaster loom, that some one else should be there, some one to offer a covering movement or a flank support wherever it might be most needed. And among all our smiling faces disaster did come, or the cold premonition of it. We were all perfect, but Somers's lip trembled. Deprived for a fortnight he was eager for the draft, and he was only twenty-six. His lip trembled, and there, under the flickering station-lamps, suddenly stood that of which there never could be again any denial, for those of us who saw.

Did we make, I wonder, even a pretense of disguising the consternation that sprang up among us, like an armed thing, ready to kill any further suggestion of the truth? I don't know. Anna Chichele's unfinished sentence dropped as if someone had given her a blow upon the mouth. Coolies were piling the luggage into a hired carriage at the edge of the platform. She walked mechanically after them, and would have stepped in with it but for the sight of her own gleaming landau drawn up within a yard or two, and the General waiting. We all got home somehow, taking it with us, and I gave Lady Chichele twenty-four hours to come to me with her face all one question and her heart all one fear. She came in twelve.

"Have you seen it– long?" Prepared as I was her directness was demoralizing.

"It isn't a mortal disease."

"Oh, for Heaven's sake—"

"Well, not with certainty, for more than a month."

She made a little spasmodic movement with her hands, then dropped them pitifully. "Couldn't you do *anything*?"

I looked at her, and she said at once, "No, of course you couldn't."

For a moment or two I took my share of the heavy sense of it, my trivial share, which yet was an experience sufficiently exciting. "I am afraid it will have to be faced," I said.

"What will happen?" Anna cried. "Oh, what will happen?"

"Why not the usual thing?" Lady Chichele looked up quickly as if at a reminder. "The ambiguous attachment of the country," I went on, limping but courageous, "half declared, half admitted, that leads vaguely nowhere, and finally perishes as the man's life enriches itself—the thing we have seen so often."

"Whatever Judy is capable of it won't be the usual thing. You know that."

I had to confess in silence that I did.

"It flashed at me—the difference in her—in Bombay." She pressed her lips together and then went on unsteadily. "In her eyes, her voice. She was mannered, extravagant, elaborate. With me! All the way up I wondered and worried. But I never thought—" She stopped; her voice simply shook itself into silence. I called a servant.

"I am going to give you a good stiff peg," I said. I apologize for the "peg," but not for the whisky and soda. It is a beverage on the frontier, of which the vulgarity is lost in the value. While it was coming I tried to talk of other things, but she would only nod absently in the pauses.

"Last night we dined with him, it was guest night at the mess, and she was there. I watched her, and she knew it. I don't know whether she tried, but anyway, she failed. The covenant between them was written on her forehead whenever she looked at him, though that was seldom. She dared not look at him. And the little conversation that they had—you would have laughed—it was a comedy of stutters. The facile Mrs. Harbottle!''

''You do well to be angry, naturally,'' I said; ''but it would be fatal to let yourself go, Anna.''

''Angry? Oh, I am *sick*. The misery of it! The terror of it! If it were anybody but Judy! Can't you imagine the passion of a temperament like that in a woman who has all these years been feeding on herself? I tell you she will take him from my very arms. And he will go—to I dare not imagine what catastrophe! Who can prevent it? Who can prevent it?''

''There is you,'' I said.

Lady Chichele laughed hysterically. ''I think you ought to say, 'There are you.' I—what can I do? Do you realize that it's *Judy*? My friend—my other self? Do you think we can drag all that out of it? Do you think a tie like that can be broken by an accident—by a misfortune? With it all I *adore* Judy Harbottle. I love her, as I have always loved her, and—it's damnable, but I don't know whether, whatever happened, I wouldn't go on loving her.''

''Finish your peg,'' I said. She was sobbing.

''Where I blame myself most,'' she went on, ''is for not seeing in him all that makes him mature to her—that makes her forget the· absurd difference between them, and take him simply and sincerely as I know she does, as the contemporary of her soul if not of her body. I saw none of that. Could I, as his mother? Would he show it to me? I thought him just a charming boy, clever, too, of course, with nice instincts and well plucked; we were always proud of that, with his delicate physique. Just a boy! I haven't yet stopped thinking how different he looks without his curls. And I thought she would be just kind and gracious and delightful to him because he was my son.''

''There, of course,'' I said, ''is the only chance.''

''Where—what?''

''He is your son.''

''Would you have me appeal to her? Do you know I don't think I could?''

''Dear me, no. Your case must present itself. It must spring upon her and grow before her out of your silence, and if you can manage it, your confidence. There is a great deal, after all, remember, to hold her in that. I can't somehow imagine her failing you. Otherwise—''

Lady Chichele and I exchanged a glance of candid admission.

''Otherwise she would be capable of sacrificing everything—everything. Of gathering her life into an hour. I know. And do you know if the thing were less impossible, less grotesque, I should not be so much afraid? I mean that the *absolute* idefensibility of it might bring her a recklessness and a momentum which might—"

"Send her over the verge," I said. "Well, go home and ask her to dinner."

There was a good deal more to say, of course, than I have thought proper to put down here, but before Anna went I saw that she was keyed up to the heroic part. This was none the less to her credit because it was the only part, the dictation of a sense of expediency that despaired while it dictated. The noble thing was her capacity to take it, and, amid all that warred in her, to carry it out on the brave high lines of her inspiration. It seemed a literal inspiration, so perfectly calculated that it was hard not to think sometimes, when one saw them together, that Anna had been lulled into a simple resumption of the old relation. Then from the least thing possible—the lift of an eyelid—it flashed upon one that between these two every moment was dramatic, and one took up the word with a curious sense of detachment and futility, but with one's heart beating like a trip-hammer with the mad excitement of it. The acute thing was the splendid sincerity of Judy Harbottle's response. For days she was profoundly on her guard, then suddenly she seemed to become practically, vividly aware of what I must go on calling the great chance, and passionately to fling herself upon it. It was the strangest co-operation without a word or a sign to show it conscious—a playing together for stakes that could not be admitted, a thing to hang upon breathless. It was there between them—the tenable ground of what they were to each other: they occupied it with almost an equal eye upon the tide that threatened, while I from my mainland tower also made an anguished calculation of the chances. I think in spite of the menace, they found real beatitudes; so keenly did they set about the business that it brought them moments finer than any they could count in the years that were behind them, the flat and colorless years that were gone. Once or twice the wild idea even visited me that it was, after all, the projection of his mother in Somers that had so seized Judy Harbottle, and that the original was all that was needed to help the happy process of detachment. Somers himself at the time was a good deal away on escort duty: they had a clear field.

I can not tell exactly when—between Mrs. Harbottle and myself—it became a matter for reference more or less overt, I mean her defined problem, the thing that went about between her and the sun. It will be imagined that it did not come up like the weather; indeed, it was hardly ever to be envisaged and never to be held; but it was always there, and out of our joint consciousness it would sometimes leap and pass, without shape or face. It might slip between two sentences, or it might remain, a dogging shadow, for an hour. Or a week would go by while, with a strong hand, she held it out of sight altogether and talked of Anna—always of Anna. Her eyes shone with the things she told me then: she seemed to keep herself under the influence of them as if they had the power of narcotics. At the end of a time like this she turned to me in the door as she was going and stood silent, as if she could neither go nor stay. I had been able to make nothing of her that afternoon: she had seemed preoccupied with the pattern of the carpet which she traced continually with her riding crop, and finally I, too, had relapsed. She sat haggard, with the fight forever in her eyes, and the day seemed to sombre about her in her corner. When she turned in the door, I looked up with sudden prescience of a crisis.

"Don't jump," she said, "it was only to tell you that I have persuaded Robert to apply for furlough. Eighteen months. From the first of April. Don't touch me." I suppose I made a movement towards her. Certainly I wanted to throw my arms about her; with the instinct, I suppose, to steady her in her great resolution.

"At the end of that time, as you know, he will be retired. I had some trouble, he is so keen on the regiment, but I think—I have succeeded. You might mention it to Anna."

"Haven't you?" sprang past my lips.

"I can't. It would be like taking an oath to tell her, and—I can't take an oath to go. But I mean to."

"There is nothing to be said," I brought out, feeling indeed that there was not. "But I congratulate you, Judy."

"No, there is nothing to be said. And you congratulate me, no doubt!"

She stood for a moment quivering in the isolation she made for herself; and I felt a primitive angry revolt against the delicate trafficking of souls that could end in such ravage and disaster. The price was too heavy; I would have denuded her, at the moment, of all that had led her into this, and turned her out a clod with fine shoulders like fifty other women in Peshawur. Then, perhaps, because I held myself silent and remote and she had no emotion of fear from me, she did not immediately go.

"It will beat itself away, I suppose, like the rest of the unreasonable pain of the world," she said at last; and that, of course, brought me to her side. "Things will go back to their proportions. This," she touched an open rose, "will claim its beauty again. And life will become—perhaps—what it was before." Still I found nothing to say, I could only put my arm in hers and walk with her to the edge of the veranda where the syce was holding her horse. She stroked the animal's neck. "Everything in me answered him," she informed me, with the grave intelligence of a patient who relates a symptom past. As she took the reins she turned to me again. "His spirit came to mine like a homing bird,'' she said, and in her smile even the pale reflection of happiness was sweet and stirring. It left me hanging in imagination over the source and the stream, a little blessed in the mere understanding.

Too much blessed for confidence, or any safe feeling that the source was bound. Rather I saw it leaping over every obstacle, flashing to its destiny. As I drove to the Club next day I decided that I would not tell Anna Chichele of Colonel Harbottle's projected furlough. If to Judy telling her would be like taking an oath that they would go, to me it would at least be like assuming sponsorship for their intention. That would be heavy indeed. From the first of April—we were then in March. Anna would hear it soon enough from the General, would see it soon enough, almost, in the *Gazette*, when it would have passed into irrecoverable fact. So I went by her with locked lips, kept out of the way of those eyes of the mother that asked and asked, and would have seen clear to any depth, any hiding-place of knowledge like that. As I pulled up at the Club I saw Colonel Harbottle talking concernedly to the wife of our Second-in-Command, and was reminded that I had not heard for some days how Major Watkins was going on. So I, too, approached Mrs. Watkins in her victoria to ask. Robert Harbottle kindly forestalled her reply. ''Hard luck, isn't it? Watkins has been ordered home at once. Just settled into their new house, too—last of the kit came up from Calcutta yesterday, didn't it, Mrs. Watkins? But it's sound to go—Peshawur is the worst hole in Asia to shake off dysentery in.''

We agreed upon this and discussed the sale-list of her new furniture that Mrs. Watkins would have to send round the station, and considered the chances of a trooper—to the Watkinses with two children and not a penny but his pay it did make it easier not to have to go by a liner—and Colonel Harbottle and I were half-way to the reading-room before the significance of Major Watkin's sick-leave flashed upon me.

''But this,'' I cried, ''will make a difference to your plans. You won't—''

''Be able to ask for that furlough Judy wants. Rather not. I'm afraid she's disappointed—she was tremendously set on going—but it doesn't matter tuppence to me.''

I sought out Mrs. Harbottle, at the end of the room. She looked radiant; she sat on the edge of the table and swung a light-hearted heel. She was talking to people who in themselves were a witness to high spirits, Captain the Hon. Freddy Gisborne, Mrs. Flamboys.

At sight of me her face clouded, fell suddenly into the old weary lines. It made me feel somehow a little sick; I went back to my cart and drove home.

For more than a week I did not see her except when I met her riding with Somers Chichele along the peach-bordered road that leads to the Wazir-Bagh. The trees were all in blossom and made a picture that might well catch dreaming hearts into a beatitude that would correspond. The air was full of spring and the scent of violets, those wonderful Peshawur violets that grow in great clumps, tall and double. Gracious clouds came and trailed across the frontier barrier; blue as an idyll it rose about us; the city smiled in her gardens.

She had it all in her face, poor Judy, all the spring softness and more, the morning she came, intensely controlled, to announce her defeat. I was in the drawing-room doing the flowers; I put them down to look at her. The wonderful telegram from Simla arrived— that was the wonderful part—at the same time; I remembered how the red, white, and blue turban of the telegraph peon bobbed up behind her shoulder in the veranda. I signed and laid it on the table; I suppose it seemed hardly likely that anything could be important enough to interfere at the moment with my impression of what love, unbound and victorious, could do with a face I thought I knew. Love sat there careless of the issue, full of delight. Love proclaimed that between him and Judith Harbottle it was all over—she had met him, alas, in too narrow a place—and I marvelled at the paradox with which he softened every curve and underlined every vivid note of personality in token that it had just begun. He sat there in great serenity, and though I knew that somewhere behind lurked a van-quished woman, I saw her through such a radiance that I could not be sure of seeing her at all . . .

She went back to the very first of it; she seemed herself intensely interested in the facts; and there is no use in pretending that, while she talked, the moral consideration was at all present with me either; it wasn't. Her extremity was the thing that absorbed us; she even, in tender thoughtfulness, diagnosed it from its definite beautiful beginning.

"It was there, in my heart, when I woke one morning, exquisite and strange, the assurance of a gift. How had it come there, while I slept? I assure you when I closed my eyes it did not exist for me. . . . Yes, of course, I had seen him, but only somewhere at dinner . . . As the day went on it changed—it turned into a clear pool, into a flower. And I—think of my not understanding! I was pleased with it! For a long time, for days, I never dreamed that it could be anything but a little secret joy. Then, suddenly—oh, I had not been perceiving enough!—it was in all my veins, a tide, an efflorescence, a thing of my very life.

"Then—it was a little late—I understood, and since—

"I began by hating it—being furious, furious—and afraid, too. Sometimes it was like a low cloud, hovering and travelling always with me, sometimes like a beast of prey that went a little way off and sat looking at me . . .

"I have—done my best. But there is nothing to do, to kill, to abolish. How can I say, 'I will not let you in,' when it is already there? How can I assume indifference when this thing is imposed upon every moment of my day? And it has grown so sweet—the longing—that—isn't it strange?—I could more willingly give him up than the desire of him. That seems as impossible to part with as life itself."

She sat reflective for a moment, and I saw her eyes slowly fill.

"Don't—don't *cry*, Judy," I faltered, wanting to horribly, myself.

She smiled them dry.

"Not now. But I am giving myself, I suppose, to many tears."

"God help you," I said. What else was there to say?

"There is no such person," she replied, gaily. "There is only a blessed devil."

"Then you go all the way—to the logical conclusion?"

She hardly hesitated. "To the logical conclusion. What poor words!"

"May I ask—when?"

"I should like to tell you that quite definitely, and I think I can. The English mail leaves tonight."

"And you have arranged to take it?"

"We have arranged nothing. Do you know"—she smiled as if at the fresh colors of an idyll—"we have not even come to the admission? There has been between us no word, no vision. Ah, we have gone in bonds, and dumb! Hours we have had, exquisite hours of the spirit, but never a moment of the heart, a moment confessed. It was mine to give—that moment, and he has waited—I know—wondering whether perhaps it would ever come. And today—we are going for a ride today, and I do not think we shall come back."

"O Judy," I cried, catching at her sleeve, "he is only a boy!"

"There were times when I thought that conclusive. Now the misery of it has gone to sleep; don't waken it. It pleases me to believe that the years are a convention. I never had any dignity, you know, and I seem to have missed the moral deliverance. I only want—oh, you know what I want. Why don't you open your telegram?"

I had been folding and fingering the brown envelope as if it had been a scrap of waste-paper.

"It is probably from Mrs. Watkins about the victoria," I said, feeling its profound irrelevance. "I wired an offer to her in Bombay. However"—and I read the telegram, the little solving telegram from Army Headquarters. I turned my back on her to read it again, and then I replaced it very carefully and put it in my pocket. It was a moment to take hold of with both hands, crying on all one's gods for steadiness.

"How white you look!" said Mrs. Harbottle, with concern. "Not bad news?"

"On the contrary, excellent news. Judy, will you stay to lunch?"

She looked at me, hesitating. "Won't it seem rather a compromise on your part? When you ought to be rousing the city—"

"I don't intend to rouse the city," I said.

"I have given you the chance."

"Thank you," I said, grimly, "but the only real favor you can do me is to stay and lunch." It was then just on one.

"I'll stay," she said, "if you will promise not to make any sort of effort. I shouldn't mind, but it would distress you."

"I promise absolutely," I said, and ironical joy rose up in me, and the telegram burned in my pocket.

She would talk of it, though I found it hard to let her go on, knowing and knowing and knowing as I did that for that day at least it could not be. There was very little about herself that she wanted to tell me; she was there confessed a woman whom joy had overcome; it was understood that we both accepted that situation. But in the details which she asked me to take charge of it was plain that she also kept a watchful eye upon fate—matters of business.

We were in the drawing-room. The little round clock in its Amritsar case marked half-past three. Judy put down her coffee-cup and rose to go. As she glanced at the clock the light deepened in her eyes, and I, with her hand in mine, felt like an agent of the Destroyer— for it was half-past three—consumed myself with fear lest the blow had miscarried. Then as we stood, suddenly, the sound of hoofs at a gallop on the drive, and my husband threw himself off at the door and tore through the hall to his room; and in the certainty that overwhelmed me even Judy, for an instant, stood dim and remote.

"Major Jim seems to be in a hurry," said Mrs. Harbottle, lightly. "I have always liked your husband. I wonder whether he will say tomorrow that he always liked me."

"Dear Judy, I don't think he will be occupied with you tomorrow."

"Oh, surely, just a little, if I go tonight."

"You won't go tonight."

She looked at me helplessly. I felt as if I were insisting upon her abasement instead of her salvation. "I wish—"

"You're not going—you're not! You can't! Look!"

I pulled it out of my pocket and thrust it at her—the telegram. It came, against every regulation, from my good friend the deputy Adjutant-General, in Simla, and it read, "*Row Khurram 12th probably ordered front three hours' time.*"

Her face changed—how my heart leaped to see it change!—and that took command there which will command trampling, even in the women of the camp, at news like this.

"What luck that Bob couldn't take his furlough!" she exclaimed, single-thoughted. "But you have known this for hours"—there was even something of the Colonel's wife, authority, incisiveness. "Why didn't you tell me? Ah—I see."

I stood before her abashed, and that was ridiculous, while she measured me as if I presented in myself the woman I took her to be. "It wasn't like that," she said. I had to defend myself. "Judy," I said, "if you weren't in honor bound to Anna, how could I know that you would be in honor bound to the regiment? There was a train at three."

"I beg to assure you that you have overcalculated," said Mrs. Harbottle. Her eyes were hard and proud. "And I am not sure"—a deep red swept over her face, a man's blush—"in the light of this I am not sure that I am not in honor bound to Anna."

We had reached the veranda, and at her signal her coachman drove quickly up. "You have kept me here three hours when there was the whole of Bob's kit to see to," she said, as she flung herself in; "you might have thought of that."

It was a more than usually tedious campaign, and Colonel Robert Harbottle was ambushed and shot in a place where one must believe pure boredom induced him to take his men. The incident was relieved, the newspapers said—and they are seldom so clever in finding relief for such incidents—by the dash and courage shown by Lieutenant Chichele, who, in one of those feats which it has lately been the fashion to criticize, carried the mortally wounded body of his Colonel out of range at conspicuous risk of depriving the Queen of another officer. I helped Judy with her silent packing; she had forgiven me long before that; and she settled almost at once into the flat in Chelsea which has since been credited with so delightful an atmosphere, went back straight into her own world. I have always kept her first letters about it, always shall. For months after, while the expedition still raged after snipers and rifle-thieves, I discussed with Lady Chichele the probable outcome of it all. I have sometimes felt ashamed of leaping as straight as I did with Anna to what we thought the inevitable. I based no calculation on all Mrs. Harbottle had gone back to, just as I had based no calculation on her ten years' companionship in arms when I kept her from the three o'clock train. This last was a retrospection in which Anna naturally could not join me; she never knew, poor dear, how fortunate as to its moment was the campaign she deplored, and nothing to this day can have disturbed her conviction that the bond she was at such magnificent pains to strengthen, held against the strain, as long, happily, as the supreme need existed. "How right you were!" she often said. "She did, after all, love me best, dear, wonderful Judy!" Her distress about poor Robert Harbottle was genuine enough, but one could not be surprised at a certain ambiguity; one tear for Robert, so to speak, and two for her boy. It could hardly be, for him, a marriage after his mother's heart. And she laid down with some emphasis that Somers was brilliantly entitled to all he was likely to get—which was natural, too . . .

I had been from the beginning so much "in it" that Anna showed me, a year later, though I don't believe she liked doing it, the letter in part of which Mrs. Harbottle shall finally excuse herself.

"Somers will give you this," I read, "and with it take back your son. You will not find, I know, anything grotesque in the charming enthusiasm with which he has offered his life to me; you understand too well, you are too kind. And if you wonder that I can so render up a dear thing which I might keep and would once have taken, think how sweet in the desert is the pool, and how barren was the prospect from Balclutha."

It was like her to abandon in pride a happiness that asked so much less humiliation; I don't know why, but it was like her. And of course, when one thought of it, she had consulted all sorts of high expediencies. But I sat silent with remembrance, quieting a pang in my heart, trying not to calculate how much it had cost Judy Harbottle to take her second chance.

# O. HENRY
## 1862–1910

William Sidney Porter was born near Greensboro, North Carolina. His father and grandfather were doctors, his mother a graduate (with honors) of Greensboro Female College in 1850. When he was three, his mother died and, soon after, his father began a long, gradual retirement from life. His Aunt Evelina ("Miss Lina") was a school teacher of considerable skill, and she took charge of Will's education until he went into his uncle's drugstore as an apprentice in 1879. In his spare time he developed his talents for horseshoe pitching, practical joking, chess-playing, pistol-shooting, and cartoon drawing. In 1882 he went to Texas, where he worked a little and visited a lot. He was charming, irresponsible, and lacking in courage—in the eyes of those who knew him them. After marriage and some business ventures, he was found to have fiddled with his accounts and stolen money. He fled to Honduras to avoid trial, but returned to

Texas in 1897. His first story was accepted for publication that year, and in 1898 he began serving a five-year sentence for embezzlement at the Federal Penitentiary in Ohio. There he began to write in earnest, and when he was released in 1902 (with time off for good behavior), his career was launched. At this time he adopted his pen name, "O. Henry," and moved to New York, writing weekly stories for the *Sunday World*. His first book, *Cabbages and Kings*, appeared in 1904, and in the six years left in his life he wrote hundreds of stories, publishing seven more volumes during his life and having five more published posthumously.

# THE GIFT OF THE MAGI

One dollar and eighty-seven cents. That was all. And sixty cents of it was in pennies. Pennies saved one and two at a time by bulldozing the grocer and the vegetable man and the butcher until one's cheeks burned with the silent imputation of parsimony that such close dealing implied. Three times Della counted it. One dollar and eighty-seven cents. And the next day would be Christmas.

There was clearly nothing to do but flop down on the shabby little couch and howl. So Della did it. Which instigates the moral reflection that life is made up of sobs, sniffles, and smiles, with sniffles predominating.

While the mistress of the home is gradually subsiding from the first stage to the second, take a look at the home. A furnished flat at $8 per week. It did not exactly beggar description, but it certainly had that word on the lookout for the mendancy squad.

In the vestibule below was a letter-box into which no letter would go, and an electric button from which no mortal finger could coax a ring. Also appertaining thereunto was a card bearing the name "Mr. James Dillingham Young."

The "Dillingham" had been flung to the breeze during a former period of prosperity when its possessor was being paid $30 per week. Now, when the income was shrunk to $20, the letters of "Dillingham" looked blurred, as though they were thinking seriously of contracting to a modest and unassuming D. But whenever Mr. James Dillingham Young came home and reached his flat above he was called "Jim" and greatly hugged by Mrs. James Dillingham Young, already introduced to you as Della. Which is all very good.

Della finished her cry and attended to her cheeks with the powder rag. She stood by the window and looked out dully at a gray cat walking a gray fence in a gray backyard. Tomorrow would be Christmas Day, and she had only $1.87 with which to buy Jim a present. She had been saving every penny she could for months, with this result. Twenty dollars a week doesn't go far. Expenses had been greater than she had calculated. They always are. Only $1.87 to buy a present for Jim. Her Jim. Many a happy hour she had spent planning for something nice for him. Something fine and rare and sterling— something just a little bit near to being worthy of the honor of being owned by Jim.

There was a pier-glass between the windows of the room. Perhaps you have seen a pier-glass in an $8 flat. A very thin and very agile person may, by observing his reflection in a rapid sequence of longitudinal strips, obtain a fairly accurate conception of his looks. Della, being slender, had mastered the art.

Suddenly she whirled from the window and stood before the glass. Her eyes were shining brilliantly, but her face had lost its color within twenty seconds. Rapidly she pulled down her hair and let it fall to its full length.

Now, there were two possessions of the James Dillingham Youngs in which they both took a mighty pride. One was Jim's gold watch that had been his father's and his grandfather's. The other was Della's hair. Had the Queen of Sheba lived in the flat across the airshaft, Della would have let her hair hang out the window some day to dry just to depreciate Her Majesty's jewels and gifts. Had King Solomon been the janitor, with all his treasures piled up in the basement, Jim would have pulled out his watch every time he passed, just to see him pluck at his beard from envy.

So now Della's beautiful hair fell about her rippling and shining like a cascade of brown waters. It reached below her knee and made itself almost a garment for her. And then she did it up again nervously and quickly. Once she faltered for a minute and stood still while a tear or two splashed on the worn red carpet.

On went her old brown jacket; on went her old brown hat. With a whirl of skirts and with the brilliant sparkle still in her eyes, she fluttered out the door and down the stairs to the street.

Where she stopped the sign read: "Mme. Sofronie. Hair Goods of All Kinds." One flight up Della ran, and collected herself, panting. Madame, large, too white, chilly, hardly looked the "Sofronie."

"Will you buy my hair?" asked Della.

"I buy hair," said Madame. "Take yer hat off and let's have a sight at the looks of it."

Down rippled the brown cascade.

"Twenty dollars," said Madame, lifting the mass with a practised hand.

"Give it to me quick," said Della.

Oh, and the next two hours tripped by on rosy wings. Forget the hashed metaphor. She was ransacking the stores for Jim's present.

She found it at last. It surely had been made for Jim and no one else. There was no other like it in any of the stores, and she had turned all of them inside out. It was a plantinum fob chain simple and chaste in design, properly proclaiming its value by substance alone and not by meretricious ornamentation—as all good things should do. It was even worthy of The Watch. As soon as she saw it she knew that it must be Jim's. It was like him. Quietness and value—the description applied to both. Twenty-one dollars they took from her for it, and she hurried home with the 87 cents. With that chain on his watch Jim might be properly anxious about the time in any company. Grand as the watch was, he sometimes looked at it on the sly on account of the old leather strap that he used in place of a chain.

When Della reached home her intoxication gave way a little to prudence and reason. She got out her curling irons and lighted the gas and went to work repairing the ravages made by generosity added to love. Which is always a tremendous task, dear friends—a mammoth task.

Within forty minutes her head was covered with tiny, close-lying curls that made her look wonderfully like a truant schoolboy. She looked at her reflection in the mirror long, carefully, and critically.

"If Jim doesn't kill me," she said to herself, "before he takes a second look at me, he'll say I look like a Coney Island chorus girl. But what could I do—oh! what could I do with a dollar and eighty-seven cents?"

At 7 o'clock the coffee was made and the frying-pan was on the back of the stove hot and ready to cook the chops.

Jim was never late. Della doubled the fob chain in her hand and sat on the corner of the table near the door that he always entered. Then she heard his step on the stair away down on the first flight, and she turned white for just a moment. She had a habit of saying little silent prayers about the simplest everyday things, and now she whispered: "Please God, make him think I am still pretty."

The door opened and Jim stepped in and closed it. He looked thin and very serious. Poor fellow, he was only twenty-two—and to be burdened with a family! He needed a new overcoat and he was without gloves.

Jim stopped inside the door, as immovable as a setter at the scent of quail. His eyes were fixed upon Della, and there was an expression in them that she could not read, and it terrified her. It was not anger, nor surprise, nor disapproval, nor horror, nor any of the sentiments that she had been prepared for. He simply stared at her fixedly with that peculiar expression on his face.

Della wriggled off the table and went for him.

"Jim, darling," she cried, "don't look at me that way. I had my hair cut off and sold it because I couldn't have lived through Christmas without giving you a present. It'll grow out again—you won't mind, will you? I just had to do it. My hair grows awfully fast. Say 'Merry Christmas!' Jim, and let's be happy. You don't know what a nice— what a beautiful, nice gift I've got for you."

"You've cut off your hair?" asked Jim, laboriously, as if he had not arrived at that patent fact yet even after the hardest mental labor.

"Cut if off and sold it," said Della. "Don't you like me just as well, anyhow? I'm me without my hair, ain't I?"

Jim looked about the room curiously.

"You say your hair is gone?" he said, with an air almost of idiocy.

"You needn't look for it," said Della. "It's sold, I tell you—sold and gone, too. It's Christmas Eve, boy. Be good to me, for it went for you. Maybe the hairs of my head were numbered," she went on with a sudden serious sweetness, "but nobody could ever count my love for you. Shall I put the chops on, Jim?"

Out of his trance Jim seemed quickly to wake. He enfolded his Della. For ten seconds let us regard with discreet scrutiny some inconsequential object in the other direction. Eight dollars a week or a million a year—what is the difference? A mathematician or a wit would give you the wrong answer. The magi brought valuable gifts, but that was not among them. This dark assertion will be illuminated later on.

Jim drew a package from his overcoat pocket and threw it upon the table.

"Don't make any mistake, Dell," he said, "about me. I don't think there's anything in the way of a haircut or a shave or a shampoo that could make me like my girl any less. But if you'll unwrap that package you may see why you had me going a while at first."

White fingers and nimble tore at the string and paper. And then an ecstatic scream of joy; and then, alas! a quick feminine change to hysterical tears and wails, necessitating the immediate employment of all the comforting powers of the lord of the flat.

For there lay The Combs—the set of combs, side and back, that Della had worshipped for long in a Broadway window. Beautiful combs, pure tortoise shell, with jewelled rims—just the shade to wear in the beautiful vanished hair. They were expensive combs, she knew, and her heart had simply craved and yearned over them without the least hope of possession. And now, they were hers, but the tresses that should have adorned the coveted adornments were gone.

But she hugged them to her bosom, and at length she was able to look up with dim eyes and a smile and say: "My hair grows so fast, Jim!"

And then Della leaped up like a little singed cat and cried, "Oh, oh!"

Jim had not yet seen his beautiful present. She held it out to him eagerly upon her open palm. The dull precious metal seemed to flash with a reflection of her bright and ardent spirit.

"Isn't it dandy, Jim? I hunted all over town to find it. You'll have to look at the time a hundred times a day now. Give me your watch. I want to see how it looks on it."

Instead of obeying, Jim tumbled down on the couch and put his hands under the back of his head and smiled.

"Dell," said he, "let's put our Christmas presents away and keep 'em a while. They're too nice to use just at present. I sold the watch to get the money to buy your combs. And now suppose you put the chops on."

The magi, as you know, were wise men—wonderfully wise men— who brought gifts to the Babe in the manger. They invented the art of giving Christmas presents. Being wise, their gifts were no doubt wise ones, possibly bearing the privilege of exchange in case of duplication. And here I have lamely related to you the uneventful chronicle of two foolish children in a flat who most unwisely sacrificed for each other the greatest treasures of their house. But in a last word to the wise of these days let it be said that of all who give gifts these two were the wisest. Of all who give and receive gifts, such as they are wisest. Everywhere they are wisest. They are the magi.

# RUDYARD KIPLING
## 1865–1936

Born in Bombay, India, of English parents, Kipling was sent home to England at age five, where for nearly six years he lived in a foster home and was subjected to what he called "calculated torture" in the form of lectures on Hell and physical beatings. After a nervous breakdown and an attack of partial blindness, he was sent to the United Services College at Westward Ho! where the sons of British military officers serving overseas were sent for education. At the age of sixteen he completed his education at Westward Ho! and returned to India to work on a newspaper, where he acquired an unparalleled knowledge of Indian life and began writing stories at age twenty. At twenty-three he had published seven volumes of fiction and one of poetry, when he returned to England to enjoy the fame he had earned. He continued to write and to be famous, in 1907 becoming the first English writer to receive the Nobel prize for literature.

# The Bull that Thought

Westward from a town by the Mouths of the Rhône[1] runs a road so mathematically straight, so barometrically level, that it ranks among the world's measured miles and motorists use it for records.

I had attacked the distance several times, but always with a Mistral blowing, or the unchancy cattle of those parts on the move. But once, running from the East, into a high-piled, almost Egyptian, sunset, there came a night which it would have been sin to have wasted. It was warm with the breath of summer in advance; moonlit till the shadow of every rounded pebble and pointed cypress windbreak lay solid on that vast flat-floored waste; and my Mr. Leggatt, who had slipped out to make sure, reported that the road-surface was unblemished.

"*Now*," he suggested, "we might see what she'll do under strict road-conditions. She's been pullin' like the Blue de Luxe all day. Unless I'm all off, it's her night out."

We arranged the trial for after dinner—thirty kilometres as near as might be; and twenty-two of them without even a level-crossing.

There sat beside me at table d'hôte an elderly, bearded Frenchman wearing the rosette of by no means the lowest grade of the Legion of Honour, who had arrived in a talkative Citroen.[2] I gathered that he had spent much of his life in the French Colonial Service in Annam and Tonquin.[3] When the War[4] came, his years barring him from the front line, he had supervised Chinese wood-cutters who, with axe and dynamite, deforested the centre of France for trench-props. He said my chauffeur had told him that I contemplated an experiment. He was interested in cars—had admired mine—would, in short, be greatly indebted to me if I permitted him to assist as an observer. One could not well refuse; and, knowing my Mr. Leggatt, it occurred to me there might also be a bet in the background.

While he went to get his coat, I asked the proprietor his name. "Voiron—Monsieur André Voiron," was the reply. "And his business?" "Mon Dieu! He is Voiron! He is all those things, there!" The proprietor waved his hands at brilliant advertisements on the dining-room walls, which declared that Voiron Frères dealt in wines, agricultural implements, chemical manures, provisions and produce throughout that part of the globe.

He said little for the first five minutes of our trip, and nothing at

1. River in the south of France
2. Automobile
3. French Indo China—later Cambodia and Vietnam.
4. World War I.

all for the next ten—it being, as Leggatt had guessed, Esmeralda's night out. But, when her indicator climbed to a certain figure and held there for three blinding kilometres, he expressed himself satisfied, and proposed to me that we should celebrate the event at the hotel. "I keep yonder," said he, "a wine on which I should value your opinion."

On our return, he disappeared for a few minutes, and I heard him rumbling in a cellar. The proprietor presently invited me to the dining-room, where, beneath one frugal light, a table had been set with local dishes of renown. There was, too, a bottle beyond most known sizes, marked black on red, with a date. Monsieur Voiron opened it, and we drank to the health of my car. The velvety, perfumed liquor, between fawn and topaz, neither too sweet nor too dry, creamed in its generous glass. But I knew no wine composed of the whispers of angels' wings, the breath of Eden, and the foam and pulse of Youth renewed. So I asked what it might be.

"It is champagne," he said gravely.

"Then what have I been drinking all my life?"

"If you were lucky, before the War, and paid thirty shillings a bottle, it is possible you may have drunk one of our better-class tisanes." [5]

"And where does one get this?"

"Here, I am happy to say. Elsewhere, perhaps, it is not so easy. We growers exchange these real wines among ourselves."

I bowed my head in admiration, surrender, and joy. There stood the most ample bottle, and it was not yet eleven o'clock. Doors locked and shutters banged throughout the establishment. Some last servant yawned on his way to bed. Monsieur Voiron opened a window and the moonlight flooded in from a small pebbled court outside. One could almost hear the town of Chambres breathing in its first sleep. Presently, there was a thick noise in the air, the passing of feet and hooves, lowings, and a stifled bark or two. Dust rose over the courtyard wall, followed by the strong smell of cattle.

"They are moving some beasts," said Monsieur Voiron, cocking an ear. "Mine, I think. Yes, I hear Christophe. Our beasts do not like automobiles—so we move at night. You do not know our country—the Crau, here, or the Camargue? I was—I am now, again—of it. All France is good; but this is the best." He spoke, as only a Frenchman can, of his own loved part of his own lovely land.

"For myself, if I were not so involved in all these affairs"—he pointed to the advertisements—"I would live on our farm with my

5. A kind of herb tea.

cattle, and worship them like a Hindu. You know our cattle of the Camargue, Monsieur? No? It is not an acquaintance to rush upon lightly. There are no beasts like them. They have a mentality superior to that of most. They graze and they ruminate, by choice, facing our Mistral,[6] which is more than some automobiles will do. Also they have in them the potentiality of thought—and when cattle think—I have seen what arrives."

"Are they so clever as all that?" I asked idly.

"Monsieur, when your *sportif* chauffeur camouflaged your limousine so that she resembled one of your Army lorries, I would not believe her capacities. I bet him—ah—two to one—she would not touch ninety kilometres. It was proved that she could. I can give you no proof, but will you believe me if I tell you what a beast who thinks can achieve?"

"After the War," said I spaciously, "everything is credible."

"That is true! Everything inconceivable has happened; but still we learn nothing and we believe nothing. When I was a child in my father's house—before I became a Colonial Administrator—my interest and my affection were among our cattle. We of the old rock live here—have you seen?—in big farms like castles. Indeed, some of them may have been Saracenic. The barns group round them—great white-walled barns, and yards solid as our houses. One gate shuts all. It is a world apart; an administration of all that concerns beasts. It was there I learned something about cattle. You see, they are our playthings in the Camargue and the Crau. The boy measures his strength against the calf that butts him in play among the manure-heaps. He moves in and out among the cows, who are—not so amiable. He rides with the herdsmen in the open to shift the herds. Sooner or later, he meets as bulls the little calves that knocked him over. So it was with me—till it became necessary that I should go to our Colonies." He laughed. "*Very* necessary. That is a good time in youth, Monsieur, when one does those things which shock our parents. Why is it always Papa who is so shocked and has never heard of such affairs—and Mama who supplies the excuses? . . . And when my brother—my elder who stayed and created the business—begged me to return and help him, I resigned my Colonial career gladly enough. I returned to our own lands, and my well-loved, wicked white and yellow cattle of the Camargue and the Crau. My Faith, I could talk of them all night, for this stuff unlocks the heart, without making repentance in the morning. . . . Yes! It was after the War that this happened. There was a calf, among Heaven knows how many of

6. Powerful, steady wind from the north.

ours—a bull-calf—an infant indistinguishable from his companions. He was sick, and he had been taken up with his mother into the big farmyard at home with us. Naturally the children of our herdsmen practised on him from the first. It is in their blood. The Spaniards make a cult of bull-fighting. Our little devils down here bait bulls as automatically as the English child kicks or throws balls. This calf would chase them with his eyes open, like a cow when she hunts a man. They would take refuge behind our tractors and wine-carts in the centre of the yard: he would chase them in and out as a dog hunts rats. More than that, he would study their psychology, his eyes in their eyes. Yes, he watched their faces to divine which way they would run. He himself, also, would pretend sometimes to charge directly at a boy. Then he would wheel right or left—one could never tell—and knock over some child pressed against a wall who thought himself safe. After this, he would stand over him, knowing that his companions must come to his aid; and when they were all together, waving their jackets across his eyes and pulling his tail, he would scatter them. How he would scatter them! He could kick, too, sideways, like a cow. He knew his ranges as well as our gunners, and he was as quick on his feet as our Carpentier.[7] I observed him often. Christophe—the man who passed just now—our chief herdsman, who had taught me to ride with our beasts when I was ten—Christophe told me that he was descended from a yellow cow of those days that had chased us once into the marshes. "He kicks just like her," said Christophe. "He can side-kick as he jumps. Have you seen, too, that he is not deceived by the jacket when a boy waves it? He uses it to find the boy. They think they are fooling him. He is fooling them always. He thinks, that one." I had come to the same conclusion. Yes—the creature was a thinker along the lines necessary to his sport; and he was a humorist also, like so many natural murderers. One knows the type among beasts as well as among men. It possesses a curious truculent mirth—almost indecent but infallibly significant——"

Monsieur Voiron replenished our glasses with the great wine that went better at each descent.

"They kept him for some time in the yards to practise upon. Naturally, he became a little brutal; so Christophe turned him out to learn manners among his equals in the grazinglands, where the Camargue joins the Crau. How old was he then? About eight or nine months, I think. We met again a few months later—he and I. I was riding one of our little half-wild horses, along a road of the Crau, when I found myself almost unseated. It was he! He had

7. An excellent light heavyweight boxer.

hidden himself behind a wind-break till we passed, and had then charged my horse from behind. Yes, he had deceived even my little horse! But I recognised him. I gave him the whip across the nose, and I said: 'Apis, for this thou goest to Arles! It was unworthy of thee, between us two.' But that creature had no shame. He went away laughing, like an Apache. If he had dismounted me, I do not think it is I who would have laughed—yearling as he was."

"Why did you want to send him to Arles?" I asked.

"For the bull-ring. When your charming tourists leave us, we institute our little amusements there. Not a real bull-fight, you understand, but young bulls with padded horns, and our boys from hereabouts and in the city go to play with them. Naturally, before we send them we try them in our yards at home. So we brought up Apis from his pastures. He knew at once that he was among the friends of his youth—he almost shook hands with them—and he submitted like an angel to padding his horns. He investigated the carts and tractors in the yards, to choose his lines of defence and attack. And then—he attacked with an *élan*, and he defended with a tenacity and forethought that delighted us. In truth, we were so pleased that I fear we trespassed on his patience. We desired him to repeat himself, which no true artist will tolerate. But he gave us fair warning. He went out to the centre of the yard, where there was some dry earth; he kneeled down and—you have seen a calf whose horns fret him thrusting and rooting into a bank? He did just that, very deliberately, till he had rubbed the pads off his horns. Then he rose, dancing on those wonderful feet that twinkled, and he said: 'Now, my friends, the buttons are off the foils. Who begins?' We understood. We finished at once. He was turned out again on the pastures till it should be time to amuse them at our little metropolis. But, some time before he went to Arles—yes, I think I have it correctly—Christophe, who had been out on the Crau, informed me that Apis had assassinated a young bull who had given signs of developing into a rival. That happens, of course, and our herdsmen should prevent it. But Apis had killed in his own style—at dusk, from the ambush of a wind-break—by an oblique charge from behind which knocked the other over. He had then disembowelled him. All very possible, *but*—the murder accomplished—Apis went to the bank of a wind-break, knelt, and carefully, as he had in our yard, cleaned his horns in the earth. Christophe, who had never seen such a thing, at once borrowed (do you know, it is most efficacious when taken that way?) some Holy Water from our little chapel in those pastures, sprinkled Apis (whom it did not affect), and rode in to tell me. It was obvious that a thinker of that bull's type would also be meticulous in his toilette; so, when he was sent to Arles, I warned our consignees to exercise caution with him. Happily, the change of scene, the music, the general attention, and the meeting again with old friends—all our bad boys attended—agreeably distracted him. He became for the time a pure *farceur* again; but his wheelings, his rushes, his rat-huntings were more superb than ever. There was in them now, you understand, a breadth of technique that comes of reasoned art, and, above all, the passion that arrives after experience. Oh, he had learned, out there on the Crau! At the end of his little turn, he was, according to local rules, to be handled in all respects except for the sword, which was a stick, as a professional bull who must die. He was manœuvred into, or he posed himself in, the proper attitude; made his rush; received the point on his shoulder and then—turned about and cantered toward the door by which he had entered the arena. He said to the world: 'My friends, the representation is ended. I thank you for your applause. I go to repose myself.' But our Arlesians, who are—not so clever as some, demanded an encore, and Apis was headed back again. We others from his country, we knew what would happen. He went to the centre of the ring, kneeled, and, slowly, with full parade, plunged his horns alternately in the dirt till the pads came off. Christophe shouts: 'Leave him alone, you straight-nosed imbeciles! Leave him before you must.' But they required emotion; for Rome has always debauched her loved Provincia with bread and circuses. It was given. Have you, Monsieur, ever seen a servant, with pan and broom, sweeping round the baseboard of a room? In a half-minute Apis has them all swept out and over the barrier. Then he demands once more that the door shall be opened to him. It is opened and he retires as though—which, truly, is the case—loaded with laurels."

Monsieur Voiron refilled the glasses, and allowed himself a cigarette, which he puffed for some time.

"And afterwards?" I said.

"I am arranging it in my mind. It is difficult to do it justice. Afterwards—yes, afterwards—Apis returned to his pastures and his mistresses and I to my business. I am no longer a scandalous old *sportif* in shirt-sleeves howling encouragement to the yellow son of a cow. I revert to Voiron Frères—wines, chemical manures, *et cetera*. And next year, through some chicane which I have not the leisure to unravel, and also, thanks to our patriarchal system of paying our older men out of the increase of the herds, old Christophe possesses himself of Apis. Oh, yes, he proves it through descent from a certain cow that my father had given his father before the Republic. Beware, Monsieur, of the memory of the illiterate man! An ancestor of Christophe had been a soldier under our Soult against your Beresford, near Bayonne. He fell into the hands of Spanish guerrillas. Christophe and his wife used to tell me the details on certain Saints' Days when I was a child. Now, as compared with our recent war, Soult's campaign and retreat across the Bidassoa—"

"But did you allow Christophe just to annex the bull?" I demanded.

"You do not know Christophe. He had sold him to the Spaniards before he informed me. The Spaniards pay in coin—douros of very pure silver. Our peasants mistrust our paper. You know the saying: 'A thousand francs paper; eight hundred metal, and the cow is yours.' Yes, Christophe sold Apis, who was then two and a half years old, and to Christophe's knowledge thrice at least an assassin."

"How was that?" I said.

"Oh, his own kind only; and always, Christophe told me, by the same oblique rush from behind, the same sideways overthrow, and the same swift disembowelment, followed by this levitical cleaning of the horns. In human life he would have kept a manicurist—this Minotaur.[8] And so, Apis disappears from our country. That does not trouble me. I know in due time I shall be advised. Why? Because, in this land, Monsieur, not a hoof moves between Berre and the Saintes Maries without the knowledge of specialists such as Christophe. The beasts are the substance and the drama of their lives to them. So when Christophe tells me, a little before Easter Sunday, that Apis makes his début in the bull-ring of a small Catalan town on the road to Barcelona, it is only to pack my car and trundle there across the frontier with him. The place lacked importance and manufactures, but it had produced a matador of some reputation, who was condescending to show his art in his native town. They were even running one special train to the place. Now our French railway system is only execrable, but the Spanish——"

"You went down by road, didn't you?" said I.

"Naturally. It was not too good. Villamarti was the matador's name. He proposed to kill two bulls for the honour of his birthplace. Apis, Christophe told me, would be his second. It was an interesting trip, and that little city by the sea was ravishing. Their bull-ring dates from the middle of the seventeenth century. It is full of feeling. The ceremonial too—when the horsemen enter and ask the Mayor in his box to throw down the keys of the bull-ring—that was exquisitely conceived. You know, if the keys are caught in the horseman's hat, it is considered a good omen. They were perfectly caught. Our seats were in the front row beside the gates where the bulls enter, so we saw everything.

"Villamarti's first bull was not too badly killed. The second matador, whose name escapes me, killed his without distinction—a foil

8. Mythical beast, half man, half bull. "Levitical" means priestly.

to Villamarti. And the third, Chisto, a laborious, middle-aged professional who had never risen beyond a certain dull competence, was equally of the background. Oh, they are as jealous as the girls of the Comédie Française, these matadors! Villamarti's troupe stood ready for his second bull. The gates opened, and we saw Apis, beautifully balanced on his feet, peer coquettishly round the corner, as though he were at home. A picador—a mounted man with the long lance-goad—stood near the barrier on his right. He had not even troubled to turn his horse, for the capeadors—the men with the cloaks—were advancing to play Apis—to feel his psychology and intentions, according to the rules that are made for bulls who do not think. . . . I did not realise the murder before it was accomplished! The wheel, the rush, the oblique charge from behind, the fall of horse and man were simultaneous. Apis leaped the horse, with whom he had no quarrel, and alighted, all four feet together (it was enough), between the man's shoulders, changed his beautiful feet on the body, and was away, pretending to fall nearly on his nose. Do you follow me? In that instant, by that stumble, he produced the impression that his adorable assassination was a mere bestial blunder. Then, Monsieur, I began to comprehend that it was an artist we had to deal with. He did not stand over the body to draw the rest of the troupe. He chose to reserve that trick. He let the attendants bear out the dead, and went on to amuse himself among the capeadors. Now to Apis, trained among our children in the yards, the cloak was simply a guide to the boy behind it. He pursued, you understand, the person, not the propaganda—the proprietor, not the journal. If a third of our electors of France were as wise, my friend! . . . But it was done leisurely, with humour and a touch of truculence. He romped after one man's cloak as a clumsy dog might do, but I observed that he kept the man on his terrible left side. Christophe whispered to me: 'Wait for his mother's kick. When he has made the fellow confident it will arrive.' It arrived in the middle of a gambol. My God! He lashed out in the air as he frisked. The man dropped like a sack, lifted one hand a little towards his head, and—that was all. So you see, a body was again at his disposition; a second time the cloaks ran up to draw him off, but, a second time, Apis refused his grand scene. A second time he acted that his murder was accident and—he convinced his audience! It was as though he had knocked over a bridge-gate in the marshes by mistake. Unbelievable? I saw it."

The memory sent Monsieur Voiron again to the champagne, and I accompanied him.

"But Apis was not the sole artist present. They say Villamarti comes of a family of actors. I saw him regard Apis with a new eye. He, too, began to understand. He took his cloak and moved out to play him before they should bring on another picador. He had his reputation. Perhaps Apis knew it. Perhaps Villamarti reminded him of some boy with whom he had practised at home. At any rate Apis permitted it—up to a certain point; but he did not allow Villamarti the stage. He cramped him throughout. He dived and plunged clumsily and slowly, but always with menace and always closing in. We could see that the man was conforming to the bull—not the bull to the man; for Apis was playing him towards the centre of the ring, and, in a little while—I watched his face—Villamarti knew it. But I could not fathom the creature's motive. 'Wait,' said old Christophe. 'He wants that picador on the white horse yonder. When he reaches his proper distance he will get him. Villamarti is his cover. He used me once that way.' And so it was, my friend! With the clang of one of our own Seventy-fives, Apis dismissed Villamarti with his chest—breasted him over—and had arrived at his objective near the barrier. The same oblique charge; the head carried low for the sweep of the horns; the immense sideways fall of the horse, broken-legged and half-paralysed; the senseless man on the ground, and—behold Apis between them, backed against the barrier—his right covered by the horse; his left by the body of the man at his feet. The simplicity of it! Lacking the carts and tractors of his early parade-grounds he, being a genius, had extemporised with the materials at hand, and dug himself in. The troupe closed up again, their left wing broken by the kicking horse, their right immobilised by the man's body which Apis bestrode with significance. Villamarti almost threw himself between the horns, but—it was more an appeal than an attack. Apis refused him. He held his base. A picador was sent at him—necessarily from the front, which alone was open. Apis charged—he who, till then, you realise, had not used the horn! The horse went over backwards, the man half beneath him. Apis halted, hooked him under the heart, and threw him to the barrier. We heard his head crack, but he was dead before he hit the wood. There was no demonstration from the audience. They, also, had begun to realise this Foch among bulls! The arena occupied itself again with the dead. Two of the troupe irresolutely tried to play him—God knows in what hope!—but he moved out to the centre of the ring. 'Look!' said Christophe. 'Now he goes to clean himself. That always frightened me.' He knelt down; he began to clean his horns. The earth was hard. He worried at it in an ecstasy of absorption. As he laid his head along and rattled his ears, it was as though he were interrogating the Devils themselves upon their secrets, and always saying impatiently: 'Yes, I know that—and *that*— and *that*! Tell me more—*more*!' In the silence that covered us, a woman cried: 'He digs a grave! Oh, Saints, he digs a grave!' Some others echoed this—not loudly—as a wave echoes in a grotto of the sea.

"And when his horns were cleaned, he rose up and studied poor Villamarti's troupe, eyes in eyes, one by one, with the gravity of an equal in intellect and the remote and merciless resolution of a master in his art. This was more terrifying than his toilette."

"And they—Villamarti's men?" I asked.

"Like the audience, were dominated. They had ceased to posture, or stamp, or address insults to him. They conformed to him. The two other matadors stared. Only Chisto, the oldest, broke silence with some call or other, and Apis turned his head towards him. Otherwise he was isolated, immobile—sombre—meditating on those at his mercy. Ah!

"For some reason the trumpet sounded for the *banderillas*—those gay hooked darts that are planted in the shoulders of bulls who do not think, after their neck-muscles are tired by lifting horses. When such bulls feel the pain, they check for an instant, and, in that instant, the men step gracefully aside. Villamarti's banderillero answered the trumpet mechanically—like one condemned. He stood out, poised the darts and stammered the usual patter of invitation. . . . And after? I do not assert that Apis shrugged his shoulders, but he reduced the episode to its lowest elements, as could only a bull of Gaul. With his truculence was mingled always—owing to the shortness of his tail—a certain Rabelaisian abandon, especially when viewed from the rear. Christophe had often commented upon it. Now Apis brought that quality into play. He circulated round that boy, forcing him to break up his beautiful poses. He studied him from various angles, like an incompetent photographer. He presented to him every portion of his anatomy except his shoulders. At intervals he feigned to run in upon him. My God, he was cruel! But his motive was obvious. He was playing for a laugh from the spectators which should synchronise with the fracture of the human morale. It was achieved. The boy turned and ran towards the barrier. Apis was on him before the laugh ceased; passed him; headed him—what do I say?—herded him off to the left, his horns beside and a little in front of his chest: he did not intend him to escape into a refuge. Some of the troupe would have closed in, but Villamarti cried: 'If he wants him he will take him. Stand!' They stood. Whether the boy slipped or Apis nosed him over I could not see. But he dropped, sobbing. Apis halted like a car with four brakes, struck a pose, smelt him very completely and turned away. It was dismissal more ignominious than degradation at the head of one's battalion. The representation was finished. Remained only for Apis to clear his stage of the subordinate characters.

"Ah! His gesture then! He gave a dramatic start—this Cyrano of the Camargue—as though he was aware of them for the first time. He moved. All their beautiful breeches twinkled for an instant along the top of the barrier. He held the stage alone! But Christophe and I, we trembled! For, observe, he had now involved himself in a stupendous drama of which he only could supply the third act. And, except for an audience on the razor-edge of emotion, he had exhausted his material. Molière[9] himself—we have forgotten, my friend, to drink to the health of that great soul—might have been at a loss. And Tragedy is but a step behind Failure. We could see the four or five Civil Guards, who are sent always to keep order, fingering the breeches of their rifles. They were but waiting a word from the Mayor to fire on him, as they do sometimes at a bull who leaps the barrier among the spectators. They would, of course, have killed or wounded several people—but that would not have saved Apis."

Monsieur Voiron drowned the thought at once, and wiped his beard.

"At that moment Fate—the Genius of France, if you will—sent to assist in the incomparable finale, none other than Chisto, the eldest, and I should have said (but never again will I judge!) the least inspired of all; mediocrity itself, but at heart—and it is the heart that conquers always, my friend—at heart an artist. He descended stiffly into the arena, alone and assured. Apis regarded him, his eyes in his eyes. The man took stance, with his cloak, and called to the bull as to an equal: 'Now, Señor, we will show these honourable caballeros something together.' He advanced thus against this thinker who at a plunge—a kick—a thrust—could, we all knew, have extinguished him. My dear friend, I wish I could convey to you something of the unaffected bonhomie, the humour, the delicacy, the consideration bordering on respect even, with which Apis, the supreme artist, responded to this invitation. It was the Master, wearied after a strenuous hour in the atelier, unbuttoned and at ease with some not inexpert but limited disciple. The telepathy was instantaneous between them. And for good reason! Christophe said to me: 'All's well. That Chisto began among the bulls. I was sure of it when I heard him call just now. He has been a herdsman. He'll pull it off.' There was a little feeling and adjustment, at first, for mutual distances and allowances.

"Oh yes! And here occurred a gross impertinence of Villamarti. He had, after an interval, followed Chisto—to retrieve his reputation. My Faith! I can conceive the elder Dumas slamming his door on an intruder precisely as Apis did. He raced Villamarti into the nearest refuge at once. He stamped his feet outside it, and he

9. The greatest of French comic playwrights.

snorted: 'Go! I am engaged with an artist.' Villamarti went—his reputation left behind for ever.

"Apis returned to Chisto saying: 'Forgive the interruption. I am not always master of my time, but you were about to observe, my dear confrère[10] . . . ?' Then the play began. Out of compliment to Chisto, Apis chose as his objective (every bull varies in this respect) the inner edge of the cloak—that nearest to the man's body. This allows but a few millimetres clearance in charging. But Apis trusted himself as Chisto trusted him, and, this time, he conformed to the man, with inimitable judgment and temper. He allowed himself to be played into the shadow or the sun, as the delighted audience demanded. He raged enormously; he feigned defeat; he despaired in statuesque abandon, and thence flashed into fresh paroxyms of wrath—but always with the detachment of the true artist who knows he is but the vessel of an emotion whence others, not he, must drink. And never once did he forget that honest Chisto's cloak was to him the gauge by which to spare even a hair on the skin. He inspired Chisto too. My God! His youth returned to that meritorious beef-sticker—the desire, the grace, and the beauty of his early dreams. One could almost see that girl of the past for whom he was rising, rising to these present heights of skill and daring. It was *his* hour too—a miraculous hour of dawn returned to gild the sunset. All he knew was at Apis' disposition. Apis acknowledged it with all that he had learned at home, at Arles and in his lonely murders on our grazing-grounds. He flowed round Chisto like a river of death—round his knees, leaping at his shoulders, kicking just clear of one side or the other of his head; behind his back, hissing as he shaved by; and once or twice—inimitable!—he reared wholly up before him while Chisto slipped back from beneath the avalanche of that instructed body. Those two, my dear friend, held five thousand people dumb with no sound but of their breathings—regular as pumps. It was unbearable. Beast and man realised together that we needed a change of note—a *détente*. They relaxed to pure buffoonery. Chisto fell back and talked to him outrageously. Apis pretended he had never heard such language. The audience howled with delight. Chisto slapped him; he took liberties with his short tail, to the end of which he clung while Apis pirouetted; he played about him in all postures; he had become the herdsman again—gross, careless, brutal, but comprehending. Yet Apis was always the more consummate clown. All that time (Christophe and I saw it) Apis drew off towards the gates of the *toril* where so many bulls enter but—have

10. Colleague.

you ever heard of one that returned? *We* knew that Apis knew that as he had saved Chisto, so Chisto would save him. Life is sweet to us all; to the artist who lives many lives in one, sweetest. Chisto did not fail him. At the last, when none could laugh any longer, the man threw his cape across the bull's back, his arm round his neck. He flung up a hand at the gate, as Villamarti, young and commanding but *not* a herdsman, might have raised it, and he cried: 'Gentlemen, open to me and my honourable little donkey.' They opened—I have misjudged Spaniards in my time!—those gates opened to the man and the bull together, and closed behind them. And then? From the Mayor to the Civil Guard they went mad for five minutes, till the trumpets blew and the fifth bull rushed out—an unthinking black Andalusian. I suppose some one killed him. My friend, my very dear friend, to whom I have opened my heart, I confess that I did not watch. Christophe and I, we were weeping together like children of the same Mother. Shall we drink to Her?''

# H. G. WELLS
## 1866–1946

Herbert George Wells was born in Bromley, Kent, England. His father was a semi-professional cricket player who kept various kinds of shops not too successfully, and his mother worked from time to time as a lady's maid. He had an irregular education, but made the most of the chance to read in the library of a great house where his mother worked. Later he failed as a draper's apprentice and was lucky enough to get some good instruction and win a scholarship to the Royal College of Science in London, where he studied under Thomas H. Huxley. But he did not develop as a scientist, turning gradually to journalism and fiction as a way of supporting himself. His "scientific romances" —*The Time Machine* (1895), *The War of the Worlds* (1898), etc.—made him immensely popular and he continued to write, trying his hand at realistic fiction, popular science, social criticism, and history in a perpetual effort to educate the English people and finally the whole world. It is ironic that his early stories and short novels are now his best known works, while his later more "serious" productions are largely ignored.

## The Country of the Blind

Three hundred miles and more from Chimborazo, one hundred from the snows of Cotopaxi, in the wildest wastes of Ecuador's Andes, there lies that mysterious mountain valley, cut off from the world of men, the Country of the Blind. Long years ago that valley lay so far open to the world that men might come at last through frightful gorges and over an icy pass into its equable meadows; and thither indeed men came, a family or so of Peruvian half-breeds fleeing from the lust and tyranny of an evil Spanish ruler. Then came the stupendous outbreak of Mindobamba, when it was night in Quito for seventeen days, and the water was boiling at Yaguachi and all the fish floating dying even as far as Guayaquil; everywhere along the Pacific slopes there were landslips and swift thawings and sudden floods, and one whole side of the old Arauca crest slipped and came down in thunder, and cut off the Country of the Blind for ever from the exploring feet of men. But one of these early settlers had chanced to be on the hither side of the gorges when the world had so terribly shaken itself, and he perforce had to forget his wife and his child and all the friends and possessions he had left up there, and start life over again in the lower world. He started it again but ill, blindness overtook him, and he died of punishment in the mines; but the story he told begot a legend that lingers along the length of the Cordilleras of the Andes to this day.

He told of his reason for venturing back from that fastness, into which he had first been carried lashed to a llama, beside a vast bale of gear, when he was a child. The valley, he said, had in it all that the heart of man could desire—sweet water, pasture, an even climate, slopes of rich brown soil with tangles of a shrub that bore an excellent fruit, and on one side great hanging forests of pine that held the avalanches high. Far overhead, on three sides, vast cliffs of grey-green rock were capped by cliffs of ice; but the glacier stream came not to them but flowed away by the farther slopes, and only now and then huge ice masses fell on the valley side. In this valley it neither rained nor snowed, but the abundant springs gave a rich green pasture, that irrigation would spread over all the valley space. The settlers did well indeed there. Their beasts did well and multiplied, and but one thing marred their happiness. Yet it was enough to mar it greatly. A strange disease had come upon them, and had made all the children born to them there—and indeed, several older children also—blind. It was to seek some charm or antidote against this plague of blindness that he had with fatigue and danger and difficulty returned down the gorge. In those days, in such cases, men did not think of germs and infections but of sins; and it seemed to him that the reason of this affliction must lie in the negligence of these priestless immigrants to set up a shrine so soon as they entered the valley. He wanted a shrine—a handsome, cheap, effectual shrine—to be erected in the valley; he wanted relics and such-like potent things of faith, blessed objects and mysterious medals and prayers. In his wallet he had a bar of native silver for which he would not account; he insisted there was none in the valley with something of the insistence of an inexpert liar. They had all clubbed their money and ornaments together, having little need for such treasure up there, he said, to buy them holy help against their ill. I figure this dim-eyed young mountaineer, sunburnt, gaunt, and anxious, hat-brim clutched feverishly, a man all unused to the ways of the lower world, telling this story to some keen-eyed, attentive priest before the great convulsion; I can picture him presently seeking to return with pious and infallible remedies against that trouble, and the infinite dismay with which he must have faced the tumbled vastness where the gorge had once come out. But the rest of his story of mischances is lost to me, save that I know of his evil death after several years. Poor stray from that remoteness! The stream that had once made the gorge now bursts from the mouth of a rocky cave, and the legend his poor, ill-told story set going developed into the legend of a race of blind men somewhere 'over there' one may still hear to-day.

And amidst the little population of that now isolated and forgotten valley the disease ran its course. The old became groping and purblind, the young saw but dimly, and the children that were born to them saw never at all. But life was very easy in that snow-rimmed basin, lost to all the world, with neither thorns nor briars, with no evil insects nor any beasts save the gentle breed of llamas they had lugged and thrust and followed up the beds of the shrunken rivers in the gorges up which they had come. The seeing had become purblind so gradually that they scarcely noted their loss. They guided the sightless youngsters hither and thither until they knew the whole valley marvellously, and when at last sight died out among them the race lived on. They had even time to adapt themselves to the blind control of fire, which they made carefully in stoves of stone. They were a simple strain of people at the first, unlettered, only slightly touched with the Spanish civilisation, but with something of a tradition of the arts of old Peru and of its lost philosophy. Generation followed generation. They forgot many things; they devised many things. Their tradition of the greater world they came from became mythical in colour and uncertain. In all things save sight they were strong and able; and presently the chance of birth and heredity sent one who had an original mind and who could talk and persuade among them, and then afterwards another. These two passed, leaving their effects, and the little community grew in numbers and in understanding, and met and settled social and economic problems that arose. Generation followed generation. There came a time when a child was born who was fifteen generations from that ancestor who went out of the valley with a bar of silver to seek God's aid, and who never returned. Thereabouts it chanced that a man came into this community from the outer world. And this is the story of that man.

He was a mountaineer from the country near Quito, a man who had been down to the sea and had seen the world, a reader of books in an original way, an acute and enterprising man, and he was taken on by a party of Englishmen who had come out to Ecuador to climb mountains, to replace one of their three Swiss guides who had fallen ill. He climbed here and he climbed there, and then came the attempt on Parascotopetl, the Matterhorn of the Andes, in which he was lost to the outer world. The story of the accident has been written a dozen times. Pointer's narrative is the best. He tells how the party worked their difficult and almost vertical way up to the very foot of the last and greatest precipice, and how they built a night shelter amidst the snow upon a little shelf of rock, and, with a touch of real dramatic power, how presently they found Núñez had gone from them. They shouted, and there was no reply; shouted and whistled, and for the rest of that night they slept no more.

As the morning broke they saw the traces of his fall. It seems impossible he could have uttered a sound. He had slipped eastward towards the unknown side of the mountain; far below he had struck a steep slope of snow, and ploughed his way down it in the midst of a snow avalanche. His track went straight to the edge of a frightful precipice, and beyond that everything was hidden. Far, far below, and hazy with distance, they could see trees rising out of a narrow, shut-in valley—the lost Country of the Blind. But they did not know it was the lost Country of the Blind, nor distinguish it in any way from any other narrow streak of upland valley. Unnerved by this disaster, they abandoned their attempt in the afternoon, and Pointer was called away to the war before he could make another attack. To this day Parascotopetl lifts an unconquered crest, and Pointer's shelter crumbles unvisited amidst the snows.

And the man who fell survived.

At the end of the slope he fell a thousand feet, and came down in the midst of a cloud of snow upon a snow slope even steeper than the one above. Down this he was whirled, stunned and insensible, but without a bone broken in his body; and then at last came to gentler slopes, and at last rolled out and lay still, buried amidst a softening heap of the white masses that had accompanied and saved him. He came to himself with a dim fancy that he was ill in bed; then realised his position with a mountaineer's intelligence, and worked himself loose, and after a rest or so, out until he saw the stars. He rested flat upon his chest for a space, wondering where he was and what had happened to him. He explored his limbs, and discovered that several of his buttons were gone and his coat turned over his head. His knife had gone from his pocket and his hat was lost, though he had tied it under his chin. He recalled that he had been looking for loose stones to raise his piece of the shelter wall. His ice-axe had disappeared.

He decided he must have fallen, and looked up to see, exaggerated by the ghastly light of the rising moon, the tremendous flight he had taken. For a while he lay, gazing blankly at that vast pale cliff towering above, rising moment by moment out of a subsiding tide of darkness. Its phantasmal mysterious beauty held him for a space, and then he was seized with a paroxysm of sobbing laughter. . . .

After a great interval of time he became aware that he was near the lower edge of the snow. Below, down what was now a moonlit and practicable slope, he saw the dark and broken appearance of rock-strewn turf. He struggled to his feet aching in every joint and limb, got down painfully from the heaped loose snow about him, went downward until he was on the turf, and there dropped rather than lay beside a boulder, drank deep from the flask in his inner pocket, and instantly fell asleep. . . .

He was awakened by the singing of birds in the trees far below.

He sat up and perceived he was on a little alp at the foot of a vast precipice, that was grooved by the gully down which he and his snow had come. Over against him another wall of rock reared itself against the sky. The gorge between these precipices ran east and west and was full of the morning sunlight, which lit to the westward the mass of fallen mountain that closed the descending gorge. Below him it seemed there was a precipice equally steep, but behind the snow in the gully he found a sort of chimney-cleft dripping with snow-water down which a desperate man might venture. He found it easier than it seemed, and came at last to another desolate alp, and then after a rock climb of no particular difficulty to a steep slope of trees. He took his bearings and turned his face up the gorge, for he saw it opened out above upon green meadows, among which he now glimpsed quite distinctly a cluster of stone huts of unfamiliar fashion. At times his progress was like clambering along the face of a wall, and after a time the rising sun ceased to strike along the gorge, the voices of the singing birds died away, and the air grew cold and dark about him. But the distant valley with its houses was all the brighter for that. He came presently to talus, and among the rocks he noted—for he was an observant man—an unfamiliar fern that seemed to clutch out of the crevices with intense green hands. He picked a frond or so and gnawed its stalk and found it helpful.

About midday he came at last out of the throat of the gorge into the plain and the sunlight. He was stiff and weary; he sat down in the shadow of a rock, filled up his flask with water from a spring and drank it down, and remained for a time resting before he went on to the houses.

They were very strange to his eyes, and indeed the whole aspect of that valley became, as he regarded it, queerer and more unfamiliar. The greater part of its surface was lush green meadow, starred with many beautiful flowers, irrigated with extraordinary care, and bearing evidence of systematic cropping piece by piece. High up and ringing the valley about was a wall, and what appeared to be a circumferential water-channel, from which the little trickles of water that fed the meadow plants came, and on the higher slopes above this flocks of llamas cropped the scanty herbage. Sheds, apparently shelters or feeding-places for the llamas, stood against the boundary wall here and there. The irrigation streams ran together into a main channel down the centre of the valley, and this was enclosed on either side by a wall breast high. This gave a singularly urban quality to this secluded place, a quality that was greatly enhanced by the fact that a number of paths paved with black and white stones, and each with a curious little kerb at the side, ran hither and thither in an orderly manner. The houses of the central village were quite unlike the casual and higgledy-piggledy agglomeration of the mountain villages he knew; they stood in a continuous row on either side of a central street of astonishing cleanness; here and there their parti-coloured façade was pierced by a door, and not a solitary window broke their even frontage. They were parti-coloured with extraordinary irregularity; smeared with a sort of plaster that was sometimes grey, sometimes drab, sometimes slate-coloured or dark brown; and it was the sight of this wild plastering that first brought the word "blind" into the thoughts of the explorer. "The good man who did that," he thought, "must have been as blind as a bat."

He descended a steep place, and so came to the wall and channel that ran about the valley, near where the latter spouted out its surplus contents into the deeps of the gorge in a thin and wavering thread of cascade. He could now see a number of men and women resting on piled heaps of grass, as if taking a siesta, in the remoter part of the meadow, and nearer the village a number of recumbent children, and then nearer at hand three men carrying pails on yokes along a little path that ran from the encircling wall towards the houses. These latter were clad in garments of llama cloth and boots and belts of leather, and they wore caps of cloth with back and ear flaps. They followed one another in single file, walking slowly and yawning as they walked, like men who have been up all night. There was something so reassuringly prosperous and respectable in their bearing that after a moment's hesitation Núñez stood forward as conspicuously as possible upon his rock, and gave vent to a mighty shout that echoed round the valley.

The three men stopped, and moved their heads as though they were looking about them. They turned their faces this way and that, and Núñez gesticulated with freedom. But they did not appear to see him for all his gestures, and after a time, directing themselves towards the mountains far away to the right, they shouted as if in answer. Núñez bawled again, and then once more, and as he gestured ineffectually the word "blind" came up to the top of his thoughts. "The fools must be blind," he said.

When at last, after much shouting and wrath, Núñez crossed the stream by a little bridge, came through a gate in the wall, and approached them, he was sure that they were blind. He was sure that this was the Country of the Blind of which the legends told. Conviction had sprung upon him, and a sense of great and rather enviable adventure. The three stood side by side, not looking at him, but with their ears directed towards him, judging him by his unfamiliar steps. They stood close together like men a little afraid, and he could see their eyelids closed and sunken, as though the very balls beneath had shrunk away. There was an expression near awe on their faces.

"A man," one said, in hardly recognisable Spanish—"a man it is—a man or a spirit—coming down from the rocks."

But Núñez advanced with the confident steps of a youth who enters upon life. All the old stories of the lost valley and the Country of the Blind had come back to his mind, and through his thoughts ran this old proverb, as if it were a refrain—

"In the Country of the Blind the One-eyed Man is King."

"In the Country of the Blind the One-eyed Man is King."

And very civilly he gave them greeting. He talked to them and used his eyes.

"Where does he come from, brother Pedro?" asked one.

"Down out of the rocks."

"Over the mountains I come," said Núñez, "out of the country beyond there—where men can see. From near Bogotá, where there are a hundred thousands of people, and where the city passes out of sight."

"Sight?" muttered Pedro. "Sight?"

"He comes," said the second blind man, "out of the rocks."

The cloth of their coats Núñez saw was curiously fashioned, each with a different sort of stitching.

They startled him by a simultaneous movement towards him,

each with a hand outstretched. He stepped back from the advance of these spread fingers.

"Come hither," said the third blind man, following his motion and clutching him neatly.

And they held Núñez and felt him over, saying no word further until they had done so.

"Carefully," he cried, with a finger in his eye, and found they thought that organ, with its fluttering lids, a queer thing in him. They went over it again.

"A strange creature, Correa," said the one called Pedro. "Feel the coarseness of his hair. Like a llama's hair."

"Rough he is as the rocks that begot him," said Correa, investigating Núñez's unshaven chin with a soft and slightly moist hand. "Perhaps he will grow finer." Núñez struggled a little under their examination, but they gripped him firm.

"Carefully," he said again.

"He speaks," said the third man. "Certainly he is a man."

"Ugh!" said Pedro, at the roughness of his coat.

"And you have come into the world?" asked Pedro.

"*Out* of the world. Over mountains and glaciers; right over above there, halfway to the sun. Out of the great big world that goes down, twelve days' journey to the sea."

They scarcely seemed to heed him. "Our fathers have told us men may be made by the forces of Nature," said Correa. "It is the warmth of things and moisture, and rottenness—rottenness."

"Let us lead him to the elders," said Pedro.

"Shout first," said Correa, "lest the children be afraid. This is a marvellous occasion."

So they shouted, and Pedro went first and took Núñez by the hand to lead him to the houses.

He drew his hand away. "I can see," he said.

"See?" said Correa.

"Yes, see," said Núñez, turning towards him, and stumbled against Pedro's pail.

"His senses are still imperfect," said the third blind man. "He stumbles, and talks unmeaning words. Lead him by the hand."

"As you will, " said Núñez, and was led along, laughing.

It seemed they knew nothing of sight.

Well, all in good time he would teach them.

He heard people shouting, and saw a number of figures gathering together in the middle roadway of the village.

He found it taxed his nerve and patience more than he had anticipated, that first encounter with the population of the Country of the

Blind. The place seemed larger as he drew near to it, and the smeared plasterings queerer, and a crowd of children and men and women (the women and girls, he was pleased to note, had some of them quite sweet faces, for all that their eyes were shut and sunken) came about him holding on to him, touching him with soft, sensitive hands, smelling at him, and listening at every word he spoke. Some of the maidens and children, however, kept aloof as if afraid, and indeed his voice seemed coarse and rude beside their softer notes. They mobbed him. His three guides kept close to him with an effect of proprietorship, and said again and again, "A wild man out of the rocks."

"Bogotá," he said. "Bogotá. Over the mountain crests."

"A wild man—using wild words," said Pedro. "Did you hear that—*Bogotá*? His mind is hardly formed yet. He has only the beginnings of speech."

A little boy nipped his hand. "Bogotá!" he said mockingly.

"Ay! A city to your village, I come from the great world—where men have eyes and see."

"His name's Bogotá," they said.

"He stumbled," said Correa, "stumbled twice as we came hither."

"Bring him to the elders."

And they thrust him suddenly through a doorway into a room as black as pitch, save at the end there faintly glowed a fire. The crowd closed in behind him and shut out all but the faintest glimmer of day, and before he could arrest himself he had fallen headlong over the feet of a seated man. His arm, out-flung, struck the face of someone else as he went down; he felt the soft impact of features and heard a cry of anger, and for a moment he struggled against a number of hands that clutched him. It was a one-sided fight. An inkling of the situation came to him, and he lay quiet.

"I fell down," he said; "I couldn't see in this pitchy darkness."

There was a pause as if the unseen persons about him tried to understand his words. Then the voice of Correa said: "He is but newly formed. He stumbles as he walks and mingles words that mean nothing with his speech."

Others also said things about him that he heard or understood imperfectly.

"May I sit up?" he asked, in a pause. "I will not struggle against you again."

They consulted and let him rise.

The voice of an older man began to question him, and Núñez found himself trying to explain the great world out of which he had fallen, and the sky and mountains and sight and such-like marvels, to these elders who sat in darkness in the Country of the Blind. And they would believe and understand nothing whatever he told them, a thing quite outside his expectation. They would not even understand many of his words. For fourteen generations these people had been blind and cut off from all the seeing world; the names for all the things of sight had faded and changed; the story of the outer world was faded and changed to a child's story; and they had ceased to concern themselves with anything beyond the rocky slopes above their circling wall. Blind men of genius had arisen among them and questioned the shreds of belief and tradition they had brought with them from their seeing days, and had dismissed all these things as idle fancies, and replaced them with new and saner explanations. Much of their imagination had shrivelled with their eyes, and they had made for themselves new imaginations with their ever more sensitive ears and finger-tips. Slowly Núñez realised this; that his expectation of wonder and reverence at his origin and his gifts was not to be borne out; and after his poor attempt to explain sight to them had been set aside as the confused version of a new-made being describing the marvels of his incoherent sensations, he subsided, a little dashed, into listening to their instruction. And the eldest of the blind men explained to him life and philosophy and religion, how that the world (meaning their valley) had been first an empty hollow in the rocks, and then had come, first, inanimate things without the gift of touch, and llamas and a few other creatures that had little sense, and then men, and at last angels, whom one could hear singing and making fluttering sounds, but whom no one could touch at all, which puzzled Núñez greatly until he thought of the birds.

He went on to tell Núñez how this time had been divided into the warm and the cold, which are the blind equivalents of day and night, and how it was good to sleep in the warm and work during the cold, so that now, but for his advent, the whole town of the blind would have been asleep. He said Núñez must have been specially created to learn and serve the wisdom they had acquired, and for that all his mental incoherency and stumbling behavior he must have courage and do his best to learn, and at that all the people in the doorway murmured encouragingly. He said the night—for the blind call their day night—was now far gone, and it behooved everyone to go back to sleep. He asked Núñez if he knew how to sleep, and Núñez said he did, but that before sleep he wanted food.

They brought him food—llama's milk in a bowl, and rough salted bread—and led him to a lonely place to eat out of their hearing, and afterwards to slumber until the chill of the mountain evening roused them to begin their day again. But Núñez slumbered not at all.

Instead, he sat up in the place where they had left him, resting his limbs and turning the unanticipated circumstances of his arrival over and over in his mind.

Every now and then he laughed, sometimes with amusement, and sometimes with indignation.

"Unformed mind!" he said. "Got no senses yet! They little know they've been insulting their heaven-sent king and master. I see I must bring them to reason. Let me think—let me think."

He was still thinking when the sun set.

Núñez had an eye for all beautiful things, and it seemed to him that the glow upon the snowfields and glaciers that rose about the valley on every side was the most beautiful thing he had ever seen. His eyes went from that inaccessible glory to the village and irrigated fields, fast sinking into the twilight, and suddenly a wave of emotion took him, and he thanked God from the bottom of his heart that the power of sight had been given him.

He heard a voice calling to him from out of the village.

"Ya ho there, Bogotá! Come hither!"

At that he stood up smiling. He would show these people once and for all what sight would do for a man. They would seek him, but not find him.

"You move not, Bogotá," said the voice.

He laughed noiselessly, and made two stealthy steps aside from the path.

"Trample not on the grass, Bogotá; that is not allowed."

Núñez had scarcely heard the sound he made himself. He stopped, amazed.

The owner of the voice came running up the piebald path towards him.

He stepped back into the pathway. "Here I am," he said.

"Why did you not come when I called you?" said the blind man. "Must you be led like a child? Cannot you hear the path as you walk?"

Núñez laughed. "I can see it," he said.

"There is no such word as *see*," said the blind man, after a pause. "Cease this folly, and follow the sound of my feet."

Núñez followed, a little annoyed.

"My time will come," he said.

"You'll learn," the blind man answered. "There is much to learn in the world."

"Has no one told you, 'In the Country of the Blind the One-eyed Man is King'?"

"What is blind?" asked the blind man carelessly over his shoulder.

Four days passed, and the fifth found the King of the Blind still incognito, as a clumsy and useless stranger among his subjects.

It was, he found, much more difficult to proclaim himself than he had supposed, and in the meantime, while he meditated his *coup d'état*, he did what he was told and learned the manners and customs of the Country of the Blind. He found working and going about at night a particularly irksome thing, and he decided that that should be the first thing he would change.

They led a simple, laborious life, these people, with all the elements of virtue and happiness, as these things can be understood by men. They toiled, but not oppressively; they had food and clothing sufficient for their needs; they had days and seasons of rest; they made much of music and singing, and there was love among them, and little children.

It was marvellous with what confidence and precision they went about their ordered world. Everything, you see, had been made to fit their needs; each of the radiating paths of the valley area had a constant angle to the others, and was distinguished by a special notch upon its kerbing; all obstacles and irregularities of path or meadow had long since been cleared away; all their methods and procedure arose naturally from their special needs. Their senses had become marvellously acute; they could hear and judge the slightest gesture of a man a dozen paces away—could hear the very beating of his heart. Intonation had long replaced expression with them, and touches gesture, and their work with hoe and spade and fork was as free and confident as garden work can be. Their sense of smell was extraordinarily fine; they could distinguish individual differences as readily as a dog can, and they went about the tending of the llamas, who lived among the rocks above and came to the wall for food and shelter, with ease and confidence. It was only when at last Núñez sought to assert himself that he found how easy and confident their movements could be.

He rebelled only after he had tried persuasion.

He tried at first on several occasions to tell them of sight. "Look you here, you people," he said. "There are things you do not understand in me."

Once or twice one or two of them attended to him; they sat with faces downcast and ears turned intelligently towards him, and he did his best to tell them what it was to see. Among his hearers was a girl, with eyelids less red and sunken than the others, so that one could almost fancy she was hiding eyes, whom especially he hoped to persuade. He spoke of the beauties of sight, of watching the mountains, of the sky and the sunrise, and they heard him with amused incredulity that presently became condemnatory. They told him there were indeed no mountains at all, but that the end of the rocks where the llamas grazed was indeed the end of the world;

thence sprang a cavernous roof of the universe, from which the dew and the avalanches fell; and when he maintained stoutly the world had neither end nor roof such as they supposed, they said his thoughts were wicked. So far as he could describe sky and clouds and stars to them it seemed to them a hideous void, a terrible blankness in the place of the smooth roof to things in which they believed—it was an article of faith with them that the cavern roof was exquisitely smooth to the touch. He saw that in some manner he shocked them, and gave up that aspect of the matter altogether, and tried to show them the practical value of sight. One morning he saw Pedro in the path called Seventeen and coming towards the central houses, but still too far off for hearing or scent and he told them as much. "In a little while," he prophesied, "Pedro will be here." An old man remarked that Pedro had no business on Path Seventeen, and then, as if in confirmation, that individual as he drew near turned and went transversely into Path Ten, and so back with nimble paces towards the outer wall. They mocked Núñez when Pedro did not arrive, and afterwards, when he asked Pedro questions to clear his character, Pedro denied and outfaced him, and was afterwards hostile to him.

Then he induced them to let him go a long way up the sloping meadows towards the wall with one complacent individual, and to him he promised to describe all that happened among the houses. He noted certain goings and comings, but the things that really seemed to signify to these people happened inside of or behind the windowless houses—the only things they took note of to test him by—and of these he could see or tell nothing; and it was after the failure of this attempt, and the ridicule they could not repress, that he resorted to force. He thought of seizing a spade and suddenly smiting one or two of them to earth, and so in fair combat showing the advantage of eyes. He went so far with that resolution as to seize his spade, and then he discovered a new thing about himself, and that was that it was impossible for him to hit a blind man in cold blood.

He hesitated, and found them all aware that he snatched up the spade. They stood alert, with their heads on one side, and bent ears towards him for what he would do next.

"Put that spade down," said one, and he felt a sort of helpless horror. He came near obedience.

Then he thrust one backwards against a house wall, and fled past him and out of the village.

He went athwart one of their meadows, leaving a track of trampled grass behind his feet, and presently sat down by the side of one of their ways. He felt something of the buoyancy that comes to all men in the beginning of a fight, but more perplexity. He began to realise that you cannot even fight happily with creatures who stand upon a different mental basis to yourself. Far away he saw a number of men carrying spades and sticks come out of the street of houses, and advance in a spreading line along the several paths towards him. They advanced slowly, speaking frequently to one another, and ever and again the whole cordon would halt and sniff the air and listen.

The first time they did this Núñez laughed. But afterwards he did not laugh.

One struck his trail in the meadow grass, and came stooping and feeling his way along it.

For five minutes he watched the slow extension of the cordon, and then his vague disposition to do something forthwith became frantic. He stood up, went a pace or so towards the circumferential wall, turned, and went back a little way. There they all stood in a crescent, still and listening.

He also stood still, gripping his spade very tightly in both hands. Should he charge them?

The pulse in his ears ran into the rhythm of "In the Country of the Blind the One-eyed Man is King!"

Should he charge them?

He looked back at the high and unclimbable wall behind—unclimbable because of its smooth plastering, but withal pierced with many little doors, and at the approaching line of seekers. Behind these, others were now coming out of the street of houses.

Should he charge them?

"Bogotá!" called one. "Bogotá! where are you?"

He gripped his spade still tighter, and advanced down the meadows towards the place of habitations, and directly he moved they converged upon him. "I'll hit them if they touch me," he swore; "by Heaven, I will. I'll hit." He called aloud, "Look here, I'm going to do what I like in this valley. Do you hear? I'm going to do what I like and go where I like!"

They were moving in upon him quickly, groping, yet moving rapidly. It was like playing blind man's buff, with everyone blindfolded except one. "Get hold of him!" cried one. He found himself in the arc of a loose curve of pursuers. He felt suddenly he must be active and resolute.

"You don't understand," he cried in a voice that was meant to be great and resolute, and which broke. "You are blind, and I can see. Leave me alone!"

"Bogotá! Put down that spade, and come off the grass!"

The last order, grotesque in its urban familiarity, produced a gust of anger.

"I'll hurt you," he said, sobbing with emotion. "By Heaven, I'll hurt you. Leave me alone!"

He began to run, not knowing clearly where to run. He ran from the nearest blind man, because it was a horror to hit him. He stopped, and then made a dash to escape from their closing ranks. He made for where a gap was wide, and the men on either side, with a quick perception of the approach of his paces, rushed in on one another. He sprang forward, and then saw he must be caught, and *swish!* the spade had struck. He felt the soft thud of hand and arm, and the man was down with a yell of pain, and he was through.

Through! And then he was close to the street of houses again, and blind men, whirling spades and stakes, were running with a sort of reasoned swiftness hither and thither.

He heard steps behind him just in time, and found a tall man rushing forward and swiping at the sound of him. He lost his nerve, hurled his spade a yard wide at his antagonist, and whirled about and fled, fairly yelling as he dodged another.

He was panic-stricken. He ran furiously to and fro, dodging when there was no need to dodge, and in his anxiety to see on every side of him at once, stumbling. For a moment, he was down and they heard his fall. Far away in the circumferential wall a little doorway looked like heaven, and he set off in a wild rush for it. He did not even look round at his pursuers until it was gained, and he had stumbled across the bridge, clambered a little way among the rocks, to the surprise and dismay of a young llama, who went leaping out of sight, and lay down sobbing for breath.

And so his *coup d'état* came to an end.

He stayed outside the wall of the valley of the Blind for two nights and days without food or shelter, and meditated upon the unexpected. During these meditations he repeated very frequently and always with a profounder note of derision the exploded proverb: "In the Country of the Blind the One-Eyed Man is King." He thought chiefly of ways of fighting and conquering these people, and it grew clear that for him no practicable way was possible. He had no weapons, and now it would be hard to get one.

The canker of civilisation had got to him even in Bogotá, and he could not find it in himself to go down and assassinate a blind man. Of course, if he did that, he might then dictate terms on the threat of assassinating them all. But—sooner or later he must sleep! . . .

He tried also to find food among the pine trees, to be comfortable under pine boughs while the frost fell at night, and—with less con-

fidence—to catch a llama by artifice in order to try to kill it—
perhaps by hammering it with a stone—and so finally, perhaps, to
eat some of it. But the llamas had a doubt of him and regarded him
with distrustful brown eyes, and spat when he drew near. Fear
came on him the second day and fits of shivering. Finally he
crawled down to the wall of the Country of the Blind and tried to
make terms. He crawled along by the stream shouting, until two
blind men came out to the gate and talked to him.

"I was mad," he said. "But I was only newly made."

They said that was better.

He told them he was wiser now, and repented of all he had done.

Then he wept without intention, for he was very weak and ill
now, and they took that as a favourable sign.

They asked him if he still thought he could "see."

"No," he said. "That was folly. The word means nothing—less
than nothing!"

They asked him what was overhead.

"About ten times ten the height of a man there is a roof above the
world—of rock—and very, very smooth." . . . He burst again into
hysterical tears. "Before you ask me any more, give me some food or
I shall die."

He expected dire punishments, but these blind people were capable of toleration. They regarded his rebellion as but one more proof
of his general idiocy and inferiority; and after they had whipped
him they appointed him to do the simplest and heaviest work they
had for anyone to do, and he, seeing no other way of living, did
submissively what he was told.

He was ill for some days, and they nursed him kindly. That refined his submission. But they insisted on his lying in the dark, and
that was a great misery. And blind philosophers came and talked to
him of the wicked levity of his mind, and reproved him so impressively for his doubts about the lid of rock that covered their cosmic
casserole that he almost doubted whether indeed he was not the
victim of hallucination in not seeing it overhead.

So Núñez became a citizen of the Country of the Blind, and these
people ceased to be a generalised people and became individualities
and familiar to him, while the world beyond the mountains became
more and more remote and unreal. There was Yacob, his master, a
kindly man when not annoyed; there was Pedro, Yacob's nephew;
and there was Medina-saroté, who was the youngest daughter of
Yacob. She was little esteemed in the world of the Blind, because
she had a clear-cut face, and lacked that satisfying, glossy smoothness that is the blind man's ideal of feminine beauty; but Núñez
thought her beautiful at first, and presently the most beautiful thing

in the whole creation. Her closed eyelids were not sunken and red after the common way of the valley, but lay as though they might open again at any moment; and she had long eyelashes, which were considered a grave disfigurement. And her voice was strong, and did not satisfy the acute hearing of the valley swains. So that she had no lover.

There came a time when Núñez thought that, could he win her, he would be resigned to live in the valley for all the rest of his days.

He watched her; he sought opportunities of doing her little services, and presently he found that she observed him. Once at a rest-day gathering they sat side by side in the dim starlight, and the music was sweet. His hand came upon hers and he dared to clasp it. Then very tenderly she returned his pressure. And one day, as they were at their meal in the darkness, he felt her hand very softly seeking him, and as it chanced the fire leaped then and he saw the tenderness of her face.

He sought to speak to her.

He went to her one day when she was sitting in the summer moonlight spinning. The light made her a thing of silver and mystery. He sat down at her feet and told her he loved her, and told her how beautiful she seemed to him. He had a lover's voice, he spoke with a tender reverence that came near to awe, and she had never before been touched by adoration. She made him no definite answer, but it was clear his words pleased her.

After that he talked to her whenever he could take an opportunity. The valley became the world for him, and the world beyond the mountains where men lived in sunlight seemed no more than a fairy tale he would some day pour into her ears. Very tentatively and timidly he spoke to her of sight.

Sight seemed to her the most poetical of fancies, and she listened to his descriptions of the stars and the mountains and her own sweet white-lit beauty as though it was a guilty indulgence. She did not believe, she could only half understand, but she was mysteriously delighted, and it seemed to him that she completely understood.

His love lost its awe and took courage. Presently he was for demanding her of Yacob and the elders in marriage, but she became fearful and delayed. And it was one of her elder sisters who first told Yacob that Medina-saroté and Núñez were in love.

There was from the first very great opposition to the marriage of Núñez and Medina-saroté; not so much because they valued her as because they held him as a being apart, an idiot, incompetent thing below the permissible level of a man. Her sisters opposed it bitterly as bringing discredit on them all; and old Yacob, though he had formed a sort of liking for his clumsy, obedient serf, shook his head and said the thing could not be. The young men were all angry at the idea of corrupting the race, and one went so far as to revile and strike Núñez. He struck back. Then for the first time he found an advantage in seeing, even by twilight, and after that fight was over no one was disposed to raise a hand against him. But they still found his marriage impossible.

Old Yacob had a tenderness for his last little daughter, and was grieved to have her weep upon his shoulder.

"You see, my dear, he's an idiot. He has delusions; he can't do anything right."

"I know," wept Medina-saroté. "But he's better than he was. He's getting better. And he's strong, dear father, and kind—stronger and kinder than any other man in the world. And he loves me—and, Father, I love him."

Old Yacob was greatly distressed to find her inconsolable, and, besides—what made it more distressing—he liked Núñez for many things. So he went and sat in the windowless council-chamber with the other elders and watched the trend of the talk, and said, at the proper time, "He's better than he was. Very likely; some day, we shall find him as sane as ourselves."

Then afterwards one of the elders, who thought deeply, had an idea. He was the great doctor among these people, their medicine-man, and he had a very philosophical and inventive mind, and the idea of curing Núñez of his peculiarities appealed to him. One day when Yacob was present he returned to the topic of Núñez.

"I have examined Bogotá," he said, "and the case is clearer to me. I think very probably he might be cured."

"That is what I have always hoped," said old Yacob.

"His brain is affected," said the blind doctor.

The elders murmured assent.

"Now *what* affects it?"

"Ah!" said old Yacob.

"*This*," said the doctor, answering his own question. "Those queer things that are called the eyes, and which exist to make an agreeable soft depression in the face, are diseased, in the case of Bogotá, in such a way as to affect his brain. They are greatly distended, he has eyelashes, and his eyelids move, and consequently his brain is in a state of constant irritation and distraction."

"Yes?" said old Yacob. "Yes?"

"And I think I may say with reasonable certainty that, in order to cure him completely, all we need do is a simple and easy surgical operation—namely, to remove these irritant bodies."

"And then he will be sane?"

"Then he will be perfectly sane, and a quite admirable citizen."

"Thank Heaven for science!" said old Yacob, and went forth at once to tell Núñez of his happy hopes.

But Núñez's manner of receiving the good news struck him as being cold and disappointing.

"One might think," he said, "from the tone you take, that you did not care for my daughter."

It was Medina-saroté who persuaded Núñez to face the blind surgeons.

"*You* do not want me," he said, "to lose my gift of sight?"

She shook her head.

"My world is sight."

Her head drooped lower.

"There are the beautiful things, the beautiful little things—the flowers, the lichens among the rocks, the lightness and softness on a piece of fur, the far sky with its drifting down of clouds, the sunsets and the stars. And there is *you*. For you alone it is good to have sight, to see your sweet, serene face, your kindly lips, your dear, beautiful hands folded together. . . . It is these eyes of mine you won, these eyes that hold me to you, that these idiots seek. I must touch you, hear you, and never see you again. I must come under that roof of rock and stone and darkness, that horrible roof under which your imagination stoops. . . . No; you would not have me do that?"

A disagreeable doubt had arisen in him. He stopped, and left the thing a question.

"I wish," she said, "sometimes——" She paused.

"Yes?" said he, a little apprehensively.

"I wish sometimes—you would not talk like that."

"Like what?"

"I know it's pretty—it's your imagination. I love it, but *now*——"

He felt cold. "*Now?*" he said faintly.

She sat still.

"You mean—you think—I should be better, better perhaps——"

He was realising things very swiftly. He felt anger, indeed, anger at the dull course of fate, but also sympathy for her lack of understanding—sympathy near akin to pity.

"*Dear*," he said, and he could see by her whiteness how intensely her spirit pressed against the things she could not say. He put his arms about her, he kissed her ear, and they sat for a time in silence.

"If I were to consent to this?" he said at last, in a voice that was very gentle.

She flung her arms about him, weeping wildly. "Oh, if you would," she sobbed, "if only you would!"

For a week before the operation that was to raise him from his servitude and inferiority to the level of a blind citizen Núñez knew nothing of sleep, and all through the warm sunlit hours, while the others slumbered happily, he sat brooding or wandered aimlessly, trying to bring his mind to bear on his dilemma. He had given his answer, he had given his consent, and still he was not sure. And at last work-time was over, the sun rose in splendour over the golden crests, and his last day of vision began for him. He had a few minutes with Medina-saroté before she went apart to sleep.

"To-morrow," he said, "I shall see no more."

"Dear heart!" she answered, and pressed his hands with all her strength.

"They will hurt you but little," she said; "and you are going through this pain—you are going through it, dear lover, for *me*. . . . Dear, if a woman's heart and life can do it, I will repay you. My dearest one, my dearest with the tender voice, I will repay."

He was drenched in pity for himself and her.

He held her in his arms, and pressed his lips to hers, and looked on her sweet face for the last time. "Good-bye!" he whispered at that dear sight, "good-bye!"

And then in silence he turned away from her.

She could hear his slow retreating footsteps, and something in the rhythm of them threw her into a passion of weeping.

He had fully meant to go to a lonely place where the meadows were beautiful with white narcissus, and there remain until the hour of his sacrifice should come, but as he went he lifted up his eyes and saw the morning, the morning like an angel in golden armour, marching down the steeps. . . .

It seemed to him that before this splendour he, and this blind world in the valley, and his love, and all, were no more than a pit of sin.

He did not turn aside as he had meant to do, but went on, and passed through the wall of the circumference and out upon the rocks, and his eyes were always upon the sunlit ice and snow.

He saw their infinite beauty, and his imagination soared over them to the things beyond he was now to resign for ever.

He thought of that great free world he was parted from, the world that was his own, and he had a vision of those further slopes, distance beyond distance, with Bogotá, a place of multitudinous stirring beauty, a glory by day, a luminous mystery by night, a place of palaces and fountains and statues and white houses, lying beautifully in the middle distance. He thought how for a day or so one might come down through passes, drawing ever nearer and nearer to its busy streets and ways. He thought of the river journey, day by day, from great Bogotá to the still vaster world beyond, through towns and villages, forest and desert places, the rushing river day by day, until its banks receded and the big steamers came splashing by, and one had reached the sea—the limitless sea, with its thousand islands, its thousands of islands, and its ships seen dimly far away in their incessant journeyings round and about that greater world. And there, unpent by mountains, one saw the sky— the sky, not such a disc as one saw it here, but an arch of immeasurable blue, a deep of deeps in which the circling stars were floating. . . .

His eyes scrutinised the great curtain of the mountains with a keener inquiry.

For example, if one went so, up that gully and to that chimney there, then one might come out high among those stunted pines that ran round in a sort of shelf and rose still higher and higher as it passed above the gorge. And then? That talus might be managed. Thence perhaps a climb might be found to take him up to the precipice that came below the snow; and if that chimney failed, then another farther to the east might serve his purpose better. And then? Then one would be out upon the amber-lit snow there, and halfway up to the crest of those beautiful desolations.

He glanced back at the village, then turned right round and regarded it steadfastly.

He thought of Medina-saroté, and she had become small and remote.

He turned again towards the mountain wall, down which the day had come to him.

Then very circumspectly he began to climb.

When sunset came he was no longer climbing, but he was far and high. He had been higher, but he was still very high. His clothes were torn, his limbs were blood-stained, he was bruised in many places, but he lay as if he were at his ease, and there was a smile on his face.

From where he rested the valley seemed as if it were in a pit and nearly a mile below. Already it was dim with haze and shadow, though the mountain summits around him were things of light and fire, and the little details of the rocks near at hand were drenched with subtle beauty—a vein of green mineral piercing the grey, the flash of crystal faces here and there, a minute, minutely beautiful orange lichen close beside his face. There were deep mysterious shadows in the gorge, blue deepening into purple, and purple into a luminous darkness, and overhead was the illimitable vastness of the sky. But he heeded these things no longer, but lay quite inactive there, smiling as if he were satisfied merely to have escaped from the valley of the Blind in which he had thought to be King.

The glow of the sunset passed, and the night came, and still he lay peacefully contented under the cold stars.

# STEPHEN LEACOCK
1869–1944

Born in Swanmore, Hampshire, Leacock came with his parents to Canada in 1876 and settled on a farm several miles south of Lake Simcoe. He attended Upper Canada College and, in 1887, entered University College, the University of Toronto, on scholarship. That year his father deserted the family and, to help support his ten sisters and brothers, Leacock left university to teach, first at Uxbridge High School and, from 1890–99, at Upper Canada College. He completed his degree in Modern Languages at McGill in 1891. In 1899, inspired by Thorstein Veblen's *Theory of the Leisure Class*, he enrolled at the University of Chicago to study economics under Veblen, received his Ph.D. in 1903, and became professor of economics at McGill University. He was appointed chairman of his department in 1908, a position he held until his retirement in 1936. He published his first and most profitable book—*Elements of Political Science*—in 1906, which became a standard textbook translated into several languages. His career as a humorist began casually. Against the advice of a friend who thought he would damage his scholarly reputation, Leacock collected humorous sketches he had earlier written for magazines and published them at his own expense as *Literary Lapses* in 1910. The book was an immediate international success. His best book, *Sunshine Sketches of a Little Town* (1912), was based on his summer holidays in Orillia, where he had bought a farm in 1908. Once established as a writer, Leacock averaged a book of humor a year, as well as biographies, social commentaries, and popular histories. A great lecturer and raconteur, he travelled on many speaking tours, which assured his reputation as Canada's greatest humorist. He died of cancer in 1944.

## The Marine Excursion of the Knights of Pythias

Half-past six on a July morning! The *Mariposa Belle* is at the wharf, decked in flags, with steam up ready to start.

Excursion day!

Half-past six on a July morning, and Lake Wissanotti lying in the sun as calm as glass. The opal colours of the morning light are shot from the surface of the water.

Out on the lake the last thin threads of the mist are clearing away like flecks of cotton wool.

The long call of the loon echoes over the lake. The air is cool and fresh. There is in it all the new life of the land of the silent pine and the moving waters. Lake Wissanotti in the morning sunlight! Don't talk to me of the Italian lakes, or the Tyrol or the Swiss Alps. Take them away. Move them somewhere else. I don't want them.

Excursion Day, at half-past six of a summer morning! With the boat all decked in flags and all the people in Mariposa on the wharf, and the band in peaked caps with big cornets tied to their bodies ready to play at any minute! I say! Don't tell me about the Carnival of Venice and the Delhi Durbar. Don't! I wouldn't look at them. I'd shut my eyes! For light and colour give me every time an excursion out of Mariposa down the lake to the Indian's Island out of sight in the morning mist. Talk of your Papal Zouaves and your Buckingham Palace Guard! I want to see the Mariposa band in uniform and the Mariposa Knights of Pythias with their aprons and their insignia and their picnic baskets and their five-cent cigars!

Half-past six in the morning, and all the crowd on the wharf and the boat due to leave in half an hour. Notice it!—in half an hour. Already she's whistled twice (at six, and at six fifteen), and at any minute now, Christie Johnson will step into the pilot house and pull the string for the warning whistle that the boat will leave in half an hour. So keep ready. Don't think of running back to Smith's Hotel for the sandwiches. Don't be fool enough to try to go up to the Greek Store, next to Netley's, and buy fruit. You'll be left behind for sure if you do. Never mind the sandwiches and the fruit! Anyway, here comes Mr. Smith himself with a huge basket of provender that would feed a factory. There must be sandwiches in that. I think I can hear them clinking. And behind Mr. Smith is the German waiter from the caff with another basket—indubitably lager beer; and behind him, the bartender of the hotel, carrying nothing, as far as one can see. But of course if you know Mariposa you will understand that why he looks so nonchalant and empty-handed is because he has two bottles of rye whisky under his linen duster. You know, I think, the peculiar walk of a man with two bottles of whisky in the inside pockets of a linen coat. In Mariposa, you see, to bring beer to an excursion is quite in keeping with public opinion. But, whisky— well, one has to be a little careful.

Do I say that Mr. Smith is here? Why, everybody's here. There's Hussell the editor of the *Newspacket*, wearing a blue ribbon on his coat, for the Mariposa Knights of Pythias are, by their constitution, dedicated to temperance; and there's Henry Mullins, the manager of the Exchange Bank, also a Knight of Pythias, with a small flask of Pogram's Special in his hip pocket as a sort of amendment to the constitution. And there's Dean Drone, the Chaplain of the Order, with a fishing-rod (you never saw such green bass as lie among the rocks at Indian's Island), and with a trolling line in case of maskinonge, and a landing-net in case of pickerel, and with his eldest daughter, Lilian Drone, in case of young men. There never was such a fisherman as the Rev. Rupert Drone.

\*     \*     \*

Perhaps I ought to explain that when I speak of the excursion as being of the Knights of Pythias, the thing must not be understood in any narrow sense. In Mariposa practically everybody belongs to the Knights of Pythias just as they do to everything else. That's the great thing about the town and that's what makes it so different from the city. Everybody is in everything.

You should see them on the seventeenth of March, for example, when everybody wears a green ribbon and they're all laughing and glad—you know what the Celtic nature is—and talking about Home Rule.

On St. Andrew's Day every man in town wears a thistle and shakes hands with everybody else, and you see the fine old Scotch honesty beaming out of their eyes.

And on St. George's Day!—well, there's no heartiness like the good old English spirit, after all; why shouldn't a man feel glad that he's an Englishman?

Then on the Fourth of July there are stars and stripes flying over half the stores in town, and suddenly all the men are seen to smoke cigars, and to know all about Roosevelt and Bryan and the Philippine Islands. Then you learn for the first time that Jeff Thorpe's people came from Massachusetts and that his uncle fought at Bunker Hill (anyway Jefferson will swear it was in Dakota all right enough); and you find that George Duff has a married sister in Rochester and that her husband is all right; in fact, George was down there as recently as eight years ago. Oh, it's the most American town imaginable is Mariposa—on the fourth of July.

But wait, just wait, if you feel anxious about the solidity of the British connexion, till the twelfth of the month, when everybody is wearing an orange streamer in his coat and the Orangemen (every man in town) walk in the big procession. Allegiance! Well, perhaps you remember the address they gave to the Prince of Wales on the platform of the Mariposa station as he went through on his tour to the west. I think that pretty well settled that question.

So you will easily understand that of course everybody belongs to the Knights of Pythias and the Masons and Oddfellows, just as they all belong to the Snow Shoe Club and the Girls' Friendly Society.

And meanwhile the whistle of the steamer has blown again for a quarter to seven—loud and long this time, for anyone not here now is late for certain, unless he should happen to come down in the last fifteen minutes.

What a crowd upon the wharf and how they pile onto the steamer!

It's a wonder that the boat can hold them all. But that's just the marvellous thing about the *Mariposa Belle.*

I don't know—I have never known—where the steamers like the *Mariposa Belle* come from. Whether they are built by Harland and Wolff of Belfast, or whether, on the other hand, they are not built by Harland and Wolff of Belfast, is more than one would like to say offhand.

The *Mariposa Belle* always seems to me to have some of those strange properties that distinguish Mariposa itself. I mean, her size seems to vary so. If you see her there in the winter, frozen in the ice beside the wharf with a snowdrift against the windows of the pilot house, she looks a pathetic little thing the size of a butternut. But in the summer time, especially after you've *been* in Mariposa for a month or two, and have paddled alongside of her in a canoe, she gets larger and taller, and with a great sweep of black sides, till you see no difference between the *Mariposa Belle* and the *Lusitania.* Each one is a big steamer and that's all you can say.

Nor do her measurements help you much. She draws about eighteen inches forward, and more than that—at least half an inch more, astern, and when she's loaded down with an excursion crowd she draws a good two inches more. And above the water—why, look at all the decks on her! There's the deck you walk onto, from the wharf, all shut in, with windows along it, and the after cabin with the long table, and above that the deck with all the chairs piled upon it, and the deck in front where the band stand round in a circle, and the pilot house is higher than that, and above the pilot house is the board with the gold name and the flag pole and the steel ropes and the flags; and fixed in somewhere on the different levels is the lunch counter where they sell the sandwiches, and the engine room, and down below the deck level, beneath the water line, is the place where the crew sleep. What with steps and stairs and passages and piles of cordwood for the engine—oh, no, I guess Harland and Wolff didn't build her. They couldn't have.

Yet even with a huge boat like the *Mariposa Belle,* it would be impossible for her to carry all of the crowd that you see in the boat and on the wharf. In reality, the crowd is made up of two classes— all of the people in Mariposa who are going on the excursion and all those who are not. Some come for the one reason and some for the other.

The two tellers of the Exchange Bank are both there standing side by side. But one of them—the one with the cameo pin and the long face like a horse—is going, and the other—with the other cameo pin and the face like another horse—is not. In the same way, Hussell of the *Newspacket* is going, but his brother, beside him, isn't. Lilian

Drone is going, but her sister can't; and so on all through the crowd.

\*     \*     \*

And to think that things should look like that on the morning of a steamboat accident.

How strange life is!

To think of all these people so eager and anxious to catch the steamer, and some of them running to catch it, and so fearful that they might miss it—the morning of a steamboat accident. And the captain blowing his whistle, and warning them so severely that he would leave them behind—leave them out of the accident! And everybody crowding so eagerly to be in the accident.

Perhaps life is like that all through.

Strangest of all to think, in a case like this, of the people who were left behind, or in some way or other prevented from going, and always afterwards told of how they had escaped being on board the *Mariposa Belle* that day!

Some of the instances were certainly extraordinary.

Nivens, the lawyer, escaped from being there merely by the fact that he was away in the city.

Towers, the tailor, only escaped owing to the fact that, not intending to go on the excursion he had stayed in bed till eight o'clock and so had not gone. He narrated afterwards that waking up that morning at half-past five, he had thought of the excursion and for some unaccountable reason had felt glad that he was not going.

\*     \*     \*

The case of Yodel, the auctioneer, was even more inscrutable. He had been to the Oddfellows' excursion on the train the week before and to the Conservative picnic the week before that, and had decided not to go on this trip. In fact, he had not the least intention of going. He narrated afterwards how the night before someone had stopped him on the corner of Nippewa and Tecumseh Streets (he indicated the very spot) and asked: "Are you going to take in the excursion tomorrow?" and he had said, just as simply as he was talking when narrating it: "No." And ten minutes after that, at the corner of Dalhousie and Brock Streets (he offered to lead a party of verification to the precise place) somebody else had stopped him and asked: "Well, are you going on the steamer trip tomorrow?" Again he had answered: "No," apparently almost in the same tone as before.

He said afterwards that when he heard the rumour of the accident it seemed like the finger of Providence, and he fell on his knees in thankfulness.

There was the similar case of Morison (I mean the one in Glover's

hardware store that married one of the Thompsons). He said afterwards that he had read so much in the papers about accidents
lately—mining accidents, and aeroplanes and gasoline—that he had
grown nervous. The night before his wife had asked him at supper:
"Are you going on the excursion?" He had answered: "No, I don't
think I feel like it," and had added: "Perhaps your mother might like
to go." And the next evening just at dusk, when the news ran
through the town, he said the first thought that flashed through his
head was: "Mrs. Thompson's on that boat."

He told this right as I say it—without the least doubt or confusion.
He never for a moment imagined she was on the *Lusitania* or the
*Olympic* or any other boat. He knew she was on this one. He said
you could have knocked him down where he stood. But no one had.
Not even when he got halfway down—on his knees, and it would
have been easier still to knock him down or kick him. People do miss
a lot of chances.

Still, as I say, neither Yodel nor Morison nor anyone thought
about there being an accident until just after sundown when they—

Well, have you ever heard the long booming whistle of a steamboat two miles out on the lake in the dusk, and while you listen and
count and wonder, seen the crimson rockets going up against the
sky and then heard the fire bell ringing right there beside you in the
town, and seen the people running to the town wharf?

That's what the people of Mariposa saw and felt that summer
evening as they watched the Mackinaw lifeboat go plunging out into
the lake with seven sweeps to a side and the foam clear to the
gunwale with the lifting stroke of fourteen men!

But, dear me, I am afraid that this is no way to tell a story. I
suppose the true art would have been to have said nothing about the
accident till it happened. But when you write about Mariposa, or
hear of it, if you know the place, it's all so vivid and real, that a thing
like the contrast between the excursion crowd in the morning and
the scene at night leaps into your mind and you must think of it.

\*    \*    \*

But never mind about the accident—let us turn back again to the
morning.

The boat was due to leave at seven. There was no doubt about the
hour—not only seven, but seven sharp. The notice in the *Newspacket*
said: "The boat will leave sharp at seven"; and the advertising
posters on the telegraph poles on Missinaba Street that began, "Ho,
for Indian's Island!" ended up with the words: "Boat leaves at seven
sharp." There was a big notice on the wharf that said: "Boat leaves
sharp on time."

So at seven, right on the hour, the whistle blew loud and long, and then at seven-fifteen three short peremptory blasts, and at seven-thirty one quick angry call—just one—and very soon after that they cast off the last of the ropes and the *Mariposa Belle* sailed off in her cloud of flags, and the band of the Knights of Pythias, timing it to a nicety, broke into the "Maple Leaf for Ever!"

I suppose that all excursions when they start are much the same. Anyway, on the *Mariposa Belle* everybody went running up and down all over the boat with deck chairs and camp stools and baskets, and found places, splendid places to sit, and then got scared that there might be better ones and chased off again. People hunted for places out of the sun and when they got them swore that they weren't going to freeze to please anybody; and the people in the sun said that they hadn't paid fifty cents to get roasted. Others said that they hadn't paid fifty cents to get covered with cinders, and there were still others who hadn't paid fifty cents to get shaken to death with the propeller.

Still, it was all right presently. The people seemed to get sorted out into the places on the boat where they belonged. The women, the older ones, all gravitated into the cabin on the lower deck and by getting round the table with needlework, and with all the windows shut, they soon had it, as they said themselves, just like being at home.

All the young boys and the toughs and the men in the band got down on the lower deck forward, where the boat was dirtiest and where the anchor was and the coils of rope.

And upstairs on the after deck there were Lilian Drone and Miss Lawson, the high-school teacher, with a book of German poetry—Gothey I think it was—and the bank teller and the young men.

In the centre, standing beside the rail, were Dean Drone and Dr. Gallagher, looking through binocular glasses at the shore.

Up in front on the little deck forward of the pilot house was a group of the older men, Mullins and Duff and Mr. Smith in a deck chair, and beside him Mr. Golgotha Gingham, the undertaker of Mariposa, on a stool. It was part of Mr. Gingham's principles to take in an outing of this sort, a business matter, more or less—for you never know what may happen at these water parties. At any rate, he was there in a neat suit of black, not, of course, his heavier or professional suit, but a soft clinging effect as of burnt paper that combined gaiety and decorum to a nicety.

*    *    *

"Yes," said Mr. Gingham, waving his black glove in a general way towards the shore, "I know the lake well, very well. I've been pretty much all over it in my time."

"Canoeing?" asked somebody.

"No," said Mr. Gingham, "not in a canoe." There seemed a peculiar and quiet meaning in his tone.

"Sailing, I suppose," said somebody else.

"No," said Mr. Gingham. "I don't understand it."

"I never knowed that you went onto the water at all, Gol," said Mr. Smith, breaking in.

"Ah, not now," explained Mr. Gingham; "it was years ago, the first summer I came to Mariposa. I was on the water practically all day. Nothing like it to give a man an appetite and keep him in shape."

"Was you camping?" asked Mr. Smith.

"We camped at night," assented the undertaker, "but we put in practically the whole day on the water. You see, we were after a party that had come up here from the city on his vacation and gone out in a sailing canoe. We were dragging. We were up every morning at sunrise, lit a fire on the beach and cooked breakfast, and then we'd light our pipes and be off with the net for a whole day. It's a great life," concluded Mr. Gingham wistfully.

"Did you get him?" asked two or three together.

There was a pause before Mr. Gingham answered.

"We did," he said "—down in the reeds past Horseshoe Point. But it was no use. He turned blue on me right away."

After which Mr. Gingham fell into such a deep reverie that the boat had steamed another half-mile down the lake before anybody broke the silence again. Talk of this sort—and after all what more suitable for a day on the water?—beguiled the way.

*     *     *

Down the lake, mile by mile over the calm water, steamed the *Mariposa Belle.* They passed Poplar Point where the high sand-banks are with all the swallows' nests in them, and Dean Drone and Dr. Gallagher looked at them alternately through the binocular glasses, and it was wonderful how plainly one could see the swallows and the banks and the shrubs—just as plainly as with the naked eye.

And a little farther down they passed the Shingle Beach, and Dr. Gallagher, who knew Canadian history, said to Dean Drone that it was strange to think that Champlain had landed there with his French explorers three hundred years ago; and Dean Drone, who didn't know Canadian history, said it was stranger still to think that the hand of the Almighty had piled up the hills and rocks long before that; and Dr. Gallagher said it was wonderful how the French had found their way through such a pathless wilderness; and Dean Drone said that it was wonderful also to think that the Almighty had placed even the smallest shrub in its appointed place. Dr. Gallagher said it filled him with admiration. Dean Drone said it filled him with awe. Dr. Gallagher said he'd been full of it ever since he was a boy and Dean Drone said so had he.

Then a little further, as the *Mariposa Belle* steamed on down the lake, they passed the Old Indian Portage where the great grey rocks are; and Dr. Gallagher drew Dean Drone's attention to the place where the narrow canoe track wound up from the shore to the woods, and Dean Drone said he could see it perfectly well without the glasses.

Dr. Gallagher said that it was just here that a party of five hundred French had made their way with all their baggage and accoutrements across the rocks of the divide and down to the Great Bay. And Dean Drone said that it reminded him of Xenophon leading his ten thousand Greeks over the hill passes of Armenia down to the sea. Dr. Gallagher said that he had often wished he could have seen and spoken to Champlain, and Dean Drone said how much he regretted to have never known Xenophon.

And then after that they fell to talking of relics and traces of the past, and Dr. Gallagher said that if Dean Drone would come round to his house some night he would show him some Indian arrow heads that he had dug up in his garden. And Dean Drone said that if Dr. Gallagher would come round to the rectory any afternoon he would show him a map of Xerxes' invasion of Greece. Only he must come some time between the Infant Class and the Mothers' Auxiliary.

So presently they both knew that they were blocked out of one another's houses for some time to come, and Dr. Gallagher walked forward and told Mr. Smith, who had never studied Greek, about Champlain crossing the rock divide.

Mr. Smith turned his head and looked at the divide for half a second and then said he had crossed a worse one up north back of the Wahnipitae and that the flies were Hades—and then went on playing freezeout poker with the two juniors in Duff's bank.

So Dr. Gallagher realized that that's always the way when you try to tell people things, and that as far as gratitude and appreciation goes one might as well never read books or travel anywhere or do anything.

In fact, it was at this very moment that he made up his mind to give the arrows to the Mariposa Mechanics' Institute—they afterwards became, as you know, the Gallagher Collection. But, for the time being, the doctor was sick of them and wandered off round the boat and watched Henry Mullins showing George Duff how to make a John Collins without lemons, and finally went and sat down among the Mariposa band and wished that he hadn't come.

So the boat steamed on and the sun rose higher and higher, and the freshness of the morning changed into the full glare of noon, and pretty soon the *Mariposa Belle* had floated out onto the lake again and they went on to where the lake began to narrow in at its foot, just where the Indian's Island is—all grass and trees and with a log wharf running into the water. Below it the Lower Ossawippi runs out of the lake, and quite near are the rapids, and you can see down among the trees the red brick of the power house and hear the roar of the leaping water.

The Indian's Island itself is all covered with trees and tangled vines, and the water about it is so still that it's all reflected double and looks the same either way up. Then when the steamer's whistle blows as it comes into the wharf, you hear it echo among the trees of the island, and reverberate back from the shores of the lake.

The scene is all so quiet and still and unbroken, that Miss Cleghorn—the sallow girl in the telephone exchange, that I spoke of—said she'd like to be buried there. But all the people were so busy getting their baskets and gathering up their things that no one had time to attend to it.

I mustn't even try to describe the landing and the boat crunching against the wooden wharf and all the people running to the same side of the deck and Christie Johnson calling out to the crowd to keep to the starboard and nobody being able to find it. Everyone who has been on a Mariposa excursion knows all about that.

Nor can I describe the day itself and the picnic under the trees. There were speeches afterwards, and Judge Pepperleigh gave such offence by bringing in Conservative politics that a man called Patriotus Canadiensis wrote and asked for some of the invaluable space of the *Mariposa Times-Herald* and exposed it.

I should say that there were races too, on the grass on the open side of the island, graded mostly according to ages—races for boys under thirteen and girls over nineteen and all that sort of thing. Sports are generally conducted on that plan in Mariposa. It is realized that a woman of sixty has an unfair advantage over a mere child.

Dean Drone managed the races and decided the ages and gave out the prizes; the Wesleyan minister helped, and he and the young student, who was relieving in the Presbyterian Church, held the string at the winning point.

They had to get mostly clergymen for the races because all the men had wandered off, somehow, to where they were drinking lager beer out of two kegs stuck on pine logs among the trees.

But if you've ever been on a Mariposa excursion you know all about these details anyway.

So the day wore on and presently the sun came through the trees on a slant and the steamer whistle blew with a great puff of white steam and all the people came straggling down to the wharf and pretty soon the *Mariposa Belle* had floated out onto the lake again and headed for the town, twenty miles away.

*    *    *

I suppose you have often noticed the contrast there is between an excursion on its way out in the morning and what it looks like on the way home.

In the morning everybody is so restless and animated and moves to and from all over the boat and asks questions. But coming home, as the afternoon gets later and later and the sun sinks beyond the hills, all the people seem to get so still and quiet and drowsy.

So it was with the people on the *Mariposa Belle*. They sat there on the benches and the deck chairs in little clusters, and listened to the regular beat of the propeller and almost dozed off asleep as they sat. Then when the sun set and the dusk drew on, it grew almost dark on the deck and so still that you could hardly tell there was anyone on board.

And if you had looked at the steamer from the shore or from one of the islands, you'd have seen the row of lights from the cabin windows shining on the water and the red glare of the burning hemlock from the funnel, and you'd have heard the soft thud of the propeller miles away over the lake.

Now and then, too, you could have heard them singing on the steamer—the voices of the girls and the men blended into unison by the distance, rising and falling in long-drawn melody: "O—Can-a-da—O—Can-a-da."

You may talk as you will about the intoning choirs of your European cathedrals, but the sound of "O Can-a-da", borne across the waters of a silent lake at evening is good enough for those of us who know Mariposa.

I think that it was just as they were singing like this: "O—Can-a-da", that word went round that the boat was sinking.

If you have ever been in any sudden emergency on the water, you will understand the strange psychology of it—the way in which what is happening seems to become known all in a moment without a word being said. The news is transmitted from one to the other by some mysterious process.

At any rate, on the *Mariposa Belle* first one and then the other heard that the steamer was sinking. As far as I could ever learn the first of it was that George Duff, the bank manager, came very quietly to Dr. Gallagher and asked him if he thought that the boat was sinking. The doctor said no, that he had thought so earlier in the day but that he didn't now think that she was.

After that Duff, according to his own account, had said to Macart-

ney, the lawyer, that the boat was sinking, and Macartney said that
he doubted it very much.

Then somebody came to Judge Pepperleigh and woke him up and
said that there was six inches of water in the steamer and that she
was sinking. And Pepperleigh said it was perfect scandal and passed
the news on to his wife and she said that they had no business to
allow it and that if the steamer sank that was the last excursion she'd
go on.

So the news went all round the boat and everywhere the people
gathered in groups and talked about it in the angry and excited way
that people have when a steamer is sinking on one of the lakes like
Lake Wissanotti.

Dean Drone, of course, and some others were quieter about it, and
said that one must make allowances and that naturally there were
two sides to everything. But most of them wouldn't listen to reason
at all. I think, perhaps, that some of them were frightened. You see
the last time but one that the steamer had sunk, there had been a
man drowned and it made them nervous.

What? Hadn't I explained about the depth of Lake Wissanotti? I
had taken it for granted that you knew; and in any case parts of it are
deep enough, though I don't suppose in this stretch of it from the
big reed beds up to within a mile of the town wharf, you could find
six feet of water in it if you tried. Oh, pshaw! I was not talking about
a steamer sinking in the ocean and carrying down its screaming
crowds of people into the hideous depths of green water. Oh, dear
me, no! That kind of thing never happens on Lake Wissanotti.

But what does happen is that the *Mariposa Belle* sinks every now and
then, and sticks there on the bottom till they get things straightened
up.

On the lakes round Mariposa, if a person arrives late anywhere
and explains that the steamer sank, everybody understands the situation.

You see when Harland and Wolff built the *Mariposa Belle*, they left
some cracks in between the timbers that you fill up with cotton
waste every Sunday. If this is not attended to, the boat sinks. In fact,
it is part of the law of the province that all the steamers like the
*Mariposa Belle* must be properly corked—I think that is the word—
every season. There are inspectors who visit all the hotels in the
province to see that it is done.

So you can imagine now that I've explained it a little straighter, the
indignation of the people when they knew that the boat had come
uncorked and that they might be stuck out there on a shoal or a
mud-bank half the night.

I don't say either that there wasn't any danger; anyway, it doesn't feel very safe when you realize that the boat is settling down with every hundred yards that she goes, and you look over the side and see only the black water in the gathering night.

Safe! I'm not sure now that I come to think of it that it isn't worse than sinking in the Atlantic. After all, in the Atlantic there is wireless telegraphy, and a lot of trained sailors and stewards. But out on Lake Wissanotti—far out, so that you can only just see the lights of the town away off to the south—when the propeller comes to a stop— and you can hear the hiss of steam as they start to rake out the engine fires to prevent an explosion—and when you turn from the red glare that comes from the furnace doors as they open them, to the black dark that is gathering over the lake—and there's a night wind beginning to run among the rushes—and you see the men going forward to the roof of the pilot house to send up the rockets to rouse the town—safe? Safe yourself, if you like; as for me, let me once get back into Mariposa again, under the night shadow of the maple trees, and this shall be the last, last time I'll go on Lake Wissanotti.

Safe! Oh, yes! Isn't it strange how safe other people's adventures seem after they happen? But you'd have been scared, too, if you'd been there just before the steamer sank, and seen them bringing up all the women on to the top deck.

I don't see how some of the people took it so calmly; how Mr. Smith, for instance, could have gone on smoking and telling how he'd had a steamer "sink on him" on Lake Nipissing and a still bigger one, a side-wheeler, sink on him in Lake Abbitibbi.

Then, quite suddenly, with a quiver, down she went. You could feel the boat sink, sink—down, down—would it never get to the bottom? The water came flush up to the lower deck, and then— thank heaven—the sinking stopped and there was the *Mariposa Belle* safe and tight on a reed bank.

Really, it made one positively laugh! It seemed so queer and, any-way, if a man has a sort of natural courage, danger makes him laugh. Danger? pshaw! fiddlesticks! everybody scouted the idea. Why, it is just the little things like this that give zest to a day on the water.

Within half a minute they were all running round looking for sandwiches and cracking jokes and talking of making coffee over the remains of the engine fires.

*    *    *

I don't need to tell at length how it all happened after that.

I suppose the people on the *Mariposa Belle* would have had to settle down there all night or till help came from the town, but some of the men who had gone forward and were peering out into the dark said that it couldn't be more than a mile across the water to Miller's Point. You could almost see it over there to the left—some of them, I think, said "off on the port bow," because you know when you get mixed up in these marine disasters, you soon catch the atmosphere of the thing.

So pretty soon they had the davits swung out over the side and were lowering the old lifeboat from the top deck into the water.

There were men leaning out over the rail of the *Mariposa Belle* with lanterns that threw the light as they let her down, and the glare fell on the water and the reeds. But when they got the boat lowered, it looked such a frail, clumsy thing as one saw it from the rail above, that the cry was raised: "Women and children first!" For what was the sense, if it should turn out that the boat wouldn't even hold women and children, of trying to jam a lot of heavy men into it?

So they put in mostly women and children and the boat pushed out into the darkness so freighted down it would hardly float.

In the bow of it was the Presbyterian student who was relieving the minister, and he called out that they were in the hands of Providence. But he was crouched and ready to spring out of them at the first moment.

So the boat went and was lost in the darkness except for the lantern in the bow that you could see bobbing on the water. Then presently it came back and they sent another load, till pretty soon the decks began to thin out and everybody got impatient to be gone.

It was about the time that the third boat-load put off that Mr. Smith took a bet with Mullins for twenty-five dollars, that he'd be home in Mariposa before the people in the boats had walked round the shore.

No one knew just what he meant, but pretty soon they saw Mr. Smith disappear down below into the lowest part of the steamer with a mallet in one hand and a big bundle of marline in the other.

They might have wondered more about it, but it was just at this time that they heard the shouts from the rescue boat—the big Mackinaw lifeboat—that had put out from the town with fourteen men at the sweeps when they saw the first rockets go up.

I suppose there is always something inspiring about a rescue at sea, or on the water.

After all, the bravery of the lifeboat man is the true bravery—expended to save life, not to destroy it.

Certainly they told for months after of how the rescue boat came out to the *Mariposa Belle*.

I suppose that when they put her in the water the lifeboat touched it for the first time since the old Macdonald Government placed her on Lake Wissanotti.

Anyway, the water poured in at every seam. But not for a moment—even with two miles of water between them and the steamer—did the rowers pause for that.

By the time they were halfway there the water was almost up to the thwarts, but they drove her on. Panting and exhausted (for mind you, if you haven't been in a fool boat like that for years, rowing takes it out of you), the rowers stuck to their task. They threw the ballast over and chucked into the water the heavy cork jackets and lifebelts that encumbered their movements. There was no thought of turning back. They were nearer to the steamer than the shore.

"Hang to it, boys," called the crowd from the steamer's deck, and hang they did.

They were almost exhausted when they got them; men leaning from the steamer threw them ropes and one by one every man was hauled aboard just as the lifeboat sank under their feet.

Saved! by heaven, saved by one of the smartest pieces of rescue work ever seen on the lake.

There's no use describing it; you need to see rescue work of this kind by lifeboats to understand it.

Nor were the lifeboat crew the only ones that distinguished themselves.

Boat after boat and canoe after canoe had put out from Mariposa to the help of the steamer. They got them all.

Pupkin, the other bank teller with a face like a horse, who hadn't gone on the excursion—as soon as he knew that the boat was signalling for help and that Miss Lawson was sending up rockets—rushed for a row boat, grabbed an oar (two would have hampered him)—and paddled madly out into the lake. He struck right out into the dark with the crazy skiff almost sinking beneath his feet. But they got him. They rescued him. They watched him, almost dead with exhaustion, make his way to the steamer, where he was hauled up with ropes. Saved! Saved!

*    *    *

They might have gone on that way half the night, picking up the rescuers, only, at the very moment when the tenth load of people left for the shore—just as suddenly and saucily as you please, up came the *Mariposa Belle* from the mud bottom and floated.

*Floated?*

Why, of course she did. If you take a hundred and fifty people off
a steamer that has sunk, and if you get a man as shrewd as Mr.
Smith to plug the timber seams with mallet and marline, and if you
turn ten bandsmen of the Mariposa band onto your hand pump on
the bow of the lower decks—float? why, what else can she do?

Then, if you stuff in hemlock into the embers of the fire that you
were raking out, till it hums and crackles under the boiler, it won't
be long before you hear the propeller thud—thudding at the stern
again, and before the long roar of the steam whistle echoes over to
the town.

And so the *Mariposa Belle*, with all steam up again and with the
long train of sparks careering from the funnel, is heading for the
town.

But no Christie Johnson at the wheel in the pilot house this time.
"Smith! Get Smith!" is the cry.

Can he take her in? Well, now! Ask a man who has had steamers
sink on him in half the lakes from Temiscaming to the Bay, if he can
take her in? Ask a man who has run a York boat down the rapids of
the Moose when the ice is moving, if he can grip the steering wheel
of the *Mariposa Belle?* So there she steams safe and sound to the town
wharf!

Look at the lights and the crowds! If only the federal census taker
could count us now! Hear them calling and shouting back and forward from the deck to the shore! Listen! There is the rattle of the
shore ropes as they get them ready, and there's the Mariposa band—
actually forming in a circle on the upper deck just as she docks, and
the leader with his baton—one—two—ready now—

"O CAN-A-DA!"


# STEPHEN CRANE
## 1871–1900

Born in Newark, New Jersey, Crane was the fourteenth child of a method-
ist minister, who named him after an ancestor who had signed the Declaration of Independence. He was a delicate child, whose health improved
when his family moved to Port Jervis, New York, in 1879. After his father
died he went to the Hudson River Institute at Caverack, New York, and
then to Lafayette College and Syracuse University, shifting his interests
from engineering to literature. He was an excellent baseball player—once
considering a professional career—and a good boxer as well. While in
school he began work as a journalist, a profession which he pursued for
most of his life. But his reporting always suffered from an excess of art. A

poetic image would distract him from journalistic details. He wrote an ironic novel *(Maggie: A Girl of the Streets)* when he was twenty-two, and a masterful novel of the Civil War *(The Red Badge of Courage)* two years later. He had not been to war but had heard the accounts of soldiers and he had read Tolstoy. Later, he became a war correspondent and confirmed his guesses first hand. Like many of America's best writers, he was cynical and sentimental at the same time. His blunt manner and indifference to public opinion offended many of his contemporaries, but Henry James and Joseph Conrad admired his work and came to pay their respects to the younger man as he was dying in England of tuberculosis.

# The Bride Comes to Yellow Sky

### I

The great Pullman was whirling onward with such dignity of motion that a glance from the window seemed simply to prove that the plains of Texas were pouring eastward. Vast flats of green grass, dull-hued spaces of mesquit and cactus, little groups of frame houses, woods of light and tender trees, all were sweeping into the east, sweeping over the horizon, a precipice.

A newly married pair had boarded this coach at San Antonio. The man's face was reddened from many days in the wind and sun, and a direct result of his new black clothes was that his brick-coloured hands were constantly performing in a most conscious fashion. From time to time he looked down respectfully at his attire. He sat with a hand on each knee, like a man waiting in a barber's shop. The glances he devoted to other passengers were furtive and shy.

The bride was not pretty, nor was she very young. She wore a dress of blue cashmere, with small reservations of velvet here and there, and with steel buttons abounding. She continually twisted her head to regard her puff sleeves, very stiff, straight, and high. They embarrassed her. It was quite apparent that she had cooked, and that she expected to cook, dutifully. The blushes caused by the careless scrutiny of some passengers as she had entered the car were strange to see upon this plain, under-class countenance, which was drawn in placid, almost emotionless lines.

They were evidently very happy. "Ever been in a parlour-car before?" he asked, smiling with delight.

"No," she answered; "I never was. It's fine, ain't it?"

"Great! And then after a while we'll go forward to the diner, and get a big lay-out. Finest meal in the world. Charge a dollar."

'Oh, do they?" cried the bride. "Charge a dollar? Why, that's too much—for us—ain't it, Jack?"

"Not this trip, anyhow," he answered bravely. "We're going to go the whole thing."

Later he explained to her about the trains. "You see, it's a thousand miles from one end of Texas to the other; and this train runs right across it, and never stops but four times." He had the pride of an owner. He pointed out to her the dazzling fittings of the coach; and in truth her eyes opened wider as she contemplated the sea-green figured velvet, the shining brass, silver, and glass, the wood that gleamed as darkly brilliant as the surface of a pool of oil. At one end a bronze figure sturdily held a support for a separated chamber, and at convenient places on the ceiling were frescos in olive and silver.

To the minds of the pair, their surroundings reflected the glory of their marriage that morning in San Antonio; this was the environment of their new estate; and the man's face in particular beamed with an elation that made him appear ridiculous to the negro porter. This individual at times surveyed them from afar with an amused and superior grin. On other occasions he bullied them with skill in ways that did not make it exactly plain to them that they were being bullied. He subtly used all the manners of the most unconquerable kind of snobbery. He oppressed them; but of this oppression they had small knowledge, and they speedily forgot that infrequently a number of travellers covered them with stares of derisive enjoyment. Historically there was supposed to be something infinitely humorous in their situation.

"We are due in Yellow Sky at 3:42," he said, looking tenderly into her eyes.

"Oh, are we?" she said, as if she had not been aware of it. To evince surprise at her husband's statement was part of her wifely amiability. She took from a pocket a little silver watch; and as she held it before her, and stared at it with a frown of attention, the new husband's face shone.

"I bought it in San Anton' from a friend of mine," he told her gleefully.

"It's seventeen minutes past twelve," she said, looking up at him with a kind of shy and clumsy coquetry. A passenger, noting this play, grew excessively sardonic, and winked at himself in one of the numerous mirrors.

At last they went to the dining-car. Two rows of negro waiters, in glowing white suits, surveyed their entrance with the interest, and also the equanimity, of men who had been forewarned. The pair fell to the lot of a waiter who happened to feel pleasure in steering them through their meal. He viewed them with the manner of a fatherly pilot, his countenance radiant with benevolence. The patronage, entwined with the ordinary deference, was not plain to them. And yet, as they returned to their coach, they showed in their faces a sense of escape.

To the left, miles down a long purple slope, was a little ribbon of mist where moved the keening Rio Grande. The train was approaching it at an angle, and the apex was Yellow Sky. Presently it was apparent that, as the distance from Yellow Sky grew shorter, the husband became commensurately restless. His brick-red hands were more insistent in their prominence. Occasionally he was even rather absent-minded and far-away when the bride leaned forward and addressed him.

As a matter of truth, Jack Potter was beginning to find the shadow of a deed weigh upon him like a leaden slab. He, the town marshal of Yellow Sky, a man known, liked, and feared in his corner, a prominent person, had gone to San Antonio to meet a girl he believed he loved, and there, after the usual prayers, had actually induced her to marry him, without consulting Yellow Sky for any part of the transaction. He was now bringing his bride before an innocent and unsuspecting community.

Of course people in Yellow Sky married as it pleased them in accordance with a general custom; but such was Potter's thought of his duty to his friends, or of their idea of his duty, or of an unspoken form which does not control men in these matters, that he felt he was heinous. He had committed an extraordinary crime. Face to face with this girl in San Antonio, and spurred by his sharp impulse, he had gone headlong over all the social hedges. At San Antonio he was like a man hidden in the dark. A knife to sever any friendly duty, any form, was easy to his hand in that remote city. But the hour of Yellow Sky—the hour of daylight—was approaching.

He knew full well that his marriage was an important thing to his town. It could only be exceeded by the burning of the new hotel. His friends could not forgive him. Frequently he had reflected on the advisability of telling them by telegraph, but a new cowardice had been upon him. He feared to do it. And now the train was hurrying him toward a scene of amazement, glee, and reproach. He glanced out of the window at the line of haze swinging slowly in toward the train.

Yellow Sky had a kind of brass band, which played painfully, to the delight of the populace. He laughed without heart as he thought of it. If the citizens could dream of his prospective arrival with his bride, they would parade the band at the station and escort them, amid cheers and laughing congratulations, to his adobe home.

He resolved that he would use all the devices of speed and plainscraft in making the journey from the station to his house. Once within that safe citadel, he could issue some sort of vocal bulletin, and then not go among the citizens until they had time to wear off a little of their enthusiasm.

The bride looked anxiously at him. "What's worrying you, Jack?"

He laughed again. "I'm not worrying, girl; I'm only thinking of Yellow Sky."

She flushed in comprehension.

A sense of mutual guilt invaded their minds and developed a finer tenderness. They looked at each other with eyes softly aglow. But Potter often laughed the same nervous laugh; the flush upon the bride's face seemed quite permanent.

The traitor to the feelings of Yellow Sky narrowly watched the speeding landscape. "We're nearly there," he said.

Presently the porter came and announced the proximity of Potter's home. He held a brush in his hand, and, with all his airy superiority gone, he brushed Potter's new clothes as the latter slowly turned this way and that way. Potter fumbled out a coin and gave it to the porter, as he had seen others do. It was a heavy and muscle-bound business, as that of a man shoeing his first horse.

The porter took their bag, and as the train began to slow they moved forward to the hooded platform of the car. Presently the two engines and their long string of coaches rushed into the station of Yellow Sky.

"They have to take water here," said Potter, from a constricted throat and in mournful cadence, as one announcing death. Before the train stopped his eye had swept the length of the platform, and he was glad and astonished to see there was none upon it but the station-agent, who, with a slightly hurried and anxious air, was walking toward the water-tanks. When the train had halted, the porter alighted first, and placed in position a little temporary step.

"Come on, girl," said Potter, hoarsely. As he helped her down they each laughed on a false note. He took the bag from the negro, and bade his wife cling to his arm. As they slunk rapidly away, his hang-dog glance perceived that they were unloading the two trunks, and also that the station-agent, far ahead near the baggage-car, had turned and was running toward him, making gestures. He laughed, and groaned as he laughed, when he noted the first effect of his marital bliss upon Yellow Sky. He gripped his wife's arm firmly to his side, and they fled. Behind them the porter stood, chuckling fatuously.

II

The California express on the Southern Railway was due at Yellow Sky in twenty-one minutes. There were six men at the bar of the Weary Gentleman saloon. One was a drummer who talked a great deal and rapidly; three were Texans who did not care to talk at that time; and two were Mexican sheep-herders, who did not talk as a general practice in the Weary Gentleman saloon. The barkeeper's dog lay on the board walk that crossed in front of the door. His head was on his paws, and he glanced drowsily here and there with the constant vigilance of a dog that is kicked on occasion. Across the sandy street were some vivid green grass-plots, so wonderful in appearance, amid the sands that burned near them in a blazing sun, that they caused a doubt in the mind. They exactly resembled the grass mats used to represent lawns on the stage. At the cooler end of the railway station, a man without a coat sat in a tilted chair and smoked his pipe. The fresh-cut bank of the Rio Grande circled near the town, and there could be seen beyond it a great plum-coloured plain of mesquit.

Save for the busy drummer and his companions in the saloon, Yellow Sky was dozing. The new-comer leaned gracefully upon the bar, and recited many tales with the confidence of a bard who has come upon a new field.

"—and at the moment that the old man fell downstairs with the bureau in his arms, the old woman was coming up with two scuttles of coal, and of course—"

The drummer's tale was interrupted by a young man who suddenly appeared in the open door. He cried: "Scratchy Wilson's drunk, and has turned loose with both hands." The two Mexicans at once set down their glasses and faded out of the rear entrance of the saloon.

The drummer, innocent and jocular, answered: "All right, old man. S'pose he has? Come in and have a drink, anyhow."

But the information had made such an obvious cleft in every skull in the room that the drummer was obliged to see its importance. All had become instantly solemn. "Say," said he, mystified, "what is this?" His three companions made the introductory genture of eloquent speech; but the young man at the door forestalled them.

"It means, my friend," he answered, as he came into the saloon, "that for the next two hours this town won't be a health resort."

The barkeeper went to the door, and locked and barred it; reaching out of the window, he pulled in heavy wooden shutters, and barred them. Immediately a solemn, chapel-like gloom was upon the place. The drummer was looking from one to another.

"But say," he cried, "what is this, anyhow? You don't mean there is going to be a gun-fight?"

"Don't know whether there'll be a fight or not," answered one man, grimly; "but there'll be some shootin'—some good shootin'."

The young man who had warned them waved his hand. "Oh, there'll be a fight fast enough, if any one wants it. Anybody can get a fight out there in the street. There's a fight just waiting."

The drummer seemed to be swayed between the interest of a foreigner and a perception of personal danger.

"What did you say his name was?" he asked.

"Scratchy Wilson," they answered in chorus.

"And will he kill anybody? What are you going to do? Does this happen often? Does he rampage around like this once a week or so? Can he break in that door?"

"No; he can't break down that door," replied the barkeeper. "He's tried it three times. But when he comes you'd better lay down on the floor, stranger. He's dead sure to shoot at it, and a bullet may come through."

Thereafter the drummer kept a strict eye upon the door. The time had not yet called for him to hug the floor, but, as a minor precaution, he sidled near the wall. "Will he kill anybody?" he said again.

The men laughed low and scornfully at the question.

"He's out to shoot, and he's out for trouble. Don't see any good in experimentin' with him."

"But what do you do in a case like this? What do you do?"

A man responded: "Why, he and Jack Potter—"

"But," in chorus the other men interrupted, "Jack Potter's in San Anton."

"Well, who is he? What's he got to do with it?"

"Oh, he's the town marshal. He goes out and fights Scratchy when he gets on one of these tears."

"Wow!" said the drummer, mopping his brow. "Nice job he's got."

The voices had toned away to mere whisperings. The drummer wished to ask further questions, which were born of an increasing anxiety and bewilderment; but when he attempted them, the men merely looked at him in irritation and motioned him to remain silent. A tense waiting hush was upon them. In the deep shadows of the room their eyes shone as they listened for sounds from the street. One man made three gestures at the barkeeper; and the latter, moving like a ghost, handed him a glass and a bottle. The man poured a full glass of whisky, and set down the bottle noiselessly. He gulped the whisky in a swallow, and turned again toward the door in immovable silence. The drummer saw that the barkeeper, without a sound, had taken a Winchester from beneath the bar. Later he saw this individual beckoning to him, so he tiptoed across the room.

"You better come with me back of the bar."

"No, thanks," said the drummer, perspiring; "I'd rather be where I can make a break for the back door."

Whereupon the man of bottles made a kindly but peremptory gesture. The drummer obeyed it, and, finding himself seated on a box with his head below the level of the bar, balm was laid upon his soul at sight of various zinc and copper fittings that bore a resemblance to armour-plate. The barkeeper took a seat comfortably upon an adjacent box.

"You see," he whispered, "this here Scratchy Wilson is a wonder with a gun—a perfect wonder; and when he goes on the war-trail, we hunt our holes—naturally. He's about the last one of the old gang that used to hang out along the river here. He's a terror when he's drunk. When he's sober he's all right—kind of simple—wouldn't hurt a fly— nicest fellow in town. But when he's drunk—whoo!"

There were periods of stillness. "I wish Jack Potter was back from San Anton'," said the barkeeper. "He shot Wilson up once—in the leg—and he would sail in and pull out the kinks in this thing."

Presently they heard from a distance the sound of a shot, followed by three wild yowls. It instantly removed a bond from the men in the darkened saloon. There was a shuffling of feet. They looked at each other. "Here he comes," they said.


III

A man in a maroon-coloured flannel shirt, which had been purchased for purposes of decoration, and made principally by some Jewish women on the East Side of New York, rounded a corner and walked into the middle of the main street of Yellow Sky. In either hand the man held a long, heavy, blue-black revolver. Often he yelled, and these cries rang through a semblance of a deserted village, shrilly flying over the roofs in a volume that seemed to have no relation to the ordinary vocal strength of a man. It was as if the surrounding stillness formed the arch of a tomb over him. These cries of ferocious challenge rang against walls of silence. And his boots had red tops with gilded imprints, of the kind beloved in winter by little sledding boys on the hillsides of New England.

The man's face flamed in a rage begot of whisky. His eyes, rolling, and yet keen for ambush, hunted the still doorways and windows. He walked with the creeping movement of the midnight cat. As it occurred to him, he roared menacing information. The

long revolvers in his hands were as easy as straws; they were removed with an electric swiftness. The little fingers of each hand
played sometimes in a musician's way. Plain from the low collar of
the shirt, the cords of his neck straightened and sank, straightened
and sank, as passion moved him. The only sounds were his terrible
invitations. The calm adobes preserved their demeanour at the passing of this small thing in the middle of the street.

There was no offer of fight—no offer of fight. The man called to
the sky. There were no attractions. He bellowed and fumed and
swayed his revolvers here and everywhere.

The dog of the barkeeper of the Weary Gentleman saloon had not
appreciated the advance of events. He yet lay dozing in front of his
master's door. At sight of the dog, the man paused and raised his
revolver humorously. At sight of the man, the dog sprang up and
walked diagonally away, with a sullen head, and growling. The man
yelled, and the dog broke into a gallop. As it was about to enter the
alley, there was a loud noise, a whistling, and something spat the
ground directly before it. The dog screamed, and, wheeling in terror, galloped headlong in a new direction. Again there was a noise,
a whistling, and sand was kicked viciously before it. Fear-stricken,
the dog turned and flurried like an animal in a pen. The man stood
laughing, his weapons at his hips.

Ultimately the man was attracted by the closed door of the Weary
Gentleman saloon. He went to it and, hammering with a revolver,
demanded drink.

The door remaining imperturbable, he picked a bit of paper from
the walk, and nailed it to the framework with a knife. He then
turned his back contemptuously upon this popular resort and, walking to the opposite side of the street and spinning there on his heel
quickly and lithely, fired at the bit of paper. He missed it by a half
inch. He swore at himself, and went away. Later he comfortably
fusilladed the windows of his most intimate friend. The man was
playing with this town; it was a toy for him.

But still there was no offer of fight. The name of Jack Potter, his
ancient antagonist, entered his mind, and he concluded that it
would be a glad thing if he should go to Potter's house, and by
bombardment induce him to come out and fight. He moved in the
direction of his desire, chanting Apache scalp-music.

When he arrived at it, Potter's house presented the same still front
as had the other adobes. Taking up a strategic position, the man
howled a challenge. But this house regarded him as might a great
stone god. It gave no sign. After a decent wait, the man howled
further challenges, mingling with them wonderful epithets.

Presently there came the spectacle of a man churning himself into deepest rage over the immobility of a house. He fumed at it as the winter wind attacks a prairie cabin in the North. To the distance there should have gone the sound of a tumult like the fighting of two hundred Mexicans. As necessity bade him, he paused for breath or to reload his revolvers.


IV

Potter and his bride walked sheepishly and with speed. Sometimes they laughed together shamefacedly and low.

"Next corner, dear," he said finally.

They put forth the efforts of a pair walking bowed against a strong wind. Potter was about to raise a finger to point the first appearance of the new home when, as they circled the corner, they came face to face with a man in a maroon-coloured shirt, who was feverishly pushing cartridges into a large revolver. Upon the instant the man dropped his revolver to the ground and, like lightning, whipped another from its holster. The second weapon was aimed at the bridegroom's chest.

There was a silence. Potter's mouth seemed to be merely a grave for his tongue. He exhibited an instinct to at once loosen his arm from the woman's grip, and he dropped the bag to the sand. As for the bride, her face had gone as yellow as old cloth. She was a slave to hideous rites, gazing at the apparitional snake.

The two men faced each other at a distance of three paces. He of the revolver smiled with a new and quiet ferocity.

"Tried to sneak up on me," he said. "Tried to sneak up on me!" His eyes grew more baleful. As Potter made a slight movement, the man thrust his revolver venomously forward "No; don't you do it, Jack Potter. Don't you move a finger toward a gun just yet. Don't you move an eyelash. The time has come for me to settle with you and I'm goin' to do it my own way, and loaf along with no interferin'. So if you don't want a gun bent on you, just mind what I tell you."

Potter looked at his enemy. "I ain't got a gun on me Scratchy," he said. "Honest, I ain't." He was stiffening and steadying, but yet somewhere at the back of his mind a vision of the Pullman floated: the sea-green figured velvet, the shining brass, silver, and glass, the wood that gleamed as darkly brilliant as the surface of a pool of oil— all the glory of marriage, the environment of the new estate. "You know I fight when it comes to fighting, Scratchy Wilson; but I ain't got a gun on me. You'll have to do all the shootin' yourself."

His enemy's face went livid. He stepped forward, and lashed his weapon to and fro before Potter's chest. "Don't you tell me you ain't got no gun on you, you whelp. Don't tell me no lie like that. There ain't a man in Texas ever seen you without no gun. Don't take me for no kid." His eyes blazed with light, and his throat worked like a pump.

"I ain't takin' you for no kid," answered Potter. His heels had not moved an inch backward. "I'm takin' you for a damn fool. I tell you I ain't got a gun, and I ain't. If you're goin' to shoot me up, you better begin now; you'll never get a chance like this again."

So much enforced reasoning had told on Wilson's rage; he was calmer. "If you ain't got a gun, why ain't you got a gun?" he sneered. "Been to Sunday-school?"

"I ain't got a gun because I've just come fron San Anton' with my wife. I'm married," said Potter. "And if I'd thought there was going to be any galoots like you prowling around when I brought my wife home, I'd had a gun, and don't you forget it."

"Married!" said Scratchy, not at all comprehending.

"Yes, married. I'm married," said Potter, distinctly.

"Married?" said Scratchy. Seemingly for the first time, he saw the drooping, drowning woman at the other man's side. "No!" he said. He was like a creature allowed a glimpse of another world. He moved a pace backward, and his arm, with the revolver, dropped to his side. "Is this the lady?" he asked.

"Yes; this is the lady," answered Potter.

There was another period of silence.

"Well," said Wilson at last, slowly, "I s'pose it's all off now."

"It's all off if you say so, Scratchy. You know I didn't make the trouble." Potter lifted his valise.

"Well, I 'low it's off, Jack," said Wilson. He was looking at the ground. "Married!" He was not a student of chivalry; it was merely that in the presence of this foreign condition he was a simple child of the earlier plains. He picked up his starboard revolver, and, placing both weapons in their holsters, he went away. His feet made funnel-shaped tracks in the heavy sand.

# SHERWOOD ANDERSON
## 1876–1941

Born in Camden, Ohio, Anderson grew up in a variety of small towns, as his talkative, unreliable father moved from job to job. The boy also did odd jobs, and was known for a while as "Jobby." He worked in the fields and at race tracks before serving in the Army—in Cuba—during the Spanish American war. Afterward he wrote advertising copy and ran a paint factory before turning seriously to the writing of fiction. After 1912 essays, poems, and stories by Anderson began appearing regularly, but today his reputation rests upon the stories of small-town America that appeared in *Winesburg, Ohio* (1919) and *Horses and Men* (1923). In his later years he influenced and befriended such younger writers as Hemingway and Faulkner, who parodied him for his pains.

## I'm a Fool

It was a hard jolt for me, one of the most bitterest I ever had to face. And it all came about through my own foolishness, too. Even yet sometimes, when I think of it, I want to cry or swear or kick myself. Perhaps, even now, after all this time, there will be a kind of satisfaction in making myself look cheap by telling of it.

It began at three o'clock one October afternoon as I sat in the grandstand at the fall trotting and pacing meet at Sandusky, Ohio.

To tell the truth, I felt a little foolish that I should be sitting in the grandstand at all. During the summer before I had left my home town with Harry Whitehead and, with a nigger named Burt, had taken a job as swipe with one of the two horses Harry was campaigning through the fall race meets that year. Mother cried and my sister Mildred, who wanted to get a job as a school teacher in our town that fall, stormed and scolded about the house all during the week before I left. They both thought it something disgraceful that one of our family should take a place as a swipe with race horses. I've an idea Mildred thought my taking the place would stand in the way of her getting the job she'd been working so long for.

But after all I had to work, and there was no other work to be got. A big lumbering fellow of nineteen couldn't just hang around the house and I had got too big to mow people's lawns and sell newspapers. Little chaps who could get next to people's sympathies by their sizes were always getting jobs away from me. There was one fellow who kept saying to everyone who wanted a lawn mowed or a cistern cleaned, that he was saving money to work his way through college, and I used to lay awake nights thinking up ways to injure him without being found out. I kept thinking of wagons running over him and bricks falling on his head as he walked along the street. But never mind him.

I got the place with Harry and I liked Burt fine. We got along splendid together. He was a big nigger with a lazy sprawling body and soft, kind eyes, and when it came to a fight he could hit like Jack Johnson. He had Bucephalus, a big black pacing stallion that could do 2.09 or 2.10, if he had to, and I had a little gelding named Doctor Fritz that never lost a race all fall when Harry wanted him to win.

We set out from home late in July in a box car with the two horses and after that, until late November, we kept moving along to the race meets and the fairs. It was a peachy time for me, I'll say that. Sometimes now I think that boys who are raised regular in houses, and never have a fine nigger like Burt for best friend, and go to high schools and college, and never steal anything, or get drunk a little, or learn to swear from fellows who know how, or come walking up in front of a grandstand in their shirt sleeves and with dirty horsey pants on when the races are going on and the grandstand is full of people all dressed up—What's the use of talking about it? Such fellows don't know nothing at all. They've never had no opportunity.

But I did. Burt taught me how to rub down a horse and put the bandages on after a race and steam a horse out and a lot of valuable things for any man to know. He could wrap a bandage on a horse's leg so smooth that if it had been the same color you would think it was his skin, and I guess he'd have been a big driver, too, and got to the top like Murphy and Walter Cox and the others if he hadn't been black.

Gee whizz, it was fun. You got to a county seat town, maybe say on a Saturday or Sunday, and the fair began the next Tuesday and lasted until Friday afternoon. Doctor Fritz would be, say in the 2.25 trot on Tuesday afternoon and on Thursday afternoon Bucephalus would knock 'em cold in the "free-for-all" pace. It left you a lot of time to hang around and listen to horse talk, and see Burt knock some yap cold that got too gay, and you'd find out about horses and men and pick up a lot of stuff you could use all the rest of your life, if you had some sense and salted down what you heard and felt and saw.

And then at the end of the week when the race meet was over, and Harry had run home to tend up to his livery stable business, you and Burt hitched the two horses to carts and drove slow and steady across the country, to the place for the next meeting, so as to not overheat the horses, etc., etc., you know.

Gee whizz, Gosh amighty, the nice hickorynut and beechnut and oaks and other kinds of trees along the roads, all brown and red, and the good smells, and Burt singing a song that was called Deep River, and the country girls at the windows of houses and everything. You can stick your colleges up your nose for all me. I guess I know where I got my education.

Why, one of those little burgs of towns you come to on the way, say now on a Saturday afternoon, and Burt says, "let's lay up here." And you did.

And you took the horses to a livery stable and fed them, and you got your good clothes out of a box and put them on.

And the town was full of farmers gaping, because they could see you were race-horse people, and the kids maybe never see a nigger before and was afraid and run away when the two of us walked down their main street.

And that was before prohibition and all that foolishness, and so you went into a saloon, the two of you, and all the yaps come and stood around, and there was always someone pretended he was horsey and knew things and spoke up and began asking questions, and all you did was to lie and lie all you could about what horses you had, and I said I owned them, and then some fellow said, "will you have a drink of whisky," and Burt knocked his eye out the way he could say, offhandlike, "Oh well, all right, I'm agreeable to a little nip. I'll split a quart with you." Gee whizz.

But that isn't what I want to tell my story about. We got home late in November and I promised mother I'd quit the race horses for good. There's a lot of things you've got to promise a mother because she don't know any better.

And so, there not being any work in our town any more than when I left there to go to the races, I went off to Sandusky and got a pretty good place taking care of horses for a man who owned a teaming and delivery and storage coal and real estate business there. It was a pretty good place with good eats, and a day off each week, and sleeping on a cot in a big barn, and mostly just shoveling in hay and oats to a lot of big good-enough skates of horses, that couldn't have trotted a race with a toad. I wasn't dissatisfied and I could send money home.

And then, I started to tell you, the fall races comes to Sandusky and I got the day off and I went. I left the job at noon and had on my good clothes and my new brown derby hat, I'd just bought the Saturday before, and a stand-up collar.

First of all I went downtown and walked about with the dudes. I've always thought to myself, "put up a good front" and so I did it. I had forty dollars in my pocket and so I went into the West House, a big hotel, and walked up to the cigar stand. "Give me three twenty-five cent cigars," I said. There was a lot of horsemen and strangers and dressed-up people from other towns standing around in the lobby and in the bar, and I mingled amongst them. In the bar there was a fellow with a cane and a Windsor tie on, that it made me sick to look at him. I like a man to be a man and dress up, but not to go put on that kind of airs. So I pushed him aside, kind of rough, and had me a drink of whisky. And then he looked at me, as though he thought maybe he'd get gay, but he changed his mind and didn't say anything. And then I had another drink of whisky, just to show him something, and went out and had a hack out to the races, all to myself, and when I got there I bought myself the best seat I could get up in the grandstand, but didn't go in for any of these boxes. That's putting on too many airs.

And so there I was, sitting up in the grandstand as gay as you please and looking down on the swipes coming out with their horses, and with their dirty horsey pants on and the horse blankets swung over their shoulders, same as I had been doing all the year before. I liked one thing about the same as the other, sitting up there and feeling grand and being down there and looking up at the yaps and feeling grander and more important, too. One thing's about as good as another, if you take it just right. I've often said that.

Well, right in front of me, in the grandstand that day, there was a fellow with a couple of girls and they was about my age. The young fellow was a nice guy all right. He was the kind maybe that goes to college and then comes to be a lawyer or maybe a newspaper editor or something like that, but he wasn't stuck on himself. There are some of that kind are all right and he was one of the ones.

He had his sister with him and another girl and the sister looked around over his shoulder, accidental at first, not intending to start anything—she wasn't that kind—and her eyes and mine happened to meet.

You know how it is. Gee, she was a peach! She had on a soft dress, kind of a blue stuff and it looked carelessly made, but was well sewed and made and everything. I knew that much. I blushed when she looked right at me and so did she. She was the nicest girl I've ever seen in my life. She wasn't stuck on herself and she could talk proper grammar without being like a school teacher or something like that. What I mean is she was O.K. I think maybe her father was well-to-do, but not rich to make her chesty because she was his daughter, as some are. Maybe he owned a drugstore or a drygoods store in their home town, or something like that. She never told me and I never asked.

My own people are all O.K. too, when you come to that. My grandfather was Welsh and over in the old country, in Wales he was—But never mind that.

The first heat of the first race come off and the young fellow setting there with the two girls left them and went down to make a bet. I knew what he was up to, but he didn't talk big and noisy and let everyone around know he was a sport, as some do. He wasn't that kind. Well, he come back and I heard him tell the two girls what horse he'd bet on, and when the heat was trotted they all half got to their feet and acted in the excited, sweaty way people do when they've got money down on a race, and the horse they bet on is up there pretty close at the end, and they think maybe he'll come on with a rush, but he never does because he hasn't got the old juice in him, come right down to it.

And then, pretty soon, the horses came out for the 2.18 pace and there was a horse in it I knew. He was a horse Bob French had in his string but Bob didn't own him. He was a horse owned by a Mr. Mathers down at Marietta, Ohio.

This Mr. Mathers had a lot of money and owned some coal mines or something, and he had a swell place out in the country, and he was stuck on race horses, but was a Presbyterian or something, and I think more than likely his wife was one, too, maybe a stiffer one than himself. So he never raced his horses hisself, and the story round the Ohio race tracks was that when one of his horses got ready to go to the races he turned him over to Bob French and pretended to his wife he was sold.

So Bob had the horses and he did pretty much as he pleased and you can't blame Bob, at least, I never did. Sometimes he was out to win and sometimes he wasn't. I never cared much about that when I was swiping a horse. What I did want to know was that my horse had the speed and could go out in front, if you wanted him to.

And, as I'm telling you, there was Bob in this race with one of Mr. Mather's horses, was named "About Ben Ahem" or something like that, and was fast as a streak. He was a gelding and had a mark of 2.21, but could step in .08 or .09.

Because when Burt and I were out, as I've told you, the year before, there was a nigger, Burt knew, worked for Mr. Mathers and we went out there one day when we didn't have no race on at the Marietta Fair and our boss Harry was gone home.

And so everyone was gone to the fair but just this one nigger and he took us all through Mr. Mather's swell house and he and Burt tapped a bottle of wine Mr. Mathers had hid in his bedroom, back in a closet, without his wife knowing, and he showed us this Ahem horse. Burt was always stuck on being a driver but didn't have much chance to get to the top, being a nigger, and he and the other nigger gulped that whole bottle of wine and Burt got a little lit up.

So the nigger let Burt take this About Ben Ahem and step him a mile in a track Mr. Mathers had all to himself, right there on the farm. And Mr. Mathers had one child, a daughter, kinda sick, and not very good-looking, and she came home and we had to hustle to get About Ben Ahem stuck back in the barn.

I'm only telling you to get everything straight. At Sandusky, that afternoon I was at the fair, this young fellow with the two girls was fussed, being with the girls and losing his bet. You know how a fellow is that way. One of them was his girl and the other his sister. I had figured that out.

"Gee whizz," I says to myself, "I'm going to give him the dope."

He was mighty nice when I touched him on the shoulder. He and the girls were nice to me right from the start and clear to the end. I'm not blaming them.

And so he leaned back and I give him the dope on About Ben Ahem. "Don't bet a cent on this first heat because he'll go like an oxen hitched to a plow, but when the first heat is over go right down and lay on your pile." That's what I told him.

Well, I never saw a fellow treat anyone sweller. There was a fat man sitting beside the little girl, that had looked at me twice by this time, and I at her, and both blushing, and what did he do but have the nerve to turn and ask the fat man to get up and change places with me so I could set with his crowd.

Gee whizz, craps amighty. There I was. What a chump I was to go and get gay up there in West House bar, and just because that dude was standing there with a cane and that kind of a necktie on, to go and get all balled up and drink that whisky just to show off.

Of course she would know, me setting right beside her and letting her smell of my breath. I could have kicked myself right down out of that grandstand and all around that race track and made a faster record than most of the skates of horses they had there that year.

Because that girl wasn't any mutt of a girl. What wouldn't I have give right then for a stick of chewing gum to chew, or a lozenger, or some liquorice, or most anything. I was glad I had those twenty-five cent cigars in my pocket and right away I give that fellow one and lit one myself. Then that fat man got up and we changed places and there I was, plunked right down beside her.

They introduced themselves and the fellow's best girl, he had with him, was named Miss Elinor Woodbury, and her father was a manufacturer of barrels from a place called Tiffin, Ohio. And the fellow himself was named Wilbur Wessen and his sister was Miss Lucy Wessen.

I suppose it was their having such swell names got me off my trolley. A fellow, just because he has been a swipe with a race horse, and works taking care of horses for a man in the teaming, delivery, and storage business, isn't any better or worse than anyone else. I've often thought that, and said it too.

But you know how a fellow is. There's something in that kind of nice clothes, and the kind of nice eyes she had, and the way she looked at me, awhile before, over her brother's shoulder, and me looking back at her, and both of us blushing.

I couldn't show her up for a boob, could I?

I made a fool of myself, that's what I did. I said my name was

Walter Mathers from Marietta, Ohio, and then I told all three of them the smashingest lie you ever heard. What I said was that my father owned the horse About Ben Ahem and that he had let him out to this Bob French for racing purposes, because our family was proud and had never gone into racing that way, in our own name, I mean. Then I had got started and they were all leaning over and listening, and Miss Lucy Wessen's eyes were shining and I went the whole hog.

I told about our place down at Marietta, and about the big stables and the grand brick house we had on a hill, up above the Ohio River, but I knew enough not to do it in no bragging way. What I did was to start things and then let them drag the rest out of me. I acted just as reluctant to tell as I could. Our family hasn't got any barrel factory, and, since I've known us, we've always been pretty poor, but not asking anything of anyone at that, and my grand-father, over in Wales—But never mind that.

We set there talking like we had known each other for years and years, and I went and told them that my father had been expecting maybe this Bob French wasn't on the square, and had sent me up to Sandusky on the sly to find out what I could.

And I bluffed it through I had found out all about the 2.18 pace, in which About Ben Ahem was to start.

I said he would lose the first heat by pacing like a lame cow and then he would come back and skin 'em alive after that. And to back up what I said I took thirty dollars out of my pocket and handed it to Mr. Wilbur Wessen and asked him, would he mind, after the first heat, to go down and place it on About Ben Ahem for whatever odds he could get. What I said was that I didn't want Bob French to see me and none of the swipes.

Sure enough the first heat come off and About Ben Ahem went off his stride, up the back stretch, and looked like a wooden horse or a sick one, and come in to be last. Then this Wilbur Wessen went down to the betting place under the grandstand and there I was with the two girls, and when that Miss Woodbury was looking the other way once, Lucy Wessen kinda, with her shoulder you know, kinda touched me. Not just tucking down, I don't mean. You know how a woman can do. They get close, but not getting gay either. You know what they do. Gee whizz.

And then they give me a jolt. What they had done, when I didn't know, was to get together, and they had decided Wilbur Wessen would bet fifty dollars, and the two girls had gone and put in ten dollars each, of their own money, too. I was sick then, but I was sicker later.

About the gelding, About Ben Ahem, and their winning their

money, I wasn't worried a lot about that. It come out O.K. Ahem stepped the next three heats like a bushel of spoiled eggs going to market before they could be found out, and Wilbur Wessen had got nine to two for the money. There was something else eating me.

Because Wilbur come back, after he had bet the money, and after that he spent most of his time talking to that Miss Woodbury, and Lucy Wessen and I was left alone together like on a desert island. Gee, if I'd only been on the square or if there had been any way of getting myself on the square. There ain't any Walter Mathers, like I said to her and them, and there hasn't ever been one, but if there was, I bet I'd go to Marietta, Ohio, and shoot him tomorrow.

There I was, big boob that I am. Pretty soon the race was over, and Wilbur had gone down and collected our money, and we had a hack downtown, and he stood us a swell supper at the West House, and a bottle of champagne beside.

And I was with that girl and she wasn't saying much, and I wasn't saying much either. One thing I know. She wasn't stuck on me because of the lie about my father being rich and all that. There's a way you know. . . . Craps amighty. There's a kind of girl, you see just once in your life, and if you don't get busy and make hay, then you're gone for good and all, and might as well go jump off a bridge. They give you a look from inside of them somewhere, and it ain't no vamping, and what it means is—you want that girl to be your wife, and you want nice things around her like flowers and swell clothes, and you want her to have the kids you're going to have, and you want good music played and no rag-time. Gee whizz.

There's a place over near Sandusky, across a kind of bay, and it's called Cedar Point. And after we had supper we went over to it in a launch, all by ourselves. Wilbur and Miss Lucy and that Miss Woodbury had to catch a ten o'clock train back to Tiffin, Ohio, because, when you're out with girls like that you can't get careless like with some kinds of Janes.

And Wilbur blowed himself to the launch and it cost him fifteen cold plunks, but I wouldn't never have knew if I hadn't listened. He wasn't no tin horn kind of a sport.

Over at Cedar Point place, we didn't stay around where there was a gang of common kind of cattle at all.

There was big dance halls and dining places for yaps, and there was a beach you could walk along and get where it was dark, and we went there.

She didn't talk hardly at all and neither did I, and I was thinking how glad I was my mother was all right, and always made us kids learn to eat with a fork at table, and not swill soup, and not be noisy and rough like a gang you see around a race track that way.

Then Wilbur and his girl went away up the beach and Lucy and I sat down in a dark place, where there was some roots of old trees, the water had washed up, and after that the time, till we had to go back in the launch and they had to catch their trains, wasn't nothing at all. It went like winking your eye.

Here's how it was. The place we were setting in was dark, like I said, and there was the roots from that old stump sticking up like arms, and there was a watery smell, and the night was like—as if you could put your hand out and feel it—so warm and soft and dark and sweet like an orange.

I most cried and I most swore and I most jumped up and danced I was so mad and happy and sad.

When Wilbur come back from being alone with his girl, and she saw him coming, Lucy she says, "we got to go to the train now", and she was most crying too, but she never knew nothing I knew, and she couldn't be so all busted up. And then, before Wilbur and Miss Woodbury got up to where we was, she put her face up and kissed me quick and put her head up against me and she was all quivering and—Gee whizz.

Sometimes I hope I have cancer and die. I guess you know what I mean. We went in the launch across the bay to the train like that, and it was dark, too. She whispered and said it was like she and I could get out of the boat and walk on the water, and it sounded foolish, but I knew what she meant.

And then quick we were right at the depot, and there was a big gang of yaps, the kind that goes to the fairs, and crowded and milling around like cattle, and how could I tell her? "It won't be long because you'll write and I'll write to you." That's all she said.

I got a chance like a hay barn afire. A swell chance I got.

And maybe she would write me, down at Marietta that way, and the letter would come back, and stamped on the front of it by the U.S.A. "there ain't any such guy," or something like that, whatever they stamp on a letter that way.

And me trying to pass myself off for a bigbug and a swell—to her, as decent a little body as God ever made. Craps amighty—a swell chance I got!

And then the train come in, and she got on it, and Wilbur Wessen he come and shook hands with me, and that Miss Woodbury was nice too and bowed to me, and I at her, and the train went and I busted out and cried like a kid.

Gee, I could have run after that train and made Dan Patch look like a freight train after a wreck but, socks amighty, what was the use? Did you ever see such a fool?

I'll bet you what—if I had an arm broke right now or a train had run over my foot—I wouldn't go to no doctor at all. I'd go set down and let her hurt and hurt—that's what I'd do.

I'll bet you what—if I hadn't a drunk that booze I'd a never been such a boob as to go tell such a lie—that couldn't never be made straight to a lady like her.

I wish I had that fellow right here that had on a Windsor tie and carried a cane. I'd smash him for fair. Gosh darn his eyes. He's a big fool—that's what he is.

And if I'm not another you just go find me one and I'll quit working and be a bum and give him my job. I don't care nothing for working, and earning money, and saving it for no such boob as myself.

# JAMES JOYCE
## 1882–1941

Joyce was born near Dublin, Ireland, and educated by the Jesuits at Belvedere and University College. He went into self-imposed exile in 1904, taking with him a young woman named Nora Barnacle. "She'll never leave him," said Joyce's father, and she didn't. In Italy and Switzerland Joyce earned a precarious living teaching English while trying to become a great writer. His short stories were all designed for a collection called *Dubliners*, which spent ten years finding a publisher and then sold less than five hundred copies in 1914. His autobiographical novel, *A Portrait of the Artist as a Young Man* (1916) attracted the attention of T. S. Eliot and Ezra Pound, who helped him get support for his major project, *Ulysses* (1922), which took realism to its logical conclusion and beyond. *Finnegans Wake* (1939) is all beyond—a book to keep the professors busy, as Joyce observed, and busy they are. But, as Joyce's work becomes more familiar, the technical breakthroughs and the difficulties seem less noticeable and the comic spirit and humanity come through more clearly.

# The Boarding House

Mrs Mooney was a butcher's daughter. She was a woman who was quite able to keep things to herself: a determined woman. She had married her father's foreman and opened a butcher's shop near Spring Gardens. But as soon as his father-in-law was dead Mr Mooney began to go to the devil. He drank, plundered the till, ran headlong into debt. It was no use making him take the pledge: he was sure to break out again a few days after. By fighting his wife in the presence of customers and by buying bad meat he ruined his business. One night he went for his wife with the cleaver and she had to sleep in a neighbour's house.

After that they lived apart. She went to the priest and got a separation from him with care of the children. She would give him neither money nor food nor house-room; and so he was obliged to enlist himself as a sheriff's man. He was a shabby stooped little drunkard with a white face and a white moustache and white eyebrows, pencilled above his little eyes, which were pink-veined and raw; and all day long he sat in the bailiff's room, waiting to be put on a job. Mrs Mooney, who had taken what remained of her money out of the butcher business and set up a boarding house in Hardwicke Street, was a big imposing woman. Her house had a floating population made up of tourists from Liverpool and the Isle of Man and, occasionally, *artistes* from the music halls. Its resident population was made up of clerks from the city. She governed the house cunningly and firmly, knew when to give credit, when to be stern and when to let things pass. All the resident young men spoke of her as *The Madam*.

Mrs Mooney's young men paid fifteen shillings a week for board and lodgings (beer or stout at dinner excluded). They shared in common tastes and occupations and for this reason they were very chummy with one another. They discussed with one another the chances of favourites and outsiders. Jack Mooney, the Madam's son, who was clerk to a commission agent in Fleet Street, had the reputation of being a hard case. He was fond of using soldiers' obscenities: usually he came home in the small hours. When he met his friends he had always a good one to tell them and he was always sure to be on to a good thing—that is to say, a likely horse or a likely *artiste*. He was also handy with the mits and sang comic songs. On Sunday nights there would often be a reunion in Mrs Mooney's front drawing-room. The music-hall *artistes* would oblige; and Sheridan played waltzes and polkas and vamped accompaniments. Polly Mooney, the Madam's daughter, would also sing. She sang:

> I'm a . . . naughty girl.
> You needn't sham:
> You know I am.

Polly was a slim girl of nineteen; she had light soft hair and a small full mouth. Her eyes, which were grey with a shade of green through them, had a habit of glancing upwards when she spoke with anyone, which made her look like a little perverse madonna. Mrs Mooney had first sent her daughter to be a typist in a corn-factor's office but, as a disreputable sheriff's man used to come every other day to the office, asking to be allowed to say a word to his daughter, she had taken her daughter home again and set her to do housework. As Polly was very lively the intention was to give her the run of the young men. Besides, young men like to feel that there is a young woman not very far away. Polly, of course, flirted with the young men but Mrs Mooney, who was a shrewd judge, knew that the young men were only passing the time away: none of them meant business. Things went on so for a long time and Mrs Mooney began to think of sending Polly back to typewriting when she noticed that something was going on between Polly and one of the young men. She watched the pair and kept her own counsel.

Polly knew that she was being watched, but still her mother's persistent silence could not be misunderstood. There had been no open complicity between mother and daughter, no open understanding but, though people in the house began to talk of the affair, still Mrs Mooney did not intervene. Polly began to grow a little strange in her manner and the young man was evidently perturbed. At last, when she judged it to be the right moment, Mrs Mooney intervened. She dealt with moral problems as a cleaver deals with meat: and in this case she had made up her mind.

It was a bright Sunday morning of early summer, promising heat, but with a fresh breeze blowing. All the windows of the boarding house were open and the lace curtains ballooned gently towards the street beneath the raised sashes. The belfry of George's Church sent out constant peals and worshippers, singly or in groups, traversed the little circus before the church, revealing their purpose by their self-contained demeanour no less than by the little volumes in their gloved hands. Breakfast was over in the boarding house and the table of the breakfast-room was covered with plates on which lay yellow streaks of eggs with morsels of bacon-fat and bacon-rind. Mrs Mooney sat in the straw arm-chair and watched the servant Mary remove the breakfast things. She made Mary collect the crusts and pieces of broken bread to help to make Tuesday's bread-pudding. When the table was cleared, the broken bread collected, the sugar and butter safe under lock and key, she began to reconstruct the interview which she had had the night before with Polly. Things were as she had suspected: she had been frank in her questions and Polly had been frank in her answers. Both had been somewhat awkward, of course. She had been made awkward by her not wishing to receive the news in too cavalier a fashion or to seem to have connived and Polly had been made awkward not merely because allusions of that kind always made her awkward but also because she did not wish it to be thought that in her wise innocence she had divined the intention behind her mother's tolerance.

Mrs Mooney glanced instinctively at the little gilt clock on the mantelpiece as soon as she had become aware through her revery that the bells of George's Church had stopped ringing. It was seventeen minutes past eleven: she would have lots of time to have the matter out with Mr Doran and then catch short twelve at Marlborough Street. She was sure she would win. To begin with she had all the weight of social opinion on her side: she was an outraged mother. She had allowed him to live beneath her roof, assuming that he was a man of honour, and he had simply abused her hospitality. He was thirty-four or thirty-five years of age, so that youth could not be pleaded as his excuse; nor could ignorance be his excuse since he was a man who had seen something of the world. He had simply taken advantage of Polly's youth and inexperience: that was evident. The question was: What reparation would he make?

There must be reparation made in such cases. It is all very well for the man: he can go his ways as if nothing had happened, having had his moment of pleasure, but the girl has to bear the brunt. Some mothers would be content to patch up such an affair for a sum of money; she had known cases of it. But she would not do so. For her only one reparation could make up for the loss of her daughter's honour: marriage.

She counted all her cards again before sending Mary up to Mr Doran's room to say that she wished to speak with him. She felt sure she would win. He was a serious young man, not rakish or loud-voiced like the others. If it had been Mr Sheridan or Mr Meade or Bantam Lyons her task would have been much harder. She did not think he would face publicity. All the lodgers in the house knew something of the affair; details had been invented by some. Besides, he had been employed for thirteen years in a great Catholic wine-merchant's office and publicity would mean for him, perhaps, the loss of his sit. Whereas if he agreed all might be well. She knew he had a good screw for one thing and she suspected he had a bit of stuff put by.

Nearly the half-hour! She stood up and surveyed herself in the pier-glass. The decisive expression of her great florid face satisfied her and she thought of some mothers she knew who could not get their daughters off their hands.

Mr Doran was very anxious indeed this Sunday morning. He had made two attempts to shave but his hand had been so unsteady that he had been obliged to desist. Three days' reddish beard fringed his jaws and every two or three minutes a mist gathered on his glasses so that he had to take them off and polish them with his pocket-handkerchief. The recollection of his confession of the night before was a cause of acute pain to him; the priest had drawn out every ridiculous detail of the affair and in the end had so magnified his sin that he was almost thankful at being afforded a loophole of reparation. The harm was done. What could he do now but marry her or run away? He could not brazen it out. The affair would be sure to be talked of and his employer would be certain to hear of it. Dublin is such a small city: everyone knows everyone else's business. He felt his heart leap warmly in his throat as he heard in his excited imagination old Mr Leonard calling out in his rasping voice: *Send Mr Doran here, please.*

All his long years of service gone for nothing! All his industry and diligence thrown away! As a young man he had sown his wild oats, of course; he had boasted of his free-thinking and denied the existence of God to his companions in public-houses. But that was all passed and done with . . . nearly. He still bought a copy of *Reynolds's Newspaper* every week but he attended to his religious duties and for nine-tenths of the year lived a regular life. He had money enough to settle down on; it was not that. But the family would look down on her. First of all there was her disreputable father and then her mother's boarding house was beginning to get a certain fame. He had a notion that he was being had. He could imagine his friends talking of the affair and laughing. She *was* a little vulgar; some times she said *I seen* and *If I had've known*. But what would grammar matter if he really loved her? He could not make up his mind whether to like her or despise her for what she had done. Of course he had done it too. His instinct urged him to remain free, not to marry. Once you are married you are done for, it said.

While he was sitting helplessly on the side of the bed in shirt and trousers she tapped lightly at his door and entered. She told him all, that she had made a clean breast of it to her mother and that her mother would speak with him that morning. She cried and threw her arms round his neck, saying:

—O Bob! Bob! What am I to do? What am I to do at all?

She would put an end to herself, she said.

He comforted her feebly, telling her not to cry, that it would be all right, never fear. He felt against his shirt the agitation of her bosom.

It was not altogether his fault that it had happened. He remembered well, with the curious patient memory of the celibate, the first casual caresses her dress, her breath, her fingers had given him. Then late one night as he was undressing for bed she had tapped at his door, timidly. She wanted to relight her candle at his for hers had been blown out by a gust. It was her bath night. She wore a loose open combing-jacket of printed flannel. Her white instep shone in the opening of her furry slippers and the blood glowed warmly behind her perfumed skin. From her hands and wrists too as she lit and steadied her candle a faint perfume arose.

On nights when he came in very late it was she who warmed up his dinner. He scarcely knew what he was eating, feeling her beside him alone, at night, in the sleeping house. And her thoughtfulness! If the night was anyway cold or wet or windy there was sure to be a little tumbler of punch ready for him. Perhaps they could be happy together. . . .

They used to go upstairs together on tiptoe, each with a candle, and on the third landing exchange reluctant goodnights. They used to kiss. He remembered well her eyes, the touch of her hand and his delirium. . . .

But delirium passes. He echoed her phrase, applying it to himself: *What am I to do?* The instinct of the celibate warned him to hold back. But the sin was there; even his sense of honour told him that reparation must be made for such a sin.

While he was sitting with her on the side of the bed Mary came to the door and said that the missus wanted to see him in the parlour. He stood up to put on his coat and waistcoat, more helpless than ever. When he was dressed he went over to her to comfort her. It would be all right, never fear. He left her crying on the bed and moaning softly: *O my God!*

Going down the stairs his glasses became so dimmed with moisture that he had to take them off and polish them. He longed to ascend through the roof and fly away to another country where he would never hear again of his trouble, and yet a force pushed him downstairs step by step. The implacable faces of his employer and of the Madam stared upon his discomfiture. On the last flight of stairs he passed Jack Mooney who was coming up from the pantry nursing two bottles of *Bass.* They saluted coldly; and the lover's eyes rested for a second or two on a thick bulldog face and a pair of thick short arms. When he reached the foot of the staircase he glanced up and saw Jack regarding him from the door of the return-room.

Suddenly he remembered the night when one of the music-hall *artistes,* a little blond Londoner, had made a rather free allusion to Polly. The reunion had been almost broken up on account of Jack's violence. Everyone tried to quiet him. The music-hall *artiste,* a little paler than usual, kept smiling and saying that there was no harm meant: but Jack kept shouting at him that if any fellow tried that sort of a game on with *his* sister he'd bloody well put his teeth down his throat, so he would.

. . . . . . . . . . . .

Polly sat for a little time on the side of the bed, crying. Then she dried her eyes and went over to the looking-glass. She dipped the end of the towel in the water-jug and refreshed her eyes with the cool water. She looked at herself in profile and readjusted a hairpin above her ear. Then she went back to the bed again and sat at the foot. She regarded the pillows for a long time and the sight of them awakened in her mind secret, amiable memories. She rested the nape of her neck against the cool iron bed-rail and fell into a revery. There was no longer any perturbation visible on her face.

She waited on patiently, almost cheerfully, without alarm, her memories gradually giving place to hopes and visions of the future. Her hopes and visions were so intricate that she no longer saw the white pillows on which her gaze was fixed or remembered that she was waiting for anything.

At last she heard her mother calling. She started to her feet and ran to the banisters.

—Polly! Polly!

—Yes, mamma?

—Come down, dear. Mr Doran wants to speak to you.

Then she remembered what she had been waiting for.

# D. H. LAWRENCE
## 1885–1930

David Herbert Lawrence was born at Eastwood, a coal-mining village in the English Midlands. His father was a miner, his mother a woman from the middle class who never accepted her husband's way of life. Lawrence was torn between them: close to his mother during her life, appreciating his father only after his death. The story of this family struggle is told in one of Lawrence's finest works, his novel *Sons and Lovers* (1913). In 1901 Lawrence nearly died of pneumonia. His health was delicate after this until his death of tuberculosis at the age of forty-five. In 1904 he took the King's Scholarship examination and came out first in all England and Wales. He seems to have been good at all academic subjects from mathematics to botany, painting, and writing. He began a career as a teacher, but trouble with his health and his early success as a writer took him away from teaching. In 1912 he ran off with the wife of a former professor of his at Nottingham University, and in 1914, when her divorce became final, he married her. From then on the Lawrences traveled, staying in England at times, but also living in Germany, Italy, Ceylon, Australia, the United States, and Mexico. After Lawrence died in southern France, his body was cremated and the ashes were brought to the United States and buried on a hill near Taos, New Mexico.

Lawrence's personality has drawn almost as much attention as his books. He spoke and wrote informally with the same vitality that animates all his literary work. And some of the informality of talk and personal correspondence can be found in his poetry and fiction. For a time censorship of his works and controversy over the supposed immorality of his views on sex obscured the seriousness and beauty of his work for many readers. But now his books are in print and his place in English letters is secure.

# The Rocking-Horse Winner

There was a woman who was beautiful, who started with all the advantages, yet she had no luck. She married for love, and the love turned to dust. She had bonny children, yet she felt they had been thrust upon her, and she could not love them. They looked at her coldly, as if they were finding fault with her. And hurriedly she felt she must cover up some fault in herself. Yet what it was that she must cover up she never knew. Nevertheless, when her children were present, she always felt the centre of her heart go hard. This troubled her, and in her manner she was all the more gentle and anxious for her children, as if she loved them very much. Only she herself knew that at the centre of her heart was a hard little place that could not feel love, no, not for anybody. Everybody else said of her: "She is such a good mother. She adores her children." Only she herself, and her children themselves, knew it was not so. They read it in each other's eyes.

There were a boy and two little girls. They lived in a pleasant house, with a garden, and they had discreet servants, and felt themselves superior to anyone in the neighbourhood.

Although they lived in style, they felt always an anxiety in the house. There was never enough money. The mother had a small income, and the father had a small income, but not nearly enough for the social position which they had to keep up. The father went into town to some office. But though he had good prospects, these prospects never materialised. There was always the grinding sense of the shortage of money, though the style was always kept up.

At last the mother said: "I will see if I can't make something." But she did not know where to begin. She racked her brains, and tried this thing and the other, but could not find anything successful. The failure made deep lines come into her face. Her children were growing up, they would have to go to school. There must be more money, there must be more money. The father, who was always very handsome and expensive in his tastes, seemed as if he never *would* be able to do anything worth doing. And the mother, who had a great belief in herself, did not succeed any better, and her tastes were just as expensive.

And so the house came to be haunted by the unspoken phrase: *There must be more money! There must be more money!* The children could hear it all the time, though nobody said it aloud. They heard it at Christmas, when the expensive and splendid toys filled the nursery. Behind the shining modern rocking-horse, behind the smart doll's house, a voice would start whispering: "There *must* be more money! There *must* be more money!" And the children would stop playing, to listen for a moment. They would look into each other's eyes, to see if they had all heard. And each one saw in the eyes of the other two that they too had heard. "There *must* be more money! There *must* be more money!"

It came whispering from the springs of the still-swaying rocking-horse, and even the horse, bending his wooden, champing head, heard it. The big doll, sitting so pink and smirking in her new pram, could hear it quite plainly, and seemed to be smirking all the more self-consciously because of it. The foolish puppy, too, that took the place of the teddy-bear, he was looking so extraordinarily foolish for no other reason but that he heard the secret whisper all over the house: "There *must* be more money!"

Yet nobody ever said it aloud. The whisper was everywhere, and therefore no one spoke it. Just as no one ever says: "We are breathing!" in spite of the fact that breath is coming and going all the time.

"Mother," said the boy Paul one day, "why don't we keep a car of our own? Why do we always use uncle's, or else a taxi?"

"Because we're the poor members of the family," said the mother.

"But why *are* we, mother?"

"Well—I suppose," she said slowly and bitterly, "it's because your father has no luck."

The boy was silent for some time.

"Is luck money, mother?" he asked, rather timidly.

"No, Paul. Not quite. It's what causes you to have money."

"Oh!" said Paul vaguely. "I thought when Uncle Oscar said *filthy lucker*, it meant money."

"*Filthy lucre* does mean money," said the mother. "But it's lucre, not luck."

"Oh!" said the boy. "Then what *is* luck, mother?"

"It's what causes you to have money. If you're lucky you have money. That's why it's better to be born lucky than rich. If you're rich, you may lose your money. But if you're lucky, you will always get more money."

"Oh! Will you? And is father not lucky?"

"Very unlucky, I should say," she said bitterly.

The boy watched her with unsure eyes.

"Why?" he asked.

"I don't know. Nobody ever knows why one person is lucky and another unlucky."

"Don't they? Nobody at all? Does *nobody* know?"

"Perhaps God. But He never tells."

"He ought to, then. And aren't you lucky either, mother?"

"I can't be, if I married an unlucky husband."

"But by yourself, aren't you?"

"I used to think I was, before I married. Now I think I am very unlucky indeed."

"Why?"

"Well—never mind! Perhaps I'm not really," she said.

The child looked at her to see if she meant it. But he saw, by the lines of her mouth, that she was only trying to hide something from him.

"Well, anyhow," he said stoutly, "I'm a lucky person."

"Why?" said his mother, with a sudden laugh.

He stared at her. He didn't even know why he had said it.

"God told me," he asserted, brazening it out.

"I hope He did, dear!" she said, again with a laugh, but rather bitter.

"He did, mother!"

"Excellent!" said the mother, using one of her husband's exclamations.

The boy saw she did not believe him; or rather, that she paid no attention to his assertion. This angered him somewhere, and made him want to compel her attention.

He went off by himself, vaguely, in a childish way, seeking for the clue to "luck." Absorbed, taking no heed of other people, he went about with a sort of stealth, seeking inwardly for luck. He wanted luck, he wanted it, he wanted it. When the two girls were playing dolls in the nursery, he would sit on his big rocking-horse, charging madly into space, with a frenzy that made the little girls peer at him uneasily. Wildly the horse careered, the waving dark hair of the boy tossed, his eyes had a strange glare in them. The little girls dared not speak to him.

When he had ridden to the end of his mad little journey, he climbed down and stood in front of his rocking-horse, staring fixedly into its lowered face. Its red mouth was slightly open, its big eye was wide and glassy-bright.

"Now!" he would silently command the snorting steed. "Now, take me to where there is luck! Now take me!"

And he would slash the horse on the neck with the little whip he had asked Uncle Oscar for. He *knew* the horse could take him to where there was luck, if only he forced it. So he would mount again and start on his furious ride, hoping at last to get there. He knew he could get there.

"You'll break your horse, Paul!" said the nurse.

"He's always riding like that! I wish he'd leave off!" said his elder sister Joan.

But he only glared down on them in silence. Nurse gave him up. She could make nothing of him. Anyhow, he was growing beyond her.

One day his mother and his Uncle Oscar came in when he was on one of his furious rides. He did not speak to them.

"Hallo, you young jockey! Riding a winner?" said his uncle.

"Aren't you growing too big for a rocking-horse? You're not a very little boy any longer, you know," said his mother.

But Paul only gave a blue glare from his big, rather close-set eyes. He would speak to nobody when he was in full tilt. His mother watched him with an anxious expression on her face.

At last he suddenly stopped forcing his horse into the mechanical gallop and slid down.

"Well, I got there!" he announced fiercely, his blue eyes still flaring, and his sturdy long legs straddling apart.

"Where did you get to?" asked his mother.

"Where I wanted to go," he flared back at her.

"That's right, son!" said Uncle Oscar. "Don't you stop till you get there. What's the horse's name?"

"He doesn't have a name," said the boy.

"Gets on without all right?" asked the uncle.

"Well, he has different names. He was called Sansovino last week."

"Sansovino, eh? Won the Ascot. How did you know this name?"

"He always talks about horse-races with Bassett," said Joan.

The uncle was delighted to find that his small nephew was posted with all the racing news. Bassett, the young gardener, who had been wounded in the left foot in the war and had got his present job through Oscar Cresswell, whose batman he had been, was a perfect blade of the "turf." He lived in the racing events, and the small boy lived with him.

Oscar Cresswell got it all from Bassett.

"Master Paul comes and asks me, so I can't do more than tell him, sir," said Bassett, his face terribly serious, as if he were speaking of religious matters.

"And does he ever put anything on a horse he fancies?"

"Well—I don't want to give him away—he's a young sport, a fine sport, sir. Would you mind asking him himself? He sort of takes a pleasure in it, and perhaps he'd feel I was giving him away, sir, if you don't mind."

Bassett was serious as a church.

The uncle went back to his nephew and took him off for a ride in the car.

"Say, Paul, old man, do you ever put anything on a horse?" the uncle asked.

The boy watched the handsome man closely.

"Why, do you think I oughtn't to?" he parried.

"Not a bit of it! I thought perhaps you might give me a tip for the Lincoln."

The car sped on into the country, going down to Uncle Oscar's place in Hampshire.

"Honour bright?" said the nephew.

"Honour bright, son!" said the uncle.

"Well, then, Daffodil."

"Daffodil! I doubt it, sonny. What about Mirza?"

"I only know the winner," said the boy. "That's Daffodil."

"Daffodil, eh?"

There was a pause. Daffodil was an obscure horse comparatively.

"Uncle!"

"Yes, son?"

"You won't let it go any further, will you? I promised Bassett."

"Bassett be damned, old man! What's he got to do with it?"

"We're partners. We've been partners from the first. Uncle, he lent me my first five shillings, which I lost. I promised him, honour bright, it was only between me and him; only you gave me that ten-shilling note I started winning with, so I thought you were lucky. You won't let it go any further, will you?"

The boy gazed at his uncle from those big, hot, blue eyes, set rather close together. The uncle stirred and laughed uneasily.

"Right you are, son! I'll keep your tip private. Daffodil, eh? How much are you putting on him?"

"All except twenty pounds," said the boy. "I keep that in reserve."

The uncle thought it a good joke.

"You keep twenty pounds in reserve, do you, you young romancer? What are you betting, then?"

"I'm betting three hundred," said the boy gravely. "But it's between you and me, Uncle Oscar! Honour bright?"

The uncle burst into a roar of laughter.

"It's between you and me all right, you young Nat Gould," he said, laughing. "But where's your three hundred?"

"Bassett keeps it for me. We're partners."

"You are, are you! And what is Bassett putting on Daffodil?"

"He won't go quite as high as I do, I expect. Perhaps he'll go a hundred and fifty."

"What, pennies?" laughed the uncle.

"Pounds," said the child, with a surprised look at his uncle. "Bassett keeps a bigger reserve than I do."

Between wonder and amusement Uncle Oscar was silent. He pursued the matter no further, but he determined to take his nephew with him to the Lincoln races.

"Now, son," he said, "I'm putting twenty on Mirza, and I'll put five on for you on any horse you fancy. What's your pick?"

"Daffodil, uncle."

"No, not the fiver on Daffodil!"

"I should if it was my own fiver," said the child.

"Good! Good! Right you are! A fiver for me and a fiver for you on Daffodil."

The child had never been to a race-meeting before, and his eyes were blue fire. He pursed his mouth tight and watched. A Frenchman just in front had put his money on Lancelot. Wild with excitement, he flayed his arms up and down, yelling "*Lancelot! Lancelot!*" in his French accent.

Daffodil came in first, Lancelot second, Mirza third. The child, flushed and with eyes blazing, was curiously serene. His uncle brought him four five-pound notes, four to one.

"What am I do with these?" he cried, waving them before the boy's eyes.

"I suppose we'll talk to Bassett," said the boy. "I expect I have fifteen hundred now; and twenty in reserve; and this twenty."

His uncle studied him for some moments.

"Look here, son!" he said. "You're not serious about Bassett and that fifteen hundred, are you?"

"Yes, I am. But it's between you and me, uncle. Honour bright?"

"Honour bright all right, son! But I must talk to Bassett."

"If you'd like to be a partner, uncle, with Bassett and me, we could all be partners. Only, you'd have to promise, honour bright, uncle, not to let it go beyond us three. Bassett and I are lucky, and you must be lucky, because it was your ten shillings I started winning with. . . ."

Uncle Oscar took both Bassett and Paul into Richmond Park for an afternoon, and there they talked.

"It's like this, you see, sir," Bassett said. "Master Paul would get me talking about racing events, spinning yarns, you know, sir. And he was always keen on knowing if I'd made or if I'd lost. It's about a year since, now, that I put five shillings on Blush of Dawn for him: and we lost. Then the luck turned, with that ten shillings he had from you: that we put on Singhalese. And since that time, it's been pretty steady, all things considering. What do you say, Master Paul?"

"We're all right when we're sure," said Paul. "It's when we're not quite sure that we go down."

"Oh, but we're careful then," said Bassett.

"But when are you *sure?*" smiled Uncle Oscar.

"It's Master Paul, sir," said Bassett in a secret, religious voice. "It's as if he had it from heaven. Like Daffodil, now, for the Lincoln. That was as sure as eggs."

"Did you put anything on Daffodil?" asked Oscar Cresswell.

"Yes, sir. I made my bit."

"And my nephew?"

Bassett was obstinately silent, looking at Paul.

"I made twelve hundred, didn't I, Bassett? I told uncle I was putting three hundred on Daffodil."

"That's right," said Bassett, nodding.

"But where's the money?" asked the uncle.

"I keep it safe locked up, sir. Master Paul he can have it any minute he likes to ask for it."

"What, fifteen hundred pounds?"

"And twenty! And *forty*, that is, with the twenty he made on the course."

"It's amazing!" said the uncle.

"If Master Paul offers you to be partners, sir, I would, if I were you: if you'll excuse me," said Bassett.

Oscar Cresswell thought about it.

"I'll see the money," he said.

They drove home again, and, sure enough, Bassett came round to the garden-house with fifteen hundred pounds in notes. The twenty pounds reserve was left with Joe Glee, in the Turf Commission deposit.

"You see, it's all right, uncle, when I'm *sure!* Then we go strong, for all we're worth. Don't we, Bassett?"

"We do that, Master Paul."

"And when are you sure?" said the uncle, laughing.

"Oh, well, sometimes I'm *absolutely* sure, like about Daffodil," said the boy; "and sometimes I have an idea; and sometimes I haven't even an idea, have I, Bassett? Then we're careful, because we mostly go down."

"You do, do you! And when you're sure, like about Daffodil, what makes you sure, sonny?"

"Oh, well, I don't know," said the boy uneasily. "I'm sure, you know, uncle; that's all."

"It's as if he had it from heaven, sir," Bassett reiterated.

"I should say so!" said the uncle.

But he became a partner. And when the Leger was coming on Paul was "sure" about Lively Spark, which was a quite inconsiderable horse. The boy insisted on putting a thousand on the horse, Bassett was for five hundred, and Oscar Cresswell two hundred. Lively Spark came in first, and the betting had been ten to one against him. Paul had made ten thousand.

"You see," he said, "I was absolutely sure of him."

Even Oscar Cresswell had cleared two thousand.

"Look here, son," he said, "this sort of thing makes me nervous."

"It needn't, uncle! Perhaps I shan't be sure again for a long time."

"But what are you going to do with your money?" asked the uncle.

"Of course," said the boy, "I started it for mother. She said she had no luck, because father is unlucky, so I thought if *I* was lucky, it might stop whispering."

"What might stop whispering?"

"Our house. I *hate* our house for whispering."

"What does it whisper?"

"Why—why"—the boy fidgeted—"why, I don't know. But it's always short of money, you know, uncle."

"I know it, son, I know it."

"You know people send mother writs, don't you, uncle?"

"I'm afraid I do," said the uncle.

"And then the house whispers, like people laughing at you behind your back. It's awful, that is! I thought if I was lucky——"

"You might stop it," added the uncle.

The boy watched him with big blue eyes, that had an uncanny cold fire in them, and he said never a word.

"Well, then!" said the uncle. "What are we doing?"

"I shouldn't like mother to know I was lucky," said the boy.

"Why not, son?"

"She'd stop me."

"I don't think she would."

"Oh!"—and the boy writhed in an odd way—"I *don't* want her to know, uncle."

"All right, son! We'll manage it without her knowing."

They managed it very easily. Paul, at the other's suggestion, handed over five thousand pounds to his uncle, who deposited it with the family lawyer, who was then to inform Paul's mother that a relative had put five thousand pounds into his hands, which sum was to be paid out a thousand pounds at a time, on the mother's birthday, for the next five years.

"So she'll have a birthday present of a thousand pounds for five successive years," said Uncle Oscar. "I hope it won't make it all the harder for her later."

Paul's mother had her birthday in November. The house had been "whispering" worse than ever lately, and, even in spite of his luck, Paul could not bear up against it. He was very anxious to see the effect of the birthday letter, telling his mother about the thousand pounds.

When there were no visitors, Paul now took his meals with his parents, as he was beyond the nursery control. His mother went into town nearly every day. She had discovered that she had an odd knack of sketching furs and dress materials, so she worked secretly in the studio of a friend who was the chief "artist" for the leading drapers. She drew the figures of ladies in furs and ladies in silk and sequins for the newspaper advertisements. This young woman artist earned several thousand pounds a year, but Paul's mother only made several hundreds, and she was again dissatisfied. She so wanted to be first in something, and she did not succeed, even in making sketches for drapery advertisements.

She was down to breakfast on the morning of her birthday. Paul watched her face as she read her letters. He knew the lawyer's letter. As his mother read it, her face hardened and became more expressionless. Then a cold, determined look came on her mouth. She hid the letter under the pile of others, and said not a word about it.

"Didn't you have anything nice in the post for your birthday, mother?" said Paul.

"Quite moderately nice," she said, her voice cold and absent.

She went away to town without saying more.

But in the afternoon Uncle Oscar appeared. He said Paul's mother had had a long interview with the lawyer, asking if the whole five thousand could not be advanced at once, as she was in debt.

"What do you think, uncle?" said the boy.

"I leave it to you, son."

"Oh, let her have it, then! We can get some more with the other," said the boy.

"A bird in the hand is worth two in the bush, laddie!" said Uncle Oscar.

"But I'm sure to *know* for the Grand National; or the Lincolnshire; or else the Derby. I'm sure to know for *one* of them," said Paul.

So Uncle Oscar signed the agreement, and Paul's mother touched the whole five thousand. Then something very curious happened. The voices in the house suddenly went mad, like a chorus of frogs on a spring evening. There were certain new furnishings, and Paul had a .tutor. He was *really* going to Eton, his father's school, in the following autumn. There were flowers in the winter, and a blossoming of the luxury Paul's mother had been used to. And yet the voices in the house, behind the sprays of mimosa and almondblossom, and from under the piles of iridescent cushions, simply trilled and screamed in a sort of ecstasy: "There *must* be more money! Oh-h-h; there *must* be more money. Oh, now, now-w! Now-w-w—there *must* be more money!—more than ever! More than ever!"

It frightened Paul terribly. He studied away at his Latin and Greek with his tutor. But his intense hours were spent with Bassett. The Grand National had gone by: he had not "known," and had lost a hundred pounds. Summer was at hand. He was in agony for the Lincoln. But even for the Lincoln he didn't "know," and he lost fifty pounds. He became wild-eyed and strange, as if something were going to explode in him.

"Let it alone, son! Don't you bother about it!" urged Uncle Oscar.

But it was as if the boy couldn't really hear what his uncle was saying.

"I've got to know for the Derby! I've got to know for the Derby!" the child reiterated, his big blue eyes blazing with a sort of madness.

His mother noticed how overwrought he was.

"You'd better go to the seaside. Wouldn't you like to go now to the seaside, instead of waiting? I think you'd better," she said, looking down at him anxiously, her heart curiously heavy because of him.

But the child lifted his uncanny blue eyes.

"I couldn't possibly go before the Derby, mother!" he said. "I couldn't possibly!"

"Why not?" she said, her voice becoming heavy when she was opposed. "Why not? You can still go from the seaside to see the Derby with your Uncle Oscar, if that's what you wish. No need for you to wait here. Besides, I think you care too much about these races. It's a bad sign. My family has been a gambling family, and you won't know till you grow up how much damage it has done. But it has done damage. I shall have to send Bassett away, and ask Uncle Oscar not to talk racing to you, unless you promise to be reasonable about it: go away to the seaside and forget it. You're all nerves!"

"I'll do what you like, mother, so long as you don't send me away till after the Derby," the boy said.

"Send you away from where? Just from this house?"

"Yes," he said, gazing at her.

"Why, you curious child, what makes you care about this house so much, suddenly? I never knew you loved it."

He gazed at her without speaking. He had a secret within a secret, something he had not divulged, even to Bassett or to his Uncle Oscar.

But his mother, after standing undecided and a little bit sullen for some moments, said:

"Very well, then! Don't go to the seaside till after the Derby, if you don't wish it. But promise me you won't let your nerves go to pieces. Promise you won't think so much about horse-racing and *events,* as you call them!"

"Oh no," said the boy casually. "I won't think much about them, mother. You needn't worry. I wouldn't worry, mother, if I were you."

"If you were me and I were you," said his mother, "I wonder what we *should* do!"

"But you know you needn't worry, mother, don't you?" the boy repeated.

"I should be awfully glad to know it," she said wearily.

"Oh, well, you *can,* you know. I mean, you *ought* to know you needn't worry," he insisted.

"Ought I? Then I'll see about it," she said.

Paul's secret of secrets was his wooden horse, that which had no name. Since he was emancipated from a nurse and a nursery-governess, he had had his rocking-horse removed to his own bedroom at the top of the house.

"Surely you're too big for a rocking-horse!" his mother had remonstrated.

"Well, you see, mother, till I can have a *real* horse, I like to have *some* sort of animal about," had been his quaint answer.

"Do you feel he keeps you company?" she laughed.

"Oh yes! He's very good, he always keeps me company, when I'm there," said Paul.

So the horse, rather shabby, stood in an arrested prance in the boy's bedroom.

The Derby was drawing near, and the boy grew more and more tense. He hardly heard what was spoken to him, he was very frail, and his eyes were really uncanny. His mother had sudden strange seizures of uneasiness about him. Sometimes, for half an hour, she would feel a sudden anxiety about him that was almost anguish. She wanted to rush to him at once, and know he was safe.

Two nights before the Derby, she was at a big party in town, when one of her rushes of anxiety about her boy, her first-born, gripped her heart till she could hardly speak. She fought with the feeling, might and main, for she believed in common sense. But it was too strong. She had to leave the dance and go downstairs to telephone to the country. The children's nursery-governess was terribly surprised and startled at being rung up in the night.

"Are the children all right, Miss Wilmot?"

"Oh yes, they are quite all right."

"Master Paul? Is he all right?"

"He went to bed as right as a trivet. Shall I run up and look at him?"

"No," said Paul's mother reluctantly. "No! Don't trouble. It's all right. Don't sit up. We shall be home fairly soon." She did not want her son's privacy intruded upon.

"Very good," said the governess.

It was about one o'clock when Paul's mother and father drove up to their house. All was still. Paul's mother went to her room and slipped off her white fur cloak. She had told her maid not to wait up for her. She heard her husband downstairs, mixing a whisky and soda.

And then, because of the strange anxiety at her heart, she stole upstairs to her son's room. Noiselessly she went along the upper corridor. Was there a faint noise? What was it?

She stood, with arrested muscles, outside his door, listening. There was a strange, heavy, and yet not loud noise. Her heart stood still. It was a soundless noise, yet rushing and powerful. Something huge, in violent, hushed motion. What was it? What in God's name was it? She ought to know. She felt that she knew the noise. She knew what it was. Yet she could not place it. She couldn't say what it was. And on and on it went, like a madness.

Softly, frozen with anxiety and fear, she turned the doorhandle.

The room was dark. Yet in the space near the window, she heard and saw something plunging to and fro. She gazed in fear and amazement.

Then suddenly she switched on the light, and saw her son, in his green pyjamas, madly surging on the rocking-horse. The blaze of light suddenly lit him up, as he urged the wooden horse, and lit her up, as she stood, blonde, in her dress of pale green and crystal, in the doorway.

"Paul!" she cried. "Whatever are you doing?"

"It's Malabar!" he screamed in a powerful, strange voice. "It's Malabar!"

His eyes blazed at her for one strange and senseless second, as he ceased urging his wooden horse. Then he fell with a crash to the ground, and she, all her tormented motherhood flooding upon her, rushed to gather him up.

But he was unconscious, and unconscious he remained, with some brain-fever. He talked and tossed, and his mother sat stonily by his side.

"Malabar! It's Malabar! Bassett, Bassett, I *know!* It's Malabar!"

So the child cried, trying to get up and urge the rocking-horse that gave him his inspiration.

"What does he mean by Malabar?" asked the heart-frozen mother.

"I don't know," said the father stonily.

"What does he mean by Malabar?" she asked her brother Oscar.

"It's one of the horses running for the Derby," was the answer.

And, in spite of himself, Oscar Cresswell spoke to Bassett, and himself put a thousand on Malabar: at fourteen to one.

The third day of the illness was critical: they were waiting for a change. The boy, with his rather long, curly hair, was tossing ceaselessly on the pillow. He neither slept nor regained consciousness, and his eyes were like blue stones. His mother sat, feeling her heart had gone, turned actually into a stone.

In the evening, Oscar Cresswell did not come, but Bassett sent a message, saying could he come up for one moment, just one moment? Paul's mother was very angry at the intrusion, but on second thoughts she agreed. The boy was the same. Perhaps Bassett might bring him to consciousness.

The gardener, a shortish fellow with a little brown moustache and sharp little brown eyes, tiptoed into the room, touched his imaginary cap to Paul's mother, and stole to the bedside, staring with glittering, smallish eyes at the tossing, dying child.

"Master Paul!" he whispered. "Master Paul! Malabar came in first all right, a clean win. I did as you told me. You've made over seventy thousand pounds, you have; you've got over eighty thousand. Malabar came in all right, Master Paul."

"Malabar! Malabar! Did I say Malabar, mother? Did I say Malabar? Do you think I'm lucky, mother? I knew Malabar, didn't I? Over eighty thousand pounds! I call that lucky, don't you, mother? Over eighty thousand pounds! I knew, didn't I know I knew? Malabar came in all right. If I ride my horse till I'm sure, then I tell you, Bassett, you can go as high as you like. Did you go for all you were worth, Bassett?"

"I went a thousand on it, Master Paul."

"I never told you, mother, that if I can ride my horse, and *get there*, then I'm absolutely sure—oh, absolutely! Mother, did I ever tell you? I *am* lucky!"

"No, you never did," said his mother.

But the boy died in the night.

And even as he lay dead, his mother heard her brother's voice saying to her: "My God, Hester, you're eighty-odd thousand to the good, and a poor devil of a son to the bad. But, poor devil, poor devil, he's best gone out of a life where he rides his rocking-horse to find a winner."

# KATHERINE MANSFIELD
## 1888–1923

She was born in Wellington, New Zealand, where her father was a success-ful merchant. She went to the village school, the Girl's High School, to a private school for young ladies, and finally for four years, to Queens Col-lege, London. It is a long way from London to New Zealand. When she returned from school, she bullied her parents until they allowed her to return to England to be a writer. She returned, with an allowance from her father that continued until her death, in search of experience. She was nineteen when she left home. Within a year she had become pregnant, married a man (not the father of her unborn child), gone to Germany, had a miscarriage, and returned to England despising Germans and men about equally. Her early stories came out of this experience. Later, after a happy marriage and the death in WWI of her younger brother, her fictional range widened and her second book *Bliss and Other Stories* (1920) had a consid-erable success. The short story was her form, and she worked well in it until her death from tuberculosis, at the age of thirty-five.

# Six Years After

It was not the afternoon to be on deck—on the contrary. It was exactly the afternoon when there is no snugger place than a warm cabin, a warm bunk. Tucked up with a rug, a hot-water bottle and a piping hot cup of tea she would not have minded the weather in the least. But he—hated cabins, hated to be inside anywhere more than was absolutely necessary. He had a passion for keeping, as he called it, above board, especially when he was travelling. And it wasn't surprising, considering the enormous amount of time he spent cooped up in the office. So, when he rushed away from her as soon as they got on board and came back five minutes later to say he had secured two deck chairs on the lee side and the steward was undoing the rugs, her voice through the high sealskin collar murmured "Good"; and because he was looking at her, she smiled with bright eyes and blinked quickly, as if to say, "Yes, perfectly all right—absolutely," and she meant it.

"Then we'd better—" said he, and he tucked her hand inside his arm and began to rush her off to where the two chairs stood. But she just had time to breathe, "Not so fast, Daddy, please," when he remembered too and slowed down.

Strange! They had been married twenty-eight years, and it was still an effort to him, each time, to adapt his pace to hers.

"Not cold, are you?" he asked, glancing sideways at her. Her little nose, geranium pink above the dark fur, was answer enough. But she thrust her free hand into the velvet pocket of her jacket and murmured gaily, "I shall be glad of my rug."

He pressed her tighter to his side—a quick, nervous pressure. He knew, of course, that she ought to be down in the cabin; he knew that it was no afternoon for her to be sitting on deck, in this cold and raw mist, lee side or no lee side, rugs or no rugs, and he realized how she must be hating it. But he had come to believe that it really was easier for her to make these sacrifices than it was for him. Take their present case, for instance. If he had gone down to the cabin with her, he would have been miserable the whole time, and he couldn't have helped showing it. At any rate, she would have found him out. Whereas, having made up her mind to fall in with his ideas, he would have betted anybody she would even go so far as to enjoy the experience. Not because she was without personality of her own. Good Lord! She was absolutely brimming with it. But because . . . but here his thoughts always stopped. Here they always felt the need of a cigar, as it were. And, looking at the cigar-tip, his fine blue eyes narrowed. It was a law of marriage, he supposed. . . . All the same, he always felt guilty when meant. His being said to her being: "You do understand, don't you?" and there was an answering tremor of her fingers, "I *understand*."

Certainly, the steward—good little chap—had done all in his power to make them comfortable. He had put up their chairs in whatever warmth there was and out of the smell. She did hope he would be tipped adequately. It was on occasions like these (and her life seemed to be full of such occasions) that she wished it was the woman who controlled the purse.

"Thank you, steward. That will do beautifully."

"Why are stewards so often delicate-looking?" she wondered, as her feet were tucked under. "This poor little chap looks as though he'd got a chest, and yet one would have thought . . . the sea air. . . ."

The button of the pigskin purse was undone. The tray was tilted. She saw sixpences, shillings, half-crowns.

"I should give him five shillings," she decided, "and tell him to buy himself a good nourishing—"

He was given a shilling, and he touched his cap and seemed genuinely grateful.

Well, it might have been worse. It might have been sixpence. It might, indeed. For at that moment Father turned towards her and said, half-apologetically, stuffing the purse back, "I gave him a shilling. I think it was worth it, don't you?"

"Oh, quite! Every bit!" said she.

It is extraordinary how peaceful it feels on a little steamer once the bustle of leaving port is over. In a quarter of an hour one might have been at sea for days. There is something almost touching, childish, in the way people submit themselves to the new conditions. They go to bed in the early afternoon, they shut their eyes and "it's night" like little children who turn the table upside down and cover themselves with the table-cloth. And those who remain on deck—they seem to be always the same, those few hardened men travellers—pause, light their pipes, stamp softly, gaze out to sea, and their voices are subdued as they walk up and down. The long-legged little girl chases after the red-cheeked boy, but soon both are captured; and the old sailor, swinging an unlighted lantern, passes and disappears. . . .

He lay back, the rug up to his chin and she saw he was breathing deeply. Sea air! If anyone believed in sea air, it was he. He had the strongest faith in its tonic qualities. But the great thing was, according to him, to fill the lungs with it the moment you came on board. Otherwise, the sheer strength of it was enough to give you a chill. . . .

She gave a small chuckle, and he turned to her quickly. "What is it?"

"It's your cap," she said. "I never can get used to you in a cap. You look such a thorough burglar."

"Well, what the deuce am I to wear?" He shot up one grey eyebrow and wrinkled his nose. "It's a very good cap, too. Very fine specimen of its kind. It's got a very rich white satin lining." He paused. He declaimed, as he had hundreds of times before at this stage, "Rich and rare were the gems she wore."

But she was thinking he really was childishly proud of the white satin lining. He would like to have taken off his cap and made her feel it. "Feel the quality!" How often had she rubbed between finger and thumb his coat, his shirt cuff, tie, sock, linen handkerchief, while he said that.

She slipped down more deeply into her chair.

And the little steamer pressed on, pitching gently, over the grey, unbroken, gently-moving water, that was veiled with slanting rain.

Far out, as though idly, listlessly, gulls were flying. Now they settled on the waves, now they beat up into the rainy air, and shone against the pale sky like the lights within a pearl. They looked cold and lonely. How lonely it will be when we have passed by, she thought. There will be nothing but the waves and those birds and rain falling.

She gazed through the rust-spotted railing along which big drops trembled, until suddenly she shut her lids. It was as if a warning voice inside her had said, "Don't look!"

"No, I won't," she decided. "It's too depressing, much too depressing."

But immediately, she opened her eyes and looked again. Lonely birds, water lifting, white pale sky—how were they changed?

And it seemed to her there was a presence far out there, between the sky and the water; someone very desolate and longing watched them pass and cried as if to stop them—but cried to her alone.

"Mother!"

"Don't leave me," sounded the cry. "Don't forget me! You are forgetting me, you know you are!" And it was as though from her own breast there came the sound of childish weeping.

"My son—my precious child—it isn't true!"

*Sh!* How was it possible that she was sitting there on that quiet steamer beside Father and at the same time she was hushing and holding a little slender boy—so pale—who had just waked out of a dreadful dream?

"I dreamed I was in a wood—somewhere far away from everybody,—and I was lying down and a great blackberry vine grew over me. And I called and called to you—and you wouldn't come—you wouldn't come—so I had to lie there for ever."

What a terrible dream! He had always had terrible dreams. How often, years ago, when he was small, she had made some excuse and escaped from their friends in the dining-room or the drawing-room to come to the foot of the stairs and listen. "Mother!" And when he was asleep, his dream had journeyed with her back into the circle of lamplight; it had taken its place there like a ghost. And now—

Far more often—at all times—in all places—like now, for instance—she never settled down, she was never off her guard for a moment but she heard him. He wanted her. "I am coming as fast as I can! As fast as I can!" But the dark stairs have no ending, and the worst dream of all—the one that is always the same—goes for ever and ever uncomforted.

This is anguish! How is it to be borne? Still, it is not the idea of her suffering which is unbearable—it is his. Can one do nothing for the dead? And for a long time the answer had been— Nothing!

. . . But softly without a sound the dark curtain has rolled down. There is no more to come. That is the end of the play. But it can't end like that—so suddenly. There must be more. No, it's cold, it's still. There is nothing to be gained by waiting.

But—did he go back again? Or, when the war was over, did he come home for good? Surely, he will marry—later on—not for several years. Surely, one day I shall remember his wedding and my first grandchild—a beautiful dark-haired boy born in the early morning— a lovely morning—spring!

"Oh, Mother, it's not fair to me to put these ideas into my head! Stop, Mother, stop! When I think of all I have missed, I can't bear it."

"I can't bear it!" She sits up breathing the words and tosses the dark rug away. It is colder than ever, and now the dusk is falling, falling like ash upon the pallid water.

And the little steamer, growing determined, throbbed on, pressed on, as if at the end of the journey there waited. . . .

# KATHERINE ANNE PORTER
1890-1980

She was born in Indian Creek, Texas, and educated both at home and in a series of girls' schools in Texas and Louisiana. She was married at sixteen, but it didn't take, and she began to support herself by doing newspaper work in Chicago. Her unusual beauty enabled her to play small parts in films as a means of support while she wrote, destroyed, and rewrote stories without seeking to publish them. She began publishing fiction when she was thirty and achieved recognition with her first collection,

*Flowering Judas*, in 1930. Since then a slow, steady output of polished fiction has solidified a reputation that has fluctuated little for fifty years.

# Rope

On the third day after they moved to the country he came walking back from the village carrying a basket of groceries and a twenty-four-yard coil of rope. She came out to meet him, wiping her hands on her green smock. Her hair was tumbled, her nose was scarlet with sunburn; he told her that already she looked like a born country woman. His gray flannel shirt stuck to him, his heavy shoes were dusty. She assured him he looked like a rural character in a play.

Had he brought the coffee? She had been waiting all day long for coffee. They had forgot it when they ordered at the store the first day.

Gosh, no, he hadn't. Lord, now he'd have to go back. Yes, he would if it killed him. He thought, though, he had everything else. She reminded him it was only because he didn't drink coffee himself. If he did he would remember it quick enough. Suppose they ran out of cigarettes? Then she saw the rope. What was that for? Well, he thought it might do to hang clothes on, or something. Naturally she asked him if he thought they were going to run a laundry? They already had a fifty-foot line hanging right before his eyes? Why, hadn't he noticed it, really? It was a blot on the landscape to her.

He thought there were a lot of things a rope might come in handy for. She wanted to know what, for instance. He thought a few seconds, but nothing occurred. They could wait and see, couldn't they? You need all sorts of strange odds and ends around a place in the country. She said, yes, that was so; but she thought just at that time when every penny counted, it seemed funny to buy more rope. That was all. She hadn't meant anything else. She hadn't just seen, not at first, why he felt it was necessary.

Well, thunder, he had bought it because he wanted to, and that was all there was to it. She thought that was reason enough, and couldn't understand why he hadn't said so, at first. Undoubtedly it would be useful, twenty-four yards of rope, there were hundreds of things, she couldn't think of any at the moment, but it would come in. Of course. As he had said, things always did in the country.

But she was a little disappointed about the coffee, and oh, look, look, look at the eggs! Oh, my, they're all running! What had he put on top of them? Hadn't he known eggs mustn't be squeezed? Squeezed, who had squeezed them, he wanted to know. What a silly thing to say. He had simply brought them along in the basket with the other things. If they got broke it was the grocer's fault. He should know better than to put heavy things on top of eggs.

She believed it was the rope. That was the heaviest thing in the pack, she saw him plainly when he came in from the road, the rope was a big package on top of everything. He desired the whole wide world to witness that this was not a fact. He had carried the rope in one hand and the basket in the other, and what was the use of her having eyes if that was the best they could do for her?

Well, anyhow, she could see one thing plain: no eggs for breakfast. They'd have to scramble them now, for supper. It was too damned bad. She had planned to have steak for supper. No ice, meat wouldn't keep. He wanted to know why she couldn't finish breaking the eggs in a bowl and set them in a cool place.

Cool place! if he could find one for her, she'd be glad to set them there. Well, then, it seemed to him they might very well cook the meat at the same time they cooked the eggs and then warm up the meat for tomorrow. The idea simply choked her. Warmed-over meat, when they might as well have had it fresh. Second best and scraps and makeshifts, even to the meat! He rubbed her shoulder a little. It doesn't really matter so much, does it, darling? Sometimes when they were playful, he would rub her shoulder and she would arch and purr. This time she hissed and almost clawed. He was getting ready to say that they could surely manage somehow when she turned on him and said, if he told her they could manage somehow she would certainly slap his face.

He swallowed the words red hot, his face burned. He picked up the rope and started to put it on the top shelf. She would not have it on the top shelf, the jars and tins belonged there; positively she would not have the top shelf cluttered up with a lot of rope. She had borne all the clutter she meant to bear in the flat in town, there was space here at least and she meant to keep things in order.

Well, in that case, he wanted to know what the hammer and nails were doing up there? And why had she put them there when she knew very well he needed that hammer and those nails upstairs to fix the window sashes? She simply slowed down everything and made double work on the place with her insane habit of changing things around and hiding them.

She was sure she begged his pardon, and if she had had any reason to believe he was going to fix the sashes this summer she would have left the hammer and nails right where he put them; in the middle of the bedroom floor where they could step on them in the dark. And now if he didn't clear the whole mess out of there she would throw them down the well.

Oh, all right, all right—could he put them in the closet? Naturally not, there were brooms and mops and dustpans in the closet, and why couldn't he find a place for his rope outside her kitchen? Had he stopped to consider there were seven God-forsaken rooms in the house, and only one kitchen?

He wanted to know what of it? And did she realize she was making a complete fool of herself? And what did she take him for, a three-year-old idiot? The whole trouble with her was she needed something weaker than she was to heckle and tyrannize over. He wished to God now they had a couple of children she could take it out on. Maybe he'd get some rest.

Her face changed at this, she reminded him he had forgot the coffee and had bought a worthless piece of rope. And when she thought of all the things they actually needed to make the place even decently fit to live in, well, she could cry, that was all. She looked so forlorn, so lost and despairing he couldn't believe it was only a piece of rope that was causing all the racket. What *was* the matter, for God's sake?

Oh, would he please hush and go away, and *stay* away, if he could, for five minutes? By all means, yes, he would. He'd stay away indefinitely if she wished. Lord, yes, there was nothing he'd like better than to clear out and never come back. She couldn't for the life of her see what was holding him, then. It was a swell time. Here she was, stuck, miles from a railroad, with a half-empty house on her hands, and not a penny in her pocket, and everything on earth to do; it seemed the God-sent moment for him to get out from under. She was surprised he hadn't stayed in town as it was until she had come out and done the work and got things straightened out. It was his usual trick.

It appeared to him that this was going a little far. Just a touch out of bounds, if she didn't mind his saying so. Why the hell had he stayed in town the summer before? To do a half-dozen extra jobs to get the money he had sent her. That was it. She knew perfectly well they couldn't have done it otherwise. She had agreed with him at the time. And that was the only time so help him he had ever left her to do anything by herself.

Oh, he could tell that to his great-grandmother. She had her notion of what had kept him in town. Considerably more than a notion, if he wanted to know. So, she was going to bring all that up again, was she? Well, she could just think what she pleased. He was tired of explaining. It may have looked funny but he had simply got hooked in, and what could he do? It was impossible to believe that she was going to take it seriously. Yes, yes, she knew how it was with a man: if he was left by himself a minute, some woman was certain to kidnap him. And naturally he couldn't hurt her feelings by refusing!

Well, what was she raving about? Did she forget she had told him those two weeks alone in the country were the happiest she had known for four years? And how long had they been married when she said that? All right, shut up! If she thought that hadn't stuck in his craw.

She hadn't meant she was happy because she was away from him. She meant she was happy getting the devilish house nice and ready for him. That was what she had meant, and now look! Bringing up something she had said a year ago simply to justify himself for forgetting her coffee and breaking the eggs and buying a wretched piece of rope they couldn't afford. She really thought it was time to drop the subject, and now she wanted only two things in the world. She wanted him to get that rope from underfoot, and go back to the village and get her coffee, and if he could remember it, he might bring a metal mitt for the skillets, and two more curtain rods, and if there were any rubber gloves in the village, her hands were simply raw, and a bottle of milk of magnesia from the drugstore.

He looked out at the dark blue afternoon sweltering on the slopes, and mopped his forehead and sighed heavily and said, if only she could wait a minute for *anything*, he was going back. He had said so, hadn't he, the very instant they found he had overlooked it?

Oh, yes, well . . . run along. She was going to wash windows. The country was so beautiful! She doubted they'd have a moment to enjoy it. He meant to go, but he could not until he had said that if she wasn't such a hopeless melancholiac she might see that this was only for a few days. Couldn't she remember anything pleasant about the other summers? Hadn't they ever had any fun? She hadn't time to talk about it, and now would he please not leave that rope lying around for her to trip on? He picked it up, somehow it had toppled off the table, and walked out with it under his arm.

Was he going this minute? He certainly was. She thought so. Sometimes it seemed to her he had second sight about the precisely perfect moment to leave her ditched. She had meant to put the mattresses out to sun, if they put them out this minute they would get at least three hours, he must have heard her say that morning she meant to put them out. So of course he would walk off and leave her to it. She supposed he thought the exercise would do her good.

Well, he was merely going to get her coffee. A four-mile walk for two pounds of coffee was ridiculous, but he was perfectly willing to do it. The habit was making a wreck of her, but if she wanted to wreck herself there was nothing he could do about it. If he thought it was coffee that was making a wreck of her, she congratulated him: he must have a damned easy conscience.

Conscience or no conscience, he didn't see why the mattresses couldn't very well wait until tomorrow. And anyhow, for God's sake, were they living *in* the house, or were they going to let the house ride them to death? She paled at this, her face grew livid about the mouth, she looked quite dangerous, and reminded him that housekeeping was no more her work than it was his: she had other work to do as well, and when did he think she was going to find time to do it at this rate?

Was she going to start on that again? She knew as well as he did that his work brought in the regular money, hers was only occasional, if they depended on what *she* made—and she might as well get straight on this question once for all!

That was positively not the point. The question was, when both of them were working on their own time, was there going to be a division of the housework, or wasn't there? She merely wanted to know, she had to make her plans. Why, he thought that was all arranged. It was understood that he was to help. Hadn't he always, in summers?

Hadn't he, though? Oh, just hadn't he? And when, and where, and doing what? Lord, what an uproarious joke!

It was such a very uproarious joke that her face turned slightly purple, and she screamed with laughter. She laughed so hard she had to sit down, and finally a rush of tears spurted from her eyes and poured down into the lifted corners of her mouth. He dashed towards her and dragged her up to her feet and tried to pour water on her head. The dipper hung by a string on a nail and he broke it loose. Then he tried to pump water with one hand while she struggled in the other. So he gave it up and shook her instead.

She wrenched away, crying out for him to take his rope and go to hell, she had simply given him up: and ran. He heard her high-heeled bedroom slippers clattering and stumbling on the stairs.

He went out around the house and into the lane; he suddenly realized he had a blister on his heel and his shirt felt as if it were on fire. Things broke so suddenly you didn't know where you were. She could work herself into a fury about simply nothing. She was terrible, damn it: not an ounce of reason. You might as well talk to a sieve as that woman when she got going. Damned if he'd spend his life humoring her! Well, what to do now? He would take back the rope and exchange it for something else. Things accumulated, things were mountainous, you couldn't move them or sort them out or get rid of them. They just lay and rotted around. He'd take it back. Hell, why should he? He wanted it. What was it anyhow? A piece of rope. Imagine anybody caring more about a piece of rope than about a man's feelings. What earthly right had she to say a word about it? He remembered all the useless, meaningless things she bought for herself: Why? because I wanted it, that's why! He stopped and selected a large stone by the road. He would put the rope behind it. He would put it in the tool-box when he got back. He'd heard enough about it to last him a life-time.

When he came back she was leaning against the post box beside the road waiting. It was pretty late, the smell of broiled steak floated nose high in the cooling air. Her face was young and smooth and fresh-looking. Her unmanageable funny black hair was all on end. She waved to him from a distance, and he speeded up. She called out that supper was ready and waiting, was he starved?

You bet he was starved. Here was the coffee. He waved it at her. She looked at his other hand. What was that he had there?

Well, it was the rope again. He stopped short. He had meant to exchange it but forgot. She wanted to know why he should exchange it, if it was something he really wanted. Wasn't the air sweet now, and wasn't it fine to be here?

She walked beside him with one hand hooked into his leather belt. She pulled and jostled him a little as he walked, and leaned against him. He put his arm clear around her and patted her stomach. They exchanged wary smiles. Coffee, coffee for the Ootsum-Wootsums! He felt as if he were bringing her a beautiful present.

He was a love, she firmly believed, and if she had had her coffee in the morning, she wouldn't have behaved so funny . . . There was a whippoorwill still coming back, imagine, clear out of season, sitting in the crab-apple tree calling all by himself. Maybe his girl stood him up. Maybe she did. She hoped to hear him once more, she loved whippoorwills . . . He knew how she was, didn't he?

Sure, he knew how she was.


# DOROTHY PARKER
## 1893–1967

Born the daughter of J. Henry and Eliza Rothschild in West End, New Jersey, she went to school at Blessed Sacrament Convent in New York City and Miss Dana's School in Morristown, N.J. At twenty she had a job with *Vogue* magazine and had begun to publish light verse. A few years later she married Edwin Parker, keeping his name though divorcing him eleven years later. Writing was her trade from the beginning, and New York City was her territory. She worked for sophisticated magazines like *Vanity Fair* and the *New Yorker*. She wrote plays for Broadway and film scripts for Hollywood. In her youth she was the only woman who belonged to a select circle of New York wits, whose base was a table in the bar of the Algonquin Hotel. She squandered her talent collaborating with clever men who were not her equals. In her later years, she stopped writing and drank too much. But for a brief period in the twenties and thirties she was the talk of the town, and her stories, verse, and even casual remarks will go on being remembered.

## You Were Perfectly Fine

The pale young man eased himself carefully into the low chair, and rolled his head to the side, so that the cool chintz comforted his cheek and temple.

"Oh, dear," he said. "Oh, dear, oh, dear, oh, dear. Oh."

The clear-eyed girl, sitting light and erect on the couch, smiled brightly at him.

"Not feeling so well today?" she said.

"Oh, I'm great," he said. "Corking, I am. Know what time I got up? Four o'clock this afternoon, sharp. I kept trying to make it, and every time I took my head off the pillow, it would roll under the bed. This isn't my head I've got on now. I think this is something that used to belong to Walt Whitman. Oh, dear, oh, dear, oh, dear."

"Do you think maybe a drink would make you feel better?" she said.

"The hair of the mastiff that bit me?" he said. "Oh, no, thank you. Please never speak of anything like that again. I'm through. I'm all, all through. Look at that hand; steady as a humming-bird. Tell me, was I very terrible last night?"

"Oh, goodness," she said, "everybody was feeling pretty high. You were all right."

"Yeah," he said. "I must have been dandy. Is everybody sore at me?"

"Good heavens, no," she said. "Everyone thought you were terribly funny. Of course, Jim Pierson was a little stuffy, there for a minute at dinner. But people sort of held him back in his chair, and got him calmed down. I don't think anybody at the other tables noticed it at all. Hardly anybody."

"He was going to sock me?" he said. "Oh, Lord. What did I do to him?"

"Why, you didn't do a thing," she said. "You were perfectly fine. But you know how silly Jim gets, when he thinks anybody is making too much fuss over Elinor."

"Was I making a pass at Elinor?" he said. "Did I do that?"

"Of course you didn't," she said. "You were only fooling, that's all. She thought you were awfully amusing. She was having a marvelous time. She only got a little tiny bit annoyed just once, when you poured the clam-juice down her back."

"My God," he said. "Clam-juice down that back. And every vertebra a little Cabot. Dear God. What'll I ever do?"

"Oh, she'll be all right," she said. "Just send her some flowers, or something. Don't worry about it. It isn't anything."

"No, I won't worry," he said. "I haven't got a care in the world. I'm sitting pretty. Oh, dear, oh, dear. Did I do any other fascinating tricks at dinner?"

"You were fine," she said. "Don't be so foolish about it. Everybody was crazy about you. The maître d'hôtel was a little worried because you wouldn't stop singing, but he really didn't mind. All he said was, he was afraid they'd close the place again, if there was so much noise. But he didn't care a bit, himself. I think he loved seeing you have such a good time. Oh, you were just singing away, there, for about an hour. It wasn't so terribly loud, at all."

"So I sang," he said. "That must have been a treat. I sang."

"Don't you remember?" she said. "You just sang one song after another. Everybody in the place was listening. They loved it. Only you kept insisting that you wanted to sing some song about some kind of fusiliers or other, and everybody kept shushing you, and you'd keep trying to start it again. You were wonderful. We were all trying to make you stop singing for a minute, and eat something, but you wouldn't hear of it. My, you were funny."

"Didn't I eat any dinner?" he said.

"Oh, not a thing," she said. "Every time the waiter would offer you something, you'd give it right back to him, because you said that he was your long-lost brother, changed in the cradle by a gypsy band, and that anything you had was his. You had him simply roaring at you."

"I bet I did," he said. "I bet I was comical. Society's Pet, I must have been. And what happened then, after my overwhelming success with the waiter?"

"Why, nothing much," she said. "You took a sort of dislike to some old man with white hair, sitting across the room, because you didn't like his necktie and you wanted to tell him about it. But we got you out, before he got really mad."

"Oh, we got out," he said. "Did I walk?"

"Walk? Of course you did," she said. "You were absolutely all right. There was that nasty stretch of ice on the sidewalk, and you did sit down awfully hard, you poor dear. But good heavens, that might have happened to anybody."

"Oh, surely," he said. "Mrs. Hoover or anybody. So I fell down on the sidewalk. That would explain what's the matter with my— Yes. I see. And then what, if you don't mind?"

"Ah, now, Peter!" she said. "You can't sit there and say you don't remember what happened after that! I did think that maybe you were just a little tight at dinner—oh, you were perfectly all right, and all that, but I did know you were feeling pretty gay. But you were so serious, from the time you fell down—I never knew you to be that way. Don't you know, how you told me I had never seen your real self before? Oh, Peter, I just couldn't bear it, if you didn't remember that lovely long ride we took together in the taxi! Please, you do remember that, don't you? I think it would simply kill me, if you didn't."

"Oh, yes," he said. "Riding in the taxi. Oh, yes, sure. Pretty long ride, hmm?"

"Round and round and round the park," she said. "Oh, and the trees were shining so in the moonlight. And you said you never knew before that you really had a soul."

"Yes," he said. "I said that. That was me."

"You said such lovely, lovely things," she said. "And I'd never known, all this time, how you had been feeling about me, and I'd never dared to let you see how I felt about you. And then last night—oh, Peter dear, I think that taxi ride was the most important thing that ever happened to us in our lives."

"Yes," he said. "I guess it must have been."

"And we're going to be so happy," she said. "Oh, I just want to tell everybody! But I don't know—I think maybe it would be sweeter to keep it all to ourselves."

"I think it would be," he said.

"Isn't it lovely?" she said.

"Yes," he said. "Great."

"Lovely!" she said.

"Look here," he said, "do you mind if I have a drink? I mean, just medicinally, you know. I'm off the stuff for life, so help me. But I think I feel a collapse coming on."

"Oh, I think it would do you good," she said. "You poor boy, it's a shame you feel so awful. I'll go make you a highball."

"Honestly," he said, "I don't see how you could ever want to speak to me again, after I made such a fool of myself, last night. I think I'd better go join a monastery in Tibet."

"You crazy idiot!" she said. "As if I could ever let you go away now! Stop talking like that. You were perfectly fine."

She jumped up from the couch, kissed him quickly on the forehead, and ran out of the room.

The pale young man looked after her and shook his head long and slowly, then dropped it in his damp and trembling hands.

"Oh, dear," he said. "Oh, dear, oh, dear, oh dear."

# ISAAC BABEL
## 1894–1939 or 1940

Babel was born in the Moldovanka, the Jewish ghetto of Odessa, a Russian port city on the Black Sea. At this time Jews in Russia were officially persecuted by the Tsarist government, but in the Moldovanka life was robust and vital, with great musicians and notable gangsters in profusion. Babel detested the terrible discipline of his Jewish education and feared that either it or his natural bent would turn him into an effete intellectual—a man with "spectacles on his nose and autumn in his heart." He left Odessa as soon as he could and when he was twenty-one arrived in St. Petersburg without a residence certificate. He made Maupassant his guide in literary matters and began to get some stories published. In 1920 he joined the army and by an irony worthy of Maupassant was assigned to a regiment of the Jews' bitter enemies, the Cossacks. He had seen his father kneel before an indifferent Cossack years before. He was fascinated and repelled by the brutality and the grace of his new companions, and these experiences led to his first important collection of fiction, *Red Cavalry*, in 1926, by which time he had fought in the army of the Tsar and the army of the Soviets. As Stalin consolidated his power, Babel learned a new literary form: silence. Even so, he was arrested in 1937 and died several years later in a Soviet concentration camp.

# Guy de Maupassant

In the winter of 1916 I found myself in St. Petersburg with a forged passport and not a cent to my name. Alexey Kazantsev, a teacher of Russian literature, took me into his house.

He lived on a yellow, frozen, evil-smelling street in the Peski district. The miserable salary he received was padded out a bit by doing translations from the Spanish. Blasco Ibáñez was just becoming famous at that time. Kazantsev had never so much as passed through Spain, but his love for that country filled his whole being. He knew every castle, every garden, and every river in Spain. There were many other people huddling around Kazantsev, all of them, like myself, flung out of the round of ordinary life. We were half-starved. From time to time the yellow press would publish, in the smallest print, unimportant news-items we had written.

I spent my mornings hanging around the morgues and police stations.

Kazantsev was happier than any of us, for he had a country of his own—Spain.

In November I was given the chance to become a clerk at the Obukhov Mills. It was a rather good position, and would have exempted me from military service.

I refused to become a clerk.

Even in those days, when I was twenty years old, I had told myself: better starve, go to jail, or become a bum than spend ten hours every day behind a desk in an office.

There was nothing particularly laudable in my resolve, but I have never broken it and I never will. The wisdom of my ancestors was firmly lodged in my head: we are born to enjoy our work, our fights, and our love; we are born for that and for nothing else.

Listening to my bragging, Kazantsev ruffled the short yellow fluff on the top of his head. The horror in his stare was mixed with admiration.

At Christmastime we had luck. Bendersky the lawyer, who owned a publishing house called "Halcyon," decided to publish a new edition of Maupassant's works. His wife Raïsa tried her hand at the translation, but nothing came of her lofty ambition.

Kazantsev, who was known as a translator of Spanish, had been asked whether he could recommend someone to assist Raïsa Mikhaylovna. He told them of me.

The next day, in someone else's coat, I made my way to the Benderskys'. They lived at the corner of the Nevsky and the Moyka, in a house of Finland granite adorned with pink columns, crenellations and coats-of-arms worked in stone.

Bankers without a history and catapulted out of nowhere, converted Jews who had grown rich selling materials to the army, they put up these pretentious mansions in St. Petersburg before the war.

There was a red carpet on the stairs. On the landings, upon their hind legs, stood plush bears. Crystal lamps burned in their open mouths.

The Benderskys lived on the second floor. A high-breasted maid with a white cap on her head opened the door. She led me into a drawing-room decorated in the old Slav style. Blue paintings by Roerich depicting prehistoric stones and monsters hung on the walls. On stands in the corners stood ancestral icons.

The high-breasted maid moved smoothly and majestically. She had an excellent figure, was nearsighted and rather haughty. In her open gray eyes one saw a petrified lewdness. She moved slowly. I thought: when she makes love she must move with unheard-of agility. The brocade portiere over the doorway suddenly swayed, and a black-haired woman with pink eyes and a wide bosom entered the room. It was easy to recognize in Raïsa Bendersky one of those charming Jewesses who have come to us from Kiev and Poltava, from the opulent steppe-towns full of chestnut trees and acacias. The money made by their clever husbands is transformed by these women into a pink layer of fat on the belly, the back of the neck, and the well-rounded shoulders. Their subtle sleepy smiles drive officers from the local garrisons crazy.

"Maupassant," Raïsa said to me, "is the only passion of my life."

Trying to keep the swaying of her great hips under control, she left the room and returned with a translation of "Miss Harriet." In her translation not even a trace was left of Maupassant's free-flowing sentences with their fragrance of passion. Raïsa Bendersky took pains to write correctly and precisely, and all that resulted was something loose and lifeless, the way Jews wrote Russian in the old days.

I took the manuscript with me, and in Kazantsev's attic, among my sleeping friends, spent the night cutting my way through the tangled undergrowth of her prose. It was not such dull work as it might seem. A phrase is born into the world both good and bad at the same time. The secret lies in a slight, an almost invisible twist. The lever should rest in your hand, getting warm, and you can only turn it once not twice.

Next morning I took back the corrected manuscript. Raïsa wasn't lying when she told me that Maupassant was her sole passion. She sat motionless, her hands clasped, as I read it to her. Her satin hands drooped to the floor, her forehead paled, and the lace between her constricted breasts danced and heaved.

"How did you do it?"

I began to speak of style, of the army of words, of the army in which all kinds of weapons may come into play. No iron can stab the heart with such force as a period put just at the right place. She listened with her head down and her painted lips half open. In her hair, pressed smooth, divided by a parting and looking like patent leather, shone a dark gleam. Her legs in tight-fitting stockings, with their strong soft calves, were planted wide apart on the carpet.

The maid, glancing to the side with her petrified wanton eyes, brought in breakfast on a tray.

The glassy rays of the Petersburg sun lay on the pale and uneven carpet. Twenty-nine volumes of Maupassant stood on the shelf above the desk. The sun with its fingers of melting dissolution touched the morocco backs of the books—the magnificent grave of a human heart.

Coffee was served in blue cups, and we started translating "Idyl." Everyone remembers the story of the youthful, hungry carpenter who sucked the breast of the stout nursing-mother to relieve her of the milk with which she was overladen. It happened in a train going from Nice to Marseille, at noon on a very hot day, in the land of roses, the birthplace of roses, where beds of flowers flow down to the seashore.

I left the Banderskys with a twenty-five rouble advance. That night our crowd at Peski got as drunk as a flock of drugged geese. Between drinks we spooned up the best caviar, and then changed over to liver sausage. Half-soused, I began to berate Tolstoy.

"He turned yellow, your Count; he was afraid. His religion was all fear. He was frightened by the cold, by old age, by death; and he made himself a warm coat out of his faith."

"Go on, go on," Kazantsev urged, swaying his birdlike head.

We fell asleep on the floor beside our beds. I dreamed of Katya, a forty-year-old washerwoman who lived a floor below us. We went to her every morning for our hot water. I had never seen her face distinctly, but in my dream we did god-awful things together. We almost destroyed each other with kisses. The very next morning I couldn't restrain myself from going to her for hot water.

I saw a wan woman, a shawl across her chest, with ash-gray hair and labor-worn, withered hands.

From then on I took my breakfast at the Benderskys' every day. A new stove, herrings, and chocolate appeared in our attic. Twice Raïsa took me out in her carriage for drives to the islands. I couldn't prevent myself from telling her all about my childhood. To my amazement the story turned out to be very sordid. From under her moleskin cowl her gleaming, frightened eyes stared at me. The rusty fringe of her eyelashes quivered with pity.

I met Raïsa's husband, a yellow-faced Jew with a bald skull and a flat, powerful body that seemed always poised obliquely, ready for flight.

There were rumors about his being close to Rasputin. The enormous profits he made from war supplies drove him almost crazy, giving him the expression of a person with a fixed hallucination. His eyes never remained still: it seemed that reality was lost to him for ever. Raïsa was embarrassed whenever she had to introduce him to new acquaintances. Because of my youth I noticed this a full week later than I should have.

After the New Year Raisa's two sisters arrived from Kiev. One day I took along the manuscript of "L'Aveu" and, not finding Raïsa at home, returned that evening. They were at dinner. Silvery, neighing laughter and excited male voices came from the dining-room. In rich houses without tradition dinners are always noisy. It was a Jewish noise, rolling and tripping and ending up on a melodious, singsong note. Raïsa came out to me in evening dress, her back bare. Her feet stepped awkwardly in wavering patent-leather slippers.

"I'm drunk, darling," she said, and held out her arms, loaded with chains of platinum and emerald stars.

Her body swayed like a snake's dancing to music. She tossed her marcelled hair about, and suddenly, with a tinkle of rings, slumped into a chair with ancient Russian carvings. Scars glowed on her powdered back.

Women's laughter again came from the dining-room. Raïsa's sisters, with delicate mustaches and as full-bosomed and round-bodied as Raïsa herself, entered the room. Their busts jutted out and their black hair fluttered. Both of them had their own Bender-skys for husbands. The room was filled with disjointed, chaotic feminine merriment, the hilarity of ripe women. The husbands wrapped the sisters in their sealskins and Orenburg shawls and shod them in black boots. Beneath the snowy visors of their shawls only painted glowing cheeks, marble noses, and eyes with their myopic Jewish glitter could be seen. After making some more happy noise they left for the theater, where Chaliapin was singing *Judith*.

"I want to work," Raïsa lisped, stretching her bare arms to me, "we've skipped a whole week."

She brought a bottle and two glasses from the dining room. Her breasts swung free beneath the sacklike gown, the nipples rose beneath the clinging silk.

"It's very valuable," said Raïsa, pouring out the wine. "Muscatel '83. My husband will kill me when he finds out."

I had never drunk Muscatel '83, and tossed off three glasses one after the other without thinking. They carried me swiftly away into alleys where an orange flame danced and sounds of music could be heard.

"I'm drunk, darling. What are we doing today?"

"Today it's 'L'Aveu.' 'The Confession,' then. The sun is the hero of this story, *le soleil de France*. Molten drops of it pattering on the red-haired Céleste changed into freckles. The sun's direct rays and wine and apple-cider burnished the face of the coachman Polyte. Twice a week Céleste drove into town to sell cream, eggs and chickens. She gave Polyte ten sous for herself and four for her basket. And every time Polyte would wink at the red-haired Céleste and ask: 'When are we going to have some fun, *ma belle?*'—'What do you mean, Monsieur Polyte?' Jogging up and down on the box, the coachman explained: 'To have some fun means . . . why, what the hell, to have some fun! A lad with a lass; no music necessary . . .'

" 'I do not care for such jokes, Monsieur Polyte,' replied Céleste, moving further away the skirts that hung over her mighty calves in red stockings.

"But that devil Polyte kept right on guffawing and coughing: 'Ah, but one day we shall have our bit of fun, *ma belle*,' while tears of delight rolled down a face the color of brick-red wine and blood."

I downed another glass of the rare muscatel. Raïsa touched glasses with me. The maid with the stony eyes crossed the room and disappeared.

"*Ce diable de Polyte* . . . In the course of two years Céleste had paid him forty-eight francs; that is, two francs short of fifty! At the end of the second year, when they were alone in the carriage, Polyte, who had some cider before setting out, asked her his usual question: 'What about having some fun today, Mamselle Céleste?' And she replied, lowering her eyes: 'I am at your disposal, Monsieur Polyte.' "

Raïsa flung herself down on the table, laughing. "*Ce diable de Poltye* . . ."

"A white spavined mare was harnessed to the carriage. The white hack, its lips pink with age, went forward at a walking pace. The gay sun of France poured down on the ancient coach, screened from the world by a weatherbeaten hood. A lad with a lass; no music necessary . . ."

Raïsa held out a glass to me. It was the fifth.

"*Mon vieux*, to Maupassant."

"And what about having some fun today, *ma belle?*"

I reached over to Raïsa and kissed her on the lips. They quivered and swelled.

"You're funny," she mumbled through her teeth, recoiling.

She pressed herself against the wall, stretching out her bare arms. Spots began to glow on her arms and shoulders. Of all the gods ever put on the crucifix, this was the most ravishing.

"Be so kind as to sit down, Monsieur Polyte."

She pointed to an oblique blue armchair done in Slavonic style. Its back was constructed of carved interlacing bands with colorful pendants. I groped my way to it, stumbling as I went.

Night had blocked the path of my famished youth with a bottle of Muscatel '83 and twenty-nine books, twenty-nine bombs stuffed with pity, genius and passion. I sprang up, knocking over the chair and banging against the shelf. The twenty-nine volumes crashed to the floor, their pages flew open, they fell on their edges . . . and the white mare of my fate went on at a walking pace.

"You are funny," growled Raïsa.

I left the granite house on the Moyka between eleven and twelve, before the sisters and the husband returned from the theater. I was sober and could have walked a chalk line, but it was pleasanter to stagger, so I swayed from side to side, singing in a language I had just invented. Through the tunnels of the streets bounded by lines of street lights the steamy fog billowed. Monsters roared behind the boiling walls. The roads amputated the legs of those walking on them.

Kazantsev was asleep when I got home. He slept sitting up, his thin legs extended in their felt boots. The canary fluff rose on his head. He had fallen asleep by the stove bending over a volume of *Don Quixote*, the edition of 1624. On the title-page of the book was a dedication to the Duc de Broglie. I got into bed quietly, so as not to wake Kazantsev; moved the lamp close to me and began to read a book by Edouard Maynial on Guy de Maupassant's life and work.

Kazantsev's lips moved; his head kept keeling over.

That night I learned from Edouard Maynial that Maupassant was born in 1850, the child of a Normandy gentleman and Laure Lepoiteven, Flaubert's cousin. He was twenty-five when he was first attacked by congenital syphilis. His productivity and *joie de vivre* withstood the onsets of the disease. At first he suffered from headaches and fits of hypochondria. Then the specter of blindness arose before him. His sight weakened. He became suspicious of everyone, unsociable and pettily quarrelsome. He struggled furiously, dashed about the Mediterranean in a yacht, fled to Tunis, Morocco, Central Africa . . . and wrote ceaselessly. He attained fame, and at forty years of age cut his throat; lost a great deal of blood, yet lived through it. He was then put away in a madhouse. There he crawled about on his hands and knees, devouring his own excrement. The last line in his hospital report read: *Monsieur de Maupassant va s'animaliser.*[1] He died at the age of forty-two, his mother surviving him.

I read the book to the end and got out of bed. The fog came close to the window, the world was hidden from me. My heart contracted as the foreboding of some essential truth touched me with light fingers.

# F. SCOTT FITZGERALD
1896–1940

Francis Scott Key Fitzgerald was born in St. Paul, Minnesota, to a genteel but ineffectual father and a doting and eccentric mother. A delicate child, he was reluctant to go to school but finally went to a small Catholic school,

---

1. "Mr. Maupassant is becoming an animal."

then to St. Paul Academy, to Newman, and finally to Princeton. He was unpopular at most of these places for most of the time, and unhappy as well, but his talent for writing and his remarkable good looks began to count for more as he grew up; so that at college he received much of the adulation for which he hungered so deeply. He was concerned to the point of obsession with social standing and prestige. Only his gift for writing and his capacity for ruthless self-criticism prevented him from sliding into a life of empty snobbery. He had to marry a beautiful girl, and he did. He had to become rich and famous—and he did. But his wife's mental health was precarious, and the fame and riches were more than he could handle. After a breakdown and painful recovery, that he described with a typical lack of self-protectiveness, he lived and worked in Hollywood, never quite recapturing the grace and beauty of his early work. He was the poet laureate of the jazz age, and in his finest novels (*The Great Gatsby*, 1925, and *Tender is the Night*,1934) and his remarkable short stories, we can find the best epitaph for that era as well as for Fitzgerald himself.


# Babylon Revisited

"And where's Mr. Campbell?" Charlie asked.

"Gone to Switzerland. Mr. Campbell's a pretty sick man, Mr. Wales."

"I'm sorry to hear that. And George Hardt?" Charlie inquired.

"Back in America, gone to work."

"And where is the Snow Bird?"

"He was in here last week. Anyway, his friend, Mr. Schaeffer, is in Paris."

Two familiar names from the long list of a year and a half ago. Charlie scribbled an address in his notebook and tore out the page.

"If you see Mr. Schaeffer, give him this," he said. "It's my brother-in-law's address. I haven't settled on a hotel yet."

He was not really disappointed to find Paris was so empty. But the stillness in the Ritz bar was strange and portentous. It was not an American bar any more—he felt polite in it, and not as if he owned it. It had gone back into France. He felt the stillness from the moment he got out of the taxi and saw the doorman, usually in a frenzy of activity at this hour, gossiping with a *chasseur* by the servants' entrance.

Passing through the corridor, he heard only a single, bored voice in the once-clamorous women's room. When he turned into the bar he traveled the twenty feet of green carpet with his eyes fixed straight ahead by old habit; and then, with his foot firmly on the rail, he turned and surveyed the room, encountering only a single pair of eyes that fluttered up from a newspaper in the corner. Charlie asked for the head barman, Paul, who in the latter days of the bull market had come to work in his own custom-built car—disembarking, however, with due nicety at the nearest corner. But Paul was at his country house today and Alix giving him information.

"No, no more," Charlie said, "I'm going slow these days."

Alix congratulated him: "You were going pretty strong a couple of years ago."

"I'll stick to it all right," Charlie assured him. "I've stuck to it for over a year and a half now."

"How do you find conditions in America?"

"I haven't been to America for months. I'm in business in Prague, representing a couple of concerns there. They don't know about me down there."

Alix smiled.

"Remember the night of George Hardt's bachelor dinner here?" said Charlie. "By the way, what's become of Claude Fessenden?"

Alix lowered his voice confidentially: "He's in Paris, but he doesn't come here any more. Paul doesn't allow it. He ran up a bill of thirty thousand francs, charging all his drinks and his lunches, and usually his dinner, for more than a year. And when Paul finally told him he had to pay, he gave him a bad check."

Alix shook his head sadly.

"I don't understand it, such a dandy fellow. Now he's all bloated up—" He made a plump apple of his hands.

Charlie watched a group of strident queens installing themselves in a corner.

"Nothing affects them," he thought. "Stocks rise and fall, people loaf or work, but they go on forever." The place oppressed him. He called for the dice and shook with Alix for the drink.

"Here for long, Mr. Wales?"

"I'm here for four or five days to see my little girl."

"Oh-h! You have a little girl?"

Outside, the fire-red, gas-blue, ghost-green signs shone smokily through the tranquil rain. It was late afternoon and the streets were in movement; the *bistros* gleamed. At the corner of the Boulevard des Capucines he took a taxi. The Place de la Concorde moved by in pink majesty; they crossed the logical Seine, and Charlie felt the sudden provincial quality of the Left Bank.

Charlie directed his taxi to the Avenue de l'Opéra, which was out of his way. But he wanted to see the blue hour spread over the magnificent façade, and imagine that the cab horns, playing endlessly the first few bars of *Le Plus que Lent*, were the trumpets of the Second Empire. They were closing the iron grill in front of Brentano's Book-store, and people were already at dinner behind the trim little bourgeois hedge of Duval's. He had never eaten at a really cheap restaurant in Paris. Five-course dinner, four francs fifty, eighteen cents, wine included. For some odd reason he wished that he had.

As they rolled on to the Left Bank and he felt its sudden provincialism, he thought, "I spoiled this city for myself. I didn't realize it, but the days came along one after another, and then two years were gone, and everything was gone, and I was gone."

He was thirty-five, and good to look at. The Irish mobility of his face was sobered by a deep wrinkle between his eyes. As he rang his brother-in-law's bell in the Rue Palatine, the wrinkle deepened till it pulled down his brows; he felt a cramping sensation in his belly. From behind the maid who opened the door darted a lovely little girl of nine who shrieked "Daddy!" and flew up, struggling like a fish, into his arms. She pulled his head around by one ear and set her cheek against his.

"My old pie," he said.

"Oh, daddy, daddy, daddy, daddy, dads, dads, dads!"

She drew him into the salon, where the family waited, a boy and a girl his daughter's age, his sister-in-law and her husband. He greeted Marion with his voice pitched carefully to avoid either feigned enthusiasm or dislike, but her response was more frankly tepid, though she minimized her expression of unalterable distrust by directing her regard toward his child. The two men clasped hands in a friendly way and Lincoln Peters rested his for a moment on Charlie's shoulder.

The room was warm and comfortably American. The three children moved intimately about, playing through the yellow oblongs that led to other rooms; the cheer of six o'clock spoke in the eager smacks of the fire and the sounds of French activity in the kitchen. But Charlie did not relax; his heart sat up rigidly in his body and he drew confidence from his daughter, who from time to time came close to him, holding in her arms the doll he had brought.

"Really extremely well," he declared in answer to Lincoln's question. "There's a lot of business there that isn't moving at all, but we're doing even better than ever. In fact, damn well. I'm bringing my sister over from America next month to keep house for me. My income last year was bigger than it was when I had money. You see, the Czechs—"

His boasting was for a specific purpose; but after a moment, seeing a faint restiveness in Lincoln's eye, he changed the subject:

"Those are fine children of yours, well brought up, good manners."

"We think Honoria's a great little girl too."

Marion Peters came back from the kitchen. She was a tall woman with worried eyes, who had once possessed a fresh American loveliness. Charlie had never been sensitive to it and was always surprised when people spoke of how pretty she had been. From the first there had been an instinctive antipathy between them.

"Well, how do you find Honoria?" she asked.

"Wonderful. I was astonished how much she's grown in ten months. All the children are looking well."

"We haven't had a doctor for a year. How do you like being back in Paris?"

"It seems very funny to see so few Americans around."

"I'm delighted," Marion said vehemently. "Now at least you can go into a store without their assuming you're a millionaire. We've suffered like everybody, but on the whole it's a good deal pleasanter."

"But it was nice while it lasted," Charlie said. "We were a sort of royalty, almost infallible, with a sort of magic around us. In the bar this afternoon"—he stumbled, seeing his mistake—"there wasn't a man I knew."

She looked at him keenly. "I should think you'd have had enough of bars."

"I only stayed a minute. I take one drink every afternoon, and no more."

"Don't you want a cocktail before dinner?" Lincoln asked.

"I take only one drink every afternoon, and I've had that."

"I hope you keep to it," said Marion.

Her dislike was evident in the coldness with which she spoke, but Charlie only smiled; he had larger plans. Her very aggressiveness gave him an advantage, and he knew enough to wait. He wanted them to initiate the discussion of what they knew had brought him to Paris.

At dinner he couldn't decide whether Honoria was most like him or her mother. Fortunate if she didn't combine the traits of both that had brought them to disaster. A great wave of protectiveness went over him. He thought he knew what to do for her. He believed in character; he wanted to jump back a whole generation and trust in character again as the eternally valuable element. Everything else wore out.

He left soon after dinner, but not to go home. He was curious to see Paris by night with clearer and more judicious eyes than those of other days. He bought a *strapontin* for the Casino and watched Josephine Baker go through her chocolate arabesques.

After an hour he left and strolled toward Montmartre, up the Rue Pigalle into the Place Blanche. The rain had stopped and there were a few people in evening clothes disembarking from taxis in front of cabarets, and *cocottes* prowling singly or in pairs, and many Negroes. He passed a lighted door from which issued music, and stopped with the sense of familiarity; it was Bricktop's, where he had parted with so many hours and so much money. A few doors farther on he found another ancient rendezvous and incautiously put his head inside.

Immediately an eager orchestra burst into sound, a pair of professional dancers leaped to their feet and a maître d'hôtel swooped toward him, crying, "Crowd just arriving, sir!" But he withdrew quickly.

"You have to be damn drunk," he thought.

Zelli's was closed, the bleak and sinister cheap hotels surrounding it were dark; up in the Rue Blanche there was more light and a local, colloquial French crowd. The Poet's Cave had disappeared, but the two great mouths of the Café of Heaven and the Café of Hell still yawned—even devoured; as he watched, the meager contents of a tourist bus—a German, a Japanese, and an American couple who glanced at him with frightened eyes.

So much for the effort and ingenuity of Montmartre. All the catering to vice and waste was on an utterly childish scale, and he suddenly realized the meaning of the word "dissipate"—to dissipate into thin air; to make nothing out of something. In the little hours of the night every move from place to place was an enormous human jump, an increase of paying for the privilege of slower and slower motion.

He remembered thousand-franc notes given to an orchestra for playing a single number, hundred-franc notes tossed to a doorman for calling a cab.

But it hadn't been given for nothing.

It had been given, even the most wildly squandered sum, as an offering to destiny that he might not remember the things most worth remembering, the things that now he would always remember—his child taken from his control, his wife escaped to a grave in Vermont.

In the glare of a *brasserie* a woman spoke to him. He bought her some eggs and coffee, and then, eluding her encouraging stare, gave her a twenty-franc note and took a taxi to his hotel.

II

He woke upon a fine fall day—football weather. The depression of yesterday was gone and he liked the people on the streets. At noon he sat opposite Honoria at Le Grand Vatel, the only restaurant he could think of not reminiscent of champagne dinners and long luncheons that began at two and ended in a blurred and vague twilight.

"Now, how about vegetables? Oughtn't you to have some vegetables?"

"Well, yes."

"Here's *épinards* and *chou-fleur* and carrots and *haricots*."

"I'd like *chou-fleur*."

"Wouldn't you like to have two vegetables?"

"I usually only have one at lunch."

The waiter was pretending to be inordinately fond of children. *"Qu'elle est mignonne la petite! Elle parle exactement comme une Française."*

"How about dessert? Shall we wait and see?"

The waiter disappeared. Honoria looked at her father expectantly.

"What are we going to do?"

"First, we're going to that toy store in the Rue Saint-Honoré and buy you anything you like. And then we're going to the vaudeville at the Empire."

She hesitated. "I like it about the vaudeville, but not the toy store."

"Why not?'

"Well, you brought me this doll." She had it with her. "And I've got lots of things. And we're not rich any more, are we?"

"We never were. But today you are to have anything you want."

"All right," she agreed resignedly.

When there had been her mother and a French nurse he had been inclined to be strict; now he extended himself, reached out for a new tolerance; he must both parents to her and not shut any of her out of communication.

"I want to get to know you," he said gravely. "First let me introduce myself. My name is Charles J. Wales, of Prague."

"Oh, daddy!" her voice cracked with laughter.

"And who are you, please?" he persisted, and she accepted a rôle immediately: "Honoria Wales, Rue Palatine, Paris."

"Married or single?"

"No, not married. Single."

He indicated the doll. "But I see you have a child, madame."

Unwilling to disinherit it, she took it to her heart and thought quickly: "Yes, I've been married, but I'm not married now. My husband is dead."

He went on quickly, "And the child's name?"

"Simone. That's after my best friend at school."

"I'm very pleased that you're doing so well at school."

"I'm third this month," she boasted. "Elsie"—that was her cousin—"is only about eighteenth, and Richard is about at the bottom."

"You like Richard and Elsie, don't you?"

"Oh, yes. I like Richard quite well and I like her all right."

Cautiously and casually he asked: "And Aunt Marion and Uncle Lincoln—which do you like best?"

"Oh, Uncle Lincoln, I guess."

He was increasingly aware of her presence. As they came in, a murmur of ". . . adorable" followed them, and now the people at the next table bent all their silences upon her, staring as if she were something no more conscious than a flower.

"Why don't I live with you?" she asked suddenly. "Because mamma's dead?"

"You must stay here and learn more French. It would have been hard for daddy to take care of you so well."

"I don't really need much taking care of any more. I do everything for myself."

Going out of the restaurant, a man and a woman unexpectedly hailed him.

"Well, the old Wales!"

"Hello there, Lorraine. . . . Dunc."

Sudden ghosts out of the past: Duncan Schaeffer, a friend from college. Lorraine Quarrles, a lovely, pale blonde of thirty; one of a crowd who had helped them make months into days in the lavish times of three years ago.

"My husband couldn't come this year," she said, in answer to his question. "We're poor as hell. So he gave me two hundred a month and told me I could do my worst on that. . . . This your little girl?"

"What about coming back and sitting down?" Duncan asked.

"Can't do it." He was glad for an excuse. As always, he felt Lorraine's passionate, provocative attraction, but his own rhythm was different now.

"Well, how about dinner?" she asked.

"I'm not free. Give me your address and let me call you."

"Charlie, I believe you're sober," she said judicially. "I honestly believe he's sober, Dunc. Pinch him and see if he's sober."

Charlie indicated Honoria with his head. They both laughed.

"What's your address?" said Duncan skeptically.

He hesitated, unwilling to give the name of his hotel.

"I'm not settled yet. I'd better call you. We're going to see the vaudeville at the Empire."

"There! That's what I want to do," Lorraine said. "I want to see some clowns and acrobats and jugglers. That's just what we'll do, Dunc."

"We've got to do an errand first," said Charlie. "Perhaps we'll see you there."

"All right, you snob. . . . Good-by, beautiful little girl."

"Good-by."

Honoria bobbed politely.

Somehow, an unwelcome encounter. They liked him because he was functioning, because he was serious; they wanted to see him, because he was stronger than they were now, because they wanted to draw a certain sustenance from his strength.

At the Empire, Honoria proudly refused to sit upon her father's folded coat. She was already an individual with a code of her own, and Charlie was more and more absorbed by the desire of putting a little of himself into her before she crystallized utterly. It was hopeless to try to know her in so short a time.

Between the acts they came upon Duncan and Lorraine in the lobby where the band was playing.

"Have a drink?"

"All right, but not up at the bar. We'll take a table."

"The perfect father."

Listening abstractedly to Lorraine, Charlie watched Honoria's eyes leave their table, and he followed them wistfully about the room, wondering what they saw. He met her glance and she smiled.

"I liked that lemonade," she said.

What had she said? What had he expected? Going home in a taxi afterward, he pulled her over until her head rested against his chest.

"Darling, do you ever think about your mother?"

"Yes, sometimes," she answered vaguely.

"I don't want you to forget her. Have you got a picture of her?"

"Yes, I think so. Anyhow, Aunt Marion has. Why don't you want me to forget her?"

"She loved you very much."

"I loved her too."

They were silent for a moment.

"Daddy, I want to come and live with you," she said suddenly.

His heart leaped; he had wanted it to come like this.

"Aren't you perfectly happy?"

"Yes, but I love you better than anybody. And you love me better than anybody, don't you, now that mummy's dead?"

"Of course I do. But you won't always like me best, honey. You'll grow up and meet somebody your own age and go marry him and forget you ever had a daddy."

"Yes, that's true," she agreed tranquilly.

He didn't go in. He was coming back at nine o'clock and he wanted to keep himself fresh and new for the thing he must say then.

"When you're safe inside, just show yourself in that window."

"All right. Good-by, dads, dads, dads, dads."

He waited in the dark street until she appeared, all warm and glowing, in the window above and kissed her fingers out into the night.

### III

They were waiting. Marion sat behind the coffee service in a dignified black dinner dress that just faintly suggested mourning. Lincoln was walking up and down with the animation of one who had already been talking. They were as anxious as he was to get into the question. He opened it almost immediately:

"I suppose you know what I want to see you about—why I really came to Paris."

Marion played with the black stars on her necklace and frowned.

"I'm awfully anxious to have a home," he continued. "And I'm awfully anxious to have Honoria in it. I appreciate your taking in Honoria for her mother's sake, but things have changed now"—he hesitated and then continued more forcibly—"changed radically with me, and I want to ask you to reconsider the matter. It would be silly for me to deny that about three years ago I was acting badly—"

Marion looked up at him with hard eyes.

"—but all that's over. As I told you, I haven't had more than a drink a day for over a year, and I take that drink deliberately, so that the idea of alcohol won't get too big in my imagination. You see the idea?"

"No," said Marion succinctly.

"It's a sort of stunt I set myself. It keeps the matter in proportion."

"I get you," said Lincoln. "You don't want to admit it's got any attraction for you."

"Something like that. Sometimes I forget and don't take it. But I try to take it. Anyway, I couldn't afford to drink in my position. The people I represent are more than satisfied with what I've done, and I'm bringing my sister over from Burlington to keep house for me, and I want awfully to have Honoria too. You know that even when her mother and I weren't getting along well we never let anything that happened touch Honoria. I know she's fond of me and I know I'm able to take care of her and—well, there you are. How do you feel about it?"

He knew that now he would have to take a beating. It would last an hour or two hours, and it would be difficult, but if he modulated his inevitable resentment to the chastened attitude of the reformed sinner, he might win his point in the end.

Keep your temper, he told himself. You don't want to be justified. You want Honoria.

Lincoln spoke first: "We've been talking it over ever since we got your letter last month. We're happy to have Honoria here. She's a dear little thing, and we're glad to be able to help her, but of course that isn't the question—"

Marion interrupted suddenly. "How long are you going to stay sober, Charlie?" she asked.

"Permanently, I hope."

"How can anybody count on that?"

"You know I never did drink heavily until I gave up business and came over here with nothing to do. Then Helen and I began to run around with—"

"Please leave Helen out of it. I can't bear to hear you talk about her like that."

He stared at her grimly; he had never been certain how fond of each other the sisters were in life.

"My drinking only lasted about a year and a half—from the time we came over until I—collapsed."

"It was time enough."

"It was time enough," he agreed.

"My duty is entirely to Helen," she said. "I try to think what she would have wanted me to do. Frankly, from the night you did that terrible thing you haven't really existed for me. I can't help that. She was my sister."

"Yes."

"When she was dying she asked me to look out for Honoria. If you hadn't been in a sanitarium then, it might have helped matters."

He had no answer.

"I'll never in my life be able to forget that morning when Helen knocked at my door, soaked to the skin and shivering and said you'd locked her out."

Charlie gripped the sides of the chair. This was more difficult than he expected; he wanted to launch out into a long expostulation and explanation, but he only said: "The night I locked her out—" and she interrupted, "I don't feel up to going over that again."

After a moment's silence Lincoln said: "We're getting off the subject. You want Marion to set aside her legal guardianship and give you Honoria. I think the main point for her is whether she has confidence in you or not."

"I don't blame Marion," Charlie said slowly, "but I think she can have entire confidence in me. I had a good record up to three years ago. Of course, it's within human possibilities I might go wrong any time. But if we wait much longer I'll lose Honoria's childhood and my chance for a home." He shook his head, "I'll simply lose her, don't you see?"

"Yes, I see," said Lincoln.

"Why didn't you think of all this before?" Marion asked.

"I suppose I did, from time to time, but Helen and I were getting along badly. When I consented to the guardianship, I was flat on my back in a sanitarium and the market had cleaned me out. I knew I'd acted badly, and I thought if it would bring any peace to Helen, I'd agree to anything. But now it's different. I'm functioning, I'm behaving damn well, so far as—"

"Please don't swear at me," Marion said.

He looked at her, startled. With each remark the force of her dislike became more and more apparent. She had built up all her fear of life into one wall and faced it toward him. This trivial reproof was possibly the result of some trouble with the cook several hours before. Charlie became increasingly alarmed at leaving Honoria in this atmosphere of hostility against himself; sooner or later it would come out, in a word here, a shake of the head there, and some of that distrust would be irrevocably implanted in Honoria. But he pulled his temper down out of his face and shut it up inside him; he had won a point, for Lincoln realized the absurdity of Marion's remark and asked her lightly since when she had objected to the word "damn."

"Another thing," Charlie said: "I'm able to give her certain advantages now. I'm going to take a French governess to Prague with me. I've got a lease on a new apartment—"

He stopped, realizing that he was blundering. They couldn't be expected to accept with equanimity the fact that his income was again twice as large as their own.

"I suppose you can give her more luxuries than we can," said Marion. "When you were throwing away money we were living along watching every ten francs. . . . I suppose you'll start doing it again."

"Oh, no," he said. "I've learned. I worked hard for ten years, you know—until I got lucky in the market, like so many people. Terribly lucky. It won't happen again."

There was a long silence. All of them felt their nerves straining, and for the first time in a year Charlie wanted a drink. He was sure now that Lincoln Peters wanted him to have his child.

Marion shuddered suddenly; part of her saw that Charlie's feet were planted on the earth now, and her own maternal feeling recognized the naturalness of his desire; but she had lived for a long time with a prejudice—a prejudice founded on a curious disbelief in her sister's happiness, and which, in the shock of one terrible night, had turned to hatred for him. It had all happened at a point in her life where the discouragement of ill health and adverse circumstances made it necessary for her to believe in tangible villainy and a tangible villain.

"I can't help what I think!" she cried out suddenly. "How much you were responsible for Helen's death, I don't know. It's something you'll have to square with your own conscience."

An electric current of agony surged through him; for a moment he was almost on his feet, an unuttered sound echoing in his throat. He hung on to himself for a moment, another moment.

"Hold on there," said Lincoln uncomfortably. "I never thought you were responsible for that."

"Helen died of heart trouble," Charlie said dully.

"Yes, heart trouble." Marion spoke as if the phrase had another meaning for her.

Then, in the flatness that followed her outburst, she saw him plainly and she knew he had somehow arrived at control over the situation. Glancing at her husband, she found no help from him, and as abruptly as if it were a matter of no importance, she threw up the sponge.

"Do what you like!" she cried, springing up from her chair. "She's your child. I'm not the person to stand in your way. I think if it were my child I'd rather see her—" She managed to check herself. "You two decide it. I can't stand this. I'm sick. I'm going to bed."

She hurried from the room; after a moment Lincoln said:

"This has been a hard day for her. You know how strongly she feels—" His voice was almost apologetic: "When a woman gets an idea in her head."

"Of course."

"It's going to be all right. I think she sees now that you—can provide for the child, and so we can't very well stand in your way or Honoria's way."

"Thank you, Lincoln."

"I'd better go along and see how she is."

"I'm going."

He was still trembling when he reached the street, but a walk down the Rue Bonaparte to the *quais* set him up, and as he crossed the Seine, fresh and new by the *quai* lamps, he felt exultant. But back in his room he couldn't sleep. The image of Helen haunted him. Helen whom he had loved so until they had senselessly begun to abuse each other's love, tear it into shreds. On that terrible February night that Marion remembered so vividly, a slow quarrel had gone on for hours. There was a scene at the Florida, and then he attempted to take her home, and then she kissed young Webb at a table; after that there was what she had hysterically said. When he arrived home alone he turned the key in the lock in wild anger. How could he know she would arrive an hour later alone, that there would be a snowstorm in which she wandered about in slippers, too confused to find a taxi? Then the aftermath, her escaping pneumonia by a miracle, and all the attendant horror. They were "reconciled," but that was the beginning of the end, and Marion, who had seen with her own eyes and who imagined it to be one of many scenes from her sister's martyrdom, never forgot.

Going over it again brought Helen nearer, and in the white, soft light that steals upon half sleep near morning he found himself talking to her again. She said that he was perfectly right about Honoria and that she wanted Honoria to be with him. She said she was glad he was being good and doing better. She said a lot of other things—very friendly things—but she was in a swing in a white dress, and swinging faster and faster all the time, so that at the end he could not hear clearly all that she said.

IV

He woke up feeling happy. The door of the world was open again. He made plans, vistas, futures for Honoria and himself, but suddenly he grew sad, remembering all the plans he and Helen had made. She had not planned to die. The present was the thing—work to do and someone to love. But not to love too much, for he knew the injury that a father can do to a daughter or a mother to a son by attaching them too closely: afterward, out in the world, the child would seek in the marriage partner the same blind tenderness and, failing probably to find it, turn against love and life.

It was another bright, crisp day. He called Lincoln Peters at the bank where he worked and asked if he could count on taking Honoria when he left for Prague. Lincoln agreed that there was no reason for delay. One thing—the legal guardianship. Marion wanted to retain that a while longer. She was upset by the whole matter, and it would oil things if she felt that the situation was still in her control for another year. Charlie agreed, wanting only the tangible, visible child.

Then the question of a governess. Charlie sat in a gloomy agency and talked to a cross Béarnaise and to a buxom Breton peasant, neither of whom he could have endured. There were others whom he would see tomorrow.

He lunched with Lincoln Peters at Griffons, trying to keep down his exultation.

"There's nothing quite like your own child," Lincoln said. "But you understand how Marion feels too."

"She's forgotten how hard I worked for seven years there," Charlie said. "She just remembers one night."

"There's another thing." Lincoln hesitated. "While you and Helen were tearing around Europe throwing money away, we were just getting along. I didn't touch any of the prosperity because I never got ahead enough to carry anything but my insurance. I think Marion felt there was some kind of injustice in it—you not even working toward the end, and getting richer and richer."

"It went just as quick as it came," said Charlie.

"Yes, a lot of it stayed in the hands of *chasseurs* and saxophone players and maîtres d'hôtel—well, the big party's over now. I just said that to explain Marion's feeling about those crazy years. If you drop in about six o'clock tonight before Marion's too tired, we'll settle the details on the spot."

Back at his hotel, Charlie found a *pneumatique* that had been redirected from the Ritz bar where Charlie had left his address for the purpose of finding a certain man.

> DEAR CHARLIE: You were so strange when we saw you the other day that I wondered if I did something to offend you. If so, I'm not conscious of it. In fact, I have thought about you too much for the last

year, and it's always been in the back of my mind that I might see you if I came over here. We *did* have such good times that crazy spring, like the night you and I stole the butcher's tricycle, and the time we tried to call on the president and you had the old derby rim and the wire cane. Everybody seems so old lately, but I don't feel old a bit. Couldn't we get together some time today for old time's sake? I've got a vile hang-over for the moment, but will be feeling better this afternoon and will look for you about five in the sweatshop at the Ritz.

Always devotedly,

LORRAINE.

His first feeling was one of awe that he had actually, in his mature years, stolen a tricycle and pedaled Lorraine all over the Étoile between the small hours and dawn. In retrospect it was a nightmare. Locking out Helen didn't fit in with any other act of his life, but the tricycle incident did—it was one of many. How many weeks or months of dissipation to arrive at that condition of utter irresponsibility?

He tried to picture how Lorraine had appeared to him then—very attractive; Helen was unhappy about it, though she said nothing. Yesterday, in the restaurant, Lorraine had seemed trite, blurred, worn away. He emphatically did not want to see her, and he was glad Alix had not given away his hotel address. It was a relief to think, instead, of Honoria, to think of Sundays spent with her and of saying good morning to her and of knowing she was there in his house at night, drawing her breath in the darkness.

At five he took a taxi and bought presents for all the Peters—a piquant cloth doll, a box of Roman soldiers, flowers for Marion, big linen handkerchiefs for Lincoln.

He saw, when he arrived in the apartment, that Marion had accepted the inevitable. She greeted him now as though he were a recalcitrant member of the family, rather than a menacing outsider. Honoria had been told she was going; Charlie was glad to see that her tact made her conceal her excessive happiness. Only on his lap did she whisper her delight and the question "When?" before she slipped away with the other children.

He and Marion were alone for a minute in the room, and on an impulse he spoke out boldly:

"Family quarrels are bitter things. They don't go according to any rules. They're not aches or wounds; they're more like splits in the skin that won't heal because there's not enough material. I wish you and I could be on better terms."

"Some things are hard to forget," she answered. "It's a question of confidence." There was no answer to this and presently she asked, "When do you propose to take her?"

"As soon as I can get a governess. I hoped the day after tomorrow."

"That's impossible. I've got to get her things in shape. Not before Saturday."

He yielded. Coming back into the room, Lincoln offered him a drink.

"I'll take my daily whisky," he said.

It was warm here, it was a home, people together by a fire. The children felt very safe and important; the mother and father were serious, watchful. They had things to do for the children more important than his visit here. A spoonful of medicine was, after all, more important than the strained relations between Marion and himself. They were not dull people, but they were very much in the grip of life and circumstances. He wondered if he couldn't do something to get Lincoln out of his rut at the bank.

A long peal at the door-bell; the *bonne à tout faire* passed through and went down the corridor. The door opened upon another long ring, and then voices, and the three in the salon looked up expectantly; Richard moved to bring the corridor within his range of vision, and Marion rose. Then the maid came back along the corridor, closely followed by the voices, which developed under the light into Duncan Schaeffer and Lorraine Quarrles.

They were gay, they were hilarious, they were roaring with laughter. For a moment Charlie was astounded; unable to understand how they ferreted out the Peters' address.

"Ah-h-h-!" Duncan wagged his finger roguishly at Charlie. "Ah-h-h!"

They both slid down another cascade of laughter. Anxious and at a loss, Charlie shook hands with them quickly and presented them to Lincoln and Marion. Marion nodded, scarcely speaking. She had drawn back a step toward the fire; her little girl stood beside her, and Marion put an arm about her shoulder.

With growing annoyance at the intrusion, Charlie waited for them to explain themselves. After some concentration Duncan said:

"We came to invite you out to dinner. Lorraine and I insist that all this shishi, cagy business 'bout your address got to stop."

Charlie came closer to them, as if to force them backward down the corridor.

"Sorry, but I can't. Tell me where you'll be and I'll phone you in half an hour."

This made no impression. Lorraine sat down suddenly on the side of a chair, and focusing her eyes on Richard, cried, "Oh, what a nice little boy! Come here, little boy." Richard glanced at his mother, but did not move. With a perceptible shrug of her shoulders, Lorraine turned back to Charlie:

"Come and dine. Sure your cousins won' mine. See you so sel'om. Or solemn."

"I can't," said Charlie sharply. "You two have dinner and I'll phone you."

Her voice became suddenly unpleasant. "All right, we'll go. But I remember once when you hammered on my door at four A.M. I was enough of a good sport to give you a drink. Come on, Dunc."

Still in slow motion, with blurred, angry faces, with uncertain feet, they retired along the corridor.

"Good night," Charlie said.

"Good night!" responded Lorraine emphatically.

When he went back into the salon Marion had not moved, only now her son was standing in the circle of her other arm. Lincoln was still swinging Honoria back and forth like a pendulum from side to side.

"What an outrage!" Charlie broke out. "What an absolute outrage!"

Neither of them answered. Charlie dropped into an armchair, picked up his drink, set it down again and said:

"People I haven't seen for two years having the colossal nerve—"

He broke off. Marion had made the sound "Oh!" in one swift, furious breath, turned her body from him with a jerk and left the room.

Lincoln set down Honoria carefully.

"You children go in and start your soup," he said, and when they obeyed, he said to Charlie:

"Marion's not well and she can't stand shocks. That kind of people make her really physically sick."

"I didn't tell them to come here. They wormed your name out of somebody. They deliberately—"

"Well, it's too bad. It doesn't help matters. Excuse me a minute."

Left alone, Charlie sat tense in his chair. In the next room he could hear the children eating, talking in monosyllables, already oblivious to the scene between their elders. He heard a murmur of conversation from a farther room and then the ticking bell of a telephone receiver picked up, and in a panic he moved to the other side of the room and out of earshot.

In a minute Lincoln came back. "Look here, Charlie. I think we'd better call off dinner for tonight. Marion's in bad shape."

"Is she angry with me?"

"Sort of," he said, almost roughly. "She's not strong and—"

"You mean she's changed her mind about Honoria?"

"She's pretty bitter right now. I don't know. You phone me at the bank tomorrow."

"I wish you'd explain to her I never dreamed these people would come here. I'm just as sore as you are."

"I couldn't explain anything to her now."

Charlie got up. He took his coat and hat and started down the corridor. Then he opened the door of the dining room and said in a strange voice, "Good night, children."

Honoria rose and ran around the table to hug him.

"Good night, sweetheart," he said vaguely, and then trying to make his voice more tender, trying to conciliate something, "Good night, dear children."

v

Charlie went directly to the Ritz bar with the furious idea of finding Lorraine and Duncan, but they were not there, and he realized that in any case there was nothing he could do. He had not touched his drink at the Peters, and now he ordered a whisky-and-soda. Paul came over to say hello.

"It's a great change," he said sadly. "We do about half the business we did. So many fellows I hear about back in the States lost everything, maybe not in the first crash, but then in the second. Your friend George Hardt lost every cent, I hear. Are you back in the States?"

"No, I'm in business in Prague."

"I heard that you lost a lot in the crash."

"I did," and he added grimly, "but I lost everything I wanted in the boom."

"Selling short."

"Something like that."

Again the memory of those days swept over him like a nightmare—the people they had met travelling; then people who couldn't add a row of figures or speak a coherent sentence. The little man Helen had consented to dance with at the ship's party, who had insulted her ten feet from the table; the women and girls carried screaming with drink or drugs out of public places—

—The men who locked their wives out in the snow, because the snow of twenty-nine wasn't real snow. If you didn't want it to be snow, you just paid some money.

He went to the phone and called the Peters' apartment; Lincoln answered.

"I called up because this thing is on my mind. Has Marion said anything definite?"

"Marion's sick," Lincoln answered shortly. "I know this thing isn't altogether your fault, but I can't have her go to pieces about it. I'm afraid we'll have to let it slide for six months; I can't take the chance of working her up to this state again."

"I see."

"I'm sorry, Charlie."

He went back to his table. His whisky glass was empty, but he shook his head when Alix looked at it questioningly. There wasn't much he could do now except send Honoria some things; he would send her a lot of things tomorrow. He thought rather angrily that this was just money—he had given so many people money. . . .

"No, no more," he said to another waiter. "What do I owe you?"

He would come back some day; they couldn't make him pay forever. But he wanted his child, and nothing was much good now, beside that fact. He wasn't young any more, with a lot of nice thoughts and dreams to have by himself. He was absolutely sure Helen wouldn't have wanted him to be so alone.

# WILLIAM FAULKNER
## 1897–1962

Faulkner was born in Union County, Mississippi. His family had been important in the political, economic, and cultural life of northern Mississippi for three generations, but their power and influence were declining, and for a time it looked as if young William might be its least distinguished member. He spent most of his youth hunting, fishing, and playing baseball. But he was gifted at drawing and telling stories, and maintained from an early age that he wanted to be a writer like his great-grandfather, William Cuthbert Faulkner, whose *White Rose of Memphis* had gone through thirty-five editions after its publication in 1880. During World War I Faulkner was turned down by the U.S. Army Air Corps because he was too short, but was accepted for flight training in the Royal Canadian Air Force. He wanted to fly in combat, but the war ended too soon, and he was injured when he and a friend celebrated Armistice Day by stunting over the field and crashing through a hangar roof.

Returning to Oxford, Mississippi, he continued to read and to write, and took courses at the University of Mississippi. But he was neither a regular nor a successful student. Nor was he having any luck trying to place his fiction and poetry with magazines. Finally, a friend subsidized a private printing of a volume of Faulkner's poetry, *The Marble Faun*, in 1924. In later life Faulkner spoke of himself as a "failed poet," who had turned to fiction only because his poetry was not good enough.

In 1925 he moved to New Orleans, where he was admitted to the circle of writers that gathered around Sherwood Anderson, and began to publish sketches in the Sunday feature section of the New Orleans *Times-Picayune*. Then, with the help of Anderson, he was able to get his first novel, *Soldier's Pay*, published in 1926. In his third novel, *Sartoris* (1929), he began to find his proper material and realize his strength as a writer. With this work he began his immense chronicle of an imaginary Mississippi county, based on the history of the area around his home in Oxford, Mississippi. His Yoknapatawpha County has become a permanent feature in the international literary landscape. Among his most highly regarded works are *Light in August* (1932) and *Absalom, Absalom!* (1936), and two collections of short fiction which have the shape and movement of a novel: *The Unvanquished* (1938) and *Go Down, Moses* (1942). In 1950 he received the Nobel Prize for literature.

# A Rose for Emily

## I

When Miss Emily Grierson died, our whole town went to her funeral: the men through a sort of respectful affection for a fallen monument, the women mostly out of curiosity to see the inside of her house, which no one save an old manservant—a combined gardener and cook—had seen in at least ten years.

It was a big, squarish frame house that had once been white, decorated with cupolas and spires and scrolled balconies in the heavily lightsome style of the seventies, set on what had once been our most select street. But garages and cotton gins had encroached and obliterated even the august names of that neighborhood; only Miss Emily's house was left, lifting its stubborn and coquettish decay above the cotton wagons and the gasoline pumps—an eyesore among eyesores. And now Miss Emily had gone to join the representatives of those august names where they lay in the cedar-bemused cemetery among the ranked and anonymous graves of Union and Confederate soldiers who fell at the battle of Jefferson.

Alive, Miss Emily had been a tradition, a duty, and a care; a sort of hereditary obligation upon the town, dating from that day in 1894 when Colonel Sartoris, the mayor—he who fathered the edict that no Negro woman should appear on the streets without an apron—

remitted her taxes, the dispensation dating from the death of her father on into perpetuity. Not that Miss Emily would have accepted charity. Colonel Sartoris invented an involved tale to the effect that Miss Emily's father had loaned money to the town, which the town, as a matter of business, preferred this way of repaying. Only a man of Colonel Sartoris' generation and thought could have invented it, and only a woman could have believed it.

When the next generation, with its more modern ideas, became mayors and aldermen, this arrangement created some little dissatisfaction. On the first of the year they mailed her a tax notice. February came, and there was no reply. They wrote her a formal letter, asking her to call at the sheriff's office at her convenience. A week later the mayor wrote her himself, offering to call or to send his car for her, and received in reply a note on paper of an archaic shape, in a thin, flowing calligraphy in faded ink, to the effect that she no longer went out at all. The tax notice was also enclosed, without comment.

They called a special meeting of the Board of Aldermen. A deputation waited upon her, knocked at the door through which no visitor had passed since she ceased giving china-painting lessons eight or ten years earlier. They were admitted by the old Negro into a dim hall from which a stairway mounted into still more shadow. It smelled of dust and disuse—a close, dank smell. The Negro led them into the parlor. It was furnished in heavy, leather-covered furniture. When the Negro opened the blinds of one window, they could see that the leather was cracked; and when they sat down, a faint dust rose sluggishly about their thighs, spinning with slow motions in the single sun-ray. On a tarnished gilt easel before the fireplace stood a crayon portrait of Miss Emily's father.

They rose when she entered—a small, fat woman in black, with a thin gold chain descending to her waist and vanishing into her belt, leaning on an ebony cane with a tarnished gold head. Her skeleton was small and spare; perhaps that was why what would have been merely plumpness in another was obesity in her. She looked bloated, like a body long submerged in motionless water, and of that pallid hue. Her eyes, lost in the fatty ridges of her face, looked like two small pieces of coal pressed into a lump of dough as they moved from one face to another while the visitors stated their errand.

She did not ask them to sit. She just stood in the door and listened quietly until the spokesman came to a stumbling halt. Then they could hear the invisible watch ticking at the end of the gold chain.

Her voice was dry and cold. "I have no taxes in Jefferson. Colonel Sartoris explained it to me. Perhaps one of you can gain access to the city records and satisfy yourselves."

"But we have. We are the city authorities, Miss Emily. Didn't you get a notice from the sheriff, signed by him?"

"I received a paper, yes," Miss Emily said. "Perhaps he considers himself the sheriff . . . I have no taxes in Jefferson."

"But there is nothing on the books to show that, you see. We must go by the—"

"See Colonel Sartoris." (Colonel Sartoris had been dead almost ten years.) "I have no taxes in Jefferson. Tobe!" The Negro appeared. "Show these gentlemen out."

## II

So she vanquished them, horse and foot, just as she had vanquished their fathers thirty years before about the smell. That was two years after her father's death and a short time after her sweetheart—the one we believed would marry her—had deserted her. After her father's death she went out very little; after her sweetheart went away, people hardly saw her at all. A few of the ladies had the temerity to call, but were not received, and the only sign of life about the place was the Negro man—a young man then—going in and out with a market basket.

"Just as if a man—any man—could keep a kitchen properly," the ladies said; so they were not surprised when the smell developed. It was another link between the gross, teeming world and the high and mighty Griersons.

A neighbor, a woman, complained to the mayor, Judge Stevens, eighty years old.

"But what will you have me do about it, madam?" he said.

"Why, send her word to stop it," the woman said. "Isn't there a law?"

"I'm sure that won't be necessary," Judge Stevens said. "It's probably just a snake or a rat that nigger of hers killed in the yard. I'll speak to him about it."

The next day he received two more complaints, one from a man who came in diffident deprecation. "We really must do something about it, Judge. I'd be the last one in the world to bother Miss Emily, but we've got to do something." That night the Board of Aldermen met—three graybeards and one younger man, a member of the rising generation.

"It's simple enough," he said. "Send her word to have her place cleaned up. Give her a certain time to do it in, and if she don't . . ."

"Dammit, sir," Judge Stevens said, "will you accuse a lady to her face of smelling bad?"

So the next night, after midnight, four men crossed Miss Emily's lawn and slunk about the house like burglars, sniffing along the base of the brickwork and at the cellar openings while one of them performed a regular sowing motion with his hand out of a sack slung from his shoulder. They broke open the cellar door and sprinkled lime there, and in all the outbuildings. As they recrossed the lawn, a window that had been dark was lighted and Miss Emily sat in it, the light behind her, and her upright torso motionless as that of an idol. They crept quietly across the lawn and into the shadow of the locusts that lined the street. After a week or two the smell went away.

That was when people had begun to feel really sorry for her. People in our town, remembering how old lady Wyatt, her great-aunt, had gone completely crazy at last, believed that the Griersons held themselves a little too high for what they really were. None of the young men were quite good enough for Miss Emily and such. We had long thought of them as a tableau, Miss Emily a slender figure in white in the background, her father a spraddled silhouette in the foreground, his back to her and clutching a horsewhip, the two of them framed by the back-flung front door. So when she got to be thirty and was still single, we were not pleased exactly, but vindicated; even with insanity in the family she wouldn't have turned down all of her chances if they had really materialized.

When her father died, it got about that the house was all that was left to her; and in a way, people were glad. At last they could pity Miss Emily. Being left alone, and a pauper, she had become humanized. Now she too would know the old thrill and the old despair of a penny more or less.

The day after his death all the ladies prepared to call at the house and offer condolence and aid, as is our custom. Miss Emily met them at the door, dressed as usual and with no trace of grief on her face. She told them that her father was not dead. She did that for three days, with the ministers calling on her, and the doctors, trying to persuade her to let them dispose of the body. Just as they were about to resort to law and force, she broke down, and they buried her father quickly.

We did not say she was crazy then. We believed she had to do that. We remembered all the young men her father had driven away, and we knew that with nothing left, she would have to cling to that which had robbed her, as people will.

### III

She was sick for a long time. When we saw her again, her hair was cut short, making her look like a girl, with a vague resemblance to those angels in colored church windows—sort of tragic and serene.

The town had just let the contracts for paving the sidewalks, and in the summer after her father's death they began the work. The construction company came with niggers and mules and machinery; and a foreman named Homer Barron, a Yankee—a big, dark, ready man, with a big voice and eyes lighter than his face. The little boys would follow in groups to hear him cuss the niggers, and the niggers singing in time to the rise and fall of picks. Pretty soon he knew everybody in town. Whenever you heard a lot of laughing anywhere about the square, Homer Barron would be in the center of the group. Presently we began to see him and Miss Emily on Sunday afternoons driving in the yellow-wheeled buggy and the matched team of bays from the livery stable.

At first we were glad that Miss Emily would have an interest, because the ladies all said, "Of course a Grierson would not think seriously of a Northerner, a day laborer." But there were still others, older people, who said that even grief could not cause a real lady to forget *noblesse oblige*—without calling it *noblesse oblige*. They just said, "Poor Emily. Her kinsfolk should come to her." She had some kin in Alabama; but years ago her father had fallen out with them over the estate of old lady Wyatt, the crazy woman, and there was no communication between the two families. They had not even been represented at the funeral.

And as soon as the old people said, "Poor Emily," the whispering began. "Do you suppose it's really so?" they said to one another. "Of course it is. What else could . . ." This behind their hands; rustling of craned silk and satin behind jalousies closed upon the sun of Sunday afternoon as the thin, swift clop-clop-clop of the matched team passed: "Poor Emily."

She carried her head high enough—even when we believed that she was fallen. It was as if she demanded more than ever the recognition of her dignity as the last Grierson; as if it had wanted that touch of earthiness to reaffirm her imperviousness. Like when she bought the rat poison, the arsenic. That was over a year after they had begun to say "Poor Emily," and while the two female cousins were visiting her.

"I want some poison," she said to the druggist. She was over thirty then, still a slight woman, though thinner than usual, with cold, haughty black eyes in a face the flesh of which was strained across the temples and about the eye-sockets as you imagine a lighthouse-keeper's face ought to look. "I want some poison," she said.

"Yes, Miss Emily. What kind? For rats and such? I'd recom—"

"I want the best you have. I don't care what kind."

The druggist named several. "They'll kill anything up to an elephant. But what you want is—"

"Arsenic," Miss Emily said. "Is that a good one?"

"Is . . . arsenic? Yes, ma'am. But what you want—"

"I want arsenic."

The druggist looked down at her. She looked back at him, erect, her face like a strained flag. "Why, of course," the druggist said. "If that's what you want. But the law requires you to tell what you are going to use it for."

Miss Emily just stared at him, her head tilted back in order to look him eye for eye, until he looked away and went and got the arsenic and wrapped it up. The Negro delivery boy brought her the package; the druggist didn't come back. When she opened the package at home there was written on the box, under the skull and bones: "For rats."

IV

So the next day we all said, "She will kill herself"; and we said it would be the best thing. When she had first begun to be seen with Homer Barron, we had said, "She will marry him." Then we said, "She will persuade him yet," because Homer himself had remarked—he liked men, and it was known that he drank with the younger men in the Elks' Club—that he was not a marrying man. Later we said, "Poor Emily" behind the jalousies as they passed on Sunday afternoon in the glittering buggy, Miss Emily with her head high and Homer Barron with his hat cocked and a cigar in his teeth, reins and whip in a yellow glove.

Then some of the ladies began to say that it was a disgrace to the town and a bad example to the young people. The men did not want to interfere, but at last the ladies forced the Baptist minister—Miss Emily's people were Episcopal—to call upon her. He would never divulge what happened during that interview, but he refused to go back again. The next Sunday they again drove about the streets, and the following day the minister's wife wrote to Miss Emily's relations in Alabama.

So she had blood-kin under her roof again and we sat back to watch developments. At first nothing happened. Then we were sure that they were to be married. We learned that Miss Emily had been to the jeweler's and ordered a man's toilet set in silver, with the letters H.B. on each piece. Two days later we learned that she had bought a complete outfit of men's clothing, including a nightshirt, and we said, "They are married." We were really glad. We were glad because the two female cousins were even more Grierson than Miss Emily had ever been.

So we were not surprised when Homer Barron—the streets had been finished some time since—was gone. We were a little disappointed that there was not a public blowing-off, but we believed that he had gone on to prepare for Miss Emily's coming, or to give her a chance to get rid of the cousins. (By that time it was a cabal, and we were all Miss Emily's allies to help circumvent the cousins.) Sure enough, after another week they departed. And, as we had expected all along, within three days Homer Barron was back in town. A neighbor saw the Negro man admit him at the kitchen door at dusk one evening.

And that was the last we saw of Homer Barron. And of Miss Emily for some time. The Negro man went in and out with the market basket, but the front door remained closed. Now and then we would see her at a window for a moment, as the men did that night when they sprinkled the lime, but for almost six months she did not appear on the streets. Then we knew that this was to be expected too; as if that quality of her father which had thwarted her woman's life so many times had been too virulent and too furious to die.

When we next saw Miss Emily, she had grown fat and her hair was turning gray. During the next few years it grew grayer and grayer until it attained an even pepper-and-salt iron-gray, when it ceased turning. Up to the day of her death at seventy-four it was still that vigorous iron-gray, like the hair of an active man.

From that time on her front door remained closed, save for a period of six or seven years, when she was about forty, during which she gave lessons in china-painting. She fitted up a studio in one of the downstairs rooms, where the daughters and granddaughters of Colonel Sartoris' contemporaries were sent to her with the same regularity and in the same spirit that they were sent to church on Sundays with a twenty-five-cent piece for the collection plate. Meanwhile her taxes had been remitted.

Then the newer generation became the backbone and the spirit of the town, and the painting pupils grew up and fell away and did not send their children to her with boxes of color and tedious brushes and pictures cut from the ladies' magazines. The front door closed upon the last one and remained closed for good. When the town got free postal delivery, Miss Emily alone refused to let them fasten the metal numbers above her door and attach a mailbox to it. She would not listen to them.

Daily, monthly, yearly we watched the Negro grow grayer and more stooped, going in and out with the market basket. Each December we sent her a tax notice, which would be returned by the post office a week later, unclaimed. Now and then we would see her in one of the downstairs windows—she had evidently shut up the top floor of the house—like the carven torso of an idol in a niche, looking or not looking at us, we could never tell which. Thus she passed from generation to generation—dear, inescapable, impervious, tranquil, and perverse.

And so she died. Fell ill in the house filled with dust and shadows, with only a doddering Negro man to wait on her. We did not even know she was sick; we had long since given up trying to get any information from the Negro. He talked to no one, probably not even to her, for his voice had grown harsh and rusty, as if from disuse.

She died in one of the downstairs rooms, in a heavy walnut bed with a curtain, her gray head propped on a pillow yellow and moldy with age and lack of sunlight.

v

The Negro met the first of the ladies at the front door and let them in, with their hushed, sibilant voices and their quick, curious glances, and then he disappeared. He walked right through the house and out the back and was not seen again.

The two female cousins came at once. They held the funeral on the second day, with the town coming to look at Miss Emily beneath a mass of bought flowers, with the crayon face of her father musing profoundly above the bier and the ladies sibilant and macabre; and the very old men—some in their brushed Confederate uniforms—on the porch and the lawn, talking of Miss Emily as if she had been a contemporary of theirs, believing that they had danced with her and courted her perhaps, confusing time with its mathematical progression, as the old do, to whom all the past is not a diminishing road but, instead, a huge meadow which no winter ever quite touches, divided from them now by the narrow bottle-neck of the most recent decade of years.

Already we knew that there was one room in that region above stairs which no one had seen in forty years, and which would have to be forced. They waited until Miss Emily was decently in the ground before they opened it.

The violence of breaking down the door seemed to fill this room with pervading dust. A thin, acrid pall as of the tomb seemed to lie everywhere upon this room decked and furnished as for a bridal: upon the valance curtains of faded rose color, upon the rose-shaded lights, upon the dressing table, upon the delicate array of crystal and the man's toilet things backed with tarnished silver, silver so tarnished that the monogram was obscured. Among them lay a collar and tie, as if they had just been removed, which, lifted, left upon the surface a pale crescent in the dust. Upon a chair hung the suit, carefully folded; beneath it the two mute shoes and the discarded socks.

The man himself lay in the bed.

For a long while we just stood there, looking down at the profound and fleshless grin. The body had apparently once lain in the attitude of an embrace, but now the long sleep that outlasts love, that conquers even the grimace of love, had cuckolded him. What was left of him, rotted beneath what was left of the nightshirt, had become inextricable from the bed in which he lay; and upon him and upon the pillow beside him lay that even coating of the patient and biding dust.

Then we noticed that in the second pillow was the indentation of a head. One of us lifted something from it, and leaning forward, that faint and invisible dust dry and acrid in the nostrils, we saw a long strand of iron-gray hair.

# ERNEST HEMINGWAY

## 1899–1961

Born in Oak Park, Illinois, the son of a doctor and a music teacher, Ernest Hemingway went to school in Oak Park and spent his summers in the upper peninsula of Michigan, where his father taught him early to hunt and fish. He was a physically active and popular boy, good at writing but bored with school. A couple of times he simply left and went on the road, but he worked on the school newspaper, graduated, and tried to enlist in the Army for World War I. A bad eye prevented that, so he went into newspaper work and then enlisted as an ambulance driver for the Red Cross in Italy, where he saw plenty of combat, was badly wounded and showed genuine heroism under fire. After the war and some newspaper work in Chicago and Toronto, Hemingway moved to Europe where he lived with his first wife, mostly in Paris. There he met Ezra Pound and Gertrude Stein, who christened Hemingway and his young friends a "lost generation." There, too, Hemingway began to write the stories and novels that made his reputation, beginning with *In Our Time* (1925) and *The Sun Also Rises* (1926). In later years he became more of a public figure and less of a writer, as he hardened into a symbol of patriarchal machismo known as "Papa." But he had a fine success with *The Old Man and the Sea* (1952) and won the Nobel Prize in 1954. In 1961, in ill health and unable to write, he loaded his silver-inlaid double-barreled shotgun, put both barrels in his mouth and pulled the triggers.

## Hills Like White Elephants

The hills across the valley of the Ebro were long and white. On this side there was no shade and no trees and the station was between two lines of rails in the sun. Close against the side of the station there was the warm shadow of the building and a curtain, made of strings of bamboo beads, hung across the open door into the bar, to keep out flies. The American and the girl with him sat at a table in the shade, outside the building. It was very hot and the express from Barcelona would come in forty minutes. It stopped at this junction for two minutes and went on to Madrid.

"What should we drink?" the girl asked. She had taken off her hat and put it on the table.

"It's pretty hot," the man said.

"Let's drink beer."

"Dos cervezas," the man said into the curtain.

"Big ones?" a woman asked from the doorway.

"Yes. Two big ones."

The woman brought two glasses of beer and two felt pads. She put the felt pads and the beer glasses on the table and looked at the man and the girl. The girl was looking off at the line of hills. They were white in the sun and the country was brown and dry.

"They look like white elephants," she said.

"I've never seen one," the man drank his beer.

"No, you wouldn't have."

"I might have," the man said. "Just because you say I wouldn't have doesn't prove anything."

The girl looked at the bead curtain. "They've painted something on it," she said. "What does it say?"

"Anis del Toro. It's a drink."

"Could we try it?"

The man called "Listen" through the curtain. The woman came out from the bar.

"Four reales."

"We want two Anis del Toro."

"With water?"

"Do you want it with water?"

"I don't know," the girl said. "Is it good with water?"

"It's all right."

"You want them with water?" asked the woman.

"Yes, with water."

"It tastes like licorice," the girl said and put the glass down.

"That's the way with everything."

"Yes," said the girl. "Everything tastes of licorice. Especially all the things you've waited so long for, like absinthe."

"Oh, cut it out."

"You started it," the girl said. "I was being amused. I was having a fine time."

"Well, let's try and have a fine time."

"All right. I was trying. I said the mountains looked like white elephants. Wasn't that bright?"

"That was bright."

"I wanted to try this new drink. That's all we do, isn't it—look at things and try new drinks?"

"I guess so."

The girl looked across at the hills.

"They're lovely hills," she said. "They don't really look like white elephants. I just meant the coloring of their skin through the trees."

"Should we have another drink?"

"All right."

The warm wind blew the bead curtain against the table.

"The beer's nice and cool," the man said.

"It's lovely," the girl said.

"It's really an awfully simple operation, Jig," the man said. "It's not really an operation at all."

The girl looked at the ground the table legs rested on.

"I know you wouldn't mind it, Jig. It's really not anything. It's just to let the air in."

The girl did not say anything.

"I'll go with you and I'll stay with you all the time. They just let the air in and then it's all perfectly natural."

"Then what will we do afterward?"

"We'll be fine afterward. Just like we were before."

"What makes you think so?"

"That's the only thing that bothers us. It's the only thing that's made us unhappy."

The girl looked at the bead curtain, put her hand out and took hold of two of the strings of beads.

"And you think then we'll be all right and be happy."

"I know we will. You don't have to be afraid. I've known lots of people that have done it."

"So have I," said the girl. "And afterward they were all so happy."

"Well," the man said, "if you don't want to you don't have to. I wouldn't have you do it if you didn't want to. But I know it's perfectly simple."

"And you really want to?"

"I think it's the best thing to do. But I don't want you to do it if you don't really want to."

"And if I do it you'll be happy and things will be like they were and you'll love me?"

"I love you now. You know I love you."

"I know. But if I do it, then it will be nice again if I say things are like white elephants, and you'll like it?"

"I'll love it. I love it now but I just can't think about it. You know how I get when I worry."

"If I do it you won't ever worry?"

"I won't worry about that because it's perfectly simple."

"Then I'll do it. Because I don't care about me."

"What do you mean?"

"I don't care about me."

"Well, I care about you."

"Oh, yes. But I don't care about me. And I'll do it and then everything will be fine."

"I don't want you to do it if you feel that way."

The girl stood up and walked to the end of the station. Across, on the other side, were fields of grain and trees along the banks of the Ebro. Far away, beyond the river, were mountains. The shadow of a cloud moved across the field of grain and she saw the river through the trees.

"And we could have all this," she said. "And we could have everything and every day we make it more impossible."

"What did you say?"

"I said we could have everything."

"We can have everything."

"No, we can't."

"We can have the whole world."

"No, we can't."

"We can go everywhere."

"No, we can't. It isn't ours any more."

"It's ours."

"No, it isn't. And once they take it away, you never get it back."

"But they haven't taken it away."

"We'll wait and see."

"Come on back in the shade," he said. "You mustn't feel that way."

"I don't feel any way," the girl said. "I just know things."

"I don't want you to do anything that you don't want to do—"

"Nor that isn't good for me," she said. "I know. Could we have another beer?"

"All right. But you've got to realize—"

"I realize," the girl said. "Can't we maybe stop talking?"

They sat down at the table and the girl looked across at the hills on the dry side of the valley and the man looked at her and at the table.

"You've got to realize," he said, "that I don't want you to do it if you don't want to. I'm perfectly willing to go through with it if it means anything to you."

"Doesn't it mean anything to you? We could get along."

"Of course it does. But I don't want anybody but you. I don't want any one else. And I know it's perfectly simple."

"Yes, you know it's perfectly simple."

"It's all right for you to say that, but I do know it."

"Would you do something for me now?"

"I'd do anything for you."

"Would you please please please please please please please stop talking?"

He did not say anything but looked at the bags against the wall of the station. There were labels on them from all the hotels where they had spent nights.

"But I don't want you to," he said, "I don't care anything about it."

"I'll scream," the girl said.

The woman came out through the curtains with two glasses of beer and put them down on the damp felt pads. "The train comes in five minutes," she said.

"What did she say?" asked the girl.

"That the train is coming in five minutes."

The girl smiled brightly at the woman, to thank her.

"I'd better take the bags over to the other side of the station," the man said. She smiled at him.

"All right. Then come back and we'll finish the beer."

He picked up the two heavy bags and carried them around the station to the other tracks. He looked up the tracks but could not see the train. Coming back, he walked through the barroom, where people waiting for the train were drinking. He drank an Anis at the bar and looked at the people. They were all waiting reasonably for the train. He went out through the bead curtain. She was sitting at the table and smiled at him.

"Do you feel better?" he asked.

"I feel fine," she said. "There's nothing wrong with me. I feel fine."

# ELIZABETH BOWEN
## 1899–1973

The only child of Henry and Isabel Bowen, of County Cork, Ireland, she was raised at the family mansion, Bowen's Court, in Ireland, until her father went insane, when she moved, with her mother, to East Kent, England. From childhood on she was handicapped by a pronounced stammer. She went to school at Downe House in Westerham (West Kent), where she was quite happy. She began writing fiction early, publishing her first collection of stories in 1923, the year in which she married. She traveled in Europe and America, building a reputation for sensitive, witty fiction with novels like *The House in Paris* (1938) and *The Death of the Heart* (1938) and stories, sometimes with a touch of the supernatural like those in *The Demon Lover* collection of 1945.

# The Demon Lover

Towards the end of her day in London Mrs. Drover went round to her shut-up house to look for several things she wanted to take away. Some belonged to herself, some to her family, who were by now used to their country life. It was late August; it had been a steamy, showery day: at the moment the trees down the pavement glittered in an escape of humid yellow afternoon sun. Against the next batch of clouds, already piling up ink-dark, broken chimneys and parapets stood out. In her once familiar street, as in any unused channel, an unfamiliar queerness had silted up; a cat wove itself in and out of railings, but no human eye watched Mrs. Drover's return. Shifting some parcels under her arm, she slowly forced round her latchkey in an unwilling lock, then gave the door, which had warped, a push with her knee. Dead air came out to meet her as she went in.

The staircase window having been boarded up, no light came down into the hall. But one door, she could just see, stood ajar, so she went quickly through into the room and unshuttered the big window in there. Now the prosaic woman, looking about her, was more perplexed than she knew by everything that she saw, by traces of her long former habit of life—the yellow smoke-stain up the white marble mantelpiece, the ring left by a vase on the top of the escritoire; the bruise in the wallpaper where, on the door being thrown open widely, the china handle had always hit the wall. The piano, having gone away to be stored, had left what looked like claw-marks on its part of the parquet. Though not much dust had seeped in, each object wore a film of another kind; and, the only ventilation being the chimney, the whole drawing-room smelled of the cold hearth. Mrs. Drover put down her parcels on the escritoire and left the room to proceed upstairs; the things she wanted were in a bedroom chest.

She had been anxious to see how the house was—the part-time caretaker she shared with some neighbours was away this week on his holiday, known to be not yet back. At the best of times he did not look in often, and she was never sure that she trusted him. There were some cracks in the structure, left by the last bombing, on which she was anxious to keep an eye. Not that one could do anything—

A shaft of refracted daylight now lay across the hall. She stopped dead and stared at the hall table—on this lay a letter addressed to her.

She thought first—then the caretaker *must* be back. All the same, who, seeing the house shuttered, would have dropped a letter in at the box? It was not a circular, it was not a bill. And the post office redirected, to the address in the country, everything for her that came through the post. The caretaker (even if he *were* back) did not know she was due in London to-day—her call here had been planned to be a surprise—so his negligence in the manner of this letter, leaving it to wait in the dusk and the dust, annoyed her. Annoyed, she picked up the letter, which bore no stamp. But it cannot be important, or they would know . . . She took the letter rapidly upstairs with her, without a stop to look at the writing till she reached what had been her bedroom, where she let in light. The room looked over the garden and other gardens: the sun had gone in; as the clouds sharpened and lowered, the trees and rank lawns seemed already to smoke with dark. Her reluctance to look again at the letter came from the fact that she felt intruded upon—and by someone contemptuous of her ways. However, in the tenseness preceding the fall of rain she read it: it was a few lines.

> DEAR KATHLEEN,
>     You will not have forgotten that to-day is our anniversary, and the day we said. The years have gone by at once slowly and fast. In view of the fact that nothing has changed, I shall rely upon you to keep your promise. I was sorry to see you leave London, but was satisfied that you would be back in time. You may expect me, therefore, at the hour arranged.
>
>                                             Until then . . .
>                                                     K.

Mrs. Drover looked for the date: it was to-day's. She dropped the letter on to the bed-springs, then picked it up to see the writing again—her lips, beneath the remains of lipstick, beginning to go white. She felt so much the change in her own face that she went to the mirror, polished a clear patch in it and looked at once urgently and stealthily in. She was confronted by a woman of forty-four, with eyes starting out under a hat-brim that had been rather carelessly pulled down. She had not put on any more powder since she left the shop where she ate her solitary tea. The pearls her husband had given her on their marriage hung loose round her now rather thinner throat, slipping into the V of the pink wool jumper her sister knitted last autumn as they sat round the fire. Mrs. Drover's most normal expression was one of controlled worry, but of assent. Since the birth of the third of her little boys, attended by a quite serious illness, she had had an intermittent muscular flicker to the left of her mouth, but in spite of this she could always sustain a manner that was at once energetic and calm.

Turning from her own face as precipitately as she had gone to meet it, she went to the chest where the things were, unlocked it, threw up the lid and knelt to search. But as rain began to come crashing down she could not keep from looking over her shoulder at the stripped bed on which the letter lay. Behind the blanket of rain the clock of the church that still stood struck six—with rapidly heightening apprehension, she counted each of the slow strokes. "The hour arranged . . . My God," she said, "*what* hour? How should I . . . ? After twenty-five years. . . ."

The young girl talking to the soldier in the garden had not ever completely seen his face. It was dark; they were saying good-bye under a tree. Now and then—for it felt, from not seeing him at this intense moment, as though she had never seen him at all—she verified his presence for these few moments longer by putting out a hand, which he each time pressed, without very much kindness, and painfully, on to one of the breast buttons of his uniform. That cut of the button on the palm of her hand was, principally, what she was to carry away. This was so near the end of a leave from France that she could only wish him already gone. It was August 1916. Being not kissed, being drawn away from and looked at intimidated Kathleen till she imagined spectral glitters in the place of his eyes. Turning away and looking back up the lawn she saw, through branches of trees, the drawing-room window alight: she caught a breath for the moment when she could go running back there into the safe arms of her mother and sister, and cry: "What shall I do, what shall I do? He has gone."

Hearing her catch her breath, her fiancé said, without feeling: "Cold?"

"You're going away such a long way."

"Not so far as you think."

"I don't understand?"

"You don't have to," he said. "You will. You know what we said."

"But that was—suppose you—I mean, suppose."

"I shall be with you," he said, "sooner or later. You won't forget that. You need do nothing but wait."

Only a little more than a minute later she was free to run up the silent lawn. Looking in through the window at her mother and sister, who did not for the moment perceive her, she already felt that unnatural promise drive down between her and the rest of all human kind. No other way of having given herself could have made her feel so apart, lost and foresworn. She could not have plighted a more sinister troth.

Kathleen behaved well when, some months later, her fiancé was reported missing, presumed killed. Her family not only supported her but were able to praise her courage without stint because they could not regret, as a husband for her, the man they knew almost nothing about. They hoped she would, in a year or two, console herself—and had it been only a question of consolation things might have gone much straighter ahead. But her trouble, behind just a little grief, was a complete dislocation from everything. She did not reject other lovers, for these failed to appear: for years she failed to attract men—and with the approach of her thirties she became natural enough to share her family's anxiousness on this score. She began to put herself out, to wonder; and at thirty-two she was very greatly relieved to find herself being courted by William Drover. She married him, and the two of them settled down in this quiet, arboreal part of Kensington: in this house the years piled up, her children were born and they all lived till they were driven out by the bombs of the next war. Her movements as Mrs. Drover were circumscribed, and she dismissed any idea that they were still watched.

As things were—dead or living the letter-writer sent her only a threat. Unable, for some minutes, to go on kneeling with her back exposed to the empty room, Mrs. Drover rose from the chest to sit on an upright chair whose back was firmly against the wall. The desuetude of her former bedroom, her married London home's whole air of being a cracked cup from which memory, with its reassuring power, had either evaporated or leaked away, made a crisis—and at just this crisis the letter-writer had, knowledgeably, struck. The hollowness of the house this evening cancelled years on years of voices, habits and steps. Through the shut windows she only heard rain fall on the roofs around. To rally herself, she said she was in a mood—and, for two or three seconds shutting her eyes, told herself that she had imagined the letter. But she opened them—there it lay on the bed.

On the supernatural side of the letter's entrance she was not permitting her mind to dwell. Who, in London, knew she meant to call at the house to-day? Evidently, however, this had been known. The caretaker, *had* he come back, had had no cause to expect her: he would have taken the letter in his pocket, to forward it, at his own time, through the post. There was no other sign that the caretaker had been in—but, if not? Letters dropped in at doors of deserted houses do not fly or walk to tables in halls. They do not sit on the dust of empty tables with the air of certainty that they will be found. There is needed some human hand—but nobody but the caretaker had a key. Under circumstances she did not care to consider, a house can be entered without a key. It was possible that she was not alone now. She might be being waited for, downstairs. Waited for—until when? Until "the hour arranged." At least that was not six o'clock: six has struck.

She rose from the chair and went over and locked the door.

The thing was, to get out. To fly? No, not that: she had to catch her train. As a woman whose utter dependability was the keystone of her family life she was not willing to return to the country, to her husband, her little boys and her sister, without the objects she had come up to fetch. Resuming work at the chest she set about making up a number of parcels in a rapid, fumbling-decisive way. These, with her shopping parcels, would be too much to carry; these meant a taxi—at the thought of the taxi her heart went up and her normal breathing resumed. I will ring up the taxi now; the taxi cannot come too soon: I shall hear the taxi out there running its engine, till I walk calmly down to it through the hall. I'll ring up—But no: the telephone is cut off . . . She tugged at a knot she had tied wrong.

The idea of flight . . . He was never kind to me, not really. I don't remember him kind at all. Mother said he never considered me. He was set on me, that was what it was—not love. Not love, not meaning a person well. What did he do, to make me promise like that? I can't remember— But she found that she could.

She remembered with such dreadful acuteness that the twenty-five years since then dissolved like smoke and she instinctively looked for the weal left by the button on the palm of her hand. She remembered not only all that he said and did but the complete suspension of *her* existence during that August week. I was not myself—they all told me so at the time. She remembered—but with one white burning blank as where acid has dropped on a photograph: *under no conditions* could she remember his face.

So, wherever he may be waiting, I shall not know him. You have no time to run from a face you do not expect.

The thing was to get to the taxi before any clock struck what could be the hour. She would slip down the street and round the side of the square to where the square gave on the main road. She would return in the taxi, safe, to her own door, and bring the solid driver into the house with her to pick up the parcels from room to room. The idea of the taxi driver made her decisive, bold: she unlocked her door, went to the top of the staircase and listened down.

She heard nothing—but while she was hearing nothing the *passé* air of the staircase was disturbed by a draught that travelled up to her face. It emanated from the basement: down there a door or window was being opened by someone who chose this moment to leave the house.

The rain had stopped; the pavements steamily shone as Mrs. Drover let herself out by inches from her own front door into the empty street. The unoccupied houses opposite continued to meet her look with their damaged stare. Making towards the thoroughfare and the taxi, she tried not to keep looking behind. Indeed, the silence was so intense—one of those creeks of London silence exaggerated this summer by the damage of war—that no tread could have gained on her unheard. Where her street debouched on the square where people went on living she grew conscious of and checked her unnatural pace. Across the open end of the square two buses impassively passed each other; women, a perambulator, cyclists, a man wheeling a barrow signalized, once again, the ordinary flow of life. At the square's most populous corner should be—and was—the short taxi rank. This evening, only one taxi—but this, although it presented its blank rump, appeared already to be alertly waiting for her. Indeed, without looking round the driver started his engine as she panted up from behind and put her hand on the door. As she did so, the clock struck seven. The taxi faced the main road: to make the trip back to her house it would have to turn—she had settled back on the seat and the taxi *had* turned before she, surprised by its knowing movement, recollected that she had not "said where." She leaned forward to scratch at the glass panel that divided the driver's head from her own.

The driver braked to what was almost a stop, turned round and slid the glass panel back: the jolt of this flung Mrs. Drover forward till her face was almost into the glass. Through the aperture driver and passenger, not six inches between them, remained for an eternity eye to eye. Mrs. Drover's mouth hung open for some seconds before she could issue her first scream. After that she continued to scream freely and to beat with her gloved hands on the glass all round at the taxi, accelerating without mercy, made off with her into the hinterland of deserted streets.

# JORGE LUIS BORGES
## 1899–

Borges (pronounced Bor'hace) was born in the heart of Buenos Aires, Argentina, where his father was a lawyer and a teacher of psychology. Borges's grandmother was English and this language was much used in the family, so that most of his early reading was in English. He began writing in Spanish and English when he was six, and had a translation of an Oscar Wilde story published in a Buenos Aires newspaper when he was nine, after which he began to go to school. When he was fifteen his family moved to Switzerland, where he studied at the college founded by John Calvin. Here all his classes were in French and the most important subject was Latin. On his own, he studied German and Italian. He was always destined to be a writer, it seems, and his love of languages was a part of his equipment. After a stay in Spain, where he wrote political poems and essays which he destroyed before leaving, he returned to Buenos Aires in 1921. He has been called a leader of the "ultraist" movement in Hispanic literature, but he says now that ultraism was obsessed with modernity and gadgets. He regrets his brief flirtation with it. Back in Buenos Aires he began to write the plainer poems and the philosophical fables that have made him famous. He has since lived a quiet life as a librarian (except for a time when dictator Perón made him a chicken inspector) and teacher of Old English literature, with his eyesight failing and his reputation growing.

# The Lottery in Babylon

Like all men in Babylon, I have been proconsul; like all, a slave. I have also known omnipotence, opprobrium, imprisonment. Look: the index finger on my right hand is missing. Look: through the rip in my cape you can see a vermilion tatoo on my stomach. It is the second symbol, Beth. This letter, on nights when the moon is full, gives me power over men whose mark is Gimmel, but it subordinates me to the men of Aleph, who on moonless nights owe obedience to those marked with Gimmel. In the half light of dawn, in a cellar, I have cut the jugular vein of sacred bulls before a black stone. During a lunar year I have been declared invisible. I shouted and they did not answer me; I stole bread and they did not behead me. I have known what the Greeks do not know, incertitude. In a bronze chamber, before the silent handkerchief of the strangler, hope has been faithful to me, as has panic in the river of pleasure. Heraclides Ponticus tells with amazement that Pythagoras remembered having been Pyrrhus and before that Euphorbus and before that some other mortal. In order to remember similar vicissitudes I do not need to have recourse to death or even to deception.

I owe this almost atrocious variety to an institution which other republics do not know or which operates in them in an imperfect and secret manner: the lottery. I have not looked into its history; I know that the wise men cannot agree. I know of its powerful purposes what a man who is not versed in astrology can know about the moon. I come

Translated by John M. Fein.

from a dizzy land where the lottery is the basis of reality. Until today I have thought as little about it as I have about the conduct of indecipherable divinities or about my heart. Now, far from Babylon and its beloved customs, I think with a certain amount of amazement about the lottery and about the blasphemous conjectures which veiled men murmur in the twilight.

My father used to say that formerly—a matter of centuries, of years?—the lottery in Babylon was a game of plebeian character. He recounted (I don't know whether rightly) that barbers sold, in exchange for copper coins, squares of bone or of parchment adorned with symbols. In broad daylight a drawing took place. Those who won received silver coins without any other test of luck. The system was elementary, as you can see.

Naturally these "lotteries" failed. Their moral virtue was nil. They were not directed at all of man's faculties, but only at hope. In the face of public indifference, the merchants who founded these venal lotteries began to lose money. Someone tried a reform: The interpolation of a few unfavorable tickets in the list of favorable numbers. By means of this reform, the buyers of numbered squares ran the double risk of winning a sum and of paying a fine that could be considerable. This slight danger (for every thirty favorable numbers there was one unlucky one) awoke, as is natural, the interest of the public. The Babylonians threw themselves into the game. Those who did not acquire chances were considered pusillanimous, cowardly. In time, that justified disdain was doubled. Those who did not play were scorned, but also the losers who paid the fine were scorned. The Company (as it came to be known then) had to take care of the winners, who could not cash in their prizes if almost the total amount of the fines was unpaid. It started a lawsuit against the losers. The judge condemned them to pay the original fine and costs or spend several days in jail. All chose jail in order to defraud the Company. The bravado of a few is the source of the omnipotence of the Company and of its metaphysical and ecclesiastical power.

A little while afterward the lottery lists omitted the amounts of fines and limited themselves to publishing the days of imprisonment that each unfavorable number indicated. That laconic spirit, almost unnoticed at the time, was of capital importance. *It was the first appearance in the lottery of nonmonetary elements.* The success was tremendous. Urged by the clientele, the Company was obliged to increase the unfavorable numbers.

Everyone knows that the people of Babylon are fond of logic and even of symmetry. It was illogical for the lucky numbers to be computed in round coins and the unlucky ones in days and nights of imprisonment. Some moralists reasoned that the possession of money does not always determine happiness and that other forms of happiness are perhaps more direct.

Another concern swept the quarters of the poorer classes. The members of the college of priests multiplied their stakes and enjoyed all the vicissitudes of terror and hope; the poor (with reasonable or unavoidable envy) knew that they were excluded from that notoriously delicious rhythm. The just desire that all, rich and poor, should participate equally in the lottery, inspired an indignant agitation, the memory of which the years have not erased. Some obstinate people did not understand (or pretended not to understand) that it was a question of a new order, of a necessary historical stage. A slave stole a crimson ticket, which in the drawing credited him with the burning of his tongue. The legal code fixed that same penalty for the one who stole a ticket. Some Babylonians argued that he deserved the burning irons in his status of a thief; others, generously, that the executioner should apply it to him because chance had determined it that way. There were disturbances, there were lamentable drawings of blood, but the masses of Babylon finally imposed their will against the opposition of the rich. The people achieved amply its generous purposes. In the first place, it caused the Company to accept total power. (That unification was necessary, given the vastness and complexity of the new operations.) In the second place, it made the lottery secret, free and general. The mercenary sale of chances was abolished. Once initiated in the mysteries of Baal, every free man automatically participated in the sacred drawings, which took place in the labyrinths of the god every sixty nights and which determined his destiny until the next drawing. The consequences were incalculable. A fortunate play could bring about his promotion to the council of wise men or the imprisonment of an enemy (public or private) or finding, in the peaceful darkness of his room, the woman who begins to excite him and whom he never expected to see again. A bad play: mutilation, different kinds of infamy, death. At times one single fact—the vulgar murder of C, the mysterious apotheosis of B—was the happy solution of thirty or forty drawings. To combine the plays was difficult, but one must remember that the individuals of the Company were (and are) omnipotent and astute. In many cases the knowledge that certain happinesses were the simple product of chance would have diminished their virtue. To avoid that obstacle, the agents of the Company made use of the power of suggestion and magic. Their steps, their maneuverings, were secret. To find out about the intimate hopes and terrors of each individual, they had astrologists and spies. There were certain stone lions, there was a sacred latrine called

Qaphqa, there were fissures in a dusty aqueduct which, according to general opinion, *led to the Company;* malignant or benevolent persons deposited information in these places. An alphabetical file collected these items of varying truthfulness.

Incredibly, there were complaints. The Company, with its usual discretion, did not answer directly. It preferred to scrawl in the rubbish of a mask factory a brief statement which now figures in the sacred scriptures. This doctrinal item observed that the lottery is an interpolation of chance in the order of the world and that to accept errors is not to contradict chance: it is to corroborate it. It likewise observed that those lions and that sacred receptacle, although not disavowed by the Company (which did not abandon the right to consult them), functioned without official guarantee.

This declaration pacified the public's restlessness. It also produced other effects, perhaps unforeseen by its writer. It deeply modified the spirit and the operations of the Company. I don't have much time left; they tell us that the ship is about to weigh anchor. But I shall try to explain it.

However unlikely it might seem, no one had tried out before then a general theory of chance. Babylonians are not very speculative. They revere the judgments of fate, they deliver to them their lives, their hopes, their panic, but it does not occur to them to investigate fate's labyrinthine laws nor the gyratory spheres which reveal it. Nevertheless, the *unofficial* declaration that I have mentioned inspired many discussions of judicial-mathematical character. From some one of them the following conjecture was born: if the lottery is an intensification of chance, a periodical infusion of chaos in the cosmos, would it not be right for chance to intervene in all stages of the drawing and not in one alone? Is it not ridiculous for chance to dictate someone's death and have the circumstances of that death—secrecy, publicity, the fixed time of an hour or a century—not subject to chance? These just scruples finally caused a considerable reform, whose complexities (aggravated by centuries' practice) only a few specialists understand, but which I shall try to summarize, at least in a symbolic way.

Let us imagine a first drawing, which decrees the death of a man. For its fulfillment one proceeds to another drawing, which proposes (let us say) nine possible executors. Of these executors, four can initiate a third drawing which will tell the name of the executioner, two can replace the adverse order with a fortunate one (finding a treasure, let us say), another will intensify the death penalty (that is, will make it infamous or enrich it with tortures), others can refuse to fulfill it. This is the symbolic scheme. In reality *the number of drawings is infinite.* No decision is final, all branch into others. Ignorant people suppose that infinite drawings require an infinite time; actually it is sufficient for time to be infinitely subdivisible, as the famous parable of the contest with the tortoise teaches. This infinity harmonizes admirably with the sinuous numbers of Chance and with the Celestial Archetype of the Lottery, which the Platonists adore. Some warped echo of our rites seems to have resounded on the Tiber: Ellus Lampridius, in the *Life of Antoninus Heliogabalus*, tells that this emperor wrote on shells the lots that were destined for his guests, so that one received ten pounds of gold and another ten flies, ten dormice, ten bears. It is permissible to recall that Heliogabalus was brought up in Asia Minor, among the priests of the eponymous god.

There are also impersonal drawings, with an indefinite purpose. One decrees that a sapphire of Taprobana be thrown into the waters of the Euphrates; another, that a bird be released from the roof of a tower; another, that each century there be withdrawn (or added) a grain of sand from the innumerable ones on the beach. The consequences are, at times, terrible.

Under the beneficent influence of the Company, our customs are saturated with chance. The buyer of a dozen amphoras of Damascene wine will not be surprised if one of them contains a talisman or a snake. The scribe who writes a contract almost never fails to introduce some erroneous information. I myself, in this hasty declaration, have falsified some splendor, some atrocity. Perhaps, also, some mysterious monotony . . . Our historians, who are the most penetrating on the globe, have invented a method to correct chance. It is well known that the operations of this method are (in general) reliable, although, naturally, they are not divulged without some portion of deceit. Furthermore, there is nothing so contaminated with fiction as the history of the Company. A paleographic document, exhumed in a temple, can be the result of yesterday's lottery or of an age-old lottery. No book is published without some discrepany in each one of the copies. Scribes take a secret oath to omit, to interpolate, to change. The indirect lie is also cultivated.

The Company, with divine modesty, avoids all publicity. Its agents, as is natural, are secret. The orders which it issues continually (perhaps incessantly) do not differ from those lavished by imposters. Moreover, who can brag about being a mere imposter? The drunkard who improvises an absurd order, the dreamer who awakens suddenly and strangles the woman who sleeps at his side, do they not execute, perhaps, a secret decision of the Company? That silent functioning, comparable to God's, gives rise to all sorts of conjectures. One abominably insinuates that the Company has not existed for centuries and that the sacred disorder of our lives is purely hereditary, traditional. Another judges it eternal and teaches that it will last until the last night, when the last god annihilates the world. Another declares that the Company is omnipotent, but that it only has influence in tiny things: in a bird's call, in the shadings of rust and of dust, in the half dreams of dawn. Another, in the words of masked heresiarchs, *that it has never existed and will not exist*. Another, no less vile, reasons that it is indifferent to affirm or deny the reality of the shadowy corporation, because Babylon is nothing else than an infinite game of chance.

# MORLEY CALLAGHAN
## 1903-

Born in Toronto of Irish parents, Morley Callaghan was educated at St. Michael's College of the University of Toronto and at Osgoode Law School. During the summer of 1923 he worked as a reporter on the *Toronto Star*, where he met Ernest Hemingway, who was with the paper at the time. Encouraged by Hemingway, he began to publish his first short stories in the Paris avant-garde magazines *transition* and *This Quarter*. In 1928 he was admitted to the bar, though he never practiced law. That same year his first novel, *A Native Argosy*, was published by Scribner's of New York (Maxwell Perkins, a famous editor there, described Callaghan as one of the best writers of his generation). In 1929 he travelled to Paris, where he met Gertrude Stein, F. Scott Fitzgerald and James Joyce—encounters he later recorded in his memoir, *That Summer in Paris* (1963). After eight months he returned to Toronto, where he has since lived. In 1933 he met Jacques Maritain, the French Catholic philosopher, whose Christian humanism greatly influenced his work. His best novels—*Such is My Beloved* (1934) and *More Joy in Heaven* (1937)—explore, in deceptively simple style, moments of spiritual illumination in the lives of ordinary men and women.

# Ancient Lineage

The young man from the Historical Club with a green magazine under his arm got off the train at Clintonville. It was getting dark but the station lights were not lit. He hurried along the platform and jumped down on the sloping cinder path to the sidewalk.

Trees were on the lawns alongside the walk, branches drooping low, leaves scraping occasionally against the young man's straw hat. He saw a cluster of lights, bluish-white in the dusk across a river, many lights for a small town. He crossed the lift-lock bridge and turned onto the main street. A hotel was at the corner.

At the desk a bald-headed man in a blue shirt, the sleeves rolled up, looked critically at the young man while he registered. "All right, Mr Flaherty," he said, inspecting the signature carefully.

"Do you know many people around here?" Mr Flaherty asked.

"Just about everybody."

"The Rowers?"

"The old lady?"

"Yeah, an old lady."

"Sure, Mrs Anna Rower. Around the corner to the left, then turn to the right on the first street, the house opposite the Presbyterian church on the hill."

"An old family," suggested the young man.

"An old-timer all right." The hotel man made it clear by a twitching of his lips that he was a part of the new town, canal, water-power, and factories.

Mr Flaherty sauntered out and turned to the left. It was dark and the street had the silence of small towns in the evening. Turning a corner he heard girls giggling in a doorway. He looked at the church on the hill, the steeple dark against the sky. He had forgotten whether the man had said beside the church or across the road, but could not make up his mind to ask the fellow who was watering the wide church lawn. No lights in the shuttered windows of the rough-cast house beside the church. He came down the hill and had to yell three times at the man because the water swished strongly against the grass.

"All right, thanks. Right across the road," Mr Flaherty repeated.

Tall trees screened the square brick house. Looking along the hall to a lighted room, Mr Flaherty saw an old lady standing at a sideboard. "She's in all right," he thought, rapping on the screen door. A large woman of about forty, dressed in blue skirt and blue waist, came down the stairs. She did not open the screen door.

"Could I speak to Mrs Anna Rower?"

"I'm Miss Hilda Rower."

"I'm from the University Historical Club."

"What did you want to see Mother for?"

Mr Flaherty did not like talking through the screen door. "I wanted to talk to her," he said firmly.

"Well, maybe you'd better come in."

He stood in the hall while the large woman lit the gas in the front room. The gas flared up, popped, showing fat hips and heavy lines on her face. Mr Flaherty, disappointed, watched her swaying down the hall to get her mother. He carefully inspected the front room, the framed photographs of dead Conservative politicians, the group of military men hanging over the old-fashioned piano, the faded greenish wallpaper and the settee in the corner.

An old woman with a knot of white hair and good eyes came into the room, walking erectly. "This is the young man who wanted to see you, Mother," Miss Hilda Rower said. They all sat down. Mr Flaherty explained he wanted to get some information concerning the Rower genealogical tree for the next meeting of his society. The Rowers, he knew, were a pioneer family in the district, and descended from William the Conqueror, he had heard.

The old lady laughed thinly, swaying from side to side. "It's true enough, but I don't know who told you. My father was Daniel Rower, who came to Ontario from Cornwall in 1830."

Miss Hilda Rower interrupted. "Wait, Mother, you may not want to tell about it." Brusque and businesslike, she turned to the young man. "You want to see the family tree, I suppose."

"Oh, yes."

"My father was a military settler here," the old lady said.

"I don't know but what we might be able to give you some notes." Miss Hilda spoke generously.

"Thanks awfully, if you will."

"Of course you're prepared to pay something if you're going to print it," she added, smugly adjusting her big body in the chair.

Mr Flaherty got red in the face; of course he understood, but to tell the truth he had merely wanted to chat with Mrs Rower. Now he knew definitely he did not like the heavy nose and unsentimental assertiveness of the lower lip of this big woman with the wide shoulders. He couldn't stop looking at her thick ankles. Rocking back and forth in the chair she was primly conscious of lineal superiority; a proud unmarried woman, surely she could handle a young man, half-closing her eyes, a young man from the University indeed. "I don't want to talk to her about the University," he thought.

Old Mrs Rower went into the next room and returned with a framed genealogical tree of the house of Rower. She handed it graciously to Mr Flaherty, who read, "The descent of the family of Rower, from William the Conqueror, from Malcom 1st, and from the Capets, Kings of France." It bore the *imprimatur* of the College of Arms, 1838.

"It's wonderful to think you have this," Mr Flaherty said, smiling at Miss Hilda, who watched him suspiciously.

"A brother of mine had it all looked up," old Mrs Rower said.

"You don't want to write about that," Miss Hilda said, crossing her ankles. The ankles looked much thicker crossed. "You just want to have a talk with Mother."

"That's it," Mr Flaherty smiled agreeably.

"We may write it up ourselves some day." Her heavy chin dipped down and rose again.

"Sure, why not?"

"But there's no harm in you talking to Mother if you want to, I guess."

"You could write a good story about that tree," Mr Flaherty said, feeling his way.

"We may do it some day but it'll take time," she smiled complacently at her mother, who mildly agreed.

Mr Flaherty talked pleasantly to this woman, who was so determined he would not learn anything about the family tree without paying for it. He tried talking about the city, then tactfully asked old Mrs Rower what she remembered of the Clintonville of seventy years ago. The old lady talked willingly, excited a little. She went into the next room to get a book of clippings. "My father, Captain Rower, got a grant of land from the Crown and cleared it," she said, talking over her shoulder. "A little way up the Trent River. Clintonville was a small military settlement then—"

"Oh, Mother, he doesn't want to know all about that," Miss Hilda said impatiently.

"It's very interesting indeed."

The old woman said nervously, "My dear, what difference does it make? You wrote it all up for the evening at the church."

"So I did too," she hesitated, thinking the young man ought to see how well it was written. "I have an extra copy." She looked at him thoughtfully. He smiled. She got up and went upstairs.

The young man talked very rapidly to the old lady and took many notes.

Miss Rower returned. "Would you like to see it?" She handed Mr Flaherty a small grey booklet. Looking quickly through it, he saw it contained valuable information about the district.

"The writing is simply splendid. You must have done a lot of work on it."

"I worked hard on it," she said, pleased and more willing to talk.

"Is this an extra copy?"

"Yes, it's an extra copy."

"I suppose I might keep it," he said diffidently.

She looked at him steadily. "Well . . . I'll have to charge you twenty-five cents."

"Sure, sure, of course, that's fine." He blushed.

"Just what it costs to get them out," the old lady explained apologetically.

"Can you change a dollar?" He fumbled in his pocket, pulling the dollar out slowly.

They could not change it but Miss Rower would be pleased to go down to the corner grocery store. Mr Flaherty protested. No trouble, he would go. She insisted on asking the next-door neighbour to change it. She went across the room, the dollar in hand.

Mr Flaherty chatted with the nice old lady and carefully examined the family tree, and wrote quickly in a small book till the screen door banged, the curtains parted, and Miss Hilda Rower came into the room. He wanted to smirk, watching her walking heavily, so conscious of her ancient lineage, a virginal mincing sway to her large hips, seventy-five cents change held loosely in drooping fingers.

"Thank you," he said, pocketing the change, pretending his work was over. Sitting back in the chair he praised the way Miss Rower had written the history of the neighbourhood and suggested she might write a splendid story of the family tree, if she had the material, of course.

"I've got the material, all right," she said, trying to get comfortable again. How would Mr Flaherty arrange it and where should she try to sell it? The old lady was dozing in the rocking-chair. Miss Rower began to talk rather nervously about her material. She talked of the last title in the family and the Sir Richard who had been at the court of Queen Elizabeth.

Mr Flaherty chimed in gaily, "I suppose you know the O'Flahertys were kings in Ireland, eh?"

She said vaguely, "I daresay, I daresay," conscious only of an interruption to the flow of her thoughts. She went on talking with hurried eagerness, all the fine talk about her ancestors bringing her peculiar satisfaction. A soft light came into her eyes and her lips were moist.

Mr Flaherty started to rub his cheek, and looked at her big legs, and felt restive, and then embarrassed, watching her closely, her firm lower lip hanging loosely. She was talking slowly, lazily, relaxing in her chair, a warm fluid oozing through her veins, exhausting but satisfying her.

He was uncomfortable. She was liking it too much. He did not know what to do. There was something immodest about it. She was close to forty, her big body relaxed in the chair. He looked at his watch and suggested he would be going. She stretched her legs graciously, pouting, inviting him to stay a while longer, but he was standing up, tucking his magazine under his arm. The old lady was still dozing. "I'm so comfortable," Miss Rower said, "I hate to move."

The mother woke up and shook hands with Mr Flaherty. Miss Rower got up to say goodbye charmingly.

Half-way down the path Mr Flaherty turned. She was standing in the doorway partly shadowed by the tall trees, bright moonlight filtering through leaves touching soft lines on her face and dark hair.

He went down the hill to the hotel unconsciously walking with a careless easy stride, wondering at the change that had come over the heavy, strong woman. He thought of taking a walk along the river in the moonlight, the river on which old Captain Rower had drilled troops on the ice in the winter of 1837 to fight the rebels. Then he thought of having a western sandwich in the café across the road from the hotel. That big woman in her own way had been hot stuff.

In the hotel he asked to be called early so he could get the first train to the city. For a long time he lay awake in the fresh, cool bed, the figure of the woman whose ancient lineage had taken the place of a lover in her life drifting into his thoughts and becoming important, while he watched on the wall the pale moonlight that had softened the lines of her face, and wondered if it was still shining on her bed, and on her throat, and on her contented, lazily relaxed body.

## KAY BOYLE
### 1903–

Born in St. Paul, Minnesota, Kay Boyle left there at the age of six months and travelled in Europe with her parents and her sister. Later she went to school in Washington, D.C. When her father suffered business reverses and opened a garage in Cincinnati, she moved there and studied violin at the Cincinnati Conservatory and architecture at the Ohio Mechanics Institute. Then she worked as a telephone operator in her father's garage, living in the building, writing poems and stories steadily. She married a French student in 1921 and went to live with him in Le Havre in 1922. When she was threatened by tuberculosis she moved south to a gentler climate. Her first daughter was born in Nice and her second in Paris in 1929, the year her first collection of stories was published. She continued to live abroad, in Austria and England as well as France, marrying a second time in 1932. After a stay in the U.S. during World War II, she returned to Europe and lived in Germany before coming back to this country. Since then she has held a number of positions teaching creative writing. She has written many novels and some poetry, but she is best known for her carefully crafted short stories. A volume of her collected stories was published in 1980.

## Winter Night

There is a time of apprehension which begins with the beginning of darkness, and to which only the speech of love can lend security. It is there, in abeyance, at the end of every day, not urgent enough to be given the name of fear but rather of concern for how the hours are to be reprieved from fear, and those who have forgotten how it was when they were children can remember nothing of this. It may begin around five o'clock on a winter afternoon when the light outside is dying in the windows. At that hour the New York apartment in which Felicia lived was filled with shadows, and the little girl would wait alone in the living room, looking out at the winter-stripped trees that stood black in the park against the isolated ovals of unclean snow. Now it was January, and the day had been a cold one; the water of the artificial lake was frozen fast, but because of the cold and the coming darkness, the skaters had ceased to move across its surface. The street that lay between the park and the apartment house was wide, and the two-way streams of cars and busses, some with their headlamps already shining, advanced and halted, halted and poured swiftly on to the tempo of the traffic signals' altering lights. The time of apprehension had set in, and Felicia, who was seven, stood at the window in the evening and waited before she asked the question. When the signals below would change from red to green again, or when the double-decker bus would turn the corner below, she would ask it. The words of it were already there, tentative in her mouth, when the answer came from the far end of the hall.

"Your mother," said the voice among the sound of kitchen things, "she telephoned up before you came in from nursery school. She won't be back in time for supper. I was to tell you a sitter was coming in from the sitting parents' place."

Felicia turned back from the window into the obscurity of the living room, and she looked toward the open door, and into the hall beyond it where the light from the kitchen fell in a clear yellow angle across the wall and onto the strip of carpet. Her hands were cold, and she put them in her jacket pockets as she walked carefully across the living-room rug and stopped at the edge of light.

"Will she be home late?" she said.

For a moment there was the sound of water running in the kitchen, a long way away, and then the sound of the water ceased, and the high, Southern voice went on:

"She'll come home when she gets ready to come home. That's all I have to say. If she wants to spend two dollars and fifty cents and ten cents' carfare on top of that three or four nights out of the week for a sitting parent to come in here and sit, it's her own business. It certainly ain't nothing to do with you or me. She makes her money, just like the rest of us does. She works all day down there in the office, or whatever it is, just like the rest of us works, and she's entitled to spend her money like she wants to spend it. There's no law in the world against buying your own freedom. Your mother and me, we're just buying our own freedom, that's all we're doing. And we're not doing nobody no harm."

"Do you know who she's having supper with?" said Felicia from the edge of dark. There was one more step to take, and then she would be standing in the light that fell on the strip of carpet, but she did not take the step.

"Do I know who she's having supper with?" the voice cried out in what might have been derision, and there was the sound of dishes striking the metal ribs of the drainboard by the sink. "Maybe it's Mr. Van Johnson, or Mr. Frank Sinatra, or maybe it's just the Duke of Wincers for the evening. All I know is you're having soft-boiled egg and spinach and applesauce for supper, and you're going to have it quick now because the time is getting away."

The voice from the kitchen had no name. It was as variable as the faces and figures of the women who came and sat in the evenings. Month by month the voice in the kitchen altered to another voice, and the sitting parents were no more than lonely aunts of an evening or two who sometimes returned and sometimes did not to this apartment in which they had sat before. Nobody stayed anywhere very long any more, Felicia's mother told her. It was part of the time in which you lived, and part of the life of the city, but when the fathers came back, all this would be miraculously changed. Perhaps you would live in a house again, a small one, with fir trees on either side of the short brick walk, and Father would drive up every night from the station just after darkness set in. When Felicia thought of this, she stepped quickly into the clear angle of light, and she left the dark of the living room behind her and ran softly down the hall.

The drop-leaf table stood in the kitchen between the refrigerator and the sink, and Felicia sat down at the place that was set. The voice at the sink was speaking still, and while Felicia ate it did not cease to speak until the bell of the front door rang abruptly. The girl walked around the table and went down the hall, wiping her dark palms in her apron, and, from the drop-leaf table, Felicia watched her step from the angle of light into darkness and open the door.

"You put in an early appearance," the girl said, and the woman who had rung the bell came into the hall. The door closed behind her, and the girl showed her into the living room, and lit the lamp on the bookcase, and the shadows were suddenly bleached away. But when the girl turned, the woman turned from the living room too and followed her, humbly and in silence, to the threshold of the kitchen. "Sometimes they keep me standing around waiting after it's time for me to be getting on home, the sitting parents do," the girl said, and she picked up the last two dishes from the table and put them in the sink. The woman who stood in the doorway was a small woman, and when she undid the white silk scarf from around her head, Felicia saw that her hair was black. She wore it parted in the middle, and it had not been cut, but was drawn back loosely into a knot behind her head. She had very clean white gloves on, and her face was pale, and there was a look of sorrow in her soft black eyes. "Sometimes I have to stand out there in the hall with my hat and coat on, waiting for the sitting parents to turn up," the girl said, and, as she turned on the water in the sink, the contempt she had for them hung on the kitchen air. "But you're ahead of time," she said, and she held the dishes, first one and then the other, under the flow of steaming water.

The woman in the doorway wore a neat black coat, not a new-looking coat, and it had no fur on it, but it had a smooth velvet collar and velvet lapels. She did not move, or smile, and she gave no sign that she had heard the girl speaking above the sound of water at the sink. She simply stood looking at Felicia, who sat at the table with the milk in her glass not finished yet.

"Are you the child?" she said at last, and her voice was low, and the pronunciation of the words a little strange.

"Yes, this here's Felicia," the girl said, and the dark hands dried the dishes and put them away. "You drink up your milk quick now, Felicia, so's I can rinse your glass."

"I will wash the glass," said the woman. "I would like to wash the glass for her," and Felicia sat looking across the table at the face in the doorway that was filled with such unspoken grief. "I will wash the glass for her and clean off the table," the woman was saying quietly. "When the child is finished, she will show me where her night things are."

"The others, they wouldn't do anything like that," the girl said, and she hung the dishcloth over the rack. "They wouldn't put their hand to housework, the sitting parents. That's where they got the name for them," she said.

Whenever the front door closed behind the girl in the evening, it would usually be that the sitting parent who was there would take up a book of fairy stories and read aloud for a while to Felicia; or else would settle herself in the big chair in the living room and begin to tell the words of a story in drowsiness to her, while Felicia took off her clothes in the bedroom, and folded them, and put her pajamas on, and brushed her teeth, and did her hair. But this time, that was not the way it happened. Instead, the woman sat down on the other chair at the kitchen table, and she began at once to speak, not of good fairies or bad, or of animals endowed with human speech, but to speak quietly, in spite of the eagerness behind her words, of a thing that seemed of singular importance to her.

"It is strange that I should have been sent here tonight," she said, her eyes moving slowly from feature to feature of Felicia's face, "for you look like a child that I knew once, and this is the anniversary of that child."

"Did she have hair like mine?" Felicia asked quickly, and she did not keep her eyes fixed on the unfinished glass of milk in shyness any more.

"Yes, she did. She had hair like yours," said the woman, and her glance paused for a moment on the locks which fell straight and thick on the shoulders of Felicia's dress. It may have been that she thought to stretch out her hand and touch the ends of Felicia's hair, for her fingers stirred as they lay clasped together on the table, and then they relapsed into passivity again. "But it is not the hair alone, it is the delicacy of your face, too, and your eyes the same, filled with the same spring lilac color," the woman said, pronouncing the words carefully. "She had little coats of golden fur on her arms and legs," she said, "and when we were closed up there, the lot of us in the cold, I used to make her laugh when I told her that the fur that was so pretty, like a little fawn's skin on her arms, would always help to keep her warm."

"And did it keep her warm?" asked Felicia, and she gave a little jerk of laughter as she looked down at her own legs hanging under the table, with the bare calves thin and covered with a down of hair.

"It did not keep her warm enough," the woman said, and now the mask of grief had come back upon her face. "So we used to take everything we could spare from ourselves, and we would sew them into cloaks and other kinds of garments for her and for the other children. . . ."

"Was it a school?" said Felicia when the woman's voice had ceased to speak.

"No," said the woman softly, "it was not a school, but still there were a lot of children there. It was a camp—that was the name the place had; it was a camp. It was a place where they put people until they could decide what was to be done with them." She sat with her hands clasped, silent a moment, looking at Felicia. "That little dress you have on," she said, not saying the words to anybody, scarcely saying them aloud. "Oh, she would have liked that little dress, the little buttons shaped like hearts, and the white collar——"

"I have four school dresses," Felicia said. "I'll show them to you. How many dresses did she have?"

"Well, there, you see, there in the camp," said the woman, "she did not have any dresses except the little skirt and the pullover. That was all she had. She had brought just a handkerchief of her belongings with her, like everybody else—just enough for three days away from home was what they told us, so she did not have enough to last the winter. But she had her ballet slippers," the woman said,

and her clasped fingers did not move. "She had brought them because she thought during her three days away from home she would
have the time to practice her ballet."

"I've been to the ballet," Felicia said suddenly, and she said it so
eagerly that she stuttered a little as the words came out of her
mouth. She slipped quickly down from the chair and went around
the table to where the woman sat. Then she took one of the
woman's hands away from the other that held it fast, and she pulled
her toward the door. "Come into the living room and I'll do a pirouette for you," she said, and then she stopped speaking, her eyes
halted on the woman's face. "Did she—did the little girl—could she
do a pirouette very well?" she said.

"Yes, she could. At first she could," said the woman, and Felicia
felt uneasy now at the sound of sorrow in her words. "But after that
she was hungry. She was hungry all winter," she said in a low
voice. "We were all hungry, but the children were the hungriest.
Even now," she said, and her voice went suddenly savage, "when I
see milk like that, clean, fresh milk standing in a glass, I want to cry
out loud, I want to beat my hands on the table, because it did not
have to be . . ." She had drawn her fingers abruptly away from
Felicia now, and Felicia stood before her, cast off, forlorn, alone
again in the time of apprehension. "That was three years ago," the
woman was saying, and one hand was lifted, as in weariness, to
shade her face. "It was somewhere else, it was in another country,"
she said, and behind her hand her eyes were turned upon the substance of a world in which Felicia had played no part.

"Did—did the little girl cry when she was hungry?" Felicia asked,
and the woman shook her head.

"Sometimes she cried," she said, "but not very much. She was
very quiet. One night when she heard the other children crying, she
said to me, 'You know, they are not crying because they want something to eat. They are crying because their mothers have gone
away.' "

Did the mothers have to go out to supper?" Felicia asked, and she
watched the woman's face for the answer.

"No," said the woman. She stood up from her chair, and now that
she put her hand on the little girl's shoulder, Felicia was taken into
the sphere of love and intimacy again. "Shall we go into the other
room, and you will do your pirouette for me?" the woman said, and
they went from the kitchen and down the strip of carpet on which
the clear light fell. In the front room, they paused hand in hand in
the glow of the shaded lamp, and the woman looked about her, at
the books, the low tables with the magazines and ash trays on them,
the vase of roses on the piano, looking with dark, scarcely seeing
eyes at these things that had no reality at all. It was only when she

saw the little white clock on the mantelpiece that she gave any sign, and then she said quickly: "What time does your mother put you to bed?"

Felicia waited a moment, and in the interval of waiting the woman lifted one hand and, as if in reverence, touched Felicia's hair.

"What time did the little girl you knew in the other place go to bed?" Felicia asked.

"Ah, God, I do not know, I do not remember," the woman said.

"Was she your little girl?" said Felicia softly, stubbornly.

"No," said the woman. "She was not mine. At least, at first she was not mine. She had a mother, a real mother, but the mother had to go away."

"Did she come back late?" asked Felicia.

"No, ah, no, she could not come back, she never came back," the woman said, and now she turned, her arm around Felicia's shoulders, and she sat down in the low soft chair. "Why am I saying all this to you, why am I doing it?" she cried out in grief, and she held Felicia close against her. "I had thought to speak of the anniversary to you, and that was all, and now I am saying these other things to you. Three years ago today, exactly, the little girl became my little girl because her mother went away. That is all there is to it. There is nothing more."

Felicia waited another moment, held close against the woman, and listening to the swift, strong heartbeats in the woman's breast.

"But the mother," she said then in the small, persistent voice, "did she take a taxi when she went?"

"This is the way it used to happen," said the woman, speaking in hopelessness and bitterness in the softly lighted room. "Every week they used to come into the place where we were and they would read a list of names out. Sometimes it would be the names of children they would read out, and then a little later they would have to go away. And sometimes it would be the grown people's names, the names of the mothers or big sisters, or other women's names. The men were not with us. The fathers were somewhere else, in another place."

"Yes," Felicia said. "I know."

"We had been there only a little while, maybe ten days or maybe not so long," the woman went on, holding Felicia against her still, "when they read the name of the little girl's mother out, and that afternoon they took her away."

"What did the little girl do?" Felicia said.

"She wanted to think up the best way of getting out so that she could go find her mother," said the woman, "but she could not think of anything good enough until the third or fourth day. And then she tied her ballet slippers up in the handkerchief again, and she went up to the guard standing at the door." The woman's voice was gentle, controlled now. "She asked the guard please to open the door so that she could go out. 'This is Thrusday,' she said, 'and every Tuesday and Thursday I have my ballet lessons. If I miss a ballet lesson, they do not count the money off, so my mother would be just paying for nothing, and she cannot afford to pay for nothing. I missed my ballet lesson on Tuesday,' she said to the guard, 'and I must not miss it again today.' "

Felicia lifted her head from the woman's shoulder, and she shook her hair back and looked in question and wonder at the woman's face.

"And did the man let her go?" she said.

"No, he did not. He could not do that," said the woman. "He was a soldier and he had to do what he was told. So every evening after her mother went, I used to brush the little girl's hair for her," the woman went on saying. "And while I brushed it, I used to tell her the stories of the ballets. Sometimes I would begin with *Narcissus*," the woman said, and she parted Felicia's locks with her fingers, "so if you will go and get your brush now, I will tell it while I brush your hair."

"Oh, yes," said Felicia, and she made two whirls as she went quickly to the bedroom. On the way back, she stopped and held on to the piano with the fingers of one hand while she went up on her toes. "Did you see me? Did you see me standing on my toes?" she called the woman, and the woman sat smiling in love and contentment at her.

"Yes, wonderful, really wonderful," she said. "I am sure I have never seen anyone do it so well." Felicia came spinning toward her, whirling in pirouette after pirouette, and she flung herself down in the chair close to her, with her thin bones pressed against the woman's soft, wide hip. The woman took the silver-backed, monogrammed brush and the tortoise-shell comb in her hands, and now she began to brush Felicia's hair. "We did not have any soap at all and not very much water to wash in, so I never could fix her as nicely and prettily as I wanted to," she said, and the brush stroked regularly, carefully down, caressing the shape of Felicia's head.

"If there wasn't very much water, then how did she do her teeth?" Felicia said.

"She did not do her teeth," said the woman, and she drew the comb through Felicia's hair. "There were not any toothbrushes or tooth paste, or anything like that."

Felicia waited a moment, constructing the unfamiliar scene of it in silence, and then she asked the tentative question.

"Do I have to do my teeth tonight?" she said.

"No," said the woman, and she was thinking of something else, "you do not have to do your teeth."

"If I am your little girl tonight, can I pretend there isn't enough water to wash?" said Felicia.

"Yes," said the woman, "you can pretend that if you like. You do not have to wash," she said, and the comb passed lightly through Felicia's hair.

"Will you tell me the story of the ballet?" said Felicia, and the rhythm of the brushing was like the soft, slow rocking of sleep.

"Yes," said the woman. "In the first one, the place is a forest glade with little pale birches growing in it, and they have green veils over their faces and green veils drifting from their fingers, because it is the springtime. There is the music of a flute," said the woman's voice softly, softly, "and creatures of the wood are dancing——"

"But the mother," Felicia said as suddenly as if she had been awaked from sleep. "What did the little girl's mother say when she didn't do her teeth and didn't wash at night?"

"The mother was not there, you remember," said the woman, and the brush moved steadily in her hand. "But she did send one little letter back. Sometimes the people who went away were able to do that. The mother wrote it in a train, standing up in a car that had no seats," she said, and she might have been telling the story of the ballet still, for her voice was gentle and the brush did not falter on Felicia's hair. "There were perhaps a great many other people standing up in the train with her, perhaps all trying to write their little letters on the bits of paper they had managed to hide on them, or that they had found in forgotten corners as they traveled. When they had written their letters, then they must try to slip them out through the boards of the car in which they journeyed, standing up," said the woman, "and these letters fell down on the tracks under the train, or they were blown into the fields or onto the country roads, and if it was a kind person who picked them up, he would seal them in envelopes and send them to where they were addressed to go. So a letter came back like this from the little girl's mother," the woman said, and the brush followed the comb, the comb the brush in steady pursuit through Felicia's hair. "It said good-by to the little girl, and it said please to take care of her. It said: 'Whoever reads this letter in the camp, please take good care of my little girl for me, and please have her tonsils looked at by a doctor if this is possible to do.' "

"And then," said Felicia softly, persistently, "what happened to the little girl?"

"I do not know. I cannot say," the woman said. But now the brush and comb had ceased to move, and in the silence Felicia turned her thin, small body on the chair, and she and the woman suddenly put their arms around each other. "They must all be asleep now, all of them," the woman said, and in the silence that fell on them again, they held each other closer. "They must be quietly asleep somewhere, and not crying all night because they are hungry and because they are cold. For three years I have been saying 'They must all be asleep, and the cold and the hunger and the seasons or night or day or nothing matters to them——' "

It was after midnight when Felicia's mother put her key in the lock of the front door, and pushed it open, and stepped into the hallway. She walked quickly to the living room, and just across the threshold she slipped the three blue foxskins from her shoulders and dropped them, with her little velvet bag, upon the chair. The room was quiet, so quiet that she could hear the sound of breathing in it, and no one spoke to her in greeting as she crossed toward the bedroom door. And then, as startling as a slap across her delicately tinted face, she saw the woman lying sleeping on the divan, and Felicia, in her school dress still, asleep within the woman's arms.

# ISAAC BASHEVIS SINGER
## 1904–

He was born in Radzymin, Poland, where his father was a rabbi, and he himself went to school at Tachenioni Rabbinical Seminary in Poland. But instead of becoming a rabbi, he began to write in Yiddish (a dialect of German spoken by Jews in Europe and America) for the Yiddish press in Poland. Coming to America in 1935, he continued this work, keeping a job with the *Jewish Daily Forward* in New York for over forty years. During this time his novels and short stories in Yiddish began to make his reputation. Translations into English and other languages followed. He was recently awarded the Nobel Prize in literature—a remarkable feat for a writer whose subject matter has always been found in his own narrow but deep cultural tradition. His three collections of short stories are *Gimpel the Fool* (1957), *The Spinoza of Market Street* (1961), and *A Friend of Kafka* (1970).

## The Third One

It was sweltering outside, but the cafeteria was cool. During the day, between three and five, it was almost empty. I took a table near the wall, drank coffee, nibbled a piece of apple cake, and looked into an occult magazine. In the letters to the editor, a woman wrote that her cat had been run over by a car and she had buried it but still it came to visit her every night. The woman gave her name and her address in a Texas village. There was sincerity in the letter; surely it could not have been made up. But does the astral body really exist? I wondered. And do animals possess it, too? If so, my whole philosophy must be revised.

Before I could undertake so large an order, I went to the counter and got another cup of coffee. "One reality has nothing to do with the other," I said to myself.

I looked at the few people sitting around me. A young man in a pink shirt was studying a racing form, smoking one cigarette after another; his ashtray overflowed with butts and ashes. Two tables away a girl was reading the want ads in the daily paper. To the left near the door sat a tall man with a white beard and long white hair—a relic of old America. I often saw him. He looked poor but clean, and he always carried a book with him. Was he religious? Was he a freethinker of the old school, a pacifist, a vegetarian, a spiritualist, an anarchist? I had been curious about him for some time, but I never made an effort to find out who he was.

The door opened and in came someone I recognized, although I could not recall his name or where I had met him. He was a small man with a shock of hair the color of sand. His head was too big for his body. He could have been anywhere from forty to fifty-five. There was a withered haggardness in his face. He had high cheek-bones, a flat nose, a long upper lip, and the tiny chin of a baby. He wore a sports shirt and linen trousers. At the check machine he hesitated. His yellow eyes darted from right to left as if he were searching for someone. Then he saw me and his face lit up. He pulled a check out vigorously, and the machine gave a loud ring. He approached my table with mincing steps. He was wearing sandals with two straps. He seemed to have adjusted to the heat of New York, while I wore a suit, hat, and tie. When he got to my table, he said in the familiar Polish Yiddish of the Lublin region, "What are you doing here in the middle of the day? Cooling off? May I sit with you? Can I bring you something?" His voice was slightly nasal.

"Thank you. Nothing. Sit down."

"You once promised to call me," he said. "But that's how things are in this city—no one has the time or the patience. You probably lost my number anyway. I do it myself—I write down addresses and numbers and they disappear. Do you come here often? I used to be a steady customer, but not lately. My wife has asked about you several times. Do you live nearby?"

Before I could answer him, he ran over to the counter with quick little steps. "Who is he?" I asked myself. The truth was that I had hoped to be alone.

He came back with a glass of iced coffee and blueberry pie. "I wanted to go to a movie," he said, "but who wants to go alone? I don't know what they're playing, but perhaps you'd like to go with me. You'd be my guest."

"Thank you, but I haven't the slightest desire for a movie."

"No? As a rule I don't go to the movies unless my wife forces me, but today I was ready to sit for a few hours and forget the daily grind. I don't even look at the screen most of the time. I let them talk, shoot, sing, or whatever they please, without me. Since you know that you can't change anything that goes on up there, you become a fatalist. Sometimes I imagine that reality is just another movie. Do you ever feel that?"

"Yes, but in the real movie we all take part and have a little choice—we can play either right or wrong."

"So you believe in free will. I don't believe in it—absolutely not. We are marionettes—nothing more. Someone pulls a string and we dance. I'm a complete determinist."

"Just the same, when you cross the street and a car is coming you run."

"That's determined, too. I read in the paper once that a young man and his girl had supper and then sat down to play Russian roulette. Between yes and no, he killed himself. Everyone wants to test fate. Why haven't I seen your name in the papers lately?"

"I haven't had anything published."

"That's the reason I became a landlord, if you can call it that. I bought a building with furnished rooms and make my living from it. Some weeks are better, some are worse, but at least I don't have to listen to the opinions of an editor. People pay me in advance. I get all kinds. The man may be a murderer, a thief, or a pimp, but he gives me the five dollars and I give him the key. Today I wanted one of the rooms for a few hours myself, but they are all taken. You never know." He took a sip of his coffee, raised his eyebrows, and said, "You don't know who I am, do you?"

"I know you, but I'm sorry to say I don't remember your name. It's a kind of amnesia with me."

"I saw it at once. Fingerbein—Zelig Fingerbein. This is my pen name. No one calls me by my real name any more. We were intro-duced at the Café Royal."

"Of course. Now I know everything," I said "You have a very pretty wife—Genia."

"So you do remember! I often forget faces and events. I used to write poems and I published, too, but who needs poetry today? It's unnecessary merchandise. Still, there are emotions that only a poem can express. Imagine the Song of Songs in any other form! But it's obsolete: Love is strong as death. Jealousy is cruel as the grave.

Othello, too. To be jealous and strangle someone isn't such an accomplishment any more. True love is forgiveness. Civilized man has to learn the greatest of all arts: to overcome jealousy. Do you smoke?"

"No."

"Why not? A cigarette helps sometimes. Women had to suffer for generations—polygamy, harems, men who came back from war with concubines. Now men will have to take their medicine. Women have the same appetites as we do—maybe bigger. Don't laugh at me, but the underworld is a lot more advanced about these things than we are, though I hear that Europeans have made big steps forward. When a king of England gives up his throne to marry an American divorcée, it isn't just stuff for a headline, but a symbol of the new time and the new men."

Zelig Fingerbein put his little fist on the table. He tasted the blueberry pie and pushed the plate away. He asked, "Do you have some time?"

"Yes, I have time."

"I know I'll regret what I'm going to do. But since I didn't go to the movies and met you here, I want to tell you something that has a connection with you."

"With me? How?"

"Actually with your writing—not with you personally."

The little man who called himself Zelig Fingerbein turned his head, as if suspicious of being listened to. His yellow eyes watched me, half smiling, half questioning. He said, "No one else must ever know what I'm about to tell you. We all need to confide in someone. If no one knows your secret, it's not a secret but just a hidden thing. It has to do with my wife. There's a great love between us. When I was a bachelor, I always thought there could not be any love between people who stood under the wedding canopy and shared a bedroom. No institution is so much spat on and laughed at as the institution of marriage. But most of these jokers sooner or later go to a rabbi or a pastor and tie the knot. If one marriage fails, they try a second, a third—a fifth. Of course, there are a lot of old bachelors and spinsters, but they want to marry, too. They keep searching until they die.

"You just said that my wife is beautiful. Thank you. I cannot tell you how beautiful she was as a girl. We both come from Kielce. We belonged to the Youths of Zion—that's how we met. All the young men were in love with her—some desperately. I'm not much of a man physically—that's obvious—but I was more intelligent than the others, and Genia and I developed a strong love for each other. I would not serve in the Polish Army, so we came to America in 1924, the very day before America closed its doors on free immigration. We were poor as the night, and Genia went to work in a shop so that I could scribble my poems. She thought I was going to become a second Slowacki or Byron. Well, as my mother used to say, 'Those who think fool themselves.' I don't have to tell you what it means to be a Yiddish poet in New York. In my circumstances, Lord Byron would have become a landlord, too.

"I grew disenchanted with my creative powers slowly. But our love didn't suffer from this. What a woman sees in a man and what a man sees in a woman no third person can ever make out. No matter how difficult the day was, our evenings were always a holiday. No matter where we lived—Broome Street, Ocean Avenue, Brighton Beach—our apartment was always lovely. We both liked pretty things, and in those days you could get antiques on Third Avenue for a song. To our regret, we had no children. I became a Yiddish teacher and I earned a decent living. Once in a while, when an editor had to fill a hole, I got something published in a magazine. Genia became a forelady at her shop. We didn't spend every penny we earned. In the summer, we went to a hotel in the Catskills. We traveled through the United States. We even went to Europe. Still, I never made peace with my failure as a poet, and Genia suffered from it. One of our great pleasures was reading. I loved literature, and Genia couldn't exist without books. In the beginning, we read Yiddish and Polish, and later English, after we learned the language. I'm not boasting, but we both have good taste—remember the cantor who said, 'I can't sing, but I understand singing'? Genia's taste is even better than mine. It's curious how people who are dull and deaf are critics and professors of literature, while Genia, who has a perfect ear for words, is a shop worker. Well, it's all part of the hypocrisy of this world. Actually, neither Genia nor I overworked; her job left her plenty of free time, and in a Yiddish school there's not much to do. We had people for supper; we had little parties, usually with the same few friends. But we liked to be together best of all, and we often thanked God when our guests left. How many couples have such a life?

"But no matter how much I loved my wife, I was never indifferent to other women. I don't have to explain it to you. What defense do modern people have against indulgence? I wasn't pious, and even if I had been, having more than one woman was not a real sin according to the Jews. The interdiction against polygamy was forced on us by the Christians. I might not have been a Byron, but my appetite for women was as strong as his. You know our milieu. There were always opportunities. I never got seriously involved, but from time to time I made love to another woman. In the beginning, I kept it a secret from Genia, but Genia's instincts are sharp—sometimes I think she's a mind reader. When I finally confessed, she didn't make a big tragedy out of it. 'Do what you like, only come back to me,' she said. 'No woman can give you what I can.' Typical feminine talk. I also began to realize that my so-called adventures aroused a new desire in her. Nothing new in that, either.

"This is how it was for a good many years. Our evenings and nights were spent talking—fantasies, facts, the things we read in books. Like most men, I wanted my freedom when it came to other women, and at the same time I wanted my wife chaste. In the beginning Genia warned me that if I ran around she would try it, too. But time passed, and everything remained as it was. By nature, Genia is shy—the shyness that's inherited from God knows how many grandmothers. The thought of having anybody else made her shudder—she told me herself. 'What would happen if—' was a game we used to play. 'Suppose you found yourself in this situation—what would you do?' We often drew the situations from your stories in the Yiddish papers. I wonder if you realize how much literature influences life. We probably pondered your heroes more than you did yourself.

"I could sit with you until tomorrow and not tell you a thousandth of what happened. But I'll keep it short. Genia began to insist that there was no basic difference between the psychology of women and men, and she even talked about finding herself a man. I didn't take it seriously. Her banter excited me, and it's good to be stimulated. She wanted to know how I would feel if she met someone who attracted her and she succumbed in a heated moment. Would I run away from her—stop loving her? If I did, wouldn't that prove that I had a double standard? I assured her that I would not; as they say in English, what's sauce for the goose is sauce for the gander. But it didn't mean anything—Genia was constantly being propositioned and she constantly said no. She confessed that she had decided to get even with me—once, at least—just to convince herself that she was a modern woman and not a sleepy yenta from behind the stove.

"She developed a real complex. Why couldn't she do what Mme. Bovary, Anna Karenina, or your Hadassa and Clara did? In her shop, the girls kept boasting about their successes. Nowadays Satan doesn't need to strain his voice to tempt us. The nine muses do his work for him. And there was Genia, walking around like a sort of holy virgin. She started talking in a jargon she picked up from books by doctors and love experts about how backward she was.

"Don't laugh, but Genia demanded my help in getting a lover.

Isn't that crazy? She said, 'I can't do it without you. Find someone for me.' She wanted just once to taste what being 'progressive' is like. One night we sat down and actually wrote out a whole list of candidates. It was a game. I'm already past fifty and Genia's not much younger. We could be grandparents. Instead, there we were, awake at night making lists of possible lovers. Funny, isn't it?"

"Not so funny."

"Wait. I'm going to get myself a coffee."

Zelig Fingerbein brought two cups of coffee, one for himself and one for me. He took a sip and said, "In my reading, I often came on the word '*Hausfreund*'[1]—the wife's lover. I could never get the sense of it. Why would a man allow his wife to betray him? Why let him into the house to begin with? An invention of novelists and playwrights, I used to think. In Kielce, no one had this kind of arrangement. But here in America I saw that it exists—actors, doctors, businessmen. There actually are men who make friends of their wife's lover. They eat together, drink together, and go to the theater together. It was beyond my wildest imagining that it could happen to me, but I have a *Hausfreund* now, and that's why I'm sitting here with you. That's why I wanted to go to a movie. When he comes, I leave. I even leave before he comes. Perhaps he's not exactly a *Hausfreund*, but he comes to the house and I know about it.

"It began like this. A few years ago, a refugee from Poland turned up. You might know him, so I'll just use his first name—Max. He was supposed to be completely Polandized, but he spoke good Yiddish. He's a painter—that's what he claims, anyway. He makes a few smudges on a canvas and it's supposed to be a sunset in Zakopane or a bullfight in Mexico. The main thing is that people buy it. The modern consumer is as much a charlatan as the producer. If a figure stands on its feet, it's banal. But if you put it on its head it's original. I met him in the Café Royal. He's a slippery fellow, with eager eyes that beg for love, friendship—the devil knows what. We were introduced and he fell over me as if I had been his long-lost brother. Right away he wanted to paint my portrait. He told me he had family in Kielce, and it came out that I was a distant relative. As a rule, when men act overly friendly to me it's because of Genia and they don't make a secret of it, but Genia wasn't around when Max and I met, and when he finally saw her he acted indifferent. Genia was insulted. She's not accustomed to being ignored by men.

"Max painted my portrait and made me look half ape, half crocodile. That's all they can do. It turned out that he was a shrewd

1. Literally, house-friend.

businessman. He dealt in antiques and jewelry. He'd come to America only yesterday, and already he knew everybody and everybody knew him. He started offering us bargains: silver spice salvers, ivory pointers, ethrog boxes, snuffboxes, whatnot. Genia's crazy for bric-a-brac, and he sold them unusually cheap. Gradually, I realized that something wasn't right about him. It took him months to finish my portrait. He looked at me with longing eyes, and every chance he got he touched me. Once, he tried to kiss me. I was shocked. After a while, he told me straight out that he was in love with me. I wanted to vomit. I said to him, 'Max, don't make a fool of yourself. I'm as far from that sort of madness as Heaven is from Hell.' He began to sigh like a rejected lover.

"I told it all to Genia and she didn't know whether to laugh or cry. You read about such things, but it seems unbelievable when you meet them. Now we had a new topic to chatter about at night. Genia was outraged that I could be more attractive to a man than she. I decided to get rid of him—but how? Max is not a man to let go. He kept coming to see us, and every time he came he brought a present. He knew all the theater people—Broadway, not just Second Avenue—and he got us theater tickets. There we'd be, the three of us, sitting together in the first row watching a play we would have had to wait months to see. He took us to Lindy's and every place else. Is this the way one becomes a *Hausfreund*, I wondered. He tried to take my hand in the theater, but I told him that if he did anything like that again I would be through with him. The whole business disgusted me.

"But suddenly a kind of competition arose between me and Genia. It almost amused me. Here was a beautiful woman trying to get that goon's attention, and he kept gaping at me. When Genia spoke to him, he pretended not to hear; when I said even the most trivial thing, he cried out with enthusiasm. Can you imagine anything more ridiculous? But I began to realize that he was spoiling our family life. Every night, Genia and I figured out different excuses for getting him out of our lives. We made firm decisions. The next day, Max would call to say that he had a gift or a great bargain for us or some sensational story we had to hear. Before I could say no, Genia would have asked him for supper. I found out later that his antiques came from a factory that turned out reproductions. I also learned that most of his paintings were copies. This man was a fraud all the way through.

"I'm not going to draw it out. Genia started to meet him alone. She had given up her full-time job and worked only two days a week. In the meantime, I'd bought the building with the furnished rooms, and that took my attention. I no longer had any patience for that phony with his lovesick gazes. Genia still said terrible things about him, but apparently she wanted to steal him away from me. Actually, he acted like a woman. He gossiped, he loved gadgets, he wore rings with stones on almost all his fingers. His hair was long and shiny from hair oil. He was obsessed with clothes. I am the short one, not he, but he wore shoes with lifts. And his ties! What woman could put up with this? You'll say I'm naïve, but it never occurred to me that Genia would have an affair with him."

"An affair? Even though he's a homosexual?" I asked.

"The devil knows what he is. Since everything else about him is a fake, maybe that is, too. Maybe his flirtation with me was only a way of getting to Genia. He's a sly fox. Slowly, as I drew away from him, Genia and he became cronies. They had lunch, supper; they went to the theater and the movies together, to exhibitions. If I protested, Genia said, 'Who are you jealous of? He's more interested in you than he is in me.' The truth is, every time they went anywhere, I was invited, but I always refused. Genia swore to me that he never touched her, and I believed her. It went on like this for months. It's astonishing how capable men are of self-deceit. Besides, I was tired of all these movies, theaters, bargains. The apartment had to be painted, and where were we going to put the junk? Millions of things have been invented, but no one has found a way to avoid the crisis of painting an apartment. Suddenly all your belongings are moved out. Your paintings are taken down. Your books are in heaps on the floor. You become a stranger in your own house. The stench of the paint makes you sick. You see the bitter truth: that a home, like everything else, is just illusion.

"I began to feel that everything was falling apart, and then one night Genia confessed to me that she was having an affair with him."

Zelig Fingerbein finished off his cold coffee in one gulp. He looked at me reproachfully. "Why are you so shocked? You write like a modern man, but here you are with the old morals and prejudices. I had them once, but I freed myself. You can't condemn a modern woman to live her whole life with the same man even if she adores him. You couldn't find a more retiring woman than Genia, but she's living in the twentieth century and you can't require her to believe that Zelig Fingerbein is the only male in New York. Just the same, when Genia told me about her affair, it made me sick. I felt as if my whole life was destroyed. If I could, I would have dragged her to the Sanhedrin and had her stoned—the way it was done in ancient times. But there's no Sanhedrin in New York. I could have packed my belongings and left—but where would I have gone? And who would I have gone to? The night she told me, I lay in bed with Genia and she cried like a little girl. 'What should I do? If you are ready to die, I'll die with you—just to show you that I belong to you and not to anyone else.' She wailed and trembled so that the bed shook and—you can call me an idiot—I comforted her. I told her it was no tragedy, but my teeth were chattering.

"That night, we swore that our association with Max was over and done with, but I knew it wasn't. The creators of religion did not know God, but human nature they did know. It's written in Aboth that one sin drags another sin after it. One step off the accepted path and all taboos are broken.

"You write about religion, marriage, and sex. You seem to understand modern man with all his complexities and pitfalls. But all you can do is criticize—you can't show the way back to faith. It's impossible for us to conduct ourselves like our parents and grandparents without having their piety. I will tell you something, though I'm ashamed to admit it. That night, Genia finally fell asleep after she took a couple of pills, but I couldn't sleep a wink. I put on my robe and slippers and went into my study. I looked at my books and I knew that not one of them could give me direction. How can Tolstoy or Dickens or Balzac teach you? They had talent, but they were as confused as we are. Suddenly I saw a volume of the Talmud and I thought, Since worldliness has failed me so miserably, perhaps I should return to God. I took out the tractate of Betzah, opened it, and began to hum as in the old times. 'If an egg was laid on festival day, the school of Shammai say: It may be eaten. And the school of Hillel say: It may not be eaten.' I kept on nodding and humming like a yeshiva boy for a good half hour. In the beginning, it was nostalgically sweet, but the more I went on, the heavier my spirit felt. As long as one believed that these laws were given to Moses on Mount Sinai, there was meaning. Without this faith, it's all sheer scholasticism. I got tired and went back to Genia. We have one bed. That night, I came to the conclusion that men must kill in themselves their strongest instinct: the possession of a woman as a piece of property. If there is a God, maybe He's leading us in this direction."

"And what happened later?"

"There was no later. Genia had promised, although I hadn't demanded it of her, that she would never see Max again. But she still meets him. She has given up her work entirely. She doesn't need it any more, and I can't be with her day and night anyhow. Lately, I lost patience with everything: with Genia's guilt and with what we call culture. I can't make a fetish out of plays on Broadway and Picasso's paintings. Even good literature doesn't interest me any more. The wall that separates the world from the underworld has become too thin. The judge, the lawyer, and the murderer all nurture the same ideas, read the same books, visit the same nightclubs, talk the same gibberish. We're returning to the cave, even though it's a cave provided with telephone, electricity, and TV. I used to think that I knew Genia through and through, but since this freak invaded our house I keep discovering new traits in her. Even her voice doesn't seem the same. As for Max, I can't even hate him, and this really surprises me. I don't know what he is, and I don't care. All I know is that he wants the same thing we all want—as much pleasure as possible before disappearing forever."

"He's not a homosexual?"

"Who knows what he is! Perhaps we're all homosexuals. I've forgotten to tell you the main thing: Genia began to go to a psychoanalyst. Max has been going to him for years. They wanted to make me a member of the club with them, but I'd rather study about the egg that is laid on a festival day."

I hadn't noticed that the cafeteria had filled up. I said to Zelig, "Let's go. They'll throw us out."

We walked out on Broadway and the heat hit me like a furnace. It was still daylight but the neon signs were already lit, announcing in fiery language the bliss to be brought by Pepsi-Cola, Bond suits, Camel cigarettes, Wrigley's chewing gum. A tepid stench came up from the subway gratings. Over a movie house hung a billboard of a half-naked woman four stories high, lit up by spotlights—her hair disheveled, her eyes wild, her legs spread out, a gun in each hand. Around her waist was a fringed scarf that covered her private parts. A mob had collected to gape at her. Men made jokes, women giggled. I look at Zelig. Half his face was green, the other red—like a modern painting. He stared, moved his lips, one eye laughing and one tearing. I said to him, "If there is no God, she is our god."

Zelig Fingerbein shook as if he had been awakened from a trance. "What *she* is promising she can deliver."

# SINCLAIR ROSS
## 1908-

Sinclair Ross was born in Shellbrook, Saskatchewan, near Prince Albert, where his parents were homesteading. After his father's death in 1920, he moved with his mother and two other children to a series of small prairie towns. At sixteen he dropped out of school and took a job with the Royal Bank of Canada in Abbey, Saskatchewan. This became a permanent job, with subsequent postings to Winnipeg and Montreal. He retired in 1968, eventually settling in Europe, living in Athens, Barcelona, and most recently in Malaga, on Spain's southern coast. He published his first short story in 1934 but had continual difficulty establishing himself as a writer. He lives a rather reclusive life as a bachelor, avoiding literary circles and publishing little. *The Lamp at Noon and Other Stories* (1968), from which the following story is taken, explores the psychological effects of a hostile prairie environment on the small communities and farms of Ross's native province. He is at his best when writing of the tragic history of the 1930's Depression and drought.

# The Lamp at Noon

A little before noon she lit the lamp. Demented wind fled keening past the house: a wail through the eaves that died every minute or two. Three days now without respite it had held. The dust was thickening to an impenetrable fog.

She lit the lamp, then for a long time stood at the window motionless. In dim, fitful outline the stable and oat granary still were visible; beyond, obscuring fields and landmarks, the lower of dust clouds made the farmyard seem an isolated acre, poised aloft above a sombre void. At each blast of wind it shook, as if to topple and spin hurtling with the dust-reel into space.

From the window she went to the door, opening it a little, and peering toward the stable again. He was not coming yet. As she watched there was a sudden rift overhead, and for a moment through the tattered clouds the sun raced like a wizened orange. It shed a soft, diffused light, dim and yellow as if it were the light from the lamp reaching out through the open door.

She closed the door, and going to the stove tried the potatoes with a fork. Her eyes all the while were fixed and wide with a curious immobility. It was the window. Standing at it, she had let her forehead press against the pane until the eyes were strained apart and rigid. Wide like that they had looked out to the deepening ruin of the storm. Now she could not close them.

The baby started to cry. He was lying in a homemade crib over which she had arranged a tent of muslin. Careful not to disturb the folds of it, she knelt and tried to still him, whispering huskily in a singsong voice that he must hush and go to sleep again. She would have liked to rock him, to feel the comfort of his little body in her arms, but a fear had obsessed her that in the dust-filled air he might contract pneumonia. There was dust sifting everywhere. Her own throat was parched with it. The table had been set less than ten minutes, and already a film was gathering on the dishes. The little cry continued, and with wincing, frightened lips she glanced around as if to find a corner where the air was less oppressive. But while the lips winced the eyes maintained their wide, immobile stare. "Sleep," she whispered again. "It's too soon for you to be hungry. Daddy's coming for his dinner."

He seemed a long time. Even the clock, still a few minutes off noon, could not dispel a foreboding sense that he was longer than he should be. She went to the door again—and then recoiled slowly to stand white and breathless in the middle of the room. She mustn't. He would only despise her if she ran to the stable looking for him. There was too much grim endurance in his nature ever to let him understand the fear and weakness of a woman. She must stay quiet and wait. Nothing was wrong. At noon he would come—and perhaps after dinner stay with her awhile.

Yesterday, and again at breakfast this morning, they had quarrelled bitterly. She wanted him now, the assurance of his strength and nearness, but he would stand aloof, wary, remembering the words she had flung at him in her anger, unable to understand it was only the dust and wind that had driven her.

Tense, she fixed her eyes upon the clock, listening. There were two winds: the wind in flight, and the wind that pursued. The one sought refuge in the eaves, whimpering, in fear; the other assailed it there, and shook the eaves apart to make it flee again. Once as she listened this first wind sprang inside the room, distraught like a bird that has felt the graze of talons on its wing; while furious the other wind shook the walls, and thudded tumbleweeds against the window till its quarry glanced away again in fright. But only to return—to return and quake among the feeble eaves, as if in all this dust-mad wilderness it knew no other sanctuary.

Then Paul came. At his step she hurried to the stove, intent upon the pots and frying-pan. "The worst wind yet," he ventured, hanging up his cap and smock. "I had to light the lantern in the tool shed, too."

They looked at each other, then away. She wanted to go to him, to feel his arms supporting her, to cry a little just that he might soothe her, but because his presence made the menace of the wind seem less, she gripped herself and thought, "I'm in the right. I won't give in. For his sake, too, I won't."

He washed, hurriedly, so that a few dark welts of dust remained to indent upon his face a haggard strength. It was all she could see as she wiped the dishes and set the food before him: the strength, the grimness, the young Paul growing old and hard, buckled against a desert even grimmer than his will. "Hungry?" she asked, touched to a twinge of pity she had not intended. "There's dust in everything. It keeps coming faster than I can clean it up."

He nodded. "Tonight, though, you'll see it go down. This is the third day."

She looked at him in silence a moment, and then as if to herself muttered broodingly, "Until the next time. Until it starts again."

There was a dark resentment in her voice now that boded another quarrel. He waited, his eyes on her dubiously as she mashed a potato with her fork. The lamp between them threw strong lights and shadows on their faces. Dust and drought, earth that betrayed alike his labour and his faith, to him the struggle had given sternness, an impassive courage. Beneath the whip of sand his youth had been effaced. Youth, zest, exuberance—there remained only a harsh and clenched virility that yet became him, that seemed at the cost of more engaging qualities to be fulfilment of his inmost and essential nature. Whereas to her the same debts and poverty had brought a plaintive indignation, a nervous dread of what was still to come. The eyes were hollowed, the lips pinched dry and colourless. It was the face of a woman that had aged without maturing, that had loved the little vanities of life, and lost them wistfully.

"I'm afraid, Paul," she said suddenly. "I can't stand it any longer. He cries all the time. You will go, Paul—say you will. We aren't living here—not really living—"

The pleading in her voice now, after its shrill bitterness yesterday, made him think that this was only another way to persuade him. He answered evenly, "I told you this morning, Ellen; we keep on right where we are. At least I do. It's yourself you're thinking about, not the baby."

This morning such an accusation would have stung her to rage; now, her voice swift and panting, she pressed on, "Listen, Paul— I'm thinking of all of us—you, too. Look at the sky—what's happening. Are you blind? Thistles and tumbleweeds—it's a desert. You won't have a straw this fall. You won't be able to feed a cow or a chicken. Please, Paul, say we'll go away—"

"Go where?" His voice as he answered was still remote and even, inflexibly in unison with the narrowed eyes and the great hunch of muscle-knotted shoulder. "Even as a desert it's better than sweeping out your father's store and running his errands. That's all I've got ahead of me if I do what you want."

"And here—" she faltered. "What's ahead of you here? At least we'll get enough to eat and wear when you're sweeping out his store. Look at it—look at it, you fool. Desert—the lamp lit at noon—"

"You'll see it come back. There's good wheat in it yet."

"But in the meantime—year after year—can't you understand, Paul? We'll never get them back—"

He put down his knife and fork and leaned toward her across the table. "I can't go, Ellen. Living off your people—charity—stop and think of it. This is where I belong. I can't do anything else."

"Charity!" she repeated him, letting her voice rise in derision. "And this—you call this independence! Borrowed money you can't even pay the interest on, seed from the government—grocery bills— doctor bills—"

"We'll have crops again," he persisted. "Good crops—the land will come back. It's worth waiting for."

"And while we're waiting, Paul!" It was not anger now, but a kind of sob. "Think of me—and him. It's not fair. We have our lives, too, to live."

"And you think that going home to your family—taking your husband with you—"

"I don't care—anything would be better than this. Look at the air he's breathing. He cries all the time. For his sake, Paul. What's ahead of him here, even if you do get crops?"

He clenched his lips a minute, then, with his eyes hard and contemptuous, struck back, "As much as in town, growing up a pauper. You're the one who wants to go, it's not for his sake. You think that in town you'd have a better time—not so much work—more clothes—"

"Maybe—" She dropped her head defencelessly. "I'm young still. I like pretty things."

There was silence now—a deep fastness of it enclosed by rushing wind and creaking walls. It seemed the yellow lamplight cast a hush upon them. Through the haze of dusty air the walls receded, dimmed, and came again. At last she raised her head and said listlessly, "Go on—your dinner's getting cold. Don't sit and stare at me. I've said it all."

The spent quietness in her voice was even harder to endure than her anger. It reproached him, against his will insisted that he see and understand her lot. To justify himself he tried, "I was a poor man when you married me. You said you didn't mind. Farming's never been easy, and never will be."

"I wouldn't mind the work or the skimping if there was something to look forward to. It's the hopelessness—going on—watching the land blow away."

"The land's all right," he repeated. "The dry years won't last forever."

"But it's not just dry years, Paul!" The little sob in her voice gave way suddenly to a ring of exasperation. "Will you never see? It's the land itself—the soil. You've plowed and harrowed it until there's not a root or fibre left to hold it down. That's why the soil drifts—that's why in a year or two there'll be nothing left but the bare clay. If in the first place you farmers had taken care of your land—if you hadn't been so greedy for wheat every year—"

She had taught school before she married him, and of late in her anger there had been a kind of disdain, an attitude almost of condescension, as if she no longer looked upon the farmers as her equals. He sat still, his eyes fixed on the yellow lamp flame, and seeming to know how her words had hurt him, she went on softly, "I want to help you, Paul. That's why I won't sit quiet while you go on wasting your life. You're only thirty—you owe it to yourself as well as me."

He sat staring at the lamp without answering, his mouth sullen. It seemed indifference now, as if he were ignoring her, and stung to anger again she cried, "Do you ever think what my life is? Two rooms to live in—once a month to town, and nothing to spend when I get there. I'm still young—I wasn't brought up this way."

"You're a farmer's wife now. It doesn't matter what you used to be, or how you were brought up. You get enough to eat and wear. Just now that's all I can do. I'm not to blame that we've been dried out five years."

"Enough to eat!" she laughed back shrilly. "Enough salt pork— enough potatoes and eggs. And look—" Springing to the middle of the room she thrust out a foot for him to see the scuffed old slipper. "When they're completely gone I suppose you'll tell me I can go barefoot—that I'm a farmer's wife—that it's not your fault we're dried out—"

"And what about these?" He pushed his chair away from the table now to let her see what he was wearing. "Cowhide—hard as boards—but my feet are so calloused I don't feel them any more."

Then he stood up, ashamed of having tried to match her hardships with his own. But frightened now as he reached for his smock she pressed close to him. "Don't go yet. I brood and worry when I'm left alone. Please, Paul—you can't work on the land anyway."

"And keep on like this? You start before I'm through the door. Week in and week out—I've troubles enough of my own."

"Paul—please stay—" The eyes were glazed now, distended a little as if with the intensity of her dread and pleading. "We won't quarrel any more. Hear it! I can't work—I just stand still and listen—"

The eyes frightened him, but responding to a kind of instinct that he must withstand her, that it was his self-respect and manhood against the fretful weakness of a woman, he answered unfeelingly, "In here safe and quiet—you don't know how well off you are. If you were out in it—fighting it—swallowing it—"

"Sometimes, Paul, I wish I was. I'm caged—if I could only break away and run. See—I stand like this all day. I can't relax. My throat's so tight it aches—

With a jerk he freed his smock from her clutch. "If I stay we'll only keep on all afternoon. Wait till tomorrow—we'll talk things over when the wind goes down."

Then without meeting her eyes again he swung outside, and doubled low against the buffets of the wind, fought his way slowly toward the stable. There was a deep hollow calm within, a vast darkness engulfed beneath the tides of moaning wind. He stood breathless a moment, hushed almost to a stupor by the sudden extinction of the storm and the stillness that enfolded him. It was a long, far-reaching stillness. The first dim stalls and rafters led the way into cavern-like obscurity, into vaults and recesses that extended far beyond the stable walls. Nor in these first quiet moments did he forbid the illusion, the sense of release from a harsh, familiar world into one of peace and darkness. The contentious mood that his stand against Ellen had roused him to, his tenacity and clenched despair before the ravages of wind, it was ebbing now, losing itself in the cover of darkness. Ellen and the wheat seemed remote, unimportant. At a whinny from the bay mare, Bess, he went forward and into her stall. She seemed grateful for his presence, and thrust her nose deep between his arm and body. They stood a long time motionless, comforting and assuring each other.

For soon again the first deep sense of quiet and peace was shrunken to the battered shelter of the stable. Instead of release or escape from the assaulting wind, the walls were but a feeble stand against it. They creaked and sawed as if the fingers of a giant hand were tightening to collapse them; the empty loft sustained a pipelike cry that rose and fell but never ended. He saw the dust-black sky again, and his fields blown smooth with drifted soil.

But always, even while listening to the storm outside, he could feel the tense and apprehensive stillness of the stable. There was not a hoof that clumped or shifted, not a rub of halter against manger. And yet, though it had been a strange stable, he would have known, despite the darkness, that every stall was filled. They, too, were all listening.

From Bess he went to the big grey gelding, Prince. Prince was twenty years old, with rib-grooved sides, and high, protruding hipbones. Paul ran his hand over the ribs, and felt a sudden shame, a sting of fear that Ellen might be right in what she said. For wasn't it true—nine years a farmer now on his own land, and still he couldn't even feed his horses? What, then, could he hope to do for his wife and son?

There was much he planned. And so vivid was the future of his planning, so real and constant, that often the actual present was but half felt, but half endured. Its difficulties were lessened by a confidence in what lay beyond them. A new house—land for the boy—land and still more land—or education, whatever he might want.

But all the time was he only a blind and stubborn fool? Was Ellen right? Was he trampling on her life, and throwing away his own? The five years since he married her, were they to go on repeating themselves, five, ten, twenty, until all the brave future he looked forward to was but a stark and futile past?

She looked forward to no future. She had no faith or dream with which to make the dust and poverty less real. He understood suddenly. He saw her face again as only a few minutes ago it had begged him not to leave her. The darkness round him now was as a slate on which her lonely terror limned itself. He went from Prince to the other horses, combing their manes and forelocks with his fingers, but always it was her face before him, its staring eyes and twisted suffering. "See Paul—I stand like this all day. I just stand still—My throat's so tight it aches—"

And always the wind, the creak of walls, the wild lipless wailing through the loft. Until at last as he stood there, staring into the livid face before him, it seemed that this scream of wind was a cry from her parched and frantic lips. He knew it couldn't be, he knew that she was safe within the house, but still the wind persisted as a woman's cry. The cry of a woman with eyes like those that watched him through the dark. Eyes that were mad now—lips that even as they cried still pleaded, "See, Paul—I stand like this all day. I just stand still—so caged! If I could only run!"

He saw her running, pulled and driven headlong by the wind, but when at last he returned to the house, compelled by his anxiety, she was walking quietly back and forth with the baby in her arms. Careful, despite his concern, not to reveal a fear or weakness that she might think capitulation to her wishes, he watched a moment through the window, and then went off to the tool shed to mend harness. All afternoon he stitched and riveted. It was easier with the lantern lit and his hands occupied. There was a wind whining high past the tool shed too, but it was only wind. He remembered the arguments with which Ellen had tried to persuade him away from the farm, and one by one he defeated them. There would be rain again—next year or the next. Maybe in his ignorance he had farmed his land the wrong way, seeding wheat every year, working the soil till it was lifeless dust—but he would do better now. He would plant clover and alfalfa, breed cattle, acre by acre and year by year restore his land its fibre and fertility. That was something to work for, a way to prove himself. It was ruthless wind, blackening the sky with his earth, but it was not his master. Out of his land it had made a wilderness. He now, out of the wilderness, would make a farm and home again.

Tonight he must talk with Ellen. Patiently, when the wind was down, and they were both quiet again. It was she who had told him to grow fibrous crops, who had called him an ignorant fool because he kept on with summer fallow and wheat. Now she might be gratified to find him acknowledging her wisdom. Perhaps she would begin to feel the power and steadfastness of the land, to take a pride in it, to understand that he was not a fool, but working for her future and their son's.

And already the wind was slackening. At four o'clock he could sense a lull. At five, straining his eyes from the tool shed doorway, he could make out a neighbour's buildings half a mile away. It was over—three days of blight and havoc like a scourge—three days so bitter and so long that for a moment he stood still, unseeing, his senses idle with a numbness of relief.

But only for a moment. Suddenly he emerged from the numbness; suddenly the fields before him struck his eyes to comprehension. They lay black, naked. Beaten and mounded smooth with dust as if a sea in gentle swell had turned to stone. And though he had tried to prepare himself for such a scene, though he had known since yesterday that not a blade would last the storm, still now, before the utter waste confronting him, he sickened and stood cold. Suddenly like the fields he was naked. Everthing that had sheathed him a little from the realities of existence: vision and purpose, faith in the land, in the future, in himself—it was all rent now, stripped away. "Desert," he heard her voice begin to sob. "Desert, you fool—the lamp lit at noon!"

In the stable again, measuring out their feed to the horses, he wondered what he would say to her tonight. For so deep were his instincts of loyalty to the land that still, even with the images of his betrayal stark upon his mind, his concern was how to withstand her, how to go on again and justify himself. It had not occurred to him yet that he might or should abandon the land. He had lived with it too long. Rather was his impulse still to defend it—as a man defends against the scorn of strangers even his most worthless kin.

He fed his horses, then waited. She too would be waiting, ready to cry at him, "Look now—that crop was to feed and clothe us! And you'll still keep on! You'll still say 'Next year—there'll be rain next year'!"

But she was gone when he reached the house. The door was open the lamp blown out, the crib empty. The dishes from their meal at noon were still on the table. She had perhaps begun to sweep, for the broom was lying in the middle of the floor. He tried to call, but a terror clamped upon on his throat. In the wan, returning light it seemed that even the deserted kitchen was straining to whisper what it had seen. The tatters of the storm still whimpered through the eaves, and in their moaning told the desolation of the miles they had traversed. On tiptoe at last he crossed to the adjoining room; then at the threshold, without even a glance inside to satisfy himself that she was really gone, he wheeled again and plunged outside.

He ran a long time—distraught and headlong as a few hours ago he had seemed to watch her run—around the farmyard, a little distance into the pasture, back again blindly to the house to see whether she had returned—and then at a stumble down the road for help.

They joined him in the search, rode away for others, spread calling across the fields in the direction she might have been carried by the wind—but nearly two hours later it was himself who came upon her. Crouched down against a drift of sand as if for shelter, her hair in matted strands around her neck and face, the child clasped tighly in her arms.

The child was quite cold. It had been her arms, perhaps, too frantic to protect him, or the smother of dust upon his throat and lungs. "Hold him," she said as he knelt beside her. "So—with his face away from the wind. Hold him until I tidy my hair."

Her eyes were still wide in an immobile stare, but with her lips she smiled at him. For a long time he knelt transfixed, trying to speak to her, touching fearfully with his fingertips the dust-grimed cheeks and eyelids of the child. At last she said, "I'll take him again. Such clumsy hands—you don't know how to hold a baby yet. See how his head falls forward on your arm."

Yet it all seemed familiar—a confirmation of what he had known since noon. He gave her the child, then, gathering them up in his arms, struggled to his feet, and turned toward home.

It was evening now. Across the fields a few spent clouds of dust still shook and fled. Beyond, as if through smoke, the sunset smouldered like a distant fire.

He walked with a long dull stride, his eyes before him, heedless of her weight. Once he glanced down with her eyes she still was smiling, "Such strong arms, Paul—and I was so tired just carrying him. . . ."

He tried to answer, but it seemed that now the dusk was drawn apart in breathless waiting, a finger on its lips until they passed. "You were right, Paul. . . ." Her voice came whispering, as if she too could feel the hush. "You said tonight we'd see the storm go down. So still now, and a red sky—it means tomorrow will be fine."

# EUDORA WELTY

1909–

Born in Jackson, Mississippi, where her father was president of an insurance company, she went to schools there, then to the Mississippi College for Women. She broke out of her home region to finish college at the University of Wisconsin in 1929, after which she studied at the Columbia University School of Advertising in 1930 and 1931. She returned to Mississippi and worked for various radio stations and newspapers, as well as for the WPA. She began writing fiction in the 1930's, publishing her first collection, *A Curtain of Green*, in 1941. Since then she has led a quiet life in Mississippi, writing and publishing her uniquely perceptive and humorous stories and novels at regular intervals.

## Why I Live at the P.O.

I was getting along fine with Mama, Papa-Daddy and Uncle Rondo until my sister Stella-Rondo just separated from her husband and came back home again. Mr. Whitaker! Of course I went with Mr. Whitaker first, when he first appeared here in China Grove, taking "Pose Yourself" photos, and Stella-Rondo broke us up. Told him I was one-sided. Bigger on one side than the other, which is a deliberate, calculated falsehood: I'm the same. Stella-Rondo is exactly twelve months to the day younger than I am and for that reason she's spoiled.

She's always had anything in the world she wanted and then she'd throw it away. Papa-Daddy gave her this gorgeous Add-a-Pearl necklace when she was eight years old and she threw it away playing baseball when she was nine, with only two pearls.

So as soon as she got married and moved away from home the first thing she did was separate! From Mr. Whitaker! This photographer with the popeyes she said she trusted. Came home from one of those towns up in Illinois and to our complete surprise brought this child of two.

Mama said she like to make her drop dead for a second. "Here you had this marvelous blond child and never so much as wrote your mother a word about it," says Mamma. "I'm thoroughly ashamed of you." But of course she wasn't.

Stella-Rondo just calmly takes off this *hat*, I wish you could see it. She says, "Why, Mama, Shirley-T.'s adopted, I can prove it."

"How?" says Mama, but all I says was, "H'm!" There I was over the hot stove, trying to stretch two chickens over five people and a completely unexpected child into the bargain, without one moment's notice.

"What do you mean—'H'm!'?" says Stella-Rondo, and Mama says, "I heard that, Sister."

I said that oh, I didn't mean a thing, only that whoever Shirley-T. was, she was the spit-image of Papa-Daddy if he'd cut off his beard, which of course he'd never do in the world. Papa-Daddy's Mama's papa and sulks.

Stella-Rondo got furious! She said, "Sister, I don't need to tell you you got a lot of nerve and always did have and I'll thank you to make no future reference to my adopted child whatsoever."

"Very well," I said. "Very well, very well. Of course I noticed at once she looks like Mr. Whitaker's side too. That frown. She looks like a cross between Mr. Whitaker and Papa-Daddy."

"Well, all I can say is she isn't."

"She looks exactly like Shirley Temple to me," says Mama, but Shirley-T. just ran away from her.

So the first thing Stella-Rondo did at the table was turn Papa-Daddy against me.

"Papa-Daddy," she says. He was trying to cut up his meat. "Papa-Daddy!" I was taken completely by surprise. Papa-Daddy is about a million years old and's got this long-long beard. "Papa-Daddy, Sister says she fails to understand why you don't cut off your beard."

So Papa-Daddy l-a-y-s down his knife and fork! He's real rich. Mama says he is, he says he isn't. So he says, "Have I heard correctly? You don't understand why I don't cut off my beard?"

"Why," I says, "Papa-Daddy, of course I understand, I did not say any such of a thing, the idea!"

He says, "Hussy!"

I says, "Papa-Daddy, you know I wouldn't any more want you to cut off your beard than the man in the moon. It was the farthest thing from my mind! Stella-Rondo sat there and made that up while she was eating breast of chicken."

But he says, "So the postmistress fails to understand why I don't cut off my beard. Which job I got you through my influence with the government. 'Bird's nest'—is that what you call it?"

Not that it isn't the next to smallest P.O. in the entire state of Mississippi.

I says, "Oh, Papa-Daddy," I says, "I didn't say any such of a thing, I never dreamed it was a bird's nest, I have always been grateful though this is the next to smallest P.O. in the state of Mississippi, and I do not enjoy being referred to as a hussy by my own grandfather."

But Stella-Rondo says, "Yes, you did say it too. Anybody in the world could of heard you, that had ears."

"Stop right there," says Mama, looking at *me*.

So I pulled my napkin straight back through the napkin ring and left the table.

As soon as I was out of the room Mama says, "Call her back, or she'll starve to death," but Papa-Daddy says, "This is the beard I started growing on the Coast when I was fifteen years old." He would of gone on till nightfall if Shirley-T. hadn't lost the Milky Way she ate in Cairo.

So Papa-Daddy says, "I am going out and lie in the hammock, and you can all sit here and remember my words: I'll never cut off my beard as long as I live, even one inch, and I don't appreciate it in you at all." Passed right by me in the hall and went straight out and got in the hammock.

It would be a holiday. It wasn't five minutes before Uncle Rondo suddenly appeared in the hall in one of Stella-Rondo's flesh-colored kimonos, all cut on the bias, like something Mr. Whitaker probably thought was gorgeous.

"Uncle Rondo!" I says. "I didn't know who that was! Where are you going?"

"Sister," he says, "get out of my way, I'm poisoned."

"If you're poisoned stay away from Papa-Daddy," I says. "Keep out of the hammock, Papa-Daddy will certainly beat you on the head if you come within forty miles of him. He thinks I deliberately said he ought to cut off his beard after he got me the P.O., and I've told him and told him and told him, and he acts like he just don't hear me. Papa-Daddy must of gone stone deaf."

"He picked a fine day to do it then," says Uncle Rondo, and before you could say "Jack Robinson" flew out in the yard.

What he'd really done, he'd drunk another bottle of that prescription. He does it every single Fourth of July as sure as shooting, and it's horribly expensive. Then he falls over in the hammock and snores. So he insisted on zigzagging right on out to the hammock, looking like a half-wit.

Papa-Daddy woke up with this horrible yell and right there without moving an inch he tried to turn Uncle Rondo against me. I heard every word he said. Oh, he told Uncle Rondo I didn't learn to read till I was eight years old and he didn't see how in the world I ever got the mail put up at the P.O., much less read it all, and he said if Uncle Rondo could only fathom the lengths he had gone to to get me that job! And he said on the other hand he thought Stella-Rondo had a brilliant mind and deserved credit for getting out of town. All the time he was just lying there swinging as pretty as you please and looping out his beard, and poor Uncle Rondo was *pleading* with him to slow down the hammock, it was making him as dizzy as a witch to watch it. But that's what Papa-Daddy likes about a hammock. So Uncle Rondo was too dizzy to get turned against me for the time being. He's Mama's only brother and is a good case of a one-track mind. Ask anybody. A certified pharmacist.

Just then I heard Stella-Rondo raising the upstairs window. While she was married she got this peculiar idea that it's cooler with the windows shut and locked. So she has to raise the window before she can make a soul hear her outdoors.

So she raises the window and says, "*Oh!*" You would have thought she was mortally wounded.

Uncle Rondo and Papa-Daddy didn't even look up, but kept right on with what they were doing. I had to laugh.

I flew up the stairs and threw the door open! I says, "What in the wide world's the matter, Stella-Rondo? You mortally wounded?"

"No," she says, "I'm not mortally wounded but I wish you would do me the favor of looking out that window there and telling me what you see."

So I shade my eyes and look out the window.

"I see the front yard," I says.

"Don't you see any human beings?" she says.

"I see Uncle Rondo trying to run Papa-Daddy out of the hammock," I says. "Nothing more. Naturally, it's so suffocating-hot in the house, with all the windows shut and locked, everybody who cares to stay in their right mind will have to go out and get in the hammock before the Fourth of July is over."

"Don't you notice anything different about Uncle Rondo?" asks Stella-Rondo.

"Why, no, except he's got on some terrible-looking flesh-colored contraption I wouldn't be found dead in, is all I can see," I says.

"Never mind, you won't be found dead in it, because it happens to be part of my trousseau, and Mr. Whitaker took several dozen photographs of me in it," says Stella-Rondo. "What on earth could Uncle Rondo *mean* by wearing part of my trousseau out in the broad open daylight without saying so much as 'Kiss my foot,' *knowing* I only got home this morning after my separation and hung my negligee up on the bathroom door, just as nervous as I could be?"

"I'm sure I don't know, and what do you expect me to do about it?" I says. "Jump out the window?"

"No, I expect nothing of the kind. I simply declare that Uncle Rondo looks like a fool in it, that's all," she says. "It makes me sick to my stomach."

"Well, he looks as good as he can," I says. "As good as anybody in reason could." I stood up for Uncle Rondo, please remember. And I said to Stella-Rondo, "I think I would do well not to criticize so freely if I were you and came home with a two-year-old child I had never said a word about, and no explanation whatever about my separation."

"I asked you the instant I entered this house not to refer one more time to my adopted child, and you gave me your word of honor you would not," was all Stella-Rondo would say, and started pulling out every one of her eyebrows with some cheap Kress tweezers.

So I merely slammed the door behind me and went down and made some green-tomato pickle. Somebody had to do it. Of course Mama had turned both the niggers loose; she always said no earthly power could hold one anyway on the Fourth of July, so she wouldn't even try. It turned out that Jaypan fell in the lake and came within a very narrow limit of drowning.

So Mama trots in. Lifts up the lid and says, "H'm! Not very good for your Uncle Rondo in his precarious condition, I must say. Or poor little adopted Shirley-T. Shame on you!"

That made me tired. I says, "Well, Stella-Rondo had better thank her lucky stars it was her instead of me came trotting in with that very peculiar-looking child. Now if it had been me that trotted in from Illinois and brought a peculiar-looking child of two, I shudder to think of ̀he reception I'd of got, much less controlled the diet of an entire family."

"But you must remember, Sister, that you were never married to Mr. Whitaker in the first place and didn't go up to Illinois to live," says Mama, shaking a spoon in my face. "If you had I would of been just as overjoyed to see you and your little adopted girl as I was to see Stella-Rondo, when you wound up with your separation and came on back home."

"You would not," I says.

"Don't contradict me, I would," says Mama.

But I said she couldn't convince me though she talked till she was blue in the face. Then I said, "Besides, you know as well as I do that that child is not adopted."

"She most certainly is adopted," says Mama, stiff as a poker.

I says, "Why, Mama, Stella-Rondo had her just as sure as anything in this world, and just too stuck up to admit it."

"Why, Sister," said Mama. "Here I thought we were going to have a pleasant Fourth of July, and you start right out not believing a word your own baby sister tells you!"

"Just like Cousin Annie Flo. Went to her grave denying the facts of life," I remind Mama.

"I told you if you ever mentioned Annie Flo's name I'd slap your face," says Mama, and slaps my face.

"All right, you wait and see," I says.

"I," says Mama, "I prefer to take my children's word for anything when it's humanly possible." You ought to see Mama, she weighs two hundred pounds and has real tiny feet.

Just then something perfectly horrible occurred to me.

"Mama," I says, "can that child talk?" I simply had to whisper! "Mama, I wonder if that child can be—you know—in any way? Do you realize," I says, "that she hasn't spoken one single, solitary word to a human being up to this minute? This is the way she looks," I says, and I looked like this.

Well, Mama and I just stood there and stared at each other. It was horrible!

"I remember well that Joe Whitaker frequently drank like a fish," says Mama. "I believed to my soul he drank *chemicals*." And without another word she marches to the foot of the stairs and calls Stella-Rondo.

"Stella-Rondo? O-o-o-o-o! Stella-Rondo!"

"What?" says Stella-Rondo from upstairs. Not even the grace to get up off the bed.

"Can that child of yours talk?" asks Mama.

Stella-Rondo says, "Can she what?"

"Talk! Talk!" says Mama. "Burdyburdyburdyburdy!"

So Stella-Rondo yells back, "Who says she can't talk?"

"Sister says so," says Mama

"You didn't have to tell me, I know whose word of honor don't mean a thing in this house," says Stella-Rondo.

And in a minute the loudest Yankee voice I ever heard in my life yells out, "OE'm Pop-OE the Sailor-r-r-r Ma-a-an!" and then somebody jumps up and down in the upstairs hall. In another second the house would of fallen down.

"Not only talks, she can tap-dance!" calls Stella-Rondo. "Which is more than some people I won't name can do."

"Why, the little precious darling thing!" Mama says, so surprised. "Just as smart as she can be!" Starts talking baby talk right there. Then she turns on me. "Sister, you ought to be thoroughly ashamed! Run upstairs this instant and apologize to Stella-Rondo and Shirley-T."

"Apologize for what?" I says. "I merely wondered if the child was normal, that's all. Now that she's proved she is, why, I have nothing further to say."

But Mama just turned on her heel and flew out, furious. She ran right upstairs and hugged the baby. She believed it was adopted. Stella-Rondo hadn't done a thing but turn her against me from upstairs while I stood there helpless over the hot stove. So that made Mama, Papa-Daddy and the baby all on Stella-Rondo's side.

Next, Uncle Rondo.

I must say that Uncle Rondo has been marvelous to me at various times in the past and I was completely unprepared to be made to jump out of my skin, the way it turned out. Once Stella-Rondo did something perfectly horrible to him—broke a chain letter from Flanders Field—and he took the radio back he had given her and gave it to me. Stella-Rondo was furious! For six months we all had to call her

Stella instead of Stella-Rondo, or she wouldn't answer. I always thought Uncle Rondo had all the brains of the entire family. Another time he sent me to Mammoth Cave, with all expenses paid.

But this would be the day he was drinking that prescription, the Fourth of July.

So at supper Stella-Rondo speaks up and says she thinks Uncle Rondo ought to try to eat a little something. So finally Uncle Rondo said he would try a little cold biscuits and ketchup, but that was all. So *she* brought it to him.

"Do you think it wise to disport with ketchup in Stella-Rondo's flesh-colored kimono?" I says. Trying to be considerate! If Stella-Rondo couldn't watch out for her trousseau, somebody had to.

"Any objections?" asks Uncle Rondo, just about to pour out all the ketchup.

"Don't mind what she says, Uncle Rondo," says Stella-Rondo. "Sister has been devoting this solid afternoon to sneering out my bedroom window at the way you look."

"What's that?" says Uncle Rondo. Uncle Rondo has got the most terrible temper in the world. Anything is liable to make him tear the house down if it comes at the wrong time.

So Stella-Rondo says, "Sister says, 'Uncle Rondo certainly does look like a fool in that pink kimono!' "

Do you remember who it was really said that?

Uncle Rondo spills out all the ketchup and jumps out of his chair and tears off the kimono and throws it down on the dirty floor and puts his foot on it. It had to be sent all the way to Jackson to the cleaners and re-pleated.

"So that's your opinion of your Uncle Rondo, is it?" he says. "I look like a fool, do I? Well, that's the last straw. A whole day in this house with nothing to do, and then to hear you come out with a remark like that behind my back!"

"I didn't say any such of a thing, Uncle Rondo," I says, "and I'm not saying who did, either. Why, I think you look all right. Just try to take care of yourself and not talk and eat at the same time," I says. "I think you better go lie down."

"Lie down my foot," says Uncle Rondo. I ought to of known by that he was fixing to do something perfectly horrible.

So he didn't do anything that night in the precarious state he was in—just played Casino with Mama and Stella-Rondo and Shirley-T. and gave Shirley-T. a nickel with a head on both sides. It tickled her nearly to death, and she called him "Papa." But at 6:30 A.M. the next morning, he threw a whole five-cent package of some unsold one-inch firecrackers from the store as hard as he could into my bedroom and they every one went off. Not one bad one in the string. Anybody else, there'd be one that wouldn't go off.

Well, I'm just terribly susceptible to noise of any kind, the doctor has always told me I was the most sensitive person he had ever seen in his whole life, and I was simply prostrated. I couldn't eat! People tell me they heard it as far as the cemetery, and old Aunt Jep Patterson, that had been holding her own so good, thought it was Judgment Day and she was going to meet her whole family. It's usually so quiet here.

And I'll tell you it didn't take me any longer than a minute to make up my mind what to do. There I was with the whole entire house on Stella-Rondo's side and turned against me. If I have anything at all I have pride.

So I just decided I'd go straight down to the P.O. There's plenty of room there in the back, I says to myself.

Well! I made no bones about letting the family catch on to what I was up to. I didn't try to conceal it.

The first thing they knew, I marched in where they were all playing Old Maid and pulled the electric oscillating fan out by the plug, and everything got real hot. Next I snatched the pillow I'd done the needlepoint on right off the davenport from behind Papa-Daddy. He went "Ugh!" I beat Stella-Rondo up the stairs and finally found my charm bracelet in her bureau drawer under a picture of Nelson Eddy.

"So that's the way the land lies," says Uncle Rondo. There he was, piecing on the ham. "Well, Sister, I'll be glad to donate my army cot if you got any place to set it up, providing you'll leave right this minute and let me get some peace." Uncle Rondo was in France.

"Thank you kindly for the cot and 'peace' is hardly the word I would select if I had to resort to firecrackers at 6:30 A.M. in a young girl's bedroom," I says back to him. "And as to where I intend to go, you seem to forget my position as postmistress of China Grove, Mississippi," I says. "I've always got the P.O."

Well, that made them all sit up and take notice.

I went out front and started digging up some four-o'clocks to plant around the P.O.

"Ah-ah-ah!" says Mama, raising the window. "Those happen to be my four-o'clocks. Everything planted in that star is mine. I've never known you to make anything grow in your life."

"Very well," I says. "But I take the fern. Even you, Mama, can't stand there and deny that I'm the one watered that fern. And I happen to know where I can send in a box top and get a packet of one thousand mixed seeds, no two the same kind, free."

"Oh, where?" Mama wants to know.

But I says, "Too late. You 'tend to your house, and I'll 'tend to mine. You hear things like that all the time if you know how to listen to the radio. Perfectly marvelous offers. Get anything you want free."

So I hope to tell you I marched in and got that radio, and they could of all bit a nail in two, especially Stella-Rondo, that it used to belong to, and she well knew she couldn't get it back, I'd sue for it like a shot. And I very politely took the sewing-machine motor I helped pay the most on to give Mama for Christmas back in 1929, and a good big calendar, with the first-aid remedies on it. The thermometer and the Hawaiian ukulele certainly were rightfully mine, and I stood on the step-ladder and got all my watermelon-rind preserves and every fruit and vegetable I'd put up, every jar. Then I began to pull the tacks out of the bluebird wall vases on the archway to the dining room.

"Who told you you could have those, Miss Priss?" says Mama, fanning as hard as she could.

"I bought 'em and I'll keep track of 'em," I says. "I'll tack 'em up one on each side the post-office window, and you can see 'em when you come to ask me for your mail, if you're so dead to see 'em."

"Not I! I'll never darken the door to that post office again if I live to be a hundred," Mama says. "Ungrateful child! After all the money we spent on you at the Normal."

"Me either," says Stella-Rondo. "You can just let my mail lie there and *rot*, for all I care. I'll never come and relieve you of a single, solitary piece."

"I should worry," I says. "And who you think's going to sit down and write you all those big fat letters and postcards, by the way? Mr. Whitaker? Just because he was the only man ever dropped down in China Grove and you got him—unfairly—is he going to sit down and write you a lengthy correspondence after you come home giving no rhyme nor reason whatsoever for your separation and no explanation for the presence of that child? I may not have your brilliant mind, but I fail to see it."

So Mama says, "Sister, I've told you a thousand times that Stella-Rondo simply got homesick, and this child is far too big to be hers," and she says, "Now, why don't you all just sit down and play Casino?"

Then Shirley-T. sticks out her tongue at me in this perfectly horrible way. She has no more manners than the man in the moon. I told her she was going to cross her eyes like that some day and they'd stick.

"It's too late to stop me now," I says. "You should have tried that yesterday. I'm going to the P.O. and the only way you can possibly see me is to visit me there."

So Papa-Daddy says, "You'll never catch me setting foot in that post office, even if I should take a notion into my head to write a letter some place." He says, "I won't have you reachin' out of that little old window with a pair of shears and cuttin' off any beard of mine. I'm too smart for you!"

"We all are," says Stella-Rondo.

But I said, "If you're so smart, where's Mr. Whitaker?"

So then Uncle Rondo says, "I'll thank you from now on to stop reading all the orders I get on postcards and telling everybody in China Grove what you think is the matter with them," but I says, "I draw my own conclusions and will continue in the future to draw them." I says, "If people want to write their inmost secrets on penny postcards, there's nothing in the wide world you can do about it, Uncle Rondo."

"And if you think we'll ever *write* another postcard you're sadly mistaken," says Mama.

"Cutting off your nose to spite your face then," I says. "But if you're all determined to have no more to do with the U.S. mail, think of this: What will Stella-Rondo do now, if she wants to tell Mr. Whitaker to come after her?"

"Wah!" says Stella-Rondo. I knew she'd cry. She had a conniption fit right there in the kitchen.

"It will be interesting to see how long she holds out," I says. "And now--I am leaving."

"Good-bye," says Uncle Rondo.

"Oh, I declare," says Mama, "to think that a family of mine should quarrel on the Fourth of July, or the day after, over Stella-Rondo leaving old Mr. Whitaker and having the sweetest little adopted child! It looks like we'd all be glad!"

"Wah!" says Stella-Rondo, and has a fresh conniption fit.

"*He* left *her*—you mark my words," I says. "That's Mr. Whitaker. I know Mr. Whitaker. After all, I knew him first. I said from the beginning he'd up and leave her. I foretold every single thing that's happened."

"Where did he go?" asks Mama.

"Probably to the North Pole, if he knows what's good for him," I says.

But Stella-Rondo just bawled and wouldn't say another word. She flew to her room and slammed the door.

"Now look what you've gone and done, Sister," says Mama. "You go apologize."

"I haven't got time, I'm leaving," I says.

"Well, what are you waiting around for?" asks Uncle Rondo.

So I just picked up the kitchen clock and marched off, without saying "Kiss my foot" or anything, and never did tell Stella-Rondo good-bye.

There was a nigger girl going along on a little wagon right in front.

"Nigger girl," I says, "come help me haul these things down the hill, I'm going to live in the post office."

Took her nine trips in her express wagon. Uncle Rondo came out on the porch and threw her a nickel.

And that's the last I've laid eyes on any of my family or my family laid eyes on me for five solid days and nights. Stella-Rondo may be telling the most horrible tales in the world about Mr. Whitaker, but I haven't heard them. As I tell everybody, I draw my own conclusions.

But oh, I like it here. It's ideal, as I've been saying. You see, I've got everything cater-cornered, the way I like it. Hear the radio? All the war news. Radio, sewing machine, book ends, ironing board and that great big piano lamp—peace, that's what I like. Butter-bean vines planted all along the front where the strings are.

Of course, there's not much mail. My family are naturally the main people in China Grove, and if they prefer to vanish from the face of the earth, for all the mail they get or the mail they write, why, I'm not going to open my mouth. Some of the folks here in town are taking up for me and some turned against me. I know which is which. There are always people who will quit buying stamps just to get on the right side of Papa-Daddy.

But here I am, and here I'll stay. I want the world to know I'm happy.

And if Stella-Rondo should come to me this minute, on bended knees, and *attempt* to explain the incidents of her life with Mr. Whitaker, I'd simply put my fingers in both my ears and refuse to listen.

# JOHN CHEEVER
## 1912–1982

He was born in Quincy, Massachusetts, where his father owned a shoe factory until the economic disaster of 1929 wiped him out. His father's ancestors were seafarers, going back to the Revolution. His mother was English. After the crash she opened a gift shop that was quite successful. He went to school in Massachusetts until he was expelled from Thayer Academy for bad behavior. His first story, "Expelled," appeared in the *New Republic* a few months later in 1930. He was a writer from the beginning, living and working in Boston, New York, and the Yaddo writer's colony in Saratoga Springs. He was poor, surviving with help from his brother and by doing odd jobs. But he had published almost forty stories when he joined the U.S. Army for World War II. His first collection of stories was published during the war, but his first real success came with his second collection, *The Enormous Radio*, in 1953. By then he was writing for the *New Yorker*, where he has placed well over a hundred stories since his first acceptance in 1940. He married in 1941 and is the father of three children. He lives in upstate New York. His reputation as a writer has grown steadily, so that the publication of his collected *Stories of John Cheever* in 1979 was a major literary event. He has written novels, but the short story is his form.

# The Swimmer

It was one of those midsummer Sundays when everyone sits around saying, "I *drank* too much last night." You might have heard it whispered by the parishioners leaving church, heard it from the lips of the priest himself, struggling with his cassock in the *vestiarium*, heard it from the golf links and the tennis courts, heard it from the wild-life preserve where the leader of the Audubon group was suffering from a terrible hangover. "I *drank* too much," said Donald Westerhazy. "We all *drank* too much," said Lucinda Merrill. "It must have been the wine," said Helen Westerhazy. "I *drank* too much of that claret."

This was at the edge of the Westerhazy's pool. The pool, fed by an artesian well with a high iron content, was a pale shade of green. It was a fine day. In the west there was a massive stand of cumulus cloud so like a city seen from a distance—from the bow of an approaching ship—that it might have had a name. Lisbon. Hackensack. The sun was hot. Neddy Merrill sat by the green water, one hand in it, one around a glass of gin. He was a slender man—he seemed to have the especial slenderness of youth—and while he was far from young he had slid down his banister that morning and given the bronze backside of Aphrodite on the hall table a smack, as he jogged toward the smell of coffee in his dining room. He might have been compared to a summer's day, particularly the last hours of one, and while he lacked a tennis racket or a sail bag the impression was definitely one of youth, sport, and clement weather. He had been swimming and now he was breathing deeply, stertorously as if he could gulp into his lungs the components of that moment, the heat of the sun, the intenseness of his pleasure. It all seemed to flow into his chest. His own house stood in Bullet Park, eight miles to the south, where his four beautiful daughters would have had their lunch and might be playing tennis. Then it occurred to him that by taking a dogleg to the southwest he could reach his home by water.

His life was not confining and the delight he took in this observation could not be explained by its suggestion of escape. He seemed to see, with a cartographer's eye, that string of swimming pools, that quasi-subterranean stream that curved across the county. He had made a discovery, a contribution to modern geography; he would name the stream Lucinda after his wife. He was not a practical joker nor was he a fool but he was determinedly original and had a vague and modest idea of himself as a legendary figure. The day was beautiful and it seemed to him that a long swim might enlarge and celebrate its beauty.

He took off a sweater that was hung over his shoulders and dove in. He had an inexplicable contempt for men who did not hurl themselves into pools. He swam a choppy crawl, breathing either with every stroke or every fourth stroke and counting somewhere well in the back of his mind the one-two one-two of a flutter kick. It was not a serviceable stroke for long distances but the domestication of swimming had saddled the sport with some customs and in his part of the world a crawl was customary. To be embraced and sustained by the light green water was less a pleasure, it seemed, than the resumption of a natural condition, and he would have liked to swim without trunks, but this was not possible, considering his project. He hoisted himself up on the far curb—he never used the ladder—and started across the lawn. When Lucinda asked where he was going he said he was going to swim home.

The only maps and charts he had to go by were remembered or imaginary but these were clear enough. First there were the Grahams, the Hammers, the Lears, the Howlands, and the Crosscups. He would cross Ditmar Street to the Bunkers and come, after a short portage, to the Levys, the Welvhers, and the public pool in Lancaster. Then there were the Hallorans, the Sachses, the Biswangers, Shirley Adams, the Gilmartins, and the Clydes. The day was lovely, and that he lived in a world so generously supplied with water seemed like a clemency, a beneficence. His heart was high and he ran across the grass. Making his way home by an uncommon route gave him the feeling that he was a pilgrim, an explorer, a man with a destiny, and he knew that he would find friends all along the way; friends would line the banks of the Lucinda River.

He went through a hedge that separated the Westerhazy's land from the Grahams', walked under some flowering apple trees, passed the shed that housed their pump and filter, and came out at the Grahams' pool. "Why, Neddy," Mrs. Graham said, "what a marvelous surprise. I've been trying to get you on the phone all morning. Here, let me get you a drink." He saw then, like any explorer, that the hospitable customs and traditions of the natives would have to be handled with diplomacy if he was ever going to reach his destination. He did not want to mystify or seem rude to the Grahams nor did he have the time to linger there. He swam the length of their pool and joined them in the sun and was rescued, a few minutes later, by the arrival of two carloads of friends from Connecticut. During the uproarious reunions he was able to slip away. He went down by the front of the Graham's house, stepped over a thorny hedge, and crossed a vacant lot to the Hammers'. Mrs. Hammer, looking up from her roses, saw him swim by although she wasn't quite sure who it was. The Lears heard him splashing past the open windows of their living room. The Howlands and the Crosscups were away. After leaving the Howlands' he crossed Ditmar Street and started for the Bunkers', where he could hear, even at that distance, the noise of a party.

The water refracted the sound of voices and laughter and seemed to suspend it in midair. The Bunkers' pool was on a rise and he climbed some stairs to a terrace where twenty-five or thirty men and women were drinking. The only person in the water was Rusty Towers, who floated there on a rubber raft. Oh, how bonny and lush were the banks of the Lucinda River! Prosperous men and women gathered by the sapphire-colored waters while caterer's men in white coats passed them cold gin. Overhead a red de Haviland trainer was circling around and around and around in the sky with something like the glee of a child in a swing. Ned felt a passing affection for the scene, a tenderness for the gathering, as if it was something he might touch. In the distance he heard thunder. As soon as Enid Bunker saw him she began to scream: "Oh, look who's here! What a marvelous surprise! When Lucinda said that you couldn't come I thought I'd *die.*" She made her way to him through the crowd, and when they had finished kissing she led him to the bar, a progress that was slowed by the fact that he stopped to kiss eight or ten other women and shake the hands of as many men. A smiling bartender he had seen at a hundred parties gave him a gin and tonic and he stood by the bar for a moment, anxious not to get stuck in any conversation that would delay his voyage. When he seemed about to be surrounded he dove in and swam close to the side to avoid colliding with Rusty's raft. At the far end of the pool he bypassed the Tomlinsons with a broad smile and jogged up the garden path. The gravel cut his feet but this was the only unpleasantness. The party was confined to the pool, and as he went toward the house he heard the brilliant, watery sound of voices fade, heard the noise of a radio from the Bunkers' kitchen, where someone was listening to a ball game. Sunday afternoon. He made his way through the parked cars and down the grassy border of their driveway to Alewives Lane. He did not want to be seen on the road in his bathing trunks but there was no traffic and he made the short distance to the Levys' driveway, marked with a PRIVATE PROPERTY sign and a green tube for *The New York Times.* All the doors and windows of the big house were open but there were no signs of life; not even a dog barked. He went around the side of the house to the pool and saw that the Levys had only recently left. Glasses and bottles and dishes of nuts were on a table at the deep end, where there was a bathhouse or gazebo, hung with Japanese lanterns. After swimming the pool he got himself a glass and poured a drink.

It was his fourth or fifth drink and he had swum nearly half the length of the Lucinda River. He felt tired, clean, and pleased at that moment to be alone; pleased with everything.

It would storm. The stand of cumulus cloud—that city—had risen and darkened, and while he sat there he heard the percussiveness of thunder again. The de Haviland trainer was still circling overhead and it seemed to Ned that he could almost hear the pilot laugh with pleasure in the afternoon; but when there was another peal of thunder he took off for home. A train whistle blew and he wondered what time it had gotten to be. Four? Five? He thought of the provincial station at that hour, where a waiter, his tuxedo concealed by a raincoat, a dwarf with some flowers wrapped in newspaper, and a woman who had been crying would be waiting for the local. It was suddenly growing dark; it was that moment when the pinheaded birds seemed to organize their song into some acute and knowledgeable recognition of the storm's approach. Then there was a fine noise of rushing water from the crown of an oak at his back, as if a spigot there had been turned. Then the noise of fountains came from the crowns of all the tall trees. Why did he love storms, what was the meaning of his excitement when the door sprang open and the rain wind fled rudely up the stairs, why had the simple task of shutting the windows of an old house seemed fitting and urgent, why did the first watery notes of a storm wind have for him the unmistakable sound of good news, cheer, glad tidings? Then there was an explosion, a smell of cordite, and rain lashed the Japanese lanterns that Mrs. Levy had bought in Kyoto the year before last, or was it the year before that?

He stayed in the Levys' gazebo until the storm had passed. The rain had cooled the air and he shivered. The force of the wind had stripped a maple of its red and yellow leaves and scattered them over the grass and the water. Since it was midsummer the tree must be blighted, and yet he felt a peculiar sadness at this sign of autumn. He braced his shoulders, emptied his glass, and started for the Welchers' pool. This meant crossing the Lindleys' riding ring and he was surprised to find it overgrown with grass and all the jumps dismantled. He wondered if the Lindleys had sold their horses or gone away for the summer and put them out to board. He seemed to remember having heard something about the Lindleys and their horses but the memory was unclear. On he went, barefoot through the wet grass, to the Welchers', where he found their pool was dry.

This breach in his chain of water disappointed him absurdly, and he felt like some explorer who seeks a torrential headwater and finds a dead stream. He was disappointed and mystified. It was common enough to go away for the summer but no one ever drained his pool. The Welchers had definitely gone away. The pool furniture was folded, stacked, and covered with a tarpaulin. The bathhouse was locked. All the windows of the house were shut, and when he went around to the driveway in front he saw a FOR SALE sign nailed to a tree. When had he last heard from the Welchers—when, that is, had he and Lucinda last regretted an invitation to dine with them? It seemed only a week or so ago. Was his memory failing or had he so disciplined it in the repression of unpleasant facts that he had damaged his sense of the truth? Then in the distance he heard the sound of a tennis game. This cheered him, cleared away all his apprehensions and let him regard the overcast sky and the cold air with indifference. This was the day that Neddy Merrill swam across the county. That was the day! He started off then for his most difficult portage.

Had you gone for a Sunday afternoon ride that day you might have seen him, close to naked, standing on the shoulders of Route 424, waiting for a chance to cross. You might have wondered if he was the victim of foul play, had his car broken down, or was he merely a fool. Standing barefoot in the deposits of the highway— beer cans, rags, and blowout patches—exposed to all kinds of ridicule, he seemed pitiful. He had known when he started that this was a part of his journey—it had been on his maps—but confronted with the lines of traffic, worming through the summery light, he found himself unprepared. He was laughed at, jeered at, a beer can was thrown at him, and he had no dignity or humor to bring to the situation. He could have gone back, back to the Westerhazys', where Lucinda would still be sitting in the sun. He had signed nothing, vowed nothing, pledged nothing, not even to himself. Why, believing as he did, that all human obduracy was susceptible to common sense, was he unable to turn back? Why was he determined to complete his journey even if it meant putting his life in danger? At what point had this prank, this joke, this piece of horseplay become serious? He could not go back, he could not even recall with any clearness the green water at the Westerhazys', the sense of inhaling the day's components, the friendly and relaxed voices saying that they had *drunk* too much. In the space of an hour, more or less, he had covered a distance that made his return impossible.

An old man, tooling down the highway at fifteen miles an hour, let him get to the middle of the road, where there was a grass divider. Here he was exposed to the ridicule of the northbound traffic, but after ten or fifteen minutes he was able to cross. From here he had only a short walk to the Recreation Center at the edge of the village of Lancaster, where there were some handball courts and a public pool.

The effect of the water on voices, the illusion of brilliance and suspense, was the same here as it has been at the Bunkers' but the sounds here were louder, harsher, and more shrill, and as soon as he entered the crowded enclosure he was confronted with regimentation. "ALL SWIMMERS MUST TAKE A SHOWER BEFORE USING THE POOL. ALL SWIMMERS MUST USE THE FOOTBATH. ALL SWIMMERS MUST WEAR THEIR IDENTIFICATION DISKS." He took a shower, washed his feet in a cloudy and bitter solution, and made his way to the edge of the water. It stank of chlorine and looked to him like a sink. A pair of lifeguards in a pair of towers blew police whistles at what seemed to be regular intervals and abused the swimmers through a public address system. Neddy remembered the sapphire water at the Bunkers' with longing and thought that he might contaminate himself—damage his own prosperousness and charm—by swimming in this murk, but he reminded himself that he was an explorer, a pilgrim, and that this was merely a stagnant bend in the Lucinda River. He dove, scowling with distaste, into the chlorine and had to swim with his head above water to avoid collisions, but even so he was bumped into, splashed, and jostled. When he got to the shallow end both lifeguards were shouting at him: "Hey, you, you without the identification disk, get outa the water." He did, but they had no way of pursuing him and he went through the reek of suntan oil and chlorine out through the hurricane fence and passed the handball courts. By crossing the road he entered the wooded part of the Halloran estate. The woods were not cleared and the footing was treacherous and difficult until he reached the lawn and the clipped beech hedge that encircled their pool.

The Hallorans were friends, an elderly couple of enormous wealth who seemed to bask in the suspicion that they might be Communists. They were zealous reformers but they were not Communists, and yet when they were accused, as they sometimes were, of subversion, it seemed to gratify and excite them. Their beech hedge was yellow and he guessed this had been blighted like the Levys' maple. He called hullo, hullo, to warn the Hallorans of his approach, to palliate his invasion of their privacy. The Hallorans, for reasons that had never been explained to him, did not wear bathing suits. No explanations were in order, really. Their nakedness was a detail in their uncompromising zeal for reform and he stepped politely out of his trunks before he went through the opening in the hedge.

Mrs. Halloran, a stout woman with white hair and a serene face, was reading the *Times*. Mr. Halloran was taking beech leaves out of the water with a scoop. They seemed not surprised or displeased to see him. Their pool was perhaps the oldest in the country, a fieldstone rectangle, fed by a brook. It had no filter or pump and its waters were the opaque gold of the stream.

"I'm swimming across the county," Ned said.

"Why, I didn't know one could," exclaimed Mrs. Halloran.

"Well, I've made it from the Westerhazys'," Ned said. "That must be about four miles."

He left his trunks at the deep end, walked to the shallow end, and swam this stretch. As he was pulling himself out of the water he heard Mrs. Halloran say, "We've been *terribly* sorry to hear about all your misfortunes, Neddy."

"My misfortunes?" Ned asked. "I don't know what you mean."

"Why, we heard that you'd sold the house and that your poor children . . ."

"I don't recall having sold the house," Ned said, "and the girls are at home."

"Yes," Mrs. Halloran sighed. "Yes . . ." Her voice filled the air with an unseasonable melancholy and Ned spoke briskly. "Thank you for the swim."

"Well, have a nice trip," said Mrs. Halloran.

Beyond the hedge he pulled on his trunks and fastened them. They were loose and he wondered if, during the space of an afternoon, he could have lost some weight. He was cold and he was tired and the naked Hallorans and their dark water had depressed him. The swim was too much for his strength but how could he have guessed this, sliding down the banister that morning and sitting in the Westerhazys' sun? His arms were lame. His legs felt rubbery and ached at the joints. The worst of it was the cold in his bones and the feeling that he might never be warm again. Leaves were falling down around him and he smelled wood smoke on the wind. Who would be burning wood at this time of year?

He needed a drink. Whiskey would warm him, pick him up, carry him through the last of his journey, refresh his feeling that it was original and valorous to swim across the county. Channel swimmers took brandy. He needed a stimulant. He crossed the lawn in front of the Hallorans' house and went down a little path to where they had built a house for their only daughter, Helen, and her husband, Eric Sachs. The Sachses' pool was small and he found Helen and her husband there.

"Oh, *Neddy*," Helen said. "Did you lunch at Mother's?"

"Not *really*," Ned said. "I *did* stop to see your parents." This seemed to be explanation enough. "I'm terribly sorry to break in on you like this but I've taken a chill and I wonder if you'd give me a drink."

"Why, I'd *love* to," Helen said, "but there hasn't been anything in this house to drink since Eric's operation. That was three years ago."

Was he losing his memory, had his gift for concealing painful facts let him forget that he had sold his house, that his children were in trouble, and that his friend had been ill? His eyes slipped from Eric's face to his abdomen, where he saw three pale, sutured scars, two of them at least a foot long. Gone was his navel, and what, Neddy thought, would the roving hand, bed-checking one's gifts at 3 A.M., make of a belly with no navel, no link to birth, this breach in the succession?

"I'm sure you can get a drink at the Biswangers'," Helen said. "They're having an enormous do. You can hear it from here. Listen!"

She raised her head and from across the road, the lawns, the gardens, the woods, the fields, he heard again the brilliant noise of voices over water. "Well, I'll get wet," he said, still feeling that he had no freedom of choice about his means of travel. He dove into the Sachses' cold water and, gasping, close to drowning, made his way from one end of the pool to the other. "Lucinda and I want *terribly* to see you," he said over his shoulder, his face set toward the Biswangers'. "We're sorry it's been so long and we'll call you *very* soon."

He crossed some fields to the Biswangers' and the sounds of revelry there. They would be honored to give him a drink, they would be happy to give him a drink. The Biswangers invited him and Lucinda for dinner four times a year, six weeks in advance. They were always rebuffed and yet they continued to send out their invitations, unwilling to comprehend the rigid and undemocratic realities of their society. They were the sort of people who discussed the price of things at cocktails, exchanged market tips during dinner, and after dinner told dirty stories to mixed company. They did not belong to Neddy's set—they were not even on Lucinda's Christmas card list. He went toward their pool with feelings of indifference, charity, and some unease, since it seemed to be getting dark and these were the longest days of the year. The party when he joined it was noisy and large. Grace Biswanger was the kind of hostess who asked the optometrist, the veterinarian, the real-estate dealer, and the dentist. No one was swimming and the twilight, reflected on the water of the pool, had a wintry gleam. There was a bar and he started for this. When Grace Biswanger saw him she came toward him, not affectionately as he had every right to expect, but bellicosely.

"Why, this party has everything," she said loudly, "including a gate crasher."

She could not deal him a social blow—there was no question about this and he did not flinch. "As a gate crasher," he asked politely, "do I rate a drink?"

"Suit yourself," she said. "You don't seem to pay much attention to invitations."

She turned her back on him and joined some guests, and he went to the bar and ordered a whiskey. The bartender served him but he served him rudely. His was a world in which the caterer's men kept the social score, and to be rebuffed by a part-time barkeep meant that he had suffered some loss of social esteem. Or perhaps the man was new and uninformed. The he heard Grace at his back say: "They went for broke overnight—nothing but income—and he showed up drunk one Sunday and asked us to loan him five thousand dollars. . . ." She was always talking about money. It was worse than eating your peas off a knife. He dove into the pool, swam its length and went away.

The next pool on his list, the last but two, belonged to his old mistress, Shirley Adams. If he had suffered any injuries at the Biswangers' they would be cured here. Love—sexual roughhouse in fact—was the supreme elixir, the pain killer, the brightly colored pill that would put the spring back into his step, the joy of life in his heart. They had had an affair last week, last month, last year. He couldn't remember. It was he who had broken it off, his was the upper hand, and he stepped through the gate of the wall that surrounded her pool with nothing so considered as self-confidence. It seemed in a way to be his pool, as the lover, particularly the illicit lover, enjoys the possessions of his mistress with an authority unknown to holy matrimony. She was there, her hair the color of brass, but her figure, at the edge of the lighted, cerulean water, excited in him no profound memories. It had been, he thought, a lighthearted affair, although she had wept when he broke it off. She seemed confused to see him and he wondered if she was still wounded. Would she, God forbid, weep again?

"What do you want?" she asked.

"I'm swimming across the county."

"Good Christ. Will you ever grow up?"

"What's the matter?"

"If you've come here for money," she said, "I won't give you another cent."

"You could give me a drink."

"I could but I won't. I'm not alone."

"Well, I'm on my way."

He dove in and swam the pool, but when he tried to haul himself up onto the curb he found that the strength in his arms and shoulders had gone, and he paddled to the ladder and climbed out. Looking over his shoulder he saw, in the lighted bathhouse, a young man. Going out onto the dark lawn he smelled chrysanthemums or marigolds—some stubborn autumnal fragrance—on the night air, strong as gas. Looking overhead he saw that the stars had come out, but why should he seem to see Andromeda, Cepheus, and Cassiopeia? What had become of the constellations of midsummer? He began to cry.

It was probably the first time in his adult life that he had ever cried, certainly the first time in his life that he had ever felt so miserable, cold, tired, and bewildered. He could not understand the rudeness of the caterer's barkeep or the rudeness of a mistress who had come to him on her knees and showered his trousers with tears. He had swum too long, he had been immersed too long, and his nose and his throat were sore from the water. What he needed then was a drink, some company, and some clean, dry clothes, and while he could have cut directly across the road to his home he went on to the Gilmartins' pool. Here, for the first time in his life, he did not dive but went down the steps into the icy water and swam a hobbled sidestroke that he might have learned as a youth. He staggered with fatigue on his way to the Clydes' and paddled the length of their pool, stopping again and again with his hand on the curb to rest. He climbed up the ladder and wondered if he had the strength to get home. He had done what he wanted, he had swum the county, but he was so stupefied with exhaustion that his triumph seemed vague. Stooped, holding on to the gateposts for support, he turned up the driveway of his own house.

The place was dark. Was it so late that they had all gone to bed? Had Lucinda stayed at the Westerhazys' for supper? Had the girls joined her there or gone someplace else? Hadn't they agreed, as they usually did on Sunday, to regret all their invitations and stay at home? He tried the garage doors to see what cars were in but the doors were locked and rust came off the handles onto his hands. Going toward the house, he saw that the force of the thunderstorm had knocked one of the rain gutters loose. It hung down over the front door like an umbrella rib, but it could be fixed in the morning. The house was locked, and he thought that the stupid cook or the stupid maid must have locked the place up until he remembered that it had been some time since they had employed a maid or a cook. He shouted, pounded on the door, tried to force it with his shoulder, and then, looking in at the windows, saw that the place was empty.

# TILLIE OLSEN

1912–

She was born in Omaha, Nebraska, and lived there until her twenties. When she was nineteen she began a novel about a poor family living through the depression, working on the book as she lived through the depression herself, moving to California, working in factories and offices. She left it unfinished in 1936 or 1937. She married, had children, and found it difficult to write until the 1950's, when she published four extraordinary stories, collected in *Tell Me a Riddle* (1961). The publication of this volume established her as an important American writer. In 1974 she published what could be salvaged of the novel she had been forced to abandon in the 1930's, *Yonnondio*.

## I Stand Here Ironing

I stand here ironing, and what you asked me moves tormented back and forth with the iron.

"I wish you would manage the time to come in and talk with me about your daughter. I'm sure you can help me understand her. She's a youngster who needs help and whom I'm deeply interested in helping."

"Who needs help." Even if I came, what good would it do? You think because I am her mother I have a key, or that in some way you could use me as a key? She has lived for nineteen years. There is all that life that has happened outside of me, beyond me.

And when is there time to remember, to sift, to weigh, to estimate, to total? I will start and there will be an interruption and I will have to gather it all together again. Or I will become engulfed with all I did or did not do, with what should have been and what cannot be helped.

She was a beautiful baby. The first and only one of our five that was beautiful at birth. You do not guess how new and uneasy her tenancy in her now-loveliness. You did not know her all those years she was thought homely, or see her poring over her baby pictures, making me tell her over and over how beautiful she had been—and would be, I would tell her—and was now, to the seeing eye. But the seeing eyes were few or non-existent. Including mine.

I nursed her. They feel that's important nowadays. I nursed all the children, but with her, with all the fierce rigidity of first motherhood, I did like the books then said. Though her cries battered me to trembling and my breasts ached with swollenness, I waited till the clock decreed.

Why do I put that first? I do not even know if it matters, or if it explains anything.

She was a beautiful baby. She blew shining bubbles of sound. She loved motion, loved light, loved color and music and textures. She would lie on the floor in her blue overalls patting the surface so hard in ecstasy her hands and feet would blur. She was a miracle to me, but when she was eight months old I had to leave her daytimes with the woman downstairs to whom she was no miracle at all, for I worked or looked for work and for Emily's father, who "could no longer endure" (he wrote in his good-bye note) "sharing want with us."

I was nineteen. It was the pre-relief, pre-WPA world of the depression. I would start running as soon as I got off the streetcar, running up the stairs, the place smelling sour, and awake or asleep to startle awake, when she saw me she would break into a clogged weeping that could not be comforted, a weeping I can hear yet.

After a while I found a job hashing at night so I could be with her days, and it was better. But it came to where I had to bring her to his family and leave her.

It took a long time to raise the money for her fare back. Then she got chicken pox and I had to wait longer. When she finally came, I hardly knew her, walking quick and nervous like her father, looking like her father, thin, and dressed in a shoddy red that yellowed her skin and glared at the pockmarks. All the baby loveliness gone.

She was two. Old enough for nursery school they said, and I did not know then what I know now—the fatigue of the long day, and the lacerations of group life in the kinds of nurseries that are only parking places for children.

Except that it would have made no difference if I had known. It was the only place there was. It was the only way we could be together, the only way I could hold a job.

And even without knowing, I knew. I knew the teacher that was evil because all these years it has curdled into my memory, the little boy hunched in the corner, her rasp, "why aren't you outside, because Alvin hits you? that's no reason, go out, scaredy." I knew Emily hated it even if she did not clutch and implore "don't go Mommy" like the other children, mornings.

She always had a reason why we should stay home. Momma, you look sick, Momma. I feel sick. Momma, the teachers aren't there today, they're sick. Momma, we can't go, there was a fire there last night. Momma, it's a holiday today, no school, they told me.

But never a direct protest, never rebellion. I think of our others in their three, four-year-oldness—the explosions, the tempers, the denunciations, the demands—and I feel suddenly ill. I put the iron down. What in me demanded that goodness in her? And what was the cost, the cost to her of such goodness?

The old man living in the back once said in his gentle way: "You should smile at Emily more when you look at her." What *was* in my face when I looked at her? I loved her. There were all the acts of love.

It was only with the others I remembered what he said, and it was the face of joy, and not of care or tightness or worry I turned to them—too late for Emily. She does not smile easily, let alone almost always as her brothers and sisters do. Her face is closed and sombre, but when she wants, how fluid. You must have seen it in her pantomimes, you spoke of her rare gift for comedy on the stage that rouses a laughter out of the audience so dear they applaud and applaud and do not want to let her go.

Where does it come from, that comedy? There was none of it in her when she came back to me that second time, after I had had to send her away again. She had a new daddy now to learn to love, and I think perhaps it was a better time.

Except when we left her alone nights, telling ourselves she was old enough.

"Can't you go some other time, Mommy, like tomorrow?" she would ask. "Will it be just a little while you'll be gone? Do you promise?"

The time we came back, the front door open, the clock on the floor in the hall. She rigid awake. "It wasn't just a little while. I didn't cry. Three times I called you, just three times, and then I ran downstairs to open the door so you could come faster. The clock talked loud. I threw it away, it scared me what it talked."

She said the clock talked loud again that night I went to the hospital to have Susan. She was delirious with the fever that comes before red measles, but she was fully conscious all the week I was gone and the week after we were home when she could not come near the new baby or me.

She did not get well. She stayed skeleton thin, not wanting to eat, and night after night she had nightmares. She would call for me, and I would rouse from exhaustion to sleepily call back: "You're all right, darling, go to sleep, it's just a dream," and if she still called, in a sterner voice, "now go to sleep, Emily, there's nothing to hurt you." Twice, only twice, when I had to get up for Susan anyhow, I went in to sit with her.

Now when it is too late (as if she would let me hold and comfort her like I do the others) I get up and go to her at once at her moan or restless stirring. "Are you awake, Emily? Can I get you something?" And the answer is always the same: "No, I'm all right, go back to sleep, Mother."

They persuaded me at the clinic to send her away to a convalescent home in the country where "she can have the kind of food and care you can't manage for her, and you'll be free to concentrate on the new baby." They still send children to that place. I see pictures on the society page of sleek young women planning affairs to raise money for it, or dancing at the affairs, or decorating Easter eggs or filling Christmas stockings for the children.

They never have a picture of the children so I do not know if the girls still wear those gigantic red bows and the ravaged looks on the every other Sunday when parents can come to visit "unless otherwise notified"—as we were notified the first six weeks.

Oh it is a handsome place, green lawns and tall trees and fluted flower beds. High up on the balconies of each cottage the children stand, the girls in their red bows and white dresses, the boys in white suits and giant red ties. The parents stand below shrieking up to be heard and the children shriek down to be heard, and between them the invisible wall "Not To Be Contaminated by Parental Germs or Physical Affection."

There was a tiny girl who always stood hand in hand with Emily. Her parents never came. One visit she was gone. "They moved her to Rose College," Emily shouted in explanation. "They don't like you to love anybody here."

She wrote once a week, the labored writing of a seven-year-old. "I am fine. How is the baby. If I write my leter nicly I will have a star. Love." There never was a star. We wrote every other day, letters she could never hold or keep but only hear read—once. "We simply do not have room for children to keep any personal possessions," they patiently explained when we pieced one Sunday's shrieking together to plead how much it would mean to Emily, who loved so to keep things, to be allowed to keep her letters and cards.

Each visit she looked frailer. "She isn't eating," they told us.

(They had runny eggs for breakfast or mush with lumps, Emily said later, I'd hold it in my mouth and not swallow. Nothing ever tasted good, just when they had chicken.)

It took us eight months to get her released home, and only the fact that she gained back so little of her seven lost pounds convinced the social worker.

I used to try to hold and love her after she came back, but her body would stay stiff, and after a while she'd push away. She ate little. Food sickened her, and I think much of life too. Oh she had physical lightness and brightness, twinkling by on skates, bouncing like a ball up and down up and down over the jump rope, skimming over the hill; but these were momentary.

She fretted about her appearance, thin and dark and foreign-looking at a time when every little girl was supposed to look or thought she should look a chubby blonde replica of Shirley Temple.

The doorbell sometimes rang for her, but no one seemed to come and play in the house or be a best friend. Maybe because we moved so much.

There was a boy she loved painfully through two school semesters. Months later she told me how she had taken pennies from my purse to buy him candy. "Licorice was his favorite and I brought him some every day, but he still liked Jennifer better'n me. Why, Mommy?" The kind of question for which there is no answer.

School was a worry to her. She was not glib or quick in a world where glibness and quickness were easily confused with ability to learn. To her overworked and exasperated teachers she was an over-conscientious "slow learner" who kept trying to catch up and was absent entirely too often.

I let her be absent, though sometimes the illness was imaginary. How different from my now-strictness about attendance with the others. I wasn't working. We had a new baby, I was home anyhow. Sometimes, after Susan grew old enough, I would keep her home from school, too, to have them all together.

Mostly Emily had asthma, and her breathing, harsh and labored, would fill the house with a curiously tranquil sound. I would bring the two old dresser mirrors and her boxes of collections to her bed. She would select beads and single earrings, bottle tops and shells, dried flowers and pebbles, old postcards, and scraps, all sorts of oddments; then she and Susan would play Kingdom, setting up landscapes and furniture, peopling them with action.

Those were the only times of peaceful companionship between her and Susan. I have edged away from it, that poisonous feeling between them, that terrible balancing of hurts and needs I had to do between the two, and did so badly, those earlier years.

Oh there are conflicts between the others too, each one human, needing, demanding, hurting, taking—but only between Emily and Susan, no, Emily toward Susan that corroding resentment. It seems so obvious on the surface, yet it is not obvious. Susan, the second child, Susan, golden- and curly-haired and chubby, quick and articulate and assured, everything in appearance and manner Emily was not; Susan, not able to resist Emily's precious things, losing or sometimes clumsily breaking them; Susan telling jokes and riddles to company for applause while Emily sat silent (to say to me later: that was *my* riddle, Mother, I told it to Susan); Susan, who for all the five years' difference in age was just a year behind Emily in developing physically.

I am glad for that slow physical development that widened the difference between her and her contemporaries, though she suffered over it. She was too vulnerable for that terrible world of youthful competition, of preening and parading, of constant measuring of yourself against every other, of envy, "If I had that copper hair," "If I had that skin . . . " She tormented herself enough about not looking like the others, there was enough of the unsureness, the having to be conscious of words before you speak, the constant caring—what are they thinking of me? without having it all magnified by the merciless physical drives.

Ronnie is calling. He is wet and I change him. It is rare there is such a cry now. That time of motherhood is almost behind me when the ear is not one's own but must always be racked and listening for the child cry, the child call. We sit for a while and I hold him, looking out over the city spread in charcoal with its soft aisles of light. *"Shoogily,"* he breathes and curls closer. I carry him back to bed, asleep. *Shoogily.* A funny word, a family word, inherited from Emily, invented by her to say: *comfort.*

In this and other ways she leaves her seal, I say aloud. And startle at my saying it. What do I mean? What did I start to gather together, to try and make coherent? I was at the terrible, growing years. War years. I do not remember them well. I was working, there were four smaller ones now, there was not time for her. She had to help be a mother, and housekeeper, and shopper. She had to set her seal. Mornings of crisis and near hysteria trying to get lunches packed, hair combed, coats and shoes found, everyone to school or Child Care on time, the baby ready for transportation. And always the paper scribbled on by a smaller one, the book looked at by Susan then mislaid, the homework not done. Running out to that huge school where she was one, she was lost, she was a drop; suffering over the unpreparedness, stammering and unsure in her classes.

There was so little time left at night after the kids were bedded down. She would struggle over books, always eating (it was in those years she developed her enormous appetite that is legendary in our family) and I would be ironing, or preparing food for the next day, or writing V-mail to Bill, or tending the baby. Sometimes, to make me laugh, or out of her despair, she would imitate happenings or types at school.

I think I said once: "Why don't you do something like this in the school amateur show?" One morning she phoned me at work, hardly understandable through the weeping: "Mother, I did it. I won, I won; they gave me first prize; they clapped and clapped and wouldn't let me go."

Now suddenly she was Somebody, and as imprisoned in her difference as she had been in anonymity.

She began to be asked to perform at other high schools, even in colleges, then at city and statewide affairs. The first one we went to, I only recognized her that first moment when thin, shy, she almost drowned herself into the curtains. Then: Was this Emily? The control, the command, the convulsing and deadly clowning, the spell, then the roaring, stamping audience, unwilling to let this rare and precious laughter out of their lives.

Afterwards: You ought to do something about her with a gift like that—but without money or knowing how, what does one do? We have left it all to her, and the gift has as often eddied inside, clogged and clotted, as been used and growing.

She is coming. She runs up the stairs two at a time with her light graceful step, and I know she is happy tonight. Whatever it was that occasioned your call did not happen today.

"Aren't you ever going to finish the ironing, Mother? Whistler painted his mother in a rocker. I'd have to paint mine standing over an ironing board." This is one of her communicative nights and she tells me everything and nothing as she fixes herself a plate of food out of the icebox.

She is so lovely. Why did you want me to come in at all? Why were you concerned? She will find her way.

She starts up the stairs to bed. "Don't get me up with the rest in the morning." "But I thought you were having midterms." "Oh, those," she comes back in, kisses me, and says quite lightly," in a couple of years when we'll all be atom-dead they won't matter a bit."

She has said it before. She *believes* it. But because I have been developing the past, and all that compounds a human being is so heavy and meaningful in me, I cannot endure it tonight.

I will never total it all. I will never come in to say: She was a child seldom smiled at. Her father left me before she was a year old. I had to work her first six years when there was work, or I sent her home and to his relatives. There were years she had care she hated. She was dark and thin and foreign-looking in a world where the prestige went to blondeness and curly hair and dimples, she was slow where glibness was prized. She was a child of anxious, not proud, love. We were poor and could not afford for her the soil of easy growth. I was a young mother, I was a distracted mother. There were the other children pushing up, demanding. Her younger sister seemed all that she was not. There were years she did not let me touch her. She kept too much in herself, her life was such she had to keep too much in herself. My wisdom came too late. She has much to her and probably little will come of it. She is a child of her age, of depression, of war, of fear.

Let her be. So all that is in her will not bloom—but in how many does it? There is still enough left to live by. Only help her to know—help make it so there is cause for her to know—that she is more than this dress on the ironing board, helpless before the iron.

# BERNARD MALAMUD
## 1914–

A city boy, of Jewish background, Malamud was born and raised in Brooklyn, New York. He went to City College, for his B.A. and to Columbia University for his M.A. He taught in night school for almost ten years before taking a job at Oregon State University. His experiences in Oregon from 1949 to 1961 became the basis for his novel A New Life (1961). As a short story writer he has continued the tradition of Babel and Singer. Since 1961 he has taught at Bennington College in Vermont. Among his most admired works are a novel, The Assistant (1957), and the stories in The Magic Barrel (1958).

## The Magic Barrel

Not long ago there lived in uptown New York, in a small, almost meager room, though crowded with books, Leo Finkle, a rabbinical student in the Yeshivah University. Finkle, after six years of study, was to be ordained in June and had been advised by an acquaintance that he might find it easier to win himself a congregation if he were married. Since he had no present prospects of marriage, after two tormented days of turning it over in his mind, he called in Pinye Salzman, a marriage broker whose two-line advertisement he had read in the Forward.

The matchmaker appeared one night out of the dark fourth-floor hallway of the graystone rooming house where Finkle lived, grasping a black, strapped portfolio that had been worn thin with use. Salzman, who had been long in the business, was of slight but dignified build, wearing an old hat, and an overcoat too short and tight for him. He smelled frankly of fish, which he loved to eat, and although he was missing a few teeth, his presence was not displeasing, because of an amiable manner curiously contrasted with mournful eyes. His voice, his lips, his wisp of beard, his bony fingers were animated, but give him a moment of repose and his mild blue eyes revealed a depth of sadness, a characteristic that put Leo a little at ease although the situation, for him, was inherently tense.

He at once informed Salzman why he had asked him to come, explaining that his home was in Cleveland, and that but for his parents, who had married comparatively late in life, he was alone in the world. He had for six years devoted himself almost entirely to his studies, as a result of which, understandably, he had found himself without time for a social life and the company of young women. Therefore he thought it the better part of trial and error—of embarrassing fumbling—to call in an experienced person to advise him on these matters. He remarked in passing that the function of the marriage broker was ancient and honorable, highly approved in the Jewish community, because it made practical the necessary without hindering joy. Moreover, his own parents had been brought together by a matchmaker. They had made, if not a financially profitable marriage—since neither had possessed any worldly goods to speak of—at least a successful one in the sense of their everlasting devotion to each other. Salzman listened in embarrassed surprise, sensing a sort of apology. Later, however, he experienced a glow of pride in his work, an emotion that had left him years ago, and he heartily approved of Finkle.

The two went to their business. Leo had led Salzman to the only clear place in the room, a table near a window that overlooked the lamp-lit city. He seated himself at the matchmaker's side but facing him, attempting by an act of will to suppress the unpleasant tickle in his throat. Salzman eagerly unstrapped his portfolio and removed a loose rubber band from a thin packet of much-handled cards. As he flipped through them, a gesture and sound that physically hurt Leo, the student pretended not to see and gazed steadfastly out the window. Although it was still February, winter was on its last legs, signs of which he had for the first time in years begun to notice. He now observed the round white moon, moving high in the sky through a cloud menagerie, and watched with half-open mouth as it penetrated a huge hen, and dropped out of her like an egg laying itself. Salzman, though pretending through eyeglasses he had just slipped on to be engaged in scanning the writing on the cards, stole occasional glances at the young man's distinguished face, noting with pleasure the long, severe scholar's nose, brown eyes heavy with learning, sensitive yet ascetic lips, and a certain, almost hollow quality of the dark cheeks. He gazed around at shelves upon shelves of books and let out a soft, contented sigh.

When Leo's eyes fell upon the cards, he counted six spread out in Salzman's hand.

"So few?" he asked in disappointment.

"You wouldn't believe me how much cards I got in my office," Salzman replied. "The drawers are already filled to the top, so I keep them now in a barrel, but is every girl good for a new rabbi?"

Leo blushed at this, regretting all he had revealed of himself in a curriculum vitae he had sent to Salzman. He had thought it best to acquaint him with his strict standards and specifications, but in having done so, felt he had told the marriage broker more than was absolutely necessary.

He hesitantly inquired, "Do you keep photographs of your clients on file?"

"First comes family, amount of dowry, also what kind promises,"

Salzman replied, unbuttoning his tight coat and settling himself in the chair. "After comes pictures, rabbi."

"Call me Mr. Finkle. I'm not yet a rabbi."

Salzman said he would, but instead called him doctor, which he changed to rabbi when Leo was not listening too attentively.

Salzman adjusted his horn-rimmed spectacles, gently cleared his throat and read in an eager voice the contents of the top card:

"Sophie P. Twenty four years. Widow one year. No children. Educated high school and two years college. Father promises eight thousand dollars. Has wonderful wholesale business. Also real estate. On the mother's side comes teachers, also one actor. Well known on Second Avenue."

Leo gazed up in surprise. "Did you say a widow?"

"A widow don't mean spoiled, rabbi. She lived with her husband maybe four months. He was a sick boy she made a mistake to marry him."

"Marrying a widow has never entered my mind."

"This is because you have no experience. A widow, especially if she is young and healthy like this girl, is a wonderful person to marry. She will be thankful to you the rest of her life. Believe me, if I was looking now for a bride, I would marry a widow."

Leo reflected, then shook his head.

Salzman hunched his shoulders in an almost imperceptible gesture of disappointment. He placed the card down on the wooden table and began to read another:

"Lily H. High school teacher. Regular. Not a substitute. Has savings and new Dodge car. Lived in Paris one year. Father is successful dentist thirty-five years. Interested in professional man. Well Americanized family. Wonderful opportunity."

"I knew her personally," said Salzman. "I wish you could see this girl. She is a doll. Also very intelligent. All day you could talk to her about books and theyater and what not. She also knows current events."

"I don't believe you mentioned her age?"

"Her age?" Salzman said, raising his brows. "Her age is thirty-two years."

Leo said after a while, "I'm afraid that seems a little too old."

Salzman let out a laugh. "So how old are you, rabbi?"

"Twenty-seven."

"So what is the difference, tell me, between twenty-seven and thirty-two? My own wife is seven years older than me. So what did I suffer?—Nothing. If Rothschild's daughter wants to marry you, would you say on account her age, no?"

"Yes," Leo said dryly.

Salzman shook off the no in the yes. "Five years don't mean a thing. I give you my word that when you will live with her for one week you will forget her age. What does it mean five years—that she lived more and knows more than somebody who is younger? On this girl, God bless her, years are not wasted. Each one that it comes makes better the bargain."

"What subject does she teach in high school?"

"Languages. If you heard the way she speaks French, you will think it is music. I am in the business twenty-five years, and I recommend her with my whole heart. Believe me, I know what I'm talking, rabbi."

"What's on the next card?" Leo said abruptly.

Salzman reluctantly turned up the third card:

"Ruth K. Nineteen years. Honor student. Father offers thirteen thousand cash to the right bridegroom. He is a medical doctor. Stomach specialist with marvelous practice. Brother in law owns own garment business. Particular people."

Salzman looked as if he had read his trump card.

"Did you say nineteen?" Leo asked with interest.

"On the dot."

"Is she attractive?" He blushed. "Pretty?"

Salzman kissed his finger tips. "A little doll. On this I give you my word. Let me call the father tonight and you will see what means pretty."

But Leo was troubled. "You're sure she's that young?"

"This I am positive. The father will show you the birth certificate."

"Are you positive there isn't something wrong with her?" Leo insisted.

"Who says there is wrong?"

"I don't understand why an American girl her age should go to a marriage broker."

A smile spread over Salzman's face.

"So for the same reason you went, she comes."

Leo flushed. "I am pressed for time."

Salzman, realizing he had been tactless, quickly explained. "The father came, not her. He wants she should have the best, so he looks around himself. When we will locate the right boy he will introduce him and encourage. This makes a better marriage than if a young girl without experience takes for herself. I don't have to tell you this."

"But don't you think this young girl believes in love?" Leo spoke uneasily.

Salzman was about to guffaw but caught himself and said soberly, "Love comes with the right person, not before."

Leo parted dry lips but did not speak. Noticing that Salzman had snatched a glance at the next card, he cleverly asked, "How is her health?"

"Perfect," Salzman said, breathing with difficulty. "Of course, she is a little lame on her right foot from an auto accident that it happened to her when she was twelve years, but nobody notices on account she is so brilliant and also beautiful."

Leo got up heavily and went to the window. He felt curiously bitter and upbraided himself for having called in the marriage broker. Finally, he shook his head.

"Why not?" Salzman persisted, the pitch of his voice rising.

"Because I detest stomach specialists."

"So what do you care what is his business? After you marry her do you need him? Who says he must come every Friday night in your house?"

Ashamed of the way the talk was going, Leo dismissed Salzman, who went home with heavy, melancholy eyes.

Though he had felt only relief at the marriage broker's departure, Leo was in low spirits the next day. He explained it as arising from Salzman's failure to produce a suitable bride for him. He did not care for his type of clientele. But when Leo found himself hesitating whether to seek out another matchmaker, one more polished than Pinye, he wondered if it could be—his protestations to the contrary, and although he honored his father and mother—that he did not, in essence, care for the matchmaking institution? This thought he quickly put out of mind yet found himself still upset. All day he ran around in the woods—missed an important appointment, forgot to give out his laundry, walked out of a Broadway cafeteria without paying and had to run back with the ticket in his hand; had even not recognized his landlady in the street when she passed with a friend and courteously called out, "A good evening to you, Doctor Finkle." By nightfall, however, he had regained sufficient calm to sink his nose into a book and there found peace from his thoughts.

Almost at once there came a knock on the door. Before Leo could say enter, Salzman, commercial cupid, was standing in the room. His face was gray and meager, his expression hungry, and he looked as if he would expire on his feet. Yet the marriage broker managed, by some trick of the muscles, to display a broad smile.

"So good evening. I am invited?"

Leo nodded, disturbed to see him again, yet unwilling to ask the man to leave.

Beaming still, Salzman laid his portfolio on the table. "Rabbi, I got for you tonight good news."

"I've asked you not to call me rabbi. I'm still a student."

"Your worries are finished. I have for you a first-class bride."

"Leave me in peace concerning this subject." Leo pretended lack of interest.

"The world will dance at your wedding."

"Please, Mr. Salzman, no more."

"But first must come back my strength," Salzman said weakly. He fumbled with the portfolio straps and took out of the leather case an oily paper bag, from which he extracted a hard, seeded roll and a small, smoked white fish. With a quick motion of his hand he stripped the fish out of its skin and began ravenously to chew. "All day in a rush," he muttered.

Leo watched him eat.

"A sliced tomato you have maybe?" Salzman hesitantly inquired.

"No."

The marriage broker shut his eyes and ate. When he had finished he carefully cleaned up the crumbs and rolled up the remains of the fish, in the paper bag. His spectacled eyes roamed the room until he discovered, amid some piles of books, a one-burner gas stove. Lifting his hat he humbly asked, "A glass tea you got, rabbi?"

Conscience-stricken, Leo rose and brewed the tea. He served it with a chunk of lemon and two cubes of lump sugar, delighting Salzman.

After he had drunk his tea, Salzman's strength and good spirits were restored.

"So tell me, rabbi," he said amiably, "you considered some more the three clients I mentioned yesterday?"

"There was no need to consider."

"Why not?"

"None of them suits me."

"What then suits you?"

Leo let it pass because he could give only a confused answer.

Without waiting for a reply, Salzman asked, "You remember this girl I talked to you—the high school teacher?"

"Age thirty-two?"

But, surprisingly, Salzman's face lit in a smile. "Age twenty-nine."

Leo shot him a look. "Reduced from thirty-two?"

"A mistake," Salzman avowed. "I talked today with the dentist. He took me to his safety deposit box and showed me the birth certificate. She was twenty-nine years last August. They made her a party in the mountains where she went for her vacation. When her father spoke to me the first time I forgot to write the age and I told you thirty-two, but now I remember this was a different client, a widow."

"The same one you told me about? I thought she was twenty-four?"

"A different. Am I responsible that the world is filled with widows?"

"No, but I'm not interested in them, nor for that matter, in school teachers."

Salzman pulled his clasped hands to his breast. Looking at the ceiling he devoutly exclaimed, "Yiddishe kinder, what can I say to somebody that he is not interested in high school teachers? So what then you are interested?"

Leo flushed but controlled himself.

"In what else will you be interested," Salzman went on, "if you not interested in this fine girl that she speaks four languages and has personally in the bank ten thousand dollars? Also her father guarantees further twelve thousand. Also she has a new car, wonderful clothes, talks on all subjects, and she will give you a first-class home and children. How near do we come in our life to paradise?"

"If she's so wonderful, why wasn't she married ten years ago?"

"Why?" said Salzman with a heavy laugh. "—Why? Because she is *partikiler*. This is why. She wants the *best*."

Leo was silent, amused at how he had entangled himself. But Salzman had aroused his interest in Lily H., and he began seriously to consider calling on her. When the marriage broker observed how intently Leo's mind was at work on the facts he had supplied, he felt certain they would soon come to an agreement.

Late Saturday afternoon, conscious of Salzman, Leo Finkle walked with Lily Hirschorn along Riverside Drive. He walked briskly and erectly, wearing with distinction the black fedora he had that morning taken with trepidation out of the dusty hat box on his closet shelf, and the heavy black Saturday coat he had thoroughly whisked clean. Leo also owned a walking stick, a present from a distant relative, but quickly put temptation aside and did not use it. Lily, petite and not unpretty, had on something signifying the approach of spring She was au courant, animatedly, with all sorts of subjects, and he weighed her words and found her surprisingly sound—score another for Salzman, whom he uneasily sensed to be somewhere around, hiding perhaps high in a tree along the street, flashing the lady signals with a pocket mirror; or perhaps a cloven-hoofed Pan, piping nuptial ditties as he danced his invisible way before them, strewing wild buds on the walk and purple grapes in their path, symbolizing fruit of a union, though there was of course still none.

Lily startled Leo by remarking, "I was thinking of Mr. Salzman, a curious figure, wouldn't you say?"

Not certain what to answer, he nodded.

She bravely went on, blushing, "I for one am grateful for his introducing us. Aren't you?"

He courteously replied, "I am."

"I mean," she said with a little laugh—and it was all in good taste, or at least gave the effect of being not in bad—"do you mind that we came together so?"

He was not displeased with her honesty, recognizing that she meant to set the relationship aright, and understanding that it took a certain amount of experience in life, and courage, to want to do it quite that way. One had to have some sort of past to make that kind of beginning.

He said that he did not mind. Salzman's function was traditional and honorable—valuable for what it might achieve, which, he pointed out, was frequently nothing.

Lily agreed with a sigh. They walked on for a while and she said after a long silence, again with a nervous laugh, "Would you mind if I asked you something a little bit personal? Frankly, I find the subject fascinating." Although Leo shrugged, she went on half embarrassedly, "How was it that you came to your calling? I mean was it a sudden passionate inspiration?"

Leo after a time, slowly replied, "I was always interested in the Law."

"You saw revealed in it the presence of the Highest?"

He nodded and changed the subject. "I understand that you spent a little time in Paris, Miss Hirschorn?"

"Oh, did Mr. Salzman tell you, Rabbi Finkle?" Leo winced but she went on, "It was ages ago and almost forgotten. I remember I had to return for my sister's wedding."

And Lily would not be put off. "When," she asked in a trembly voice, "did you become enamored of God?"

He stared at her. Then it came to him that she was talking not about Leo Finkle, but of a total stranger, some mystical figure, perhaps even passionate prophet that Salzman had dreamed up for her—no relation to the living or dead. Leo trembled with rage and weakness. The trickster had obviously sold her a bill of goods, just as he had him, who'd expected to become acquainted with a young lady of twenty-nine, only to behold, the moment he laid eyes upon her strained and anxious face, a woman past thirty-five and aging rapidly. Only his self-control had kept him this long in her presence.

"I am not," he said gravely, "a talented religious person," and in seeking words to go on, found himself possessed by shame and fear. "I think," he said in a strained manner, "that I came to God not because I loved Him, but because I did not."

This confession he spoke harshly because its unexpectedness shook him.

Lily wilted. Leo saw a profusion of loaves of bread go flying like ducks high over his head, not unlike the winged loaves by which he had counted himself to sleep last night. Mercifully, then, it snowed, which he would not put past Salzman's machinations.

He was infuriated with the marriage broker and swore he would throw him out of the room the minute he reappeared. But Salzman did not come that night; and when Leo's anger had subsided, an unaccountable despair grew in its place. At first he thought this was caused by his disappointment in Lily, but before long it became evident that he had involved himself with Salzman without a true knowledge of his own intent. He gradually realized—with an emptiness that seized him with six hands—that he had called in the broker to find him a bride because he was incapable of doing it himself. This terrifying insight he had derived as a result of his meeting and conversation with Lily Hirschorn. Her probing questions had somehow irritated him into revealing—to himself more than her—the true nature of his relationship to God, and from that it had come upon him, with shocking force, that apart from his parents, he had never loved anyone. Or perhaps it went the other way, that he did not love God so well as he might, because he had not loved man. It seemed to Leo that his whole life stood starkly revealed and he saw himself for the first time as he truly was—unloved and loveless. This bitter but somehow not fully unexpected revelation brought him to a point of panic, controlled only by extraordinary effort. He covered his face with his hands and cried.

The week that followed was the worst of his life. He did not eat and lost weight. His beard darkened and grew ragged. He stopped attending seminars and almost never opened a book. He seriously considered leaving the Yeshivah, although he was deeply troubled at the thought of the loss of all his years of study—saw them like pages torn from a book, strewn over the city—and at the devastating effect of this decision upon his parents. But he had lived without knowledge of himself, and never in the Five Books and all the Commentaries—mea culpa—had the truth been revealed to him. He did not know where to turn, and in all this desolating loneliness there was no *to whom*, although he often thought of Lily but not once could bring himself to go downstairs and make the call. He became touchy and irritable, especially with his landlady, who asked him all manner of personal questions; on the other hand, sensing his own disagreeableness, he waylaid her on the stairs and apologized abjectly, until mortified, she ran from him. Out of this, however, he drew the consolation that he was a Jew and that a Jew suffered. But gradually, as the long and terrible week drew to a close, he regained his composure and some idea of purpose in life: to go on as planned. Although he was imperfect, the ideal was not. As for his quest of a bride, the thought of continuing afflicted him with anxiety and heartburn, yet perhaps with this new knowledge of himself he would be more successful than in the past. Perhaps love would now come to him and a bride to that love. And for this sanctified seeking who needed a Salzman?

The marriage broker, a skeleton with haunted eyes, returned that very night. He looked, withal, the picture of frustrated expectancy—as if he had steadfastly waited the week at Miss Lily Hirschorn's side for a telephone call that never came.

Casually coughing, Salzman came immediately to the point: "So how did you like her?"

Leo's anger rose and he could not refrain from chiding the matchmaker: "Why did you lie to me, Salzman?"

Salzman's pale face went dead white, the world had snowed on him.

"Did you not state that she was twenty-nine?" Leo insisted.

"I give you my word—"

"She was thirty-five, if a day. *At least* thirty-five."

"Of this don't be too sure. Her father told me—"

"Never mind. The worst of it was that you lied to her."

"How did I lie to her, tell me?"

"You told her things about me that weren't true. You made me out to be more, consequently less than I am. She had in mind a totally different person, a sort of semi-mystical Wonder Rabbi."

"All I said, you was a religious man."

"I can imagine."

Salzman sighed. "This is my weakness that I have," he confessed. "My wife says to me I shouldn't be a salesman, but when I have two fine people that they would be wonderful to be married, I am so happy that I talk too much." He smiled wanly. "This is why Salzman is a poor man."

Leo's anger left him. "Well, Salzman, I'm afraid that's all."

The marriage broker fastened hungry eyes on him.

"You don't want any more a bride?"

"I do," said Leo, "but I have decided to seek her in a different way. I am no longer interested in an arranged marriage. To be frank, I now admit the necessity of premarital love. That is, I want to be in love with the one I marry."

"Love?" said Salzman, astounded. After a moment he remarked, "For us, our love is our life, not for the ladies. In the ghetto they—"

"I know, I know," said Leo. "I've thought of it often. Love, I have said to myself, should be a by-product of living and worship rather than its own end. Yet for myself I find it necessary to establish the level of my need and fulfill it."

Salzman shrugged but answered, "Listen, rabbi, if you want love, this I can find for you also. I have such beautiful clients that you will love them the minute your eyes will see them."

Leo smiled unhappily. "I'm afraid you don't understand."

But Salzman hastily unstrapped his portfolio and withdrew a manila packet from it.

"Pictures," he said, quickly laying the envelope on the table.

Leo called after him to take the pictures away, but as if on the wings of the wind, Salzman had disappeared.

March came. Leo had returned to his regular routine. Although he felt not quite himself yet—lacked energy—he was making plans for a more active social life. Of course it would cost something, but he was an expert in cutting corners; and when there was no corners left he would make circles rounder. All the while Salzman's pictures had lain on the table, gathering dust. Occasionally as Leo sat studying, or enjoying a cup of tea, his eyes fell on the manila envelope, but he never opened it.

The days went by and no social life to speak of developed with a member of the opposite sex—it was difficult, given the circumstances of his situation. One morning Leo toiled up the stairs to his room and stared out the window at the city. Although the day was bright his view of it was dark. For some time he watched the people in the street below hurrying along and then turned with a heavy heart to his little room. On the table was the packet. With a sudden relentless gesture he tore it open. For a half-hour he stood by the table in a state of excitement, examining the photographs of the ladies Salzman had included. Finally, with a deep sigh he put them down. There were six, of varying degrees of attractiveness, but look at them long enough and they all became Lily Hirschorn: all past their prime, all starved behind bright smiles, not a true personality in the lot. Life, despite their frantic yoohooings, had passed them by; they were pictures in a brief case that stank of fish. After a while, however, as Leo attempted to return the photographs into the envelope, he found in it another, a snapshot of the type taken by a machine for a quarter. He gazed at it a moment and let out a cry.

Her face deeply moved him. Why, he could at first not say. It gave him the impression of youth—spring flowers, yet age—a sense of having been used to the bone, wasted; this came from the eyes, which were hauntingly familiar, yet absolutely strange. He had a vivid impression that he had met her before, but try as he might he could not place her although he could almost recall her name, as if he had read it in her own handwriting. No, this couldn't be; he would have remembered her. It was not, he affirmed, that she had an extraordinary beauty—no, though her face was attractive enough; it was that *something* about her moved him. Feature for feature, even some of the ladies of the photographs could do better; but she leaped forth to his heart—had *lived*, or wanted to—more than just wanted, perhaps regretted how she had lived—had somehow deeply suffered: it could be seen in the depths of those reluctant eyes, and from the way the light enclosed and shone from her, and within her, opening realms of possibility: this was her own. Her he desired. His head ached and eyes narrowed with the intensity of his gazing, then as if an obscure fog had blown up in the mind, he experienced fear of her and was aware that he had received an impression, somehow, of evil. He shuddered, saying softly, it is thus with us all. Leo brewed some tea in a small pot and sat sipping it without sugar, to calm himself. But before he had finished drinking, again with excitement he examined the face and found it good: good for Leo Finkle. Only such a one could understand him and help him seek whatever he was seeking. She might, perhaps, love him. How she had happened to be among the discards in Salzman's barrel he could never guess, but he knew he must urgently go find her.

Leo rushed downstairs, grabbed up the Bronx telephone book, and searched for Salzman's home address. He was not listed, nor was his office. Neither was he in the Manhattan book. But Leo remembered having written down the address on a slip of paper after he had read Salzman's advertisement in the "personals" column of the *Forward*. He ran up to his room and tore through his papers, without luck. It was exasperating. Just when he needed the matchmaker he was nowhere to be found. Fortunately Leo remembered to look in his wallet. There on a card he found his name written and a Bronx address. No phone number was listed, the reason—Leo now recalled—he had originally communicated with Salzman by letter. He got on his coat, put a hat on over his skull cap and hurried to the subway station. All the way to the far end of the Bronx he sat on the edge of his seat. He was more than once tempted to take out the picture and see if the girl's face was as he remembered it, but he refrained, allowing the snapshot to remain in his inside coat pocket, content to have her so close. When the train pulled into the station he was waiting at the door and bolted out. He quickly located the street Salzman had advertised.

The building he sought was less than a block from the subway, but it was not an office building, nor even a loft, nor a store in which one could rent office space. It was a very old tenement house. Leo found Salzman's name in pencil on a soiled tag under the bell and climbed three dark flights to his apartment. When he knocked, the door was opened by a thin, asthmatic, gray-haired woman, in felt slippers.

"Yes?" she said, expecting nothing. She listened without listening. He could have sworn he had seen her, too, before but knew it was an illusion.

"Salzman—does he live here? Pinye Salzman," he said, "the matchmaker?"

She stared at him a long minute. "Of course."

He felt embarrassed. "Is he in?"

"No." Her mouth, though left open, offered nothing more.

"The matter is urgent. Can you tell me where his office is?"

"In the air." She pointed upward.

"You mean he has no office?" Leo asked.

"In his socks."

He peered into the apartment. It was sunless and dingy, one large room divided by a half-open curtain, beyond which he could see a sagging metal bed. The near side of a room was crowded with rickety chairs, old bureaus, a three-legged table, racks of cooking utensils, and all the apparatus of a kitchen. But there was no sign of Salzman or his magic barrel, probably also a figment of the imagination. An odor of frying fish made Leo weak to the knees.

"Where is he?" he insisted. "I've got to see your husband."

At length she answered, "So who knows where he is? Every time he thinks a new thought he runs to a different place. Go home, he will find you."

"Tell him Leo Finkle."

She gave no sign she had heard.

He walked downstairs, depressed.

But Salzman, breathless, stood waiting at his door.

Leo was astounded and overjoyed. "How did you get here before me?"

"I rushed."

"Come inside."

They entered. Leo fixed tea, and a sardine sandwich for Salzman. As they were drinking he reached behind him for the packet of pictures and handed them to the marriage broker.

Salzman put down his glass and said expectantly, "You found somebody you like?"

"Not among these."

The marriage broker turned away.

"Here is the one I want." Leo held forth the snapshot.

Salzman slipped on his glasses and took the picture into his trembling hand. He turned ghastly and let out a groan.

"What's the matter?" cried Leo.

"Excuse me. Was an accident this picture. She isn't for you."

Salzman frantically shoved the manila packet into his portfolio. He thrust the snapshot into his pocket and fled down the stairs.

Leo, after momentary paralysis, gave chase and cornered the marriage broker in the vestibule. The landlady made hysterical outcries but neither of them listened.

"Give me back the picture, Salzman."

"No." The pain in his eyes was terrible.

"Tell me who she is then."

"This I can't tell you. Excuse me."

He made to depart, but Leo, forgetting himself, seized the match-maker by his tight coat and shook him frenziedly.

"Please," sighed Salzman. "*Please.*"

Leo ashamedly let him go. "Tell me who she is," he begged. "It's very important for me to know."

"She is not for you. She is a wild one—wild, without shame. This is not a bride for a rabbi."

"What do you mean wild?"

"Like an animal. Like a dog. For her to be poor was a sin. This is why to me she is dead now."

"In God's name, what do you mean?"

"Her I can't introduce to you," Salzman cried.

"Why are you so excited?"

"Why, he asks," Salzman said, bursting into tears. "This is my baby, my Stella, she should burn in hell."

Leo hurried up to bed and hid under the covers. Under the covers he thought his life through. Although he soon fell asleep he could not sleep her out of his mind. He woke, beating his breast. Though he prayed to be rid of her, his prayers went unanswered. Through days of torment he endlessly struggled not to love her; fearing success, he escaped it. He then concluded to convert her to goodness, himself to God. The idea alternately nauseated and exalted him.

He perhaps did not know that he had come to a final decision until he encountered Salzman in a Broadway cafeteria. He was sitting alone at a rear table, sucking the bony remains of a fish. The marriage broker appeared haggard, and transparent to the point of vanishing.

Salzman looked up at first without recognizing him. Leo had grown a pointed beard and his eyes were weighted with wisdom.

"Salzman," he said, "love has at last come to my heart."

"Who can love from a picture?" mocked the marriage broker.

"It is not impossible."

"If you can love her, then you can love anybody. Let me show you some new clients that they just sent me their photographs. One is a little doll."

"Just her I want," Leo murmured.

"Don't be a fool, doctor. Don't bother with her."

"Put me in touch with her, Salzman," Leo said humbly. "Perhaps I can be of service."

Salzman had stopped eating and Leo understood with emotion that it was now arranged.

Leaving the cafeteria, he was, however, afflicted by a tormenting suspicion that Salzman had planned it all to happen this way.

Leo was informed by letter that she would meet him on a certain corner, and she was there one spring night, waiting under a street lamp. He appeared, carrying a small bouquet of violets and rosebuds. Stella stood by the lamp post, smoking. She wore white with red shoes, which fitted his expectations, although in a troubled moment he had imagined the dress red, and only the shoes white. She waited uneasily and shyly. From afar he saw that her eyes—clearly her father's—were filled with desperate innocence. He pictured, in her, his own redemption. Violins and lit candles revolved in the sky. Leo ran forward with flowers outthrust.

Around the corner, Salzman, leaning against a wall, chanted prayers for the dead.

# JULIO CORTÁZAR
## 1914–

He was born in Brussels, Belgium, of Argentinian parents. When he was four, the family returned to Buenos Aires, where he was raised by his mother and an aunt after his father left home. His ancestors were Basques on his father's side, French and German on his mother's. In Argentina he read fantasy and dutifully attended schools, earning qualification as an elementary school teacher in 1932 and a high school teacher in 1935. While teaching in Bolívar he began to write stories and poems. In 1945 he was invited to teach French at the University of Cuba. There he was arrested briefly for participating in a protest against Perónism. After working as a public translator he received a scholarship for study in Paris. He left Argentina for France in 1951 and has remained there ever since, writing in Spanish his surrealistic novels and stories. He has continued to travel and translate. He is six feet six inches tall and collects Charlie Parker records.

# Blow-Up

It'll never be known how this has to be told, in the first person or in the second, using the third person plural or continually inventing modes that will serve for nothing. If one might say: I will see the moon rose, or: we hurt me at the back of my eyes, and especially: you the blond woman was the clouds that race before my your his our yours their faces. What the hell.

Seated ready to tell it, if one might go to drink a bock over there, and the typewriter continue by itself (because I use the machine), that would be perfection. And that's not just a manner of speaking. Perfection, yes, because here is the aperture which must be counted also as a machine (of another sort, a Contax 1.1.2) and it is possible that one machine may know more about another machine than I, you,

Translated by Paul Blackburn.

she—the blond—and the clouds. But I have the dumb luck to know that if I go this Remington will sit turned to stone on top of the table with the air of being twice as quiet that mobile things have when they are not moving. So, I have to write. One of us all has to write, if this is going to get told. Better that it be me who am dead, for I'm less compromised than the rest; I who see only the clouds and can think without being distracted, write without being distracted (there goes another, with a grey edge) and remember without being distracted, I who am dead (and I'm alive, I'm not trying to fool anybody, you'll see when we get to the moment, because I have to begin some way and I've begun with this period, the last one back the one at the beginning, which in the end is the best of the periods when you want to tell something).

All of a sudden I wonder why I have to tell this, but if one begins to wonder why he does all he does do, if one wonders why he accepts an invitation to lunch (now a pigeon's flying by and it seems to me a sparrow), or why when someone has told us a good joke immediately there starts up something like a tickling in the stomach and we are not at peace until we've gone into the office across the hall and told the joke over again; then it feels good immediately, one is fine, happy, and can get back to work. For I imagine that no one has explained this, that really the best thing is to put aside all decorum and tell it, because, after all's done, nobody is ashamed of breathing or of putting on his shoes; they're things that you do, and when something weird happens, when you find a spider in your shoe or if you take a breath and feel like a broken window, then you have to tell what's happening, tell it to the guys at the office or to the doctor. Oh, doctor, every time I take a breath . . . Always tell it, always get rid of that tickle in the stomach that bothers you.

And now that we're finally going to tell it, let's put things a little bit in order, we'd be walking down the staircase in this house as far as Sunday, November 7, just a month back. One goes down five floors and stands then in the Sunday in the sun one would not have suspected of Paris in November, with a large appetite to walk around, to see things, to take photos (because we were photographers, I'm a photographer). I know that the most difficult thing is going to be finding a way to tell it, and I'm not afraid of repeating myself. It's going to be difficult because nobody really knows who it is telling it, if I am I or what actually occurred or what I'm seeing (clouds, and once in a while a pigeon) or if, simply, I'm telling a truth which is only my truth, and then is the truth only for my stomach, for this impulse to go running out and to finish up in some manner with this, whatever it is.

We're going to tell it slowly, what happens in the middle of what I'm writing is coming already. If they replace me, if, so soon, I don't know what to say, if the clouds stop coming and something else starts (because it's impossible that this keep coming, clouds passing continually and occasionally a pigeon), if something out of all this . . . . And after the "if" what am I going to put if I'm going to close the sentence structure correctly? But if I begin to ask questions, I'll never tell anything, maybe to tell would be like an answer, at least for someone who's reading it.

Roberto Michel, French-Chilean, translator and in his spare time an amateur photographer, left number 11, rue Monsieur-le-Prince Sunday November 7 of the current year (now there're two small ones passing, with silver linings). He had spent three weeks working on the French version of a treatise on challenges and appeals by José Norberto Allende, professor at the University of Santiago. It's rare that there's wind in Paris, and even less seldom a wind like this that swirled around corners and rose up to whip at old wooden venetian blinds behind what astonished ladies commented variously on how unreliable the weather had been these last few years. But the sun was out also, riding the wind and friend of the cats, so there was nothing that would keep me from taking a walk along the docks of the Seine and taking photos of the Conservatoire and Sainte-Chapelle. It was hardly ten o'clock, and I figured that by eleven the light would be good, the best you can get in the fall; to kill some time I detoured around by the Isle Saint-Louis and started to walk along the quai d'Anjou. I stared for a bit at the hôtel de Lauzun, I recited bits from Apollinaire which always get into my head whenever I pass in front of the hôtel de Lauzun (and at that I ought to be remembering the other poet, but Michel is an obstinate beggar), and when the wind stopped all at once and the sun came out at least twice as hard (I mean warmer, but really it's the same thing), I sat down on the parapet and felt terribly happy in the Sunday morning.

One of the many ways of contesting level-zero, and one of the best, is to take photographs, an activity in which one should start becoming an adept very early in life, teach it to children since it requires discipline, aesthetic education, a good eye and steady fingers. I'm not talking about waylaying the lie like any old reporter, snapping the stupid silhouette of the VIP leaving number 10 Downing Street, but in all ways when one is walking about with a camera, one has almost a duty to be attentive, to not lose that abrupt and happy rebound of sun's rays off an old stone, or the pigtails-flying run of a small girl going home with a loaf of bread or a bottle of milk. Michel knew that the photographer always worked as a permutation of his personal way of seeing the world as other than the camera insidiously imposed upon it (now a large cloud is by, almost black), but he lacked no confidence in himself, knowing that he had only to go out without the Contax to recover the keynote of distraction, the sight without a frame around it, light without the diaphragm aperture or 1/250 sec. **Right now** (what a word, *now,* what a dumb lie) I was able to sit quietly on the railing overlooking the river watching the red and black motor-boats passing below without it occurring to me to think photo-graphically of the scenes, nothing more than letting myself go in the letting go of objects, running immobile in the stream of time. And then the wind was not blowing.

After, I wandered down the quai de Bourbon until getting to the end of the isle where the intimate square was (intimate because it was small, not that it was hidden, it offered its whole breast to the river and the sky), I enjoyed it, a lot. Nothing there but a couple and, of course, pigeons; maybe even some of those which are flying past now so that I'm seeing them. A leap up and I settled on the wall, and let myself turn about and be caught and fixed by the sun, giving it my face and ears and hands (I kept my gloves in my pocket). I had no desire to shoot pictures, and lit a cigarette to be doing something; I think it was that moment when the match was about to touch the tobacco that I saw the young boy for the first time.

What I'd thought was a couple seemed much more now a boy with his mother, although at the same time I realized that it was not a kid and his mother, and that it was a couple in the sense that we always allegate to couples when we see them leaning up against the parapets or embracing on the benches in the squares. As I had nothing else to do, I had more than enough time to wonder why the boy was so nervous, like a young colt or a hare, sticking his hands into his pockets, taking them out immediately, one after the other, running his fingers through his hair, changing his stance, and especially why was he afraid, well, you could guess that from every gesture, a fear suffocated by his shyness, an impulse to step backwards which he telegraphed, his body standing as if it were on the edge of flight, holding itself back in a final, pitiful decorum.

All this was so clear, ten feet away—and we were alone against the parapet at the tip of the island—that at the beginning the boy's fright didn't let me see the blond very well. Now, thinking back on it, I see her much better at that first second when I read her face (she'd turned around suddenly, swinging like a metal weathercock, and the eyes, the eyes were there), when I vaguely understood what might have been occurring to the boy and figured it would be worth the trouble to stay and watch (the wind was blowing their words away and they were speaking in a low murmur). I think that I know how to look, if it's something I know, and also that every looking oozes with mendacity, because it's that which expels us furthest outside ourselves, without the least guarantee, whereas to smell, or (but Michel rambles on to himself easily enough, there's no need to let him harangue on this way). In any case, if the likely inaccuracy can be seen beforehand, it becomes possible again to look; perhaps it suffices to choose between looking and the reality looked at, to strip things of all their unnecessary clothing. And surely all this is difficult besides.

As for the boy I remember the image before his actual body (that will clear itself up later), while now I am sure that I remember the woman's body much better than the image. She was thin and willowy, two unfair words to describe what she was, and was wearing an almost-black fur coat, almost long, almost handsome. All the morning's wind (now it was hardly a breeze and it wasn't cold) had blown through her blond hair which pared away her white, bleak face—two unfair words—and put the world at her feet and horribly alone in front of her dark eyes, her eyes fell on things like two eagles, two leaps into nothingness, two puffs of greem slime. I'm not describing anything, it's more a matter of trying to understand it. And I said two puffs of green slime.

Let's be fair, the boy was well enough dressed and was sporting yellow gloves which I would have sworn belonged to his older brother, a student of law or sociology; it was pleasant to see the fingers of the gloves sticking out of his jacket pocket. For a long time I didn't see his face, barely a profile, not stupid—a terrified bird, a Fra Filippo angel, rice pudding with milk—and the back of an adolescent who wants to take up judo and has had a scuffle or two in defense of an idea or his sister. Turning fourteen, perhaps fifteen, one would guess that he was dressed and fed by his parents but without a nickel in his pocket, having to debate with his buddies before making up his mind to buy a coffee, a cognac, a pack of cigarettes. He'd walk through the streets thinking of the girls in his class, about how good it would be to go to the movies and see the latest film, or to buy novels or neckties or bottles of liquor with green and white labels on them. At home (it would be a respectable home, lunch at noon and romantic landscapes on the walls, with a dark entryway and a mahogany umbrella stand inside the door) there'd be the slow rain of time, for studying, for being mama's hope, for looking like dad, for writing to his aunt in Avignon. So that there was a lot of walking the streets, the whole of the river for him (but without a nickel) and the mysterious city of fifteen-year-olds with its signs in doorways, its terrifying cats, a paper of fried potatoes for thirty francs, the pornographic magazine folded four ways, a solitude like the emptiness of his pockets, the eagerness for so much that was incomprehensible but illumined by a total love, by the availability analogous to the wind and the streets.

This biography was of the boy and of any boy whatsoever, but this particular one now, you could see he was insular, surrounded solely by the blond's presence as she continued talking with him. (I'm tired of insisting, but two long ragged ones just went by. That morning I don't think I looked at the sky once, because what was happening with the boy and the woman appeared so soon I could do nothing but look at them and wait, look at them and . . .) To cut it short, the boy was agitated and one could guess without too much trouble what had just occurred a few minutes before, at most half-an-hour. The boy had come onto the tip of the island, seen the woman and thought her marvelous. The woman was waiting for that because she was there waiting for that, or maybe the boy arrived before her and she saw him from one of the balconies or from a car and got out to meet him, starting the conversation with whatever, from the beginning she was sure that he was going to be afraid and want to run off, and that, naturally, he'd stay, stiff and sullen, pretending experience and the pleasure of the adventure. The rest was easy because it was happening ten feet away from me, and anyone could have gauged the stages of the game, the derisive, competitive fencing; its major attraction was not that it was happening but in foreseeing its denouement. The boy would try to end it by pretending a date, an obligation, whatever, and would go stumbling off disconcerted, wishing he were walking with some assurance, but naked under the mocking glance which would follow him until he was out of sight. Or rather, he would stay there, fascinated or simply incapable of taking the initiative, and the woman would begin to touch his face gently, muss his hair, still talking to him voicelessly, and soon would take him by the arm to lead him off, unless he, with an uneasiness beginning to tinge the edge of desire, even his stake in the adventure, would rouse himself to put his arm around her waist and to kiss her. Any of this could have happened, though it did not, and perversely Michel waited, sitting on the railing, making the settings almost without looking at the camera, ready to take a picturesque shot of a corner of the island with an uncommon couple talking and looking at one another.

Strange how the scene (almost nothing: two figures there mismatched in their youth) was taking on a disquieting aura. I thought it was I imposing it, and that my photo, if I shot it, would reconstitute things in their true stupidity. I would have liked to know what he was thinking, a man in a grey hat sitting at the wheel of a car parked on the dock which led up to the footbridge, and whether he was reading the paper or asleep. I had just discovered him because people inside a parked car have a tendency to disappear, they get lost in that wretched, private cage stripped of the beauty that motion and danger give it. And nevertheless, the car had been there the whole time, forming part (or deforming that part) of the isle. A car: like saying a lighted streetlamp, a park bench. Never like saying wind, sunlight, those elements always new to the skin and the eyes, and also the boy and the woman, unique, put there to change the island, to show it to me in another way. Finally, it may have been that the man with the newspaper also became aware of what was happening and would, like me, feel that malicious sensation of waiting for everything to happen. Now the woman had swung around smoothly, putting the young boy between herself and the wall, I saw them almost in profile, and he was taller, though not much taller, and yet she dominated him, it seemed like she was hovering over him (her laugh, all at once, a whip of feathers), crushing him just by being there, smiling, one hand taking a stroll though the air. Why wait any longer? Aperture at sixteen, a sighting which would not include the horrible black car, but yes, that tree, necessary to break up too much grey space . . .

I raised the camera, pretended to study a focus which did not include them, and waited and watched closely, sure that I would finally catch the revealing expression, one that would sum it all up, life that is rhythmed by movement but which a stiff image destroys, taking time in cross section, if we do not choose the essential imperceptible fraction of it. I did not have to wait long. The woman was getting on with the job of handcuffing the boy smoothly, stripping from him what was left of his freedom a hair at a time, in an incredibly slow and delicious torture. I imagined the possible endings (now a small fluffy cloud appears, almost alone in the sky), I saw their arrival at the house (a basement apartment probably, which she would have filled with large cushions and cats) and conjectured the boy's terror and his desperate decision to play it cool and to be led off pretending there was nothing new in it for him. Closing my eyes, if I did in fact close my eyes, I set the scene: the teasing kisses, the woman mildly repelling the hands which were trying to undress her, like in novels, on a bed that would have a lilac-colored comforter, on the other hand she taking off his clothes, plainly mother and son under a milky yellow light, and everything would end up as usual, perhaps, but maybe everything would go otherwise, and the initiation of the adolescent would not happen, she would not let it happen, after a long prologue wherein the awkwardnesses, the exasperating caresses, the running of hands over bodies would be resolved in who knows what, in a separate and solitary pleasure, in a petulant denial mixed with the art of tiring and disconcerting so much poor innocence. It might go like that, it might very well go like that; that woman was not looking for the boy as a lover, and at the same time she was dominating him toward some end impossible to understand if you do not imagine it as a cruel game, the desire to desire without satisfaction, to excite herself for someone else, someone who in no way could be that kid.

Michel is guilty of making literature, of indulging in fabricated unrealities. Nothing pleases him more than to imagine exceptions to the rule, individuals outside the species, not-always-repugnant monsters. But that woman invited speculation, perhaps giving clues enough for the fantasy to hit the bullseye. Before she left, and now that she would fill my imaginings for several days, for I'm given to ruminating, I decided not to lose a moment more. I got it all into the view-finder (with the tree, the railing, the eleven-o'clock sun) and took the shot. In time to realize that they both had noticed and stood there looking at me, the boy surprised and as though questioning, but she was irritated, her face and body flat-footedly hostile, feeling robbed, ignominiously recorded on a small chemical image.

I might be able to tell it in much greater detail but it's not worth the trouble. The woman said that no one had the right to take a picture without permission, and demanded that I hand her over the film. All this in a dry, clear voice with a good Parisian accent, which rose in color and tone with every phrase. For my part, it hardly mattered whether she got the roll of film or not, but anyone who knows me will tell you, if you want anything from me, ask nicely. With the result that I restricted myself to formulating the opinion that not only was photography in public places not prohibited, but it was looked upon with decided favor, both private and official. And while that was getting said, I noticed on the sly how the boy was falling back, sort of actively backing up though without moving, and all at once (it seemed almost incredible) he turned and broke into a run, the poor kid, thinking that he was walking off and in fact in full flight, running past the side of the car, disappearing like a gossamer filament of angel-spit in the morning air.

But filaments of angel-spittle are also called devil-spit, and Michel had to endure rather particular curses, to hear himself called meddler and imbecile, taking great pains meanwhile to smile and to abate with simple movements of his head such a hard sell. As I was beginning to get tired, I heard the car door slam. The man in the grey hat was there, looking at us. It was only at that point that I realized he was playing a part in the comedy.

He began to walk toward us, carrying in his hand the paper he had been pretending to read. What I remember best is the grimace that twisted his mouth askew, it covered his face with wrinkles, changed somewhat both in location and shape because his lips trembled and the grimace went from one side of his mouth to the other as though it were on wheels, independent and involuntary. But the rest stayed fixed, a flour-powdered clown or bloodless man, dull dry skin, eyes deepset, the nostrils black and prominently visible, blacker than the eyebrows or hair or the black necktie. Walking cautiously as though the pavement hurt his feet; I saw patent-leather shoes with such thin soles that he must have felt every roughness in the pavement. I don't know why I got down off the railing, nor very well why I decided to not give them the photo, to refuse that demand in which I guessed at their fear and cowardice. The clown and the woman consulted one another in silence: we made a perfect and unbearable triangle, something I felt compelled to break with a crack of a whip. I laughed in their faces and began to walk off, a little more slowly, I imagine, than the boy. At the level of the first houses, beside the iron footbridge, I turned around to look at them. They were not moving, but the man had dropped his newspaper; it seemed to me that the woman, her back to the parapet, ran her hands over the stone with the classical and absurd gesture of someone pursued looking for a way out.

What happened after that happened here, almost just now, in a room on the fifth floor. Several days went by before Michel developed the photos he'd taken on Sunday; his shots of the Conservatoire and of Sainte-Chapelle were all they should be. Then he found two or three proof-shots he'd forgotten, a poor attempt to catch a cat perched astonishingly on the roof of a rambling public urinal, and also the shot of the blond and the kid. The negative was so good that he made an enlargement; the enlargement was so good that he made one very much larger, almost the size of a poster. It did not occur to him (now one wonders and wonders) that only the shots of the Conservatoire were worth so much work. Of the whole series, the snapshot of the tip of the island was the only one which interested him; he tacked up the enlargement on one wall of the room, and the first day he spent some time looking at it and remembering, that gloomy operation of comparing the memory with the gone reality; a frozen memory, like any photo, where nothing is missing, not even, and especially, nothingness, the true solidifier of the scene. There was the woman, there was the boy, the tree rigid above their heads, the sky as sharp as the stone of the parapet, clouds and stones melded into a single substance and inseparable (now one with sharp edges is going by, like a thunderhead). The first two days I accepted what I had done, from the photo itself to the enlargement on the wall, and didn't even question that every once in a while I would interrupt my translation of José Norberto Allende's treatise to encounter once more the woman's face, the dark splotches on the railing. I'm such a jerk; it had never occurred to me that when we look at a photo from the front, the eyes reproduce exactly the position and the vision of the lens; it's these things that are taken for granted and it never occurs to anyone to think about them. From my chair, with the typewriter directly in front of me, I looked at the photo ten feet away, and then it occurred to me that I had hung it exactly at the point of view of the lens. It looked very good that way; no doubt, it was the best way to appreciate a photo, though the angle from the diagonal doubtless has its pleasures and might even divulge different aspects. Every few minutes, for example when I was unable to find the way to say in good French what José Norberto Allende was saying in very good Spanish, I raised my eyes and looked at the photo; sometimes the woman would catch my eye, sometimes the boy, sometimes the pavement where a dry leaf had fallen admirably situated to heighten a lateral section. Then I rested a bit from my labors, and I enclosed myself again happily in that morning in which the photo was drenched, I recalled ironically the angry picture of the woman demanding I give her the photograph, the boy's pathetic and ridiculous flight, the entrance on the scene of the man with the white face. Basically, I was satisfied with myself; my part had not been too brilliant, and since the French have been given the gift of the sharp response, I did not see very well why I'd chosen to leave without a complete demonstration of the rights, privileges and prerogatives of citizens. The important thing, the really important thing was having helped the kid to escape in time (this in case my theorizing was correct, which was not sufficiently proven, but the running away itself seemed to show it so). Out of plain meddling, I had given him the opportunity finally to take advantage of his fright to do something useful; now he would be regretting it, feeling his honor impaired, his manhood diminished. That was better than the attentions of a woman capable of looking as she had looked at him on that island. Michel is something of a puritan at times, he believes that one should not seduce someone from a position of strength. In the last analysis, taking that photo had been a good act.

Well, it wasn't because of the good act that I looked at it between paragraphs while I was working. At that moment I didn't know the reason, the reason I had tacked the enlargement onto the wall; maybe all fatal acts happen that way, and that is the condition of their fulfillment. I don't think the almost-furtive trembling of the leaves on the tree alarmed me. I was working on a sentence and rounded it out successfully. Habits are like immense herbariums, in the end an enlargement of 32 x 28 looks like a movie screen, where, on the tip of the island, a woman is speaking with a boy and a tree is shaking its dry leaves over their heads.

But her hands were just too much. I had just translated: "In that case, the second key resides in the intrinsic nature of difficulties which societies . . ." —when I saw the woman's hand beginning to stir slowly, finger by finger. There was nothing left of me, a phrase in French which I would never have to finish, a typewriter on the floor, a chair that squeaked and shook, fog. The kid had ducked his head like boxers do when they've done all they can and are waiting for the final blow to fall; he had turned up the collar of his overcoat and seemed more a prisoner than ever, the perfect victim helping promote the catastrophe. Now the woman was talking into his ear, and her hand opened again to lay itself against his cheekbone, to caress and caress it, burning it, taking her time. The kid was less startled than he was suspicious, once or twice he poked his head over the woman's shoulder and she continued talking, saying something that made him look back every few minutes toward that area where Michel knew the car was parked and the man in the grey hat, carefully eliminated from the photo but present in the boy's eyes (how doubt that now) in the words of the woman, in the woman's hands, in the vicarious presence of the woman. When I saw the man come up, stop near them and look at them, his hands in his pockets and a stance somewhere between disgusted and demanding, the master who is about to whistle in his dog after a frolic in the square, I understood, if that was to understand, what had to happen now, what had to have happened then, what would have to happen at that moment, among these people, just where I had poked my nose in to upset an established order, interfering innocently in that which had not happened, but which was now going to happen, now was going to be fulfilled. And what I had imagined earlier was much less horrible than the reality, that woman, who was not there by herself, she was not caressing or propositioning or encouraging for her own pleasure, to lead the angel away with his tousled hair and play the tease with his terror and his eager grace. The real boss was waiting there, smiling petulantly, already certain of the business; he was not the first to send a woman in the vanguard, to bring him the prisoners manacled with flowers. The rest of it would be so simple, the car, some house or another, drinks, stimulating engravings, tardy tears, the awakening in hell. And there was nothing I could do, this time I could do absolutely nothing. My strength had been a photograph, that, there, where they were taking their revenge on me, demonstrating clearly what was going to happen. The photo had been taken, the time had run out, gone; we were so far from one another, the abusive act had certainly already taken place, the tears already shed, and the rest conjecture and sorrow. All at once the order was inverted, they were alive, moving, they were deciding and had decided, they were going to their future; and I on this side, prisoner of another time, in a room on the fifth floor, to not know who they were, that woman, that man, and that boy, to be only the lens of my camera, something fixed, rigid, incapable of intervention. It was horrible, their mocking me, deciding it before my impotent eye, mocking me, for the boy again was looking at the flour-faced clown and I had to accept the fact that he was going to say yes, that the proposition carried money with it or a gimmick, and I couldn't yell for him to run, or even open the road to him again with a new photo, a small and almost meek intervention which would ruin the framework of drool and perfume. Everything was going to resolve itself right there, at that moment; there was like an immense silence which had nothing to do with physical silence. It was stretching it out, setting itself up. I think I screamed, I screamed terribly, and that at that exact second I realized that I was beginning to move toward them, four inches, a step, another step, the tree swung its branches rhythmically in the foreground, a place where the railing was tarnished emerged from the frame, the woman's face turned toward me as though surprised, was enlarging, and then I turned a bit, I mean that the camera turned a little, and without losing sight of the woman, I began to close in on the man who was looking at me with the black holes he had in places of eyes, surprised and angered both, he looked, wanting to nail me onto the air, and at that instant I happened to see something like a large bird outside the focus that was flying in a single swoop in front of the picture, and I leaned up against the wall of my room and was happy because the boy had just managed to escape, I saw him running off, in focus again, sprinting with his hair flying in the wind, learning finally to fly across the island, to arrive at the footbridge, return to the city. For the second time he'd escaped them, for the second time I was helping him to escape, returning him to his precarious paradise. Out of breath, I stood in front of them; no need to step closer, the game was played out. Of the woman you could see just maybe a shoulder and a bit of the hair, brutally cut off by the frame of the picture; but the man was directly center, his mouth half open, you could see a shaking black tongue, and he lifted his hands slowly, bringing them into the foreground, an instant still in perfect focus, and then all of him a lump that blotted out the island, the tree, and I shut my eyes, I didn't want to see any more, and I covered my face and broke into tears like an idiot.

Now there's a big white cloud, as on all these days, all this untellable time. What remains to be said is always a cloud, two clouds, or long hours of a sky perfectly clear, a very clean, clear rectangle tacked up with pins on the wall of my room. That was what I saw when I opened my eyes and dried them with my fingers: the clear sky, and then a cloud that drifted in from the left, passed gracefully and slowly across and disappeared on the right. And then another, and for a change sometimes, everything gets grey, all one enormous cloud, and suddenly the splotches of rain cracking down, for a long spell you can see it raining over the picture, like a spell of weeping reversed, and little by little, the frame becomes clear, perhaps the sun comes out, and again the clouds begin to come, two at a time, three at a time. And the pigeons once in a while, and a sparrow or two.

# ANNE HÉBERT
1916–

Born at Sainte-Catherine-de-Fossambault, near Quebec City, she was the eldest of three children. Childhood illness left her an invalid for many years, and she was educated at home by her father, the respected poet and critic Maurice Hébert, and later at the Collège Notre-Dame-de-Bellevue and the College Mérici, Quebec. As a child she formed a close literary friendship with her cousin, Saint-Denys-Garneau, one of Quebec's finest poets. From 1950 to 1954 she worked as a script writer for both Radio-Canada and the National Film Board of Canada. In 1954 Hébert went to Paris to live as a writer, and since then she has spent a great deal of time in France. Best known as a poet for such books as *Le tombeau des rois* (1953), she has also written several collections of short stories as well as novels, most notably *Kamouraska* (1970), which was made into a film.

## The House on the Esplanade[1]

Stephanie de Bichette was a curious little creature with frail limbs that seemed badly put together. Only her starched collarette kept her head from falling over on her shoulder; it was too heavy for her long, slender neck. If the head of Stephanie de Bichette looked so heavy, it was because all the pomp of her aristocratic ancestors was symbolized in her coiffure, a high up-swept style, with padded curls arranged in rows on her narrow cranium, an architectural achievement in symmetrical silvery blobs.

Mademoiselle de Bichette had passed, without transition period, without adolescence, from the short frocks of her childhood to this everlasting ash-grey dress, trimmed at neck and wrists with a swirl of lilac braiding. She owned two parasols with carved ivory handles—one lilac and the other ash-grey. When she went out driving in the carriage she chose her parasol according to the weather, and everyone in the little town could tell the weather by the colour of Mademoiselle de Bichette's parasol. The lilac one appeared on days of brilliant sunshine, the ash-grey one whenever it was slightly cloudy. In winter, and when it rained, Stephanie simply never went out at all.

I have spoken at length about her parasols because they were the outward and visible signs of a well-regulated life, a perfect edifice of regularity. Unchanging routine surrounded and supported this innocent old creature. The slightest crack in this extraordinary construc-

<hr>

[1]Translated by Morna Scott Stoddart.

tion, the least change in this stern programme would have been enough to make Mademoiselle de Bichette seriously ill.

Fortunately, she had never had to change her maid. Geraldine served and cared for her mistress with every evidence of complete respect for tradition. The whole life of Stephanie de Bichette was a tradition, or rather a series of traditions, for apart from the tradition of the well-known parasols and the complicated coiffure, there was the ritual of getting up, of going to bed, of lace-making, of meal-times, and so on.

Stephanie Hortense Sophie de Bichette lived facing the Esplanade, in a grey stone house dating back to the days of the French occupation. You know the sort of house *that* implies—a tall, narrow edifice with a pointed roof and several rows of high windows, where the ones at the top look no bigger than swallows' nests, a house with two or three large attics that most old maids would have delighted in. But, believe it or not, Mademoiselle de Bichette never climbed up to her attics to sentimentalize over souvenirs, to caress treasured old belongings, or to plan meticulous orgies of housecleaning amid the smell of yellowing paper and musty air that even the best-kept attics seem to possess.

No, she occupied the very heart of the house, scarcely one room on each floor. On the fourth story, only Geraldine's room remained open, among the rooms of all the former servants. It was part of the family tradition to close off rooms that were no longer used. One after another, bedroom after bedroom had been condemned: the room where the little brothers had died of scarlet fever, when Stephanie was only ten years old; the bedroom of their mother, who had passed away soon after her two children; the room of Irénée, the elder brother who had been killed in an accident, out hunting; the room of the elder sister, Desneiges, who had entered the Ursuline convent; then the bedroom of Monsieur de Bichette, the father, who had succumbed to a long illness; to say nothing of the room belonging to Charles, the only surviving brother, which had been closed ever since his marriage.

The ritual was always the same: once the occupant of the room had departed for the cemetery, the convent, or the adventure of matrimony, Geraldine would tidy everything away, carefully leaving each piece of furniture exactly in place; then she would draw the shutters, put dust-covers on the arm-chairs, and lock the door for good. No one ever set foot in that room again. One more member of the family was finally disposed of.

Geraldine took a distinct pleasure in this solemn, unvarying rite, just as a gravedigger may take pride in a neat row of graves, with well-kept mounds and smoothly raked grass above them. Sometimes she remembered that one day she would have to close Mademoiselle Stephanie's room, too, and live on for a while, the only living creature among all the dead. She looked forward to that moment, not with horror, but with pleasant anticipation, as a rest and a reward. After so many years of housework in that great house, all its rooms would be fixed at last in order, for all eternity. Mildew and dust could take possession then; Geraldine would have no more cleaning to do then. The rooms of the dead are not "done up."

This was not the calculation of a lazy woman. Geraldine dreamed of the last door closed and the last key turned in the lock just as the harvester dreams of the last sheaf of corn, or the needlewoman of the last stitch in her embroidery. It would be the crowning achievement of her long life, the goal of her destiny.

It was strange that the old servant reckoned two living people among the dead: Mademoiselle Desneiges, the nun, and Monsieur Charles, a married man and the father of a family. They had both left the family roof, that was enough for Geraldine to class them as non-existent. The heavy door of the cloister had closed forever on one, while Charles, by marrying a common little seamstress from the Lower Town, had so grieved his father that the old house and all it contained had been left to Stephanie. Charles came to see his sister every evening, but Geraldine never spoke a word to him. For her, Stephanie was the whole of the de Bichette family.

On the third floor, all the bedrooms were closed, with the exception of Mademoiselle de Bichette's. On the second, only the small blue boudoir lived on, a life of dimness and disuse. On the first floor, an immense drawing-room stretched from front to back, cluttered with furniture of different periods, each piece bristling with fussy elaborate knick-knacks. The ground-floor doors were always open, with high, carved portals to the vestibule, the parlour, the dining-room. In the basement was the old-fashioned kitchen, uncomfortable and always damp. Geraldine was the cook as well as the maid-of-all-work, but was never addressed as such.

If her mistress lived by tradition until it became a religion, Geraldine, too had her tradition, the collecting of bright-coloured buttons. Her black skirt and her white apron never changed, but she used her imagination in trimming her blouses. Red buttons sparkled on blue blouses, yellow ones on green, and so on, not to mention buttons in gold and silver and crystal. In the attic, she had discovered great chests of ancient garments which she had stripped, shamelessly, of their trimmings. Apart from this innocent craze for buttons, the big woman with the ruddy complexion made no objections to touring the wine cellar every evening before going to bed, as the last of her duties, conscientiously and even devotedly performed. But where she excelled, was in the observance of tradition where her mistress was concerned.

Every morning, at seven o'clock in summer and eight in winter, she climbed the three flights of stairs and knocked at the bedroom door. . . . Two taps, two firm, decided taps, no more, no less. This was the signal for the ceremonial to begin.

Geraldine opened the bedroom curtains, then the window curtains, and finally the shutters. Her ageing mistress preferred to sleep in complete darkness, requiring several thicknesses of material and polished wood between herself and the wicked witchcraft of the night. She was afraid of the first rays of sunlight as well, not knowing what to do about them, since they might easily wake you long before the proper time for getting up.

Then Geraldine would return to the passage to fetch a kind of wagon equipped with everything Stephanie might need for the first few hours of the day. Two white pills in a glass of water, coffee and toast, toothbrush and toothpowder, a copper bathtub, white towels, white, starched underwear. Also a feather duster, a broom, a dustpan . . . all that she used for tidying up the room. This wagon was as wide as a single bed, four feet wide, with three shelves. Geraldine had made it herself out of old packing cases.

When Stephanie's breakfast was finished, the maid would bathe, dress, and powder her mistress, then do her hair. Stephanie allowed her to do everything, silent, inert, trusting. After that, there was sometimes a moment of painful indecision, an anguished knot in the brain of Mademoiselle de Bichette, when Geraldine leaned over to look out of the window, examining the sky and frowning as she declared:

"I really don't know what sort of weather we're going to have today."

Then the old lady would stare at her maid with such forlorn eyes that Geraldine would say, hurriedly:

"It's going to rain. You're not going to be able to go out this morning. I'll let the coachman know."

Stephanie would grow calm again after that, but she would not be entirely herself until Geraldine had settled her carefully in the blue drawing-room, on her high-backed chair of finely carved wood, near the window, her half-finished lace on her knee and her crochet hook in her hand. Only then would the idea take firm root in her brain:

"It's going to rain. I can't go out. . . . All I have to do is to handle this hook and this thread as my mother taught me to do when I was seven years old. . . . If it had been a fine day, it would have been different, I would have gone out in the carriage. There are only two realities in the world . . . only two realities I can rely on . . . and close my eyes, deep inside them: the reality of going out in the carriage, the reality of making my lace. . . . How lost and strange I am when Geraldine cannot tell what the weather is going to do, and I am left in suspense with no solid ground beneath my feet. . . . It just *wracks* my brain! Oh! Not to have to think about it, to let myself be carried away by one or the other of these my only two sure and certain realities going out for a drive or sitting here, making my lace. . . ."

Even if the day turned out fine in the end, Geraldine never said so. It would have been too much of a shock for her mistress. Imagine what confusion in such a patterned existence if someone had suddenly announced a change, after she had firmly established herself for the day in the reality of lace-making, and dared to tell her she had taken the wrong road? She could never again have believed in any reality at all.

Since her childhood, Mademoiselle de Bichette had been making lace doilies of different sizes, which Geraldine used in many different ways. These doilies flowed from her fingers at the steady rate of four per week, small pieces of white lace that resembled each other like peas in a pod. They were everywhere in the house—five or six on the piano, seven or eight on all the tables, as many as ten on every armchair, one or two on all the smaller chairs. Every knick-knack rested on a piece of delicate openwork, so that the furniture all seemed powdered with snowflakes, enlarged as if under a microscope.

In winter, and in summer, on the days when Geraldine had decided the weather was not fit for going out, Mademoiselle de Bichette would crochet all the morning, in her blue boudoir, sitting up so straight and still that she scarcely seemed real, her feet resting on a stool covered by something that was strangely like the work the old lady held in her hands.

At five minutes to twelve, Geraldine would announce:

"Mademoiselle Stephanie's luncheon is served."

At the mention of her name, the old lady would rise at once; the ritual phrase had touched a switch somewhere within her, so that without effort, without thinking, without even understanding, she would put herself slowly and ceremoniously in motion, descend the staircase and take her place at the table.

If Stephanie did go out, she invariably returned home at a quarter to twelve, so she had ample time to receive the announcement that luncheon was served with the necessary calm.

The outings of Madmoiselle de Bichette were governed by just as incredible a routine. She came out on the sidewalk with tiny steps, her frail little body bending under the weight of that enormous pile of scaffolded curls. Geraldine helped her mistress into the carriage, the coachman whipped up his horse, and the victoria started on its slow, quiet drive, invariably the same, through the streets of the little town. The horse knew the road by heart, so the coachman seized the opportunity for a short nap, his cap pulled down over his eyes, his legs stretched out, his hands folded on his stomach. He always waked up in time, as if by magic, when the drive came to an end, crying out and stretching himself, with a jolly air of surprise:

"Well, well, Mamzelle, here we are back again!"

Just as if the old fellow, when he went to sleep as the drive started, had not been quite sure he would come back when he awoke, or if his return would be to the country of the living!

Mademoiselle de Bichette would disappear into the house, on Geraldine's arm; the coachman would unharness the horse and put the carriage away; and it was all over. With regret, the townsfolk watched the disintegration of this strange conveyance, like a ghostly apparition cutting through the clear morning light . . . the ancient nag, pulling an antique carriage, with a sleepy coachman and a tiny figure like a mummy, swathed in ash-grey and lilac.

After luncheon, Geraldine would lead her mistress into the long drawing-room on the first floor, where, without ever laying her crochet aside, Stephanie would receive a few callers, and the maid would serve dandelion wine and madeleines.

The old lady never left her chair, forcing herself to hold her head high, though her neck felt as if it were breaking under the weight of her monumental coiffure. Sometimes, this constant, painful effort was betrayed by a twitch of the lips, the only change of expression that callers could ever distinguish upon that small, powdered face. Then Stephanie would ask: "How is Madame your mother?" in a voice so white and colourless that it might have come from one of the closed rooms, where, according to the gossips of the town, some of the original inhabitants still lived on.

This phrase of Stephanie's had to do for greeting, for farewell, for conversation; indeed, it had to do for everthing, for the wine was sour and the madeleines stale and hard as stones. The callers were all so aged and unsteady that the most utter stranger would have had the tact never to ask that preposterous question, but Mademoiselle de Bichette knew no other formula, and in any case, she attached no importance whatever to the words she was saying. If she finished a lace doily while her callers were present, she simply let it fall at her feet, like a pebble into a pool, and began another identical piece of lace. The visiting ladies never stayed very long, and Stephanie seemed to notice their departure as little as she did their presence.

At a quarter past six, Geraldine would announce that Monsieur Charles was waiting below. The programme of the day was ticking on like the mechanism of a good Swiss watch, and the invisible wheels of Mademoiselle de Bichette responded perfectly, warning the limbs of this strange little creature that they must immediately convey her to the ground floor.

Her brother would kiss her brow and smile, rubbing his stubby-fingered hands together and remarking:

"Um-phm! It feels good in the house."

Then he would hang his overcoat up on a hall stand, while Geraldine followed his every movement with her look of triumphant disdain. With her arms crossed upon her swelling chest, she doubtless thought she looked like the statue of the Commendatore, bound on revenge. She would cast a glance of scorn on the threadbare coat, as if to say:

"Well, what did you expect? Monsieur Charles *would* get married to a chit of a girl from the Lower Town, so naturally, his father cut him off, and I locked up his room as if he were dead. If Mademoiselle Stephanie wants him here every evening, it's her own business, but I'*m* going to let him know that I'm *glad* he was thrown out, if I *am* only the servant. I know he's poor and that's his punishment for disobeying his father. He comes here because there isn't enough to eat at home. So he gobbles up our dinners and carries away on his nasty skin a bit of the warmth from our fires. . . . The good-for-nothing!"

If it were true that Charles had only one decent meal a day, it was astonishing that he was not at all thin. He was even fat, very fat, flabby and yellow-complexioned, with a bald head and a shiny face, colourless lips and almost colourless eyes. Geraldine said he had eyes like a codfish and his clothes always smelt of stale grease. Apart from that, she could not forgive a de Bichette for forgetting his table manners.

"To think that his slut of a wife has made him lose all he ever learned in decent society. . . . You wouldn't believe it possible," she would grumble to herself.

As dinner-time drew near, Charles became more and more noisily jolly. He never stopped rubbing his hands together; he got up, sat down, got up again, went from window to door and back a dozen times, while Stephanie's eyes ignored him. Then the brother and sister took their places, one at each end of the long table in the dining-room. There was no gas chandelier in this room, so it seemed even longer and darker, lit only by two tall candles in silver candlesticks. The corners of the room disappeared into the dimness, and the shadows of the brother and sister danced like black flames on the curiously carved oak panelling of the walls.

Every evening, the atmosphere of this dining-room seemed more impressive to Charles. Perhaps he felt unseen forms hiding in the darkness, invisible spectators of this singular repast; perhaps he feared to find the ghosts that haunted the bedrooms above, to see them take their places at the huge dining-table, where an old creature presided, small as a cat, white as the table-linen, who seemed already to be living in the uneasy world of phantoms.

As soon as Stephanie's brother had swallowed a few mouthfuls of soup, his good humour fell away, lifeless, utterly destroyed. When he entered the house, the smell of cooking would stimulate him, would intoxicate him with its marvellous promise, but now that the promise was kept, the man became gloomy again. Through his own bitter thoughts, he stared at the lace cloth, the heavy silverware, the fine china, and at this sister of his, who was still alive in spite of her look of belonging to some other world. What mysterious thread was keeping Stephanie here on earth? To look at her, you would have thought the slightest breath might carry her away, yet there she was, still alive.

Geraldine came and went around the table and her sharp eyes seemed to plumb the very depths of the man's thoughts. The brother sat there, knowing himself watched and understood, telling himself, in his embarrassment, that his sister would have joined her ancestors long ago had it not been for this fiendish servant, who by some diabolical process had contrived to keep the dying thing alive in her father's mansion, simply in order to enjoy as long as possible the spectacle of his own failure. In what dread "No Man's Land" of the spirit had the old witch made a pact with Monsieur de Bichette—and with Satan himself? Geraldine had inherited all the father's anger against his son, and faithful to that anger as if to a sacred promise, she was constantly reminding Charles of the curse that lay heavy upon him. At that moment he raised his head, resenting the eyes he felt fixed upon his every movement, but Geraldine was no longer there, Charles could hear the tinkle of her keys, in the passage between the staircase and the kitchen. He shuddered, for he knew very well which keys she carried at her waist. No cupboard, no inhabited room possessed a key. It chilled his heart strangely to know that the key of his room was there, along with those of the rooms of the dead. It scared him. Then he took hold of himself again and muttered:

"This damned house! . . . Enough to drive a man crazy to sit here night after night with two cracked old fools of women. . . . The wine must have gone to my head."

But Stephanie had just got up from the table, and Charles followed her as usual.

The evening began like all the rest. Stephanie took up her lace again, while her brother walked to and fro in the long drawing-room, his hands behind his back.

And so, night after night, in complete silence, without a single word exchanged between brother and sister, the time passed until the old clock chimed ten. Then Charles, having laid up a store of warmth for the night, kissed his sister's brow, slipped on his overcoat, and with his hands in his pockets, made for Ireland Street, walking slowly along, like an idle fellow accustomed to musing as he walked.

The man followed his shadow as it flickered on the walls. The same thoughts were turning and twisting in his brain; he was used to them, as a man gets used to animals he tends every day. He knew them too well to be surprised by them; he had stopped looking at them straight in the face; they passed to and fro behind his pale eyes without ever changing his passive stare.

As he came near his own home, Charles thought of his wife. He was going back to her, in no hurry, but with a certain feeling of security, as if to a piece of property he knew belonged to him.

Suddenly, he noticed that he was nearly there. Two low houses, identical twins in misery and poverty, stood waiting for him, their tumbledown grey "stoops" jutting out to meet the sidewalk. He rented rooms on the second floor of one of these houses.

He climbed the stairs, lit a candle and went into the bedroom. A hoarse, veiled voice, a well-known voice, that could still charm him in spite of himself, said wearily:

"That you Charles?"

He set the candle on the night table. The woman shaded her eyes with her hand. He sat down on the foot of the bed.

"How's your sister?"

"Just the same."

This question, this reply, as on every other night, fell heavily into a dull silence. Beneath the words was stirring in the shadows the real meaning, unexpressed:

"Do you think your sister will last much longer?"

"'Fraid so. . . . She's still hanging on. . . ."

At that moment, in the house on the Esplanade, Stephanie de Bichette was crossing her tiny cold hands on her breast and abandoning to the great empty gulf of night the small emptiness that was herself, ridiculous as an old fashion plate and dry as a pressed fig.

And Geraldine lay awake, dreaming that death had closed the last door in the old house.

# DORIS LESSING

## 1919–

Doris Taylor was born in Kermanshah, Persia (now Iran), where her father had a managerial post in the Imperial Bank of Persia. He was an Englishman who had lost a leg in World War I and married his nurse. In 1925 the family moved to Southern Rhodesia (now Zimbabwe), where Alfred Taylor got a loan from the government land bank to buy 3,000 acres of land recently taken away from Africans, who had been put onto reservations. With cheap native labor the Taylors raised corn on the land and never made enough money to get off it. Doris Taylor went to a Catholic convent school and Girls' High School in the small city of Salisbury, but left school at fourteen and worked as a nursemaid and then as a secretary. She was married twice (acquiring the name of Lessing) and had children, before deciding that marriage was not one of her talents. She had been writing for some time but got serious about it only in her late twenties. She left Rhodesia with her first novel and some stories complete, and moved to England, where she joined the Communist Party briefly and began her five-volume sequence of autobiographical novels, *Children of Violence.* Her most ambitious book is *The Golden Notebook* (1962). Recently, her concern for the human future has led her to writing science fiction. She is one of England's most important writers at the present time.

## Sunrise on the Veld

Every night that winter he said aloud into the dark of the pillow: Half-past four! Half-past four! till he felt his brain had gripped the words and held them fast. Then he fell asleep at once, as if a shutter had fallen; and lay with his face turned to the clock so that he could see it first thing when he woke.

It was half-past four to the minute, every morning. Triumphantly pressing down the alarm-knob of the clock, which the dark half of his mind had outwitted, remaining vigilant all night and counting the hours as he lay relaxed in sleep, he huddled down for a last warm moment under the clothes, playing with the idea of lying abed for this once only. But he played with it for the fun of knowing that it was a weakness he could defeat without effort; just as he set the alarm each night for the delight of the moment when he woke and stretched his limbs, feeling the muscles tighten, and thought: Even my brain— even that! I can control every part of myself.

Luxury of warm rested body, with the arms and legs and fingers waiting like soldiers for a word of command! Joy of knowing that the precious hours were given to sleep voluntarily!—for he had once stayed awake three nights running, to prove that he could, and then worked all day, refusing even to admit that he was tired; and now sleep seemed to him a servant to be commanded and refused.

The boy stretched his frame full-length, touching the wall at his head with his hands, and the bedfoot with his toes; then he sprang out, like a fish leaping from water. And it was cold, cold.

He always dressed rapidly, so as to try and conserve his night-warmth till the sun rose two hours later; but by the time he had on his clothes his hands were numbed and he could scarcely hold his shoes. These he could not put on for fear of waking his parents, who never came to know how early he rose.

As soon as he stepped over the lintel, the flesh of his soles contracted on the chilled earth, and his legs began to ache with cold. It was night: the stars were glittering, the trees standing black and still. He looked for signs of day, for the greying of the edge of a stone, or a lightening in the sky where the sun would rise, but there was nothing yet. Alert as an animal he crept past the dangerous window, standing poised with his hand on the sill for one proudly fastidious moment, looking in at the stuffy blackness of the room where his parents lay.

Feeling for the grass-edge of the path with his toes, he reached inside another window further along the wall, where his gun had been set in readiness the night before. The steel was icy, and numbed fingers slipped along it, so that he had to hold it in the crook of his arm for safety. Then he tiptoed to the room where the dogs slept, and was fearful that they might have been tempted to go before him; but they were waiting, their haunches crouched in reluctance at the cold, but ears and swinging tails greeting the gun ecstatically. His warning undertone kept them secret and silent till the house was a hundred yards back: then they bolted off into the bush, yelping excitedly. The boy imagined his parents turning in their beds and muttering: Those dogs again! before they were dragged back in sleep; and he smiled scornfully. He always looked back over his shoulder at the house before he passed a wall of trees that shut it from sight. It looked so low and small, crouching there under a tall and brilliant sky. Then he turned his back on it, and on the frowsting sleepers, and forgot them.

He would have to hurry. Before the light grew strong he must be four miles away; and already a tint of green stood in the hollow of a leaf, and the air smelled of morning and the stars were dimming.

He slung the shoes over his shoulder, veld *skoen* that were crinkled and hard with the dews of a hundred mornings. They would be necessary when the ground became too hot to bear. Now he felt the chilled dust push up between his toes, and he let the muscles of his feet spread and settle into the shapes of the earth; and he thought: I could walk a hundred miles on feet like these! I could walk all day, and never tire!

He was walking swiftly through the dark tunnel of foliage that in day-time was a road. The dogs were invisibly ranging the lower travelways of the bush, and he heard them panting. Sometimes he felt a cold muzzle on his leg before they were off again, scouting for a trail to follow. They were not trained, but free-running companions of the hunt, who often tired of the long stalk before the final shots, and went off on their own pleasure. Soon he could see them, small and wild-looking in a wild strange light, now that the bush stood trembling on the verge of colour, waiting for the sun to paint earth and grass afresh.

The grass stood to his shoulders; and the trees were showering a faint silvery rain. He was soaked; his whole body was clenched in a steady shiver.

Once he bent to the road that was newly scored with animal trails, and regretfully straightened, reminding himself that the pleasure of tracking must wait till another day.

He began to run along the edge of a field, noting jerkily how it was filmed over with fresh spiderweb, so that the long reaches of great black clods seemed netted in glistening grey. He was using the steady lope he had learned by watching the natives, the run that is a dropping of the weight of the body from one foot to the next in a slow balancing movement that never tires, nor shortens the breath; and he felt the blood pulsing down his legs and along his arms, and the exultation and pride of body mounted in him till he was shutting his teeth hard against a violent desire to shout his triumph.

Soon he had left the cultivated part of the farm. Behind him the bush was low and black. In front was a long vlei, acres of long pale grass that sent back a hollowing gleam of light to a satiny sky. Near him thick swathes of grass were bent with the weight of water, and diamond drops sparkled on each frond.

The first bird woke at his feet and at once a flock of them sprang into the air calling shrilly that day had come; and suddenly, behind him, the bush woke into song, and he could hear the guinea fowl calling far ahead of him. That meant they would now be sailing down from their trees into thick grass, and it was for them he had come: he was too late. But he did not mind. He forgot he had come to shoot. He set his legs wide, and balanced from foot to foot, and swung his gun up and down in both hands horizontally, in a kind of improvised exercise, and let his head sink back till it was pillowed in his neck muscles, and watched how above him small rosy clouds floated in a lake of gold.

Suddenly it all rose in him: it was unbearable. He leapt up into the air, shouting and yelling wild, unrecognisable noises. Then he began to run, not carefully, as he had before, but madly, like a wild thing. He was clean crazy, yelling mad with the joy of living and a superfluity of youth. He rushed down the vlei under a tumult of crimson and gold, while all the birds of the world sang about him. He ran in great leaping strides, and shouted as he ran, feeling his body rise into the crisp rushing air and fall back surely on to sure feet; and thought briefly, not believing that such a thing could happen to him, that he could break his ankle any moment, in this thick tangled grass. He cleared bushes like a duiker, leapt over rocks; and finally came to a dead stop at a place where the ground fell abruptly away below him to the river. It had been a two-mile-long dash through waist-high growth, and he was breathing hoarsely and could no longer sing. But he poised on a rock and looked down at stretches of water that gleamed through stooping trees, and thought suddenly, I am fifteen! Fifteen! The words came new to him; so that he kept repeating them wonderingly, with swelling excitement; and he felt the years of his life with his hands, as if he were counting marbles, each one hard and separate and compact, each one a wonderful shining thing. That was what he was: fifteen years of this rich soil, and this slow-moving water, and air that smelt like a challenge whether it was warm and sultry at noon, or as brisk as cold water, like it was now.

There was nothing he couldn't do, nothing! A vision came to him, as he stood there, like when a child hears the word "eternity" and tries to understand it, and time takes possession of the mind. He felt his life ahead of him as a great and wonderful thing, something that was his; and he said aloud, with the blood rising to his head: all the great men of the world have been as I am now, and there is nothing I can't become, nothing I can't do; there is no country in the world I cannot make part of myself, if I choose. I contain the world. I can make of it what I want. If I choose, I can change everything that is going to happen: it depends on me, and what I decide now.

The urgency, and the truth and the courage of what his voice was saying exulted him so that he began to sing again, at the top of his voice, and the sound went echoing down the river gorge. He stopped for the echo, and sang again: stopped and shouted. That was what he was!—he sang, if he chose; and the world had to answer him.

And for minutes he stood there, shouting and singing and waiting for the lovely eddying sound of the echo; so that his own new strong thoughts came back and washed round his head, as if someone were answering him and encouraging him; till the gorge was full of soft voices clashing back and forth from rock to rock over the river. And then it seemed as if there was a new voice. He listened, puzzled, for it was not his own. Soon he was leaning forward, all his nerves alert, quite still: somewhere close to him there was a noise that was no joyful bird, nor tinkle of falling water, nor ponderous movement of cattle.

There it was again. In the deep morning hush that held his future and his past, was a sound of pain, and repeated over and over: it was a kind of shortened scream, as if someone, something, had no breath to scream. He came to himself, looked about him, and called for the dogs.

They did not appear: they had gone off on their own business, and he was alone. Now he was clean sober, all the madness gone. His heart beating fast, because of that frightened screaming, he stepped carefully off the rock and went towards a belt of trees. He was moving cautiously, for not so long ago he had seen a leopard in just this spot.

At the edge of the trees he stopped and peered, holding his gun ready; he advanced, looking steadily about him, his eyes narrowed. Then, all at once, in the middle of a step, he faltered, and his face was puzzled. He shook his head impatiently, as if he doubted his own sight.

There, between two trees, against a background of gaunt black rocks, was a figure from a dream, a strange beast that was horned and drunken-legged, but like something he had never even imagined. It seemed to be ragged. It looked like a small buck that had black ragged tufts of fur standing up irregularly all over it, with patches of raw flesh beneath . . . but the patches of rawness were disappearing under moving black and came again elsewhere; and all the time the creature screamed, in small gasping screams, and leaped drunkenly from side to side, as if it were blind.

Then the boy understood: it *was* a buck. He ran closer, and again stood still, stopped by a new fear. Around him the grass was whispering and alive. He looked wildly about, and then down. The ground was black with ants, great energetic ants that took no notice of him, but hurried and scurried towards the fighting shape, like glistening black water flowing through the grass.

And, as he drew in his breath and pity and terror seized him, the beast fell and the screaming stopped. Now he could hear nothing but one bird singing, and the sound of the rustling, whispering ants.

He peered over at the writhing blackness that jerked convulsively with the jerking nerves. It grew quieter. There were small twitches from the mass that still looked vaguely like the shape of a small animal.

It came into his mind that he should shoot it and end its pain; and he raised the gun. Then he lowered it again. The buck could no longer feel; its fighting was a mechanical protest of the nerves. But it was not that which made him put down the gun. It was a swelling feeling of rage and misery and protest that expressed itself in the thought: if I had not come it would have died like this: so why should I interfere? All over the bush things like this happen; they happen all the time; this is how life goes on, by living things dying in anguish. He gripped the gun between his knees and felt in his own limbs the myriad swarming pain of the twitching animal that could no longer feel, and set his teeth, and said over and over again under his breath: I can't stop it. I can't stop it. There is nothing I can do.

He was glad that the buck was unconscious and had gone past suffering so that he did not have to make a decision to kill it even when he was feeling with his whole body: this is what happens, this is how things work.

*It was right*—that was what he was feeling. *It was right and nothing could alter it.*

The knowledge of fatality, of what has to be, had gripped him and for the first time in his life; and he was left unable to make any movement of brain or body, except to say: "Yes, yes. That is what living is." It had entered his flesh and his bones and grown in to the furthest corners of his brain and would never leave him. And at that moment he could not have performed the smallest action of mercy, knowing as he did, having lived on it all his life, the vast unalterable, cruel veld, where at any moment one might stumble over a skull or crush the skeleton of some small creature.

Suffering, sick, and angry, but also grimly satisfied with his new stoicism, he stood there leaning on his rifle, and watched the seething black mound grow smaller. At his feet, now, were ants trickling back with pink fragments in their mouths, and there was a fresh acid smell in his nostrils. He sternly controlled the uselessly convulsing muscles of his empty stomach, and reminded himself: the ants must eat too! At the same time he found that the tears were streaming down his face, and his clothes were soaked with the sweat of that other creature's pain.

The shape had grown small. Now it looked like nothing recognisable. He did not know how long it was before he saw the blackness thin, and bits of white showed through, shining in the sun—yes, there was the sun, just up, glowing over the rocks. Why, the whole thing could not have taken longer than a few minutes.

He began to swear, as if the shortness of the time was in itself unbearable, using the words he had heard his father say. He strode forward, crushing ants with each step, and brushing them off his clothes, till he stood above the skeleton, which lay sprawled under a small bush. It was clean-picked. It might have been lying there years, save that on the white bone were pink fragments of gristle. About the bones ants were ebbing away, their pincers full of meat.

The boy looked at them, big black ugly insects. A few were standing and gazing up at him with small glittering eyes.

"Go away!" he said to the ants, very coldly. "I am not for you—not just yet, at any rate. Go away." And he fancied that the ants turned and went away.

He bent over the bones and touched the sockets in the skull; that was where the eyes were, he thought incredulously, remembering the liquid dark eyes of a buck. And then he bent the slim foreleg bone, swinging it horizontally in his palm.

That morning, perhaps an hour ago, this small creature had been stepping proud and free through the bush, feeling the chill on its hide even as he himself had done, exhilarated by it. Proudly stepping the earth, tossing its horns, frisking a pretty white tail, it had sniffed the cold morning air. Walking like kings and conquerors it had moved through this free-held bush, where each blade of grass grew for it alone, and where the river ran pure sparkling water for its slaking.

And then—what had happened? Such a swift surefooted thing could surely not be trapped by a swarm of ants?

The boy bent curiously to the skeleton. Then he saw that the back leg that lay uppermost and strained out in the tension of death, was snapped midway in the thigh, so that broken bones jutted over each other uselessly. So that was it! Limping into the ant-masses it could not escape, once it had sensed the danger. Yes, but how had the leg been broken? Had it fallen, perhaps? Impossible, a buck was too light and graceful. Had some jealous rival horned it?

What could possibly have happened? Perhaps some Africans had thrown stones at it, as they do, trying to kill it for meat, and had broken its leg. Yes, that must be it.

Even as he imagined the crowd of running, shouting natives, and the flying stones, and the leaping buck, another picture came into his mind. He saw himself, on any one of these bright ringing mornings, drunk with excitement, taking a snap shot at some half-seen buck. He saw himself with the gun lowered, wondering whether he had missed or not; and thinking at last that it was late, and he wanted his breakfast, and it was not worth while to track miles after an animal that would very likely get away from him in any case.

For a moment he would not face it. He was a small boy again, kicking sulkily at the skeleton, hanging his head, refusing to accept the responsibility.

Then he straightened up, and looked down at the bones with an odd expression of dismay, all the anger gone out of him. His mind went quite empty: all around him he could see trickles of ants disappearing into the grass. The whispering noise was faint and dry, like the rustling of a cast snakeskin.

At last he picked up his gun and walked homewards. He was telling himself half defiantly that he wanted his breakfast. He was telling himself that it was getting very hot, much too hot to be out roaming the bush.

Really, he was tired. He walked heavily, not looking where he put his feet. When he came within sight of his home he stopped, knitting his brows. There was something he had to think out. The death of that small animal was a thing that concerned him, and he was by no means finished with it. It lay at the back of his mind uncomfortably.

Soon, the very next morning, he would get clear of everybody and go to the bush and think about it.

# GRACE PALEY
1922–

Grace Goodside was born in New York City, the daughter of Isaac (a doctor) and Mary Goodside. She went to city schools, including Hunter College, and has done some teaching at Syracuse and Sarah Lawrence. She has been married twice and had two children. During the Vietnam War she was active in the peace movement, taking part in delegations to Hanoi and Moscow. She began to publish stories in the 1950's, and her reputation as a writer with a unique voice and vision has grown steadily. Her two collections of short shories are *The Little Disturbances of Man* (1959) and *Enormous Changes at the Last Minute* (1974).

## The Long-Distance Runner

One day, before or after forty-two, I became a long-distance runner. Though I was stout and in many ways inadequate to this desire, I wanted to go far and fast, not as fast as bicycles and trains, not as far as Taipei, Hingwen, places like that, islands of the slant-eyed cunt, as sailors in bus stations say when speaking of travel, but round and round the county from the sea side to the bridges, along the old neighborhood streets a couple of times, before old age and urban renewal ended them and me.

I tried the country first, Connecticut, which being wooded is always full of buds in spring. All creation is secret, isn't that true? So I trained in the wide-zoned suburban hills where I wasn't known. I ran all spring in and out of dogwood bloom, then laurel.

People sometimes stopped and asked me why I ran, a lady in silk shorts halfway down over her fat thighs. In training, I replied and rested only to answer if closely questioned. I wore a white sleeveless undershirt as well, with excellent support, not to attract the attention of old men and prudish children.

Then summer came, my legs seemed strong. I kissed the kids goodbye. They were quite old by then. It was near the time for parting anyway. I told Mrs. Raftery to look in now and then and give them some of that rotten Celtic supper she makes.

I told them they could take off any time they wanted to. Go lead your private life, I said. Only leave me out of it.

A word to the wise . . . said Richard.

You're depressed Faith, Mrs. Raftery said. Your boy friend Jack, the one you think's so hotsy-totsy, hasn't called and you're as gloomy as a tick on Sunday.

Cut the folkshit with me, Raftery, I muttered. Her eyes filled with tears because that's who she is: folkshit from bunion to topknot. That's how she got liked by me, loved, invented and endured.

When I walked out the door they were all reclining before the television set, Richard, Tonto and Mrs. Raftery, gazing at the news. Which proved with moving pictures that there *had* been a voyage to the moon and Africa and South America hid in a furious whorl of clouds.

I said, Goodbye. They said, Yeah, O.K., sure.

If that's how it is, forget it, I hollered and took the Independent subway to Brighton Beach.

At Brighton Beach I stopped at the Salty Breezes Locker Room to change my clothes. Twenty-five years ago my father invested $500 in its future. In fact he still clears about $3.50 a year, which goes directly (by law) to the Children of Judea to cover their deficit.

No one paid too much attention when I started to run, easy and light on my feet. I ran on the boardwalk first, past my mother's leafleting station—between a soft-ice-cream stand and a degenerated dune. There she had been assigned by her comrades to halt the tides of cruel American enterprise with simple socialist sense.

I wanted to stop and admire the long beach. I wanted to stop in order to think admiringly about New York. There aren't many rotting cities so tan and sandy and speckled with citizens at their salty edges. But I had already spent a lot of life lying down or standing and staring. I had decided to run.

After about a mile and a half I left the boardwalk and began to trot into the old neighborhood. I was running well. My breath was long and deep. I was thinking pridefully about my form.

Suddenly I was surrounded by about three hundred blacks.

Who you?

Who that?

Look at her! Just look! When you seen a fatter ass?

Poor thing. She ain't right. Leave her, you boys, you bad boys.

I used to live here, I said.

Oh yes, they said, in the white old days. That time too bad to last.

But we loved it here. We never went to Flatbush Avenue or Times Square. We loved our block.

Tough black titty.

I like your speech, I said. Metaphor and all.

Right on. We get that from talking.

Yes my people also had a way of speech. And don't forget the Irish. The gift of gab.

Who they? said a small boy.

Cops.

Nowadays, I suggested, there's more than Irish on the police force.

You right, said two ladies. More more, much much more. They's French Chinamen Russkies Congoleans. Oh missee, you too right.

I lived in that house, I said. That apartment house. All my life. Till I got married.

Now that *is* nice. Live in one place. My mother live that way in South Carolina. One place. Her daddy farmed. She said. They ate. No matter winter war bad times. Roosevelt. Something! Ain't that wonderful! And it weren't cold! Big trees!

*That* apartment. I looked up and pointed. There. The third floor.

They all looked up. So what! You blubrous devil! said a dark young man. He wore horn-rimmed glasses and had that intelligent look that City College boys used to have when I was eighteen and first looked at them.

He seemed to lead them in contempt and anger, even the littlest ones who moved toward me with dramatic stealth singing, Devil, Oh Devil. I don't think the little kids had bad feeling because they poked a finger into me, then laughed.

Still I thought it might be wise to keep my head. So I jumped right in with some facts. I said, How many flowers' names do you know? Wild flowers, I mean. My people only knew two. That's what they say now anyway. Rich or poor, they only had two flowers' names. Rose and violet.

Daisy, said one boy immediately.

Weed, said another. That *is* a flower, I thought. But everyone else got the joke.

Saxifrage, lupine, said a lady. Viper's bugloss, said a small Girl Scout in medium green with a dark green sash. She held up a *Handbook of Wild Flowers.*

How many you know, fat mama? a boy asked warmly. He wasn't against my being a mother or fat. I turned all my attention to him.

Oh sonny, I said, I'm way ahead of my people. I know in yellows alone: common cinquefoil, trout lily, yellow adder's-tongue, swamp buttercup and common buttercup, golden sorrel, yellow or hop clover, devil's-paintbrush, evening primrose, black-eyed Susan, golden aster, also the yellow pickerelweed growing down by the water if not in the water, and dandelions of course. I've seen all these myself. Seen them.

You could see China from the boardwalk, a boy said. When it's nice.

I know more flowers than countries. Mostly young people these days have traveled in many countries.

Not me. I ain't been nowhere.

Not me either, said about seventeen boys.

*I'm* not allowed, said a little girl. There's drunken junkies.

But *I! I!* cried out a tall black youth, very handsome and well dressed. I am an African. My father came from the high stolen plains. *I* have been everywhere. I was in Moscow six months, learning machinery. I was in France, learning French. I was in Italy, observing the peculiar Renaissance and the people's sweetness. I was in England, where I studied the common law and the urban blight. I was at the Conference of Dark Youth in Cuba to understand our passion. I am now here. Here am I to become an engineer and return to my people, around the Cape of Good Hope in a Norwegian sailing vessel. In this way I will learn the fine old art of sailing in case the engines of the new society of my old inland country should fail.

We had an extraordinary amount of silence after that. Then one old lady in a black dress and high white lace collar said to another old lady dressed exactly the same way, Glad tidings when someone got brains in the head not fish juice. Amen, said a few.

Whyn't you go up to Mrs. Luddy living in your house, you lady, huh? The Girl Scout asked this.

Why she just groove to see you, said some sarcastic snickerer.

She got palpitations. Her man, he give it to her.

That ain't all, he a natural gift-giver.

I'll take you, said the Girl Scout. My name is Cynthia. I'm in Troop 355, Brooklyn.

I'm not dressed, I said, looking at my lumpy knees.

You shouldn't wear no undershirt like that without no runnin number or no team writ on it. It look like a undershirt.

Cynthia! Don't take her up there, said an important boy. Her head strange. Don't you take her. Hear?

Lawrence, she said softly, you tell me once more what to do I'll wrap you round that lamppost.

Git! she said, powerfully addressing *me*.

In this way I was led into the hallway of the whole house of my childhood.

The first door I saw was still marked in flaky gold, 1A. That's where the janitor lived, I said. He was a Negro.

How come like that? Cynthia made an astonished face. How come the janitor was a black man?

Oh Cynthia, I said. Then I turned to the opposite door, first floor front, 1B. I remembered. Now, here, this was Mrs. Goreditsky, very very fat lady. All her children died at birth. Born, then one, two, three. Dead. Five children, then Mr. Goreditsky said, I'm bad luck on you Tessie and he went away. He sent $15 a week for seven years. Then no one heard.

I know her, poor thing, said Cynthia. The city come for her summer before last. The way they knew, it smelled. They wrapped her up in a canvas. They couldn't get through the front door. It scraped off a piece of her. My uncle Ronald had to help them, but he got disgusted.

Only two years ago. She was still here! Wasn't she scared?

So we all, said Cynthia. White ain't everything.

Who lived up here, she asked, 2B. Right now, my best friend Nancy Rosalind lives here. She got two brothers, and her sister married and got a baby. She very light-skinned. Not her mother. We got all colors amongst us.

Your best friend? That's funny. Because it was *my* best friend. Right in that apartment. Joanna Rosen.

What become of her? Cynthia asked. She got a running shirt too?

Come on Cynthia, if you really want to know, I'll tell you. She married this man, Marvin Steirs.

Who's he?

I recollected his achievements. Well, he's the president of a big corporation, JoMar Plastics. This corporation owns a steel company, a radio station, a new Xerox-type machine that lets you do twenty-five different pages at once. This corporation has a foundation, The JoMar Fund for Research in Conservation. Capitalism is like that, I added, in order to be politically useful.

How come you know? You go over their house a lot?

No. I happened to read all about them on the financial page, just last week. It made me think: a different life. That's all.

Different spokes for different folks, said Cynthia.

I sat down on the cool marble steps and remembered Joanna's cousin Ziggie. He was older than we were. He wrote a poem which told us we were lovely flowers and our legs were petals, which nature would force open no matter how many times we said no.

Then I had several other interior thoughts that I couldn't share with a child, the kind that give your face a blank or melancholy look.

Now you're not interested, said Cynthia. Now you're not gonna say a thing. Who lived here, 2A? Who? Two men lives here now. Women coming and women going. My mother says, Danger sign: Stay away, my darling, stay away.

I don't remember, Cynthia. I really don't.

You got to. What'd you come for, anyways?

Then I tried. 2A. 2A. Was it the twins? I felt a strong obligation as though remembering was in charge of the *existence* of the past. This is not so.

Cynthia, I said, I don't want to go any further. I don't even want to remember.

Come on, she said, tugging at my shorts, don't you want to see
Mrs. Luddy, the one lives in your old house? That be fun, no?

No. No, I don't want to see Mrs. Luddy.

Now you shouldn't pay no attention to those boys downstairs.
She will like you. I mean, she is kind. She don't like most white
people, but she might like you.

No Cynthia, it's not that, but I don't want to see my father and
mother's house now.

I didn't know what to say. I said, Because my mother's dead. This
was a lie, because my mother lives in her own room with my father
in the Children of Judea. With her hand over her socialist heart, she
reads the paper every morning after breakfast. Then she says sadly
to my father, Every day the same. Dying . . . dying, dying from
killing.

My mother's dead Cynthia. I can't go in there.

Oh . . . oh, the poor thing, she said, looking into my eyes. Oh, if
my mother died, I don't know what I'd do. Even if I was old as you.
I could kill myself. Tears filled her eyes and started down her
cheeks. If my mother died, what would I do? She is my protector,
she won't let the pushers get me. She hold me tight. She gonna hide
me in the cedar box if my Uncle Rudford comes try to get me back.
She *can't* die, my mother.

Cynthia—honey—she won't die. She's young. I put my arm out to
comfort her. You could come live with me, I said. I got two boys,
they're nearly grown up. I missed it, not having a girl.

What? What you mean now, live with you and boys. She pulled
away and ran for the stairs. Stay way from me, honky lady. I know
them white boys. They just gonna try and jostle my black woman-
hood. My mother told me about that, keep you white honky devil
boys to your devil self, you just leave me be you old bitch you.
Somebody help me, she started to scream, you hear. Somebody
help. She gonna take me away.

She flattened herself to the wall, trembling. I was too frightened
by her fear of me to say, honey, I wouldn't hurt you, it's me. I heard
her helpers, the voices of large boys crying. We coming, we coming,
hold your head up, we coming. I ran past her fear to the stairs and
up them two at a time. I came to my old own door. I knocked like
the landlord, loud and terrible.

Mama not home, a child's voice said. No, no, I said. It's me! a
lady! Someone's chasing me, let me in. Mama not home, I ain't
allowed to open up for nobody.

It's me! I cried out in terror. Mama! Mama! let me in!

The door opened. A slim woman whose age I couldn't invent
looked at me. She said, Get in and shut that door tight. She took a
hard pinching hold on my upper arm. Then she bolted the door

herself. Them hustlers after you. They make me pink. Hide this white lady now, Donald. Stick her under your bed, you got a high bed.

Oh that's O.K. I'm fine now, I said. I felt safe and at home.

You in my house, she said. You do as I say. For two cents, I throw you out.

I squatted under a small kid's pissy mattress. Then I heard the knock. It was tentative and respectful. My mama don't allow me to open. Donald! someone called. Donald!

Oh no, he said. Can't do it. She gonna wear me out. You know her. She already tore up my ass this morning once. Ain't *gonna* open up.

I lived there for about three weeks with Mrs. Luddy and Donald and three little baby girls nearly the same age. I told her a joke about Irish twins. Ain't Irish, she said.

Nearly every morning the babies woke us at about 6:45. We gave them all a bottle and went back to sleep till 8:00. I made coffee and she changed diapers. Then it really stank for a while. At this time I usually said, Well listen, thanks really, but I've got to go I guess. I guess I'm going. She'd usually say, Well, guess again. *I* guess you ain't. Or if she was feeling disgusted she'd say, Go on now! Get! You wanna go, I guess by now I have snorted enough white lady stink to choke a horse. Go on!

I'd get to the door and then I'd hear voices. I'm ashamed to say I'd become fearful. Despite my wide geographical love of mankind, I would be attacked by local fears.

There was a sentimental truth that lay beside all that going and not going. It *was* my house where I'd lived long ago my family life. There was a tile on the bathroom floor that I myself had broken, dropping a hammer on the toe of my brother Charles as he stood dreamily shaving, his prick halfway up his undershorts. Astonishment and knowledge first seized me right there. The kitchen was the same. The table was the enameled table common to our class, easy to clean, with wooden undercorners for indigent and old cockroaches that couldn't make it to the kitchen sink. (However, it was not the same table, because I have inherited that one, chips and all.)

The living room was something like ours, only we had less plastic. There may have been less plastic in the world at that time. Also, my mother had set beautiful cushions everywhere, on beds and chairs. It was the way she expressed herself, artistically, to embroider at night or take strips of flowered cotton and sew them across ordinary white or blue muslin in the most delicate designs, the way women have always used materials that live and die in hunks and tatters to say: This is my place.

Mrs. Luddy said, Uh huh!

Of course, I said, men don't have that outlet. That's how come they run around so much.

Till they drunk enough to lay down, she said.

Yes, I said, on a large scale you can see it in the world. First they make something, then they murder it. Then they write a book about how interesting it is.

You got something there, she said. Sometimes she said, Girl, you don't know *nothing*.

We often sat at the window looking out and down. Little tufts of breeze grew on that windowsill. The blazing afternoon was around the corner and up the block.

You say men, she said. Is that men? she asked. What you call—a Man?

Four flights below us, leaning on the stoop, were about a dozen people and around them devastation. Just a minute, I said. I had seen devastation on my way, running, gotten some of the pebbles of it in my running shoe and the dust of it in my eyes. I had thought with the indignant courtesy of a citizen, This is a disgrace to the City of New York which I love and am running through.

But now, from the commanding heights of home, I saw it clearly. The tenement in which Jack my old and present friend had come to gloomy manhood had been destroyed, first by fire, then by demolition (which is a swinging ball of steel that cracks bedrooms and kitchens). Because of this work, we could see several blocks wide and a block and a half long. Crazy Eddy's house still stood, famous 1510 gutted, with black window frames, no glass, open laths. The stubbornness of the supporting beams! Some persons or families still lived on the lowest floors. In the lots between a couple of old sofas lay on their fat faces, their springs sticking up into the air. Just as in wartime a half-dozen ailanthus trees had already found their first quarter inch of earth and begun a living attack on the dead yards. At night I knew animals roamed the place, squalling and howling, furious New York dogs and street cats and mighty rats. You would think you were in Bear Mountain Park, the terror of venturing forth.

Someone ought to clean that up, I said.

Mrs. Luddy said, Who you got in mind? Mrs. Kennedy?—

Donald made a stern face. He said, That just what I gonna do when I get big. Gonna get the Sanitary Man in and show it to him. You see that, you big guinea you, you clean it up right now! Then he stamped his feet and fierced his eyes.

Mrs. Luddy said, Come here, you little nigger. She kissed the top of his head and gave him a whack on the backside all at one time.

Well, said Donald, encouraged, look out there now you all! Go on

I say, look! Though we had already seen, to please him we looked. On the stoop men and boys lounged, leaned, hopped about, stood on one leg, then another, took their socks off, and scratched their toes, talked, sat on their haunches, heads down, dozing.

Donald said, Look at them. They ain't got self-respect. They got Afros *on* their heads, but they don't know they black *in* their heads.

I thought he ought to learn to be more sympathetic. I said, There are reasons that people are that way.

Yes, ma'am, said Donald.

Anyway, how come you never go down and play with the other kids, how come you're up here so much?

My mama don't like me do that. Some of them is bad. Bad. I might become a dope addict. I got to stay clear.

You just a dope, that's a fact, said Mrs. Luddy.

He ought to be with kids his age more, I think.

He see them in school, miss. Don't trouble your head about it if you don't mind.

Actually, Mrs. Luddy didn't go down into the street either. Donald did all the shopping. She let the welfare investigator in, the meterman came into the kitchen to read the meter. I saw him from the back room, where I hid. She did pick up her check. She cashed it. She returned to wash the babies, change their diapers, wash clothes, iron, feed people, and then in free half hours she sat by that window. She was waiting.

I believed she was watching and waiting for a particular man. I wanted to discuss this with her, talk lovingly like sisters. But before I could freely say, Forget about that son of a bitch, he's a pig, I did have to offer a few solid facts about myself, my kids, about fathers, husbands, passers-by, evening companions, and the life of my father and mother in this room by this exact afternoon window.

I told her for instance, that in my worst times I had given myself one extremely simple physical pleasure. This was cream cheese for breakfast. In fact, I insisted on it, sometimes depriving the children of very important articles and foods.

Girl, you don't know nothing, she said.

Then for a little while she talked gently as one does to a person who is innocent and insane and incorruptible because of stupidity.She had had two such special pleasures for hard times she said. The first, men, but they turned rotten, white women had ruined the best, give them the idea their dicks made of solid gold. The second pleasure she had tried was wine. She said, I do like wine. You *has* to have something just for yourself by yourself. Then she said, But you can't raise a decent boy when you liquor-dazed every night.

White or black, I said, returning to men, they did think they were bringing a rare gift, whereas it was just sex, which is common like bread, though essential.

Oh, you can do without, she said. There's folks does without.

I told her Donald deserved the best. I loved him. If he had flaws, I hardly noticed them. It's one of my beliefs that children do not have flaws, even the worst do not.

Donald was brilliant—like my boys except that he had an easier disposition. For this reason I decided, almost the second moment of my residence in that household, to bring him up to reading level at once. I told him we would work with books and newspapers. He went immediately to his neighborhood library and brought some hard books to amuse me, *Black Folktales* by Julius Lester and *The Pushcart War*, which is about another neighborhood but relevant.

Donald always agreed with me when we talked about reading and writing. In fact, when I mentioned poetry, he told me he knew all about it, that David Henderson, a known black poet, had visited his second-grade class. So Donald was, as it turned out, well ahead of my nosy tongue. He was usually very busy shopping. He also had to spend a lot of time making faces to force the little serious baby girls into laughter. But if the subject came up, he could take *the* poem right out of the air into which language and event had just gone.

An example: That morning, his mother had said, Whew, I just got too much piss and diapers and wash. I wanna just sit down by that window and rest myself. He wrote a poem:

> *Just got too much pissy diapers*
> *and wash and wash*
> *just wanna sit down by that window*
> *and look out*
> > *ain't nothing there.*

Donald, I said, you are plain brilliant. I'm never going to forget you. For God's sakes don't you forget me.

You fool with him too much, said Mrs. Luddy. He already don't even remember his grandma, you never gonna meet someone like her, a curse never come past her lips.

I do remember, Mama, I remember. She lying in bed, right there. A man standing in the door. She say, Esdras, I put a curse on you head. You worsen tomorrow. How come she said like that?

Gomorrah, I believe Gomorrah, she said. She know the Bible inside out.

Did she live with you?

No. No, she visiting. She come up to see us all, her children, how we doing. She come up to see sights. Then she lay down and died. She was old.

I remained quiet because of the death of mothers. Mrs. Luddy looked at me thoughtfully, then she said:

My mama had stories to tell, she raised me on. *Her* mama was a little thing, no sense. Stand in the door of the cabin all day, sucking her thumb. It was slave times. One day a young field boy come storming along. He knock on the door of the first cabin hollering, Sister, come out, it's freedom. She come out. She say, Yeah? When? He say, Now! It's freedom now! Then he knock at the next door and say, Sister! It's freedom! Now! From one cabin he run to the next cabin, crying out, Sister, it's freedom now!

Oh I remember that story, said Donald. Freedom now! Freedom now! He jumped up and down.

You don't remember nothing boy. Go on, get Eloise, she want to get into the good times.

Eloise was two but undersized. We got her like that, said Donald. Mrs. Luddy let me buy her ice cream and green vegetables. She was waiting for kale and chard, but it was too early. The kale liked cold. You not about to be here November, she said. No, no. I turned away, lonesomeness touching me and sang our Eloise song:

> Eloise loves the bees
> the bees they buzz
> like Eloise does.

Then Eloise crawled all over the splintery floor, buzzing wildly.

Oh you crazy baby, said Donald, buzz buzz buzz.

Mrs. Luddy sat down by the window.

You all make a lot of noise, she said sadly. You just right on noisy.

The next morning Mrs. Luddy woke me up.

Time to go, she said.

What?

Home.

What? I said.

Well, don't you think your little spoiled boys crying for you? Where's Mama? They standing in the window. Time to go lady. This ain't Free Vacation Farm. Time we was by ourself a little.

Oh Ma, said Donald, she ain't a lot of trouble. Go on, get Eloise, she hollering. And button up your lip.

She didn't offer me coffee. She looked at me strictly all the time. I tried to look strictly back, but I failed because I loved the sight of her.

Donald was teary, but I didn't dare turn my face to him, until the parting minute at the door. Even then, I kissed the top of his head a little too forcefully and said, Well, I'll see you.

On the front stoop there were about half a dozen mid-morning family people and kids arguing about who had dumped garbage out of which window. They were very disgusted with one another.

Two young men in handsome dashikis stood in counsel and agreement at the street corner. They divided a comment. How come white womens got rotten teeth? And look so old? A young woman waiting at the light said, Hush . . .

I walked past them and didn't begin my run till the road opened up somewhere along Ocean Parkway. I was a little stiff because my way of life had used only small movements, an occasional stretch to put a knife or teapot out of reach of the babies. I ran about ten, fifteen blocks. Then my second wind came, which is classical, famous among runners, it's the beginning of flying.

In the three weeks I'd been off the street, jogging had become popular. It seemed that I was only one person doing her thing, which happened like most American eccentric acts to be the most "in" thing I could have done. In fact, two young men ran alongside of me for nearly a mile. They ran silently beside me and turned off at Avenue H. A gentleman with a mustache, running poorly in the opposite direction, waved. He called out, Hi, senora.

Near home I ran through our park, where I had aired my children on weekends and late-summer afternoons. I stopped at the northeast playground, where I met a dozen young mothers intelligently handling their little ones. In order to prepare them, meaning no harm, I said, In fifteen years, you girls will be like me, wrong in everything.

At home it was Saturday morning. Jack had returned looking as grim as ever, but he'd brought cash and a vacuum cleaner. While the coffee perked, he showed Richard how to use it. They were playing tick tack toe on the dusty wall.

Richard said, Well! Look who's here! Hi!

Any news? I asked.

Letter from Daddy, he said. From the lake and water country in Chile. He says it's like Minnesota.

He's never been to Minnesota, I said. Where's Anthony?

Here I am, said Tonto, appearing. But I'm leaving.

Oh yes, I said. Of course. Every Saturday he hurries through breakfast or misses it. He goes to visit his friends in institutions. These are well-known places like Bellevue, Hillside, Rockland State, Central Islip, Manhattan. These visits take him all day and sometimes half the night.

I found some chocolate-chip cookies in the pantry. Take them, Tonto, I said. I remember nearly all his friends as little boys and girls always hopping, skipping, jumping and cookie-eating. He was annoyed. He said, No! Chocolate cookies is what the commissaries are full of. How about money?

Jack dropped the vacuum cleaner. He said, No! They have parents for that.

I said, Here, five dollars for cigarettes, one dollar each.

Cigarettes! said Jack. Goddamnit! Black lungs and death! Cancer! Emphysema! He stomped out of the kitchen, breathing. He took the bike from the back room and started for Central Park, which had been closed to cars but opened to bicycle riders. When he'd been gone about ten minutes, Anthony said, It's really open only on Sundays.

Why didn't you say so? Why can't you be decent to him? I asked. It's important to me.

Oh Faith, he said, patting me on the head because he'd grown so tall, all that air. It's good for his lungs. And his muscles! He'll be back soon.

You should ride too, I said. You don't want to get mushy in your legs. You should go swimming once a week.

I'm too busy, he said. I have to see my friends.

Then Richard, who had been vacuuming under his bed, came into the kitchen. You still here, Tonto?

Going going gone, said Anthony, don't bat your eye.

Now listen, Richard said, here's a note. It's for Judy, if you get as far as Rockland. Don't forget it. Don't open it. Don't read it. I know he'll read it.

Anthony smiled and slammed the door.

Did I lose weight? I asked. Yes, said Richard. You look O.K. You never look too bad. But where were you? I got sick of Raftery's boiled potatoes. Where were you, Faith?

Well! I said. Well! I stayed a few weeks in my old apartment, where Grandpa and Grandma and me and Hope and Charlie lived, when we were little. I took you there long ago. Not so far from the ocean where Grandma made us very healthy with sun and air.

What are you talking about? said Richard. Cut the baby talk.

Anthony came home earlier than expected that evening because some people were in shock therapy and someone else had run away. He listened to me for a while. Then he said, I don't know what she's talking about either.

Neither did Jack, despite the understanding often produced by love after absence. He said, Tell me again. He was in a good mood. He said, You can even tell it to me twice.

I repeated the story. They all said, What?

Because it isn't usually so simple. Have you known it to happen

much nowadays? A woman inside the steamy energy of middle age
runs and runs. She finds the houses and streets where her childhood happened. She lives in them. She learns as though she was
still a child what in the world is coming next.

## MAVIS GALLANT

1922–

Born in Montreal, Gallant was educated at convent and public schools in Quebec
and the eastern United States. She worked briefly for the National Film board
and as a writer for the *Montreal Standard* before leaving for France in 1950.
Although she returned to Canada in 1983–4 as writer-in-residence at the University of Toronto, she has lived most of her life in Paris. One of the most persistent
themes in her work evident in her first collection of stories, *The Other Paris* (1956)
is the dilemma of exile; she also continues to be fascinated by the contrasts
between the European and North American sensibilities. She has published two
novels and six collections of stories. *Home Truths: Selected Canadian Stories*
(1981) won a Governor General's award. Gallant is noted also for her distinguished non-fiction, a selection of which appears in *Paris Notebooks: Essays and
Reviews* (1986).

## The Ice Wagon Going Down the Street

Now that they are out of world affairs and back where they started,
Peter Frazier's wife says, "Everybody else did well in the international thing except us."

"You have to be crooked," he tells her.

"Or smart. Pity we weren't."

It is Sunday morning. They sit in the kitchen, drinking their coffee,
slowly, remembering the past. They say the names of people as if they
were magic. Peter thinks, *Agnes Brusen*, but there are hundreds of
other names. As a private married joke, Peter and Sheilah wear the
silk dressing gowns they bought in Hong Kong. Each thinks the other
a peacock, rather splendid, but they pretend the dressing gowns are
silly and worn in fun.

Peter and Sheilah and their two daughters, Sandra and Jennifer,
are visiting Peter's unmarried sister, Lucille. They have been Lucille's
guests seventeen weeks, ever since they returned to Toronto from the

Far East. Their big old steamer trunk blocks a corner of the kitchen, making a problem of the refrigerator door; but even Lucille says the trunk may as well stay where it is, for the present. The Fraziers' future is so unsettled; everything is still in the air.

Lucille has given her bedroom to her two nieces, and sleeps on a camp cot in the hall. The parents have the living-room divan. They have no privileges here; they sleep after Lucille has seen the last television show that interests her. In the hall closet their clothes are crushed by winter overcoats. They know they are being judged for the first time. Sandra and Jennifer are waiting for Sheilah and Peter to decide. They are waiting to learn where these exotic parents will fly to next. What sort of climate will Sheilah consider? What job will Peter consent to accept? When the parents are ready, the children will make a decision of their own. It is just possible that Sandra and Jennifer will choose to stay with their aunt.

The peacock parents are watched by wrens. Lucille and her nieces are much the same—sandy-colored, proudly plain. Neither of the girls has the father's insouciance or the mother's appearance—her height, her carriage, her thick hair, and sky-blue eyes. The children are more cautious than their parents; more Canadian. When they saw their aunt's apartment they had been away from Canada nine years, ever since they were two and four; and Jennifer, the elder, said, "Well, now we're home." Her voice is nasal and flat. Where did she learn that voice? And why should this be home? Peter's answer to anything about his mystifying children is, "It must be in the blood."

On Sunday morning Lucille takes her nieces to church. It seems to be the only condition she imposes on her relations: the children must be decent. The girls go willingly, with their new hats and purses and gloves and coral bracelets and strings of pearls. The parents, ramshackle, sleepy, dim in the brain because it is Sunday, sit down to their coffee and privacy and talk of the past.

"We weren't crooked," says Peter. "We weren't even smart."

Sheilah's head bobs up; she is no drowner. It is wrong to say they have nothing to show for time. Sheilah has the Balenciaga. It is a black afternoon dress, stiff and boned at the waist, long for the fashions of now, but neither Sheilah nor Peter would change a thread. The Balenciaga is their talisman, their treasure; and after they remember it they touch hands and think that the years are not behind them but hazy and marvelous and still to be lived.

The first place they went to was Paris. In the early 'fifties the pick of the international jobs was there. Peter had inherited the last scrap of money he knew he was ever likely to see, and it was enough to get them over: Sheilah and Peter and the babies and the steamer trunk. To their joy and astonishment they had money in the bank. They said to each other, "It should last a year." Peter was fastidious about the new job; he hadn't come all this distance to accept just anything. In Paris he met Hugh Taylor, who was earning enough smuggling gasoline to keep his wife in Paris and a girl in Rome. That impressed Peter, because he remembered Taylor as a sour scholarship student without the slightest talent for life. Taylor had a job, of course. He hadn't said to himself, I'll go over to Europe and smuggle gasoline. It gave Peter an idea; he saw the shape of things. First you catch your fish. Later, at an international party, he met Johnny Hertzberg, who told him Germany was the place. Hertzberg said that anyone who came out of Germany broke now was too stupid to be here, and deserved to be back home at a desk. Peter nodded, as if he had already thought of that. He began to think about Germany. Paris was fine for a holiday, but it had been picked clean. Yes, Germany. His money was running low. He thought about Germany quite a lot.

That winter was moist and delicate; so fragile that they daren't speak of it now. There seemed to be plenty of everything and plenty of time. They were living the dream of a marriage, the fabric uncut, nothing slashed or spoiled. All winter they spent their money, and went to parties, and talked about Peter's future job. It lasted four months. They spent their money, lived in the future, and were never as happy again.

After four months they were suddenly moved away from Paris, but not to Germany—to Geneva. Peter thinks it was because of the incident at the Trudeau wedding at the Ritz. Paul Trudeau was a French-Canadian Peter had known at school and in the Navy. Trudeau had turned into a snob, proud of his career and his Paris connections. He tried to make the difference felt, but Peter thought the difference was only for strangers. At the wedding reception Peter lay down on the floor and said he was dead. He held a white azalea in a brass pot on his chest, and sang, "Oh, hear us when we cry to Thee for those in peril on the sea." Sheilah bent over him and said, "Peter, darling, get up. Pete, listen, every single person who can do something for you is in this room. If you love me, you'll get up."

"I do love you," he said, ready to engage in a serious conversation. "She's so beautiful," he told a second face. "She's nearly as tall as I am. She was a model in London. I met her over in London in the war. I met her there in the war." He lay on his back with the azalea on his chest, explaining their history. A waiter took the brass pot away, and after Peter had been hauled to his feet he knocked the waiter down. Trudeau's bride, who was freshly out of an Ursuline convent, became hysterical; and even though Paul Trudeau and Peter were old acquaintances, Trudeau never spoke to him again. Peter says now that French-Canadians always have that bit of spite. He says Trudeau asked the Embassy to interfere. Luckily, back home there were still a few people to whom the name "Frazier" meant something, and it was to these people that Peter appealed. He wrote letters saying that a French-Canadian combine was preventing his getting a decent job, and could anything be done? No one answered directly, but it was clear that what they settled for was exile to Geneva: a season of meditation and remorse, as he explained to Sheilah, and it was managed tactfully, through Lucille. Lucille wrote that a friend of hers, May Fergus, now a secretary in Geneva, had heard about a job. The job was filing pictures in the information service of an international agency in the Palais des Nations. The pay was so-so, but Lucille thought Peter must be getting fed up doing nothing.

Peter often asks his sister now who put her up to it—what important person told her to write that letter suggesting Peter go to Geneva?

"Nobody," says Lucille. "I mean, nobody in the way *you* mean. I really did have this girl friend working there, and I knew you must be running through your money pretty fast in Paris."

"It must have been somebody pretty high up," Peter says. He looks at his sister admiringly, as he has often looked at his wife.

Peter's wife had loved him in Paris. Whatever she wanted in marriage she found that winter, there. In Geneva, where Peter was a file clerk and they lived in a furnished flat, she pretended they were in Paris and life was still the same. Often, when the children were at supper, she changed as though she and Peter were dining out. She wore the Balenciaga, and put candles on the card table where she and Peter ate their meal. The neckline of the dress was soiled with make-up. Peter remembers her dabbing on the make-up with a wet sponge. He remembers her in the kitchen, in the soiled Balenciaga, patting on the make-up with a filthy sponge. Behind her, at the kitchen table, Sandra and Jennifer, in buttonless pajamas and bunny slippers, ate their supper of marmalade sandwiches and milk. When the children were asleep, the parents dined solemnly, ritually, Sheilah sitting straight as a queen.

It was a mysterious period of exile, and he had to wait for signs, or signals, to know when he was free to leave. He never saw the job any other way. He forgot he had applied for it. He thought he had been sent to Geneva because of a misdemeanor and had to wait to be released. Nobody pressed him at work. His immediate boss had resigned, and he was alone for months in a room with two desks. He read the *Herald-Tribune*, and tried to discover how things were here—how the others ran their lives on the pay they were officially getting. But it was a closed conspiracy. He was not dealing with adventurers now but civil servants waiting for pension day. No one ever answered his questions. They pretended to think his questions were a form of wit. His only solace in exile was the few happy weekends he had in the late spring and early summer. He had met another old acquaintance, Mike Burleigh. Mike was a serious liberal who had married a serious heiress. The

Burleighs had two guest lists. The first was composed of stuffy people they felt obliged to entertain, while the second was made up of their real friends, the friends they wanted. The real friends strove hard to become stuffy and dull and thus achieve the first guest list, but few succeeded. Peter went on the first list straight away. Possibly Mike didn't understand, at the beginning, why Peter was pretending to be a file clerk. Peter had such an air—he might have been sent by a universal inspector to see how things in Geneva were being run.

Every Friday in May and June and part of July, the Fraziers rented a sky-blue Fiat and drove forty miles east of Geneva to the Burleighs' summer house. They brought the children, a suitcase, the children's tattered picture books, and a token bottle of gin. This, in memory, is a period of water and water birds; swans, roses, and singing birds. The children were small and still belonged to them. If they remember too much, their mouths water, their stomachs hurt. Peter says, "It was fine while it lasted." Enough. While it lasted Sheilah and Madge Burleigh were close. They abandoned their husbands and spent long summer afternoons comparing their mothers and praising each other's skin and hair. To Madge, and not to Peter, Sheilah opened her Liverpool childhood with the words "rat poor." Peter heard about it later, from Mike. The women's friendship seemed to Peter a bad beginning. He trusted women but not with each other. It lasted ten weeks. One Sunday, Madge said she needed the two bedrooms the Fraziers usually occupied for a party of sociologists from Pakistan, and that was the end. In November, the Fraziers heard that the summer house had been closed, and that the Burleighs were in Geneva, in their winter flat; they gave no sign. There was no help for it, and no appeal.

Now Peter began firing letters to anyone who had ever known his late father. He was living in a mild yellow autumn. Why does he remember the streets of the city dark, and the windows everywhere black with rain? He remembers being with Sheilah and the children as if they clung together while just outside their small shelter it rained and rained. The children slept in the bedroom of the flat because the window gave on the street and they could breathe air. Peter and Sheilah had the living-room couch. Their window was not a real window but a square on a wall of cement. The flat seemed damp as a cave. Peter remembers steam in the kitchen, pools under the sink, sweat on the pipes. Water streamed on him from the children's clothes, washed and dripping overhead. The trunk upended in the children's room, was not quite unpacked. Sheilah had not signed her name to this life; she had not given in. Once Peter heard her drop her aitches. "You kids are lucky," she said to the girls. "I never 'ad so much as a sit-down meal. I ate chips out of a paper or I 'ad a butty out on the stairs." He never asked her what a butty was. He thinks it means bread and cheese.

The day he heard "You kids are lucky" he understood they were becoming in fact something they had only *appeared* to be until now— the shabby civil servant and his brood. If he had been European he would have ridden to work on a bicycle, in the uniform of his class and condition. He would have worn a tight coat, a turned collar, and a dirty tie. He wondered then if coming here had been a mistake, and if he should not, after all, still be in a place where his name meant something. Surely Peter Frazier should live where "Frazier" counts? In Ontario even now when he says "Frazier" an absent look comes over his hearer's face, as if its owner were consulting an interior guide. What is Frazier? What does it mean? Oil? Power? Politics? Wheat? Real estate? The creditors had the house sealed when Peter's father died. His aunt collapsed with a heart attack in somebody's bachelor apartment, leaving three sons and a widower to surmise they had never known her. Her will was a disappointment. None of that generation left enough. One made it: the granite Presbyterian immigrants from Scotland. Their children, a generation of daunted women and maiden men, held still. Peter's father's crowd spent: they were not afraid of their fathers, and their grandfathers were old. Peter and his sister and his cousins lived on the remains. They were left the rinds of income, of notions, and the memories of ideas rather than ideas intact. If Peter can choose his reincarnation, let him be the oppressed son of a Scottish parson. Let Peter grow up on cuffs and iron principles. Let him make the fortune! Let him flee the manse! When he was small his patrimony was squandered under his nose. He remembers people dancing in his father's house. He remembers seeing and nearly understanding adultery in a guest room, among a pile of wraps. He thought he had seen a murder; he never told. He remembers licking glasses wherever he found them—on window sills, on stairs, in the pantry. In his room he listened while Lucille read Beatrix Potter. The bad rabbit stole the carrot from the good rabbit without saying please, and downstairs was the noise of the party—the roar of the crouched lion. When his father died he saw the chairs upside down and the bailiff's chalk marks. Then the doors were sealed.

He has often tried to tell Sheilah why he cannot be defeated. He remembers his father saying, "Nothing can touch us," and Peter believed it and still does. It has prevented his taking his troubles too seriously. "Nothing can be as bad as this," he will tell himself. "It is happening to me." Even in Geneva, where his status was file clerk, where he sank and stopped on the level of the men who never emigrated, the men on the bicycles—even there he had a manner of strolling to work as if his office were a pastime, and his real life a secret so splendid he could share it with no one except himself.

In Geneva Peter worked for a woman—a girl. She was a Norwegian from a small town in Saskatchewan. He supposed they had been put together because they were Canadians; but they were as strange to each other as if "Canadian" meant any number of things, or had no real meaning. Soon after Agnes Brusen came to the office she hung her framed university degree on the wall. It was one of the gritty, prideful gestures that stand for push, toil,and family sacrifice. He thought,then, that she must be one of a family of immigrants for whom education is everything. Hugh Taylor had told him that in some families the older children never marry until the youngest have finished school. Sometimes every second child is sacrificed and made to work for the education of the next born. Those who finish college spend years paying back. They are white-hot Protestants, and they live with a load of work and debt and obligation. Peter placed his new colleague on scraps of information. He had never been in the West.

She came to the office on a Monday morning in October. The office was overheated and painted cream. It contained two desks, the filing cabinets, a map of the world as it had been in 1945, and the Charter of the United Nations left behind by Agnes Brusen's predecessor. (She took down the Charter without asking Peter if he minded, with the impudence of gesture you find in women who wouldn't say boo to a goose; and then she hung her college degree on the nail where the Charter had been.) Three people brought her in—a whole committee. One of them said, "Agnes, this is Pete Frazier. Pete, Agnes Brusen. Pete's Canadian, too, Agnes. He knows all about the office, so ask him anything."

Of course he knew all about the office: he knew the exact spot where the cord of the venetian blind was frayed, obliging one to give an extra tug to the right.

The girl might have been twenty-three: no more. She wore a brown tweed suit with bone buttons, and a new silk scarf and new shoes. She clutched an unscratched brown purse. She seemed dressed in going-away presents. She said, "Oh, I never smoke," with a convulsive movement of her hand, when Peter offered his case. He was courteous, hiding his disappointment. The people he worked with had told him a Scandinavian girl was arriving, and he had expected a stunner. Agnes was a mole: she was small and brown, and round-shouldered as if she had always carried parcels or younger children in her arms. A mole's profile was turned when she said goodbye to her committee. If she had been foreign, ill-favored though she was, he might have flirted a little, just to show that he was friendly; but their being Canadian, and suddenly left together, was a sexual damper. He sat down and lit his own cigarette. She smiled at him, questioningly, he thought, and sat as if she had never seen a chair before. He wondered if his smoking was annoying her. He wondered if she was fidgety about drafts, or allergic to anything, and whether she would want the blind up or down. His social compass was out of order because the others couldn't tell Peter and Agnes apart. There was a world of difference between them, yet it was she who had been brought in to sit at the larger of the two desks.

While he was thinking this she got up and walked around the office, almost on tiptoe, opening the doors of closets and pulling out the filing trays. She looked inside everything except the drawers of Peter's desk. (In any case, Peter's desk was locked. His desk is locked wherever he works. In Geneva he went into Personnel one morning, early, and pinched his application form. He had stated on the form that he had seven years' experience in public relations and could speak French, German, Spanish, and Italian. He has always collected anything important about himself—anything useful. But he can never get on with the final act, which is getting rid of the information. He has kept papers about for years, a constant source of worry.)

"I know this looks funny, Mr Ferris," said the girl. "I'm not really snooping or anything. I just can't feel easy in a new place unless I know where everything is. In a new place everything seems so hidden."

If she had called him 'Ferris' and pretended not to know he was Frazier, it could only be because they had sent her here to spy on him and see if he had repented and was fit for a better place in life. "You'll be all right here," he said. "Nothing's hidden. Most of us haven't got brains enough to have secrets. This is Rainbow Valley." Depressed by the thought that they were having him watched now, he passed his hand over his hair and looked outside to the lawn and the parking lot and the peacocks someone gave the Palais des Nations years ago. The peacocks love no one. They wander about the parked cars looking elderly, bad-tempered, mournful, and lost.

Agnes had settled down again. She folded her silk scarf and placed it just so, with her gloves beside it. She opened her new purse and took out a notebook and a shiny gold pencil. She may have written

> Duster for desk
> Kleenex
> Glass jar for flowers
> Air-Wick because he smokes
> Paper for lining drawers

because the next day she brought each of these articles to work. She also brought a large black Bible, which she unwrapped lovingly and placed on the left-hand corner of her desk. The flower vase—empty—stood in the middle, and the Kleenex made a counterpoise for the Bible on the right.

When he saw the Bible he knew she had not been sent to spy on his work. The conspiracy was deeper. She might have been dispatched by ghosts. He knew everything about her, all in a moment: he saw the ambition, the terror, the dry pride. She was the true heir of the men from Scotland; she was at the start. She had been sent to tell him, "You can begin, but not begin again." She never opened the Bible, but she dusted it as she dusted her desk, her chair, and any surface the cleaning staff had overlooked. And Peter, the first days, watching her timid movements, her insignificant little face, felt, as you feel the approach of a storm, the charge of moral certainty round her, the belief in work, the faith in undertakings, the bread of the Black Sunday. He recognized and tasted all of it: ashes in the mouth.

After five days their working relations were settled. Of course, there was the Bible and all that went with it, but his tongue had never held the taste of ashes long. She was an inferior girl of poor quality. She had nothing in her favor except the degree on the wall. In the real world, he would not have invited her to his house except to mind the children. That was what he said to Sheilah. He said that Agnes was a mole, and a virgin, and that her tics and mannerisms were sending him round the bend. She had an infuriating habit of covering her mouth when she talked. Even at the telephone she put up her hand as if afraid of losing anything, even a word. Her voice was nasal and flat. She had two working costumes, both dull as the wall. One was the brown suit, the other a navy-blue dress with changeable collars. She dressed for no one; she dressed for her desk, her jar of flowers, her Bible, and her box of Kleenex. One day she crossed the space between the two desks and stood over Peter, who was reading a newspaper. She could have spoken to him from her desk, but she may have felt that being on her feet gave her authority. She had plenty of courage, but authority was something else.

"I thought—I mean, they told me you were the person . . ." She got on with it bravely: "If you don't want to do the filing or any work, all right, Mr Frazier. I'm not saying anything about that. You might have poor health or your personal reasons. But it's got to be done, so if you'll kindly show me about the filing I'll do it. I've worked in Information before, but it was a different office, and every office is different."

"My dear girl," said Peter. He pushed back his chair and looked at her, astonished. "You've been sitting there fretting, worrying. How insensitive of me. How trying for you. Usually I file on the last Wednesday of the month, so you see, you just haven't been around long enough to see a last Wednesday. Not another word, please. And let us not waste another minute." He emptied the heaped baskets of photographs so swiftly, pushing "Iran—Smallpox Control" into "Irish Red Cross" (close enough), that the girl looked frightened, as if she had raised a whirlwind. She said slowly, "If you'll only show me, Mr Frazier, instead of doing it so fast, I'll gladly look after it, because you might want to be doing other things, and I feel the filing should be done every day.'' But Peter was too busy to answer, and so she sat down, holding the edge of her desk.

"There,'' he said, beaming. "All done.'' His smile, his sunbrust, was wasted, for the girl was staring round the room as if she feared she had not inspected everything the first day after all; some drawer, some cupboard, hid a monster. That evening Peter unlocked one of the drawers of his desk and took away the application form he had stolen from Personnel. The girl had not finished her search.

"How could you *not* know?'' wailed Sheilah. "You sit looking at her every day. You must talk about *something*. She must have told you.''

"She did tell me,'' said Peter, "and I've just told you.''

It was this: Agnes Brusen was on the Burleighs' guest list. How had the Burleighs met her? What did they see in her? Peter could not reply. He knew that Agnes lived in a bed-sitting room with a Swiss family and had her meals with them. She had been in Geneva three months, but no one had ever seen her outside the office. "You *should* know,'' said Sheilah. "She must have something, more than you can see. Is she pretty? Is she brilliant? What is it?''

"We don't really talk,'' Peter said. They talked in a way: Peter teased her and she took no notice. Agnes was not a sulker. She had taken her defeat like a sport. She did her work and a good deal of his. She sat behind her Bible, her flowers, and her Kleenex, and answered when Peter spoke. That was how he learned about the Burleighs—just by teasing and being bored. It was a January afternoon. He said, "*Miss* Brusen. Talk to me. Tell me everything. Pretend we have perfect rapport. Do you like Geneva?''

"It's a nice clean town,'' she said. He can see to this day the red and blue anemones in the glass jar, and her bent head, and her small untended hands.

"Are you learning beautiful French with your Swiss family?''

"They speak English.''

"Why don't you take an apartment of your own?'' he said. Peter was not usually impertinent. He was bored. "You'd be independent then.''

"I am independent,'' she said. "I earn my living. I don't think it proves anything if you live by yourself. Mrs Burleigh wants me to live alone, too. She's looking for something for me. It mustn't be dear. I send money home.''

Here was the extraordinary thing about Agnes Brusen: she refused the use of Christian names and never spoke to Peter unless he spoke first, but she would tell anything, as if to say, "Don't waste time fishing. Here it is.''

He learned all in one minute that she sent her salary home, and that she was a friend of the Burleighs. The first he had expected; the second knocked him flat.

"She's got to come to dinner," Sheilah said. "We should have had her right from the beginning. If only I'd known! But *you* were the one. You said she looked like—oh, I don't even remember. A Norwegian mole."

She came to dinner one Saturday night in January, in her navy-blue dress, to which she had pinned an organdy gardenia. She sat upright on the edge of the sofa. Sheilah had ordered the meal from a restaurant. There was lobster, good wine, and a *pièce-montée* full of kirsch and cream. Agnes refused the lobster; she had never eaten anything from the sea unless it had been sterilized and tinned, and said so. She was afraid of skin poisoning. Someone in her family had skin poisoning after having eaten oysters. She touched her cheeks and neck to show where the poisoning had erupted. She sniffed her wine and put the glass down without tasting it. She could not eat the cake because of the alcohol it contained. She ate an egg, bread and butter, a sliced tomato, and drank a glass of ginger ale. She seemed unaware she was creating disaster and pain. She did not help clear away the dinner plates. She sat, adequately nourished, decently dressed, and waited to learn why she had been invited here—that was the feeling Peter had. He folded the card table on which they had dined, and opened the window to air the room.

"It's not the same cold as Canada, but you feel it more," he said, for something to say.

"Your blood has gotten thin," said Agnes.

Sheilah returned from the kitchen and let herself fall into an armchair. With her eyes closed she held out her hand for a cigarette. She was performing the haughty-lady act that was a family joke. She flung her head back and looked at Agnes through half-closed lids; then she suddenly brought her head forward, widening her eyes.

"Are you skiing madly?" she said.

"Well, in the first place there hasn't been any snow," said Agnes. "So nobody's doing any skiing so far as I know. All I hear is people complaining because there's no snow. Personally, I don't ski. There isn't much skiing in the part of Canada I come from. Besides, my family never had that kind of leisure."

"Heavens," said Sheilah, as if her family had every kind.

I'll bet they had, thought Peter. On the dole.

Sheilah was wasting her act. He had a suspicion that Agnes knew it was an act but did not know it was a joke. If so, it made Sheilah seem a fool, and he loved Sheilah too much to enjoy it.

"The Burleighs have been wonderful to me," said Agnes. She seemed to have divined why she was here, and decided to give them all the information they wanted, so that she could put on her coat and go home to bed. "They had me out to their place on the lake every weekend until the weather got cold and they moved back to town. They've rented a chalet for the winter, and they want me to come there, too. But I don't know if I will or not. I don't ski, and, oh, I don't know—I don't drink, either, and I don't always see the point. Their friends are too rich and I'm too Canadian."

She had delivered everything Sheilah wanted and more: Agnes was on the first guest list and didn't care. No, Peter corrected; doesn't know. Doesn't care and doesn't know.

"I thought with you Norwegians it was in the blood, skiing. And drinking," Sheilah murmured.

"Drinking, maybe," said Agnes. She covered her mouth and said behind her spread fingers, "In our family we were religious. We didn't drink or smoke. My brother was in Norway in the war. He saw some cousins. Oh," she said, unexpectedly loud, "Harry said it was just terrible. They were so poor. They had flies in their kitchen. They gave him something to eat a fly had been on. They didn't have a real toilet, and they'd been in the same house about two hundred years. We've only recently built our own home, and we have a bathroom and two toilets. I'm from Saskatchewan," she said. "I'm not from any other place."

Surely one winter here had been punishment enough? In the spring they would remember him and free him. He wrote Lucille, who said he was lucky to have a job at all. The Burleighs had sent the Fraziers a second-guest list Christmas card. It showed a Moslem refugee child weeping outside a tent. They treasured the card and left it standing long after the others had been given the children to cut up. Peter had discovered by now what had gone wrong in the friendship—Sheilah had charged a skirt at a dressmaker to Madge's account. Madge had told her she might, and then changed her mind. Poor Sheilah! She was new to this part of it—to the changing humors of independent friends. Paris was already a year in the past. At Mardi Gras, the Burleighs gave their annual party. They invited everyone, the damned and the dropped, with the prodigality of a child at prayers. The invitation said "in costume," but the Fraziers were too happy to wear a disguise. They might not be recognized. Like many of the guests they expected to meet at the party, they had been disgraced, forgotten, and rehabili-tated. They would be anxious to see one another as they were.

On the night of the party, the Fraziers rented a car they had never seen before and drove through the first snowstorm of the year. Peter had not driven since last summer's blissful trips in the Fiat. He could not find the switch for the windshield wiper in this car. He leaned over the wheel. "Can you see on your side?" he asked. "Can I make a left turn here? Does it look like a one-way?"

"I can't imagine why you took a car with a right-hand drive," said Sheilah.

He had trouble finding a place to park; they crawled up and down unknown streets whose curbs were packed with snow-covered cars. When they stood at last on the pavement, safe and sound, Peter said. "This is the first snow."

"I can see that," said Sheilah. "Hurry, darling. My hair."

"It's the first snow."

"You're repeating yourself," she said. "Please hurry, darling. Think of my poor shoes. My *hair*."

She was born in an ugly city, and so was Peter, but they have this difference: she does not know the importance of the first snow—the first clean thing in a dirty year. He would have told her that this storm, which was wetting her feet and destroying her hair, was like the first day of the English spring, but she made a frightened gesture, trying to shield her head. The gesture told him he did not understand her beauty.

"Let me," she said. He was fumbling with the key, trying to lock the car. She took the key without impatience and locked the door on the driver's side; and then, to show Peter she treasured him and was not afraid of wasting her life or her beauty, she took his arm and they walked in the snow down a street and around a corner to the apartment house where the Burleighs lived. They were, and are, a united couple. They were afraid of the party, and each of them knew it. When they walk together, holding arms, they give each other whatever each can spare.

Only six people had arrived in costume. Madge Burliegh was disguised as Manet's "Lola de Valence," which everyone mistook for Carmen. Mike was an Impressionist painter, with a straw hat and a glued-on beard. "I am all of them," he said. He would rather have dressed as a dentist, he said, welcoming the Fraziers as if he had parted from them the day before, but Madge wanted him to look as if he had created her. "You know?" he said.

"Perfectly," said Sheilah. Her shoes were stained and the snow had softened her lacquered hair. She was not wasted; she was the most beautiful woman here.

About an hour after their arrival, Peter found himself with no one to talk to. He had told about the Trudeau wedding in Paris and the pot of azaleas, and after he mislaid his audience he began to look around for Sheilah. She was on a window seat, partly concealed by a green velvet curtain. Facing her, so that their profiles were neat and perfect against the night, was a man. Their conversation was private and enclosed, as if they had in minutes covered leagues of time and arrived at the place where everything was implied, understood. Peter began working his way across the room, toward his wife, when he saw Agnes. He was granted the sight of her drowning face. She had dressed with comic intention, obviously with care, and now she was a ragged hobo, half tramp, half clown. Her hair was tucked up under a bowler hat. The six costumed guests who had made the same mistake—the ghost, the gypsy, the Athenian maiden, the geisha, the Martian, and the apache—were delighted to find a seventh; but Agnes was not amused; she was gasping for life. When a waiter passed with a crowded tray, she took a glass without seeing it; then a wave of the party took her away.

Sheilah's new friend was named Simpson. After Simpson said he thought perhaps he'd better circulate, Peter sat down where he had been. "Now look, Sheilah," he began. Their most intimate conversations have taken place at parties. Once at a party she told him she was leaving him; she didn't, of course. Smiling, blue-eyed, she gazed lovingly at Peter and said rapidly, "Pete, shut up and listen. That man. The man you scared away. He's a big wheel in a company out in India or someplace like that. It's gorgeous out there. Pete, the *servants*. And it's warm. It never snows. He says there's heaps of jobs. You pick them off the trees like . . . orchids. He says it's even easier now than when we owned all those places, because now the poor pets can't run anything and they'll pay *fortunes*. Pete, he says it's warm, it's heaven, and Pete, they pay."

A few minutes later, Peter was alone again and Sheilah part of a closed, laughing group. Holding her elbow was the man from the place where jobs grew like orchids. Peter edged into the group and laughed at a story he hadn't heard. He heard only the last line, which was, "Here comes another tunnel." Looking out from the tight laughing ring, he saw Agnes again, and he thought, I'd be like Agnes if I didn't have Sheilah. Agnes put her glass down on a table and lurched toward the doorway, head forward. Madge Burleigh, who never stopped moving around the room and smiling, was still smiling when she paused and said in Peter's ear, "Go with Agnes, Pete. See that she gets home. People will notice if Mike leaves."

"She probably just wants to walk around the block," said Peter. "She'll be back."

"Oh, stop thinking about yourself, for once, and see that that poor girl gets home," said Madge. "You've still got your Fiat, haven't you?"

He turned away as if he had been pushed. Any command is a release, in a way. He may not want to go in that particular direction, but at least he is going somewhere. And now Sheilah, who had moved inches nearer to hear what Madge and Peter were murmuring, said, "Yes, go, darling," as if he were leaving the gates of Troy.

Peter was to find Agnes and see that she reached home: this he repeated to himself as he stood on the landing, outside the Burleighs' flat, ringing for the elevator. Bored with waiting for it, he ran down the stairs, four flights,and saw that Agnes had stalled the lift by leaving the door open. She was crouched on the floor, propped on her fingertips. Her eyes were closed.

"Agnes," said Peter. "*Miss* Brusen, I mean. That's no way to leave a party. Don't you know you're supposed to curtsey and say thanks? My God, Agnes, anybody going by here just now might have seen you! Come on, be a good girl. Time to go home."

She got up without his help and, moving between invisible crevasses, shut the elevator door. Then she left the building and Peter followed, remembering he was to see that she got home. They walked along the snowy pavement, Peter a few steps behind her. When she turned right for no reason, he turned, too. He had no clear idea where they were going. Perhaps she lived close by. He had forgotten where the hired car was parked, or what it looked like; he could not remember its make or its color. In any case, Sheilah had the key. Agnes walked on steadily, as if she knew their destination, and he thought, Agnes Brusen is drunk in the street in Geneva and dressed like a tramp. He wanted to say, "This is the best thing that ever happened to you, Agnes; it will help you understand how things are for some of the rest of us." But she stopped and turned and, leaning over a low hedge, retched on a frozen lawn. He held her clammy forehead and rested his hand on her arched back, on muscles as tight as a fist. She straightened up and drew a breath but the cold air made her cough. "Don't breath too deeply," he said. "It's the worst thing you can do. Have you got a handkerchief?" He passed his own handkerchief over her wet weeping face, upturned like the face of one of his little girls. "I'm out without a coat," he said, noticing it. "We're a pair."

"I never drink," said Agnes. "I'm just not used to it." Her voice was sweet and quiet. He had never seen her so peaceful, so composed. He thought she must surely be all right, now, and perhaps he might leave her here. The trust in her tilted face had perplexed him. He wanted to get back to Sheilah and have her explain something. He had forgotten what it was, but Sheilah would know. "Do you live around here?" he said. As he spoke, she let herself fall. He had wiped her face and now she trusted him to pick her up, set her on her feet, take her wherever she ought to be. He pulled her up and she stood, wordless, humble, as he brushed the snow from her tramp's clothes. Snow horizontally crossed the lamplight. The street was silent. Agnes had lost her hat. Snow, which he tasted, melted on her hands. His gesture of licking snow from her hands was formal as a handshake. He tasted snow on her hands and then they walked on.

"I never drink," she said. They stood on the edge of a broad avenue. The wrong turning now could lead them anywhere; it was the changeable avenue at the edge of towns that loses its houses and becomes a highway. She held his arm and spoke in a gentle voice. She said, "In our house we didn't smoke or drink. My mother was ambitious for me, more than for Harry and the others." She said, "I've never been alone before. When I was a kid I would get up in the summer before the others, and I'd see the ice wagon going down the street. I'm alone now. Mrs Burleigh's found me an apartment. It's only one room. She likes it because it's in the old part of town. I don't like old houses. Old houses are dirty. You don't know who was there before.'

"I should have a car somewhere," Peter said. "I'm not sure where we are."

He remembers that on this avenue they climbed into a taxi, but nothing about the drive. Perhaps he fell asleep. He does remember that when he paid the driver Agnes clutched his arm, trying to stop him. She pressed extra coins into the driver's palm. The driver was paid twice.

"I'll tell you one thing about us," said Peter. "We pay everything twice." This was part of a much longer theory concerning North American behavior, and it was not Peter's own. Mike Burleigh had held forth about it on summer afternoons.

Agnes pushed open a door between a stationer's shop and a grocery, and led the way up a narrow inside stair. They climbed one flight, frightening beetles. She had to search every pocket for the latchkey. She was shaking with cold. Her apartment seemed little warmer than the street. Without speaking to Peter she turned on all the lights. She looked inside the kitchen and the bathroom and then got down on her hands and knees and looked under the sofa. The room was neat and belonged to no one. She left him standing in this unclaimed room—she had forgotten him—and closed a door behind her. He looked for something to do—some useful action he could repeat to Madge. He turned on the electric radiator in the fireplace. Perhaps Agnes wouldn't thank him for it; perhaps she would rather undress in the cold. "I'll be on my way.' he called to the bathroom door.

She had taken off the tramp's clothes and put on a dressing gown of orphanage wool. She came out of the bathroom and straight toward him. She pressed her face and rubbed her cheek on his shoulder as if hoping the contact would leave a scar. He saw her back and her profile and his own face in the mirror over the fireplace. He thought, This is how disasters happen. He saw floods of sea water moving with perfect punitive justice over reclaimed land; he saw lava covering vineyards and overtaking of dogs and stragglers. A bridge over an abyss snapped in two and the long express train, suddenly V-shaped, floated like snow. He thought amiably of every kind of disaster and thought, This is how they occur.

Her eyes were closed. She said, "I shouldn't be over here. In my family we didn't drink or smoke. My mother wanted a lot from me, more than from Harry and the others." But he knew all that; he had known from the day of the Bible, and because once, at the beginning, she had made him afraid. He was not afraid of her now.

She said, "It's no use staying here, is it?"

"If you mean what I think, no."

"It wouldn't be better anywhere."

She let him see full on her blotched face. He was not expected to do anything. He was not required to pick her up when she fell or wipe her tears. She was poor quality, really—he remembered having thought that once. She left him and went quietly in to the bathroom and locked the door. He heard taps running and supposed it was a hot bath. He was pretty certain there would be no more tears. He looked at his watch: Sheilah must be home, now, wondering what had become of him. He descended the beetles' staircase and for forty minutes crossed the city under a windless fall of snow.

The neighbor's child who had stayed with Peter's children was asleep on the living-room sofa. Peter woke her and sent her, sleep-walking, to her own door. He sat down, wet to the bone, thinking, I'll call the Burleighs. In half an hour I'll call the police. He heard a car stop and the engine running and a confusion of two voices laughing and calling goodnight. Presently Sheilah let herself in, rosy-faced, smiling. She carried his trenchcoat over her arm. She said, "How's Agnes?"

"Where were you?" he said. "Whose car was that?"

Sheilah had gone into the children's room. He heard her shutting their window. She returned, undoing her dress, and said, "Was Agnes all right?"

"Agnes is all right. Sheilah, this is about the worst . . ."

She stepped out of the Balenciaga and threw it over a chair. She stopped and looked at him and said, "Poor old Pete, are you in love with Agnes?" And then, as if the answer were of so little importance she hadn't time for it, she locked her arms around him and said, "My love, we're going to Ceylon."

Two days later, when Peter strolled into his office, Agnes was at her desk. She wore the blue dress, with a spotless collar. White and yellow freesias were symmetrically arranged in the glass jar. The room was hot, and the spring snow, glued for a second when it touched the window, blurred the view of parked cars.

"Quite a party," Peter said.

She did not look up. He sighed, sat down, and thought if the snow held he would be skiing at the Burleighs' very soon. Impressed by his kindness to Agnes, Madge had invited the family for the first possible weekend.

Presently Agnes said, "I'll never drink again or go to a house where people are drinking. And I'll never bother anyone the way I bothered you."

"You didn't bother me," he said. "I took you home. You were alone and it was late. It's normal."

"Normal for you, maybe, but I'm used to getting myself home by myself. Please never tell what happened."

He stared at her. He can still remember the freesias and the Bible and the heat in the room. She looked as if the elements had no power. She felt neither heat nor cold. "Nothing happened," he said.

"I behaved in a silly way. I had no right to. I led you to think I might do something wrong."

"*I* might have tried something," he said gallantly. "But that would be my fault and not yours."

She put her knuckle to her mouth and he could scarcely hear. "It was because of you. I was afraid you might be blamed, or else you'd blame yourself."

"There's no question of any blame," he said. "Nothing happened. We'd both had a lot to drink. Forget about it. Nothing *happened*. You'd remember if it had."

She put down her hand. There was an expression on her face. Now she sees me, he thought. She had never looked at him after the first day. (He has since tried to put a name to the look on her face; but how can he, now, after so many voyages, after Ceylon, and Hong Kong, and Sheilah's nearly leaving him, and all their difficulties—the money owed, the rows with hotel managers, the lost and found steamer trunk, the children throwing up the foreign food?) She sees me now, he thought. What does she see?

She said, "I'm from a big family. I'm not used to being alone. I'm not a suicidal person, but I could have done something after that party, just not to see any more, or think or listen or expect anything. What can I think when I see these people? All my life I heard, Educated people don't do this, educated people don't do that. And now I'm here, and you're all educated people, and you're nothing but pigs. You're educated and you drink and do everything wrong and you know what you're doing, and that makes you worse than pigs. My family worked to make me an educated person, but they didn't know you. But what if I didn't see and hear and expect anything any more? It wouldn't change anything. You'd all be still the same. Only *you* might have thought it was your fault. You might have thought you were to blame. It could worry you all your life. It would have been wrong for me to worry you."

He remembered that the rented car was still along a snowy curb somewhere in Geneva. He wondered if Sheilah had the key in her purse and if she remembered where they'd parked.

"I told you about the ice wagon," Agnes said. "I don't remember everything, so you're wrong about remembering. But I remember telling you that. That was the best. It's the best you can hope to have. In a big family, if you want to be alone, you have to get up before the rest of them. You get up early in the morning in the summer and it's you, you, once in your life alone in the universe. You think you know everything that can happen . . . Nothing is ever like that again."

He looked at the smeared window and wondered if this day could end without disaster. In his mind he saw her falling in the snow wearing a tramp's costume, and he saw her coming to him in the orphanage dressing gown. He saw her drowning face at the party. He was afraid for himself. The story was still unfinished. It had to come to a climax, something threatening to him. But there was no climax. They talked that day, and afterward nothing else was said. They went on in the same office for a short time, until Peter left for Ceylon; until somebody read the right letter, passed it on for the right initials, and the Fraziers began the Oriental tour that should have made their fortune. Agnes and Peter were too tired to speak after that morning. They were like a married couple in danger, taking care.

But what were they talking about that day, so quietly, such old friends? They talked about dying, about being ambitious, about being religious, about different kinds of love. What did she see when she looked at him—taking her knuckle slowly away from her mouth, bringing her hand down to the desk, letting it rest there? They were both Canadians, so they had this much together—the knowledge of the little you dare admit. Death, near-death, the best thing, the wrong thing—God knows what they were telling each other. Anyway, nothing happened.

When, on Sunday mornings, Sheilah and Peter talk about those times, they take on the glamor of something still to come. It is then he remembers Agnes Brusen. He never says her name. Sheilah wouldn't remember Agnes. Agnes is the only secret Peter has from his wife, the only puzzle he pieces together without her help. He thinks about families in the West as they were fifteen, twenty years ago—the iron-cold ambition, and every member pushing the next one on. He thinks of his father's parties. When he thinks of his father he imagines him with Sheilah, in a crowd. Actually, Sheilah and Peter's father never met, but they might have liked each other. His father admired good-looking women. Peter wonders what they were doing over there in Geneva—not Sheilah and Peter, *Agnes* and Peter. It is almost as if they had once run away together, silly as children, irresponsible as lovers. Peter and Sheilah are back where they started. While they were out in world affairs picking up microbes and debts, always on the fringe of disaster, the fringe of a fortune, Agnes went on and did—what? They lost each other. He thinks of the ice wagon going down the street. He sees something he had never seen in his life—a Western town that belongs to Agnes. Here is Agnes—small, mole-faced, round-shouldered because she has always carried a younger child. She watches the ice wagon and the trail of ice water in a morning invented for her: hers. He sees the weak prairie trees and the shadows on the sidewalk. Nothing moves except the shadows and the ice wagon and the changing amber of the child's eyes. The child is Peter. He has seen the grain of the cement sidewalk and the grass in the cracks, and the dust, and the dandelions at the edge of the road. He is there. He has taken the morning that belongs to Agnes, he is up before the others, and he knows everything. There is nothing he doesn't know. He could keep the morning, if he wanted to, but what can Peter do with the start of a summer day? Sheilah is here, it is a true Sunday morning, with its dimness and headache and remorse and regrets and this is life. He says, "We have the Balenciaga." He touches Sheilah's hand. The children have their aunt now, and he and Sheilah have each other. Everything works out, somehow or other. Let Agnes have the start of the day. Let Agnes think it was invented for her. Who wants to be alone in the universe? No, begin at the beginning: Peter lost Agnes. Agnes says to herself somewhere, Peter is lost.

# ITALO CALVINO
## 1923–1985

He was born in Cuba, in a little town near Havana. His father was a soil scientist, from San Remo, Italy. His mother also had scientific training. In 1925 the family returned to San Remo, where he went to school until enrolling in the agriculture school of the University of Torino in 1941. His parents were free thinkers, who taught him the taxonomy of plants and animals instead of the religious catechism. He did not answer his draft notice for the Italian fascist army during World War II but joined the partisans in the mountains of northwest Italy and became a member of the Communist Party. In 1947 he took his university degree in literature with a thesis on Joseph Conrad, and he published his neo-realistic novel *The Path to the Nest of Spiders*, based on his wartime experiences. In the years that followed he moved away from neo-realism and began to develop his unique kind of fiction. The publication of *Cosmicomics* (1965) and *T-Zero* (1967) made him internationally known as a writer of philosophical and scientific fables.

# Meiosis

Narrating things as they are means narrating them from the beginning, and even if I start the story at a point where the characters are multicellular organisms, for example the story of my relationship with Priscilla, I have first to define clearly what I mean when I say me and what I mean when I say Priscilla, then I can go on to establish what this relationship was. So I'll begin by saying that Priscilla is an individual of my same species and of the sex opposite mine, multicellular as I now find myself, too; but having said this I still haven't said anything, because I must specify that by multicellular individual is meant a complex of about fifty trillion cells very different among themselves but marked by certain chains of identical acids in the chromosomes of each cell of each individual, acids that determine various processes in the proteins of the cells themselves.

So narrating the story of me and Priscilla means first of all defining the relations established between my proteins and Priscilla's proteins, commanded, both mine and hers, by chains of nucleic acids arranged in identical series in each of her cells and in each of mine. Then narrating this story becomes still more complicated than when it was a question of a single cell, not only because the description of the relationship must take into account so many things that happen at the same time but above all because it's necessary to establish who is having relations with whom, before specifying what sort of relations they are. Actually, when you come right down to it, defining the sort of relations isn't after all as important as it seems, because saying we have mental relations, for example, or else, for example, physical relations doesn't change much, since a mental relationship involves several billion special cells called neurons which, however, function by receiving stimuli from such a great number of other cells that we might just as well consider all the trillions of cells of the organism at once as we do when we talk about a physical relationship.

In saying how difficult it is to establish who's having relations with whom we must first clear the decks of a subject that often crops up in conversation: namely, the fact that from one moment to the next I am no longer the same I nor is Priscilla any longer the same Priscilla, because of the continuous renewal of the protein molecules in our cells through, for example, digestion or also respiration which fixes the oxygen in the bloodstream. This kind of argument takes us completely off our course because while it's true that the cells are renewed, in renewing themselves they go on following the program established by those that were there before and so in this sense you could reasonably insist that I continue to be I and Priscilla, Priscilla. This in other words is not the problem, but perhaps it was of some use to raise it because it helps us realize that things aren't as simple as they seem and so we slowly approach the point where we will realize how complicated they are.

Well then, when I say I, or when I say Priscilla, what do I mean? I mean that special configuration which my cells and her cells assume through a special relationship between the environment and a special genetic heritage which from the beginning seemed invented on purpose to cause my cells to be mine and Priscilla's cells to be Priscilla's. As we proceed we'll see that nothing is made on purpose, that nobody has invented anything, that the way I am and Priscilla is really doesn't matter in the least to anyone: all a genetic heritage has to do is to transmit what was transmitted to it for transmitting, not giving a damn about how it's received. But for the moment let's limit ourselves to answering the question if I, in quotes, and Priscilla, in quotes, are our genetic heritage, in quotes, or our form, in quotes. And when I say form I mean both what is seen and what isn't seen, namely, all her way of being Priscilla, the fact that fuchsia or orange is becoming to her, the scent emanating from her skin not only because she was born with a glandular constitution suited to giving off that scent but also because of everything she has eaten in her life and the brands of soap she has used, in other words because of what is called, in quotes, culture, and also her way of walking and of sitting down which comes to her from the way she has moved among those who move in the cities and houses and streets where she's lived, all this but also the things she has in her memory, after having seen them perhaps just once and perhaps at the movies, and also the forgotten things which still remain recorded somewhere in the back of the neurons like all the psychic trauma a person has to swallow from infancy on.

Now, both in the form you see and don't see and in our genetic heritage, Priscilla and I have absolutely identical elements—common to the two of us, or to the environment, or to the species—and also elements which establish a difference. Then the problem begins to arise whether the relationship between me and Priscilla is the relationship only between the differential elements, because the common ones can be overlooked in both—that is, whether by "Priscilla" we must understand "what is peculiar to Priscilla as far as the other members of the species are concerned"—or whether the relationship is between the common elements, and then we must decide if it's the ones common to the species or to the environment or to the two of us as distinct from the rest of the species and perhaps more beautiful than the others.

On closer examination, if individuals of opposite sex enter into a particular relationship it clearly isn't we who decide but the species, or rather not so much the species as the animal condition, or the vegetable-animal condition of the animal-vegetives distinguished into distinct sexes. Now, in the choice I make of Priscilla to have with her relations whose nature I don't yet know—and in the choice that Priscilla makes of me, assuming that she does choose me and doesn't change her mind at the last moment—no one knows what order of priority comes first into play, therefore no one knows how many I's precede the I that I think I am, and how many Priscillas precede the Priscilla toward whom I believe I am running.

In short, the more you simplify the terms of the question the more they become complicated: once we've established that what I call "I" consists of a certain number of amino acids which line up in a certain way, it's logical that inside these molecules all possible relations are foreseen, and from outside we have nothing but the exclusion of some of the possible relations in the form of certain enzymes which block certain processes. Therefore you can say that it's as if everything possible had already happened to me, including the possibility of its not happening: once I am I the cards are all dealt, I dispose of a finite number of possibilities and no more, what happens outside counts for me only if it's translated into operations already foreseen by my nucleic acids, I'm walled up within myself, chained to my molecular program: outside of me I don't have and won't have relations with anything or with anybody. And neither will Priscilla; I mean the *real* Priscilla, poor thing. If around me and around her there's some stuff that seems to have relations with other stuff, these are facts that don't concern us: in reality for me and for her nothing substantial can happen.

Hardly a cheerful situation, therefore: and not because I was expecting to have a more complex individuality than the one given me, beginning with a special arrangement of an acid and of four basic substances which in their turn command the disposition of about twenty amino acids in the forty-six chromosomes of each cell I have; but because this individuality repeated in each of my cells is mine only after a manner of speaking, since out of forty-six chromosomes twenty-three come to me from my father and twenty-three from my mother, that is, I continue carrying my parents with me in all my cells, and I'll never be able to free myself of this burden.

What my parents programmed me to be in the beginning is what I am: that and nothing else. And in my parents' instructions are contained the instructions of my parents' parents handed down in turn from parent to parent in an endless chain of obedience. The story I wanted to narrate therefore is not only impossible to narrate but first of all impossible to live, because it's all there already, contained in a past that can't be narrated since, in turn, it's included in its own past, in the many individual pasts—so many that we can't really be sure they aren't the past of the species and of what existed before the species, a general past to which all individual pasts refer but which no matter how far you go back doesn't exist except in the form of individual cases, such as Priscilla and I might be, between which, however, nothing happens, individual or general.

What each of us really is and has is the past; all we are and have is the catalogue of the possibilities that didn't fail, of the experiences that are ready to be repeated. A present doesn't exist, we proceed blindly toward the outside and the afterward, carrying out an established program with materials we fabricate ourselves, always the same. We don't tend toward any future, there's nothing awaiting us, we're shut within the system of a memory which foresees no task but remembering itself. What now leads me and Priscilla to seek each other isn't an impulse toward the afterward: it's the final action of the past that is fulfilled through us. Good-by, Priscilla, our encounter, our embrace are useless, we remain distant, or finally near, in other words forever apart.

Separation, the impossibility of meeting, has been in us from the very beginning. We were born not from a fusion but from a juxtaposition of distinct bodies. Two cells grazed each other: one is lazy and all pulp, the other is only a head and a darting tail. They are egg and seed: they experience a certain timidity; then they rush—at their different speeds—and hurry toward each other. The seed plunges headlong into the egg; the tail is left outside; the head—all full of nucleus— is shot at the nucleus of the egg; the two nuclei are shattered: you might expect heaven knows what fusion or mingling or exchange of selves; instead, what was written in one nucleus and in the other, those spaced lines, fall in and arrange themselves, on each side, in the new nucleus, very closely printed; the words of both nuclei fit in, whole and clearly separate. In short, nobody was lost in the other, nobody has given in or has given himself; the two cells now one are packaged together but just as they were before: the first thing they feel is a slight disappointment. Meanwhile the double nucleus has begun its sequence of duplications, printing the combined messages of father and mother in each of the offspring cells, perpetuating not so much the union as the unbridgeable distance that separates in each couple the two companions, the failure, the void that remains in the midst of even the most successful couple.

Of course, on every disputed issue our cells can follow the instructions of a single parent and thus feel free of the other's command, but we know what we claim to be in our exterior form counts for little compared to the secret program we carry printed in each cell, where the contradictory orders of father and mother continue arguing. What really counts is this incompatible quarrel of father and mother that each of us drags after him, with the rancor of every point where one partner has had to give way to the other, who then raises his voice still louder in his victory as dominant mate. So the characteristics that determine my interior and exterior form, when they are not the sum or the average of the orders received from father and mother together, are orders denied in the depth of cells, counterbalanced by different orders which have remained latent, sapped by the suspicion that perhaps the other orders were better. So at times I'm seized with uncertainty as to whether I am really the sum of the dominant characteristics of the past, the result of a series of operations that produced always a number bigger than zero, or whether instead my true essence isn't rather what descends from the succession of defeated characteristics, the total of the terms with the minus sign, of everything that in the tree of derivations has remained excluded, stifled, interrupted: the weight of what hasn't been weighs on me, no less crushing than what has been and couldn't not be.

Void, separation and waiting, that's what we are. And such we remain even on the day when the past inside us rediscovers its original forms, clustering into swarms of seed-cells or concentrated ripening of the egg-cells, and finally the words written in the nuclei are no longer the same as before but are no longer part of us either, they're a message beyond us, which already belongs to us no more. In a hidden point in ourselves the double series of orders from the past is divided in two and the new cells find themselves with a simple past, no longer double, which gives them lightness and the illusion of being really new, of having a new past that almost seems a future.

Now, I've said it hastily like this but it's a complicated process, there in the darkness of the nucleus, in the depth of the sex organs, a succession of phases some a bit jumbled with others, but from which there's no turning back. At first the pairs of maternal and paternal messages which thus far had remained separate seem to remember they're couples and they join together two by two, so many fine little threads that become interwoven and confused; the desire to copulate outside myself now leads me to copulate within myself, at the depths of the extreme roots of the matter I'm made of, to couple the memory of the ancient pair I carry within me, the first couple, that is both the one that comes immediately before me, mother and father, and absolute first one, the couple at the animal-vegetal origins of the first coupling on Earth, and so the forty-six filaments that an obscure and secret cell bears in the nucleus are knotted two by two, still not giving up their old disagreement, since in fact they immediately try to disentangle themselves but remain stuck at some point in the knot, so when in the end they do suc-ceed, with a wrench, in separating—because meanwhile the mech-anism of separation has taken possession of the whole cell, stretch-ing out its pulp—each chromosome discovers it's changed, made of segments that first belonged some to one and some to the other, and it moves from the other, now changed too, marked by the alternate exchanges of the segments, and already two cells are being detached each with twenty-three chromosomes, one cell's different from the other's, and different from those that were in the previous cell, and at the next doubling there will be four cells all different, each with twenty-three chromosomes, in which what was the father's and the mother's, or rather the fathers' and the mothers', is mingled.

So finally the encounter of the pasts which can never take place in the present of those who believe they are meeting does take place in the form of the past of him who comes afterward and who cannot live that encounter in his own present. We believe we're going toward our marriage, but it is still the marriage of the fathers and the mothers which is celebrated through our expectation and our desire. What seems to us our happiness is perhaps only the happi-ness of the others' story which ends just where we thought ours began.

And it's pointless for us to run, Priscilla, to meet each other and follow each other: the past disposes of us with blind indifference, and once it has moved those fragments of itself and of us, it doesn't bother afterward how we spend them. We were only the prepara-tion, the envelope, for the encounter of pasts which happens through us but which is already part of another story, the story of the afterward: the encounters always take place before us and after us, and in them the elements of the new, forbidden to us, are active: chance, risk, improbability.

This is how we live, not free, surrounded by freedom, driven, acted on by this constant wave which is the combination of the possible cases and which passes through those points of space and of time in which the rose of the pasts is joined to the rose of the futures. The primordial sea was a soup of beringed molecules tra-versed at intervals by the messages of the similarity and of the difference that surrounded us and imposed new combinations. So the ancient tide rises at intervals in me and in Priscilla following the course of the Moon; so the sexed species respond to the old conditioning which prescribes ages and seasons of loves and also grants extensions and postponements to the ages and the seasons and at times becomes involved in obstinacies and coercions and vices.

In other words, Priscilla and I are only meeting places for messages from the past: not only for messages among themselves, but for messages meeting answers to messages. And as the different elements and molecules answer messages in different ways—imperceptibly or boundlessly different—so the messages vary according to the world that receives them and interprets them, or else, to remain the same, they are forced to change. You might say, then, that the messages are not messages at all, that a past to transmit doesn't exist, and only so many futures exist which correct the course of the past, which give it form, which invent it.

The story I wanted to tell is the encounter of two individuals who don't exist, since they are definable only with regard to a past or a future, past and future whose reality is reciprocally doubted. Or else it's a story that cannot be separated from the story of all the rest of what exists, and therefore from the story of what doesn't exist and, not existing, causes what does exist to exist. All we can say is that in certain points and moments that interval of void which is our individual presence is grazed by the wave which continues to renew the combinations of molecules and to complicate them or erase them, and this is enough to give us the certitude that somebody is "I" and somebody is "Priscilla" in the temporal and spatial distribution of the living cells, and that something happens or has happened or will happen which involves us directly and—I would dare say—happily and totally. This is in itself enough, Priscilla, to cheer me, when I bend my outstretched neck over yours and I give you a little nip on your yellow fur and you dilate your nostrils, bare your teeth, and kneel on the sand, lowering your hump to the level of my breast so that I can lean on it and press you from behind, bearing down on my rear legs, oh how sweet those sunsets in the oasis you remember when they loosen the burden from the packsaddle and the caravan scatters and we camels feel suddenly light and you break into a run and I trot after you, overtaking you in the grove of palm trees.

# FLANNERY O'CONNOR

## 1925–1964

Mary Flannery O'Connor was born in Savannah, Georgia. Her parents were Roman Catholics from families that had lived in the south for generations. She went to parochial schools in Savannah. When the girls were taught to sew and told to make clothes for dolls, she made a fancy coat for a pet chicken and brought him to school to show off his new outfit. When she was thirteen her father developed a fatal disease called "disseminated lupus," in which antibodies attack the blood vessels, joints, and internal organs. The family moved to Milledgeville, Georgia, to live with relatives, and Mary went to Peabody High School and Georgia State College for Women. She drew cartoons for the college paper and her yearbook. She also edited the literary magazine and won a fellowship to the Writers Workshop at the University of Iowa. At Iowa she began to publish her fiction, deciding to drop the "Mary" from her name. After receiving her MFA she went to Yaddo, a writers' colony at Saratoga Springs, New York, where she met people who encouraged her and helped her arrange publication for more of her work. In 1950 she was stricken with the disease that had killed her father nine years earlier. She moved to a farm near Milledgeville and continued writing there until her death in 1964, with her reputation growing steadily, even after her death. Most of her fiction can be found in *Collected Stories* (1971), which includes early versions of her two novels.

## Everything That Rises Must Converge

Her doctor had told Julian's mother that she must lose twenty pounds on account of her blood pressure, so on Wednesday nights Julian had to take her downtown on the bus for a reducing class at the Y. The reducing class was designed for working girls over fifty, who weighed from 165 to 200 pounds. His mother was one of the slimmer ones, but she said ladies did not tell their age or weight. She would not ride the buses by herself at night since they had been integrated, and because the reducing class was one of her few pleasures, necessary for her health, and *free*, she said Julian could at least put himself out to take her, considering all she did for him. Julian did not like to consider all she did for him, but every Wednesday night he braced himself and took her.

She was almost ready to go, standing before the hall mirror, putting on her hat, while he, his hands behind him, appeared pinned to the door frame, waiting like Saint Sebastian for the arrows to begin piercing him. The hat was new and had cost her seven dollars and a half. She kept saying, "Maybe I shouldn't have paid that for it. No, I shouldn't have. I'll take it off and return it tomorrow. I shouldn't have bought it."

Julian raised his eyes to heaven. "Yes, you should have bought it," he said. "Put it on and let's go." It was a hideous hat. A purple velvet flap came down on one side of it and stood up on the other; the rest of it was green and looked like a cushion with the stuffing out. He decided it was less comical than jaunty and pathetic. Everything that gave her pleasure was small and depressed him.

She lifted the hat one more time and set it down slowly on top of her head. Two wings of gray hair protruded on either side of her florid face, but her eyes, sky-blue, were as innocent and untouched by experience as they must have been when she was ten. Were it not that she was a widow who had struggled fiercely to feed and clothe and put him through school and who was supporting him still, "until he got on his feet," she might have been a little girl that he had to take to town.

"It's all right, it's all right," he said. "Let's go." He opened the door himself and started down the walk to get her going. The sky was a dying violet and the houses stood out darkly against it, bulbous liver-colored monstrosities of a uniform ugliness though no two were alike. Since this had been a fashionable neighborhood forty years ago, his mother persisted in thinking they did well to have an apartment in it. Each house had a narrow collar of dirt around it in which sat, usually, a grubby child. Julian walked with his hands in his pockets, his head down and thrust forward and his eyes glazed with the determination to make himself completely numb during the time he would be sacrificed to her pleasure.

The door closed and he turned to find the dumpy figure, surmounted by the atrocious hat, coming toward him. "Well," she said, "you only live once and paying a little more for it, I at least won't meet myself coming and going."

"Some day I'll start making money," Julian said gloomily—he knew he never would—"and you can have one of those jokes whenever you take the fit." But first they would move. He visualized a place where the nearest neighbors would be three miles away on either side.

"I think you're doing fine," she said, drawing on her gloves. "You've only been out of school a year. Rome wasn't built in a day."

She was one of the few members of the Y reducing class who arrived in hat and gloves and who had a son who had been to college. "It takes time," she said, "and the world is in such a mess. This hat looked better on me than any of the others, though when she brought it out I said, 'Take that thing back. I wouldn't have it on my head,' and she said, 'Now wait till you see it on,' and when she put it on me, I said, 'We-ull,' and she said, 'If you ask me, that hat does something for you and you do something for the hat, and besides,' she said, 'with that hat, you won't meet yourself coming and going.'"

persuaded

Julian thought he could have stood his lot better if she had been un- selfish, if she had been an old hag who drank and screamed at him. He walked along, saturated in depression, as if in the midst of his martyrdom he had lost his faith. Catching sight of his long, hopeless, irritated face, she stopped suddenly with a grief-stricken look, and pulled back on his arm. "Wait on me," she said. "I'm going back to the house and take this thing off and tomorrow I'm going to return it. I was out of my head. I can pay the gas bill with the seven-fifty."

He caught her arm in a vicious grip. "You are not going to take it back," he said. "I like it."

"Well," she said, "I don't think I ought . . ."

"Shut up and enjoy it," he muttered, more depressed than ever.

"With the world in the mess it's in," she said, "it's a wonder we can enjoy anything. I tell you, the bottom rail is on the top."

Julian sighed.

"Of course," she said, "if you know who you are, you can go anywhere." She said this every time he took her to the reducing class. "Most of them in it are not our kind of people," she said, "but I can be gracious to anybody. I know who I am."

"They don't give a damn for your graciousness," Julian said savagely. "Knowing who you are is good for one generation only. You haven't the foggiest idea where you stand now or who you are."

She stopped and allowed her eyes to flash at him. "I most certainly do know who I am," she said, "and if you don't know who you are, I'm ashamed of you."

"Oh hell," Julian said.

"Your great-grandfather was a former governor of this state," she said. "Your grandfather was a prosperous landowner. Your grandmother was a Godhigh."

"Will you look around you," he said tensely, "and see where you are now?" and he swept his arm jerkily out to indicate the neighborhood, which the growing darkness at least made less dingy.

"You remain what you are," she said. "Your great-grandfather had a plantation and two hundred slaves."

"There are no more slaves," he said irritably.

"They were better off when they were," she said. He groaned to see that she was off on that topic. She rolled onto it every few days like a train on an open track. He knew every stop, every junction, every swamp along the way, and knew the exact point at which her conclusion would roll majestically into the station: "It's ridiculous. It's simply not realistic. They should rise, yes, but on their own side of the fence."

"Let's skip it," Julian said.

"The ones I feel sorry for," she said, "are the ones that are half white. They're tragic."

"Will you skip it?"

"Suppose we were half white. We would certainly have mixed feelings."

"I have mixed feelings now," he groaned.

"Well let's talk about something pleasant," she said. "I remember going to Grandpa's when I was a little girl. Then the house had double stairways that went up to what was really the second floor—all the cooking was done on the first. I used to like to stay down in the kitchen on account of the way the walls smelled. I would sit with my nose pressed against the plaster and take deep breaths. Actually the place belonged to the Godhighs but your grandfather Chestny paid the mortgage and saved it for them. They were in reduced circumstances," she said, "but reduced or not, they never forgot who they were."

"Doubtless that decayed mansion reminded them," Julian muttered. He never spoke of it without contempt or thought of it without longing. He had seen it once when he was a child before it had been sold. The double stairways had rotted and been torn down. Negroes were living in it. But it remained in his mind as his mother had known it. It appeared in his dreams regularly. He would stand on the wide porch, listening to the rustle of oak leaves, then wander through the high-ceilinged hall into the parlor that opened onto it and gaze at the worn rugs and faded draperies. It occurred to him that it was he, not she, who could have appreciated it. He preferred its threadbare elegance to anything he could name and it was because of it that all the neighborhoods they had lived in had been a torment to him—whereas she had hardly known the difference. She called her insensitivity "being adjustable."

"And I remember the old darky who was my nurse, Caroline. There was no better person in the world. I've always had a great respect for my colored friends," she said. "I'd do anything in the world for them and they'd . . ."

"Will you for God's sake get off that subject?" Julian said. When he got on a bus by himself, he made it a point to sit down beside a Negro, in reparation as it were for his mother's sins.

"You're mighty touchy tonight," she said. "Do you feel all right?"

"Yes I feel all right," he said. "Now lay off."

She pursed her lips. "Well, you certainly are in a vile humor," she observed. "I just won't speak to you at all."

They had reached the bus stop. There was no bus in sight and Julian, his hands still jammed in his pockets and his head thrust forward, scowled down the empty street. The frustration of having to wait on the bus as well as ride on it began to creep up his neck like a hot hand. The presence of his mother was borne in upon him as she gave a pained sigh. He looked at her bleakly. She was holding herself very erect under the preposterous hat, wearing it like a banner of her imaginary dignity. There was in him an evil urge to break her spirit. He suddenly unloosened his tie and pulled it off and put it in his pocket.

She stiffened. "Why must you look like *that* when you take me to town?" she said. "Why must you deliberately embarrass me?"

"If you'll never learn where you are," he said, "you can at least learn where I am."

"You look like a—thug," she said.

"Then I must be one," he murmured.

"I'll just go home," she said. "I will not bother you. If you can't do a little thing like that for me . . ."

Rolling his eyes upward, he put his tie back on. "Restored to my class," he muttered. He thrust his face toward her and hissed, "True culture is in the mind, the *mind*," he said, and tapped his head, "the mind."

"It's in the heart," she said, "and in how you do things and how you do things is because of who you *are*."

"Nobody in the damn bus cares who you are."

"I care who I am," she said icily.

The lighted bus appeared on top of the next hill and as it approached, they moved out into the street to meet it. He put his hand under her elbow and hoisted her up on the creaking step. She entered with a little smile, as if she were going into a drawing room where everyone had been waiting for her. While he put in the tokens, she sat down in one of the broad front seats for three which faced the aisle. A thin woman with protruding teeth and long yellow hair was sitting on the end of it. His mother moved up beside her and left room for Julian besides herself. He sat down and looked at the floor across the aisle where a pair of thin feet in red and white canvas sandals were planted.

His mother immediately began a general conversation meant to attract anyone who felt like talking. "Can it get any hotter?" she said and removed from her purse a folding fan, black with a Japanese scene on it, which she began to flutter before her.

"I reckon it might could," the woman with the protruding teeth said, "but I know for a fact my apartment couldn't get no hotter."

"It must get the afternoon sun," his mother said. She sat forward and looked up and down the bus. It was half filled. Everybody was white. "I see we have the bus to ourselves," she said. Julian cringed.

"For a change," said the woman across the aisle, the owner of the red and white canvas sandals. "I come on one the other day and they were thick as fleas—up front and all through."

"The world is in a mess everywhere," his mother said. "I don't know how we've let it get in this fix."

"What gets my goat is all those boys from good families stealing automobile tires," the woman with the protruding teeth said. "I told my boy, I said you may not be rich but you been raised right and if I ever catch you in any such mess, they can send you on to the reformatory. Be exactly where you belong."

"Training tells," his mother said. "Is your boy in high school?"

"Ninth grade," the woman said.

"My son just finished college last year. He wants to write but he's selling typewriters until he gets started," his mother said.

The woman leaned forward and peered at Julian. He threw her such a malevolent look that she subsided against the seat. On the floor across the aisle there was an abandoned newspaper. He got up and got it and opened it out in front of him. His mother discreetly continued the conversation in a lower tone but the woman across the aisle said in a loud voice, "Well that's nice. Selling typewriters is close to writing. He can go right from one to the other."

"I tell him," his mother said, "that Rome wasn't built in a day."

Behind the newspaper Julian was withdrawing into the inner compartment of his mind where he spent most of his time. This was a kind of mental bubble in which he established himself when he could not bear to be a part of what was going on around him. From it he could see out and judge but in it he was safe from any kind of penetration from without. It was the only place where he felt free of the general idiocy of his fellows. His mother had never entered it but from it he could see her with absolute clarity.

The old lady was clever enough and he thought that if she had started from any of the right premises, more might have been expected of her. She lived according to the laws of her own fantasy world, outside of which he had never seen her set foot. The law of it was to sacrifice herself for him after she had first created the necessity to do so by making a mess of things. If he had permitted her sacrifices, it was only because her lack of foresight had made them necessary. All of her life had been a struggle to act like a Chestny without the Chestny goods, and to give him everything she thought a Chestny ought to have; but since, said she, it was fun to struggle, why complain? And when you had won, as she had won, what fun to look back on the hard times! He could not forgive her that she had enjoyed the struggle and that she thought *she* had won.

What she meant when she said she had won was that she had brought him up successfully and had sent him to college and that he had turned out so well—good looking (her teeth had gone unfilled so that his could be straightened), intelligent (he realized he was too intelligent to be a success), and with a future ahead of him (there was of course no future ahead of him). She excused his gloominess on the grounds that he was still growing up and his radical ideas on his lack of practical experience. She said he didn't yet know a thing about "life," that he hadn't even entered the real world—when already he was as disenchanted with it as a man of fifty.

The further irony of all this was that in spite of her, he had turned out so well. In spite of going to only a third-rate college, he had, on his own initiative, come out with a first-rate education; in spite of growing up dominated by a small mind, he had ended up with a large one; in spite of all her foolish views, he was free of prejudice and unafraid to face facts. Most miraculous of all, instead of being blinded by love for her as she was for him, he had cut himself emotionally free of her and could see her with complete objectivity. He was not dominated by his mother.

The bus stopped with a sudden jerk and shook him from his meditation. A woman from the back lurched forward with little steps and barely escaped falling in his newspaper as she righted herself. She got off and a large Negro got on. Julian kept his paper lowered to watch. It gave him a certain satisfaction to see injustice in daily operation. It confirmed his view that with a few exceptions there was no one worth knowing within a radius of three hundred miles. The Negro was well dressed and carried a briefcase. He looked around and then sat down on the other end of the seat where the woman with the red and white canvas sandals was sitting. He immediately unfolded a newspaper and obscured himself behind it. Julian's mother's elbow at once prodded insistently into his ribs. "Now you see why I won't ride on these buses by myself," she whispered.

The woman with the red and white canvas sandals had risen at the same time the Negro sat down and had gone further back in the bus and taken the seat of the woman who had got off. His mother leaned forward and cast her an approving look.

Julian rose, crossed the aisle, and sat down in the place of the woman with the canvas sandals. From this position, he looked serenely across at his mother. Her face had turned an angry red. He stared at her, making his eyes the eyes of a stranger. He felt his tension suddenly lift as if he had openly declared war on her.

He would have liked to get in conversation with the Negro and to talk with him about art or politics or any subject that would be above the comprehension of those around them, but the man remained entrenched behind his paper. He was either ignoring the change of seating or had never noticed it. There was no way for Julian to convey his sympathy.

His mother kept her eyes fixed reproachfully on his face. The woman with the protruding teeth was looking at him avidly as if he were a type of monster new to her.

"Do you have a light?" he asked the Negro.

Without looking away from his paper, the man reached in his pocket and handed him a packet of matches.

"Thanks," Julian said. For a moment he held the matches foolishly. A NO SMOKING sign looked down upon him from over the door. This alone would not have deterred him; he had no cigarettes. He had quit smoking some months before because he could not afford it. "Sorry," he muttered and handed back the matches. The Negro lowered the paper and gave him an annoyed look. He took the matches and raised the paper again.

His mother continued to gaze at him but she did not take advantage of his momentary discomfort. Her eyes retained their battered look. Her face seemed to be unnaturally red, as if her blood pressure had risen. Julian allowed no glimmer of sympathy to show on his face. Having got the advantage, he wanted desperately to keep it and carry it through. He would have liked to teach her a lesson that would last her a while, but there seemed no way to continue the point. The Negro refused to come out from behind his paper.

Julian folded his arms and looked stolidly before him, facing her but as if he did not see her, as if he had ceased to recognize her existence. He visualized a scene in which the bus having reached their stop, he would remain in his seat and when she said, "Aren't you going to get off?" he would look at her as at a stranger who had rashly addressed him. The corner they got off on was usually deserted, but it was well lighted and it would not hurt her to walk by herself the four blocks to the Y. He decided to wait until the time came and then decide whether or not he would let her get off by herself. He would have to be at the Y at ten to bring her back, but he could leave her wondering if he was going to show up. There was no reason for her to think she could always depend on him.

He retired again into the high-ceilinged room sparsely settled with large pieces of antique furniture. His soul expanded momentarily but then he became aware of his mother across from him and the vision shriveled. He studied her coldly. Her feet in little pumps dangled like a child's and did not quite reach the floor. She was training on him an exaggerated look of reproach. He felt completely detached from her. At that moment he could with pleasure have slapped her as he would have slapped a particularly obnoxious child in his charge.

He began to imagine various unlikely ways by which he could teach her a lesson. He might make friends with some distinguished Negro professor or lawyer and bring him home to spend the evening. He would be entirely justified but her blood pressure would rise to 300. He could not push her to the extent of making her have a stroke, and moreover, he had never been successful at making any Negro friends. He had tried to strike up an acquaintance on the bus with some of the better types, with ones that looked like professors or ministers or lawyers. One morning he had sat down next to a distinguished-looking dark brown man who had answered his questions with a sonorous solemnity but who had turned out to be an undertaker. Another day he had sat down beside a cigar-smoking Negro with a diamond ring on his finger, but after a few stilted pleasantries, the Negro had rung the buzzer and risen, slipping two lottery tickets into Julian's hand as he climbed over him to leave.

He imagined his mother lying desperately ill and his being able to secure only a Negro doctor for her. He toyed with that idea for a few minutes and then dropped it for a momentary vision of himself participating as a sympathizer in a sit-in demonstration. This was possible but he did not linger with it. Instead, he approached the ultimate horror. He brought home a beautiful suspiciously Negroid woman. Prepare yourself, he said. There is nothing you can do about it. This is the woman I've chosen. She's intelligent, dignified, even good, and she's suffered and she hasn't thought it *fun*. Now persecute us, go ahead and persecute us. Drive her out of here, but remember, you're driving me too. His eyes were narrowed and through the indignation he had generated, he saw his mother across the aisle, purple-faced, shrunken to the dwarf-like proportions of her moral nature, sitting like a mummy beneath the ridiculous banner of her hat.

He was tilted out of his fantasy again as the bus stopped. The door opened with a sucking hiss and out of the dark a large, gaily dressed, sullen-looking colored woman got on with a little boy. The child, who might have been four, had on a short plaid suit and a Tyrolean hat with a blue feather in it. Julian hoped that he would sit down beside him and that the woman would push in beside his mother. He could think of no better arrangement.

As she waited for her tokens, the woman was surveying the seating possibilities—he hoped with the idea of sitting where she was least wanted. There was something familiar-looking about her but Julian could not place what it was. She was a giant of a woman. Her face was set not only to meet opposition but to seek it out. The downward tilt of her large lower lip was like a warning sign: DON'T TAMPER WITH ME. Her bulging figure was encased in a green crepe dress and her feet overflowed in red shoes. She had on a hideous hat. A purple velvet flap came down on one side of it and stood up on the other; the rest of it was green and looked like a cushion with the stuffing out. She carried a mammoth red pocketbook that bulged throughout as if it were stuffed with rocks.

To Julian's disappointment, the little boy climbed up on the empty seat beside his mother. His mother lumped all children, black and white, into the common category, "cute," and she thought little Negroes were on the whole cuter than little white children. She smiled at the little boy as he climbed on the seat.

Meanwhile the woman was bearing down upon the empty seat beside Julian. To his annoyance, she squeezed herself into it. He saw his mother's face change as the woman settled herself next to him and he realized with satisfaction that this was more objectionable to her than it was to him. Her face seemed almost gray and there was a look of dull recognition in her eyes, as if suddenly she had sickened at some awful confrontation. Julian saw that it was because she and the woman had, in a sense, swapped sons. Though his mother would not realize the symbolic significance of this, she would feel it. His amusement showed plainly on his face.

The woman next to him muttered something unintelligible to herself. He was conscious of a kind of bristling next to him, muted growling like that of an angry cat. He could not see anything but the red pocketbook upright on the bulging green thighs. He visualized the woman as she had stood waiting for her tokens—the ponderous figure, rising from the red shoes upward over the solid hips, the mammoth bosom, the haughty face, to the green and purple hat.

His eyes widened.

The vision of the two hats, identical, broke upon him with the radiance of a brilliant sunrise. His face was suddenly lit with joy. He could not believe that Fate had thrust upon his mother such a lesson. He gave a loud chuckle so that she would look at him and see that he saw. She turned her eyes on him slowly. The blue in them seemed to have turned a bruised purple. For a moment he had an uncomfortable sense of her innocence, but it lasted only a second before principle rescued him. Justice entitled him to laugh. His grin hardened until it said to her as plainly as if he were saying aloud: Your punishment exactly fits your pettiness. This should teach you a permanent lesson.

Her eyes shifted to the woman. She seemed unable to bear looking at him and to find the woman preferable. He became conscious again of the bristling presence at his side. The woman was rumbling like a volcano about to become active. His mother's mouth began to twitch slightly at one corner. With a sinking heart, he saw incipient signs of recovery on her face and realized that this was going to strike her suddenly as funny and was going to be no lesson at all. She kept her eyes on the woman and an amused smile came over her face as if the woman were a monkey that had stolen her hat. The little Negro was looking up at her with large fascinated eyes. He had been trying to attract her attention for some time.

"Carver!" the woman said suddenly. "Come heah!"

When he saw that the spotlight was on him at last, Carver drew his feet up and turned himself toward Julian's mother and giggled.

"Carver!" the woman said. "You heah me? Come heah!"

Carver slid down from the seat but remained squatting with his back against the base of it, his head turned slyly around toward Julian's mother, who was smiling at him. The woman reached a hand across the aisle and snatched him to her. He righted himself and hung backwards on her knees, grinning at Julian's mother. "Isn't he cute?" Julian's mother said to the woman with the protruding teeth.

"I reckon he is," the woman said without conviction.

The Negress yanked him upright but he eased out of her grip and shot across the aisle and scrambled, giggling wildly, onto the seat beside his love.

"I think he likes me," Julian's mother said, and smiled at the woman. It was the smile she used when she was being particularly gracious to an inferior. Julian saw everything lost. The lesson had rolled off her like rain on a roof.

The woman stood up and yanked the little boy off the seat as if she were snatching him from contagion. Julian could feel the rage in her at having no weapon like his mother's smile. She gave the child a sharp slap across his leg. He howled once and then thrust his head into her stomach and kicked his feet against her shins. "Behave," she said vehemently.

The bus stopped and the Negro who had been reading the newspaper got off. The woman moved over and set the little boy down with a thump between herself and Julian. She held him firmly by the knee. In a moment he put his hands in front of his face and peeped at Julian's mother through his fingers.

"I see yoooooooo!" she said and put her hand in front of her face and peeped at him.

The woman slapped his hand down. "Quit yo' foolishness," she said, "before I knock the living Jesus out of you!"

Julian was thankful that the next stop was theirs. He reached up and pulled the cord. The woman reached up and pulled it at the same time. Oh my God, he thought. He had the terrible intuition that when they got off the bus together, his mother would open her purse and give the little boy a nickel. The gesture would be as natural to her as breathing. The bus stopped and the woman got up and lunged to the front, dragging the child, who wished to stay on, after her. Julian and his mother got up and followed. As they neared the door, Julian tried to relieve her of her pocketbook.

"No," she murmured, "I want to give the little boy a nickel."

"No!" Julian hissed. "No!"

She smiled down at the child and opened her bag. The bus door opened and the woman picked him up by the arm and descended with him, hanging at her hip. Once in the street she set him down and shook him.

Julian's mother had to close her purse while she got down the bus step but as soon as her feet were on the ground, she opened it again and began to rummage inside. "I can't find but a penny," she whispered, "but it looks like a new one."

"Don't do it!" Julian said fiercely between his teeth. There was a streetlight on the corner and she hurried to get under it so that she could better see into her pocketbook. The woman was heading off rapidly down the street with the child still hanging backward on her hand.

"Oh little boy!" Julian's mother called and took a few quick steps and caught up with them just beyond the lamppost. "Here's a bright new penny for you," and she held out the coin, which shone bronze in the dim light.

The huge woman turned and for a moment stood, her shoulders lifted and her face frozen with frustrated rage, and stared at Julian's mother. Then all at once she seemed to explode like a piece of machinery that had been given one ounce of pressure too much. Julian saw the black fist swing out with the red pocketbook. He shut his eyes and cringed as he heard the woman shout, "He don't take nobody's pennies!" When he opened his eyes, the woman was disappearing down the street with the little boy staring wide-eyed over her shoulder. Julian's mother was sitting on the sidewalk.

"I told you not to do that," Julian said angrily. "I told you not to do that!"

He stood over her for a minute, gritting his teeth. Her legs were stretched out in front of her and her hat was on her lap. He squatted down and looked her in the face. It was totally expressionless. "You got exactly what you deserved," he said. "Now get up."

He picked up her pocketbook and put what had fallen out back in it. He picked the hat up off her lap. The penny caught his eye on the sidewalk and he picked that up and let it drop before her eyes into the purse. Then he stood up and leaned over and held his hands out to pull her up. She remained immobile. He sighed. Rising about them on either side were black apartment buildings, marked with irregular rectangles of light. At the end of the block a man came out of a door and walked off in the opposite direction. "All right," he said, "suppose somebody happens by and wants to know why you're sitting on the sidewalk?"

She took the hand and, breathing hard, pulled heavily up on it and then stood for a moment, swaying slightly as if the spots of light in the darkness were circling around her. Her eyes, shadowed and confused, finally settled on his face. He did not try to conceal his irritation. "I hope this teaches you a lesson," he said. She leaned forward and her eyes raked his face. She seemed trying to determine his identity. Then, as if she found nothing familiar about him, she started off with a headlong movement in the wrong direction.

"Aren't you going on to the Y?" he asked.

"Home," she muttered.

"Well, are we walking?"

For answer she kept going. Julian followed along, his hands behind him. He saw no reason to let the lesson she had had go without backing it up with an explanation of its meaning. She might as well be made to understand what had happened to her. "Don't think that was just an uppity Negro woman," he said. "That was the whole colored race which will no longer take your condescending pennies. That was your black double. She can wear the same hat as you, and to be sure," he added gratuitously (because he thought it was funny), "it looked better on her than it did on you. What all this means," he said, "is that the old world is gone. The old manners are obsolete and your graciousness is not worth a damn." He thought bitterly of the house that had been lost for him. "You aren't who you think you are," he said.

She continued to plow ahead, paying no attention to him. Her hair had come undone on one side. She dropped her pocketbook and took no notice. He stooped and picked it up and handed it to her but she did not take it.

"You needn't act as if the world had come to an end," he said, "because it hasn't. From now on you've got to live in a new world and face a few realities for a change. Buck-up," he said, "it won't kill you."

She was breathing fast.

"Let's wait on the bus," he said.

"Home," she said thickly.

"I hate to see you behave like this," he said. "Just like a child. I should be able to expect more of you." He decided to stop where he was and make her stop and wait for a bus. "I'm not going any farther," he said, stopping. "We're going on the bus."

She continued to go on as if she had not heard him. He took a few steps and caught her arm and stopped her. He looked into her face and caught his breath. He was looking into a face he had never seen before. "Tell Grandpa to come get me," she said.

He stared, stricken.

"Tell Caroline to come get me," she said.

Stunned, he let her go and she lurched forward again, walking as if one leg were shorter than the other. A tide of darkness seemed to be sweeping her from him. "Mother!" he cried. "Darling, sweetheart, wait!" Crumpling, she fell to the pavement. He dashed forward and fell at her side, crying, "Mamma, Mamma!" He turned her over. Her face was fiercely distorted. One eye, large and staring, moved slightly on the left as if it had become unmoored. The other remained fixed on him, raked his face again, found nothing and closed.

"Wait here, wait here!" he cried and jumped up and began to run for help toward a cluster of lights he saw in the distance ahead of him. "Help, help!" he shouted, but his voice was thin, scarcely a thread of sound. The lights drifted farther away the faster he ran and his feet moved numbly as if they carried him nowhere. The tide of darkness seemed to sweep him back to her, postponing from moment to moment his entry into the world of guilt and sorrow.

## MARGARET LAURENCE
1926-1986

Margaret Wemyss Laurence was born in Neepawa, Manitoba, where her family had lived for several generations. In 1930 her mother died suddenly and a sister came to look after the family, marrying Robert Wemyss a year later (he died of pneumonia within two years). Margaret Laurence was brought up by her step-mother. Against the veto of her grandfather, who supported the family financially, she entered the University of Manitoba in 1944. She graduated in Honours English in 1947 and worked as a reporter on the *Winnipeg Citizen*. In 1948 she married Jack Laurence, a civil engineer whom she met at the university, and they moved to England in 1949, to Somaliland (now Somalia) in 1950, and then to the Gold Coast (now Ghana) where they lived until their return to Vancouver in 1957. The Laurences had two children. After separating from her husband in the late 50's, Laurence took her children to London, England, where they remained for the next ten years. She lived for many years in Lakefield, Ontario. Her best novel, *The Stone Angel* (1964), begins her saga of the fictional town of Manawaka, which is the setting of four other books.

## Horses of the Night

I never knew I had distant cousins who lived up north, until Chris came down to Manawaka to go to high school. My mother said he belonged to a large family, relatives of ours, who lived at Shallow Creek, up north. I was six, and Shallow Creek seemed immeasurably far, part of a legendary winter country where no leaves grow and where the breath of seals and polar bears snuffled out steamily and turned to ice.

"Could plain people live there?" I asked my mother, meaning people who were not Eskimos. "Could there be a farm?"

"How do you mean?" she said, puzzled. "I told you. That's where they live. On the farm. Uncle Wilf—that was Chris's father, who died a few years back—he got the place as a homestead, donkey's years ago."

"But how could they grow anything? I thought you said it was up north."

"Mercy," my mother said, laughing, "it's not *that* far north, Vanessa. It's about a hundred miles beyond Galloping Mountain. You be nice to Chris, now, won't you? And don't go asking him a whole lot of questions the minute he steps inside the door."

How little my mother knew of me, I thought. Chris had been fifteen. He could be expected to feel only scorn towards me. I detested the fact that I was so young. I did not think I would be able to say anything at all to him.

"What if I don't like him?"

"What if you don't?" my mother responded sharply. "You're to watch your manners, and no acting up, understand? It's going to be quite difficult enough without that."

"Why does he have to come here, anyway?" I demanded crossly. "Why can't he go to school where he lives?"

"Because there isn't any high school up there," my mother said. "I hope he gets on well here, and isn't too homesick. Three years is a long time. It's very good of your grandfather to let him stay at the Brick House."

She said this last accusingly, as though she suspected I might be thinking differently. But I had not thought of it one way or another. We were all having dinner at the Brick House because of Chris's arrival. It was the end of August, and sweltering. My grandfather's house looked huge and cool from outside, the high low-sweeping spruce trees shutting out the sun with their dusky out-fanned branches. But inside it wasn't cool at all. The woodstove in the kitchen was going full blast, and the whole place smelled of roasting meat.

Grandmother Connor was wearing a large mauve apron. I thought it was a nicer colour than the dark bottle-green of her dress, but she believed in wearing sombre shades lest the spirit give way to vanity, which in her case was certainly not much of a risk. The apron came up over her shapeless bosom and obscured part of her cameo brooch, the only jewellery she ever wore, with its portrait of a fiercely bearded man whom I imagined to be either Moses or God.

"Isn't it nearly time for them to be getting here, Beth?" Grandmother Connor asked.

"Train's not due until six," my mother said. "It's barely five-thirty, now. Has Father gone to the station already?"

"He went an hour ago," my grandmother said.

"He would," my mother commented.

"Now, now, Beth," my grandmother cautioned and soothed.

At last the front screen door was hurled open and Grandfather Connor strode into the house, followed by a tall lanky boy. Chris was wearing a white shirt, a tie, grey trousers. I thought, unwillingly, that he looked handsome. His face was angular, the bones showing through the brown skin. His grey eyes were slightly slanted, and his hair was the colour of couchgrass at the end of summer when it has been bleached to a light yellow by the sun. I had not planned to like him, not even a little, but somehow I wanted to defend him when I heard what my mother whispered to my grandmother before they went into the front hall.

"Heavens, look at the shirt and trousers—must've been his father's, the poor kid."

I shot out into the hall ahead of my mother, and then stopped and stood there.

"Hi, Vanessa," Chris said.

"How come you knew who I was?" I asked.

"Well, I knew your mother and dad only had one of a family, so I figured you must be her," he replied, grinning.

The way he spoke did not make me feel I had blundered. My mother greeted him warmly but shyly. Not knowing if she were expected to kiss him or to shake hands, she finally did neither. Grandmother Connor, however, had no doubts. She kissed him on both cheeks and then held him at arm's length to have a proper look at him.

"Bless the child," she said.

Coming from anyone else, this remark would have sounded ridiculous, especially as Chris was at least a head taller. My grandmother was the only person I have ever known who could say such things without appearing false.

"I'll show you your room, Chris," my mother offered.

Grandfather Connor, who had been standing in the living room doorway in absolute silence, looking as granite as a statue in the cemetery, now followed Grandmother out to the kitchen.

"Train was forty minutes late," he said weightily.

"What a shame," my grandmother said. "But I thought it wasn't due until six, Timothy."

"Six!" my grandfather cried. "That's the mainline train. The local's due at five-twenty."

This was not correct, as both my grandmother and I knew. But neither of us contradicted him.

"What on earth are you cooking a roast for, on a night like this?" my grandfather went on. "A person could fry an egg on the sidewalk, it's that hot. Potato salad would've gone down well."

Privately I agreed with this opinion, but I could never permit myself to acknowledge agreement with him on anything. I automatically and emotionally sided with Grandmother in all issues, not because she was inevitably right but because I loved her.

"It's not a roast," my grandmother said mildly. "It's mock-duck. The stove's only been going for an hour. I thought the boy would be hungry after the trip."

My mother and Chris had come downstairs and were now in the living room. I could hear them there, talking awkwardly, with pauses.

"Potato salad," my grandfather declaimed, "would've been plenty good enough. He'd have been lucky to get it, if you ask me anything. Wilf's family hasn't got two cents to rub together. It's me that's paying for the boy's keep."

The thought of Chris in the living room, and my mother unable to explain, was too much for me. I sidled over to the kitchen door, intending to close it. But my grandmother stopped me.

"No," she said, with unexpected firmness. "Leave it open, Vanessa."

I could hardly believe it. Surely she couldn't want Chris to hear? She herself was always able to move with equanimity through a hurricane because she believed that a mighty fortress was her God. But the rest of us were not like that, and usually she did her best to protect us. At that time I felt only bewilderment. I think now that she must have realised Chris would have to learn the Brick House sooner or later, and he might as well start right away.

I had to go into the living room. I had to know how Chris would take my grandfather. Would he, as I hoped, be angry and perhaps even speak out? Or would he, meekly, only be embarrassed?

"Wilf wasn't much good, even as a young man," Grandfather Connor was trumpeting. "Nobody but a simpleton would've taken up a homestead in a place like that. Anybody could've told him that land's no use for a thing except hay."

Was he going to remind us again how well he had done in the hardware business? Nobody had ever given him a hand, he used to tell me. I am sure he believed that this was true. Perhaps it even was true.

"If the boy takes after his father, it's a poor lookout for him," my grandfather continued.

I felt the old rage of helplessness. But as for Chris—he gave no sign of feeling anything. He was sitting on the big wing-backed sofa that curled into the bay window like a black and giant seashell. He began to talk to me, quite easily, just as though he had not heard a word my grandfather was saying.

This method proved to be the one Chris always used in any dealings with my grandfather. When the bludgeoning words came, which was often, Chris never seemed, like myself, to be holding back with a terrible strained force for fear of letting go and speaking out and having the known world unimaginably fall to pieces. He would not argue or defend himself, but he did not apologise, either. He simply appeared to be absent, elsewhere. Fortunately there was very little need for response, for when Grandfather Connor pointed out your shortcomings, you were not expected to reply.

But this aspect of Chris was one which I noticed only vaguely at the time. What won me was that he would talk to me and wisecrack as though I were his same age. He was—although I didn't know the phrase then—a respecter of persons.

On the rare evenings when my parents went out, Chris would come over to mind me. These were the best times, for often when he was supposed to be doing his homework, he would make fantastic objects for my amusement, or his own—pipecleaners twisted into the shape of wildly prancing midget men, or an old set of Christmas-tree lights fixed onto a puppet theatre with a red velvet curtain that really pulled. He had skill in making miniature things of all kinds. Once for my birthday he gave me a leather saddle no bigger than a matchbox, which he had sewn himself, complete in every detail, stirrups and horn, with the criss-cross lines that were the brand name of his ranch, he said, explaining it was a reference to his own name.

"Can I go to Shallow Creek sometime?" I asked one evening.

"Sure. Some summer holidays, maybe. I've got a sister about your age. The others are all grownup."

I did not want to hear. His sisters—for Chris was the only boy—did not exist for me, not even as photographs, because I did not want them to exist. I wanted him to belong only here. Shallow Creek existed, though, no longer filled with ice mountains in my mind but as some beckoning country beyond all ordinary considerations.

"Tell me what it's like there, Chris."

"My gosh, Vanessa, I've told you before, about a thousand times."

"You never told me what your house is like."

"Didn't I? Oh well—it's made out of trees grown right there beside the lake."

"Made out of trees? Gee. Really?"

I could see it. The trees were still growing, and the leaves were firmly and greenly on them. The branches had been coaxed into formations of towers and high-up nests where you could look out and see for a hundred miles or more.

"That lake, you know," Chris said. "It's more like an inland sea. It goes on for ever and ever amen, that's how it looks. And you know what? Millions of years ago, before there were any human beings at all, that lake was full of water monsters. All different kinds of dinosaurs. Then they all died off. Nobody knows for sure why. Imagine them—all those huge creatures, with necks like snakes, and some of them had hackles on their heads, like a rooster's comb only very tough, like hard leather. Some guys from Winnipeg came up a few years back, there, and dug up dinosaur bones, and they found footprints in the rocks."

"Footprints in the *rocks*?"

"The rocks were mud, see, when the dinosaurs went trampling through, but after trillions of years the mud turned into stone and there were these mighty footprints with the claws still showing. Amazing, eh?"

I could only nod, fascinated and horrified. Imagine going swimming in those waters. What if one of the creatures had lived on?

"Tell me about the horses," I said.

"Oh, them. Well, we've got these two riding horses. Duchess and Firefly. I raised them, and you should see them. Really sleek, know what I mean? I bet I could make racers out of them."

He missed the horses, I thought with selfish satisfaction, more than he missed his family. I could visualise the pair, one sorrel and one black, swifting through all the meadows of summer.

"When can I go, Chris?"

"Well, we'll have to see. After I get through high school, I won't be at Shallow Creek much."

"Why not?"

"Because," Chris said, "what I am going to be is an engineer, civil engineer. You ever seen a really big bridge, Vanessa? Well, I haven't either, but I've seen pictures. You take the Golden Gate Bridge in San Francisco, now. Terrifically high—all those thin ribs of steel, joined together to go across this very wide stretch of water. It doesn't seem possible, but it's there. That's what engineers do. Imagine doing something like that, eh?"

I could not imagine it. It was beyond me.

"Where will you go?" I asked. I did not want to think of his going anywhere.

"Winnipeg, to college," he said with assurance.

The Depression did not get better, as everyone had been saying it would. It got worse, and so did the drought. That part of the prairies where we lived was never dustbowl county. The farms around Manawaka never had a total crop failure, and afterwards, when the drought was over, people used to remark on this fact proudly, as though it had been due to some virtue or special status, like the Children of Israel being afflicted by Jehovah but never in real danger of annihilation. But although Manawaka never knew the worst, what it knew was bad enough. Or so I learned later. At the time I saw none of it. For me, the Depression and drought were external and abstract, malevolent gods whose names I secretly learned although they were concealed from me, and whose evil I sensed only superstitiously, knowing they threatened us but not how or why. What I really saw was only what went on in our family.

"He's done quite well all through, despite everything," my mother said. She sighed, and I knew she was talking about Chris.

"I know," my father said. "We've been over all this before, Beth. But quite good just isn't good enough. Even supposing he managed to get a scholarship, which isn't likely, it's only tuition and books. What about room and board? Who's going to pay for that? Your father?"

"I see I shouldn't have brought up the subject at all," my mother said in an aloof voice.

"I'm sorry," my father said impatiently. "But you know, yourself, he's the only one who might possibly—"

"I can't bring myself to ask Father about it, Ewen. I simply cannot do it."

"There wouldn't be much point in asking," my father said, "when the answer is a foregone conclusion. He feels he's done his share, and actually you know, Beth, he has, too. Three years, after all. He may not have done it gracefully, but he's done it."

We were sitting in the living room, and it was evening. My father was slouched in the grey armchair that was always his. My mother was slenderly straight-backed in the blue chair in which nobody else ever sat. I was sitting on the footstool, beige needlepoint with mathematical roses, to which I had staked my own claim. This seating arrangement was obscurely satisfactory to me, perhaps because predictable, like the three bears. I was pretending to be colouring into a scribbler on my knee, and from time to time my lethargic purple crayon added a feather to an outlandish swan. To speak would be to invite dismissal. But their words forced questions in my head.

"Chris isn't going away, is he?"

My mother swooped, shocked at her own neglect.

"My heavens—are you still up, Vanessa? What am I thinking of?"

"Where is Chris going?"

"We're not sure yet," my mother evaded, chivvying me up the stairs. "We'll see."

He would not go, I thought. Something would happen, miraculously, to prevent him. He would remain, with his long loping walk and his half-slanted grey eyes and his talk that never excluded me. He would stay right here. And soon, because I desperately wanted to, and because every day mercifully made me older, quite soon I would be able to reply with such a lightning burst of knowingness that it would astound him, when he spoke of the space or was it some black sky that never ended anywhere beyond this earth. Then I would not be innerly belittled for being unable to figure out what he would best like to hear. At that good and imagined time, I would not any longer be limited. I would not any longer be young.

I was nine when Chris left Manawaka. The day before he was due to go, I knocked on the door of his room in the Brick House.

"Come in," Chris said. "I'm packing. Do you know how to fold socks, Vanessa?"

"Sure. Of course."

"Well, get folding on that bunch there, then."

I had come to say goodbye, but I did not want to say it yet. I got to work on the socks. I did not intend to speak about the matter of college, but the knowledge that I must not speak about it made me uneasy. I was afraid I would blurt out a reference to it in my anxiety not to. My mother had said, "He's taken it amazingly well—he doesn't even mention it, so we mustn't either."

"Tomorrow night you'll be in Shallow Creek," I ventured.

"Yeh." He did not look up. He went on stuffing clothes and books into his suitcase.

"I bet you'll be glad to see the horses, eh?" I wanted him to say he didn't care about the horses any more and that he would rather stay here.

"It'll be good to see them again," Chris said. "Mind handing over those socks now, Vanessa? I think I can just squash them in at the side here. Thanks. Hey, look at that, will you? Everything's in. Am I an expert packer or am I an expert packer?"

I sat on his suitcase for him so it would close, and then he tied a piece of rope around it because the lock wouldn't lock.

"Ever thought what it would be like to be a traveller, Vanessa?" he said.

I thought of Richard Halliburton, taking an elephant over the Alps and swimming illicitly in the Taj Mahal lily pool by moonlight.

"It would be keen," I said, because this was the word Chris used to describe the best possible. "That's what I'm going to do someday."

He did not say, as for a moment I feared he might, that girls could not be travellers.

"Why not?" he said. "Sure you will, if you really want to. I got this theory, see, that anybody can do anything at all, anything, if they really set their minds to it. But you have to have this total concentration. You have to focus on it with your whole mental powers, and not let it slip away by forgetting to hold it in your mind. If you hold it in your mind, like, then it's real, see? You take most people, now. They can't concentrate worth a darn."

"Do you think I can?" I enquired eagerly, believing that this was what he was talking about.

"What?" he said. "Oh—sure. Sure I think you can. Naturally."

Chris did not write after he left Manawaka. About a month later we had a letter from his mother. He was not at Shallow Creek. He had not gone back. He had got off the northbound train at the first stop after Manawaka, cashed in his ticket, and thumbed a lift with a truck to Winnipeg. He had written to his mother from there, but had given no address. She had not heard from him since. My mother read Aunt Tess's letter aloud to my father. She was too upset to care whether I was listening or not.

"I can't think what possessed him, Ewen. He never seemed irresponsible. What if something should happen to him? What if he's broke? What do you think we should do?"

"What can we do? He's nearly eighteen. What he does is his business. Simmer down, Beth, and let's decide what we're going to tell your father."

"Oh, Lord," my mother said. "There's that to consider, of course."

I went out without either of them noticing. I walked to the hill at the edge of the town, and down into the valley where the scrub oak and poplar grew almost to the banks of the Wachakwa River. I found the oak where we had gone last autumn, in a gang, to smoke cigarettes made of dried leaves and pieces of newspaper. I climbed to the lowest branch and stayed there for a while.

I was not consciously thinking about Chris. I was not thinking of anything. But when at last I cried, I felt relieved afterwards and could go home again.

Chris departed from my mind, after that, with a quickness that was due to the other things that happened. My Aunt Edna, who was a secretary in Winnipeg, returned to Manawaka to live because the insurance company cut down on staff and she could not find another job. I was intensely excited and jubilant about her return, and could not see why my mother seemed the opposite, even though she was as fond of Aunt Edna as I was. Then my brother Roderick was born, and that same year Grandmother Connor died. The strangeness, the unbelievability, of both these events took up all of me.

When I was almost eleven, almost two years after Chris had left, he came back without warning. I came home from school and found him sitting in our living room. I could not accept that I had nearly forgotten him until this instant. Now that he was present, and real again, I felt I had betrayed him by not thinking of him more.

He was wearing a navy-blue serge suit. I was old enough now to notice that it was a cheap one and had been worn a considerable time. Otherwise, he looked the same, the same smile, the same knife-boned face with no flesh to speak of, the same unresting eyes.

"How come you're here?" I cried. "Where have you been, Chris?"

"I'm a traveller," he said. "Remember?"

He was a traveller all right. One meaning of the word *traveller* in our part of the world, was a travelling salesman. Chris was selling vacuum cleaners. That evening he brought out his line and showed us. He went through his spiel for our benefit, so we could hear how it sounded.

"Now look, Beth," he said, turning the appliance on and speaking loudly above its moaning roar, "see how it brightens up this old rug of yours? Keen, eh?"

"Wonderful," my mother laughed. "Only we can't afford one."

"Oh well—" Chris said quickly, "I'm not trying to sell one to you. I'm only showing you. Listen, I've only been in this job for a month, but I figure this is really a going thing. I mean, it's obvious, isn't it? You can take all those old wire carpet-beaters of yours, Beth. You could kill yourself over them and your carpet isn't going to look one-tenth as good as it does with this."

"Look, I don't want to seem—" my father put in, "but, hell, they're not exactly a new invention, and we're not the only ones who can't afford—"

"This is a pretty big outfit, you know?" Chris insisted. "Listen, I don't plan to stay, Ewen. But a guy could work at it for a year or so, and save—right? Lots of guys work their way through university like that."

I needed to say something really penetrating, something that would show him I knew the passionate truth of his conviction.

"I bet—" I said, "I bet you could sell a thousand, Chris."

Two years ago, this statement would have seemed self-evident, unquestionable. Yet now, when I had spoken, I knew that I did not believe it.

The next time Chris visited Manawaka, he was selling magazines. He had the statistics worked out. If every sixth person in town would get a subscription to *Country Guide*, he could make a hundred dollars in a month. We didn't learn how he got on. He didn't stay in Manawaka a full month. When he turned up again, it was winter. Aunt Edna phoned.

''Nessa? Listen, kiddo, tell your mother she's to come down if it's humanly possible. Chris is here, and Father's having fits.''

So in five minutes we were scurrying through the snow, my mother and I, with our overshoes not even properly done up and our feet getting wet. We need not have worried. By the time we reached the Brick House, Grandfather Connor had retired to the basement, where he sat in the rocking chair beside the furnace, making occasional black pronouncements like a subterranean oracle. These loud utterances made my mother and aunt wince, but Chris didn't seem to notice any more than he ever had. He was engrossed in telling us about the mechanism he was holding. It had a cranker handle like an old-fashioned sewing machine.

"You attach the ball of wool here, see? Then you set this little switch here, and adjust this lever, and you're away to the races. Neat, eh?"

It was a knitting machine. Chris showed us the finished products. The men's socks he had made were coarse wool, one pair in grey heather and another in maroon. I was impressed.

"Gee—can I do it, Chris?"

"Sure. Look, you just grab hold of the handle right here."

"Where did you get it?" my mother asked.

"I've rented it. The way I figure it, Beth, I can sell these things at about half the price you'd pay in a store, and they're better quality."

"Who are you going to sell them to?" Aunt Edna enquired.

"You take all these guys who do outside work—they need heavy socks all year round, not just in the winter. I think this thing could be quite a gold mine."

"Before I forget," my mother said, "how's your mother and the family keeping?"

"They're okay," Chris said in a restrained voice. "They're not short of hands, if that's what you mean, Beth. My sisters have their husbands there."

Then he grinned, casting away the previous moment, and dug into his suitcase.

"Hey, I haven't shown you—these are for you, Vanessa, and this pair is for Roddie."

My socks were cherry-coloured. The very small ones for my brother were turquoise.

Chris only stayed until after dinner, and then he went away again.

After my father died, the whole order of life was torn. Nothing was known or predictable any longer. For months I lived amost entirely within myself, so when my mother told me one day that Chris couldn't find any work at all because there were no jobs and so he had gone back to Shallow Creek to stay, it made scarcely any impression on me. But that summer, my mother decided I ought to go away for a holiday. She hoped it might take my mind off my father's death. What, if anything, was going to take her mind off his death, she did not say.

"Would you like to go to Shallow Creek for a week or so?" she asked me. "I could write to Chris's mother."

Then I remembered, all in a torrent, the way I had imagined it once, when he used to tell me about it—the house fashioned of living trees, the lake like a sea where monsters had dwelt, the grass that shone like green wavering light while the horses flew in the splendour of their pride.

"Yes," I said. "Write to her."

The railway did not go through Shallow Creek, but Chris met me at Challoner's Crossing. He looked different, not only thinner, but— what was it? Then I saw that it was the fact that his face and neck were tanned red-brown, and he was wearing denims, farm pants, and a blue plaid shirt open at the neck. I liked him like this. Perhaps the change was not so much in him as in myself, now that I was thirteen. He looked masculine in a way I had not been aware of, before.

"C'mon, kid," he said. "The limousine's over here."

It was a wagon and two horses, which was what I had expected, but the nature of each was not what I had expected. The wagon was a long and clumsy one, made of heavy planking, and the horses were both plough horses, thick in the legs, and badly matched as a team. The mare was short and stout, matronly. The gelding was very tall and gaunt, and he limped.

"Allow me to introduce you," Chris said. "Floss—Trooper—this is Vanessa."

He did not mention the other horses, Duchess and Firefly, and neither did I, not all the fortnight I was there. I guess I had known for some years now, without realising it, that the pair had only ever existed in some other dimension.

Shallow Creek wasn't a town. It was merely a name on a map. There was a grade school a few miles away, but that was all. They had to go to Challoner's Crossing for their groceries. We reached the farm, and Chris steered me through the crowd of aimless cows and wolfish dogs in the yard, while I flinched with panic.

It was perfectly true that the house was made out of trees. It was a fair-sized but elderly shack, made out of poplar poles and chinked with mud. There was an upstairs, which was not so usual around here, with three bedrooms, one of which I was to share with Chris's sister, Jeannie, who was slightly younger than I, a pallid-eyed girl who was either too shy to talk or who had nothing to say. I never discovered which, because I was so reticent with myself, wanting to push her away, not to recognise her, and at the same time experiencing a shocked remorse at my own unacceptable feelings.

Aunt Tess, Chris's mother, was severe in manner and yet wanting to be kind, worrying over it, making tentative overtures which were either ignored or repelled by her older daughters and their monosyl- labic husbands. Youngsters swam in and out of the house like shoals of nameless fishes. I could not see how so many people could live here, under the one roof, but then I learned they didn't. The married daughters had their own dwelling places, nearby, but some kind of communal life was maintained. They wrangled endlessly but they never left one another alone, not even for a day.

Chris took no part at all, none. When he spoke, it was usually to the children, and they would often follow him around the yard or to the barn, not pestering but just trailing along in clusters of three or four. He never told them to go away. I liked him for this, but it bothered me, too. I wished he would return his sisters' bickering for once, or tell them to clear out, or even yell at one of the kids. But he never did. He closed himself off from squabbling voices just as he used to do with Grandfather Connor's spearing words.

The house had no screens on the doors or windows, and at meal times the flies were so numerous you could hardly see the food for the iridescent-winged blue-black bodies squirming all over it. Nobody noticed my squeamishness except Chris, and he was the only one from whom I really wanted to conceal it.

"Fan with your hand," he murmured.

"It's okay," I said quickly.

For the first time in all years we had known each other, we could not look the other in the eye. Around the table, the children stabbed and snivelled, until Chris's oldest sister, driven frantic, shrieked, *Shut up shut up shut up.* Chris began asking me about Manawaka then, as though nothing were going on around him.

They were due to begin haying, and Chris announced that he was going to camp out in the bluff near the hayfields. To save himself the long drive in the wagon each morning, he explained, but I felt this wasn't the real reason.

"Can I go, too?" I begged. I could not bear the thought of living in the house with all the others who were not known to me, and Chris not here.

"Well, I don't know—"

"Please. Please, Chris. I won't be any trouble. I promise."

Finally, he agreed. We drove out in the big hayrack, its slatted sides rattling, its old wheels jolting metallically. The road was narrow and dirt, and around it the low bushes grew, wild rose and blueberry and wolf willow with silver leaves. Sometimes we would come to a bluff of pale-leaved popular trees, and once a red-winged blackbird flew up out of the branches and into the hot dusty blue of the sky.

Then we were there. The hayfields lay beside the lake. It was my first view of the water which had spawned saurian giants so long ago. Chris drove the hayrack through the fields of high coarse grass and on down almost to the lake's edge, where there was no shore but only the green rushes like floating meadows in which the water birds nested. Beyond the undulating reeds the open lake stretched, deep, green-grey, out and out, beyond sight.

No human word could be applied. The lake was not lonely or untamed. These words relate to people, and there was nothing of people here. There was no feeling about the place. It existed in some world in which man was not yet born. I looked at the grey reaches of it and felt threatened. It was like the view of God which I had held since my father's death. Distant, indestructible, totally indifferent.

Chris had jumped down off the hayrack.

"We're not going to camp *here*, are we?" I asked and pleaded.

"No. I just want to let the horses drink. We'll camp up there in the bluff."

I looked. "It's still pretty close to the lake, isn't it?"

"Don't worry," Chris said, laughing. "You won't get your feet wet."

"I didn't mean that."

Chris looked at me.

"I know you didn't," he said. "But let's learn to be a little tougher, and not let on, eh? It's necessary."

Chris worked through the hours of the sun, while I lay on the half-formed stack of hay and looked up at the sky. The blue air trembled and spun with the heat haze, and the hay on which I was lying held the scents of grass and dust and wild mint.

In the evening, Chris took the horses to the lake again, and then he drove the hayrack to the edge of the bluff and we spread out our blankets underneath it. He made a fire and we had coffee and a tin of stew, and then we went to bed. We did not wash, and we slept in our clothes. It was only when I was curled up uncomfortably with the itching blanket around me that I felt a sense of unfamiliarity at being here, with Chris only three feet away, a self-consciousness I would not have felt even the year before. I do not think he felt this sexual strangeness. If he wanted me not to be a child—and he did— it was not with the wish that I would be a woman. It was something else.

"Are you asleep, Vanessa?" he asked.

"No. I think I'm lying on a tree root."

"Well, shift yourself, then," he said. "Listen, kid, I never said anything before, because I didn't really know what to say, but—you know how I felt about your dad dying, and that, don't you?"

"Yes," I said chokingly. "It's okay. I know."

"I used to talk with Ewen sometimes. He didn't see what I was driving at, mostly, but he'd always listen, you know? You don't find many guys like that."

We were both silent for a while.

"Look," Chris said finally. "Ever noticed how much brighter the stars are when you're completely away from the houses? Even the lamps up at the farm, there, make enough of a glow to keep you from seeing properly like you can out here. What do they make you think about, Vanessa?"

"Well—"

"I guess most people don't give them much thought at all, except maybe to say—*very pretty*—or like that. But the point is, they aren't like that. The stars and planets, in themselves, are just not like that, not *pretty*, for heaven's sake. They're gigantic—some of them burning—imagine those worlds tearing through space and made of pure fire. Or the ones that are absolutely dead—just rock or ice and no warmth in them. There must be some, though, that have living creatures. You wonder what *they* could look like, and what they feel. We won't ever get to know. But somebody will know, someday. I really believe that. Do you ever think about this kind of thing at all?"

He was twenty-one. The distance between us was still too great. For years I had wanted to be older so I might talk with him, but now I felt unready.

"Sometimes," I said, hesitantly, making it sound like *Never*.

"People usually say there must be a God," Chris went on, "because otherwise how did the universe get here? But that's ridiculous. If the stars and planets go on to infinity, they could have existed forever, for no reason at all. Maybe they weren't ever created. Look—what's the alternative? To believe in a God who is brutal. What else could he be? You've only got to look anywhere around you. It would be an insult to Him to believe in a God like that. Most people don't like talking about this kind of thing—it embarrasses them, you know? Or else they're not interested. I don't mind. I can always think about things myself. You don't actually need anyone to talk to. But about God, though—if there's a war, like it looks there will be, would people claim that was planned? What kind of a God would pull a trick like that? And yet, you know, plenty of guys would think it was a godsend, and who's to say they're wrong? It would be a job, and you'd get around and see places."

He paused, as though waiting for me to say something. When I did not, he resumed.

"Ewen told me about the last war, once. He hardly ever talked about it, but this once he told me about seeing the horses in the mud, actually going under, you know? And the way their eyes looked when they realised they weren't going to get out. Ever seen horses' eyes when they're afraid, I mean really berserk with fear, like in a bush-fire? Ewen said a guy tended to concentrate on the horses because he didn't dare think what was happening to the men. Including himself. Do you ever listen to the news at all, Vanessa?"

"I—"

I could only feel how foolish I must sound, still unable to reply as I would have wanted, comprehendingly. I felt I had failed myself utterly. I could not speak even the things I knew. As for the other things, the things I did not know, I resented Chris's facing me with them. I took refuge in pretending to be asleep, and after a while Chris stopped talking.

Chris left Shallow Creek some months after the war began, and joined the Army. After his basic training he was sent to England. We did not hear from him until about a year later, when a letter arrived for me.

"Vanessa—what's wrong?" my mother asked.

"Nothing."

"Don't fib," she said firmly. "What did Chris say in his letter, honey?"

"Oh—not much."

She gave me a curious look and then she went away. She would never have demanded to see the letter. I did not show it to her and she did not ask about it again.

Six months later my mother heard from Aunt Tess. Chris had been sent home from England and discharged from the Army because of a mental breakdown. He was now in the provincial mental hospital and they did not know how long he would have to remain there. He had been violent, before, but now he was not violent. He was, the doctors had told his mother, passive.

*Violent.* I could not associate the word with Chris, who had been so much the reverse. I could not bear to consider what anguish must have catapulted him into that even greater anguish. But the way he was now seemed almost worse. How might he be? Sitting quite still, wearing the hospital's grey dressing-gown, the animation gone from his face?

My mother cared about him a great deal, but her immediate thought was not for him.

"When I think of you, going up to Shallow Creek that time," she said, "and going out camping with him, and what might have happened—"

I, also, was thinking of what might have happened. But we were not thinking of the same thing. For the first time I recognised, at least a little, the dimensions of his need to talk that night. He must have understood perfectly well how impossible it would be, with a thirteen-year-old. But there was no one else. All his life's choices had grown narrower and narrower. He had been forced to return to the alien lake of home, and when finally he saw a means of getting away, it could only be into a turmoil which appalled him and which he dreaded even more than he knew. I had listened to his words, but I had not really heard them, not until now. It would not have made much difference to what happened, but I wished it were not too late to let him know.

Once when I was on holiday from college, my mother got me to help her clean out the attic. We sifted through boxes full of junk, old clothes, schoolbooks, bric-a-brac that once had been treasures. In one of the boxes I found the miniature saddle that Chris had made for me a long time ago.

"Have you heard anything recently?" I asked, ashamed that I had not asked sooner.

She glanced up at me. "Just the same. It's always the same. They don't think there will be much improvement."

Then she turned away.

"He always used to seem so—hopeful. Even when there was really nothing to be hopeful about. That's what I find so strange. He *seemed* hopeful, didn't you think?"

"Maybe it wasn't hope," I said.

"How do you mean?"

I wasn't certain myself. I was thinking of all the schemes he'd had, the ones that couldn't possibly have worked, the unreal solutions to which he'd clung because there were no others, the brave and useless strokes of fantasy against a depression that was both the world's and his own.

"I don't know," I said. "I just think things were always more difficult for him than he let on, that's all. Remember that letter?"

"Yes."

"Well—what it said was that they could force his body to march and even to kill, but what they didn't know was that he'd fooled them. He didn't live inside it any more."

"Oh Vanessa—" my mother said, "You must have suspected right then."

"Yes, but—"

I could not go on, could not say that the letter seemed only the final heartbreaking extension of that way he'd always had of distancing himself from the absolute unbearability of battle.

I picked up the tiny saddle and turned it over in my hand.

"Look. His brand, the name of his ranch. The Criss-Cross."

"What ranch?" my mother said, bewildered.

"The one where he kept his racing horses. Duchess and Firefly."

Some words came into my head, a single line from a poem I had once heard. I knew it referred to a lover who did not want the morning to come, but to me it had another meaning, a different relevance.

*Slowly, slowly, horses of the night—*

The night must move like this for him, slowly, all through the days and nights. I could not know whether the land he journeyed through was inhabited by terrors, the old monster-kings of the lake, or whether he had discovered at last a way for himself to make the necessary dream perpetual.

I put the saddle away once more, gently and ruthlessly, back into the cardboard box.

# GABRIEL GARCÍA MÁRQUEZ
## 1928–

The oldest of a telegraph operator's twelve children, he was born in the small town of Aracataca, Columbia, and raised there by his mother's parents. After his grandfather's death in 1936 he was educated by the Jesuits in Barranquilla and Zipaquirá, entering the National University in Bogotá to study law in 1941. At this time he began to publish fiction in newspapers and gradually shifted his career from law to journalism. Since then he has been active in left wing causes while living in Spain and Latin America. His novel *One Hundred Years of Solitude* (1969) was instantly recognized in Europe and the Western Hemisphere as one of the major works of this century.

## Tuesday Siesta

The train emerged from the quivering tunnel of sandy rocks, began to cross the symmetrical, interminable banana plantations, and the air became humid and they couldn't feel the sea breeze any more. A stifling blast of smoke came in the car window. On the narrow road parallel to the railway there were oxcarts loaded with green bunches of bananas. Beyond the road, in uncultivated spaces set at odd intervals there were offices with electric fans, red-brick buildings, and residences with chairs and little white tables on the terraces among dusty palm trees and rosebushes. It was eleven in the morning, and the heat had not yet begun.

"You'd better close the window," the woman said. "Your hair will get full of soot."

The girl tried to, but the shade wouldn't move because of the rust.

They were the only passengers in the lone third-class car. Since the smoke of the locomotive kept coming through the window, the girl left her seat and put down the only things they had with them: a plastic sack with some things to eat and a bouquet of flowers wrapped in newspaper. She sat on the opposite seat, away from the window, facing her mother. They were both in severe and poor mourning clothes.

The girl was twelve years old, and it was the first time she'd ever been on a train. The woman seemed too old to be her mother, because of the blue veins on her eyelids and her small, soft, and shapeless body, in a dress cut like a cassock. She was riding with her spinal column braced firmly against the back of the seat, and held a peeling patent-leather handbag in her lap with both hands. She bore the conscientious serenity of someone accustomed to poverty.

By twelve the heat had begun. The train stopped for ten minutes to take on water at a station where there was no town. Outside, in the mysterious silence of the plantations, the shadows seemed clean. But the still air inside the car smelled like untanned leather. The train did not pick up speed. It stopped at two identical towns with wooden houses painted bright colors. The woman's head nodded and she sank into sleep. The girl took off her shoes. Then she went to the washroom to put the bouquet of flowers in some water.

When she came back to her seat, her mother was waiting to eat. She gave her a piece of cheese, half a corn-meal pancake, and a cookie, and took an equal portion out of the plastic sack for herself. While they ate, the train crossed an iron bridge very slowly and passed a town just like the ones before, except that in this one there was a crowd in the plaza. A band was playing a lively tune under the oppressive sun. At the other side of town the plantations ended in a plain which was cracked from the drought.

The woman stopped eating.

"Put on your shoes," she said.

The girl looked outside. She saw nothing but the deserted plain, where the train began to pick up speed again, but she put the last piece of cookie into the sack and quickly put on her shoes. The woman gave her a comb.

"Comb your hair," she said.

The train whistle began to blow while the girl was combing her hair. The woman dried the sweat from her neck and wiped the oil from her face with her fingers. When the girl stopped combing, the train was passing the outlying houses of a town larger but sadder than the earlier ones.

"If you feel like doing anything, do it now," said the woman. "Later, don't take a drink anywhere even if you're dying of thirst. Above all, no crying."

The girl nodded her head. A dry, burning wind came in the window, together with the locomotive's whistle and the clatter of the old cars. The woman folded the plastic bag with the rest of the food and put it in the handbag. For a moment a complete picture of the town, on that bright August Tuesday, shone in the window. The girl wrapped the flowers in the soaking-wet newspapers, moved a little farther away from the window, and stared at her mother. She received a pleasant expression in return. The train began to whistle and slowed down. A moment later it stopped.

There was no one at the station. On the other side of the street, on the sidewalk shaded by the almond trees, only the pool hall was open. The town was floating in the heat. The woman and the girl got off the train and crossed the abandoned station—the tiles split apart by the grass growing up between—and over to the shady side of the street.

It was almost two. At that hour, weighted down by drowsiness, the town was taking a siesta. The stores, the town offices, and the public school were closed at eleven, and didn't reopen until a little before four, when the train went back. Only the hotel across from the station, with its bar and pool hall, and the telegraph office at one side of the plaza stayed open. The houses most of them built on the banana company's model, had their doors locked from inside and their blinds drawn. In some of them it was so hot that the residents ate lunch in the patio. Others leaned a chair against the wall, in the shade of the almond trees, and took their siesta right out in the street.

Keeping to the protective shade of the almond trees, the woman and the girl entered the town without disturbing the siesta. They went directly to the parish house. The woman scratched the metal grating on the door with her fingernail, waited a moment, and scratched again. An electric fan was humming inside. They did not hear the steps. They hardly heard the slight creaking of a door, and immediately a cautious voice, right next to the metal grating: "Who is it?" The woman tried to see through the grating.

"I need the priest," she said.

"He's sleeping now."

"It's an emergency," the woman insisted.

Her voice showed a calm determination.

The door was opened a little way, noiselessly, and a plump, older woman appeared, with very pale skin and hair the color of iron. Her eyes seemed too small behind her thick eyeglasses.

"Come in," she said, and opened the door all the way.

They entered a room permeated with an old smell of flowers. The woman of the house led them to a wooden bench and signaled them to sit down. The girl did so, but her mother remained standing, absent-mindedly, with both hands clutching the handbag. No noise could be heard above the electric fan.

The woman of the house reappeared at the door at the far end of the room. "He says you should come back after three," she said in a very low voice. "He just lay down five minutes ago."

"The train leaves at three-thirty," said the woman.

It was a brief and self-assured reply, but her voice remained pleasant, full of undertones. The woman of the house smiled for the first time.

"All right," she said.

When the far door closed again, the woman sat down next to her daughter. The narrow waiting room was poor, neat, and clean. On the other side of the wooden railing which divided the room, there was a worktable, a plain one with an oilcloth cover, and on top of the table a primitive typewriter next to a vase of flowers. The parish records were beyond. You could see that it was an office kept in order by a spinster.

The far door opened and this time the priest appeared, cleaning his glasses with a handkerchief. Only when he put them on was it evident that he was the brother of the woman who had opened the door.

"How can I help you?" he asked.

"The keys to the cemctery," said the woman.

The girl was seated with the flowers in her lap and her feet crossed under the bench. The priest looked at her, then looked at the woman, and then through the wire mesh of the window at the bright, cloudless sky.

"In this heat," he said. "You could have waited until the sun went down."

The woman moved her head silently. The priest crossed to the other side of the railing, took out of the cabinet a notebook covered with oilcloth, a wooden penholder, and an inkwell, and sat down at the table. There was more than enough hair on his hands to account for what was missing on his head.

"Which grave are you going to visit?" he asked.

"Carlos Centeno's," said the woman.

"Who?"

"Carlos Centeno," the woman repeated.

The priest still did not understand.

"He's the thief who was killed here last week," said the woman in the same tone of voice. "I am his mother."

The priest scrutinized her. She stared at him with quiet selfcontrol, and the Father blushed. He lowered his head and began to write. As he filled the page, he asked the woman to identify herself, and she replied unhesitatingly, with precise details, as if she were reading them. The Father began to sweat. The girl unhooked the buckle of her left shoe, slipped her heel out of it, and rested it on the bench rail. She did the same with the right one.

It had all started the Monday of the previous week, at three in the morning, a few blocks from there. Rebecca, a lonely widow who lived in a house full of odds and ends, heard above the sound of the drizzling rain someone trying to force the front door from outside. She got up, rummaged around in her closet for an ancient revolver that no one had fired since the days of Colonel Aureliano Buendía, and went into the living room without turning on the lights. Orienting herself not so much by the noise at the lock as by a terror developed in her by twenty-eight years of loneliness, she fixed in her imagination not only the spot where the door was but also the exact height of the lock. She clutched the weapon with both hands, closed her eyes, and squeezed the trigger. It was the first time in her life that she had fired a gun. Immediately after the explosion, she could hear nothing except the murmur of the drizzle on the galvanized roof. Then she heard a little metallic bump on the cement porch, and a very low voice, pleasant but terribly exhausted: "Ah, Mother." The man they found dead in front of the house in the morning, his nose blown to bits, wore a flannel shirt with colored stripes, everyday pants with a rope for a belt, and was barefoot. No one in town knew him.

"So his name was Carlos Centeno," murmured the Father when he finished writing.

"Centeno Ayala," said the woman. "He was my only boy."

The priest went back to the cabinet. Two big rusty keys hung on the inside of the door; the girl imagined, as her mother had when she was a girl and as the priest himself must have imagined at some time, that they were Saint Peter's keys. He took them down, put them on the open notebook on the railing, and pointed with his forefinger to a place on the page he had just written, looking at the woman.

"Sign here."

The woman scribbled her name, holding the handbag under her arm. The girl picked up the flowers, came to the railing shuffling her feet, and watched her mother attentively.

The priest sighed.

"Didn't you ever try to get him on the right track?"

The woman answered when she finished signing.

"He was a very good man."

The priest looked first at the woman and then at the girl, and realized with a kind of pious amazement that they were not about to cry. The woman continued in the same tone:

"I told him never to steal anything that anyone needed to eat, and he minded me. On the other hand, before, when he used to box, he used to spend three days in bed, exhausted from being punched."

"All his teeth had to be pulled out," interrupted the girl.

"That's right," the woman agreed. "Every mouthful I ate those days tasted of the beatings my son got on Saturday nights."

"God's will is inscrutable," said the Father.

But he said it without much conviction, partly because experience had made him a little skeptical and partly because of the heat. He suggested that they cover their heads to guard against sunstroke. Yawning, and now almost completely asleep, he gave them instructions about how to find Carlos Centeno's grave. When they came back, they didn't have to knock. They should put the key under the door; and in the same place, if they could, they should put an offering for the Church. The woman listened to his directions with great attention, but thanked him without smiling.

The Father had noticed that there was someone looking inside, his nose pressed against the metal grating, even before he opened the door to the street. Outside was a group of children. When the door was opened wide, the children scattered. Ordinarily, at that hour there was no one in the street. Now there were not only children. There were groups of people under the almond trees. The Father scanned the street swimming in the heat and then he understood. Softly, he closed the door again.

"Wait a moment," he said without looking at the woman.

His sister appeared at the far door with a black jacket over her nightshirt and her hair down over her shoulders. She looked silently at the Father.

"What was it?" he asked.

"The people have noticed," murmured his sister.

"You'd better go out by the door to the patio," said the Father.

"It's the same there," said his sister. "Everybody is at the windows."

The woman seemed not to have understood until then. She tried to look into the street through the metal grating. Then she took the bouquet of flowers from the girl and began to move toward the door. The girl followed her.

"Wait until the sun goes down," said the Father.

"You'll melt," said his sister, motionless at the back of the room. "Wait and I'll lend you a parasol."

"Thank you," replied the woman. "We're all right this way."

She took the girl by the hand and went into the street.

# JOHN BARTH

1930–

John Barth and his twin sister Jill were born in Cambridge, on the eastern shore of Maryland. As a boy he was a serious musician, organizing his own band and starting study at the Juilliard School of Music. His interest shifted to literature and he transferred to Johns Hopkins, where he received his M.A. in 1952. He supported himself, his wife, and children by his music until he got his first teaching job in 1953. He has taught ever since, publishing his first novel in 1956 and establishing himself as a major writer with *The Sot-Weed Factor* in 1960 and his collection of short fiction *Lost in the Funhouse* in 1968.

## Lost in the Funhouse

For whom is the funhouse fun? Perhaps for lovers. For Ambrose it is *a place of fear and confusion.* He has come to the seashore with his family for the holiday, *the occasion of their visit is Independence Day, the most important secular holiday of the United States of America.* A single straight underline is the manuscript mark for italic type, *which in turn* is the printed equivalent to oral emphasis of words and phrases as well as the customary type for titles of complete works, not to mention. Italics are also employed, in fiction stories especially, for "outside," intrusive, or artificial voices, such as radio announcements, the texts of telegrams and newspaper articles, et cetera. They should be used *sparingly.* If passages originally in roman type are italicized by someone repeating them, it's customary to acknowledge the fact. *Italics mine.*

Ambrose was "at that awkward age." His voice came out high-pitched as a child's if he let himself get carried away; to be on the safe side, therefore, he moved and spoke with *deliberate calm* and *adult gravity.* Talking soberly of unimportant or irrelevant matters and listening consciously to the sound of your own voice are useful habits for maintaining control in this difficult interval. *Enroute* to Ocean City he sat in the back seat of the family car with his brother Peter, age fifteen, and Magda G——, age fourteen, a pretty girl and exquisite young lady, who lived not far from them on B—— Street in the town of D——, Maryland. Initials, blanks, or both were often substituted for proper names in nineteenth-century fiction to enhance the illusion of reality. It is as if the author felt it necessary to delete the names for reasons of tact or legal liability. Interestingly, as with other aspects of realism, it is an *illusion* that is being enhanced, by purely artificial means. Is it likely, does it violate the principle of verisimilitude, that a thirteen-year-old boy could make such a sophisticated observation? A girl of fourteen is *the psychological coeval* of a boy of fifteen or sixteen; a thirteen-year-old boy, therefore, even one precocious in some other respects, might be three years *her emotional junior*.

Thrice a year—on Memorial, Independence, and Labor Days—the family visits Ocean City for the afternoon and evening. When Ambrose and Peter's father was their age, the excursion was made by train, as mentioned in the novel *The 42nd Parallel* by John Dos Passos. Many families from the same neighborhood used to travel together, with dependent relatives and often with Negro servants; schoolfuls of children swarmed through the railway cars; everyone shared everyone else's Maryland fried chicken, Virginia ham, deviled eggs, potato salad, beaten biscuits, iced tea. Nowadays (that is, in 19—, the year of our story) the journey is made by automobile—more comfortably and quickly though without the extra fun though without the *camaraderie* of a general excursion. It's all part of the deterioration of American life, their father declares; Uncle Karl supposes that when the boys take *their* families to Ocean City for the holidays they'll fly in Autogiros. Their mother, sitting in the middle of the front seat like Magda in the second, only with her arms on the seat-back behind the men's shoulders, wouldn't want the good old days back again, the steaming trains and stuffy long dresses; on the other hand she can do without Autogiros, too, if she has to become a grandmother to fly in them.

Description of physical appearance and mannerisms is one of several standard methods of characterization used by writers of fiction. It is also important to "keep the senses operating"; when a detail from one of the five senses, say visual, is "crossed" with a detail from another, say auditory, the reader's imagination is oriented to the scene, perhaps unconsciously. This procedure may be compared to the way surveyors and navigators determine their positions by two or more compass bearings, a process known as triangulation. The brown hair on Ambrose's mother's forearms gleamed in the sun like. Though right-handed, she took her left arm from the seat-back to press the dashboard cigar lighter for Uncle Karl. When the glass bead in its handle glowed red, the lighter was ready for use. The smell of Uncle Karl's cigar smoke reminded one of. The fragrance of the ocean came strong to the picnic ground where they always stopped for lunch, two miles inland from Ocean City. Having to pause for a full hour almost within sound of the breakers was difficult for Peter and Ambrose when they were younger; even at their present age it was not easy to keep their anticipation, *stimulated by the briny spume*, from turning into short temper. The Irish author James Joyce, in his unusual novel entitled *Ulysses*, now available in this country, uses the adjectives *snot-green* and *scrotum-tightening* to describe the sea. Visual; auditory; tactile; olfactory; gustatory. Peter and Ambrose's father, while steering their black 1936 LaSalle sedan with one hand, could with the other remove the first cigarette from a white pack of Lucky Strikes and, more remarkably, light it with a match forefingered from its book and thumbed against the flint paper without being detached. The matchbook cover merely advertised U. S. War Bonds and Stamps. A fine metaphor, simile, or other figure of speech, in addition to its obvious "first-order" relevance to the thing it describes, will be seen upon reflection to have a second order of significance: it may be drawn from the *milieu* of the action, for example, or be particularly appropriate to the sensibility of the narrator, even hinting to the reader things of which the narrator is unaware; or it may cast further and subtler lights upon the things it describes, sometimes ironically qualifying the more evident sense of the comparison.

To say that Ambrose's and Peter's mother was *pretty* is to accomplish nothing; the reader may acknowledge the proposition, but his imagination is not engaged. Besides, Magda was also pretty, yet in an altogether different way. Although she lived on B—— Street she had very good manners and did better than average in school. Her figure was very well developed for her age. Her right hand lay casually on the plush upholstery of the seat, very near Ambrose's left leg, on which his own hand rested. The space between their legs, between her right and his left leg, was out of the line of sight of anyone sitting on the other side of Magda, as well as anyone glancing into the rear-view mirror. Uncle Karl's face resembled Peter's—rather, vice versa. Both had dark hair and eyes, short husky statures, deep voices. Magda's left hand was probably in a similar position on her left side. The boys' father is difficult to describe; no particular feature of his appearance or manner stood out. He wore glasses and was principal of a T—— County grade school. Uncle Karl was a masonry contractor.

Although Peter must have known as well as Ambrose that the latter, because of his position in the car, would be the first to see the electrical towers of the power plant at V——, the halfway point of their trip, he leaned forward and slightly toward the center of the car and pretended to be looking for them through the flat pinewoods and tuckahoe creeks along the highway. For as long as the boys could remember, "looking for the Towers" had been a feature of the first half of their excursions to Ocean City, "looking for the standpipe" of the second. Though the game was childish, their mother preserved the tradition of rewarding the first to see the Towers with a candy-bar or piece of fruit. She insisted now that Magda play the game; the prize, she said, was "something hard to get nowadays." Ambrose decided not to join in; he sat far back in his seat. Magda, like Peter, leaned forward. Two sets of straps were discernible through the shoulders of her sun dress; the inside right one, a brassiere-strap, was fastened or shortened with a small safety pin. The right armpit of her dress, presumably the left as well, was damp with perspiration. The simple strategy for being first to espy the Towers, which Ambrose had understood by the age of four, was to sit on the right-hand side of the car. Whoever sat there, however, had also to put up with the worst of the sun, and so Ambrose, without mentioning the matter, chose sometimes the one and sometimes the other. Not impossibly Peter had never caught on to the trick, or thought that his brother hadn't simply because Ambrose on occasion preferred shade to a Baby Ruth or tangerine.

The shade-sun situation didn't apply to the front seat, owing to the windshield; if anything the driver got more sun, since the person on the passenger side not only was shaded below by the door and dashboard but might swing down his sunvisor all the way too.

"Is that them?" Magda asked. Ambrose's mother teased the boys for letting Magda win, insinuating that "somebody [had] a girlfriend." Peter and Ambrose's father reached a long thin arm across their mother to butt his cigarette in the dashboard ashtray, under the lighter. The prize this time for seeing the Towers first was a banana. Their mother bestowed it after chiding their father for wasting a half-smoked cigarette when everything was so scarce. Magda, to take the prize, moved her hand from so near Ambrose's that he could have touched it as though accidentally. She offered to share the prize, things like that were so hard to find; but everyone insisted it was hers alone. Ambrose's mother sang an iambic trimeter couplet from a popular song, femininely rhymed:

> "What's good is in the Army;
> What's left will never harm me."

Uncle Karl tapped his cigar ash out the ventilator window; some particles were sucked by the slipstream back into the car through the rear window on the passenger side. Magda demonstrated her ability to hold a banana in one hand and peel it with her teeth. She still sat forward; Ambrose pushed his glasses back onto the bridge of his nose with his left hand, which he then negligently let fall to the seat cushion immediately behind her. He even permitted the single hair, gold, on the second joint of his thumb to brush the fabric of her skirt. Should she have sat back at that instant, his hand would have been caught under her.

Plush upholstery prickles uncomfortably through gabardine slacks in the July sun. The function of the *beginning* of a story is to introduce the principal characters, establish their initial relationships, set the scene for the main action, expose the background of the situation if necessary, plant motifs and foreshadowings where appropriate, and initiate the first complication or whatever of the "rising action." Actually, if one imagines a story called "The Funhouse," or "Lost in the Funhouse," the details of the drive to Ocean City don't seem especially relevant. The *beginning* should recount the events between Ambrose's first sight of the funhouse early in the afternoon and his entering it with Magda and Peter in the evening. The *middle* would narrate all relevant events from the time he goes in to the time he loses his way; middles have the double and contradictory function of delaying the climax while at the same time preparing the reader for it and fetching him to it. Then the *ending* would tell what Ambrose does while he's lost, how he finally finds his way out, and what everybody makes of the experience. So far there's been no real dialogue, very little sensory detail, and nothing in the way of a *theme*. And a long time has gone by already without anything happening; it makes a person wonder. We haven't even reached Ocean City yet: we will never get out of the funhouse.

The more closely an author identifies with the narrator, literally or metaphorically, the less advisable it is, as a rule, to use the first-person narrative viewpoint. Once three years previously the young people *aforementioned* played Niggers and Masters in the backyard; when it was Ambrose's turn to be Master and theirs to be Niggers Peter had to go serve his evening papers; Ambrose was afraid to punish Magda alone, but she led him to the whitewashed Torture Chamber between the woodshed and the privy in the Slaves Quarters; there she knelt sweating among bamboo rakes and dusty Mason jars, pleadingly embraced his knees, and while bees droned in the lattice as if on an ordinary summer afternoon, purchased clemency at a surprising price set by herself. Doubtless she remembered nothing of this event; Ambrose on the other hand seemed unable to forget the least detail of his life. He even recalled how, standing beside himself with awed impersonality in the reeky heat, he'd stared the while at an empty cigar box in which Uncle Karl kept stone-cutting chisels: beneath the words *El Producto* a laureled, loose-toga'd lady regarded the sea from a marble bench; beside her, forgotten or not yet turned to, was a five-stringed lyre. Her chin reposed on the back of her right hand; her left depended negligently from the bench-arm. The lower half of the scene and lady was peeled away; the words EXAMINED BY _____ were inked there into the wood. Nowadays cigar boxes are made of pasteboard. Ambrose wondered what Magda would have done, Ambrose wondered what Magda would do when she sat back on his hand as he resolved she should. Be angry. Make a teasing joke of it. Give no sign at all. For a long time she leaned forward, playing cow-poker with Peter against Uncle Karl and Mother and watching for the first sign of Ocean City. At nearly the same instant, picnic ground and Ocean City standpipe hove into view; an Amoco filling station on their side of the road cost Mother and Uncle Karl fifty cows and the game; Magda bounced back, clapping her right hand on Mother's right arm; Ambrose moved clear "in the nick of time."

At this rate our hero, at this rate our protagonist will remain in the funhouse forever. Narrative ordinarily consists of alternating dramatization and summarization. One symptom of nervous tension, paradoxically, is repeated and violent yawning; neither Peter nor Magda nor Uncle Karl nor Mother reacted in this manner. Although they were no longer small children, Peter and Ambrose were each given a dollar to spend on boardwalk amusements in addition to what money of their own they'd brought along. Magda too, though she protested she had ample spending money. The boys' mother made a little scene out of distributing the bills; she pretended that her sons and Magda were small children and cautioned them not to spend the sum too quickly or in one place. Magda promised with a merry laugh and, having both hands free, took the bill with her left. Peter laughed also and pledged in a falsetto to be a good boy. His imitation of a child was not clever. The boys' father was tall and thin, balding, fair-complexioned. Assertions of that sort are not effective; the reader may acknowledge the proposition, but. We should be much farther along than we are; something has gone wrong; not much of this preliminary rambling seems relevant. Yet everyone begins in the same place; how is it that most go along without difficulty but a few lose their way?

"Stay out from under the boardwalk," Uncle Karl growled from the side of his mouth. The boys' mother pushed his shoulder *in mock annoyance*. They were all standing before Fat May the Laughing Lady who advertised the funhouse. Larger than life, Fat May mechanically shook, rocked on her heels, slapped her thighs, while recorded laughter—uproarious, female—came amplified from a hidden loudspeaker. It chuckled, wheezed, wept; tried in vain to catch its breath; tittered, groaned, exploded raucous and anew. You couldn't hear it without laughing yourself, no matter how you felt. Father came back from talking to a Coast-Guardsman on duty and reported that the surf was spoiled with crude oil from tankers recently torpedoed offshore. Lumps of it, difficult to remove, made tarry tidelines on the beach and stuck on swimmers. Many bathed in the surf nevertheless and came out speckled; others paid to use a municipal pool and only sunbathed on the beach. We would do the latter. We would do the latter. We would do the latter.

Under the boardwalk, matchbook covers, grainy other things. What is the story's theme? Ambrose is ill. He perspires in the dark passages; candied apples-on-a-stick, delicious-looking, disappointing to eat. Funhouses need men's and ladies' rooms at intervals. Others perhaps have also vomited in corners and corridors; may even have had bowel movements liable to be stepped in in the dark. The word *fuck* suggests suction and/or and/or flatulence. Mother and Father; grandmothers and grandfathers on both sides; great-grandmothers and great-grandfathers on four sides, et cetera. Count a generation as thirty years: in approximately the year when Lord Baltimore was granted charter to the province of Maryland by Charles I, five hundred twelve women—English, Welsh, Bavarian, Swiss—of every class and character, received into themselves the penises the intromittent organs of five hundred twelve men, ditto, in every circumstance and posture, to conceive the five hundred twelve ancestors of the two hundred fifty-six ancestors of the et cetera et cetera et cetera et cetera et cetera et cetera et cetera et cetera of the author, of the narrator, of this story, *Lost in the Funhouse*. In alleyways, ditches, canopy beds, pinewoods, bridal suites, ship's cabins, coach-and-fours, coaches-and-four, sultry toolsheds; on the cold sand under boardwalks, littered with *El Producto* cigar butts, treasured with Lucky Strike cigarette stubs, Coca-Cola caps, gritty turds, cardboard lollipop sticks, matchbook covers warning that A Slip of the Lip Can Sink a Ship. The shluppish whisper, continuous as seawash round the globe, tidelike falls and rises with the circuit of dawn and dusk.

Magda's teeth. She *was* left-handed. Perspiration. They've gone all the way, through, Magda and Peter, they've been waiting for hours with Mother and Uncle Karl while Father searches for his lost son; they draw french-fried potatoes from a paper cup and shake their heads. They've named the children they'll one day have and bring to Ocean City on holidays. Can spermatozoa properly be thought of as male animalcules when there are no female spermatozoa? They grope through hot, dark windings, past Love's Tunnel's fearsome obstacles. Some perhaps lose their way.

Peter suggested then and there that they do the funhouse; he had been through it before, so had Magda, Ambrose hadn't and suggested, his voice cracking on account of Fat May's laughter, that they swim first. All were chuckling, couldn't help it; Ambrose's father, Ambrose's and Peter's father came up grinning like a lunatic with two boxes of syrup-coated popcorn, one for Mother, one for Magda; the men were to help themselves. Ambrose walked on Magda's right; being by nature left-handed, she carried the box in her left hand. Up front the situation was reversed.

"What are you limping for?" Magda inquired of Ambrose. He supposed in a husky tone that his foot had gone to sleep in the car. Her teeth flashed. "Pins and needles?" It was the honeysuckle on the lattice of the former privy that drew the bees. Imagine being stung there. How long is this going to take?

The adults decided to forego the pool; but Uncle Karl insisted they change into swimsuits and do the beach. "He wants to watch the pretty girls," Peter teased, and ducked behind Magda from Uncle Karl's pretended wrath. "You've got all the pretty girls you need right here," Magda declared, and Mother said: "Now that's the gospel truth." Magda scolded Peter, who reached over her shoulder to sneak some popcorn. "Your brother and father aren't getting any." Uncle Karl wondered if they were going to have fireworks that night, what with the shortages. It wasn't the shortages, Mr. M____ replied; Ocean City had fireworks from pre-war. But it was too risky on account of the enemy submarines, some people thought.

"Don't seem like Fourth of July without fireworks," said Uncle Karl. The inverted tag in dialogue writing is still considered permissible with proper names or epithets, but sounds old-fashioned with personal pronouns. "We'll have 'em again soon enough," predicted the boys' father. Their mother declared she could do without fireworks: they reminded her too much of the real thing. Their father said all the more reason to shoot off a few now and again. Uncle Karl asked *rhetorically* who needed reminding, just look at people's hair and skin.

"The oil, yes," said Mrs. M____.

Ambrose had a pain in his stomach and so didn't swim but enjoyed watching the others. He and his father burned red easily. Magda's figure was exceedingly well developed for her age. She too declined to swim, and got mad, and became angry when Peter attempted to drag her into the pool. She always swam, he insisted; what did she mean not swim? Why did a person come to Ocean City?

"Maybe I want to lay here with Ambrose," Magda teased.

Nobody likes a pedant.

"Aha," said Mother. Peter grabbed Magda by one ankle and ordered Ambrose to grab the other. She squealed and rolled over on the beach blanket. Ambrose pretended to help hold her back. Her tan was darker than even Mother's and Peter's. "Help out, Uncle Karl!" Peter cried. Uncle Karl went to seize the other ankle. Inside the top of her swimsuit, however, you could see the line where the sunburn ended and, when she hunched her shoulders and squealed again, one nipple's auburn edge. Mother made them behave themselves. *"You* should certainly know," she said to Uncle Karl. Archly. "That when a lady says she doesn't feel like swimming, a gentleman doesn't ask questions." Uncle Karl said excuse *him;* Mother winked at Magda; Ambrose blushed; stupid Peter kept saying "Phooey on *feel like!"* and tugging at Magda's ankle; then even he got the point, and cannon-balled with a holler into the pool.

"I swear," Magda said, in mock *in feigned* exasperation.

The diving would make a suitable literary symbol. To go off the high board you had to wait in a line along the poolside and up the ladder. Fellows tickled girls and goosed one another and shouted to the ones at the top to hurry up, or razzed them for bellyfloppers. Once on the springboard some took a great while posing or clowning or deciding on a dive or getting up their nerve; others ran right off. Especially among the younger fellows the idea was to strike the funniest pose or do the craziest stunt as you fell; a thing that got harder to do as you kept on and kept on. But whether you hollered *Geronimo!* or *Sieg heil!*, held your nose or "rode a bicycle," pretended to be shot or did a perfect jacknife or changed your mind halfway down and ended up with nothing, it was over in two seconds, after all that wait. Spring, pose, splash. Spring, neat-o, splash. Spring, aw fooey, splash.

The grown-ups had gone on; Ambrose wanted to converse with Magda; she was remarkably well developed for her age; it was said that that came from rubbing with a turkish towel, and there were other theories. Ambrose could think of nothing to say except how good a diver Peter was, who was showing off for her benefit. You could pretty well tell by looking at their bathing suits and arm muscles how far along the different fellows were. Ambrose was glad he hadn't gone in swimming, the cold water shrank you up so. Magda pretended to be uninterested in the diving; she probably weighed as much as he did. If you knew your way around in the funhouse like your own bedroom, you could wait until a girl came along and then slip away without ever getting caught, even if her boyfriend was right with her. She'd think *he* did it! It would be better to be the boyfriend, and act outraged, and tear the funhouse apart.

Not act; *be*.

"He's a master diver," Ambrose said. In feigned admiration. "You really have to slave away at it to get that good." What would it matter anyhow if he asked her right out whether she remembered, even teased her with it as Peter would have?

There's no point in going farther; this isn't getting anybody anywhere; they haven't even come to the funhouse yet. Ambrose is off the track, in some new or old part of the place that's not supposed to be used; he strayed into it by some one-in-a-million chance, like the time the roller coaster car left the tracks in the nineteen-teens against all the laws of physics and sailed over the boardwalk in the dark. And they can't locate him because they don't know where to look. Even the designer and operator have forgotten this other part, that winds around on itself like a whelk shell. That winds around the right part like the snakes on Mercury's caduceus. Some people, perhaps, don't "hit their stride" until their twenties, when the growing-up business is over and women appreciate other things besides wisecracks and teasing and strutting. Peter didn't have one-tenth the imagination *he* had, not one-tenth. Peter did this naming-their-children thing as a joke, making up names like Aloysius and Murgatroyd, but Ambrose knew *exactly* how it would feel to be married and have children of your own, and be a loving husband and father, and go comfortably to work in the mornings and to bed with your wife at night, and wake up with her there. With a breeze coming through the sash and birds and mockingbirds singing in the Chinese-cigar trees. His eyes watered, there aren't enough ways to say that. He would be quite famous in his line of work. Whether Magda was his wife or not, one evening when he was wise-lined and gray at the temples he'd smile gravely, at a fashionable dinner party, and remind her of his youthful passion. The time they went with his family to Ocean City; the *erotic fantasies* he used to have about her. How long ago it seemed, and childish! Yet tender, too, *n'est-ce pas?* Would she have imagined that the world-famous whatever remembered how many strings were on the lyre on the bench beside the girl on the label of the cigar box he'd stared at in the toolshed at age ten while she, age eleven. Even then he had felt *wise beyond his years;* he'd stroked her hair and said in his deepest voice and correctest English, as to a dear child: "I shall never forget this moment."

But though he had breathed heavily, groaned as if ecstatic, what he'd really felt throughout was an odd detachment, as though some one else were Master. Strive as he might to be transported, he heard his mind take notes upon the scene: *This is what they call* passion. *I am experiencing it.* Many of the digger machines were out of order in the penny arcades and could not be repaired or replaced for the duration. Moreover the prizes, made now in USA, were less interesting than formerly, pasteboard items for the most part, and some of the machines wouldn't work on white pennies. The gypsy fortune-teller machine might have provided a foreshadowing of the climax of this story if Ambrose had operated it. It was even dilapidateder than most: the silver coating was worn off the brown metal handles, the glass windows around the dummy were cracked and taped, her kerchiefs and silks long-faded. If a man lived by himself, he could take a department-store mannequin with flexible joints and modify her in certain ways. *However:* by the time he was that old he'd have a real woman. There was a machine that stamped your name around a white-metal coin with a star in the middle: A____. His son would be the second, and when the lad reached thirteen or so he would put a strong arm around his shoulder and tell him calmly: "It is perfectly normal. We have all been through it. It will not last forever." Nobody knew how to be what they were right. He'd smoke a pipe, teach his son how to fish and softcrab, assure him he needn't worry about himself. Magda would certainly give, Magda would certainly yield a great deal of milk, although guilty of occasional solecisms. It don't taste so bad. Suppose the lights came on now!

*The day wore on.* You think you're yourself, but there are other persons in you. Ambrose gets hard when Ambrose doesn't want to, *and obversely.* Ambrose watches them disagree; Ambrose watches him watch. In the funhouse mirror-room you can't see yourself go on forever, because no matter how you stand, your head gets in the way.

Even if you had a glass periscope, the image of your eye would cover up the thing you really wanted to see. The police will come; there'll be a story in the papers. That must be where it happened. Unless he can find a surprise exit, an unofficial backdoor or escape hatch opening on an alley, say, and then stroll up to the family in front of the funhouse and ask where everybody's been; *he's* been out of the place for ages. That's just where it happened, in that last lighted room: Peter and Magda found the right exit; he found one that you weren't supposed to find and strayed off into the works somewhere. In a perfect funhouse you'd be able to go only one way, like the divers off the highboard; getting lost would be impossible; the doors and halls would work like minnow traps or the valves in veins.

On account of German U-boats, Ocean City was "browned out": streetlights were shaded on the seaward side; shop-windows and boardwalk amusement places were kept dim, not to silhouette tankers and Liberty-ships for torpedoing. In a short story about Ocean City, Maryland, during World War II, the author could make use of the image of sailors on leave in the penny arcades and shooting galleries, sighting through the crosshairs of toy machine guns at swastika'd subs, while out in the black Atlantic a U-boat skipper squints through his periscope at real ships outlined by the glow of penny arcades. After dinner the family strolled back to the amusement end of the boardwalk. The boys' father had burnt red as always and was masked with Noxema, a minstrel in reverse. The grown-ups stood at the end of the boardwalk where the Hurricane of '33 had cut an inlet from the ocean to Assawoman Bay.

"Pronounced with a long *o*," Uncle Karl reminded Magda with a wink. His shirt sleeves were rolled up; Mother punched his brown biceps with the arrowed heart on it and said his mind was naughty. Fat May's laugh came suddenly from the funhouse, as if she'd just got the joke; the family laughed too at the coincidence. Ambrose went under the boardwalk to search for out-of-town matchbook covers with the aid of his pocket flashlight; he looked out from the edge of the North American continent and wondered how far their laughter carried over the water. Spies in rubber rafts; survivors in lifeboats. If the joke had been beyond his understanding, he could have said: *"The laughter was over his head."* And let the reader see the serious wordplay on second reading.

He turned the flashlight on and then off at once even before the woman whooped. He sprang away, heart athud, dropping the light. What had the man grunted? Perspiration drenched and chilled him by the time he scrambled up to the family. "See anything?" his father asked. His voice wouldn't come; he shrugged and violently brushed sand from his pants legs.

"Let's ride the old flying horses!" Magda cried. I'll never be an author. It's been forever already, everybody's gone home, Ocean City's deserted, the ghost-crabs are tickling across the beach and down the littered cold streets. And the empty halls of clapboard hotels and abandoned funhouses. A tidal wave; an enemy air raid; a monster-crab swelling like an island from the sea. *The inhabitants fled in terror.* Magda clung to his trouser leg; he alone knew the maze's secret. "He gave his life that we might live," said Uncle Karl with a scowl of pain, as he. The fellow's hands had been tattooed; the woman's legs, the woman's fat white legs had. *An astonishing coincidence.* He yearned to tell Peter. He wanted to throw up for excitement. They hadn't even chased him. He wished he were dead.

One possible ending would be to have Ambrose come across another lost person in the dark. They'd match their wits together against the funhouse, struggle like Ulysses past obstacle after obstacle, help and encourage each other. Or a girl. By the time they found the exit they'd be closest friends, sweethearts if it were a girl; they'd know each other's inmost souls, be bound together *by the cement of shared adventure;* then they'd emerge into the light and it would turn out that his friend was a Negro. A blind girl. President Roosevelt's son. Ambrose's former archenemy.

Shortly after the mirror room he'd groped along a musty corridor, his heart already misgiving him at the absence of phosphorescent arrows and other signs. He's found a crack of light—not a door, it turned out, but a seam between the plyboard wall panels—and squinting up to it, espied a small old man, *in appearance not unlike* the photographs at home of Ambrose's late grandfather, nodding upon a stool beneath a bare, speckled bulb. A crude panel of toggle- and knife-switches hung beside the open fuse box near his head; elsewhere in the little room were wooden levers and ropes belayed to boat cleats. At the time, Ambrose wasn't lost enough to rap or call; later he couldn't find that crack. Now it seemed to him that he'd possibly dozed off for a few minutes somewhere along the way; certainly he was exhausted from the afternoon's sunshine and the evening's problems; he couldn't be sure he hadn't dreamed part or all of the sight. Had an old black wall fan droned like bees and shimmied two flypaper streamers? Had the funhouse operator—gentle, somewhat sad and tired-appearing, in expression not unlike the photographs at home of Ambrose's late Uncle Konrad—murmured in his sleep? Is there really such a person as Ambrose, or is he a figment of the author's imagination? Was it Assawoman Bay or Sinepuxent? Are there other errors of fact in this fiction? Was there another sound besides the little slap slap of thigh on ham, like water sucking at the chine-boards of a skiff?

When you're lost, the smartest thing to do is stay put till you're found, hollering if necessary. But to holler guarantees humiliation as well as rescue; keeping silent permits some saving of face—you can act surprised at the fuss when your rescuers find you and swear you weren't lost, if they do. What's more you might find your own way yet, *however belatedly*.

"Don't tell me your foot's still asleep!" Magda exclaimed as the three young people walked from the inlet to the area set aside for ferris wheels, carrousels, and other carnival rides, they having decided in favor of the vast and ancient merry-go-round instead of the funhouse. What a sentence, everything was wrong from the outset. People don't know what to make of him, he doesn't know what to make of himself, he's only thirteen, *athletically and socially inept*, not astonishingly bright, but there are antennae; he has . . . some sort of receivers in his head; things speak to him, he understands more than he should, the world winks at him through its objects, grabs grinning at his coat. Everybody else is in on some secret he doesn't know; they've forgotten to tell him. Through simple *procrastination* his mother put off his baptism until this year. Everyone else had it done as a baby; he'd assumed the same of himself, as had his mother, so she claimed, until it was time for him to join Grace Methodist-Protestant and the oversight came out. He was mortified, but pitched sleepless through his private catechizing, intimidated by the ancient mysteries, a thirteen year old would never say that, resolved to experience conversion like St. Augustine. When the water touched his brow and Adam's sin left him, he contrived by a strain like defecation to bring tears into his eyes—but felt nothing. There was some simple, radical difference about him; he hoped it was genius, feared it was madness, devoted himself to amiability and inconspicuousness. Alone on the seawall near his house he was seized by the terrifying transports he'd thought to find in toolshed, in Communion-cup. The grass was alive! The town, the river, himself, were not imaginary; time roared in his ears like wind; the world was *going on!* This part ought to be dramatized. The Irish author James Joyce once wrote. Ambrose M____ is going to scream.

There is no *texture of rendered sensory detail*, for one thing. The fad ed distorting mirrors beside Fat May; the impossibility of choosing a mount when one had but a single ride on the great carrousel; the *vertigo attendant on his recognition* that Ocean City was worn out, the place of fathers and grandfathers, straw-boatered men and parasoled ladies survived by their amusements. Money spent, the three paused at Peter's insistence beside Fat May to watch the girls get their skirts blown up. The object was to tease Magda, who said: "I swear, Peter M____, you've got a one-track mind! Amby and me aren't *interested* in such things." In the tumbling-barrel, too, just inside the Devil's-mouth entrance to the funhouse, the girls were upended and their boyfriends and others could see up their dresses if they cared to.

Which was the whole point, Ambrose realized. Of the entire funhouse! If you looked around, you noticed that almost all the people on the boardwalk were paired off into couples except the small children; in a way, that was the whole point of Ocean City! If you had X-ray eyes and could see everything going on at that instant under the boardwalk and in all the hotel rooms and cars and alleyways, you'd realize that all that normally showed, like restaurants and dance halls and clothing and test-your-strength machines, was merely preparation and intermission. Fat May screamed.

Because he watched the goings-on from the corner of his eye, it was Ambrose who spied the half-dollar on the boardwalk near the tumbling-barrel. Losers weepers. The first time he'd heard some people moving through a corridor not far away, just after he'd lost sight of the crack of light, he'd decided not to call to them, for fear they'd guess he was scared and poke fun; it sounded like roughnecks; he'd hoped they'd come by and he could follow in the dark without their knowing. Another time he'd heard just one person, unless he imagined it, bumping along as if on the other side of the plywood; perhaps Peter coming back for him, or Father, or Magda lost too. Or the owner and operator of the funhouse. He'd called out once, as though merrily: "Anybody know where the heck we are?" But the query was too stiff, his voice cracked, when the sounds stopped he was terrified: maybe it was a queer who waited for fellows to get lost, or a longhaired filthy monster that lived in some cranny of the funhouse. He stood rigid for hours it seemed like, scarcely respiring. His future was shockingly clear, in outline. He tried holding his breath to the point of unconsciousness. There ought to be a button you could push to end your life absolutely without pain; disappear in a flick, like turning out a light. He would push it instantly! He despised Uncle Karl. But he despised his father too, for not being what he was supposed to be. Perhaps his father hated his father, and so on, and his son would hate him, and so on. Instantly!

Naturally he didn't have nerve enough to ask Magda to go through the funhouse with him. With incredible nerve and to everyone's surprise he invited Magda, quietly and politely, to go through the funhouse with him. "I warn you, I've never been through it before," he added, laughing easily; "but I reckon we can manage somehow. The important thing to remember, after all, is that it's meant to be a funhouse; that is, a place of amusement. If people really got lost or injured or too badly frightened in it, the owner'd go out of business. There'd even be lawsuits. No character in a work of fiction can make a speech this long without interruption or acknowledgment from the other characters."

Mother teased Uncle Karl: "Three's a crowd, I always heard." But actually Ambrose was relieved that Peter now had a quarter too.

Nothing was what it looked like. Every instant, under the surface of the Atlantic Ocean, millions of living animals devoured one another. Pilots were falling in flames over Europe; women were being forcibly raped in the South Pacific. His father should have taken him aside and said: "There is a simple secret to getting through the funhouse, as simple as being first to see the Towers. Here it is. Peter does not know it; neither does your Uncle Karl. You and I are different. Not surprisingly, you've often wished you weren't. Don't think I haven't noticed how unhappy your childhood has been! But you'll understand, when I tell you, why it had to be kept secret until now. And you won't regret not being like your brother and your uncle. *On the contrary!*" If you knew all the stories behind all the people on the boardwalk, you'd see that *nothing* was what it looked like. Husbands and wives often hated each other; parents didn't necessarily love their children; et cetera. A child took things for granted because he had nothing to compare his life to and everybody acted as if things were as they should be. Therefore each saw himself as the hero of the story, when the truth might turn out to be that he's the villain, or the coward. And there wasn't one thing you could do about it!

Hunchbacks, fat ladies, fools—that no one chose what he was was unbearable. In the movies he'd meet a beautiful young girl in the funhouse; they'd have hairs-breadth escapes from real dangers; he'd do and say the right things; she also; in the end they'd be lovers; their dialogue lines would match up; he'd be perfectly at ease; she'd not only like him well enough, she'd think he was *marvelous;* she'd lie awake thinking about *him,* instead of vice versa—the way *his* face looked in different lights and how he stood and exactly what he'd said—and yet that would be only one small episode in his wonderful life, among many many others. Not a *turning point* at all. What had happened in the toolshed was nothing. He hated, he loathed his parents! One reason for not writing a lost-in-the-funhouse story is that either everybody's felt what Ambrose feels, in which case it goes without saying, or else no normal person feels such things, in which case Ambrose is a freak. "Is anything more tiresome, in fiction, than the problems of sensitive adolescents?" And it's all too long and rambling, as if the author. For all a person knows the first time through, the end could be just around any corner; perhaps, *not impossibly* it's been within reach any number of times. On the other hand he may be scarcely past the start, with everything yet to get through, an intolerable idea.

*Fill in:* His father's raised eyebrows when he announced his decision to do the funhouse with Magda. Ambrose understands now, but didn't then, that his father was wondering whether he knew what the funhouse was *for*—especially since he didn't object, as he should have, when Peter decided to come along too. The ticket-woman, witchlike, mortifying him when inadvertently he gave her his name-coin instead of the half-dollar, then unkindly calling Magda's attention to the birthmark on his temple: "Watch out for him, girlie, he's a marked man!" She wasn't even cruel, he understood, only vulgar and insensitive. Somewhere in the world there was a young woman with such splendid understanding that she'd see him entire, like a poem or story, and find his words so valuable after all that when he confessed his apprehensions she would explain why they were in fact the very things that made him precious to her . . . and to Western Civilization! There was no such girl, the simple truth being. Violent yawns as they approached the mouth. Whispered advice from an old-timer on a bench near the barrel: "Go crabwise and ye'll get an eyeful without upsetting!" Composure vanished at the first pitch: Peter hollered joyously, Magda tumbled, shrieked, clutched her skirt; Ambrose scrambled crabwise, tight-lipped with terror, was soon out, watched his dropped name-coin slide among the couples. Shamefaced he saw that to get through expeditiously was not the point; Peter feigned assistance in order to trip Magda up, shouted "I see Christmas!" when her legs went flying. The old man, his latest betrayer, cackled approval. A dim hall then of black-thread cobwebs and recorded gibber: he took Magda's elbow to steady her against revolving discs set in the slanted floor to throw your feet out from under, and explained to her in a calm, deep voice his theory that each phase of the funhouse was triggered either automatically, by a series of photoelectric devices, or else manually by operators stationed at peepholes. But he lost his voice thrice as the discs unbalanced him; Magda was anyhow squealing; but at one point she clutched him about the waist to keep from falling, and her right cheek pressed for a moment against his belt-buckle. Heroically he drew her up, it was his chance to clutch her close as if for support and say: "I love you." He even put an arm lightly about the small of her back before a sailor-and-girl pitched into them from behind, sorely treading his left big toe and knocking Magda asprawl with them. The sailor's girl was a string-haired hussy with a loud laugh and light blue drawers; Ambrose realized that he wouldn't have said "I love you" anyhow, and was smitten with self-contempt. How much better it would be to be that common sailor! A wiry little Seaman 3rd, the fellow squeezed a girl to each side and stumbled hilarious into the mirror room, closer to Magda in thirty seconds than Ambrose had got in thirteen years. She giggled at something the fellow said to Peter; she drew her hair from her eyes with a movement so womanly it struck Ambrose's heart; Peter's smacking her backside then seemed particularly coarse. But Magda made a pleased indignant face and cried, "All right for *you*, mister!" and pursued Peter into the maze without a backward glance. The sailor followed after, leisurely, drawing his girl against his hip;

Ambrose understood not only that they were all so relieved to be rid of his burdensome company that they didn't even notice his absence, but that he himself shared their relief. Stepping from the treacherous passage at last into the mirror-maze, he saw once again, more clearly than ever, how readily he deceived himself into supposing he was a person. He even foresaw, wincing at his dreadful self-knowledge, that he would repeat the deception, at ever-rarer intervals, all his wretched life, so fearful were the alternatives. Fame, madness, suicide; perhaps all three. It's not believable that so young a boy could articulate that reflection, and in fiction the merely true must always yield to the plausible. Moreover, the symbolism is in places heavy-footed. Yet Ambrose M— understood, as few adults do, that the famous loneliness of the great was no popular myth but a general truth— furthermore, that it was as much cause as effect.

All the preceding except the last few sentences is exposition that should've been done earlier or interspersed with the present action instead of lumped together. No reader would put up with so much with such *prolixity*. It's interesting that Ambrose's father, though presumably an intelligent man (as indicated by his role as grade-school principal), neither encouraged nor discouraged his sons at all in any way—as if he either didn't care about them or cared all right but didn't know how to act. If this fact should contribute to one of them's becoming a celebrated but wretchedly unhappy scientist, was it a good thing or not? He too might someday face the question; it would be useful to know whether it had tortured his father for years, for example, or never once crossed his mind.

In the maze two important things happened. First, our hero found a name-coin someone else had lost or discarded: *AMBROSE,* suggestive of the famous lightship and of his late grandfather's favorite dessert, which his mother used to prepare on special occasions out of coconut, oranges, grapes, and what else. Second, as he wondered at the endless replication of his image in the mirrors, second, as he *lost himself in the reflection* that the necessity for an observer makes perfect observation impossible, better make him eighteen at least, yet that would render other things unlikely, he heard Peter and Magda chuckling some-where together in the maze. "Here!" "No, here!" they shouted to each other; Peter said, "Where's Amby?" Magda murmured. "Amb?" Peter called. In a pleased, friendly voice. He didn't reply. The truth was, his brother was a *happy-go-lucky youngster* who'd've been better off with a regular brother of his own, but who seldom complained of his lot and was generally cordial. Ambrose's throat ached; there aren't enough different ways to say that. He stood quietly while the two young people giggled and thumped through the glittering maze, hurrah'd their discovery of its exit, cried out in joyful alarm at what next beset them. Then he set his mouth and followed after, as he supposed, took a wrong turn, strayed into the pass *wherein he lingers yet*.

The action of conventional dramatic narrative may be represented by a diagram called Freitag's Triangle:

or more accurately by a variant of that diagram:

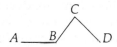

in which *AB* represents the exposition, *B* the introduction of conflict, *BC* the "rising action," complication, or development of the conflict, *C* the climax, or turn of the action, *CD* the dénoucment, or resolution of the conflict. While there is no reason to regard this pattern as an absolute necessity, like many other conventions it became conventional because great numbers of people over many years learned by trial and error that it was effective; one ought not to forsake it, therefore, unless one wishes to forsake as well the effect of drama or has clear cause to feel that deliberate violation of the "normal" pattern can better can better effect that effect. This can't go on much longer; it can go on forever. He died telling stories to himself in the dark; years later, when that vast unsuspected area of the funhouse came to light, the first expedition found his skeleton in one of its labyrinthine corridors and mistook it for part of the entertainment. He died of starvation telling himself stories in the dark; but unbeknownst unbeknownst to him, an assistant operator of the funhouse, happening to overhear him, crouched just behind the plyboard partition and wrote down his every word. The operator's daughter, an exquisite young woman with a figure unusually well developed for her age, crouched just behind the partition and transcribed his every word. Though she had never laid eyes on him, she recognized that here was one of Western Culture's truly great imaginations, the eloquence of whose suffering would be an inspiration to unnumbered. And her. heart was torn between her love for the misfortunate young man (yes, she loved him, though she had never laid though she knew him only—but how well!—through his words, and the deep, calm voice in which he spoke them) between her love et cetera and her womanly intuition that only in suffering and isolation could he give voice et cetera. Lone dark dying. Quietly she kissed the rough plyboard, and a tear fell upon the page. Where she had written in shorthand *Where she had written in shorthand* Where she had written in shorthand *Where she* et cetera. A long time ago we should have passed the apex of Freitag's Triangle and made brief work of the *dénouement*; the plot doesn't rise by meaningful steps but winds upon itself, digresses, retreats, hesitates, sighs, collapses, expires. The climax of the story must be its protagonist's discovery of a way to get through the funhouse. But he has found none, may have ceased to search.

What relevance does the war have to the story? Should there be fireworks outside or not?

Ambrose wandered, languished, dozed. Now and then he fell into his habit of rehearsing to himself the unadventurous story of his life, narrated from the third-person point of view, from his earliest memory parenthesis of maple leaves stirring in the summer breath of tidewater Maryland end of parenthesis to the present moment. Its principle events, on this telling, would appear to have been *A, B, C,* and *D*.

He imagined himself years hence, successful, married, at ease in the world, the trials of his adolescence far behind him. He has come to the seashore with his family for the holiday: how Ocean City has changed! But at one seldom at one ill-frequented end of the boardwalk a few derelict amusements survive from times gone by: the great carrousel from the turn of the century, with its monstrous griffins and mechanical concert band; the roller coaster rumored since 1916 to have been condemned; the mechanical shooting gallery in which only the image of our enemies changed. His own son laughs with Fat May and wants to know what a funhouse is; Ambrose hugs the sturdy lad close and smiles around his pipestem at his wife.

The family's going home. Mother sits between Father and Uncle Karl, who teases him good-naturedly who chuckles over the fact that the comrade with whom he'd fought his way shoulder to shoulder through the funhouse had turned out to be a blind Negro girl—to their mutual discomfort, as they'd opened their souls. But such are the walls of custom, which even. Whose arm is where? How must it feel. He dreams of a funhouse vaster by far than any yet constructed; but by then they may be out of fashion, like steamboats and excursion trains. Already quaint and seedy: the draperied ladies on the frieze of the carrousel are his father's father's mooncheeked dreams; if he thinks of it more he will vomit his apple-on-a-stick.

He wonders: will he become a regular person? Something has gone wrong; his vaccination didn't take; at the Boy-Scout initiation campfire he only pretended to be deeply moved, as he pretends to this hour that it is not so bad after all in the funhouse, and that he has a little limp. How long will it last? He envisions a truly astonishing funhouse, incredibly complex yet utterly controlled from a great central switchboard like the console of a pipe organ. Nobody had enough imagination. He could design such a place himself, wiring and all, and he's only thirteen years old. He would be its operator: panel lights would show what was up in every cranny of its cunning of its multifarious vastness; a switch-flick would ease this fellow's way, complicate that's, to balance things out; if anyone seemed lost or frightened, all the operator had to do was.

He wishes he had never entered the funhouse. But he has. Then he wishes he were dead. But he's not. Therefore he will construct funhouses for others and be their secret operator—though he would rather be among the lovers for whom funhouses are designed.

# TIMOTHY FINDLEY
## 1930–

Born and educated in Toronto, Findley turned first to theater as a career. He worked for the Stratford (Ontario) Shakespeare Festival in its first season in 1953, and then moved to London, England, to study at the Central School of Speech and Drama. Between 1953 and 1956 he toured England, Europe, and the United States as a contract player with H. M. Tennant. In New York he met Thornton Wilder while performing in his play *The Matchmaker* and, with Wilder's encouragement, began to write fiction. After returning to Canada, Findley began to write plays and documentaries for radio and television, choosing writing as his full-time career in 1962. He has written five novels. His third, *The Wars* (1977), won a Governor General's award and was made into a feature film.

# Dinner Along the Amazon

*For Robin Phillips*

Perhaps the house was to blame. Once, it had been Olivia's pride; her safe, good place. Everyone else—including Michael—found it charming. Prestigious. Practical. North Seton Drive was a great location. Running out of Rosedale down towards the ravine, all its back yards were set with trees and rolling lawns. Autumn and spring, Olivia could happily walk or ride her bicycle to Branksome Hall, where she had been teaching now for six years. She really had no right to complain. Number 38 was handsome enough—its glass all shining; its paint unchipped.

Recently, however, Olivia had begun to balk at the physical act of arriving there; of being on the sidewalk and turning in towards the house, admitting that she belonged on that cement and was meant to walk through that front door. There was always something lying on the grass she would not allow was hers: a torn, wet *Star* or a bit of orange peel—(*I didn't put that there!*)—something left by a neighbor's child or someone else's dog. And even, once, a sinister pair of men's blue undershorts.

Inside, the house gave off the smell of discontent; of ashes in the sink and slippers prowling through the halls at night; of schisms rusting like a set of knives. Also the odor—faintly underarm—of Michael's petulance and Olivia's silence hiding in the closets. *Boo. . . .*

Today, on the twenty-eighth of April, Olivia entered the house with her arms full of flowers at five in the afternoon. The flowers were done up in green paper cones, but still the smell of them was rampant under her chin and she stood in the middle of the hall not speaking—only listening—dizzy with the scent of freesia.

Michael was in here somewhere. Up in the sun room, probably. Drunk. Conrad's car was in the driveway, rubbing its already damaged bumper up against the garage. This could only signal they would both be drunk: not only Michael but Conrad, too. Old friends and empty bottles. Poor deadly Conrad, dragging the unwelcome past with all its frayed address books and stringy love affairs behind him, had come to "visit for a while"—i.e. to crash until he'd pulled himself together. God damn old friends.

It could not be borne. There wasnt' time for the past in their lives. Not now. Not ever. All it did was crowd you into corners and turn out the lights. Then it rattled you with guilt and regret and left you inarticulate and incapacitated. Who needs that? *I'm taking enough of a beating from the present, thank you very much*; Olivia thought. *Damn you, Conrad. Much as I love you, if you hadn't come, I could talk to Michael. Now. Tonight. I could tell him and get it over with.*

*No I couldn't.*

Olivia peered to her left, into the dim shuttered light of Michael's den. She tried to imagine the thing in her belly running through that doorway into those shadows to find its father. It was impossible. He would slam the door in its face. *Get out!*

She knew this was only a coward's excuse. Michael didn't hate children: he hated the future—and that was different. He hated anything he couldn't control: he hated anything he didn't know. Certainty was the only ally you could trust, in Michael's books. Certainty and literature. History—(maybe)—and a few poems written on the backs of envelopes. He *wanted* children, but he didn't want their lives to run beyond his own. He couldn't bear to inject them into the future—only into the past. Michael would like it best if his children had preceded him. Then he could say to them; "Everything I told you was the truth. I have never lied. It is all borne out by what you have seen: the known—the safe." The future was his enemy.

In Michael's den, there were piles and piles of notebooks and reams of paper. These were his diatribes—some of them four or six or ten years old. They were covered with marmalade fungi and peanut butter mushrooms. Olivia smiled. The rug was stained with his solipsisms. She had listened to him roaring there, amongst his books—knocking over his drinks—jabbing his fingers at her: ''Just you wait, Olivia! Every word I say is true. . . . '' Then he would have to verify every word—dragging down all the pertinent books, drawing out all the pertinent pieces of paper, going crazy—ranting—when he couldn't find what he wanted. In its way, it was a sad, dead room. Echoes hiding in the curtains. The roll-top desk had pigeon holes that smelled, Olivia swore, of pigeons: all the pigeons flown away with their messages—the words that Michael couldn't find. In a bowl, he kept all his paper clips attached to rubber bands—ready to fire at the passing parade or at any rash intruder who brought the future into his presence: man, woman or child . . .

No. There could be no child.

Olivia turned towards the kitchen, leaning her ear in the direction of the stairwell, hoping to hear the sound of sober conversation. Even of laughter. But there was nothing. Only the silence between drinks. Up there, sitting in the sun room, they were probably holding their breath: Michael and Conrad, hiding from Olivia. *Don't give away our secret, Connie.* Mustn't let her know we're only ten years old, when she thinks we're twelve, at least.

It *was* the house: its airlessness; its *culs-de-sac*; its bear pits waiting for the bears. It had lost its capacity to generate dreams. All it reflected, as you moved from room to room, was the tidy horror of what was really going to happen.

As Olivia entered the kitchen, the sun room made a creaking noise above her head. She looked up, thinking; *they're walking on tiptoe. How ridiculous. Two grown men* . . .

She crossed to the sink, making sure her heels could be heard as she went. Still clothed in all her outer garments, her tweed coat; her three layers of scarves; her soft, rich sweater; her wool lined boots— she set her briefcase on one cutting board and the packets of flowers on the other. She turned on the tap for a glass of water and reached to the left for a thick, red tumbler with a crack in it. Habit. It was always there, the last of its kind. There had once been eight—a gift from Conrad. Pinned to the curtain above the sink was one of Mrs. Kemp's inimitable notes:

> Mrs. Penny I done the back room up for Mr. Fastbinder and put a towel and a wash cloth on his burow. You run out of blue sheets so he only got one and the other ones yellow. Grennel is loss again. Hiden.

Olivia, reading, was holding the tumbler under the tap.

> I could not find no more OLD DUTCH so have put down OLD DUTCH on the list. 4

large ones please as the bathroom really eats them up. Mr. Fastbinder near creamed the garage. Dont let them tell you different. I will be in tomorrow to clean up after.

Lilah Kemp.

The cold water ran on Olivia's hands, comforting, numbing.

Ps Prof Penny did not eat his sandwich. Toona if you want one.

All the usual digs at Michael were intact. Mortal enemies—Michael Penny and Mrs. Kemp. And Grendel. Grendel was Michael's beloved dog and, like his master, he always hid from Mrs. Kemp and her dreaded vacuum cleaner and her dreadful tuna sandwiches, the edges of which she always left in Grendel's dish.

Olivia set aside the tumbler and took down the note, threw it into the garbage pail and replaced the pin in the folds of the curtain. As she drank her water, she wondered where the dog might be this time. Lying poisoned, perhaps, in someone's flower bed—the victim of Mrs. Kemp's "toona". The detritus of neglect. Poor old Grendel.

Poor old Grendel had a habit of lying dead in other people's flowerbeds, but his favorite place of all was in behind the curtain of the shower stall, where he portrayed with alarming veracity the corpses of his master and his mistress—one and then the other. Michael and Olivia, dead.

Olivia's hand went down to rest on her belly and the red tumbler, in the other hand, shook. *Michael first and then Olivia—dead*. I am not a murderer. Not. I am doing what is right. The only right thing: the only possible thing.

She began to cry—(*oh why am I crying?*)—her gaze shifting sideways, awash—(*please: it's so shaming*)—towards the flowers—(*and stupid: stop*). What had the flowers been for, she wondered, setting the tumbler aside. To get her past the front door without throwing up? Not that. No. She could tolerate the tension one more week—so what had the flowers been for? Perhaps, she decided, they were for Grendel, always "dying." Or for Michael, still alive. Or for the undug grave in her belly. Pick a card—any card. Now put it back in the deck. Just don't tell me which card it was. . . .

"Hallo."

Olivia grabbed the sink and nearly fell before she turned.

Standing in the doorway was a man she had never seen before. A man—a "boy." He was in his early twenties.

"Yes?" she said.

His arms were full of brown paper packages.

"Who are you?" he said, with casual, inbred impertinence.

Olivia was flabbergasted. "I'm . . . Olivia Penny," she said. *And this is my house*, she almost added. But didn't.

"Are you Professor Penny's sister, then?" The young man barged completely into the kitchen. The brown paper packages were clinking suspiciously like future toasts, and the young man was trying not to spill them before they could be proposed.

"No, I am not Professor Penny's God damn sister. I am Professor Penny's God damn wife," said Olivia, stepping aside to avoid being trampled. "And who the hell are you?"

"I'm with Conrad," the young man said. He laid his loot—eight bottles of wine, four bottles of scotch—beside and on top of the flowers and turned to smile at Olivia. "You're a scream," he said, and put out his hand. "Conrad didn't tell me you were *funny*," he added. "I'm Rodney Farquhar." (His grip was like the proverbial vise.) "Or should I say I'm Conrad's God damn lover?"

"Why are you here?" said Olivia.

Rodney Farquhar's face was emptied of all expression. Perhaps he didn't know the answer to the question.

"You've just set all your things on top of my flowers," Olivia continued. "Would you please find some other place?"

Rodney moved in on the bottles and began to shift them, two by two, onto the kitchen table.

"Why are you here?" Olivia repeated.

"I was sent to get the booze," he said. "I've just come back. . . ."

"I can see that. Booze for what?"

"For the party," said Rodney. His back was to her.

*Party?*

"What party?" said Olivia. Her eyes had narrowed. Her blood was rising.

"Conrad's party," said Rodney.

"Conrad is giving a party? Where?"

"Here, of course."

Olivia ground her teeth and was speechless for a moment. Then she said, "Am I invited?"

Conrad was lying in the bath. The bathroom was full of steam and the steam was scented with Conrad's favorite cologne: *Chanel 19.* Michael was seated on the toilet, the lid down—its grey fur cover slightly damp beneath him. Conrad could barely be seen in the fog.

"Aren't you going to boil yourself to death in there?" Michael asked.

"Never," said Conrad. "The heat is wonderful. It spreads the alcohol faster through the system. Give me another. . . ."

Conrad's hand, with goblet, appeared from the steam.

Michael poured more scotch and the hand withdrew and then Michael poured more scotch into his own Waterford goblet and took a great, raw mouthful; "ahhhh . . . " He set the goblet on the floor, fingering its cut design. "Always drink the best from the best," he said. "So, who have you invited?"

"Fabiana Holbach," said Conrad.

"Yes. And who else?"

"Who cares who else? Fabiana Holbach. That's all that matters."

"So I gather," Michael sighed. He lighted a damp cigarette, with a damp recalcitrant match. "Are you sure this is really a good idea? Inviting Fabiana after all these years?"

"All these years number precisely three," said Conrad. "Give me a cigarette."

Michael handed over the one already lit and lighted another.

"You realize, of course," he said, "she's married, now."

"People can always be convinced their current marriages don't work," said Conrad.

Michael muttered "yes" and "amen" to this, but not loud enough for Conrad to hear.

"What's her name, now?" said Conrad.

"Mrs. Jackman Powell."

The bath fell silent. Not a ripple.

"You don't approve, I take it," said Michael.

"It's neither here nor there," said Conrad. "Truth is, I always thought that *Jackman* had to be the most pretentious name a man could have. Isn't his brother's name plain old Tom?"

"Yes."

"Maybe their mother's name was Jackman."

"No. Their mother's name was Tompkins."

Conrad laughed. Then sobered. "Son-of-a-bitch," he said. "So she married Jackman Powell."

"That's right." Michael was watching all he could see of Conrad— the arm that lay along the rim of the tub; the shape of the neck; the thrust of the head as it bent to the glass to drink; above all, the tension in the hand that held the cigarette so hard against the tub, the cigarette broke and the lighted end of it fell to the floor. Conrad didn't even notice. All he did was mutter: "sons-of-bitches."

"Who?"

"All of them," Conrad said with a kind of vehemence Michael had never heard from his friend before. "All of the God damn Powells. God damn sons-of-bitches." Conrad sat disconsolate, still barely visible.

What, Michael wondered, could have happened to Conrad—usually so resilient and now, apparently, defeated by the mention of a mere name. They had spent all their school days laughing. Not that a person could go on laughing forever. Michael was perfectly aware of this and of the darker things that had affected Conrad's life. But this was something new; unknown. As if the laughter had escaped and Conrad could not locate it.

"I suppose," Conrad said, "this means Fabiana will actually bring him with her. Jackman. I suppose this means I'll have to face him . . . stand there and actually shake his God damn hand."

"I suppose so. Does it matter?"

"Yes. It matters."

"Why?"

"Won't go into it. Later, maybe. After they've gone. Not now. The son-of-a-bitch. . . . "

"You've said that. Several times."

"I know I have. Leave me alone."

"You know I can't leave you alone, Con. . . . " (Michael was using a swishy, sibilant voice—the one he always used to tease Conrad.) "I adore you."

"Don't," said Conrad. "This isn't funny."

"I'm sorry." Michael lighted another cigarette and handed it through the mist to Conrad. Ever since Conrad's father had died, three years ago, there were things you couldn't talk about. Not always having to do with Fastbinder senior (whose name had been Karl). Sometimes with mysteries Michael wasn't privy to. The causes of Conrad's silence: the long sojourn abroad in Italy and Spain; his sudden reappearance; Rodney Farquhar; Fabiana Holbach Powell. . . . God knew, any or all of these things could and should be the centers of conversation. But, more often than not, they were the cause of snapping jaws and bitten tongues.

"Change the subject," said Conrad. "Help me understand what's wrong between you and Olivia. Give me something to laugh about."

"You think we're going to laugh about *that*?" said Michael.

"Maybe," said Conrad. "Is there another woman?"

"No," said Michael. "I wish there was."

"What do you mean? Is there someone you love?"

"Yes."

"Someone you can't have?"

"Yes. I suppose you could put it that way."

"Who?"

"Olivia."

"Oh." Conrad drank from his glass and took a drag from his cigarette. "Have you ever seriously thought of falling in love with me?" he said.

"I wouldn't know how to behave in bed," said Michael, trying to be funny: failing. "What *do* you do with Rodney?"

"I admire him, dear," said Conrad. "He adores it. I tell him he has the most beautiful pudendum known to man or boy. A palpable lie of course. But Rodney believes it. Sometimes I pull it for him."

"Don't be so God damn crude. That's disgusting."

"Well—you asked."

"It's so childish."

"Precisely. And Rodney is a child."

"And you? What do you get out of all this?"

"Notoriety. Open doors. Rodney's connections are quite spectacular, you know."

"But you don't need open doors, Con. Every door is open to you."

Conrad was silent. Then he said: "*was*."

"You mean to tell me you've taken up with that young man just to get through a few doors? It's grotesque."

"How the hell else am I supposed to get through? Who else would take me? I'm a forty-year-old faggot without a cent to my name."

"That's only temporary, Con."

"You're damn right it is. Any minute now, I'm going to be a forty-*one*-year-old faggot without a cent to my name. And stop laughing! Rodney's getting restless. The young always do. They wake up one morning and they *see* you. That's why I always insist on separate rooms. Never let your lover see you, Michael. It's death." Conrad held out his goblet. "If anyone turns up here tonight, it's only going to be because Rodney Farquhar asked them. I may be the attraction— but it's Rodney's circus."

Michael said, "That's ridiculous" and poured more scotch.

"It's not ridiculous. Alas," said Conrad, lying back in the bath. "I overheard him on the phone. '*Do come and see old Conrad again. He's so amusing. Tells such wonderful funny stories. Even gets drunk and falls down . . . but never loses consciousness. I tell you, it's a scream. He once had a whole conversation with the Princess of Rheims lying flat on his back in the middle of the floor. The whole room flocked to him. People were actually introduced while he lay there. The footmen brought him drinks and got on their knees to serve him.*' I heard him, Michael. He could sell tickets. But I can't. I'm the one they all come to see, lying down on the rug. You do have a rug, I hope."

Michael could see Conrad, now. The steam was beginning to dissipate. His skin was alarmingly pale; his arms and shoulders lacked entirely the tension of muscles; his neck was like a girl's, stretching to hold the tremulous chin in place and the large, round head with its dank, stringy hair seemed unable to contain his skull which pushed against the skin like a swollen melon about to burst. His hands were almost ridiculously fine; waxen, beautifully shaped and manicured. . . .

"Please stop staring," said Conrad. "Tell me about Olivia."

Michael did not say all of this that follows. He only said the parts he could articulate. The rest—the precision and the syntax—were in his mind, but silent under a cloud of scotch and daydreams. Downstairs, he could hear Olivia setting the table in the dining room—telling Rodney she didn't have anything that matched by way of crystal and china—all because Mrs. Kemp had her own definition of the word "set": "*break eight and leave four. . . .*" Rodney could also be heard on the telephone, ordering food from Fenton's. Grendel was found in the hall closet and came up the stairs to lie outside the bathroom door.

Michael said: "When you said you always insisted on separate rooms. I understood. Our bed—Olivia's and mine—is divided down the middle by the Grand Canyon. We might as well live in separate hotels."

Conrad glanced at Michael, huge and majestic, just a shape in the steam: backlit—hovering on the toilet seat—holding both the bottle and his goblet—his head turned sideways, looking for the words. Michael was six foot four and he had a club foot that no one ever talked about. It affected his walk, of course, but not outrageously and on the occasions when it pained him, he would remove the boot and rest the foot on a table or a chair. He was resting it now on the edge of the tub.

*She's gone away somewhere*, Con: *gone without going, of course.*

Conrad waved his hand in the soapy water, watching it vanish.

*Now what am I? A sort of bachelor, living in her house: always on the periphery of Olivia's life. "Goodbye, Michael." "Goodbye, Olivia." "I'm going to the other end of the sofa, now." Gone. Like that.*

I saw a movie once. One of those "Nature of Things" on the CBC. It was a film about some tribe in Borneo. One of those primitive tribes—still living almost a prehistoric existence. Ceremonial killings. Sexual segregation. Ritual circumcision. Unbelievable savagery. The way they treated one another—slaughtered their animals—slaughtered their enemies. Three things stood out: three I will never forget. One was the pig thing.

The women with children lived in special houses—groups of women and children—until the children grew to be a certain age. And they had these pigs, you see, as pets. The women and the babies and pigs all lived together and, the way it was shown, they seemed to be quite happy. Then the men would decide it was time to have a nice feast of pork and they would come and drag away the pigs and they would kill them. The women's pets, you see. The children's pets. But it was only the men who got to eat them. Pork was supposed to induce some special kind of magic. So off they went—the men—to their bachelors' quarters where they'd roast these pigs and sit around having magic dreams.

Another thing was the women killing their babies. But only their boy babies. Only their boys. But it wasn't always . . . I mean, they didn't necessarily kill every boy.

What you have to know is, the women did all the work. The only thing they didn't do was hunt. But everything else was left up to them and they had to do it all with their babies on their backs and their children dragging along behind them. You could see it must drive them mad; all these children and all this work and, all of a sudden, there would be this moment when one of them would take off down to the river. Where she would drown her baby son. Not quite dispassionately—certainly with anger—but suddenly: coldly—methodically—without remorse. It was awful. You knew it was revenge for how the men had made them live and for what the men had done to their pigs.

And then there was this other thing—the third thing I remember.

This is about the bachelors. Even the husbands were "bachelors." And they moved in and out of the women's lives—mating with them—not "making love" but truly mating, animal style. And stealing their pigs and watching the women—always from a distance. There were these huts—retreats—high up in the mountains where the bachelors went. Also, there were these compounds where the growing boys were kept. Not just kept with the men—but, really, kept apart from the women. And this was some kind of privilege. Different, you see, from the dowdy huts and the little, crowded farmyards where the women lived with all the pigs and babies. The men and boys had contests. They played games and laughed. They created a culture of male totems. . . .

"Why?" said Conrad.

"Fear," said Michael.

That was the basis of it. Fear. Partly disgust and a sort of mystical distrust of the women because of menstruation. But also a childlike fear of the power of women to give birth. And this fear was real and so tacit that, even though the men had segregated the women—even though they had succeeded in debasing them and disinheriting them, the women taunted the men. And they got away with it. They stood on the hillsides in groups and they laughed at the men in the compounds and they dared the boys to come out and have sexual intercourse. Dared them with all kinds of lewd, graphic gestures and always laughing. And, of course, the boys wouldn't go. They were afraid. They backed off. They hid. Or else, they came outside the compound in an army and they'd kill the pigs. Sometimes, too, they made war on their neighbors. Anything, rather than go to the women.

"Are you sure it was really the women they were afraid of?"

Michael did not answer this.

Conrad pulled the plug and the water began to surge toward the drain. He lay back watching it ebbing, revealing his pallid, hairless body.

"Anyhow, that's how I see myself now," Michael said. "A kind of ritual bachelor, living in retreat. Taunted from the hillsides. Being watched and listened to. But silently . . . "

"What about her pigs?"

Michael thought of the yelling matches and the slamming doors and the undone, promised things. He also thought of the silence with which Olivia seemed to be rebuking him. "I guess I've killed a few," he said. "But I haven't had the benefit of any God damn magic dreams."

The last of the water drew away with a great, loud sucking noise and was gone. Conrad lay there in the empty tub, with his goblet in his hand and his toes sticking up.

After a moment, he spoke and he said, "This is how they found my father. Just exactly three years ago. The twenty-ninth of April. With his wrists slashed."

"Today's the twenty-eighth," said Michael.

Outside the bathroom door, Grendel threw up the remnants of Mrs. Kemp's toona sandwich. It was now 6:45. The guests would arrive at eight and still no one knew—but Rodney—who they would be.

"Conrad wants an egg."

"But we're going to eat in an hour-and-a-half."

"I don't think he wants it to eat," said Michael."

"He's going to throw it at someone, is that it?" Olivia was undoing the boxes from Fenton's and setting the contents in bowls and soufflé dishes. Rodney was arranging her flowers in crystal vases on the cutting board.

"All I know is, he wants an egg."

"He wants it to lift his face with," said Rodney. "If you have a pastry brush, you'd better send that up, too. And a nice little dish to separate the egg in."

"Has he been doing this long?" Michael asked.

"About a year," said Rodney. "And only at parties. It makes him look Chinese."

"All we need," said Michael. "The Empress of China."

They arrived in the first warm rain.

There was a girl whose name was Louellen Potts who had once been one of Michael's students. She was now out taking care of other people's children in a daycare center, wasting her talents as a first rate critic. She had come, this evening, ostensibly as Rodney's "date"—but she seemed to have an ulterior motive: at least, in Michael's view. She was one of those dreadful women who hound you with their beauty while they beat you with their mind. Michael cringed from the thought of what lay ahead: Louellen attempting to best him at every turn in the conversation, opening one and then two more buttons of her blouse and thrusting her breasts into the lamplight. If only she were less attractive, he could be sure of winning.

Olivia rather liked Louellen Potts. She was one of perhaps six students both she and Michael had encountered in the classroom and the lecture hall over the years. What Olivia instilled from *Heart of Darkness*, Michael destroyed with *Frankenstein*. Kurtz and the Monster, walking hand in hand: *that* was the future, according to Michael.

When Fabiana Holbach Powell arrived, she was not with her husband, but her husband's brother Tom and Tom's wife Betty. Fabiana's husband, Jackman, was enigmatically "abroad." The word "abroad" was delivered by Tom, while Fabiana looked the other way.

They had drunk for half-an-hour, waiting for Conrad to come downstairs. Michael put on some passable tapes (acceptable to everyone, that is, except Louellen) and the atmosphere was actually bearable. Under the influence of Cleo Laine, things loosened up a bit. The sailing voice cut through the dreadful, early chit-chat and very soon people were asking freely for "another scotch" or another glass of white wine. If only Louellen would stop exposing herself, life might be endurable.

Tom Powell was a cold-eyed blond who had just come back from Nassau. He had one of those infuriating tans and an even more infuriating physique. He didn't say much. The eyes said it all. They never left Fabiana, unless they were turned on Michael (perhaps "*through*" Michael would be more accurate) during the course of such questions as: "When was the last time we saw you?" and statements, such as the patently ridiculous: "You're looking well, Mike."

Betty Powell just sat on the sofa and rummaged in her pocket book for something she never found.

Fabiana, on the other hand, was radiant—as always. She carried with her—just as she had as a child—that wonderful and wondrous sense of someone always on the verge of imparting the secret of life, if only she could remember the wording. Her gaze would drift away towards the answer—beautiful and oddly heartbreaking—only to return yet again with the words; "no—that's not it . . . " implicit in the wounded, blue confusion of her eyes. She had once been kidnapped and the ransom had been a million dollars. Lucien Holbach, her father, had refused to pay it—even though he had sixty millions and his wife twenty millions more. Fabiana had escaped, unharmed.

Or had she? Michael wondered.

At any rate, she had escaped and, shortly thereafter, she had been married to Jackman Powell—who was currently "abroad." She claimed to have never seen her captors, having been forced to wear a blindfold the whole time. It was when, after hours of silence, she had discovered she was standing in the middle of an empty house that she made her escape. All of this had happened in Jamaica: a place to which Fabiana had never returned.

Years and years and years ago—when they were children—Conrad Fastbinder had fallen in love with Fabiana Holbach and, for a while—in later years, before the kidnap, it seemed that Fabiana might return his love. But three things had happened in rapid succession, dashing all those hopes forever: until now. Fastbinder's father had died, leaving him penniless: Fabiana had been kidnapped and Jackman Powell—("that son-of-a-bitch!")—had married her.

Tonight, through some fortuitous twist of fate, she had turned up in Michael and Olivia Penny's living room without her husband—and only her brother-in-law ("that other son-of-a-bitch!") to watch over her.

Conrad waited for Cleo to begin singing "*Traces*" before he made his entrance.

"*A faded photograph,*
*Covered, now, with lines and creases . . .*"

Fabiana claimed not to recognize him.

Michael, never having seen his friend in lacquer before, tended to agree with Fabiana. Conrad, decked out in summer whites and with his hair plastered back, looked like someone trying to escape from a Somerset Maugham short story. His tie was a florid pink (admittedly, in fashion, if you glanced at the right magazines) and he reeked of Chanel 19. As for the face—it was true. Conrad Fastbinder had descended from the upper reaches in a Chinese mask.

The trouble was, he couldn't speak—whether because of all the scotch he had drunk in the afternoon, or because of the strictures of his "facelift" or, perhaps, because of both. As a consequence, he merely bowed over Fabiana's hand, and kissed it—after which, they all went in to dinner.

Michael sat at the head of the table, leaning back in his chair. He was turned to one side in order to accommodate his foot which increasingly troubled him as the evening wore on. He watched his guests—or rather, Conrad's guests, through a haze of pain and liquor.

Far off, he could just make out Olivia seated at the other end of the table. She was smiling—oh rare event—and, though the smile was somewhat fixed, it appeared to be genuine. What could she be smiling about? Michael regretted he had not begun to count as soon as the smile had turned up—just to see how long it would stay. It was rather like a visitor: another guest at the table: a stranger. He should keep a little book, like Hamlet: "My tables—meet it is, I set it down . . . Olivia smiled today for twenty seconds."

Why?

Michael looked around the table.

See who's here; he thought. All the bachelors. This is a bachelors' dinner. Rodney, Conrad, me. And Tom Powell—*he's* a bachelor. So's his wife. Look at them! I bet they touch each other with tongs. Or perhaps they wear gloves. Louellen Potts is a bachelor. (Damn it.) So is Fabiana.

So is Olivia.

Every damn one of us, living alone.

Here we are on the hillside—having killed the pig—and about to fall beneath the spell of the magic dream, perhaps.

Louellen Potts was sitting beside him: green eyed and green in tailored tweed. Breathtaking: youthful. Budding. Hair that falls—every hair in place and smelling of skin and flesh, no perfumes, only air and apples and sitting with one hand near his own, turned up—so innocent—or was that innocence? Maybe it was disdain. Knowing the harmless impotence of pockmarked hosts in their cups . . .

*Not pockmarked.* No. Do not go cruel into that good face. Be kinder. Kinder to yourself. Be kind.

Then, on the other side of the table, next to that blazered booby—Rodney Farquhar, pal and pudendum to the fallen Conrad—there was someone weeping.

Fabiana.

Was it true? Was she weeping?

Tom had told the tale at dinner—the dinner just finished, the one whose little bones were scattered under the grape seeds even now mounting on the plates as the bachelors lingered over their wine.

Tom, without saying so, had made it clear that Fabiana was waiting for a divorce. Her husband, his brother Jackman, had disappeared. He was a civil engineer—or something—and, though Fabiana's lawyers (working, of course for *him*) had told her he had "left her" and had gone somewhere, they would not say where. Not precisely. Only "into the Amazon region." That was all. That was how they had put it to her: "Jackman has gone"—into roughly speaking one million square green miles of rain forest. Now, he had been gone eight months and the lawyers had said, "he is probably not coming back."

So she could not get a divorce. She could only wait the mandatory seven years, after which she could declare herself a widow. Not that Jackman would be dead. He had gone there with her money. It was the money that was dead.

There was more, of course. Money. Enough for Conrad to cultivate, if he'd only take that egg off his face.

Michael watched Fabiana.

Just as Olivia's badge was neatness, Fabiana's badge was a restless wrist—her left—which she constantly massaged with her right hand, adjusting her watch and her bracelets and her bones, while the wrist turned slowly, this way and that. She also never looked at whoever was speaking, but set her eyes on those who were listening, watching perhaps for some clue as to the importance and meaning of what was being said. Now, it was Olivia who was speaking and Fabiana was watching Betty Powell, her sister-in-law. Betty Powell was cutting up an apple with a knife and there was blood on her napkin, of which she seemed to be entirely unaware.

Olivia was still smiling.

The subject under discussion had been famous mistresses and who had performed that function best in history. Olivia had just said something startling and amusing and even Michael was laughing.

Olivia had suggested that Antinous, the beloved of the Emperor Hadrian, had been the world's greatest mistress.

"Why?" Louellen Potts has asked.

"Because," Olivia had answered, "he couldn't bear children."

"Do you mean he couldn't stand them?" Betty asked. "Or just that he couldn't have them . . . "

She was ignored.

It was then that disaster struck, as it will out of silence.

Thinking he spoke in a confidential tone, and being quite drunk, Conrad turned towards Michael and reached out his hand as if to emphasize his words. As a result of the gesture, he knocked over Betty Powell's glass. Wine and blood and an apple core.

But that was not the disaster. The disaster was in what he said.

What he said was, "There's your answer, Michael. You and Olivia should have a baby."

Michael said: "Thanks for the advice and shut up."

Conrad said; "Oh, I see . . . " and he laughed. "You're afraid Olivia will kill it."

For a moment, there was only the sound of dripping wine and of someone breathing and then Louellen Potts turned down the table in Conrad's direction and said, "Do you think that's funny, Mr. Fastbinder? Do you really think that's funny?" Then she turned to Michael and she said, "Why don't you hit him? If I were you, I'd hit him."

"You are not me, Miss Potts," said Michael. He was looking at Olivia, who looked away.

Now, Louellen turned to her and she said, "Mrs. Penny? Don't you want to be defended?"

Olivia didn't answer her. She was looking at her napkin.

"Really, Professor Penny," Louellen said—still standing—"I think it is outrageous. And if you won't hit him, I will!''

"Sit down, Potts." (Michael)

"I will not sit down! This appalling man has just said the most appalling thing about your wife and . . . "

"SIT DOWN!"

"Michael . . . " This was Olivia. "Leave her alone."

"I beg your pardon," said Michael, alarmed, his voice rising. "I beg your bloody pardon?"

"You heard her," said Louellen—somewhat tipsy herself. "She says you're to leave me alone."

Michael said, "You condescending green-eyed bitch!"

"Michael!" said Olivia.

"Don't you 'Michael' me—you down there in the dark! What the hell right has she to put herself in my shoes?"

"She's only expressing her feelings, Michael. And whether or not they're valid, she has a right to express them."

"Not at my table, she hasn't!"

"This is our table, Michael. Not your table. Ours." Olivia did not even raise her voice.

Michael snapped. "Well she's sitting at my end."

And Louellen said, with great vehemence, "*Standing!*"

And suddenly, everyone was laughing. Everyone, that is, except the Powells. They did not seem to know what to do in the presence of laughter.

Louellen Potts sat down and there was then a second, but minor disaster. Her hand had fallen onto the table rather near Michael's. And now, unthinking, Michael took it—merely as a gesture of forgiveness. Except that he did not let go.

Louellen looked at the table, not quite focusing on her upturned fingers resting under Michael's hand. Her main awareness was of Olivia's eyes.

Michael felt the reverberation and he, too, became aware of Olivia's eyes. He turned his hand away slowly and withdrew it all the way back to his head, where he pushed back his hair.

"Conrad," he said.

"Yes, sir," said Conrad.

"Tell us about the time you got lost in that hotel and ended up in Princess Diana's bedroom."

In the living room, Conrad was lying on the rug, smoking a cigarette and staring at the ceiling. Michael, limping as unobtrusively as possible, was going about the room and bestowing second brandies into upheld glasses, including Conrad's.

Beyond them, the dining room glowed in the flickering light of its guttering candles. The table was an ordered ruin, with its eight distinct place settings, each distinctly destroyed by a separate pair of hands; the eight plates marred with the elegant parings of apples and cheese and pears; the wine glasses emptied to an exact degree, each one a signature; and the napkins, folded or thrown down and the chairs pushed back, reflective or violent or simply dispensed with—and the low, silver bowl of freesia, the flowers drooping as if they had been assaulted—and the mirrors that reflected mirrors that reflected mirrors—each one holding its perfect image a further remove, like sign posts down a road that led into darkness.

Rodney was playing the piano.

Otherwise—silence.

Olivia returned from the hallway, having opened the front door to let in some air. Outside, there was a spring rain and the strong smell of budding. She picked up her glass—allowed Michael to fill it—touched him with her pensiveness as he passed—and leaned against the door jamb, neither here nor there.

It was warm—and Fabiana's wrist was moving.

Slowly—it was imperceptible at first—as if a butterfly had entered the room and caught their attention only by degrees—Fabiana began to talk. She began in the middle of some interior monologue that perhaps had occupied her for some time—which yet seemed pertinent to the monologue of each of the others; one long sentence describing their mutual apprehension, whether it be about the past or the present or the future; arising out of that common literature which is the mind, peopled with common characters, moving over a common landscape, like a book they had all read—from which now one of their voices began to quote aloud:

" . . . I know he went there without me in order to escape me. And yet I never bothered or pursued him. I was always standing still, it seems. I hadn't wanted him at first; but only let myself be wanted. The way a dog will let itself be wanted, not understanding why, except that out of being wanted—wanting comes. And out of being chosen—choosing. And out of being longed for—longing. Con knows. I never gave my loving. Never trusted myself to give. Never let it happen. I was always the little sister—sitting in the front seat, watching in the mirror. Until I met him—Jackman Powell. He was like a drug you take at a party, for fun. And then you wonder what it was. And then you ask for more. And then you realize you're hooked. And you never stop to think they've hooked you on purpose. You only think what a lovely feeling it is—and all you want is more. Until one day, they refuse. *There isn't any more.* Or worse, *there is—but I'm not going to let you have it.* And then they hold it up—they keep on holding it up where you can see it—and saying to you: *no; no more, Fabiana. Never any more.* And then they shoot it into the air, they waste it before your eyes. And they walk away—and they leave you with this empty syringe—and nothing to fill it with. And nothing to fill your veins with. And they haven't told you what it was—so you don't know how to ask for more. Because it was unique; it was *theirs*—they grew it, manufactured it or conjured it out of the air. And then they get on a boat and they don't even wave good-bye. And they're gone. And then you get a message—telling you they've disappeared forever."

Nobody watched her while she finished.

Instead, they each one welcomed the anaesthetic that prevented, if only for the moment, the idea that hope itself—anticipation—had disappeared for all of them into the Amazon region along with Jackman Powell.

Michael looked with a dreadful panic at Olivia.

Louellen Potts—the briefest of his dreams—got up to leave the room.

"It's time to go," she whispered, having lost her voice in Fabiana's recitation. "Late," she said. And went upstairs to collect her coat.

3:00 a.m. and Grendel made a tour of the house, making his presence known to all the mice and to all the ghosts who haunted the dark, including the dark at the edge of everyone's dreams. Finally, he settled at the foot of the stairs, intermittently waking to stare out the open door through the screen at the sidewalks sparkling with rain—and to listen to the droning in the den, which to Grendel was like a cave, inhabited by bears or perhaps by giant, cave-dwelling birds whose wings were lifted in constant repetition, casting their immense shadows across the floor towards his paws. Michael's curtains. He eyed them with a careful wariness. He never completely slept. When there was thunder, the piano would echo its dying reverberations and the cello, in its corner, would hum a low, solemn note. The crystal prisms that hung from the candlesticks also sang and the dying fire in the grate made another song and the floorboards creaked in the faraway sun room and the windows sighed all over the house.

His ears hurt—chewed in a week-old battle—and his gums were tender, having been torn. All along his back, he ached. No position was comfortable.

Everyone had gone upstairs—and he was alone. All the food—anything of real interest—was locked away. Except . . .

One bone, he remembered—put down by Michael under the kitchen table.

Grendel got up and fetched the bone and brought it back to the foot of the stairs. All through the next hour, he held it tenderly between his paws and wrecked it—very slowly—with his chipped and broken teeth.

The sound of gnawing—bone against bone—was all that could be heard. That, and the sluicing of the rain. And Olivia's voice, as she lay in the bed with her gaze on the patterns running down the walls.

"Michael . . . ?"

She was smiling.

Far in the Amazon region, a pin dropped.

# MORDECAI RICHLER

1931–

Mordecai Richler was born on St. Urbain Street in the Jewish quarter of Montreal. His father, an immigrant from Galicia, was a junk dealer. Richler attended Baron Byng High School (identified in his fiction as Fletcher's Field) and Sir George Williams University, but left before graduating. He went to Paris in 1951 and began his first novel. He returned to Canada in 1953, worked briefly for the CBC, and left again in 1954 for England, where he lived for the next eighteen years. Supporting himself as a freelance writer, Richler wrote scripts for television and such films as *Life at the Top* and *No Love for Johnny*. In 1972 he returned to live permanently in Canada. His best novels, *The Apprenticeship of Duddy Kravitz*, (1959) and *St. Urbain's Horseman* (1971), are based on his experiences of growing up in poverty in Montreal.

## Benny, the War in Europe, and Myerson's Daughter Bella

When Benny was sent overseas in the autumn of 1941 his father, Mr. Garber, thought that if he had to give up one son to the army, it might as well be Benny who was a quiet boy, and who wouldn't push where he shouldn't; and Mrs. Garber thought: "my Benny he'll take care, he'll watch out;" and Benny's brother Abe thought "when he comes back, I'll have a garage of my own, you bet, and I'll be able to give him a job." Benny wrote every week, and every week the Garbers sent him parcels full of good things that a Jewish boy should always have, like salami and pickled herring and *shtrudel*. The food parcels were always the same, and the letters—coming from Camp Borden and Aldershot and Normandy and Holland—were always the same too. They began—"I hope you are all well and good"—and ended—"don't worry, all the best to everybody, thank you for the parcel."

When Benny came home from the war in Europe, the Garbers

didn't make much of a fuss. They met him at the station, of course, and they had a small dinner for him.

Abe was thrilled to see Benny again. "Atta boy," was what he kept saying all evening, "Atta boy, Benny."

"You shouldn't go back to the factory," Mr. Garber said. "You don't need the old job. You can be a help to your brother Abe in his garage."

"Yes," Benny said.

"Let him be, let him rest," Mrs. Garber said, "What'll happen if he doesn't work for two weeks?"

"Hey, when Artie Segal came back," Abe said, "he said that in Italy there was nothing that a guy couldn't get for a couple of Sweet Caps. Was he shooting me the bull, or what?"

Benny had been discharged and sent home, not because the war was over, but because of the shrapnel in his leg, but he didn't limp too badly and he didn't talk about his wound or the war, so at first nobody noticed that he had changed. Nobody, that is, except Myerson's daughter Bella.

Myerson was the proprietor of Pop's Cigar & Soda, on Laurier Street, and any day of the week, you could find him there seated on a worn, peeling kitchen chair playing poker with the men of the neighbourhood. He had a glass-eye and when a player hesitated on a bet, he would take it out and polish it, a gesture that never failed to intimidate. His daughter, Bella, worked behind the counter. She had a club foot and mousy hair and some more hair on her face, and although she was only twenty-six, it was generally supposed that she would end up an old maid. Anyway she was the one—the first one—who noticed that the war in Europe had changed Benny. And, as a matter of fact, the very first time he came into the store after his homecoming she said to him: "What's wrong, Benny? Are you afraid?"

"I'm all right," he said.

Benny was a quiet boy. He was short and skinny with a long narrow face, a pulpy mouth that was somewhat crooked, and soft black eyes. He had big conspicuous hands, which he preferred to keep out of sight in his pockets. In fact, he seemed to want to keep out of sight altogether and whenever possible, he stood behind a chair or in a dim light so that people wouldn't notice him—and, noticing him, chase him away. When he failed the ninth grade at Baron Byng High School, his class-master, a Mr. Perkins, had sent him home with a note saying: "Benjamin is not a student, but he has all the makings of a good citizen. He is honest and attentive in class and a hard worker. I recommend that he learn a trade."

And when Mr. Garber had read what his son's teacher had written, he had shaken his head and crumpled up the bit of paper and said,—"A trade?"—he had looked at his boy and shaken his head and said—"A trade?"

Mrs. Garber had said stoutly, "Haven't you got a trade?"

"Shapiro's boy will be a doctor," Mr. Garber had said.

"Shapiro's boy," Mrs. Garber said.

And afterwards, Benny had retrieved the note and smoothed out the creases and put it in his pocket, where it had remained. For Benny was sure that one day a policeman, or perhaps even a Mountie, would try to arrest him, and then the paper that Mr. Perkins had written so long ago might prove helpful.

Benny figured that he had been lucky, truly lucky, to get away with living for so long. Oh, he had his dreams. He would have liked to have been an aeroplane pilot, or still better, to have been born rich or intelligent. Those kind of people, he had heard, slept in mornings until as late as nine o'clock. But he had been born stupid, people could tell that, just looking at him, and one day they would come to take him away. They would, sure as hell they would.

The day after his return to Montreal, Benny showed up at Abe's garage having decided that he didn't want two weeks off. That pleased Abe a lot. "I can see that you've matured since you've been away," Abe said. "That's good. That counts for you in this world."

Abe worked very hard, he worked night and day, and he believed that having Benny with him would give his business an added kick. "That's my kid brother Benny," Abe used to tell the cabbies. "Four years in the infantry, two of them up front. A tough hombre, let me tell you."

For the first few weeks Abe was very pleased with Benny. "He's slow," he thought, "no genius of a mechanic, but the customers like him and he'll learn." Then Abe began to notice things. When business was slow, Benny—instead of taking advantage of the lull to clean up the shop—used to sit shivering in a dim corner, with his hands folded tight on his lap. The first time Abe noticed his brother behaving like that, he said: "What's wrong? You got a chill?"

"No. I'm all right."

"You want to go home, or something?"

"No."

Then, when Abe began to notice him sitting like that more and more, he pretended not to see. "He needs time," he thought. But whenever it rained, and it rained often that spring, Benny was not to be found around the garage, and that put Abe in a bad temper. Until one day during a thunder shower, Abe tried the toilet door and found that it was locked. "Benny," he yelled, "come on out, I know you're in there."

Benny didn't answer, so Abe got the key. He found Benny huddled up in a corner with his head buried in his knees, trembling, with sweat running down his face in spite of the cold.

"It's raining," Benny said.

"Benny, get up. What's wrong?"

"Go away," Benny said. "It's raining."

"I'll get a doctor, Benny. I'll. . . ."

"Don't—you mustn't. Go away. Please, Abe."

"But Benny. . . ."

A terrible chill must have overcome Benny just then for he began to shake violently, just as if an inner whip had been cracked. Then, after it had passed, he looked up at Abe dumbly, his mouth hanging open. "It's raining," he said.

His discovery that afternoon gave Abe a good scare, and the next morning he went to see his father. "It was awful spooky, Paw," Abe said. "I don't know what to do with him."

"The war left him with a bad taste," Mrs. Garber said. "It made him something bad."

"Other boys went to war," Abe said.

"Shapiro's boy," Mr. Garber said, "was an officer."

"Shapiro's boy," Mrs. Garber said. "You give him a vacation, Abe. You insist. He's a good boy. From the best. He'll be all right."

Benny did not know what to do with his vacation so he tried sleeping in late like the rich and the intelligent, but in the late morning hours he dreamed bad dreams and that made him very frightened so he gave up that kind of thing. He did not dare go walking because he was sure people could tell, just looking at him, that he was not working, and he did not want others to think that he was a bum. So he began to do odd jobs for people in the neighbourhood. He repaired bicycles and toasters and lamps. But he did not take any money for his work and that made people a little afraid. "Isn't our money good enough for him? All right, he was wounded, so maybe I was the one who shot him?"

Benny began to hang around Pop's Cigar & Soda.

"I don't like it, Bella," Mr. Myerson said, admiring the polish of his glass eye against the light. "I need him here like I need a cancer."

"Something's wrong with him psychologically," one of the card players said.

But obviously Bella liked having Benny around, and after a while Mr. Myerson stopped complaining. "Maybe the boy is serious," he thought, "and what with her club-foot and all that stuff on her face, I can't start picking and choosing. Beside, it's not as if he was a crook!"

Bella and Benny did not talk much when they were together,

afraid, perhaps, that whatever it was that was "starting" up between them, was rich in delicacy, and would be soiled by ordinary words. She used to knit, he used to smoke. He would watch silently as she limped about the store, silently, with longing, and burning hope and consternation. The letter from Mr. Perkins was in his pocket. He wanted to tell her about the war—about things.

"I was walking with the sergeant. He reached into his pocket to show me a letter from his wife when. . . ."

There he would stop. A twitching would start around his eyes and he would swallow hard and stop.

Bella would look up from her knitting, waiting for him the way a mother waits for a child to be reasonable, knowing that it is only a question of time. But Benny would begin to shiver, and, looking down at the floor, grip his hands together until the knuckles went white. Around five in the afternoon he would get up and leave without saying a word. Bella would give him a stack of magazines to take home and at night he would read them all from cover to cover and the next morning he would bring them back as clean as new. Then he would sit with her in the store again, looking down at the floor or at his hands, as though he were in great pain. Time passed, and one day instead of going home around five in the afternoon he went upstairs with her. Mr. Myerson, who was watching, smiled happily. He turned to Mr. Shub and said: "If I had a boy of my own, I couldn't wish for a better one than Benny."

"Look who's counting his chickens already," Mr. Shub said.

Benny's vacation continued for several weeks and every morning he sat down in the store and stared at his hands, as if he expected them to have changed overnight, and every evening he went upstairs with Bella pretending not to have heard the remarks, the good-natured observations that had been made by the card-players as they passed.

Until, one afternoon, she said to him: "I'm going to have a baby."

"All right," Benny said.

"Aren't you even going to say luck or something?"

Benny got up and bit his lower lip and gripped his hands together hard. "If you only knew what I have seen," he said.

They had a very simple wedding without speeches in a small synagogue and after the ceremony was over Abe slapped his younger brother's back and said, "Atta boy, Benny. Atta boy."

"Can I come back to work?"

"Sure, of course you can. You're the old Benny again," Abe said. "I can see that."

And when Mr. Garber got home, without much more to expect but getting older, and more tired earlier in the day, he turned to his wife and said: "Shapiro's boy married into the Segals."

"Shapiro's boy," Mrs. Garber said.

Benny went back to the garage but this time he settled down to work hard and that pleased Abe a good deal. "That's my kid brother, Benny," Abe used to tell the cabbies, "married six weeks and he's already got one in the oven. A quick worker, I'll tell you."

Benny settled down to work hard and when the baby was born he even laughed a little and began to save money and plan things, but every now and then, usually when there was a slack period at the garage, Benny would shut up tight and sit in a chair in a dark corner and stare at his hands. Bella was good with him. She never raised her voice to say an ugly thing, and when he woke up screaming from a dream about the war in Europe she would stroke his neck and say tender things. He, on the other hand, began to speak to her confidentially.

"Bella?"

"Yes."

"I killed a man."

"What? You what? When did you. . . ."

"In the war."

"Oh, in the war. For a moment I—A German you mean. . . ."

"Yes, a German."

"If you ask me it's too bad you didn't kill a dozen. Those Germans I. . . ."

"I killed him with my hands."

"Go to sleep."

"Bella?"

"Yes."

"Are you ashamed that I. . . ."

"Go to sleep."

"I saw babies killed," he said. "What if. . . ."

"There won't be another war. Don't worry about our baby."

"But. . . ."

"Sleep. Go to sleep."

The baby grew into a fine, husky boy, and whenever there was a parade Benny used to hoist him on his shoulders so that he could see better. He was amazed, truly amazed, that he could have had such a beautiful child. He hardly had nightmares at all any more and he became talkative and somewhat shrewd. One night he came home and said: "Abe is going to open a branch on Mount Royal Street. I'm going to manage it. I'm going to be a partner in it."

So Benny finally threw away the paper that Mr. Perkins had written for him so long ago. They bought a car and planned, the following year, to have enough money saved so that Bella could go to a clinic in the United States to have an operation on her club foot. "I can assure you that I'm not going to spend such a fortune to make myself beautiful," Bella said, "and plainly speaking I'm not doing it for you. But I don't want that when the boy is old enough to go to school that he should be teased because his mother is a cripple."

Then, a month before Bella was to go to the clinic, they went to see their first cinemascope film. Now, previous to that evening, Bella had made a point never to take Benny along to see a war film, no matter who was playing in it. So as soon as the newsreel came on—it was that special one about the hydrogen bomb tests—she knew that she had made a mistake in bringing Benny with her, cinemascope or no cinemascope. She turned to him quickly. "Don't look," she said.

But Benny was enthralled. He watched the explosion, and he watched as the newsreel showed by means of diagrams what a hydrogen bomb could do to a city the size of New York—never mind Montreal.

Then he got up and left.

When Bella got home that night she found Benny huddled up in a dark corner with his head buried in his knees, trembling, with sweat running down his face. She tried to stroke his neck but he moved away from her.

"Should I send for a doctor?"

"Bella," he said. "Bella, Bella."

"Try to relax," she said. "Try to think about something pretty. Flowers, or something. Try for the boy's sake."

"Bella," he said. "Bella, Bella."

When she woke up the next morning he was still crouching there in the dark corner gripping his hand together tight, and he wouldn't eat or speak—not even to the boy.

The living-room was in a mess, papers spilled everywhere, as if he had been searching for something.

Finally—it must have been around noon—he put on his hat and walked out of the house. She knew right then that she should have stopped him. That she shouldn't have let him go. She knew.

Her father came around at five o'clock and she could tell from the expression on his face that she had guessed right. Mr. and Mrs. Garber were with him.

"He's dead?" Bella asked.

"Shapiro's boy, the doctor," Mr. Garber said, "said it was quick."

"Shapiro's boy," Mrs. Garber said.

"It wasn't the driver's fault," Mr. Myerson said.

"I know," Bella said.

# ALICE MUNRO

1931–

Born in the farming community of Wingham in southeastern Ontario, Alice Laidlaw Munro was the eldest of three children. She attended the University of Western Ontario, graduating in Honours English in 1952. She moved to British Columbia with her husband, James Munro, a classmate she had married the previous year, living first in Vancouver, where she worked as an assistant in the Vancouver Public Library, and then in Victoria, where she and her husband owned a book store. They had three children. When the Munroes separated, she returned to Ontario, where she now lives with her second husband, Gerald Fremlin. Her fiction is deeply rooted in the environment of rural eastern Ontario, a part of the country Munro has described as "gothic." She has written four collections of short stories with interrelated characters and locations.

## Something I've Been Meaning to Tell You

"Anyway he knows how to fascinate the women," said Et to Char. She could not tell if Char went paler, hearing this, because Char was pale in the first place as anybody could get. She was like a ghost now, with her hair gone white. But still beautiful, she couldn't lose it.

"No matter to him the age or the size," Et pressed on. "It's natural to him as breathing, I guess. I only hope the poor things aren't taken in by it."

"I wouldn't worry," Char said.

The day before, Et had taken Blaikie Noble up on his invitation to go along on one of his tours and listen to his spiel. Char was asked too, but of course she didn't go. Blaikie Noble ran a bus. The bottom part of it was painted red and the top part was striped, to give the effect of an awning. On the side was painted: LAKESHORE TOURS, INDIAN GRAVES, LIMESTONE GARDENS, MILLIONAIRE'S MANSION, BLAIKIE NOBLE, DRIVER, GUIDE. Blaikie had a room at the hotel, and he also worked on the grounds, with one helper, cutting grass and clipping hedges and digging the borders. What a comedown, Et had said at the beginning of the summer when they first found out he was back. She and Char had known him in the old days.

So Et found herself squeezed into his bus with a lot of strangers, though before the afternoon was over she had made friends with a number of them and had a couple of promises of jackets needing letting out, as if she didn't have enough to do already. That was beside the point, the thing on her mind was watching Blaikie.

And what did he have to show? A few mounds with grass growing on them, covering dead Indians, a plot full of odd-shaped, grayish-white, dismal-looking limestone things—far-fetched imitations of plants (there could be the cemetery, if that was what you wanted)—and an old monstrosity of a house built with liquor money. He made the most of it. A historical discourse on the Indians, then a scientific discourse on the Limestone. Et had no way of knowing how much of it was true. Arthur would know. But Arthur wasn't there; there was nobody there but silly women, hoping to walk beside Blaikie to and from the sights, chat with him over their tea in the Limestone Pavilion, looking forward to having his strong hand under their elbows, the other hand brushing somewhere around the waist, when he helped them down off the bus ("I'm not a tourist," Et whispered sharply when he tried it on her).

He told them the house was haunted. The first Et ever heard of it, living ten miles away all her life. A woman had killed her husband, the son of the millionaire, at least it was believed she had killed him.

"How?" cried some lady, thrilled out of her wits.

"Ah, the ladies are always anxious to know the means, said Blaikie, in a voice like cream, scornful and loving,. "It was a slow—poison. Or that's what they said. This is all hearsay, all local gossip." (*Local my foot*, said Et to herself.) "She didn't appreciate his lady friends. The wife didn't. No."

He told them the ghost walked up and down in the garden, between two rows of blue spruce. It was not the murdered man who walked, but the wife, regretting. Blaikie smiled ruefully at the busload. At first Et had thought his attentions were all false, an ordinary commercial flirtation, to give them their money's worth. But gradually she was getting a different notion. He bent to each woman he talked to—it didn't matter how fat or scrawny or silly she was—as if there was one thing in her he would like to find. He had a gentle and laughing but ultimately serious, narrowing look (was that the look men finally had when they made love, that Et would never see?) that made him seem to want to be a deepsea diver diving down, down through all the emptiness and cold and wreckage to discover the one thing he had set his heart on, something small and precious, hard to locate, as a ruby maybe on the ocean floor. That was a look she would like to have described to Char. No doubt Char had seen it. But did she know how freely it was being distributed?

Char and Arthur had been planning a trip that summer to see Yellow-stone Park and the Grand Canyon, but they did not go. Arthur suffered a series of dizzy spells just at the end of school, and the doctor put him to bed. Several things were the matter with him. He was anemic, he had an irregular heartbeat, there was trouble with his kidneys. Et worried about leukemia. She woke at night, worrying.

"Don't be silly," said Char serenely. "He's overtired."

Arthur got up in the evenings and sat in his dressing gown. Blaikie Noble came to visit. He said his room at the hotel was a hole above the kitchen, they were trying to steam-cook him. It made him appreciate the cool of the porch. They played the games that Arthur loved, schoolteacher's games. They played a geography game, and they tried to see who could make the most words out of the name Beethoven. Arthur won. He got thirty-four. He was immensely delighted.

"You'd think you'd found the Holy Grail," Char said.

They played "Who Am I?" Each of them had to choose somebody to be—real or imaginary, living or dead, human or animal—and the others had to try to guess it in twenty questions. Et got who Arthur was on the thirteenth question. Sir Galahad.

"I never thought you'd get it so soon."

"I thought back to Char saying about the Holy Grail."

*"My strength is as the strength of ten,"* said Blaikie Noble, *"Because my heart is pure.* I didn't know I remembered that."

"You should have been King Arthur," Et said. "King Arthur is your namesake."

"I should have. King Arthur was married to the most beautiful woman in the world."

"Ha," said Et. "We all know the end of that story."

Char went into the living room and played the piano in the dark.

> The flowers that bloom in the spring, tra-la,
> Have nothing to do with the case. . . .

When Et arrived, out of breath, that past June, and said, "Guess who I saw downtown on the street?" Char, who was on her knees picking strawberries, said "Blaikie Noble."

"You've seen him."

"No," said Char. "I just knew. I think I knew by your voice."

A name that had not been mentioned between them for thirty years. Et was too amazed then to think of the explanation that came to her later. Why did it need to be a surprise to Char? There was a postal service in this country, there had been all along.

"I asked him about his wife," she said, "The one with the dolls." (As if Char wouldn't remember.) "He says she died a long time ago.

Not only that. He married another one and she's dead. Neither could have been rich. And where is all the Nobles' money, from the hotel?"

"We'll never know," said Char, and ate a strawberry.

The hotel had just recently been opened up again. The Nobles had given it up in the twenties and the town had operated it for a while as a hospital. Now some people from Toronto had bought it, renovated the dining room, put in a cocktail lounge, reclaimed the lawns and garden, though the tennis court seemed to be beyond repair. There was a croquet set put out again. People came to stay in the summers, but they were not the sort of people who used to come. Retired couples. Many widows and single ladies. Nobody would have walked a block to see them get off the boat, Et thought. Not that there was a boat any more.

The first time she met Blaikie Noble on the street she had made a point of not being taken aback. He was wearing a creamy suit and his hair, that had always been bleached by the sun, was bleached for good now, white.

"Blaikie, I knew either it was you or a vanilla ice-cream cone. I bet you don't know who I am."

"You're Et Desmond and the only thing different about you is you cut off your braids." He kissed her forehead, nervy as always.

"So you're back visiting old haunts," said Et, wondering who had seen that.

"Not visiting. Haunting." He told her then how he had got wind of the hotel opening up again, and how he had been doing this sort of thing, driving tour buses, in various places, in Florida and Banff. And when she asked he told her about his two wives. He never asked was she married, taking for granted she wasn't. He never asked if Char was, till she told him.

Et remembered the first time she understood that Char was beautiful. She was looking at a picture taken of them, of Char and herself and their brother who was drowned. Et was ten in the picture, Char fourteen and Sandy seven, just a couple of weeks short of all he would ever be. Et was sitting in an armless chair and Char was behind her, arms folded on the chair-back, with Sandy in his sailor suit cross-legged on the floor—or marble terrace, you would think, with the effect made by what had been nothing but a dusty, yellowing screen, but came out in the picture a pillar and draped curtain, a scene of receding poplars and fountains. Char had pinned her front hair up for the picture and was wearing a bright blue, ankle-length silk dress—of course the color did not show—with complicated black velvet piping. She was smiling slightly, with great composure. She could have been eighteen, she could have been twenty-two. Her beauty was not of the fleshy timid sort most often featured on calendars and cigar boxes of the period, but was sharp and delicate, intolerant, challenging.

Et took a long look at this picture and then went and looked at Char, who was in the kitchen. It was washday. The woman who came to help was pulling clothes through the wringer, and their mother was sitting down resting and staring through the screen door (she never got over Sandy, nobody expected her to). Char was starching her father's collars. He had a tobacco and candy store on the Square and wore a fresh collar every day. Et was prepared to find that some metamorphosis had taken place, as in the background, but it was not so. Char, bending over the starch basin, silent and bad-humored (she hated washday, the heat and steam and flapping sheets and chugging commotion of the machine—in fact, she was not fond of any kind of housework), showed in her real face the same almost disdainful harmony as in the photograph. This made Et understand, in some not entirely welcome way, that the qualities of legend were real, that they surfaced where and when you least expected. She had almost thought beautiful women were a fictional invention. She and Char would go down to watch the people get off the excursion boat, on Sundays, walking up to the Hotel. So much white it hurt your eyes, the ladies' dresses and parasols and the men's summer suits and Panama hats, not to speak of the sun dazzling on the water and the band playing. But looking closely at those ladies, Et found fault. Coarse skin or fat behind or chicken necks or dull nests of hair, probably ratted. Et did not let anything get by her, young as she was. At school she was respected for her self-possession and her sharp tongue. She was the one to tell you if you had been at the blackboard with a hole in your stocking or a ripped hem. She was the one who imitated (but in a safe corner of the schoolyard, out of earshot, always) the teacher reading "The Burial of Sir John Moore."

All the same it would have suited her better to have found one of those ladies beautiful, not Char. It would have been more appropriate. More suitable than Char in her wet apron with her cross expression, bent over the starch basin. Et was a person who didn't like contradictions, didn't like things out of place, didn't like mysteries or extremes.

She didn't like the bleak notoriety of having Sandy's drowning attached to her, didn't like the memory people kept of her father carrying the body up from the beach. She could be seen at twilight,

in her gym bloomers, turning cartwheels on the lawn of the
stricken house. She made a wry mouth, which nobody saw, one
day in the park when Char said, "That was my little brother who
was drowned."

The park overlooked the beach. They were standing there with
Blaikie Noble, the hotel owner's son, who said, "Those waves can be
dangerous. Three or four years ago there was a kid drowned."

And Char said—to give her credit, she didn't say it tragically, but
almost with amusement, that he should know so little about Mock
Hill people—"That was my little brother who was drowned."

Blaikie Noble was not any older than Char—if he had been, he
would have been fighting in France—but he had not had to live all
his life in Mock Hill. He did not know the real people there as well
as he knew the regular guests at his father's hotel. Every winter he
went with his parents to California, on the train. He had seen the
Pacific surf. He had pledged allegiance to their flag. His manners
were democratic, his skin was tanned. This was at a time when
people were not usually tanned as a result of leisure, only work. His
hair was bleached by the sun. His good looks were almost as notable
as Char's but his were corrupted by charm, as hers were not.

It was the heyday of Mock Hill and all the other towns around the
lakes, of all the hotels which in later years would become Sunshine
Camps for city children, T.B. sanatoriums, barracks for R.A.F. training pilots in World War II. The white paint on the hotel was renewed
every spring, hollowed-out logs filled with flowers were set on the
railings, pots of flowers swung on chains above them. Croquet sets
and wooden swings were set out on the lawns, the tennis court
rolled. People who could not afford the hotel, young workingmen,
shop clerks and factory girls from the city, stayed in a row of tiny
cottages, joined by latticework that hid their garbage pails and communal outhouses, stretching far up the beach. Girls from Mock Hill,
if they had mothers to tell them what to do, were told not to walk
out there. Nobody told Char what to do, so she walked along the
boardwalk in front of them in the glaring afternoon, taking Et with
her for company. The cottages had no glass in their windows, they
had only propped-up wooden shutters that were closed at night.
From the dark holes came one or two indistinct, sad or drunk invitations, that was all. Char's looks and style did not attract men, perhaps intimidated them. All through high school in Mock Hill she had
not one boy friend. Noble was her first, if that was what he was.

What did this affair of Char's and Blaikie Noble's amount to in the
summer of 1918? Et was never sure. He did not call at the house, at
least no more than once or twice. He was kept busy, working at the

hotel. Every afternoon he drove an open excursion wagon, with an awning on top of it, up the lakeshore road, taking people to look at the Indian graves and the limestone garden and to glimpse through the trees the Gothic stone mansion, built by a Toronto distiller and known locally as Grog Castle. He was also in charge of the variety show the hotel put on once a week, with a mixture of local talent, recruited guests, and singers and comedians brought in especially for the performance.

Late mornings seemed to be the time he and Char had. "Come on," Char would say, "I have to go downtown," and she would in fact pick up the mail and walk part way round the Square before veering off into the park. Soon Blaikie Noble would appear from the side door of the hotel and come bounding up the steep path. Sometimes he would not even bother with the path but jump over the back fence, to amaze them. None of this, the bounding or jumping, was done the way some boy from Mock Hill High School might have done it, awkwardly yet naturally. Blaikie Noble behaved like a man imitating a boy; he mocked himself but was graceful, like an actor.

"Isn't he stuck on himself?" said Et to Char, watching. The position she had taken up right away on Blaikie was that she didn't like him.

"Of course he is," said Char.

She told Blaikie. "Et says you're stuck on yourself."

"What did you say?"

"I told her you had to be, nobody else is."

Blaikie didn't mind. He had taken the position that he liked Et. He would with a quick tug loosen and destroy the arrangement of looped-up braids she wore. He told them things about the concert artists. He told them the Scottish ballad singer was a drunk and wore corsets, that the female impersonator even in his hotel room donned a blue nightgown with feathers, that the lady ventriloquist talked to her dolls—they were named Alphonse and Alicia—as if they were real people, and had them sitting up in bed one on each side of her.

"How would you know that?" Char said.

"I took her up her breakfast."

"I thought you had maids to do that."

"The morning after the show I do it. That's when I hand them their pay envelope and give them their walking papers. Some of them would stay all week if you didn't inform them. She sits up in bed trying to feed them bits of bacon and talking to them and doing them answering back, you'd have a fit if you could see."

"She's cracked I guess," Char said peacefully.

One night that summer Et woke up and remembered she had left her pink organdy dress on the line, after handwashing it. She thought she heard rain, just the first few drops. She didn't, it was just leaves rustling, but she was confused, waking up like that. She thought it was far on in the night, too, but thinking about it later she decided it might have been only around midnight. She got up and went downstairs, turned on the back kitchen light, and let herself out the back door, and standing on the stoop pulled the clothesline towards her. Then almost under her feet, from the grass right beside the stoop, where there was a big lilac bush that had grown and spread, untended, to the size of a tree, two figures lifted themselves, didn't stand or even sit up, just roused their heads as if from bed, still tangled together some way. The back kitchen light didn't shine directly out but lit the yard enough for her to see their faces. Blaikie and Char.

She never did get a look at what state their clothes were in, to see how far they had gone or were going. She wouldn't have wanted to. To see their faces was enough for her. Their mouths were big and swollen, their cheeks flattened, coarsened, their eyes holes. Et left her dress, she fled into the house and into her bed where she surprised herself by falling asleep. Char never said a word about it to her next day. All she said was, "I brought your dress in, Et. I thought it might rain." As if she had never seen Et out there pulling on the clothesline. Et wondered. She knew if she said, "You saw me," Char would probably tell her it had been a dream. She let Char think she had been fooled into believing that, if that was what Char was thinking. That way, Et was left knowing more; she was left knowing what Char looked like when she lost her powers, abdicated. Sandy drowned, with green stuff clogging his nostrils, couldn't look more lost than that.

Before Christmas the news came to Mock Hill that Blaikie Noble was married. He had married the lady ventriloquist, the one with Alphonse and Alicia. Those dolls, who wore evening dress and had sleek hairdos in the style of Vernon and Irene Castle, were more clearly remembered than the lady herself. The only thing people recalled for sure about her was she could not have been under forty. A nineteen-year-old boy. It was because he had not been brought up like other boys, had been allowed the run of the hotel, taken to California, let mix with all sorts of people. The result was depravity, and could have been predicted.

Char swallowed poison. Or what she thought was poison. It was laundry-blueing. The first thing she could reach down from the shelf in the back kitchen. Et came home after school—she had heard the news at noon, from Char herself in fact, who had laughed and said,

"Wouldn't that kill you?"—and she found Char vomiting into the toilet. "Go get the Medical Book," Char said to her. A terrible involuntary groan came out of her. "Read what it says about poison." Et went instead to phone the doctor. Char came staggering out of the bathroom holding the bottle of bleach they kept behind the tub. "If you don't put up the phone I'll drink the whole bottle," she said in a harsh whisper. Their mother was presumably asleep behind her closed door.

Et had to hang up the phone and look in the ugly old book where she had read long ago about childbirth and signs of death, and had learned about holding a mirror to the mouth. She was under the mistaken impression that Char had been drinking from the bleach bottle already, so she read all about that. Then she found it was the blueing. Blueing was not in the book, but it seemed the best thing to do would be to induce vomiting, as the book advised for most poisons—Char was at it already, didn't need to have it induced—and then drink a quart of milk. When Char got the milk down she was sick again.

"I didn't do this on the account of Blaikie Noble," she said between spasms. "Don't you ever think that. I wouldn't be such a fool. A pervert like him. I did it because I'm sick of living."

"What are you sick of about living?" said Et sensibly when Char had wiped her face.

"I'm sick of this town and all the stupid people in it and Mother and her dropsy and keeping house and washing sheets every day. I don't think I'm going to vomit any more. I think I could drink some coffee. It says coffee."

Et made a pot and Char got out two of the best cups. They began to giggle as they drank.

"I'm sick of Latin," Et said, "I'm sick of Algebra. I think I'll take blueing."

"Life is a burden," Char said. "O Life, where is thy sting?"

"O Death. O Death, where is thy sting?"

"Did I say Life? I meant Death. O Death, where is thy sting? Pardon me."

One afternoon Et was staying with Arthur while Char shopped and changed books at the Library. She wanted to make him an eggnog, and she went searching in Char's cupboard for the nutmeg. In with the vanilla and the almond extract and the artificial rum she found a small bottle of a strange liquid. *Zinc phosphide.* She read the label and turned it around in her hands. A rodenticide. Rat poison, that must mean. She had not known Char and Arthur were troubled with rats. They kept a cat, old Tom, asleep now around Arthur's feet. She unscrewed the top and sniffed at it, to know what it smelled like.

Like nothing. Of course. It must taste like nothing too, or it wouldn't fool the rats.

She put it back where she had found it. She made Arthur his eggnog and took it in and watched him drink it. A slow poison. She remembered that from Blaikie's foolish story. Arthur drank with an eager noise, like a child, more to please her, she thought, than because he was so pleased himself. He would drink anything you handed him. Naturally.

"How are you these days, Arthur?"

"Oh, Et. Some days a bit stronger, and then I seem to slip back. It takes time."

But there was none gone, the bottle seemed full. What awful nonsense. Like something you read about, Agatha Christie. She would mention it to Char and Char would tell her the reason.

"Do you want me to read to you?" she asked Arthur, and he said yes. She sat by the bed and read to him from a book about the Duke of Wellington. He had been reading it by himself but his arms got tired holding it. All those battles, and wars, and terrible things, what did Arthur know about such affairs, why was he so interested? He knew nothing. He did not know why things happened, why people could not behave sensibly. He was too good. He knew about history but not about what went on, in front of his eyes, in his house, anywhere. Et differed from Arthur in knowing that something went on, even if she could not understand why; she differed from him in knowing there were those you could not trust.

She did not say anything to Char after all. Every time she was in the house she tried to make some excuse to be alone in the kitchen, so that she could open the cupboard and stand on tiptoe and look in, to see it over the tops of the other bottles, to see that the level had not gone down. She did think maybe she was going a little strange, as old maids did; this fear of hers was like the absurd and harmless fears young girls sometimes have, that they will jump out a window, or strangle a baby, sitting in its buggy. Though it was not her own acts she was frightened of.

Et looked at Char and Blaikie and Arthur, sitting on the porch, trying to decide if they wanted to go in and put the light on and play cards. She wanted to convince herself of her silliness. Char's hair, and Blaikie's too, shone in the dark. Arthur was almost bald now and Et's own hair was thin and dark. Char and Blaikie seemed to her the same kind of animal—tall, light, powerful, with a dangerous luxuriance. They sat apart but shone out together. *Lovers.* Not a soft word, as people thought, but cruel and tearing. There was Arthur in the rocker with a quilt over his knees, foolish as something that hasn't grown its final, most necessary, skin. Yet in a way the people like

Arthur were the most trouble-making of all.

"I love my love with an R, because he is ruthless. His name is Rex, and he lives in a—restaurant."

"I love my love with an A, because he is absent minded. His name is Arthur, and he lives in an ashcan."

"Why Et," Arthur said. "I never suspected. But I don't know if I like about the ashcan."

"You would think we were all twelve years old," said Char.

After the blueing episode Char became popular. She became involved in the productions of the Amateur Dramatic Society and the Oratorio Society, although she was never much of an actress or a singer. She was always the cold and beautiful heroine in the plays, or the brittle exquisite young society woman. She learned to smoke, because of having to do it onstage. In one play Et never forgot, she was a statue. Or rather, she played a girl who pretended to be a statue, so that a young man fell in love with her and later discovered, to his confusion and perhaps disappointment, that she was only human. Char had to stand for eight minutes perfectly still on stage, draped in white crepe and showing the audience her fine indifferent profile. Everyone marveled at how she did it.

The moving spirit behind the Amateur Dramatic Society and the Oratorio Society was a high school teacher new to Mock Hill, Arthur Comber. He taught Et history in her last year. Everybody said he gave her A's because he was in love with her sister, but Et knew it was because she worked harder than she ever had before; she learned the History of North America as she had never learned anything in her life. Missouri Compromise. Mackenzie to the Pacific, 1793–She never forgot.

Arthur Comber was thirty or so, with a high bald forehead, a red face in spite of not drinking (that later paled) and a clumsy, excited manner. He knocked a bottle of ink off his desk and permanently stained the History Room floor. "Oh dear, oh dear," he said, crouching down to the spreading ink, flapping at it with his handkerchief. Et imitated that. "Oh dear, oh dear!" "Oh good heavens!" All his flustery exclamations and miscalculated gestures. Then, when he took her essay at the door, his red face shining with eagerness, giving her work and herself such a welcome, she felt sorry. That was why she worked so hard, she thought, to make up for mocking him.

He had a black scholar's gown he wore over his suit, to teach in. Even when he wasn't wearing it, Et could see it on him. Hurrying along the street to one of his innumerable, joyfully undertaken obligations, flapping away at the Oratorio singers, jumping on stage—so the whole floor trembled—to demonstrate something to the actors in

a play, he seemed to her to have those lo
flapping after him, to be as different from
intriguing, as the priest from Holy Cross. (
the gown altogether, after they were married.
tripped in it, running up the steps of the s
sprawling. That finished it, she ripped it up.

"I was afraid one of these days you'd really get

But Arthur said, "Ah. You thought I looked like a

Char didn't deny it, though his eyes on her, his w
begging her to. Her mouth twitched at the corners, in
self. Contempt. Fury. Et saw, they both saw, a great wav
over her before she could smile at him and say, "Don'
Then her smile and her eyes were trying to hold on to him,
clutch onto his goodness (which he saw, as much as anybo
did, but which finally only enraged her, Et believed, like ever
else about him, like his sweaty forehead and his galloping
mism), before that boiling wave could come back again, altoget
carry her away.

Char had a miscarriage during the first year of her marriage and
was sick for a long time afterwards. She was never pregnant again.
Et by this time was not living in the house, she had her own place on
the Square, but she was there one time on washday, helping Char
haul the sheets off the line. Their parents were both dead by that
time—their mother had died before and their father after the wedding—but it looked to Et like sheets for two beds.

"It gives you plenty of wash."

"What does?"

"Changing sheets like you do."

Et was often there in the evening, playing rummy with Arthur
while Char, in the other room, picked at the piano in the dark. Or
talking and reading library books with Char, while Arthur marked
his papers. Arthur walked her home. "Why do you have to go off
and live by yourself anyway?" he scolded her. "You ought to come
back and live with us."

"Three's a crowd."

"It wouldn't be for long. Some man is going to come along some
day and fall hard."

"If he was such a fool as to do that I'd never fall for him, so we'd
be back where we started."

"I was a fool that fell for Char, and she ended up having me."

Just the way he said her name indicated that Char was above,
outside, all ordinary considerations—a marvel, a mystery. No one
could hope to solve her, they were lucky just being allowed to contemplate her. Et was on the verge of saying, "She swallowed blueing

r," but she thought what
 seem more splendid to
queezed Et's waist as if
voluntary obeisance,
py pressure of his
her skirt fastened.
ut the keys of a

 long narrow
d all her fitting,
in, her sleeping and
ne squares of pressed tin
er own. Arthur had not liked
 he thought she was too smart for
 done in History had given him an
rains. "Besides," she told him, "it takes
d fit, if you do it right, than to teach people
812. Because, once you learn that, it's learned and
change you. Whereas every article of clothing you
 entirely new proposition."

 it's a surprise," said Arthur, "to see the way you settle
wn."

It surprised everybody, but not Et herself. She made the change easily, from a girl turning cartwheels to a town fixture. She drove the other dressmakers out of business. They had been meek, unimportant creatures anyway, going around to people's houses, sewing in back rooms and being grateful for meals. Only one serious rival appeared in all Et's years, and that was a Finnish woman who called herself a designer. Some people gave her a try, because people are never satisfied, but it soon came out she was all style and no fit. Et never mentioned her, she let people find out for themselves; but afterwards, when this woman had left town and gone to Toronto—where, from what Et had seen on the streets, nobody knew a good fit from a bad—Et did not restrain herself. She would say to a customer she was fitting, "I see you're still wearing that herringbone my foreigner friend tacked together for you. I saw you on the street."

"Oh, I know," the woman would say. "But I do have to wear it out."

"You can't see yourself from behind anyway, what's the difference."

Customers took this kind of thing from Et, came to expect it, even. She's a terror, they said about her, Et's a terror. She had them at a disadvantage, she had them in their slips and corsets. Ladies who looked quite firm and powerful, outside, were here immobilized, apologetic, exposing such trembly, meek-looking thighs squeezed together by corsets, such long sad breast creases, bellies blown up and torn by children and operations.

"Et always closed her front curtains tight, pinning the crack.

"That's to keep the men from peeking."

Ladies laughed nervously.

"That's to keep Jimmy Saunders from stumping over to get an eyeful."

Jimmy Saunders was a World War I veteran who had a little shop next to Et's, harness and leather goods.

"Oh, Et. Jimmy Saunders has a wooden leg."

"He hasn't got wooden eyes. Or anything else that I know of."

"Et you're terrible."

Et kept Char beautifully dressed. The two steadiest criticisms of Char, in Mock Hill, were that she dressed too elegantly, and that she smoked. It was because she was a teacher's wife that she should have refrained from doing either of these things, but Arthur of course let her do anything she liked, even buying her a cigarette holder so she could look like a lady in a magazine. She smoked at a high school dance, and wore a backless satin evening dress, and danced with a boy who had got a high school girl pregnant, and it was all the same to Arthur. He did not get to be Principal. Twice the school board passed him over and brought in somebody from outside, and when they finally gave him the job, in 1942, it was only temporarily and because so many teachers were away at war.

Char fought hard all these years to keep her figure. Nobody but Et and Arthur knew what effort that cost her. Nobody but Et knew it all. Both of their parents had been heavy, and Char had inherited the tendency, though Et was always as thin as a stick. Char did exercises and drank a glass of warm water before every meal. But sometimes she went on eating binges. Et had known her to eat a dozen cream puffs one after the other, a pound of peanut brittle, or a whole lemon meringue pie. Then pale and horrified she took down Epsom salts, three or four or five times the prescribed amount. For two or three days she would be sick, dehydrated, purging her sins, as Et said. During these periods she could not look at food. Et would have to come and cook Arthur's supper. Arthur did not know about the pie or the peanut brittle or whatever it was, or about the Epsom salts. He thought she had gained a pound or two and was going through a fanatical phase of dieting. He worried about her.

"What is the difference, what does it matter?" he would say to Et. "She would still be beautiful."

"She won't do herself any harm," said Et, enjoying her food, and glad to see that worry hadn't put him off his. She always made him good suppers.

It was the week before the Labor Day weekend. Blaikie had gone to Toronto, for a day or two he said.

"It's quiet without him," said Arthur.

"I never noticed he was such a conversationalist," Et said.

"I only mean in the way that you get used to somebody."

"Maybe we ought to get unused to him," said Et.

Arthur was unhappy. He was not going back to the school; he had obtained a leave of absence until after Christmas. Nobody believed he would go back then.

"I suppose he has his own plans for the winter," he said.

"He may have his own plans for right now. You know I have my customers from the hotel. I have my friends. Ever since I went on that excursion, I hear things."

She never knew where she got the inspiration to say what she said, where it came from. She had not planned it at all, yet it came so easily, believably.

"I hear he's taken up with a well-to-do woman down at the hotel."

Arthur was the one to take an interest, not Char.

"A widow?"

"Twice, I believe. The same as he is. And she has the money from both. It's been suspected for some time and she was talking about it openly. He never said anything, though. He never said anything to you, did he, Char?"

"No," said Char.

"I heard this afternoon that now he's gone, and she's gone. It wouldn't be the first time he pulled something like this. Char and I remember."

Then Arthur wanted to know what she meant and she told him the story of the lady ventriloquist, remembering even the names of the dolls, though of course she left out all about Char. Char sat through this, even contributing a bit.

"They might come back but my guess is they'd be embarrassed. He'd be embarrassed. He'd be embarrassed to come here, anyway."

"Why?" said Arthur, who had cheered up a little through the ventriloquist story. "We never set down any rule against a man getting married."

Char got up and went into the house. After a while they heard the sound of the piano.

The question often crossed Et's mind in later years—what did she mean to do about this story when Blaikie got back? For she had no reason to believe he would not come back. The answer was that she had not made any plans at all. She had not planned anything. She supposed she might have wanted to make trouble between him and Char—make Char pick a fight with him, her suspicions roused even if rumors had not been borne out, make Char read what he might do again in the light of what he had done before. She did not know what she wanted. Only to throw things into confusion, for she believed then that somebody had to, before it was too late.

Arthur made as good a recovery as could be expected at his age, he went back to teaching history to the senior classes, working half-days until it was time for him to retire. Et kept up her own place on the Square and tried to get up and do some cooking and cleaning for Arthur, as well. Finally, after he retired, she moved back into the house, keeping the other place only for business purposes. "Let people jaw all they like," she said. "At our age."

Arthur lived on and on, though he was frail and slow. He walked down to the Square once a day, dropped in on Et, went and sat in the park. The hotel closed down and was sold again. There was a story that it was going to be opened up and used as a rehabilitation center for drug addicts, but the town got up a petition and that fell through. Eventually it was torn down.

Et's eyesight was not as good as it used to be, she had to slow down. She had to turn people away. Still she worked, every day. In the evenings Arthur watched television or read, but she sat out on the porch, in the warm weather, or in the dining room in winter, rocking and resting her eyes. She came and watched the news with him, and made him his hot drink, cocoa or tea.

There was no trace of the bottle. Et went and looked in the cupboard as soon as she could—having run to the house in response to Arthur's early morning call, and found the doctor, old McClain, coming in at the same time. She ran out and looked in the garbage, but she never found it. Could Char have found the time to bury it? She was lying on the bed, fully and nicely dressed, her hair piled up. There was no fuss about the cause of death as there is in stories. She had complained of weakness to Arthur the night before, after Et had gone, she had said she thought she was getting the flu. So the old doctor said heart, and let it go. Nor could Et ever know. Would what was in that bottle leave a body undisfigured, as Char's was? Perhaps what was in the bottle was not what it said. She was not even sure that it had been there that last evening, she had been too carried away with what she was saying to go and look, as she usually did. Perhaps it had been thrown out earlier and Char had taken something else, pills maybe. Perhaps it really was her heart. All that purging would have weakened anybody's heart.

Her funeral was on Labor Day and Blaikie Noble came, cutting out his bus tour. Arthur in his grief had forgotten about Et's story, was not surprised to see Blaikie there. He had come back to Mock Hill on the day Char was found. A few hours too late, like some story. Et in her natural confusion could not remember what it was. Romeo and Juliet, she thought later. But Blaikie of course did not do away with himself afterwards, he went back to Toronto. For a year or two he sent Christmas cards, then was not heard of any more. Et would not be surprised if her story of his marrying had not come true in the end. Only her timing was mistaken.

Sometimes Et had it on the tip of her tongue to say to Arthur, "There's something I've been meaning to tell you." She didn't believe she was going to let him die without knowing. He shouldn't be allowed. He kept a picture of Char on his bureau. It was the one taken of her in her costume for that play, where she played the statue girl. But Et let it go, day to day. She and Arthur still played rummy and kept up a bit of garden, along with raspberry canes. If they had been married, people would have said they were very happy.

# JOHN UPDIKE
## 1932–

John Updike was born in Shillington, Pennsylvania, where his father was a teacher. His mother, a writer, encouraged him to write and paint. He went to Harvard University, where he excelled in his academic work and became a cartoonist for the *Harvard Lampoon*. After graduating in 1954 he spent a year in England at the Ruskin School of Drawing and Fine Art, and returned to a job with the *New Yorker*, where his stories had begun to appear in 1954. After 1957 he moved to Massachusetts, where he has lived with his wife and children most of the time since then.

## Ace in the Hole

No sooner did his car touch the boulevard heading home than Ace flicked on the radio. He needed the radio, especially today. In the seconds before the tubes warmed up, he said aloud, doing it just to hear a human voice, "Jesus. She'll pop her lid." His voice, though familiar, irked him; it sounded thin and scratchy, as if the bones in his head were picking up static. In a deeper register Ace added, "She'll murder me." Then the radio came on, warm and strong, so he stopped worrying. The Five Kings were doing "Blueberry Hill"; to hear them made Ace feel so sure inside that from the pack pinched between the car roof and the sun shield he plucked a cigarette, hung it on his lower lip, snapped a match across the rusty place on the dash, held the flame in the instinctive spot near the tip of his nose, dragged, and blew out the match, all in time to the music. He rolled down the window and snapped the match so it spun end-over-end into the gutter. "Two points," he said, and cocked the cigarette toward the roof of the car, sucked powerfully, and exhaled two plumes through his nostrils. He was beginning to feel like himself, Ace Anderson, for the first time that whole day, a bad day. He beat time on the accelerator. The car jerked crazily. "On Blueberry Hill," he sang, "My heart stood still. The wind in the wil-low tree"—he braked for a red light—"played love's suh-*weet* melodee—"

"Go, Dad, bust your lungs!" a kid's voice blared. The kid was riding in a '52 Pontiac that had pulled up beside Ace at the light. The profile of the driver, another kid, was dark over his shoulder.

Ace looked over at him and smiled slowly, just letting one side of his mouth lift a little, "Shove it," he said, goodnaturedly, across the little gap of years that separated them. He knew how they felt, young and mean and shy.

But the kid, who looked Greek, lifted his thick upper lip and spat out the window. The spit gleamed on the asphalt like a half-dollar.

"Now isn't that pretty?" Ace said, keeping one eye on the light. "You miserable wop. You are *miserable*." While the kid was trying to think of some smart comeback, the light changed. Ace dug out so hard he smelled burned rubber. In his rear-view mirror he saw the Pontiac lurch forward a few yards, then stop dead, right in the middle of the intersection.

The idea of them stalling their fat tin Pontiac kept him in a good humor all the way home. He decided to stop at his mother's place and pick up the baby, instead of waiting for Evey to do it. His mother must have seen him drive up. She came out on the porch holding a plastic spoon and smelling of cake.

"You're out early," she told him.

"Friedman fired me," Ace told her.

"Good for you," his mother said. "I always said he never treated you right." She brought a cigarette out of her apron pocket and tucked it deep into one corner of her mouth, the way she did when something pleased her.

Ace lighted it for her. "Friedman was O.K. personally," he said. "He just wanted too much for his money. I didn't mind working Saturdays, but until eleven, twelve Friday nights was too much. Everybody has a right to some leisure."

"Well, I don't dare think what Evey will say, but I, for one, thank dear God you had the brains to get out of it. I always said that job had no future to it—no future of any kind, Freddy."

"I guess," Ace admitted. "But I wanted to keep at it, for the family's sake."

"Now, I know I shouldn't be saying this, but any time Evey—this is just between us—any time Evey thinks she can do better, there's room for you *and* Bonnie right in your father's house." She pinched her lips together. He could almost hear the old lady think, *There, I've said it.*

"Look, Mom, Evey tries awfully hard, and anyway you know she can't work that way. Not that *that*—I mean, she's a realist, too . . . " He let the rest of the thought fade as he watched a kid across the street dribbling a basketball around a telephone pole that had a backboard and net nailed on it.

"Evey's a wonderful girl of her own kind. But I've always said, and your father agrees, Roman Catholics ought to marry among themselves. Now I know I've said it before, but when they get out in the greater world—"

"*No,* Mom."

She frowned, smoothed herself, and said, "Your name was in the paper today."

Ace chose to let that go by. He kept watching the kid with the basketball. It was funny how, though the whole point was to get the ball up into the air, kids grabbed it by the sides and squeezed. Kids just didn't think.

"Did you hear?" his mother asked.

"Sure, but so what?" Ace said. His mother's lower lip was coming at him, so he changed the subject. "I guess I'll take Bonnie."

His mother went into the house and brought back his daughter, wrapped in a blue blanket. The baby looked dopey. "She fussed all day," his mother complained. "I said to your father, 'Bonnie is a dear little girl, but without a doubt she's her mother's daughter.' You were the best-natured boy."

"Well I *had* everything," Ace said with an impatience that made his mother blink. He nicely dropped his cigarette into a brown flowerpot on the edge of the porch and took his daughter into his arms. She was getting heavier, solid. When he reached the end of the cement walk, his mother was still on the porch, waving to him. He was so close he could see the fat around her elbow jiggle, and he only lived a half block up the street, yet here she was, waving to him as if he was going to Japan.

At the door of his car, it seemed stupid to him to drive the measly half block home. His old coach, Bob Behn, used to say never to ride where you could walk. Cars were the death of legs. Ace left the ignition keys in his pocket and ran along the pavement with Bonnie laughing and bouncing at his chest. He slammed the door of his landlady's house open and shut, pounded up the two flights of stairs, and was panting so hard when he reached the door of his apartment that it took him a couple of seconds to fit the key into the lock.

The run must have tuned Bonnie up. As soon as he lowered her into the crib, she began to shout and wave her arms. He didn't want to play with her. He tossed some blocks and a rattle into the crib and walked into the bathroom, where he turned on the hot water and began to comb his hair. Holding the comb under the faucet before every stroke, he combed his hair forward. It was so long, one strand curled under his nose and touched his lips. He whipped the whole mass back with a single pull. He tucked in the tufts around his ears, and ran the comb straight back on both sides of his head. With his fingers he felt for the little ridge at the back where the two sides met. It was there, as it should have been. Finally, he mussed the hair in front enough for one little lock to droop over his forehead, like Alan Ladd. It made the temple seem lower than it was. Every day, his hairline looked higher. He had observed all around him how blond men went bald first. He remembered reading somewhere, though, that baldness shows virility.

On his way to the kitchen he flipped the left-hand knob of the television. Bonnie was always quieter with the set on. Ace didn't see how she could understand much of it, but it seemed to mean something to her. He found a can of beer in the refrigerator behind some brownish lettuce and those hot dogs Evey never got around to cooking. She'd be home any time. The clock said 5:12. She'd pop her lid.

Ace didn't see what he could do but try and reason with her. "Evey," he'd say, "you ought to thank God I got out of it. It had no future to it at all." He hoped she wouldn't get too mad, because when she was mad he wondered if he should have married her, and doubting that made him feel crowded. It was bad enough, his mother always crowding him. He punched the two triangles in the top of the beer can, the little triangle first, and then the big one, the one he drank from. He hoped Evey wouldn't say anything that couldn't be forgotten. What women didn't seem to realize was that there were things you knew but shouldn't say.

He felt sorry he called the kid in the car a wop.

Ace balanced the beer on a corner where two rails of the crib met and looked under the chairs for the morning paper. He had trouble finding his name, because it was at the bottom of a column on an inside sports page, in a small article about the county basketball statistics:

> "Dusty" Tremwick, Grosvenor Park's sure-fingered center, copped the individual scoring honors with a season's grand (and we do mean grand) total of 376 points. This is within eighteen points of the all-time record of 394 racked up in the 1949-1950 season by Olinger High's Fred Anderson.

Ace angrily sailed the paper into an armchair. Now it was Fred Anderson; it used to be Ace. He hated being called Fred, especially in print, but then the sportswriters were all office boys anyway, Behn used to say.

"Do not just ask for shoe polish," a man on television said, "but ask for *Emu Shoe Gloss*, the *only* polish that absolutely *guarantees* to make your shoes look shinier than new." Ace turned the sound off, so that the man moved his mouth like a fish blowing bubbles. Right away, Bonnie howled, so Ace turned it up loud enough to drown her out and went into the kitchen, without knowing what he wanted there. He wasn't hungry; his stomach was tight. It used to be like that when he walked to the gymnasium alone in the dark before a game and could see the people from town, kids and parents, crowding in at the lighted doors. But once he was inside, the locker room would be bright and hot, and the other guys would be there, laughing it up and towel-slapping, and the tight feeling would leave. Now there were whole days when it didn't leave.

A key scratched at the door lock. Ace decided to stay in the kitchen. Let *her* find *him*. Her heels clicked on the floor for a step or two; then the television set went off. Bonnie began to cry. "Shut up, honey," Evey said. There was a silence.

"I'm home," Ace called.

"No kidding. I thought Bonnie got the beer by herself."

Ace laughed. She was in a sarcastic mood, thinking she was Lauren Bacall. That was all right, just so she kept funny. Still smiling, Ace eased into the living room and got hit with, "What are *you* smirking about? Another question: What's the idea running up the street with Bonnie like she was a football?"

"You saw that?"

"Your mother told me."

"You saw her?"

"Of course I saw her. I dropped by to pick up Bonnie. What the hell do you think?—I read her tiny mind?"

"Take it easy," Ace said, wondering if Mom had told her about Friedman.

"Take it easy? Don't coach *me*. Another question: Why's the car out in front of her place? You give the car to her?"

"Look, I parked it there to pick up Bonnie, and I thought I'd leave it there."

"Why?"

"Whaddeya mean, why? I just did. I just thought I'd walk. It's not that far, you know."

"No, I don't know. If you'd been on your feet all day a block would look like one hell of a long way."

"Okay. I'm sorry."

She hung up her coat and stepped out of her shoes and walked around the room picking up things. She stuck the newspaper in the wastebasket.

Ace said, "My name was in the paper today."

"They spell it right?" She shoved the paper deep into the basket with her foot. There was no doubt; she knew about Friedman.

"They called me Fred."

"Isn't that your name? What *is* your name anyway? Hero J. Great?"

There wasn't any answer, so Ace didn't try any. He sat down on the sofa, lighted a cigarette, and waited.

Evey picked up Bonnie. "Poor thing stinks. What does your mother do, scrub out the toilet with her?"

"Can't you take it easy? I know you're tired."

"You should. I'm always tired."

Evey and Bonnie went into the bathroom; when they came out, Bonnie was clean and Evey was calm. Evey sat down in an easy chair beside Ace and rested her stocking feet on his knees. "Hit me," she said, twiddling her fingers for the cigarette.

The baby crawled up to her chair and tried to stand, to see what he gave her. Leaning over close to Bonnie's nose, Evey grinned, smoke leaking through her teeth, and said, "Only for grownups, honey."

"Eve," Ace began, "there was no future in that job. Working all Saturday, and then Friday nights on top of it."

"I know. Your mother told *me* all that, too. All I want from you is what happened."

She was going to take it like a sport, then. He tried to remember how it did happen. "It wasn't my fault," he said. "Friedman told me to back this '51 Chevvy into the line that faces Church Street. He just bought it from an old guy this morning who said it only had thirteen thousand on it. So in I jump and start her up. There was a knock in the engine like a machine gun. I almost told Friedman he'd bought a squirrel, but you know I cut that smart stuff out ever since Palotta laid me off."

"You told me that story. What happens in this one?"

"Look, Eve. I *am* telling ya. Do you want me to go out to a movie or something?"

"Suit yourself."

"So I jump in the Chevvy and snap it back in line, and there was a kind of scrape and thump. I get out and look and Friedman's running over, his arms going like *this'*—Ace whirled his own arms and laughed—" and here was the whole back fender of a '49 Merc mashed in. Just looked like somebody took a planer and shaved off the bulge, you know, there at the back." He tried to show her with his hands. "The Chevvy, though, didn't have a dent. It even gained some paint. But *Friedman*, to *hear* him—Boy, they can rave when their pocketbook's hit. He said"—Ace laughed again—"never mind."

Evey said, "You're proud of yourself."

"No, listen, I'm not happy about it. But there wasn't a thing I could *do*. It wasn't my driving at all. I looked over on the other side, and there was just two or three inches between the Chevvy and a Buick. *Nobody* could have gotten into that hole. Even if it had hair on it." He thought this was pretty good.

She didn't. "You could have looked."

"There just wasn't the *space*. Friedman said stick it in; I stuck it in."

"But you could have looked and moved the other cars to make more room."

"I guess that would have been the smart thing."

"I guess, too. Now what?"

"What do you mean?"

"I mean now what? Are you going to give up? Go back to the Army? Your mother? Be a basketball pro? What?"

"You know I'm not tall enough. Anybody under six-six they don't want."

"Is that so? Six-six? Well, please listen to this, Mr. Six-Foot-Five-and-a-Half: I'm fed up. I'm ready as Christ to let you run." She stabbed her cigarette into an ashtray on the arm of the chair so hard the ashtray jumped to the floor. Evey flushed and shut up.

What Ace hated most in their arguments was these silences after Evey had said something so ugly she wanted to take it back. "Better ask the priest first," he murmured.

She sat right up. "If there's one thing I don't want to hear about from you it's priests. You let the priests to me. You don't know a damn thing about it. Not a damn thing."

"Hey, look at Bonnie," he said, trying to make a fresh start with his tone.

Evey didn't hear him. "If you think," she went on, "if for one rotten moment you think, Mr. Fred, that the be-all and end-all of my life is you and your hot-shot stunts—"

"Look, Mother," Ace pleaded, pointing at Bonnie. The baby had picked up the ashtray and put it on her head for a hat and was waiting for praise.

Evey glanced down sharply at the child. "Cute," she said. "Cute as her daddy."

The ashtray slid from Bonnie's head and she patted where it had been and looked around puzzled.

"Yeah, but watch," Ace said. "Watch her hands. They're really terrific hands."

"You're nuts," Evey said.

"No, honest. Bonnie's great. She's a natural. Get the rattle for her. Never mind, I'll get it." In two steps, Ace was at Bonnie's crib, picking the rattle out of the mess of blocks and plastic rings and beanbags. He extended the rattle toward his daughter, shaking it delicately. Made wary by this burst of attention, Bonnie reached with both hands; like two separate animals they approached from opposite sides and touched the smooth rattle simultaneously. A smile bubbled up on her face. Ace tugged weakly. She held on, and then tugged back. "She's a natural," Ace said, "and it won't do her any good because she's a baby girl. Baby, we got to have a boy."

"I'm not your baby," Evey said, closing her eyes.

Saying "Baby" over and over again, Ace backed up to the radio and, without turning around, switched on the volume knob. In the moment before the tubes warmed up, Evey had time to say, "Wise up, Freddy. What shall we do?"

The radio came in on something slow: dinner music. Ace picked Bonnie up and set her in the crib. "Shall we dance?" he asked his wife, bowing.

"I want to talk."

"Baby. It's the cocktail hour."

"This is getting us no place," she said, rising from her chair, though.

"Fred Junior. I can see him now," he said, seeing nothing.

"We will have no Juniors."

In her crib, Bonnie whimpered at the sight of her mother being seized. Ace fitted his hand into the natural place on Evey's back and she shuffled stiffly into his lead. When, with a sudden injection of saxophones, the tempo quickened, he spun her out carefully, keeping the beat with his shoulders. Her hair brushed his lips as she minced in, then swung away, to the end of his arm; he could feel her toes dig into the carpet. He flipped his own hair back from his eyes. The music ate through his skin and mixed with the nerves and small veins; he seemed to be great again, and all the other kids were around them, in a ring, clapping time.

## RUDY WIEBE

1934–

Born near Fairholm, Saskatchewan, of Mennonite parents who fled religious persecution in the Soviet Union in 1930, Wiebe moved with his family to a farm in Coaldale, Alberta, when he was twelve. He was educated at the Mennonite High School in Coaldale and at the Universities of Alberta and Tübingen, West Germany. He completed a theological degree at the Mennonite Brethren Bible College in Winnipeg, and an M.A. from the University of Alberta in 1960. Now a professor of English at the University of Alberta, he has published five novels, including *The Blue Mountains of China* (1970) and *The Temptations of Big Bear* (1973), and a collection of short stories, *Where is the Voice Coming From?* (1974). Attracted to historical subjects for his fiction, he often writes about the prairies and also draws on his Mennonite background.

## The Naming of Albert Johnson

1. *The Eagle River, Yukon:*    Wednesday, February 17, 1932
                                 Tuesday, February 16

There is arctic silence at last, after the long snarl of rifles. As if all the stubby trees within earshot had finished splitting in the cold. Then the sound of the airplane almost around the river's bend begins to return, turning as tight a spiral as it may up over bank and trees and back down, over the man crumpled on the bedroll, over the frantic staked dogteams, spluttering, down, glancing down off the wind-ridged river. Tail leaping, almost cartwheeling over its desperate roar for skis, immense sound rocketing from that bouncing black dot on the level glare but stopped finally, its prop whirl staggering out motionless just behind the man moving inevitably forward on snowshoes, not looking back, step by step up the river with his rifle ready. Hesitates, lifts one foot, then the other, stops, and moves forward again to the splotch in the vast whiteness before him.

The pack is too huge, and apparently worried by rats with very long, fine teeth. Behind it a twisted body. Unbelievably small. One outflung hand still clutching a rifle, but no motion, nothing, the airplane dead and only the distant sounds of dogs somewhere, of men moving at the banks of the river. The police rifle points down, steadily extending the police arm until it can lever the body, already stiffening, up. A red crater for hip. As if one small part of that incredible toughness had rebelled at last, exploded red out of itself, splattering itself with itself when everything but itself was at last unreachable. But the face is turning up. Rime, and clots of snow ground into whiskers, the fur hat hurled somewhere by bullets perhaps and the whipped cowlick already a mat frozen above half-open eyes showing only white, nostrils flared, the concrete face wiped clean of everything but snarl. Freezing snarl and teeth. As if the long clenched jaws had tightened down beyond some ultimate cog and openly locked their teeth into their own torn lips in one final wordlessly silent scream.

The pilot blunders up, gasping. "By god, we got the son, of a bitch!" stumbles across the back of the snowshoes and recovers beside the policeman. Gagging a little, "My g—" All that sudden colour propped up by the rifle barrel on the otherwise white snow. And the terrible face.

The one necessary bullet, in the spine where its small entry cannot be seen at this moment, and was never felt as six others were, knocked the man face down in the snow. Though that would never loosen his grip on his rifle. The man had been working himself over on his side, not concerned as it seemed for the bullets singing to him from the level drifts in front of him or the trees on either bank. With his left hand he was reaching into his coat pocket to reload his Savage .30–.30, almost warm on the inside of his other bare hand, and he knew as every good hunter must that he had exactly thirty-nine bullets left besides the one hidden under the rifle's butt plate. If they moved in any closer he also had the Winchester .22 with sixty-four bullets, and closer still there will be the sawed-off shotgun, though he had only a few shells left, he could not now be certain exactly how many. He had stuffed snow tight into the hole where one or perhaps even two shells had exploded in his opposite hip pocket. A man could lose his blood in a minute from a hole that size but the snow was still white and icy the instant he had to glance at it, packing it in. If they had hit him there before forcing him down behind his pack in the middle of the river, he could not have moved enough to pull out of the pack straps, leave alone get behind it for protection. Bullets twitch it, whine about his tea tin like his axe handle snapping once at his legs as he ran from the eastern river bank too steep to clamber up, a very bad mistake to have to discover after spending several minutes and a hundred yards of strength running his snowshoes towards it. Not a single rock, steep and bare like polished planks. But he had gained a little on them, he saw that as he curved without stopping towards the centre of the river and the line of trees beyond it. That bank is easily climbed, he knows because he climbed it that morning, but all the dogs and men so suddenly around the hairpin turn surprised him toward the nearest bank, and he sees the teams spreading to outflank him, three towards the low west bank. And two of them bending over the one army radioman he got.

Instantly the man knew it was the river that had betrayed him. He had outlegged their dogs and lost the plane time and again on glareice and in fog and brush and between the endless trails of caribou herds, but the sluggish loops of this river doubling back on itself have betrayed him. It is his own best move, forward and then back, circle forward and further back, backwards, so the ones following his separate tracks will suddenly confront each other in cursing bewilderment. But this river, it cannot be named the Porcupine, has outdoubled him. For the dogs leaping towards him around the bend, the roaring radioman heaving at his sled, scrabbling for his rifle, this is clearly what he saw when he climbed the tree on the far bank, one of the teams he saw then across a wide tongue of land already ahead of him, as it seemed, and he started back to get further behind them before he followed and picked them off singly in whatever tracks of his they thought they were following. These dogs and this driver rounding to face him as he walks so carefully backwards in his snowshoes on the curve of his own tracks.

Whatever this river is spiralling back into the Yukon hills, his rifle will not betray him. Words are bellowing out of the racket of teams hurtling around the bend. His rifle speaks easily, wordlessly to the army radioman kneeling, sharpshooter position, left elbow propped on left knee. The sights glided together certain and deadly, and long before the sound had returned that one kneeling was already flung back clean as frozen wood bursting at his axe.

He has not eaten, he believes it must be two days, and the rabbit tracks are so old they give no hope for his snares. The squirrel burrow may be better. He is scraping curls from tiny spruce twigs, watching them tighten against the lard pail, watching the flames as it seems there licking the tin blacker with their gold tongues. The fire lives with him, and he will soon examine the tinfoil of matches in his pocket, and the tinfoil bundle in his pack and also the other two paper-wrapped packages. That must be done daily, if possible. The pack, unopened, with the .22 laced to its side is between his left shoulder and the snow hollow; the moose hides spread under and behind him; the snowshoes stuck erect into the snow on the right, the long axe lying there and the rifle also, in its cloth cover but on the moosehide pouch. He has already worked carefully on his feet, kneading as much of the frost out of one and then the other as he can before the fire though two toes on the left are black and the heel of the right is rubbed raw. Bad lacing when he walked backwards, and too numb for him to notice. The one toe can only be kept another day, perhaps, but he has only a gun-oily rag for his heel. Gunoil? Spruce gum? Wait. His feet are wrapped and ready to move instantly and he sits watching warmth curl around the pail. Leans his face down into it. Then he puts the knife away in his clothes and pulls out a tiny paper. His hard fingers unfold it carefully, he studies the crystals a moment, and then as the flames tighten the blackened spirals of spruce he pours that into the steaming pail. He studies the paper, the brownness of it; the suggestion of a word beginning, or perhaps ending, that shines through its substance. He lowers it steadily then until it darkens, smiling as a spot of deep brown breaks through the possible name and curls back a black empty circle towards his fingers. He lets it go, feeling warmth like a massage in its final flare and dying. There is nothing left but a smaller fold of pepper and a bag of salt so when he drinks it is very slowly, letting each mouthful move for every part of his tongue to hold a moment this last faint sweetness.

He sits in the small yellow globe created by fire. Drinking. The wind breathes through the small spruce, his body rests motionlessly; knowing that dug into the snow with drifts and spruce tips above him they could see his smokeless fire only if they flew directly over him. And the plane cannot fly at night. They are somewhere very close now, and their plane less than a few minutes behind. It has flown straight in an hour, again and again, all he had overlaid with tangled tracks in five weeks, but the silent land is what it is. He is now resting motionlessly. And waiting.

And the whisky-jacks are suddenly there. He had not known them before to come after dark, but grey and white tipped with black they fluffed themselves at the grey edge of his light, watching, and then one hopped two hops. Sideways. The first living thing he had seen since the caribou. But he reaches for the bits of babiche he had cut and rubbed in salt, laid ready on the cloth of the riflebutt. He throws, the draggle-tail is gone but the other watches, head cocked, then jumps so easily the long space his stiff throw had managed, and the bit is gone. He does not move his body, tosses another bit, and another, closer, closer, and then draggle-tail is there scrabbling for the bit, and he twitches the white string lying beside the bits of babiche left by the rifle, sees the bigger piece tug from the snow and draggle-tail leap to it. Gulp. He tugs, feels the slight weight as the thread lifts from the snow in the firelight, and now the other is gone while draggle-tail comes towards him inevitably, string pulling the beak soundlessly agape, wings desperate in snow, dragged between rifle and fire into the waiting claw of his hand. He felt the bird's blood beat against his palm, the legs and tail and wings thud an instant, shuddering and then limp between his relentless fingers.

Wings. Noiselessly he felt the beautiful muscles shift, slip over bones delicate as twigs. He could lope circles around any dogs they set on his trail but that beast labelled in letters combing the clouds, staring everywhere until its roar suddenly blundered up out of a canyon or over a ridge, laying its relentless shadow like words on the world: he would have dragged every tree in the Yukon together to build a fire and boil that. Steel pipes and canvas and wires and name, that stinking noise. In the silence under the spruce he skims the tiny fat bubbles from the darkening soup; watches them coagulate yellow on the shavings. Better than gunoil, or gum. He began to unwrap his feet again but listening, always listening. The delicate furrow of the bird pointed toward him in the snow.

2. *The Richardson Mountains, N.W.T.:*      Tuesday, February 9, 1932
                                            Saturday, January 30

Though it means moving two and three miles to their one, the best trail to confuse them in the foothill ravines was a spiral zig-zag. West of the mountains he has not seen them; he has outrun them so far in crossing the Richardson Mountains during the blizzard that when he reaches a river he thought it must be the Porcupine because he seems at last to be inside something that is completely alone. But the creeks draining east lay in seemingly parallel but eventually converging canyons with tundra plateaus glazed under wind between them, and when he paused on one leg of his zag he sometimes saw them, across one plateau or in a canyon, labouring with their dogs and sleds as it seems ahead of him. In the white scream of the mountain pass where no human being has ever ventured in winter he does not dare pause to sleep for two days and the long night between them, one toe and perhaps another frozen beyond saving and parts of his face dead, but in the east he had seen the trackers up close, once been above them and watched them coming along his trails towards each other unawares out of two converging canyons with their sleds and drivers trailing, and suddenly round the cliff to face each other in cursing amazement. He was far enough not to hear their words as they heated water for tea, wasting daylight minutes, beating their hands to keep warm.

The police drive the dog teams now, and the Indians sometimes; the ones who best track him on the glazed snow, through zags and bends, always wary of ambush, are the two army radiomen. One of the sleds is loaded with batteries when it should be food, but they

sniff silently along his tracks, loping giant circles ahead of the heaving dogs and swinging arms like semaphores when they find a trail
leading as it seems directly back towards the sleds they have just
left. He would not have thought them so relentless at unravelling his
trails, these two who every morning tried to raise the police on their
frozen radio, and when he was convinced they would follow him as
certainly as Millen and the plane roared up, dropping supplies, it
was time to accept the rising blizzard over the mountains and find at
last, for certain, the Porcupine River.

It is certainly Millen who brought the plane north just before the
blizzard, and it was Millen who saw his smoke and heard him
coughing, whistling in that canyon camp hidden in trees under a cliff
so steep he has to chop handholds in the frozen rock to get out of
there. Without dynamite again, or bombs, they could not dig him
out; even in his unending alert his heart jerks at the sound of what
was a foot slipping against a frozen tree up the ridge facing him. His
rifle is out of its sheath, the shell racking home in the cold like
precise steel biting. There is nothing more; an animal? A tree burst
ing? He crouches motionless, for if they are there they should be all
around him, perhaps above on the cliff, and he will not move until
he knows. Only the wind worrying spruce and snow, whining
wordlessly. There, twenty yards away a shadow moves, Millen certainly, and his shot snaps as his rifle swings up, as he drops. Bullets
snick from everywhere, their sound booming back and forth along
the canyon. He has only fired once and is down, completely aware,
on the wrong side of his fire and he shoots carefully again to draw
their shots and they come, four harmlessly high and nicely spaced
out: there are two—Millen and another—below him in the canyon
and two a bit higher on the right ridge, one of them that slipped.
Nothing up the canyon or above on the cliff. With that knowledge he
gathered himself and leaped over the fire against the cliff and one on
the ridge made a good shot that cut his jacket and he could fall as if
gut-shot in the hollow or deadfall. Until the fire died, he was almost
comfortable.

In the growing dusk he watches the big Swede, who drove dogs
very well, crawl toward Millen stretched out, face down. He watches
him tie Millen's legs together with the laces of his mukluks and drag
him backwards, plowing a long furrow and leaving the rifle sunk in
the snow. He wastes no shot at their steady firing, and when they
stop there are Millen's words still

You're surrounded. King isn't dead. Will you give

waiting, frozen in the canyon. He lay absolutely motionless behind the deadfall against the cliff, as if he were dead, knowing they would have to move finally. He flexed his feet continuously, and his fingers as he shifted the rifle no more quickly than a clock hand, moving into the position it would have to be when they charged him. They almost outwait him; it is really a question between the coming darkness and his freezing despite his invisible motions, but before darkness Millen had to move. Two of them were coming and he shifted his rifle slightly on the log to cover the left one—it must have been the long cold that made him mistake that for Millen—who dived out of sight, his shot thundering along the canyon, but Millen did not drop behind anything. Simply down on one knee, firing. Once, twice bullets tore the log and then he had his head up with those eyes staring straight down his sights and he fired two shots so fast the roar in the canyon sounded as one and Millen stood up, the whole length over him, whirled in that silent unmistakable way and crashed face down in the snow. He hears them dragging and chopping trees for a stage cache to keep the body, and in the darkness he chops handholds up the face of the cliff, step by step as he hoists himself and his pack out of another good shelter. As he has had to leave others.

3. *The Rat River, N.W.T..*   Saturday, January 10, 1932
                              Thursday, December 31, 1931
                              Tuesday, July 28

In his regular round of each loophole he peers down the promontory toward their fires glaring up from behind the riverbank. They surround him on three sides, nine of them with no more than forty dogs, which in this cold means they already need more supplies than they can have brought with them. They will be making plans for something, suddenly, beyond bullets against his logs and guns and it will have to come soon. In the long darkness, and he can wait far easier than they. Dynamite. If they have any more to thaw out very carefully after blowing open the roof and stovepipe as darkness settled, a hole hardly big enough for one of them—a Norwegian, they were everywhere with their long noses—to fill it an instant, staring down at him gathering himself from the corner out of roof-sod and pipes and snow: the cabin barely stuck above the drifts but that one was gigantic to lean in like that, staring until he lifted his rifle and the long face vanished an instant before his bullet passed through that space. But the hole was large enough for the cold to slide down along the wall and work itself into his trench, which would be all that saved him when they used the last of their dynamite. He began to feel what they had stalked him with all day: cold tightening steadily as steel around toes, face, around fingers.

In the clearing still nothing stirs. There is only the penumbra of light along the circle of the bank as if they had laid a trench-fire to thaw the entire promontory and were soundlessly burrowing in under him. Their flares were long dead, the sky across the river flickering with orange lights to vanish down into spruce and willows again, like the shadow blotting a notch in the eastern bank and he thrust his rifle through the chink and had almost got a shot away when a projectile arced against the sky and he jerked the gun out, diving, into the trench deep under the wall among the moose hides that could not protect him from the roof and walls tearing apart so loud it seemed most of himself had been blasted to the farthest granules of sweet, silent, earth. The sods and foot-thick logs he had built together where the river curled were gone and he would climb out and walk away as he always had, but first he pulled himself up and out between the splinters, still holding the rifle, just in time to see yellow light humpling through the snow toward him and he fired three times so fast it sounded in his ears as though his cabin was continuing to explode. The shadows around the light dance in one spot an instant but come on in a straight black line, lengthening down, faster, and the light cuts straight across his eyes and he gets away the fourth shot and the light tears itself into bits. He might have been lying on his back staring up into night and had the stars explode into existence above him. And whatever darkness is left before him then blunders away, desperately plowing away from him through the snow like the first one who came twice with a voice repeating at his door

I am Constable Alfred King, are you in there?

fist thudding the door the second time with a paper creaking louder than his voice so thin in the cold silence

I have a search warrant now, we have had complaints and if you don't open

and then plowing away in a long desperate scrabble through the sun-shot snow while the three others at the riverbank thumped their bullets hopelessly high into the logs but shattering the window again and again until they dragged King and each other head first over the edge while he placed lead carefully over them, snapping willow bits on top of them and still seeing, strangely, the tiny hole that had materialized up into his door when he flexed the trigger, still hearing the grunt that had wormed in through the slivers of the board he had whipsawn himself. Legs and feet wrapped in moose hide lay a

moment across his window, level in the snow, jerking as if barely
attached to a body knocked over helpless, a face somewhere twisted
in gradually developing pain that had first leaned against his door,
fist banging while that other one held the dogs at the edge of the
clearing, waiting

Hallo? Hallo? This is Constable Alfred King of the Royal Canadian
Mounted Police. I want to talk to you. Constable Millen

and they looked into each other's eyes, once, through his tiny window. The eyes peering down into his—could he be seen from out of
the blinding sun?—squinted blue from a boy's round face with a
bulging nose bridged over pale with cold. King, of the Royal
Mounted. Like a silly book title, or the funny papers. He didn't look
it as much as Spike Millen, main snooper and tracker at Arctic Red
River who baked pies and danced, everybody said, better than any
man in the north. Let them dance hipped in snow, get themselves
dragged away under spruce and dangling traps, asking, laying
words on him, naming things

You come across from the Yukon? You got a trapper's licence? The
Loucheaux trap the Rat, up towards the Richardson Mountains.
You'll need a licence, why not

Words. Dropping out of nothing into advice. Maybe he wanted a
kicker to move that new canoe against the Rat River? Loaded down
as it is. The Rat drops fast, you have to hand-line the portage anyway to get past Destruction City where those would-be Klondikers
wintered in '98. He looked up at the trader above him on the wedge
of gravel. He had expected at least silence. From a trader standing
with the bulge of seven hundred dollars in his pocket; in the south a
man could feed himself with that for two years. Mouths always full
of words, pushing, every mouth falling open and dropping words
from nothing into meaning. The trader's eyes shifted finally, perhaps
to the junction of the rivers behind them, south and west, the united
river clicking under the canoe. As he raised his paddle. The new rifle
oiled and ready with its butt almost touching his knees as he kneels,
ready to pull the canoe around.

4. *Above Fort McPherson, N.W.T.:* Tuesday, July 7, 1931

The Porcupine River, as he thought it was then, chuckled between
the three logs of his raft. He could hear that below him, under the
mosquitoes probing the mesh about his head, and see the gold
lengthen up the river like the canoe that would come toward him

from the north where the sun just refused to open the spiky horizon. Gilded, hammered out slowly, soundlessly toward him the thick gold. He sat almost without breathing, watching it come like silence. And then imperceptibly the black spired riverbend grew pointed, stretched itself in a thin straight line double-bumped, gradually spreading a straight wedge below the sun through the golden river. When he had gathered that slowly into anger it was already too late to choke his fire; the vee had abruptly bent toward him, the bow man already raised his paddle; hailed. Almost it seemed as if a name had been blundered into the silence, but he did not move in his fury. The river chuckled again.

" . . . o-o-o-o . . . " the point of the wedge almost under him now. And the sound of a name, that was so clear he could almost distinguish it. Perhaps he already knew what it was, had long since lived this in that endlessly enraged chamber of himself, even to the strange Indian accent mounded below him in the canoe bow where the black hump of the stern partner moved them straight toward him out of the fanned ripples, crumpling gold. To the humps of his raft below on the gravel waiting to anchor them.

"What d'ya want."

"You Albert Johnson?"

It could have been the sternman who named him. The sun like hatchet-strokes across slanted eyes, the gaunt noses below him there holding the canoe against the current, their paddles hooked in the logs of his raft. Two Loucheaux half-faces, black and red kneeling in the roiled gold of the river, the words thudding softly in his ears.

You Albert Johnson?

One midnight above the Arctic Circle to hear again the inevitability of name. He has not heard it in four years, it could be to the very day since that Vancouver garden, staring into the evening sun and hearing this quiet sound from these motionless—perhaps they are men kneeling there, perhaps waiting for him to accept again what has now been laid inevitably upon him, the name come to meet him in his journey north, come out of north around the bend and against the current of the Peel River, as they name that too, to confront him on a river he thought another and aloud where he would have found after all his years, at long last, only nameless silence.

You Albert Johnson?

"Yes," he said finally.

And out of his rage he begins to gather words together. Slowly, every word he can locate, as heavily as he would gather stones on a Saskatchewan field, to hold them for one violent moment against himself between his two hands before he heaves them up and hurls them—but they are gone. The ripples of their passing may have been smoothing out as he stares at where they should have been had they been there. Only the briefly golden river lies before him, whatever its name may be since it must have one, bending back somewhere beyond that land, curling back upon itself in its giant, relentless spirals down to the implacable, and ice-choked, arctic sea.

## LEON ROOKE
1934–

Born in North Carolina, Leon Rooke has lived in Victoria, British Columbia, since 1969. He has taught in the creative writing programs at several universities in Canada and the United States. Since his first collection of stories appeared in 1968, Rooke has published more than a dozen books, including novels, stories, and plays. His novel *Shakespeare's Dog* (1983) won a Governor General's award. He is often described as a "post-modernist" writer because of his willingness to move his narratives to the level of the surreal, as was clear in the stories in *A Bolt of White Cloth* (1984). The following is the title story from that collection.

# A Bolt of White Cloth

A man came by our road carrying an enormous bolt of white cloth on his back. Said he was from the East. Said whoever partook of this cloth would come to know true happiness. Innocence without heartbreak, he said, if that person proved worthy. My wife fingered his cloth, having in mind something for new curtains. It was good quality, she said. Beautifully woven, of a fine, light texture, and you certainly couldn't argue with the color.

"How much is it?" he asked.

"Before I tell you that," the man said, "you must tell me truthfully if you've ever suffered."

"Oh, I've suffered," she said. "I've known suffering of some description every day of my natural life."

I was standing over by the toolshed, with a big smile. My wife is a real joker, who likes nothing better than pulling a person's leg. She's known hardships, this and that upheaval, but nothing I would call down-and-out suffering. Mind you, I don't speak for her. I wouldn't pretend to speak for another person.

This man with the bolt of cloth, however, he clearly had no sense of my wife's brand of humor. She didn't get an itch of a smile out of him. He kept the cloth neatly balanced on his shoulder, wincing a little from the weight and from however far he'd had to carry it, staring hard and straight at my wife the whole time she fooled with him, as if he hoped to peer clear through to her soul. His eyes were dark and brooding and hollowed out some. He was like no person either my wife or me had ever seen before.

"Yes," he said, "but suffering of what kind?"

"Worse than I hope forever to carry, I'll tell you that," my wife said. "But why are you asking me these questions? I like your cloth and if the price is right I mean to buy it."

"You can only buy my cloth with love," he said.

We began right then to understand that he was some kind of oddity. He was not like anybody we'd ever seen and he didn't come from around here. He'd come from a place we'd never heard of, and if that was the East, or wherever, then he was welcome to it.

"Love?" she said. "Love? There's *love* and there's *love*, mister. What kind are you talking about?" She hitched a head my way, rolling her eyes, as if to indicate that if it was *passionate* love he was talking about then he'd first have to do something with me. He'd have to get me off my simmer and onto full boil. That's what she was telling him, with this mischief in her eyes.

I put down my pitchfork about here, and strolled nearer. I liked seeing my wife dealing with difficult situations. I didn't want to miss anything. My life with that woman has been packed with the unusual. Unusual circumstances, she calls them. Any time she's ever gone out anywhere without me, whether for a day or an hour or for five minutes, she's come back with whopping good stories about what she's seen and heard and what's happened to her. She's come back with reports on these unusual circumstances, these little adventures in which so many people have done so many extraordinary things or behaved in such fabulous or foolish ways. So what was rare this time, I thought, was that it had come visiting. She hadn't had to go out and find it.

"Hold these," my wife told me. And she put this washtub of clothes in my hands, and went back to hanging wet pieces on the line, which is what she'd been doing when this man with the bolt of cloth ventured up into our yard.

"Love," she told him. "You tell me what kind I need, if I'm to buy that cloth. I got good ears and I'm listening."

The man watched her stick clothespins in her mouth, slap out a good wide sheet, and string it up. He watched her hang two of these, plus a mess of towels, and get her mouth full again before he spoke. He looked about the unhappiest I've ever seen any man look. He didn't have any joy in him. I wondered why he didn't put down that heavy bolt of cloth, and why he didn't step around into a spot of shade. The sun was lick-killing bright in that yard. I was worried he'd faint.

"The ordinary kind," he said. "Your ordinary kind of love will buy this cloth."

My wife flapped her wash and laughed. He was really tickling her. She was having herself a wonderful time.

"What's ordinary?" she said. "I've never known no *ordinary* love."

He jumped right in. He got excited just for a second.

"The kind such as might exist between the closest friends," he said. "The kind such as might exist between a man and his wife or between parents and children or for that matter the love a boy might have for his dog. That kind of love."

"I've got that," she said. "I've had all three. Last year this time I had me a fourth, but it got run over. Up on the road there, by the tall trees, by a man in a car who didn't even stop."

"That would have been your cat," he said. "I don't know much about cats."

I put down the washtub. My wife let her arms drop. We looked at him, wondering how he knew about that cat. Then I laughed, for I figured someone down the road must have told him of my wife's mourning over that cat. She'd dug it a grave under the grapevine and said sweet words over it. She sorely missed that cat.

"What's wrong with loving cats?" she asked him. "Or beasts of the fields? I'm surprised at you."

The man shifted his burden and worked one shoe into the ground. He stared off at the horizon. He looked like he knew he'd said something he shouldn't.

She pushed me out of the way. She wanted to get nearer to him. She had something more to say.

"Now listen to me," she said. "I've loved lots of things in my life. Lots and lots. *Him*!" she said (pointing at me), "*it*" (pointing to our house), "*them*!" (pointing to the flower beds), "*that*" (pointing to the sky), "*those*" (pointing to the woods), "*this*" (pointing to the ground)—"practically *everything*! There isn't any of it I've hated, and not much I've been indifferent to. Including cats. So put that in your pipe and smoke it."

Then swooping up her arms and laughing hard, making it plain she bore no grudge but wasn't just fooling.

Funny thing was, hearing her say it, I felt the same way. *It, them, that, those*—they were all beautiful. I couldn't deny it was love I was feeling.

The man with the cloth had turned each way she'd pointed. He'd staggered a time or two but he'd kept up. In fact, it struck me that he'd got a little ahead of her. That he knew where her arm was next going. Some trickle of pleasure was showing in his face. And something else was happening, something I'd never seen. He had his face lifted up to this burning sun. It was big and orange, that sun, and scorching-hot, but he was staring smack into it. He wasn't blinking or squinting. His eyes were wide open.

Madness or miracle, I couldn't tell which.

He strode over to a parcel of good grass.

"I believe you mean it," he said. "How much could you use?"

He placed the bolt of white cloth down on the grass and pulled out shiny scissors from his back pocket.

"I bet he's blind," I whispered to my wife. "I bet he's got false eyes."

My wife shushed me. She wasn't listening. She had her excitement hat on; her *unusual circumstances* look. He was offering free cloth for love, ordinary love, and she figured she'd go along with the gag.

How much?

"Oh," she said, "maybe eight yards. Maybe ten. It depends on how many windows I end up doing, plus what hang I want, plus the pleating I'm after."

"You mean to make these curtains yourself?" he asked. He was already down on his knees, smoothing the bolt. Getting set to roll it out.

"Why, sure," she said. "I don't know who else would do it for me. I don't know who else I would ask."

He nodded soberly, not thinking about it. "That's so," he said casually. "Mend your own fences first." He was perspiring in the sun, and dishevelled, as though he'd been on the road a long time. His shoes had big holes in them and you could see the blistered soles of his feet, but he had an air of exhilaration now. His hair fell down over his eyes and he shoved the dark locks back. I got the impression that some days he went a long time between customers; that he didn't find cause to give away this cloth every day.

He got a fair bit unrolled. It certainly did look like prime goods, once you saw it spread out on the grass in that long expanse.

"It's so pretty!" My wife said. "Heaven help me, but I think it is *prettier* than grass!"

"It's pretty, all right," he said. "It's a wing-dinger. Just tell me when to stop," he said. "Just shout yoo-hoo."

"Hold up a minute," she said. "I don't want to get greedy. I don't want you rolling off more than we can afford."

"You can afford it," he said.

He kept unrolling. He was up past the well house by now, whipping it off fast, though the bolt didn't appear to be getting any smaller. My wife had both hands up over her mouth. Half of her wanted to run into the house and get her purse so she could pay; the other half wanted to stay and watch this man unfurl his beautiful cloth. She whipped around to me, all agitated.

"I believe he means it," she said. "He means us to have this cloth. What do I do?"

I shook my head. This was her territory. It was the kind of adventure constant to her nature and necessary to her well-being.

"Honey," I said, "you deal with it."

The sun was bright over everything. It was whipping-hot. There wasn't much wind but I could hear the clothes flapping on the line. A woodpecker had himself a pole somewhere and I could hear him pecking. The sky was wavy blue. The trees seemed to be swaying.

He was up by the front porch now, still unrolling. It surprised us both that he could move so fast.

"Yoo-hoo," my wife said. It was no more than a peep, the sound you might make if a butterfly lands on your hand.

"Wait," he said. "One thing. One question I meant to ask. All this talk of love, your *it*, your *those* and *them*, it slipped my mind."

"Let's hear it," my wife said. "Ask away." It seemed to me that she spoke out of a trance. That she was as dazzled as I was.

"You two got no children," he said. "Why is that? You're out here on this nice farm, and no children to your name. Why is that?"

We hadn't expected this query from him. It did something to the light in the yard and how we saw it. It was as if some giant dark bird had fluttered between us and the sun. Without knowing it, we sidled closer to each other. We fumbled for the other's hand. We stared off every which way. No one on our road had asked that question in a long, long time; they hadn't asked it in some years.

"We're not able," we said. Both of us spoke at the same time. It seemed to me that it was my wife's voice which carried; mine was some place down in my chest, and dropping, as if it meant to crawl on the ground.

"We're not able," we said. That time it came out pure, without any grief to bind it. It came out the way we long ago learned how to say it.

"Oh," he said. "I see." He mumbled something else. He kicked the ground and took a little walk back and forth. He seemed angry, though not at us. "Wouldn't you know it?" he said. "Wouldn't you know it?"

He swore a time or two. He kicked the ground. He surely didn't like it."

"We're over that now," my wife said. "We're past that caring."

"I bet you are," he said. "You're past that little misfortune."

He took to unrolling his bolt again, working with his back to the sun. Down on his knees, scrambling, smoothing the material. Sweating and huffing. He was past the front porch now, and still going, getting on toward that edge where the high weeds grew.

"About here, do you think?" he asked.

He'd rolled off about fifty yards.

My wife and I slowly shook our heads, not knowing what to think.

"Say the word," he told us. "I can give you more if more is what you want."

"I'd say you were giving us too much," my wife said. "I'd say we don't need nearly that much."

"Never mind that," he said. "I'm feeling generous today."

He nudged the cloth with his fingers and rolled off a few yards more. He would have gone on unwinding his cloth had the weeds not stopped him. He stood and looked back over the great length he had unwound.

"Looks like a long white road, don't it?" he said. "You could walk that road and your feet never get dirty."

My wife clenched my hand; it was what we'd both been thinking.

*SnipSnipSnip.* He began snipping. His scissors raced over the material. *SnipSnipSnip.* The cloth was sheared clear and clean of his bolt, yet it seemed to me the size of that bolt hadn't lessened any. My wife saw it too.

"He's got cloth for all eternity," she said. "He could unroll that cloth till doomsday."

The man laughed. We were whispering this, but way up by the weeds he heard us. "There's doom and there's doom," he said. "*Which* doomsday?"

I had the notion he'd gone through more than one. That he knew the picture from both sides.

"It *is* smart as grass," he said. "Smarter. It never needs watering." He chuckled at that, spinning both arms. Dancing a little. "You could make *nighties* out of this," he said. "New bedsheets. Transform your whole bedroom."

My wife made a face. She wasn't too pleased, talking *nighties* with another man.

Innocence without heartbreak, I thought. That's what we're coming to.

He nicely rolled up the cloth he'd sheared off and presented it to my wife. "I hope you like it," he said. "No complaints yet. Maybe you can make yourself a nice dress as well. Maybe two or three. Make him some shirts. I think you'll find there's plenty here.'

"Goodness, it's light," she said.

"Not if you've been carrying it long as I have," he said. He pulled a blue bandanna from his pocket and wiped his face and neck. He ran his hand through his hair and slicked it back. He looked up at the sky. His dark eyes seemed to have cleared up some. They looked less broody now. "Gets hot," he said, "working in this sun. But a nice day. I'm glad I found you folks home."

"Oh, we're most always home," my wife said.

I had to laugh at that. My wife almost never *is* home. She's forever gallivanting over the countryside, checking up on this person and that, taking them her soups and jams and breads.

"We're homebodies, us two."

She kept fingering the cloth and sighing over it. She held it up against her cheek and with her eyes closed rested herself on it. The man hoisted his own bolt back on his shoulder; he seemed ready to be going. I looked at my wife's closed lids, at the soft look she had.

I got trembly, fearful of what might happen if that cloth didn't work out.

"Now look," I said to him, "what's wrong with this cloth? Is it going to rot inside a week? Tomorrow is some *other* stranger going to knock on our door saying we owe him a hundred or five hundred dollars for this cloth? Mister, I don't understand you," I said.

He hadn't bothered with me before; now he looked me dead in the eye. "I can't help being a stranger," he said. "If you never set eyes on me before, I guess that's what I would have to be. Don't you like strangers? Don't you trust them?"

My wife jumped in. Her face was fiery, like she thought I had wounded him. "We like strangers just fine," she said. "We've helped out many a-one. No, I can't say our door has ever been closed to whoever it is comes by. Strangers can sit in our kitchen just the same as our friends."

He smiled at her but kept his stern look for me. "As to your questions," he said, "You're worried about the golden goose, I can see that. Fair enough. No, your cloth will not rot. It will not shred, fade, or tear. Nor will it ever need cleaning, either. This cloth requires no upkeep whatsoever. Though a sound heart helps. A sweet disposition, too. Innocence without heartbreak, as I told you. And your wife, if it's her making the curtains or making herself a dress, she will find it to be an amazingly easy cloth to work with. It will practically do the job itself. No, I don't believe you will ever find you have any reason to complain of the quality of that cloth."

My wife had it up to her face again. She had her face sunk in it.

"Goodness," she said, "it's *soft*! It smells so fresh. It's like someone singing a song to me."

The man laughed. "It is soft," he said. "But it can't sing a note, or has never been known to."

It was my wife singing. She had this little hum under the breath.

"This is the most wonderful cloth in the world," she said.

He nodded. "I can't argue with you on that score," he said. Then he turned again to me. "I believe your wife is satisfied," he said. "But if you have any doubts, if you're worried someone is going to knock on your door tomorrow asking you for a hundred or five hundred dollars, I suppose I could write you up a guarantee. I could give you a PAID IN FULL."

He was making me feel ashamed of myself. They both were. "No, no," I said, "if she's satisfied then I am. And I can see she's tickled pink. No, I beg your pardon. I meant no offense."

"No offense taken," he said.

But his eyes clouded a token. He gazed off at our road and up along the stand of trees and his eyes kept roaming until they snagged the sun. He kept his eyes there, unblinking, open, staring at the sun. I could see the red orbs reflected in his eyes.

"There is one thing," he said.

I caught my breath and felt my wife catch hers. The hitch? A hitch, after all? Coming so late?

He waited.

He shuffled his feet. He brought out his bandanna and wiped his face again. He stared at the ground.

"Should you ever stop loving," he said, "you shall lose this cloth and all else. You shall wake up one morning and it and all else will no longer be where you left it. It will all be gone and you will not know where you are. You will not know what to do with yourself. You will wish you'd never been born."

My wife's eyes went saucer-size.

He had us in some kind of spell.

Hocus-pocus, I thought. He is telling us some kind of hocus-pocus. Yet I felt my skin shudder; I felt the goose bumps rise.

"That's it?" my wife said. "That's the only catch?"

He shrugged. "That's it," he said. "Not much, is it? Not a whisper of menace for a pair such as yourselves."

My wife's eyes were gauzed over; there was a wetness in them.

"Hold on," she said. "Don't you be leaving yet. Hold this, honey."

She put the cloth in my arms. Then she hastened over to the well, pitched the bucket down, and drew it up running over with fresh water.

"Here," she said, coming back with a good dipperful. "Here's a nice drink of cool water. You need it on a day like this."

The man drank. He held the dipper in both hands, with the tips of his fingers, and drained the dipper dry, then wiped his chin with the back of a hand.

"I did indeed," he said. "That's very tasty water. I thank you."

"That's good water," she said. "That well has been here lo a hundred years. You could stay on for supper," she said. "It's getting on toward that time and I have a fine stew on the stove, with plenty to spare."

"That's kind of you," he said back, "and I'm grateful. But I'd best pass on up your road while there's still daylight left, and see who else might have need of this cloth."

My wife is not normally a demonstrative woman, not in public. Certainly not with strangers. You could have knocked me over with a feather when she up and kissed him full on the mouth, with a nice hug to boot.

"There's payment," she said, "if our money's no good."

He blushed, trying to hide his pleasure. It seemed to me she had him wrapped around her little finger . . . or the other way around.

"You kiss like a woman," he said. "Like one who knows what kissing is for, and can't hardly stop herself."

It was my wife's turn to blush.

I took hold of her hand and held her down to grass, because it seemed to me another kiss or two and she'd fly right away with him.

He walked across the yard and up by the well house, leaving by the same route he had come. Heading for the road. At the turn, he spun around and waved.

"You could try the Hopkins place!" my wife called. "There's a fat woman down that road got a sea of troubles. She could surely use some of that cloth."

He smiled and again waved. Then we saw his head and his bolt of white cloth bobbing along the weeds as he took the dips and rises in the road. Then he went on out of sight.

"There's that man with some horses down that road!" my wife called. "You be careful of him!"

It seemed we heard some sound come back, but whether it was his we couldn't say.

My wife and I stood a long time in the yard, me holding the dipper and watching her, while she held her own bolt of cloth in her arms, staring off to where he'd last been.

Then she sighed dreamily and went inside. I went on down to the barn and looked after the animals. Getting my feeding done. I talked a spell to them. Talking to animals is soothing to me, and they like it too. They pretend to stare at the walls or the floor as they're munching their feed down, but I know they listen to me. We had us an *unusual circumstances* chat. "That man with the cloth," I said. "Maybe you can tell me what you make of him."

Thirty minutes later I heard my wife excitedly calling me. She was standing out on the back doorstep, with this incredulous look.

"I've finished," she said. "I've finished the windows. *Nine* windows. It beats me how."

I started up to the house. Her voice was all shaky. Her face flushed, flinging her arms about. Then she got this new look on.

"Wait!" she said. "Stay there! Give me ten minutes!"

And she flung herself back inside, banging the door. I laughed. It always gave me a kick how she ordered me around.

I got the milk pail down under the cow. Before I'd touched and drained all four teats she was calling again.

*"Come look, come look, oh come look!"*

She was standing in the open doorway, with the kitchen to her back. Behind her, through the windows, I could see the streak of a red sunset and how it lit up the swing of trees. But I wasn't looking there. I was looking at her. Looking and swallowing hard and trying to remember how a body produced human speech. I had never thought of white as a color she could wear. White, it pales her some. It leaves her undefined and washes out what parts I like best. But she looked beautiful now. In her new dress she struck me down to my bootstraps. She made my chest break.

"Do you like it?" she said.

I went running up to her. I was up against her, hugging her and lifting her before she'd even had a chance to get set. I'd never held on so tightly or been so tightly held back.

Truth is, it was the strangest thing. Like we were both so innocent we hadn't yet shot up out of new ground.

"Come see the curtains," she whispered. "Come see the new sheets. Come see what else I've made. You'll see it all. You'll see how our home has been transformed."

I crept inside. There was something holy about it. About it and about us and about those rooms and the whole wide world. Something radiant. Like you had to put your foot down easy and hold it down or you'd float on up.

"That's it," she said. "That's how I feel too."

That night in bed, trying to figure it out, we wondered how Ella Mae down the road had done. How the people all along our road had made out.

"No worry," my wife said. "He'll have found a bonanza around here. There's heaps of decent people in this neck of the woods."

"Wonder where he is now?" we said.

"Wonder where he goes next?"

"Where he gets that cloth?"

"Who he *is*?"

We couldn't get to sleep, wondering about that.

# JACK HODGINS
1938–

Born in the Comox Valley on Vancouver Island, Jack Hodgins grew up on a stump ranch in a logging and farming community. He attended the University of British Columbia, graduating in 1961. He taught English at the Nanaimo District Senior Secondary School until 1979, and was writer-in-residence at Simon Fraser University in 1977. Now writer-in-residence at the University of Ottawa, he is married and has three children. His first collection of stories—*Spit Delaney's Island*—was published in 1976, and Hodgins has written three novels since then—*The Invention of the World* (1977), *The Resurrection of Joseph Bourne* (1979), and *The Barclay Family Theatre* (1981).

## Separating

People driving by don't notice Spit Delaney. His old gas station is nearly hidden now behind the firs he's let grow up along the road, and he doesn't bother to whitewash the scalloped row of half-tires someone planted once instead of fence. And rushing by on the Island highway today, heading north or south, there's little chance that anyone will notice Spit Delaney seated on the big rock at the side of his road-end, scratching at his narrow chest, or hear him muttering to the flat grey highway and to the scrubby firs and to the useless old ears of his neighbour's dog that he'll be damned if he can figure out what it is that is happening to him.

Hitch-hikers do notice, however; they can hear his muttering. Walking past the sheep sorrel and buttercup on the gravel shoulder, they see him suddenly, they turn alarmed eyes his way. Nodding, half smiling at this long-necked man with the striped engineer's cap, they move on through the shade-stripes of trees, their own narrow shadows like knives shaving the pavement beside them. And all he gives back, all they can take away with them, is a side-tilted look they have seen a hundred times in family snapshots, in the eyes of people out at the edge of group photos unsure they belong. Deference. *Look at the camera, son, this is all being done for you, it has nothing to do with me.* He does not accept their attention, he admits only to being a figure on the edge of whatever it is they are really looking at: his gas station perhaps, or his rusty old tow truck, or his wife piling suitcases into the trunk of her car. He relocates his cap, farther back on his head; his Adam's apple slides up his long throat like a bubble in a tube, then pushes down.

Spit Delaney cannot remember a time when he was not fascinated by the hitch-hikers. His property is close to a highway junction where they are often dropped off by the first ride that picked them up back near the ferry terminal. On these late-summer days, they line up across the front of his place like a lot of shabby refugees to wait for their second ride. Some walk past to get right out beyond the others, but most space themselves along the gravel, motionless, expressionless, collapsed. In pairs or clusters they drape themselves over their canvas packsacks and their sleeping bags. Some stretch out level on the ground, using their gear as head-rests with only an arm and an upright thumb to show that they're awake, or alive. They are heading for the west coast of the Island, he knows, the Pacific, where they have heard it is still possible to live right down on the beach under driftwood shelters and go everywhere naked from morning until night. The clothes they are so eager to shed are patched jeans and wide braces and shirts made to look like flags and big floppy hats. There is a skinny boy with a panting St Bernard tied to his pack with a length of clothes line; there is a young frizzy-haired couple with a whining baby they pass back and forth; there is a grizzled old man, a hunched-over man with a stained-yellow beard, who must be at least in his seventies though he is dressed the same as the others. Stupid old fool, thinks Spit Delaney, and grins. Sitting on his rock, at the foot of the old paint-peeled sign saying B/A, he isn't afraid to envy.

There are ninety miles of road, of this road and another, between the rock at his road-end and the west-coast beaches they are heading for. It runs grey-silver over hills and along bays and through villages and around mountains and along river banks, and is alive already with traffic: tourists set loose from a ferry and racing for campsites, salesmen released from motels and rushing for appointments. Beginnings are hard, and endings, but the long grey ribbon that joins them runs smooth and mindless along the surface of things. In his head Spit Delaney can follow it, can see every turn, can feel himself coming over the last hill to find the ocean laid out in the wide blue haze beneath him. The long curving line of sand that separates island from sea and man from whale is alive with the quickflashing movements of people.

Behind him the trunk lid slams shut. His wife's footsteps crunch down the gravel towards him. He can tell without looking that she is wearing the crepe-soled shoes she bought in a fire sale and tried to return the next day. Spit Delaney's heavy brows sink, as if he is straining to see something forty miles across the road, deep into brush. He dispatches a wad of throat-phlegm in a clean arc out onto a stalk of dog-daisy, and doesn't bother watching it slide to the ground.

She stops a few feet behind. "There's enough in the fridge to last you a week," she says.

He ducks his head, to study the wild sweet-pea that twists in the grass between his boots.

She is going, now.

That is what they have agreed on.

"Sit down when you eat," she says. "Don't go standing up at the counter, the way you will."

The boy with the St Bernard gets a ride at this moment, a green GMC pickup. They leap into the back, dog and boy, and scramble up close to the cab. Then the boy slaps his hand on the roof, signal to start, and settles back with an arm around the dog's neck, laughing. For a moment his eyes meet Spit's, the laugh dies; they watch each other until the pickup has gone on past the other hitch-hikers, on up the road out of sight behind trees.

I am a wifeless man, Spit tells the disappeared youth. This is the day of our separation. I am a wifeless man.

In his fortieth year Spit Delaney was sure he'd escaped all the pitfalls that seemed to catch everyone else in their thirties. He was a survivor.

"This here's one bugger you don't catch with his eyes shut," was his way of putting it.

And wasn't it obvious? While all his friends were getting sick of the jobs they'd worked at ever since they quit high school and were starting to hop around from one new job to another, Spit Delaney was still doing the same thing he'd been doing for twenty years, the thing he loved: operating Old Number One steam locomotive in the paper mill, shunting up and down the tracks, pushing flatcars and boxcars and tankcars off and onto barges. "Spit and Old Number One, a marriage made in heaven," people joked. "Him and that machine was made for each other, a kid and his toy. That train means more to him than any other human could hope to." Only it wasn't a joke, it was true, he was glad to admit it. Who else in all that mill got out of bed at four o'clock in the morning to fire up a head of steam for the day's work? Who else hung around after the shift was over, cleaning and polishing? Roy Rogers and Trigger, that's what they were. Spit and Old Number One. He couldn't name another person whose job was so much a part of himself, who was so totally committed to what he did for a living.

In the family department, too, he was a survivor. While everyone else's kids in their teens seemed to be smashing up the old man's car or getting caught at pot parties or treating their parents like slaves or having quiet abortions on the mainland, Jon and Cora looked as if they were going to sail right through their adolescence without a hitch: Cora would rather watch television and eat chocolate cake than fool around with boys or go to parties; Jon would rather read a book than do anything else at all. The two of them looked safe enough. It was a sign that they respected their father, Spit would say, though he admitted some of the credit had to go to his wife.

Stella. That was one more thing. All through his thirties it seemed as if every time he turned around someone else was splitting up. Everybody except him and Stella. Friends broke up, divorced, couples fell apart and regrouped into new couples. The day came when Stella Delaney looked at him out of her flat, nearly colourless eyes and said, "You and me are just about the only people we know that are still married." You couldn't count on the world being the same two weekends in a row. It was a hazard of their age, boredom was doing it, Stella told him, boredom and the new morality. People suddenly realized what they didn't have to put up with. There was no sense inviting anybody over for Saturday night, she said, they could be separated by then. But, miraculously, by the time Spit reached his fortieth year, he and Stella were still married, still together. However, if they intended to continue with their marriage, she told him, they'd have to make some new friends. Everyone else their age was newly single or newly remarried or shacking up with people half their age; what would they have in common?

The secret of his successful marriage, Spit insisted, was the way it started. Stella was a long-legged bony-faced woman of twenty-two, already engaged to some flat-assed logger from Tahsis, when Spit came into the kitchen at the back of her father's store. She was doing peach preserves for her first married winter, and admiring the logger's dinky little diamond ring up on the windowsill in front of her. Her big hands, in the orange mess of peel and juice and carved-out bruises, reminded him of the hands of a fisherman gouging out fish guts. The back of her cotton dress dipped up at the hem, to show the tiny blue veins behind her knees and the pink patches of skin where she'd pressed one leg to the other. He touched. She told him "Get lost mister, I got work to do," and he said "That logger musta been bushed and desperate is all I can say" but stayed to win her anyway, and to rush her off to a preacher's house on the day before her intended wedding. With a start like that, he said, how could anything go wrong?

It couldn't. He was sure of it. Things that were important to him, things that were real—his job, his family, his marriage—these things were surely destined to survive even the treacherous thirties.

But before he had time to congratulate himself, things began to fall apart. He insisted later that it was all because the stupidest goddamned question he ever heard just popped into his head all of a sudden. He didn't look for it, he didn't ask for it, it just came.

He was lying on his back in the sand at Wickanninish Bay, soaking up sun. He'd driven over with the family to the west coast for the weekend, had parked the camper up in the trees above the high-tide line. Stella was lying beside him on her giant towel, reading a magazine, oiled and gleaming like a beached eel. The question just popped into his head, all of a sudden: *Where is the dividing line?*

He was so surprised that he answered out loud. "Between what and what?"

Stella turned a page and folded it back. Most of the new page was taken up with a photograph of a woman who'd increased her bust measurement in a matter of days and wanted to show Stella how to do the same.

"Wha'd you say?"

"Nothing," he said, and rolled over onto his side to face away from her. Between what and what? he asked himself. Maybe he was beginning to crack up. He'd heard of the things that happened to some men at his age.

*Between what is and what isn't.*

Spit sat up, cursing.

Stella slid her dark glasses down her nose and peered at him. "What's the matter with you?"

"Nothing," he said. *Where is the dividing line?* When the words hit him again like that he jumped to his feet and shook his head, like a cow shaking off flies.

"Sand fleas?" she said.

"It's nothing," he said, and stomped around to shake the sand out of the hair on his legs.

"Too much sun," she said, and pushed herself up. "We better move up into shade."

But when they settled down by a log, cool in the shade of the wind-crippled spruce, she told him it might just be this beach that was spooking him. "This Indian Lady at Lodge," she said, "told me her people get uneasy along this beach." Spit knew Sophie Jim by name, but Stella always referred to her as This Indian Lady at Lodge. It was some kind of triumph, apparently, when Sophie was finally persuaded to join the Daughters, their first native. "She said there's a story that some kind of Sea-Wolf monster used to come whanging up out of the Pacific here to gobble up people. It came up to sire wolves for the land too, but went back into the sea to live. She says they're all just a little nervous of this place."

Spit's brain itched from the slap of the sudden question. He wanted to go home, but the kids were far out on the sand at the water's edge and he could holler at them till he was blue in the face without being heard above the roar of the waves.

"She said all up and down the coast there are stories. About monsters that come out and change people into things. To hear her tell it there must've been a whole lot of traffic back and forth between sea and land."

"A whole lot of bull," he said, and put on his shirt. It was cold up here, and what did he care about a lot of Indian stuff? He knew Indians. When he was a boy the people up the road adopted a little Indian kid, a girl, and told it around that nobody, *nobody* was to dare tell her what she was. When she was ten years old she still hadn't figured out that she wasn't the same as everybody else, so Spit sat her down on the step and told her. He had to tell her three times before she believed him and then she started to howl and cry and throw herself around. But she dried out eventually and went Indian with a vengeance, to make up for lost time. He couldn't go near her without having to listen to a whole lot of stuff she'd got soaked up into her brain from hanging around the Reserve. So he knew all about Wasgo, Stella couldn't tell him anything new about that guy. He knew about Kanikiluk too, which was worse. That son of a bitch would think nothing of stepping out of the ocean and turning a man into a fish or making a piece of seaweed think it was human. He knew all about the kind of traffic she meant.

"They say we crawled up out of there ourselves," she said. "Millions of years ago."

"Let's go home," he said. "Let's get out of here."

Within fifteen minutes they had Cora and Jon herded up off that beach and pushed into the back of the camper and had started on their way across the island to their little house behind the gas station. It wasn't really a gas station any more, though he had never bothered to pull the pumps out; the shed was a good place to store the car parts and engine pieces he kept against the day they would be needed, and the roof out over the pumps was a good place to park the tow truck. Nor was it a real business—his job at the paper mill was enough for anyone to handle—but he'd fixed up the tow truck himself out of parts and used it to pull people out of snowbanks in winter or to help friends when they got their tractors mired in swamp.

When he got home from the coast he did not go into the gas station to brood, as he might have done, nor did he sit behind the wheel of his tow truck. This was too serious for that. He drove all the way down to the paper mill, punched himself in at the gate, and climbed up into the cab of Old Number One. He knew even then that something was starting to go wrong. *Where is the dividing line?* He sat there with his hands on the levers deep into night, all the way through the early morning when it was time to fire up her boilers and start getting ready for the day's work ahead. *And what does it take to see it?*

And, naturally, that was the day the company picked to tell him what they'd done with Old Number One.

Sold her to the National Museum in Ottawa.

For tourists to gawk at.

Sons of bitches. They might as well have lopped off half of his brain. Why didn't they sell the government his right arm too while they were at it?

The hundred-and-thirty-ton diesel-electric they offered was no consolation. "A dummy could run that rig!" he shouted. "It takes a man to put life into Old Number One!"

He ought to be glad, they told him. That shay was long past her usefulness, the world had changed, the alternative was the junkyard. You can't expect *things* to last for ever.

But this was one uncoupling that would not be soon forgiven.

First he hired a painter to come into the mill and do a four-foot oil of her to hang over the fireplace. And unscrewed the big silver 1 from the nose to hang on the bedroom door. And bought himself a good-quality portable recorder to get the locomotive's sounds immortalized on tape. While there was some small comfort in knowing the old girl at least wasn't headed for the scrapyard, it was no easy thing when he had to bring her out on that last day, sandblasted and repainted a gleaming black, to be taken apart and shipped off in a boxcar. But at least he knew that while strangers four thousand miles away were staring at her, static and soundless as a stuffed grizzly, he would be able to sit back, close his eyes, and let the sounds of her soul shake through him full-blast just whenever he felt like it.

Stella allowed him to move her Tom Thomson print to the side wall to make room for the new painting; she permitted him to hang the big number 1 on the bedroom door; but she forbade him to play his tape when she was in the house. Enough is enough, she said. Wives who only had infidelity to worry about didn't know how lucky they were.

She was president of her Lodge, and knew more than she could ever tell of the things women had to put up with.

"Infidelity?" he said. It had never occurred to him. He rolled his eyes to show it was something he was tempted to think about, now that she'd brought it up, then kissed the top of her head to show he was joking.

"A woman my age," she said, "starts to ask what has she got and where is she headed."

"What you need is some fun out of life," he said, and gathered the family together. How did a world tour sound?

It sounded silly, they said.

It sounded like a waste of good money.

Good money or bad, he said, who'd been the one to go out and earn it? Him and Old Number One, that's who. Hadn't he got up at four o'clock every damn morning to get the old girl fired up, and probably earned more overtime that way than anybody else on this island? Well, was there a better way to spend money than taking his family to Europe at least?

They left her mother behind to keep an eye on the house. An old woman who had gone on past movement and caring and even speech, she could spend the time primly waiting in an armchair, her face in the only expression she seemed to have left: dark brows lowered in a scowl, eyes bulging as if in behind them she was planning to push until they popped out and rolled on the floor. Watching was the one thing she did well, she looked as if she was trying with the sheer force of those eyes to make things stay put. With her in the house it was safe to leave everything behind.

If they thought he'd left Old Number One behind him, however, if they thought he'd abandoned his brooding, they were very much mistaken; but they got all the way through Spain and Italy and Greece before they found it out. They might have suspected if they'd been more observant; they might have noticed the preoccupied, desperate look in his eyes. But they were in Egypt before that desperation became intense enough to risk discovery.

They were with a group of tourists, standing in desert, looking at a pyramid. Cora whined about the heat, and the taste of dry sand in the air.

"It's supposed to be hot, stupid," Jon said. "This is Egypt." He spent most of the trip reading books about the countries they were passing through, and rarely had time for the real thing. It was obvious to Spit that his son was cut out for a university professor.

And Cora, who hated everything, would get married. "I can't see why they don't just tear it down. A lot of hot stone."

Jon sniffed his contempt. "It's a monument. It's something they can look at to remind them of their past."

"Then they ought to drag it into a museum somewhere under a roof. With air conditioning."

Stella said, "Where's Daddy?"

He wasn't anywhere amongst the tourists. No one in the family had seen him leave.

"Maybe he got caught short," Jon said, and sniggered.

Cora stretched her fat neck, to peer. "And he's not in the bus."

The other tourists, too, appeared uneasy. Clearly something was sensed, something was wrong. They shifted, frowned, looked out where there was nothing to see. Stella was the first to identify it:

somewhere out there, somewhere out on that flat hot sand, that desert, a train was chugging, my God, a steam engine was chugging and hissing. People frowned at one another, craned to see. Uneasy feet shifted. Where in all that desert was there a train?

But invisible or not it got closer, louder. Slowing. *Humph humph humph humph.* Then speeding up, clattering, hissing. When it could have been on top of them all, cutting their limbs off on invisible tracks, the whistle blew like a long clarion howl summoning them to death.

Stella screamed. "Spit! Spit!" She ran across sand into the noise, forgetting to keep her arms clamped down against the circles of sweat.

She found him where in the shrill moment of the whistle she'd realized he would be, at the far side of the pyramid, leaning back against the dusty base with his eyes closed. The tape recorder was clutched with both hands against his chest. Old Number One rattled through him like a fever.

When it was over, when he'd turned the machine off, he raised his eyes to her angry face.

"Where is the line?" he said, and raised an eyebrow.

"You're crazy," she said. "Get a hold of yourself." Her eyes banged around in her bony head as if they'd gone out of control. There were witnesses all over this desert, she appeared to be saying, who knew what kind of a fool she had to put up with. He expected her to kick at him, like someone trying to rout a dog. Her mouth gulped at the hot air; her throat pumped like desperate gills. Lord, you're an ugly woman, he thought.

The children, of course, refused to speak to him through Israel, Turkey, and France. They passed messages through their mother— "We're starved, let's eat" or "I'm sick of this place"—but they kept their faces turned from him and pretended, in crowds, that they had come alone, without parents. Cora cried a great deal, out of shame. And Jon read a complete six-volume history of Europe. Stella could not waste her anxiety on grudges, for while the others brooded over the memory of his foolishness she saw the same symptoms building up again in his face. She only hoped that this time he would choose some place private.

He chose Anne Hathaway's Cottage in Stratford. They wouldn't have gone there at all if it hadn't been for Jon, who'd read a book on Shakespeare and insisted on seeing the place. "You've dragged me from one rotten dump to another," he said, "now let me see one thing I want to see. She was twenty-six and Shakespeare was only my age when he got her pregnant. That's probably the only reason he married her. Why else would a genius marry an old woman?"

Spit bumped his head on the low doorway and said he'd rather stay outside. He couldn't see any point in a monument to a woman like *that*, anyway. The rest of them were upstairs in the bedroom, looking at the underside of the thatched roof, when Old Number One started chugging her way towards them from somewhere out in the garden.

By the time they got to Ireland, where they would spend the next two weeks with one of her distant cousins, Stella Delaney was beginning to suffer from what she called a case of nerves. She had had all she could take of riding in foreign trains, she said, she was sure she'd been on every crate that ran on tracks in every country of Europe and northern Africa; and now she insisted that they rent a car in Dublin for the drive down to her cousin's, who lived about as far as you get on that island, way out at the end of one of those south-western peninsulas. "For a change let's ride in style," she said, and pulled her chin to show she meant business. She was missing an important Lodge convention for this. The least he could do, she said, was make it comfortable.

The cousin, a farmer's wife on a mountain slope above Ballinskelligs Bay, agreed. "'Tis a mad life you've been living, sure. Is it some kind of race you're in?"

"It is," Stella said. "But I haven't the foggiest idea who or what we're racing against. Or what is chasing us."

"Ah well," said the cousin, wringing her hands. "God is good. That is one thing you can be certain of. Put your feet up and relax so."

She knew about American men, the cousin told them. You had to watch them when they lost their playthings, or their jobs, they just shrivelled up and died.

Stella looked frightened.

Oh yes, the cousin said. She knew. She'd been to America once as a girl, to New York, and saw all she needed to see of American men.

Spit Delaney thought he would go mad. He saw soon enough that he could stare out this farmhouse window all he wanted and never find what he needed. He could look at sheep grazing in their little hedged-in patches, and donkey carts passing by, and clumps of furze moving in the wind, he could look at the sloping farms and the miles and miles of flat green bog with its brown carved-out gleaming beds and piled-up bricks of turf and at the deep curved bay of Atlantic ocean with spray standing up around the jagged rocks until he was blind from looking, but he'd never see a train of any kind. Nor find an answer. Old Number One was in Ottawa by now, being polished and dusted by some uniformed pimple-faced kid who wouldn't know a piston from a lever.

"We'd've been better off spending the money on a swimming pool," Stella told her cousin. "We might as well have flushed it down the toilet."

"That's dumb," Cora said. She buttered a piece of soda bread and scooped out a big spoonful of gooseberry jam.

"Feeding your pimples," Jon said. He had clear skin, not a single adolescent blemish, nor any sign of a whisker. Sexually he was a late developer, he explained, and left you to conclude the obvious: he was a genius. Brilliant people didn't have time for a messy adolescence. They were too busy thinking.

"Don't pick on your sister," Stella said. "And be careful or you'll get a prissy mouth. There's nothing worse on a man."

A hollow ache sat in Spit's gut. He couldn't believe these people belonged to him. This family he'd been dragging around all over the face of the earth was as foreign to him as the little old couple who lived in this house. What did the prim sneery boy have to do with him? Or that fat girl. And Stella: behind those red swollen eyes she was as much a stranger to him now as she was on the day he met her. If he walked up behind her and touched her leg, he could expect her to say Get lost mister I got work to do, just as she had then. They hadn't moved a single step closer.

I don't know what's going on, he thought, but something's happening. If we can't touch, in our minds, how can I know you are there? How can I know who you are? If two people can't overlap, just a little, how the hell can they be sure of a god-damn thing?

The next day they asked him to drive in to Cahirciveen, the nearest village, so Jon could have a look around the library and Stella could try on sweaters, which she said were bound to be cheaper since the sheep were so close at hand. Waiting for them, sitting in the little rented car, he watched the people on the narrow crooked street. Fat red-faced women chatted outside shop doors; old men in dark suits stood side by side in front of a bar window looking into space; a tall woman in a black shawl threaded her way down the sidewalk; a fish woman with a cigarette stuck in the middle of her mouth sat with her knees locked around a box of dried mackerel; beside the car a cripple sat right on the concrete with his back to the store-front wall and his head bobbing over a box for tossed coins.

The temptation was too much to resist. He leaned back and closed his eyes, pressed the button, and turned the volume up full. Old Number One came alive again, throbbed through him, swelled to become the whole world. His hand shifted levers, his foot kicked back from a back-spray of steam, his fingers itched to yank the whistle-cord. Then, when it blew, when the old steam whistle cut right through to his core, he could have died happily.

But he didn't die. Stella was at the window, screaming at him, clawing at the recorder against his chest. A finger caught at the strap and it went flying out onto the street. The whistle died abruptly, all sound stopped. Her face, horrified, glowing red, appeared to be magnified a hundred times. Other faces, creased and toothless, whiskered, stared through glass. It appeared that the whole street had come running to see him, this maniac.

Stella, blushing, tried to be pleasant, dipped apologies, smiled grimly as she went around to her side of the car.

If her Lodge should hear of this.

Or her mother.

The chin, tucked back, was ready to quiver. She would cry this time, and that would be the worst of all. Stella, crying, was unbearable.

But she didn't cry. She was furious. "You stupid stupid man," she said, as soon as she'd slammed the door. "You stupid stupid man."

He got out to rescue his recorder, which had skidded across the sidewalk almost to the feet of the bobbing cripple. When he bent to pick it up, the little man's eyes met his, dully, for a moment, then shifted away.

Jon refused to ride home with them. He stuck his nose in the air, swung his narrow shoulders, and headed down the street with a book shoved into his armpit. He'd walk the whole way back to the cousin's, he said, before he'd ride with *them*.

She sat silent and bristling while he drove out past the last grey buildings and the Co-op dairy and the first few stony farms. She scratched scales of skin off the dry eczema patches that were spreading on her hands. Then, when they were rushing down between rows of high blooming fuchsia bushes, she asked him what he thought she was supposed to be getting out of this trip.

"Tomorrow," he said. "Tomorrow we go home."

Spit Delaney had never travelled off the Island more than twice before in his life, both those times to see a doctor on the mainland about the cast in his eye. Something told him a once-in-a-lifetime trip to Europe ought to have been more than it was. Something told him he'd been cheated. Cheated in a single summer out of Old Number One, his saved-up overtime money, the tourist's rightfully expected fun, and now out of wife as well. For the first thing she told him when the plane landed on home territory was this: "Maybe we ought to start thinking about a separation. This is no marriage at all any more."

He stopped at the house only long enough to drop them off, then fled for the coast, his ears refusing the sounds of her words.

But it was a wet day, and the beach was almost deserted. A few seagulls slapped around on the sand, or hovered by tide pools. Trees, already distorted and one-sided from a lifetime of assaults, bent even farther away from the wind. A row of yellowish seaweed, rolled and tangled with pieces of bark and chunks of wood, lay like a continuous window along the uneven line of last night's highest tide. Far out on the sand an old couple walked, leaning on each other, bundled up in toques and Cowichan sweaters and gum boots. The ocean was first a low lacy line on sand, then sharp chopped waves like ploughed furrows, then nothing but haze and mist, a thick blending with uncertain sky.

There was no magic here. No traffic, no transformations. No Kanikiluk in sight. He'd put ninety miles on the camper for nothing. He might as well have curled up in a corner of the old gas station, amongst the car parts, or sat in behind the wheel of his tow truck to brood. The world was out to cheat him wherever he turned.

Still, he walked out, all the way out in the cold wind to the edge of the sea, and met a naked youth coming up out of the waves to greet him.

"Swimming?" Spit said, and frowned. "Don't you tell me it's warm when you get used to it, boy, I can see by the way you're all shrivelled up that you're nearly froze."

The youth denied nothing. He raised both arms to the sky as if expecting to ascend, water streaming from his long hair and beard and his crotch, forming beads in the hairs, shining on goose-bumped skin. Then he tilted his head.

"Don't I know you?"

"Not me," Spit said. "I don't live here."

"Me neither," the youth said. "Me and some other guys been camping around that point over there all summer, I go swimming twice a day."

Spit put both hands in his pockets, planted his feet apart, and stretched his long neck. He kept his gaze far out to sea, attempting to bore through that mist. "I just come down for a look at this here ocean."

"Sure, man," the youth said. "I *do* know you. You let me use your can."

"What? What's that?" Why couldn't the kid just move on? You had to be alone sometimes, other people only complicated things.

"I was waiting for a ride, to come up here, and I come to your house to use the can. Hell, man, you gave me a beer and sat me down and told me your whole life story. When I came out my friend had gone on without me."

Spit looked at the youth's face. He remembered someone, he remembered the youth on that hot day, but there was nothing in his face that he recognized. It was as if when he'd stripped off his clothes he'd also stripped off whatever it was that would make his face different from a thousand others.

"You know what they found out there, don't you?" the youth said. He turned to face the ocean with Spit. "Out there they found this crack that runs all around the ocean floor. Sure, man, they say it's squeezing lava out like toothpaste all the time. Runs all the way around the outside edge of this ocean."

"What?" Spit said. "What are you talking about?"

"Squirting lava up out of the centre of the earth! Pushing the continents farther and farther apart! Don't that blow your mind?"

"Look," Spit said. But he lost the thought that had occurred.

"Pushing and pushing. Dividing the waters. Like that what-was-it right back there at the beginning of things. And there it is, right out there somewhere, a bloody big seam. Spreading and pushing."

"You can't believe them scientists," Spit said. "They like to scare you."

"I thought I recognized you. You pulled two beer out of the fridge, snapped off the caps, and put them on the table. Use the can, you said, and when you come out this'll wash the dust from your throat. You must've kept me there the whole afternoon, talking."

"Well, nobody's stopping you now. Nobody's forcing you to stay. Go on up and get dressed." If all he came up out of that ocean to tell about was a crack, he might as well go back in.

Which he did, on the run.

Straight back through ankle-foam, into breakers, out into waves. A black head, bobbing; he could be a seal, watching the shore.

Go looking for your crack, he wanted to shout. Go help push the continents apart. Help split the god-damned world in two.

"There's no reason why we can't do this in a friendly fashion," Stella said when he got home. "It's not as if we hate each other. We simply want to make a convenient arrangement. I phoned a lawyer while you were out."

She came down the staircase backwards, on her hands and knees, scrubbing, her rear end swinging to the rhythm of her arm. Stella was death on dirt, especially when she was upset.

"Don't be ridiculous," Spit said. "This isn't Hollywood, this is *us*. We survived all that crap."

She turned on the bottom step, sat back, and pushed her hair away from her eyes. "Not quite survived. It just waited until we were off guard, until we thought we were home-safe."

He could puke.

Or hit her.

"But there isn't any home-safe, Spit. And this *is* Hollywood, the world has shrunk, it's changed, even here." She tapped the pointed wooden scrub brush on the step, to show where here was.

Spit fingered the cassette in his pocket. She'd smashed his machine. He'd have to buy a new one, or go without.

"Lady," he said, "that flat-assed logger don't know what a close call he had. If he'd've known he'd be thanking me every day of his life."

Though he didn't mean it.

Prying him loose from Stella would be like prying off his arm. He'd got used to her, and couldn't imagine how he'd live without her.

Her mother sat in her flowered armchair and scowled out over her bulging eyeballs at him as if she were trying to see straight to his centre and burn what she found. Her mouth chewed on unintelligible sounds.

"This is my bad year," he said. "First they take away Old Number One, and now this. The only things that mattered to me. Real things."

"Real!" the old woman screeched, threw up her hands, and slapped them down again on her skinny thighs. She laughed, squinted her eyes at the joke, then blinked them open again, bulged them out, and pursed her lips. Well, have we got news for you, she seemed to be saying. She could hardly wait for Stella's answer.

"The only things you can say that about," Stella said, "are the things that people can't touch, or wreck. Truth is like that, I imagine, if there is such a thing."

The old woman nodded, nodded: That'll show you, that'll put you in your place. Spit could wring her scrawny neck.

"You!" he said. "What do you know about anything?"

The old woman pulled back, alarmed. Her big eyes filled with tears, her hands dug into the folds of her dress. The lips moved, muttered, mumbled things at the window, at the door, at her own pointed knees. Then suddenly she leaned ahead again, seared a scowl into him. "All a mirage!" she shrieked, and looked frightened by her own words. She drew back, swallowed, gathered courage again. "Blink your eyes and it's gone, or moved!"

Spit and Stella looked at each other. Stella raised an eyebrow. "That's enough, Mother," she said. Gently.

"Everybody said we had a good marriage," he said. "Spit and Stella, solid as rocks."

"If you had a good marriage," the old woman accused, "it was with your train, not a woman." And looked away, pointed her chin elsewhere.

Stella leapt up, snorting, and hurried out of the room with her bucket of soapy water.

Spit felt, he said, like he'd been dragged under the house by a couple of dogs and fought over. He had to lie down. And, lying down, he had to face up to what was happening. She came into the bedroom and stood at the foot of her bed. She puffed up her cheeks like a blowfish and fixed her eyes on him.

"I told the lawyer there was no fighting involved. I told him it was a friendly separation. But he said one of us better get out of the house all the same, live in a motel or something until it's arranged. He said you."

"Not me," he said. "I'll stay put, thank you."

"Then I'll go." Her face floated back, wavered in his watery vision, then came ahead again.

"I'd call that desertion," he said.

"You wouldn't dare."

And of course he wouldn't. It was no more and no less then what he'd expected, after everything else, if he thought about it.

All he wanted to do was put his cassette tape into a machine, lie back, close his eyes, and let the sounds of Old Number One rattle through him. That was all he wanted. When she'd gone he would drive in to town and buy a new machine.

"I'll leave the place clean," she said. "I'll leave food in the fridge when I go, in a few days. Do you think you can learn how to cook?"

"I don't know," he said. "How should I know? I don't even believe this is happening. I can't even think what it's going to be like."

"You'll get used to it. You've had twenty years of one kind of life, you'll get used to another."

Spit put his head back on the pillow. There wasn't a thing he could reach out and touch and be sure of.

At the foot of his obsolete B/A sign, Spit on his rock watches the hitch-hikers spread out along the roadside like a pack of ragged refugees. Between him and them there is a ditch clogged with dry podded broom and a wild tangle of honeysuckle and blackberry vines. They perch on their packs, lean against the telephone pole, lie out flat on the gravel; every one of them indifferent to the sun, the traffic, to one another. We have all day, their postures say, we have for ever. If you won't pick us up, someone else just as good will do it, nobody needs you.

Spit can remember a time when he tried to have a pleading look on his face whenever he was out on the road. A look that said Please pick me up I may die if I don't get where I'm going on time. And made obscene gestures at every driver that passed him by. Sometimes hollered insults. These people, though, don't care enough to look hopeful. It doesn't matter to them if they get picked up or not, because they think where they're going isn't the slightest bit different from where they are now. Like bits of dry leaves, letting the wind blow them whatever way it wants.

The old bearded man notices Spit, raises a hand to his forehead in greeting. His gaze runs up the pole, flickers over the weathered sign, and runs down again. He gives Spit a grin, a slight shake of his head, turns away. Old fool, Spit thinks. At your age. And lifts his engineer cap to settle it farther back.

Spit cannot bear to think where these people are going, where their rides will take them. His mind touches, slides away from the boy with the St Bernard, sitting up against the back of that green pickup cab. He could follow them, in his mind he could go the whole distance with them, but he refuses, slides back from it, holds onto the things that are happening here and now.

The sound of Stella's shoes shifting in gravel. The scent of the pines, leaking pitch. The hot smell of sun on the rusted pole.

"I've left my phone number on the memo pad, on the counter."

The feel of the small pebbles under his boots.

"Jon and Cora'll take turns, on the weekends. Don't be scared to make Cora do your shopping when she's here. She knows how to look for things, you'll only get yourself cheated."

He'd yell *Okay!*

He holds on. He thinks of tourists filing through the National Museum, looking at Old Number One. People he'll never see, from Ottawa and Toronto and New York and for all he knows from Africa and Russia, standing around Old Number One, talking about her, pointing, admiring the black shine of her finish. Kids wondering what it would be like to ride in her, feel the thudding of her pistons under you.

He'd stand at the edge of the water and yell *Okay you son of a bitch, okay!*

"It don't look like there's going to be any complications. My lawyer can hardly believe how friendly all this's been. It'll all go by smooth as sailing."

Spit Delaney sees himself get up into the pickup with the youth and the St Bernard, sees himself slide his ass right up against the cab, slam his hand in a signal on the hot metal roof. Sees himself going down the silver-grey road, heading west. Sees himself laughing.

He says, "My lawyer says if it's all so god-damned friendly how come you two are splitting up."

"That's just it," she says. "Friends are one thing. You don't have to be married to be a friend."

"I don't know what you're talking about," Spit says. It occurs to him that he has come home from a trip through Europe and northern Africa and can't remember a thing. Something happened there, but what was it?

He sees himself riding in that pickup all up through the valley farmlands, over the mountains in the centre of the island, down along the lakes and rivers, snaking across towards Pacific. Singing, maybe, with that boy. Throwing his arm around the floppy dog's ugly neck. Feeling the air change gradually to damp, and colder. Straining his neck to see.

"I got my Lodge tonight, so I better get going, it'll give me the day to get settled in, it takes time to unpack. You'll be all right?"

Sees himself hopping off the green pickup, amongst the distorted combed-back spruce, the giant salal, sees himself touching the boy goodbye, patting the dog. Sees himself go down through the logs, through the white dry sand, over the damp brown sand and the seaweed. Sees himself at the water's edge on his long bony legs like someone who's just grown them, unsteady, shouting.

Shouting into the blind heavy roar.

*Okay!*

*Okay you son of a bitch!*

*I'm stripped now, okay, now where is that god-damned line?*

# RAYMOND CARVER

1938–

Born in Clatskanie, Oregon, Carver was educated at Humboldt State College (now California State University, Humboldt) and at the University of Iowa. He has worked as an editor for Science Research Associates, Inc., and as a professor of English and creative writing at various universities, including the University of California at Berkeley, the University of Iowa, the University of Texas at El Paso, and Syracuse University. Carver has published over fifteen books of poetry and fiction, and is often credited with having helped to revive the short story as a literary form in the United States.

## Cathedral

This blind man, an old friend of my wife's, he was on his way to spend the night. His wife had died. So he was visiting the dead wife's relatives in Connecticut. He called my wife from his in-laws'. Arrangements were made. He would come by train, a five-hour trip, and my wife would meet him at the station. She hadn't seen him since she worked for him one summer in Seattle ten years ago. But she and the blind man had kept in touch. They made tapes and mailed them back and forth. I wasn't enthusiastic about his visit. He was no one I knew. And his being blind bothered me. My idea of blindness came from the movies. In the movies, the blind moved slowly and never laughed. Sometimes they were led by seeing-eye dogs. A blind man in my house was not something I looked forward to.

That summer in Seattle she had needed a job. She didn't have any money. The man she was going to marry at the end of the summer was in officers' training school. He didn't have any money, either. But she was in love with the guy, and he was in love with her, etc. She'd seen something in the paper: HELP WANTED—*Reading to Blind Man*, and a telephone number. She phoned and went over, was hired on the spot. She'd worked with this blind man all summer. She read stuff to him, case studies, reports, that sort of thing. She helped him organize his little office in the county social-service department. They'd become good friends, my wife and the blind man. How do I know these things? She told me. And she told me something else. On her last day in the office, the blind man asked if he could touch her face. She agreed to this. She told me he touched his fingers to every part of her face, her nose—even her neck! She never forgot it. She even tried to write a poem about it. She was always trying to write a poem. She wrote a poem or two every year, usually after something really important had happened to her.

When we first started going out together, she showed me the poem. In the poem, she recalled his fingers and the way they had moved around over her face. In the poem, she talked about what she had felt at the time, about what went through her mind when the blind man touched her nose and lips. I can remember I didn't think much of the poem. Of course, I didn't tell her that. Maybe I just don't understand poetry. I admit it's not the first thing I reach for when I pick up something to read.

Anyway, this man who'd first enjoyed her favors, the officer-to-be, he'd been her childhood sweetheart. So okay. I'm saying that at the end of the summer she let the blind man run his hands over her face, said goodbye to him, married her childhood etc., who was now a commissioned officer, and she moved away from Seattle. But they'd kept in touch, she and the blind man. She made the first contact after a year or so. She called him up one night from an Air Force base in Alabama. She wanted to talk. They talked. He asked her to send him a tape and tell him about her life. She did this. She sent the tape. On the tape, she told the blind man about her husband and about their life together in the military. She told the blind man she loved her husband but she didn't like it where they lived and she didn't like it that he was a part of the military-industrial thing. She told the blind man she'd written a poem and he was in it. She told him that she was writing a poem about what it was like to be an Air Force officer's wife. The poem wasn't finished yet. She was still writing it. The blind man made a tape. He sent her the tape. She made a tape. This went on for years. My wife's officer was posted to one base and then another. She sent tapes from Moody AFB, McGuire, McConnell, and finally Travis, near Sacramento, where one night she got to feeling lonely and cut off from people she kept losing in that moving-around life. She got to feeling she couldn't go it another step. She went in and swallowed all the pills and capsules in the medicine chest and washed them down with a bottle of gin. Then she got into a hot bath and passed out.

But instead of dying, she got sick. She threw up. Her officer—why should he have a name? he was the childhood sweetheart, and what more does he want?—came home from somewhere, found her, and called the ambulance. In time, she put it all on a tape and sent the tape to the blind man. Over the years, she put all kinds of stuff on tapes and sent the tapes off lickety-split. Next to writing a poem every year, I think it was her chief means of recreation. On one tape, she told the blind man she'd decided to live away from her officer for a time. On another tape, she told him about her divorce. She and I began going out, and of course she told her blind man about it. She told him everything, or so it seemed to me. Once she asked me if I'd like to hear the latest tape from the blind man. This was a year ago. I was on the tape, she said. So I said okay, I'd listen to it. I got us drinks and we settled down in the living room. We made ready to listen. First she inserted the tape into the player and adjusted a couple of dials. Then she pushed a lever. The tape squeaked and someone began to talk in this loud voice. She lowered the volume. After a few minutes of harmless chitchat, I heard my own name in the mouth of this stranger, this blind man I didn't even know! And then this: "From all you've said about him, I can only conclude—" But we were interrupted, a knock at the door, something, and we didn't ever get back to the tape. Maybe it was just as well. I'd heard all I wanted to.

Now this same blind man was coming to sleep in my house.

"Maybe I could take him bowling," I said to my wife. She was at the draining board doing scalloped potatoes. She put down the knife she was using and turned around.

"If you love me," she said, "you can do this for me. If you don't love me, okay. But if you had a friend, any friend, and the friend came to visit, I'd make him feel comfortable." She wiped her hands with the dish towel.

"I don't have any blind friends," I said.

"You don't have any friends," she said. "Period. Besides," she said, "goddamn it, his wife's just died! Don't you understand that? The man's lost his wife?

I didn't answer. She'd told me a little about the blind man's wife. Her name was Beulah. Beulah! That's a name for a colored woman.

"Was his wife a Negro?" I asked.

"Are you crazy?" my wife said. "Have you just flipped or something?" She picked up a potato. I saw it hit the floor, then roll under the stove. "What's wrong with you?" she said. "Are you drunk?"

"I'm just asking," I said.

Right then my wife filled me in with more detail than I cared to know. I made a drink and sat at the kitchen table to listen. Pieces of the story began to fall into place.

Beulah had gone to work for the blind man the summer after my wife had stopped working for him. Pretty soon Beulah and the blind man had themselves a church wedding. It was a little wedding— who'd want to go to such a wedding in the first place?—just the two of them, plus the minister and the minister's wife. But it was a church wedding just the same. It was what Beulah had wanted, he'd said. But even then Beulah must have been carrying the cancer in her glands. After they had been inseparable for eight years—my wife's word, *inseparable*—Beulah's health went into a rapid decline. She died in a Seattle hospital room, the blind man sitting beside the bed and holding on to her hand. They'd married, lived and worked together, slept together—had sex, sure—and then the blind man had to bury her. All this without his having ever seen what the goddamned woman looked like. It was beyond my understanding. Hearing this, I felt sorry for the blind man for a little bit. And then I found myself thinking what a pitiful life this woman must have led. Imagine a woman who could never see herself as she was seen in the eyes of her loved one. A woman who could go on day after day and never receive the smallest compliment from her beloved. A woman whose husband could never read the expression on her face, be it misery or something better. Someone who could wear makeup or not—what difference to him? She could, if she wanted, wear green eye-shadow around one eye, a straight pin in her nostril, yellow slacks and purple shoes, no matter. And then to slip off into death, the blind man's hand on her hand, his blind eyes streaming tears—I'm imagining now—her last thought maybe this: that he never even knew what she looked like, and she on an express to the grave. Robert was left with a small insurance policy and half of a twenty-peso Mexican coin. The other half of the coin went into the box with her. Pathetic.

So when the time rolled around, my wife went to the depot to pick him up. With nothing to do but wait—sure, I blamed him for that— I was having a drink and watching the TV when I heard the car pull into the drive. I got up from the sofa with my drink and went to the window to have a look.

I saw my wife laughing as she parked the car. I saw her get out of the car and shut the door. She was still wearing a smile. Just amazing. She went around to the other side of the car to where the blind man was already starting to get out. This blind man, feature this, he was wearing a full beard! A beard on a blind man! Too much, I say. The blind man reached into the back seat and dragged out a suitcase. My wife took his arm, shut the car door, and, talking all the way, moved him down the drive and then up the steps to the front porch. I turned off the TV. I finished my drink, rinsed the glass, dried my hands. Then I went to the door.

My wife said, "I want you to meet Robert. Robert, this is my husband. I've told you all about him." She was beaming. She had this blind man by his coat sleeve.

The blind man let go of his suitcase and up came his hand.

I took it. He squeezed hard, held my hand, and then he let it go. "I feel like we've already met," he boomed.

"Likewise," I said. I didn't know what else to say. Then I said, "Welcome. I've heard a lot about you." We began to move then, a little group, from the porch into the living room, my wife guiding him by the arm. The blind man was carrying his suitcase in his other hand. My wife said things like, "To your left here, Robert. That's right. Now watch it, there's a chair. That's it. Sit down right here. This is the sofa. We just bought the sofa two weeks ago."

I started to say something about the old sofa. I'd liked that old sofa. But I didn't say anything. Then I wanted to say something else, small-talk, about the scenic ride along the Hudson. How going *to* New York, you should sit on the right-hand side of the train, and coming *from* New York, the left-hand side.

"Did you have a good train ride?" I said. "Which side of the train did you sit on, by the way?"

"What a question, which side!" my wife said. "What's it matter which side?" she said.

"I just asked," I said.

"Right side," the blind man said. "I hadn't been on a train in nearly forty years. Not since I was a kid. With my folks. That's been a long time. I'd nearly forgotten the sensation. I have winter in my beard now," he said. "So I've been told, anyway. Do I look distinguished, my dear?" the blind man said to my wife.

"You look distinguished, Robert," she said. "Robert," she said. "Robert, it's just so good to see you."

My wife finally took her eyes off the blind man and looked at me. I had the feeling she didn't like what she saw. I shrugged.

I've never met, or personally known, anyone who was blind. This blind man was late forties, a heavy-set, balding man with stooped shoulders, as if he carried a great weight there. He wore brown slacks, brown shoes, a light-brown shirt, a tie, a sports coat. Spiffy. He also had this full beard. But he didn't use a cane and he didn't wear dark glasses. I'd always thought dark glasses were a must for the blind. Fact was, I wished he had a pair. At first glance, his eyes looked like anyone else's eyes. But if you looked close, there was something different about them. Too much white in the iris, for one thing, and the pupils seemed to move around in the sockets without his knowing it or being able to stop it. Creepy. As I stared at his face, I saw the left pupil turn in toward his nose while the other made an effort to keep in one place. But it was only an effort, for that eye was on the roam without his knowing it or wanting it to be.

I said, "Let me get you a drink. What's your pleasure? We have a little of everything. It's one of our pastimes."

"Bub, I'm a Scotch man myself," he said fast enough in this big voice.

"Right," I said. Bub! "Sure you are. I knew it."

He let his fingers touch his suitcase, which was sitting alongside the sofa. He was taking his bearings. I didn't blame him for that.

"I'll move that up to your room," my wife said.

"No, that's fine," the blind man said loudly. "It can go up when I go up."

"A little water with the Scotch?" I said.

"Very little," he said.

"I knew it," I said.

He said, "Just a tad. The Irish actor, Barry Fitzgerald? I'm like that fellow. When I drink water, Fitzgerald said, I drink water. When I drink whiskey, I drink whiskey." My wife laughed. The blind man brought his hand up under his beard. He lifted his beard slowly and let it drop.

I did the drinks, three big glasses of Scotch with a splash of water in each. Then we made ourselves comfortable and talked about Robert's travels. First the long flight from the West Coast to Connecticut, we covered that. Then from Connecticut up here by train. We had another drink concerning that leg on the trip.

I remembered having read somewhere that the blind didn't smoke because, as speculation had it, they couldn't see the smoke they exhaled. I thought I knew that much and that much only about blind people. But this blind man smoked his cigarette down to the nubbin and then lit another one. This blind man filled his ashtray and my wife emptied it.

When we sat down at the table for dinner, we had another drink. My wife heaped Robert's plate with cube steak, scalloped potatoes, green beans. I buttered him up two slices of bread. I said, "Here's bread and butter for you." I swallowed some of my drink. "Now let us pray," I said, and the blind man lowered his head. My wife looked at me, her mouth agape. "Pray the phone won't ring and the food doesn't get cold," I said.

We dug in. We ate everything there was to eat on the table. We ate like there was no tomorrow. We didn't talk. We ate. We scarfed. We grazed that table. We were into serious eating. The blind man had right away located his foods, he knew just where everything was on his plate. I watched with admiration as he used his knife and fork on the meat. He'd cut two pieces of meat, fork the meat into his mouth, and then go all out for the scalloped potatoes, the beans next, and then he'd tear off a hunk of buttered bread and eat that. He'd follow this up with a big drink of milk. It didn't seem to bother him to use his fingers once in a while, either.

We finished everything, including half a strawberry pie. For a few moments, we sat as if stunned. Sweat beaded on our faces. Finally, we got up from the table and left the dirty plates. We didn't look back. We took ourselves into the living room and sank into our places again. Robert and my wife sat on the sofa. I took the big chair. We had us two or three more drinks while they talked about the major things that had come to pass for them in the past ten years. For the most part, I just listened. Now and then I joined in. I didn't want him to think I'd left the room, and I didn't want her to think I was feeling left out. They talked of things that had happened to them— to them!—these past ten years. I waited in vain to hear my name on my wife's sweet lips: "And then my dear husband came into my life"—something like that. But I heard nothing of the sort. More talk of Robert. Robert had done a little of everything, it seemed, a regular blind jack-of-all-trades. But most recently he and his wife had had an Amway distributorship, from which, I gathered, they'd earned their living, such as it was. The blind man was also a ham radio operator. He talked in his loud voice about conversations he'd had with fellow operators in Guam, in the Philippines, in Alaska, and even in Tahiti. He said he'd have a lot of friends there if he ever wanted to go visit those places. From time to time, he'd turn his blind face toward me, put his hand under his beard, ask me something. How long had I been in my present position? (Three years) Did I like my work? (I didn't.) Was I going to stay with it? (What were the options?) Finally, when I thought he was beginning to run down, I got up and turned on the TV.

My wife looked at me with irritation. She was heading toward a boil. Then she looked at the blind man and said, "Robert, do you have a TV?"

The blind man said, "My dear, I have two TVs. I have a color set and a black-and-white thing, an old relic. It's funny, but if I turn the

TV on, and I'm always turning it on, I turn on the color set. It's funny, don't you think?''

I didn't know what to say to that. I had absolutely nothing to say to that. No opinion. So I watched the news program and tried to listen to what the announcer was saying.

"This is a color TV," the blind man said. "Don't ask me how, but I can tell."

"We traded up a while ago," I said.

The blind man had another taste of his drink. He lifted his beard, sniffed it, and let it fall. He leaned forward on the sofa. He positioned his ashtray on the coffee table, then put the lighter to his cigarette. He leaned back on the sofa and crossed his legs at the ankles.

My wife covered her mouth, and then she yawned. She stretched. She said, "I think I'll go upstairs and put on my robe. I think I'll change into something else. Robert, you make yourself comfortable," she said.

"I'm comfortable," the blind man said.

"I want you to feel comfortable in this house," she said.

"I am comfortable," the blind man said.

After she'd left the room, he and I listened to the weather report and then to the sports roundup. By that time, she'd been gone so long I didn't know if she was going to come back. I thought she might have gone to bed. I wished she'd come back downstairs. I didn't want to be left alone with a blind man. I asked him if he wanted another drink, and he said sure. Then I asked if he wanted to smoke some dope with me. I said I'd just rolled a number. I hadn't, but I planned to do so in about two shakes.

"I'll try some with you," he said.

"Damn right," I said. "That's the stuff."

I got our drinks and sat down on the sofa with him. Then I rolled us two fat numbers. I lit one and passed it. I brought it to his fingers. He took it and inhaled.

"Hold it as long as you can," I said. I could tell he didn't know the first thing.

My wife came back downstairs wearing her pink robe and her pink slippers.

"What do I smell?" she said.

"We thought we'd have us some cannabis," I said.

My wife gave me a savage look. Then she looked at the blind man and said, "Robert, I didn't know you smoked."

He said, "I do now, my dear. There's a first time for everything. But I don't feel anything yet."

"This stuff is pretty mellow," I said. "This stuff is mild. It's dope you can reason with," I said. "It doesn't mess you up."

"Not much it doesn't, bub," he said, and laughed.

My wife sat on the sofa between the blind man and me. I passed her the number. She took it and toked and then passed it back to me. "Which way is this going?" she said. Then she said, "I shouldn't be smoking this. I can hardly keep my eyes open as it is. That dinner did me in. I shouldn't have eaten so much."

"It was the strawberry pie," the blind man said. "That's what did it," he said, and he laughed his big laugh. Then he shook his head.

"There's more strawberry pie," I said.

"Do you want some more, Robert?" my wife said.

"Maybe in a little while," he said.

We gave our attention to the TV. My wife yawned again. She said, "Your bed is made up when you feel like going to bed, Robert. I know you must have had a long day. When you're ready to go to bed, say so." She pulled his arm. "Robert?"

He came to and said, "I've had a real nice time. This beats tapes, doesn't it?"

I said, "Coming at you," and I put the number between his fingers. He inhaled, held the smoke, and then let it go. It was like he'd been doing it since he was nine years old.

"Thanks, bub," he said. "But I think this is all for me. I think I'm beginning to feel it," he said. He held the burning roach out for my wife.

"Same here," she said. "Ditto. Me, too." She took the roach and passed it to me. "I may just sit here for a while between you two guys with my eyes closed. But don't let me bother you, okay? Either one of you. If it bothers you, say so. Otherwise, I may just sit here with my eyes closed until you're ready to go to bed," she said. "Your bed's made up, Robert, when you're ready. It's right next to our room at the top of the stairs. We'll show you up when you're ready. You wake me up now, you guys, if I fall asleep." She said that and then she closed her eyes and went to sleep.

The news program ended. I got up and changed the channel. I sat back down on the sofa. I wished my wife hadn't pooped out. Her head lay across the back of the sofa, her mouth open. She'd turned so that her robe had slipped away from her legs, exposing a juicy thigh. I reached to draw her robe back over her, and it was then that I glanced at the blind man. What the hell! I flipped the robe open again.

"You say when you want some strawberry pie," I said.

"I will," he said.

I said, "Are you tired? Do you want me to take you up to your bed? Are you ready to hit the hay?"

"Not yet," he said. "No, I'll stay up with you, bub. If that's all right. I'll stay up until you're ready to turn in. We haven't had a chance to talk. Know what I mean? I feel like me and her monopolized the evening." He lifted his beard and he let it fall. He picked up his cigarettes and his lighter.

"That's all right," I said. Then I said, "I'm glad for the company."

And I guess I was. Every night I smoked dope and stayed up as long as I could before I fell asleep. My wife and I hardly ever went to bed at the same time. When I did go to sleep, I had these dreams. Sometimes I'd wake up from one of them, my heart going crazy.

Something about the church and the Middle Ages was on the TV. Not your run-of-the-mill TV fare. I wanted to watch something else. I turned to the other channels. But there was nothing on them, either. So I turned back to the first channel and apologized.

"Bub, it's all right," the blind man said. "It's fine with me. Whatever you want to watch is okay. I'm always learning something. Learning never ends. It won't hurt me to learn something tonight. I got ears," he said.

We didn't say anything for a time. He was leaning forward with his head turned at me, his right ear aimed in the direction of the set. Very disconcerting. Now and then his eyelids drooped and then they snapped open again. Now and then he put his fingers into his beard and tugged, like he was thinking about something he was hearing on the television.

On the screen, a group of men wearing cowls was being set upon and tormented by men dressed in skeleton costumes and men dressed as devils. The men dressed as devils wore devil masks, horns, and long tails. This pageant was part of a procession. The Englishman who was narrating the thing said it took place in Spain once a year. I tried to explain to the blind man what was happening.

"Skeletons," he said. "I know about skeletons," he said, and he nodded.

The TV showed this one cathedral. Then there was a long, slow look at another one. Finally, the picture switched to the famous one in Paris, with its flying buttresses and its spires reaching up to the clouds. The camera pulled away to show the whole of the cathedral rising above the skyline.

There were times when the Englishman who was telling the thing would shut up, would simply let the camera move around over the cathedrals. Or else the camera would tour the countryside, men in fields walking behind oxen. I waited as long as I could. Then I felt I had to say something. I said, "They're showing the outside of this cathedral now. Gargoyles. Little statues carved to look like monsters. Now I guess they're in Italy. Yeah, they're in Italy. There's paintings on the walls of this one church."

"Are those fresco paintings, bub?" he asked, and he sipped from his drink.

I reached for my glass. But it was empty. I tried to remember what I could remember. "You're asking me are those frescoes?" I said. "That's a good question. I don't know."

The camera moved to a cathedral outside Lisbon. The differences in the Portuguese cathedral compared with the French and Italian were not that great. But they were there. Mostly the interior stuff. Then something occurred to me, and I said, "Something has occurred to me. Do you have any idea what a cathedral is? What they look like, that is? Do you follow me? If somebody says cathedral to you, do you have any notion what they're talking about? Do you know the difference between that and a Baptist church, say?"

He let the smoke dribble from his mouth. "I know they took hundreds of workers fifty or a hundred years to build," he said. "I just heard the man say that, of course. I know generations of the same families worked on a cathedral. I heard him say that, too. The men who began their life's work on them, they never lived to see the completion of their work. In that wise, bub, they're no different from the rest of us, right?" He laughed. Then his eyelids drooped again. His head nodded. He seemed to be snoozing. Maybe he was imagining himself in Portugal. The TV was showing another cathedral now. This one was in Germany. The Englishman's voice droned on. "Cathedrals," the blind man said. He sat up and rolled his head back and forth. "If you want the truth, bub, that's about all I know. What I just said. What I heard him say. But maybe you could describe one to me? I wish you'd do it. I'd like that. If you want to know, I really don't have a good idea."

I stared hard at the shot of the cathedral on the TV. How could I even begin to describe it? But say my life depended on it. Say my life was being threatened by an insane guy who said I had to do it or else.

I stared some more at the cathedral before the picture flipped off into the countryside. There was no use. I turned to the blind man and said, "To begin with, they're very tall." I was looking around the room for clues. "They reach way up. Up and up. Toward the sky. They're so big, some of them, they have to have these supports. To help hold them up, so to speak. These supports are called buttresses. They remind me of viaducts, for some reason. But maybe you don't know viaducts, either? Sometimes the cathedrals have devils and such carved into the front. Sometimes lords and ladies. Don't ask me why this is," I said.

He was nodding. The whole upper part of his body seemed to be moving back and forth.

"I'm not doing so good, am I?" I said.

He stopped nodding and leaned forward on the edge of the sofa. As he listened to me, he was running his fingers through his beard. I wasn't getting through to him, I could see that. But he waited for me to go on just the same. He nodded, like he was trying to encourage me. I tried to think what else to say. "They're really big," I said. "They're massive. They're built of stone. Marble, too, sometimes. In those olden days, when they built cathedrals, men wanted to be close to God. In those olden days, God was an important part of everyone's life. You could tell this from their cathedral-building. I'm sorry," I said, "but it looks like that's the best I can do for you. I'm just no good at it."

"That's all right, bub," the blind man said. "Hey, listen. I hope you don't mind my asking you. Can I ask you something? Let me ask you a simple question, yes or no. I'm just curious and there's no offense. You're my host. But let me ask if you are in any way religious? You don't mind my asking?"

I shook my head. He couldn't see that, though. A wink is the same as a nod to a blind man. "I guess I don't believe in it. In anything. Sometimes it's hard. You know what I'm saying?"

"Sure, I do," he said.

"Right," I said.

The Englishman was still holding forth. My wife sighed in her sleep. She drew a long breath and went on with her sleeping.

"You'll have to forgive me," I said. "But I can't tell you what a cathedral looks like. It just isn't in me to do it. I can't do any more than I've done."

The blind man sat very still, his head down, as he listened to me.

I said, "The truth is, cathedrals don't mean anything special to me. Nothing. Cathedrals. They're something to look at on late-night TV. That's all they are."

It was then that the blind man cleared his throat. He brought something up. He took a handkerchief from his back pocket. Then he said, "I get it, bub. It's okay. It happens. Don't worry about it," he said. "Hey, listen to me. Will you do me a favor? I got an idea. Why don't you find us some heavy paper? And a pen. We'll do something. We'll draw one together. Get us a pen and some heavy paper. Go on, bub, get the stuff," he said.

So I went upstairs. My legs felt like they didn't have any strength in them. They felt like they did after I'd done some running. In my wife's room, I looked around. I found some ballpoints in a little basket on her table. And then I tried to think where to look for the kind of paper he was talking about.

Downstairs, in the kitchen, I found a shopping bag with onion skins in the bottom of the bag. I emptied the bag and shook it. I brought it into the living room and sat down with it near his legs. I moved some things, smoothed the wrinkles from the bag, spread it out on the coffee table.

The blind man got down from the sofa and sat next to me on the carpet.

He ran his fingers over the paper. He went up and down the sides of the paper. The edges, even the edges. He fingered the corners.

"All right," he said. "All right, let's do her."

He found my hand, the hand with the pen. He closed his hand over my hand. "Go ahead, bub, draw," he said. "Draw. You'll see. I'll follow along with you. It'll be okay. Just begin now like I'm telling you. You'll see. Draw," the blind man said.

So I began. First I drew a box that looked like a house. It could have been the house I lived in. Then I put a roof on it. At either end of the roof, I drew spires. Crazy.

"Swell," he said. "Terrific. You're doing fine," he said. "Never thought anything like this could happen in your lifetime, did you, bub? Well, it's a strange life, we all know that. Go on now. Keep it up."

I put in windows with arches. I drew flying buttresses. I hung great doors. I couldn't stop. The TV station went off the air. I put down the pen and closed and opened my fingers. The blind man felt around over the paper. He moved the tips of his fingers over the paper, all over what I had drawn, and he nodded.

"Doing fine," the blind man said.

I took up the pen again, and he found my hand. I kept at it. I'm no artist. But I kept drawing just the same.

My wife opened up her eyes and gazed at us. She sat up on the sofa, her robe hanging open. She said, "What are you doing? Tell me, I want to know."

I didn't answer her.

The blind man said, "We're drawing a cathedral. Me and him are working on it. Press hard," he said to me. "That's right. That's good," he said. "Sure. You got it, bub. I can tell. You didn't think you could. But you can, can't you? You're cooking with gas now. You know what I'm saying? We're going to really have us something here in a minute. How's the old arm?" he said. "Put some people in there now. What's a cathedral without people?"

My wife said, "What's going on? Robert, what are you doing? What's going on?"

"It's all right," he said to her. "Close your eyes now," the blind man said to me.

I did it. I closed them just like he said.

"Are they closed?" he said. "Don't fudge."

"They're closed," I said.

"Keep them that way," he said. He said, "Don't stop now. Draw."

So we kept on with it. His fingers rode my fingers as my hand went over the paper. It was like nothing else in my life up to now.

Then he said, "I think that's it. I think you got it," he said. "Take a look. What do you think?"

But I had my eyes closed. I thought I'd keep them that way for a little longer. I thought it was something I ought to do.

"Well?" he said. "Are you looking?"

My eyes were still closed. I was in my house. I knew that. But I didn't feel like I was inside anything.

"It's really something," I said.


# MARGARET ATWOOD
## 1939–

Born in Ottawa, Margaret Atwood moved with her family to Sault Ste Marie in 1945 and to Toronto a year later. The daughter of an entomologist who specialized in forest insects, she came to know the bush country of northern Ontario and Quebec intimately. She graduated from Victoria College, the University of Toronto, in 1961, and received an M.A. from Radcliffe College, Harvard, in 1962. She has worked as a senior editor at the House of Anansi, as an executive member of the Writers' Union of Canada, and has taught English at a number of Canadian universities. At present she lives in Toronto with her husband, Graeme Gibson (also a writer) and daughter. She has written nine books of poetry, four novels and a collection of short stories, as well as a thematic guide to Canadian literature, *Survival*.


## The Grave of the Famous Poet

There are a couple of false alarms before we actually get there, towns we pass through that might be it but aren't, uninformative stores and houses edging the road, no signs. Even when we've arrived we aren't sure; we peer out, looking for a name, an advertisement. The bus pauses.

"This has to be it," I say. I have the map.

"Better ask the driver," he says, not believing me.

"Have I ever been wrong?" I say, but I ask the driver anyway. I'm right again and we get off.

We're in a constricted street of grey flat-fronted houses, their white lace curtains pulled closed, walls rising cliff-straight and lawnless from the narrow sidewalk. There are no other people; at least it isn't a tourist trap. I have to eat, we've been travelling all morning, but he wants to find a hotel first, he always needs a home base.

Right in front of us there's a building labelled HOTEL. We hesitate outside it, patting down our hair, trying to look acceptable. When he finally grits up the steps with our suitcases the doors are locked. Maybe it's a pub.

Hoping there may be a place further along, we walk down the hill, following the long stone wall, crossing the road when the sidewalk disappears at the corners. Cars pass us, driving fast as though on their way to somewhere else.

At the bottom of the hill near the beach there's a smattering of shops and a scarred, listing inn. Radio music and hilarious voices from inside.

"It seems local," I say, pleased.

"What does 'Inn' mean here?" he asks, but I don't know. He goes in to see; then he comes out, dispirited. I'm too tired to think up solutions; I'm scarcely noticing the castle on the hill behind us, the sea.

"No wonder he drank," he says.

"I'll ask," I say, aggrieved: it was his idea, he should do the finding. I try the general store. It's full of people, women mostly, with scarves on their heads and shopping baskets. They say there is no hotel; one woman says her mother has some rooms free though, and she gives me directions while the others gaze pityingly, I'm so obviously a tourist.

The house, when we find it, is eighteenth century and enormous, a summer residence when the town was fashionable. It offers Bed and Breakfast on a modest sign We're glad to have something spelled out for us. The door is open, we go into the hall, and the woman emerges from the parlour as though startled; she has a forties bobby-soxer hairdo with curious frontal lobes, only it's grey. She's friendly to us, almost sprightly, and yes, she has a room for us. I ask, in a lowered voice, if she can tell us where the grave is.

"You can almost see it from the window," she says, smiling—she knew we would ask that—and offers to lend us a book with a map in it of the points of interest, his house and all. She gets the book, scampers up the wide maroon-carpeted staircase to show us our room. It's vast, chill, high-ceilinged, with floral wallpaper and white-painted woodwork; instead of curtains the windows have inside shutters. There are three beds and numerous dressers and cupboards, crowded into the room as though in storage, a chunky bureau blocking the once-palatial fireplace. We say it will be fine.

"The grave is just up the hill, that way," she says, pointing through the window. We can see the tip of a church. "I'm sure you'll enjoy it."

I change into jeans and boots while he opens and closes the drawers on all the pieces of furniture, searching for ambushes or reading matter. He discovers nothing and we set out.

We ignore the church—he once said it was unremarkable—and head for the graveyard. It must rain a lot: ivy invades everything, and the graveyard is lush with uncut grass, succulent and light green. Feet have beaten animal-trail paths among the tombstones. The graves themselves are neatly tended, most of them have the grass clipped and fresh flowers in the teastrainer-shaped flower holders. There are three old ladies in the graveyard now, sheaves of flowers in their arms, gladioli, chrysanthemums; they are moving among the graves, picking out the old flowers and distributing the new ones impartially, like stewardesses. They take us for granted, neither approaching nor avoiding us: we are strangers and as such part of this landscape.

We find the right grave easily enough; as the book says, it's the only one with a wooden cross instead of a stone. The cross has been recently painted and the grave is planted with a miniature formal-garden arrangement of moss roses and red begonias; the sweet alyssum intended for a border hasn't quite worked. I wonder who planned it, surely it wouldn't have been her. The old ladies have been here and have left a vase, yellowish glassware of the kind once found in cereal boxes, with orange dahlias and spikes of an unknown pink flower. We've brought nothing and have no ceremonies to perform; we muse for an acceptable length of time, then retreat to the scroll-worked bench up the hill and sit in the sun, listening to the cows in the field across the road and the murmur of the ladies as they stoop and potter below us, their print dresses fluttering in the easy wind.

"It's not such a bad place," I say.

"But dull," he answers.

We have whatever it was we came for, the rest of the day is our own. After a while we leave the graveyard and stroll back down the main street, holding hands absentmindedly, looking in the windows of the few shops: an overpriced antique store, a handicrafts place with pottery and Welsh weaving, a nondescript store that sells everything, including girlie joke magazines and copies of his books. In the window, half-hidden among souvenir cups, maps and faded pennants, is a framed photograph of his face, three-quarters profile. We buy a couple of ice-cream bars; they are ancient and soapy.

We reach the bottom of the winding hill and decide to walk along to his house, which we can see, an indistinct white square separated from us by half a mile of rough beach. It's his house all right, it was marked on the map. At first we have no trouble; there's a wide uneven pathway, broken asphalt, the remains or perhaps the beginning of a road. Above us at the edge of the steep, leaf-covered cliff, what is left of the castle totters down, slowly, one stone a year. For him, turrets are irresistible. He finds a scrabbly trail, a children's entrance up sheer mud.

He goes up sideways, crabwise, digging footholds with the sides of his boots. "Come on!" he shouts down. I'm hesitant but I follow. At the top he reaches his hand to me, but, perpendicular and with the earth beside me, afraid of losing my balance, I avoid it and scramble the last few feet, holding on to roots. In wet weather it would be impossible.

He's ahead, eager to explore. The tunnel through the undergrowth leads to a gap in the castle wall; I follow his sounds, rustlings, the soft thud of his feet. We're in the skeleton of a garden, the beds marked by brick borders now grass-infested, a few rose bushes still attempting to keep order in spite of the aphids, nothing else paying any attention. I bend over a rose, ivory hearted, browning at the edges; I feel like a usurper. He's already out of sight again, hidden by an archway.

I catch up to him in the main courtyard. Everything is crumbling, stairways, ramparts, battlements; so much has fallen it's hard for us to get our bearings, translate this rubbish back into its earlier clear plan.

"That must have been the fireplace," I say, "and that's the main gate. We must have come round from the back." For some reason we speak in whispers; he tosses a fragment of stone and I tell him to be careful.

We go up the remnants of a stairway into the keep. It's almost totally dark; the floors are earth-covered. People must come here though, there's an old sack, an unidentifiable piece of clothing. We don't stay long inside: I'm afraid of getting lost, though it's not likely, and I would rather be able to see him. I don't like the thought of finding his hand suddenly on me unannounced. Besides, I don't trust the castle; I expect it to thunder down on us at the first loud laugh or false step. But we make it outside safely.

We pass beneath the gateway, its Norman curve still intact. Outside is another, larger courtyard, enclosed by the wall we have seen from outside and broken through; it has trees, recent trees not more than a hundred years old, dark-foliaged as etchings. Someone must come here to cut the grass: it's short, hair-textured. He lies down on it and draws me down beside him and we rest on our elbows, surveying. From the front the castle is more complete; you can see how it could once have been lived in by real people.

He lies down, closing his eyes, raising his hand to shade them from the sun. He's pale and I realize he must be tired too. I've been thinking of my own lack of energy as something he has caused and must therefore be immune from.

"I'd like to have a castle like that," he says. When he admires something he wants to own it. For an instant I pretend that he does have the castle, he's always been here, he has a coffin hidden in the crypt, if I'm not careful I'll be trapped and have to stay with him forever. If I'd had more sleep last night I'd be able to frighten myself this way but as it is I give up and lean back on the grass beside him, looking up at the trees as their branches move in the wind, every leaf sharpened to a glass-clear edge by my exhaustion.

I turn my head to watch him. In the last few days he's become not more familiar to me as he should have but more alien. Close up, he's a strange terrain, pores and hairs; but he isn't nearer, he's further away, like the moon when you've finally landed on it. I move back from him so I can see him better, he misinterprets, thinking I'm trying to get up, and stretches himself over me to prevent me. He kisses me, teeth digging into my lower lip; when it hurts too much I pull away. We lie side by side, both suffering from unrequited love.

This is an interval, a truce; it can't last, we both know it, there have been too many differences, of opinion we called it but it was more than that, the things that mean safety for him mean danger for me. We've talked too much or not enough: for what we have to say to each other there's no language, we've tried them all. I think of old science-fiction movies, the creature from another galaxy finally encountered after so many years of signals and ordeals only to be destroyed because he can't make himself understood. Actually it's less a truce than a rest, those silent black-and-white comedians hitting each other until they fall down, then getting up after a pause to begin again. We love each other, that's true whatever it means, but we aren't good at it; for some it's a talent, for others only an addiction. I wonder if they ever came here while he was still alive.

Right now though there's neither love nor anger, no resentment; it's a suspension, of fear even, like waiting for the dentist. But I don't want him to die. I feel nothing but I concentrate, somebody's version of God, I will him to exist, right now on the vacant lawn of this castle whose name we don't know in this foreign town we're in only because dead people are more real to him than living ones. Despite the mistakes I want everything to stay the way it is; I want to hold it.

He sits up: he's heard voices. Two little girls, baskets over their arms as though for a picnic or a game, have come into the grounds and are walking towards the castle. They stare at us curiously and decide we are harmless. "Let's play in the tower," one calls and they run and disappear among the walls. For them the castle is ordinary as a backyard.

He gets up, brushing of bits of grass. We haven't visited the house

yet but we still have time. We find our break in the wall, our pathway, and slide back down to sealevel. The sun has moved, the green
closes behind us.

The house is further than it looked from the village. The semi-road
gives out and we pick our way along the stoney beach. The tide is
out; the huge bay stretches as far as we can see, a solid mud-flat
except for the thin silty river that cuts along beside us. The dry part
narrows and vanishes, we are stranded below the tide line, clambering over slippery masses of purplish-brown rock or squelching
through the mud, thick as clotted cream. All around us is an odd
percolating sound: it's the mud, drying in the sun. There are gulls
too, and wind bending the unhealthy-coloured rushes by the bank.

"How the hell did he get back and forth?" he says. "Think of
doing this drunk on a dark night."

"There must be a road further up," I say.

We reach the house at last. Like everything else here it has a wall;
this one is to keep out the waves at high tide. The house itself is on
stilts, jammed up against the cliff, painted stone with a spindly-
railed two-decker porch. It hasn't been lived in for many years: one
window is broken and the railings are beginning to go. The yard is
weed-grown, but maybe it always was. I sit on the wall, dangling my
legs, while he pokes around, examining the windows, the outhouse
(which is open), the shed once used perhaps for a boat. I don't want
to see any of it. Graves are safely covered and the castle so derelict it
has the status of a tree or a stone, but the house is too recent, it is
still partly living. If I looked in the window there would be a table
with dishes not yet cleared away, or a fresh cigarette or a coat just
taken off. Or maybe a broken plate: they used to have fights, apparently. She never comes back and I can see why. He wouldn't leave
her alone.

He's testing the railing on the second-storey porch; he's going to
pull himself up by it.

"Don't do that," I say wearily.

"Why not?" he says. "I want to see the other side."

"Because you'll fall and I don't want to have to scrape you off the
rocks."

"Don't be like that," he says.

How did she manage? I turn my head away, I don't want to
watch. It will be such an effort, the police, I'll have to explain what I
was doing here, why he was climbing and fell. He should be more
considerate. But for once he thinks better of it.

There is another road, we discover it eventually, along the beach
and up an asphalt walk beside a neat inhabited cottage. Did they see
us coming, are they wondering who we are? The road above is

paved, it has a railing and a sign with the poet's name on it, wired to the fence.

"I'd like to steal that," he says.

We pause to view the house from above. There's an old lady in a garden-party hat and gloves, explaining things to an elderly couple. "He always kept to himself, he did," she is saying. "No one here ever got to know him really." She goes on to detail the prices that have been offered for the house: America wanted to buy it and ship it across the ocean, she says, but the town wouldn't let them.

We start back towards our room. Halfway along we sit down on a bench to scrape the mud from our boots; it clings like melted marshmallow. I lean back; I'm not sure I can make it to the house, whatever reserves my body has been drawing on are almost gone. My hearing is blurred and it's hard to breathe.

He bends over to kiss me. I don't want him to, I'm not calm now, I'm irritated, my skin prickles, I think of case histories, devoted wives who turn kleptomaniac two days a month, the mother who threw her baby out into the snow, it was in *Reader's Digest*, she had a hormone disturbance, love is all chemical. I want it to be over, this long abrasive competition for the role of victim; it used to matter that it should finish right, with grace, but not now. One of us should just get up from the bench, shake hands and leave, I don't care who is last, it would sidestep the recriminations, the totalling up of scores, the reclaiming of possessions, your key, my book. But it won't be that way, we'll have to work through it, boring and foreordained though it is. What keeps me is a passive curiosity, it's like an Elizabethan tragedy or a horror movie, I know which ones will be killed but not how. I take his hand and stroke the back of it gently, the fine hairs rasping my fingertips like sandpaper.

We'd been planning to change and have dinner, it's almost six, but back in the room I have only strength enough to pull off my boots. Then with my clothes still on I crawl into the enormous, creaking bed, cold as porridge and hammock-saggy. I float for an instant in the open sky on the backs of my eyelids, free fall, until sleep rushes up to meet me like the earth.

I wake up suddenly in total darkness. I remember where I am. He's beside me but he seems to be lying outside the blankets, furled in the bedspread. I get stealthily out of the bed, grope to the window and open one of the wooden shutters. It's almost as dark outside, there are no streetlights, but by straining I can read my watch; two o'clock. I've had my eight hours and my body thinks it's time for breakfast. I notice I still have my clothes on, take them off and get back in bed, but my stomach won't let me sleep. I hesitate, then decide it won't do him any harm and turn on the bedside lamp. On the dresser there's a crumpled paper bag; inside it is a Welsh cake, a soft white biscuit with currants in it. I bought it yesterday near the train station, asking in bakeries crammed with English buns and French pastries, running through the streets in a crazed search for local colour that almost made us late for the bus. Actually I bought two of them. I ate mine yesterday, this one is his, but I don't care; I take it out of the bag and devour it whole.

In the mirror I'm oddly swollen, as though I've been drowned, my eyes are purple-circled, my hair stands out from my head like a second-hand doll's, there's a diagonal scar-like mark across my cheek where I've been sleeping on my face. This is what it does to you. I estimate the weeks, months, it will take me to recuperate. Fresh air, good food and plenty of sun.

We have so little time and he just lies there, rolled up like a rug, not even twitching. I think of waking him, I want to make love, I want all there is because there's not much left. I start to think what he will do after I'm over and I can't stand that, maybe I should kill him, that's a novel idea, how melodramatic; nevertheless I look around the room for a blunt instrument; there's nothing but the bedside lamp, a grotesque woodland nymph with metal tits and a lightbulb coming out of her head. I could never kill anyone with that. Instead I brush my teeth, wondering if he'll ever know how close he came to being murdered, resolving anyway never to plant flowers for him, never to come back, and slide in among the chilly furrows and craters of the bed. I intend to watch the sun rise but I fall asleep by accident and miss it.

Breakfast, when the time for it finally comes, is shabby, decorous, with mended linens and plentiful but dinted silver. We have it in an ornate, dilapidated room whose grandiose mantelpiece now supports only china spaniels and tinted family photos. We're brushed and combed, thoroughly dressed; we speak in subdued voices.

The food is the usual: tea and toast, fried eggs and bacon and the inevitable grilled tomato. It's served by a different woman, grey-haired also but with a corrugated perm and red lipstick. We unfold our map and plan the route back; it's Sunday and there won't be a bus to the nearest railway town till after one, we may have trouble getting out.

He doesn't like fried eggs and he's been given two of them. I eat one for him and tell him to hack the other one up so it will look nibbled at least, it's only polite. He is grateful to me, he knows I'm taking care of him, he puts his hand for a moment over mine, the one not holding the fork. We tell each other our dreams: his of men with armbands, later of me in a cage made of frail slat-like bones, mine of escaping in winter through a field.

I eat his grilled tomato as an afterthought and we leave.

Upstairs in our room we pack; or rather I pack, he lies on the bed.

"What're we going to do till the bus comes?" he says. Being up so early unsettles him.

"Go for a walk," I say.

"We went for a walk yesterday," he says.

I turn around and he's holding out his arms, he wants me to come and lie down beside him. I do and he gives me a perfunctory initial kiss and starts to undo my buttons. He's using only his left hand, the right one is underneath me. He's having trouble. I stand up and take off, reluctantly, the clothes I've so recently put on. It's time for sex; he missed out on it last night.

He reaches up and hauls me in among the tangled sheets. I tense; he throws himself on me with the utilitarian urgency of a man running to catch a train, but it's more than that, it's different, he's biting down on my mouth, this time he'll get blood if it kills him. I pull him into me, wanting him to be with me, but for the first time I feel it's just flesh, a body, a beautiful machine, an animated corpse, he isn't in it any more, I want him so much and he isn't here. The bedsprings mourn beneath us.

"Sorry about that," he says.

"It's all right."

"No, shit, I really am sorry. I don't like it when that happens."

"It's all right," I say. I smooth his back, distancing him: he's back by the deserted house, back lying on the grass, back in the graveyard, standing in the sun looking down, thinking of his own death.

"We better get up," I say, "she might want to make up the room."

We're waiting for the bus. They lied to me in the general store, there is a hotel, I can see it now, it's just around the corner. We've had our quarrel, argument, fight, the one we were counting on. It was a routine one, a small one comparatively, its only importance the fact that it was the last. It carries the weight of all the other, larger things we said we forgave each other for but didn't. If there were separate buses we'd take them. As it is we wait together, standing a little apart.

We have over half an hour. "Let's go down to the beach," I say. "We can see the bus from there; it has to go the other way first." I cross the road and he follows me at a distance.

There's a wall; I climb it and sit down. The top is scattered with sharp flakes of broken stone, flint possibly, and bleached thumbnail-sized cockleshells, I know what they are because I saw them in the museum two days ago, and the occasional piece of broken glass. He leans against the wall near me, chewing on a cigarette. We say what we have to say in even, conversational voices, discussing how we'll get back, the available trains. I wasn't expecting it so soon.

After a while he looks at his watch, then walks away from me towards the sea, his boots crunching on the shells and pebbles. At the edge of the reed bank by the river he stops, back to me, one leg slightly bent. He holds his elbows, wrapped in his clothes as though in a cape, the storm breaks, his cape billows, thick leather boots sprout up his legs, a sword springs to attention in his hand. He throws his head back, courage, he'll meet them alone. Flash of lightning. Onward.

I wish I could do it so quickly. I sit calmed, frozen, not yet sure whether I've survived, the words we hurled at each other lying spread in fragments around me, solidified. It's the pause during the end of the world; how does one behave? The man who said he'd continue to tend his garden, does that make sense to me? It would if it were only a small ending, my own. But we aren't more doomed than anything else, it's dead already, at any moment the bay will vaporize, the hills across will lift into air, the space between will scroll itself up and vanish; in the graveyard the graves will open to show the dry puffball skulls, his wooden cross will flare like a match, his house collapse into itself, cardboard and lumber, no more language. He will stand revealed, history scaling away from him, the versions of him I made up and applied, stripped down to what he really is for a last instant before he flames up and goes out. Surely we should be holding each other, absolving, repenting, saying goodbye to each other, to everything because he will never find it again.

Above us the gulls wheel and ride, crying like drowning puppies or disconsolate angels. They have black rims around their eyes; they're a new kind, I've never seen any like that before. The tide is going out; the fresh wet mud gleams in the sun, miles of it, a level field of pure glass, pure gold. He stands outlined against it; a dark shape, faceless, light catching the edges of his hair.

I turn aside and look down at my hands. They are covered with greyish dust: I've been digging among the shells, gathering them together. I arrange them in a border, a square, each white shell overlapping the next. Inside I plant the flints, upright in tidy rows, like teeth, like flowers.

## BHARATI MUKHERJEE

1940–

Born in Calcutta, Mukherjee lived in Montreal and Toronto from 1966 to 1980; she is currently living in the United States. She has published two novels, *The Tiger's Daughter* (1972) and *Wife* (1975) and *Darkness* (1985), a collection of stories. With her husband, Clark Blaise she has published two works of non-fiction: *Days and Nights in Calcutta* (1977) and *The Sorrow and the Terror: The Haunting Legacy of the Air India Disaster* (1986). Finding herself labeled "ethnic" in the North American context has led Mukherjee to a persistent fascination, in her fiction, with the theme of cultural displacement.

# The Lady from Lucknow

When I was four, one of the girls next door fell in love with a Hindu. Her father intercepted a love note from the boy, and beat her with his leather sandals. She died soon after. I was in the room when my mother said to our neighbor, "The Nawab-*sahib* had no choice, but Husseina's heart just broke, poor dear." I was an army doctor's daughter, and I pictured the dead girl's heart—a rubbery squeezable organ with auricles and ventricles—first swelling, then bursting and coating the floor with thick, slippery blood.

We lived in Lucknow at the time, where the Muslim community was large. This was just before the British took the fat, diamond-shaped subcontinent and created two nations, a big one for the Hindus and a littler one for us. My father moved us to Rawalpindi in Pakistan two months after Husseina died. We were a family of soft, voluptuous children, and my father wanted to protect us from the Hindus' shameful lust.

I have fancied myself in love many times since, but never enough for the emotions to break through tissue and muscle. Husseina's torn heart remains the standard of perfect love.

At seventeen I married a good man, the fourth son of a famous poet-cum-lawyer in Islamabad. We have a daughter, seven, and a son, four. In the Muslim communities we have lived in, we are admired, Iqbal works for IBM, and because of his work we have made homes in Lebanon, Brazil, Zambia, and France. Now we live in Atlanta, Georgia, in a wide, new house with a deck and a backyard that runs into a golf course. IBM has been generous to us. We expect to pass on this good, decent life to our children. Our children are ashamed of the dingy cities where we got our start.

Some Sunday afternoons when Iqbal isn't at a conference halfway across the world, we sit together on the deck and drink gin and tonics as we have done on Sunday afternoons in a dozen exotic cities. But here, the light is different somehow. A gold haze comes off the golf course and settles on our bodies, our new house. When the light shines right in my eyes, I pull myself out of the canvas deck chair and lean against the railing that still smells of forests. Everything in Atlanta is so new!

"Sit," Iqbal tells me. "You'll distract the golfers. Americans are crazy for sex, you know that."

He half rises out of his deck chair. He lunges for my breasts in mock passion. I slip out of his reach.

At the bottom of the backyard, the golfers, caddies, and carts are too minute to be bloated with lust.

But, who knows? One false thwock! of their golfing irons, and my little heart, like a golf ball, could slice through the warm air and vanish into the jonquil-yellow beyond.

It isn't trouble that I want, though I do have a lover. He's an older man, an immunologist with the Center for Disease Control right here in town. He comes to see me when Iqbal is away at high-tech conferences in sunny, remote resorts. Just think, Beirut was once such a resort! Lately my lover comes to me on Wednesdays even if Iqbal's in town.

"I don't expect to live till ninety-five," James teases on the phone. His father died at ninety-three in Savannah. "But I don't want a bullet in the brain from a jealous husband right now."

Iqbal owns no firearms. Jealously would inflame him.

Besides, Iqbal would never come home in the middle of the day. Not even for his blood-pressure pills. The two times he forgot them last month, I had to take the bottle downtown. One does not rise through the multinational hierarchy coming home in midday, arriving late, or leaving early. Especially, he says, if you're a "not-quite" as we are. It is up to us to set the standards.

Wives who want to be found out will be found out. Indiscretions are deliberate. The woman caught in mid-shame is a woman who wants to get out. The rest of us carry on.

James flatters me indefatigably; he makes me feel beautiful, exotic, responsive. I am a creature he has immunized of contamination. When he is with me, the world seems a happy enough place.

Then he leaves. He slips back into his tweed suit and backs out of my driveway.

I met James Beamish at a reception for foreign students on the Emory University campus. Iqbal avoids these international receptions because he thinks of them as excuses for looking back when we should be looking forward. These evenings are almost always tedious, but I like to go; just in case there's someone new and fascinating.

The last two years, I've volunteered as host in the "hospitality pro-gram." At Thanksgiving and Christmas, two lonely foreign students are sent to our table.

That first evening at Emory we stood with name tags on lapels, white ones for students and blue ones for hosts. James was by a long table, pouring Chablis into a plastic glass. I noticed him right off. He was dressed much like the other resolute, decent men in the room. But whereas the other men wore white or blue shirts under their dark wool suits, James's shirt was bright red.

His wife was with him that evening, a stoutish woman with slender ankles and expensive shoes.

"Darling," she said to James. "See if you can locate our Palestin-ian." Then she turned to me, and smiling, peered into my name tag.

"I'm Nafeesa Hafeez," I helped out.

"Na-fee-sa," she read out. "Did I get that right?"

"Yes, perfect," I said.

"What a musical name," she said. "I hope you'll be very happy here. Is this your first time abroad?"

James came over with a glass of Chablis in each hand. "Did we draw this lovely lady? Oops, I'm sorry, you're a *host*, of course." A mocking blue light was in his eyes. "Just when I thought we were getting lucky, dear."

"Darling, ours is a Palestinian. I told you that in the car. This one is obviously not Palestinian, are you dear?" She took a bright orange notebook out of her purse and showed me a name.

I had to read it upside-down. Something Waheed. School of Dentistry.

"What are you drinking?" James asked. He kept a glass for himself and gave me the other one.

Maybe James Beamish said nothing fascinating that night, but he was attentive, even after the Beamishes' Palestinian joined us. Mrs. Beam-ish was brave, she asked the dentist about his family and hometown. The dentist described West Beirut in detail. The shortage of bread and vegetables, the mortar poundings, the babies bleeding. I wonder when aphasia sets in. When does a dentist, even a Palestinian dentist, decide it's time to cut losses.

Then my own foreign student arrived. She was an Indian Muslim from Lucknow, a large, bold woman who this far from our common hometown claimed me as a countrywoman. India, Pakistan, she said, not letting go of my hand, what does it matter?

I'd rather have listened to James Beamish but I couldn't shut out the woman's voice. She gave us her opinions on Thanksgiving rit-uals. She said, "It is very odd that the pumpkin vegetable should be used for dessert, no? We are using it as vegetable only. Chhi!

Pumpkin as a sweet. The very idea is horrid."

I promised that when she came to our house for Thanksgiving, I'd make sweetmeats out of ricotta cheese and syrup. When you live in as many countries as Iqbal had made me, you can't tell if you pity, or if you envy, the women who stayed back.

I didn't hear from James Beamish for two weeks. I thought about him. In fact I couldn't get him out of my mind. I went over the phrases and gestures, the mocking light in the eyes, but they didn't add up to much. After the first week, I called Amina and asked her to lunch. I didn't know her well but her husband worked at the Center for Disease Control. Just talking to someone connected with the Center made me feel good. I slipped his name into the small talk with Amina and her eyes popped open, "Oh, he's famous!" she exclaimed, and I shrugged modestly. I stayed home in case he should call. I sat on the deck and in spite of the cold, pretended to read Barbara Pym novels. Lines from Donne and Urdu verses about love floated in my skull.

I wasn't sure Dr. Beamish would call me. Not directly, that is. Perhaps he would play a subtler game, get his wife to invite Iqbal and me for drinks. Maybe she'd even include their Palestinian and my Indian and make an international evening out of it. It sounded plausible.

Finally James Beamish called me on a Tuesday afternoon, around four. The children were in the kitchen, and a batch of my special chocolate sludge cookies was in the oven.

"Hi," he said, then nothing for a bit. Then he said, "This is James Beamish from the CDC. I've been thinking of you."

He was between meetings, he explained. Wednesday was the only flexible day in his week, his day for paperwork. Could we have lunch on Wednesday?

The cookies smelled gooey hot, not burned. My daughter had taken the cookie sheet out and put in a new one. She'd turned the cold water faucet on so she could let the water drip on a tiny rosebud burn on her arm.

I felt all the warm, familiar signs of lust and remorse. I dabbed the burn with an ice cube wrapped in paper towel and wondered if I'd have time to buy a new front-closing bra after Iqbal got home.

James and I had lunch in a Dekalb County motel lounge.

He would be sixty-five in July, but not retire till sixty-eight. Then he would live in Tonga, in Fiji, see the world, travel across Europe and North America in a Winnebago. He wouldn't be tied down. He had five daughters and two grandsons, the younger one aged four, a month older than my son. He had been in the navy during the war (*his* war), and he had liked that.

I said, " 'Goodbye, Mama, I'm off to Yokohama.' " It was silly, but it was the only war footage I could come up with, and it made him laugh.

"You're special," he said. He touched my knee under the table. "You've already been everywhere."

"Not because I've wanted to."

He squeezed my knee again, then paid with his MasterCard card.

As we were walking through the parking lot to his car (it was a Cougar or a Buick, and not German or British as I'd expected), James put his arm around my shoulders. I may have seen the world but I haven't gone through the American teenage rites of making out in parked cars and picnic grounds, so I walked briskly out of his embrace. He let his hand slide off my shoulder. The hand slid down my back. I counted three deft little patts to my bottom before he let his hand fall away.

Iqbal and I are sensual people, but secretive. The openness of James Beamish's advance surprised me.

I got in his car, wary, expectant.

"Do up the seatbelt," he said.

He leaned into his seatbelt and kissed me lightly on the lips. I kissed him back, hard. "You don't panic easily, do you?" he said. The mocking blue light was in his eyes again. His tongue made darting little thrusts and probes past my lips.

Yes, I do, I would have said if he'd let me.

We held hands on the drive to my house. In the driveway he parked behind my Honda. "Shall I come in?"

I said nothing. Love and freedom drop into our lives. When we have to beg or even agree, it's already too late.

"Let's go in." He said it very softly.

I didn't worry about the neighbors. In his grey wool slacks and tweed jacket, he looked too old, too respectable, for any sordid dalliance with a not-quite's wife.

Our house is not that different in size and shape from the ones on either side. Only the inside smells of heavy incense, and the walls are hung with rows of miniature paintings from the reign of Emperor Akbar. I took James's big wrinkled hand in mine. Adultery in my house is probably no different, no quieter, than in other houses in this neighborhood.

Afterwards it wasn't guilt I felt (guilt comes with desire not acted), but wonder that while I'd dashed out Tuesday night and bought myself silky new underwear, James Beamish had worn an old T-shirt and lemon-pale boxer shorts. Perhaps he hadn't planned on seducing a Lucknow lady that afternoon. Adventure and freedom had come to him out of the blue, too. Or perhaps only younger men like Iqbal make a fetish of doing sit-ups and dieting and renewing their membership at the racquet club when they're on the prowl.

October through February our passion held. When we were together, I felt cherished. I only played at being helpless, hysterical, cruel. When James left, I'd spend the rest of the afternoon with a Barbara Pym novel. I kept the novels open at pages in which excellent British women recite lines from Marvell to themselves. I didn't read. I watched the golfers trudging over brown fairways instead. I let the tiny golfers—clumsy mummers—tell me stories of ambitions unfulfilled. Golf carts lurched into the golden vista. I felt safe.

In the first week of March we met in James's house for a change. His wife was in Madison to babysit a grandson while his parents flew to China for a three-week tour. It was a thrill to be in his house. I fingered the book spines, checked the color of sheets and towels, the brand names of cereals and detergents. Jane Fonda's Workout record was on the VCR. He was a man who took exceptional care of himself, this immunologist. Real intimacy, at last. The lust of the winter months had been merely foreplay. I felt at home in his house, in spite of the albums of family photographs on the coffee table and the brutish metal vulvas sculpted by a daughter in art school and stashed in the den. James was more talkative in his own house. He showed me the photos he wanted me to see, named real lakes and mountains. His family was real, and not quite real. The daughters were hardy, outdoor types. I saw them hiking in Zermatt and bicycling through Europe. They had red cheeks and backpacks. Their faces were honest and marvellously ordinary. What would they say if they knew their father, at sixty-five, was in bed with a married woman from Lucknow? I feared and envied their jealousy more than any violence in my husband's heart.

Love on the decline is hard to tell from love on the rise. I have lived a life perched on the edge of ripeness and decay. The traveller feels at home everywhere, because she is never at home anywhere. I felt the hot red glow of blood rushing through capillaries.

His wife came back early, didn't call, caught a ride from Hartsfield International with a friend. She had been raised in Saskatchewan, and she'd remained thrifty.

We heard the car pull into the driveway, the loud "thank yous" and "no, I couldn'ts" and then her surprised shout, "James? Are you ill? What're you doing home?" as she shut the front door.

We were in bed, sluggish cozy and still moist under the goosedown quilt that the daughter in Madison had sent them as a fortieth anniversary gift some years before. His clothes were on top of a long dresser; mine were on the floor, the stockings wrinkled and looking legless.

James didn't go to pieces. I had to admire that. He said. "Get in the bathroom. Get dressed. I'll take care of this."

I am submissive by training. To survive, the Asian wife will usually do as she is told. But this time I stayed in bed.

"How are you going to explain me away, James? Tell her I'm the new cleaning woman?" I laughed, and my laugh tinkled flirtatiously, at least to me.

"Get in the bathroom." This was the fiercest I'd ever heard him.

"I don't think so," I said. I jerked the quilt off my body but didn't move my legs.

So I was in bed with the quilt at my feet, and James was by the dresser buttoning his shirt when Kate Beamish stood at the door.

She didn't scream. She didn't leap for James's throat—or mine. I'd wanted passion, but Kate didn't come through. I pulled the quilt over me.

I tried insolence. "Is your wife not the jealous kind?" I asked.

"Let's just get over this as quietly and quickly as we can, shall we?" she said. She walked to the window in her brown Wallabies. "I don't see any unfamiliar cars, so I suppose you'll expect James to drive you home."

"She's the jealous type," James said. He moved towards his wife and tried to guide her out of the bedroom.

"I'm definitely the jealous kind," Kate Beamish said. "I might have stabbed you if I could take you seriously. But you are quite ludicrous lounging like a Goya nude on my bed." She gave a funny little snort. I noticed straggly hairs in her nostrils and looked away.

James was running water in the bathroom sink. Only the panicky ones fall apart and call their lawyers from the bedroom.

She sat on my side of the bed. She stared at me. If that stare had made me feel secretive and loathsome, I might not have wept, later. She plucked the quilt from my breasts as an internist might, and snorted again. "Yes," she said, "I don't deny a certain interest he might have had," but she looked through my face to the pillow behind, and dropped the quilt as she stood. I was shadow without depth or color, a shadow-temptress who would float back to a city of teeming millions when the affair with James had ended.

I had thought myself provocative and fascinating. What had begun as an adventure had become shabby and complex. I was just another involvement of a white man in a pokey little outpost, something that "men do" and then come to their senses while the *memsahibs* drink gin and tonic and fan their faces. I didn't merit a stab wound through the heart.

It wasn't the end of the world. It was humorous, really. Still. I let

James call me a cab. That half-hour wait for the cab, as Kate related tales of the grandson to her distracted husband was the most painful. It came closest to what Husseina must have felt. At least her father, the Nawab-*sahib*, had beaten her.

I have known all along that perfect love has to be fatal. I have survived on four of the five continents. I get by because I am at least moderately charming and open-minded. From time to time, James Beamish calls me. "She's promised to file for divorce." Or "Let's go away for a weekend. Let's go to Bermuda. Have lunch with me this Wednesday." Why do I hear a second voice? She has laughed at me. She has mocked my passion.

I want to say yes. I want to beg him to take me away to Hilton Head in his new, retirement Winnebago. The golden light from the vista is too yellow. Yes, *please*, let's run away, keep this new and simple.

I can hear the golfballs being thwocked home by clumsy mummers far away where my land dips. My arms are numb, my breathing loud and ugly from pressing hard against the cedar railing. The pain in my chest will not go away. I should be tasting blood in my throat by now.

## SANDRA BIRDSELL

### 1947–

Born in Morris, Manitoba, Birdsell now lives in Winnipeg where she is an active member of the Manitoba Writers' Guild. She has written plays and scripts for the National film Board, including dramatizations of her own work. Her first collection of stories, *Night Travellers* (1982), is powerful in its evocation of the rural background of her childhood. *Ladies of the House* (1984), which contains stories set in the urban working-class environment of Winnipeg, won the Gerald Lampert Award for fiction.

## The Wednesday Circle

Betty crosses the double planks that span the ditch in front of Joys' yard. Most people have only one plank. But Mrs. Joy needs two. Mrs. Joy is a possible candidate for the circus. Like sleeping with an elephant, Betty's father says often. But Mr. and Mrs. Joy, the egg people, don't sleep together. Betty knows this even though she's never gone further than inside their stale smelling kitchen.

The highway is a smeltering strip of gunmetal grey at her back. It leads to another town like the one she lives in. If you kept on going south, you would get to a place called Pembina in the States and a small dark tavern where a woman will serve under-age kids beer. Laurence, Betty's friend, knows about this. But if you turn from the highway and go west, there are dozens of villages and then the Pembina Hills which Betty has seen on one occasion, a school trip to the man-made lake at Morden. Home of the rich and the godly, Betty's father calls these villages. Wish the godly would stay home. Can't get a seat in the parlor on Friday nights.

Beyond her lies a field in summer fallow and a dirt road rising to a slight incline and then falling as it meets the highway. Before her is the Joys' crumbling yellow cottage, flanked on all sides by greying bales of straw which have swollen and broken free from their bindings and are scattered about the yard. Behind the cottage is the machine shed. Behind the machine shed and bumping up against the prairie is the chicken coop.

Because Mika, Betty's mother, sends her for the eggs instead of having them delivered by Mr. Joy, she gets them cheaper.

Betty balances the egg cartons beneath her chin and pushes open the gate. It shrieks on its rusty hinges. The noise doesn't affect her as it usually does. Usually, the noise is like a door opening into a dark room and she is filled with dread. Today, she is prepared for it. Today is the day for the Wednesday Circle. The church ladies are meeting at her home. Even now, they're there in the dining room, sitting in a circle with their Bibles in their laps. It's like women and children in the center. And arrows flying. Wagons are going up in flames and smoke. The goodness and matronly wisdom of the Wednesday Circle is a newly discovered thing. She belongs with them now. They can reach out to protect her even here, by just being what they are. And although she wants nothing to happen today, she is prepared for the worst.

"Come on in," Mrs. Joy calls from the kitchen.

Betty sets the egg cartons down on the steps and enters the house. Mrs. Joy's kitchen resembles a Woolworth store. There are porcelain dogs and cats in every corner on knick-knack shelves. Once upon a time, she used to love looking at those figurines but now she thinks they're ugly.

The woman sits in her specially made chair which is two chairs wired together. Her legs are stretched out in front resting up on another chair. Out of habit, Betty's heart constricts because she knows the signs. Mrs. Joy is not up to walking back to the chicken coop with her. And that's how it all began.

"Lo, I am with you always even unto the end of the world," her mind recites.

These verses rise unbidden. She has memorized one hundred of them and won a trip to a summer Bible camp at Lake Winnipeg. She has for the first time seen the ocean on the prairie and tried to walk on water. The waves have lifted and pulled her out where her feet couldn't touch the sandy bottom and she has been swept beneath that mighty sea and heard the roaring of the waves in her head and felt the sting of fish water in her nostrils. Like a bubble of froth she is swept beneath the water, back and forth by the motion of the waves. She is drowning. What happens is just as she's heard. Her whole life flashes by. Her head becomes a movie screen playing back every lie and swearing, malicious and unkind deeds, thoughts, words. There is not one thing that makes her look justified for having done or said them. And then her foot touches a rock and she pushes herself forward in desperation, hoping it's the right direction.

Miraculously, it is. She bounces forward from the depths to where she can tip-toe to safety, keeping her nose above the waves. She runs panting with fear to her cabin. She pulls the blankets over her. She tells no one. But that evening in the chapel during devotions, the rustling wind in the poplars against the screen causes her to think of God. When they all sing, "Love Lifted Me," the sunset parts the clouds above the water so there is a crack of gold where angels hover, watching. So she goes forward to the altar with several others and has her name written in the Book of Life. They tell her the angels are clapping and she thinks she can hear them there at that crack of gold which is the door to heaven. She confesses every sin she's been shown in the water except for one. For some reason, it wasn't there in the movie. And they are such gentle, smiling nice people who have never done what she's done. So she can't bring herself to tell them that Mr. Joy puts his hands in her pants.

"Rainin' today, ain't it child?" Mrs. Joy asks.

"No, not yet," Betty says. "It's very muggy."

"Don't I know it," she says.

"Are your legs sore?" Betty asks.

"Oh Lord, yes, how they ache," Mrs. Joy says and rolls her eyes back into her head. Her jersey dress is a tent stretched across her knees. She cradles a cookie tin in her lap.

"That's too bad," Betty says.

A chuckle comes from deep inside her mammoth chest. "You sound just like your mother," she says. "And you're looking more and more like her each time I see you. You're just like an opal, always changing."

God's precious jewels, Mrs. Joy calls them when she visits Mika. She lines them up verbally, Betty and her sisters and brothers, comparing chins, noses. This one here, she says about Betty, she's an opal. You oughta keep a watch over that one. Always changing. But it just goes to show, His mysteries does He perform. Not one of them the same.

"Thank you," Betty says, but she hates being told she looks like her mother. Mika has hazel eyes and brown hair. She is blonde and blue-eyed like her Aunt Elizabeth.

"Well, you know where the egg pail is," Mrs. Joy says, dismissing her with a flutter of her pudgy hand.

"Aren't you coming?" Betty asks.

"Not today, girl. It aches me so to walk. You collect the eggs and then you jest find Mr. Joy and you pay him. He gets it in the end anyhow."

Betty looks around the kitchen. His jacket is missing from its hook on the wall. She goes over to the corner by the window and feigns interest in the procelain figures. She picks one up, sets it down. His truck is not in the yard.

"Where is he?"

"Went to town for something," Mrs. Joy says. "But I thought he'd be back by now. Doesn't matter though, jest leave the money in the back porch."

The egg pail thumps against her leg as she crosses the yard to the chicken coop. She walks toward the cluttered wire enclosure, past the machine shed. The doors are open wide. The hens scratch and dip their heads in her direction as she approaches. Hope rises like an erratic kite as she passes the shed and there are no sounds coming from it. She stamps her feet and the hens scatter before her, then circle around and approach her from behind, silently. She quickly gathers three dozen of the warm, straw-flecked eggs, and then steps free of the stifling smelly coop out into the fresh moist air. She is almost home-free. She won't have to face anything today. It has begun to rain. Large spatters spot her white blouse, feel cool on her back. She sets the pail down on the ground beside the egg cartons and begins to transfer the eggs.

"Here, you don't have to do that outside." His sudden voice, as she fills the egg cartons, brings blood to her face, threatens to pitch her foward over the pail.

He strides across the yard from the shed. "Haven't got enough sense to come in out of the rain," he says. "Don't you know you'll melt? Be nothing left of you but a puddle."

He carries the pail, she carries the cartons. He has told her: Mrs. Joy is fat and lazy, you are my sunshine, my only sunshine. I would like six little ones running around my place too, but Mrs. Joy is fat and lazy. His thin hand has gone from patting her on the head with affection, to playfully slapping her on the behind, graduated then to tickling her armpits and ribs and twice now, his hands have been inside her underpants.

"Be not afraid," a verse leaps into her head. "For I am with you." She will put her plan into action. The Wednesday Circle women are strong and mighty. She knows them all, they're her mother's friends.

She'll just go to them and say, Mr. Joy feels me up, and that will be the end of it.

She walks behind him, her heart pounding. He has an oil rag hanging from his back pocket and his boots are caked with clay, adding inches to his height.

"I'm waiting for my parts," he says over his shoulder. "Can't do anything until I get that truck fixed." Sometimes he talks to her as though she were an adult. Sometimes as though she were ten again and just coming for the eggs for the first time. How old are you, he'd asked the last time and was surprised when she said, fourteen. My sunshine has grown up.

They enter the machine shed and he slides the doors closed behind them, first one and then the other, leaving a sliver of daylight beaming through where the doors join. A single light bulb dangles from a wire, shedding a circle of weak yellow light above the truck, not enough to clear the darkness from the corners.

"Okay-dokey," he says and puts the pail of eggs on the workbench. "You can work here. I've got things to do." He goes over to the truck, disappears beneath its raised hood.

Then he's back at the workbench, searching through his tool box. "Seen you with your boyfriend the other day," he says. "That Anderson boy."

"He's not my boyfriend," she says.

"I saw you," he says. His usual bantering tone is missing. "The two of you were in the coulee." Then his breath is warm on the side of her face as he reaches across her. His arms knock against her breast, sending pain shooting through her chest. I need a bra, she has told Mika. Whatever for? Wear an undershirt if you think you really need to.

"Do you think it's a good idea to hang around in the coulee with your boyfriend?"

"He's not my boyfriend," she says. "I told you."

He sees her flushed cheeks, senses her discomfort. "Aha," he says. "So he is. You can't fool me."

She moves away from him. Begins to stack the cartons up against her chest, protection against his nudgings. Why is it that everyone but her own mother notices that she has breasts now?

"Don't rush off," he says. "Wait until the rain passes." The sound of it on the tin roof is like small pebbles being dropped one by one.

He takes the cartons from her and sets them back on the workbench. He smiles and she can see that perfect decayed circle between his front teeth. His hair is completely grey even though he's not as old as her father. He starts to walk past her, back towards the truck and then suddenly he grasps her about the waist and begins to tickle her ribs. She is slammed up against him and gasping for breath. His whiskers prickle against her neck. She tastes the bitterness of his flannel shirt.

She pushes away. "Stop."

He holds her tighter. "You're so pretty," he says. "No wonder the boys are chasing you. When I'm working in here, know what I'm thinking all the time?'

"Let me go." She continues to push against his bony arms.

"I'm thinking about all the things I could do to you."

Against her will, she has been curious to know. She feels desire rising when he speaks of what he would like to do. He has drawn vivid word-pictures that she likes to reconstruct until her face burns. Only it isn't Mr. Joy in the pictures, it's Laurence. It's what made her pull aside her underpants so he could fumble inside her moist crevice with his grease-stained fingers.

"Show me your tits," he whispers into her neck. "I'll give you a dollar if you do."

She knows the only way out of this is to tell. When the whole thing is laid out before the Wednesday Circle, she will become whiter than snow. "No," she says.

"What do you mean, no," he says, jabbing her in the ribs once again.

"I'm going to tell," she says. "You can't make me do anything anymore because I'm going to tell on you." She feels as though a rock has been taken from her stomach. He is ugly. He is like a salamander dropping from the sky after a rainstorm into a mincemeat pail. She doesn't know how she could ever have liked him.

"Make you?" he says. "Make you? Listen here, girlie, I've only done what you wanted me to do."

She knows this to be true and not true. She isn't certain how she has come to accept and even expect his fondling. It has happened over a course of four years, gradually, like growing.

She walks to the double doors where the light shines through. "Open them, please," she says.

"Open them yourself," he says. She can feel the presence of the Wednesday Circle. The promise of their womanly strength is like a lamp unto her feet. They will surround her and protect her. Freedom from his word-pictures will make her a new person.

"You say anything," he says. "You say one thing and I'll have some pretty stories to tell about you. You betcha."

"That woman," Mika is saying to the Wednesday Circle as Betty enters the dining room. "That woman. She has absolutely no knowledge of the scriptures. She takes everything out of context." Mika is standing at the buffet with a china tea cup in her hand. Betty steps into the circle of chairs and sits down in Mika's empty one. Mika stops talking, throws her a look of surprise and question. The other women greet her with smiles, nods.

"Did you get the eggs?" Mika asks.

Betty feels her mouth stretching, moving of its own accord into a silly smile. She knows the smile irritates Mika but she can't help it. At times like these, her face moves on its own. She can hear her own heartbeat in her ears, like the ocean, roaring.

"What now?" Mika asks, worried.

"What do you mean, she takes everything out of context?" Mrs. Brawn asks, ignoring Betty. It's her circle. She started it off, arranging for the church women to meet in each others' homes twice a month to read scripture and sew things which they send to a place in the city where they are distributed to the poor. The women are like the smell of coffee to Betty and at the same time, they are like the cool opaque squares of Mika's lemon slice which is arranged on bread and butter plates on the table. They are also like the sturdy varnished chairs they sit on. To be with them now is the same as when she was a child and thought that if you could always be near an adult when you were ill, you wouldn't die.

"My, my," Mika mimicks someone to demonstrate to Mrs. Brawn what she means. She places her free hand against her chest in a dramatic gesture. "They are different, ain't they? God's precious jewels. Just goes to show, His mysteries does He perform."

Betty realizes with a sudden shock that her mother is imitating Mrs. Joy.

Mrs. Brawn takes in Mika's pose with a stern expression and immediately Mika looks guilty, drops her hand from her breast and begins to fill cups with coffee.

"I suppose that we really can't expect much from Mrs. Joy," Mika says with her back to them. Betty hears the slight mocking tone in her voice that passes them by.

Heads bent over needlework nod their understanding. The women's stitches form thumbs, forest-green fingers; except for the woman who sits beside Betty. With a hook she shapes intricate spidery patterns to lay across varnished surfaces, the backs of chairs. What the poor would want with those, I'll never know, Mika has said privately. But they include the doilies in their parcels anyway because they have an understanding. They whisper that this white-haired woman has known suffering.

She works swiftly. It seems to Betty as though the threads come from the ends of her fingers, white strings with a spot of red every few inches. It looks as though she's cut her finger and secretly bleeds the color into the lacy scallops. The women all unravel and knit and check closely for evenness of tension.

Mika enters the circle of chairs then, carrying the tray of coffee, and begins to make her way around it. She continues to speak of Mrs. Joy.

"Are you looking forward to school?" the white-haired woman asks Betty. Her voice is almost a whisper, a knife peeling skin from a taut apple. Betty senses that it has been difficult for her to speak, feels privileged that she has.

"Yes, I miss school."

The woman blinks as she examines a knot in her yarn. She scrapes at it with her large square thumbnail which is flecked oddly with white fish-hook-shaped marks. "Your mother tells us you were at camp," she says. "What did you do there?"

Mika approaches them with the tray of coffee. "I just wish she hadn't picked me out, that's all," Mika says. "She insists on coming over here in the morning and it's impossible to work with her here. And Mr. Joy is just as bad. I send Betty for the eggs now because he used to keep me at the door talking."

Mr. Joy is just as bad. Mr. Joy makes me ashamed of myself and I let him do it. The woman shakes loose the doily; it unfolds into the shape of a star as she holds it up.

"You like it?" the white-haired woman asks Betty.

"It's pretty."

"Maybe I give it to you."

"Ah, Mika," a woman across the circle says, "she just knows where she can find the best baking in town."

Then they all laugh; even the quiet woman beside Betty has a dry chuckle over the comment, only Mrs. Brawn doesn't smile. She stirs her coffee with more force than necessary and sets the spoon alongside it with a clang.

"Obesity is no laughing matter," she says. "Mrs. Joy is a glutton and that's to be pitied. We don't laugh at sin, the wages of sin is death."

"But the gift of God is eternal life through Jesus Christ our Lord," the woman says so softly, the words are nail filings dropping into her lap. If Betty hadn't seen her lips moving, she wouldn't have heard it. "God forgives," the woman says then, louder. She is an odd combination of young and old. Her voice and breasts are young but her hair is white.

Mika stands before them with the tray of coffee. "Not always," Mika says. "There's the unpardonable sin, don't forget about that." She seems pleased to have remembered this.

"Which is?" the woman asks.

"Well, suicide," Mika says. "It has to be, because when you think of it, it's something you can't repent of once the deed is done." Mika smiles around the circle as if to say to them, I'm being patient with this woman who has known suffering.

"Perhaps there is no need to repent," the woman says.

"Pardon?"

"In Russia," the woman begins and then stops to set her thread down into her lap. She folds her hands one on top of the other and closes her eyes. The others, sensing a story, fall silent.

"During the revolution in Russia, there was once a young girl who was caught by nine soldiers and was their prisoner for two weeks. She was only thriteen. These men had their way with her many times, each one taking their turn, every single night. In the end, she shot herself. What about her?"

"I've never heard of such a case," Mika says. She sounds as though she resents hearing of it now.

"There are always such cases," the woman says. "If God knows the falling of a single sparrow, He is also merciful. He knows we're only human."

Mrs. Brawn sets her knitting down on the floor in front of her chair, leans forward slightly. "Oh, He knows," she says. "But He never gives us more than we can bear. When temptation arises, He gives us the strength to resist." She closes her statement with her hands, like a conductor pinching closed the last sound.

Betty watches as the white-haired woman twists and untwists her yarn into a tight ring around her finger. "I don't believe for one moment," she says finally, "that God would condemn such a person to hell. Jesus walked the earth and so He knows."

"No, no," Mika says from the buffet. "He doesn't condemn us, don't you see? That's where you're wrong. We condemn ourselves. We make that choice."

"And what choice did that young girl have?" the woman asks. "It was her means of escape. God provided the gun."

Mika holds the tray of lemon squares up before her as though she were offering them to the sun. She looks stricken. Deep lines cut a shart V above her nose. "You don't mean that," she says. "Suicide is unpardonable. I'm sure of it. Knowing that keeps me going. Otherwise, I would have done it myself long ago."

There is shocked silence and a rapid exchange of glances around the circle, at Betty, to see if she's heard.

"You shouldn't say such things," Mrs. Brawn says quietly. "For shame. You have no reason to say that."

The white-haired woman speaks with a gaunt smile. "Occasionally," she says, "in this room, someone dares to speak the truth."

"What do you mean?" asks Mrs. Brawn.

"Look at us," the woman says. "We're like filthy rags to Him in our self-righteousness. We obey because we fear punishment, not because we love."

Betty sees the grease spot on her blouse where his arm has brushed against her breast. Her whole body is covered with handprints. The stone is back in her stomach. She feels betrayed. For a moment the women are lost inside their own thoughts and they don't notice as she rises from her chair and sidles over to the door. Then, as if on some signal, their conversation resumes its usual level, each one waiting impatiently for the other to be finished so they can speak their words. Their laughter and goodwill have a feeling of urgency, of desperation. Betty stands at the door; a backward glance and she sees the white-haired woman bending over her work once again, eyes blinking rapidly, her fingers moving swiftly and the doily, its flecked pattern spreading like a web across her lap.

## ANN BEATTIE

1947–

Born in Washington, D.C., Beattie was educated at American University and the University of Connecticut. She has taught at the University of Virginia and Harvard. Since her first appearance in *The New Yorker* in 1974, she has been recognized as one of the best new American writers. She has published three novels and four collections of stories, *Distortions*, *Secrets and Surprises*, *The Burning House*, and *Where You'll Find Me*, which includes the following story. Beattie lives in Charlottesville, Virginia.

## Janus

The bowl was perfect. Perhaps it was not what you'd select if you faced a shelf of bowls, and not the sort of thing that would inevitably attract a lot of attention at a crafts fair, yet it had real presence. It was as predictably admired as a mutt who has no reason to suspect he might be funny. Just such a dog, in fact, was often brought out (and in) along with the bowl.

Andrea was a real-estate agent, and when she thought that some prospective buyers might be dog lovers, she would drop off her dog at the same time she placed the bowl in the house that was up for sale. She would put a dish of water in the kitchen for Mondo, take his squeaking plastic frog out of her purse and drop it on the floor. He would pounce delightedly, just as he did every day at home, batting around his favorite toy. The bowl usually sat on a coffee table, though recently she had displayed it on top of a pine blanket chest and on a lacquered table. It was once placed on a cherry table beneath a Bonnard still life, where it held its own.

Everyone who has purchased a house or who has wanted to sell a house must be familiar with some of the tricks used to convince a buyer that the house is quite special: a fire in the fireplace in early evening; jonquils in a pitcher on the kitchen counter, where no one ordinarily has space to put flowers; perhaps the slight aroma of spring, made by a single drop of scent vaporizing from a lamp bulb.

The wonderful thing about the bowl, Andrea thought, was that it was both subtle and noticeable—a paradox of a bowl. Its glaze was the color of cream and seemed to glow no matter what light it was placed in. There were a few bits of color in it—tiny geometric flashes— and some of these were tinged with flecks of silver. They were as mysterious as cells seen under a microscope; it was difficult not to study them, because they shimmered, flashing for a split second, and then resumed their shape. Something about the colors and their random placement suggested motion. People who liked country furniture always commented on the bowl, but then it turned out that people who felt comfortable with Biedermeier loved it just as much. But the bowl was not at all ostentatious, or even so noticeable that anyone would suspect that it had been put in place deliberately. They might notice the height of the ceiling on first entering a room, and only when their eye moved down from that, or away from the refraction of sunlight on a pale wall, would they see the bowl. Then they would go immediately to it and comment. Yet they always faltered when they tried to say something. Perhaps it was because they were in the house for a serious reason, not to notice some object.

Once Andrea got a call from a woman who had not put in an offer on a house she had shown her. That bowl, she said—would it be possible to find out where the owners had bought that beautiful bowl? Andrea pretended that she did not know what the woman was referring to. A bowl, somewhere in the house? Oh, on a table under the window. Yes, she would ask, of course. She let a couple of days pass, then called back to say that the bowl had been a present and the people did not know where it had been purchased.

When the bowl was not being taken from house to house, it sat on Andrea's coffee table at home. She didn't keep it carefully wrapped (although she transported it that way, in a box); she kept it on the table, because she liked to see it. It was large enough so that it didn't seem fragile or particularly vulnerable if anyone sideswiped the table or Mondo blundered into it at play. She had asked her husband to please not drop his house key in it. It was meant to be empty.

When her husband first noticed the bowl, he had peered into it and smiled briefly. He always urged her to buy things she liked. In recent years, both of them had acquired many things to make up for all the lean years when they were graduate students, but now that they had been comfortable for quite a while, the pleasure of new possessions dwindled. Her husband had pronounced the bowl "pretty," and he had turned away without picking it up to examine it. He had no more interest in the bowl than she had in his new Leica.

She was sure that the bowl brought her luck. Bids were often put in on houses where she had displayed the bowl. Sometimes the owners, who were always asked to be away or to step outside when the house was being shown, didn't even know that the bowl had been in their house. Once—she could not imagine how—she left it behind, and then she was so afraid that something might have happened to it that she rushed back to the house and sighed with relief when the woman owner opened the door. The bowl, Andrea explained—she had purchased a bowl and set it on the chest for safekeeping while she toured the house with the prospective buyers, and she . . . She felt like rushing past the frowning woman and seizing her bowl. The owner stepped aside, and it was only when Andrea ran to the chest that the lady glanced at her a little strangely. In the few seconds before Andrea picked up the bowl, she realized that the owner must have just seen that it had been perfectly placed, that the sunlight struck the bluer part of it. Her pitcher had been moved to the far side of the chest, and the bowl predominated. All the way home, Andrea wondered how she could have left the bowl behind. It was like leaving a friend at an outing—just walking off. Sometimes there were stories in the paper about families forgetting a child somewhere and driving to the next city. Andrea had only gone a mile down the road before she remembered.

In time, she dreamed of the bowl. Twice, in a waking dream—early in the morning, between sleep and a last nap before rising—she had a clear vision of it. It came into sharp focus and startled her for a moment—the same bowl she looked at every day.

She had a very profitable year selling real estate. Word spread, and she had more clients than she felt comfortable with. She had the foolish thought that if only the bowl were an animate object she could thank it. There were times when she wanted to talk to her husband about the bowl. He was a stockbroker, and sometimes told people that he was fortunate to be married to a woman who had such a fine aesthetic sense and yet could also function in the real world. They were a lot alike, really—they had agreed on that. They were both quiet people—reflective, slow to make value judgments, but almost intractable once they had come to a conclusion. They both liked details, but while ironies attracted her, he was more impatient and dismissive when matters became many-sided or unclear. They both knew this, and it was the kind of thing they could talk about when they were alone in the car together, coming home from a party or after a weekend with friends. But she never talked to him about the bowl. When they were at dinner, exchanging their news of the day, or while they lay in bed at night listening to the stereo and murmuring sleepy disconnections, she was often tempted to come right out and say that she thought that the bowl in the living room, the cream-colored bowl, was responsible for her success. But she didn't say it. She couldn't begin to explain it. Sometimes in the morning, she would look at him and feel guilty that she had such a constant secret.

Could it be that she had some deeper connection with the bowl—a relationship of some kind? She corrected her thinking: how could she imagine such a thing, when she was a human being and it was a bowl? It was ridiculous. Just think of how people lived together and loved each other . . . But was that always so clear, always a relationship? She was confused by these thoughts, but they remained in her mind. There was something within her now, something real, that she never talked about.

The bowl was a mystery, even to her. It was frustrating, because her involvement with the bowl contained a steady sense of unrequited good fortune; it would have been easier to respond if some sort of demand were made in return. But that only happened in fairy tales. The bowl was just a bowl. She did not believe that for one second. What she believed was that it was something she loved.

In the past, she had sometimes talked to her husband about a new property she was about to buy or sell—confiding some clever strategy she had devised to persuade owners who seemed ready to sell. Now she stopped doing that, for all her strategies involved the bowl. She became more deliberate with the bowl, and more possessive. She put it in houses only when no one was there, and removed it when she left the house. Instead of just moving a pitcher or a dish, she would remove all the other objects from a table. She had to force herself to handle them carefully, because she didn't really care about them. She just wanted them out of sight.

She wondered how the situation would end. As with a lover, there was no exact scenario of how matters would come to a close. Anxiety became the operative force. It would be irrelevant if the lover rushed into someone else's arms, or wrote her a note and departed to another city. The horror was the possibility of the disappearance. That was what mattered.

She would get up at night and look at the bowl. It never occurred to her that she might break it. She washed and dried it without anxiety, and she moved it often, from coffee table to mahogany corner table or wherever, without fearing an accident. It was clear that she would not be the one who would do anything to the bowl. The bowl was only handled by her, set safely on one surface or another; it was not very likely that anyone would break it. A bowl was a poor conductor of electricity: it would not be hit by lightning. Yet the idea of damage persisted. She did not think beyond that—to what her life would be without the bowl. She only continued to fear that some accident would happen. Why not, in a world where people set plants where they did not belong, so that visitors touring a house would be fooled into thinking that dark corners got sunlight—a world full of tricks?

She had first seen the bowl several years earlier, at a crafts fair she had visited half in secret, with her lover. He had urged her to buy the bowl. She didn't *need* any more things, she told him. But she had been drawn to the bowl, and they had lingered near it. Then she went on to the next booth, and he came up behind her, tapping the rim against her shoulder as she ran her fingers over a wood carving. "You're still insisting that I buy that?" she said. "No," he said. "I bought it for you." He had bought her other things before this— things she liked more, at first—the child's ebony-and-turquoise ring that fitted her little finger; the wooden box, long and thin, beautifully dovetailed, that she used to hold paper clips; the soft gray sweater with a pouch pocket. It was his idea that when he could not be there to hold her hand she could hold her own—clasp her hands inside the lone pocket that stretched across the front. But in time she became more attached to the bowl than to any of his other presents. She tried to talk herself out of it. She owned other things that were more striking or valuable. It wasn't an object whose beauty jumped out at you; a lot of people must have passed it by before the two of them saw it that day.

Her lover had said that she was always too slow to know what she really loved. Why continue with her life the way it was? Why be two-faced, he asked her. He had made the first move toward her. When she would not decide in his favor, would not change her life and come to him, he asked her what made her think she could have it both ways. And then he made the last move and left. It was a decision meant to break her will, to shatter her intransigent ideas about honoring previous commitments.

Time passed. Alone in the living room at night, she often looked at the bowl sitting on the table, still and safe, unilluminated. In its way, it was perfect: the world cut in half, deep and smoothly empty. Near the rim, even in dim light, the eye moved toward one small flash of blue, a vanishing point on the horizon.

# 3
## THE
## MODERN
## NOVELLA

# Introduction

The novella is a difficult literary form. Unlike the short story, it is not limited by concentration on a crucial moment in people's lives or the achievement of a single affect. It attempts, in fact, to do what the full scale novel does, to give us the pattern and movement of a whole life—but without using the scope of the full scale novel to document and illustrate that life. To be rich and full and satisfying as a novel, but as tightly constructed and efficient as a short story—that is the novella's goal. Not surprisingly, the number of masterworks in this form is small.

The three novellas in this section are perhaps the most widely acclaimed works ever written in this form. That is why they were selected. Taken together they do not constitute a history of the form as the previous stories constitute a kind of history of the short story. A history of the novella would require much more space than is available here. But note that the first two novellas here were written almost at the same time by two authors who knew one another and shared certain principles of art and certain ethical values, though their lives had been very different. The third novella, by a man of different background, race, and language, written a dozen years later on the eve of the first World War (in 1912), seems to come from another world. Here the Flaubertian modernism of James and Conrad is replaced by one of the first voices of the post-modernist movement, Franz Kafka. These novellas can be read in many ways. One of them is with an eye toward what they can tell us about the history of literature and the history of culture in the twentieth century.

# HENRY JAMES
## 1843–1916

James was born into a wealthy and cultured New York family, and received all the advantages of travel and private education that such a family could afford. His older brother William became an important American philosopher/psychologist, and Henry turned to the arts, writing about the painters and writers of Europe. Gradually, he began to publish his own fiction, with the same care for artistic perfection that had motivated Flaubert, but with a more American, slightly Puritanical moral tone. Refined, elliptical, leisurely—his work never reached a wide audience, and when he tried for popular success as a playwright he suffered a humiliating rejection by the public. But his dedication to the art of fiction kept him from despair, so that he finally left behind a body of novels and stories impressive in both its size and its achievement. His greatest novels—*Portrait of a Lady* (1881) and *The Ambassadors* (1903)—are much admired, and even some of his lesser works have been made into excellent films, giving him posthumously the popular success that escaped him in life. He spent most of his adult life in England and finally became a British citizen just before his death.

## The Turn of the Screw

The story had held us, round the fire, sufficiently breathless, but except the obvious remark that it was gruesome, as, on Christmas eve in an old house, a strange tale should essentially be, I remember no comment uttered till somebody happened to say that it was the only case he had met in which such a visitation had fallen on a child. The case, I may mention, was that of an apparition in just such an old house as had gathered us for the occasion—an appearance, of a dreadful kind, to a little boy sleeping in the room with his mother and waking her up in the terror of it; waking her not to dissipate his dread and soothe him to sleep again, but to encounter also, herself, before she had succeeded in doing so, the same sight that had shaken him. It was this observation that drew from Douglas—not immediately, but later in the evening—a reply that had the interesting consequence to which I call attention. Someone else told a story not particularly effective, which I saw he was not following. This I took for a sign that he had himself something to produce and that we should only have to wait. We waited in fact till two nights later; but that same evening, before we scattered, he brought out what was in his mind.

"I quite agree—in regard to Griffin's ghost, or whatever it was—

that its appearing first to the little boy, at so tender an age, adds a particular touch. But it's not the first occurrence of its charming kind that I know to have involved a child. If the child gives the effect another turn of the screw, what do you say to *two* children——?"

"We say, of course," somebody exclaimed, "that they give two turns! Also that we want to hear about them."

I can see Douglas there before the fire, to which he had got up to present his back, looking down at his interlocutor with his hands in his pockets. "Nobody but me, till now, has ever heard. It's quite too horrible." This, naturally, was declared by several voices to give the thing the utmost price, and our friend, with quiet art, prepared his triumph by turning his eyes over the rest of us and going on: "It's beyond everything. Nothing at all that I know touches it."

"For sheer terror?" I remember asking.

He seemed to say it was not so simple as that; to be really at a loss how to qualify it. He passed his hand over his eyes, made a little wincing grimace. "For dreadful—dreadfulness!"

"Oh, how delicious!" cried one of the women.

He took no notice of her; he looked at me, but as if, instead of me, he saw what he spoke of. "For general uncanny ugliness and horror and pain."

"Well then," I said, "Just sit right down and begin."

He turned round to the fire, gave a kick to a log, watched it an instant. Then as he faced us again: "I can't begin. I shall have to send to town." There was a unanimous groan at this, and much reproach; after which, in his preoccupied way, he explained. "The story's written. It's in a locked drawer—it has not been out for years. I could write to my man and enclose the key; he could send down the packet as he finds it." It was to me in particular that he appeared to propound this—appeared almost to appeal for aid not to hesitate. He had broken a thickness of ice, the formation of many a winter; had had his reasons for a long silence. The others resented postponement, but it was just his scruples that charmed me. I adjured him to write by the first post and to agree with us for an early hearing; then I asked him if the experience in question had been his own. To this his answer was prompt. "Oh, thank God, no!"

"And is the record yours? You took the thing down?"

"Nothing but the impression. I took that *here*"—he tapped his heart. "I've never lost it."

"Then your manuscript——?"

"Is in old, faded ink, and in the most beautiful hand." He hung fire again. "A woman's. She has been dead these twenty years. She sent me the pages in question before she died." They were all listening now, and of course there was somebody to be arch, or at any rate to draw the inference. But if he put the inference by without a smile it was also without irritation. "She was a most charming person, but she was ten years older than I. She was my sister's governess," he quietly said. "She was the most agreeable woman I've ever known in her position; she would have been worthy of any whatever. It was long ago, and this episode was long before. I was at Trinity, and I found her at home on my coming down the second summer. I was much there that year—it was a beautiful one; and we had, in her off-hours, some strolls and talks in the garden—talks in which she struck me as awfully clever and nice. Oh yes; don't grin: I liked her extremely and am glad to this day to think she liked me too. If she hadn't she wouldn't have told me. She had never told anyone. It wasn't simply that she said so, but that I knew she hadn't. I was sure; I could see. You'll easily judge why when you hear."

"Because the thing had been such a scare?"

He continued to fix me. "You'll easily judge," he repeated: "*you will*."

I fixed him too. "I see. She was in love."

He laughed for the first time. "You *are* acute. Yes, she was in love. That is, she had been. That came out—she couldn't tell her story without its coming out. I saw it, and she saw I saw it; but neither of us spoke of it. I remember the time and the place—the corner of the lawn, the shade of the great beeches and the long, hot summer afternoon. It wasn't a scene for a shudder; but oh——!" He quitted the fire and dropped back into his chair.

"You'll receive the packet Thursday morning?" I inquired.

"Probably not till the second post."

"Well then; after dinner——"

"You'll all meet me here?" He looked us round again. "Isn't anybody going?" It was almost the tone of hope.

"Everybody will stay!"

*I* will—and *I* will!" cried the ladies whose departure had been fixed. Mrs. Griffin, however, expressed the need for a little more light. "Who was it she was in love with?"

"The story will tell," I took upon myself to reply.

"Oh, I can't wait for the story!"

"The story *won't* tell," said Douglas; "not in any literal, vulgar way."

"More's the pity, then. That's the only way I ever understand."

"Won't *you* tell, Douglas?" somebody else inquired.

He sprang to his feet again. "Yes—tomorrow. Now I must go to bed. Good-night." And quickly catching up a candlestick, he left us slightly bewildered. From our end of the great brown hall we heard his step on the stair; whereupon Mrs. Griffin spoke. "Well, if I don't know who she was in love with, I know who *he* was."

"She was ten years older," said her husband.

"*Raison de plus*[1]——at that age! But it's rather nice, his long reticence."

"Forty years!" Griffin put in.

"With this outbreak at last."

"The outbreak," I returned, "will make a tremendous occasion of Thursday night"; and everyone so agreed with me that, in the light of it, we lost all attention for everything else. The last story, however incomplete and like the mere opening of a serial, had been told; we handshook and "candlestuck," as somebody said, and went to bed.

I knew the next day that a letter containing the key had, by the first post, gone off to his London apartments; but in spite of—or perhaps just on account of—the eventual diffusion of this knowledge we quite let him alone until after dinner, till such an hour of the evening, in fact, as might best accord with the kind of emotion on which our hopes were fixed. Then he became as communicative as we could desire and indeed gave us his best reason for being so. We had it from him again before the fire in the hall, as we had had our mild wonders of the previous night. It appeared that the narrative he had promised to read us really required for a proper intelligence a few words of prologue. Let me say here distinctly, to have done with it, that this narrative, from an exact transcript of my own made much later, is what I shall presently give. Poor Douglas, before his death—when it was in sight—committed to me the manuscript that reached him on the third of these days and that, on the same spot, with immense effect, he began to read to our hushed little circle on the night of the fourth. The departing ladies who had said they would stay didn't, of course, thank heaven, stay: they departed, in consequence of arrangements made, in a rage of curiosity, as they professed, produced by the touches with which he had already worked us up. But that only made his little final auditory more compact and select, kept it, round the hearth, subject to a common thrill.

The first of these touches conveyed that the written statement took up the tale at a point after it had, in a manner, begun. The fact to be in possession of was therefore that his old friend, the youngest of several daughters of a poor country parson, had, at the age of twenty, on taking service for the first time in the schoolroom, come up to London, in trepidation, to answer in person an advertisement

---

1. All the more reason

that had already placed her in brief correspondence with the adver-
tiser. This person proved, on her presenting herself, for judgment,
at a house in Harley Street, that impressed her as vast and imposing—this prospective patron proved a gentleman, a bachelor in the
prime of life, such a figure as had never risen, save in a dream or an
old novel, before a fluttered, anxious girl out of a Hampshire vicarage. One could easily fix his type; it never, happily, dies out. He
was handsome and bold and pleasant, off-hand and gay and kind.
He struck her, inevitably, as gallant and spendid, but what took her
most of all and gave her the courage she afterwards showed was that
he put the whole thing to her as a kind of favour, an obligation he
should gratefully incur. She conceived him as rich, but as fearfully
extravagant—saw him all in a glow of high fashion, of good looks,
of expensive habits, of charming ways with women. He had for his
own town residence a big house filled with the spoils of travel and
the trophies of the chase; but it was to his country home, an old
family place in Essex, that he wished her immediately to proceed.

He had been left, by the death of their parents in India, guardian
to a small nephew and a small niece, children of a younger, a military brother, whom he had lost two years before. These children
were, by the strangest of chances for a man in his position,—a lone
man without the right sort of experience or a grain of patience,—
very heavily on his hands. It had all been a great worry and, on his
own part doubtless, a series of blunders, but he immensely pitied
the poor chicks and had done all he could; had in particular sent
them down to his other house, the proper place for them being of
course the country, and kept them there, from the first, with the
best people he could find to look after them, parting even with his
own servants to wait on them and going down himself, whenever
he might, to see how they were doing. The awkward thing was that
they had practically no other relations and that his own affairs took
up all his time. He had put them in possession of Bly, which was
healthy and secure, and had placed at the head of their little establishment—but below stairs only—an excellent woman, Mrs. Grose,
whom he was sure his visitor would like and who had formerly
been maid to his mother. She was now housekeeper and was also
acting for the time as superintendent to the little girl, of whom,
without children of her own, she was, by good luck, extremely fond.
There were plenty of people to help, but of course the young lady
who should go down as governess would be in supreme authority.
She would also have, in holidays, to look after the small boy, who
had been for a term at school—young as he was to be sent, but what
else could be done?—and who, as the holidays were about to begin,

would be back from one day to the other. There had been for the two children at first a young lady whom they had had the misfortune to lose. She had done for them quite beautifully—she was a most respectable person—till her death, the great awkwardness of which had, precisely, left no alternative but the school for little Miles. Mrs. Grose, since then, in the way of manners and things, had done as she could for Flora; and there were, further, a cook, a housemaid, a dairywoman, an old pony, an old groom, and an old gardener, all likewise thoroughly respectable.

So far had Douglas presented his picture when someone put a question. "And what did the former governess die of?—of so much respectability?"

Our friend's answer was prompt. "That will come out. I don't anticipate."

"Excuse me—I thought that was just what you *are* doing."

"In her successor's place," I suggested, "I should have wished to learn if the office brought with it——"

"Necessary danger to life?" Douglas completed my thought. "She did wish to learn, and she did learn. You shall hear tomorrow what she learnt. Meanwhile, of course, the prospect struck her as slightly grim. She was young, untried, nervous: it was a vision of serious duties and little company, of really great loneliness. She hesitated—took a couple of days to consult and consider. But the salary offered much exceeded her modest measure, and on a second interview she faced the music, she engaged." And Douglas, with this, made a pause that, for the benefit of the company, moved me to throw in—

"The moral of which was of course the seduction exercised by the splendid young man. She succumbed to it."

He got up and, as he had done the night before, went to the fire, gave a stir to a log with his foot, then stood a moment with his back to us. "She saw him only twice."

"Yes, but that's just the beauty of her passion."

A little to my surprise, on this, Douglas turned round to me. "It *was* the beauty of it. There were others," he went on, "who hadn't succumbed. He told her frankly all his difficulty—that for several applicants the conditions had been prohibitive. They were, somehow, simply afraid. It sounded dull—it sounded strange; and all the more so because of his main condition."

"Which was——?"

"That she should never trouble him—but never, never: neither appeal nor complain nor write about anything; only meet all questions herself, receive all moneys from his solicitor, take the whole thing over and let him alone. She promised to do this, and she mentioned to me that when, for a moment, disburdened, delighted, he held her hand, thanking her for the sacrifice, she already felt rewarded."

"But was that all her reward?" one of the ladies asked.

"She never saw him again."

"Oh!" said the lady; which, as our friend immediately left us again, was the only other word of importance contributed to the subject till, the next night, by the corner of the hearth, in the best chair, he opened the faded red cover of a thin old-fashioned gilt-edged album. The whole thing took indeed more nights than one, but on the first occasion the same lady put another question. "What is your title?"

"I haven't one."

"Oh, I have!" I said. But Douglas, without needing me, had begun to read with a fine clearness that was like a rendering to the ear of the beauty of his author's hand.


I

I remember the whole beginning as a succession of flights and drops, a little see-saw of the right throbs and the wrong. After rising, in town, to meet his appeal, I had at all events a couple of very bad days—found myself doubtful again, felt indeed sure I had made a mistake. In this state of mind I spent the long hours of a bumping, swinging coach that carried me to the stopping-place at which I was to be met by a vehicle from the house. This convenience, I was told, had been ordered, and I found, toward the close of the June afternoon, a commodious fly waiting for me. Driving at that hour, on a lovely day, through a country to which the summer sweetness seemed to offer me a friendly welcome, my fortitude mounted afresh and, as we turned into the avenue, encountered a reprieve that was probably but a proof of the point to which it had sunk. I suppose I had expected, or had dreaded, something so melancholy that what greeted me was a good surprise. I remember as a most pleasant impression the broad, clear front, its open windows and fresh curtains and the pair of maids looking out; I remember the lawn and the bright flowers and the crunch of my wheels on the gravel and the clustered tree-tops over which the rooks circled and cawed in the golden sky. The scene had a greatness that made it a different affair from my own scant home, and there immediately appeared at the door, with a little girl in her hand, a civil person who dropped me as decent a curtsey as if I had been the mistress or a distinguished visitor. I had received in Harley Street a narrower notion of the place, and that, as I recalled it, made me think the proprietor still more of a gentleman, suggested that what I was to enjoy might be something beyond his promise.

I had no drop again till the next day, for I was carried triumphantly through the following hours by my introduction to the younger of my pupils. The little girl who accompanied Mrs. Grose appeared to me on the spot a creature so charming as to make it a great fortune to have to do with her. She was the most beautiful child I had ever seen, and I afterwards wondered that my employer had not told me more of her. I slept little that night—I was too much excited; and this astonished me too, I recollect, remained with me, adding to my sense of the liberality with which I was treated. The large, impressive room, one of the best in the house, the great state bed, as I almost felt it, the full, figured draperies, the long glasses in which, for the first time, I could see myself from head to foot, all struck me—like the extraordinary charm of my small charge—as so many things thrown in. It was thrown in as well, from the first moment, that I should get on with Mrs. Grose in a relation over which, on my way, in the coach, I fear I had rather brooded. The only thing indeed that in this early outlook might have made me shrink again was the clear circumstance of her being so glad to see me. I perceived within half an hour that she was so glad—stout, simple, plain, clean, wholesome woman—as to be positively on her guard against showing it too much. I wondered even then a little why she should wish not to show it, and that, with reflection, with suspicion, might of course have made me uneasy.

But it was a comfort that there could be no uneasiness in a connection with anything so beatific as the radiant image of my little girl, the vision of whose angelic beauty had probably more than anything else to do with the restlessness that, before morning, made me several times rise and wander about my room to take in the whole picture and prospect; to watch, from my open window, the faint summer dawn, to look at such portions of the rest of the house as I could catch, and to listen, while, in the fading dusk, the first birds began to twitter, for the possible recurrence of a sound or two, less natural and not without, but within, that I had fancied I heard. There had been a moment when I believed I recognised, faint and far, the cry of a child; there had been another when I found myself just consciously starting as at the passage, before my door, of a light footstep. But these fancies were not marked enough not to be thrown off, and it is only in the light, or the gloom, I should rather say, of other and subsequent matters that they now come back to me. To watch, teach, "form" little Flora would too evidently be the making of a happy and useful life. It had been agreed between us downstairs that after this first occasion I should have her as a matter of course at night, her small white bed being already arranged, to that end, in my room. What I had undertaken was the whole care of her, and she had remained, just this last time, with Mrs. Grose only as an effect of our consideration for my inevitable strangeness and her natural timidity. In spite of this timidity—which the child herself, in the oddest way in the world, had been perfectly frank and brave about, allowing it, without a sign of uncomfortable consciousness, with the deep, sweet serenity indeed of one of Raphael's holy infants, to be discussed, to be imputed to her and to determine us— I felt quite sure she would presently like me. It was part of what I already liked Mrs. Grose herself for, the pleasure I could see her feel in my admiration and wonder as I sat at supper with four tall candles and with my pupil, in a high chair, and a bib, brightly facing me, between them, over bread and milk. There were naturally things that in Flora's presence could pass between us only as prodigious and gratified looks, obscure and roundabout allusions.

"And the little boy—does he look like her? Is he too so very remarkable?"

One wouldn't flatter a child. "Oh, Miss, *most* remarkable. If you think well of this one!"—and she stood there with a plate in her hand, beaming at our companion, who looked from one of us to the other with placid heavenly eyes that contained nothing to check us.

"Yes; if I do——?"

"You *will* be carried away by the little gentleman!"

"Well, that, I think, is what I came for—to be carried away. I'm afraid, however," I remember feeling the impulse to add, "I'm rather easily carried away. I was carried away in London!"

I can still see Mrs. Grose's broad face as she took this in. "In Harley Street?"

"In Harley Street."

"Well, Miss, you're not the first—and you won't be the last."

"Oh, I've no pretension," I could laugh, "to being the only one. My other pupil, at any rate, as I understand, comes back tomorrow?"

"Not tomorrow—Friday, Miss. He arrives, as you did, by the coach, under care of the guard, and is to be met by the same carriage."

I forthwith expressed that the proper as well as the pleasant and friendly thing would be therefore that on the arrival of the public conveyance I should be waiting for him with his little sister; an idea in which Mrs. Grose concurred so heartily that I somehow took her manner as a kind of comforting pledge—never falsified, thank heaven!—that we should on every question be quite at one. Oh, she was glad I was there!

What I felt the next day was, I suppose, nothing that could be fairly called a reaction from the cheer of my arrival; it was probably at the most only a slight oppression produced by a fuller measure of the scale, as I walked round them, gazed up at them, took them in, of my new circumstances. They had, as it were, an extent and mass for which I had not been prepared and in the presence of which I found myself, freshly, a little scared as well as a little proud. Lessons, in this agitation, certainly suffered some delay; I reflected that my first duty was, by the gentlest arts I could contrive, to win the child into the sense of knowing me. I spent the day with her out of doors; I arranged with her, to her great satisfaction, that it should be she, she only, who might show me the place. She showed it step by step and room by room and secret by secret, with droll, delightful, childish talk about it and with the result, in half an hour, of our becoming immense friends. Young as she was, I was struck, throughout our little tour, with her confidence and courage with the way, in empty chambers and dull corridors, on crooked staircases that made me pause and even on the summit of an old machicolated square tower that made me dizzy, her morning music, her disposition to tell me so many more things than she asked, rang out and led me on. I have not seen Bly since the day I left it, and I dare say that to my older and more informed eyes it would now appear sufficiently contracted. But as my little conductress, with her hair of gold and her frock of blue, danced before me round corners and pattered down passages, I had the view of a castle of romance inhabited by a rosy sprite, such a place as would somehow, for diversion of the young idea, take all colour out of storybooks and fairy-tales. Wasn't it just a storybook over which I had fallen a-doze and a-dream? No; it was a big, ugly, antique, but convenient house, embodying a few features of a building still older, half replaced and half utilised, in which I had the fancy of our being almost as lost as a handful of passengers in a great drifting ship. Well, I was, strangely, at the helm!

## II

This came home to me when, two days later, I drove over with Flora to meet, as Mrs. Grose said, the little gentleman; and all the more for an incident that, presenting itself the second evening, had deeply disconcerted me. The first day had been, on the whole, as I have expressed, reassuring; but I was to see it wind up in keen apprehension. The postbag, that evening,—it came late,—contained a letter for me, which, however, in the hand of my employer, I found to be composed but of a few words enclosing another, addressed to himself, with a seal still unbroken. "This, I recognise, is from the headmaster, and the head-master's an awful bore. Read him, please; deal with him; but mind you don't report. Not a word. I'm off!" I broke the seal with a great effort—so great a one that I was a long time coming to it; took the unopened missive at last up to my room and only attacked it just before going to bed. I had better have let it wait till morning, for it gave me a second sleepless night. With no counsel to take, the next day, I was full of distress; and it finally got so the better of me that I determined to open myself at least to Mrs. Grose.

"What does it mean? The child's dismissed his school."

She gave me a look that I remarked at the moment; then, visibly, with a quick blankness, seemed to try to take it back. "But aren't they all——?"

"Sent home—yes. But only for the holidays. Miles may never go back at all."

Consciously, under my attention, she reddened. "They won't take him?"

"They absolutely decline."

At this she raised her eyes, which she had turned from me; I saw them fill with good tears. "What has he done?"

I hesitated; then I judged best simply to hand her my letter— which, however, had the effect of making her, without taking it, simply put her hands behind her. She shook her head sadly. "Such things are not for me, Miss."

My counsellor couldn't read! I winced at my mistake, which I attenuated as I could, and opened my letter again to repeat it to her; then, faltering in the act and folding it up once more, I put it back in my pocket. "Is he really *bad*?"

The tears were still in her eyes. "Do the gentlemen say so?"

"They go into no particulars. They simply express their regret that it should be impossible to keep him. That can have only one mean-ing." Mrs. Grose listened with dumb emotion; she forbore to ask me what this meaning might be; so that, presently, to put the thing with some coherence and with the mere aid of her presence to my own mind, I went on: "That he's an injury to the others."

At this, with one of the quick turns of simple folk, she suddenly flamed up. "Master Miles! *him* an injury?"

There was such a flood of good faith in it that, though I had not yet seen the child, my very fears made me jump to the absurdity of the idea. I found myself, to meet my friend the better, offering it, on the spot, sarcastically: "To his poor little innocent mates!"

"It's too dreadful," cried Mrs. Grose, "to say such cruel things! Why, he's scarce ten years old."

"Yes, yes; it would be incredible."

She was evidently grateful for such a profession. "See him, Miss, first. *Then* believe it!" I felt forthwith a new impatience to see him; it was the beginning of a curiosity that, for all the next hours, was to deepen almost to pain. Mrs. Grose was aware, I could judge, of what she had produced in me, and she followed it up with assurance. "You might as well believe it of the little lady. Bless her," she added the next moment—"*look* at her!"

I turned and saw that Flora, whom, ten minutes before, I had established in the schoolroom with a sheet of white paper, a pencil, and a copy of nice "round O's," now presented herself to view at the open door. She expressed in her little way an extraordinary detachment from disagreeable duties, looking to me, however, with a great childish light that seemed to offer it as a mere result of the affection she had conceived for my person, which had rendered necessary that she should follow me. I needed nothing more than this to feel the full force of Mrs. Grose's comparison, and, catching my pupil in my arms, covered her with kisses in which there was a sob of atonement.

None the less, the rest of the day, I watched for further occasion to approach my colleague, especially as, toward evening, I began to fancy she rather sought to avoid me. I overtook her, I remember, on the staircase; we went down together, and at the bottom I detained her, holding her there with a hand on her arm. "I take what you said to me at noon as a declaration that *you've* never known him to be bad."

She threw back her head; she had clearly, by this time, and very honestly, adopted an attitude. "Oh, never known him—I don't pretend *that*!"

I was upset again. "Then you *have* known him——?"

"Yes indeed, Miss, thank God!"

On reflection I accepted this. "You mean that a boy who never is——?"

"Is no boy for *me*!"

I held her tighter. "You like them with the spirit to be naughty?" Then, keeping pace with her answer, "So do I!" I eagerly brought out. "But not to the degree to contaminate——"

"To contaminate?"—my big word left her at a loss. I explained it. "To corrupt."

She stared, taking my meaning in; but it produced in her an odd laugh. "Are you afraid he'll corrupt *you*?" She put the question with such a fine bold humour that, with a laugh, a little silly doubtless, to match her own, I gave way for the time to the apprehension of ridicule.

But the next day, as the hour for my drive approached, I cropped up in another place. "What was the lady who was here before?"

"The last governess? She was also young and pretty—almost as young and almost as pretty, Miss, even as you."

"Ah, then, I hope her youth and her beauty helped her!" I recollect throwing off. "He seems to like us young and pretty!"

"Oh, he *did*," Mrs. Grose assented: "it was the way he liked everyone!" She had no sooner spoken indeed than she caught herself up. "I mean that's *his* way—the master's."

I was struck. "But of whom did you speak first?"

She looked blank, but she coloured. "Why, of *him*."

"Of the master?"

"Of who else?"

There was so obviously no one else that the next moment I had lost my impression of her having accidentally said more than she meant; and I merely asked what I wanted to know. "Did *she* see anything in the boy——?"

"That wasn't right? She never told me."

I had a scruple, but I overcame it. "Was she careful—particular?"

Mrs. Grose appeared to try to be conscientious. "About some things—yes."

"But not about all?"

Again she considered. "Well, Miss—she's gone. I won't tell tales."

"I quite understand your feeling," I hastened to reply; but I thought it, after an instant, not opposed to this concession to pursue: "Did she die here?"

"No—she went off."

I don't know what there was in this brevity of Mrs. Grose's that struck me as ambiguous. "Went off to die?" Mrs. Grose looked straight out of the window, but I felt that, hypothetically, I had a right to know what young persons engaged for Bly were expected to do. "She was taken ill, you mean, and went home?"

"She had not taken ill, so far as appeared, in this house. She left it, at the end of the year, to go home, as she said, for a short holiday, to which the time she had put in had certainly given her a right. We had then a young woman—a nurse-maid who had stayed on and who was a good girl and clever; and *she* took the children altogether for the interval. But our young lady never came back and at the very moment I was expecting her I heard from the master that she was dead."

I turned this over. "But of what?"

"He never told me! But please, Miss," said Mrs. Grose, "I must get to my work."

III

Her thus turning her back on me was fortunately not, for my just preoccupations, a snub that could check the growth of our mutual esteem. We met, after I had brought home little Miles, more intimately than ever on the ground of my stupefaction, my general emotion: so monstrous was I then ready to pronounce it that such a child as had now been revealed to me should be under an interdict. I was a little late on the scene, and I felt, as he stood wistfully looking out for me before the door of the inn at which the coach had put him down, that I had seen him, on the instant, without and within, in the great glow of freshness, the same positive fragrance of purity, in which I had, from the first moment, seen his little sister. He was incredibly beautiful, and Mrs. Grose had put her finger on it: everything but a sort of passion of tenderness for him was swept away by his presence. What I then and there took him to my heart for was something divine that I have never found to the same degree in any child—his indescribable little air of knowing nothing in the world but love. It would have been impossible to carry a bad name with a greater sweetness of innocence, and by the time I had got back to Bly with him I remained merely bewildered—so far, that is, as I was not outraged—by the sense of the horrible letter locked up in my room, in a drawer. As soon as I could compass a private word with Mrs. Grose I declared to her that it was grotesque.

She promptly understood me. "You mean the cruel charge——?"

"It doesn't live an instant. My dear woman, *look* at him!"

She smiled at my pretension to have discovered his charm. "I assure you, Miss, I do nothing else! What will you say, then?" she immediately added.

"In answer to the letter?" I had made up my mind. "Nothing."

"And to his uncle?"

I was incisive. "Nothing."

"And to the boy himself?"

I was wonderful. "Nothing."

She gave with her apron a great wipe to her mouth. "Then I'll stand by you. We'll see it out."

"We'll see it out!" I ardently echoed, giving her my hand to make it a vow.

She held me there a moment, then whisked up her apron again with her detached hand. "Would you mind, Miss, if I used the freedom——"

"To kiss me? No!" I took the good creature in my arms and, after we had embraced like sisters, felt still more fortified and indignant.

This, at all events, was for the time: a time so full that, as I recall the way it went, it reminds me of all the art I now need to make it a little distinct. What I look back at with amazement is the situation I accepted. I had undertaken, with my companion, to see it out, and I

was under a charm, apparently, that could smooth away the extent
and the far and difficult connections of such an effort. I was lifted
aloft on a great wave of infatuation and pity. I found it simple, in
my ignorance, my confusion, and perhaps my conceit, to assume
that I could deal with a boy whose education for the world was all
on the point of beginning. I am unable even to remember at this day
what proposal I framed for the end of his holidays and resumption
of his studies. Lessons with me indeed, that charming summer, we
all had a theory that he was to have; but I now feel that, for weeks,
the lessons must have been rather my own. I learnt something—at
first certainly—that had not been one of the teachings of my small,
smothered life; learnt to be amused, and even amusing, and not to
think for the morrow. It was the first time, in a manner, that I had
known space and air and freedom, all the music of summer and all
the mystery of nature. And then there was consideration—and consideration was sweet. Oh, it was a trap—not designed, but deep—to
my imagination, to my delicacy, perhaps to my vanity; to whatever,
in me, was most excitable. The best way to picture it all is to say
that I was off my guard. They gave me so little trouble—they were of
a gentleness so extraordinary. I used to speculate—but even this
with a dim disconnectedness—as to how the rough future (for all
futures are rough!) would handle them and might bruise them. They
had the bloom of health and happiness; and yet, as if I had been in
charge of a pair of little grandees, of princes of the blood, for whom
everything, to be right, would have to be enclosed and protected,
the only form that, in my fancy, the after-years could take for them
was that of a romantic, a really royal extension of the garden and the
park. It may be, of course, above all, that what suddenly broke into
this gives the previous time a charm of stillness—that hush in which
something gathers or crouches. The change was actually like the
spring of a beast.

   In the first weeks the days were long; they often, at their finest,
gave me what I used to call my own hour, the hour when, for my
pupils, tea-time and bed-time having come and gone, I had, before
my final retirement, a small interval alone. Much as I liked my
companions, this hour was the thing in the day I liked most; and I
liked it best of all when, as the light faded—or rather, I should say,
the day lingered and the last calls of the last birds sounded, in a
flushed sky, from the old trees—I could take a turn into the grounds
and enjoy, almost with a sense of property that amused and flattered
me, the beauty and dignity of the place. It was a pleasure at these
moments to feel myself tranquil and justified; doubtless, perhaps,
also to reflect that by my discretion, my quiet good sense and general high propriety, I was giving pleasure—if he ever thought of

it!—to the person to whose pressure I had responded. What I was doing was what he had earnestly hoped and directly asked of me, and that I *could*, after all, do it proved even a greater joy than I had expected. I dare say I fancied myself, in short, a remarkable young woman and took comfort in the faith that this would more publicly appear. Well, I needed to be remarkable to offer a front to the remarkable things that presently gave their first sign.

It was plump, one afternoon, in the middle of my very hour: the children were tucked away and I had come out for my stroll. One of the thoughts that, as I don't in the least shrink now from noting, used to be with me in these wanderings was that it would be as charming as a charming story suddenly to meet someone. Someone would appear there at the turn of a path and would stand before me and smile and approve. I didn't ask more than that—I only asked that he should *know* ; and the only way to be sure he knew would be to see it, and the kind light of it, in his handsome face. That was exactly present to me—by which I mean the face was—when, on the first of these occasions, at the end of a long June day, I stopped short on emerging from one of the plantations and coming into view of the house. What arrested me on the spot—and with a shock much greater than any vision had allowed for—was the sense that my imagination had, in a flash, turned real. He did stand there!—but high up, beyond the lawn and at the very top of the tower to which, on that first morning, little Flora had conducted me. This tower was one of a pair—square, incongruous, crenelated structures—that were distinguished, for some reason, though I could see little difference, as the new and the old. They flanked opposite ends of the house and were probably architectural absurdities, redeemed in a measure indeed by not being wholly disengaged nor of a height too pretentious, dating, in their gingerbread antiquity, from a romantic revival that was already a respectable past. I admired them, had fancies about them, for we could all profit in a degree, especially when they loomed through the dusk, by the grandeur of their actual battlements; yet it was not at such an elevation that the figure I had so often invoked seemed most in place.

It produced in me, this figure, in the clear twilight, I remember, two distinct gasps of emotion, which were, sharply, the shock of my first and that of my second surprise. My second was a violent perception of the mistake of my first: the man who met my eyes was not the person I had precipitately supposed. There came to me thus a bewilderment of vision of which, after these years, there is no living view that I can hope to give. An unknown man in a lonely place is a permitted object of fear to a young woman privately bred; and the figure that faced me was—a few more seconds assured me—as little anyone else I knew as it was the image that had been in my mind. I had not seen it in Harley Street—I had not seen it anywhere. The place, moreover, in the strangest way in the world, had, on the instant, and by the very fact of its appearance, become a solitude. To me at least, making my statement here with a deliberation with which I have never made it, the whole feeling of the moment returns. It was as if, while I took in—what I did take in—all the rest of the scene had been stricken with death. I can hear again, as I write, the intense hush in which the sounds of evening dropped. The rooks stopped cawing in the golden sky and the friendly hour lost, for the minute, all its voice. But there was no other change in nature, unless indeed it were a change that I saw with a stranger sharpness. The gold was still in the sky, the clearness in the air, and the man who looked at me over the battlements was as definite as a picture in a frame. That's how I thought, with extraordinary quickness, of each person that he might have been and that he was not. We were confronted across our distance quite long enough for me to ask myself with intensity who then he was and to feel, as an effect of my inability to say, a wonder that in a few instants more become intense.

The great question, or one of these is, afterwards, I know, with regard to certain matters, the question of how long they have lasted. Well, this matter of mine, think what you will of it, lasted while I caught at a dozen possibilities, none of which made a difference for the better, that I could see, in there having been in the house—and for how long, above all?—a person of whom I was in ignorance. It lasted while I just bridled a little with the sense that my office demanded that there should be no such ignorance and no such person. It lasted while this visitant, at all events,—and there was a touch of the strange freedom, as I remember, in the sign of familiarity of his wearing no hat,—seemed to fix me, from his position, with just the question, just the scrutiny through the fading light, that his own presence provoked. We were too far apart to call to each other, but there was a moment at which, at shorter range, some challenge between us, breaking the hush, would have been the right result of our straight mutual stare. He was in one of the angles, the one away from the house, very erect, as it struck me, and with both hands on the ledge. So I saw him as I see the letters I form on this page; then, exactly, after a minute, as if to add to the spectacle, he slowly changed his place—passed, looking at me hard all the while, to the opposite corner of the platform. Yes, I had the sharpest sense that during this transit he never took his eyes from me, and I can see at this moment the way his hand, as he went, passed from one of the crenelations to the next. He stopped at the other corner, but less long, and even as he turned away still markedly fixed me. He turned away; that was all I knew.

IV

It was not that I didn't wait, on this occasion, for more, for I was rooted as deeply as I was shaken. Was there a "secret" at Bly—a mystery of Udolpho or an insane, an unmentionable relative kept in unsuspected confinement? I can't say how long I turned it over, or how long, in a confusion of curiosity and dread, I remained where I had had my collision; I only recall that when I re-entered the house darkness had quite closed in. Agitation, in the interval, certainly had held me and driven me, for I must, in circling about the place, have walked three miles; but I was to be, later on, so much more overwhelmed that this mere dawn of alarm was a comparatively human chill. The most singular part of it in fact—singular as the rest had been—was the part I became, in the hall, aware of in meeting Mrs. Grose. This picture comes back to me in the general train—the impression, as I received it on my return, of the wide white pan-elled space, bright in the lamplight and with its portraits and red carpet, and of the good surprised look of my friend, which immedi-ately told me she had missed me. It came to me straightway, under her contact, that, with plain heartiness, mere relieved anxiety at my appearance, she knew nothing whatever that could bear upon the incident I had there ready for her. I had not suspected in advance that her comfortable face would pull me up, and I somehow mea-sured the importance of what I had seen by my thus finding myself hesitate to mention it. Scarce anything in the whole history seems to me so odd as this fact that my real beginning of fear was one, as I may say, with the instinct of sparing my companion. On the spot, accordingly, in the pleasant hall and with her eyes on me, I, for a reason that I couldn't then have phrased, achieved an inward revo-lution—offered a vague pretext for my lateness and, with the plea of the beauty of the night and of the heavy dew and wet feet, went as soon as possible to my room.

Here it was another affair; here, for many days after, it was a queer affair enough. There were hours, from day to day,—or at least there were moments, snatched even from clear duties,—when I had to shut myself up to think. It was not so much yet that I was more nervous than I could bear to be as that I was remarkably afraid of becoming so; for the truth I had now to turn over was, simply and clearly, the truth that I could arrive at no account whatever of the visitor with whom I had been so inexplicably and yet, as it seemed to me, so intimately concerned. It took little time to see that I could sound without forms of inquiry and without exciting remark any domestic complication. The shock I had suffered must have sharpened all my senses; I felt sure, at the end of three days and as the result of mere closer attention, that I had not been practised upon by the servants nor made the object of any "game." Of whatever it was that I knew nothing was known around me. There was but one sane inference: someone had taken a liberty rather gross. That was what, repeatedly, I dipped into my room and locked the door to say to myself. We had been, collectively, subject to an intrusion; some unscrupulous traveller, curious in old houses, had made his way in unobserved, enjoyed the prospect from the best point of view, and then stolen out as he came. If he had given me such a bold hard stare, that was but a part of his indiscretion. The good thing, after all, was that we should surely see no more of him.

This was not so good a thing, I admit, as not to leave me to judge that what, essentially, made nothing else much signify was simply my charming work. My charming work was just my life with Miles and Flora, and through nothing could I so like it as through feeling that I could throw myself into it in trouble. The attraction of my small charges was a constant joy, leading me to wonder afresh at the vanity of my original fears, the distaste I had begun by entertaining for the probable grey prose of my office. There was to be no grey prose, it appeared, and no long grind; so how could work not be charming that presented itself as daily beauty? It was all the romance of the nursery and the poetry of the schoolroom. I don't mean by this, of course, that we studied only fiction and verse; I mean I can express not otherwise the sort of interest my companions inspired. How can I describe that except by saying that instead of growing used to them—and it's a marvel for a governess: I call the sisterhood to witness!—I made constant fresh discoveries. There was one direction, assuredly, in which these discoveries stopped: deep obscurity continued to cover the region of the boy's conduct at school. It had been promptly given me, I have noted, to face that mystery without a pang. Perhaps even it would be nearer the truth to say that—without a word—he himself had cleared it up. He had made the whole charge absurd. My conclusion bloomed there with the real rose-flush of his innocence: he was only too fine and fair for the little horrid, unclean school-world, and he had paid a price for it. I reflected acutely that the sense of such differences, such superiorities of quality, always, on the part of the majority—which could include even stupid, sordid head-masters—turns infallibly to the vindictive.

Both the children had a gentleness (it was their only fault, and it never made Miles a muff) that kept them—how shall I express it?—

almost impersonal and certainly quite unpunishable. They were like the cherubs of the anecdote, who had—morally at any rate—nothing to whack! I remember feeling with Miles in especial as if he had had, as it were, no history. We expect of a small child a scant one, but there was in this beautiful little boy something extraordinarily sensitive, yet extraordinarily happy, that, more than in any creature of his age I have seen, struck me as beginning anew each day. He had never for a second suffered. I took this as a direct disproof of his having really been chastised. If he had been wicked he would have "caught" it, and I should have caught it by the rebound—I should have found the trace. I found nothing at all, and he was therefore an angel. He never spoke of his school, never mentioned a comrade or a master; and I, for my part, was quite too much disgusted to allude to them. Of course I was under the spell, and the wonderful part is that, even at the time, I perfectly knew I was. But I gave myself up to it; it was an antidote to any pain, and I had more pains than one. I was in receipt in these days of disturbing letters from home, where things were not going well. But with my children, what things in the world mattered? That was the question I used to put to my scrappy retirements. I was dazzled by their loveliness.

There was a Sunday—to get on—when it rained with such force and for so many hours that there could be no procession to church; in consequence of which, as the day declined, I had arranged with Mrs. Grose that, should the evening show improvement, we would attend together the late service. The rain happily stopped, and I prepared for our walk, which through the park and by the good road to the village, would be a matter of twenty minutes. Coming downstairs to meet my colleague in the hall, I remembered a pair of gloves that had required three stitches and that had received them— with a publicity perhaps not edifying—while I sat with the children at their tea, served on Sundays, by exception, in that cold, clean temple of mahogany and brass, the "grown-up" dining-room. The gloves had been dropped there, and I turned in to recover them. The day was grey enough, but the afternoon light still lingered, and it enabled me, on crossing the threshold, not only to recognise, on a chair near the wide window, then closed, the articles I wanted, but to become aware of a person on the other side of the window and looking straight in. One step into the room had sufficed; my vision was instantaneous; it was all there. The person looking straight in was the person who had already appeared to me. He appeared thus again with I won't say greater distinctness, for that was impossible, but with a nearness that represented a forward stride in our inter-course and made me, as I met him, catch my breath and turn cold. He was the same—he was the same, and seen, this time, as he had

been seen before, from the waist up, the window, though the dining-room was on the ground-floor, not going down to the terrace on
which he stood. His face was close to the glass, yet the effect of this
better view was, strangely, only to show me how intense the former
had been. He remained but a few seconds—long enough to convince me he also saw and recognised; but it was as if I had been
looking at him for years and had known him always. Something,
however, happened this time that had not happened before; his
stare into my face, through the glass and across the room, was as
deep and hard as then, but it quitted me for a moment during
which I could still watch it, see it fix successively several other
things. On the spot there came to me the added shock of a certitude
that it was not for me he had come there. He had come for someone
else.

The flash of this knowledge—for it was knowledge in the midst of
dread—produced in me the most extraordinary effect, started, as I
stood there, a sudden vibration of duty and courage. I say courage
because I was beyond all doubt already far gone. I bounded straight
out of the door again, reached that of the house, got, in an instant,
upon the drive, and, passing along the terrace as fast as I could
rush, turned a corner and came full in sight. But it was in sight of
nothing now—my visitor had vanished. I stopped, I almost
dropped, with the real relief of this; but I took in the whole scene—I
gave him time to reappear. I call it time, but how long was it? I can't
speak to the purpose today of the duration of these things. That
kind of measure must have left me: they couldn't have lasted as they
actually appeared to me to last. The terrace and the whole place, the
lawn and the garden beyond it, all I could see of the park, were
empty with a great emptiness. There were shrubberies and big
trees, but I remember the clear assurance I felt that none of them
concealed him. He was there or was not there: not there if I didn't
see him. I got hold of this; then, instinctively, instead of returning
as I had come, went to the window. It was confusedly present to me
that I ought to place myself where he had stood. I did so; I applied
my face to the pane and looked, as he had looked, into the room. As
if, at this moment, to show me exactly what his range had been,
Mrs. Grose, as I had done for himself just before, came in from the
hall. With this I had the full image of a repetition of what had
already occurred. She saw me as I had seen my own visitant; she
pulled up short as I had done; I gave her something of the shock
that I had received. She turned white, and this made me ask myself
if I had blanched as much. She stared, in short, and retreated on just
*my* lines, and I knew she had then passed out and come round to me
and that I should presently meet her. I remained where I was, and

while I waited I thought of more things than one. But there's only
one I take space to mention. I wondered why *she* should be scared.


V

Oh, she let me know as soon as, round the corner of the house, she
loomed again into view. "What in the name of goodness is the
matter—?" She was now flushed and out of breath.

I said nothing till she came quite near. "With me?" I must have
made a wonderful face. "Do I show it?"

"You're as white as a sheet. You look awful."

I considered; I could meet on this, without scruple, any innocence. My need to respect the bloom of Mrs. Grose's had dropped,
without a rustle, from my shoulders, and if I wavered for the instant
it was not with what I kept back. I put out my hand to her and she
took it; I held her hard a little, liking to feel her close to me. There
was a kind of support in the shy heave of her surprise. "You came
for me for church, of course, but I can't go."

"Has anything happened?"

"Yes. You must know now. Did I look very queer?"

"Through this window? Dreadful!"

"Well," I said, "I've been frightened." Mrs. Grose's eyes expressed plainly that *she* had no wish to be, yet also that she knew
too well her place not to be ready to share with me any marked
inconvenience. Oh, it was quite settled that she *must* share! "Just
what you saw from the dining-room a minute ago was the effect of
that. What *I* saw—just before—was much worse."

Her hand tightened. "What was it?"

"An extraordinary man. Looking in."

"What extraordinary man?"

"I haven't the least idea."

Mrs. Grose gazed around us in vain. "Then where is he gone?"

"I know still less."

"Have you seen him before?"

"Yes—once. On the old tower."

She could only look at me harder. "Do you mean he's a stranger?"

"Oh, very much!"

"Yet you didn't tell me?"

"No—for reasons. But now that you've guessed—"

Mrs. Grose's round eyes encountered this charge. "Ah, I haven't
guessed!" she said very simply. "How can I if *you* don't imagine?"

"I don't in the very least."

"You've seen him nowhere but on the tower?"

"And on this spot just now."

Mrs. Grose looked round again. "What was he doing on the tower?"

"Only standing there and looking down at me."

She thought a minute. "Was he a gentleman?"

I found I had no need to think. "No." She gazed in deeper wonder. "No."

"Then nobody about the place? Nobody from the village?"

"Nobody—nobody. I didn't tell you, but I made sure."

She breathed a vague relief: this was, oddly, so much to the good. It only went indeed a little way. "But if he isn't a gentleman—"

"What *is* he? He's a horror."

"A horror?"

"He's—God help me if I know *what* he is!"

Mrs. Grose looked round once more; she fixed her eyes on the duskier distance, then, pulling herself together, turned to me with abrupt inconsequence. "It's time we should be at church."

"Oh, I'm not fit for church!"

"Won't it do you good?"

"It won't do *them*—!" I nodded at the house.

"The children?"

"I can't leave them now."

"You're afraid—?"

I spoke boldly. "I'm afraid of *him*. "

Mrs. Grose's large face showed me, at this, for the first time, the far-away faint glimmer of a consciousness more acute: I somehow made out in it the delayed dawn of an idea I myself had not given her and that was as yet quite obscure to me. It comes back to me that I thought instantly of this as something I could get from her; and I felt it to be connected with the desire she presently showed to know more. "When was it—on the tower?"

"About the middle of the month. At this same hour."

"Almost at dark," said Mrs. Grose.

"Oh no, not nearly. I saw him as I see you."

"Then how did he get in?"

"And how did he get out?" I laughed. "I had no opportunity to ask him! This evening, you see," I pursued, "he has not been able to get in."

"He only peeps?"

"I hope it will be confined to that!" She had now let go my hand; she turned away a little. I waited an instant; then I brought out: "Go to church. Good-bye. I must watch."

Slowly she faced me again. "Do you fear for them?"

We met in another long look. "Don't *you* ?" Instead of answering she came nearer to the window and, for a minute, applied her face to the glass. "You see how he could see," I meanwhile went on.

She didn't move. "How long was he here?"

"Till I came out. I came to meet him."

Mrs. Grose at last turned round, and there was still more in her face. "*I* couldn't have come out."

"Neither could I!" I laughed again. "But I did come. I have my duty."

"So have I mine," she replied; after which she added: ".What is he like?"

"I've been dying to tell you. But he's like nobody."

"Nobody?" she echoed.

"He has no hat." Then seeing in her face that she already, in this, with a deeper dismay, found a touch of picture, I quickly added stroke to stroke. "He has red hair, very red, close-curling, and a pale face, long in shape, with straight, good features and little, rather queer whiskers that are as red as his hair. His eyebrows are, somehow, darker; they look particularly arched and as if they might move a good deal. His eyes are sharp, strange—awfully; but I only know clearly that they're rather small and very fixed. His mouth's wide, and his lips are thin, and except for his little whiskers he's quite clean-shaven. He gives me a sort of sense of looking like an actor."

"An actor!" It was impossible to resemble one less, at least, than Mrs. Grose at that moment.

"I've never seen one, but so I suppose them. He's tall, active, erect," I continued, "but never—no, never!—a gentleman."

My companion's face had blanched as I went on; her round eyes started and her mild mouth gaped. "A gentleman?" she gasped, confounded, stupefied: "a gentleman *he*?"

"You know him then?"

She visibly tried to hold herself. "But he *is* handsome?"

I saw the way to help her. "Remarkably!"

"And dressed—?"

"In somebody's clothes. They're smart, but they're not his own."

She broke into a breathless affirmative groan. "They're the master's!"

I caught it up. "You *do* know him?"

She faltered but a second. "Quint!" she cried.

"Quint?"

"Peter Quint—his own man, his valet, when he was here!"

"When the master was?"

Gaping still, but meeting me, she pieced it all together. "He never wore his hat, but he did wear—well, there were waistcoats missed! They were both here—last year. Then the master went and Quint was alone."

I followed, but halting a little. "Alone?"

"Alone with *us.* " Then, as from a deeper depth, "In charge," she added.

"And what became of him?"

She hung fire so long that I was still more mystified. "He went too," she brought out at last.

"Went where?"

Her expression, at this, became extraordinary. "God knows where! He died."

"Died?" I almost shrieked.

She seemed fairly to square herself, plant herself more firmly to utter the wonder of it. "Yes. Mr. Quint is dead."

### VI

It took of course more than that particular passage to place us together in presence of what we had now to live with as we could— my dreadful liability to impressions of the order so vividly exemplified, and my companion's knowledge, henceforth,—a knowledge half consternation and half compassion,—of that liability. There had been, this evening, after the revelation that left me, for an hour, so prostrate—there had been, for either of us, no attendance on any service but a little service of tears and vows, of prayers and promises, a climax to the series of mutual challenges and pledges that had straightway ensued on our retreating together to the schoolroom and shutting ourselves up there to have everything out. The result of our having everything out was, simply to reduce our situation to the last rigour of its elements. She herself had seen nothing, not the shadow of a shadow, and nobody in the house but the governess was in the governess's plight; yet she accepted without directly impugning my sanity the truth as I gave it to her, and ended by showing me, on this ground, an awe-struck tenderness, an expression of the sense of my more than questionable privilege, of which the very breath has remained with me as that of the sweetest of human charities.

What was settled between us, accordingly, that night, was that we thought we might bear things together; and I was not even sure that, in spite of her exemption, it was she who had the best of the burden. I knew at this hour, I think, as well as I knew later what I was capable of meeting to shelter my pupils; but it took me some time to be wholly sure of what my honest ally was prepared for to keep terms with so compromising a contract. I was queer company enough—quite as queer as the company I received; but as I trace over what we went through I see how much common ground we must have found in the one idea that, by good fortune, *could* steady us. It was the idea, the second movement, that led me straight out, as I may say, of the inner chamber of my dread. I could take the air in the court, at least, and there Mrs. Grose could join me. Perfectly can I recall now the particular way strength came to me before we separated for the night. We had gone over and over every feature of what I had seen.

"He was looking for someone else, you say—someone who was not you?"

"He was looking for little Miles." A portentous clearness now possessed me. "*That's* whom he was looking for."

"But how do you know?"

"I know, I know, I know!" My exaltation grew. "And *you* know, my dear!"

She didn't deny this, but I required, I felt, not even so much telling as that. She resumed in a moment, at any rate: "What if *he* should see him?"

"Little Miles? That's what he wants!"

She looked immensely scared again. "The child?"

"Heaven forbid! The man. He wants to appear to *them*. " That he might was an awful conception, and yet, somehow, I could keep it at bay; which, moreover, as we lingered there, was what I succeeded in practically proving. I had an absolute certainty that I should see again what I had already seen, but something within me said that by offering myself bravely as the sole subject of such experience, by accepting, by inviting, by surmounting it all, I should serve as an expiatory victim and guard the tranquillity of my companions. The children, in especial, I should thus fence about and absolutely save. I recall one of the last things I said that night to Mrs. Grose.

"It does strike me that my pupils have never mentioned——"

She looked at me hard as I musingly pulled up. "His having been here and the time they were with him?"

"The time they were with him, and his name, his presence, his history, in any way."

"Oh, the little lady doesn't remember. She never heard or knew."

"The circumstances of his death?" I thought with some intensity. "Perhaps not. But Miles would remember—Miles would know."

"Ah, don't try him!" broke from Mrs. Grose.

I returned her the look she had given me. "Don't be afraid." I continued to think. "It *is* rather odd."

"That he has never spoken of him?"

"Never by the least allusion. And you tell me that were 'great friends'?"

"Oh, it wasn't *him!*" Mrs. Grose with emphasis declared. "It was Quint's own fancy. To play with him, I mean—to spoil him." She paused a moment; then she added: "Quint was much too free."

This gave me, straight from my vision of his face—*such* a face!—a sudden sickness of disgust. "Too free with *my* boy?"

"Too free with everyone!"

I forbore, for the moment, to analyse this description further than by the reflection that a part of it applied to several of the members of the household, of the half-dozen maids and men who were still of our small colony. But there was everything, for our apprehension, in the lucky fact that no discomfortable legend, no perturbation of scullions, had ever, within anyone's memory, attached to the kind old place. It had neither bad name nor ill fame, and Mrs. Grose, most apparently, only desired to cling to me and to quake in silence. I even put her, the very last thing of all, to the test. It was when, at midnight, she had her hand on the schoolroom door to take leave. "I have it from you then—for it's of great importance—that he was definitely and admittedly bad?"

"Oh, not admittedly. *I* knew it—but the master didn't."

"And you never told him?"

"Well, he didn't like tale-bearing—he hated complaints. He was terribly short with anything of that kind; and if people were all right to *him*—"

"He wouldn't be bothered with more?" This squared well enough with my impression of him: he was not a trouble-loving gentleman, nor so very particular perhaps about some of the company *he* kept. All the same, I pressed my interlocutress. "I promise you *I* would have told!"

She felt my discrimination. "I dare say I was wrong. But, really, I was afraid."

"Afraid of what?"

"Of things that man could do. Quint was so clever—he was so deep."

I took this in still more than, probably, I showed. "You weren't afraid of anything else? Not of his effect——?"

"His effect?" she repeated with a face of anguish and waiting while I faltered.

"On innocent little precious lives. They were in your charge."

"No, they were not in mine!" she roundly and distressfully returned. "The master believed in him and placed him here because he was supposed not to be well and the country air so good for him.

So he had everything to say."Yes"—she let me have it—"even about
*them.* "

"Them—that creature?" I had to smother a kind of howl. "And
you could bear it!"

"No. I couldn't—and I can't now!" And the poor woman burst
into tears.

A rigid control, from the next day, was, as I have said, to follow
them; yet how often and how passionately, for a week, we came
back together to the subject! Much as we had discussed it that Sunday night, I was, in the immediate later hours in especial—for it
may be imagined whether I slept—still haunted with the shadow of
something she had not told me. I myself had kept back nothing, but
there was a word Mrs. Grose had kept back. I was sure, moreover,
by morning, that this was not from a failure of frankness, but because on every side there were fears. It seems to me indeed, in
retrospect, that by the time the morrow's sun was high I had restlessly read into the facts before us almost all the meaning they were
to receive from subsequent and more cruel occurrences. What they
gave me above all was just the sinister figure of the living man—the
dead one would keep awhile!—and of the months he had continuously passed at Bly, which, added up, made a formidable stretch.
The limit of this evil time had arrived only when, on the dawn of a
winter's morning, Peter Quint was found, by a labourer going to
early work, stone dead on the road from the village: a catastrophe
explained—superficially at least—by a visible wound to his head;
such a wound as might have been produced—and as, on the final
evidence, *had* been—by a fatal slip; in the dark and after leaving the
public house, on the steepish icy slope, a wrong path altogether, at
the bottom of which he lay. The icy slope, the turn mistaken at
night and in liquor, accounted for much—practically, in the end and
after the inquest and boundless chatter, for everything; but there
had been matters in his life—strange passages and perils, secret
disorders, vices more than suspected—that would have accounted
for a good deal more.

I scarcely know how to put my story into words that shall be a
credible picture of my state of mind; but I was in these days literally
able to find a joy in the extraordinary flight of heroism the occasion
demanded of me. I now saw that I had been asked for a service
admirable and difficult; and there would be a greatness in letting it
be seen—oh, in the right quarter! that I could succeed where many
another girl might have failed. It was an immense help to me—I
confess I rather applaud myself as I look back!—that I saw my service so strongly and so simply. I was there to protect and defend the
little creatures in the world the most bereaved and the most love-

able, the appeal of whose helplessness had suddenly become only too explicit, a deep, constant ache of one's own committed heart. We were cut off, really, together; we were united in our danger. They had nothing but me, and I—well, I had *them*. It was in short a magnificent chance. This chance presented itself to me in an image richly material. I was a screen—I was to stand before them. The more I saw, the less they would. I began to watch them in a stifled suspense, a disguised excitement that might well, had it continued too long, have turned to something like madness. What saved me, as I now see, was that it turned to something else altogether. It didn't last as suspense—it was superseded by horrible proofs. Proofs, I say, yes—from the moment I really took hold.

This moment dated from an afternoon hour that I happened to spend in the grounds with the younger of my pupils alone. We had left Miles indoors, on the red cushion of a deep window-seat; he had wished to finish a book, and I had been glad to encourage a purpose so laudable in a young man whose only defect was an occasional excess of the restless. His sister, on the contrary, had been alert to come out, and I strolled with her half an hour, seeking the shade, for the sun was still high and the day exceptionally warm. I was aware afresh, with her, as we went, of how, like her brother, she contrived—it was the charming thing in both children—to let me alone without appearing to drop me and to accompany me without appearing to surround. They were never importunate and yet never listless. My attention to them all really went to seeing them amuse themselves immensely without me: this was a spectacle they seemed actively to prepare and that engaged me as an active admirer. I walked in a world of their invention—they had no occasion whatever to draw upon mine; so that my time was taken only with being, for them, some remarkable person or thing that the game of the moment required, and that was merely, thanks to my superior, my exalted stamp, a happy and highly distinguished sinecure. I forget what I was on the present occasion; I only remember that I was something very important and very quiet and that Flora was playing very hard. We were on the edge of the lake, and, as we had lately begun geography, the lake was the Sea of Azof.

Suddenly, in these circumstances, I became aware that, on the other side of the Sea of Azof, we had an interested spectator. The way this knowledge gathered in me was the strangest thing in the world—the strangest, that is, except the very much stranger in which it quickly merged itself. I had sat down with a piece of work—for I was something or other that could sit—on the old stone bench which overlooked the pond; and in this position I began to take in with certitude, and yet without direct vision, the presence, at a distance, of a third person. The old trees, the thick shrubbery, made a great and pleasant shade, but it was all suffused with the brightness of the hot, still hour. There was no ambiguity in anything; none whatever, at least, in the conviction I from one moment to another found myself forming as to what I should see straight before me and across the lake as a consequence of raising my eyes. They were attached at this juncture to the stitching in which I was engaged, and I can feel once more the spasm of my effort not to move them till I should so have steadied myself as to be able to make up my mind what to do. There was an alien object in view— a figure whose right of presence I instantly, passionately questioned. I recollect counting over perfectly the possibilities, reminding myself that nothing was more natural, for instance, than the appearance of one of the men about the place, or even of a messenger, a postman or a tradesman's boy, from the village. That reminder had as little effect on my practical certitude as I was conscious—still even without looking—of its having upon the character and attitude of our visitor. Nothing was more natural than that these things should be the other things that they absolutely were not.

Of the positive identity of the apparition I would assure myself as soon as the small clock of my courage should have ticked out the right second; meanwhile, with an effort that was already sharp enough, I transferred my eyes straight to little Flora, who, at the moment, was about ten yards away. My heart had stood still for an instant with the wonder and terror of the question whether she too would see; and I held my breath while I waited for what a cry from her, what some sudden innocent sign either of interest or of alarm, would tell me. I waited, but nothing came; then, in the first place— and there is something more dire in this, I feel, than in anything I have to relate—I was determined by a sense that, within a minute, all sounds from her had previously dropped; and, in the second, by the circumstance that, also within the minute, she had, in her play, turned her back to the water. This was her attitude when I at last looked at her—looked with the confirmed conviction that we were still, together, under direct personal notice. She had picked up a small flat piece of wood, which happened to have in it a little hole that had evidently suggested to her the idea of sticking in another fragment that might figure as a mast and make the thing a boat. This second morsel, as I watched her, she was very markedly and intently attempting to tighten in its place. My apprehension of what she was doing sustained me so that after some seconds I felt I was ready for more. Then I again shifted my eyes—I faced what I had to face.

VII

I got hold of Mrs. Grose as soon after this as I could; and I can give no intelligible account of how I fought out the interval. Yet I still hear myself cry as I fairly threw myself into her arms: "They *know*— it's too monstrous: they know, they know!"

"And what on earth——?" I felt her incredulity as she held me.

"Why, all that *we* know—and heaven knows what else besides!" Then, as she released me, I made it out to her, made it out perhaps only now with full coherency even to myself. "Two hours ago, in the garden" —I could scarce articulate—"Flora *saw!*"

Mrs. Grose took it as she might have taken a blow in the stomach. "She has told you?" she panted.

"Not a word—that's the horror. She kept it to herself! The child of eight, *that* child!" Unutterable still, for me, was the stupefaction of it.

Mrs. Grose, of course, could only gape the wider. "Then how do you know?"

"I was there—I saw with my eyes: saw that she was perfectly aware."

"Do you mean aware of *him?*"

"No—of *her.*" I was conscious as I spoke that I looked prodigious things, for I got the slow reflection of them in my companion's face. "Another person—this time; but a figure of quite as unmistakeable horror and evil: a woman in black, pale and dreadful—with such an air also, and such a face!—on the other side of the lake. I was there with the child—quiet for the hour; and in the midst of it she came."

"Came how—from where?"

"From where they come from! She just appeared and stood there—but not so near."

"And without coming nearer?"

"Oh, for the effect and the feeling, she might have been as close as you!"

My friend, with an odd impulse, fell back a step. "Was she some-one you've never seen?"

"Yes. But someone the child has. Someone *you* have." Then, to show how I had thought it all out: "My predecessor—the one who died."

"Miss Jessel?"

"Miss Jessel. You don't believe me?" I pressed.

She turned right and left in her distress. "How can you be sure?"

This drew from me, in the state of my nerves, a flash of impa-tience. "Then ask Flora—*she's* sure!" But I had no sooner spoken than I caught myself up. "No, for God's sake, *don't* ! She'll say she isn't—she'll lie!"

Mrs. Grose was not too bewildered instinctively to protest. "Ah, how *can* you?"

"Because I'm clear. Flora doesn't want me to know."

"It's only then to spare you."

"No, no—there are depths, depths! The more I go over it, the more I see in it, and the more I see in it the more I fear. I don't know what I *don't* see—what I *don't* fear!"

Mrs. Grose tried to keep up with me. "You mean you're afraid of seeing her again?"

"Oh, no; that's nothing—now!" Then I explained. "It's of *not* seeing her."

But my companion only looked wan. "I don't understand you."

"Why, it's that the child may keep it up—and that the child assuredly *will* —without my knowing it."

At the image of this possibility Mrs. Grose for a moment collapsed, yet presently began to pull herself together again, as if from the positive force of the sense of what, should we yield an inch, there would really be to give way to. "Dear, dear—we must keep our heads! And after all, if she doesn't mind it——!" She even tried a grim joke. "Perhaps she likes it!"

"Likes *such* things— a scrap of an infant!"

"Isn't it just a proof of her blessed innocence?" my friend bravely inquired.

She brought me, for the instant, almost round. "Oh, we must clutch at *that* —we must cling to it! If it isn't a proof of what you say, it's a proof of—God knows what! For the woman's a horror of horrors."

Mrs. Grose, at this, fixed her eyes a minute on the ground; then at last raising them, "Tell me how you know," she said.

"Then you admit it's what she was?" I cried.

"Tell me how you know," my friend simply repeated.

"Know? By seeing her! By the way she looked."

"At you, do you mean—so wickedly?"

"Dear me, no—I could have borne that. She gave me never a glance. She only fixed the child."

Mrs. Grose tried to see it. "Fixed her?"

"Ah, with such awful eyes!"

She stared at mine as if they might really have resembled them. "Do you mean of dislike?"

"God help us, no. Of something much worse."

"Worse than dislike?"—this left her indeed at a loss.

"With a determination—indescribable. With a kind of fury of intention."

I made her turn pale. "Intention?"

"To get hold of her." Mrs. Grose—her eyes just lingering on mine—gave a shudder and walked to the window; and while she stood there looking out I completed my statement. *"That's* what Flora knows."

After a little she turned round. "The person was in black, you say?"

"In mourning—rather poor, almost shabby. But—yes—with extraordinary beauty." I now recognised to what I had at last, stroke by stroke, brought the victim of my confidence, for she quite visibly weighed this. "Oh, handsome,—very, very," I insisted; "wonderfully handsome. But infamous."

She slowly came back to me. "Miss Jessel—*was* infamous." She once more took my hand in both her own, holding it as tight as if to fortify me against the increase of alarm I might draw from this disclosure. "They were both infamous," she finally said.

So, for a little, we faced it once more together; and I found absolutely a degree of help in seeing it now so straight. "I appreciate," I said, "the great decency of your not having hitherto spoken; but the time has certainly come to give me the whole thing." She appeared to assent to this, but still only in silence; seeing which I went on: "I must have it now. Of what did she die? Come, there was something between them."

"There was everything."

"In spite of the difference—?"

"Oh, of their rank, their condition"—she brought it woefully out. *"She* was a lady."

I turned it over; I again saw. "Yes—she was a lady."

"And he so dreadfully below," said Mrs. Grose.

I felt that I doubtless needn't press too hard, in such company, on the place of a servant in the scale; but there was nothing to prevent an acceptance of my companion's own measure of my predecessor's abasement. There was a way to deal with that, and I dealt; the more readily for my full vision—on the evidence—of our employer's late clever, good-looking "own" man; impudent, assured, spoiled, depraved. "The fellow was a hound."

Mrs. Grose considered as if it were perhaps a little a case for a sense of shades. "I've never seen one like him. He did what he wished."

"With *her* ?"

"With them all."

It was as if now in my friend's own eyes Miss Jessel had again appeared. I seemed at any rate, for an instant, to see their evocation of her as distinctly as I had seen her by the pond; and I brought out with decision: "It must have been also what *she* wished!"

Mrs. Grose's face signified that it had been indeed, but she said at the same time: "Poor woman—she paid for it!"

"Then you do know what she died of?" I asked.

"No—I know nothing. I wanted not to know; I was glad enough I didn't; and I thanked heaven she was well out of this!"

"Yet you had, then, your idea——"

"Of her real reason for leaving? Oh, yes—as to that. She couldn't have stayed. Fancy it here—for a governess! And afterwards I imagined—and I still imagine. And what I imagine is dreadful."

"Not so dreadful as what *I* do," I replied; on which I must have shown her—as I was indeed but too conscious—a front of miserable defeat. It brought out again all her compassion for me, and at the renewed touch of her kindess my power to resist broke down. I burst, as I had, the other time, made her burst, into tears; she took me to her motherly breast, and my lamentation overflowed. "I don't do it!" I sobbed in despair; "I don't save or shield them! It's far worse than I dreamed—they're lost!"

VIII

What I had said to Mrs. Grose was true enough: there were in the matter I had put before her depths and possibilities that I lacked resolution to sound; so that when we met once more in the wonder of it we were of a common mind about the duty of resistance to extravagant fancies. We were to keep our heads if we should keep nothing else—difficult indeed as that might be in the face of what, in our prodigious experience, was least to be questioned. Late that night, while the house slept, we had another talk in my room, when she went all the way with me as to its being beyond doubt that I had seen exactly what I had seen. To hold her perfectly in the pinch of that, I found I had only to ask her how, if I had "made it up," I came to be able to give, of each of the persons appearing to me, a picture disclosing, to the last detail, their special marks—a portrait on the exhibition of which she had instantly recognised and named them. She wished, of course,—small blame to her!—to sink the whole subject; and I was quick to assure her that my own interest in it had now violently taken the form of a search for the way to escape from it. I encountered her on the ground of a probability that with recurrence—for recurrence we took for granted—I should get used to my danger, distinctly professing that my personal exposure had suddenly become the least of my discomforts. It was my new suspicion that was intolerable; and yet even to this complication the later hours of the day had brought a little ease.

On leaving her, after my first outbreak, I had of course returned to my pupils, associating the right remedy for my dismay with that sense of their charm which I had already found to be a thing I could positively cultivate and which had never failed me yet. I had simply, in other words, plunged afresh into Flora's special society and there become aware—it was almost a luxury!—that she could put her little conscious hand straight upon the spot that ached. She had looked at me in sweet speculation and then had accused me to my face of having "cried." I had supposed I had brushed away the ugly signs; but I could literally—for the time, at all events—rejoice under this fathomless charity, that they had not entirely disappeared. To gaze into the depths of blue of the child's eyes and pronounce their loveliness a trick of premature cunning was to be guilty of a cynicism in preference to which I naturally preferred to abjure my judgment and, so far as might be, my agitation. I couldn't abjure for merely wanting to, but I could repeat to Mrs. Grose—as I did there, over and over, in the small hours—that with their voices in the air, their pressure on one's heart and their fragrant faces against one's cheek, everything fell to the ground but their incapacity and their beauty. It was a pity that, somehow, to settle this once for all, I had equally to re-enumerate the signs of subtlety that, in the afternoon, by the lake, had made a miracle of my show of self-possession. It was a pity to be obliged to re-investigate the certitude of the moment itself and repeat how it had come to me as a revelation that the inconceivable communion I then surprised was a matter, for either party, of habit. It was a pity that I should have had to quaver out again the reasons for my not having, in my delusion, so much as questioned that the little girl saw our visitant even as I actually saw Mrs. Grose herself, and that she wanted, by just so much as she did thus see, to make me suppose she didn't, and at the same time without showing anything, arrive at a guess as to whether I myself did! It was a pity that I needed once more to describe the portentous little activity by which she sought to divert my attention—the perceptible increase of movement, the greater intensity of play, the singing, the gabbling of nonsense, and the invitation to romp.

Yet if I had not indulged, to prove there was nothing in it, in this review, I should have missed the two or three dim elements of comfort that still remained to me. I should not for instance have been able to asseverate to my friend that I was certain—which was so much to the good—that *I* at least had not betrayed myself. I should not have been prompted, by stress of need, by desperation of mind,—I scarce know what to call it,—to invoke such further aid to intelligence as might spring from pushing my colleague fairly to the wall. She had told me, bit by bit, under pressure, a great deal; but a small shifty spot on the wrong side of it all still sometimes brushed my brow like the wing of a bat; and I remember how on this occasion—for the sleeping house and the concentration alike of our danger and our watch seemed to help—I felt the importance of giving the last jerk to the curtain. "I don't believe anything so horrible," I recollect saying; "no, let us put it definitely, my dear, that I don't. But if I did, you know, there's a thing I should require now, just without sparing you the least bit more—oh, not a scrap, come!—to get out of you. What was it you had in mind when, in our distress, before Miles came back, over the letter from his school, you said, under my insistance, that you didn't pretend for him that he had not literally *ever* been 'bad'? He has *not* literally 'ever,' in these weeks that I myself have lived with him and so closely watched him; he has been an imperturbable little prodigy of delightful, loveable goodness. Therefore you might perfectly have made the claim for him if you had not, as it happened, seen an exception to take. What was your exception, and to what passage in your personal observation of him did you refer?"

It was a dreadfully austere inquiry, but levity was not our note, and, at any rate, before the grey dawn admonished us to separate I had got my answer. What my friend had had in mind proved to be immensely to the purpose. It was neither more nor less than the circumstance that for a period of several months Quint and the boy had been perpetually together. It was in fact the very appropriate truth that she had ventured to criticise the propriety, to hint at the incongruity, of so close an alliance, and even to go so far on the subject as a frank overture to Miss Jessel. Miss Jessel had, with a most strange manner, requested her to mind her business, and the good woman had, on this, directly approached little Miles. What she had said to him, since I pressed, was that *she* liked to see young gentlemen not forget their station.

I pressed again, of course, at this. "You reminded him that Quint was only a base menial?"

"As you might say! And it was his answer, for one thing, that was bad."

"And for another thing?" I waited. "He repeated your words to Quint?"

"No, not that. It's just what he *wouldn't*!" she could still impress upon me. "I was sure, at any rate," she added, "that he didn't. But he denied certain occasions."

"What occasions?"

"When they had been about together quite as if Quint were his tutor—and a very grand one—and Miss Jessel only for the little lady. When he had gone off with the fellow, I mean, and spent hours with him."

"He then prevaricated about it—he said he hadn't?" Her assent was clear enough to cause me to add in a moment: "I see. He lied."

"Oh!" Mrs. Grose mumbled. This was a suggestion that it didn't matter; which indeed she backed up by a further remark. "You see, after all, Miss Jessel didn't mind. She didn't forbid him."

I considered. "Did he put that to you as a justification?"

At this she dropped again. "No, he never spoke of it."

"Never mentioned her in connection with Quint?"

She saw, visibly flushing where I was coming out. "Well, he didn't show anything. He denied," she repeated; "he denied."

Lord, how I pressed her now! "So that you could see he knew what was between the two wretches?"

"I don't know—I don't know!" the poor woman groaned.

"You do know, you dear thing," I replied; "only you haven't my dreadful boldness of mind, and you keep back, out of timidity and modesty and delicacy, even the impression that, in the past, when you had, without my aid, to flounder about in silence, most of all made you miserable. But I shall get it out of you yet! There was something in the boy that suggested to you," I continued, "that he covered and concealed their relation."

"Oh, he couldn't prevent——"

"Your learning the truth? I dare say! But, heavens," I fell, with vehemence, a-thinking, "what it shows that they must, to that extent have succeeded in making of him!"

"Ah, nothing that's not nice *now!*" Mrs. Grose lugubriously pleaded.

"I don't wonder you looked queer," I persisted, "when I mentioned to you the letter from his school!"

"I doubt if I looked as queer as you!" she retorted with homely force. "And if he was so bad then as that comes to, how is he such an angel now?"

"Yes, indeed—and if he was a fiend at school! How, how, how? Well," I said in my torment, "you must put it to me again, but I shall not be able to tell you for some days. Only, put it to me again!" I cried in a way that made my friend stare. "There are directions in which I must not for the present let myself go." Meanwhile I returned to her first example—the one to which she had just previously referred—of the boy's happy capacity for an occasional slip. "If Quint—on your remonstrance at the time you speak of—was a base menial, one of the things Miles said to you, I find myself guessing, was that you were another." Again her admission was so adequate that I continued: "and you forgave him that?"

"Wouldn't *you* ?"

'Oh, yes !'' And we exchanged there, in the stillness, a sound of the oddest amusement. Then I went on: "At all events, while he was with the man——"

"Miss Flora was with the woman. It suited them all!"

It suited me too, I felt, only too well; by which I mean that it suited exactly the particularly deadly view I was in the very act of forbidding myself to entertain. But I so far succeeded in checking the expression of this view that I will throw, just here, no further light on it than may be offered by the mention of my final observation to Mrs. Grose. "His having lied and been impudent are, I confess, less engaging specimens than I had hoped to have from you of the outbreak in him of the little natural man. Still," I mused, "they must do, for they make me feel more than ever that I must watch."

It made me blush, the next minute, to see in my friend's face how much more unreservedly she had forgiven him than her anecdote struck me as presenting to my own tenderness an occasion for doing. This came out when, at the schoolroom door, she quitted me. "Surely you don't accuse *him* —"

"Of carrying on an intercourse that he conceals from me? Ah, remember that, until further evidence, I now accuse nobody." Then, before shutting her out to go, by another passage, to her own place, "I must just wait," I wound up.

IX

I waited and waited, and the days, as they elapsed, took something from my consternation. A very few of them, in fact, passing, in constant sight of my pupils, without a fresh incident, sufficed to give to grievous fancies and even to odious memories a kind of brush of the sponge. I have spoken of the surrender to their extraordinary childish grace as a thing I could actively cultivate, and it may be imagined if I neglected now to address myself to this source for whatever it would yield. Stranger than I can express, certainly, was the effort to struggle against my new lights! it would doubtless have been, however, a greater tension still had it not been so frequently successful. I used to wonder how my little charges could help guessing that I thought strange things about them; and the circumstance that these things only made them more interesting was not by itself a direct aid to keeping them in the dark. I trembled lest they should see that they *were* so immensely more interesting. Putting things at the worst, at all events, as in meditation I so often did, any clouding of their innocence could only be—blameless and foredoomed as they were—a reason the more for taking risks. There were moments

when, by an irresistible impulse, I found myself catching them up
and pressing them to my heart. As soon as I had done so I used to
say to myself: "What will they think of that? Doesn't it betray too
much?" It would have been easy to get into a sad, wild tangle about
how much I might betray; but the real account, I feel, of the hours of
peace that I could still enjoy was that the immediate charm of my
companions was a beguilement still effective even under the
shadow of the possibility that it was studied. For if it occurred to me
that I might occasionally excite suspicion by the little outbreaks of
my sharper passion for them, so too I remember wondering if I
mightn't see a queerness in the traceable increase of their own demonstrations.

They were at this period extravagantly and preternaturally fond of
me; which, after all, I could reflect, was no more than a graceful
response in children perpetually bowed over and hugged. The homage of which they were so lavish succeeded, in truth, for my nerves,
quite as well as if I never appeared to myself, as I may say, literally
to catch them at a purpose in it. They had never, I think, wanted to
do so many things for their poor protectress; I mean—though they
got their lessons better and better, which was naturally what would
please her most—in the way of diverting, entertaining, surprising
her; reading her passages, telling her stories, acting her charades,
pouncing out at her, in disguises, as animals and historical characters, and above all astonishing her by the "pieces" they had secretly got by heart and could interminably recite. I should never get
to the bottom—were I to let myself go even now—of the prodigious
private commentary, all under still more private correction, with
which, in these days, I overscored their full hours. They had shown
me from the first a facility for everything, a general faculty which,
taking a fresh start, achieved remarkable flights. They got their little
tasks as if they loved them, and indulged, from the mere exuberance
of the gift, in the most unimposed little miracles of memory. They
not only popped out at me as tigers and as Romans, but as Shake-
speareans, astronomers, and navigators. This was so singularly the
case that it had presumably much to do with the fact as to which, at
the present day, I am at a loss for a different explanation: I allude to
my unnatural composure on the subject of another school for Miles.
What I remember is that I was content not, for the time, to open the
question, and that contentment must have sprung from the sense of
his perpetually striking show of cleverness. He was too clever for a
bad governess, for a parson's daughter, to spoil; and the strangest if
not the brightest thread in the pensive embroidery I just spoke of
was the impression I might have got, if I had dared to work it out,
that he was under some influence operating in his small intellectual
life as a tremendous incitement.

If it was easy to reflect, however, that such a boy could postpone school, it was at least as marked that for such a boy to have been "kicked out" by a school-master was a mystification without end. Let me add that in their company now—and I was careful almost never to be out of it—I could follow no scent very far. We lived in a cloud of music and love and success and private theatricals. The musical sense in each of the children was of the quickest, but the elder in especial had a marvellous knack of catching and repeating. The schoolroom piano broke into all gruesome fancies; and when that failed there were confabulations in corners, with a sequel of one of them going out in the highest spirits in order to "come in" as something new. I had had brothers myself, and it was no revelation to me that little girls could be slavish idolaters of little boys. What surpassed everything was that there was a little boy in the world who could have for the inferior age, sex, and intelligence so fine a consideration. They were extraordinarily at one, and to say that they never either quarrelled or complained is to make the note of praise coarse for their quality of sweetness. Sometimes, indeed, when I dropped into coarseness, I perhaps came across traces of little understandings between them by which one of them should keep me occupied while the other slipped away. There is a naïf side, I suppose, in all diplomacy; but if my pupils practiced upon me, it was surely with the minimum of grossness. It was all in the other quarter that, after a lull, the grossness broke out.

I find that I really hang back; but I must take my plunge. In going on with the record of what was hideous at Bly, I not only challenge the most liberal faith—for which I little care; but—and this is another matter—I renew what I myself suffered, I again push my way through it to the end. There came suddenly an hour after which, as I look back, the affair seems to me to have been all pure suffering; but I have at least reached the heart of it, and the straightest road out is doubtless to advance. One evening—with nothing to lead up or to prepare it—I felt the cold touch of the impression that had breathed on me the night of my arrival and which, much lighter than, as I have mentioned, I should probably have made little of in memory had my subsequent sojourn been less agitated. I had not gone to bed; I sat reading by a couple of candles. There was a roomfull of old books at Bly—last-century fiction, some of it, which, to the extent of a distinctly deprecated renown, but never to so much as that of a stray specimen, had reached the sequestered home and appealed to the unavowed curiosity of my youth. I remember that the book I had in my hand was Fielding's *Amelia*; also that I was wholly awake. I recall further both a general conviction that it was horribly late and a particular objection to looking at my watch. I figure, finally, that the white curtain draping, in the fashion of those days, the head of Flora's little bed, shrouded, as I had assured myself long before, the perfection of childish rest. I recollect in short that, though I was deeply interested in my author, I found myself, at the turn of a page and with his spell all scattered, looking straight up from him and hard to the door of my room. There was a moment during which I listened, reminded of the faint sense I had had, the first night, of there being something undefineably astir in the house, and noted the soft breath of the open casement just move the half-drawn blind. Then, with all the marks of a deliberation that must have seemed magnificent had there been anyone to admire it, I laid down my book, rose to my feet, and, taking, a candle, went straight out of the room, and, from the passage, on which my light made little impression, noiselessly closed and locked the door.

I can say now neither what determined nor what guided me, but I went straight along the lobby, holding my candle high, till I came within sight of the tall window that presided over the great turn of the staircase. At this point I percipitately found myself aware of three things. They were practically simultaneous, yet they had flashes of succession. My candle, under a bold flourish, went out, and I perceived, by the uncovered window, that the yielding dusk of earliest morning rendered it unnecessary. Without it, the next instant, I saw that there was someone on the stair. I speak of sequences, but I required no lapse of seconds to stiffen myself for a third encounter with Quint. The apparition had reached the landing half-way up and was therefore on the spot nearest the window, where at sight of me, it stopped short and fixed me exactly as it had fixed me from the tower and from the garden. He knew me as well as I knew him; and so, in the cold, faint twilight, with a glimmer in the high glass and another on the polish of the oak stair below, we faced each other in our common intensity. He was absolutely, on this occasion, a living, detestable, dangerous presence. But that was not the wonder of wonders; I reserve this distinction for quite another circumstance: the circumstance that dread had unmistakeably quitted me and there was nothing in me there that didn't meet and measure him.

I had plenty of anguish after that extraordinary moment, but I had, thank God, no terror. And he knew I had not—I found myself at the end of an instant magnificently aware of this. I felt, in a fierce rigour of confidence, that if I stood my ground a minute I should cease—for the time, at least—to have him to reckon with; and during the minute, accordingly, the thing was as human and hideous as a real interview: hideous just because it *was* human, as human as to have met alone, in the small hours, in a sleeping house, some enemy, some adventurer, some criminal. It was the dead silence of our long gaze at such close quarters that gave the whole horror, huge as it was, its only note of the unnatural. If I had met a murderer in such a place and at such an hour, we still at least would have spoken. Something would have passed in life, between us; if nothing had passed one of us would have moved. The moment was so prolonged that it would have taken but little more to make me doubt if even *I* were in life. I can't express what followed it save by saying that the silence itself—which was indeed in a manner an attestation of my strength—became the element into which I saw the figure disappear; in which I definitely saw it turn as I might have seen the low wretch to which it had once belonged turn on receipt of an order, and pass, with my eyes on the villainous back that no hunch could have more disfigured, straight down the staircase and into the darkness in which the next bend was lost.

### X

I remained awhile at the top of the stair, but with the effect presently of understanding that when my visitor had gone, he had gone: then I returned to my room. The foremost thing I saw there by the light of the candle I had left burning was that Flora's little bed was empty; and on this I caught my breath with all the terror that, five minutes before, I had been able to resist. I dashed at the place in which I had left her lying and over which (for the small silk counterpane and the sheets were disarranged) the white curtains had been deceivingly pulled forward; then my step, to my unutterable relief, produced an answering sound: I perceived an agitation of the window-blind, and the child, ducking down, emerged rosily from the other side of it. She stood there in so much of her candour and so little of her nightgown, with her pink bare feet and the golden glow of her curls. She looked intensely grave, and I had never had such a sense of losing an advantage acquired (the thrill of which had just been so prodigious) as on my consciousness that she addressed me with a reproach. "You naughty: where *have* you been?"—instead of challenging her own irregularity I found myself arraigned and explaining. She herself explained, for that matter, with the loveliest, eagerest simplicity. She had known suddenly, as she lay there, that I was out of the room, and had jumped up to see what had become of me. I had dropped, with the joy of her reappearance, back into my chair—feeling then, and then only, a little faint; and she had pattered straight over to me, thrown herself upon my knee, given herself to be held with the flame of the candle full in the wonderful little face that was still flushed with sleep. I remember closing my eyes an instant, yieldingly, consciously, as before the excess of something beautiful that shone out of the blue of her own. "You were looking for me out of the window?" I said. "You thought I might be walking in the grounds?"

"Well, you know, I thought someone was"—she never blanched as she smiled out that at me.

Oh, how I looked at her now! "And did you see anyone?"

"Ah, *no!*" she returned, almost with the full privilege of childish inconsequence, resentfully, though with a long sweetness in her little drawl of the negative.

At that moment, in the state of my nerves, I absolutely believed she lied; and if I once more closed my eyes it was before the dazzle of the three or four possible ways in which I might take this up. One of these, for a moment, tempted me with such singular intensity that, to withstand it, I must have gripped my little girl with a spasm that, wonderfully, she submitted to without a cry or a sign of fright. Why not break out at her on the spot and have it all over?— give it to her straight in her lovely little lighted face? "You see, you see, you *know* that you do and that you already quite suspect I believe it; therefore why not frankly confess it to me, so that we may at least live with it together and learn perhaps, in the strangeness of our fate, where we are and what it means?" This solicitation dropped, alas, as it came: if I could immediately have succumbed to it I might have spared myself—well you'll see what. Instead of succumbing I sprang again to my feet, looked at her bed, and took a helpless middle way. "Why did you pull the curtain over the place to make me think you were still there?"

Flora luminously considered; after which, with her little divine smile: "Because I don't like to frighten you!"

"But if I had, by your idea, gone out——?"

She absolutely declined to be puzzled; she turned her eyes to the flame of the candle as if the question were as irrelevant, or at any rate as impersonal, as Mrs. Marcet or nine-times-nine. "Oh, but you know," she quite adequately answered, "that you might come back, you dear, and that you *have* !" And after a little, when she had got into bed, I had, for a long time, by almost sitting on her to hold her hand, to prove that I recognised the pertinence of my return.

You may imagine the general complexion, from that moment, of my nights. I repeatedly sat up till I didn't know when; I selected moments when my room-mate unmistakeably slept, and, stealing out, took noiseless turns in the passage and even pushed as far as to where I had last met Quint. But I never met him there again; and I may as well say at once that I on no other occasion saw him in the house. I just missed, on the staircase, on the other hand, a different adventure. Looking down it from the top I once recognised the

presence of a woman seated on one of the lower steps with her back
presented to me, her body half bowed and her head, in an attitude
of woe, in her hands. I had been there but an instant, however,
when she vanished without looking round at me. I knew, none the
less, exactly what dreadful face she had to show; and I wondered
whether, if instead of being above I had been below. I should have
had, for going up, the same nerve I had lately shown Quint. Well,
there continued to be plenty of chance for nerve. On the eleventh
night after my latest encounter with that gentleman—they were all
numbered now—I had an alarm that perilously skirted it and that
indeed, from the particular quality of its unexpectedness, proved
quite my sharpest shock. It was precisely the first night during this
series that, weary with watching, I had felt that I might again without laxity lay myself down at my old hour. I slept immediately and,
as I afterwards knew, till about one o'clock; but when I woke it was
to sit straight up, as completely roused as if a hand had shook me. I
had left a light burning, but it was now out, and I felt an instant
certainty that Flora had extinguished it. This brought me to my feet
and straight, in the darkness, to her bed, which I found she had left.
A glance at the window enlightened me further, and the striking of
a match completed the picture.

The child had again got up—this time blowing out the taper, and
had again, for some purpose of observation or response, squeezed
in behind the blind and was peering out into the night. That she
now saw—as she had not, I had satisfied myself, the previous
time—was proved to me by the fact that she was disturbed neither
by my re-illumination nor by the haste I made to get into slippers
and into a wrap. Hidden, protected, absorbed, she evidently rested
on the sill—the casement opened forward—and gave herself up.
There was a great still moon to help her, and this fact had counted
in my quick decision. She was face to face with the apparition we
had met at the lake, and could now communicate with it as she had
not then been able to do. What I, on my side, had to care for was,
without disturbing her, to reach, from the corridor, some other window in the same quarter. I got to the door without her hearing me; I
got out of it, closed it and listened, from the other side, for some
sound from her. While I stood in the passage I had my eyes on her
brother's door, which was but ten steps off and which, indescriba-
bly, produced in me a renewal of the strange impulse that I lately
spoke of as my temptation. What if I should go straight in and
march to *his* window?—what if, by risking to his boyish bewilderment a revelation of my motive, I should throw across the rest of the
mystery the long halter of my boldness?

This thought held me sufficiently to make me cross to his threshold and pause again. I preternaturally listened: I figured to myself what might portentously be; I wondered if his bed were also empty and he too were secretly at watch. It was a deep, soundless minute, at the end of which my impulse failed. He was quiet; he might be innocent; the risk was hideous; I turned away. There was a figure in the grounds—a figure prowling for a sight, the visitor with whom Flora was engaged; but it was not the visitor most concerned with my boy. I hesitated afresh, but on the other grounds and only a few seconds; then I had made my choice. There were empty rooms at Bly, and it was only a question of choosing the right one. The right one suddenly presented itself to me as the lower one—though high above the gardens—in the solid corner of the house that I have spoken of as the old tower. This was a large, square chamber, arranged with some state as a bedroom, the extravagant size of which made it so inconvenient that it had not for years, though kept by Mrs. Grose in exemplary order, been occupied. I had often admired it and I knew my way about in it; I had only, after just faltering at the first chill gloom of its disuse, to pass across it and unbolt as quietly as I could one of the shutters. Achieving this transit, I uncovered the glass without a sound and, applying my face to the pane, was able, the darkness without being much less than within, to see that I commanded the right direction. Then I saw something more. The moon made the night extraordinarily penetrable and showed me on the lawn a person, diminished by distance, who stood there motionless and as if fascinated, looking up to where I had appeared—looking, that is, not so much straight at me as at something that was apparently above me. There was clearly another person above me—there was a person on the tower; but the presence on the lawn was not in the least what I had conceived and had confidently hurried to meet. The presence on the lawn—I felt sick as I made it out—was poor little Miles himself.

## XI

It was not till late next day that I spoke to Mrs. Grose; the rigour with which I kept my pupils in sight making it often difficult to meet her privately, and the more as we each felt the importance of not provoking—on the part of the servants quite as much as on that of the children—any suspicion of a secret flurry or of a discussion of mysteries. I drew a great security in this particular from her mere smooth aspect. There was nothing in her fresh face to pass on to others my horrible confidences. She believed me, I was sure, absolutely: if she hadn't I don't know what would have become of me for I couldn't have borne the business alone. But she was a magnificent monument to the blessing of a want of imagination, and if she could see in our little charges nothing but their beauty and amiability, their happiness and cleverness, she had no direct communication with the sources of my trouble. If they had been at all visibly blighted or battered, she would doubtless have grown, on tracing it back, haggard enough to match them; as matters stood, however, I could feel her, when she surveyed them, with her large white arms folded and the habit of serenity in all her look, thank the Lord's mercy that if they were ruined the pieces would still serve. Flights of fancy gave place, in her mind, to a steady fireside glow, and I had already begun to perceive how, with the development of the conviction that—as time went on without a public accident—our young things could, after all, look out for themselves, she addressed her greatest solicitude to the sad case presented by their instructress. That, for myself, was a sound simplification: I could engage that, to the world, my face should tell no tales, but it would have been, in the conditions, an immense added strain to find myself anxious about hers.

At the hour I now speak of she had joined me, under pressure, on the terrace, where, with the lapse of the season, the afternoon sun was now agreeable; and we sat there together while, before, us, at a distance, but within call if we wished, the children strolled to and fro in one of their most manageable moods. They moved slowly, in unison, below us, over the lawn, the boy, as they went, reading aloud from a storybook and passing his arm round his sister to keep her quite in touch. Mrs. Grose watched them with positive placidity; then I caught the suppressed intellectual creak with which she conscientiously turned to take from me a view of the back of the tapestry. I had made her a receptacle of lurid things, but there was an odd recognition of my superiority—my accomplishments and my function—in her patience under my pain. She offered her mind to my disclosures as, had I wished to mix a witch's broth and proposed it with assurance, she would have held out a large saucepan. This had become thoroughly her attitude by the time that, in my recital of the events of the night, I reached the point of what Miles had said to me when, after seeing him, at such a monstrous hour, almost on the very spot where he happened now to be, I had gone down to bring him in; choosing then, at the window, with a concentrated need of not alarming the house, rather that method than a signal more resonant. I had left her meanwhile in little doubt of my small hope of representing with success even to her actual sympathy my sense of the real splendour of the little inspiration with which, after I had got him into the house, the boy met my final articulate challenge. As soon as I appeared in the moonlight on the terrace, he had come to me as straight as possible; on which I had taken his hand without a word and led him, through the dark spaces, up the staircase where Quint had so hungrily hovered for him, along the lobby where I had listened and trembled, and so to his forsaken room.

Not a sound, on the way, had passed between us, and I had wondered—oh, *how* I had wondered!—if he were groping about in his little mind for something plausible and not too grotesque. It would tax his invention, certainly, and I felt this time, over his real embarrassment, a curious thrill of triumph. It was sharp trap for the inscrutable! He couldn't play any longer at innocence; so how the deuce would he get out of it? There beat in me indeed, with the passionate throb of this question, an equal dumb appeal as to how the deuce *I* should. I was confronted at last, as never yet, with all the risk attached even now to sounding my own horrid note. I remember in fact that as we pushed into his little chamber, where the bed had not been slept in at all and the window, uncovered to the moonlight, made the place so clear that there was no need of striking a match—I remember how I suddenly dropped, sank upon the edge of the bed from the force of the idea that he must know how he really, as they say, "had" me. He could do what he liked, with all his cleverness to help him, so long as I should continue to defer to the old tradition of the criminality of those caretakers of the young who minister to superstitions and fears. He "had" me indeed, and in a cleft stick; for who would ever absolve me, who would consent that I should go unhung, if, by the faintest tremor of an overture, I were the first to introduce into our perfect intercourse an element so dire? No, no: it was useless to attempt to convey to Mrs. Grose, just as it is scarcely less so to attempt to suggest here, how, in our short, stiff brush in the dark, he fairly shook me with admiration. I was of course thoroughly kind and merciful; never, never yet had I placed on his little shoulders hands of such tenderness as those with which, while I rested against the bed, I held him there well under fire. I had no alternative but, in form at least, to put it to him.

"You must tell me now—and all the truth. What did you go out for? What were you doing there?"

I can still see his wonderful smile, the whites of his beautiful eyes, and the uncovering of his little teeth shine to me in the dusk. "If I tell you why, will you understand?" My heart, at this, leaped into my mouth. *Would* he tell me why? I found no sound on my lips to press it, and I was aware of replying only with a vague, repeated, grimacing nod. He was gentleness itself, and while I wagged my head at him he stood there more than ever a little fairy prince. It was his brightness indeed that gave me a respite. Would it be so great if he were really going to tell me? "Well," he said at last, "just exactly in order that you should do this."

"Do what?"

"Think me—for a change—*bad!*" I shall never forget the sweetness and gaiety with which he brought out the word, nor how, on top of it, he bent forward and kissed me. It was practically the end of everything. I met his kiss and I had to make, while I folded him for a minute in my arms, the most stupendous effort not to cry. He had given exactly the account of himself that permitted least of my going behind it, and it was only with the effect of confirming my acceptance of it that, as I presently glanced about the room, I could say—

"Then you didn't undress at all?"

He fairly glittered in the gloom. "Not at all. I sat up and read."

"And when did you go down?"

"At midnight. When I'm bad I *am* bad!"

"I see, I see—it's charming. But how could you be sure I would know it?"

"Oh, I arranged that with Flora." His answers rang out with a readiness! "She was to get up and look out."

"Which is what she did do." It was I who fell into the trap!

"So she disturbed you, and, to see what she was looking at, you also looked—you saw."

"While you," I concurred, "caught your death in the night air!"

He literally bloomed so from this exploit that he could afford radiantly to assent. "How otherwise should I have been bad enough?" he asked. Then, after another embrace, the incident and our interview closed on my recognition of all the reserves of goodness, that, for his joke, he had been able to draw upon.

## XII

The particular impression I had received proved in the morning light, I repeat, not quite successfully presentable to Mrs. Grose, though I reinforced it with the mention of still another remark that he had made before we separated. "It all lies in half-a-dozen words," I said to her, "words that really settle the matter. 'Think, you know, what I *might* do!' He threw that off to show me how good he is. He knows down to the ground what he 'might' do. That's what he gave them a taste of at school."

"Lord, you do change!" cried my friend.

"I don't change—I simply make it out. The four, depend upon it, perpetually meet. If on either of these last nights you had been with either child, you would clearly have understood. The more I've watched and waited the more I've felt that if there were nothing else to make it sure it would be made so by the systematic silence of each. *Never*, by a slip of the tongue, have they so much as alluded to either of their old friends, any more than Miles has alluded to his expulsion. Oh yes, we may sit here and look at them, and they may show off to us there to their fill; but even while they pretend to be lost in their fairy-tale they're steeped in their vision of the dead restored. He's not reading to her," I declared; "they're talking of *them*—they're talking horrors! I go on, I know, as if I were crazy; and it's a wonder I'm not. What I've seen would have made *you* so; but it has only made me more lucid, made me get hold of still other things."

My lucidity must have seemed awful, but the charming creatures who were victims of it, passing and repassing in their interlocked sweetness, gave my colleague something to hold on by; and I felt how tight she held as, without stirring in the breath of my passion, she covered them still with her eyes. "Of what other things have you got hold?"

"Why, of the very things that have delighted, fascinated, and yet, at bottom, as I now so strangely see, mystified and troubled me. Their more than earthly beauty, their absolutely and unnatural goodness. It's a game," I went on; "it's a policy and a fraud!"

"On the part of little darlings——?"

"As yet mere lovely babies? Yes, mad as that seems!" The very act of bringing it out really helped me to trace it—follow it all up and piece it all together. "They haven't been good—they've only been absent. It has been easy to live with them, because they're simply leading a life of their own. They're not mine—they're not ours. They're his and they're hers!"

"Quint's and that woman's?"

"Quint's and that woman's. They want to get to them."

Oh, how, at this, poor Mrs. Grose appeared to study them! "But for what?"

"For the love of all the evil that, in those dreadful days, the pair put into them. And to ply them with that evil still, to keep up the work of demons, is what brings the others back."

"Laws!" said my friend under her breath. The exclamation was homely, but it revealed a real acceptance of my further proof of what, in the bad time—for there had been a worse even than this!— must have occurred. There could have been no such justification for me as the plain assent of her experience to whatever depth of depravity I found credible in our brace of scoundrels. It was in obvious submission of memory that she brought out after a moment: "They *were* rascals! But whan can they now do?" she pursued.

"Do?" I echoed so loud that Miles and Flora, as they passed at their distance, paused an instant in their walk and looked at us. "Don't they do enough?" I demanded in a lower tone, while the children, having smiled and nodded and kissed hands to us, resumed their exhibition. We were held by it a minute; then I answered: "They can destroy them!" At this my companion did turn, but the inquiry she launched was a silent one, the effect of which was to make me more explicit. "They don't know, as yet, quite how—but they're trying hard. They're seen only across, as it were, and beyond—in strange places and on high places, the top of towers, the roof of houses, the outside of windows, the further edge of pools; but there's a deep design, on either side, to shorten the distance and overcome the obstacle; and the success of the tempters is only a question of time. They've only to keep to their suggestions of danger."

"For the children to come?"

"And perish in the attempt!" Mrs. Grose slowly got up, and I scrupulously added: "Unless, of course, we can prevent!"

Standing there before me while I kept my seat, she visibly turned things over. "Their uncle must do the preventing. He must take them away."

"And who's to make him?"

She had been scanning the distance, but she now dropped on me a foolish face. "You, Miss."

"By writing to him that his house is poisoned and his little nephew and niece mad?"

"But if they *are*, Miss?"

"And if I am myself, you mean? That's charming news to be sent him by a governess whose prime undertaking was to give him no worry."

Mrs. Grose considered, following the children again. "Yes, he do hate worry. That was the great reason——"

"Why those fiends took him in so long? No doubt, though his indifference must have been awful. As I'm not a fiend, at any rate, I shouldn't take him in."

My companion, after an instant and for all answer, sat down again and grasped my arm. "Make him at any rate come to you."

I stared. "To *me*?" I had a sudden fear of what she might do. " 'Him'?"

"He ought to *be* here—he ought to help."

I quickly rose, and I think I must have shown her a queerer face than ever yet. "You see me asking him for a visit?" No, with her eyes on my face she evidently couldn't. Instead of it even—as a woman reads another—she could see what I myself saw: his derision, his amusement, his contempt for the break-down of my resignation at being left alone and for the fine machinery I had set in motion to attract his attention to my slighted charms. She didn't know—no one knew—how proud I had been to serve him and to stick to our terms; yet she none the less took the measure, I think, of the warning I now gave her. "If you should so lose your head as to appeal to him for me——"

She was really frightened. "Yes, Miss?"

"I would leave, on the spot, both him and you."

XIII

It was all very well to join them, but speaking to them proved quite as much as ever an effort beyond my strength—offered, in close quarters, difficulties as insurmountable as before. This situation continued a month, and with new aggravations and particular notes, the note above all, sharper and sharper, of the small ironic consciousness on the part of my pupils. It was not, I am as sure today as I was sure then, my mere infernal imagination: it was absolutely traceable that they were aware of my predicament and that this strange relation made, in a manner, for a long time, the air in which we moved. I don't mean that they had their tongues in their cheeks or did anything vulgar, for that was not one of their dangers: I do mean, on the other hand, that the element of the unnamed and untouched became, between us, greater than any other, and that so much avoidance could not have been so success-fully effected without a great deal of tacit arrangement. It was as if, at moments, we were perpetually coming into sight of subjects be-fore which we must stop short, turning suddenly out of alleys that we perceived to be blind, closing with a little bang that made us look at each other—for, like all bangs, it was something louder than we had intended—the doors we had indiscreetly opened. All roads lead to Rome, and there were times when it might have struck us that almost every branch of study or subject of conversation skirted forbidden ground. Forbidden ground was the question of the return of the dead in general and of whatever, in especial, might survive, in memory, of the friends little children had lost. There were days when I could have sworn that one of them had, with a small invisi-ble nudge, said to the other: "She thinks she'll do it this time—but she *won't!*" To "do it" would have been to indulge for instance—and for once in a way—in some direct reference to the lady who had prepared them for my discipline. They had a delightful endless ap-petite for passages in my own history, to which I had again and again treated them; they were in possession of everything that had ever happened to me, had had, with every circumstance the story of my smallest adventures and of those of my brothers and sisters and of the cat and the dog at home, as well as many particulars of the eccentric nature of my father, of the furniture and arrangement of our house, and of the conversation of the old women of our village. There were things enough, taking one with another, to chatter about, if one went very fast and knew by instinct when to go round. They pulled with an art of their own the strings of my invention and my memory; and nothing else perhaps, when I thought of such occasions afterwards, gave me so the suspicion of being watched from under cover. It was in any case over *my* life, *my* past, and *my* friends alone that we could take anything like our ease—a state of affairs that led them sometimes without the least pertinence to break out into sociable reminders. I was invited—with no visible connection—to repeat afresh Goody Gosling's celebrated *mot* or to confirm the details already supplied as to the cleverness of the vicarage pony.

It was partly at such junctures as these and partly at quite different ones that, with the turn my matters had now taken, my predicament, as I have called it, grew most sensible. The fact that the days passed for me without another encounter ought, it would have appeared, to have done something toward soothing my nerves. Since the light brush, that second night on the upper landing, of the presence of a woman at the foot of the stair, I had seen nothing, whether in or out of the house, that one had better not have seen. There was many a corner round which I expected to come upon Quint, and many a situation that, in a merely sinister way, would have favoured the appearance of Miss Jessel. The summer had turned, the summer had gone; the autumn had dropped upon Bly and had blown out half our lights. The place, with its grey sky and withered garlands, its bared spaces and scattered dead leaves, was like a theatre after the performance—all strewn with crumpled playbills. There were exactly states of the air, conditions of sound and of stillness, unspeakable impressions of the *kind* of ministering moment, that brought back to me, long enough to catch it, the feeling of the medium in which, that June evening out-of-doors, I had had my first sight of Quint, and in which, too, at those other instants, I had, after seeing him through the window, looked for him in vain in the circle of the shrubbery. I recognised the signs, the portents—I recognised the moment, the spot. But they remained unaccompanied and empty, and I continued unmolested; if unmolested one could call a young woman whose sensibility had, in the most extraordinary fashion, not declined but deepened. I had said in my talk with Mrs. Grose on that horrid scene of Flora's by the lake—and had perplexed her by so saying—that it would from that moment distress me much more to lose my power than to keep it. I had then expressed what was vividly in my mind: the truth that, whether the children really saw or not—since, that is, it was not yet definitely proved—I greatly preferred, as a safeguard, the fulness of my own exposure. I was ready to know the very worst that was to be known. What I had then had an ugly glimpse of was that my eyes might be sealed just while theirs were most opened. Well, my eyes *were* sealed, it appeared, at present—a consummation for which it seemed blasphemous not to thank God. There was, alas, a difficulty about that: I would have thanked him with all my soul had I not had in a proportionate measure this conviction of the secret of my pupils.

How can I retrace today the strange steps of my obsession? There were times of our being together when I would have been ready to swear that, literally, in my presence, but with my direct sense of it closed, they had visitors who were known and were welcome. Then it was that, had I not been deterred by the very chance that such an injury might prove greater than the injury to be averted, my exultation would have broken out. "They're here, they're here, you little wretches, " I would have cried, "and you can't deny it now!" The little wretches denied it with all the added volume of their sociability and their tenderness, in just the crystal depths of which—like the flash of fish in a stream—the mockery of their advantage peeped up. The shock, in truth, had sunk into me still deeper than I knew on the night when, looking out to see either Quint or Miss Jessel under the stars, I had beheld the boy over whose rest I watched and who had immediately brought in with him—had straightway, there, turned it on me—the lovely upward look with which, from the battlements above me, the hideous apparition of Quint had played. If it was a question of a scare, my discovery on this occasion had scared me more than any other, and it was in the condition of nerves produced by it that I made my actual inductions. They harassed me so that sometimes, at odd moments, I shut myself up audibly to rehearse—it was at once a fantastic relief and a renewed despair—the manner in which I might come to the point. I approached it from one side and the other while, in my room, I flung myself about, but I always broke down in the monstrous utterance of names. As they died away on my lips, I said to myself that I should indeed help them to represent something infamous if, by pronouncing them, I should violate as rare a little case of instinctive delicacy as any schoolroom, probably, had ever known. When I said to myself: "*They* have the manners to be silent, and you, trusted as you are, the baseness to speak!" I felt myself crimson and I covered my face with my hands. After these secret scenes I chattered more than ever, going on volubly enough till one of our prodigious, palpable hushes occurred—I can call them nothing else—the strange, dizzy lift or swim (I try for terms!) into a stillness, a pause of all life, that had nothing to do with the more or less noise that at the moment we might be engaged in making and that I could hear through any deepened exhilaration or quickened recitation or louder strum of the piano. Then it was that the others, the outsiders, were there. Though they were not angels, they "passed," as the French say, causing me, while they stayed, to tremble with the fear of their addressing to their younger victims some yet more infernal message or more vivid image than they had thought good enough for myself.

What it was most impossible to get rid of was the cruel idea that, whatever I had seen, Miles and Flora saw *more*—things terrible and unguessable and that sprang from dreadful passages of intercourse in the past. Such things naturally left on the surface, for the time, a chill which we vociferously denied that we felt; and we had, all three, with repetition, got into such splendid training that we went, each time, almost automatically, to mark the close of the incident, through the very same movements. It was striking of the children, at all events, to kiss me inveterately with a kind of wild irrelevance and never to fail—one or the other—of the precious question that had helped us through many a peril. "When do you think he *will* come? Don't you think we *ought* to write?" —there was nothing like that inquiry, we found by experience, for carrying off an awkwardness. "He" of course was their uncle in Harley Street; and we lived in much profusion of theory that he might at any moment arrive to mingle in our circle. It was impossible to have given less encouragement than he had done to such a doctrine, but if we had not had the doctrine to fall back upon we should have deprived each other of some of our finest exhibitions. He never wrote to them—that may have been selfish, but it was a part of the flattery of his trust of me; for the way in which a man pays his highest tribute to a woman is apt to be but the more festal celebration of one of the sacred laws of his comfort; and I held that I carried out the spirit of the pledge given not to appeal to him when I let my charges understand that their own letters were but charming literary exercises. They were too beautiful to be posted; I kept them myself; I have them all to this hour. This was a rule indeed which only added to the satiric effect of my being plied with the supposition that he might at any moment be among us. It was exactly as if my charges knew how almost more awkward than anything else that might be for me. There appears to me, moreover, as I look back, no note in all this more extraordinary than the mere fact that, in spite of my tension and of their triumph, I never lost patience with them. Adorable they must in truth have been, I now reflect, that I didn't in these days hate

them! Would exasperation, however, if relief had longer been post-
poned, finally have betrayed me? It little matters, for relief arrived. I
call it relief, though it was only the relief that a snap brings to a
strain or the burst of a thunderstorm to a day of suffocation. It was
at least change, and it came with a rush.


### XIV

Walking to church a certain Sunday morning, I had little Miles at my
side and his sister, in advance of us and at Mrs. Grose's, well in
sight. It was a crisp, clear day, the first of its order for some time;
the night had brought a touch of frost, and the autumn air, bright
and sharp, made the church-bells almost gay. It was an odd accident
of thought that I should have happened at such a moment to be
particularly and very gratefully struck with the obedience of my
little charges. Why did they never resent my inexorable, my perpetual society? Something or other had brought nearer home to me that
I had all but pinned the boy to my shawl and that, in the way our
companions were marshalled before me, I might have appeared to
provide against some danger of rebellion. I was like a gaoler with an
eye to possible surprises and escapes. But all this belonged—I mean
their magnificent little surrender—just to the special array of the
facts that were most abysmal. Turned out for Sunday by his uncle's
tailor, who had had a free hand and a notion of pretty waistcoats
and of his grand little air, Miles's whole title to independence, the
rights of his sex and situation, were so stamped upon him that if he
had suddenly struck for freedom I should have had nothing to say. I
was by the strangest of chances wondering how I should meet him
when the revolution unmistakeably occurred. I call it a revolution
because I now see how, with the word he spoke, the curtain rose on
the last act of my dreadful drama and the catastrophe was precipi-
tated. "Look here, my dear, you know," he charmingly said, "when
in the world, please, am I going back to school?"

Transcribed here the speech sounds harmless enough, particularly
as uttered in the sweet, high, casual pipe with which, at all inter-
locutors, but above all at his eternal governess, he threw off intona-
tions as if he were tossing roses. There was something in them that
always made one "catch," and I caught, at any rate, now so effectually that I stopped as short as if one of the trees of the park had
fallen across the road. There was something new, on the spot, between us, and he was perfectly aware that I recognised it, though, to
enable me to do so, he had no need to look a whit less candid and
charming than usual. I could feel in him how he already, from my at
first finding nothing to reply, perceived the advantage he had
gained. I was so slow to find anything that he had plenty of time,

after a minute, to continue with his suggestive but inconclusive smile: "You know, my dear, that for a fellow to be with a lady *always*——!" His "my dear" was constantly on his lips for me, and nothing could have expressed more the exact shade of the sentiment with which I desired to inspire my pupils than its fond familiarity. It was so respectfully easy.

But, oh, how I felt that at present I must pick my own phrases! I remember that, to gain time, I tried to laugh, and I seemed to see in the beautiful face with which he watched me how ugly and queer I looked. "And always with the same lady?" I returned.

He neither blenched nor winked. The whole thing was virtually out between us. "Ah, of course, she's a jolly, 'perfect' lady; but, after all, I'm a fellow, don't you see? that's—well, getting on."

I lingered there with him an instant ever so kindly. "Yes, you're getting on." Oh, but I felt helpless!

I have kept to this day the heartbreaking little idea of how he seemed to know that and to play with it. "And you can't say I've not been awfully good, can you?"

I laid my hand on his shoulder, for, though I felt how much better it would have been to walk on, I was not yet quite able. "No, I can't say that, Miles."

"Except just that one night, you know——!"

"That one night?" I couldn't look as straight as he.

"Why, when I went down—went out of the house."

"Oh, yes. But I forget what you did it for."

"You forget?"—he spoke with the sweet extravagance of childish reproach. "Why, it was to show you I could!"

"Oh, yes, you could."

"And I can again."

I felt that I might, perhaps, after all, succeed in keeping my wits about me. "Certainly. But you won't."

"No, not *that* again. It was nothing."

"It was nothing," I said. "But we must go on."

He resumed our walk with me, passing his hand into my arm. "Then when *am* I going back?"

I wore, in turning it over, my most responsible air. "Were you very happy at school?"

He just considered. "Oh, I'm happy enough anywhere!"

"Well, then," I quavered, "if you're just as happy here——!"

"Ah, but that isn't everything! Of course *you* know a lot——"

"But you hint that you know almost as much?" I risked as he paused.

"Not half I want to!" Miles honestly professed. "But it isn't so much that."

"What is it, then?"

"Well—I want to see more life."

"I see; I see." We had arrived within sight of the church and of various persons, including several of the household of Bly, on their way to it and clustered about the door to see us go in. I quickened our step; I wanted to get there before the question between us opened up much further; I reflected hungrily that, for more than an hour, he would have to be silent; and I thought with envy of the comparative dusk of the pew and of the almost spiritual help of the hassock on which I might bend my knees. I seemed literally to be running a race with some confusion to which he was about to reduce me, but I felt that he had got in first when, before we had even entered the churchyard, he threw out——

"I want my own sort!"

It literally made me bound forward. "There are not many of your own sort, Miles!" I laughed. "Unless perhaps dear little Flora!"

"You really compare me to a baby girl?"

This found me singularly weak. "Don't you, then, *love* our sweet Flora?"

"If I didn't—and you too; if I didn't——!" he repeated as if retreating for a jump, yet leaving his thought so unfinished that, after we had come into the gate, another stop, which he imposed on me by the pressure of his arm, had become inevitable. Mrs. Grose and Flora had passed into the church, the other worshippers had followed, and we were, for the minute, alone among the old, thick graves. We had paused, on the path from the gate, by a low, oblong, tablelike tomb.

"Yes, if you didn't——?"

He looked, while I waited, about at the graves. "Well, you know what!" But he didn't move, and he presently produced something that made me drop straight down on the stone slab, as if suddenly to rest. "Does my uncle think what *you* think?"

I markedly rested. "How do you know what I think?"

"Ah, well, of course I don't; for it strikes me you never tell me. But I mean does *he* know?"

"Know what, Miles?"

"Why, the way I'm going on."

I perceived quickly enough that I could make, to this inquiry, no answer that would not involve something of a sacrifice of my employer. Yet it appeared to me that we were all, at Bly, sufficiently sacrificed to make that venial. "I don't think your uncle much cares."

Miles, on this, stood looking at me. "Then don't you think he can be made to?"

"In what way?"

"Why, by his coming down."

"But who'll get him to come down?"

"*I* will!" the boy said with extraordinary brightness and emphasis. He gave me another look charged with that expression and then marched off alone into church.

## XV

The business was practically settled from the moment I never followed him. It was a pitiful surrender to agitation, but my being aware of this had somehow no power to restore me. I only sat there on my tomb and read into what my little friend had said to me the fulness of its meaning; by the time I had grasped the whole of which I had also embraced, for absence, the pretext that I was ashamed to offer my pupils and the rest of the congregation such an example of delay. What I said to myself above all was that Miles had got something out of me and that the proof of it, for him, would be just this awkward collapse. He had got out of me that there was something I was much afraid of and that he should probably be able to make use of my fear to gain, for his own purpose, more freedom. My fear was of having to deal with the intolerable question of the grounds of his dismissal from school, for that was really but the question of the horrors gathered behind. That his uncle should arrive to treat with me of these things was a solution that, strictly speaking, I ought now to have desired to bring on; but I could so little face the ugliness and the pain of it that I simply procrastinated and lived from hand to mouth. The boy, to my deep discomposure, was immensely in the right, was in a position to say to me: "Either you clear up with my guardian the mystery of this interruption of my studies, or you cease to expect me to lead with you a life that's so unnatural for a boy." What was so unnatural for the particular boy I was concerned with was this sudden revelation of a consciousness and a plan.

That was what really overcame me, what prevented my going in. I walked round the church, hesitating, hovering; I reflected that I had already, with him, hurt myself beyond repair. Therefore I could patch up nothing, and it was too extreme an effort to squeeze beside him into the pew: he would be so much more sure then ever to pass his arm into mine and make me sit there for an hour in close, silent contact with his commentary on our talk. For the first minute since his arrival I wanted to get away from him. As I paused beneath the high east window and listened to the sounds of worship, I was taken with an impulse that might master me, I felt, completely should I give it the least encouragement. I might easily put an end to my predicament by getting away altogether. Here was my chance;

there was no one to stop me; I could give the whole thing up—turn my back and retreat. It was only a question of hurrying again, for a few preparations, to the house which the attendance at church of so many of the servants would practically have left unoccupied. No one, in short, could blame me if I should just drive desperately off. What was it to get away if I got away only till dinner? That would be in a couple of hours, at the end of which—I had the acute prevision—my little pupils would play at innocent wonder about my non-appearance in their train.

"What *did* you do, you naughty, bad thing? Why in the world, to worry us so—and take our thoughts off too, don't you know?—did you desert us at the very door?" I couldn't meet such questions nor, as they asked them, their false little lovely eyes; yet it was all so exactly what I should have to meet that, as the prospect grew sharp to me, I at last let myself go.

I got, so far as the immediate moment was concerned, away; I came straight out of the churchyard and, thinking hard, retraced my steps through the park. It seemed to me that by the time I reached the house I had made up my mind I would fly. The Sunday stillness both of the approaches and of the interior, in which I met no one, fairly excited me with a sense of opportunity. Were I to get off quickly, this way, I should get off without a scene, without a word. My quickness would have to be remarkable, however, and the question of a conveyance was the great one to settle. Tormented, in the hall, with difficulties and obstacles, I remember sinking down at the foot of the staircase—suddenly collapsing there on the lowest step and then, with a revulsion, recalling that it was exactly where more than a month before, in the darkness of the night and just so bowed with evil things, I had seen the spectre of the most horrible of women. At this I was able to straighten myself; I went the rest of the way up; I made, in my bewilderment, for the schoolroom, where there were objects belonging to me that I should have to take. But I opened the door to find again, in a flash, my eyes unsealed. In the presence of what I saw I reeled straight back upon my resistance.

Seated at my own table in clear noonday light I saw a person whom, without my previous experience, I should have taken at the first blush for some housemaid who might have stayed at home to look after the place and who, availing herself of rare relief from observation and of the schoolroom table and my pens, ink, and paper, had applied herself to the considerable effort of a letter to her sweetheart. There was an effort in the way that, while her arms rested on the table, her hands with evident weariness supported her head; but at the moment I took this in I had already become aware that, in spite of my entrance, her attitude strangely persisted. Then it was—with the very act of its announcing itself—that her identity flared up in a change of posture. She rose, not as if she had heard me, but with an indescribable grand melancholy of indifference and detachment, and, within a dozen feet of me, stood there as my vile predecessor. Dishonoured and tragic, she was all before me; but even as I fixed and, for memory, secured it, the awful image passed away. Dark as midnight in her black dress, her haggard beauty and her unutterable woe, she had looked at me long enough to appear to say that her right to sit at my table was as good as mine to sit at hers. While these instants lasted indeed I had the extraordinary chill of a feeling that it was I who was the intruder. It was as a wild protest against it that, actually addressing her—"You terrible, miserable woman!"—I heard myself break into a sound that, by the open door, rang through the long passage and the empty house. She looked at me as if she heard me, but I had recovered myself and cleared the air. There was nothing in the room the next minute but the sunshine and a sense that I must stay.

XVI

I had so perfectly expected that the return of my pupils would be marked by a demonstration that I was freshly upset at having to take into account that they were dumb about my absence. Instead of gaily denouncing and caressing me, they made no allusion to my having failed them, and I was left, for the time, on perceiving that she too said nothing, to study Mrs. Grose's odd face. I did this to such purpose that I made sure they had in some way bribed her to silence; a silence that, however, I would engage to break down on the first private opportunity. This opportunity came before tea: I secured five minutes with her in the housekeeper's room, where, in the twilight, amid a smell of lately-baked bread, but with the place all swept and garnished, I found her sitting in pained placidity before the fire. So I see her still, so I see her best: facing the flame from her straight chair in the dusky, shining room, a large clean image of the "put away"—of drawers closed and locked and rest without a remedy.

"Oh, yes, they asked me to say nothing; and to please them—so long as they were there—of course I promised. But what had happened to you?"

"I only went with you for the walk," I said. "I had then to come back to meet a friend."

She showed her surprise. "A friend—*you*?"

"Oh, yes, I have a couple!" I laughed. "But did the children give you a reason?"

"For not alluding to your leaving us? Yes; they said you would like it better. Do you like it better?"

My face had made her rueful. "No, I like it worse!" But after an instant I added: "Did they say why I should like it better?"

"No; Master Miles only said,'We must do nothing but what she likes!' "

"I wish indeed he would! And what did Flora say?"

"Miss Flora was too sweet. She said, 'Oh, of course, of course!'— and I said the same."

I thought a moment. "You were too sweet too—I can hear you all. But none the less, between Miles and me, it's now all out."

"All out?" My companion stared. "But what, Miss?"

"Everything. It doesn't matter. I've made up my mind. I came home, my dear," I went on, "for a talk with Miss Jessel."

I had by this time formed the habit of having Mrs. Grose literally well in hand in advance of my sounding that note; so that even now, as she bravely blinked under the signal of my word, I could keep her comparatively firm. "A talk! Do you mean she spoke?"

"It came to that. I found her, on my return, in the schoolroom."

"And what did she say?" I can hear the good woman still, and the candour of her stupefaction.

"That she suffers the torments——!"

It was this, of a truth, that made her, as she filled out my picture, gape. "Do you mean," she faltered, "—of the lost?"

"Of the lost. Of the damned. And that's why, to share them——" I faltered myself with the horror of it.

But my companion, with less imagination, kept me up. "To share them——?"

"She wants Flora." Mrs. Grose might, as I gave it to her, fairly have fallen away from me had I not been prepared. I still held her there, to show I was. "As I've told you, however, it doesn't matter."

"Because you've made up your mind? But to what?"

"To everything."

"And what do you call 'everything'?"

"Why, sending for their uncle."

"Oh, Miss, in pity do," my friend broke out.

"Ah, but I will, I *will*! I see it's the only way. What's 'out,' as I told you, with Miles is that if he thinks I'm afraid to—and has ideas of what he gains by that—he shall see he's mistaken. Yes, yes; his uncle shall have it here from me on the spot (and before the boy himself if necessary) that if I'm to be reproached with having done nothing again about more school——"

"Yes, Miss—" my companion pressed me.

"Well, there's that awful reason."

There were now clearly so many of these for my poor colleague that she was excusable for being vague. "But—a—which?"

"Why, the letter from his old place."

"You'll show it to the master?"

"I ought to have done so on the instant."

"Oh, no!" said Mrs. Grose with decision.

"I'll put it before him," I went on inexorably, "that I can't undertake to work the question on behalf of a child who has been expelled——"

"For we've never in the least known what!" Mrs. Grose declared.

"For wickedness. For what else—when he's so clever and beautiful and perfect? Is he stupid? Is he untidy? Is he infirm? Is he ill-natured? He's exquisite—so it can be only *that*; and that would open up the whole thing. After all," I said, "it's their uncle's fault. If he left here such people——!"

"He didn't really in the least know them. The fault's mine." She had turned quite pale.

"Well, you shan't suffer," I answered.

"The children shan't!" she emphatically returned.

I was silent awhile; we looked at each other. "Then what am I to tell him?"

"You needn't tell him anything. *I'll* tell him."

I measured this. "Do you mean you'll write——?" Remembering she couldn't, I caught myself up. "How do you communicate?"

"I tell the bailiff. *He* writes."

"And should you like him to write our story?"

My question had a sarcastic force that I had not fully intended, and it made her, after a moment, inconsequently break down. The tears were again in her eyes. "Ah, Miss, *you* write!"

"Well—tonight," I at last answered; and on this we separated.

XVII

I went so far, in the evening, as to make a beginning. The weather had changed back, a great wind was abroad, and beneath the lamp, in my room, with Flora at peace beside me, I sat for a long time before a blank sheet of paper and listened to the lash of the rain and the batter of the gusts. Finally I went out, taking a candle; I crossed the passage and listened a minute at Miles's door. What, under my endless obsession, I had been impelled to listen for was some betrayal of his not being at rest, and I presently caught one, but not in the form I had expected. His voice tinkled out. "I say, you there—come in." It was a gaiety in the gloom!

I went in with my light and found him, in bed, very wide awake, but very much at his ease. "Well, what are *you* up to?" he asked with a grace of sociability in which it occurred to me that Mrs. Grose, had she been present, might have looked in vain for proof that anything was "out."

I stood over him with my candle. "How did you know I was there?"

"Why, of course I heard you. Did you fancy you made no noise? You're like a troop of cavalry!" he beautifully laughed.

"Then you weren't asleep?"

"Not much! I lie awake and think."

I had put my candle, designedly, a short way off, and then, as he held out his friendly old hand to me, had sat down on the edge of his bed. "What is it," I asked, "that you think of?"

"What in the world, my dear, but *you*?"

"Ah, the pride I take in your appreciation doesn't insist on that! I had so far rather you slept."

"Well, I think also, you know, of this queer business of ours."

I marked the coolness of his little hand. "Of what queer business, Miles?"

"Why, the way you bring me up. And all the rest!"

I fairly held my breath a minute, and even from my glimmering taper there was light enough to show how he smiled up at me from his pillow. "What do you mean by all the rest?"

"Oh, you know, you know!"

I could say nothing for a minute, though I felt, as I held his hand and our eyes continued to meet, that my silence had all the air of admitting his charge and that nothing in the whole world of reality was perhaps at that moment so fabulous as our actual relation. "Certainly you shall go back to school," I said, "if it be that that troubles you. But not to the old place—we must find another, a better. How could I know it did trouble you, this question, when you never told me so, never spoke of it at all?" His clear, listening face, framed in its smooth whiteness, made him for the minute as appealing as some wistful patient in a children's hospital; and I would have given, as the resemblance came to me, all I possessed on earth really to be the nurse or the sister of charity who might have helped to cure him. Well, even as it was, I perhaps might help! "Do you know you've never said a word to me about your school—I mean the old one; never mentioned it in any way?"

He seemed to wonder; he smiled with the same loveliness. But he clearly gained time; he waited, he called for guidance. "Haven't I?" It wasn't for *me* to help him—it was for the thing I had met!

Something in his tone and the expression on his face, as I got this from him, set my heart aching with such a pang as it had never yet known; so unutterably touching was it to see his little brain puzzled and his little resources taxed to play, under the spell laid on him, a part of innocence and consistency. "No, never—from the hour you came back. You've never mentioned to me one of your masters, one of your comrades, nor the least little thing that ever happened to you at school. Never, little Miles—no, never—have you given me an inkling of anything that *may* have happened there. Therefore you can fancy how much I'm in the dark. Until you came out, that way, this morning, you had, since the first hour I saw you, scarce even made a reference to anything in your previous life. You seemed so perfectly to accept the present." It was extraordinary how my absolute conviction of his secret precocity (or whatever I might call the poison of an influence that I dared but half to phrase) made him, in spite of the faint breath of his inward trouble, appear as accessible as an older person—imposed him almost as an intellectual equal. "I thought you wanted to go on as you are."

It struck me that at this he just faintly coloured. He gave, at any rate, like a convalescent slightly fatigued, a languid shake of his head. "I don't—I don't. I want to get away."

"You're tired of Bly?"

"Oh, no, I like Bly."

"Well, then——?"

"Oh, *you* know what a boy wants!"

I felt that I didn't know so well as Miles, and I took temporary refuge. "You want to go to your uncle?"

Again, at this, with his sweet ironic face, he made a movement on the pillow. "Ah, you can't get off with that!"

I was silent a little, and it was I, now, I think, who changed colour. "My dear, I don't want to get off!"

"You can't, even if you do. You can't, you can't!"—he lay beautifully staring. "My uncle must come down, and you must completely settle things."

"If we do," I returned with some spirit, "you may be sure it will be to take you quite away."

"Well, don't you understand that that's exactly what I'm working for? You'll have to tell him—about the way you've let it all drop: you'll have to tell him a tremendous lot!"

The exultation with which he uttered this helped me somehow, for the instant, to meet him rather more. "And how much will *you*, Miles, have to tell him? There are things he'll ask you!"

He turned it over. "Very likely. But what things?"

"The things you've never told me. To make up his mind what to do with you. He can't send you back——"

"Oh, I don't want to go back!" he broke in. "I want a new field."

He said it with admirable serenity, with positive unimpeachable gaiety; and doubtless it was that very note that most evoked for me the poignancy, the unnatural childish tragedy, of his probable reappearance at the end of three months with all this bravado and still more dishonour. It overwhelmed me now that I should never be able to bear that, and it made me let myself go. I threw myself upon him and in the tenderness of my pity I embraced him. "Dear little Miles, dear little Miles——!"

My face was close to his, and he let me kiss him, simply taking it with indulgent good-humour. "Well, old lady?"

"Is there nothing—nothing at all that you want to tell me?"

He turned off a little, facing round toward the wall and holding up his hand to look at as one had seen sick children look. "I've told you—I told you this morning."

Oh, I was sorry for him! "That you just want me not to worry you?"

He looked round at me now, as if in recognition of my understanding him; then ever so gently, "To let me alone," he replied.

There was even a singular little dignity in it, something that made me release him, yet, when I had slowly risen, linger beside him. God knows I never wished to harass him, but I felt that merely, at this, to turn my back on him was to abandon or, to put it more truly, to lose him. "I've just begun a letter to your uncle," I said.

"Well, then, finish it!"

I waited a minute. "What happened before?

He gazed up at me again. "Before what?"

"Before you came back. And before you went away."

For some time he was silent, but he continued to meet my eyes. "What happened?"

It made me, the sound of the words, in which it seemed to me that I caught for the very first time a small faint quaver of consenting consciousness—it made me drop on my knees beside the bed and seize once more the chance of possessing him. "Dear little Miles, dear little Miles, if you *knew* how I want to help you! It's only that, it's nothing but that, and I'd rather die than give you a pain or do you a wrong—I'd rather die than hurt a hair of you. Dear little Miles"—oh, I brought it out now even if I *should* go too far—"I just want you to help me to save you!" But I knew in a moment after this that I had gone too far. The answer to my appeal was instantaneous, but it came in the form of an extraordinary blast and chill, a gust of frozen air and a shake of the room as great as if, in the wild wind, the casement had crashed in. The boy gave a loud, high shriek, which, lost in the rest of the shock of sound, might have seemed, indistinctly, though I was so close to him, a note either of jubilation or of terror. I jumped to my feet again and was conscious of darkness. So for a moment we remained, while I stared about me and saw that the drawn curtains were unstirred and the window tight. "Why, the candle's out!" I then cried.

"It was I who blew it, dear!" said Miles.

### XVIII

The next day, after lessons, Mrs. Grose found a moment to say to me quietly: "Have you written, Miss?"

"Yes—I've written." But I didn't add—for the hour—that my letter, sealed and directed, was still in my pocket. There would be time enough to send it before the messenger should go to the village. Meanwhile there had been, on the part of my pupils, no more brilliant, more exemplary morning. It was exactly as if they had both had at heart to gloss over any recent little friction. They performed the dizziest feats of arithmetic, soaring quite out of *my* feeble range, and perpetrated, in higher spirits than ever, geographical and historical jokes. It was conspicuous of course in Miles in particular that he appeared to wish to show how easily he could let me down. This child, to my memory, really lives in a setting of beauty and misery that no words can translate; there was a distinction all his own in every impulse he revealed; never was a small natural creature, to the uninitiated eye all frankness and freedom, a more ingenious, a more extraordinary little gentleman. I had perpetually to guard against the wonder of contemplation into which my initiated view betrayed me; to check the irrelevant gaze and discouraged sigh in which I constantly both attacked and renounced the enigma of what such a little gentleman could have done that deserved a penalty. Say that, by the dark prodigy I knew, the imagination of all evil *had* been opened up to him: all the justice within me ached for the proof that it could ever have flowered into an act.

He had never, at any rate, been such a little gentleman as when, after our early dinner on this dreadful day, he came round to me and asked if I shouldn't like him, for half an hour, to play to me. David playing to Saul could never have shown a finer sense of the occasion. It was literally a charming exhibition of tact, of magnanimity, and quite tantamount to his saying outright: "The true knights we love to read about never push an advantage too far. I know what you mean now: you mean that—to be let alone yourself and not followed up—you'll cease to worry and spy upon me, won't keep me so close to you, will let me go and come. Well, I 'come, ' you see—but I don't go! There'll be plenty of time for that. I do really delight in your society, and I only want to show you that I contended for a principle." It may be imagined whether I resisted this appeal or failed to accompany him again, hand in hand, to the schoolroom. He sat down at the old piano and played as he had never played, and if there are those who think he had better have been kicking a football I can only say that I wholly agree with them. For at the end of a time that under his influence I had quite ceased to measure I started up with a strange sense of having literally slept at my post. It was after luncheon, and by the schoolroom fire, and yet I hadn't really, in the least, slept: I had only done something much worse—I had forgotten. Where, all this time, was Flora? When I put the question to Miles he played on a minute before answering, and then could only say: "Why, my dear, how do *I* know ?" breaking moreover into a happy laugh which, immediately after, as if it were a vocal accompaniment, he prolonged into incoherent, extravagant song.

I went straight to my room, but his sister was not there; then, before going downstairs, I looked in several others. As she was nowhere about she would surely be with Mrs. Grose, whom, in the comfort of that theory, I accordingly proceeded in quest of. I found her where I had found her the evening before, but she met my quick challenge with blank, scared ignorance. She had only supposed that, after the repast, I had carried off both the children; as to which she was quite right, for it was the very first time I had allowed the little girl out of my sight without some special provision. Of course now indeed she might be with the maids, so that the immediate thing was to look for her without an air of alarm. This we promptly arranged between us; but when, ten minutes later and in pursuance of our arrangment, we met in the hall, it was only to report on either side that after guarded inquiries we had altogether failed to trace her. For a minute there, apart from observation, we exchanged mute alarms, and I could feel with what high interest my friend returned me all those I had from the first given her.

"She'll be above," she presently said—"in one of the rooms you haven't searched."

"No, she's at a distance." I had made up my mind. "She has gone out."

"Mrs. Grose stared. "Without a hat?"

I naturally also looked volumes. "Isn't that woman always without one?"

"She's with *her*?"

"She's with *her*!" I declared. "We must find them."

My hand was on my friend's arm, but she failed for the moment, confronted with such an account of the matter, to respond to my pressure. She communed, on the contrary, on the spot, with her uneasiness. "And where's Master Miles?"

"Oh, *he's* with Quint. They're in the schoolroom."

"Lord, Miss!" My view, I was myself aware—and therefore I suppose my tone—had never yet reached so calm an assurance.

"The trick's played," I went on; "they've successfully worked their plan. He found the most divine little way to keep me quiet while she went off."

"Divine?" Mrs. Grose bewilderedly echoed.

"Infernal, then!" I almost cheerfully rejoined. "He has provided for himself as well. But come!"

She had helplessly gloomed at the upper regions. "You leave him—?"

"So long with Quint? Yes—I don't mind that now."

She always ended, at these moments, by getting possession of my hand, and in this manner she could at present still stay me. But after gasping an instant at my sudden resignation, "Because of your letter?" she eagerly brought out.

I quickly, by way of answer, felt for my letter, drew it forth, held it up, and then, freeing myself, went and laid it on the great hall-table. "Luke will take it," I said as I came back. I reached the house-door and opened it; I was already on the steps.

My companion still demurred: the storm of the night and the early morning had dropped, but the afternoon was damp and grey. I came down to the drive while she stood in the doorway. "You go with nothing on?"

"What do I care when the child has nothing? I can't wait to dress," I cried, "and if you must do so, I leave you. Try meanwhile, yourself, upstairs."

"With *them?*" Oh, on this, the poor woman promptly joined me!

### XIX

We went straight to the lake, as it was called at Bly, and I dare say rightly called, though I reflect that it may in fact have been a sheet of water less remarkable than it appeared to my untravelled eyes. My acquaintance with sheets of water was small, and the pool of Bly, at all events on the few occasions of my consenting, under the protection of my pupils, to affront its surface in the old flatbottomed boat moored there for our use, had impressed me both with its extent and its agitation. The usual place of embarkation was half a mile from the house, but I had an intimate conviction that wherever Flora might be, she was not near home. She had not given me the slip for any small adventure, and, since the day of the very great one that I had shared with her by the pond, I had been aware, in our walks, of the quarter to which she most inclined. This was why I had now given to Mrs. Grose's steps so marked a direction—a direction that made her, when she perceived it, oppose a resistance that showed me she was freshly mystified. "You're going to the water, Miss?— you think she's *in*—?"

"She may be, though the depth is, I believe, nowhere very great. But what I judge most likely is that she's on the spot from which, the other day, we saw together what I told you."

"When she pretended not to see—?"

"With that astounding self-possession! I've always been sure she wanted to go back alone. And now her brother has managed it for her."

Mrs. Grose still stood where she had stopped. "You suppose they really *talk* of them?"

I could meet this with a confidence! "They say things that, if we heard them, would simply appal us."

"And if she *is* there—?"

"Yes?"

"Then Miss Jessel is?"

"Beyond a doubt. You shall see."

"Oh, thank you!" my friend cried, planted so firm that, taking it in, I went straight on without her. By the time I reached the pool, however, she was close behind me, and I knew that, whatever, to her apprehension, might befall me, the exposure of my society struck her as her least danger. She exhaled a moan of relief as we at last came in sight of the greater part of the water without a sight of the child. There was no trace of Flora on that nearer side of the bank where my observation of her had been most startling, and none on the opposite edge, where, save for a margin of some twenty yards, a thick copse came down to the water. The pond, oblong in shape, had a width so scant compared to its length that, with its ends out of view, it might have been taken for a scant river. We looked at the empty expanse, and then I felt the suggestion of my friend's eyes. I knew what she meant and I replied with a negative headshake.

"No, no; wait! She has taken the boat."

My companion stared at the vacant mooring-place and then again across the lake. "Then where is it?"

"Our not seeing it is the strongest of proofs. She has used it to go over, and then has managed to hide it."

"All alone—that child?"

"She's not alone, and at such times she's not a child: she's an old, old woman." I scanned all the visible shore while Mrs. Grose took again, into the queer element I offered her, one of her plunges of submission; then I pointed out that the boat might perfectly be in a small refuge formed by one of the recesses of the pool, an indentation masked, for the hither side, by a projection of the bank and by a clump of trees growing close to the water.

"But if the boat's there, where on earth's *she*?" my colleague anxiously asked.

"That's exactly what we must learn." And I started to walk further.

"By going all the way around?"

"Certainly, far as it is. It will take us but ten minutes, but it's far enough to have made the child prefer not to walk. She went straight over."

"Laws!" cried my friend again; the chain of my logic was ever too much for her. It dragged her at my heels even now, and when we had got half-way round— a devious, tiresome process, on ground much broken and by a path choked with overgrowth—I paused to give her breath. I sustained her with a grateful arm, assuring her that she might hugely help me; and this started us afresh, so that in the course of but few minutes more we reached a point from which we found the boat to be where I had supposed it. It had been intentionally left as much as possible out of sight and was tied to one of the stakes of a fence that came, just there, down to the brink and that had been an assistance to disembarking. I recognised, as I looked at the pair of short, thick oars, quite safely drawn up, the prodigious character of the feat for a little girl; but I had lived, by this time, too long among wonders and had panted to too many livelier measures. There was a gate in the fence, through which we passed, and that brought us, after a trifling interval, more into the open. Then, "There she is!" we both exclaimed at once.

Flora, a short way off, stood before us on the grass and smiled as if her performance was now complete. The next thing she did, however, was to stoop straight down and pluck—quite as if it were all she was there for—a big, ugly spray of withered fern. I instantly became sure she had just come out of the copse. She waited for us, not herself taking a step, and I was conscious of the rare solemnity with which we presently approached her. She smiled and smiled, and we met; but it was all done in a silence by this time flagrantly ominous. Mrs. Grose was the first to break the spell: she threw herself on her knees and, drawing the child to her breast, clasped in a long embrace the little tender, yielding body. While this dumb convulsion lasted I could only watch it—which I did the more intently when I saw Flora's face peep at me over our companion's shoulder. It was serious now—the flicker had left it; but it strengthened the pang with which I at that moment envied Mrs. Grose the simplicity of *her* relation. Still, all this while, nothing more passed between us save that Flora had let her foolish fern again drop to the ground. What she and I had virtually said to each other was that pretexts were useless now. When Mrs. Grose finally got up she kept the child's hand, so that the two were still before me; and the singular reticence of our communion was even more marked in the frank look she launched me. "I'll be hanged," it said, "if *I'll* speak!"

It was Flora who, gazing all over me in candid wonder, was the first. She was struck with our bareheaded aspect. "Why, where are your things?"

"Where yours are, my dear!" I promptly returned.

She had already got back her gaiety, and appeared to take this as an answer quite sufficient. "And where's Miles?" she went on.

There was something in the small valour of it that quite finished me: these three words from her were, in a flash like the glitter of a drawn blade, the jostle of the cup that my hand, for weeks and weeks, had held high and full to the brim and that now, even before speaking, I felt overflow in a deluge. "I'll tell you if you'll tell *me*—" I heard myself say, then heard the tremor in which it broke.

"Well, what?"

Mrs. Grose's suspense blazed at me, but it was too late now, and I brought the thing out handsomely. "Where, my pet, is Miss Jessel?"

### xx

Just as in the churchyard with Miles, the whole thing was upon us. Much as I had made of the fact that this name had never once, between us, been sounded, the quick, smitten glare with which the child's face now received it fairly likened my breach of the silence to the smash of a pane of glass. It added to the interposing cry, as if to stay the blow, that Mrs. Grose, at the same instant, uttered over my violence—the shriek of a creature scared, or rather wounded, which, in turn, within a few seconds, was completed by a gasp of my own. I seized my colleague's arm. "She's there, she's there!"

Miss Jessel stood before us on the opposite bank exactly as she had stood the other time, and I remember, strangely, as the first feeling now produced in me, my thrill of joy at having brought on a proof. She was there, and I was justified; she was there, and I was neither cruel nor mad. She was there for poor scared Mrs. Grose, but she was there most for Flora; and no moment of my monstrous time was perhaps so extraordinary as that in which I consciously threw out to her—with the sense that, pale and ravenous demon as she was, she would catch and understand it—an articulate message of gratitude. She rose erect on the spot my friend and I had lately quitted, and there was not, in all the long reach of her desire, an inch of her evil that fell short. This first vividness of vision and emotion were things of a few seconds, during which Mrs. Grose's dazed blink across to where I pointed struck me as a sovereign sign that she too at last saw, just as it carried my own eyes precipitately to the child. The revelation then of the manner in which Flora was affected startled me, in truth, far more than it would have done to find her also merely agitated, for direct dismay was of course not what I had expected. Prepared and on her guard as our pursuit had actually made her, she would repress every betrayal; and I was therefore shaken, on the spot, by my first glimpse of the particular one for which I had not allowed. To see her, without a convulsion of her small pink face, not even feign to glance in the direction of the prodigy I announced, but only, instead of that, turn at *me* an expression of hard, still gravity, an expression absolutely new and unprecedented and that appeared to read and accuse and judge me— this was a stroke that somehow converted the little girl herself into the very presence that could make me quail. I quailed even though my certitude that she thoroughly saw was never greater than at that instant, and in the immediate need to defend myself I called it passionately to witness. "She's there, you little unhappy thing— there, there, *there*, and you see her as well as you see me!" I had said shortly before to Mrs. Grose that she was not at these times a child, but an old, old woman, and that description of her could not have been anxious all day and, even while in his usual sweet little manner answer to this, she simply showed me, without a concession, an admission, of her eyes, a countenance of deeper and deeper, of indeed suddenly quite fixed reprobation. I was by this time—if I can put the whole thing at all together—more appalled at what I may properly call her manner than at anything else, though it was simultaneously with this that I became aware of having Mrs. Grose also, and very formidably, to reckon with. My elder companion, the next moment, at any rate, blotted out everything but her own flushed face and her loud, shocked protest, a burst of high disapproval. "What a dreadful turn, to be sure, Miss! Where on earth do you see anything?"

I could only grasp her more quickly yet, for even while she spoke the hideous plain presence stood undimmed and undaunted. It had already lasted a minute, and it lasted while I continued, seizing my colleague, quite thrusting her at it and presenting her to it, to insist with my pointing hand. "You don't see her exactly as *we* see?—you mean to say you don't now—*now?* She's as big as a blazing fire! Only look, dearest woman, *look*—!" She looked, even as I did, and

gave me, with her deep groan of negation, repulsion, compassion—
the mixture with her pity of her relief at her exemption—a sense,
touching to me even then, that she would have backed me up if she
could. I might well have needed that, for with this hard blow of the
proof that her eyes were hopelessly sealed I felt my own situation
horribly crumble. I felt—I saw—my livid predecessor press, from
her position, on my defeat, and I was conscious, more than all, of
what I should have from this instant to deal with in the astounding
little attitude of Flora. Into this attitude Mrs. Grose immediately and
violently entered, breaking, even while there pierced through my
sense of ruin a prodigious private triumph, into breathless reassur-
ance.

"She isn't there, little lady, and nobody's there—and you never
see nothing, my sweet! How can poor Miss Jessel—when poor Miss
Jessel's dead and buried? *We* know, don't we, love?"—and she appealed, blundering in, to the child. "It's all a mere mistake and a
worry and a joke—and we'll go home as fast as we can!"

Our companion, on this, had responded with a strange, quick
primness of propriety, and they were again, with Mrs. Grose on her
feet, united, as it were, in pained opposition to me. Flora continued
to fix me with her small mask of reprobation, and even at that
minute I prayed God to forgive me for seeming to see that, as she
stood there holding tight to our friend's dress, her incomparable
childish beauty had suddenly failed, had quite vanished. I've said it
already—she was literally, she was hideously, hard; she had turned
common and almost ugly. "I don't know what you mean. I see
nobody. I see nothing. I never *have*. I think you're cruel. I don't like
you!" Then, after this deliverance, which might have been that of a
vulgarly pert little girl in the street, she hugged Mrs. Grose more
closely and buried in her skirts the dreadful little face. In this position she produced an almost furious wail. "Take me away, take me
away—oh, take me away from *her*!"

"From *me*?" I panted.

"From you—from you!" she cried.

Even Mrs. Grose looked across at me dismayed, while I had nothing to do but communicate again with the figure that, on the opposite bank, without a movement, as rigidly still as if catching, beyond the interval, our voices, was as vividly there for my disaster as
it was not there for my service. The wretched child had spoken
exactly as if she had got from some outside source each of her
stabbing little words, and I could therefore, in the full despair of all I
had to accept, but sadly shake my head at her. "If I had ever
doubted, all my doubt would at present have gone. I've been living
with the miserable truth, and now it has only too much closed

round me. Of course I've lost you: I've interfered, and you've seen—
under *her* dictation"—with which I faced, over the pool again, our
infernal witness—"the easy and perfect way to meet it. I've done my
best, but I've lost you. Good-bye." For Mrs. Grose I had an imperative, an almost frantic "Go, go!" before which, in infinite distress,
but mutely possessed of the little girl and clearly convinced, in spite
of her blindness, that something awful had occurred and some collapse engulfed us, she retreated, by the way we had come, as fast as
she could move.

Of what first happened when I was left alone I had no subsequent
memory. I only knew that at the end of, I suppose, a quarter of an
hour, an odorous dampness and roughness, chilling and piercing
my trouble, had made me understand that I must have thrown myself, on my face, on the ground and given way to a wildness of grief.
I must have lain there long and cried and sobbed, for when I raised
my head the day was almost done. I got up and looked a moment,
through the twilight, at the grey pool and its blank, haunted edge,
and then I took, back to the house, my dreary and difficult course.
When I reached the gate in the fence the boat, to my surprise, was
gone, so that I had a fresh reflection to make on Flora's extraordinary command of the situation. She passed that night, by the most
tacit, and I should add, were not the word so grotesque a false note,
the happiest of arrangements, with Mrs. Grose. I saw neither of
them on my return, but, on the other hand as by an ambiguous
compensation, I saw a great deal of Miles. I saw—I can use no other
phrase—so much of him that it was as if it were more than it had
ever been. No evening I had passed at Bly had the portentous quality of this one; in spite of which—and in spite also of the deeper
depths of consternation that had opened beneath my feet—there
was literally, in the ebbing actual, an extraordinarily sweet sadness.
On reaching the house I had never so much as looked for the boy; I
had simply gone straight to my room to change what I was wearing
and to take in, at a glance, much material testimony to Flora's rup-
ture. Her little belongings had all been removed. When later, by the
schoolroom fire, I was served with tea by the usual maid, I indulged, on the article of my other pupil, in no inquiry whatever. He
had his freedom now—he might have it to the end! Well, he did
have it; and it consisted—in part at least—of his coming in at about
eight o'clock and sitting down with me in silence. On the removal of
the tea-things I had blown out the candles and drawn my chair
closer: I was conscious of a mortal coldness and felt as if I should
never again be warm. So, when he appeared, I was sitting in the
glow with my thoughts. He paused a moment by the door as if to
look at me; then—as if to share them—came to the other side of the

hearth and sank into a chair. We sat there in absolute stillness; yet he wanted, I felt, to be with me.

### XXI

Before a new day, in my room, had fully broken, my eyes opened to Mrs. Grose, who had come to my bedside with worse news. Flora was so markedly feverish that an illness was perhaps at hand; she had passed a night of extreme unrest, a night agitated above all by fears that had for their subject not in the least her former, but wholly her present, governess. It was not against the possible re-entrance of Miss Jessel on the scene that she protested—it was conspicuously and passionately against mine. I was promptly on my feet of course, and with an immense deal to ask; the more that my friend had discernibly now girded her loins to meet me once more. This I felt as soon as I had put to her the question of her sense of the child's sincerity as against my own. "She persists in denying to you that she saw, or has ever seen, anything?"

My visitor's trouble, truly, was great. "Ah, Miss, it isn't a matter on which I can push her! Yet it isn't either, I must say, as if I much needed to. It has made her, every inch of her, quite old."

"Oh, I see her perfectly from here. She resents, for all the world like some high little personage, the imputation on her truthfulness and, as it were, her respectability. ' Miss Jessel indeed—she! ' Ah, she's 'respectable,' the chit! The impression she gave me there yesterday was, I assure you, the very strangest of all; it was quite beyond any of the others. I *did* put my foot in it! She'll never speak to me again."

Hideous and obscure as it all was, it held Mrs. Grose briefly silent; then she granted my point with a frankness which, I made sure, had more behind it. "I think indeed, Miss, she never will. She do have a grand manner about it!"

"And that manner"—I summed it up—"is practically what's the matter with her now!"

Oh, that manner, I could see in my visitor's face, and not a little else besides! "She asks me every three minutes if I think you're coming in."

"I see—I see." I too, on my side, had so much more than worked it out. "Has she said to you since yesterday—except to repudiate her familiarity with anything so dreadful—a single other word about Miss Jessel?"

"Not one, Miss. And of course you know," my friend added, "I took it from her, by the lake, that, just then and there at least, there *was* nobody."

"Rather! And, naturally, you take it from her still."

"I don't contradict her. What else can I do?"

"Nothing in the world! You've the cleverest little person to deal with. They've made them—their two friends, I mean—still cleverer even than nature did; for it was wondrous material to play on! Flora has now her grievance, and she'll work it to the end."

"Yes, Miss; but to *what* end?"

"Why, that of dealing with me to her uncle. She'll make me out to him the lowest creature—!"

I winced at the fair show of the scene in Mrs. Grose's face; she looked for a minute as if she sharply saw them together. "And him who thinks so well of you!"

"He has an odd way—it comes over me now," I laughed, "—of proving it! But that doesn't matter. What Flora wants, of course, is to get rid of me."

My companion bravely concurred. "Never again to so much as look at you."

"So that what you've come to me now for," I asked, "is to speed me on my way?" Before she had time to reply, however, I had her in check. "I've a better idea—the result of my reflections. My going *would* seem the right thing, and on Sunday I was terribly near it. Yet that won't do. It's *you* who must go. You must take Flora."

My visitor, at this, did speculate. "But where in the world—?"

"Away from here. Away from *them*. Away, even most of all, now, from me. Straight to her uncle."

"Only to tell on you—?"

"No, not 'only'! To leave me, in addition, with my remedy."

She was still vague. "And what *is* your remedy?"

"Your loyalty, to begin with. And then Miles's."

She looked at me hard. "Do you think he—?"

"Won't if he has the chance, turn on me? Yes, I venture still to think of it. At all events, I want to try. Get off with his sister as soon as possible and leave me with him alone." I was amazed, myself, at the spirit I had still in reserve, and therefore perhaps a trifle the more disconcerted at the way in which, in spite of this fine example of it, she hesitated. "There's one thing, of course," I went on: "they mustn't, before she goes, see each other for three seconds." Then it came over me that, in spite of Flora's presumable sequestration from the instant of her return from the pool, it might already be too late. "Do you mean," I anxiously asked, "that they *have* met?"

At this she quite flushed. "Ah, Miss, I'm not such a fool as that! If I've been obliged to leave her three or four times, it has been each time with one of the maids, and at present, though she's alone, she's locked in safe. And yet—and yet!" There were too many things.

"And yet what?"

"Well, are you so sure of the little gentleman?"

"I'm not sure of anything but *you*. But I have, since last evening, a new hope. I think he wants to give me an opening. I do believe that—poor little exquisite wretch!—he wants to speak. Last evening, in the firelight and the silence, he sat with me for two hours as if it were just coming."

Mrs. Grose looked hard, through the window, at the grey, gathering day. "And did it come?"

"No, though I waited and waited, I confess it didn't, and it was without a breach of the silence or so much as a faint allusion to his sister's condition and absence that we at last kissed for good-night. All the same," I continued, "I can't, if her uncle sees her, consent to his seeing her brother without my having given the boy—and most of all because things have got so bad—a little more time."

My friend appeared on this ground more reluctant than I could quite understand. "What do you mean by more time?"

"Well, a day or two—really to bring it out. He'll then be on *my* side—of which you see the importance. If nothing comes, I shall only fail, and you will, at the worst, have helped me by doing, on your arrival in town, whatever you may have found possible." So I put it before her, but she continued for a little so inscrutably embarrassed that I came again to her aid. "Unless, indeed," I wound up, "you really want *not* to go."

I could see it, in her face, at last clear itself; she put out her hand to me as a pledge. "I'll go—I'll go. I'll go this morning."

I wanted to be very just. "If you *should* wish still to wait, I would engage she shouldn't see me."

"No, no; it's the place itself. She must leave it." She held me a moment with heavy eyes, then brought out the rest. "Your idea's the right one. I myself, Miss—"

"Well?"

"I can't stay."

The look she gave me with it made me jump at possibilities. "You mean that, since yesterday, you *have* seen—?"

She shook her head with dignity. "I've *heard* —!"

"Heard?"

"From that child—horrors! There!" she sighed with tragic relief. "On my honour, Miss, she says things —!" But at this evocation she broke down; she dropped, with a sudden sob, upon my sofa and, as I had seen her do before, gave way to all the grief of it.

It was quite in another manner that I, for my part, let myself go. "Oh, thank God!"

She sprang up again at this, drying her eyes with a groan.

" 'Thank God'?"

"It so justifies me!"

"It does that, Miss!"

I couldn't have desired more emphasis, but I just hesitated. "She's so horrible?"

I saw my colleague scarce knew how to put it. "Really shocking."

"And about me?"

"About you, Miss—since you must have it. It's beyond every-thing, for a young lady; and I can't think wherever she must have picked up—"

"The appalling language she applied to me? I can, then!' I broke in with a laugh that was doubtless significant enough.

It only, in truth, left my friend still more grave. "Well, perhaps I ought to also—since I've heard some of it before! Yet I can't bear it," the poor woman went on while, with the same movement, she glanced, on my dressing-table, at the face of my watch. "But I must go back."

I kept her, however. "Ah, if you can't bear it—!"

"How can I stop with her, you mean? Why, just *for* that: to get her away. Far from this," she pursued, "far from *them* —"

"She may be different? she may be free?" I seized her almost with joy. "Then, in spite of yesterday, you *believe* —"

"In such doings?" Her simple description of them required, in the light of her expression, to be carried no further, and she gave me the whole thing as she had never done. "I believe."

Yes, it was a joy, and we were still shoulder to shoulder: if I might continue sure of that I should care but little what else happened. My support in the presence of disaster would be the same as it had been in my early need of confidence, and if my friend would answer for my honesty, I would answer for all the rest. On the point of taking leave of her, none the less, I was to some extent embarrassed. "There's one thing of course—it occurs to me—to remember. My letter, giving the alarm, will have reached town before you."

I now perceived still more how she had been beating about the bush and how weary at last it had made her. "Your letter won't have got there. Your letter never went."

"What then became of it?"

"Goodness knows! Master Miles—"

"Do you mean *he* took it?" I gasped.

She hung fire, but she overcame her reluctance. "I mean that I saw yesterday, when I came back with Miss Flora, that it wasn't where you had put it. Later in the evening I had the chance to question Luke, and he declared that he had neither noticed nor touched it." We could only exchange, on this, one of our deeper mutual soundings, and it was Mrs. Grose who first brought up the plumb with an almost elate "You see!"

"Yes, I see that if Miles took it instead he probably will have read it and destroyed it."

"And don't you see anything else?"

I faced her a moment with a sad smile. "It strikes me that by this time your eyes are open even wider than mine."

They proved to be so indeed, but she could still blush, almost, to show it. "I make out now what he must have done at school." And she gave, in her simple sharpness, an almost droll disillusioned nod. "He stole!"

I turned it over—I tried to be more judicial. "Well—perhaps."

She looked as if she found me unexpectedly calm. "He stole *letters!*"

She couldn't know my reasons for a calmness after all pretty shallow; so I showed them off as I might. "I hope then it was to more purpose than in this case! The note, at any rate, that I put on the table yesterday," I pursued, "will have given him so scant an advantage—for it contained only the bare demand for an interview— that he is already much ashamed of having gone so far for so little, and that what he had on his mind last evening was precisely the need of confession." I seemed to myself, for the instant, to have mastered it, to see it all. "Leave us, leave us"—I was already, at the door, hurrying her off. "I'll get it out of him. He'll meet me—he'll confess. If he confesses, he's saved. And if he's saved—"

"Then *you* are?" The dear woman kissed me on this, and I took her farewell. "I'll save you without him!" she cried as she went.

### XXII

Yet it was when she had got off—and I missed her on the spot—that the great pinch really came. If I had counted on what it would give me to find myself alone with Miles, I speedily perceived, at least, that it would give me a measure. No hour of my stay in fact was so assailed with apprehensions as that of my coming down to learn that the carriage containing Mrs. Grose and my younger pupil had already rolled out of the gates. Now I *was*, I said to myself, face to face with the elements, and for much of the rest of the day, while I fought my weakness I could consider that I had been supremely rash. It was a tighter place still than I had yet turned round in; all the more that, for the first time, I could see in the aspect of others a confused reflection of the crisis. What had happened naturally caused them all to stare; there was too little of the explained, throw out whatever we might, in the suddenness of my colleague's act. The maids and the men looked blank; the effect of which on my nerves was an aggravation until I saw the necessity of making it a positive aid. It was precisely, in short, by just clutching the helm that I avoided total wreck; and I dare say that, to bear up at all, I became, that morning, very grand and very dry. I welcomed the consciousness that I was charged with much to do, and I caused it to be known as well that, left thus to myself, I was quite remarkably firm. I wandered with that manner, for the next hour or two, all over the place and looked, I have no doubt, as if I were ready for any onset. So, for the benefit of whom it might concern, I paraded with a sick heart.

The person it appeared least to concern proved to be, till dinner, little Miles himself. My perambulations had given me, meanwhile, no glimpse of him, but they had tended to make more public the change taking place in our relation as a consequence of his having at the piano, the day before, kept me, in Flora's interest, so beguiled and befooled. The stamp of publicity had of course been fully given by her confinement and departure, and the change itself was now ushered in by our non-observance of the regular custom of the schoolroom. He had already disappeared when, on my way down, I pushed open his door, and I learned below that he had breakfasted—in the presence of a couple of the maids—with Mrs. Grose and his sister. He had then gone out, as he said, for a stroll; than which nothing, I reflected, could better have expressed his frank view of the abrupt transformation of my office. What he would now permit this office to consist of was yet to be settled: there was a queer relief, at all events—I mean for myself in especial—in the renouncement of one pretension. If so much had sprung to the surface, I scarce put it too strongly in saying that what had perhaps sprung highest was the absurdity of our prolonging the fiction that I had anything more to teach him. It sufficiently stuck out that, by tacit little tricks in which even more than myself he carried out the care for my dignity, I had had to appeal to him to let me off straining to meet him on the ground of his true capacity. He had at any rate his freedom now; I was never to touch it again; as I had amply shown, moreover, when, on his joining me in the schoolroom the previous night, I had uttered, on the subject of the interval just concluded, neither challenge nor hint. I had too much, from this moment, my other ideas. Yet when he at last arrived the difficulty of applying them, the accumulations of my problem, were brought straight home to me by the beautiful little presence on which what had occurred had as yet, for the eye, dropped neither stain nor shadow.

To mark, for the house, the high state I cultivated I decreed that my meals with the boy should be served, as we called it, downstairs; so that I had been awaiting him in the ponderous pomp of the room outside of the window of which I had had from Mrs. Grose, that first scared Sunday, my flash of something it would scarce have done to call light. Here at present I felt afresh—for I had felt it again and again—how my equilibrium depended on the success of my rigid will, the will to shut my eyes as tight as possible to the truth that what I had to deal with was, revoltingly, against nature. I could only get on at all by taking "nature" into my confidence and my account, by treating my monstrous ordeal as a push in a direction unusual, of course, and unpleasant, but demanding, after all, for a fair front, only another turn of the screw of ordinary human virtue. No attempt, none the less, could well require more tact than just this attempt to supply, one's self, *all* the nature. How could I put even a little of that article into a suppression of reference to what had occurred? How, on the other hand, could I make a reference without a new plunge into the hideous obscure? Well, a sort of answer, after a time, had come to me, and it was so far confirmed as that I was met, incontestably, by the quickened vision of what was rare in my little companion. It was indeed as if he had found even now—as he had so often found at lessons—still some other delicate way to ease me off. Wasn't there light in the fact which, as we shared our solitude, broke out with a specious glitter it had never yet quite worn?—the fact that (opportunity aiding, precious opportunity which had now come) it would be preposterous, with a child so endowed, to forgo the help one might wrest from absolute intelligence? What had his intelligence been given him for but to save him? Mightn't one, to reach his mind, risk the stretch of an angular arm over his character? It was as if, when we were face to face in the dining-room, he had literally shown me the way. The roast mutton was on the table, and I had dispensed with attendance. Miles, before he sat down, stood a moment with his hands in his pockets and looked at the joint, on which he seemed on the point of passing some humorous judgment. But what he presently produced was: "I say, my dear, is she really very awfully ill?"

"Little Flora? Not so bad but that she'll presently be better. London will set her up. Bly had ceased to agree with her. Come here and take your mutton."

He alertly obeyed me, carried the plate carefully to his seat, and, when he was established, went on. "Did Bly disagree with her so terribly suddenly?"

"Not so suddenly as you might think. One had seen it coming on."

"Then why didn't you get her off before?"

"Before what?"

"Before she became too ill to travel."

I found myself prompt. "She's *not* too ill to travel: she only might have become so if she had stayed. This was just the moment to seize. The journey will dissipate the influence"—oh, I was grand!— "and carry it off."

"I see, I see"—Miles, for that matter, was grand too. He settled to his repast with the charming little "table manner" that, from the day of his arrival, had relieved me of all grossness of admonition. Whatever he had been driven from school for, it was not for ugly feeding. He was irreproachable, as always, to-day; but he was unmistakably more conscious. He was discernibly trying to take for granted more things than he found, without assistance, quite easy; and he dropped into peaceful silence while he felt his situation. Our meal was of the briefest—mine a vain pretence, and I had the things immediately removed. While this was done Miles stood again with his hands in his little pockets and his back to me—stood and looked out of the wide window through which, that other day, I had seen what pulled me up. We continued silent while the maid was with us—as silent, it whimsically occurred to me, as some young couple who, on their wedding-journey, at the inn, feel shy in the presence of the waiter. He turned round only when the waiter had left us. "Well—so we're alone!"

### XXIII

"Oh, more or less." I fancy my smile was pale. "Not absolutely. We shouldn't like that!" I went on.

"No—I suppose we shouldn't. Of course we have the others."

"We have the others—we have indeed the others," I concurred.

"Yet even though we have them," he returned, still with his hands in his pockets and planted there in front of me, "they don't much count, do they?"

I made the best of it, but I felt wan. "It depends on what you call 'much'!"

"Yes"—with all accommodation—"everything depends!" On this, however, he faced to the window again and presently reached it with his vague, restless, cogitating step. He remained there awhile, with his forehead against the glass, in contemplation of the stupid shrubs I knew and the dull things of November. I had always my hypocrisy of "work," behind which, now, I gained the sofa. Steadying myself with it there as I had repeatedly done at those moments of torment that I have described as the moments of my knowing the

children to be given to something from which I was barred, I sufficiently obeyed my habit of being prepared for the worst. But an
extraordinary impression dropped on me as I extracted a meaning
from the boy's embarrassed back—none other than the impression
that I was not barred now. This inference grew in a few minutes to
sharp intensity and seemed bound up with the direct perception
that it was positively *he* who was. The frames and squares of the
great window were a kind of image, for him, of a kind of failure. I
felt that I saw him, at any rate, shut in or shut out. He was admirable, but not comfortable: I took it in with a throb of hope. Wasn't
he looking, through the haunted pane, for something he couldn't
see?—and wasn't it the first time in the whole business that he had
known such a lapse? The first, the very first: I found it a splendid
portent. It made him anxious, though he watched himself; he had
been anxious all day and, even whle in his usual sweet little manner
he sat at table, had needed all his small strange genius to give it a
gloss. When he at last turned round to meet me, it was almost as if
this genius had succumbed. 'Well, I think I'm glad Bly agrees with
*me* !"

"You would certainly seem to have seen, these twenty-four hours,
a good deal more of it than for some time before. I hope," I went on
bravely, "that you've been enjoying yourself."

"Oh, yes, I've been ever so far; all round about—miles and miles
away. I've never been so free."

He had really a manner of his own, and I could only try to keep
up with him. "Well, do you like it?"

He stood there smiling; then at last he put into two words—"Do
*you?*"—more discrimination than I had ever heard two words contain. Before I had time to deal with that, however, he continued as if
with the sense that this was an impertinence to be softened. "Nothing could be more charming than the way you take it, for of course
if we're alone together now it's you that are alone most. But I hope,"
he threw in, "you don't particularly mind!"

"Having to do with you?"I asked. "My dear child, how can I help
minding? Though I've renounced all claim to your company,—
you're so beyond me, —I at least greatly enjoy it. What else should I
stay on for?"

He looked at me more directly, and the expression of his face,
graver now, struck me as the most beautiful I had ever found in it.
"You stay on just for *that?*"

"Certainly. I stay on as your friend and from the tremendous
interest I take in you till something can be done for you that may be
more worth your while. That needn't surprise you." My voice trembled so that I felt it impossible to suppress the shake. "Don't you

remember how I told you, when I came and sat on your bed the night of the storm, that there was nothing in the world I wouldn't do for you?"

"Yes, yes!" He, on his side, more and more visibly nervous, had a tone to master; but he was so much more successful than I that, laughing out through his gravity, he could pretend we were pleasantly jesting. "Only that, I think, was to get me to do something for *you!*"

"It was partly to get you to do something," I conceded. "But, you know, you didn't do it."

"Oh, yes," he said with the brightest superficial eagerness, "you wanted me to tell you something."

"That's it. Out, straight out. What you have on your mind, you know."

"Ah, then, is *that* what you've stayed over for?"

He spoke with a gaiety through which I could still catch the finest little quiver of resentful passion; but I can't begin to express the effect upon me of an implication of surrender even so faint. It was as if what I had yearned for had come at last only to astonish me. "Well, yes—I may as well make a clean breast of it. It was precisely for that."

He waited so long that I supposed it for the purpose of repudiating the assumption on which my action had been founded; but what he finally said was: "Do you mean now—here?"

"There couldn't be a better place or time." He looked round him uneasily, and I had the rare—oh, the queer!—impression of the very first symptom I had seen in him of the approach of immediate fear. It was as if he were suddenly afraid of me—which struck me indeed as perhaps the best thing to make him. Yet in the very pang of the effort I felt it vain to try sternness, and I heard myself the next instant so gentle as to be almost grotesque. "You want so to go out again?"

"Awfully!" He smiled at me heroically, and the touching little bravery of it was enhanced by his actually flushing with pain. He had picked up his hat, which he had brought in, and stood twirling it in a way that gave me, even as I was just nearly reaching port, a perverse horror of what I was doing. To do it in *any* way was an act of violence, for what did it consist of but the obtrusion of the idea of grossness and guilt on a small helpless creature who had been for me a revelation of the possibilities of beautiful intercourse? Wasn't it base to create for a being so exquisite a mere alien awkwardness? I suppose I now read into our situation a clearness it couldn't have had at the time, for I seem to see our poor eyes already lighted with some spark of a prevision of the anguish that was to come. So we circled about, with terrors and scruples, like fighters not daring to close. But it was for each other we feared! That kept us a little longer suspended and unbruised. "I'll tell you everything." Miles said—"I mean I'll tell you anything you like. You'll stay on with me, and we shall both be all right and I *will* tell you—I *will*. But not now."

"Why not now?"

My insistence turned him from me and kept him once more at his window in a silence during which, between us, you might have heard a pin drop. Then he was before me again with the air of a person for whom, outside, someone who had frankly to be reckoned with was waiting. "I have to see Luke."

I had not yet reduced him to quite so vulgar a lie, and I felt proportionately ashamed. But, horrible as it was, his lies made up my truth. I achieved throughtfully a few loops of my knitting. "Well, then, go to Luke, and I'll wait for what you promise. Only, in return for that, satisfy, before you leave me, one very much smaller request."

He looked as if he felt he had succeeded enough to be able still a little to bargain. "Very much smaller—?"

"Yes, a mere fraction of the whole. Tell me"—oh, my work preoccupied me, and I was offhand!—"if, yesterday afternoon, from the table in the hall, you took, you know, my letter."

XXIV

My sense of how he received this suffered for a minute from something that I can describe only as a fierce split of my attention—a stroke that at first, as I sprang straight up, reduced me to the mere blind movement of getting hold of him, drawing him close, and, while I just fell for support against the nearest piece of furniture, instinctively keeping him with his back to the window. The appearance was full upon us that I had already had to deal with here: Peter Quint had come into view like a sentinel before a prison. The next thing I saw was that, from outside, he had reached the window, and then I knew that, close to the glass and glaring in through it, he offered once more to the room his white face of damnation. It represents but grossly what took place within me at the sight to say that on the second my decision was made; yet I believed that no woman so overwhelmed ever in so short a time recovered her grasp of the *act*. It came to me in the very horror of the immediate presence that the act would be, seeing and facing what I saw and faced, to keep the boy himself unaware. The inspiration—I can call it by no other name—was that I felt how voluntarily, how transcendently, I *might*. It was like fighting with a demon for a human soul, and when I had fairly so appraised it I saw how the human soul—held out, in the tremor of my hands, at arm's length—had perfect dew of sweat on a lovely childish forehead. The face that was close to mine was as white as the face against the glass, and out of it presently came a sound, not low nor weak, but as if from much further away, that I drank like a waft of fragrance.

"Yes—I took it."

At this, with a moan of joy, I enfolded, I drew him close; and while I held him to my breast, where I could feel in the sudden fever of his little body the tremendous pulse of his little heart, I kept my eyes on the thing at the window and saw it move and shift its posture. I have likened it to a sentinel, but its slow wheel, for a moment, was rather the prowl of a baffled beast. My present quickened courage, however, was such that, not too much to let it through, I had to shade, as it were, my flame. Meanwhile the glare of the face was again at the window, the scoundrel fixed as if to watch and wait. It was the very confidence that I might now defy him, as well as the positive certitude, by this time, of the child's unconsciousness, that made me go on. "What did you take it for?"

"To see what you said about me."

"You opened the letter?"

"I opened it."

My eyes were now, as I held him off a little again, on Miles's own face, in which the collapse of mockery showed me how complete was the ravage of uneasiness. What was prodigious was that at last, by my success, his sense was sealed and his communication stopped: he knew that he was in presence, but knew not of what, and knew still less that I also was and that I did know. And what did this strain of trouble matter when my eyes went back to the window only to see that the air was clear again and—by my personal triumph—the influence quenched? There was nothing there. I felt that the cause was mine and that I should surely get all. "And you found nothing!"—I let my elation out.

He gave the most mournful, thoughtful little headshake. "Nothing."

"Nothing, nothing!" I almost shouted in my joy.

"Nothing, nothing," he sadly repeated.

I kissed his forehead; it was drenched. "So what have you done with it?"

"I've burnt it."

"Burnt it?" It was now or never. "Is that what you did at school?"

Oh, what this brought up! "At school?"

"Did you take letters!—or other things?"

"Other things?" He appeared now to be thinking of something far off and that reached him only through the pressure of his anxiety. Yet it did reach him. "Did I *steal?*"

I felt myself redden to the roots of my hair as well as wonder if it were more strange to put to a gentleman such a question or to see him take it with allowances that gave the very distance of his fall in the world. "Was it for that you mightn't go back?"

The only thing he felt was rather a dreary little surprise. "Did you know I mightn't go back?"

"I know everything."

He gave me at this the longest and strangest look. "Everything?"

"Everything. Therefore *did* you—?" But I couldn't say it again. Miles, could, very simply. "No. I didn't steal."

My face must have shown him I believed him utterly; yet my hands—but it was for pure tenderness—shook him as if to ask him why, if it was all for nothing, he had condemned me to months of torment. "What then did you do?"

He looked in vague pain all round the top of the room and drew his breath, two or three times over, as if with difficulty. He might have been standing at the bottom of the sea and raising his eyes to some faint green twilight. "Well—I said things."

"Only that?"

"They thought it was enough!"

"To turn you out for?"

Never, truly, had a person "turned out" shown so little to explain it as this little person! He appeared to weigh my question, but in a manner quite detached and almost helpless. "Well, I suppose I oughtn't."

"But to whom did you say them?"

He evidently tried to remember, but it dropped—he had lost it. "I don't know!"

He almost smiled at me in the desolation of his surrender, which was indeed practically, by this time, so complete that I ought to have left it there. But I was infatuated—I was blind with victory, though even then the very effect that was to have brought him so much nearer was already that of added separation. "Was it to everyone?" I asked.

"No; it was only to—" But he gave a sick little headshake. "I don't remember their names."

"Were they then so many?"

"No—only a few. Those I liked."

Those he liked? I seemed to float not into clearness, but into a darker obscure, and within a minute there had come to me out of my very pity the appalling alarm of his being perhaps innocent. It

was for the instant confounding and bottomless, for if he *were* innocent, what then on earth was *I?* Paralysed, while it lasted, by the
mere brush of the question, I let him go a little, so that, with a
deep-drawn sigh, he turned away from me again; which, as he
faced toward the clear window, I suffered, feeling that I had nothing
now there to keep him from. "And did they repeat what you said?"
I went on after a moment.

He was soon at some distance from me, still breathing hard and
again with the air, though now without anger for it, of being confined against his will. Once more, as he had done before, he looked
up at the dim day as if, of what had hitherto sustained him, nothing
was left but an unspeakable anxiety. "Oh, yes," he nevertheless
replied—"they must have repeated them. To those *they* liked," he
added.

There was, somehow, less of it than I had expected; but I turned it
over. "And these things came round—?"

"To the masters? Oh, yes!" he answered very simply. "But I
didn't know they'd tell."

"The masters? They didn't—they've never told. That's why I ask
you."

He turned to me again his little beautiful fevered face. "Yes, it
was too bad."

"Too bad?"

"What I suppose I sometimes said. To write home."

I can't name the exquisite pathos of the contradiction given to
such a speech by such a speaker; I only know that the next instant I
heard myself throw off with homely force: "Stuff and nonsense!"
But the next after that I must have sounded stern enough. "What
*were* these things?"

My sternness was all for his judge, his executioner; yet it made
him avert himself again, and that movement made *me*, with a single
bound and an irrepressible cry, spring straight upon him. For there
again, against the glass, as if to blight his confession and stay his
answer was the hideous author of our woe—the white face of damnation. I felt a sick swim at the drop of my victory and all the return
of my battle, so that the wildness of my veritable leap only served as
a great betrayal. I saw him, from the midst of my act, meet it with a
divination, and on the perception that even now he only guessed,
and that the window was still to his own eyes free, I let the impulse
flame up to convert the climax of his dismay into the very proof of
his liberation. "No more, no more, no more!" I shrieked, as I tried
to press him against me, to my visitant.

"Is she *here?*" Miles panted as he caught with his sealed eyes the direction of my words. Then as his strange "she" staggered me and, with a gasp, I echoed it, "Miss Jessel, Miss Jessel!" he with a sudden fury gave me back.

I seized, stupefied, his supposition—some sequel to what we had done to Flora, but this made me only want to show him that it was better still than that. "It's not Miss Jessel! But it's at the window—straight before us. It's *there*—the coward horror, there for the last time!"

At this, after a second in which his head made the movement of a baffled dog's on a scent and then gave a frantic shake for air and light, he was at me in a white rage, bewildered, glaring vainly over the place and missing wholly, though it now, to my sense, filled the room like the taste of poison, the wide, overwhelming presence. "It's *he*?"

I was so determined to have all my proof that I flashed into ice to challenge him. "Whom do you mean by 'he'?"

"Peter Quint—you devil!" His face gave again, round the room, its convulsed supplication. "*Where?*"

They are in my ears still, his supreme surrender of the name and his tribute to my devotion. "What does he matter now, my own?—what will he *ever* matter? *I* have you," I launched at the beast, "but he has lost you for ever!" Then, for the demonstration of my work, "There, *there!*" I said to Miles.

But he had already jerked straight round, stared, glared again, and seen but the quiet day. With the stroke of the loss I was so proud of he uttered the cry of a creature hurled over an abyss, and the grasp with which I recovered him might have been that of catching him in his fall. I caught him, yes, I held him—it may be imagined with what a passion; but at the end of a minute I began to feel what it truly was that I held. We were alone with the quiet day, and his little heart, dispossessed, had stopped.

# JOSEPH CONRAD
## 1857–1924

Jozef Teodor Konrad Nalecz Korzeniowski was born in Poland to a respected family of landed gentry, although Conrad's father was not typical of his class. A man of letters, he translated Shakespeare into Polish; a patriot, he worked for Polish independence and was condemned to exile in Russia. Young Joseph and his mother accompanied the head of their household into exile in 1862. Three years later the boy's mother died, and he was sent to live with an uncle in Poland. Growing up inland, he formed the unaccountable desire to make his career on the sea. With misgivings his uncle allowed him to enter the French marine service at the age of eighteen. After a disastrous attempt to run guns from Marseilles to Spain, and an even more disastrous love affair that ended in a suicide attempt, he decided he had exhausted the possibilities of France. He also wished to avoid the compulsory military service that would have been his lot in Poland or as a French citizen. Thus it was that at the age of twenty he left the Continent and sailed as an ordinary seaman on his first English ship, knowing only a few words of the language. Two years later he had his third mate papers in the British Merchant Service, and six years after that, in 1886, he obtained his master's papers and his British citizenship. In two more years he had his first command at sea. In 1890 he made a voyage up the Congo which provided the material for *Heart of Darkness*. He then began writing seriously in the English language. In 1895 his first novel was published and he left the sea to pursue his career as a writer, under the simplified version of his name which he had adopted in the course of his nautical life. His course was set for fame. Among his finest novels are *Lord Jim* (1900), *Nostromo* (1904), and *The Secret Agent* (1907).

# Heart of Darkness

The *Nellie*, a cruising yawl, swung to her anchor without a flutter of the sails, and was at rest. The flood had made, the wind was nearly calm, and being bound down the river, the only thing for it was to come to and wait for the turn of the tide.

The sea-reach of the Thames stretched before us like the beginning of an interminable waterway. In the offing the sea and the sky were welded together without a joint, and in the luminous space the tanned sails of the barges drifting up with the tide seemed to stand still in red clusters of canvas sharply peaked, with gleams of varnished spirits. A haze rested on the low shores that ran out to sea in vanishing flatness. The air was dark above Gravesend, and farther back still seemed condensed into a mournful gloom, brooding motionless over the biggest, and the greatest, town on earth.

The Director of Companies was our captain and our host. We four affectionately watched his back as he stood in the bows looking seaward. On the whole river there was nothing that looked half so nautical. He resembled a pilot, which to a seaman is trustworthiness personified. It was difficult to realize his work was not out there in the luminous estuary, but behind him, within the brooding gloom.

Between us there was, as I have already said somewhere, the bond of the sea. Besides holding our hearts together through long periods of separation, it had the effect of making us tolerant of each

other's yarns—and even convictions. The lawyer—the best of old
fellows—had, because of his many years and many virtues, the only
cushion on deck, and was lying on the only rug. The accountant had
brought out already a box of dominoes, and was toying architectur-
ally with the bones. Marlow sat cross-legged right aft, leaning
against the mizzenmast. He had sunken cheeks, a yellow complexion, a straight back, an ascetic aspect, and, with his arms dropped,
the palms of hands outwards, resembled an idol. The director, satisfied the anchor had good hold, made his way aft and sat down
amongst us. We exchanged a few words lazily. Afterwards there was
silence on board the yacht. For some reason or other we did not
begin that game of dominoes. We felt meditative, and fit for nothing
but placid staring. The day was ending in a serenity of still and
exquisite brilliance. The water shone pacifically; the sky, without a
speck, was a benign immensity of unstained light; the very mist on
the Essex marshes was like a gauzy and radiant fabric, hung from
the wooded rises inland, and draping the low shores in diaphanous
folds. Only the gloom to the west, brooding over the upper reaches,
became more somber every minute, as if angered by the approach of
the sun.

And at last, in its curved and imperceptible fall, the sun sank low,
and from glowing white changed to a dull red without rays and
without heat, as if about to go out suddenly, stricken to death by
the touch of that gloom brooding over a crowd of men.

Forthwith a change came over the waters, and the serenity became less brilliant but more profound. The old river in its broad
reach rested unruffled at the decline of day, after ages of good service done to the race that peopled its banks, spread out in the
tranquil dignity of a waterway leading to the uttermost ends of the
earth. We looked at the venerable stream not in the vivid flush of a
short day that comes and departs forever, but in the august light of
abiding memories. And indeed nothing is easier for a man who has,
as the phrase goes, "followed the sea" with reverence and affection,
than to evoke the great spirit of the past upon the lower reaches of
the Thames. The tidal current runs to and fro in its unceasing service, crowded with memories of men and ships it had borne to the
rest of home or to the battles of the sea. It had known and served all
the men of whom the nation is proud, from Sir Francis Drake to Sir
John Franklin, knights all, titled and untitled—the great knights-
errant of the sea. It had borne all the ships whose names are like
jewels flashing in the night of time, from the *Golden Hind* returning
with her round flanks full of treasure, to be visited by the Queen's
Highness and thus pass out of the gigantic tale, to the *Erebus* and
*Terror*, bound on other conquests—and that never returned. It had

known the ships and the men. They had sailed from Deptford, from Greenwich, from Erith—the adventurers and the settlers; kings' ships and ships of men on 'Change; captains, admirals, the dark "interlopers" of the Eastern trade, and the commissioned "generals" of East India fleets. Hunters for gold or pursuers of fame, they all had gone out on that stream, bearing the sword, and often the torch, messengers of the might within the land, bearers of a spark from the sacred fire. What greatness had not floated on the ebb of that river into the mystery of an unknown earth! . . . The dreams of men, the seed of commonwealths, the germs of empires.

The sun set; the dusk fell on the stream, and lights began to appear along the shore. The Chapman lighthouse, a three-legged thing erect on a mud-flat, shone strongly. Lights of ships moved in the fairway—a great stir of lights going up and going down. And farther west on the upper reaches the place of the monstrous town was still marked ominously on the sky, a brooding gloom in sunshine, a lurid glare under the stars.

"And this also," said Marlow suddenly, "has been one of the dark places of the earth."

He was the only man of us who still "followed the sea." The worse that could be said of him was that he did not represent his class. He was a seaman, but he was a wanderer, too, while most seamen lead, if one may so express it, a sedentary life. Their minds are of the stay-at-home order, and their home is always with them—the ship; and so is their country—the sea. One ship is very much like another, and the sea is always the same. In the immutability of their surroundings the foreign shores, the foreign faces, the changing immensity of life, glide past, veiled not by a sense of mystery but by a slightly disdainful ignorance; for there is nothing mysterious to a seaman unless it be the sea itself, which is the mistress of his existence and as inscrutable as destiny. For the rest, after his hours of work, a casual stroll or a casual spree on shore suffices to unfold for him the secret of a whole continent, and generally he finds the secret not worth knowing. The yarns of seamen have a direct simplicity, the whole meaning of which lies within the shell of a cracked nut. But Marlow was not typical (if his propensity to spin yarns be excepted), and to him the meaning of an episode was not inside like a kernel but outside, enveloping the tale which brought it out only as a glow brings out a haze, in the likeness of one of these misty halos that sometimes are made visible by the spectral illumination of moonshine.

His remark did not seem at all surprising. It was just like Marlow. It was accepted in silence. No one took the trouble to grunt even; and presently he said, very slow:

"I was thinking of very old times, when the Romans first came here, nineteen hundred years ago—the other day. . . . Light came out of this river since—you say knights? Yes; but it is like a running blaze on a plain, like a flash of lightning in the clouds. We live in the flicker—may it last as long as the old earth keeps rolling! But darkness was here yesterday. Imagine the feelings of a commander of a fine—what d'ye call 'em?—trireme in the Mediterranean, ordered suddenly to the north; run overland across the Gauls in a hurry; put in charge of one of these craft the legionaries—a wonderful lot of handy men they must have been, too—used to build, apparently by the hundred, in a month or two, if we may believe what we read. Imagine him here—the very end of the world, a sea the color of lead, a sky the color of smoke, a kind of ship about as rigid as a concertina—and going up this river with stores, or orders, or what you like. Sandbanks, marshes, forests, savages—precious little to eat fit for a civilized man, nothing but Thames water to drink. No Falernian wine here, no going ashore. Here and there a military camp lost in a wilderness, like a needle in a bundle of hay—cold, fog, tempests, disease, exile, and death—death skulking in the air, in the water, in the bush. They must have been dying like flies here. Oh, yes—he did it. Did it very well, too, no doubt, and without thinking much about it either, except afterwards to brag of what he had gone through in his time, perhaps. They were men enough to face the darkness. And perhaps he was cheered by keeping his eye on a chance of promotion to the fleet at Ravenna by and by, if he had good friends in Rome and survived the awful climate. Or think of a decent young citizen in a toga—perhaps too much dice, you know—coming out here in the train of some prefect, or tax-gatherer, or trader even, to mend his fortunes. Land in a swamp, march through the woods, and in some inland post feel the savagery, the utter savagery, had closed round him—all that mysterious life of the wilderness that stirs in the forest, in the jungles, in the hearts of wild men. There's no initiation either into such mysteries. He has to live in the midst of the incomprehensible, which is also detestable. And it has a fascination, too, that goes to work upon him. The fascination of the abomination—you know, imagine the growing regrets, the longing to escape, the powerless disgust, the surrender, the hate."

He paused.

"Mind," he began again, lifting one arm from the elbow, the palm of the hand outwards, so that, with his legs folded before him, he had the pose of a Buddha preaching in European clothes and without a lotus flower—"Mind, none of us would feel exactly like this. What saves us is efficiency—the devotion of efficiency. But these chaps were not much account, really. They were no colonists; their administration was merely a squeeze, and nothing more, I suspect. They were conquerors, and for that you want only brute force—nothing to boast of, when you have it, since your strength is just an accident arising from the weakness of others. They grabbed what they could get for the sake of what was to be got. It was just robbery with violence, aggravated murder on a great scale, and men going at it blind—as is very proper for those who tackle a darkness. The conquest of the earth, which mostly means the taking it away from those who have a different complexion or slightly flatter noses than ourselves, is not a pretty thing when you look into it too much. What redeems it is the idea only. An idea at the back of it; not a sentimental pretence but an idea; and an unselfish belief in the idea—something you can set up, and bow down before, and offer a sacrifice to. . . ."

He broke off. Flames glided in the river, small green flames, red flames, white flames, pursuing, overtaking, joining, crossing each other—then separating slowly or hastily. The traffic of the great city went on in the deepening night upon the sleepless river. We looked on, waiting patiently—there was nothing else to do till the end of the flood; but it was only after a long silence, when he said, in a hesitating voice, "I suppose you fellows remember I did once turn freshwater sailor for a bit," that we knew we were fated, before the ebb began to run, to hear about one of Marlow's inconclusive experiences.

"I don't want to bother you much with what happened to me personally," he began, showing in this remark the weakness of many tellers of tales who seem so often unaware of what their audience would best like to hear; "yet to understand the effect of it on me you ought to know how I got out there, what I saw, how I went up that river to the place where I first met the poor chap. It was the farthest point of navigation and the culminating point of my experience. It seemed somehow to throw a kind of light on everything about me—and into my thoughts. It was somber enough, too—and pitiful—not extraordinary in any way—not very clear either. No, not very clear. And yet it seemed to throw a kind of light.

"I had then, as you remember, just returned to London after a lot of Indian Ocean, Pacific, China Seas—a regular dose of the East—six years or so, and I was loafing about, hindering you fellows in your work and invading your homes, just as though I had got a heavenly mission to civilize you. It was very fine for a time, but after a bit I did get tired of resting. Then I began to look for a ship—I should think the hardest work on earth. But the ships wouldn't even look at me. And I got tired of that game, too.

"Now when I was a little chap I had a passion for maps. I would look for hours at South America, or Africa, or Australia, and lose myself in all the glories of exploration. At that time there were many blank spaces on the earth, and when I saw one that looked particularly inviting on a map (but they all look that) I would put my finger on it and say, 'When I grow up I will go there.' The North Pole was one of these places, I remember. Well, I haven't been there yet, and shall not try now. The glamor's off. Other places were scattered about the Equator, and in every sort of latitude all over the two hemispheres. I have been in some of them, and . . . well, we won't talk about that. But there was one yet—the biggest, the most blank, so to speak—that I had a hankering after.

"True, by this time it was not a blank space any more. It had got filled since my boyhood with rivers and lakes and names. It had ceased to be a blank space of delightful mystery—a white patch for a boy to dream gloriously over. It had become a place of darkness. But there was in it one river especially, a mighty big river, that you could see on the map, resembling an immense snake uncoiled, with its head in the sea, its body at rest curving afar over a vast country, and its tail lost in the depths of the land. And as I looked at the map of it in a shop window, it fascinated me as a snake would a bird—a silly liitle bird. Then I remembered there was a big concern, a company for trade on that river. Dash it all! I thought to myself, they can't trade without using some kind of craft on that lot of fresh water—steamboats! Why shouldn't I try to get charge of one? I went on along Fleet Street, but could not shake off the idea. The snake had charmed me.

"You understand it was a continental concern, that trading society; but I have a lot of relations living on the continent, because it's cheap and not so nasty as it looks, they say.

"I am sorry to own I began to worry them. This was already a fresh departure for me. I was not used to get things that way, you know. I always went my own road and on my own legs where I had a mind to go. I wouldn't have believed it of myself; but, then—you see—I felt somehow I must get there by hook or by crook. So I worried them. The men said 'My dear fellow,' and did nothing. Then—would you believe it?—I tried the women. I, Charlie Marlow, set the women to work—to get a job. Heavens! Well, you see, the notion drove me. I had an aunt, a dear enthusiastic soul. She wrote: 'It will be delightful. I am ready to do anything, anything for you. It is a glorious idea. I know the wife of a very high personage in the administration, and also a man who has lots of influence with,' etc., etc. She was determined to make no end of fuss to get me appointed skipper of a river steamboat, if such was my fancy.

"I got my appointment—of course; and I got it very quick. It appears the company had received news that one of their captains had been killed in a scuffle with the natives. This was my chance, and it made me the more anxious to go. It was only months and months afterwards, when I made the attempt to recover what was left of the body, that I heard the original quarrel arose from a misunderstanding about some hens. Yes, two black hens. Fresleven—that was the fellow's name, a Dane—thought himself wronged somehow in the bargain, so he went ashore and started to hammer the chief of the village with a stick. Oh, it didn't surprise me in the least to hear this, and at the same time to be told that Fresleven was the gentlest, quietest creature that ever walked on two legs. No doubt he was; but he had been a couple of years already out there engaged in the noble cause, you know, and he probably felt the need at last of asserting his self-respect in some way. Therefore he whacked the old nigger mercilessly, while a big crowd of his people watched him, thunderstruck, till some man—I was told the chief's son—in desperation at hearing the old chap yell, made a tentative jab with a spear at the white man—and of course it went quite easy between the shoulder blades. Then the whole population cleared into the forest, expecting all kinds of calamities to happen, while, on the other hand, the steamer Fresleven commanded left also in a bad panic, in charge of the engineer, I believe. Afterwards nobody seemed to trouble much about Fresleven's remains, till I got out and stepped into his shoes. I couldn't let it rest, though; but when an opportunity offered at last to meet my predecessor, the grass growing through his ribs was tall enough to hide his bones. They were all there. The supernatural being had not been touched after he fell. And the village was deserted, the huts gaped black, rotting, all askew within the fallen enclosures. A calamity had come to it, sure enough. The people had vanished. Mad terror had scattered them, men, women, and children, through the bush, and they had never returned. What became of the hens I don't know either. I should think the cause of progress got them, anyhow. However, through this glorious affair I got my appointment, before I had fairly begun to hope for it.

"I flew around like mad to get ready, and before forty-eight hours I was crossing the Channel to show myself to my employers, and sign the contract. In a very few hours I arrived in a city[1] that always makes me think of a whited sepulcher. Prejudice no doubt. I had no

---

1. Brussels, Belgium.

difficulty in finding the company's offices. It was the biggest thing in the town, and everybody I met was full of it. They were going to run an over-sea empire, and make no end of coin by trade.

"A narrow and deserted street in deep shadow, high houses, innumerable windows with venetian blinds, a dead silence, grass sprouting between the stones, imposing carriage archways right and left, immense double doors standing ponderously ajar. I slipped through one of these cracks, went up a swept and ungarnished staircase, as arid as a desert, and opened the first door I came to. Two women, one fat and the other slim, sat on straw-bottomed chairs, knitting black wool. The slim one got up and walked straight at me—still knitting with downcast eyes—and only just as I began to think of getting out of her way, as you would for a somnambulist, stood still, and looked up. Her dress was as plain as an umbrella-cover, and she turned round without a word and preceded me into a waiting room. I gave my name, and looked about. Deal table in the middle, plain chairs all round the walls, on one end a large shining map, marked with all the colors of a rainbow. There was a vast amount of red—good to see at any time, because one knows that some real work is done in there, a deuce of a lot of blue, a little green, smears of orange, and, on the East Coast, a purple patch, to show where the jolly pioneers of progress drink the jolly lager beer. However, I wasn't going into any of these. I was going into the yellow.[2] Dead in the center. And the river was there—fascinating—deadly—like a snake. Ough! A door opened, a white-haired secretarial head, but wearing a compassionate expression, appeared, and a skinny forefinger beckoned me into the sanctuary. Its light was dim, and a heavy writing desk squatted in the middle. From behind that structure came out an impression of pale plumpness in a frock coat. The great man himself. He was five feet six, I should judge, and had his grip on the handle-end of ever so many millions. He shook hands, I fancy, murmured vaguely, was satisfied with my French. *Bon voyage.*

"In about forty-five seconds I found myself again in the waiting room with the compassionate secretary, who, full of desolation and sympathy, made me sign some document. I believe I undertook amongst other things not to disclose any trade secrets. Well, I am not going to.

"I began to feel slightly uneasy. You know I am not used to such ceremonies, and there was something ominous in the atmosphere. It was just as though I had been let into some conspiracy—I don't

2. Red = English colonies; blue = French; green = Portuguese; orange = Dutch; purple = German; yellow = Belgian.

know—something not quite right; and I was glad to get out. In the outer room the two women knitted black wool feverishly. People were arriving, and the younger one was walking back and forth introducing them. The old one sat on her chair. Her flat cloth slippers were propped up on a foot-warmer, and a cat reposed on her lap. She wore a starched white affair on her head, had a wart on one cheek, and silver-rimmed spectacles hung on the tip of her nose. She glanced at me above the glasses. The swift and indifferent placidity of that look troubled me. Two youths with foolish and cheery countenances were being piloted over, and she threw at them the same quick glance of unconcerned wisdom. She seemed to know all about them and about me, too. An eerie feeling came over me. She seemed uncanny and fateful. Often far away there I thought of these two, guarding the door of darkness, knitting black wool as for a warm pall, one introducing, introducing continuously to the unknown, the other scrutinizing the cheery and foolish faces with unconcerned old eyes. *Ave!* Old knitter of black wool. *Morituri te salutant.*[3] Not many of those she looked at ever saw her again—not half, by a long way.

"There was yet a visit to the doctor. 'A simple formality,' assured me the secretary, with an air of taking an immense part in all my sorrows. Accordingly a young chap wearing his hat over the left eyebrow, some clerk I suppose—there must have been clerks in the business, though the house was as still as a house in a city of the dead—came from somewhere upstairs, and led me forth. He was shabby and careless, with inkstains on the sleeves of his jacket, and his cravat was large and billowy, under a chin shaped like the toe of an old boot. It was a little too early for the doctor, so I proposed a drink, and thereupon he developed a vein of joviality. As we sat over our vermouths he glorified the company's business, and by and by I expressed casually my surprise at him not going out there. He became very cool and collected all at one. 'I am not such a fool as I look, quoth Plato to his disciples,' he said sententiously, emptied his glass with great resolution, and we rose.

"The old doctor felt my pulse, evidently thinking of something else the while. 'Good, good for there,' he mumbled, and then with a certain eagerness asked me whether I would let him measure my head. Rather surprised, I said 'yes,' when he produced a thing like calipers and got the dimensions back and front and every way, taking notes carefully. He was an unshaven little man in a threadbare coat like a gaberdine, with his feet in slippers, and I thought

---

3. "Those who are about to die salute you"—the gladiators' greeting to Roman audiences.

him a harmless fool. 'I always ask leave, in the interests of science, to measure the crania of those going out there,' he said. 'And when they come back, too?' I asked. 'Oh, I never see them,' he remarked; 'and, moreover, the changes take place inside, you know.' He smiled, as if at some quiet joke. 'So you are going out there. Famous. Interesting, too.' He gave me a searching glance, and made another note. 'Ever any madness in your family?' he asked, in a matter-of-fact tone. I felt very annoyed. 'Is that question in the interests of science, too?' 'It would be,' he said, without taking notice of my irritation, 'interesting for science to watch the mental changes of individuals, on the spot, but . . .' 'Are you an alienist?'[4] I interrupted. 'Every doctor should be—a little,' answered that original, imperturbably. 'I have a little theory which you messieurs who go out there must help me to prove. This is my share in the advantages my country shall reap from the possession of such a magnificent dependency. The mere wealth I leave to others. Pardon my questions, but you are the first Englishman coming under my observation. . . .' I hastened to assure him I was not in the least typical. 'If I were,' said I, 'I wouldn't be talking like this with you.' 'What you say is rather profound, and probably erroneous,' he said, with a laugh. 'Avoid irritation more than exposure to the sun. Adieu. How do you English say, eh? Good-by. Ah! Good-by. Adieu. In the tropics one must before everything keep calm.' . . . He lifted a warning forefinger. . . . 'Du calme, du calme. Adieu.'

"One thing more remained to do—say good-by to my excellent aunt. I found her triumphant. I had a cup of tea—the last decent cup of tea for many days—and in a room that most soothingly looked just as you would expect a lady's drawing room to look, we had a long quiet chat by the fireside. In the course of these confidences it became quite plain to me I had been represented to the wife of the high dignitary, and goodness knows to how many more people besides, as an exceptional and gifted creature—a piece of good fortune for the company—a man you don't get hold of every day. Good heavens! and I was going to take charge of a two-penny-half-penny river steamboat with a penny whistle attached! It appeared, however, I was also one of the Workers, with a capital—you know. Something like an emissary of light, something like a lower sort of apostle. There had been a lot of such rot let loose in print and talk just about that time, and the excellent woman, living right in the rush of all that humbug, got carried off her feet. She talked about 'weaning those ignorant millions from their horrid ways,' till, upon my word, she made me quite uncomfortable. I ventured to hint that the company was run for profit.

4. Psychiatrist.

" 'You forget, dear Charlie, that the laborer is worthy of his hire,' she said, brightly. It's queer how out of touch with truth women are. They live in a world of their own, and there had never been anything like it, and never can be. It is too beautiful altogether, and if they were to set it up it would go to pieces before the first sunset. Some confounded fact we men have been living contentedly with ever since the day of creation would start up and knock the whole thing over.

"After this I got embraced, told to wear flannel, be sure to write often, and so on—and I left. In the street—I don't know why—a queer feeling came to me that I was an impostor. Odd thing that I, who used to clear out for any part of the world at twenty-four hours' notice, with less thought than most men give to the crossing of a street, had a moment—I won't say of hesitation, but of startled pause, before this commonplace affair. The best way I can explain it to you is by saying that, for a second or two, I felt as though, instead of going to the center of a continent, I were about to set off for the center of the earth.

"I left in a French steamer, and she called in every blamed port they have out there, for, as far as I could see, the sole purpose of landing soldiers and custom-house officers. I watched the coast. Watching a coast as it slips by the ship is like thinking about an enigma. There it is before you—smiling, frowning, inviting, grand, mean, insipid, or savage, and always mute with an air of whispering. Come and find out. This one was almost featureless, as if still in the making, with an aspect of monotonous grimness. The edge of a colossal jungle, so dark-green as to be almost black, fringed with white surf, ran straight, like a ruled line, far, far away along a blue sea whose glitter was blurred by a creeping mist. The sun was fierce, the land seemed to glisten and drip with steam. Here and there grayish-whitish specks showed up clustered inside the white surf, with a flag flying above them perhaps. Settlements some centuries old, and still no bigger than pinheads on the untouched expanse of their background. We pounded along, stopped, landed soldiers; went on, landed custom-house clerks to levy toll in what looked like a God-forsaken wilderness, with a tin shed and a flag-pole lost in it; landed more soldiers—to take care of the custom-house clerks, presumably. Some, I heard, got drowned in the surf; but whether they did or not, nobody seemed particularly to care. They were just flung out there, and on we went. Every day the coast looked the same, as though we had not moved; but we passed various places—trading places—with names like Gran' Bassam, Little Popo; names that seemed to belong to some sordid farce acted in front of a sinister back-cloth. The idleness of a passenger, my isolation amongst all these men with whom I had no point of contact, the oily and languid sea, the uniform somberness of the coast, seemed to keep me away from the truth of things, within the toil of a mournful and senseless delusion. The voice of the surf heard now and then was a positive pleasure, like the speech of a brother. It was something natural, that had its reason, that had a meaning. Now and then a boat from the shore gave one a momentary contact with reality. It was paddled by black fellows. You could see from afar the white of their eyeballs glistening. They shouted, sang; their bodies streamed with perspiration; they had faces like grotesque masks— these chaps; but they had bone, muscle, a wild vitality, an intense energy of movement, that was as natural and true as the surf along their coast. They wanted no excuse for being there. They were a great comfort to look at. For a time I would feel I belonged still to a world of straightforward facts; but the feeling would not last long. Something would turn up to scare it away. Once, I remember, we came upon a man-of-war anchored off the coast. There wasn't even a shed there, and she was shelling the bush. It appears the French had one of their wars going on thereabouts. Her ensign dropped limp like a rag; the muzzles of the long six-inch guns stuck out all over the low hull; the greasy, slimy swell swung her up lazily and let her down, swaying her thin masts. In the empty immensity of earth, sky, and water, there she was, incomprehensible, firing into a continent. Pop, would go one of the six-inch guns; a small flame would dart and vanish, a little white smoke would disappear, a tiny projectile would give a feeble screech—and nothing happened. Nothing could happen. There was a touch of insanity in the proceeding, a sense of lugubrious drollery in the sight; and it was not dissipated by somebody on board assuring me earnestly there was a camp of natives—he called them enemies!—hidden out of sight somewhere.

"We gave her her letters (I heard the men in that lonely ship were dying of fever at the rate of three a day) and went on. We called at some more places with farcical names, where the merry dance of death and trade goes on in a still and earthy atmosphere as of an overheated catacomb; all along the formless coast bordered by dangerous surf, as if Nature herself had tried to ward off intruders; in and out of rivers, streams of death in life, whose banks were rotting into mud, whose waters, thickened into slime, invaded the contorted mangroves, that seemed to writhe at us in the extremity of an impotent despair. Nowhere did we stop long enough to get a particularized impression, but the general sense of vague and oppressive wonder grew upon me. It was like a weary pilgrimage amongst hints for nightmares.

"It was upward of thirty days before I saw the mouth of the big river. We anchored off the seat of the government. But my work would not begin till some two hundred miles farther on. So as soon as I could I made a start for a place thirty miles higher up.

"I had my passage on a little seagoing steamer. Her captain was a Swede, and knowing me for a seaman, invited me on the bridge. He was a young man, lean, fair, and morose, with lanky hair and a shuffling gait. As we left the miserable little wharf, he tossed his head contemptuously at the shore. 'Been living there?' he asked. I said, 'Yes.' 'Fine lot these government chaps—are they not?' he went on, speaking English with great precision and considerable bitterness. 'It is funny what some people will do for a few francs a month. I wonder what becomes of that kind when it goes up country?' I said to him I expected to see that soon. 'So-o-o!' he exclaimed. He shuffled athwart, keeping one eye ahead vigilantly. 'Don't be too sure,' he continued. 'The other day I took up a man who hanged himself on the road. He was a Swede, too.' 'Hanged himself! Why, in God's name?' I cried. He kept on looking out watchfully. 'Who knows? The sun too much for him, or the country perhaps.'

"At last we opened a reach. A rocky cliff appeared, mounds of turned-up earth by the shore, houses on a hill, others with iron roofs, amongst a waste of excavations, or hanging to the declivity. A continuous noise of the rapids above hovered over this scene of inhabited devastation. A lot of people, mostly black and naked, moved about like ants. A jetty projected into the river. A blinding sunlight drowned all this at times in a sudden recrudescence of glare. 'There's your company's station,' said the Swede, pointing to three wooden barrack-like structures on the rocky slope. 'I will send your things up. Four boxes did you say? So. Farewell.'

"I came upon a boiler wallowing in the grass, then found a path leading up the hill. It turned aside for the boulders, and also for an undersized railway truck lying there on its back with its wheels in the air. One was off. The thing looked as dead as the carcass of some animal. I came upon more pieces of decaying machinery, a stack of rusty rails. To the left a clump of trees made a shady spot, where dark things seemed to stir feebly. I blinked, the path was steep. A horn tooted to the right, and I saw the black people run. A heavy and dull detonation shook the ground, a puff of smoke came out of the cliff, and that was all. No change appeared on the face of the rock. They were building a railway. The cliff was not in the way or anything, but this objectless blasting was all the work going on.

"A slight clinking behind me made me turn my head. Six black men advanced in a file, toiling up the path. They walked erect and slow, balancing small baskets full of earth on their heads, and the clink kept time with their footsteps. Black rags were wound round their loins, and the short ends behind waggled to and fro like tails. I could see every rib, the joints of their limbs were like knots in a rope; each had an iron collar on his neck, and all were connected together with a chain whose bights swung between them, rhythmically clinking. Another report from the cliff made me think suddenly of that ship of war I had seen firing into a continent. It was the same kind of ominous voice; but these men could by no stretch of the imagination be called enemies. They were called criminals, and the outraged law, like the bursting shells, had come to them, an insoluble mystery from the sea. All their meager breasts panted together, the violently dilated nostrils quivered, the eyes stared stonily uphill. They passed me within six inches, without a glance, with that complete, deathlike indifference of unhappy savages. Behind this raw matter one of the reclaimed, the product of the new forces at work, strolled despondently, carrying a rifle by its middle. He had a uniform jacket with one button off, and seeing a white man on the path, hoisted his weapon to his shoulder with alacrity. This was simple prudence, white men being so much alike at a distance that he could not tell who I might be. He was speedily reassured, and with a large, white, rascally grin, and a glance at his charge, seemed to take me into partnership in his exalted trust. After all, I also was a part of the great cause of these high and just proceedings.

"Instead of going up, I turned and descended to the left. My idea was to let that chain gang get out of sight before I climbed the hill. You know I am not particularly tender; I've had to strike and to fend off. I've had to resist and to attack sometimes—that's only one way of resisting—without counting the exact cost, according to the demands of such sort of life as I had blundered into. I've seen the devil of violence, and the devil of greed, and the devil of hot desire; but, by all the stars! these were strong, lusty, red-eyed devils, that swayed and drove men—men, I tell you. But as I stood on this hillside, I foresaw that in the blinding sunshine of that land I would become acquainted with a flabby, pretending, weak-eyed devil of a rapacious and pitiless folly. How insidious he could be, too, I was only to find out several months later and a thousand miles farther. For a moment I stood appalled, as though by a warning. Finally I descended the hill, obliquely, towards the trees I had seen.

"I avoided a vast artificial hole somebody had been digging on the slope, the purpose of which I found it impossible to divine. It wasn't a quarry or a sandpit, anyhow. It was just a hole. It might have been connected with the philanthropic desire of giving the criminals something to do. I don't know. Then I nearly fell into a very narrow ravine, almost no more than a scar in the hillside. I discovered that a lot of imported drainage pipes for the settlement had been tumbled in there. There wasn't one that was not broken. It was a wanton smashup. At last I got under the trees. My purpose was to stroll into the shade for a moment; but no sooner within than it seemed to me I had stepped into the gloomy circle of some inferno. The rapids were near, and an uninterrupted, uniform, headlong, rushing noise filled the mournful stillness of the grove, where not a breath stirred, not a leaf moved, with a mysterious sound—as though the tearing pace of the launched earth had suddenly become audible.

"Black shapes crouched, lay, sat between the trees leaning against the trunks, clinging to the earth, half coming out, half effaced within the dim light, in all the attitudes of pain, abandonment, and despair. Another mine on the cliff went off, followed by a slight shudder of the soil under my feet. The work was going on. The work! And this was the place where some of the helpers had withdrawn to die.

"They were dying slowly—it was very clear. They were not enemies, they were not criminals, they were nothing earthly now, nothing but black shadows of disease and starvation, lying confusedly in the greenish gloom. Brought from all the recesses of the coast in all the legality of time contracts, lost in uncongenial surroundings, fed on unfamiliar food, they sickened, became inefficient, and were then allowed to crawl away and rest. These moribund shapes were free as air—and nearly as thin. I began to distinguish the gleam of the eyes under the trees. Then, glancing down, I saw a face near my hand. The black bones reclined at full length with one shoulder against the tree, and slowly the eyelids rose and the sunken eyes looked up at me, enormous and vacant, a kind of blind, white flicker in the depths of the orbs, which died out slowly. The man seemed young—almost a boy—but you don't know with them it's hard to tell. I found nothing else to do but to offer him one of my good Swede's ship's biscuits I had in my pocket. The fingers closed slowly on it and held—there was no other movement and no other glance. He had tied a bit of white worsted round his neck—Why? Where did he get it? Was it a badge—an ornament—a charm—a propitiatory act? Was there any idea at all connected with it? It looked startling round his black neck, this bit of white thread from beyond the sea.

"Near the same tree two more bundles of acute angles sat with their legs drawn up. One, with his chin propped on his knees, stared at nothing, in an intolerable and appalling manner: his brother phantom rested its forehead, as if overcome with a great weariness; and all about others were scattered in every pose of contorted collapse, as in some picture of a massacre or a pestilence.

While I stood horror-struck, one of these creatures rose to his hands and knees, and went off on all fours towards the river to drink. He lapped out of his hand, then sat up in the sunlight, crossing his shins in front of him, and after a time let his wooly head fall on his breastbone.

"I didn't want any more loitering in the shade, and I made haste towards the station. When near the buildings I met a white man, in such an unexpected elegance of getup that in the first moment I took him for a sort of vision. I saw a high starched collar, white cuffs, a light alpaca jacket, snowy trousers, a clear necktie, and varnished boots. No hat. Hair parted, brushed, oiled, under a green-lined parasol held in a big white hand. He was amazing, and had a penholder behind his ear.

"I shook hands with this miracle, and I learned he was the company's chief accountant, and that all the bookkeeping was done at this station. He had come out for a moment, he said, 'to get a breath of fresh air.' The expression sounded wonderfully odd, with its suggestion of sedentary desk life. I wouldn't have mentioned the fellow to you at all, only it was from his lips that I first heard the name of the man who is so indissolubly connected with the memories of that time. Moreover, I respected the fellow. Yes; I respected his collars, his vast cuffs, his brushed hair. His appearance was certainly that of a hairdresser's dummy; but in the great demoralization of the land he kept up his appearance. That's backbone. His starched collars and got-up shirt fronts were achievements of character. He had been out nearly three years; and, later, I could not help asking him how he managed to sport such linen. He had just the faintest blush, and said modestly, 'I've been teaching one of the native women about the station. It was difficult. She had a distaste for the work.' Thus this man had truly accomplished something. And he was devoted to his books, which were in apple-pie order.

"Everything else in the station was in a muddle—heads, things, buildings. Strings of dusty niggers with splay feet arrived and departed; a stream of manufactured goods, rubbishy cottons, beads, and brass wire set into the depths of darkness, and in return came a precious trickle of ivory.

"I had to wait in the station for ten days—an eternity. I lived in a hut in the yard, but to be out of the chaos I would sometimes get into the accountant's office. It was built of horizontal planks, and so badly put together that, as he bent over his high desk, he was barred from neck to heels with narrow strips of sunlight. There was no need to open the big shutter to see. It was hot there, too; big flies buzzed fiendishly, and did not sting, but stabbed. I sat generally on the floor, while, of faultless appearance (and even slightly scented), perching on a high stool, he wrote, he wrote. Sometimes he stood up for exercise. When a truckle bed with a sick man (some invalid agent from upcountry) was put in there, he exhibited a gentle annoyance. 'The groans of this sick person,' he said, 'distract my attention. And without that it is extremely difficult to guard against clerical errors in this climate.'

"One day he remarked, without lifting his head, 'In the interior you will no doubt meet Mr. Kurtz.' On my asking who Mr. Kurtz was, he said he was a first-class agent; and seeing my disappointment at this information, he added slowly, laying down his pen, 'He is a very remarkable person.' Further questions elicited from him that Mr. Kurtz was at present in charge of a trading post, a very important one, in the true ivory-country, at 'the very bottom of there. Sends in as much ivory as all the others put together. . . .' He began to write again. The sick man was too ill to groan. The flies buzzed in a great peace.

"Suddenly there was a growing murmur of voices and a great tramping of feet. A caravan had come in. A violent babble of uncouth sounds burst out on the other side of the planks. All the carriers were speaking together, and in the midst of the uproar the lamentable voice of the chief agent was heard 'giving it up' tearfully for the twentieth time that day. . . . He rose slowly. 'What a frightful row,' he said. He crossed the room gently to look at the sick man, and returning, said to me, 'He does not hear.' 'What! Dead?' I asked, startled. 'No, not yet,' he answered, with great composure. Then, alluding with a toss of the head to the tumult in the station yard, 'When one has got to make correct entries, one comes to hate those savages—hate them to the death.' He remained thoughtful for a moment. 'When you see Mr. Kurtz,' he went on, 'tell him from me that everything here'—he glanced at the desk—'is very satisfactory. I don't like to write to him—with those messengers of ours you never know who may get hold of your letter—at that Central Station.' He stared at me for a moment with his mild, bulging eyes. 'Oh, he will go far, very far,' he began again. 'He will be a somebody in the administration before long. They, above—the council in Europe, you know—mean him to be.'

"He turned to his work. The noise outside had ceased, and presently in going out I stopped at the door. In the steady buzz of flies the homeward-bound agent was lying flushed and insensible; the other, bent over his books, was making correct entries of perfectly correct transactions; and fifty feet below the doorstep I could see the still treetops of the grove of death.

"Next day I left that station at last, with a caravan of sixty men, for a two-hundred-mile tramp.

"No use telling you much about that. Paths, paths, everywhere; a stamped-in network of paths spreading over the empty land, through long grass, through burnt grass, through thickets, down and up chilly ravines, up and down stony hills ablaze with heat; and a solitude, a solitude, nobody, not a hut. The population had cleared out a long time ago. Well, if a lot of mysterious niggers armed with all kinds of fearful weapons suddenly took to traveling on the road between Deal and Gravesend, catching the yokels right and left to carry heavy loads for them, I fancy every farm and cottage thereabouts would get empty very soon. Only here the dwellings were gone, too. Still I passed through several abandoned villages. There's something pathetically childish in the ruins of grass walls. Day after day, with the stamp and shuffle of sixty pair of bare feet behind me, each pair under a sixty-lb. load. Camp, cook, sleep, strike camp, march. Now and then a carrier dead in harness, at rest in the long grass near the path, with an empty water gourd and his long staff lying by his side. A great silence around and above. Perhaps on some quiet night the tremor of far-off drums, sinking, swelling, a tremor vast, faint; a sound weird, appealing, suggestive, and wild—and perhaps with as profound a meaning as the sound of bells in a Christian country. Once a white man in an unbuttoned uniform, camping on the path with an armed escort of lank Zanzibaris, very hospitable and festive—not to say drunk. Was looking after the upkeep of the road he declared. Can't say I saw any road or any upkeep, unless the body of a middle-aged Negro, with a bullethole in the forehead, upon which I absolutely stumbled three miles farther on, may be considered as a permanent improvement. I had a white companion, too, not a bad chap, but rather too fleshy and with the exasperating habit of fainting on the hot hillsides, miles away from the least bit of shade and water. Annoying, you know, to hold your own coat like a parasol over a man's head while he is coming to. I couldn't help asking him once what he meant by coming there at all. 'To make money, of course. What do you think?' he said, scornfully. Then he got fever, and had to be carried in a hammock slung under a pole. As he weighed 224 pounds I had no end of rows with the carriers. They jibbed, ran away, sneaked off with their loads in the night—quite a mutiny. So, one evening, I made a speech in English with gestures, not one of which was lost to the sixty pairs of eyes before me, and the next morning I started the hammock off in front all right. An hour afterwards I came upon the whole concern wrecked in a bush—man, hammock, groans, blankets, horrors. The heavy pole had skinned his poor nose. He was very anxious for me to kill somebody, but there wasn't the shadow of a carrier near. I remember the old doctor, 'It would be interesting for science to watch the mental changes of individuals, on the spot.' I felt I was becoming scientifically interesting. However, all that is to no purpose. On the fifteenth day I came in sight of the big river again, and hobbled into the Central Station. It was on a back water surrounded by scrub and forest, with a pretty border of smelly mud on one side, and on the three others enclosed by a crazy fence of rushes. A neglected gap was all the gate it had, and the first glance at the place was enough to let you see the flabby devil was running the show. White men with long staves in their hands appeared languidly from amongst the buildings, strolling up to take a look at me, and then retired out of sight somewhere. One of them, a stout, excitable chap with black mustaches, informed me with great volubility and many digressions, as soon as I told him who I was, that my steamer was at the bottom of the river. I was thunderstruck. What, how, why? Oh, it was 'all right.' The 'manager himself' was there. All quite correct. 'Everybody had behaved splendidly! splendidly!'—'you must,' he said in agitation, 'go and see the general manager at once. He is waiting!'

"I did not see the real significance of that wreck at once. I fancy I see it now, but I am not sure—not at all. Certainly the affair was too stupid—when I think of it—to be altogether natural. Still . . . But at the moment it presented itself simply as a confounded nuisance. The steamer was sunk. They had started two days before in a sudden hurry up the river with the manager on board, in charge of some volunteer skipper, and before they had been out three hours they tore the bottom out of her on stones, and she sank near the south bank. I asked myself what I was to do there, now my boat was lost. As a matter of fact, I had plenty to do in fishing my command out of the river. I had to set about it the very next day. That, and the repairs when I brought the pieces to the station, took some months.

"My first interview with the manager was curious. He did not ask me to sit down after my twenty-mile walk that morning. He was commonplace in complexion, in feature, in manners, and in voice. He was of middle size and of ordinary build. His eyes, of the usual blue, were perhaps remarkably cold, and he certainly could make his glance fall on one as trenchant and heavy as an axe. But even at these times the rest of his person seemed to disclaim the intention. Otherwise there was only an indefinable, faint expression of his lips, something stealthy—a smile—not a smile—I remember it, but I can't explain. It was unconscious, this smile was, though just after he had said something it got intensified for an instant. It came at the end of his speeches like a seal applied on the words to make the meaning of the commonest phrase appear absolutely inscrutable. He was a common trader, from his youth up employed in these parts—

nothing more. He was obeyed, yet he inspired neither love nor fear, nor even respect. He inspired uneasiness. That was it! Uneasiness. Not a definite mistrust—just uneasiness—nothing more. You have no idea how effective such a . . . a . . . faculty can be. He had no genius for organizing, for initiative, or for order even. That was evident in such things as the deplorable state of the station. He had no learning, and no intelligence. His position had come to him— why? Perhaps because he was never ill . . . He had served three terms of three years out there. . . . Because triumphant health in the general rout of constitutions is a kind of power in itself. When he went home on leave he rioted on a large scale—pompously. Jack ashore—with a difference—in externals only. This one could gather from his casual talk. He originated nothing, he could keep the routine going—that's all. But he was great. He was great by this little thing that it was impossible to tell what could control such a man. He never gave that secret away. Perhaps there was nothing within him. Such a suspicion made one pause—for out there there were no external checks. Once when various tropical diseases had laid low almost every 'agent' in the station, he was heard to say, 'Men who come out here should have no entrails.' He sealed the utterance with that smile of his, as though it had been a door opening into a darkness he had in his keeping. You fancied you had seen things— but the seal was on. When annoyed at mealtimes by the constant quarrels of the white men about precedence, he ordered an immense round table to be made, for which a special house had to be built. This was the station's messroom. Where he sat was the first place—the rest were nowhere. One felt this to be his unalterable conviction. He was neither civil nor uncivil. He was quiet. He allowed his 'boy'—an overfed young Negro from the coast—to treat the white men, under his very eyes, with provoking insolence.

"He began to speak as soon as he saw me. I had been very long on the road. He could not wait. Had to start without me. The up-river stations had to be relieved. There had been so many delays already that he did not know who was dead and who was alive, and how they got on—and so on, and so on. He paid no attention to my explanations, and, playing with a stick of sealing wax, repeated several times that the situation was 'very grave, very grave.' There were rumors that a very important station was in jeopardy, and its chief, Mr. Kurtz, was ill. Hoped it was not true. Mr. Kurtz was . . . I felt weary and irritable. Hang Kurtz, I thought. I interrupted him by saying I had heard of Mr. Kurtz on the coast. 'Ah! So they talk of him down there,' he murmured to himself. Then he began again, assuring me Mr. Kurtz was the best agent he had, an exceptional man, of the greatest importance to the company; therefore I could understand his anxiety. He was, he said, 'very, very uneasy.' Certainly he fidgeted on his chair a good deal, exclaimed, 'Ah, Mr. Kurtz!' broke the stick of sealing wax and seemed dumfounded by the accident. Next thing he wanted to know 'how long it would take to' . . . I interrupted him again. Being hungry, you know, and kept on my feet, too, I was getting savage. 'How could I tell?' I said. 'I hadn't even seen the wreck yet—some months, no doubt.' All this talk seemed to me so futile. 'Some months,' he said. 'Well, let us say three months before we can make a start. Yes. That ought to do the affair.' I flung out of his hut (he lived all alone in a clay hut with a sort of veranda) muttering to myself my opinion of him. He was a chattering idiot. Afterwards I took it back when it was borne in upon me startlingly with what extreme nicety he had estimated the time requisite for the 'affair.'

"I went to work the next day, turning, so to speak, my back on that station. In that way only it seemed to me I could keep my hold on the redeeming facts of life. Still, one must look about sometimes; and then I saw this station, these men strolling aimlessly about in the sunshine of the yard. I asked myself sometimes what it all meant. They wandered here and there with their absurd long staves in their hands, like a lot of faithless pilgrims bewitched inside a rotten fence. The word 'ivory' rang in the air, was whispered, was sighed. You would think they were praying to it. A taint of imbecile rapacity blew through it all, like a whiff from some corpse. By Jove! I've never seen anything so unreal in my life. And outside, the silent wilderness surrounding this cleared speck on the earth struck me as something great and invincible, like evil or truth, waiting patiently for the passing away of this fantastic invasion.

"Oh, these months! Well, never mind. Various things happened. One evening a grass shed full of calico, cotton prints, beads, and I don't know what else, burst into a blaze so suddenly that you would have thought the earth had opened to let an avenging fire consume all that trash. I was smoking my pipe quietly by my dismantled steamer, and saw them all cutting capers in the light with their arms lifted high, when the stout man with mustaches came tearing down to the river, a tin pail in his hand, assured me that everybody was 'behaving splendidly, splendidly,' dipped about a quart of water and tore back again. I noticed there was a hole in the bottom of his pail.

"I strolled up. There was no hurry. You see the thing had gone off like a box of matches. It had been hopeless from the very first. The flame had leaped high, driven everybody back, lighted up everything—and collapse. The shed was already a heap of embers glowing fiercely. A nigger was being beaten near by. They said he had caused the fire in some way; be that as it may, he was screeching most horribly. I saw him, later, for several days, sitting in a bit of shade looking very sick and trying to recover himself: afterwards he arose and went out—and the wilderness without a sound took him into its bosom again. As I approached the glow from the dark I found myself at the back of two men, talking. I heard the name of Kurtz pronounced, then the words, 'take advantage of this unfortunate accident.' One of the men was the manager. I wished him a good evening. 'Did you ever see anything like it—eh? It is incredible,' he said, and walked off. The other man remained. He was a first-class agent, young, gentlemanly, a bit reserved, with a forked little beard and a hooked nose. He was standoffish with the other agents, and they on their side said he was the manager's spy upon them. As to me, I had hardly ever spoken to him before. We got into talk, and by and by we strolled away from the hissing ruins. Then he asked me to his room, which was in the main building of the station. He struck a match, and I perceived that this young aristocrat had not only a silver-mounted dressing case but also a whole candle all to himself. Just at that time the manager was the only man supposed to have any right to candles. Native mats covered the clay walls; a collection of spears, assagais, shields, knives was hung up in trophies. The business intrusted to this fellow was the making of bricks—so I had been informed; but there wasn't a fragment of a brick anywhere in the station, and he had been there more than a year—waiting. It seems he could not make bricks without something, I don't know what—straw maybe. Anyways, it could not be found there, and as it was not likely to be sent from Europe, it did not appear clear to me what he was waiting for. An act of special creation perhaps. However, they were all waiting—all the sixteen or twenty pilgrims of them—for something; and upon my word it did not seem an uncongenial occupation, from the way they took it, though the only thing that ever came to them was disease—as far as I could see. They beguiled the time by backbiting and intriguing against each other in a foolish kind of way. There was an air of plotting about that station, but nothing came of it, of course. It was as unreal as everything else—as the philanthropic pretense of the whole concern, as their talk, as their government, as their show of work. The only real feeling was a desire to get appointed to a trading post where ivory was to be had, so that they could earn percentages. They intrigued and slandered and hated each other only on that account, but as to effectually lifting a little finger—oh, no. By heavens! There is something after all in the world allowing one man to steal a horse while another must not look at a halter. Steal a horse straight out. Very well. He has done it. Perhaps he can ride. But there is a way of looking at a halter that would provoke the most charitable of saints into a kick.

"I had no idea why he wanted to be sociable, but as we chatted in there it suddenly occurred to me the fellow was trying to get at something—in fact, pumping me. He alluded constantly to Europe, to the people I was supposed to know there—putting leading questions as to my acquaintances in the sepulchral city, and so on. His little eyes glittered like mica discs—with curiosity—though he tried to keep up a bit of superciliousness. At first I was astonished, but very soon I became awfully curious to see what he would find out from me. I couldn't possibly imagine what I had in me to make it worth his while. It was very pretty to see how he baffled himself, for in truth my body was full only of chills, and my head had nothing in it but that wretched steamboat business. It was evident he took me for a perfectly shameless prevaricator. At last he got angry, and, to conceal a movement of furious annoyance, he yawned. I rose. Then I noticed a small sketch in oils on a panel, representing a woman, draped and blindfolded, carrying a lighted torch. The background was somber—almost black. The movement of the woman was stately, and the effect of the torchlight on the face was sinister.

"It arrested me, and he stood by civilly, holding an empty half-pint champagne bottle (medical comforts) with the candle stuck in it. To my question he said Mr. Kurtz had painted this—in this very station more than a year ago—while waiting for means to go to his trading post. 'Tell me, pray,' said I, 'who is this Mr. Kurtz?'

" 'The chief of the Inner Station,' he answered in a short tone looking away. 'Much obliged,' I said, laughing. 'And you are the brickmaker of the Central Station. Everyone knows that.' He was silent for a while. 'He is a prodigy,' he said at last. 'He is an emissary of pity, and science, and progress, and devil knows what else. We want,' he began to declaim suddenly, 'for the guidance of the cause intrusted to us by Europe, so to speak, higher intelligence, wide sympathies, a singleness of purpose.' 'Who says that?' I asked. 'Lots of them,' he replied. 'Some even write that; and so *he* comes here, a special being, as you ought to know.' 'Why ought I to know?' I interrupted, really surprised. He paid no attention. 'Yes. Today he is chief of the best station, next year he will be assistant manager, two years more and . . . but I daresay you know what he will be in two years' time. You are of the new gang—the gang of virtue. The same people who sent him specially also recommended you. Oh, don't say no. I've my own eyes to trust.' Light dawned upon me. My dear aunt's influential acquaintances were producing an unexpected effect upon that young man. I nearly burst into a laugh. 'Do you read the company's confidential correspondence?' I asked. He hadn't a word to say. It was great fun. 'When Mr. Kurtz,' I continued, severely, 'is general manager, you won't have the opportunity.'

"He blew the candle out suddenly, and we went outside. The moon had risen. Black figures strolled about listlessly, pouring water on the glow, whence proceeded a sound of hissing; steam ascended in the moonlight, the beaten nigger groaned somewhere. 'What a row the brute makes!' said the indefatigable man with the mustaches, appearing near us. 'Serve him right. Transgression—punishment—bang! Pitiless, pitiless. That's the only way. This will prevent all conflagrations for the future. I was just telling the manage . . .' He noticed my companion, and became crestfallen all at once. 'Not in bed yet,' he said, with a kind of servile heartiness; 'it's so natural. Ha! Danger—agitation.' He vanished. I went on to the river side, and the other followed me. I heard a scathing murmur at my ear, 'Heap of muffs—go to.' The pilgrims could be seen in knots gesticulating, discussing. Several had still their staves in their hands. I truly believe they took these sticks to bed with them. Beyond the fence the forest stood up spectrally in the moonlight, and through the dim stir, through the faint sounds of that lamentable courtyard, the silence of the land went home to one's very heart—its mystery, its greatness, the amazing reality of its concealed life. The hurt nigger moaned feebly somewhere near by, and then fetched a deep sigh that made me mend my pace away from there. I felt a hand introducing itself under my arm. 'My dear sir,'' said the fellow, 'I don't want to be misunderstood, and especially by you, who will see Mr. Kurtz long before I can have that pleasure. I wouldn't like him to get a false idea of my disposition. . . .'

'I let him run on, this papier-mâché Mephistopheles, and it seemed to me that if I tried I could poke my forefinger through him, and would find nothing inside but a little loose dirt, maybe. He, don't you see, had been planning to be assistant manager by and by under the present man, and I could see that the coming of that Kurtz had upset them both not a little. He talked precipitately, and I did not try to stop him. I had my shoulders against the wreck of my steamer, hauled up on the slope like a carcass of some big river animal. The smell of mud, of primeval mud, by Jove! was in my nostrils, the high stillness of primeval forest was before my eyes; there were shiny patches on the black creek. The moon had spread over everything a thin layer of silver—over the rank grass, over the mud, upon the wall of matted vegetation standing higher than the wall of a temple, over the great river I could see through a somber gap glittering, glittering, as it flowed broadly by without a murmur. All this was great, expectant, mute, while the man jabbered about himself. I wondered whether the stillness on the face of the immensity looking at us two were meant as an appeal or as a menace. What were we who had strayed in here? Could we handle that dumb thing, or would it handle us? I felt how big, how confoundedly big, was that thing that couldn't talk, and perhaps was deaf as well. What was in there? I could see a little ivory coming out from there, and I had heard Mr. Kurtz was in there. I had heard enough about it, too—God knows! Yet somehow it didn't bring any image with it—no more than if I had been told an angel or a fiend was in there. I believed it in the same way one of you might believe there are inhabitants in the planet Mars. I knew once a Scotch sailmaker who was certain, dead sure, there were people in Mars. If you asked him for some idea how they looked and behaved, he would get shy and mutter something about 'walking on all fours.' If you as much as smiled, he would—though a man of sixty—offer to fight you. I would not have gone so far as to fight for Kurtz, but I went for him near enough to a lie. You know I hate, detest, and can't bear a lie, not because I am straighter than the rest of us, but simply because it appalls me. There is a taint of death, a flavor of mortality in lies—which is exactly what I hate and detest in the world—what I want to forget. It makes me miserable and sick, like biting something rotten would do. Temperament, I suppose. Well, I went near enough to it by letting the young fool there believe anything he liked to imagine as to my influence in Europe. I became in an instant as much of a pretense as the rest of the bewitched pilgrims. This simply because I had a notion it somehow would be of help to that Kurtz whom at the time I did not see—you understand. He was just a word for me. I did not see the man in the name any more than you do. Do you see him? Do you see the story? Do you see anything? It seems to me I am trying to tell you a dream—making a vain attempt, because no relation of a dream can convey the dream-sensation, that commingling of absurdity, surprise, and bewilderment in a tremor of struggling revolt, that notion of being captured by the incredible which is of the very essence of dreams. . . ."

He was silent for a while.

". . . No, it is impossible; it is impossible to convey the life-sensation of any given epoch of one's existence—that which makes its truth, its meaning—its subtle and penetrating essence. It is impossible. We live, as we dream—alone. . . ."

He paused again as if reflecting, then added:

"Of course in this you fellows see more than I could then. You see me, whom you know. . . ."

It had become so pitch dark that we listeners could hardly see one another. For a long time already he, sitting apart, had been no more to us than voice. There was not a word from anybody. The others might have been asleep, but I was awake. I listened, I listened on the watch for the sentence, for the word, that would give me the clue to the faint uneasiness inspired by this narrative that seemed to shape itself without human lips in the heavy night air of the river.

". . . Yes—I let him run on," Marlow began again, "and think what he pleased about the powers that were behind me. I did! And there was nothing behind me! There was nothing but that wretched, old, mangled steamboat I was leaning against, while he talked fluently about 'the necessity for every man to get on.' 'And when one comes out here, you conceive, it is not to gaze at the moon.' Mr. Kurtz was a 'universal genius,' but even a genius would find it easier to work with 'adequate tools—intelligent men.' He did not make bricks—why, there was a physical impossibility in the way— as I was well aware; and if he did secretarial work for the manager, it was because 'no sensible man rejects wantonly the confidence of his superiors.' Did I see it? I saw it. What more did I want? What I really wanted was rivets, by heaven! Rivets. To get on with the work—to stop the hole. Rivets I wanted. There were cases of them down at the coast—cases—piled up—burst—split! You kicked a loose rivet at every second step in that station yard on the hillside. Rivets had rolled into the grove of death. You could fill your pockets with rivets for the trouble of stooping down—and there wasn't one rivet to be found where it was wanted. We had plates that would do, but nothing to fasten them with. And every week the messenger, a lone Negro, letter bag on shoulder and staff in hand, left our station for the coast. And several times a week a coast caravan came in with trade goods—ghastly glazed calico that made you shudder only to look at it, glass beads, value about a penny a quart, confounded spotted cotton handkerchiefs. And no rivets. Three carriers could have brought all that was wanted to set that steamboat afloat.

"He was becoming confidential now, but I fancy my unresponsive attitude must have exasperated him at last, for he judged it necessary to inform me he feared neither God nor devil, let alone any mere man. I said I could see that very well, but what I wanted was a certain quantity of rivets—and rivets were what really Mr. Kurtz wanted, if he had only known it. Now letters went to the coast every week. . . . 'My dear sir,' he cried, 'I write from dictation.' I demanded rivets. There was a way—for an intelligent man. He changed his manner; became very cold, and suddenly began to talk about a hippopotamus; wondered whether sleeping on board the steamer (I stuck to my salvage night and day) I wasn't disturbed. There was an old hippo that had the bad habit of getting out on the bank and roaming at night over the station grounds. The pilgrims used to turn out in a body and empty every rifle they could lay hands on at him. Some even had sat up o' nights for him. All this energy was wasted, though. 'That animal has a charmed life,' he said; 'but you can say this only of brutes in this country. No man— you apprehend me?—no man here bears a charmed life.' He stood there for a moment in the moonlight with his delicate hooked nose set a little askew, and his mica eyes glittering without a wink, then, with a curt good night, he strode off. I could see he was disturbed and considerably puzzled, which made me feel more hopeful than I had been for days. It was a great comfort to turn from that chap to my influential friend, the battered, twisted, ruined, tinpot steamboat. I clambered on board. She rang under my feet like an empty Huntley and Palmer biscuit tin kicked along a gutter; she was nothing so solid in make, and rather less pretty in shape, but I had expended enough hard work on her to make me love her. No influential friend would have served me better. She had given me a chance to come out a bit—to find out what I could do. No, I don't like work. I had rather laze about and think of all the fine things that can be done. I don't like work—no man does—but I like what is in the work, the chance to find yourself. Your own reality—for yourself, not for others—what no other man can ever know. They can only see the mere show, and never can tell what it really means.

"I was not surprised to see somebody sitting aft, on the deck, with his legs dangling over the mud. You see I rather chummed with the few mechanics there were in that station, whom the other pilgrims naturally despised—on account of their imperfect manners, I suppose. This was the foreman—a boilermaker by trade—a good worker. He was a lank, bony, yellow-faced man, with big intense eyes. His aspect was worried, and his head was as bald as the palm of my hand; but his hair in falling seemed to have stuck to his chin, and had prospered in the new locality, for his beard hung down to his waist. He was a widower with six young children (he had left them in charge of a sister of his to come out there), and the passion of his life was pigeon flying. He was an enthusiast and a connoisseur. He would rave about pigeons. After work hours he used sometimes to come over from his hut for a talk about his children and his pigeons; at work, when he had to crawl in the mud under the bottom of the steamboat, he would tie up that beard of his in a kind of white serviette he brought for the purpose. It had loops to go over his ears. In the evening he could be seen squatted on the bank rinsing that wrapper in the creek with great care, then spreading it solemnly on a bush to dry.

"I slapped him on the back and shouted 'We shall have rivets!' He scrambled to his feet exclaiming 'No! Rivets!' as though he couldn't believe his ears. Then in a low voice, 'You . . . eh?' I don't know why we behaved like lunatics. I put my finger to the side of my nose and nodded mysteriously. 'Good for you!' he cried, snapped his fingers above his head, lifting one foot. I tried a jig. We capered on the iron deck. A frightful clatter came out of that hulk, and the virgin forest on the other bank of the creek sent it back in a thundering roll upon the sleeping station. It must have made some of the pilgrims sit up in their hovels. A dark figure obscured the lighted doorway of the manager's hut, vanished, then, a second or so after, the doorway itself vanished, too. We stopped, and the silence driven away by the stamping of our feet flowed back again from the recesses of the land. The great wall of vegetation, an exuberant and entangled mass of trunks, branches, leaves, boughs, festoons, motionless in the moonlight, was like a rioting invasion of soundless life, a rolling wave of plants, piled up crested, ready to topple over the creek, to sweep every little man of us out of his little existence. And it moved not. A deadened burst of mighty splashes and snorts reached us from afar, as though an ichthyosaurus had been taking a bath of glitter in the great river. 'After all,' said the boilermaker in a reasonable tone, 'why shouldn't we get the rivets?' Why not, indeed! I did not know of any reason why we shouldn't. 'They'll come in three weeks,' I said, confidently.

"But they didn't. Instead of rivets there came an invasion, an infliction, a visitation. It came in sections during the next three weeks, each section headed by a donkey carrying a white man in new clothes and tan shoes, bowing from that elevation right and left to the impressed pilgrims. A quarrelsome band of footsore sulky niggers trod on the heels of the donkey; a lot of tents, campstools, tin boxes, white cases, brown bales would be shot down in the courtyard, and the air of mystery would deepen a little over the muddle of the station. Five such installments came, with their absurd air of disorderly flight with the loot of innumerable outfit shops and provision stores, that, one would think, they were lugging, after a raid, into the wilderness for equitable division. It was an inextricable mess of things decent in themselves but that human folly made look like spoils of thieving.

"This devoted band called itself the Eldorado Exploring Expedition, and I believe they were sworn to secrecy. Their talk, however, was the talk of sordid buccaneers: it was reckless without hardihood, greedy without audacity, and cruel without courage; there was not an atom of foresight or of serious intention in the whole batch of them, and they did not seem aware these things are wanted for the work of the world. To tear treasure out of the bowels of the land was their desire, with no more moral purpose at the back of it than there is in burglars breaking into a safe. Who paid the expenses of the noble enterprise I don't know; but the uncle of our manager was leader of that lot.

"In exterior he resembled a butcher in a poor neighborhood, and his eyes had a look of sleepy cunning. He carried his fat paunch with ostentation on his short legs, and during the time his gang infested the station spoke to no one but his nephew. You could see these two roaming about all day long with their heads close together in an everlasting confab.

"I had given up worrying myself about the rivets. One's capacity for that kind of folly is more limited than you would suppose. I said Hang!—and let things slide. I had plenty of time for meditation, and now and then I would give some thought to Kurtz. I wasn't very interested in him. No. Still, I was curious to see whether this man, who had come out equipped with moral ideas of some sort, would climb to the top after all and how he would set about his work when there."

## II

"One evening as I was lying flat on the deck of my steamboat, I heard voices approaching—and there were the nephew and the uncle strolling along the bank. I laid my head on my arm again, and had nearly lost myself in a doze, when somebody said in my ear, as it were: 'I am as harmless as a little child, but I don't like to be dictated to. Am I the manager—or am I not? I was ordered to send him there. It's incredible.' . . . I became aware that the two were standing on the shore alongside the forepart of the steamboat, just below my head. I did not move; it did not occur to me to move: I was sleepy. 'It *is* unpleasant,' grunted the uncle. 'He has asked the administration to be sent there,' said the other, 'with the idea of showing what he could do; and I was instructed accordingly. Look at the influence that man must have. Is it not frightful?' They both agreed it was frightful, then made several bizarre remarks: 'Make rain and fine weather—one man—the council—by the nose'—bits of absurd sentences that got the better of my drowsiness, so that I had pretty near the whole of my wits about me when the uncle said, 'The climate may do away with this difficulty for you. Is he alone there?' 'Yes,' answered the manager; 'he sent his assistant down the river with a note to me in these terms: "Clear this poor devil out of the country, and don't bother sending more of that sort. I had rather be alone than have the kind of men you can dispose of with me." It was more than a year ago. Can you imagine such impudence!' 'Anything since then?' asked the other, hoarsely. 'Ivory,' jerked the nephew; 'lots of it—prime sort—lots—most annoying, from him.' 'And with that?' questioned the heavy rumble. 'Invoice,' was the reply fired out, so to speak. Then silence. They had been talking about Kurtz.

"I was broad awake by this time, but, lying perfectly at ease, remained still, having no inducement to change my position. 'How did that ivory come all this way?' growled the elder man, who seemed very vexed. The other explained that it had come with a fleet of canoes in charge of an English half-caste clerk Kurtz had with him; that Kurtz had apparently intended to return himself, the station being by that time bare of goods and stores, but after coming three hundred miles, had suddenly decided to go back, which he started to do alone in a small dugout with four paddlers, leaving the half-caste to continue down the river with the ivory. The two fellows there seemed astounded at anybody attempting such a thing. They were at a loss for an adequate motive. As to me, I seemed to see Kurtz for the first time. It was a distinct glimpse: the dugout, four paddling savages, and the lone white man turning his back suddenly on the headquarters, on relief, on thoughts of home— perhaps; setting his face towards the depths of the wilderness, towards his empty and desolate station. I did not know the motive. Perhaps he was just simply a fine fellow who stuck to his work for its own sake. His name, you understand, had not been pronounced once. He was 'that man.' The half-caste, who, as far as I could see, had conducted a difficult trip with great prudence and pluck, was invariably alluded to as 'that scoundrel.' The 'scoundrel' had reported that the 'man' had been very ill—had recovered imperfectly. . . . The two below me moved away then a few paces, and strolled back and forth at some little distance. I heard: 'Military post—doctor—two hundred miles—quite alone now—unavoidable delays—nine months—no news—strange rumors.' They approached again, just as the manager was saying, 'No one, as far as I know, unless a species of wandering trader—a pestilential fellow, snapping ivory from the natives.' Who was it they were talking about now? I gathered in snatches that this was some man supposed to be in Kurtz's district, and of whom the manager did not approve. 'We will not be free from unfair competition till one of these fellows is hanged for an example,' he said. 'Certainly,' grunted the other; 'get him hanged! Why not? Anything—anything can be done in this country. That's what I say; nobody here, you understand, *here*, can endanger your position. And why? You stand the climate—you outlast them all. The danger is in Europe; but there before I left I took care to—' They moved off and whispered, then their voices rose again. 'The extraordinary series of delays is not my fault. I did my best.' The fat man sighed. 'Very sad.' 'And the pestiferous absurdity of his talk,' continued the other; 'he bothered me enough when he was here. "Each station should be like a beacon on the road towards better things, a center for trade of course, but also for humanizing, improving, instructing." Conceive you—that ass! And he wants to be manager! No, it's—' Here he got choked by excessive indignation, and I lifted my head the least bit. I was surprised to see how near they were—right under me. I could have spat upon their hats. They were looking on the ground, absorbed in thought. The manager was switching his leg with a slender twig; his sagacious relative lifted his head. 'You have been well since you came out this time?' he asked. The other gave a start. 'Who? I? Oh! Like a charm—like a charm. But the rest—oh, my goodness! All sick. They die so quick, too, that I haven't the time to send them out of the country—it's incredible!' 'H'm. Just so,' grunted the uncle. 'Ah! my boy, trust to this—I say, trust to this.' I saw him extend his short flipper of an arm for a gesture that took in the forest, the creek, the mud, the river—seemed to beckon with a dishonoring flourish before the sunlit face of the land a treacherous appeal to the lurking death, to the hidden evil, to the profound darkness of its heart. It was so startling that I leaped to my feet and looked back at the edge of the forest, as though I had expected an answer of some sort to that black display of confidence. You know the foolish notions that come to one sometimes. The high stillness confronted these two figures with its ominous patience, waiting for the passing away of a fantastic invasion.

"They swore aloud together—out of sheer fright, I believe—then pretending not to know anything of my existence, turned back to the station. The sun was low; and leaning forward side by side, they seemed to be tugging painfully uphill their two ridiculous shadows of unequal length, that trailed behind them slowly over the tall grass without bending a single blade.

"In a few days the Eldorado Expedition went into the patient wilderness, that closed upon it as the sea closes over a diver. Long afterwards the news came that all the donkeys were dead. I know nothing as to the fate of the less valuable animals. They, no doubt, like the rest of us, found what they deserved. I did not inquire. I was then rather excited at the prospect of meeting Kurtz very soon. When I say very soon I mean it comparatively. It was just two months from the day we left the creek when we came to the bank below Kurtz's station.

"Going up that river was like traveling back to the earliest beginnings of the world, when vegetation rioted on the earth and the big trees were kings. An empty stream, a great silence, an impenetrable forest. The air was warm, thick, heavy, sluggish. There was no joy in the brilliance of sunshine. The long stretches of the waterway ran on, deserted, into the gloom of overshadowed distances. On silvery sandbanks hippos and alligators sunned themselves side by side. The broadening waters flowed through a mob of wooded islands; you lost your way on that river as you would in a desert, and butted all day long against shoals, trying to find the channel, till you thought yourself bewitched and cut off forever from everything you had known once—somewhere—far away—in another existence perhaps. There were moments when one's past came back to one, as it will sometimes when you have not a moment to spare to yourself; but it came in the shape of an unrestful and noisy dream, remembered with wonder amongst the overwhelming realities of this strange world of plants, and water, and silence. And this stillness of life did not in the least resemble a peace. It was the stillness of an implacable force brooding over an inscrutable intention. It looked at you with a vengeful aspect. I got used to it afterwards; I did not see it any more; I had no time. I had to keep guessing at the channel; I had to discern, mostly by inspiration, the signs of hidden banks; I watched for sunken stones; I was learning to clap my teeth smartly before my heart flew out, when I shaved by a fluke some infernal sly old snag that would have ripped the life out of the tin-pot steamboat and drowned all the pilgrims; I had to keep a lookout for the signs of dead wood we could cut up in the night for next day's steaming. When you have to attend to things of that sort, to the mere incidents of the surface, the reality—the reality, I tell you—fades. The inner truth is hidden—luckily, luckily. But I felt it all the same; I felt often its mysterious stillness watching me at my monkey tricks, just as it watches you fellows performing on your respective tightropes for—what is it? a half crown a tumble—"

"Try to be civil, Marlow," growled a voice, and I knew there was at least one listener awake besides myself.

"I beg your pardon. I forgot the heartache which makes up the rest of the price. And indeed what does the price matter, if the trick be well done? You do your tricks very well. And I didn't do badly either, since I managed not to sink that steamboat on my first trip. It's a wonder to me yet. Imagine a blindfolded man set to drive a van over a bad road. I sweated and shivered over that business considerably, I can tell you. After all, for a seaman, to scrape the bottom of the thing that's supposed to float all the time under his care is the unpardonable sin. No one may know of it, but you never forget the thump—eh? A blow on the very heart. You remember it, you dream of it, you wake up at night and think of it—years after—

and go hot and cold all over. I don't pretend to say that steamboat floated all the time. More than once she had to wade for a bit, with twenty cannibals splashing around and pushing. We had enlisted some of these chaps on the way for a crew. Fine fellows— cannibals—in their place. They were men one could work with, and I am grateful to them. And, after all, they did not eat each other before my face: they had brought along a provision of hippo meat which went rotten, and made the mystery of the wilderness stink in my nostrils. Phoo! I can sniff it now. I had the manager on board and three or four pilgrims with their staves—all complete. Sometimes we came upon a station close by the bank, clinging to the skirts of the unknown, and the white men rushing out of a tumble- down hovel, with great gestures of joy and surprise and welcome, seemed very strange—had the appearance of being held there cap- tive by a spell. The word ivory would ring in the air for a while— and on we went again into the silence, along empty reaches, round the still bends, between the high walls of our winding way, rever- berating in hollow claps the ponderous beat of the stern wheel. Trees, trees, millions of trees, massive, immense, running up high; and at their foot, hugging the bank against the stream, crept the little begrimed steamboat, like a sluggish beetle crawling on the floor of a lofty portico. It made you feel very small, very lost, and yet it was not altogether depressing, that feeling. After all, if you were small, the grimy beetle crawled on—which was just what you wanted it to do. Where the pilgrims imagined it crawled to I don't know. To some place where they expected to get something, I bet! For me it crawled towards Kurtz—exclusively; but when the steam pipes started leaking we crawled very slow. The reaches opened before us and closed behind, as if the forest had stepped leisurely across the water to bar the way for our return. We penetrated deeper and deeper into the heart of darkness. It was very quiet there. At night sometimes the roll of drums behind the curtain of trees would run up the river and remain sustained faintly, as if hovering in the air high over our heads, till the first break of day. Whether it meant war, peace, or prayer we could not tell. The dawns were heralded by the descent of a chill stillness; the woodcutters slept, their fires burned low; the snapping of a twig would make you start. We were wanderers on prehistoric earth, on an earth that wore the aspect of an unknown planet. We could have fancied ourselves the first of men taking possession of an accursed inheritance, to be subdued at the cost of profound anguish and of excessive toil. But suddenly, as we struggled round a bend, there would be a glimpse of rush walls, of peaked grass roofs, a burst of yells, a whirl of black limbs, a mass of hands clapping, of feet stamping, of bodies swaying, of eyes rolling, under the droop of heavy and motionless foliage. The steamer toiled along slowly on the edge of a black and incomprehensible frenzy. The prehistoric man was cursing us, praying to us, welcoming us—who could tell? We were cut off from the comprehension of our surroundings; we glided past like phantoms, wondering and secretly appalled, as sane men would be before an enthusiastic outbreak in a madhouse. We could not understand because we were too far and could not remember, because we were traveling in the night of first ages, of those ages that are gone, leaving hardly a sign—and no memories.

"The earth seemed unearthly. We are accustomed to look upon the shackled form of a conquered monster, but there—there you could look at a thing monstrous and free. It was unearthly, and the men were— No, they were not inhuman. Well, you know, that was the worst of it—this suspicion of their not being inhuman. It would come slowly to one. They howled and leaped, and spun, and made horrid faces; but what thrilled you was just the thought of their humanity—like yours—the thought of your remote kinship with this wild and passionate uproar. Ugly. Yes, it was ugly enough; but if you were man enough you would admit to yourself that there was in you just the faintest trace of a response to the terrible frankness of that noise, a dim suspicion of there being a meaning in it which you—you so remote from the night of first ages—could comprehend. And why not? The mind of man is capable of anything—because everything is in it, all the past as well as all the future. What was there after all? Joy, fear, sorrow, devotion, valor, rage—who can tell?—but truth—truth stripped of its cloak of time. Let the fool gape and shudder—the man knows, and can look on without a wink. But he must at least be as much of a man as these on the shore. He must meet that truth with his own true stuff—with his own inborn strength. Principles won't do. Acquisitions, clothes, pretty rags—rags that would fly off at the first good shake. No; you want a deliberate belief. An appeal to me in this fiendish row—is there? Very well; I hear; I admit, but I have a voice, too, and for good or evil mine is the speech that cannot be silenced. Of course, a fool, what with sheer fright and fine sentiments, is always safe. Who's that grunting? You wonder I didn't go ashore for a howl and a dance? Well, no—I didn't. Fine sentiments, you say? Fine sentiments, be hanged! I had no time. I had to mess about with white lead and strips of woolen blanket helping to put bandages on those leaky steam pipes—I tell you. I had to watch the steering, and circumvent those snags, and get the tin-pot along by hook or by crook. There was surface truth enough in these things to save a wiser man. And between whiles I had to look after the savage who was fireman.

He was an improved specimen; he could fire up a vertical boiler. He was there below me, and, upon my word, to look at him was as edifying as seeing a dog in a parody of breeches and a feather hat, walking on his hind legs. A few months of training has done for that really fine chap. He squinted at the steam gauge and at the water gauge with an evident effort of intrepidity—and he had filed teeth, too, the poor devil, and the wool of his pate shaved into queer patterns, and three ornamental scars on each of his cheeks. He ought to have been clapping his hands and stamping his feet on the bank, instead of which he was hard at work, a thrall to strange witchcraft, full of improving knowledge. He was useful because he had been instructed; and what he knew was this—that should the water in that transparent thing disappear, the evil spirit inside the boiler would get angry through the greatness of his thirst, and take a terrible vengeance. So he sweated and fired up and watched the glass fearfully (with an impromptu charm, made of rags, tied to his arm, and a piece of polished bone, as big as a watch, stuck flatways through his lower lip), while the wooded banks slipped past us slowly, the short noise was left behind, the interminable miles of silence—and we crept on, towards Kurtz. But the snags were thick, the water was treacherous and shallow, the boiler seemed indeed to have a sulky devil in it, and thus neither that fireman nor I had any time to peer into our creepy thoughts.

"Some fifty miles below the Inner Station we came upon a hut of reeds, an inclined and melancholy pole, with the unrecognizable tatters of what had been a flag of some sort flying from it, and a neatly stacked wood pile. This was unexpected. We came to the bank, and on the stack of firewood found a flat piece of board with some faded pencil writing on it. When deciphered it said: 'Wood for you. Hurry up. Approach cautiously.' There was a signature, but it was illegible—not Kurtz—a much longer word. Hurry up. Where? Up the river? 'Approach cautiously.' We had not done so. But the warning could not have been meant for the place where it could be only found after approach. Something was wrong above. But what— and how much? That was the question. We commented adversely upon the imbecility of that telegraphic style. The bush around said nothing, and would not let us look very far, either. A torn curtain of red twill hung in the doorway of the hut, and flapped sadly in our faces. The dwelling was dismantled; but we could see a white man had lived there not very long ago. There remained a rude table—a plank on two posts; a heap of rubbish reposed in a dark corner, and by the door I picked up a book. It had lost its covers, and the pages had been thumbed into a state of extremely dirty softness; but the back had been lovingly stitched afresh with white cotton thread, which looked clean yet. It was an extraordinary find. Its title was, *An Inquiry into Some Points of Seamanship*, by a man Tower, Towson—some such name—Master in his Majesty's Navy. The matter looked dreary reading enough, with illustrative diagrams and repulsive tables of figures, and the copy was sixty years old. I handled this amazing antiquity with the greatest possible tenderness, lest it should dissolve in my hands. Within, Towson or Towser was inquiring earnestly into the breaking strain of ships' chains and tackle, and other such matters. Not a very enthralling book; but at the first glance you could see there a singleness of intention, an honest concern for the right way of going to work, which made these humble pages, thought out so many years ago, luminous with another than a professional light. The simple old sailor, with his talk of chains and purchases, made me forget the jungle and the pilgrims in a delicious sensation of having come upon something unmistakably real. Such a book being there was wonderful enough; but still more astounding were the notes penciled in the margin, and plainly referring to the text. I couldn't believe my eyes! They were in cipher! Yes, it looked like cipher. Fancy a man lugging with him a book of that description into this nowhere and studying it—and making notes—in cipher at that! It was an extravagant mystery.

"I had been dimly aware for some time of a worrying noise, and when I lifted my eyes I saw the wood pile was gone, and the manager, aided by all the pilgrims, was shouting at me from the river side. I slipped the book into my pocket. I assure you to leave off reading was like tearing myself away from the shelter of an old and solid friendship.

"I started the lame engine ahead. 'It must be this miserable trader—this intruder,' exclaimed the manager, looking back malevolently at the place we had left. 'He must be English,' I said. 'It will not save him from getting into trouble if he is not careful,' muttered the manager darkly. I observed with assumed innocence that no man was safe from trouble in this world.

"The current was more rapid now, the steamer seemed at her last gasp, the stern wheel flopped languidly, and I caught myself listening on tiptoe for the next beat of the boat, for in sober truth I expected the wretched thing to give up every moment. It was like watching the last flickers of a life. But still we crawled. Sometimes I would pick out a tree a little way ahead to measure our progress towards Kurtz by, but I lost it invariably before we got abreast. To keep the eyes so long on one thing was too much for human patience. The manager displayed a beautiful resignation. I fretted and fumed and took to arguing with myself whether or no I would talk openly with Kurtz; but before I could come to any conclusion it occurred to me that my speech of my silence, indeed any action of mine, would be a mere futility. What did it matter what anyone knew or ignored? What did it matter who was manager? One gets sometimes such a flash of insight. The essentials of this affair lay deep under the surface, beyond my reach, and beyond my power of meddling.

"Towards the evening of the second day we judged ourselves about eight miles from Kurtz's station. I wanted to push on; but the manager looked grave, and told me the navigation up there was so dangerous that it would be advisable, the sun being very low already, to wait where we were till next morning. Moreover, he pointed out that if the warning to approach cautiously were to be followed, we must approach in daylight—not at dusk, or in the dark. This was sensible enough. Eight miles meant nearly three hours' steaming for us, and I could also see suspicious ripples at the upper end of the reach. Nevertheless, I was annoyed beyond expression at the delay, and most unreasonably, too, since one night more could not matter much after so many months. As we had plenty of wood, and caution was the word, I brought up in the middle of the stream. The reach was narrow, straight, with high sides like a railway cutting. The dusk came gliding into it long before the sun had set. The current ran smooth and swift, but a dumb immobility sat on the banks. The living trees, lashed together by the creepers and every living bush of the undergrowth, might have been changed into stone, even to the slenderest twig, to the lightest leaf. It was not sleep—it seemed unnatural, like a state of trance. Not the faintest sound of any kind could be heard. You looked on amazed, and began to suspect yourself of being deaf—then the night came suddenly, and struck you blind as well. About three in the morning some large fish leaped, and the loud splash made me jump as though a gun had been fired. When the sun rose there was a white fog, very warm and clammy, and more blinding than the night. It did not shift or drive; it was just there, standing all round you like something solid. At eight or nine, perhaps, it lifted as a shutter lifts. We had a glimpse of the towering multitude of trees, of the immense matted jungle, with the blazing little ball of the sun hanging over it—all perfectly still—and then the white shutter came down again, smoothly, as if sliding in greased grooves. I ordered the chain, which we had begun to heave in, to be paid out again. Before it stopped running with a muffled rattle, a cry, a very loud cry, as of infinite desolation, soared slowly in the opaque air. It ceased. A complaining clamor, modulated in savage discords, filled our ears. The sheer unexpectedness of it made my hair stir under my cap. I don't know how it struck the others: to me it seemed as though the mist itself had screamed, so suddenly, and apparently from all sides at once, did this tumultuous and mournful uproar arise. It culminated in a hurried outbreak of almost intolerably excessive shrieking, which stopped short, leaving us stiffened in a variety of silly attitudes, and obstinately listening to the nearly as appalling and excessive silence. 'Good God! What is the meaning—' stammered at my elbow one of the pilgrims, a little fat man, with sandy hair and red whiskers, who wore sidespring boots, and pink pajamas tucked into his socks. Two others remained openmouthed a whole minute, then dashed into the little cabin, to rush out incontinently and stand darting scared glances, with Winchesters at 'ready' in their hands. What we could see was just the steamer we were on, her outlines blurred as though she had been on the point of dissolving, and a misty strip of water, perhaps two feet broad, around her—and that was all. The rest of the world was nowhere, as far as our eyes and ears were concerned. Just nowhere. Gone, disappeared; swept off without leaving a whisper or a shadow behind.

"I went forward, and ordered the chain to be hauled in short, so as to be ready to trip the anchor and move the steamboat at once if necessary. 'Will they attack?' whispered an awed voice. 'We will be all butchered in this fog,' murmured another. The faces twitched with the strain, the hands trembled slightly, the eyes forgot to wink. It was very curious to see the contrast of expressions of the white men and of the black fellows of our crew, who were as much strangers to that part of the river as we, though their homes were only eight hundred miles away. The whites, of course greatly discomposed, had besides a curious look of being painfully shocked by such an outrageous row. The others had an alert, naturally interested expression; but their faces were essentially quiet, even those of the one or two who grinned as they hauled at the chain. Several exchanged short, grunting phrases, which seemed to settle the matter to their satisfaction. Their headman, a young, broadchested black, severely draped in dark-blue fringed cloths, with fierce nostrils and his hair all done up artfully in oily ringlets, stood near me. 'Aha!' I said, just for good fellowship's sake. 'Catch 'im,' he snapped, with a bloodshot widening of his eyes and a flash of sharp teeth—'catch 'im. Give 'im to us.' 'To you, eh?' I asked; 'what would you do with them?' 'Eat 'im!' he said, curtly, and, leaning his elbow on the rail, looked out into the fog in a dignified and profoundly pensive attitude. I would no doubt have been properly horrified, had it not occurred to me that he and his chaps must be very hungry: that they must have been growing increasingly hungry for at least this month past. They had been engaged for six months (I don't think a single one of them had any clear idea of time, as we at the end of countless ages have. They still belonged to the beginnings of time—had no inherited experience to teach them as it were), and of course, as long as there was a piece of paper written over in accordance with some farcical law or other made down the river, it didn't enter anybody's head to trouble how they would live. Certainly they had brought with them some rotten hippo meat, which couldn't have lasted very long, anyway even if the pilgrims hadn't, in the midst of a shocking hullabaloo, thrown a considerable quantity of it overboard. It looked like a high-handed proceeding; but it was really a case of legitimate self-defense. You can't breathe dead hippo waking, sleeping, and eating, and at the same time keep your precarious grip on existence. Besides that, they had given them every week three pieces of brass wire, each about nine inches long; and the theory was they were to buy their provisions with that currency in river-side villages. You can see how *that* worked. There were either no villages, or the people were hostile, or the director, who like the rest of us fed out of tins, with an occasional old he-goat thrown in, didn't want to stop the steamer for some more or less recondite reasons. So, unless they swallowed the wire itself, or made loops of it to snare the fishes with, I don't see what good their extravagant salary could be to them. I must say it was paid with a regularity worthy of a large and honorable trading company. For the rest, the only thing to eat—though it didn't look eatable in the least—I saw in their possession was a few lumps of some stuff like half-cooked dough, of a dirty lavender color, they kept wrapped in leaves, and now and then swallowed a piece of, but so small that it seemed done more for the looks of the thing than for any serious purpose of sustenance. Why in the name of all the gnawing devils of hunger they didn't go for us—they were thirty to five—and have a good tuck in for once, amazes me now when I think of it. They were big powerful men, with not much capacity to weigh the consequences, with courage, with strength, even yet, though their skins were no longer glossy and their muscles no longer hard. And I saw that something restraining, one of those human secrets that baffle probability, had come into play there. I looked at them with a swift quickening of interest—not because it occurred to me I might be eaten by them before very long, though I own to you that just then I perceived—in a new light, as it were—how unwholesome the pilgrims looked, and I hoped, yes, I positively hoped, that my aspect was not so—what shall I say?—so—unappetizing: a touch of fantastic vanity which fitted well with the dream-sensation that pervaded all my days at that time. Perhaps I had a little fever, too. One can't live with one's finger everlastingly on one's pulse. I had often 'a little fever,' or a little touch of other things—the playful paw-strokes of the wilderness, the preliminary trifling before the more serious onslaught which came in due course. Yes; I looked at them as you would on any human being, with a curiosity of their impulses, motives, capacities, weaknesses, when brought to the test of an inexorable physical necessity. Restraint! What possible restraint? Was it superstition, disgust, patience, fear—or some kind of primitive honor? No fear can stand up to hunger, no patience can wear it out, disgust simply does not exist where hunger is; and as to superstition, beliefs, and what you may call principles, they are less than chaff in a breeze. Don't you know the devilry of lingering starvation, its exasperating torment, its black thoughts, its somber and brooding ferocity? Well, I do. It takes a man all his inborn strength to fight hunger properly. It's really easier to face bereavement, dishonor, and the perdition of one's soul—than this kind of prolonged hunger. Sad, but true. And these chaps, too, had no earthly reason for any kind of scruple. Restraint! I would just as soon have expected restraint from a hyena prowling amongst the corpses of a battlefield. But there was the fact facing me—the fact dazzling, to be seen, like the foam on the depths of the sea, like a ripple on an unfathomable enigma, a mystery greater—when I thought of it— than the curious, inexplicable note of desperate grief in this savage clamor that had swept by us on the river bank, behind the blind whiteness of the fog.

"Two pilgrims were quarreling in hurried whispers as to which bank. 'Left.' 'No, no; how can you? Right, right, of course.' 'It is very serious,' said the manager's voice behind me; 'I would be desolated if anything should happen to Mr. Kurtz before we came up.' I looked at him, and had not the slightest doubt he was sincere. He was just the kind of man who would wish to preserve appearances. That was his restraint. But when he muttered something about going on at once, I did not even take the trouble to answer him. I knew, and he knew, that it was impossible. Were we to let go our hold of the bottom, we would be absolutely in the air—in space. We wouldn't be able to tell where we were going to—whether up- or down-stream, or across—till we fetched against one bank or the other, and then we wouldn't know at first which it was. Of course I made no move. I had no mind for a smashup. You couldn't imagine a more deadly place for a shipwreck. Whether drowned at once or not, we were sure to perish speedily in one way or another. 'I authorize you to take all the risks,' he said, after a short silence. 'I refuse to take any,' I said, shortly; which was just the answer he expected, though its tone might have surprised him. 'Well, I must defer to your judgment. You are captain,' he said, with marked civility. I turned my shoulder to him in sign of my appreciation, and looked into the fog. How long would it last? It was the most hope-less lookout. The approach to this Kurtz grubbing for ivory in the wretched bush was beset by as many dangers as though he had been an enchanted princess sleeping in a fabulous castle. 'Will they attack, do you think?' asked the manager, in a confidential tone.

"I did not think they would attack, for several obvious reasons. The thick fog was one. If they left the bank in their canoes they would get lost in it, as we would be if we attempted to move. Still, I had also judged the jungle of both banks quite impenetrable—and yet eyes were in it, eyes that had seen us. The riverside bushes were certainly very thick; but the undergrowth behind was evidently pe-netrable. However, during the short lift I had seen no canoes any-where in the reach—certainly not abreast of the steamer. But what made the idea of attack inconceivable to me was the nature of the noise—of the cries we had heard. They had not the fierce character boding of immediate hostile intention. Unexpected, wild, and vio-lent as they had been, they had given me an irresistible impression of sorrow. The glimpse of the steamboat had for some reason filled those savages with unrestrained grief. The danger, if any, I ex-pounded, was from our proximity to a great human passion let loose. Even extreme grief may ultimately vent itself in violence—but more generally takes the form of apathy. . . .

"You should have seen the pilgrims stare! They had no heart to grin, or even to revile me: but I believe they thought me gone mad—with fright, maybe. I delivered a regular lecture. My dear boys, it was no good bothering. Keep a lookout? Well, you may guess I watched the fog for the signs of lifting as a cat watches a mouse; but for anything else our eyes were of no more use to us than if we had been buried miles deep in a heap of cotton-wool. It felt like it, too—choking, warm, stifling. Besides, all I said, though it sounded extravagant, was absolutely true to fact. What we after-wards alluded to as an attack was really an attempt at repulse. The action was very far from being aggressive—it was not even defen-sive, in the ususal sense: it was undertaken under the stress of desperation, and in its essence was purely protective.

"It developed itself, I should say, two hours after the fog lifted, and its commencement was at a spot, roughly speaking, about a mile and a half below Kurtz's station. We had just floundered and flopped round a bend, when I saw an islet, a mere grassy hummock of bright green, in the middle of the stream. It was the only thing of the kind; but as we opened the reach more, I perceived it was the head of a long sandbank, or rather of a chain of shallow patches stretching down the middle of the river. They were discolored, just awash, and the whole lot was seen just under the water, exactly as a man's backbone is seen running down the middle of his back under the skin. Now, as far as I did see, I could go to the right or to the left of this. I didn't know either channel, of course. The banks looked pretty well alike, the depth appeared the same; but as I had been informed the station was on the west side, I naturally headed for the western passage.

"No sooner had we fairly entered it than I became aware it was much narrower than I had supposed. To the left of us there was the long uninterrupted shoal, and to the right a high, steep bank heavily overgrown with bushes. Above the bush the trees stood in serried ranks. The twigs overhung the current thickly, and from distance to distance a large limb of some tree projected rigidly over the stream. It was then well on in the afternoon, the face of the forest was gloomy, and a broad strip of shadow had already fallen on the water. In this shadow we steamed up—very slowly, as you may imagine. I sheered her well inshore—the water being deepest near the bank, as the sounding pole informed me.

"One of my hungry and forbearing friends was sounding in the bows just below me. This steamboat was exactly like a decked scow. On the deck, there were two little teakwood houses, with doors and windows. The boiler was in the fore-end, and the machinery right astern. Over the whole there was a light roof, supported on stanchions. The funnel projected through that roof, and in front of the funnel a small cabin built of light planks served for a pilot house. It contained a couch, two campstools, a loaded Martini-Henry leaning in one corner, a tiny table, and the steering wheel. It had a wide door in front and a broad shutter at each side. All these were always thrown open, of course. I spent my days perched up there on the extreme fore-end of that roof, before the door. At night I slept, or tried to, on the couch. An athletic black belonging to some coast tribe, and educated by my poor predecessor, was the helmsman. He sported a pair of brass earrings, wore a blue cloth wrapper from the waist to the ankles, and thought all the world of himself. He was the most unstable kind of fool I had ever seen. He steered with no end of a swagger while you were by; but if he lost sight of you, he became instantly the prey of an abject funk, and would let that cripple of a steamboat get the upper hand of him in a minute.

"I was looking down at the sounding pole, and feeling much annoyed to see at each try a little more of it stick out of that river, when I saw my poleman give up the business suddenly, and stretch himself flat on the deck, without even taking the trouble to haul his pole in. He kept hold on it though, and it trailed in the water. At the same time the fireman, whom I could also see below me, sat down abruptly before his furnace and ducked his head. I was amazed.

Then I had to look at the river mighty quick, because there was a snag in the fairway. Sticks, little sticks, were flying about—thick: they were whizzing before my nose, dropping below me, striking behind me against my pilot house. All this time the river, the shore, the woods, were very quiet—perfectly quiet. I could only hear the heavy splashing thump of the stern wheel and the patter of these things. We cleared the snag clumsily. Arrows, by Jove! We were being shot at! I stepped in quickly to close the shutter on the land side. That fool helmsman, his hands on the spokes, was lifting his knees high, stamping his feet, champing his mouth, like a reined-in horse. Confound him! And we were staggering within ten feet of the bank. I had to lean right out to swing the heavy shutter, and I saw a face amongst the leaves on the level with my own, looking at me very fierce and steady; and then suddenly, as though a veil had been removed from my eyes, I made out, deep in the tangled gloom, naked breasts, arms, legs, glaring eyes—the bush was swarming with human limbs in movement, glistening, of bronze color. The twigs shook, swayed, and rustled, the arrows flew out of them, and then the shutter came to. 'Steer her straight,' I said to the helmsman. He held his head rigid, face forward; but his eyes rolled, he kept on, lifting and setting down his feet gently, his mouth foamed a little. 'Keep quiet!' I said in a fury. I might just as well have ordered a tree not to sway in the wind. I darted out. Below me there was a great scuffle of feet on the iron deck; confused exclamations; a voice screamed, 'Can you turn back?' I caught sight of a V-shaped ripple on the water ahead. What? Another snag! A fusillade burst out under my feet. The pilgrims had opened with their Winchesters, and were simply squirting lead into that bush. A deuce of a lot of smoke came up and drove slowly forward. I swore at it. Now I couldn't see the ripple or the snag either. I stood in the doorway, peering, and the arrows came in swarms. They might have been poisoned, but they looked as though they wouldn't kill a cat. The bush began to howl. Our woodcutters raised a warlike whoop; the report of a rifle just at my back deafened me. I glanced over my shoulder, and the pilot house was yet full of noise and smoke when I made a dash at the wheel. The fool nigger had dropped everything, to throw the shutter open and let off that Martini-Henry. He stood before the wide opening, glaring, and I yelled at him to come back, while I straightened the sudden twist out of that steamboat. There was no room to turn even if I had wanted to, the snag was somewhere very near ahead in that confounded smoke, there was no time to lose, so I just crowded her into the bank—right into the bank, where I knew the water was deep.

"We tore slowly along the overhanging bushes in a whirl of

broken twigs and flying leaves. The fusillade below stopped short, as I had foreseen it would when the squirts got empty. I threw my head back to a glinting whizz that traversed the pilot house, in at one shutter-hole and out at the other. Looking past that mad helmsman, who was shaking the empty rifle and yelling at the shore, I saw vague forms of men running bent double, leaping, gliding, distinct, incomplete, evanescent. Something big appeared in the air before the shutter, the rifle went overboard, and the man stepped back swiftly, looked at me over his shoulder in an extraordinary, profound, familiar manner, and fell upon my feet. The side of his head hit the wheel twice, and the end of what appeared a long cane clattered round and knocked over a little campstool. It looked as though after wrenching that thing from somebody ashore he had lost his balance in the effort. The thin smoke had blown away, we were clear of the snag, and looking ahead I could see that in another hundred yards or so I would be free to sheer off, away from the bank; but my feet felt so very warm and wet that I had to look down. The man had rolled on his back and stared straight up at me; both his hands clutched that cane. It was the shaft of a spear that, either thrown or lunged through the opening, had caught him in the side just below the ribs; the blade had gone in out of sight, after making a frightful gash; my shoes were full; a pool of blood lay very still, gleaming dark-red under the wheel; his eyes shone with an amazing luster. The fusillade burst out again. He looked at me anxiously, gripping the spear like something precious, with an air of being afraid I would try to take it away from him. I had to make an effort to free my eyes from his gaze and attend to the steering. With one hand I felt above my head for the line of the steam whistle, and jerked out screech after screech hurriedly. The tumult of angry and warlike yells was checked instantly, and then from the depths of the woods went out such a tremulous and prolonged wail of mournful fear and utter despair as may be imagined to follow the flight of the last hope from the earth. There was a great commotion in the bush; the shower of arrows stopped, a few dropping shots rang out sharply—then silence, in which the languid beat of the stern wheel came plainly to my ears. I put the helm hard a-starboard at the moment when the pilgrim in pink pajamas, very hot and agitated, appeared in the doorway. 'The manager sends me—' he began in an official tone, and stopped short. 'Good God!' he said, glaring at the wounded man.

"We two whites stood over him, and his lustrous and inquiring glance enveloped us both. I declare it looked as though he would presently put to us some question in an understandable language; but he died without uttering a sound, without moving a limb, without twitching a muscle. Only in the very last moment, as though in response to some sign we could not see, to some whisper we could not hear, he frowned heavily, and that frown gave to his black death mask an inconceivably somber, brooding, and menacing expression. The luster of inquiring glance faded swiftly into vacant glassiness. 'Can you steer?' I asked the agent eagerly. He looked very dubious; but I made a grab at his arm, and he understood at once I meant him to steer whether or no. To tell you the truth, I was morbidly anxious to change my shoes and socks. 'He is dead,' murmured the fellow, immensely impressed. 'No doubt about it,' said I, tugging like mad at the shoelaces. 'And by the way, I suppose Mr. Kurtz is dead as well by this time.'

"For the moment that was the dominant thought. There was a sense of extreme disappointment, as though I had found out I had been striving after something altogether without a substance. I couldn't have been more disgusted if I had traveled all this way for the sole purpose of talking with Mr. Kurtz. Talking with . . . I flung one shoe oveboard, and became aware that that was exactly what I had been looking forward to—a talk with Kurtz. I made the strange discovery that I had never imagined him as doing, you know, but as discoursing. I didn't say to myself, 'Now I will never see him,' or 'Now I will never shake him by the hand,' but, 'now I will never hear him.' The man presented himself as a voice. Not of course that I did not connect him with some sort of action. Hadn't I been told in all the tones of jealousy and admiration that he had collected, bartered, swindled, or stolen more ivory than all the other agents together? That was not the point. The point was in his being a gifted creature, and that of all his gifts the one that stood out preeminently, that carried with it a sense of real presence, was his ability to talk, his words—the gift of expression, the bewildering, the illuminating, the most exalted and the most contemptible, the pulsating stream of light, or the deceitful flow from the heart of an impenetrable darkness.

"The other shoe went flying unto the devil-god of that river. I thought, by Jove! it's all over. We are too late; he has vanished—the gift has vanished, by means of some spear, arrow, or club. I will never hear that chap speak after all, and my sorrow had a startling extravagance of emotion, even such as I had noticed in the howling sorrow of these savages in the bush. I couldn't have felt more of lonely desolation somehow, had I been robbed of a belief or had missed my destiny in life. . . . Why do you sigh in this beastly way, somebody? Absurd? Well, absurd. Good Lord! mustn't a man ever— Here, give me some tobacco." . . .

There was a pause of profound stillness, then a match flared, and

930 THE MODERN NOVELLA

Marlow's lean face appeared, worn, hollow, with downward folds and dropped eyelids, with an aspect of concentrated attention; and as he took vigorous draws at his pipe, it seemed to retreat and advance out of the night in the regular flicker of the tiny flame. The match went out.

"Absurd!" he cried. "This is the worst of trying to tell. . . . Here you all are, each moored with two good addresses, like a hulk with two anchors, a butcher round one corner, a policeman round another, excellent appetites, and temperature normal—you hear— normal from year's end to year's end. And you say, Absurd! Absurd be—exploded! Absurd! My dear boys, what can you expect from a man who out of sheer nervousness had just flung overboard a pair of new shoes! Now I think of it, it is amazing I did not shed tears. I am, upon the whole, proud of my fortitude. I was cut to the quick at the idea of having lost the inestimable privilege of listening to the gifted Kurtz. Of course I was wrong. The privilege was waiting for me. Oh, yes, I heard more than enough. And I was right, too. A voice. He was very little more than a voice. And I heard—him—it— this voice—other voices—all of them were so little more than voices—and the memory of that time itself lingers around me, im- palpable, like a dying vibration of one immense jabber, silly, atro- cious, sordid, savage, or simply mean, without any kind of sense. Voices, voices—even the girl herself—now—"

He was silent for a long time.

"I laid the ghost of his gifts at last with a lie," he began suddenly. "Girl! What? Did I mention a girl? Oh, she is out of it—completely. They—the women I mean—are out of it—should be out of it. We must help them to stay in that beautiful world of their own, lest ours gets worse. Oh, she had to be out of it. You should have heard the disinterred body of Mr. Kurtz saying, 'My Intended.' You would have perceived directly then how completely she was out of it. And the lofty frontal bone of Mr. Kurtz! They say the hair goes on grow- ing sometimes, but this—ah—specimen, was impressively bald. The wilderness had patted him on the head, and, behold, it was like a ball—an ivory ball; it had caressed him, and—lo!—he had withered; it had taken him, loved him, embraced him, got into his veins, consumed his flesh, and sealed his soul to its own by the inconceivable ceremonies of some devilish initiation. He was its spoiled and pampered favorite. Ivory? I should think so. Heaps of it, stacks of it. The old mud shanty was bursting with it. You would think there was not a single tusk left either above or below the ground in the whole country. 'Mostly fossil,' the manager had remarked, disparagingly. It was no more fossil than I am; but they call it fossil when it is dug up. It appears these niggers do bury the tusks sometimes—but evidently they couldn't bury this parcel deep enough to save the gifted Mr. Kurtz from his fate. We filled the steamboat with it, and had to pile a lot on the deck. Thus he could see and enjoy as long as he could see, because the appreciation of his favor had remained with him to the last. You should have heard him say, 'My ivory.' Oh yes, I heard him. 'My Intended, my ivory, my station, my river, my—' everything belonged to him. It made me hold my breath in expectation of hearing the wilderness burst into a prodigious peal of laughter that would shake the fixed stars in their places. Everything belonged to him—but that was a trifle. The thing was to know what he belonged to, how many powers of darkness claimed him for their own. That was the reflection that made you creepy all over. It was impossible—it was not good for one either—trying to imagine. He had taken a high seat amongst the devils of the land—I mean literally. You can't understand. How could you?—with solid pavement under your feet, surrounded by kind neighbors ready to cheer you or to fall on you, stepping delicately between the butcher and the policeman, in the holy terror of scandal and gallows and lunatic asylums—how can you imagine what particular region of the first ages a man's untrammeled feet may take him into by the way of solitude—utter solitude without a policeman—by the way of silence—utter silence, where no warning voice of a kind neighbor can be heard whispering of public opinion? These little things make all the great difference. When they are gone you must fall back upon your own innate strength, upon your own capacity for faithfulness. Of course you may be too much of a fool to go wrong—too dull even to know you are being assaulted by the powers of darkness. I take it, no fool ever made a bargain for his soul with the devil: the fool is too much of a fool, or the devil too much of a devil—I don't know which. Or you may be such a thunderingly exalted creature as to be altogether deaf and blind to anything but heavenly sights and sounds. Then the earth for you is only a standing place—and whether to be like this is your loss or your gain I won't pretend to say. But most of us are neither one nor the other. The earth for us is a place to live in, where we must put up with sights, with sounds, with smells, too, by Jove!—breathe dead hippo, so to speak, and not be contaminated. And there, don't you see? Your strength comes in, the faith in your ability for the digging of unostentatious holes to bury the stuff in—your power of devotion, not to yourself, but to an obscure, back-breaking business. And that's difficult enough. Mind, I am not trying to excuse or even explain—I am trying to account to myself for—for—Mr. Kurtz—for the shade of Mr. Kurtz. This initiated wraith from the back of Nowhere honored me with its amazing confidence before it vanished altogether. This was because it could speak English to me. The original Kurtz had been educated partly in England, and—as he was good enough to say himself—his sympathies were in the right place. His mother was half-English, his father was half-French. All Europe contributed to the making of Kurtz; and by and by I learned that, most appropriately, the International Society for the Suppression of Savage Customs had intrusted him with the making of a report, for its future guidance. And he had written it, too. I've seen it. I've read it. It was eloquent, vibrating with eloquence, but too high-strung, I think. Seventeen pages of close writing he had found time for! But this must have been before his—let us say—nerves, went wrong, and caused him to preside at certain midnight dances ending with unspeakable rites, which—as far as I reluctantly gathered from what I heard at various times— were offered up to him—do you understand?—to Mr. Kurtz himself. But it was a beautiful piece of writing. The opening paragraph, however, in the light of later information, strikes me now as ominous. He began with the argument that we whites, from the point of development we had arrived at, 'must necessarily appear to them [savages] in the nature of supernatural beings—we approach them with the might as of a deity,' and so on, and so on. 'By the simple exercise of our will we can exert a power for good practically unbounded,' etc., etc. From that point he soared and took me with him. The peroration was magnificent, though difficult to remember, you know. It gave me the notion of an exotic Immensity ruled by an august Benevolence. It made me tingle with enthusiasm. This was the unbounded power of eloquence—of words—of burning noble words. There were no practical hints to interrupt the magic current of phrases, unless a kind of note at the foot of the last page, scrawled evidently much later, in an unsteady hand, may be regarded as the exposition of a method. It was very simple, and at the end of that moving appeal to every altruistic sentiment it blazed at you, luminous and terrifying, like a flash of lightning in a serene sky: 'Exterminate all the brutes!' The curious part was that he had apparently forgotten all about that valuable postscriptum, because, later on, when he in a sense came to himself, he repeatedly entreated me to take good care of 'my pamphlet' (he called it), as it was sure to have in the future a good influence upon his career. I had full information about all these things, and, besides, as it turned out, I was to have the care of his memory. I've done enough for it to give me the indisputable right to lay it, if I choose, for an everlasting rest in the dust bin of progress, amongst all the sweepings and, figuratively speaking, all the dead cats of civilization. But then, you see, I can't choose. He won't be forgotten. Whatever he was, he was not common. He had the power to charm or frighten rudimentary

souls into an aggravated witch dance in his honor; he could also fill
the small souls of the pilgrims with bitter misgivings: he had one
devoted friend at least, and he had conquered one soul in the world
that was neither rudimentary nor tainted with self-seeking. No; I
can't forget him, though I am not prepared to affirm the fellow was
exactly worth the life we lost in getting to him. I missed my late
helmsman awfully—I missed him even while his body was still lying in the pilot house. Perhaps you will think it passing strange this
regret for a savage who was no more account than a grain of sand in
a black Sahara. Well, don't you see, he had done something, he had
steered; for months I had him at my back—a help—an instrument. It
was a kind of partnership. He steered for me—I had to look after
him, I worried about his deficiencies, and thus a subtle bond had
been created, of which I only became aware when it was suddenly
broken. And the intimate profundity of that look he gave me when
he received his hurt remains to this day in my memory—like a claim
of distant kinship affirmed in a supreme moment.

"Poor fool! If he had only left that shutter alone. He had no restraint, no restraint—just like Kurtz—a tree swayed by the wind. As
soon as I had put on a dry pair of slippers, I dragged him out, after
first jerking the spear out of his side, which operation I confess I
performed with my eyes shut tight. His heels leaped together over
the little doorstep; his shoulders were pressed to my breast; I
hugged him from behind desperately. Oh! he was heavy, heavy;
heavier than any man on earth, I should imagine. Then without
more ado I tipped him overboard. The current snatched him as
though he had been a wisp of grass, and I saw the body roll over
twice before I lost sight of it forever. All the pilgrims and the manager were then congregated on the awning deck about the pilot
house, chattering at each other like a flock of excited magpies, and
there was a scandalized murmur at my heartless promptitude. What
they wanted to keep that body hanging about for I can't guess.
Embalm it, maybe. But I had also heard another, and a very ominous, murmur on the deck below. My friends the woodcutters were
likewise scandalized, and with a better show of reason—though I
admit that the reason itself was quite inadmissible. Oh, quite! I had
made up my mind that if my late helmsman was to be eaten, the
fishes alone should have him. He had been a very second-rate
helmsman while alive, but now he was dead he might have become
a first-class temptation, and possibly cause some startling trouble.
Besides, I was anxious to take the wheel, the man in pink pajamas
showing himself a hopeless duffer at the business.

"This I did directly the simple funeral was over. We were going
half-speed, keeping right in the middle of the stream, and I listened

to the talk about me. They had given up Kurtz, they had given up the station; Kurtz was dead, and the station had been burnt—and so on—and so on. The red-haired pilgrim was beside himself with the thought that at least this poor Kurtz had been properly avenged. 'Say! We must have made a glorious slaughter of them in the bush. Eh? What do you think? Say?' He positively danced, the bloodthirsty little gingery beggar. And he had nearly fainted when he saw the wounded man! I could not help saying, 'You made a glorious lot of smoke, anyhow.' I had seen, from the way the tops of the bushes rustled and flew, that almost all the shots had gone too high. You can't hit anything unless you take aim and fire from the shoulder; but these chaps fired from the hip with their eyes shut. The retreat, I maintained—and I was right—was caused by the screeching of the steam whistle. Upon this they forgot Kurtz, and began to howl at me with indignant protests.

"The manager stood by the wheel murmuring confidentially about the necessity of getting well away down the river before dark at all events, when I saw in the distance a clearing on the river side and the outlines of some sort of building. 'What's this?' I asked. He clapped his hands in wonder. 'That station!' he cried. I edged in at once, still going half-speed.

"Through my glasses I saw the slope of a hill interspersed with rare trees and perfectly free from undergrowth. A long decaying building on the summit was half buried in the high grass; the large holes in the peaked roof gaped black from afar; the jungle and the woods made a background. There was no enclosure or fence of any kind; but there had been one apparently, for near the house half-a-dozen slim posts remained in a row, roughly trimmed, and with their upper ends ornamented with round carved balls. The rails, or whatever there had been between, had disappeared. Of course the forest surrounded all that. The river bank was clear, and on the water side I saw a white man under a hat like a cart wheel beckoning persistently with his whole arm. Examining the edge of the forest above and below, I was almost certain I could see movements—human forms gliding here and there. I steamed past prudently, then stopped the engines and let her drift down. The man on the shore began to shout, urging us to land. 'We have been attacked,' screamed the manager. 'I know—I know. It's all right,' yelled back the other, as cheerful as you please. 'Come along. It's all right. I am glad.'

"His aspect reminded me of something I had seen—something funny I had seen somewhere. As I maneuvered to get alongside, I was asking myself, 'What does this fellow look like?' Suddenly I got it. He looked like a harlequin. His clothes had been made of some stuff that was brown holland probably, but it was covered with patches all over, with bright patches, blue, red, and yellow—patches on the back, patches on the front, patches on elbows, on knees; colored binding around his jacket, scarlet edging at the bottom of his trousers; and the sunshine made him look extremely gay and wonderfully neat withal, because you could see how beautifully all this patching had been done. A beardless, boyish face, very fair, no features to speak of, nose peeling, little blue eyes, smiles and frowns chasing each other over that open countenance like sunshine and shadow on a wind-swept plain. 'Look out, captain!' he cried; 'there's a snag lodged in here last night.' What! Another snag? I confess I swore shamefully. I had nearly holed my cripple, to finish off that charming trip. The harlequin on the bank turned his little pug nose up to me. 'You English?' he asked, all smiles. 'Are you?' I shouted from the wheel. The smiles vanished, and he shook his head as if sorry for my disappointment. Then he brightened up. 'Never mind!' he cried, encouragingly. 'Are we in time?' I asked. 'He is up there,' he replied, with a toss of the head up the hill, and becoming gloomy all of a sudden. His face was like the autumn sky, overcast one moment and bright the next.

"When the manager, escorted by the pilgrims, all of them armed to the teeth, had gone to the house this chap came on board. 'I say, I don't like this. These natives are in the bush,' I said. He assured me earnestly it was all right. 'They are simple people,' he added; 'well, I am glad you came. It took me all my time to keep them off.' 'But you said it was all right,' I cried. 'Oh, they meant no harm,' he said; and as I stared he corrected himself, 'Not exactly.' Then vivaciously, 'My faith, your pilot house wants a clean-up!' In the next breath he advised me to keep enough steam on the boiler to blow the whistle in case of any trouble. 'One good screech will do more for you than all your rifles. They are simple people,' he repeated. He rattled away at such a rate he quite overwhelmed me. He seemed to be trying to make up for lots of silence, and actually hinted, laughing, that such was the case. 'Don't you talk with Mr. Kurtz?' I said. 'You don't talk with that man—you listen to him,' he exclaimed with severe exaltation. 'But now—" He waved his arm, and in the twinkling of an eye was in the uttermost depths of despondency. In a moment he came up again with a jump, possessed himself of both my hands, shook them continuously, while he gabbled: 'Brother sailor . . . honor . . . pleasure . . . delight . . . introduce myself . . . Russian . . . son of an arch-priest . . . Government of Tambov. . . . What? Tobacco! English tobacco; the excellent English tobacco! Now, that's brotherly. Smoke? Where's a sailor that does not smoke?'

"The pipe soothed him, and gradually I made out he had run

away from school, had gone to sea in a Russian ship; ran away again; served some time in English ships; was now reconciled with the arch-priest. He made a point of that. 'But when one is young one must see things, gather experience, ideas; enlarge the mind.' 'Here!' I interrupted, 'You can never tell! Here I met Mr. Kurtz,' he said, youthfully solemn and reproachful. I held my tongue after that. It appears he had persuaded a Dutch trading house on the coast to fit him out with stores and goods, and had started for the interior with a light heart, and no more idea of what would happen to him than a baby. He had been wandering about that river for nearly two years alone, cut off from everybody and everything. 'I am not so young as I look. I am twenty-five,' he said. 'At first old Van Shuyten would tell me to go to the devil,' he narrated with keen enjoyment; 'but I stuck to him, and talked and talked, till at last he got afraid I would talk the hind leg off his favorite dog, so he gave me some cheap things and a few guns, and told me he hoped he would never see my face again. Good old Dutchman, Van Shuyten. I've sent him one small lot of ivory a year ago, so that he can't call me a little thief when I get back. I hope he got it. And for the rest I don't care. I had some wood stacked for you. That was my old house. Did you see?'

"I gave him Towson's book. He made as though he would kiss me, but restrained himself. 'The only book I had left, and I thought I had lost it,' he said, looking at it ecstatically. 'So many accidents happen to a man going about alone, you know. Canoes get upset sometimes—and sometimes you've got to clear out so quick when the people get angry.' He thumbed the pages. 'You made notes in Russian?' I asked. He nodded. 'I thought they were written in cipher,' I said. He laughed, then became serious. 'I had lots of trouble to keep these people off,' he said. 'Did they want to kill you?' I asked. 'Oh, no!' he cried, and checked himself. 'Why did they attack us?' I pursued. He hesitated, then said shamefacedly, 'They don't want him to go.' 'Don't they?' I said curiously. He nodded a nod full of mystery and wisdom. 'I tell you,' he cried, 'this man has enlarged my mind.' He opened his arms wide, staring at me with his little blue eyes that were perfectly round."

### III

"I looked at him, lost in astonishment. There he was before me, in motley, as though he had absconded from a troupe of mimes, enthusiastic, fabulous. His very existence was improbable, inexplicable, and altogether bewildering. He was an insoluble problem. It was inconceivable how he had existed, how he had succeeded in getting so far, how he had managed to remain—why he did not instantly disappear. 'I went a little farther,' he said, 'then still a little farther—till I had gone so far that I don't know how I'll ever get back. Never mind. Plenty time. I can manage. You take Kurtz away quick—quick—I tell you.' The glamor of youth enveloped his parti-colored rags, his destitution, his loneliness, the essential desolation of his futile wanderings. For months—for years—his life hadn't been worth a day's purchase; and there he was gallantly, thought-lessly alive, to all appearance indestructible solely by the virtue of his few years and of his unreflecting audacity. I was seduced into something like admiration—like envy. Glamor urged him on, gla-mor kept him unscathed. He surely wanted nothing from the wilderness but space to breathe in and to push on through. His need was to exist, and to move onwards at the greatest possible risk, and with a maximum of privation. If the absolutely pure, uncalculat-ing, unpractical spirit of adventure had ever ruled a human being, it ruled this bepatched youth. I almost envied him the possession of this modest and clear flame. It seemed to have consumed all thought of self so completely, that even while he was talking to you, you forgot that it was he—the man before your eyes—who had gone through these things. I did not envy him his devotion to Kurtz, though. He had not meditated over it. It came to him, and he ac-cepted it with a sort of eager fatalism. I must say that to me it appeared about the most dangerous thing in every way he had come upon so far.

"They had come together unavoidably, like two ships becalmed near each other, and lay rubbing sides at last. I suppose Kurtz wanted an audience, because on a certain occasion, when encamped in the forest, they had talked all night, or more probably Kurtz had talked. 'We talked of everything,' he said, quite transported at the recollection. 'I forgot there was such a thing as sleep. The night did not seem to last an hour. Everything! Everything! . . . Of love, too.' 'Ah, he talked to you of love!' I said, much amused. 'It isn't what you think,' he cried, almost passionately. 'It was in general. He made me see things—things.'

"He threw his arms up. We were on deck at the time, and the headman of my woodcutters, lounging near by, turned upon him his heavy and glittering eyes. I looked around, and I don't know why, but I assure you that never, never before, did this land, this river, this jungle, the very arch of this blazing sky, appear to me so hopeless and so dark, so impenetrable to human thought, so pitiless to human weakness. 'And, ever since, you have been with him, of course?' I said.

"On the contrary. It appears their intercourse had been very much broken by various causes. He had, as he informed me proudly, managed to nurse Kurtz through two illnesses (he alluded to it as you would to some risky feat), but as a rule Kurtz wandered alone, far in the depths of the forest. 'Very often coming to this station, I had to wait days and days before he would turn up,' he said. 'Ah, it was worth waiting for!—sometimes.' 'What was he doing? Exploring or what?' I asked. 'Oh, yes, of course'; he had discovered lots of villages, a lake, too—he did not know exactly in what direction; it was dangerous to inquire too much—but mostly his expeditions had been for ivory. 'But he had not goods to trade with by that time,' I objected. 'There's a good lot of cartridges left even yet,' he answered, looking away. 'To speak plainly, he raided the country,' I said. He nodded. 'Not alone, surely!' He muttered something about the villages round that lake. 'Kurtz got the tribe to follow him, did he?' I suggested. He fidgeted a little. 'They adored him,' he said. The tone of these words was so extraordinary that I looked at him searchingly. It was curious to see his mingled eagerness and reluctance to speak of Kurtz. The man filled his life, occupied his thoughts, swayed his emotions. 'What can you expect?' he burst out; 'he came to them with thunder and lightning, you know—and they had never seen anything like it—and very terrible. He could be very terrible. You can't judge Mr. Kurtz as you would an ordinary man. No, no, no! Now—just to give you an idea—I don't mind telling you, he wanted to shoot me, too, one day—but I don't judge him.' 'Shoot you!' I cried. 'What for?' 'Well, I had a small lot of ivory the chief of that village near my house gave me. You see I used to shoot game for them. Well, he wanted it, and wouldn't hear reason. He declared he would shoot me unless I gave him the ivory and then cleared out of the country, because he could do so, and had a fancy for it, and there was nothing on earth to prevent him killing whom he jolly well pleased. And it was true, too. I gave him the ivory. What did I care! But I didn't clear out. No, no. I couldn't leave him. I had to be careful, of course, till we got friendly again for a time. He had his second illness then. Afterwards I had to keep out of the way; but I didn't mind. He was living for the most part in those villages on the lake. When he came down to the river, sometimes he would take to me, and sometimes it was better for me to be careful. This man suffered too much. He hated all this, and somehow he couldn't get away. When I had a chance I begged him to try and leave while there was time; I offered to go back with him. And he would say yes, and then he would remain; go off on another ivory hunt; disappear for weeks; forget himself amongst these people—forget himself—you know.' 'Why! he's mad,' I said. He protested indignantly. Mr. Kurtz couldn't be mad. If I had heard him talk, only two days ago, I wouldn't dare hint at such a thing. . . . I had taken up my binoculars while we talked, and was looking at the shore, sweeping the limit of the forest at each side and at the back of the house. The consciousness of there being people in that bush, so silent, so quiet—as silent and quiet as the ruined house on the hill—made me uneasy. There was no sign on the face of nature of this amazing tale that was not so much told as suggested to me in desolate exclamations, completed by shrugs, in interrupted phrases, in hints ending in deep sighs. The woods were unmoved, like a mask—heavy, like the closed door of a prison—they looked with their air of hidden knowledge, of patient expectation, of unapproachable silence. The Russian was explaining to me that it was only lately that Mr. Kurtz had come down to the river, bringing along with him all the fighting men of that lake tribe. He had been absent for several months—getting himself adored, I suppose—and had come down unexpectedly, with the intention to all appearances of making a raid either across the river or downstream. Evidently the appetite for more ivory had got the better of the—what shall I say?—less material aspirations. However he had got much worse suddenly. 'I heard he was lying helpless, and so I came up—took my chance,' said the Russian. 'Oh, he is bad, very bad.' I directed my glass to the house. There were no signs of life, but there was the ruined roof, the long mud wall peeping above the grass, with three little square window holes, no two of the same size; all this brought within reach of my hand, as it were. And then I made a brusque movement, and one of the remaining posts of that vanished fence leaped up in the field of my glass. You remember I told you I had been struck at the distance by certain attempts at ornamentation, rather remarkable in the ruinous aspect of the place. Now I had suddenly a nearer view, and its first result was to make me throw my head back as if before a blow. Then I went carefully from post to post with my glass, and I saw my mistake. These round knobs were not ornamental but symbolic; they were expressive and puzzling, striking and disturbing—food for thought and also for the vultures if there had been any looking down from the sky; but at all events for such ants as were industrious enough to ascend the pole. They would have been even more impressive, those heads on the stakes, if their faces had not been turned to the house. Only one, the first I had made out, was facing my way. I was not so shocked as you may think. The start back I had given was really nothing but a movement of surprise. I had expected to see a knob of wood there, you know. I returned deliberately to the first I had seen—and there it was, black, dried, sunken, with closed eyelids, a head that seemed to sleep at the top of that pole, and, with the shrunken dry lips showing a narrow white line of the teeth, was smiling, too, smiling continuously at some endless and jocose dream of that eternal slumber.

"I am not disclosing any trade secrets. In fact, the manager said afterwards that Mr. Kurtz's methods had ruined the district. I have no opinion on that point, but I want you clearly to understand that there was nothing exactly profitable in these heads being there. They only showed that Mr. Kurtz lacked restraint in the gratificaiton of his various lusts, that there was something wanting in him— some small matter which, when the pressing need arose, could not be found under his magnificent eloquence. Whether he knew of this deficiency himself I can't say. I think the knowledge came to him at last—only at the very last. But the wilderness had found him out early, and had taken on him a terrible vengeance for the fantastic invasion. I think it had whispered to him things about himself which he did not know, things of which he had no conception till he took counsel with this great solitude—and the whisper had proved irresistibly fascinating. It echoed loudly within him because he was hollow at the core. . . . I put down the glass, and the head that had appeared near enough to be spoken to seemed at once to have leaped away from me into inaccessible distance.

"The admirer of Mr. Kurtz was a bit crestfallen. In a hurried, indistinct voice he began to assure me he had not dared to take these—say, symbols—down. He was not afraid of the natives; they would not stir till Mr. Kurtz gave the word. His ascendancy was extraordinary. The camps of these people surrounded the place, and the chiefs came every day to see him. They would crawl. . . . 'I don't want to know anything of the ceremonies used when approaching Mr. Kurtz,' I shouted. Curious, this feeling that came over me that such details would be more intolerable than those heads drying on the stakes under Mr. Kurtz's windows. After all, that was only a savage sight, while I seemed at one bound to have been transported into some lightless region of subtle horrors, where pure, uncompli- cated savagery was a positive relief, being something that had a right to exist—obviously—in the sunshine. The young man looked at me with surprise. I suppose it did not occur to him that Mr. Kurtz was no idol of mine. He forgot I hadn't heard any of these splendid monologues on, what was it? On love, justice, conduct of life—or whatnot. If it had come to crawling before Mr. Kurtz, he crawled as much as the veriest savage of them all. I had no idea of the condi- tions, he said: these heads were the heads of rebels. I shocked him excessively by laughing. Rebels! What would be the next definition I was to hear? There had been enemies, criminals, workers—and these were rebels. Those rebellious heads looked very subdued to me on their sticks. 'You don't know how such a life tries a man like Kurtz,' cried Kurtz's last disciple. 'Well, and you?' I said. 'I! I! I am a simple man. I have no great thoughts. I want nothing from any-body. How can you compare me to? . . .' His feelings were too much for speech, and suddenly he broke down. 'I don't under-stand,' he groaned. 'I've been doing my best to keep him alive, and that's enough. I had no hand in all this. I have no abilities. There hasn't been a drop of medicine or a mouthful of invalid food for months here. He was shamefully abandoned. A man like this, with such ideas. Shamefully! Shamefully! I—I—haven't slept for the last ten nights. . . .'

"His voice lost itself in the calm of the evening. The long shadows of the forest had slipped downhill while we talked, had gone far beyond the ruined hovel, beyond the symbolic row of stakes. All this was in the gloom, while we down there were yet in the sun-shine, and the stretch of the river abreast of the clearing glittered in a still and dazzling splendor, with a murky and overshadowed bend above and below. Not a living soul was seen on the shore. The bushes did not rustle.

"Suddenly round the corner of the house a group of men ap-peared, as though they had come up from the ground. They waded waist-deep in the grass, in a compact body, bearing an improvised stretcher in their midst. Instantly, in the emptiness of the landscape, a cry arose whose shrillness pierced the still air like a sharp arrow flying straight to the very heart of the land; and, as if by enchant-ment, streams of human beings—of naked human beings—with spears in their hands, with bows, with shields, with wild glances and savage movements, were poured into the clearing by the dark-faced and pensive forest. The bushes shook, the grass swayed for a time, and then everything stood still in attentive immobility.

" 'Now, if he does not say the right thing to them we are all done for,' said the Russian at my elbow. The knot of men with the stretcher had stopped, too, halfway to the steamer, as if petrified. I saw the man on the stretcher sit up, lank and with an uplifted arm, above the shoulders of the bearers. 'Let us hope that the man who can talk so well of love in general will find some particular reason to spare us this time,' I said. I resented bitterly the absurd danger of our situation, as if to be at the mercy of that atrocious phantom had been a dishonoring necessity. I could not hear a sound, but through my glasses I saw the thin arm extended commandingly, the lower jaw moving, the eyes of that apparition shining darkly far in its bony head that nodded with grotesque jerks. Kurtz—Kurtz—that means short in German—don't it? Well, the name was as true as everything else in his life—and death. He looked at least seven feet long. His covering had fallen off, and his body emerged from it pitiful and appalling as from a winding sheet. I could see the cage of his ribs all astir, the bones of his arm waving. It was as though an animated image of death carved out of old ivory had been shaking its hand with menaces at a motionless crowd of men made of dark and glittering bronze. I saw him open his mouth wide—it gave him a weirdly voracious aspect, as though he had wanted to swallow all the air, all the earth, all the men before him. A deep voice reached me faintly. He must have been shouting. He fell back suddenly. The stretcher shook as the bearers staggered forward again, and almost at the same time I noticed that the crowd of savages was vanishing without any perceptible movement of retreat, as if the forest that had ejected these beings so suddenly had drawn them in again as the breath is drawn in a long aspiration.

"Some of the pilgrims behind the stretcher carried his arms—two shotguns, a heavy rifle, and a light revolver carbine—the thunderbolts of that pitiful Jupiter. The manager bent over him murmuring as he walked beside his head. They laid him down in one of the little cabins—just a room for a bedplace and a camp-stool or two, you know. We had brought his belated correspondence, and a lot of torn envelopes and open letters littered his bed. His hand roamed feebly amongst these papers. I was struck by the fire of his eyes and the composed languor of his expression. It was not so much the exhaustion of disease. He did not seem in pain. This shadow looked satiated and calm, as though for the moment it had had its fill of all the emotions.

"He rustled one of the letters, and looking straight in my face said, 'I am glad.' Somebody had been writing to him about me. These special recommendations were turning up again. The volume of tone he emitted without effort, almost without the trouble of moving his lips, amazed me. A voice! a voice! It was grave, profound, vibrating, while the man did not seem capable of a whisper. However, he had enough strength in him—factitious no doubt—to very nearly make an end of us, as you shall hear directly.

"The manager appeared silently in the doorway; I stepped out at once and he drew the curtain after me. The Russian, eyed curiously by the pilgrims, was staring at the shore. I followed the direction of his glance.

"Dark human shapes could be made out in the distance, flitting indistinctly against the gloomy border of the forest, and near the river two bronze figures, leaning on tall spears, stood in the sunlight under fantastic headdresses of spotted skins, warlike and still in statuesque repose. And from right to left along the lighted shore moved a wild and gorgeous apparition of a woman.

"She walked with measured steps, draped in striped and fringed cloths, treading the earth proudly, with a slight jingle and flash of barbarous ornaments. She carried her head high; her hair was done in the shape of a helmet; she had brass leggings to the knee, brass wire gauntlets to the elbow, a crimson spot on her tawny cheek, innumerable necklaces of glass beads on her neck; bizarre things, charms, gifts of witch men, that hung about her, glittered and trembled at every step. She must have had the value of several elephant tusks upon her. She was savage and superb, wild-eyed and magnificent; there was something ominous and stately in her deliberate progress. And in the hush that had fallen suddenly upon the whole sorrowful land, the immense wilderness, the colossal body of the fecund and mysterious life seemed to look at her, pensive, as though it had been looking at the image of its own tenebrous and passionate soul.

"She came abreast of the steamer, stood still, and faced us. Her long shadow fell to the water's edge. Her face had a tragic and fierce aspect of wild sorrow and of dumb pain mingled with the fear of some struggling, half-shaped resolve. She stood looking at us without a stir, and like the wilderness itself, with an air of brooding over an inscrutable purpose. A whole minute passed, and then she made a step forward. There was a low jingle, a glint of yellow metal, a sway of fringed draperies, and she stopped as if her heart had failed her. The young fellow by my side growled. The pilgrims murmured at my back. She looked at us all as if her life had depended upon the unswerving steadiness of her glance. Suddenly she opened her bared arms and threw them up rigid above her head, as though in an uncontrollable desire to touch the sky, and at the same time the swift shadows darted out on the earth, swept around on the river, gathering the steamer into a shadowy embrace. A formidable silence hung over the scene.

"She turned away slowly, walked on, following the bank, and passed into the bushes to the left. Once only her eyes gleamed back at us in the dusk of the thickets before she disappeared.

" 'If she had offered to come aboard I really think I would have tried to shoot her,' said the man of patches, nervously. 'I had been risking my life every day for the last fortnight to keep her out of the house. She got in one day and kicked up a row about those miserable rags I picked up in the storeroom to mend my clothes with. I wasn't decent. At least it must have been that, for she talked like a fury to Kurtz for an hour, pointing at me now and then. I don't understand the dialect of this tribe. Luckily for me, I fancy Kurtz felt too ill that day to care, or there would have been mischief. I don't understand. . . . No—it's too much for me. Ah, well, it's all over now.'

"At this moment I heard Kurtz's deep voice behind the curtain:

'Save me!—save the ivory, you mean. Don't tell me. Save *me!* Why, I've had to save you. You are interrupting my plans now. Sick! Sick! Not so sick as you would like to believe. Never mind. I'll carry my ideas out yet—I will return. I'll show you what can be done. You with your little peddling notions—you are interfering with me. I will return. I . . .'

"The manager came out. He did me the honor to take me under the arm and lead me aside. 'He is very low, very low,' he said. He considered it necessary to sigh, but neglected to be consistently sorrowful. 'We have done all we could for him—haven't we? But there is no disguising the fact, Mr. Kurtz has done more harm than good to the Company. He did not see the time was not ripe for vigorous action. Cautiously, cautiously—that's my principle. We must be cautious yet. The district is closed to us for a time. Deplorable! Upon the whole, the trade will suffer. I don't deny there is a remarkable quantity of ivory—mostly fossil. We must save it, at all events—but look how precarious the position is—and why? Because the method is unsound.' 'Do you,' said I, looking at the shore, 'call it "unsound method?" ' 'Without doubt,' he exclaimed, hotly. 'Don't you?' . . .

" 'No method at all,' I murmured after a while. 'Exactly,' he exulted. 'I anticipated this. Shows a complete want of judgment. It is my duty to point it out in the proper quarter.' 'Oh,' said I, 'that fellow—what's his name?—the brickmaker, will make a readable report for you.' He appeared confounded for a moment. It seemed to me I had never breathed an atmosphere so vile, and I turned mentally to Kurtz for relief—positively for relief. 'Nevertheless I think Mr. Kurtz is a remarkable man,' I said with emphasis. He started, dropped on me a cold heavy glance, said very quietly, 'he *was*,' and turned his back on me. My hour of favor was over; I found myself lumped along with Kurtz as a partisan of methods for which the time was not ripe: I was unsound! Ah! but it was something to have at least a choice of nightmares.

"I had turned to the wilderness really, not to Mr. Kurtz, who, I was ready to admit, was as good as buried. And for a moment it seemed to me as if I also were buried in a vast grave full of unspeakable secrets. I felt an intolerable weight oppressing my breast, the smell of the damp earth, the unseen presence of victorious corruption, the darkness of an impenetrable night. . . . The Russian tapped me on the shoulder. I heard him mumbling and stammering something about 'brother seaman—couldn't conceal—knowledge of matters that would affect Mr. Kurtz's reputation.' I waited. For him evidently Mr. Kurtz was not in his grave; I suspect that for him Mr.

Kurtz was one of the immortals. 'Well!' said I at last, 'speak out. As it happens, I am Mr. Kurtz's friend—in a way.'

"He stated with a good deal of formality that had we not been 'of the same profession,' he would have kept the matter to himself without regard to consequences. 'He suspected there was an active ill will towards him on the part of these white men that—' 'You are right,' I said, remembering a certain conversation I had overheard. 'The manager thinks you ought to be hanged.' He showed a concern at this intelligence which amused me at first. 'I had better get out of the way quietly,' he said, earnestly. 'I can do no more for Kurtz now, and they would soon find some excuse. What's to stop them? There's a military post three hundred miles from here.' 'Well, upon my word,' said I, 'perhaps you had better go if you have any friends amongst the savages near by.' 'Plenty,' he said. 'They are simple people—and I want nothing, you know.' He stood biting his lip, then: 'I don't want any harm to happen to these whites here, but of course I was thinking of Mr. Kurtz's reputation—but you are a brother seaman and—' 'All right,' said I, after a time. 'Mr. Kurtz's reputation is safe with me.' I did not know how truly I spoke.

"He informed me, lowering his voice, that it was Kurtz who had ordered the attack to be made on the steamer. 'He hated sometimes the idea of being taken away—and then again . . . But I don't understand these matters. I am a simple man. He thought it would scare you away—that you would give it up, thinking him dead. I could not stop him. Oh, I had an awful time of it this last month.' 'Very well,' I said. 'He is all right now.' 'Ye-e-es,' he muttered, not very convinced apparently. 'Thanks,' said I; 'I shall keep my eyes open.' 'But quiet—eh?' he urged, anxiously. 'It would be awful for his reputation if anybody here—' I promised a complete discretion with great gravity. 'I have a canoe and three black fellows waiting not very far. I am off. Could you give me a few Martini-Henry cartridges?' I could, and did, with proper secrecy. He helped himself, with a wink at me, to a handful of my tobacco. 'Between sailors—you know—good English tobacco.' At the door of the pilot house he turned round—'I say, haven't you a pair of shoes you could spare?' He raised one leg. 'Look.' The soles were tied with knotted strings sandal-wise under his bare feet. I rooted out an old pair, at which he looked with admiration before tucking it under his left arm. One of his pockets (bright red) was bulging with cartridges, from the other (dark blue) peeped 'Towson's Inquiry,' etc., etc. He seemed to think himself excellently well equipped for a renewed encounter with the wilderness. 'Ah! I'll never, never meet such a man again. You ought to have heard him recite poetry—his own, too, it was, he told me. Poetry!' He rolled his eyes at the recollection of these delights. 'Oh, he enlarged my mind!' 'Goodby,' said I. He shook hands and vanished in the night. Sometimes I ask myself whether I had every really seen him—whether it was possible to meet such a phenomenon! . . .

"When I woke up shortly after midnight his warning came to my mind with its hint of danger that seemed, in the starred darkness, real enough to make me get up for the purpose of having a look round. On the hill a big fire burned, illuminating fitfully a crooked corner of the station house. One of the agents with a picket of a few of our blacks, armed for the purpose, was keeping guard over the ivory; but deep within the forest, red gleams that wavered, that seemed to sink and rise from the ground amongst confused columnar shapes of intense blackness, showed the exact position of the camp where Mr. Kurtz's adorers were keeping their uneasy vigil. The monotonous beating of a big drum filled the air with muffled shocks and a lingering vibration. A steady droning sound of many men chanting each to himself some weird incantation came out from the black, flat wall of the woods as the humming of bees comes out of a hive, and had a strange narcotic effect upon my half-awake senses. I believe I dozed off leaning over the rail, till an abrupt burst of yells, an overwhelming outbreak of a pent-up and mysterious frenzy, woke me up in a bewildered wonder. It was cut short all at once, and the low droning went on with an effect of audible and soothing silence. I glanced casually into the little cabin. A light was burning within, but Mr. Kurtz was not there.

"I think I would have raised an outcry if I had believed my eyes. But I didn't believe them at first—the thing seemed so impossible. The fact is I was completely unnerved by a sheer blank fright, pure abstract terror, unconnected with any distinct shape of physical danger. What made this emotion so overpowering was—how shall I define it?—the moral shock I received, as if something altogether monstrous, intolerable to thought and odious to the soul, had been thrust upon me unexpectedly. This lasted of course the merest fraction of a second, and then the usual sense of commonplace, deadly danger, the possibility of a sudden onslaught and massacre, or something of the kind, which I saw impending, was positively welcome and composing. It pacified me, in fact, so much, that I did not raise an alarm.

"There was an agent buttoned up inside an ulster and sleeping on a chair on deck within three feet of me. The yells had not awakened him; he snored very slightly; I left him to his slumbers and leaped ashore. I did not betray Mr. Kurtz—it was ordered I should never betray him—it was written I should be loyal to the nightmare of my

choice. I was anxious to deal with this shadow by myself alone—
and to this day I don't know why I was so jealous of sharing with
anyone the peculiar blackness of that experience.

"As soon as I got on the bank I saw a trail—a broad trail through
the grass. I remember the exultation with which I said to myself,
'He can't walk—he is crawling on all fours—I've got him.' The grass
was wet with dew. I strode rapidly with clenched fists. I fancy I had
some vague notion of falling upon him and giving him a drubbing.
I don't know. I had some imbecile thoughts. The knitting old
woman with the cat obtruded herself upon my memory as a most
improper person to be sitting at the other end of such an affair. I
saw a row of pilgrims squirting lead in the air out of Winchesters
held to the hip. I thought I would never get back to the steamer, and
imagined myself living alone and unarmed in the woods to an advanced age. Such silly things—you know. And I remember I confounded the beat of the drum with the beating of my heart, and was
pleased at its calm regularity.

"I kept to the track though—then stopped to listen. The night was
very clear; a dark blue space, sparkling with dew and starlight, in
which black things stood very still. I thought I could see a kind of
motion ahead of me. I was strangely cocksure of everything that
night. I actually left the track and ran in a wide semicircle (I truly
believe chuckling to myself) so as to get in front of that stir, of that
motion I had seen—if indeed I had seen anything. I was circum-
venting Kurtz as though it had been a boyish game.

"I came upon him, and, if he had not heard me coming, I would
have fallen over him, too, but he got up in time. He rose, unsteady,
long, pale, indistinct, like a vapor exhaled by the earth, and swayed
slightly, misty and silent before me; while at my back the fires
loomed between the trees, and the murmur of many voices issued
from the forest. I had cut him off cleverly; but when actually confronting him I seemed to come to my senses, I saw the danger in its
right proportion. It was by no means over yet. Suppose he began to
shout? Though he could hardly stand, there was still plenty of vigor
in his voice. 'Go away—hide yourself,' he said, in that profound
tone. It was very awful. I glanced back. We were within thirty yards
from the nearest fire. A black figure stood up, strode on long black
legs, waving long black arms, across the glow. It had horns—ante-
lope horns, I think—on its head. Some sorcerer, some witch man,
no doubt: it looked fiend-like enough. 'Do you know what you are
doing?' I whispered. 'Perfectly,' he answered, raising his voice for
that single word: it sounded to me far off and yet loud, like a hail
through a speaking trumpet. If he makes a row we are lost, I
thought to myself. This clearly was not a case for fisticuffs, even

apart from the very natural aversion I had to beat that Shadow—this wandering and tormented thing. 'You will be lost,' I said—'utterly lost.' One gets sometimes such a flash of inspiration, you know. I did say the right thing, though indeed he could not have been more irretrievably lost than he was at this very moment, when the foundations of our intimacy were being laid—to endure—to endure—even to the end—even beyond.

" 'I had immense plans,' he muttered irresolutely. 'Yes,' said I; 'but if you try to shout I'll smash your head with—' There was not a stick or a stone near. 'I will throttle you for good,' I corrected myself. 'I was on the threshold of great things,' he pleaded, in a voice of longing, with a wistfulness of tone that made my blood run cold. 'And now for this stupid scoundrel—' 'Your success in Europe is assured in any case,' I affirmed, steadily. I did not want to have the throttling of him, you understand—and indeed it would have been very little use for any practical purpose. I tried to break the spell—the heavy, mute spell of the wilderness—that seemed to draw him to its pitiless breast by the awakening of forgotten and brutal instincts, by the memory of gratified and monstrous passions. This alone, I was convinced, had driven him out to the edge of the forest, to the bush, towards the gleam of fires, the throb of drums, the drone of weird incantations; this alone had beguiled his unlawful soul beyond the bounds of permitted aspirations. And, don't you see, the terror of the position was not in being knocked on the head—though I had a very lively sense of that danger, too—but in this, that I had to deal with a being to whom I could not appeal in the name of anything high or low. I had, even like the niggers, to invoke him—himself—his own exalted and incredible degradation. There was nothing either above or below him, and I knew it. He had kicked himself loose of the earth. Confound the man! he had kicked the very earth to pieces. He was alone, and I before him did not know whether I stood on the ground or floated in the air. I've been telling you what we said—repeating the phrases we pronounced—but what's the good? They were common everyday words—the familiar, vague sounds exchanged on every waking day of life. But what of that? They had behind them, to my mind, the terrific suggestiveness of words heard in dreams, of phrases spoken in nightmares. Soul! If anybody had ever struggled with a soul, I am the man. And I wasn't arguing with a lunatic either. Believe me or not, his intelligence was perfectly clear—concentrated, it is true, upon himself with horrible intensity, yet clear; and therein was my only chance—barring, of course, the killing him there and then, which wasn't so good, on account of unavoidable noise. But his soul was mad. Being alone in the wilderness, it had looked within itself, and, by heavens! I tell you, it had gone mad. I had—for my sins, I suppose—to go through the ordeal of looking into it myself. No eloquence could have been so withering to one's belief in mankind as his final burst of sincerity. He struggled with himself, too. I saw it, I heard it. I saw the inconceivable mystery of a soul that knew no restraint, no faith, and no fear, yet struggling blindly with itself. I kept my head pretty well; but when I had him at last stretched on the couch, I wiped my forehead, while my legs shook under me as though I had carried half a ton on my back down that hill. And yet I had only supported him, his bony arm clasped round my neck—and he was not much heavier than a child.

"When next day we left at noon, the crowd, of whose presence behind the curtain of trees I had been acutely conscious all the time, flowed out of the woods again, filled the clearing, covered the slope with a mass of naked, breathing quivering, bronze bodies. I steamed up a bit, then swung downstream, and two thousand eyes followed the evolutions of the splashing, thumping, fierce river-demon beating the water with its terrible tail and breathing black smoke into the air. In front of the first rank, along the river, three men, plastered with bright red earth from head to foot, strutted to and fro restlessly. When we came abreast again, they faced the river, stamped their feet, nodded their horned heads, swayed their scarlet bodies; they shook towards the fierce river-demon a bunch of black feathers, a mangy skin with a pendent tail—something that looked like a dried gourd; they shouted periodically together strings of amazing words that resembled no sounds of human language; and the deep murmurs of the crowd, interrupted suddenly, were like the responses of some satanic litany.

"We had carried Kurtz into the pilot house: there was more air there. Lying on the couch, he stared through the open shutter. There was an eddy in the mass of human bodies, and the woman with helmeted head and tawny cheeks rushed out to the very brink of the stream. She put out her hands, shouted something, and all that wild mob took up the shout in a roaring chorus of articulated, rapid, breathless utterance.

" 'Do you understand this?' I asked.

"He kept on looking out past me with fiery, longing eyes, with a mingled expression of wistfulness and hate. He made no answer, but I saw a smile, a smile of indefinable meaning, appear on his colorless lips that a moment after twitched convulsively. 'Do I not?' he said slowly, gasping, as if the words had been torn out of him by a supernatural power. "I pulled the string of the whistle, and I did this because I saw the pilgrims on deck getting out their rifles with an air of anticipating a jolly lark. At the sudden screech there was a

movement of abject terror through that wedged mass of bodies.
'Don't! Don't you frighten them away,' cried someone on deck dis-
consolately. I pulled the string time after time. They broke and ran,
they leaped, they crouched, they swerved, they dodged the flying
terror of the sound. The three red chaps had fallen flat, face down on
the shore, as though they had been shot dead. Only the barbarous
and superb woman did not so much as flinch, and stretched tragically her bare arms after us over the somber and glittering river.

"And then that imbecile crowd down on the deck started their
little fun, and I could see nothing more for smoke.

"The brown current ran swiftly out of the heart of darkness, bearing us down towards the sea with twice the speed of our upward
progress; and Kurtz's life was running swiftly, too, ebbing, ebbing
out of his heart into the sea of inexorable time. The manager was
very placid, he had no vital anxieties now, he took us both in with a
comprehensive and satisfied glance: the 'affair' had come off as well
as could be wished. I saw the time approaching when I would be
left alone of the party of 'unsound method.' The pilgrims looked
upon me with disfavor. I was, so to speak, numbered with the dead.
It is strange how I accepted this unforeseen partnership, this choice
of nightmares forced upon me in the tenebrous land invaded by
these mean and greedy phantoms.

"Kurtz discoursed. A voice! a voice! It rang deep to the very last.
It survived his strength to hide in the magnificent folds of eloquence
the barren darkness of his heart. Oh, he struggled! he struggled!
The wastes of his weary brain were haunted by shadowy images
now—images of wealth and fame revolving obsequiously round his
unextinguishable gift of noble and lofty expression. My Intended,
my station, my career, my ideas—these were the subjects for the
occasional utterances of elevated sentiments. The shade of the original Kurtz frequented the bedside of the hollow sham, whose fate it
was to be buried presently in the mold of primeval earth. But both
the diabolic love and the unearthly hate of the mysteries it had
penetrated fought for the possession of that soul satiated with
primitive emotions, avid of lying fame, of sham distinction, of all
the appearances of success and power.

"Sometimes he was contemptibly childish. He desired to have
kings meet him at railway stations on his return from some ghastly
Nowhere, where he intended to accomplish great things. 'You show
them you have in you something that is really profitable, and then
there will be no limits to the recognition of your ability,' he would
say. 'Of course you must take care of the motives—right motives—
always.' The long reaches that were like one and the same reach,

monotonous bends that were exactly alike, slipped past the steamer with their multitude of secular trees looking patiently after this grimy fragment of another world, the forerunner of change, of conquest, of trade, of massacres, of blessings. I looked ahead—piloting. 'Close the shutter,' said Kurtz suddenly one day; 'I can't bear to look at this.' I did so. There was a silence. 'Oh, but I will wring your heart yet!' he cried at the invisible wilderness.

"We broke down—as I had expected—and had to lie-up for repairs at the head of an island. This delay was the first thing that shook Kurtz's confidence. One morning he gave me a packet of papers and a photograph—the lot tied together with a shoestring. 'Keep this for me,' he said. 'This noxious fool' (meaning the manager) 'is capable of prying into my boxes when I am not looking.' In the afternoon I saw him. He was lying on his back with closed eyes, and I withdrew quietly, but I heard him mutter, 'Live rightly, die, die. . . .' I listened. There was nothing more. Was he rehearsing some speech in his sleep, or was it a fragment of a phrase from some newspaper article? He had been writing for the papers and meant to do so again, 'for the furthering of my ideas. It's a duty.'

"His was an impenetrable darkness. I looked at him as you peer down at a man who is lying at the bottom of a precipice where the sun never shines. But I had not much time to give him, because I was helping the engine driver to take to pieces the leaky cylinders, to straighten a bent connecting rod, and in other such matters. I lived in an infernal mess of rust, filings, nuts, bolts, spanners, hammers, ratchet drills—things I abominate, because I don't get on with them. I tended the little forge we fortunately had aboard; I toiled wearily in a wretched scrapheap—unless I had the shakes too bad to stand.

"One evening coming in with a candle I was startled to hear him say a little tremulously, 'I am lying here in the dark waiting for death.' The light was within a foot of his eyes. I forced myself to murmur, 'Oh, nonsense!' and stood over him as if transfixed.

"Anything approaching the change that came over his features I have never seen before, and hope never to see again. Oh, I wasn't touched. I was fascinated. It was as though a veil had been rent. I saw on that ivory face the expression of somber pride, of ruthless power, of craven terror—of an intense and hopeless despair. Did he live his life again in every detail of desire, temptation, and surrender during that supreme moment of complete knowledge? He cried in a whisper at some image, at some vision—he cried out twice, a cry that was no more than a breath: 'The horror! The horror!'

"I blew the candle out and left the cabin. The pilgrims were dining in the messroom, and I took my place opposite the manager, who lifted his eyes to give me a questioning glance, which I successfully ignored. He leaned back, serene, with that peculiar smile of his sealing the unexpressed depths of his meanness. A continuous shower of small flies streamed upon the lamp, upon the cloth, upon our hands and faces. Suddenly the manager's boy put his insolent black head in the doorway, and said in a tone of scathing contempt—

"Mistah Kurtz—he dead.'

"All the pilgrims rushed out to see. I remained, and went on with my dinner. I believe I was considered brutally callous. However, I did not eat much. There was a lamp in there—light, don't you know—and outside it was so beastly, beastly dark. I went no more near the remarkable man who had pronounced a judgment upon the adventures of his soul on this earth. The voice was gone. What else had been there? But I am of course aware that next day the pilgrims buried something in a muddy hole.

"And then they very nearly buried me.

"However, as you see, I did not go to join Kurtz there and then. I did not. I remained to dream the nightmare out to the end, and to show my loyalty to Kurtz once more. Destiny. My destiny! Droll thing life is—that mysterious arrangement of merciless logic for a futile purpose. The most you can hope from it is some knowledge of yourself—that comes too late—a crop of unextinguishable regrets. I have wrestled with death. It is the most unexciting contest you can imagine. It takes place in an impalpable grayness, with nothing underfoot, with nothing around, without spectators, without clamor, without glory, without the great desire of victory, without the great fear of defeat, in a sickly atmosphere of tepid skepticism, without much belief in your own right, and still less in that of your adversary. If such is the form of ultimate wisdom, then life is a greater riddle than some of us think it to be. I was within a hair's-breadth of the last opportunity for pronouncement, and I found with humiliation that probably I would have nothing to say. This is the reason why I affirm that Kurtz was a remarkable man. He had something to say. He said it. Since I had peeped over the edge myself, I understand better the meaning of his stare, that could not see the flame of the candle, but was wide enough to embrace the whole universe, piercing enough to penetrate all the hearts that beat in the darkness. He had summed up—he had judged. 'The horror!' He was a remarkable man. After all, this was the expression of some sort of belief; it had candor, it had conviction, it had a vibrating note of revolt in its whisper, it had the appalling face of a glimpsed truth—the strange commingling of desire and hate. And it is not my own extremity I remember best—a vision of grayness without form filled with physical pain, and a careless contempt for the evanescence of all things—even of this pain itself. No! It is his extremity that I seem to have lived through. True, he had made that last stride, he had stepped over the edge, while I had been permitted to draw back my hesitating foot. And perhaps in this is the whole difference; perhaps all the wisdom, and all truth, and all sincerity, are just compressed into that inappreciable moment of time in which we step over the threshold of the invisible. Perhaps! I like to think my summing-up would not have been a word of careless contempt. Better his cry—much better. It was an affirmation, a moral victory paid for by innumerable defeats, by abominable terrors, by abominable satisfactions. But it was a victory! That is why I have remained loyal to Kurtz to the last, and even beyond, when a long time after I heard once more, not his own voice, but the echo of his magnificent eloquence thrown to me from a soul as translucently pure as a cliff of crystal.

"No, they did not bury me, though there is a period of time which I remember mistily, with a shuddering wonder, like a passage through some inconceivable world that had no hope in it and no desire. I found myself back in the sepulchral city resenting the sight of people hurrying through the streets to filch a little money from each other, to devour their infamous cookery, to gulp their unwholesome beer, to dream their insignificant and silly dreams. They trespassed upon my thoughts. They were intruders whose knowledge of life was to me an irritating pretense, because I felt so sure they could not possibly know the things I knew. Their bearing, which was simply the bearing of commonplace individuals going about their business in the assurance of perfect safety, was offensive to me like the outrageous flauntings of folly in the face of a danger it is unable to comprehend. I had no particular desire to enlighten them, but I had some difficulty in restraining myself from laughing in their faces, so full of stupid importance. I daresay I was not very well at that time. I tottered about the streets—there were various affairs to settle—grinning bitterly at perfectly respectable persons. I admit my behavior was inexcusable, but then my temperature was seldom normal in these days. My dear aunt's endeavors to 'nurse up my strength' seemed altogether beside the mark. It was not my strength that wanted nursing, it was my imagination that wanted soothing. I kept the bundle of papers given me by Kurtz, not knowing exactly what to do with it. His mother had died lately, watched over, as I was told, by his Intended. A clean-shaved man, with an official manner and wearing gold-rimmed spectacles, called on me one day and made inquiries, at first circuitous, afterwards suavely pressing, about what he was pleased to denominate certain 'documents.' I was not surprised, because I had had two rows with the manager on the subject out there. I had refused to give up the smallest scrap out of that package, and I took the same attitude with the spectacled man. He became darkly menacing at last, and with much heat argued that the company had the right to every bit of information about its 'territories.' And said he, 'Mr. Kurtz's knowledge of unexplored regions must have been necessarily extensive and peculiar—owing to his great abilities and to the deplorable circumstances in which he had been placed: therefore—' I assured him Mr. Kurtz's knowledge, however extensive, did not bear upon the problems of commerce or administration. He invoked then the name of science. 'It would be an incalculable loss if,' etc., etc. I offered him the report on the 'Suppression of Savage Customs,' with the postscriptum torn off. He took it up eagerly, but ended by sniffing at it with an air of contempt. 'This is not what we had a right to expect,' he remarked. 'Expect nothing else,' I said. 'There are only private letters.' He withdrew upon some threat of legal proceedings, and I saw him no more; but another fellow, calling himself Kurtz's cousin, appeared two days later, and was anxious to hear all the details about his dear relative's last moments. Incidentally he gave me to understand that Kurtz had been essentially a great musician. 'There was the making of an immense success,' said the man, who was an organist, I believe, with lank gray hair flowing over a greasy coat collar. I had no reason to doubt his statement; and to this day I am unable to say what was Kurtz's profession, whether he ever had any—which was the greatest of his talents. I had taken him for a painter who wrote for the papers, or else for a journalist who could paint—but even the cousin (who took snuff during the interview) could not tell me what he had been—exactly. He was a universal genius—on that point I agreed with the old chap, who thereupon blew his nose noisily into a large cotton handkerchief and withdrew in senile agitation, bearing off some family letters and memoranda without importance. Ultimately a journalist anxious to know something of the fate of his 'dear colleague' turned up. This visitor informed me Kurtz's proper sphere ought to have been politics 'on the popular side.' He had furry straight eyebrows, bristly hair cropped short, an eyeglass on a broad ribbon, and, becoming expansive, confessed his opinion that Kurtz really couldn't write a bit—'but heavens! how that man could talk. He electrified large meetings. He had faith—don't you see?—he had the faith. He could get himself to believe anything—anything. He would have been a splendid leader of an extreme party.' 'What party?' I asked. 'Any party,' answered the other. 'He was an—an—extremist.' Did I not think so? I assented. Did I know, he asked, with a sudden flash of curiosity, 'what it was that had induced him to go out there?' 'Yes,' said I, and forthwith handed him the famous report for publication, if he thought fit. He glanced through it hurriedly, mumbling all the time, judged 'it would do,' and took himself off with this plunder.

"Thus I was left at last with a slim packet of letters and the girl's portrait. She struck me as beautiful—I mean she had a beautiful expression. I know that the sunlight can be made to lie, too, yet one felt that no manipulation of light and pose could have conveyed the delicate shade of truthfulness upon those features. She seemed ready to listen without mental reservation, without suspicion, without a thought for herself. I concluded I would go and give her back her portrait and those letters myself. Curiosity? Yes; and also some other feeling perhaps. All that had been Kurtz's had passed out of my hands: his soul, his body, his station, his plans, his ivory, his career. There remained only his memory and his Intended—and I wanted to give that up, too, to the past, in a way—to surrender personally all that remained of him with me to that oblivion which is the last word of our common fate. I don't defend myself. I had no clear perception of what it was I really wanted. Perhaps it was an impulse of unconscious loyalty, or the fulfilment of one of these ironic necessities that lurk in the facts of human existence. I don't know. I can't tell. But I went.

"I thought his memory was like the other memories of the dead that accumulate in every man's life—a vague impress on the brain of shadows that had fallen on it in their swift and final passage; but before the high and ponderous door, between the tall houses of a street as still and decorous as a well-kept alley in a cemetery, I had a vision of him on the stretcher, opening his mouth voraciously, as if to devour all the earth with all its mankind. He lived then before me; he lived as much as he had ever lived—a shadow insatiable of splendid appearances, of frightful realities; a shadow darker than the shadow of the night, and draped nobly in the folds of a gorgeous eloquence. The vision seemed to enter the house with me—the stretcher, the phantom-bearers, the wild crowd of obedient worshipers, the gloom of the forests, the glitter of the reach between the murky bends, the beat of the drum, regular and muffled like the beating of a heart—the heart of a conquering darkness. It was a moment of triumph for the wilderness, an invading and vengeful rush which, it seemed to me, I would have to keep back alone for the salvation of another soul. And the memory of what I had heard him say afar there, with the horned shapes stirring at my back, in the glow of fires, within the patient woods, those broken phrases came back to me, were heard again in their ominous and terrifying simplicity. I remembered his abject pleading, his abject threats, the colossal scale of his vile desires, the meanness, the torment, the tempestuous anguish of his soul. And later on I seemed to see his collected languid manner, when he said one day, 'This lot of ivory now is really mine. The company did not pay for it. I collected it myself at a very great personal risk. I am afraid they will try to claim it as theirs though. H'm. It is a difficult case. What do you think I ought to do—resist? Eh? I want no more than justice. . . . He wanted no more than justice—no more than justice. I rang the bell before a mahogany door on the first floor, and while I waited he seemed to stare at me out of the glassy panel—stare with that wide and immense stare embracing, condemning, loathing all the universe. I seemed to hear the whispered cry, 'The horror! The horror!'

"The dusk was falling. I had to wait in a lofty drawing room with three long windows from floor to ceiling that were like three luminous and bedraped columns. The bent gilt legs and backs of the furniture shone in indistinct curves. The tall marble fireplace had a cold and monumental whiteness. A grand piano stood massively in a corner; with dark gleams on the flat surfaces like a somber and polished sarcophagus. A high door opened—closed, I rose.

"She came forward, all in black, with a pale head, floating towards me in the dusk. She was in mourning. It was more than a year since his death, more than a year since the news came; she seemed as though she would remember and mourn forever. She took both my hands in hers and murmured, 'I had heard you were coming.' I noticed she was not very young—I mean not girlish. She had a mature capacity for fidelity, for belief, for suffering. The room seemed to have grown darker, as if all the sad light of the cloudy evening had taken refuge on her forehead. This fair hair, this pale visage, this pure brow, seemed surrounded by an ashy halo from which the dark eyes looked out at me. Their glance was guileless, profound, confident, and trustful. She carried her sorrowful head as though she were proud of that sorrow, as though she would say, I— I alone know how to mourn for him as he deserves. But while we were still shaking hands, such a look of awful desolation came upon her face that I perceived she was one of those creatures that are not the playthings of Time. For her he had died only yesterday. And, by Jove! the impression was so powerful that for me, too, he seemed to have died only yesterday—nay, this very minute. I saw her and him in the same instant of time—his death and her sorrow—I saw her sorrow in the very moment of his death. Do you understand? I saw them together—I heard them together. She had said, with a deep catch of the breath, 'I have survived' while my strained ears seemed to hear distinctly, mingled with her tone of despairing regret, the summing-up whisper of his eternal condemnation. I asked myself what I was doing there, with a sensation of panic in my heart as though I had blundered into a place of cruel and absurd mysteries not fit for a human being to behold. She motioned me to a chair. We sat down. I laid the packet gently on the little table, and she put her hand over it. . . . 'You knew him well,' she murmured, after a moment of mourning silence.

" 'Intimacy grows quickly out there,' I said. 'I knew him as well as it is possible for one man to know another.'

" 'And you admired him,' she said. 'It was impossible to know him and not to admire him. Was it?'

" 'He was a remarkable man,' I said, unsteadily. Then before the appealing fixity of her gaze, that seemed to watch for more words on my lips, I went on, 'It was impossible not to—'

" 'Love him,' she finished eagerly, silencing me into an appalled dumbness. 'How true! how true! But when you think that no one knew him so well as I! I had all his noble confidence. I knew him best.'

" 'You knew him best,' I repeated. And perhaps she did. But with every word spoken the room was growing darker, and only her forehead, smooth and white, remained illumined by the unextinguishable light of belief and love.

" 'You were his friend,' she went on. 'His friend,' she repeated, a little louder. 'You must have been, if he had given you this, and sent you to me. I feel I can speak to you—and oh! I must speak. I want you—you who have heard his last words—to know I have been worthy of him. . . . It is not pride. . . . Yes! I am proud to know I understood him better than anyone on earth—he told me so himself. And since his mother died I have had no one—no one—to—to—'

"I listened. The darkness deepened. I was not even sure whether he had given me the right bundle. I rather suspect he wanted me to take care of another batch of his papers which, after his death, I saw the manager examining under the lamp. And the girl talked, easing her pain in the certitude of my sympathy; she talked as thirsty men drink. I had heard that her engagement with Kurtz had been disapproved by her people. He wasn't rich enough or something. And indeed I don't know whether he had not been a pauper all his life. He had given me some reason to infer that it was his impatience of comparative poverty that drove him out there.

" '. . . Who was not his friend who had heard him speak once?' she was saying. 'He drew men towards him by what was best in them.' She looked at me with intensity. 'It is the gift of the great,' she went on, and the sound of her low voice seemed to have the accompaniment of all the other sounds, full of mystery, desolation, and sorrow, I had ever heard—the ripple of the river, the soughing of the trees swayed by the wind, the murmurs of the crowds, the faint ring of incomprehensible words cried from afar, the whisper of a voice speaking from beyond the threshold of an eternal darkness. 'But you have heard him! You know! she cried.

" 'Yes, I know,' I said with something like despair in my heart, but bowing my head before the faith that was in her, before that great and saving illusion that shone with an unearthly glow in the darkness, in the triumphant darkness from which I could not have defended her—from which I could not even defend myself.

" 'What a loss to me—to us!'—she corrected herself with beautiful generosity; then added in a murmur, 'To the world.' By the last gleams of twilight I could see the glitter of her eyes, full of tears—of tears that would not fall.

" 'I have been very happy—very fortunate—very proud,' she went on. 'Too fortunate. Too happy for a little while. And now I am unhappy for—for life."

"She stood up; her fair hair seemed to catch all the remaining light in a glimmer of gold. I rose, too.

" 'And of all this,' she went on, mournfully, 'of all his promise, and of all his greatness, of his generous mind, of his noble heart, nothing remains—nothing but a memory. You and I—'

" 'We shall always remember him,' I said, hastily.

" 'No!' she cried. 'It is impossible that all this should be lost—that such a life should be sacrificed to leave nothing—but sorrow. You know what vast plans he had. I knew of them, too—I could not perhaps understand—but others knew of them. Something must remain. His words, at least have not died.'

" 'His words will remain,' I said.

" 'And his example,' she whispered to herself. 'Men looked up to him—his goodness shone in every act. His example—'

" 'True,' I said; 'his example, too. Yes, his example. I forgot that.'

" 'But I do not. I cannot—I cannot believe—not yet. I cannot believe that I shall never see him again, that nobody will see him again, never, never, never.'

"She put out her arms as if after a retreating figure, stretching them back and with clasped pale hands across the fading and narrow sheen of the window. Never see him! I saw him clearly enough then. I shall see this eloquent phantom as long as I live, and I shall see her, too, a tragic and familiar Shade, resembling in this gesture another one, tragic also, and bedecked with powerless charms, stretching bare brown arms over the glitter of the infernal stream, the stream of darkness. She said suddenly very low, 'He died as he lived.'

" 'His end,' said I, with dull anger stirring in me, 'was in every way worthy of his life.'

" 'And I was not with him,' she murmured. My anger subsided before a feeling of infinite pity.

" 'Everything that could be done—' I mumbled.

" 'Ah, but I believed in him more than anyone on earth—more than his own mother, more than—himself. He needed me! Me! I would have treasured every sigh, every word, every sign, every glance.'

"I felt like a chill grip on my chest. 'Don't,' I said, in a muffled voice.

" 'Forgive me. I—I—have mourned so long in silence—in silence. . . . You were with him—to the last? I think of his loneliness. Nobody near to understand him as I would have understood. Perhaps no one to hear. . . .'

" 'To the very end,' I said, shakily. 'I heard his very last words. . . .' I stopped in a fright.

" 'Repeat them,' she murmured in a heartbroken tone. 'I want—I want—something—something—to—to live with.'

"I was on the point of crying at her, 'Don't you hear them?' The dusk was repeating them in a persistent whisper all around us, in a whisper that seemed to swell menacingly like the first whisper of a rising wind. 'The horror! the horror!'

" 'His last word—to live with,' she insisted. 'Don't you understand I loved him—I loved him—I loved him!'

"I pulled myself together and spoke slowly.

" 'The last word he pronounced was—your name.'

"I heard a light sigh and then my heart stood still, stopped dead short by an exulting and terrible cry, by the cry of inconceivable triumph and of unspeakable pain. 'I knew it—I was sure!' . . . She knew. She was sure. I heard her weeping; she had hidden her face in her hands. It seemed to me that the house would collapse before I could escape, that the heavens would fall upon my head. But nothing happened. The heavens do not fall for such a trifle. Would they have fallen, I wonder, if I had rendered Kurtz that justice which was his due? Hadn't he said he wanted only justice? But I couldn't. I could not tell her. It would have been too dark—too dark altogether. . . ."

Marlow ceased, and sat apart, indistinct and silent, in the pose of a meditating Buddha. Nobody moved for a time. "We have lost the first of the ebb," said the director, suddenly. I raised my head. The offing was barred by a black bank of clouds, and the tranquil waterway leading to the uttermost ends of the earth flowed somber under an overcast sky—seemed to lead into the heart of an immense darkness.

# FRANZ KAFKA

1883–1924

He was born in Prague, Czechoslovakia, to Jewish parents, and went to German schools in Prague. His father, the son of a butcher, was a tall, strong patriarch, who built a large and successful wholesale clothing business in Prague. In 1901 Kafka began studying at the German University in Prague, obtaining his doctorate in jurisprudence there in 1906. Two years later he found a job with the Workers' Accident Insurance Company that allowed him some time to write. He was engaged twice and fathered a child whose existence was kept from him. He never married. In 1912 he began to write his most serious work. In 1917 he was diagnosed as tubercular, and his health declined steadily from then until his death in 1924. In 1919 two volumes of his stories were published: *A Country Doctor* and *In the Penal Colony*. On his death he left the manuscripts of three nearly finished novels and many diaries and stories, with instructions that they should all be destroyed. His wishes were not obeyed, and the novels *Amerika*, *The Castle*, and *The Trial*, along with many other works, were saved for publication, bringing him posthumous fame.

# The Metamorphosis

I

As Gregor Samsa awoke one morning from uneasy dreams he found himself transformed in his bed into a gigantic insect. He was lying on his hard, as it were armor-plated, back and when he lifted his head a little he could see his dome-like brown belly divided into stiff arched segments on top of which the bed quilt could hardly keep in position and was about to slide off completely. His numerous legs, which were pitifully thin compared to the rest of his bulk, waved helplessly before his eyes.

What has happened to me? he thought. It was no dream. His room, a regular human bedroom, only rather too small, lay quiet between the four familiar walls. Above the table on which a collection of cloth samples was unpacked and spread out—Samsa was a commercial traveler—hung the picture which he had recently cut out of an illustrated magazine and put into a pretty gilt frame. It showed a lady, with a fur cap on and a fur stole, sitting upright and holding out to the spectator a huge fur muff into which the whole of her forearm had vanished!

Gregor's eyes turned next to the window, and the overcast sky—

one could hear rain drops beating on the window gutter—made him quite melancholy. What about sleeping a little longer and forgetting all this nonsense, he thought, but it could not be done, for he was accustomed to sleep on his right side and in his present condition he could not turn himself over. However violently he forced himself towards his right side he always rolled on to his back again. He tried it at least a hundred times, shutting his eyes to keep from seeing his struggling legs, and only desisted when he began to feel in his side a faint dull ache he had never experienced before.

Oh God, he thought, what an exhausting job I've picked on! Traveling about day in, day out. It's much more irritating work than doing the actual business in the office, and on top of that there's the trouble of constant traveling, of worrying about train connections, the bed and irregular meals, casual acquaintances that are always new and never become intimate friends. The devil take it all! He felt a slight itching up on his belly; slowly pushed himself on his back nearer to the top of the bed so that he could lift his head more easily; identified the itching place which was surrounded by many small white spots the nature of which he could not understand and made to touch it with a leg, but drew the leg back immediately, for the contact made a cold shiver run through him.

He slid down again into his former position. This getting up early, he thought, makes one quite stupid. A man needs his sleep. Other commercials live like harem women. For instance, when I come back to the hotel of a morning to write up the orders I've got, these others are only sitting down to breakfast. Let me just try that with my chief; I'd be sacked on the spot. Anyhow, that might be quite a good thing for me, who can tell? If I didn't have to hold my hand because of my parents I'd have given notice long ago, I'd have gone to the chief and told him exactly what I think of him. That would knock him endways from his desk! It's a queer way of doing, too, this sitting on high at a desk and talking down to employees, especially when they have to come quite near because the chief is hard of hearing. Well, there's still hope; once I've saved enough money to pay back my parents' debts to him—that should take another five or six years—I'll do it without fail. I'll cut myself completely loose then. For the moment, though, I'd better get up, since my train goes at five.

He looked at the alarm clock ticking on the chest. Heavenly Father! he thought. It was half-past six o'clock and the hands were quietly moving on, it was even past the half-hour, it was getting on toward a quarter to seven. Had the alarm clock not gone off? From the bed one could see that it had been properly set for four o'clock; of course it must have gone off. Yes, but was it possible to sleep quietly through that ear-splitting noise? Well, he had not slept quietly, yet apparently all the more soundly for that. But what was he to do now? The next train went at seven o'clock; to catch that he would need to hurry like mad and his samples weren't even packed up, and he himself wasn't feeling particularly fresh and active. And even if he did catch the train he wouldn't avoid a row with the chief, since the firm's porter would have been waiting for the five o'clock train and would have long since reported his failure to turn up. The porter was a creature of the chief's, spineless and stupid. Well, supposing he were to say he was sick? But that would be most unpleasant and would look suspicious, since during his five years' employment he had not been ill once. The chief himself would be sure to come with the sick-insurance doctor, would reproach his parents with their son's laziness and would cut all excuses short by referring to the insurance doctor, who of course regarded all mankind as perfectly healthy malingerers. And would he be so far wrong on this occasion? Gregor really felt quite well, apart from a drowsiness that was utterly superfluous after such a long sleep, and he was even unusually hungry.

As all this was running through his mind at top speed without his being able to decide to leave his bed—the alarm clock had just struck a quarter to seven—there came a cautious tap at the door behind the head of his bed. "Gregor," said a voice—it was his mother's—"it's a quarter to seven. Hadn't you a train to catch?" That gentle voice! Gregor had a shock as he heard his own voice answering hers, unmistakably his own voice, it was true, but with a persistent horrible twittering squeak behind it like an undertone, that left the words in their clear shape only for the first moment and then rose up reverberating round them to destroy their sense, so that one could not be sure one had heard them rightly. Gregor wanted to answer at length and explain everything, but in the circumstances he confined himself to saying: "Yes, yes, thank you, Mother, I'm getting up now." The wooden door between them must have kept the change in his voice from being noticeable outside, for his mother contented herself with this statement and shuffled away. Yet this brief exchange of words had made the other members of the family aware that Gregor was still in the house, as they had not expected, and at one of the side doors his father was already knocking, gently, yet with his fist. "Gregor, Gregor," he called, "what's the matter with you?" And after a little while he called again in a deeper voice: "Gregor! Gregor!" At the other side door his sister was saying in a low, plaintive tone: "Gregor! Aren't you well? Are you needing anything?" He answered them both at once: "I'm just ready," and did his best to make his voice sound as normal as possible by enunciating the words very clearly and leaving long pauses between them. So his father went back to his breakfast, but his sister whispered: "Gregor, open the door, do." However, he was not thinking of opening the door, and felt thankful for the purdent habit he had acquired in traveling of locking all doors during the night, even at home.

His immediate intention was to get up quietly without being disturbed, to put on his clothes and above all eat his breakfast, and only then to consider what else was to be done, since in bed, he was well aware, his meditations would come to no sensible conclusion. He remembered that often enough in bed he had felt small aches and pains, probably caused by awkward postures, which had proved purely imaginary once he got up, and he looked forward eagerly to seeing this morning's delusions gradually fall away. That the change in his voice was nothing but the precursor of a severe chill, a standing ailment of commercial travelers, he had not the least possible doubt.

To get rid of the quilt was quite easy; he had only to inflate himself a little and it fell off by itself. But the next move was difficult, especially because he was so uncommonly broad. He would have needed arms and hands to hoist himself up; instead he had only the numerous little legs which never stopped waving in all directions and which he could not control in the least. When he tried to bend one of them it was the first to stretch itself straight; and did he succeed at last in making it do what he wanted, all the other legs meanwhile waved the more wildly in a high degree of unpleasant agitation. "But what's the use of lying idle in bed," said Gregor to himself.

He thought that he might get out of bed with the lower part of his body first, but this lower part, which he had not yet seen and of which he could form no clear conception, proved too difficult to move; it shifted so slowly; and when finally, almost wild with annoyance, he gathered his forces together and thrust out recklessly, he had miscalculated the direction and bumped heavily against the lower end of the bed, and the stinging pain he felt informed him that precisely this lower part of his body was at the moment probably the most sensitive.

So he tried to get the top part of himself out first, and cautiously moved his head towards the edge of the bed. That proved easy enough, and despite its breadth and mass the bulk of his body at last slowly followed the movement of his head. Still, when he finally got his head free over the edge of the bed he felt too scared to go on advancing, for after all if he let himself fall in this way it would take a miracle to keep his head from being injured. And at all costs he must not lose consciousness now, precisely now; he would rather stay in bed.

But when after a repetition of the same efforts he lay in his former position again, sighing, and watched his little legs struggling against each other more wildly than ever, if that were possible, and saw no way of bringing any order into this arbitrary confusion, he told himself again that it was impossible to stay in bed and that the most sensible course was to risk everything for the smallest hope of getting away from it. At the same time he did not forget meanwhile to remind himself that cool reflection, the coolest possible, was much better than desperate resolves. In such moments he focused his eyes as sharply as possible on the window, but, unfortunately, the prospect of the morning fog, which muffled even the other side of the narrow street, brought him little encouragement and comfort. "Seven o'clock already," he said to himself when the alarm clock chimed again, "seven o'clock already and still such a thick fog." And for a little while he lay quiet, breathing lightly, as if perhaps expecting such complete repose to restore all things to their real and normal condition.

But then he said to himself: "Before it strikes a quarter past seven I must be quite out of this bed, without fail. Anyhow, by that time someone will have come from the office to ask for me, since it opens before seven." And he set himself to rocking his whole body at once in a regular rhythm, with the idea of swinging it out of the bed. If he tipped himself out in that way he could keep his head from injury by lifting it at an acute angle when he fell. His back seemed to be hard and was not likely to suffer from a fall on the carpet. His biggest worry was the loud crash he would not be able to help making, which would probably cause anxiety, if not terror, behind all the doors. Still, he must take the risk.

When he was already half out of the bed—the new method was more a game than an effort, for he needed only to hitch himself across by rocking to and fro—it struck him how simple it would be if he could get help. Two strong people—he thought of his father and the servant girl—would be amply sufficient; they would only have to thrust their arms under his convex back, lever him out of the bed, bend down with their burden and then be patient enough to let him turn himself right over on to the floor, where it was to be hoped his legs would then find their proper function. Well, ignoring the fact that the doors were all locked, ought he really to call for help? In spite of his misery he could not suppress a smile at the very idea of it.

He had got so far that he could barely keep his equilibrium when he rocked himself strongly, and he would have to nerve himself very soon for the final decision since in five minutes' time it would be a quarter past seven—when the front door bell rang. "That's someone from the office," he said to himself, and grew almost rigid, while his little legs only jigged about all the faster. For a moment everything stayed quiet. "They're not going to open the door," said Gregor to himself, catching at some kind of irrational hope. But then of course the servant girl went as usual to the door with her heavy tread and opened it. Gregor needed only to hear the first good morning of the visitor to know immediately who it was—the chief clerk himself. What a fate, to be condemned to work for a firm where the smallest omission at once gave rise to the gravest suspicion! Were all employees in a body nothing but scoundrels, was there not among them one single loyal devoted man who, had he wasted only an hour or so of the firm's time in a morning, was so tormented by conscience as to be driven out of his mind and actually incapable of leaving his bed? Wouldn't it really have been sufficient to sent an apprentice to inquire—if any inquiry were necessary at all—did the chief clerk himself have to come and thus indicate to the entire family, an innocent family, that this suspicious circumstance could be investigated by no one less versed in affairs than himself? And more through the agitation caused by these reflections than through any act of will Gregor swung himself out of bed with all his strength. There was a loud thump, but it was not really a crash. His fall was broken to some extent by the carpet, his back, too, was less stiff than he thought, and so there was merely a dull thud, not so very startling. Only he had not lifted his head carefully enough and had hit it; he turned it and rubbed it on the carpet in pain and irritation.

"That was something falling down in there," said the chief clerk in the next room to the left. Gregor tried to suppose to himself that something like what had happened to him today might some day happen to the chief clerk; one really could not deny that it was possible. But as if in brusque reply to this supposition the chief clerk took a couple of firm steps in the next-door room and his patent leather boots creaked. From the right-hand room his sister was whispering to inform him of the situation: "Gregor, the chief clerk's here." "I know," muttered Gregor to himself; but he didn't dare to make his voice loud enough for his sister to hear it.

"Gregor," said his father now from the left-hand room, "the chief clerk has come and wants to know why you didn't catch the early train. We don't know what to say to him. Besides, he wants to talk to you in person. So open the door, please. He will be good enough to excuse the untidiness of your room." "Good morning, Mr. Samsa," the chief clerk was calling amiably meanwhile. "He's not well," said his mother to the visitor, while his father was still speaking through the door, "he's not well, sir, believe me. What else would make him miss a train! The boy thinks about nothing but his work. It makes me almost cross the way he never goes out in the evenings; he's been here the last eight days and has stayed at home every single evening. He just sits there quietly at the table reading a newspaper or looking through railway timetables. The only amusement he gets is doing fretwork. For instance, he spent two or three evenings cutting out a little picture frame; you would be surprised to see how pretty it is; it's hanging in his room; you'll see it in a minute when Gregor opens the door. I must say I'm glad you've come, sir; we should never have got him to unlock the door by ourselves; he's so obstinate; and I'm sure he's unwell, though he wouldn't have it to be so this morning." "I'm just coming," said Gregor slowly and carefully, not moving an inch for fear of losing one word of the conversation. "I can't think of any other explanation, madam," said the chief clerk, "I hope it's nothing serious. Although on the other hand I must say that we men of business— fortunately or unfortunately—very often simply have to ignore any slight indisposition, since business must be attended to." "Well, can the chief clerk come in now?" asked Gregor's father impatiently, again knocking on the door. "No," said Gregor. In the left-hand room a painful silence followed this refusal, in the right-hand room his sister began to sob.

Why didn't his sister join the others? She was probably newly out of bed and hadn't even begun to put on her clothes yet. Well, why was she crying? Because he wouldn't get up and let the chief clerk in, because he was in danger of losing his job, and because the chief would begin dunning his parents again for the old debts? Surely these were things one didn't need to worry about for the present. Gregor was still at home and not in the least thinking of deserting the family. At the moment, true, he was lying on the carpet and no one who knew the condition he was in could seriously expect him to admit the chief clerk. But for such a small discourtesy, which could plausibly be explained away somehow later on, Gregor could hardly be dismissed on the spot. And it seemed to Gregor that it would be much more sensible to leave him in peace for the present than to trouble him with tears and entreaties. Still, of course, their uncertainty bewildered them all and excused their behavior.

"Mr. Samsa," the chief clerk called now in a louder voice, "what's the matter with you? Here you are, barricading yourself in your room, giving only 'yes' and 'no' for answers, causing your parents a lot of unnecessary trouble and neglecting—I mention this only in passing—neglecting your business duties in an incredible fashion. I am speaking here in the name of your parents and of your chief, and I beg you quite seriously to give me an immediate and precise explanation. You amaze me, you amaze me. I thought you were a quiet, dependable person, and now all at once you seem bent on making a disgraceful exhibition of yourself. The chief did hint to me early this morning a possible explanation for your disappearance—with reference to the cash payments that were entrusted to you recently—but I almost pledged my solemn word of honor that this could not be so. But now that I see how incredibly obstinate you are, I no longer have the slightest desire to take your part at all. And your position in the firm is not so unassailable. I came with the intention of telling you all this in private, but since you are wasting my time so needlessly I don't see why your parents shouldn't hear it too. For some time past your work has been most unsatisfactory; this is not the season of the year for a business boom, of course, we admit that, but a season of the year for doing no business at all, that does not exist, Mr. Samsa, must not exist."

"But, sir," cried Gregor, beside himself and in his agitation forgetting everything else. "I'm just going to open the door this very minute. A slight illness, an attack of gidiness, has kept me from getting up. I'm still lying in bed. But I feel all right again. I'm getting out of bed now. Just give me a moment or two longer! I'm not quite so well as I thought. But I'm all right, really. How a thing like that can suddenly strike one down! Only last night I was quite well, my parents can tell you, or rather I did have a slight presentiment. I must have showed some sign of it. Why didn't I report it at the office! But one always thinks that an indisposition can be got over without staying in the house. Oh sir, do spare my parents! All that you're reproaching me with now has no foundation; no one has ever said a word to me about it. Perhaps you haven't looked at the last orders I sent in. Anyhow, I can still catch the eight o'clock train, I'm much the better for my few hours' rest. Don't let me detain you here, sir; I'll be attending to business very soon, and do be good enough to tell the chief so and to make my excuses to him!"

And while all this was tumbling out pell-mell and Gregor hardly knew what he was saying, he had reached the chest quite easily, perhaps because of the practice he had had in bed, and was now trying to lever himself upright by means of it. He meant actually to open the door, actually to show himself and speak to the chief clerk; he was eager to find out what the others, after all their insistence, would say at the sight of him. If they were horrified then the responsibility was no longer his and he could stay quiet. But if they took it calmly, then he had no reason either to be upset, and could really get to the station for the eight o'clock train if he hurried. At first he slipped down a few times from the polished surface of the chest, but at length with a last heave he stood upright; he paid no more attention to the pains in the lower part of his body, however they smarted. Then he let himself fall against the back of a near-by chair, and clung with his little legs to the edges of it. That brought him into control of himself again and he stopped speaking, for now he could listen to what the chief clerk was saying.

"Did you understand a word of it?" the chief clerk was asking; "surely he can't be trying to make fools of us?" "Oh dear," cried his mother, in tears, "perhaps he's terribly ill and we're tormenting him. Grete! Grete!" she called out then. "Yes Mother?" called his sister from the other side. They were calling to each other across Gregor's room. "You must go this minute for the doctor. Gregor is ill. Go for the doctor, quick. Did you hear how he was speaking?" "That was no human voice," said the chief clerk in a voice notice-ably low beside the shrillness of the mother's. "Anna! Anna!" his father was calling through the hall to the kitchen, clapping his hands, "get a locksmith at once!" And the two girls were already running through the hall with a swish of skirts—how could his sister have got dressed so quickly?—and were tearing the front door open. There was no sound of its closing again; they had evidently left it open, as one does in houses where some great misfortune has happened.

But Gregor was now much calmer. The words he uttered were no longer understandable, apparently, although they seemed clear enough to him, even clearer than before, perhaps because his ear had grown accustomed to the sound of them. Yet at any rate people now believed that something was wrong with him, and were ready to help him. The positive certainty with which these first measures had been taken comforted him. He felt himself drawn once more into the human circle and hoped for great and remarkable results from both the doctor and the locksmith, without really distinguish-ing precisely between them. To make his voice as clear as possible for the decisive conversation that was now imminent he coughed a little, as quietly as he could, of course, since this noise too might not sound like a human cough for all he was able to judge. In the next room meanwhile there was complete silence. Perhaps his parents were sitting at the table with the chief clerk, whispering, perhaps they were all leaning against the door and listening.

Slowly Gregor pushed the chair towards the door, then let go of it, caught hold of the door for support—the soles at the end of his little legs were somewhat sticky—and rested against it for a moment after his efforts. Then he set himself to turning the key in the lock with his mouth. It seemed, unhappily, that he hadn't really any teeth—

what could he grip the key with?—but on the other hand his jaws were certainly very strong; with their help he did manage to set the key in motion, heedless of the fact that he was undoubtedly damaging them somewhere, since a brown fluid issued from his mouth, flowed over the key and dripped on the floor. "Just listen to that," said the chief clerk next door; "he's turning the key." That was a great encouragement to Gregor; but they should all have shouted encouragement to him, his father and mother too: "Go on Gregor," they should have called out, "keep going, hold on to that key!" And in the belief that they were all following his efforts intently, he clenched his jaws recklessly on the key with all the force at his command. As the turning of the key progressed he circled round the lock, holding on now only with his mouth, pushing on the key, as required, or pulling it down again with all the weight of his body. The louder click of the finally yielding lock literally quickened Gregor. With a deep breath of relief he said to himself: "So I didn't need the locksmith," and laid his head on the handle to open the door wide.

Since he had to pull the door towards him, he was still invisible when it was really wide open. He had to edge himself slowly round the near half of the double door, and to do it very carefully if he was not to fall plump upon his back just on the threshold. He was still carrying out this difficult manoeuvre, with no time to observe anything else, when he heard the chief clerk utter a loud "Oh!"—it sounded like a gust of wind—and now he could see the man, standing as he was nearest to the door, clapping one hand before his open mouth and slowly backing away as if driven by some invisible steady pressure. His mother—in spite of the chief clerk's being there her hair was still undone and sticking up in all directions—first clasped her hands and looked at his father, then took two steps towards Gregor and fell on the floor among her outspread skirts, her face quite hidden on her breast. His father knotted his fist with a fierce expression on his face as if he meant to knock Gregor back into his room, covered his eyes with his hands and wept till his great chest heaved.

Gregor did not go now into the living room, but leaned against the inside of the firmly shut wing of the door, so that only half his body was visible and his head above it bending sideways to look at the others. The light had meanwhile strengthened; on the other side of the street one could see clearly a section of the endlessly long, dark gray building opposite—it was a hospital—abruptly punctuated by its row of regular windows; the rain was still falling, but only in large singly discernible and literally singly splashing drops. The breakfast dishes were set out on the table lavishly, for breakfast was the most important meal of the day to Gregor's father, who lingered it out for hours over various newspapers. Right opposite Gregor on the wall hung a photograph of himself on military service, as a lieutenant, hand on sword, a carefree smile on his face, inviting one to respect his uniform and military bearing. The door leading to the hall was open, and one could see that the front door stood open too, showing the landing beyond and the beginning of the stairs going down.

"Well," said Gregor, knowing perfectly that he was the only one who had retained any composure, "I'll put my clothes on at once, pack up my samples and start off. Will you only let me go? You see, sir, I'm not obstinate, and I'm willing to work; traveling is hard life, but I couldn't live without it. Where are you going, sir? To the office? Yes? Will you give a true account of all this? One can be temporarily incapacitated, but that's just the moment for remembering former services and bearing in mind that later on, when the incapacity has been got over, one will certainly work with all the more industry and concentration. I'm loyally bound to serve the chief, you know that very well. Besides, I have to provide for my parents and my sister. I'm in great difficulties, but I'll get out of them again. Don't make things any worse for me than they are. Stand up for me in the firm. Travelers are not popular there, I know. People think they earn sacks of money and just have a good time. A prejudice there's no particular reason for revising. But you, sir, have a more comprehensive view of affairs than the rest of the staff, yes, let me tell you in confidence, a more comprehensive view than the chief himself, who, being the owner, lets his judgment easily be swayed against one of his employees. And you know very well that the traveler, who is never seen in the office almost the whole year round, can so easily fall a victim to gossip and ill luck and unfounded complaints, which he mostly knows nothing about, except when he comes back exhausted from his rounds, and only then suffers in person from their evil consequences, which he can no longer trace back to the original causes. Sir, sir, don't go away without a word to me to show that you think me in the right at least to some extent!"

But at Gregor's very first words the chief clerk had already backed away and only stared at him with parted lips over one twitching shoulder. And while Gregor was speaking he did not stand still one moment but stole away towards the door, without taking his eyes off Gregor, yet only an inch at a time, as if obeying some secret injunction to leave the room. He was already at the hall, and the suddenness with which he took his last step out of the living room would have made one believe he had burned the sole of his foot.

Once in the hall he stretched his right arm before him towards the staircase, as if some supernatural power were waiting there to deliver him.

Gregor perceived that the chief clerk must on no account be allowed to go away in this frame of mind if his position in the firm were not to be endangered to the utmost. His parents did not understand this so well; they had convinced themselves in the course of years that Gregor was settled for life in this firm, and besides they were so preoccupied with their immediate troubles that all foresight had forsaken them. Yet Gregor had this foresight. The chief clerk must be detained, soothed, and persuaded and finally won over; the whole future of Gregor and his family depended on it! If only his sister had been there! She was intelligent; she had begun to cry while Gregor was still lying quietly on his back. And no doubt the chief clerk, so partial to ladies, would have been guided by her; she would have shut the door of the flat and in the hall talked him out of his horror. But she was not there, and Gregor would have to handle the situation himself. And without remembering that he was still unaware what powers of movement he possessed, without even remembering that his words in all possibility, indeed in all likelihood, would again be unintelligible, he let go the wing of the door, pushed himself through the opening, started to walk towards the chief clerk, who was already ridiculously clinging with both hands to the railing on the landing; but immediately, as he was feeling for a support, he fell down with a little cry upon all his numerous legs. Hardly was he down when he experienced for the first time this morning a sense of physical comfort; his legs had firm ground under them; they were completely obedient, as he noted with joy; they even strove to carry him forward in whatever direction he chose; and he was inclined to believe that a final relief from all his sufferings was at hand. But in the same moment as he found himself on the floor, rocking with suppressed eagerness to move, not far from his mother, indeed just in front of her, she, who had seemed so completely crushed, sprang all at once to her feet, her arms and fingers outspread, cried: "Help, for God's sake, help!" bent her head down as if to see Gregor better, yet on the contrary kept backing senselessly away; had quite forgotten that the laden table stood behind her; sat upon it hastily, as if in absence of mind, when she bumped into it; and seemed altogether unaware that the big coffee pot beside her was upset and pouring coffee in a flood over the carpet.

"Mother, Mother," said Gregor in a low voice, and looked up at her. The chief clerk, for the moment, had quite slipped from his mind; instead, he could not resist snapping his jaws together at the sight of the streaming coffee. That made his mother scream again, she fled from the table and fell into the arms of his father, who hastened to catch her. But Gregor had now no time to spare for his parents; the chief clerk was already on the stairs; with his chin on the banisters he was taking one last backward look. Gregor made a spring, to be as sure as possible of overtaking him; the chief clerk must have divined his intention, for he leaped down several steps and vanished; he was still yelling "Ugh!" and it echoed through the whole staircase.

Unfortunately, the flight of the chief clerk seemed completely to upset Gregor's father, who had remained relatively calm until now, for instead of running after the man himself, or at least not hindering Gregor in his pursuit, he seized in his right hand the walking stick which the chief clerk had left behind on a chair, together with a hat and greatcoat, snatched in his left hand a large newspaper from the table and began stamping his feet and flourishing the stick and the newspaper to drive Gregor back into his room. No entreaty of Gregor's availed, indeed no entreaty was even understood, however humbly he bent his head his father only stamped on the floor more loudly. Behind his father his mother had torn open a window, despite the cold weather, and was leaning far out of it with her face in her hands. A strong draught set in from the street to the staircase, the window curtains blew in, the newspapers on the table fluttered, stray pages whisked over the floor. Pitilessly Gregor's father drove him back, hissing and crying "Shoo!" like a savage. But Gregor was quite unpracticed in walking backwards, it really was a slow business. If he only had a chance to turn round he could get back to his room at once, but he was afraid of exasperating his father by the slowness of such a rotation and at any moment the stick in his father's hand might hit him a fatal blow on the back or on the head. In the end, however, nothing else was left for him to do since to his horror he observed that in moving backwards he could not even control the direction he took; and so, keeping an anxious eye on his father all the time over his shoulder, he began to turn round as quickly as he could, which was in reality very slowly. Perhaps his father noted his good intentions, for he did not interfere except every now and then to help him in the manoeuvre from a distance with the point of the stick. If only he would have stopped making that unbearable hissing noise! It made Gregor lose his head. He had turned almost completely round when the hissing noise so distracted him that he even turned a little the wrong way again. But when at last his head was fortunately right in front of the doorway, it appeared that his body was too broad simply to get through the opening. His father, of course, in his present mood was far from thinking of such a thing as opening the other half of the door, to let Gregor have enough space. He had merely the fixed idea of driving Gregor back into his room as quickly as possible. He would never have suffered Gregor to make the circumstantial preparations for standing up on end and perhaps slipping his way through the door. Maybe he was now making more noise than ever to urge Gregor forward, as if no obstacle impeded him; to Gregor, anyhow, the noise in his rear sounded no longer like the voice of one single father; this was really no joke, and Gregor thrust himself—come what might—into the doorway. One side of his body rose up, he was tilted at an angle in the doorway, his flank was quite bruised, horrid blotches stained the white door, soon he was stuck fast and, left to himself, could not have moved at all, his legs on one side fluttered trembling in the air, those on the other were crushed painfully to the floor—when from behind his father gave him a strong push which was literally a deliverance and he flew far into the room, bleeding freely. The door was slammed behind him with the stick, and then at last there was silence.

## II

Not until it was twilight did Gregor awake out of a deep sleep, more like a swoon than a sleep. He would certainly have waked up of his own accord not much later, for he felt himself sufficiently rested and well-slept, but it seemed to him as if a fleeting step and a cautious shutting of the door leading into the hall had aroused him. The electric lights in the street cast a pale sheen here and there on the ceiling and the upper surfaces of the furniture, but down below, where he lay, it was dark. Slowly, awkwardly trying out his feelers, which he now first learned to appreciate, he pushed his way to the door to see what had been happening there. His left side felt like one single long, unpleasantly tense scar, and he had actually to limp on his two rows of legs. One little leg, moreover, had been severely damaged in the course of that morning's events—it was almost a miracle that only one had been damaged—and trailed uselessly behind him.

He had reached the door before he discovered what had really drawn him to it: the smell of food. For there stood a basin filled with fresh milk in which floated little sops of white bread. He could almost have laughed with joy, since he was now still hungrier than in the morning, and he dipped his head almost over the eyes straight into the milk. But soon in disappointment he withdrew it again; not only did he find it difficult to feed because of his tender left side—and he could only feed with the palpitating collaboration of his whole body—he did not like the milk either, although milk had been his favorite drink and that was certainly why his sister had set it there for him, indeed it was almost with repulsion that he turned away from the basin and crawled back to the middle of the room.

He could see through the crack of the door that the gas was turned on in the living room, but while usually at this time his father made a habit of reading the afternoon newspaper in a loud voice to his mother and occasionally his sister as well, not a sound was now to be heard. Well, perhaps his father had recently given up this habit of reading aloud, which his sister had mentioned so often in conversation and in her letters. But there was the same silence all around, although the flat was certainly not empty of occupants. "What a quiet life our family has been leading," said Gregor to himself, and as he sat there motionless staring into the darkness he felt great pride in the fact that he had been able to provide such a life for his parents and sister in such a fine flat. But what if all the quiet, the comfort, the contentment were now to end in horror? To keep himself from being lost in such thoughts Gregor took refuge in movement and crawled up and down in the room.

Once during the long evening one of the side doors was opened a little and quickly shut again, later the other side door too; someone had apparently wanted to come in and then thought better of it. Gregor now stationed himself immediately before the living room door, determined to persuade any hesitating visitor to come in or at least to discover who it might be; but the door was not opened again and he waited in vain. In the early morning, when the doors were locked, they had all wanted to come in, now that he had opened the door and the other had apparently been opened during the day, no one came in and even the keys were on the other side of the doors.

It was late at night before the gas went out in the living room, and Gregor could easily tell that his parents and his sister had all stayed awake until then, for he could clearly hear the three of them stealing away on tiptoe. No one was likely to visit him, not until the morning, that was certain; so he had plenty of time to meditate at his leisure on how he was to arrange his life afresh. But the lofty, empty room in which he had to lie flat on the floor filled him with an apprehension he could not account for, since it had been his very own room for the past five years—and with a half-unconscious action, not without a slight feeling of shame, he scuttled under the sofa, where he felt comfortable at once, although his back was a little cramped and he could not lift his head up, and his only regret was that his body was too broad to get the whole of it under the sofa.

He stayed there all night, spending the time partly in a light slumber, from which his hunger kept waking him up with a start, and partly worrying and sketching vague hopes, which all led to the same conclusion, that he must lie low for the present and, by excercising patience and the utmost consideration, help the family to bear the inconvenience he was bound to cause them in his present condition.

Very early in the morning, it was still almost night, Gregor had the chance to test the strength of his new resolutions, for his sister, nearly fully dressed, opened the door from the hall and peered. She did not see him at once, yet when she caught sight of him under the sofa—well, he had to be somewhere, he couldn't have flown away, could he?—she was so startled that without being able to help it she slammed the door shut again. But as if regretting her behavior she opened the door again immediately and came in on tiptoe, as if she were visiting an invalid or even a stranger. Gregor had pushed his head forward to the very edge of the sofa and watched her. Would she notice that he had left the milk standing, and not for lack of hunger, and would she bring in some other kind of food more to his taste? If she did not do it of her own accord, he would rather starve than draw her attention to the fact, although he felt a wild impulse to dart out from under the sofa, throw himself at her feet and beg her for something to eat. But his sister at once noticed, with surprise, that the basin was still full, except for a little milk that had been spilt all around it, she lifted it immediately, not with her bare hands, true, but with a cloth and carried it away. Gregor was wildly curious to know what she would bring instead, and made various speculations about it. Yet what she actually did next, in the goodness of her heart, he could never have guessed at. To find out what he liked she brought him a whole selection of food, all set out on an old newspaper. There were old, half-decayed vegetables, bones from last night's supper covered with a white sauce that had thickened; some raisins and almonds; a piece of cheese that Gregor would have called uneatable two days ago; a dry roll of bread, a buttered roll, and a roll both buttered and salted. Besides all that, she set down again the same basin, into which she had poured some water, and which was apparently to be reserved for his exclusive use. And with fine tact, knowing that Gregor would not eat in her presence, she withdrew quickly and even turned the key, to let him understand that he could take his ease as much as he liked. Gregor's legs all whizzed towards the food. His wounds must have healed completely, moreover, for he felt no disability, which amazed him and made him reflect how more than a month ago he had cut one finger a little with a knife and had still suffered pain from the wound only the day before yesterday. Am I less sensitive now? he thought, and sucked greedily at the cheese, which above all the other edibles attracted him at once and strongly. One after another and with tears of satisfaction in his eyes he quickly devoured the cheese, the vegetables and the sauce; the fresh food, on the other hand, had no charms for him, he could not even stand the smell of it and actually dragged away to some little distance the things he could eat. He had long finished his meal and was only lying lazily on the same spot when his sister turned the key slowly as a sign for him to retreat. That roused him at once, although he was nearly asleep, and he hurried under the sofa again. But it took considerable self-control for him to stay under the sofa, even for the short time his sister was in the room, since the large meal had swollen his body somewhat and he was so cramped he could hardly breathe. Slight attacks of breathlessness afflicted him and his eyes were starting a little out of his head as he watched his unsuspecting sister sweeping together with a broom not the remains of what he had eaten but even the things he had not touched, as if these were now of no use to anyone, and hastily shoveling it all into a bucket, which she covered with a wooden lid and carried away. Hardly had she turned her back when Gregor came from under the sofa and stretched and puffed himself out.

In this manner Gregor was fed, once in the early morning while his parents and the servant girl were still asleep, and a second time after they had all had their midday dinner, for then his parents took a short nap and the servant girl could be sent out on some errand or other by his sister. Not that they would have wanted him to starve, of course, but perhaps they could not have borne to know more about his feeding than from hearsay, perhaps too his sister wanted to spare them such little anxieties wherever possible, since they had quite enough to bear as it was.

Under what pretext the doctor and the locksmith had been got rid of on the first morning Gregor could not discover, for since what he said was not understood by the others it never struck any of them, not even his sister, that he could understand what they said, and so whenever his sister came into his room he had to content himself with hearing her utter only a sigh now and then and an occasional appeal to the saints. Later on, when she had got a little used to the situation—of course she could never get completely used to it—she sometimes threw out a remark which was kindly meant or could be interpreted. "Well, he liked his dinner today," she would say when Gregor had made a good clearance of his food; and when he had not eaten, which gradually happened more and more often, she would say almost sadly: "Everything's been left standing again."

But although Gregor could get no news directly, he overheard a lot from the neighboring rooms, and as soon as voices were audible, he would run to the door of the room concerned and press his whole body against it. In the first few days especially there was no conversation that did not refer to him somehow, even if only indirectly. For two whole days there were family consultations at every mealtime about what should be done; but also between meals the same subject was discussed, for there were always at least two members of the family at home, since no one wanted to be alone in the flat and to leave it quite empty was unthinkable. And on the very first of these days the household cook—it was not quite clear what and how much she knew of the situation—went down on her knees to his mother and begged leave to go, and when she departed, a quarter of an hour later, gave thanks for her dismissal with tears in her eyes as if for the greatest benefit that could have been conferred on her, and without any prompting swore a solemn oath that she would never say a single word to anyone about what had happened.

Now Gregor's sister had to cook too, helping her mother; true, the cooking did not amount to much, for they ate scarcely anything. Gregor was always hearing one of the family vainly urging another to eat and getting no answer but: "Thanks, I've had all I want," or something similar. Perhaps they drank nothing either. Time and again his sister kept asking his father if he wouldn't like some beer and offered kindly to go and fetch it herself, and when he made no answer suggested that she could ask the concierge to fetch it, so that he need feel no sense of obligation, but then a round "No" came from his father and no more was said about it.

In the course of that very first day Gregor's father explained the family's financial position and prospects to both his mother and his sister. Now and then he rose from the table to get some voucher or memorandum out of the small safe he had rescued from the collapse of his business five years earlier. One could hear him opening the complicated lock and rustling papers out and shutting it again. This statement made by his father was the first cheerful information Gregor had heard since his imprisonment. He had been of the opinion that nothing at all was left over from his father's business, at least his father had never said anything to the contrary, and of course he had not asked him directly. At that time Gregor's sole desire was to do his utmost to help the family to forget as soon as possible the catastrophe which had overwhelmed the business and thrown them all into a state of complete despair. And so he had set to work with unusual ardor and almost overnight had become a commercial traveler instead of a little clerk, with of course much greater chances of earning money, and his success was immediately translated into good round coin which he could lay on the table for his amazed and happy family. These had been fine times, and they had never re-curred, at least not with the same sense of glory, although later on Gregor had earned so much money that he was able to meet the expenses of the whole household and did so. They had simply got used to it, both the family and Gregor; the money was gratefully accepted and gladly given, but there was no special uprush of warm feeling. With his sister alone had he remained intimate, and it was a secret plan of his that she, who loved music, unlike himself, and could play movingly on the violin, should be sent next year to study at the Conservatorium, despite the great expense that would entail, which must be made up in some other way. During his brief visits home the Conservatorium was often mentioned in the talks he had with his sister, but always merely as a beautiful dream which could never come true, and his parents discouraged even these innocent references to it; yet Gregor had made up his mind firmly about it and meant to announce the fact with due solemnity on Christmas Day.

Such were the thoughts, completely futile in his present condi-tion, that went through his head as he stood clinging upright to the door and listening. Sometimes out of sheer weariness he had to give up listening and let his head fall negligently against the door, but he always had to pull himself together again at once, for even the slight sound his head made was audible next door and brought all conver-sation to a stop. "What can he be doing now?" his father would say after a while, obviously turning towards the door, and only then would the interrupted conversation gradually be set going again.

Gregor was now informed as amply as he could wish—for his father tended to repeat himself in his explanations, partly because it was a long time since he had handled such matters and partly be-cause his mother could not always grasp things at once—that a certain amount of investments, a very small amount it was true, had survived the wreck of their fortunes and had even increased a little because the dividends had not been touched meanwhile. And be-sides that, the money Gregor brought home every month—had never been quite used up and now amounted to a small capital sum. Behind the door Gregor nodded his head eagerly, rejoiced at this evidence of unexpected thrift and foresight. True, he could really have paid off some more of his father's debts to the chief with this extra money, and so brought much nearer the day on which he could quit his job, but doubtless it was better the way his father had arranged it.

Yet this capital was by no means sufficient to let the family live on the interest of it; for one year, perhaps, or at the most two, they could live on the principal, that was all. It was simply a sum that ought not to be touched and should be kept for a rainy day; money for living expenses would have to be earned. Now his father was still hale enough but an old man, and he had done no work for the past five years and could not be expected to do much; during these five years, the first years of leisure in his laborious though unsuccessful life, he had grown rather fat and become sluggish. And Gregor's old mother, how was she to earn a living with her asthma, which troubled her even when she walked through the flat and kept her lying on a sofa every other day panting for breath beside an open window? And was his sister to earn her bread, she who was still a child of seventeen and whose life hitherto had been so pleasant, consisting as it did in dressing herself nicely, sleeping long, helping in the housekeeping, going out to a few modest entertainments and above all playing the violin? At first whenever the need for earning money was mentioned Gregor let go his hold on the door and threw himself down on the cool leather sofa beside it, he felt so hot with shame and grief.

Often he just lay there the long nights through without sleeping at all, scrabbling for hours on the leather. Or he nerved himself to the great effort of pushing an armchair to the window, then crawled up over the window sill and, braced against the chair, leaned against the window panes, obviously in some recollection of the sense of freedom that looking out of a window always used to give him. For in reality day by day things that were even a little way off were growing dimmer to his sight; the hospital across the street, which he used to execrate for being all too often before his eyes, was now quite beyond his range of vision, and if he had not known that he lived in Charlotte Street, a quiet street but still a city street, he might have believed that his window gave on a desert waste where gray sky and gray land blended indistinguishably into each other. His quick-witted sister only needed to observe twice that the armchair stood by the window; after that whenever she tidied the room she always pushed the chair back to the same place at the window and even left the inner casements open.

If he could have spoken to her and thanked her for all she had to do for him, he could have borne her ministrations better; as it was, they oppressed him. She certainly tried to make as light as possible of whatever was disagreeable in her task, and as time went on she succeeded, of course, more and more, but time brought more enlightenment to Gregor too. The very way she came in distressed him. Hardly was she in the room when she rushed to the window, without even taking time to shut the door, careful as she was usually to shield the sight of Gregor's room from the others, and as if she were almost suffocating tore the casements open with hasty fingers, standing then in the open draught for a while even in the bitterest cold and drawing deep breaths. This noisy scurry of hers upset Gregor twice a day; he would crouch trembling under the sofa all the time, knowing quite well that she would certainly have spared him such a disturbance had she found it at all possible to stay in his presence without opening the window.

On one occasion, about a month after Gregor's metamorphosis, when there was surely no reason for her to be still startled at his appearance, she came a little earlier than usual and found him gazing out of the window, quite motionless, and thus well placed to look like a bogey. Gregor would not have been surprised had she not come in at all, for she could not immediately open the window while he was there, but not only did she retreat, she jumped back as if in alarm and banged the door shut; a stranger might well have thought that he had been lying in wait for her there meaning to bite her. Of course he hid himself under the sofa at once, but he had to wait until midday before she came again, and she seemed more ill at ease than usual. This made him realize how repulsive the sight of him still was to her, and that it was bound to go on being repulsive, and what an effort it must cost her not to run away even from the sight of the small portion of his body that stuck out from under the sofa. In order to spare her that, therefore, one day he carried a sheet on his back to the sofa—it cost him four hours' labor—and arranged it there in such a way as to hide him completely, so that even if she were to bend down she could not see him. Had she considered the sheet unnecessary, she would certainly have stripped it off the sofa again, for it was clear enough that this curtaining and confining of himself was not likely to conduce to Gregor's comfort, but she left it where it was, and Gregor even fancied that he caught a thankful glance from her eye when he lifted the sheet carefully a very little with his head to see how she was taking the new arrangement.

For the first fortnight his parents could not bring themselves to the point of entering his room, and he often heard them expressing their appreciation of his sister's activities, whereas formerly they had frequently scolded her for being as they thought a somewhat useless daughter. But now, both of them often waited outside the door, his father and his mother, while his sister tidied his room, and as soon as she came out she had to tell exactly how things were in the room, what Gregor had eaten, how he had conducted himself this time and whether there was not perhaps some slight improvement in his condition. His mother, moreover, began relatively soon to want to visit him, but his father and sister dissuaded her at first with arguments which Gregor listened to very attentively and altogether approved. Later, however, she had to be held back by main force, and when she cried out: "Do let me in to Gregor, he is my unfortunate son! Can't you understand that I must go to him?" Gregor thought that it might be well to have her come in, not every day, of course, but perhaps once a week; she understood things, after all, much better than his sister, who was only a child despite the efforts she was making and had perhaps taken on so difficult a task merely out of childish thoughtlessness.

Gregor's desire to see his mother was soon fulfilled. During the daytime he did not want to show himself at the window, out of consideration for his parents, but he could not crawl very far around the few square yards of floor space he had, nor could he bear lying quietly at rest all during the night, while he was fast losing any interest he had ever taken in food, so that for mere recreation he had formed the habit of crawling crisscross over the walls and ceiling. He especially enjoyed hanging suspended from the ceiling; it was much better than lying on the floor; one could breathe more freely; one's body swung and rocked lightly; and in the almost blissful absorption induced by this suspension it could happen to his own surprise that he let go and fell plump on the floor. Yet he now had his body much better under control than formerly, and even such a big fall did him no harm. His sister at once remarked the new distraction Gregor had found for himself—he left traces behind him of the sticky stuff on his soles wherever he crawled—and she got the idea in her head of giving him as wide a field as possible to crawl in and of removing pieces of furniture that hindered him, above all the chest of drawers and the writing desk. But that was more than she could manage all by herself; she did not dare ask her father to help her; and as for the servant girl, a young creature of sixteen who had had the courage to stay on after the cook's departure, she could not be asked to help, for she had begged as an especial favor that she might keep the kitchen door locked and open it only on a definite summons; so there was nothing left but to apply to her mother at an hour when her father was out. And the old lady did come, with exclamations of joyful eagerness, which, however, died away at the door of Gregor's room. Gregor's sister, of course, went in first, to see that everything was in order before letting his mother enter. In great haste Gregor pulled the sheet lower and rucked it more in folds so that it really looked as if it had been thrown accidentally over the sofa. And this time he did not peer out from under it; he renounced the pleasure of seeing his mother on this occasion and was only glad that she had come at all. "Come in, he's out of sight," said his sister, obviously leading her mother in by the hand. Gregor could now hear the two women struggling to shift the heavy old chest from its place, and his sister claiming the greater part of the labor for herself, without listening to the admonitions of her mother who feared she might overstrain herself. It took a long time. After at least a quarter of an hour's tugging his mother objected that the chest had better be left where it was, for in the first place it was too heavy and could never be got out before his father came home, and standing in the middle of the room like that it would only hamper Gregor's movements, while in the second place it was not at all certain that removing the furniture would be doing a service to Gregor. She was inclined to think to the contrary; the sight of the naked walls made her own heart heavy, and why shouldn't Gregor have the same feeling, considering that he had been used to his furniture for so long and might feel forlorn without it. "And doesn't it look," she concluded in a low voice—in fact she had been almost whispering all the time as if to avoid letting Gregor, whose exact whereabouts she did not know, hear even the tones of her voice, for she was convinced that he could not understand her words— "doesn't it look as if we were showing him, by taking away his furniture, that we have given up hope of his ever getting better and are just leaving him coldly to himself? I think it would be best to keep his room exactly as it has always been, so that when he comes back to us he will find everything unchanged and be able all the more easily to forget what has happened in between."

On hearing these words from his mother Gregor realized that the lack of all direct human speech for the past two months together with the monotony of family life must have confused his mind, otherwise he could not account for the fact that he had quite earnestly looked forward to having his room emptied of furnishing. Did he really want his warm room, so comfortably fitted with old family furniture, to be turned into a naked den in which he would certainly be able to crawl unhampered in all directions but at the price of shedding simultaneously all recollection of his human background? He had indeed been so near the brink of forgetfulness that only the voice of his mother, which he had not heard for so long, had drawn him back from it. Nothing should be taken out of his room; everything must stay as it was; he could not dispense with the good influence of the furniture on his state of mind; and even if the furniture did hamper him in his senseless crawling round and round, that was no drawback but a great advantage.

Unfortunately his sister was of the contrary opinion; she had grown accustomed, and not without reason, to consider herself an expert in Gregor's affairs as against her parents, and so her mother's advice was now enough to make her determined on the removal not only of the chest and the writing desk, which had been her first intention, but of all the furniture except the indispensable sofa. This determination was not, of course, merely the outcome of childish recalcitrance and of the self-confidence she had recently developed so unexpectedly and at such cost; she had in fact perceived that Gregor needed a lot of space to crawl about in, while on the other hand he never used the furniture at all, so far as could be seen. Another factor might have been also the enthusiastic temperament of an adolescent girl, which seeks to indulge itself on every opportunity and which now tempted Grete to exaggerate the horror of her brother's circumstances in order that she might do all the more for him. In a room where Gregor lorded it all alone over empty walls no one save herself was likely ever to set foot.

And so she was not to be moved from her resolve by her mother, who seemed moreover to be ill at ease in Gregor's room and therefore unsure of herself, was soon reduced to silence and helped her daughter as best she could to push the chest outside. Now, Gregor could do without the chest, if need be, but the writing desk he must retain. As soon as the two women had got the chest out of his room, groaning as they pushed it, Gregor stuck his head out from under the sofa to see how he might intervene as kindly and cautiously as possible. But as bad luck would have it, his mother was the first to return, leaving Grete clasping the chest in the room next door where she was trying to shift it all by herself, without of course moving it from the spot. His mother however was not accustomed to the sight of him, it might sicken her and so in alarm Gregor backed quickly to the other end of the sofa, yet could not prevent the sheet from swaying a little in front. That was enough to put her on the alert. She paused, stood still for a moment and then went back to Grete.

Although Gregor kept reassuring himself that nothing out of the way was happening, but only a few bits of furniture were being changed round, he soon had to admit that all this trotting to and fro of the two women, their little ejaculations and the scraping of furniture along the floor affected him like a vast disturbance coming from all sides at once, and however much he tucked in his head and legs and cowered to the very floor he was bound to confess that he would not be able to stand it for long. They were clearing his room out; taking away everything he loved; the chest in which he kept his fret saw and other tools was already dragged off; they were now loosening the writing desk which had almost sunk into the floor, the desk at which he had done all his homework when he was at the commercial academy, at the grammar school before that, and, yes, even at the primary school—he had no more time to waste in weighing the good intentions of the two women, whose existence he had by now almost forgotten, for they were so exhausted that they were laboring in silence and nothing could be heard but the heavy scuffling of their feet.

And so he rushed out—the women were just leaning against the writing desk in the next room to give themselves a breather—and four times changed his direction, since he really did not know what to rescue first, then on the wall opposite, which was already otherwise cleared, he was struck by the picture of the lady muffled in so much fur and quickly crawled up to it and pressed himself to the glass, which was a good surface to hold on to and comforted his hot belly. This picture at least, which was entirely hidden beneath him, was going to be removed by nobody. He turned his head towards the door of the living room so as to observe the women when they came back.

They had not allowed themselves much of a rest and were already coming; Grete had twined her arm round her mother and was almost supporting her. "Well, what shall we take now?" said Grete, looking round. Her eyes met Gregor's from the wall. She kept her composure, presumably because of her mother, bent her head down to her mother, to keep her from looking up, and said, although in a fluttering, unpremeditated voice: "Come, hadn't we better go back to the living room for a moment?" Her intentions were clear enough to Gregor, she wanted to bestow her mother in safety and then chase him down from the wall. Well, just let her try it! He clung to his picture and would not give it up. He would rather fly in Grete's face.

But Grete's words had succeeded in disquieting her mother, who took a step to one side, caught sight of the huge brown mass on the flowered wallpaper, and before she was really conscious that what she saw was Gregor screamed in a loud, hoarse voice: "Oh God, oh God!" fell with outspread arms over the sofa as if giving up and did not move. "Gregor!" cried his sister, shaking her fist and glaring at him. This was the first time she had directly addressed him since his metamorphosis. She ran into the next room for some aromatic essence with which to rouse her mother from her fainting fit. Gregor wanted to help too—there was still time to rescue the picture—but he was stuck fast to the glass and had to tear himself loose; he then ran after his sister into the next room as if he could advise her, as he used to do; but then had to stand helplessly behind her; she meanwhile searched among various small bottles and when she turned round started in alarm at the sight of him; one bottle fell on the floor and broke; a splinter of glass cut Gregor's face and some kind of corrosive medicine splashed him; without pausing a moment longer Grete gathered up all the bottles she could carry and ran to her mother with them; she banged the door shut with her foot. Gregor was now cut off from his mother, who was perhaps nearly dying because of him; he dared not open the door for fear of frightening away his sister, who had to stay with her mother; there was nothing he could do but wait; and harassed by self-reproach and worry he began now to crawl to and fro, over everything, walls, furniture and ceiling, and finally, in his despair, when the whole room seemed to be reeling round him, fell down on to the middle of the big table.

A little while elapsed, Gregor was still lying there feebly and all around was quiet, perhaps that was a good omen. Then the doorbell rang. The servant girl was of course locked in her kitchen, and Grete would have to open the door. It was his father. "What's been happening?" were his first words; Grete's face must have told him everything. Grete answered in a muffled voice, apparently hiding her head on his breast: "Mother has been fainting, but she's better now. Gregor's broken loose." "Just what I expected," said his father, "just what I've been telling you, but you women would never listen." It was clear to Gregor that his father had taken the worst interpretation of Grete's all too brief statement and was assuming that Gregor had been guilty of some violent act. Therefore Gregor must now try to propitiate his father, since he had neither time nor means for an explanation. And so he fled to the door of his own room and crouched against it, to let his father see as soon as he came in from the hall that his son had the good intention of getting back into his room immediately and that it was not necessary to drive him there, but that if only the door were opened he would disappear at once.

Yet his father was not in the mood to perceive such fine distinctions. "Ah!" he cried as soon as he appeared, in a tone which sounded at once angry and exultant. Gregor drew his head back from the door and lifted it to look at his father. Truly, this was not the father he had imagined to himself; admittedly he had been too absorbed of late in his new recreation of crawling over the ceiling to take the same interest as before in what was happening elsewhere in the flat, and he ought really to be prepared for some changes. And yet, and yet, could that be his father? the man who used to lie wearily sunk in bed whenever Gregor set out on a business journey; who welcomed him back of an evening lying in a long chair in a dressing gown; who could not really rise to his feet but only lifted his arms in greeting, and on the rare occasions when he did go out with his family, on one or two Sundays a year and on high holidays, walked between Gregor and his mother, who were slow walkers anyhow, even more slowly than they did, muffled in his old greatcoat, shuffling laboriously forward with the help of his crook-handled stick which he set down most cautiously at every step and, whenever he wanted to say anything, nearly always came to a full stop and gathered his escort around him? Now he was standing there in fine shape; dressed in a smart blue uniform with gold buttons, such as bank messengers wear; his strong double chin bulged over the stiff high collar of his jacket; from under his bushy eyebrows his black eyes darted fresh and penetrating glances; his onetime tangled white hair had been combed flat on either side of a shining and carefully exact parting. He pitched his cap, which bore a gold monogram, probably the badge of some bank, in a wide sweep across the whole room on to a sofa and with the tailends of his jacket thrown back, his hands in his trouser pockets, advanced with a grim visage towards Gregor. Likely enough he did not himself know what he meant to do; at any rate he lifted his feet uncommonly high, and Gregor was dumbfounded at the enormous size of his shoe soles. But Gregor could not risk standing up to him, aware as he had been from the very first day of his new life that his father believed only the severest measures suitable for dealing with him. And so he ran before his father, stopping when he stopped and scuttling forward again when his father made any kind of move. In this way they circled the room several times without anything decisive happening, indeed the whole operation did not even look like a pursuit because it was carried out so slowly. And so Gregor did not leave the floor, for he feared that his father might take as a piece of peculiar wickedness any excursion of his over the walls or the ceiling. All the same, he could not stay this course much longer, for while his father took one step he had to carry out a whole series of movements. He was already beginning to feel breathless, just as in his former life his lungs had not been very dependable. As he was staggering along, trying to concentrate his energy on running, hardly keeping his eyes open; in his dazed state never even thinking of any other escape than simply going forward; and having almost forgotten that the walls were free to him, which in this room were well provided with finely carved pieces of furniture full of knobs and crevices—suddenly something lightly flung landed close behind him and rolled before him. It was an apple; a second apple followed immediately; Gregor came to a stop in alarm; there was no point in running on, for his father was determined to bombard him. He had filled his pockets with fruit from the dish on the sideboard and was now shying apple after apple, without taking particularly good aim for the moment. The small red apples rolled about the floor as if magnetized and cannoned into each other. An apple thrown without much force grazed Gregor's back and glanced off harmlessly. But another following immediately landed right on his back and sank in; Gregor wanted to drag himself forward, as if this startling, incredible pain could be left behind him; but he felt as if nailed to the spot and flattened himself out in a complete derangement of all his senses. With his last conscious look he saw the door of his room being torn open and his mother rushing out ahead of his screaming sister, in her underbodice, for her daughter had loosened her clothing to let her breathe more freely and recover from her swoon, he saw his mother rushing towards his father, leaving one after another behind her on the floor her loosened petticoats, stumbling over her petticoats straight to his father and embracing him, in complete union with him—but here Gregor's sight began to fail—with her hands clasped round his father's neck as she begged for her son's life.

### III

The serious injury done to Gregor, which disabled him for more than a month—the apple went on sticking in his body as a visible reminder, since no one ventured to remove it—seemed to have made even his father recollect that Gregor was a member of the family, despite his present unfortunate and repulsive shape, and ought not to be treated as an enemy, that, on the contrary, family duty required the suppression of disgust and the exercise of patience, nothing but patience.

And although his injury had impaired, probably for ever, his powers of movement, and for the time being it took him long, long minutes to creep across his room like an old invalid—there was no question now of crawling up the wall—yet in his own opinion he was sufficiently compensated for this worsening of his condition by the fact that towards evening the living-room door, which he used to watch intently for an hour or two beforehand, was always thrown open, so that lying in the darkness of his room invisible to the family, he could see them all at the lamp-lit table and listen to their talk, by general consent as it were, very different from his earlier eavesdropping.

True, their intercourse lacked the lively character of former times, which he had always called to mind with a certain wistfulness in the small hotel bedrooms where he had been wont to throw himself down, tired out, on damp bedding. They were now mostly very silent. Soon after supper his father would fall asleep in his armchair; his mother and sister would admonish each other to be silent; his mother, bending low over the lamp, stitched at fine sewing for an underwear firm; his sister, who had taken a job as a salesgirl, was learning shorthand and French in the evenings on the chance of bettering herself. Sometimes his father woke up, and as if quite unaware that he had been sleeping said to his mother: "What a lot of sewing you're doing today!" and at once fell asleep again, while the two women exchanged a tired smile.

With a kind of mulishness his father persisted in keeping his uniform on even in the house; his dressing gown hung uselessly on its peg and he slept fully dressed where he sat, as if he were ready for service at any moment and even here only at the beck and call of his superior. As a result, his uniform, which was not brand-new to start with, began to look dirty, despite all the loving care of the mother and sister to keep it clean, and Gregor often spent whole evenings gazing at the many greasy spots on the garment, gleaming with gold buttons always in a high state of polish, in which the old man sat sleeping in extreme discomfort and yet quite peacefully.

As soon as the clock struck ten his mother tried to rouse his father with gentle words and to persuade him after that to get into bed, for sitting there he could not have a proper sleep and that was what he needed most, since he had to go on duty at six. But with the mulishness that had obsessed him since he became a bank messenger he always insisted on staying longer at the table, although he regularly fell asleep again and in the end only with the greatest trouble could be got out of his armchair and into his bed. However insistently Gregor's mother and sister kept urging him with gentle reminders, he would go on slowly shaking his head for a quarter of an hour, keeping his eyes shut, and refuse to get to his feet. The mother plucked at his sleeve, whispering endearments in his ear, the sister left her lessons to come to her mother's help, but Gregor's father was not to be caught. Not until the two women hoisted him up by the armpits did he open his eyes and look at them both, one after the other, usually with the remark: "This is a life. This is the peace and quiet of my old age." And leaning on the two of them he would heave himself up, with difficulty, as if he were a great burden to himself, suffer them to lead him as far as the door and then wave them off and go on alone, while the mother abandoned her needle-work and the sister her pen in order to run after him and help him farther.

Who could find time, in this overworked and tired-out family, to bother about Gregor more than was absolutely needful? The household was reduced more and more; the servant girl was turned off; a gigantic bony charwoman with white hair flying round her head came in morning and evening to do the rough work; everything else was done by Gregor's mother, as well as great piles of sewing. Even various family ornaments, which his mother and sister used to wear with pride at parties and celebrations, had to be sold, as Gregor discovered of an evening from hearing them all discuss the prices obtained. But what they lamented most was the fact that they could not leave the flat which was much too big for their present circumstances, because they could not think of any way to shift Gregor. Yet Gregor saw well enough that consideration for him was not the main difficulty preventing the removal, for they could have easily shifted him in some suitable box with a few air holes in it; what really kept them from moving into another flat was rather their own complete hopelessness and the belief that they had been singled out for a misfortune such as had never happened to any of their relations or acquaintances. They fulfilled to the uttermost all that the world demands of poor people, the father fetched breakfast for the small clerks in the bank, the mother devoted her energy to making underwear for strangers, the sister trotted to and fro behind the counter at the behest of customers, but more than this they had not the strength to do. And the wound in Gregor's back began to nag at him afresh when his mother and sister, after getting his father into bed, came back again, left their work lying, drew close to each other and sat cheek by cheek; when his mother, pointing towards his room, said: "Shut that door now, Grete," and he was left again in darkness, while next door the women mingled their tears or perhaps sat dry-eyed staring at the table.

Gregor hardly slept at all by night or by day. He was often haunted by the idea that next time the door opened he would take the family's affairs in hand again just as he used to do; once more, after this long interval, there appeared in his thoughts the figures of the chief and the chief clerk, the commercial travelers and the apprentices, the porter who was so dull witted, two or three friends in other firms, a chambermaid in one of the rural hotels, a sweet and fleeting memory, a cashier in a milliner's shop, whom he had wooed earnestly but too slowly—they all appeared, together with strangers or people he had quite forgotten, but instead of helping him and his family they were one and all unapproachable and he was glad when they vanished. At other times he would not be in the mood to bother about his family, he was only filled with rage at the way they were neglecting him, and although he had no clear idea of what he might care to eat he would make plans for getting into the larder to take the food that was after all his due, even if he were not hungry. His sister no longer took thought to bring him what might especially please him, but in the morning and at noon before she went to business hurriedly pushed into his room with her foot any food that was available, and in the evening cleared it out again with one sweep of the broom, heedless of whether it had been merely tasted, or—as most frequently happened—left untouched. The cleaning of his room, which she now did always in the evenings, could not have been more hastily done. Streaks of dirt stretched along the walls, here and there lay balls of dust and filth. At first Gregor used to station himself in some particularly filthy corner when his sister arrived, in order to reproach her with it, so to speak. But he could have sat there for weeks without getting her to make any improvement; she could see the dirt as well as he did, but she had simply made up her mind to leave it alone. And yet, with a touchiness that was new to her, which seemed anyhow to have infected the whole family, she jealously guarded her claim to be the sole caretaker of Gregor's room. His mother once subjected his room to a thorough cleaning, which was achieved only by means of several buckets of water—all this dampness of course upset Gregor too and he lay widespread, sulky and motionless on the sofa—but she was well punished for it. Hardly had his sister noticed the changed aspect of his room that evening than she rushed in high dudgeon into the living room and, despite the imploringly raised hands of her mother, burst into a storm of weeping, while her parents—her father had of course been startled out of his chair—looked on at first in helpless amazement; then they too began to go into action; the father reproached the mother on his right for not having left the cleaning of Gregor's room to his sister; shrieked at the sister on his left that never again was she to be allowed to clean Gregor's room; while the mother tried to pull the father into his bedroom, since he was beyond himself with agitation, the sister, shaken with sobs, thei. beat upon the table with her small fists; and Gregor hissed loudly with rage because not one of them thought of shutting the door to spare him such a spectacle and so much noise.

Still, even if the sister, exhausted by her daily work, had grown tired of looking after Gregor as she did formerly, there was no need for his mother's intervention or for Gregor's being neglected at all. The charwoman was there. This old widow, whose strong bony frame had enabled her to survive the worst a long life could offer, by no means recoiled from Gregor. Without being in the least curious she had once by chance opened the door of his room and at the sight of Gregor, who, taken by surprise, began to rush to and fro although no one was chasing him, merely stood there with her arms folded. From that time she never failed to open his door a little for a moment, morning and evening, to have a look at him. At first she even used to call him to her, ʋith words which apparently she took to be friendly, such as "Come along, then, you old dung beetle!" or "Look at the old dung beetle, then!" To such allocutions Gregor made no answer, but stayed motionless where he was, as if the door had never been opened. Instead of being allowed to disturb him so senselessly whenever the whim took her, she should rather have been ordered to clean out his room daily, that charwoman! Once, early in the morning—heavy rain was lashing on the windowpanes, perhaps a sign that spring was on the way—Gregor was so exasperated when she began addressing him again that he ran at her, as if to attack her, although slowly and feebly enough. But the charwoman instead of showing fright merely lifted high a chair that happened to be beside the door, and as she stood there with her mouth wide open it was clear that she meant to shut it only when she brought the chair down on Gregor's back. "So you're not coming any nearer?" she asked, as Gregor turned away again, and quietly put the chair back into the corner.

Gregor was now eating hardly anything. Only when he happened to pass the food laid out for him did he take a bit of something in his mouth as a pastime, kept it there for an hour at a time and usually spat it out again. At first he thought it was chagrin over the state of his room that prevented him from eating, yet he soon got used to the various changes in his room. It had become a habit in the family to push into his room things there was no room for elsewhere, and there were plenty of these now, since one of the rooms had been let to three lodgers. These serious gentlemen—all three of them with full beards, as Gregor once observed through a crack in the door—had a passion for order, not only in their own room but, since they were now members of the household, in all its arrangements, especially in the kitchen. Superfluous, not to say dirty, objects they could not bear. Besides, they had brought with them most of the furnishings they needed. For this reason many things could be dispensed with that it was no use trying to sell but that should not be thrown away either. All of them found their way into Gregor's room. The ash can likewise and the kitchen garbage can. Anything that was not needed for the moment was simply flung into Gregor's room by the charwoman, who did everything in a hurry; fortunately Gregor usually saw only the object, whatever it was, and the hand that held it. Perhaps she intended to take the things away again as time and opportunity offered, or to collect them until she could throw them all out in a heap, but in fact they just lay wherever she happened to throw them, except when Gregor pushed his way through the junk heap and shifted it somewhat, at first out of necessity, because he had not room enough to crawl, but later with increasing enjoyment, although after such excursions, being sad and weary to death, he would lie motionless for hours. And since the lodgers often ate their supper at home in the common living room, the living-room door stayed shut many an evening, yet Gregor reconciled himself quite easily to the shutting of the door, for often enough on evenings when it was opened he had disregarded it entirely and lain in the darkest corner of his room, quite unnoticed by the family. But on one occasion the charwoman left the door open a little and it stayed ajar even when the lodgers came in for supper and the lamp was lit. They set themselves at the top end of the table where formerly Gregor and his father and mother had eaten their meals, unfolded their napkins and took knife and fork in hand. At once his mother appeared in the other doorway with a dish of meat and close behind her his sister with a dish of potatoes piled high. The food steamed with a thick vapor. The lodgers bent over the food set before them as if to scrutinize it before eating, in fact the man in the middle, who seemed to pass for an authority with the other two, cut a piece of meat as it lay on the dish, obviously to discover if it were tender or should be sent back to the kitchen. He showed satisfaction, and Gregor's mother and sister, who had been watching anxiously, breathed freely and began to smile.

The family itself took its meals in the kitchen. None the less, Gregor's father came into the living room before going into the kitchen and with one prolonged bow, cap in hand, made a round of the table. The lodgers all stood up and murmured something in their beards. When they were alone again they ate their food in almost complete silence. It seemed remarkable to Gregor that among the various noises coming from the table he could always distinguish the sound of their masticating teeth, as if this were a sign to Gregor that one needed teeth in order to eat, and that with toothless jaws even of the finest make one could do nothing. "I'm hungry enough," said Gregor sadly to himself, "but not for that kind of food. How these lodgers are stuffing themselves, and here am I dying of starvation!"

On that very evening—during the whole of his time there Gregor could not remember ever having heard the violin—the sound of violin-playing came from the kitchen. The lodgers had already finished their supper, the one in the middle had brought out a newspaper and given the other two a page apiece, and now they were leaning back at ease reading and smoking. When the violin began to play they pricked up their ears, got to their feet, and went on tiptoe to the hall door where they stood huddled together. Their movements must have been heard in the kitchen, for Gregor's father called out: "Is the violin-playing disturbing you, gentlemen? It can be stopped at once." "On the contrary," said the middle lodger, "could not Fräulein Samsa come and play in this room, beside us, where it is much more convenient and comfortable?" "Oh certainly," cried Gregor's father, as if he were the violin-player. The lodgers came back into the living room and waited. Presently Gregor's father arrived with the music stand, his mother carrying the music and his sister with the violin. His sister quietly made everything ready to start playing; his parents, who had never let rooms before and so had an exaggerated idea of the courtesy due to lodgers, did not venture to sit down on their own chairs; his father leaned against the door, the right hand thrust between two buttons of his livery coat, which was formally buttoned up; but his mother was offered a chair by one of the lodgers and, since she left the chair just where he had happened to put it, sat down in a corner to one side.

Gregor's sister began to play; the father and mother, from either side, intently watched the movements of her hands. Gregor, attracted by the playing, ventured to move forward a little until his head was actually inside the living room. He felt hardly any surprise at his growing lack of consideration for the others; there had been a time when he prided himself on being considerate. And yet just on this occasion he had more reason than ever to hide himself, since owing to the amount of dust which lay thick in his room and rose into the air at the slightest movement, he too was covered with dust; fluff and hair and remnants of food trailed with him, caught on his back and along his sides; his indifference to everything was much too great for him to turn on his back and scrape himself clean on the carpet, as once he had done several times a day. And in spite of his condition, no shame deterred him from advancing a little over the spotless floor of the living room.

To be sure, no one was aware of him. The family was entirely absorbed in the violin-playing; the lodgers, however, who first of all had stationed themselves, hands in pockets, much too close behind the music stand so that they could all have read the music, which must have bothered his sister, had soon retreated to the window, half-whispering with downbent heads, and stayed there while his father turned an anxious eye on them. Indeed, they were making it more than obvious that they had been disappointed in their expectation of hearing good or enjoyable violin-playing, that they had had more than enough of the performance and only out of courtesy suffered a continued disturbance of their peace. From the way they all kept blowing the smoke of their cigars high in the air through nose and mouth one could divine their irritation. And yet Gregor's sister was playing so beautifully. Her face leaned sideways, intently and sadly her eyes followed the notes of music. Gregor crawled a little farther forward and lowered his head to the ground so that it might be possible for his eyes to meet hers. Was he an animal, that music had such an effect upon him? He felt as if the way were opening before him to the unknown nourishment he craved. He was determined to push forward till he reached his sister, to pull at her skirt and so let her know that she was to come into his room with her violin, for no one here appreciated her playing as he would appreciate it. He would never let her out of his room, at least, not so long as he lived; his frightful appearance would become, for the first time, useful to him; he would watch all the doors of his room at once and spit at intruders; but his sister should need no constraint, she should stay with him of her own free will; she should sit beside him on the sofa, bend down her ear to him and hear him confide that he had had the firm intention of sending her to the Conservatorium, and that, but for his mishap, last Christmas—surely Christmas was long past?—he would have announced it to everybody without allowing a single objection. After this confession his sister would be so touched that she would burst into tears, and Gregor would then raise himself to her shoulder and kiss her on the neck, which, now that she went to business, she kept free of any ribbon or collar.

"Mr. Samsa!" cried the middle lodger, to Gregor's father, and pointed, without wasting any more words, at Gregor, now working himself slowly forwards. The violin fell silent, the middle lodger first smiled to his friends with a shake of the head and then looked at Gregor again. Instead of driving Gregor out, his father seemed to think it more needful to begin by soothing down the lodgers, although they were not at all agitated and apparently found Gregor more entertaining than the violin-playing. He hurried towards them and, spreading out his arms, tried to urge them back into their own room and at the same time to block their view of Gregor. They now began to be really a little angry, one could not tell whether because of the old man's behavior or because it had just dawned on them that all unwittingly they had such a neighbor as Gregor next door. They demanded explanations of his father, they waved their arms like him, tugged uneasily at their beards, and only with reluctance backed towards their room. Meanwhile Gregor's sister, who stood there as if lost when her playing was so abruptly broken off, came to life again, pulled herself together all at once after standing for a while holding violin and bow in nervelessly hanging hands and staring at her music, pushed her violin into the lap of her mother, who was still sitting in her chair fighting asthmatically for breath, and ran into the lodgers' room to which they were now being shepherded by her father rather more quickly than before. One could see the pillows and blankets on the beds flying under her accustomed fingers and being laid in order. Before the lodgers had actually reached their room she had finished making the beds and slipped out.

The old man seemed once more to be so possessed by his mulish self-assertiveness that he was forgetting all the respect he should show to his lodgers. He kept driving them on and driving them on until in the very door of the bedroom the middle lodger stamped his foot loudly on the floor and so brought him to a halt. "I beg to announce," said the lodger, lifting one hand and looking also at Gregor's mother and sister, "that because of the disgusting conditions prevailing in this household and family"—here he spat on the floor with emphatic brevity—"I give you notice on the spot. Naturally I won't pay you a penny for the days I have lived here, on the contrary I shall consider bringing an action for damages against you, based on claims—believe me—that will be easily susceptible of proof." He ceased and stared straight in front of him, as if he expected something. In fact his two friends at once rushed into the breach with these words: "And we too give notice on the spot." On that he seized the door-handle and shut the door with a slam.

Gregor's father, groping with his hands, staggered forward and fell into his chair; it looked as if he were stretching himself there for his ordinary evening nap, but the marked jerkings of his head, which was as if uncontrollable, showed that he was far from asleep. Gregor had simply stayed quietly all the time on the spot where the lodgers had espied him. Disappointment at the failure of his plan, perhaps also the weakness arising from extreme hunger, made it impossible for him to move. He feared, with a fair degree of certainty, that at any moment the general tension would discharge itself in a combined attack upon him, and he lay waiting. He did not react even to the noise made by the violin as it fell off his mother's lap from under her trembling fingers and gave out a resonant note.

"My dear parents," said his sister, slapping her hand on the table by way of introduction, "things can't go on like this. Perhaps you don't realize that, but I do. I won't utter my brother's name in the presence of this creature, and so all I say is: we must try to get rid of it. We've tried to look after it and to put up with it as far as is humanly possible, and I don't think anyone could reproach us in the slightest."

"She is more than right," said Gregor's father to himself. His mother, who was still choking for lack of breath, began to cough hollowly into her hand with a wild look in her eyes.

His sister rushed over to her and held her forehead. His father's thoughts seemed to have lost their vagueness at Grete's words, he sat more upright, fingering his service cap that lay among the plates still lying on the table from the lodgers' supper, and from time to time looked at the still form of Gregor.

"We must try to get rid of it," his sister now said explicitly to her father, since her mother was coughing too much to hear a word, "it will be the death of both of you, I can see that coming. When one has to work as hard as we do, all of us, one can't stand this continual torment at home on top of it. At least I can't stand it any longer." And she burst into such a passion of sobbing that her tears dropped on her mother's face, where she wiped them off mechanically.

"My dear," said the old man sympathetically, and with evident understanding, "but what can we do?"

Gregor's sister merely shrugged her shoulders to indicate the feeling of helplessness that had now overmastered her during her weeping fit, in contrast to her former confidence.

"If he could understand us," said her father, half questioningly; Grete, still sobbing, vehemently waved a hand to show how unthinkable that was.

"If he could understand us," repeated the old man, shutting his eyes to consider his daughter's conviction that understanding was impossible, "then perhaps we might come to some agreement with him. But as it is—"

"He must go," cried Gregor's sister, "that's the only solution, Father. You must just try to get rid of the idea that this is Gregor. The fact that we've believed it for so long is the root of all our trouble. But how can it be Gregor? If this were Gregor, he would have realized long ago that human beings can't live with such a creature, and he'd have gone away on his own accord. Then we wouldn't have any brother, but we'd be able to go on living and keep his memory in honor. As it is, this creature persecutes us, drives away our lodgers, obviously wants the whole apartment to himself and would have us all sleep in the gutter. Just look, Father," she shrieked all at once, "he's at it again!" And in an access of panic that was quite incomprehensible to Gregor she even quitted her mother, literally thrusting the chair from her as if she would rather sacrifice her mother than stay so near to Gregor, and rushed behind her father, who also rose up, being simply upset by her agitation, and half-spread his arms out as if to protect her.

Yet Gregor had not the slightest intention of frightening anyone, far less his sister. He had only begun to turn round in order to crawl back to his room, but it was certainly a startling operation to watch, since because of his disabled condition he could not execute the difficult turning movements except by lifting his head and then bracing it against the floor over and over again. He paused and looked round. His good intentions seemed to have been recognized; the alarm had only been momentary. Now they were all watching him in melancholy silence. His mother lay in her chair, her legs stiffly outstretched and pressed together, her eyes almost closing for sheer weariness; his father and his sister were sitting beside each other, his sister's arm around the old man's neck.

Perhaps I can go on turning round now, thought Gregor, and

began his labors again. He could not stop himself from panting with the effort, and had to pause now and then to take breath. Nor did anyone harass him, he was left entirely to himself. When he had completed the turn-round he began at once to crawl straight back. He was amazed at the distance separating him from his room and could not understand how in his weak state he had managed to accomplish the same journey so recently, almost without remarking it. Intent on crawling as fast as possible, he barely noticed that not a single word, not an ejaculation from his family, interfered with his progress. Only when he was already in the doorway did he turn his head round, not completely, for his neck muscles were getting stiff, but enough to see that nothing had changed behind him except that his sister had risen to her feet. His last glance fell on his mother, who was not quite overcome by sleep.

Hardly was he well inside his room when the door was hastily pushed shut, bolted and locked. The sudden noise in his rear startled him so much that his little legs gave beneath him. It was his sister who had shown such haste. She had been standing ready waiting and had made a light spring forward, Gregor had not even heard her coming, and she cried "At last!" to her parents as she turned the key in the lock.

"And what now?" said Gregor to himself, looking round in the darkness. Soon he made the discovery that he was now unable to stir a limb. This did not surprise him, rather it seemed unnatural that he should ever actually have been able to move on these feeble little legs. Otherwise he felt relatively comfortable. True, his whole body was aching, but it seemed that the pain was gradually growing less and would finally pass away. The rotting apple in his back and the inflamed area around it, all covered with soft dust, already hardly troubled him. He thought of his family with tenderness and love. The decision that he must disappear was one that he held to even more strongly than his sister, if that were possible. In this state of vacant and peaceful meditation he remained until the tower clock struck three in the morning. The first broadening of light in the world outside the window entered his consciousness once more. Then his head sank to the floor of its own accord and from his nostrils came the last faint flicker of his breath.

When the charwoman arrived early in the morning—what between her strength and her impatience she slammed all the doors so loudly, never mind how often she had been begged not to do so, that no one in the whole apartment could enjoy any quiet sleep after her arrival—she noticed nothing unusual as she took her customary peep into Gregor's room. She thought he was lying motionless on purpose, pretending to be in the sulks; she credited him with every kind of intelligence. Since she happened to have the long-handled broom in her hand she tried to tickle him up with it from the doorway. When that too produced no reaction she felt provoked and poked at him a little harder, and only when she had pushed him along the floor without meeting any resistance was her attention aroused. It did not take her long to establish the truth of the matter, and her eyes widened, she let out a whistle, yet did not waste much time over it but tore open the door of the Samsas' bedroom and yelled into the darkness at the top of her voice: "Just look at this, it's dead; it's lying here dead and done for!"

Mr. and Mrs. Samsa started up in their double bed and before they realized the nature of the charwoman's announcement had some difficulty in overcoming the shock of it. But then they got out of bed quickly, one on either side, Mr. Samsa throwing a blanket over his shoulders, Mrs. Samsa in nothing but her nightgown; in this array they entered Gregor's room. Meanwhile the door of the living room opened, too, where Grete had been sleeping since the advent of the lodgers; she was completely dressed as if she had not been to bed, which seemed to be confirmed also by the paleness of her face. "Dead?" said Mrs. Samsa, looking questioningly at the charwoman, although she could have investigated for herself, and the fact was obvious enough without investigation. "I should say so," said the charwoman, proving her words by pushing Gregor's corpse a long way to one side with her broomstick. Mrs. Samsa made a movement as if to stop her, but checked it. "Well," said Mr. Samsa, "now thanks be to God." He crossed himself, and the three women followed his example. Grete, whose eyes never left the corpse, said: "Just see how thin he was. It's such a long time since he's eaten anything. The food came out again just as it went in." Indeed, Gregor's body was completely flat and dry, as could only now be seen when it was no longer supported by the legs and nothing prevented one from looking closely at it.

"Come in beside us, Grete, for a little while," said Mrs. Samsa with a tremulous smile, and Grete, not without looking back at the corpse, followed her parents into their bedroom. The charwoman shut the door and opened the window wide. Although it was so early in the morning a certain softness was perceptible in the fresh air. After all, it was already the end of March.

The three lodgers emerged from their room and were surprised to see no breakfast; they had been forgotten. "Where's our breakfast?" said the middle lodger peevishly to the charwoman. But she put her finger to her lips and hastily, without a word, indicated by gestures that they should go into Gregor's room. They did so and stood, their hands in the pockets of their somewhat shabby coats, around Gregor's corpse in the room where it was now fully light.

At that the door of the Samsas' bedroom opened and Mr. Samsa appeared in his uniform, his wife on one arm, his daughter on the other. They all looked a little as if they had been crying; from time to time Grete hid her face on her father's arm.

"Leave my house at once!" said Mr. Samsa, and pointed to the door without disengaging himself from the women. "What do you mean by that?" said the middle lodger, taken somewhat aback, with a feeble smile. The two others put their hands behind them and kept rubbing them together, as if in gleeful expectation of a fine set-to in which they were bound to come off the winners. "I mean just what I say," answered Mr. Samsa, and advanced in a straight line with his two companions towards the lodger. He stood his ground at first quietly, looking at the floor as if his thoughts were taking a new pattern in his head. "Then let us go, by all means," he said, and looked up at Mr. Samsa as if in a sudden access of humility he were expecting some renewed sanction for this decision. Mr. Samsa merely nodded briefly once or twice with meaning eyes. Upon that the lodger really did go with long strides into the hall, his two friends had been listening and had quite stopped rubbing their hands for some moments and now went scuttling after him as if afraid that Mr. Samsa might get into the hall before them and cut them off from their leader. In the hall they all three took their hats from the rack, their sticks from the umbrella stand, bowed in silence and quitted the apartment. With a suspiciousness which proved quite unfounded Mr. Samsa and the two women followed them out to the landing; leaning over the banister they watched the three figures slowly but surely going down the long stairs, vanishing from sight at a certain turn of the staircase on every floor and coming into view again after a moment or so; the more they dwindled, and when a butcher's boy met them and passed them on the stairs coming up proudly with a tray on his head, Mr. Samsa and the two women soon left the landing and as if a burden had been lifted from them went back into their apartment.

They decided to spend this day in resting and going for a stroll; they had not only deserved such a respite from work, but absolutely needed it. And so they sat down at the table and wrote three notes of excuse, Mr. Samsa to his board of management, Mrs. Samsa to her employer and Grete to the head of her firm. While they were writing, the charwoman came in to say that she was going now, since her morning's work was finished. At first they only nodded without looking up, but as she kept hovering there they eyed her irritably. "Well?" said Mr. Samsa. The charwoman stood grinning in the doorway as if she had good news to impart to the family but meant not to say a word unless properly questioned. The small ostrich feather standing upright on her hat, which had annoyed Mr. Samsa ever since she was engaged, was waving gaily in all directions. "Well, what is it then?" asked Mrs. Samsa, who obtained more respect from the charwoman than the others. "Oh," said the charwoman, giggling so amiably that she could not at once continue, "just this, you don't need to bother about how to get rid of the thing next door. It's been seen to already." Mrs. Samsa and Grete bent over their letters again, as if preoccupied; Mr. Samsa, who perceived that she was eager to begin describing it all in detail, stopped her with a decisive hand. But since she was not allowed to tell her story, she remembered the great hurry she was in, being obviously deeply huffed: "Bye, everybody," she said, whirling off violently, and departed with a frightful slamming of doors.

"She'll be given notice tonight," said Mr. Samsa, but neither from his wife nor his daughter did he get any answer, for the charwoman seemed to have shattered again the composure they had barely achieved. They rose, went to the window and stayed there, clasping each other tight. Mr. Samsa turned in his chair to look at them and quietly observed them for a little. Then he called out: "Come along, now, do. Let bygones be bygones. And you might have some consideration for me." The two of them complied at once, hastened to him, caressed him and quickly finished their letters.

Then they all three left the apartment together, which was more than they had done for months, and went by tram into the open country outside the town. The tram, in which they were the only passengers, was filled with warm sunshine. Leaning comfortably back in their seats they canvassed their prospects for the future, and it appeared on closer inspection that these were not at all bad, for the jobs they had got, which so far they had never really discussed with each other, were all three admirable and likely to lead to better things later on. The greatest immediate improvement in their condition would of course arise from moving to another house; they wanted to take a smaller and cheaper but also better situated and more easily run apartment than the one they had, which Gregor had selected. While they were thus conversing, it struck both Mr. and Mrs. Samsa, almost at the same moment, as they became aware of their daughter's increasing vivacity, that in spite of all the sorrow of recent times, which had made her cheeks pale, she had bloomed into a pretty girl with a good figure. They grew quieter and half unconsciously exchanged glances of complete agreement, having come to the conclusion that it would soon be time to find a good husband for her. And it was like a confirmation of their new dreams and excellent intentions that at the end of their journey their daughter sprang to her feet first and stretched her young body.

# Glossary of Critical Terms

ALLEGORY  A story in which the events and characters are symbolic of another order of meaning, in a frame of reference outside that of the fictional world, the way killing a dragon may symbolize defeating the devil. See pp. 13–14.

CHARACTER  A name or title and a set of qualities that make a fictional person. See pp. 11–12, 38, 44, 48.

COMEDY  The story of a person's rise to a higher station in life through education or improvement of personality. See pp. 8–9.

DESIGN  The shape of a story when it is considered as a completed object rather than an ongoing process. See pp. 19–21.

DIALOGUE  The parts of a story in which the words of characters are directly reported. See p. 15.

FABLE  A story that makes a moral point through the actions of characters, often using animals to represent human behavior. See p. 25–26.

FABULATION  Fiction that violates normal probabilities to make some point about the nature of existence. See p. 79.

FACT  A thing that has been done, or a true statement. See pp. 3–4.

FANTASY  A story of events that violate our sense of natural possibilities in this world; the more extreme the violation, the more fantastic the story. See pp. 5–6.

FICTION  Something made up, usually a made-up story. See pp. 3–4.

HISTORY  The events of the past, or a re-telling of those events in the form of a story; the most factual kind of fiction. See pp. 5–7, 39.

IRONY  The result of some difference in point of view or values between a character in fiction and the narrator or reader. See pp. 15–16.

JUXTAPOSITION  The way episodes or elements of a plot are located next to one another to contribute to the design of a story. See pp. 19–21.

METAFICTION  A special kind of fabulation that calls into question the nature of fiction itself. See p. 79.

METAPHOR  The way rich and complex thoughts can be conveyed by the linking of different images and ideas. See pp. 15–19.

MYTH    A story that expresses a deep human concern, often involving the actions of gods or other superhuman figures. See pp. 22–23.

NARRATION    The parts of a story that summarize events and conversations. See p. 15.

NARRATOR    The person who tells a story. See p. 15.

PARABLE    A story that takes the form of a simple allegory, using humble characters and situations as a way of suggesting more important moral or religious concerns. See pp. 25–26.

PATHOS    The emotion generated by the story of a character's fall or persecution through no fault of his own. See p. 8–9.

PICARESQUE    A kind of story that blends comedy and satire to narrate the adventures of a rogue passing though a low or debased version of contemporary reality. See p. 9.

PLOT    The order of events in a story as an ongoing process.

POINT OF VIEW    The voice and vision through which the events of a story reach the reader. See pp. 15–19.

REALISM    A mode of fiction that is not specifically factual but presents a world recognizably bound by the same laws as the world of the author. See pp. 7, 60.

REPETITION    The way certain features or elements of a story may be presented more than once to make a thematic point. See pp. 19–21.

ROMANCE    A story that is neither wildly fantastic nor bound by the conventions of realism, but offers a heightened version of reality. See pp. 7, 60.

SATIRE    A story that offers a world that is debased in relation to the world of the author. See pp. 8–9.

STORY    A complete sequence of events, as told about a single character or group of characters. See p. 4.

STREAM OF CONSCIOUSNESS    A fictional technique in which the thoughts of a character are entirely opened to the reader, usually being presented as a flow of ideas and feelings, apparently without logical organization. See p. 11.

SYMBOL    A particular object or event in a story which acquires thematic value through its function or the way it is presented.

TALE    A story that is told for its own sake, because it has a satisfying shape. See pp. 30–31.

THEME    The ideas, values, or feelings that are developed or questioned by a work of fiction. See pp. 12–14.

TONE    The way in which attitudes are conveyed through language without being presented directly as statements, as in sarcasm.

TRAGEDY    The story of a character's fall from a high position through some flaw of personality. See pp. 8–9.

ERRATUM to page 748

He holds on. He thinks of tourists filing through the National Museum, looking at Old Number One. People he'll never see, from Ottawa and Toronto and New York and for all he knows from Africa and Russia, standing around Old Number One, talking about her, pointing, admiring the black shine of her finish. Kids wondering what it would be like to ride in her, feel the thudding of her pistons under you.

He'd stand at the edge of the water and yell *Okay you son of a bitch, okay!*

"It don't look like there's going to be any complications. My lawyer can hardly believe how friendly all this's been. It'll all go by smooth as sailing."

Spit Delaney sees himself get up into the pickup with the youth and the St Bernard, sees himself slide his ass right up against the cab, slam his hand in a signal on the hot metal roof. Sees himself going down the silver-grey road, heading west. Sees himself laughing.

He says, "My lawyer says if it's all so god-damned friendly how come you two are splitting up."

"That's just it," she says. "Friends are one thing. You don't have to be married to be a friend."

"I don't know what you're talking about," Spit says. It occurs to him that he has come home from a trip through Europe and northern Africa and can't remember a thing. Something happened there, but what was it?

He sees himself riding in that pickup all up through the valley farmlands, over the mountains in the centre of the island, down along the lakes and rivers, snaking across towards Pacific. Singing, maybe, with that boy. Throwing his arm around the floppy dog's ugly neck. Feeling the air change gradually to damp, and colder. Straining his neck to see.

"I got my Lodge tonight, so I better get going, it'll give me the day to get settled in, it takes time to unpack. You'll be all right?"

Sees himself hopping off the green pickup, amongst the distorted combed-back spruce, the giant salal, sees himself touching the boy goodbye, patting the dog. Sees himself go down through the logs, through the white dry sand, over the damp brown sand and the seaweed. Sees himself at the water's edge on his long bony legs like someone who's just grown them, unsteady, shouting.

Shouting into the blind heavy roar.

*Okay!*

*Okay you son of a bitch!*

*I'm stripped now, okay, now where is that god-damned line?*